Once Upon a Courtship

Once Upon a Courtship: A Sweet Historical Romance Collection
Mail-Order Millie © 2024 by Kit Morgan
Courting Miss Darling © 2024 by Chautona Having
The Privateer's Prize © 2024 by MaryLu Tyndall
Grace in the Storm © 2024 by Tricia Goyer
Leftover Mail-Order Bride © 2024 by Regina Lundgren
Clara's Compassion © 2024 by Marlene Bierworth
Miss Spencer Meets Her Match © 2024 by Linore Rose Burkard
Lissa and the Spy © 2024 by Camy Tang
Abiding Faith, Freedom's Call © 2024 by Louise M. Gouge
Jory's Story © 2024 by Lisa M. Prysock
Priscilla's Promise © 2024 by Teresa Slack
The Gilding of Minnie Tucker © 2024 by Marilyn Turk

Published by Forget Me Not Romances, an imprint of Winged Publications

Winged Publications
www.wingedpublications.com

Editor: Cynthia Hickey
Cover Design by Chautona Havig
Interior Design by Camy Tang

All rights reserved. No part of this publication may be reproduced, stored in a retrieval system, or transmitted in any form or by any means—electronic, mechanical, photocopying, recording, or otherwise—without the prior written permission of the publisher. The only exception is brief quotations in printed reviews. Piracy is illegal. Thank you for respecting the hard work of this author.

This book is a work of fiction. Names, characters, Places, incidents, and dialogues are either products of the author's imagination or used fictitiously.

ISBN: 978-1-965352-21-2

Once Upon A Courtship

A SWEET HISTORICAL ROMANCE COLLECTION

KIT MORGAN
CHAUTONA HAVIG
TRICIA GOYER
MARYLU TYNDALL
REGINA SCOTT

MARLENE BIERWORTH
LINORE ROSE BURKARD
CAMILLE ELLIOT
LOUISE M. GOUGE
LISA M. PRYSOCK
TERESA SLACK
MARILYN TURK

Table of Contents

- *The Privateer's Prize* 5
- *Clara's Compassion* 59
- *Miss Spencer Meets Her Match* 120
- *Lissa and the Spy* 171
- *Abiding Faith – Freedom's Call* 233
- *Grace in the Storm* 303
- *Courting Miss Darling* 340
- *Jory's Story* 410
- *Mail-Order Millie* 493
- *Leftover Mail-Order Bride* 552
- *Priscilla's Promise* 611
- *The Gilding of Minnie Tucker* 679

The Privateer's Prize

by MaryLu Tyndall

Spinster Thea Cabot has long since given up her dream of getting married and having a family. Shamed for life when her fiancé Isaac Prescott left her at the altar, she spent the past four years caring for her younger sisters and an aging father. Now they are all gone. To make matters worse, her beloved city of Savannah, Georgia is overrun by British troops, and it looks as though they are here to stay. Honoring her father's dying wish, Thea boards a merchantman carrying a secret Patriot message for a contact in Baltimore, but imagine her shock when the ship is soon captured by an American Privateer, captained by the very man who ruined her life.

And we know that all things work together for good to them that love God, to them who are the called according to his purpose

Romans 8:28

Chapter One

Savannah, Georgia. April 1780

One step. Just one step and Thea Cabot would leave behind everything she'd ever known—home, family, and friends. She bit her lip and stared at the sailor's outstretched hand and then down at the rolling deck of the merchant brig. Behind her, Ruth grunted and sighed as she made her way up the plank. The poor servant was none too pleased at having to accompany Thea to New York and then Baltimore. Especially upon such rough seas. But Thea couldn't very well travel alone without proper escort.

The slam of Ruth's portmanteau shook the plank, and Thea steadied her feet, lest she fall into the Savannah River—a fitting beginning to this dreadful journey.

"Miss?" Ruth's questioning tone and the slight nudge to her back made Thea realize it would be better to step aboard the ship of her own volition than end up on her bottom amid an immodest flurry of skirts.

For all the sailors to see.

Not that they would be interested in an old spinster like her. At five and twenty, Thea was well past her prime and well past hope of getting married and having a family of her own.

And whose fault was that? None other than Isaac Preston. Even after four years, just thinking of the man made her jaw tighten and her stomach sour.

"Move along, Miss," someone shouted from behind, and the sailor in front of her raised a brow, his hand still elevated in her direction.

Drawing a deep breath, Thea gave him her valise, clutched her skirts, and slid her gloved hand into his. With more gentleness than she would expect from a sailor, he assisted her onto the deck and then led her to the railing before returning to help Ruth.

Why was the silly boat moving so much at anchor? Thea nearly fell and quickly gripped the wooden rail as the sailor delivered Ruth to her side.

"Best t' hang on, Miss, if ye ain't used to the sea," he said. "The purser be along soon t' show ye to yer cabin."

Thea thanked the man, who tipped his floppy hat and headed back to his duties. Other sailors who'd been staring at her and Ruth since they'd first appeared on the plank also returned to their tasks, save for occasional glances their way. Mercy, were they the only women on board? Perhaps so, since it was a merchant ship, and Thea had begged *and bribed* the captain to take them on as passengers.

"Seems we are drawing a bit of unwanted attention, Miss." Ruth glanced over the deck and inched closer to Thea. "I told you this weren't a good idea. Though spring be upon us, I still feel colder than a wet hen." She drew her shawl up to her neck.

"It's no less than seventy degrees, Ruth." Thea huffed, then chastised herself. Ruth was ten years her senior and no doubt feeling the cold more than she. "I'm sure it's warmer below deck."

A blast of wind brought the scent of fish and the sea, only increasing Thea's angst. She glanced over Savannah as rays of the morning sun kissed familiar buildings and streets awake—the fort with its cannons poking through earthworks, the courthouse, public mill, stone well, the milliners, bakers, and chandlers shops lining River Street. Beyond the palisades, fields of rice surrounded the settlement, glimmering in dawn's rays. At the edge of the docks, fur traders stood haggling prices beside piles of deerskins, fishermen returned with nets full of fish, while vendors readied their carts for the day's commerce.

And the ever present red and white uniforms of British infantry marched down the streets like blood stains on a festering wound.

Unexpected emotion burned her throat at the sight of her father's bakery and the home above it, where she and her two sisters had lived for the past twenty-five years. How could she leave a place so full of happy memories? Yet they were all gone now—the memories and those who had made them. Her sisters married and moved away, her father placed in his grave nigh a month past.

A burst of chilled wind rushed in from the sea, and she wiped away a tear and held up her chin. The time for mourning was over. At least that's what her father had told her.

"Don't mourn me, precious child. I'll be in heaven. I don't want to look down on you and see you wearing black and the world denied that beautiful smile of yours."

He had made her promise. Hence the reason for the blue camlet gown she wore with ruffles across the hem and sleeves. She fingered the black ribbon tied around her wrist—the only reminder she allowed herself of her father's passing. Should he glance down upon her, she hoped he would see it and know how much she loved him.

She patted her skirts just above her knee and felt the folded parchment. Another reason her father would be pleased. She fully intended to keep her promise to deliver this one final correspondence to his contact in Baltimore.

The flap of sails drew her gaze up to sailors in the tops loosening sailcloth. Other men on deck shouted orders.

"Stand by to make sail! Lay aloft topmen, lay aloft and loose!"

"Welcome aboard, Miss Cabot."

The male voice startled her and brought her gaze down to a stout man with a tuft of gray hair, a weather-lined face, and a kind smile. "I'm Captain Henshaw, and this here is Mr. Milson, my purser." He gestured to a thin man beside him. "He will show you ladies to your cabin. We are about to get under way, and it isn't safe for you on deck."

"Thank you, Captain." She attempted a smile but couldn't resist glancing one last time over Savannah. Tears blurred her vision until it seemed the city was drowning. Would she ever see her home again? Or would she live out her days as a spinster with her aunt in Baltimore and die alone without love and without children of her own?

"Miss, I must insist," the captain pressed.

Reluctantly, she allowed the purser to escort her and Ruth below to a room no bigger than a henhouse.

An hour later, Thea regretted ever stepping on board the ship. The tiny cabin spun like churned butter, the floor bucked like a wild horse, and light from the porthole shifted up and down on the wall like a teeter-totter. Thea had already tossed what was left of the toast she'd consumed that morning, and though her stomach still lodged in her throat, she had nothing more to give.

Ruth attempted to help her as best she could with cool cloths on her forehead and words of comfort. But there was naught to be done. Instead, Thea was forced to watch her servant pace the cabin, grumbling and muttering until Thea longed to be thrown overboard just to escape her incessant complaints.

Minutes passed like hours. Sunlight leaping over the walls faded from gold to orange to gray and finally disappeared. Still Thea's agony continued. She turned down the captain's invitation to dinner and went to bed early. After tossing and turning for hours, sometime in the middle of the night, she fell into a dream state. At first, happy memories flooded her— her father and sisters sitting around the fireplace at night, sunshine sparkling like jewels on Savannah River, church socials, country dances, and the good food, laughter, and love that had always filled their home. Then, a vision of Isaac Preston down on one knee, asking for her hand. He was so handsome in his black silk waistcoat and breeches, his dark hair neatly combed, his white bubbling cravat, and his stark golden eyes that had looked at her as if she were the most precious woman in the world. She, a girl of only twenty-one and he twenty-two, both young and in love after a fairy tale romance of carriage rides, picnics, and soirees. The dashing Mr. Preston was the dream of every young girl in Savannah. And he had chosen her.

Amid rumblings of war with England, wedding plans were made. Though a mere baker, her father spared no expense in either her wedding gown or in the feast to be held after the ceremony, which included all manner of delicious food, nutmeats and candy, coffee and spiced cider.

Finally, her wedding day arrived. She stood in the church wearing a gorgeous cream silk brocade gown with embroidered roses and matching shoes, waiting, along with fifty guests, for her intended to make an appearance. A smile lit her face, a sparkle her eyes. Her heart nearly burst with love for Isaac and with the excitement that she would soon become his wife.v

Hours passed.

Guests left.

No word came.

The ground shook beneath her, then tilted back and forth. She rolled and hit her head on something. Her stomach vaulted.

The creak of wood and gurgle of waves filled her ears.

Against her better judgment, she pried open her eyes.

The merchant ship. Gray light angled in through the porthole and oscillated over the floor. Thea gripped her stomach and attempted to rise, but the room spun and forced her back.

"Ruth," she called out, but one glance told her the woman was not there.

Thunder rumbled. Wind slammed against the hull.

A storm. What else could go wrong?

The door to her cabin crashed open and in walked two sailors.

She didn't have time to protest before they gripped her arms and dragged her off her cot and out the door.

"What is the meaning of this? How dare you? Where is my maid?"

"The captain wishes to speak to you."

Speak to her? Surely there were more mannerly ways of requesting an audience. She shoved down another burst of nausea as fear took root. Something wasn't right.

The men led her down a hall and up a ladder through a hatch. A blast of wind slapped her, dislodging hair from her pins, and filling her nose with the scent of rain and brine. Dark clouds broiled on the horizon as foam-capped seas hissed and spat around them. The ship pitched over a wave. Bracing on the tilting deck, the sailors dragged her toward Captain Henshaw, who was oddly speaking to Ruth.

"Ah, here's the traitor now." He turned to face her, a snarl on his lips.

Traitor?

Heart slamming against her ribs, Thea jerked from the men's grips and, as nonchalantly as possible, patted her skirt.

The note was gone.

She shifted her gaze to Ruth, but the woman's eyes remained focused on the deck.

White hot lightning etched her doom across the horizon. Terror joined Thea's nausea. "Whatever do you mean, Captain?"

His eyes narrowed as he thrust her father's correspondence in her face. "You are a rebel spy, as was your father before you! Who were you to deliver this to in Baltimore?"

Thea met the man's gaze directly. There was no use denying it, but she would give him no further information.

"Decipher this at once!" He gripped her arm—tightly—and she withheld a scream. Instead, sorrow threatened to melt what was left of her hope as she addressed her constant companion these past ten years.

"Why, Ruth?"

The woman shuffled her feet over the deck. Wind blew her hair wildly about her cap. "I've known you and your father were spies for a long time, Miss. I love my country, and I cannot allow you to betray England."

Numbness nearly halted the beating of Thea's heart. "I trusted you. I thought you were my friend."

Tears filled the woman's eyes before she shifted them away.

A fine mist settled over the dismal scene. The deck lurched, and if not for the captain's firm clench on her arm, Thea might have ended up in the raging sea.

"Miss Cabot," he announced, tightening his grip. "You are a traitor to England. I have no recourse but to put you in irons in your cabin until we reach New York, where I will turn you and this message over to the British authorities."

One of the sailors spat at her feet. Others cursed her and growled.

Thea repressed a shudder. Gathering her resolve, she replied with a courage that was fast dwindling. "I am no traitor, Captain. I am an American Patriot, and you, sir, are the invader in *my* country."

Chuckles ensued.

"Bah!" Captain Henshaw motioned for two sailors to approach. One of them yanked Thea's arms behind her back. Pain seared across her shoulders as the cold bite of iron circled her wrists and the harsh clank of the lock sealed her fate.

Wind whipped hair in her face as the deck canted, and she struggled to remain upright.

A thunderous boom filled the air. Too close to hail from the distant storm.

Releasing her, the captain spun about and marched to the railing.

"Confound it all!" he shouted. "A privateer!"

"She's coming around fast, Captain." Another man held a telescope to his eye. "Twenty guns to our eight. Nine pounders by the looks of them."

"Max, Birch, ready the guns!" Captain Henshaw cursed, snagged the scope from the sailor, and held it to his eye. "How did she sneak up on us so fast?" He glared above at a man at the masthead who, Thea assumed, was the lookout. "Lay aloft and loose fore topsail! Loose topgallants! Clear away the jib! We will outrun her!"

Thea peered around the men dashing across the deck. A two-masted ship sailed toward them off their larboard quarter, sails bloated white against the stormy skies and foam cresting on her bow. The muzzles of ten charred cannons poked over her railing, beyond which dozens of men crowded the deck.

A privateer! A *Patriot* privateer. She didn't know whether to be frightened or relieved.

A string of curses erupted from Captain Henshaw as the merchant ship crested a swell and came sweeping down, sails thundering.

"She's windward and coming fast on our larboard side!" a sailor shouted above the wind.

A burst of yellow flared from the privateer. A thunderous roar followed. The s7.31 inhip trembled. An eerie whine scraped Thea's ears. She closed her eyes and waited to be blown to bits.

Instead, a mighty splash sounded.

"Surrender or die!" a voice bellowed over the water from the privateer.

"They'll loose a broadside, Cap'n," the first mate shouted. "We'll be sunk for sure!"

Thea looked up and almost felt sorry for the aged captain as his shoulders sank and his hands fisted at his sides. Finally, he nodded to his first mate, and the man shouted orders to lower sails and heave to.

Ruth let out a whimper as she trembled beside Thea. Were they to be boarded and forced to witness a hand-to-hand battle? Surely not. With only twenty sailors on board the merchant ship and what appeared to be double that on the privateer, Captain Henshaw would be a fool to fight.

The captain must have done the calculation as well, for he nodded to a young sailor, and the man raised a white flag. Soon, with sails lowered, the merchant brig sat lifeless on the restless sea.

The mist turned to sprinkles. Thunder rumbled overhead.

Ruth clung to Thea as if she were her last hope.

"There, there. We will be all right," Thea said, her anger at her maid abating.

Ruth wiped tears from her face. "Why are you so kind to me after…after…"

"It doesn't matter now." If there was one thing Thea had learned in four years of war, it was that divided loyalties made enemies of the best of friends.

The sailors who weren't attending sails crowded around their captain, some demanding they stand and fight, others cursing and spitting, while others gathered weapons.

Thea's heart refused to settle. She had heard privateers were nothing but glorified pirates, equally brutal and debauched. Patriots or not, most had joined the war effort purely for wealth and were loyal to none. What would they do with two women? Or maybe they'd just rob the ship and leave Thea with the British, and her lot would remain the same.

All these thoughts scrambled through her mind as the privateer slowed and halted keel to keel with the merchantmen. A boat was lowered and within minutes a dozen men popped over the railing and thumped onto the deck. All were armed with pikes, cutlasses, and axes, and all looked as frightful as she expected.

The man who must be the privateer captain approached Captain Henshaw, drew off his hat, and bowed before him. "Good quarter will be granted provided you lay down your arms and open the hatches, Sir."

Thea's heart turned to ash.

Nay, couldn't be! She blinked and then looked again.

His hair was longer, his shoulders broader beneath a black sailor's coat, his jaw stubbled, his stance commanding, and somehow, he seemed taller. But she'd know him anywhere—the man who had ruined her life—Isaac Preston.

Chapter Two

"Thea?" Isaac cleared the hot lump forming in his throat. "Miss Cabot?" He gaped at the woman he'd initially thought must be the captain's wife. But no. Couldn't be Thea. She was safely in Savannah. She would never board a ship, never venture away from home, especially during war. Not the Thea he'd known. But he'd know that silky hair the color of rich Georgia clay anywhere and those jade green eyes, now firing grapeshot at him. Not to mention the spray of freckles on her nose, which always wrinkled when she was angry.

"You know the wench?" the captain spit out. "Ah, 'course you do." The man uttered a curse no real lady should hear.

"Beware your tongue, Sir," Isaac barked, then dropped his gaze to Thea's hands locked in irons behind her back. "What is the meaning of this?"

"She's one of yours, *Captain*."

Thea, a Patriot? Isaac studied her, searching for any truth to the man's words. But all he saw in her eyes was hatred. Facing the captain, he held out his hand. "Keys."

With a mighty scowl and another curse, the man fished a key from his trouser pocket and handed it to Isaac.

A blast of rain-laden wind struck him as he called two of his crew standing nearby. "Lock the captain and his crew below decks. "Nicols, take ten men, search the ship, and bring anything of value up on deck."

"Wait!" Thea offered her first word since he'd seen her. "He has an important correspondence of mine." She nodded toward the captain.

Confusion rattled Isaac's brain, reminding him of a common condition when around this woman.

"In his coat pocket!" Pleading replaced fury in her eyes.

11

Isaac nodded toward Hastings, who searched the captain's waistcoat, plucked out a piece of parchment, and handed it to Isaac.

The words scrawled across it made no sense. It was either a foreign language he had no knowledge of, or it was gobbledygook. *Or* a code. A blast of wind nearly tore it from his hands.

"Be careful!" Thea shouted as Isaac gestured for his men to escort the prisoners away.

Folding the paper, he tucked it inside his coat, then gently turned Thea around and unlocked her irons. Only then did he recognize her maid and companion, Ruth, cowering behind her.

Thea rubbed her wrists.

"Escort Miss Cabot and her maid to the *Avenger*, Mr. Babcock. Lock them in Jeremy's cabin for now."

"Lock us?" Thea jerked from his grasp. "We are on the same side, Captain."

"That is yet to be determined, Miss Cabot."

Heart and mind spinning, Isaac watched as his purser aided Thea and Ruth down the ladder and into the boat. Of all the people from his past to encounter, it had to be the woman he once loved—still loved, if he were truthful—and yet the woman he'd mistreated more than any other.

But he couldn't think of that now. He had work to do. Glancing over the deck of the British merchant ship, watching as his men brought up barrels and crates of valuable goods, he grinned. What an easy catch! The second one this month. If his luck and God's grace continued, he'd be well on his way to capturing twenty prizes thus far this year. Not only would he rid these American waters of enemy supplies, but he'd make a name and a fortune for himself and his men.

Two hours later, after he'd brought the most valuable cargo onto his brigantine and left the rest, along with the British ship, in Mr. Babcock's charge, Isaac entered his cabin with a sigh of both relief and exhaustion.

"Where should I point her?" Marlow, his quartermaster, followed him inside, along with Nicols, his bosun, and Hastings, his first mate. Outside the small window, the setting sun cast a gray hue over the eastern sky and spread a black net over the sea, which had calmed considerably since the battle.

"We took in a fine haul, Cap'n." Nicols dragged a sleeve beneath his pointy nose. "Coffee, rice, gunpowder, shot, thirty muskets, and beans and flour."

"Excellent." Isaac nodded. All things that would bring a great price. "Furl tops, raise main and fore, and head north. Keep close to shore during the night."

"Aye, Cap'n."

"And bring Miss Cabot here at once."

Hastings grinned, a playful twinkle in his eyes. "Should I have enough supper brought for two?"

Drawing his sword, Isaac laid it across his desk, pondering the question. "Yes. Thank you. And take her maid some supper as well."

"Aye." The man slipped out, barely giving Isaac time to settle his thoughts *and* intentions before a knock on his door preceded Miss Cabot being ushered inside.

Wind had loosened strands of hair from her pins and the ruffles of her neckline were

12

ripped, but otherwise she appeared unharmed.

She stood as still as a statue, refusing to glance his way.

"Please, have a seat, Thea." Isaac leaned back against his desk.

She lifted her chin. "How dare you use my Christian name. You will address me as Miss Cabot, Sir."

Ignoring the fury in her tone, he frowned. "Indeed. Then you will address *me* as Captain."

"I will have no occasion to address you at all, *Captain*, if you would take me to the nearest patriot port forthwith, preferably Baltimore."

He studied her. "A dangerous port for a Tory."

Her jaw turned to steel, her eyes blazing. "As you so clearly saw, *Captain*, I am no Tory."

"I'm not entirely positive what I saw." Pushing from the desk, he plucked his pistol from his belt and set it on a side table, then loosened his neckerchief, which had suddenly become tight. "Your irons could have been a ruse to facilitate bringing you on board my privateer."

She laughed. "To what end, Isaa…Captain? To spy on the vast plans of a single lowly privateer? To incite the crew to mutiny?"

He repressed a grin. The woman had a point. "Your tongue has sharpened since last I saw you."

"If you mean I do not fear to speak my mind, then yes. And that is not all you will find changed."

Anger flared red across her creamy cheeks, matching the color of the loose curls dangling beside them. A long, graceful neck led down to a chest that billowed beneath breaths of fury that would match any dragon's. Despite that, he couldn't help but notice how her blue gown did naught to hide her curves. He'd not thought it possible, but Thea Cabot had grown more beautiful these past four years. Or perhaps he had missed her more than he realized.

"Then I shall look forward to getting reacquainted."

Her brows collided in battle array. "You're mad if you think I want anything to do with you."

Ignoring the pang in his heart, he retorted, "Is that any way to thank me for saving you from a British prison ship—*if* that was where you were headed?"

Clutching a dangling curl, she twirled it around her finger. "I have but moved from one prison to another. In truth, I preferred the British captain to you."

"Ouch." Grinning, he placed a hand over his heart.

"You find this amusing?"

He shook his head. "No. But I will admit that it is good to see you again."

Her eyes narrowed, the freckles on her nose wrinkling. "I do not share your sentiments, Captain." She held out her hand. "My correspondence, if you please."

"I do *not* please." Egad, he was enjoying bantering with this woman.

"It is mine and none of your affair."

"It is if it proves to be information for the British. Do you have the decipher code?"

"Of course not!"

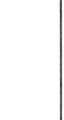

Sails flapped thunderously above them, and the ship tilted to larboard. Thea began to topple, and Isaac charged forward to catch her, but she gripped the edge of his desk and gave him a warning glare that would freeze the most valiant warrior. Moaning, she laid a hand on her belly and managed to mumble out, "Will you or will you not take me to Baltimore, Captain?"

Before he could answer, a knock sounded, and upon his "enter," Cook and two of his crew ambled inside, carrying platters of food.

"On my desk, Marlin. Thank you."

After setting down the trays and casting curious glances at Thea, the men left them alone once again.

"I am no Tory," Thea announced, chin raised. "I am as much a Patriot as you. Give me my letter and take me to Baltimore. It's of the upmost importance that I get there as soon as possible." Her gaze landed on the food, and she once again pressed a hand on her stomach. "You owe me."

He *did* owe her. A great deal. At the very least, an apology. For now, all he could offer her was a meal and safety until he could make port. "I will consider your request, Miss Cabot, but I must first stop at Philadelphia. My hold is full of prizes that I must cash in before I engage another enemy vessel."

"By then it will be too late!" She glanced at the food once again and moaned. "Once in Philadelphia, it will take days to settle your accounts. Besides, Baltimore is on the way."

Isaac crossed arms over his chest. "I have made my decision. In the meantime, you are free to roam my ship. You'll find my crew to be gentlemen."

Wind whistled against the window as the deck once again rolled over a wave. Thea lost her grip on the desk and started to fall.

Dashing forward, Isaac caught her and gently shored her up.

Just as she opened her mouth and vomited all over his coat.

Chapter Three

"What did Mr. Isaac say, Miss?" Ruth leapt from her seat as Thea entered the tiny cabin. "I cannot believe it were him. After all these years."

Closing the door, Thea faced her maid…her once friend and companion. "It matters not, Ruth. What matters is that I can no longer trust you." A lump burned in her throat as the deck tilted, and she leaned a hand on the wall…bulkhead, whatever they called it.

Clasping her hands together, Ruth approached. "I'm truly sorry, Miss. I…I…couldn't allow you to betray our country. I didn't mean you harm."

Thea huffed and held out a palm to stop Ruth's advance. "Harm? I would have been sent to one of those prison ships in England."

Tears spilled down Ruth's cheeks as she retreated and took her seat again. "I didn't realize."

"I should inform the captain of your loyalties," Thea spat out as the deck canted again.

A visible shiver coursed through Ruth.

"But I am not cruel like you," she added.

Ruth lowered her chin. "Thank you, Miss. I don't deserve your kindness."

"No, you don't."

Water made a mad dash against the hull as the ship picked up speed.

"What do we do now?" Ruth's eyes were pools of sorrow and fear.

Thea wanted to tell her there was no "we," but she bit her tongue upon seeing the woman's terror. Her loyalties were with England. Before her father had convinced Thea otherwise, hers had been as well. How could she fault Ruth for believing as she once had? The war had divided many friends and family.

"We sleep." Thea glanced at the single cot even as nausea gurgled in her belly.

"You still have mal-de-mar, Miss?"

Thea couldn't help but grin. "I fear I tossed my accounts all over Isaac."

"You did not!" Ruth giggled.

Thea nodded, still smiling at the memory. The look of disgust and horror on his face was almost worth her being sick the past few days.

An impish sparkle lit Ruth's eyes, and Thea released a heavy sigh. How easy it was to talk to her friend and forget her betrayal. But she must not. She must never trust her again. Moving to sit on the cot, she dropped her head into her hands, "I must get the captain to take me to the nearest port." The ship bucked, and her stomach mutinied yet again. "For what purpose would a privateer need to make for the nearest port?" she muttered out, seeking no answer.

"Storms, a need for supplies, repairs to the ship," Ruth said.

"I can hardly conjure up a storm or lack of supplies. However,"—Thea locked eyes with Ruth—"damage to the ship."

"Yes, Miss. They cannot sail in dangerous waters with a disabled ship, especially during war."

Then that is what Thea must do. But how? She knew nothing about ships.

"My brother works on a merchantman, Miss," Ruth added, fingering the torn edge of her sleeve. "He gave me a tour of the ship once."

Thea studied her maid, wondering if she should believe anything she said.

Ruth's eyes widened. "You could damage the rudder chain so the ship can't steer."

"But how would I do that?"

Ruth shook her head. "I don't know, Miss. I'm sure we have not the strength for such a task. Neither can we chop a hole in the hull. It's far too hard to hack through."

Thea swallowed a lump of frustration.

"The only other thing is damaging the masts or sail."

Thea frowned. "I can hardly take an ax and chop through a mast or climb aloft and rip a hole in the canvas without being seen."

Ruth glanced up at the lantern hooked above them. "A fire would do it."

Thea followed her gaze. Perhaps if given the run of the ship, she could find some gunpowder or rum and easily ignite a mast or sails. "But isn't that dangerous? What if the entire ship blazes? We would all die."

"True enough, Miss." Ruth flattened her lips. "It's a risk. More than likely, though, the

15

crew would put out the fire quickly and then they'd have to make for an inlet or port where they could fix the mast and replace the sail."

It was pure madness, but it just might work.

"Why are you helping me?" Thea asked.

"I suppose I owe you, Miss, for my betrayal. But"—she gave a sly grin—"I *am* helping you disable a Patriot privateer."

An hour later, Ruth's deep breaths filtered through the cabin, but Thea's mind refused to settle. A fire was a maniacally dangerous idea, but what choice did she have? Her father had told her the message she carried could turn the course of the war in their favor, but it had to be delivered before the end of May or it would be too late.

As if that weren't enough to keep her awake, her thoughts were consumed with the man in the captain's cabin down the hall. He had said she had changed. In truth, *he* had changed as well. He was not the young, impulsive, jovial boy she'd known. He was more serious, less playful. He wore the confidence and authority of a privateer captain well, a rather handsome captain, if she admitted it. Which she did not. *Gah!* Perhaps he was even married. She had no idea. Nor did she care.

All she cared about now was getting her message to Baltimore posthaste. And she was willing to do whatever it took to fulfill her father's last wishes and save her country. Good thing she had copied it word for word on a separate piece of parchment before she left Savannah. That copy was now safely sewn into the fabric of her skirts, and Ruth knew nothing about it.

Early in the morning, a sailor knocked on her door and brought her a pot of ginger tea, compliments of the captain, along with fresh biscuits to break their fast. While Ruth gorged herself on the biscuits, Thea drank the tea and soon found it aided much in relieving her turbulent stomach. Either that or she was growing accustomed to being tossed about like a puppet on a string. Yet what was she to think of Isaac's kindness? Especially after she'd tossed her accounts all over him?

Most likely a ploy.

Hence, feeling much better, she spent the majority of the day taking Isaac up on his offer to wander the ship at will. It was a small ship to be sure, so it took no time at all for her to find her way around the various sections—the galley where the cooking was done when not under rough seas, the capstan used to weigh and drop anchor, the various storerooms that held supplies, gunpowder, and shot. She avoided going deep in the hold, from where she could hear rats pattering about, and of course she didn't go near the officers' quarters, but she found the wardroom where they relaxed when not on duty. Isaac was right about one thing, though she felt the crew's eyes upon her, not a single lurid suggestion nor untoward action was directed her way.

Finally, after spotting Ruth above deck talking with a crewman, Thea slipped into her cabin, and lifting her skirts, drew out a flask of rum she'd stolen from the wardroom, and shoved it beneath the mattress. She'd had to wander through several times before she finally found the room empty and took her prize. In addition, the steward had given her flint and steel to keep the lantern in their cabin burning at night. Both of which were snug inside the pockets of her skirts.

Now she had one final thing to gather, and it was the hardest thing of all—the coded letter. Though she had a copy, she was responsible for the message and didn't want it to fall into the wrong hands.

Back on deck, Thea gripped the larboard railing and strained to see the distant shore blurring below a setting sun. She'd not spoken to Isaac all day, though she'd seen him on deck on several occasions, issuing orders for sails, speed, and direction to be adjusted. Did he notice her? Did he look at her? She had no idea and chastised herself for even thinking such thoughts.

Drawing a deep breath of the salty sea air, she closed her eyes for a moment and allowed the cool breeze to dance through her hair. Sails fluttered and snapped above her as the creak and groan of the ship created a soothing cadence. Waves of azure blue rolled and dipped, their foamy caps sparkling in the fading light. The sea was truly magnificent. She'd been so ill, she'd not been able to enjoy it.

"How do you like the *Avenger*?"

That voice…that voice that used to send warmth spiraling through her but now caused her blood to freeze.

Isaac appeared beside her, the wind tossing his brown hair and his golden eyes regarding her with an emotion she could not name.

"*Avenger*?"

"My brigantine." He waved an arm across the deck. "My men tell me you were wandering over the ship today."

She faced the sea. "I have never been on a privateer. I was curious."

"I see the tea has helped settle your stomach." Sunlight sparkled off a jeweled ring on his finger, catching her gaze. Isaac had never been one for such baubles.

"For now." She huffed. "Though I'm not sure whether it was mal-de-mar or merely your company which caused my illness."

A spark of pain crossed his eyes before he shifted his gaze away. His jaw tightened. "Then I suppose my invitation to dine with me tonight will be denied."

Wind tossed a curl into her face, and she snapped it aside. In truth, now that her stomach had settled, she was quite famished. And though spending time with the man who had ruined her life had no appeal, perhaps she could discover the location of her correspondence.

"I will dine with you on one condition, Captain."

One of Isaac's brows arched.

"That you give me back my message. It belongs to me, after all."

The ship plowed over a wave, and Thea gripped the railing lest she fall against Isaac.

"I will return it when I discover where your loyalties lie, Miss Cabot, and not a minute sooner." He studied her, the intensity of his gaze reminding her that he used to be able to read her thoughts. As he seemed to be doing now.

"Aye, yes." He patted the pocket of his waistcoat. "I keep it on me, so don't try to find it in my cabin."

"You say you have changed, but you haven't at all. You continue to take things from innocent women."

"Innocent? Yet to be determined." He huffed. "Do I take that as a no for dinner then?" One side of his lips quirked in that delightful way that had always made her heart leap.

"You may take that as a no for anything you want from me, Captain." She returned a tight smile before she tore her gaze from the infuriating man.

"Then if you'll excuse me." He dipped his head in her direction and stomped away, each thump of his boots stabbing her in the back. Was it her imagination, or was there a hint of sorrow in his voice?

Regardless, there was only one thing left to do. And she would have to do it tonight.

Chapter Four

Why, on this night of all nights, did Ruth remain awake until nearly dawn? The woman would not cease rambling on and on about a sailor she'd met that day—how charming he was, how handsome, how kind, smart, attentive.

Ugh. Nausea returned to Thea's stomach, threatening to reject the delicious supper a sailor had brought them earlier.

Thea had never realized her maid could be so girlishly silly. *Gah*, the woman was over thirty. Finally, however, Ruth's light snoring filled the cabin, and being as quiet as she could, Thea dressed, gathered the rum, and slipped out the door.

She expected there to be sailors on watch. What she hadn't expected was for there to be ten. Two in the crow's nest above, four on the forecastle, and four on the quarterdeck.

Making her way as casually as possible to the railing, she gripped it as the ship pitched over a wave. Topsails had been furled along with a few others she couldn't name, but at least the mainsail was still fluttering in the wind.

A few of the sailors glanced her way, one even tipping his hat in her direction, but other than that, they paid her no mind.

Now all she had to do was douse the main mast with rum and light it aflame before the men noticed. Thankfully, the moon was shrouded in clouds, thus allowing shadows to cover most of the deck.

Then why was her heart crashing against her chest and her blood racing so fast she felt she would faint? She'd always been the meek, obedient daughter, yet here she was about to set a ship on fire! A madcap drastic measure, but what else could she do?

She drew a deep breath of salty air, attempting to settle her nerves, and gazed over the ebony sea, streaked in ribbons of moonlight. Clouds drifted aside, revealing more stars than she could remember seeing, cast here and there like diamonds on velvet. Wind caressed her face, and she wondered how such a horrid war could exist beneath such beauty.

Still, there *was* a war. A war for freedom, for the right to live one's life as one chose. Surely that was what God wanted for all people? And she had a part to play in it. *She!* She waited what seemed like an eternity, waited until the sailors grew accustomed to her presence and took no note of her. Waited until a strip of gray framed the horizon. Dawn was coming. She had to move quickly.

Releasing the railing, she slowly backed up toward the main mast. Thankfully, it was still shrouded in darkness as she grabbed the bottle of rum from within her skirts, along with the flint and steel.

Perspiration dotted her forehead. She could barely hear over the riotous surge of blood through her ears. Yet when she glanced at the watchmen, they paid her no mind.

Ducking into the shadows, she uncorked the bottle and poured it all over the mast, both front and back, sprinkling the last drops as far up as she could. Then, taking the flint and steel, she struck them together. Twice. Nothing but a few impotent sparks lit the night. Her hands trembled. Dawn's light began to creep over the deck. Heart hammering, she struck them again. Several sparks shot onto the mast, and instantly a blaze started.

Shoving the flint and steel back into her pockets, she backed away from the fire, breath coming hard and fast as flaming tongues danced up the mast and licked toward the mainsail. She must leave before she was caught. Too late. A group of watchmen were already running her way.

"Fire! Fire!" one shouted.

Thea slipped into the shadows.

The shrill of a whistle pierced the air. "Battle stations! Fire!" A bell clanged. The rest of the watchmen dashed onto the main deck and began tying ropes to buckets.

Only then did Thea notice the empty bottle of rum tottering on the deck. *Gah*! But it was too late to retrieve it.

Heat from the fire seared her skin, and she inched her way to the larboard railing as men leapt up from below and mobbed the deck. Including Isaac. Bare feet and bare chested, he stormed across the ship, shouting orders.

More sailors flew from below like bees from a hive, and soon they formed two organized lines passing buckets of water from the sea and pouring it on the mast. Black smoke rose into the now gray sky and filtered over the deck.

Coughing, Thea batted it away. Still, she couldn't help but be impressed with how quickly the sailors knew exactly what to do. There was no chaos, no screaming or dashing about in fear. They just went to work as if it were any other task. Isaac had taught them well.

Dawn painted a swath of golden light across the horizon, announcing a new day. But Thea's gaze was on the mainsail. Flames had reached it, consuming the bottom section, including the yard, and releasing it to flap in the light breeze.

Even so, Isaac's crew were able to douse the flames before they destroyed the entire sail and did more damage to the yard and mast. Indeed, the mast remained standing, water dripping from the charred portion.

Would it be enough to force them to make port?

Isaac leapt down the quarterdeck ladder and made his way to the mainmast to inspect the damage. Thus far he had not seen her. Thea bit her lip. If only she could slip down one of the hatches unnoticed, but they were all exposed.

"What's this?" Isaac hefted the empty bottle of rum and cast an angry gaze over his men. "Whose is this?"

Wind whipped through his loose hair as dawn's golden light landed on the muscles of his bare chest and arms. Thea gulped. When had the boy become such an imposing man? Keeping to what remained of the shadows, she dipped her head and crept toward the quarterdeck ladder.

She felt rather than heard his footsteps pounding toward her. He leapt in front of her, forcing her to look up at him.

His eyes flashed fury.

"You did this!" Spit flew from his mouth.

Doing her best to settle her racing heart, Thea raised her chin. "How else to force you to make port? You left me no choice."

He let out a rather bestial growl. "Do you think we don't have extra sailcloth below deck, Miss Cabot? Do you think I don't have an expert carpenter on board? We can have the sail and yard fixed within an hour."

Gah! She hadn't thought of that.

Isaac took up a maddening pace in front of her. "Besides, if we hadn't caught this in time and put it out, our fate would have been to burn alive or drown!"

Thea gulped.

"A sail! A sail!" A shout blared down from the crosstrees.

Isaac marched to the starboard railing and raised the scope to his eye. "Where away?"

"Three points off our starboard side, Captain."

"Friend or foe?"

"I cannot tell."

"Blast it all! Either way I cannot outrun her with my mainsail damaged," Isaac growled.

"Raise all remaining sails, Mr. Hastings! Get ready to bring her about. We'll search for an inlet in which to hide." He fired off a string of orders, sending the men scrambling to task. "Jenkins, Smith, get below and fetch new canvas for the main. Hawkes!" he shouted, scanning the men and upon finding him added, "Get to repairing the yard and mast!"

"Aye, Cap'n," the skinny sailor replied.

"Marlin, lock Miss Cabot and her maid in their cabin!"

He finally faced Thea. "Where you will remain for the rest of our journey. Do you know what you have done? If that is a British privateer or warship, we are done for. You had better pray that ship is one of ours, or you have sent us all to our graves!"

Heart in her throat and tears flooding her eyes, Thea tore her gaze from his as the sailor gripped her arm and dragged her off.

What had she done?

Isaac had no time to be angry, no time to ponder whether Thea was utterly mad or determined to punish him for jilting her. Either way, he'd have to deal with her later. After a quick trip to his cabin, where he put on his shirt, waistcoat, and boots, and strapped on his weapons, he leapt back on deck to find the *Avenger* had successfully tacked and was hugging the coast as ordered. Fortunately, a thick fog blanketed much of the land, extending out onto the sea as well. Now to find a place to hide before the ship they'd spotted took note of them. There were dozens of islands and inlets along the coast of North Carolina where they could easily find refuge.

"She flies British colors, Cap'n!" The shout from above confirmed his worst fears.

Plucking the scope from his belt, he leveled it on his eye. Indeed, she was British, but from the looks of her, more merchantmen than privateer, for she sat low in the water, no doubt her hold full of cargo. Though no gun ports lined her hull, he could make out at least a dozen six-pounders and several larger guns perched on the deck as she rose and plunged through the sea, heading straight for them, at least a mile away and closing fast.

"Orders, Captain?" Hastings said from beside him.

"Load and run out the guns, sand the deck, and"—he glanced at the sails glutted with wind above—"reduce to battle sail."

"You intend to fight, Captain? Without a mainsail?"

"We have no choice. I can't outrun her, and I don't have time to slip into a cove to hide." He steadied his boots on the heaving deck as a blast of morning wind struck him. "If we cripple her, we may be able to slip away."

No sooner had he said the words than a mighty roar cracked the sky and a belch of fire emerged from the British ship.

"All hands down!" Isaac shouted, sending the sailors to cover.

A splash told them the shot had landed short of the *Avenger*. A warning, no doubt. If he positioned the ship just right, he'd have but one chance to return fire and hit his mark. After that, he'd be unable to maneuver quick enough to avoid return fire.

"Bring her about, Mr. Hastings! Bear off! Haul your braces, ease sheets, starboard guns standby!"

The *Avenger* creaked and groaned as she veered to larboard, bringing her guns to bear.

"Let's give them an answer, Mr. Ackland!" Isaac shouted to his master gunner. "Wait for my command." He kept a steady eye on the advancing merchantman, allowing her to come within a quarter mile while gauging the rise and fall of his brigantine in the water. "FIRE!"

With a roar and eruption of flame, the guns spoke. Black smoke swept over the deck, suffocating Isaac. Coughing, he peered through the haze, praying, hoping he'd done sufficient damage to the merchantman.

One shot pierced the ship's hull in a gaping, smoking hole above the waterline, and another punched through their outer jib, leaving a rugged tear in her sail. Blast it all. He could find no other damage. Terror clumped in his throat.

Turning, he shouted orders for the topmen to adjust sail to quickly turn the *Avenger* to larboard, but no matter how fast the sails shifted and filled with wind, the ship lumbered about like a drunken sailor at port.

The thunderous booms of guns quaked the sea as the merchantman touched off her six-pounders in rapid succession.

"Hands to the deck!" Isaac shouted as shot zipped by him, and the ship shuddered under the blows at stem and stern.

The larboard bulwark smashed in two places, splinters flying. One ball sliced through the shrouds on the foremast, still others slammed into the hull with staggering blows.

"Water in the hold!" A sailor shouted from below, and Isaac leaned over the railing to see one of the shots had struck below the water line.

They were done for.

"Orders?" For the first time since he'd sailed with the man, terror masked his first mate's face.

The same terror Isaac felt, along with a desperation that threatened to undo him.

Lifting his scope to his eye, he scanned the coastline where he knew several inlets lined the swampy land. Morning fog, not yet touched by the sun, hovered over both water and land, obscuring everything in sight.

Wind blasted over him, smelling of gun smoke, sweat, and fear. The *Avenger* completed the tack, presenting only their stern to the merchantman's guns. But she continued toward them. They'd be within boarding range within minutes.

"Mr. Ackland, load the bow chasers with langrel and grape, then fire as you bear! And have your men reload and fire all the other guns as well."

"But they ain't aimed nowhere, Cap'n."

"Just do it!"

The men rushed off to do his bidding.

He needed no spyglass to see the enemy now. They bore down upon them, white foam exploding over her bow. The sun spread golden talons through her sails, making them look like dragon wings.

Dashing to the wheel, Isaac directed the quartermaster to steer the *Avenger* around the upcoming island, while also ordering a sailor to take soundings as they went.

As if his ship had one last breath of life, Isaac ordered all guns to fire, and in a deafening roar that would wake the Kraken, the cannons belched their wicked loads, shaking the ship down to the keel and in the process creating a cloud of smoke that hopefully hid them from sight.

At least until they could slip into the fog and disappear behind the islands.

The merchantman returned fire, but thank the good Lord, the shots landed impotently in the sea beside the *Avenger*.

They slipped into the fog.

Silence invaded the ship, save for the silky purl of water against the hull and the heavy breathing of her crew. They risked running her aground, but Isaac knew these waters, had careened his ship here once, and thus knew the perfect place to hide.

Standing beside his quartermaster, he directed the ship down a large bay and then to the left into a shallow inlet. The merchantman was too large to enter or they'd risk being grounded. And it would be difficult to perfect a shot at them from the entrance.

"Very clever, Cap'n," Hastings said. "We might be able to get repairs done before he finds us."

"Let's pray so, Mr. Hastings."

Isaac spent the next hour not only praying but aiding his sailors in repairing the damage. The burned mainsail was hauled down and replaced with new canvas, the foremast shrouds were fixed. Mr. Hawkes repaired the mainmast and yard as best he could and the hole in the hull was sufficiently plugged. The *Avenger* would at least be able to sail and maneuver until they could make it to port for complete repairs.

Yet with each minute that passed, the sun rose higher in the sky, scattering the fog. He needed to find a better place to hide or attempt to sneak out onto the sea and put all canvas to the wind.

All these thoughts ran rampant through his mind when one of his men spotted the top of a mast over the tree line. Before Isaac could issue an order, the British merchantman appeared at the entrance to the inlet, all guns pointed at the *Avenger*.

Isaac's blood turned to ice.

"We'll be blown to bits, Cap'n." Hastings stared wide-eyed at their enemy.

"He raises a white flag," one of the sailors said. "He requests a parlay."

Isaac could not surrender. He would *not* lose his ship. Not after all he had done, all the risk, the battles, the years of hard work and sweat it had taken to acquire it. But what choice did he have? He would not risk the lives of his men.

"Signal him to come aboard."

"Sorry, Cap'n." His quartermaster spat onto the deck. "'Twere the woman what did this to ye. Always said it were bad luck to have a woman on board."

Bad luck, indeed.

Chapter Five

"Colonel Adley Barstow of His Royal Majesty's Armed Forces at your service." The man who led a group of British marines onto the deck swept off his tricorn and dipped his head at Isaac. Light hair, slicked back with pomade, was tied behind his neck. Clean jaw, stark blue eyes, a thin mustache, and a large hawklike nose completed a face that might be handsome except for the smug malevolence pasted upon it. "I offer a trade, Captain."

Isaac ground his teeth together, preferring to punch the man in the jaw rather than deal with him.

"Your brigantine completely unscathed," the Colonel continued, "for Miss Thea Cabot and all her belongings."

If King George himself leapt onto the deck, Isaac couldn't be more shocked. *Thea*? How did this British officer know her and, even more importantly, why was she so valuable to him?

Isaac blew out an impatient sigh. "Who? I know no Thea Cabot, Colonel."

"Come now, Captain. We both know she is on board. It is a fair trade, is it not? Your ship is damaged, your men fewer than mine." He waved a hand over the dozen or so marines he'd brought on board and the dozens more waiting in boats just off the *Avenger*. "I have already won. Hence, I offer you a gift, Captain. A reprieve if you will."

Isaac grimaced, fury at both himself and at Thea bubbling in his gut. "I could have my top shooters pick off your sailors in those boats one by one."

"And *I* could raise a simple hand signal, and the gunner on board the merchantman will rip what's left of your ship to shreds." He grinned, spreading fingers down his long mustache.

"With you on board?"

The colonel shrugged. "He has orders to shoot below deck."

"Then the lady will be harmed."

"Ah ha! You do have her."

Growling, Isaac stiffened his jaw. Could it be that Thea told the truth about her secret correspondence? Why else would the man risk so much to capture her?

"Hand her over now, and I will take her back to my ship and sail away. You have my word."

Fury tightened every muscle. The woman had done nothing but cause him trouble. Now this?

"And why should I trust you?" Isaac's pointed gaze wandered over the armed marines standing behind the colonel. "You could fight me and my men and *possibly* take my ship, regardless. Though I dare you to try."

A speck of fear appeared in the man's eyes.

"I care not for your pathetic privateer, Captain. Nor do I wish for any unnecessary deaths on the part of these merchantmen whom I have commissioned to assist me. Besides, I fight my battles on land, not on sea."

Thea stood at the bottom of the companionway, listening, or *trying* to listen over Ruth's nervous rambling behind her. The minute that snakelike hiss of a voice slid to her ears, she knew who had boarded the ship. But why was Colonel Barstow searching for her? Surely the man would not go to such lengths for a silly infatuation, one which she had spurned the past year. He must know she carried an important Patriot correspondence. But how? She'd destroyed everything of her father's before she'd left Savannah.

Her breath came hard and fast, perspiration moistened her neck as every nerve was strung tight. Isaac's ship was important to him. She'd gathered that much in their brief conversations. While she, on the other hand, was obviously *not*, something she'd known all too well these past four years.

She squeezed the edges of the ladder so tightly her fingers began to ache. Any minute now, Isaac would send one of his men to fetch her and her belongings and hand her over to that fiend of a Redcoat. And then she would not only be in enemy hands, but she'd fail her father and, more importantly, her country.

No sense in waiting for Isaac's answer, for she knew what it would be. Hence, turning, she gripped Ruth's shoulders just as Isaac's voice filtered below.

"Then you may do your worst, Colonel. For I am not handing Miss Cabot over to you."

The words jumbled into nonsense in her mind. Surely, she had misheard him.

"Ruth, go to our cabin and shut the door. Don't come out until you deem it safe to do so."

"But where are you going, Miss? Why not go with the colonel? He's always been kind to you."

"Most unfortunate," Thea heard the colonel say. "Then you have left me no recourse, Captain. In the end, I will have both your ship and Miss Cabot."

The eerie chime of several swords being plucked from their sheaths sent a tremble through Thea.

"Let us find out," Isaac returned with authority.

The ring of blade striking blade and the crack of a pistol filled the humid air.

"Do as I say, Ruth!" Thea shot over her shoulder as she rushed down the companionway.

"Yes, Miss, But what will you…"

Ruth's voice faded beneath the sounds of battle as Thea dashed down the hallway to the port side of the ship where she remembered a ladder ascending to a small hatch on the quarterdeck. She had but one chance to do this or all was lost.

Lord, I know I haven't spoken to you in a while, but I sure could use your help now.

The air was full of the incessant hiss and clangor of flying cutlasses. along with the blood-curdling sounds of battle—shouts, moans of agony, pistol shots, and horrifying screams—all sending Thea's nerves into a cyclone.

Reaching the ladder, she poked her head above deck. Sailors mobbed the ship, punching, shooting, slicing each other in a ferocious sight that nearly froze her with fear. She sought for Isaac and found him engaged with two British sailors.

No one was looking her way. No one would notice her. Rising onto the deck, she darted for the railing, took a quick glance at the distance to shore…a mere twenty yards. And then hiking up her skirts, she leapt over the railing and dropped into the water.

A strange sound met Isaac's ears. The sound of water splashing. Yet he'd not seen any sailors tossed overboard. Perhaps the colonel intended to surprise him from behind with more men creeping up his port side.

With a forward slash, he quickly felled his opponent, dashed to the railing, and glanced over the side. Thea, skirts floating atop the swampy water, swam toward shore!

What was the madcap woman doing now?

Movement caught his eye, and he shifted his gaze to a British sailor who must have come from one of the boats, swimming her way.

Blast it all!

The man would surely overtake her and bring her to the colonel. Or worse.

A sailor charged him, blade raised, and he met him with his own. Their swords clanged together back and forth in a macabre dance of death.

The rest of his men were engaged, fighting well like he'd taught them, but no matter their skill or ferocity, the marines kept pouring over the sides from boats below. Several men on both sides had fallen to the deck with bloody wounds. Still, Isaac continued his parry with the sailor, pushing him back against the bulkhead. Finally flinging the sword from his hand with a flip of his own, he knocked him out with the hilt. He'd once thought he'd fight to the death to save his ship. But what of Thea? How could he leave her defenseless against that soldier?

His precious brigantine or Thea?

Beside him, his first mate ran his blade through his opponent, and the man dropped to the deck.

"Mr. Hastings."

"Aye, Cap'n," he puffed out between heavy breaths.

"You have command."

Hasting's expression folded in confusion as he stared at Isaac.

"Save the *Avenger* at all costs. I'll meet you in Baltimore."

And before Mr. Hastings could respond, Isaac sheathed his blade, removed his boots, put one hand on the railing, and leapt into the water.

Chapter Six

Grabbing her sodden—and heavy—skirts, Thea trudged onto the sand, out of breath and out of strength. But she couldn't stop now. She must quickly dive into the brush and hide herself before anyone noticed where she had gone.

The sounds of battle raged behind her, sending a shiver through her for the men that would die this day. She lifted up a prayer for Ruth and Isaac to be safe. And for all the men. War was such a horrid affair. One she'd rather not take part in, but unfortunately, one in which she now found herself thrust into the middle.

Forcing herself to run, she slipped into a grove of trees and dared take a breath at having succeeded in her escape.

Until a rustling sound jerked her gaze to the right where a British soldier, red coat sopping wet and knife in hand, grinned at her like a panther about to catch a week's worth of meals.

She froze. Her heart seized. Was this to be her end, then?

A sudden flash came out of the brush. The hilt of a sword crashed down on the poor soldier's head, and his eyes rolled back before he collapsed in a heap to the dirt.

Isaac, blade raised, shirt open to the wind, smiled at her. Smiled? "Going somewhere?"

"What are you…" But she didn't have time to finish before he took her by the arm and dragged her farther into the forest.

"Hush," was all he said for several minutes as they tromped through sandy soil and prickly underbrush. Finally, he halted, released her, and stared longingly through the trees back toward his ship.

The sounds of battle had ceased, but what that meant, she could not say.

A look of deep sorrow tugged at his features before he swung back around and began walking. "We must get as far away as we can before the colonel finds you gone."

Rage strangled his voice, rage and sorrow. Why had he rescued her? Why had he given up his ship? So many questions rumbled through her mind, but she dared not ask any of them.

In truth, she was thankful for Isaac's sudden appearance. She'd either be dead or in the hands of the British right now if not for him. Even if she'd escaped unscathed, she had no idea how she would have travelled to Baltimore from wherever they were without any money or food.

Hours passed.

Thea's feet ached, and her wet petticoats chafed her skin through her stockings. "Stop, please." She tugged on him. "I cannot go another step."

Scanning the area, he led her to a fallen log to sit, then took a seat on a boulder across from her.

Birds fluttered about in the branches above them as the sun, high in the sky now, pierced the canopy with arrows of golden light. A lizard scrambled across the fallen leaves carpeting the forest floor, while humidity draped everything in a blanket of moisture. Still, Isaac wouldn't look at her, wouldn't speak to her. He merely sat, leaning forward, elbows on his knees, and stared at his bare feet as if they held the answers to all his problems. Strands of dark hair the color of earthy loam hung about a jaw strung so tight, she thought it would burst.

"Where are you taking me?" she finally asked.

Blazing eyes met hers. "When did you learn to swim? You were always afraid of water."

Thea batted a fly away. "Fear was not a luxury one could afford after the British took over Savannah." Her tone spiked with more fury than she intended. "Why are you so angry at me?"

His brows collided, and he gave a sordid chuckle. "How can you even ask that? I've lost my brigantine. Or didn't you notice? All because of you and your foolish antics, I've lost a ship I slaved for three years to acquire. And you come back into my life, and just like that it is all gone like a puff of smoke." He fingered a ring on his finger, turning it this way and that.

"Humph," she retorted, stiffening, "similar to how I lost everything when you left me at the altar."

He breathed a heavy sigh and rubbed the back of his neck. "Why is that colonel after you?"

"I'll answer your question when you answer mine." She lifted her chin.

His jaw clenched yet again as eyes as sharp as any sword pierced her. "A small trading post named Redding. It's not far."

"And then?"

"Answer my question first."

A spire of sunlight pierced the canopy above, landing on Isaac's shoulder as if God were trying to get his attention.

"I've already told you, Captain. I carry an important message for the Patriots in Baltimore."

"If this message is so secret, how did the colonel know about it and that you were the one who carried it?"

Throwing modesty to the wind, Thea leaned over and removed her shoes. "Honestly, I do not know. I mean, I know the man, but I don't believe he suspected my father of being a Patriot."

"Your father?"

Thea fingered the black ribbon around her wrist. "Yes. He took information he got from his British friends, coded it, and passed it along to contacts in Baltimore."

Isaac gave an incredulous huff. "I had no idea." He paused before adding, "How is he? Your father?"

"Dead." Though she thought she'd long since mourned him, tears burned in her eyes.

"I'm sorry, Thea."

The look he gave her, one of true care and sympathy, only deepened the wound in her heart. She snapped her gaze away.

Isaac dragged a hand through his damp hair and shook his head. "I always thought he was a Tory. And you, as well."

Leaning over, Thea rubbed her aching feet, only then noticing the cuts and bruises on Isaac's from their trek through the forest.

"I was at first, but my father convinced me otherwise." A breeze squeezed through the trees and wafted over her, cooling her moist skin.

"If what you say is true…." Isaac eased a piece of parchment from within his waistcoat and gently opened it. Even from where she sat, Thea could see the water had done its damage across it. "I fear the message is useless now. I forgot I had it on me when I dove into the bay."

She couldn't help but grin. "Never fear, I have a copy."

His eyes narrowed with both suspicion and confusion.

"Wrapped in leather, sealed in beeswax, and sewed into the folds of my petticoat."

A slight grin curved the right side of his lips. "You *have* truly changed." He nodded toward her skirts. "Don't you want to make sure it survived your swim?"

Why was he so anxious to see it? Perhaps he intended to steal it from her again. "I'm sure it did."

Several moments passed in silence, save for the warble of birds and flutter of leaves. Thea could hardly believe the turn of events. She could hardly believe that instead of safely arriving in Baltimore, she found herself in the forest with the one man she had hoped never to see again. Would she ever fulfill her mission? If Isaac was the type of man to leave his intended alone at the altar without a word, surely he would think nothing of abandoning her at some backwoods outpost.

Finally, he stood. "Let us be on our way."

"You didn't answer me. What are you to do with me after Redding?" Thea slipped on her shoes, wincing at the pain.

"I'll take you to Baltimore to deliver your message."

She stared at him. He'd once promised to love and protect her forever. She would never trust him again. "Why the change of heart, *Captain*?"

"I'm not doing it for you. I'm doing it for our country," he snapped back, his anger returning.

Of all the nerve. *His* anger? He might have lost a ship, but she had lost her reputation, her future, and any hope of happiness.

Redding was just as Isaac remembered. A one-road town with a trading post, horse stable, schoolhouse, grist mill, several stores, a tavern, and a ferry across the Pasquotank river. One glance over his shoulder told him that even though Thea had not once complained during their travels, she was beyond exhaustion. She had looked so beautiful sitting on that log with her damp auburn hair tumbling in curls over her shoulder and her forest green eyes, cheeks blushed with exertion, and the freckles on her pert little nose flaring. He found his anger toward her abating ever so slightly, especially after discovering she truly was a Patriot.

But he would not, *could not* allow himself to be lured into her charms again. Especially not after she cost him his brigantine, the only thing that mattered to him. Just thinking of that loss twisted the knife already plunged into his heart. Hence, he kept his thoughts on that fact as they'd trekked through the marshy woods. It helped. At least until he now saw her looking so bedraggled and miserable.

He led the way to the tavern, ignoring the strange looks they received from the townsfolk, then mounted the steps and opened the door, allowing Thea to enter.

"Help you folks?" An older gentleman entered the foyer from a door to the side. He studied them through bifocals perched on his nose. "You ain't traders, I see that." His gaze dipped to Isaac's bare feet. "What brings you to our town?"

"We need two rooms for the night, Sir, if you please," Isaac said. "And do you have a laundress to tend to the lady's clothing by morning?"

"Private rooms, did you say? I only got two of them, and they'll cost you a pretty penny." He raised thick gray eyebrows.

"I can pay." Isaac pulled out a pouch from his trouser pocket.

Emitting a huff, the clerk moved to the desk, flipped open a book, dipped a pen in ink, and handed it to Isaac. "That'll be ten shillings for the rooms and another five for a meal."

Isaac poured five gold coins onto the desk.

The clerk's eyes widened so fast his bifocals slid to the tip of his nose. "Ain't seen doubloons like this for a while."

Isaac grinned. "Of more value than your Continentals, I'd say."

The man hurriedly scooped up the coins, then glanced at Thea. "Mrs. Crandle would be happy to attend to your needs, Miss. I'll have her sent to your room right away." Then facing Isaac, he asked, "What did you say brought you to Redding, Mister…Mister…"

"Mr. Preston, and this is Miss Cabot. And we'll need a horse on the morrow."

"Grates down at the stables be happy to help you out."

Isaac nodded, anxious to get to his room, dry out his clothes, and rest. Especially anxious for the lady to do so as well.

But the nosy clerk continued talking. "A might untoward the lady traveling without female escort, wouldn't you say?" Bloodshot eyes traveled over Thea in disdain *or desire*, he couldn't tell. How he hated putting her reputation at risk, but there was naught to be done about it. "Our rooms, Sir?"

The man frowned. "Supper is served at six in the dining room. Millie!" He called for a maid who scurried into the room.

During the exchange, Thea had slunk into the shadows of the foyer, pretending to examine the divots carved into a side table laden with vase and flowers. Now, as Millie directed them up the stairs to their room, she said not a word.

"I'll call upon you at six for supper," Isaac said as Millie opened Thea's door and allowed her inside.

She waved at him over her shoulder but said nothing. Not even a thank you.

Thea had never been so tired. Nor so filthy and covered with perspiration. Her salt-encrusted gown was stiff, her hair hung in sticky strands, and blisters pained her feet. She'd also never been so conflicted. She'd hated Isaac, had loathed him for four long years, but now here he was saving her, helping her. Or perhaps he only assisted her for his country, as he said.

Regardless, by the time the rap sounded on her door at six, Thea had enjoyed a warm bath—brought up in buckets by Millie, who turned out to be a sweet young girl—had taken a two-hour nap, had given her filthy clothing to Mrs. Crandle to wash, and had donned the gown the woman had brought for her to wear in the meantime. The bodice was a bit too tight and the skirts too short, but it felt wonderful to be in clean clothes again. She'd retrieved the coded message and found it had not been water damaged at all, so she'd tucked it safely inside the pockets of her new attire.

In truth, it was her stomach that finally convinced her to dine with Isaac, for she'd been hesitant to spend any more time with him than she must. But hunger gnawed at her insides until she believed she could eat the four-poster bed in her chamber. Hence, she moved to the door and opened it. Against everything within her, her heart leapt at the sight of him, just like it used to. *Gah!*

Though he wore the same clothes, he had cleaned up nicely. He'd combed his hair and tied it behind his neck, and an attempt had been made to shave, though a light stubble still peppered his jaw. The stains on his shirt had been scrubbed out, his waistcoat was buttoned, and a clean cravat graced his neck. He must have gone out, for his breeches were stuffed within a pair of new leather boots, while the ever-present sword hung at his side.

She tried to hide her intake of breath, but, thankfully, he didn't seem to notice as his golden eyes traveled over her, a delight that surprised her sparkling within them.

He cleared his throat. "You appear to be quite refreshed, Miss Cabot." He extended his arm. "Shall we?"

Ignoring him, Thea closed her door and proceeded down the hallway to the stairs. Only a few other patrons graced the small dining room, along with a group of what looked like fur traders, from their ragged attire, hefting glasses of foamy ale at a table in the corner.

"I'm surprised you agreed to dine with me, The…Miss Cabot," Isaac said as he sat across from her. Lantern light carved his face, making him more handsome than ever.

"If I were not so famished, I would not have, Captain." She attempted to soften her tone. "However, I am grateful for the room, the clean attire, and this repast."

"Ah, a thank you!" He snorted. "But not for saving your life?" He leaned toward her, one incriminating brow arched.

Thea flattened her lips. "As you so ardently expressed, your motive was purely in getting my message to Baltimore."

"Yet, at the time, I did not know you still had the message." He leaned back in his chair, a teasing grin on his lips.

His statement incited a raging battle between her thoughts and feelings—a battle she'd rather not fight at the moment. Thankfully, it was interrupted by a tavern maid slamming two mugs of ale onto the table, followed by platters of food, the savory scent of which made Thea's stomach lurch—a Cheshire pie filled with pork, apples, and spices, fresh biscuits, and corn pudding.

They ate in silence, both of them gobbling up the food as if they hadn't eaten in a week. The traders in the corner grew louder and louder with each round of ale as a few more patrons entered the dim room, lit by lanterns hanging from the rafters above.

Thea cast furtive glances at Isaac, longing to ask him the question burning on her heart. Why had he left his ship to save her? Particularly when he hadn't known she had the secret message.

Setting down her fork, she sat back in her chair, grabbed a wayward lock of her hair and spun it around her finger. "Where did you come by so vast a fortune, Captain, that you so easily can pay for private rooms, a meal, and a horse?"

Isaac scooped one last spoonful of pudding into his mouth and winked. "Privateering has been quite lucrative."

"Yet, as firstborn, you were to inherit your father's plantation, the land and produce of which surely amounted to more than anything you can make as a pirate. Not to mention the prestige of a place in society."

Huffing, he cocked his head, lantern light hardening the sheen on his eyes. "It's privateering, not piracy. And there are some things worth more than money."

Some things worth more than her. She shifted her gaze away, not wanting to expose her pain. "I assume we leave first thing in the morning?"

Isaac held up a palm to silence her, his body instantly stiffening. Before she could protest, he tossed down his serviette, leapt to his feet, grabbed her hand, and yanked her from her seat. Glancing about the room, he darted for a door to the left, dragging her behind him.

"What are you—"

"Hush!" He raced through the door and dashed into the darkness.

Her arm stung where he clasped her. Her feet began to ache again. "Have you gone mad?"

Halting, Isaac swung her to face him and slammed the palm of his hand over her mouth. "Quiet! He's here."

She merely stared at him, eyes shifting between his.

"Barstow," he whispered. "I heard his voice asking about us from the front desk."

Air seized in her throat.

"Will you be quiet?" he asked.

She nodded, and he removed his palm.

"How could you hear that from where we were?" she whispered. "I heard no such thing."

"I have excellent hearing, Miss Cabot. Now, come."

She resisted his pull. "How do I know this is not some trick?"

His nostrils flared. "To what end?"

That, she didn't know. But she grew weary of trusting a man who had proven himself untrustworthy.

The back door of the tavern slammed open. Light from inside spilled upon a man dressed in plain attire, the features of his face hidden in the shadows. Barstow? She couldn't tell. Whoever it was, he started for them.

This time when Isaac pulled on her arm, she followed him, her heart clambering up her throat.

Moments later, after racing through the mud behind several buildings, they slipped through the back door of a large barn. The scent of horseflesh, hay, and droppings assailed her. Neighs and whinnies announced their arrival, but whoever managed the place must have stepped out.

Isaac quickly poured several coins from his pouch onto the desk, grabbed the lantern and a bridle hanging from a nail on the wall, and quietly led out the first horse from its stall.

Boots slapped the mud outside the building, and Thea thought her heart would burst through her chest. They had only seconds before the colonel, if that's who it was, would enter and find them.

Isaac shared a nervous glance with her, then slipped the bridle onto the horse, doused the lantern, and quietly led the mare out the opposite end of the stable.

No sooner had he closed the door than the colonel's voice bellowed from within. "Hold up there! In the name of His Majesty, King George!"

Before she knew what was happening, Isaac grabbed her by the waist and hoisted her onto the horse's bare back. The mare snorted and shifted, nearly jostling Thea to the ground.

Grabbing her mane, Isaac was about to haul himself up behind Thea when the stable door creaked open.

"That's far enough!" A voice emerged from the dark mist, a voice that even when friendly had always slid over Thea with the charm of a snake. The man himself stepped into the light of a lantern hanging outside the stables, pistol in hand.

Isaac froze.

"Raise your hands, Captain Preston, and back up toward me, or I'll shoot you where you stand."

The horse pawed the ground, seemingly as anxious to get away as Thea was. The eerie trill of a night heron rang through the trees. Her blood raced. She could kick the horse and possibly gallop off to safety. But how could she leave Isaac?

Isaac, his back toward the colonel, plucked a knife from his belt and hid it alongside his forearm as he lifted his hands.

Colonel Barstow stepped closer, his vile gaze traveling over Thea before he refocused on Isaac. "Now, back up, Captain. All I want is the woman."

In a movement too fast to see, Isaac spun and hurled the knife through the air. It struck the colonel's arm. He let out a yelp and bent over. The pistol fired. Isaac grabbed the horse's mane and flung himself up behind Thea. Then taking the reins in one hand and wrapping his other arm around her, he kicked the horse, and the animal took off in a gallop.

Chapter Seven

Trees, branches, and brambles sped past Thea as fast as her mind and heart raced. Wind, ripe with the scents of forest loam and spring flowers, whipped her face and hair as she tried to sort through what had just occurred. But she found both her thoughts in a knot and her heart in a twist due to Isaac's warm body pressed against her and his strong arm keeping her close. His unique scent stirred memories she'd rather forget. She'd forgotten how her body responded to his touch, and those sensations now threatened to melt the shield of hatred and animosity she'd erected around her heart.

Yet he had saved her life once again and in a rather heroic way. She'd never seen anyone toss a knife with such precision, nor be so calm while facing death. The young Isaac she'd known had grown up a pampered son of a plantation owner with very little skill for anything save ordering servants about, managing books, and playing a good game of whist.

The horse maintained a fast pace down the wooded trail, her heavy pants filling the air, her hooves slapping the moist dirt one minute, then splashing through a bog the next. How Isaac kept his balance without a saddle was beyond Thea, though she found herself thankful for his steady strength.

Moonlight sliced through leaves and branches, creating ghostly shafts of eerie silver as they continued to speed down the wooded trail. Was Colonel Barstow following them? But of course he was. The man was not the type to give up easily, evidenced by how he'd continued to pursue her in Savannah even after she'd repeatedly rejected his advances.

Finally, Isaac slowed the horse to a canter and then to a walk, his heavy breaths wafting over her. She tried to wiggle from his embrace, but he kept his hold firm. Dark clouds quickly swallowed up the moonlight, and the smell of rain stung the air.

"Do you know where we are?" she finally asked. "Will the colonel find us?"

"I know where we are heading, and no, not if I can help it." Isaac's voice came out raspy, pained.

She wanted to turn her head to see why, but that would put their faces but inches from each other, and she was already having trouble keeping her wits about her.

Warm horseflesh moistened her skirts with each bunch and roll of the animal's muscles beneath her. A low rumble of thunder quaked the forest. Soon they emerged from the trees onto a meadow, though it was hard to tell how far it extended in the darkness.

"We need to find a place to rest the horse," Isaac said. "*And* us."

She quite agreed, especially since light raindrops began to fall, tapping the ground and creating a nerve-wracking cadence on leaves.

Isaac nudged the horse into a canter once again as they headed across the meadow.

Thunder bellowed, louder this time, followed by a streak of lightning that lit a building in the distance. Raindrops pelted them, stinging Thea's face.

No light emanated from the house or the barn as Isaac brought the horse to a halt before what she could now see was a broken-down stable. Swinging his leg over the horse, he slid to the ground and attempted to reach up for her, but instead backed away with a moan.

Panic gripped her. The rain continued its relentless beating until she could hear nothing but its violent tapping. Water soaked through her gown, chilling her. Still, Isaac remained a distant shadow.

Wiggling to get her other leg over the side of the horse, Thea leapt down, landed with a jarring thud, and rushed to him.

"Isaac, are you all right?"

"Yes." But his moan indicated otherwise. "Let's get the horse in the barn." Another groan filled the air as he struggled to open the door and lead the horse within.

Thea followed and shut it behind her, closing them in darkness except for a few holes in the roof.

While Isaac settled the horse, Thea felt around the front wall for a lantern and found one hanging on a hook. Then remembering she had transferred the flint and steel to the pockets in her new attire, she retrieved them and soon a circle of light shoved the darkness aside.

A thud and a groan echoed through the barn. "Isaac?"

No response, save the patter of rain on the roof and the hiss of wind against the walls. A light breeze swept over her sodden gown, causing her to shiver.

Holding the lantern high, Thea crept across the hay-strewn floor, nerves tight.

Isaac sat, propped up against a stall, hand pressed on his shoulder and the horse nudging him with her nose.

Thea dashed to him and set down the lantern. Blood oozed from between his fingers. "You're shot!"

Isaac blinked, forcing back the dizziness threatening to send him into a black void. Before him, Thea's beautiful, yet worried face, circled in his vision. He must have lost more blood than he realized. Blast it all! How was he to protect Thea and get her message to the Patriots in Baltimore now?

"I'll be all right, Thea. Just allow me to rest a minute." He hoped to encourage her, to stop her from having one of her usual nervous fits.

But instead, she leapt to her feet, took the lantern, and returned several minutes later with a bucket of water, rags, a knife, and a cupful of crushed flowers. Isaac had no time to inquire what she was doing before she had removed his coat, sliced open his shirt, and examined the bloody opening. "The shot went clean through you," she announced as she cleaned the area front and back and pressed the crushed flowers into the wound. Rather forcefully, he might add.

"What are those?" he finally asked, struggling to speak through the pain. "Must you press so hard?"

"Ah, I thought you privateer captains were brave." Her tone was playful.

"Brave, aye, impervious to pain, nay. Besides, you seem to be enjoying this more than you should."

She gave him a sly look as she continued to press the flowery paste into his wound. "This is chamomile. I saw some by the front door when we first got here. It's good for healing."

"Ouch."

"Hush now, Captain." Taking the knife, she tore the rags into long strips, then wrapped his shoulder and tied them together. "Thank God the bleeding has stopped."

The horse leaned down and nudged Isaac once again.

"Yes, girl, I know," he said. "I think she wants some hay."

"I'll get some." Thea started to rise, but he took her hand in his.

"Thank you. When did you learn to tend wounds and not…"

One of her brows lifted as a sparkle appeared in her eyes. "And not faint?"

He smiled.

"There were many wounded in Savannah after the British…" Slamming her lips shut, she looked away.

He nodded. Of course. He hadn't considered how difficult her life had been after the British had stormed in and taken over. Not to mention the ensuing battles when the Patriots attempted to recover the city.

She'd always been such a skittish little mouse, given to high nerves and easily distraught over every unexpected turn of events. Her main concerns had centered around affording the latest fashions and attending society functions. But this woman before him now showed more courage, more ability to react well under fearful circumstances than some of his sailors.

Tugging from his hand, she rose and soon returned with a skirt full of hay and a bucket of water, which she poured into a trough nearby.

Pushing against the dirt with his good hand, Isaac struggled to rise. The barn spun, and he gripped a nearby post.

"What are you doing?" Thea asked. "You need to rest."

"We are both wet," he said as he closed the stall door to keep the mare inside. "We need to make a bed of hay and try to get some sleep."

Picking up the lantern, Thea backed away. "I cannot stay in here with you. Haven't you ruined my reputation enough?"

He winced at the pain in her tone. "There's nothing to be done for it. I'll keep my distance, I promise. You sleep, and I'll stand guard."

"You will do no such thing in your condition, Captain." She huffed and twisted a damp curl dangling about her shoulder. "We shall both stay awake until the rain ceases and you are recovered."

Egad, but she looked beautiful with her damp curls cascading over her overly tight gown, her eyes the color of forest moss, her cheeks pinked, her lips…

Isaac swallowed. She was right. The storm prevented them from further travel, and he didn't trust himself to protect her until his dizziness passed. "Very well, let's find a corner to hide in and some hay to keep warm and then try to rest."

Nodding, she approached, handed him his coat, and assisted him to stand, then led him farther into the shadowy barn. He didn't need the help, but he had no desire to free himself from her gentle touch.

"Looks like whoever once lived in the house and kept this barn has been gone awhile," she said. "Many lost their homes in this horrid war." Turning a corner at the end of the stalls, she gestured to a pile of loose hay, set down the lantern, and helped him to sit. Then, plopping down a few yards away, she leaned back and sighed.

The woman muddled his mind. One minute her tone was full of spite, the next she was tending his wounds with concern.

They lay there in silence for several minutes, listening to the drum of rain on the roof and the occasional growl of thunder.

Finally, she huffed. "Why did you give up your ship for me? Had your men already won?"

A question he continued to ask himself as well. "I saw the British soldier pursuing you, and I knew he would do you harm."

She gave a ladylike snort. "Gah! With your ship still in danger?"

Pain radiated through his shoulder, matching the sudden pain in his heart. "Listen, Thea.

I'm truly sorry for leaving you."

"At the altar, you mean?" Her tone dripped with venom. "Standing there like a fool?"

Isaac shrank at her fury, not in fear, but in shame.

"Could you not at least have informed me the day before?"

"I'm sorry, Thea. I was on board Captain Jamison's privateer and had no way to contact you. He had to leave port suddenly, leaving me unable to even send a message."

Her growl matched that of the thunder above them. "A poor excuse for a gentleman." She sat up, spearing him with her gaze, the freckles on her nose wrinkling in fury. "Do you know what you did to me? No man would even look my way after that. No courters came calling, save Colonel Barstow later on. All of society whispered about me behind raised hands. I am unwanted, a spinster, and I will never have the family I longed for." She sank back into the hay, her angry tone distorted into one of pain, *real* pain.

Isaac closed his eyes, guilt and shame ripping his soul. He had felt like a cad at the time, but he'd soon got caught up in the excitement of privateering and those feelings had dissipated. "I was the worst sort of rogue. There's no excuse for what I did, Thea."

"Then why?" Eyes brimming with angry tears shot his way. "Why? We had a great future. I thought you loved me." A sob shuddered through her.

"I did!" *I do*. In truth, now that he saw her again, he realized he had never stopped.

"There must have been something wrong with me, something that made you run."

Struggling to sit, he inched closer and reached for her hand, but she snapped it away. "There's nothing wrong with you." He released a heavy sigh, listening to the rain march across the roof. How could he explain something he wasn't sure he understood himself? "It was me, Thea. The closer I came to getting married, the more my future rose to haunt me. I couldn't see myself tied down to a life running a plantation like my father, a life of boredom, monotony, landlocked."

"So, you find me boring, is that it?" she snapped.

"No. Far from it. Being married, running a plantation, it was not the life I wanted. I craved adventure, purpose, so when Captain Jamison asked me to join him in privateering, I couldn't resist. If I could have taken you with me, I would have."

"You never gave me the choice."

Twisting the ring on his finger, he sighed. At the time, he knew she'd never agree to an adventurous life, not timid, insecure Thea. Nor did he wish to put her in danger. In truth, he'd been selfish and cruel, putting his desire for adventure and purpose above Thea, above even God.

"Admit it, Captain. Your ship and your privateering were more important than me."

He looked her way, but she stared at the hay, chin lowered. "At the time, yes. But I am not that man anymore. I hope you can forgive me."

A tear spilled down her cheek, a diamond sparkling in the lantern light, and he longed to wipe it away. If only he could wipe away the damage he'd done just as easily.

"I don't know if I can forgive you." She swiped the moisture from her face.

His shoulder throbbed, and he pressed a hand over it, hard, if only to punish himself for the pain he caused this dear lady. "I hope you can forgive me someday, for your sake, not for mine."

"If you mean that the Scriptures say God will not forgive me if I don't forgive others, I will admit I'm a bit angry at the Almighty at the moment, for I did nothing to deserve the fate which befell me."

Isaac's heart shriveled. Thea had always been a Godfearing woman, knowledgeable of Scripture, and faithful to the Word. He had loved that about her, for at the time, he had a rebellious spirit and needed her stability to keep him on the right road.

"Thea, don't give up on God. It was I who betrayed you, not Him."

She huffed, her jaw stiffening. "Your betrayal was only the beginning of the disasters God has allowed."

He wanted to ask her what disasters, but she stood, brushed the hay from her skirts, and moved to lean back against the stall wall. "You speak of God, yet you were never one to follow Him."

Isaac frowned. "Aye, but as it turns out, Captain Jamison was a very Godly man. He held studies of the Scriptures in his cabin every night, a mandatory event for his officers." Isaac pictured the aged man reading the Bible, his eyes glittering as if it were worth more than gold. He had such a deep love for Jesus, it poured out of his every word. "I learned much from him and have since repented of my sins. And they were many. The most egregious one was leaving you as I did."

She cast him a skeptical look. "Yet you never returned to apologize."

"I couldn't, Thea. The British had taken over Savannah by then."

"You could have found a way." Her voice was ice.

The rain lessened to a light rapping as the wind ceased its howling. Shivering, Thea hugged herself.

Struggling to rise, Isaac stood, approached her, and handed her his coat. "Here, put this on. I can't have you getting sick."

She waved him away. "I have no need of your chivalry, Captain."

"But you have need of warmth. Take it, The…Miss Cabot. I insist."

"You are not in charge here on land, *Captain*, and not in charge of me." Still, she took the coat and flattened her lips. "So that's why you gave up your ship to save me. Guilt. Some sort of twisted recompense."

Was that true? Isaac had no idea. "In truth, Thea, I saw you in trouble and didn't even think about what I was doing."

She huffed.

Gave up his ship? The words speared deep in his soul. He hadn't quite faced that reality. Didn't want to face it. Hopefully, Hastings and his men had defeated the British and were now on their way to Baltimore. If not, he had lost the most important thing in his life, his purpose, his reason for living.

"Let's get some sleep. We have a long way to go tomorrow to get to Norfolk."

She nodded, shifted her gaze away, and lowered once again to the hay as far away from him as she could.

Finally, after at least an hour, he heard her drift off to sleep, but sleep did not welcome him in its embrace. His mind and emotions were spinning uncontrollably between being furious at Thea for the loss of his ship and feeling guilty for the agony he'd caused her. Several times, he rose to check on the mare and look outside for any intruders heading their way. During those times, he'd sit and watch Thea sleep. She'd put on his coat and curled up like a purring cat sinking into the soft hay. Wisps of hair lay across her creamy cheek like auburn filagree as her chest rose and fell with the deep breaths of slumber. Occasionally, she'd mutter, her expression scrunching in the most adorable way as if she lived another life in her dreams.

And he began to wonder how he could have ever left such a treasure. He'd been such a young buck, ready to conquer the world and make a name for himself that he hadn't considered the trail of misery he would leave behind. And now Thea had stolen his life from him as he had stolen hers. A fair punishment, he supposed. Yet he couldn't help but dream that someday he'd sail as a privateer again.

In the meantime, he must protect this precious lady, and though he doubted she would ever return his love—a love he no longer deserved—he must fix things between them. He had not only broken her heart, but he had pushed her away from God, a far worse condition than being jilted.

"Oh, Father, I'm so sorry. Help me to make it up to her. Help me to protect her at all costs."

Chapter Eight

Once again, Thea found herself on horseback, only this time she sat behind Isaac, which made her no less uncomfortable than before. In truth, far worse, for she had to wrap her arms around his waist and press against him to keep from falling. Hence, she felt the roll and bunch of the muscles in his back, was flooded with his unique masculine scent, and enjoyed the tickle of his hair brushing her face.

They'd not found a saddle in the barn, forcing her to once again ride astride the horse. How indecent! Yet, after spending the night under the same roof with Isaac without chaperone, what did it matter? Still, she'd awoken to the sight of him standing guard at the entrance to the stall where they'd slept, giving her a chance to study him. Determination coupled with uneasiness rode on his brow as if he faced an army of hostiles and yet knew exactly how to defeat them. Brown breeches, stuffed into leather boots clung tightly to his muscular legs, where a sword hung idly from his hip. Dark hair, normally tied behind his neck, fell loose over his shoulders. His shirt hung in tatters over his left arm, where a bloody bandage marked his sacrifice to save her.

Who was this man? So much about him—his voice, his expressions, the tiny divot in the cleft of his chin, the way his lips curved on one side when he was amused—told her he was the same Isaac. Yet, he wasn't the same. The fun-loving, pampered boy had become a warrior, a champion, and by his own admission, a man of God.

Still, she couldn't trust him. He'd apologized for ruining her life, but was he sincere? Or was his selfless heroism a mere act? To what end, she could not guess. Four years ago he'd done something that had gone against everything she'd believed about him. Perhaps he would do so again. Perhaps she was the worst judge of character. Perhaps she was just a silly woman allowing her emotions and her body's reaction to him to dig yet another grave into which she would fall.

Isaac said little as he kept the horse moving at a rapid pace. The lush foliage of Virginia—for surely they had left North Carolina behind by now—passed her in various shades of green and brown, shifting from forests to meadows to prickly shrubs as the horse clomped over firm soil one minute, then sloshed through marshes the next. Fortunately, the sun crossed a cloudless sky, warming Thea and leeching the remaining moisture from her gown.

Ever so often, Isaac would halt the horse and turn about to look behind them. He'd sit for several minutes, listening carefully, no doubt for horse hooves, wagon wheels, or the sound of human voices.

"Do you think he's following us?" she asked him on one such occasion.

He swiped a sleeve over his forehead but gave no answer.

"You can be truthful with me. I can handle it."

He smiled and finally met her gaze, their eyes but inches from each other. "I'm starting to believe that, Miss Cabot. And yes, it is doubtful a man like the colonel would give up so easily."

The mare pawed the ground and snorted, and Isaac led her off the path into a shaded wood where a stream danced along merrily as if nothing were wrong with the world. If only that were so.

Dismounting with ease, he reached up for her and groaned as he placed her on the ground. "We'll rest here a moment."

"You shouldn't tax your shoulder so." Thea gestured to his wound before kneeling by the creek and bringing scoopfuls of water to her mouth. When she glanced up, Isaac was staring at her, a hint of a smile quirking his lips.

"I never thought to see the day when proper Thea Cabot would drink water in…"

"In such an unladylike way?" Rising, she stiffened her jaw, her anger simmering. "You make it sound as though I was some priggish flower."

He made no reply, merely smiled at her, his gaze soaking her in as if she were that precious flower.

Gah! What a fright she must look—her hair falling about her in tangles, her gown torn and stained, dirt smudging her skin. She spun a wayward lock around her finger, then shoved it behind her ear. What did she care, anyway?

Releasing the reins, Isaac led the horse to the creek. "What happened between you and the colonel?"

"He wished to court me. I had no interest," she said matter-of-factly, not wishing to discuss it with Isaac.

"And I take it he would not accept your refusal?"

She closed her eyes, remembering the countless times the colonel demanded her attentions, insinuating her refusals were but a coquettish game of seduction, impervious to the thought that any woman would deny him. There were times she saw a darkness in his eyes that gave her pause, caused her to never find herself alone with the man.

"As you said, he is not a man to give up easily."

"Hmm. Seems there is more to his obsession than the coded message you carry."

Above her, a pair of warblers danced among the branches of a hackberry tree, singing a happy tune, so at odds with the mood that had descended upon her as they spoke of Barstow.

Squatting by the creek, Isaac cupped water to his mouth. "How do you suppose he found out about your message?"

Thea shook her head. "He must have found some clue among my father's things at our home, though I thought I had destroyed everything." She fingered the black ribbon about her wrist, not wanting to discuss the colonel anymore.

Removing the coat Isaac had given her the night before, she handed it to him. "For when we get to Norfolk. To cover your wound, so we don't draw curious eyes."

"We are at war, my dear." He chuckled but took it. "A bloody wound is not an uncommon sight. Besides, I'm not altogether sure we will meet many people since most of the town was burned to the ground four years past."

Isaac was correct in his assessment of Norfolk, for no sooner did they arrive at the outskirts of the city than nothing but charred buildings, broken fences, loose chickens and pigs, and weed-ridden cobblestone streets met their gaze. Thea had read that over eight hundred structures had been burned, some by the British, but most by the Patriots, who were intent on destroying the city so the British would have no use for it. They started down the worn path, as worn as she was feeling at the moment. What she wouldn't give for a hot meal, a warm bath, and a soft bed.

Thankfully, a group of intact buildings rose in the distance, where surely the port was located. The pounding of hammers and grinding of saws joined the squawk of seabirds and the distant lap of waves as they moved forward, past the scorched skeletons of homes, shops, and warehouses that were once bustling with people going about their day.

Occasionally, they passed structures still standing, while others were being rebuilt by workmen hard at work. A wagon loaded with goods rattled along the road, the driver tipping his hat at them. A woman with three children in tow carried a basket of eggs down the avenue. Young trees reached for the sky past the dark remains of their predecessors. Green gardens sprang up among the blackened soil, proving the resilience of life among death.

A band of bedraggled Patriot troops marched down the road, their leader eyeing them with suspicion.

The sun sank into the western sky, spreading wings of saffron and maroon atop the trees as they entered the newly built Norfolk Port, bustling with shoppers, slaves, merchants, seamen, and sailors. A bell rang. A hawker shouted, "Fresh fish for sale," while a young boy held a stack of papers in his hand and shouted, "War news! Get yer latest news on the war."

Prying eyes cast aspersions on Thea riding astride, though none said a word as Isaac stopped the mare in front of the stables, dismounted, and reached for her.

"Your shoulder, Captain?" Thea grabbed the reins and attempted to swing her leg over the animal as gracefully as possible, but the horse leapt to the side, and she started to fall.

Right into Isaac's arms. He caught her with precision, with strength, and with a bit of glee as a sideways smile curved his lips.

She pushed against his chest. "You can let me go now."

Yet at least another minute passed before he slowly eased her down, so close to him she could feel his heat, and set her feet on the muddy ground. Her blood raced hot in her veins, her body tingled, and she found herself unable to utter a word. He glanced down at her, desire burning in his eyes and something else…something that caused her to push from him and turn aside.

Nay, nay, nay! She would not fall for this man again!

Clearing his throat, he led her inside where he sold the mare for a decent sum and then headed to the tavern for a meal. After the owner wrinkled his nose at their appearance, it took an extra coin in his hands before he allowed them to sit and order supper. Even then, other patrons cast looks of censure at them. One would think Thea would have grown accustomed to tongues wagging behind her back. All due to the man who sat across from her, gulping down his venison pie as if he hadn't a care in the world.

Her pork pottage did not look quite as good. Or smell. But starvation would make lye soap taste like sweet cream, so she took a spoonful.

"What now, Captain?" she asked him in between bites.

He'd been staring at the door, but now glanced her way. "We buy passage on a boat heading to Baltimore. If all goes well, it shouldn't take more than a day or two."

"But isn't the Chesapeake dangerous?"

"No more so than wandering about on land. Besides, there are dozens of tiny inlets where a smaller ship can hide if need be."

She nodded and took a sip of ale. To think she would be in Baltimore in just a few days where she could finally deliver her message to the right people. She could finally honor her father's last wish, along with aiding her new nation's cause.

After their meal, Isaac started for the docks. "Say nothing. Let me do the negotiating."

In truth, she was far too exhausted to argue with him. Besides, this was *his* world, not hers. Darkness had draped a black shroud over the newly erected town, sending most decent citizens inside, while the more ignoble elements of society crawled out like cockroaches. Street lanterns atop poles offered a modicum of light as they traversed the dirt road to the docks.

Though the night was warm, an odd shiver sped down Thea's back as they turned the corner around what surely was a fish warehouse. The scent burned her nose, and she reached up to rub it when a man leapt from behind the building, the tip of his sword pointed straight at Isaac.

Chapter Nine

Isaac didn't have to see the man's face or even hear his voice to know who it was. Colonel Barstow had found them, just as he'd feared. The man might be evil, but he wasn't dumb. He no doubt had discovered where Thea was heading, and he also knew Norfolk would be the best place to procure a boat.

"We meet again, Captain." Barstow pressed the tip of his blade against Isaac's chest, and he knew the man wouldn't hesitate to run him through and steal off with Thea.

Behind Isaac, the lady gasped and started forward, but he held out his arm to keep her back.

"Why can you not leave us be?" she cried.

Barstow released a heavy sigh as if bored. "Ah, my dear. As I've told you many a time, you and I are destined to be together. Besides, I make my final offer, Captain. Your ship for the lady and her message."

Isaac gripped the hilt of his blade, wishing nothing more than to draw it and run this monster through.

"Ah, ah, ah, Captain," Barstow teased, shifting his stance. "Do you truly wish to die for this wench?"

Isaac ground his teeth at the insult to the lady. "You do not have my brigantine, Colonel, so I believe I cannot agree to your bargain." He hoped *and* prayed that was true, for he could not endure the alternative.

"That's where you are wrong, Captain. Your ship, the *Avenger*, is it? sits just past this port at the head of the Chesapeake. With my men in charge, of course."

Isaac blew out a huff. "How would you know such a thing since you've been following us on land?"

"Nay, I rode through the night and made it to this decrepit city of Norfolk this morning, where I had instructed my men to meet me with your ship." He peeked around Isaac at Thea. "Your maid, my dear, has quite the loose tongue. Hence, how I knew where you were going."

"Where is she?" Thea raged. "What have you done with her?"

Colonel Barstow grinned. "Not to worry, my dear. I transferred her to the British merchantman, where she will be quite safe. I always reward loyalty."

Isaac growled, his fingers so tight on the hilt of his blade they ached. In truth, his shoulder ached as well. How was he to fight the man with such a recent wound? And where was Barstow's injury? A coat covered the damage done by Isaac's knife. He grimaced. "Still, there is no proof you have my brigantine. My men rarely lose a battle."

"Pshaw!" The colonel laughed. "Is it proof you require?" He snapped his fingers, and a moment later, a man stepped out from behind the warehouse, shuffled forward, and raised his face to the paltry light of a half-moon.

"Sorry, Cap'n."

"Jakes." Isaac frowned at the sight of his topman.

"He's got the *Avenger*, Cap'n, jist like he says. After you left, the Redcoats were too much fer us. They locked what were left of us alive in the hold an' sailed here."

No ropes bound Jakes's hands. No pistol was pointed at his back. "Why are you here with this fiend?"

Lowering his chin, Jakes shrugged. "He said after I came an' told you the truth, he'd pay me an' set me free. Sorry, Cap'n. It were more money than I ever had. Ye knows I have a sick mum an' little ones to feed."

Indeed. Jakes had always been hardworking and loyal. Isaac could hardly fault him for making a deal with the colonel. But what it meant, what it proved, caused the remainder of his hope to burn into ash. His brigantine was so close, so very close, he could almost feel her shifting deck beneath his feet, hear the thunderous snap of her sails.

And it was all Thea's fault he'd lost her.

Barstow cocked his head. "So, Captain. What'll it be? I truly do not wish to kill you in front of the lady. You have my word that my men and I will abandon your ship the minute I give the signal."

Jakes ambled off to the side but remained, no doubt awaiting his payment.

Something wasn't right. Isaac shook his head. "If what you say is true, why bring only Jakes? Why not bring a group of your marines and simply kill me and force the lady to accompany you?"

The colonel's eyes narrowed. He lowered his blade slightly. "Because you'll find me an honorable man, Captain, unlike you rebels. A successful bargain is always better than unnecessary deaths."

"Yet we are at war, and you are a soldier." Isaac studied his opponent, looking for any duplicity. "Besides, why would you allow one of the most successful privateers to continue preying on your merchantmen?"

The colonel waved a hand through the air. "I shall let the greatest navy in the world deal with you measly privateers. Egad, how much damage can a single lowly privateer accomplish?"

Isaac snorted. "You do not know me, nor my crew, Colonel."

"Perhaps it is *you* who do not know me." He peeked around Isaac once again. "Come along, my love, or do you wish more deaths on your account?"

Isaac heard Thea's footsteps, felt her touch on his back, then on his side as her fingers slid into one of his pockets. She must have given him the secret correspondence. But why?

Then stepping out from behind him, she lifted her chin. "I will go with you, Colonel, if you promise not to harm Captain Preston and return his ship as you have promised."

Isaac hesitated. *Hesitated?* He should shout *NO*. He should never agree to the colonel's bargain. Yet…a storm of thoughts, feelings, desires, and dreams raged through him. If there was any truth to the colonel's words, if his brigantine was within his reach, how could he give it up so easily, along with the privateering adventures that came with it? Especially since Thea was to blame! In truth, they had become his entire world, more important to him than anything.

Thou shalt have no idols before me.

The Holy words, though softly spoken, thundered through him. Aye, Isaac had turned back to God, had committed his life to Him, but he had never fully given Him everything. He had never put Him first. How could he justify such selfishness when Jesus had given His all, His very life, for Isaac?

He searched his mind, his heart, for any possible way to save both Thea and his ship. But there was none.

She's the reason you lost your brigantine in the first place. She deserves this.

No! The truth of the words struck him, but another truth struck him. He'd been a fool to put anything above this precious lady, and a bigger fool to put anything above God.

Tossing out his arm, he nudged Thea behind him, took a step back, and drew his blade. "You'll have to kill me first!"

"So be it." The colonel smiled and thrust his sword toward Isaac.

Thea had seen many men wounded from battle, had tended to many of those wounds, but aside from her brief encounter on board the *Avenger*, she had never witnessed a sword fight firsthand. Nor one in which her fate rested in the outcome. Nor one in which she loved one of the men who might die. Aye, *loved*. She could not deny it now, not when terror strangled her so tightly, she couldn't breathe, couldn't think, couldn't move for fear of losing him.

Isaac met the colonel's blade with a mighty *clang*, then shoved him backward and quickly swooped down upon him, slashing left then right. A look of pain etched across his face. The bullet wound! Surely it pained him terribly. Even worse, it might hinder his ability to fight.

Yet…she snapped her gaze to the colonel. Hadn't Isaac stabbed him with a knife? Perhaps, it would also hinder his ability. She could only hope.

The chime of steel against steel rang through the air, along with grunts and groans as the men battled for their very lives.

And all because of her! Horrified, Thea glanced around for anything with which to help Isaac, anything heavy to strike the colonel with, but nothing but small pebbles and rubble met her gaze. Not that she could do much as both men parried with more skill and speed than she expected.

Growling like a rabid bear, the colonel once again lunged toward Isaac, but Isaac tilted his sword down in defense, then swung it back up, snagging it hilt to hilt with the colonel's. The two men struggled to free their blades, shoving and pushing, and the colonel cursing.

Finally releasing his blade, Isaac backed away, moaning in agony.

The colonel smiled. "Had enough? Not too late to get your brig back."

"But too late for you." With a mighty and pain-filled howl, Isaac raised his sword and shoved the colonel backwards.

Stumbling, the monster flung out his arms for balance. His blade flew from his hand and clanked to the cobblestone path.

Why wasn't Jakes helping his captain? Thea searched the shadows for him, but he was gone.

Then it was up to her! Thea charged forward to grab the blade, but with lightning speed, the colonel gripped the hilt and swung it up…up…

Pain scorched a trail across her side as the sword met its mark.

She dropped to the ground.

"Thea!" Isaac shouted, then growled and rushed the colonel, hacking left, right, sending the man reeling backward.

Thea gripped her side. Warm liquid seeped through her fingers. The metallic smell of blood filled her nose. She could hear the colonel's heavy breaths, could almost feel his panic as Isaac unleashed the full storm of his fury on him.

The sound of a blade crashing to the ground brought her gaze up to see the colonel had tossed his sword and plucked a pistol from his belt. Cocking it, he pointed it at Isaac.

"Coward!" Isaac spat, still holding his blade aloft. "You dishonor yourself, Sir."

The colonel's breath came out fast and hard. "There is no honor in war."

"Only for dishonorable men," Isaac retorted.

The colonel sneered. "Say goodbye, Captain."

"No!" Thea screamed.

Ducking, Isaac rushed toward the colonel, charging him like a bull let loose from its pen.

The pistol fired. The shot echoed across the night sky.

Desperate, Thea blinked to clear her vision as gun smoke stung her nose.

The smoking gun lay on the ground.

The colonel, eyes wide, gripped his stomach and backed away. Blood dripped from Isaac's blade.

Then, after one quick glance toward her, the colonel turned and lumbered into the darkness.

Chapter Ten

The now-familiar sound of water rustling against a hull tugged on Thea, luring her from a pain-free place where she found peace and comfort. The ground moved beneath her. Or was it the deck of a ship? The scent of sodden wood, brine, and oddly, Isaac filled her nose.

Pain suddenly scored a trail down her right side.

Gasping, she opened her eyes. Above her, a white sail stood stark against a black sky where more stars than she could count winked at her as if they held a secret.

A moan escaped her lips, and Isaac's face appeared in her vision. Lantern light swayed across his look of concern.

"Thea…" His voice came out breathless. "Shh, now. You are safe, my love."

My love? "Where, how…ouch!" She pressed a hand onto her side. Her fingers met rough cloth. A bandage?

Isaac took her hand in his. "Leave it be. Mr. Atwater cleansed and stitched the wound."

"Atwater?"

"Aye, the physician at Norfolk."

Memories flashed across her mind—Isaac carrying her through the dark streets, a physician, angry at having his supper interrupted, excruciating pain as he ripped her gown and poured rum over her side. She must have fainted, for she remembered nothing else.

A flood of embarrassment heated her. "He tore my gown!?"

"Aye, a hole only large enough to dress the wound. Your modesty was preserved, Thea."

The deck shifted, and she struggled to sit. A thousand knives pierced her side. She cried out.

"Try not to move." Isaac gently caressed her hand.

A stack of cloths lay beneath her, while within her reach, the worn bulwarks of a boat protected her side. A small boat, from the looks of it, as she peered through the darkness where a lantern showered light upon the stern.

Footsteps shook the deck beneath. A shadow approached.

"How is yer lady?" A gruff voice brought Thea's gaze up to a stout man with graying hair and a thick beard staring down at her.

Isaac glanced up at him. "In pain, but well. Thank you, Captain Barnet, once again for taking us on your sloop, especially under the circumstances."

"Ah, me pleasure helpin' out a privateer an' 'is lady."

Releasing Thea's hand, Isaac stood and ushered the captain a few feet away, but she could still hear him, nonetheless.

"You've not sighted any sails, Captain? I cannot emphasize enough that this British madman may very well be in pursuit."

"I'd like to see him try, that white-livered cur!" the captain spat back. "Never fear, my men are well trained to avoid all enemy craft, dippin' into inlets, coves, canals, an' such like where they can't go."

Isaac clapped him on the back. "You're a good man, Captain."

"Just doin' me part…carryin' messages an' goods up the Chesapeake. An' now even a privateersman! Curse me for a lubber, who would have thought?"

The crash of water against the hull drowned out their next words.

Isaac returned and dropped beside her. Grabbing a flask, he slipped an arm behind her and gently tilted her head up for a drink.

"Thank you," she muttered out in between sips, noting he winced slightly. "How is your wound? You fought Barstow so bravely and furiously, I know it pained you."

He laid her back down and smiled. "Always thinking of others, Thea. You amaze me." He set down the flask and rotated his shoulder. "The doc redressed my wound in Norfolk. Said you'd done a good job tending it."

She nodded, pleased. "When will we be in Baltimore?"

"A day."

She blew out a sigh. Soon this harrowing adventure would be over. Then why did she suddenly feel sad? An ache pounded across her head, dragging a memory, a question, along with it. She gazed up at Isaac, longing to see his eyes in the shadows. "You could have had your brigantine back, your dream. Why, when I gave you the coded message?"

"Indeed." He chuckled. "I found it in my breeches' pocket. Very clever and brave of you."

"Then why not take it *and* your brigantine?"

"And leave you with that fiend? You don't know me, Thea."

She thought she'd known him once, but he'd proven otherwise. And now? How she wished she could see his expression, though his tone carried more depth of affection than she ever remembered. "You could have left me with the doctor, rowed out to your brigantine, and tried to win it back." It was why she'd given him the message, thinking he'd do just that after he defeated the colonel.

Taking her hand in his, Isaac shook his head. "Thea, I couldn't leave you. I won't leave you. Never again."

She allowed a spark of joy to lift her heart at his tender words, but painful memories quickly snuffed it out. "I heard the same promise four years ago."

"I was a fool four years ago."

Emotion burned in her throat at his loving tone, his gentle touch…but trust him? How could she be so foolish again?

She tugged her hand from his. Pain thrummed in her side and across her head, and she closed her eyes. "Do you think Barstow survived? Will he follow us?"

"Do not concern yourself with it, Thea. You are safe."

"But I heard…"

"Rest now, my love. We will be in Baltimore tomorrow."

Dawn's blessed light spread across the horizon, scattering the mist hovering over the water. Isaac drew a deep breath of the sea air, scanning the rippling bay for the sight of any ship, a certain one, in particular. Not that he could take it back with a mere one-masted sloop and a crew of ten, but one could hope. He twisted the jeweled ring on his finger, the only remnant of his ship he had left, and bowed his head. *Lord, I'm sorry I put my ship and my dreams above you. Forgive me. Please heal Thea. Help her forgive me also and bless our cause of freedom. Keep us safe.*

Wind blasted over him, tossing his loose hair and caressing his face. He truly did love the sea, the wildness of it, the freedom. But it was no longer more important to him than God, nor more important than the precious lady sleeping at his feet.

That precious lady moaned, and he glanced down at her, her hair spread over the white sailcloth in waves of auburn. He'd not left her side all night, ensuring she was as comfortable and safe as possible nestled among the sailcloth and coverlets the crew had lent them. The sloop was so small there were no cabins below deck wherein she could rest and have some privacy, at least none that had been offered to them.

Sometime after midnight, a fever had consumed her, causing her to toss and turn, moan and groan. *And* Isaac's fear to rise. That's when he'd started praying. Soon after, she fell into a deep slumber. Had God answered his prayers? He smiled.

Now, kneeling, he laid the back of his hand against her forehead. Thank God, her skin was no longer hot, and the bleeding in her side had ceased. When the colonel's blade had sliced her, it had taken a piece of his heart with it. Nothing else mattered. Not his brigantine, not his privateering, not even the secret message they carried that could possibly win the war. Nothing but quickly dispatching the colonel and getting Thea to a physician.

He could not lose her. He would not lose her! Not after he'd found her again. Not after he realized that he had never stopped loving her.

Behind him, two sailors played a card game while another took soundings over the side.

Thea's eyelids fluttered, and she sighed and moved her head slightly. Isaac took her hand in his once again.

Green eyes, clearer and more brilliant than he remembered, focused on him like emeralds on a sunny day. "You're still here…" she muttered. "I must have fallen asleep." Blinking, she gazed up at the blue sky.

"You had a fever in the night." Isaac grabbed the flask of water. "But you are well now. How do you feel?"

"Like I've fought a battle. And lost horribly." She started to laugh, but instantly winced in pain.

"Here, drink."

The sloop eased over a wavelet, and she reached for him. "Help me sit."

Setting the flask down, Isaac looped his arm behind her and gently drew her off the pile of sailcloth. Her curves pressed against his chest, and a flood of heat swamped him as he quickly helped move her to lean against the bulwarks.

"There." He steadied her, then sat back. Her expression shifted from one of pain to one of confusion as her eyes flitted between his. Had she felt the same thrill at their closeness? Nay, the lady hated him and with good cause.

Embarrassed, he dropped his gaze, grabbed the flask again, and handed it to her. "You are very brave, Thea."

Captain Barnet shouted an order to the crew, and a sailor leapt into the shrouds to adjust sail.

Uncorking the flask, she sipped the water. "I am anything but brave, as you well know."

"Nay. The old Thea would never have even ventured on this mission in the first place, nor survived a perilous journey and a sword wound, nor would be sitting here in blood-stained and ripped attire, your hair aflutter, in pain and with little sleep, yet with nary a complaint spilling from your lips."

She smiled. "Oh my, was I that bad?"

"We were both very young."

Taking another sip, she lowered the flask, her mood growing somber.

Wind wafted over them, dancing among the curls of her hair and bringing with it the scent of brine, wood, and tar. She had suffered much in his absence, and he hated himself for it.

She fingered the black ribbon on her wrist.

"Your sisters?" he asked, hoping to lighten her mood. "You never told me how they fare."

"They are both married now. Elaine has a young babe, and Mercy was with child when I left."

"But they were all younger than…" Isaac bit his tongue as guilt sliced through him.

She took another sip, then shoved the cork into the opening. "As I said, no honest man would court me after you left."

"I'm truly sorry, Thea."

She pressed a hand onto her side, her moan joining the creak and groan of timbers as the sloop mounted another wave.

"It was left to me to help my father with the bakery," she continued, her tone pained. "And to care for him when he took ill."

Isaac blew out a heavy sigh and lowered his gaze, shame swamping him as he twisted the ring on his finger.

"What is that ring to you?" she snapped. "You are always spinning it."

He stared at the gold circle, embedded with a sapphire surrounded by rubies. "This was on the first prize I ever took as captain of the *Avenger*." He couldn't help but smile as memories flooded him of the thrill of that first victory. He'd kept the ring as a reminder.

She frowned. "It obviously means a great deal to you."

That he could not deny, though he made no response.

"Would it have been such a horrible life, Isaac?" Moisture filled her eyes. "Married to me?"

Raking back his hair, he shook his head. "It wasn't you, Thea. It was the monotony of it all."

She pursed her lips, anger causing the freckles on her nose to fold. "And do you think I wish such a thing? A petty life devoid of purpose and adventure?"

He stared at her. The Thea before him was still the woman he'd always loved, but she was stronger now, more capable, confident. Which only made him love her more. "Not anymore."

Her smile warmed him. "I was a bit of a spoiled chit back then."

"Truly?" He winked.

She gave him a sly grin. "You were no mature gentleman yourself, Sir."

"That is fair. It seems we both have changed."

Several minutes passed. Thea put her hands on the deck to steady herself against the rocking of the sloop. The captain continued ordering the crew about, sending them to task, most of them completely ignoring the two guests. She finally met Isaac's gaze again, a look of understanding and almost surrender in her eyes. "Then it wasn't meant to be. For surely we would have made each other miserable."

"Does that mean you forgive me?" Hope teetered on the edge of her next words.

She bit her lip, drew a deep breath, and glanced up at the sail flapping in the wind.

He took her hand, but she snatched it away.

"I forgive you, Isaac. I do. But trust you? I doubt I could ever do that again."

Isaac swallowed the devastation clambering up his throat, threatening to explode in a sob. He deserved that and more for the pain and disgrace he'd cost this lady. "I understand," he said, doing his best to hide his agony. Best change the topic before his emotions got the best of him. "When we get to Baltimore, we'll seek out a physician to check on your wound, but since your fever has abated, I am sure it is healing well."

She nodded, a sudden sorrow claiming her features.

"I'll go gather us something to eat," he said, rising.

Shielding her eyes from the sun, she glanced up at him. "How soon until we arrive?"

"This afternoon, unless we encounter an enemy." Pivoting, he left before she saw the pain on his face. Not from the wound in his shoulder, but the one in his heart.

Nodding at the sailor at the wheel, Isaac dropped down the hatch to the galley below. He finally realized the value of this amazing lady, but he also realized it was too late, for he doubted any number of apologies, even extended with true remorse, could ever heal Thea's damaged heart.

Chapter Eleven

Baltimore harbor was everything Thea imagined it to be. Wooden docks stretched into the bay like ravenous tongues seeking their daily fare. Ships idly rocked beside them, their bare masts reaching high into the blue sky. Other ships of all sizes and shapes entered the narrow bay, lowering sails as they went. A thousand sounds met her ears—the shouts of sailors adjusting sail, the squawk of birds, clanging bells, the crank of wagon wheels, the whinny of horses, and the chatter of people running to and fro over the cobblestone streets.

The ever-attentive Isaac stood beside her, one hand pressed on her back should she stumble and fall. Even though she assured him she needed no help, he had all but hoisted her in his arms and set her on her feet when she requested to see Baltimore.

Though her side continued to throb, it had lessened somewhat. Still, she'd be thankful to be on land, for every tilt and leap of the deck shot spires of pain through her.

Isaac had not said much the rest of their journey, though he'd remained by her side and fussed over her like an anxious hen. Was his kindness a mere effort of penance for leaving her at the altar and ruining her life, or were his feelings genuine? She couldn't tell. What she *could* tell was that, even injured, her body reacted to his closeness like it used to four years ago. Perhaps even more.

Yet how could she ever trust him again? He had changed, aye. But what would happen when their adventure was over? Would he find another privateer to captain? Leave her again?

He gave up his brigantine for you.

That voice…a voice she hadn't heard in some time, eased into her thoughts, soothing her fears.

Behind her, Captain Barnet shouted orders for his crew to lower sail and ease beside a smaller dock to their left, and within minutes, the sloop was secured with ropes, and Isaac slapped a stack of Continentals into the man's hands.

An hour later, they stood at the door of a home on Lombard Street and knocked. Though they had attracted curious stares on their short walk there—no doubt due to the condition of her gown and the amount of blood splattered over them both—Thea had rather forcefully denied both Isaac's requests to first visit a physician and, second, to hire a conveyance. The bumpy ride would only cause her pain, and she must deliver her message posthaste.

Thea bit her lip. She'd only met her father's sister once when she was a young girl. Would the woman remember her? Even if she did, would she trust her instead of her father? She would soon find out as footsteps padded within and the door swung open.

A woman stood at the threshold, hair as red as Thea's father swept back in a bun beneath a white lace cap. An apron was tied at the waist of her modest gown of blue taffeta. "Yes?" She stared at Thea, then dropped her gaze to the blood on her gown. Recognition, along with horror, screamed from her face.

"Thea? Is that you?"

"Yes, Aunt Jane."

"My Lord, come in, come in. You're hurt. What happened?" She ushered them in and poked her head out the door. "Where is your father?"

Thea's head swam as Isaac led her into the front parlor and helped her lower onto a settee in the corner before facing her aunt. "Can you please send for your physician, madam?"

"Of course, but who, pray tell, are you?" Confusion and horror marred her plump, freckled face.

"This is Captain Isaac Preston, Aunt." Thea winced and grabbed her side. "He is a friend. You can trus—" The word froze in her mouth as she looked up at him. "Trust him."

He smiled and nodded as if to say, *yes, you can trust me.*

Aunt Jane hurried out of the room and returned with a maid in tow, whom she instructed to go fetch Doctor Miller.

"Lay down, my dear." She rushed to Thea to assist her.

"No, Aunt. I'm all right." Thea held up a hand. "We need to speak to you." She exchanged a glance with Isaac. "Please sit. I have some sad news."

Placing a hand on her heart, Aunt Jane lowered to a cushioned chair beside her.

There was no easy way to say it, so Thea drew a deep breath and uttered the words that still pained her to hear. "Father has died."

"Oh, my." Aunt Jane's eyes flooded with tears as she slumped into the chair. "I feared as much when I saw you at my door."

"He was ill, as you know, for a year or so…but he finally succumbed a month past. I'm so sorry." Thea fingered the black ribbon around her wrist.

"I'm sorry for *you*, my dear. To have neither of your parents. And in the middle of war."

"That is why we have come, Aunt." Thea listened for sounds of anyone else in the house. "Are we alone? We have information of great import to give you."

Drawing a handkerchief from her skirt pocket, Aunt Jane dabbed her eyes and stared at Thea with suspicion. "Yes, my maid was the only one here with me. Your uncle, as you know, passed three years ago."

Nodding, Thea bit her lip, unsure of how to proceed. "Before he died, Father told me of your…*activities* for the Patriot cause."

Aunt Jane said nothing, merely shifted a wary gaze between Thea and Isaac. Finally, she spoke up. "Of what activities do you refer? I'm sure I have no idea."

Thea could understand why her aunt wouldn't trust her. She'd been living under British rule for over a year. And the woman had no idea who Isaac was.

She nodded at Isaac, and reaching into his waistcoat pocket, he pulled out a letter and handed it to her aunt.

"Let no net ensnare us." Thea uttered the phrase her father had told her to say.

Her aunt's eyes widened as she clutched the missive, her breath coming fast. Before she could open it, the maid burst through the door. A rotund man with a round face, kind expression, and a satchel in hand, barreled in behind her. He started straight for Thea.

"Doctor Miller, this is my niece, Thea Cabot." Her aunt quickly stuffed the letter inside her sleeve.

Thea was ushered into the back room of the house—her uncle's study, she was told—and onto a large sofa. After she instructed the maid to bring them a basin of water and Isaac some tea, her aunt followed.

"Now, what have we here?" Dr. Miller began peeling off the bloody bandage around her waist.

Thea laid a hand on her aunt's arm. "Isaac…I mean, Captain Preston is injured as well."

"Now, now." Her aunt patted her hand. "I'm sure Doctor Miller will tend to him next."

"Indeed." Setting the bandages aside, the doctor peered at the wound. "Hmm. A knife, large blade? Nay, perhaps a sword did this? What happened, my dear?"

Thea thought it best not to answer the question. "How does it look, Doctor? It pains me so."

"To be expected." Dipping a cloth in a basin of water, he cleaned the wound, and it took everything within Thea not to scream out.

After finishing his ministrations, he applied some salve, then sat back and stared at her with a suspicious but kind look. "You are very brave, Miss. Whoever stitched this did a good job. It will heal nicely, but"—he glanced at Thea's aunt—"I recommend a few weeks of rest."

Her aunt nodded, smiling at Thea.

"Would you check on the captain, Doctor?" Thea pleaded.

"Of course." The doctor washed his hands, then began packing up his instruments.

After he left, her aunt scurried from the room, returning within minutes with a clean chemise, petticoats, stays, and gown. Her maid carried a basin of water behind her, and soon Thea felt refreshed with clean attire, her skin free of dirt, and her hair swept up in a bun.

Back in the parlor, the doctor was just finishing wrapping a bandage around Isaac's shoulder. But spotting her, Isaac quickly grabbed his coat for propriety's sake, shrugged into it, and stood.

Chuckling, Doctor Miller snapped his satchel closed. "Seems you two have had quite the adventure. But I declare you both will live. That is"—he raised a teasing brow—"if you avoid swords and pistols in the future." With a wink, he headed toward the door.

But Isaac's eyes were on Thea, not just *on* her, but seeping into her very soul. She swallowed a burst of emotion at the intensity of affection she saw within them.

After the doctor left, Aunt Jane pointed to her sleeve. "I must deal with this message. Remain here." And off she went.

Shifting her gaze from Isaac, Thea took a seat.

"Thank God you are not seriously hurt, Thea." Isaac slid beside her, his masculine scent flooding her nostrils and doing strange things in her belly.

For some reason she suddenly felt uncomfortable being alone with him. *Gah!* They had traveled alone together for two days. They had slept, eaten, been chased, and endured a sword fight together. And now she felt uncomfortable?

Perhaps it was because she knew their time would soon come to an end, and despite her every effort to the contrary, she had allowed this man into her heart once again.

"Your aunt seems a very capable, smart lady."

"Yes." Thea smiled and glanced around the room. "Much like my father."

"And like you." Admiration poured from his eyes as they shifted between hers.

Lowering her gaze to her lap, she ignored the compliment. "Thank you for taking care of me after I was wounded, Captain."

"Are we now back to 'Captain' after all we've been through?" He extended a hand toward her but pulled back as if he feared her rejection.

Thea reached for a lock of her hair, but they were all tucked safely in her bun. Perhaps it was best to cut ties with this man before he broke her heart again. "I'm sure it was the fear and uncertainty of our adventure that forced us together, forced us to become friends. But as we both admitted, we would surely make each other miserable."

She could almost sense his sorrow. "In the past, perhaps. But now?"

Thankfully, Thea did not have to answer, for her aunt charged into the room, her skirts fluttering about her and her face red.

"We must get this message to General Washington posthaste!"

Chapter Twelve

Isaac hurried down Lombard Street, turned on Light Street, and headed to the docks. After Thea's aunt had informed him that most of the courier routes that led to the general's secret location had been compromised—that several couriers had been caught or killed and their dispatches stolen, he recommended taking the message by ship. It would be faster and safer, especially with him on board. Now to find a vessel heading north and a captain who would take him on.

Weaving around the crowds of people, wagons, and horses, he halted at the first dock, held a hand to his eyes to shield the sun, and scanned the harbor for the most unpretentious merchantman.

That's when he saw it. In truth, he didn't believe it at first. No doubt exhaustion had finally taken over his senses. Shutting his eyes, he shook his head, believing that when he opened them, the glorious vision would be gone.

Instead of disappearing, his brigantine, *Avenger*, eased up to the last of the empty docks at the far end of the harbor. Were the British still on board? If so, how did they pass the harbor inspection and the guns at Fort Whetstone?

Isaac could care less. His ship was here, and if he had a chance of getting it back, he'd fight the entire British army if need be.

But there were no Redcoats on board. Quite the contrary. Hastings and Marlow waved at him from the deck, huge grins on their faces.

"You made it!" Isaac leapt over the bulwarks and gripped his first mate's shoulders. "You saved my ship!"

Hastings laughed. "That were yer last orders, were they not, Cap'n?"

Isaac joined his chuckle. "Sink and drown me, Hastings, you defeated those cutthroat Redcoats!"

"Aye, we did at that, though weren't easy." He thumbed behind him, where several of Isaac's crew crowded to greet him.

Isaac gave them all an appreciative nod, but sudden sorrow threatened to sink his newfound joy. "Injured? Deaths?"

"None dead. A few injured. And we 'ave prisoners in the hold."

Isaac spent the next several minutes greeting and thanking his men, so thrilled and proud, he almost forgot why he'd come to the docks. Glancing aloft, he noticed the mast, yard, and mainsail had been repaired. "I see you fixed the damage?"

"Aye, all 'cept the hole in the hull. But Hawkes patched it up good enough fer sailing until we can fix it proper."

Isaac nodded. "We'll have to wait for that. Restock the brigantine with supplies and get some rest," he ordered Hastings. "We set sail at dawn."

"Where to, Cap'n?"

"We have a very important mission to accomplish."

Thea could hardly believe she was once again aboard the *Avenger*. It seemed like years since she'd first been brought on this ship as a prisoner. And yet now that she was back, it seemed only minutes, for her heart was doing as many flips and flops as it had back then.

She watched as Isaac issued orders from behind his desk in his cabin, sending his men scrambling off to their tasks. He wore a clean linen shirt, leather waistcoat, and black breeches tucked within tall boots. His hair hung wildly about a jaw that was tight as he studied the chart spread across his desk, the lantern light oscillating over his handsome features. Behind him, moonlight trickled silver filagree over the wavelets of the harbor, creating a beauty she felt none of within her soul.

Isaac had his ship back. His *true* love. And he was leaving Thea again.

Then why had she come to see him off?

Because she was the biggest fool who ever lived. There could be no other reason.

Finally, he looked up at her and smiled that cocksure smile of his that sent a pleasurable shiver through her.

"Can you believe it?" He chuckled. "That lying snake Barstow never had my brigantine. My men tell me they defeated the Brits right after I leapt overboard."

"Truly? But what about Jakes?"

"Hastings says Barstow grabbed him, used him as a shield as he escaped into the woods after us." Isaac frowned. "Must have paid him to come with him and lie in the end."

Thea nodded, clasping her hands in front of her, angry at herself for her sudden influx of nerves.

"I'm sorry you cannot accompany me, Thea." He circled his desk and studied her curiously as if he could sense her angst.

She breathed out a sigh. "After all I've been through, I don't understand all the fuss." Even as she said the words, an ache traveled down her side.

"You must rest. You heard the doctor. And I won't risk your health."

Wouldn't risk her health or was in a hurry to be rid of her? Avoiding him, she made her way to the stern window and stared at the inky water of the bay, not wanting him to see the moisture in her eyes. "You must be thrilled to have your brigantine back."

"I admit it is a blessing from God I did not expect." She sensed him moving to stand behind her. "Never fear. I will do you, your aunt, and your father proud. I am quite familiar with the Little Egg Harbor River in New Jersey. From there, I'll personally get the message to Morristown and place it in General Washington's hands myself."

"I have no doubt, Isaac, for I'm beginning to believe there's nothing you cannot accomplish."

He laughed. "I am only a man, Thea. But I'm glad your aunt trusts me for such an important task."

"She trusts whom *I* trust."

54

Gently grabbing her shoulders, he turned her around to face him. "Do you, Thea? Do you really?"

Swallowing down a lump of sorrow, she lowered her gaze. "In this matter, aye."

"But you do not trust me with your heart?" Placing a finger beneath her chin, he raised her gaze to his. Love poured from his eyes, a love she had once trusted.

"Give me a reason to, Isaac."

He took her hands and brought them both to his lips for a kiss. "I love you, Thea Cabot. I always have and always will. And you have my word, I will return to you."

Against her own will, hope and joy spiraled through her. "But you have your ship, your privateering."

"It is nothing without you. I know that now."

No longer able to bear being so close to him, she withdrew her hands, and started to walk away. "Yet you told me you cannot tolerate a monotonous life."

"Ha, with you? Life will be anything but monotonous." He clutched her arm before she got too far. "I'm starting to see the advantage of becoming a spy. I find we make quite a good team, no?"

Halting, she stared at him.

"We could move messages faster by ship," he said, giving her that playful half-grin of his. "Besides, I think you would make a great captain's wife."

Thea's head spun. Her breath caught in her throat, even as anger brewed hot in her belly. Turning her back to him, she tore from his grip and moved away. "I believe we tried that once before, and I remember well the outcome."

He followed her, took her hand in his and spun her around, pressing her close. Before she realized it, his lips were on hers, gentle at first, then seeking, probing, caressing. Worst part, she allowed him! She could not pull away, not if her life depended on it. Life and love, hope and possibility, all swirled together in a pleasurable brew that caused all her problems to melt, her surroundings to fade, her fears to abate…until all that was left was Isaac.

He finally withdrew, his warm breath wafting over her, his unique salty scent filling her nose, filling her very lungs as she continued to tremble at his touch.

"I love you, Thea. I will never leave you again." He gently caressed her cheek with his thumb and eased a strand of her hair behind her ear.

Breathless, she backed away from him, searching his eyes for any truth to his words.

He twisted off his ring and handed it to her.

"What is this?"

"It's yours now."

"But this means so much to you. It represents your privateering success."

"Not anymore. Consider it a token of my promise to return and make you my wife."

She took it, forcing back tears. "Those were the exact words you said to me before you left me in Savannah." *Oh, Lord, do not allow me to be deceived again.* Not again with this man. She wanted to tell him she loved him too, that she'd marry him in a second if she thought his words were true. Instead, she said nothing. Merely laid her palm against his cheek for but a moment, relishing in the feel of him, and said, "Stay safe, Isaac," before she left the cabin.

Two months later

Thea stood before the docks at Baltimore harbor. As she had done every day for the past two months, fool that she was. Isaac should have returned weeks ago, yet here she stood, all alone like the lovesick, jilted woman she was, garnering the usual stares of pity and wonder from the townsfolk.

Perspiration slid down her back in the hot June sun as she adjusted her bonnet against the fierce rays. She pressed her side, where only a slight ache remained of the sword wound she'd received in Isaac's altercation with Colonel Barstow. In truth, the pain was the only thing that kept her from believing it had all been a dream, a wonderful, adventurous dream she'd made up to heal the lesions marring her shattered heart, a heart that now threatened to completely crumble to ashes.

During the long wait, Thea had spent many hours talking to God, trying to make up for lost time during the past four years. She'd repented of blaming God for Isaac's abandonment. She'd repented of her unforgiveness. All that remained was her trust. Not necessarily in Isaac, but trust in God. Trust that He had the best plan for her life. As both she and Isaac had realized, had they married four years ago, they'd have been miserable. Yet in the ensuing years, they had both grown, changed, matured. Was it God's will they get married now? If so, then Isaac would return as he'd promised. If not, then it was for the best. Hence the trust, the trust ultimately in God's plan for her and for Isaac. She'd battled this trust in God over the past weeks, tossed and turned at night, lost her appetite, wandered the streets of Baltimore until Aunt Jane's maid, who accompanied her, complained of the strenuous exercise. Did Thea trust God with her life, her love, her future? Even her heart?

Yes! She'd finally fully submitted to Him and His plan. Which was why this would be her last visit to the docks. No longer would she pine away for a man she wasn't supposed to marry. No, she would join her aunt in doing their part in the Culper Spy Ring. In addition, her aunt was close friends with Katherine Goddard, who ran the *Maryland Journal*, and the woman invited Thea to use her writing talents to propagate Patriot news and encouragement in the war. Monotonous? Boring? Never. With God, she would have an exciting, purposeful life!

She glanced over her shoulder at her aunt's maid, Maryanne, sitting on a crate in the shade. No doubt the girl would love to return home before the afternoon heat became excruciating.

Still, something compelled Thea to stay a few minutes longer.

Tugging on the chain around her neck, she pulled out Isaac's ring. Sunlight sparkled over the jewels, winking at her, almost as if they held a secret. If so, she wished they would share it. She'd not taken it off since Isaac had given it to her two months past when he'd declared his love. With a sigh, she dropped it back inside her gown and started to leave when something caught her eye. A ship rounded the corner of Fells Point, an ordinary ship, by all accounts, its crew rushing across the deck and up the ratlines to lower sail. Yet…something kept her eye upon it.

The closer it came, the more rapidly her heartbeat thrummed until she felt it would burst through her chest.

The *Avenger*! She'd know that brigantine anywhere!

Squealing like a schoolgirl, she grabbed her skirts, and rushed along the docks, following the path the ship was taking, refusing to take her eyes from it for fear it would disappear.

Oh, Lord, could it be?

The minutes crept by like hours as she waited for the *Avenger* to ease next to one of the wooden docks.

Then she saw him. Captain Isaac Preston standing amidships in his white linen shirt flapping in the breeze, his dark hair tied behind his neck, and a tricorn atop his head. He was issuing order after order but stopped suddenly when he saw her.

Before the brigantine even came to a full stop, he leapt over the railing onto the wooden dock and charged down it, halting before her.

Grinning, he swept off his hat. "My lady, I have returned as promised."

Was there a man more handsome, more chivalrous, more honorable in all the world? So overcome with joy and love, she could not find her voice.

"Do not leave me in suspense, Thea." He dropped to his knee. "Say you will marry me."

Tears of joy filled her eyes. Her throat choked with emotion. But she finally managed to squeak out a "Yes!"

Shouting with glee, he rose, swallowed her up in his arms, and showered her with kisses.

Was it all a dream? Thea could hardly believe it, so overwhelmed with happiness as she was. *Thank you, Lord*, she silently prayed as Isaac spun her around, both of them laughing and crying for joy. And she realized, with God, dreams really did come true.

Historical Note

In the summer of 1780, 6000 French soldiers were set to arrive in Rhode Island to aid the Americans. However, the British spy, Benedict Arnold, informed the British of the French landing, and plans were made to attack the French reinforcements. But due to the brave efforts of the Culper Spy Ring, George Washington received news of the British plans. After warning the French of an impending attack, he ordered his operatives to spread disinformation that he was preparing to raid New York. The British took the bait, choosing to defend the city rather than attack the arriving French forces. The French arrived safely, and with their help, the Americans were able to win the war.

About the Author

    Award-winning and best-selling author, MaryLu Tyndall dreamt of pirates and seafaring adventures during her childhood days on Florida's Coast. With more than thirty books published, she makes no excuses for the deep spiritual themes embedded within her romantic adventures. Her hope is that readers will not only be entertained but will be brought closer to the Creator who loves them beyond measure. In a culture that accepts the occult, wizards, zombies, and vampires without batting an eye, MaryLu hopes to show the awesome present and powerful acts of God in a dying world. A Christy and Maggie award nominee and two-time winner of the RWA Inspy Reader's Choice Award, MaryLu makes her home with her husband, six children, four grandchildren, and several stray cats on the California coast.

    If you enjoyed this book, one of the nicest ways to say "thank you" to an author and help them be able to continue writing is to leave a favorable review on Amazon, Barnes and Noble, Goodreads, Ibooks (And elsewhere, too!) I would appreciate it if you would take a moment to do so. Thanks so much!

    Comments? Questions? I love hearing from my readers, so feel free to contact me via my website: **https://www.marylutyndall.com/** Or email me at: marylu_tyndall@yahoo.com

Follow me on:
BLOG: https://crossandcutlass.blogspot.com/
PINTEREST: http://www.pinterest.com/mltyndall/
BOOKBUB: https://www.bookbub.com/authors/marylu-tyndall
AMAZON: https://www.amazon.com/MaryLu-Tyndall/e/B002BOG7JG
Instagram: https://www.instagram.com/marylu_tyndall/

To hear news about special prices and new releases sign up for my newsletter on my website Or follow me on Bookbub!
https://www.marylutyndall.com/
https://www.bookbub.com/authors/marylu-tyndall

Clara's Compassion

by Marlene Bierworth

Clara Stewart wants to go West. Her ticket to Cranston is a teaching certificate and a prearranged marriage. Graham Lee earns a management position to extend the Canadian Pacific Railway line through the Rocky Mountains, battling pre-conceived notions at every turn.

The courtship is tested when Clara's compassion for the frontier immigrant workers wreaks conflict and heartbreak for Graham, the railroad boss. Clara answers the call to share God's unconditional love, and when tragedy strikes at the camp, the heart of the community awakens. The lines become grayed for Graham when he is forced to choose between his conscience, his loyalties, his betrothed, and his job. Will the transformation reshape Cranston's future and bring hope to the couple who is headed for their happily ever after? Or drive them apart?

Clara's Compassion is a heartwarming pioneer adventure and a suspense-filled sweet romance in courtship, love, and compassion. Enjoy the journey as Clara and Graham seek to find a common ground to call home.

NOTE: This solo contribution will become book 1 in an upcoming series with more adventures being added starting 2025, after the limited time boxset collection has been taken down, allowing each author to republish their stories independently. Be sure to watch for author Marlene Bierworth's new Rocky Mountain Brides series in 2025.

"Jesus went, He saw, and was filled with compassion."

Clara Stewart's compassion is unleashed upon a hurting and diverse community.

Welcome to Cranston.

Chapter One

Hamilton, Ontario, Canada

"You did what?" Clara could not believe her ears.

"I found you a husband in British Columbia, just like you wanted," her father, Charles Stewart, repeated for the second time.

"I *wanted* to go to one of the railroad towns in the Rocky Mountains and educate the children, not get married to a stranger."

"The railroad manager in Cranston needs a wife. Being married will bring an element of respectability to the new train stop breaking new ground in the West. They tell me the man is a bit of a womanizer, or he would be if there were any single females in the area ripe for the picking. I have no doubt you will settle him down soon enough, daughter."

"You want me to marry a womanizer? Father, are you having a breakdown? Maybe we need to call the doctor."

Charles laughed casually. "Believe me, you can learn to co-exist with almost anyone. Your mother and I did, and I have grown quite fond of her."

"Fond of her! Really? I want the warm fuzzies, the rapid heartbeat and goosebumps, or nothing at all."

"Oh, to be young again." Charles sighed heavily. "At the very least, if the feelings don't sweep you off your feet, you can help the fellow spend the money I'm going to pay him."

"You're going to pay him to marry me?" The conversation was sounding more bizarre by the minute.

"He claims not to have great wealth to offer a woman of your station, so good old Dad will lend a helping hand to get you both started right."

"A dowry for a man that can't possibly profit your portfolio?"

"I'm doing fine on my own," Charles said. "I just want my little girl to be happy. My main reason for organizing this match was as a favor to you, Clara."

"A favor? I can't wait to hear this," Clara said, a little curious as to how he might explain himself.

Her father appeared calm as he reasoned the details of her sentencing. "It is your desire to go West, right?"

"Yes," she said, grinning despite herself and commending him for a winning opening defense. "It's very advantageous of you to begin your argument by voicing *my* wishes."

"Well, the brains behind the Canadian Pacific Railroad Company, the likes of which I admire and will support with your inheritance, requires a mail-order bride of quality breeding to court and marry—"

"Breeding!" Clara gasped. "Am I one of your prize horses now?"

Charles ignored her outburst and stated with a finality that hit Clara's defense where it mattered most. "The railroad manager is working in a location most desirable to you—the mountains. The railroad must be seen as above reproof if stakeholders are to gain loyalty from businesses and future passengers."

"I see clearly now why you don't need the manager's money," Clara stated rather indignantly. "You are padding your pockets by negotiating your daughter and the honorable Stewart name, into the deal."

"If you stay here in Hamilton, your mother will organize your coming out season, and you will end up with one of those stuffy gents you detest. Your twentieth birthday will be here before you know it."

His mention of her following year's birthday had her wanting to run for the hills. "Next December seems eons away."

"Time marches on, and you are as familiar as I with the conditions of your grandmother's will: all of the money sitting in your trust fund will go up in smoke next Christmas for no other reason than that my strong-willed daughter has refused every suitor introduced to her." It was a reality of which Father often reminded Clara. The young woman had long disapproved of the condition Granny had written into her last will and testament. She'd loved her dear old grandmother but never had a stauncher prude existed, hanging on to pre-historic practices until her dying breath. The sad reality was that Granny's son and his wife had carried on her absurdity, living only within the margins of society, never hungry enough to test the waters of change.

Traditions were one thing, but Clara drew the line at martyrdom.

"I can't stay in Hamilton and wed a fortune hunter, Father. Surely you understand." She lifted her hands in frustration. "Of course, you don't understand. *Your* parents selected the perfect match for you years ago."

"I understand that gents seeking your hand might be out for the inheritance, but you make the term *fortune hunter,* sound monstrous. Surely you would respect a man who looks for opportunities to increase his wealth, his pampered wife becoming the recipient of such an arrangement?" Charles chuckled as if it were a tasteless joke that tickled his funny bone, but Clara failed to see the humor in the situation.

Her father sobered just as quickly. "Name-calling doesn't suit you, dear, and it will not further your cause." The man seemed to melt before her, casting his best rendition of puppy-dog-eyes, knowing they had the power to soften his daughter's heart.

Clara groaned.

"I understand that love can be hard when the head is the only thing to participate, but I truly hope you will learn to care for this man and come to fully enjoy your Western adventure." Her father's words sounded genuine—she would give him that—and she realized he had her best interests at heart, as he always did. The man openly adored and spoiled his daughter whom everyone else viewed as being Daddy's little girl.

Clara succumbed to her fate. Whatever that might be, it was better than staying in Hamilton. "My groom must be a worthwhile prospect to have landed such a leading position in the expanding of the Pacific Railroad across our great country. The owner would not hire a scallywag to fulfil the promise given by the Confederation over a decade ago. It is amazing to think we will soon have our first transcontinental railway line." She paused to consider the greatness of such an undertaking. "I agree, respectability on all fronts is essential for such an endeavor to succeed."

In spouting all the positives she could muster, another bleak thought struck Clara. "He is *not* an old man, is he?"

"Mid-twenties, I'm told."

She sighed. "Good. I am not a nurse for some aging gent, but a teacher."

"Now you're sounding like the audacious daughter I know so well. The children will love you, and so will Graham Lee."

"Mrs. Clara Lee," she mused, "sounds like two first names."

"Clarissa Lee sounds just fine."

"Fancying up my first name will surely drive the man away, thinking his mail-order bride is soft, but yes, the surname has potential, and hopefully, the man does, too."

"Graham Lee knows we expect him to court you proper-like. It won't hurt to bring a refining touch to the Wild West."

"As long as it doesn't affect its spirit. That is of paramount importance, Father. The West must be tamed by courageous frontiersmen and women if it is to entice future travelers to ride the black iron beast to view nature's wonders."

"That's my girl. It's all settled, then. You shall begin to plan, and I will send a wire confirming your arrival in Cranston, via the Pacific Railroad."

"How far do the trains go presently?"

"Cranston is the end of the line, but not for long. Construction is twisting through Alberta's mountain ranges and into British Columbia as we speak, with your husband at the helm to see it to completion."

"My husband, you say? The title already sounds dreadfully confining."

Clara left her father's office and climbed the wide, regal staircase to her suite on the second floor, her fingers sliding along the cherry wood banister. The flight of steps widened at the top, dividing the east and west wings, with the exposed landing overlooking the space below. Clara's mother had hoped she would someday descend that winding trail to society's select as they awaited the bride in the great hall. The woman must be silently grieving now that her daughter's wedding would occur far from their Hamilton home. Still, Clara had siblings —let Florence Stewart transfer her expectations to Grace, the next in line.

Clara kicked off her shoes inside her bedroom and dropped dramatically onto the soft comforter covering her double bed. Winter would be long and cold that year, especially while anticipating the future she simultaneously yearned for and feared. The news her father had dropped on her that day exhausted her, and a wee rest before supper was in order. If only her mind would shut down. The mail-order bride wondered if there was a church in Cranston. If not, that would be her first order of business. A town needed a preacher to marry and bury the people as well as lead the residents of the new train stop spiritually. It was the same way entrepreneurs grew a town economically.

This opportunity would be the fruition of her frontier dream. The move West was finally sanctioned by her previously hesitant parents, not to mention the teaching position for which she'd yearned coming available in an area desperate for educators and not fussy when it came to her soon-to-be married status. It was a miracle worth celebrating, though the proposal of a paid off husband would not have been her choice. The ridiculous notion fogged her mind, threatening to squelch her dream. Clara hoped the groom would not assume a false victory before her arrival, for the choice to marry remained hers. Still, that privilege did not bring her the relief she needed. Marriage was inevitable—finishing school had groomed her for that role—and her preference to choose her mate was a foreign concept that rarely materialized within her social circles.

She wondered from where her independent streak had come. Probably her grandfather, who had been a kindred spirit, a fact that only added to Granny's torment and her doubt that their granddaughter would grow up fit for society. The deceased woman would never have agreed to Father's method of husband selection, but Charles Stewart seemed willing to stir up the grave dust and chance his mother's wrath haunting his dreams. The nightmare picture forming in her mind made Clara chuckle. She knew her daddy loved her and that he had somehow managed to find at least a partial solution for her to follow her dream to the Wild West. For that small mercy, Clara was grateful.

Clara contemplated on the Westerner picked for her by the railroad personnel, strangers who had no idea if the match would bring either of the recipients' happiness. Most likely, they couldn't care less. She prayed Graham Lee would be *the* one the Lord had set aside for her from the beginning of time. In her daydreams, she had also been so bold as to give the Ultimate Matchmaker a specific character list for her Western cowboy, and trusted that God had found him in Cranston.

Cranston: in the mountains bordering Alberta and British Columbia

Graham had been delayed at the Groger site. He pushed his horse along the winding trail between the two mountain peaks. The new teacher—more specifically, his mail-order bride—was due to arrive that day. He was late, and he knew that first impressions were important for a lady of her station. Many a contender in the courting race for a woman's hand would be disqualified based on their initial meeting, or so Caleb had informed him. His younger brother had experienced such a fate before choosing to join him in Cranston several months prior. He'd brought along his bitter attitude that Graham hoped the rugged West would replace with a new vision after healing. So far, that had not been the case. As manager of railroad construction close to the Alberta/British Columbia border and westward, Graham had enough troubles of his own, and he could neither relate, nor did he have time, to indulge Caleb's recovery from bankruptcy and lost love.

He sighed as he closed in on the stationary train, the iron beast sitting silent and deserted. Graham noted the oversized trunk and bags lying on the ground and concluded that a certain disgruntled female passenger had left them behind and headed to find people…or the one who had stood her up.

Not a good start for a bridegroom.

Graham supposed that, sooner, rather than later, she would need to learn that his life ran on the railroad's timetable. She had come from a wealthy family that was willing to pay for their daughter to discover her dream. When *his* boss had rewarded him with the promise of a lady to love for a job well done, Graham figured the unexpected bonus would fill two needs: it would pad his pocketbook so he might indulge his new wife, keeping her in her accustomed lifestyle, as well as satisfy his yearning for a family of his own. Mr. Charles Stewart from Hamilton, Ontario, had sent a fair warning to Graham that the lure of teaching and the mountains were the clincher when it came to convincing his daughter, Clarissa—who preferred the name Clara—to accept his proposal that she become a mail-order bride. He also told Graham that the result of the courtship was entirely on him, hinting that winning her affections might be a challenge. The note had ended with Charles Stewart wishing him luck.

The statement had left him wondering what he had gotten himself into.

With the downpayment, came the understanding that Clara was entrusted to Graham's hands for safekeeping, regardless of his success at romance.

Graham hoped the courtship would be swift and stress-free. His managerial position came with pros and cons, some of which were likely to hinder his romantic progress. The pay was good—the respectability, a plus—but the railroad owner operated under a rigid schedule.

When British Columbia became a province in 1871, the government promised that it would link the overpopulated East with the frontier, thus bringing scores of people their way to settle the Canadian West. The top man seemed determined to see the program come to pass—or more likely the case, pressure his field managers into completing the line on time. To win favor with the public and demonstrate their unwavering commitment, the railroad took on the logo of the beaver, proudly displaying it on their trains for everyone to see. The citizens grew to view the entire venture as a potent symbol of Canadian nationalism, connecting the idea to the hard-working nature of the company. It looked fine on paper and puffed up those who seated themselves behind oak desks as they issued unreasonable orders to those who made it happen. Regardless, Graham and his labor force determined to do their best.

It would take a remarkable woman to understand the gravity of his burden.

Graham felt sure the top guns running the project in the east had never traveled via the Rocky Mountain passes or understood the dangerous blasting and complex assembly such an endeavor entailed. Nevertheless, the boss had high expectations. He wanted to get the job done at any cost, and not simply dollars, but time and even lives, if necessary. According to the owners, everything and everyone was expendable in developing the modern era they proudly stood behind. "All for the cause" was the working man's slogan, whereas "we look after our employees" the façade they portrayed to the watching public.

Too many Chinese immigrants died carrying and fusing the explosives to make the paths through and around the Rocky Mountains, a dangerous job his white counterparts claimed was better suited for the small, agile men in the camp. Graham had taken his turn to show the new men—who arrived in the country by the scores—how to safely blast away the rock, hoping to provide a model for his disparate labor force. He was unsure if he made the impact he wanted, but time marched on, leaving no hours slated for pampering.

Graham respected the courageous immigrants who had fled China to escape British dominance after the Opium War ended in 1842. Families continued to arrive in Canada seeking a new life, many of whom were transported and hired by the railroad to help build the new line. Their presence brought out the worst and the best in the local population, but all felt the effects of a culture struggling to accept new people on Canadian soil. Graham had no doubt it would all iron out in the end. The immigrants were intelligent and willing workers, his only wish being that he had the time to make their adjustment to life in the New World a little less stressful. However, Graham was only one man, and he could not be everywhere at once.

Although Graham did not share the worldview of the rich and powerful who pushed forward the great cause of the country's prosperity and growth at any cost, his influence and convictions were not always communicated by the supervisors under him at the numerous sites already up and running. To get the massive job done in the time allotted, Graham often had to close his eyes to the daily practices when it came to the handling of the crew.

Yet, there was a price to pay for ignoring his nagging conscience: restless nights and watching his character nose-dive to a place of which he was not overly proud.

He heard the commotion ahead, dismounted, and spoke to the animal as he gently stroked his steed. "It's payday, Chet, and it looks like trouble again." He took the animal's lead rope and walked toward the train car offices. Despite the bad investments that had caused Caleb to lose his entire savings, Graham had given his brother the job of paymaster, in charge of all things financial on the Cranston site, The man's understanding of numbers made him a good fit for the job, and Graham hoped the responsibility might boost his bruised ego.

He wondered what his mail-order bride might think of the set up in Cranston. It was a rough railroad town, with cut-throat business people doing whatever was necessary to be the first choice in their trade as they strived to gain the loyalty of the shoppers in the area over their weaker competitors.

Graham stopped and stared at the scene ahead of him. A well-dressed woman was on the ground beside a Chinese worker as Caleb stood there, looking on. Graham fumed. It was likely Clara, as he knew every other female in the area. His staff had been alerted of her arrival in case of his delay, and he had specifically ordered them to be on their top behavior as he had no desire to douse his bride's adventurous spirit on her first day in town.

Clara Stewart was all class, starch, and gunpowder in one tiny frame of a woman. Apparently, her vocabulary did not include the word fear, or perhaps she needed to know more about the fine balancing wire between which these two groups of workers walked. "Come on, Chet. We'd best rescue the damsel in distress. It might even win me the favor I lost by not being here when the train arrived."

Chapter Two

The journey: Hamilton to Cranston

In Hamilton, the preparations for Clara's trip west began the week following her father's announcement of her governed fate, intensified over the cold winter, and mounted to a chaotic frenzy the week of her departure from her childhood home.

Florence Stewart declared that the beastly mountain weather demanded a new wardrobe for her departing daughter. The endless fittings made Clara impatient to shed the fuss and be on her way. Each new outfit was wrapped and placed in the trunk as if it were gold-threaded, and when spring finally arrived, the conductor hauled her carefully packed belongings aboard the first of many trains that would whisk her away from Hamilton to share a new life with her *beloved* in the Rocky Mountains.

Clara had begun to think of Graham Lee in those cherished terms, as the letters they had exchanged since her father dropped the news into her lap the previous fall had grown peculiarly intimate. The stranger seemed to have mastered the fine art of perching on the edge of familiarity while maintaining a gentleman's distance. The man had sent pencil-drawn pictures of his memories of the terrain she would travel before safely arriving in his mountainous domain. The trip excited her in a manner no one in her established society understood.

The goodbye communicated by her family on departure day, brought on a sweet mix of tears. Some of it was due to the sadness of leaving her loved ones while others were of joy for the journey ahead. Her parents ladened Clara with last-minute instructions, addressing different aspects of the venture before sending her on her way. She waved her arm furiously out the open window, but when the train rounded the bend in the tracks and the figures standing on the depot platform disappeared from view, Clara sunk into her seat. The May air was still damp, and she shivered as she pulled shut the windowpane beside her.

She withdrew the bundle of letters wrapped in a blue ribbon from her handbag and held them close to her heart. The man whom she was speeding toward had been a faithful correspondent, and she almost felt as if she knew him, sight unseen. He challenged her to think of him as she journeyed so as not to grow weary, for the trip from Ontario to British Columbia's border would be long and exhausting.

To the contrary, that first day neither taxed her mind or body. Instead, she experienced nothing but clarity as she left the city behind, and the land opened up before her like a trailing gown of beauty. The promise of luscious and dense forests budding, ready to welcome another season, filled her with new energy. She loved the spring when the dead branches came to life, blossoming and thickening under the hand of the Creator's glory. Nothing in her mind matched the miracle of nature, and she wanted to immerse herself in it as she broke free from a lifetime cocoon of endless feeding. At last, she could spread her butterfly wings and soar through the heavens. Clara smiled knowing her mother would admonish her for entertaining such silly thoughts. In that inept socialite's estimation, a young woman had far more serious issues to concern herself with other than drinking in nature.

Clara ran her manicured fingernails over the top letter and closed her eyes. She had to admit that thinking of her frontier railway man produced a flutter in her heart, not at all like the queasiness evoked after stately gentlemen in Hamilton came calling. Her unspeakable attraction to life's wild side was a feeling she endeavored to quench in her old locale, but now it stirred freely within her. Clara prayed the West would finally satisfy the craving.

The children awaited her, many of whom had never set foot inside a classroom. They fulfilled the practical side of Clara's longing. The brief classes she'd taught to youngsters at her local church would seem like a drop in a bucket compared to educating someone for life. It was a gift she felt eager to bestow upon Cranston's students.

She dozed often, and the terrain offered a new view each time she awoke. Traveling northwest introduced rocky landscapes where trees protruded from cracks at odd angles without any nourishing soil as far as she could see. The twists and turns of the firmly rooted tree trunks, while seeking to face the sun, was a marvel to behold. Nature had found an impossible path on which to grow, and trees stood fearlessly proud, shading the exposed stone from the brilliant sun. Water from the many lakes they passed surged ashore, their whitecaps shimmering in the daytime glare.

Clara caught her first glimpse of the prairies many days later. It was the stretch of land Graham had warned her against. Once the endless fields of blowing grasses began, he'd written, they would seem unending, and she should not be dismayed. Clara was not downcast, for from the midst of the fall's planting, the vibrant fresh of spring green showed the occasional promise of the golden-colored wheat stalks already reaching toward the sky. She could hear a song in the air that would not be extinguished even by the chugging train. The breeze seemed to blow continuously, whistling a sweet, melodic lullaby that brought a soothing rest to the lone traveler.

Clara gasped when she finally caught her first sight of the Rocky Mountains in the distance. She stared in awe, reaching her hand to the window ledge to retrieve the letter in which Graham had described his homeland. She brought it to her pounding heart. Under the cloudless sky, she saw the rugged mountain tips jutting into the heavens, higher than she suspected birds even dared to fly. Snowcapped peaks, shrouded in mist, drifted in and around the crests as if scanning the area for a place to rest. Indeed, its glorious magnificence stood proud, just as Graham had penned. There were wonders too magnificent for the mind to fathom.

After weeks of climbing on and off trains, she lost her bearings and was surprised when the conductor announced they were nearing Cranston. The railroad town was presently the end of the Canadian Pacific Railway line, but only for a short time, the man assured her. His voice sounded full of praise for the railroad that would bring the masses West and keep him employed for the rest of his days.

The train pulled up alongside a half-built platform, and Clara was the only passenger left to disembark at the journey's end, and to her dismay, no one awaited her arrival. The uniformed man unloaded her belongings, and still no one came. Where was her betrothed?

The conductor pointed toward clouds of smoke billowing from chimney stacks off to the west, assuring her that Cranston was a leisurely walk. She took it as an opportunity to stretch her legs.

Clara marched from the partially built train depot to the first sign of civilization with the newly found energy that feeds the fury of a woman scorned. Halting when she saw a long line of railroad workers and a man sitting at a table holding a strongbox, pen and paper, she determined it must be payday. Those awaiting their turn did not appear to be enthusiastic to receive the fruits of their labor, and silence hung in the air like a thick fog.

She had always loved it when her father presented to her a monthly allowance, finding it impossible to hold back her excitement. Unlike *her* frivolous purchases, these men must have bills to pay or families to support. Those burdens and exhaustion were, no doubt, the reason for the long faces.

A short, small-statured man was next in line to receive his monthly wage, and when his limp slowed his progress, the paymaster behind the desk bellowed, "Do you want your pay or not, Cui Wong? I don't have all day."

The employee in line behind him grabbed Wong's arm and quickened his pace toward the impatient man. He bowed his head and inched back as the paymaster scowled. "Twenty-five dollars is more than you deserve. When will that leg heal so you can do a decent day's work?"

Wong shrugged his shoulders and cast a downcast gaze at his feet. The paymaster handed the worker the currency owing but pulled his arm back when Wong leaned in to take the bills. He roared in laughter when the act caused Wong to lose his balance and grab the desk to steady himself.

"Get your filthy hands off my table!" the man roared. Wong backed off to avoid the spittle accompanying the outburst. When the bills had landed on the ground at his feet, the suffering man groaned and bent to retrieve them.

Clara could see the anguish on his face, yet no one offered to assist him. This conduct was barbaric. Instead of being grateful for the man's toil for six out of seven twelve-hour days—that information had been given her by Graham in one of his letters—the paymaster belittled his service. She scanned the area, wondering where the operations manager and her soon-to-be-husband was hiding out while the man bullied his workers.

When no one came to Wong's defense, and the fellow in charge ordered the next in line to step up, Clara rushed over to the table, cast the paymaster a disapproving glance, and crouched to help the injured man pick up his wages. The metal box nearly landed on her when the paymaster behind the desk jumped to his feet.

"Who are you?" he demanded.

She stood, pushed the loosened hat down tighter on her head, and placed both hands firmly on her hips. The stance startled the employee, but she replied gently, hoping to offset his temper. "My name is Clara Stewart. I have just arrived on the train, a short distance back down the line where the tracks ended, expecting to see my fiancé. Instead, after walking ten minutes with the sun beating on my back, I come upon this distasteful scene."

"Miss Stewart... Graham planned to be here but he ran into trouble. As for me, well, you can see I am doing my job, paying these good men for their hard work."

"Humph," she uttered. "I see no such thing and plan to report you to Graham when he returns. What is your name, sir?"

"You think I'm putting a nail in my coffin by giving my name?"

"Don't be absurd. I'm sure there is only one paymaster in the camp, and besides, I have an excellent memory for faces."

"Seeing as how you are fresh off the train, you can't hope to understand how the railroad operates, so don't jump to conclusions."

"Common courtesy for fellow employees is a standard requirement for men in your position. This worker needs to see a doctor. The wound is dirty and will become infected without ointment." She shook the bills she had picked up from the ground in the air. "Do you think this measly amount will pay for a physician to mend him properly and see to his personal needs? Surely, the chap is of more value to you alive than dead."

"That is a matter of opinion," he mumbled before catching sight of something over her head and relief flooded his face. He called out, "Graham, come get your woman. She's a wild one that needs taming."

Clara spun to see a man leading a horse toward her. He removed his hat and slapped it against the leg of his trousers, creating a cloud of dust. His smile was warm and somewhat endearing after the paymaster's cold attitude, but she spotted the worrisome vex lurking behind his deep blue eyes.

"Mr. Lee, I presume? Better late than never," she announced, not attempting to hide her irritation. "This worker has been injured and needs to see a doctor. Do you have one on staff?"

"Kind of."

"Kind of? What sort of an answer is that?"

"Doc Freeman is old school, and he's very selective about who he treats."

"But Wong's wound is festering."

Graham moved closer to study the man whose friend had stepped in to hold him upright. "Send for the town doctor, Wong. If you can't afford his fee, he might take some baking from your missus."

Clara was fuming. She inhaled deeply to calm her nerves. *This* man was her intended? The same one who had won her heart with his clever charm in his letters?

Wong politely nodded when she handed him the bills that she'd picked off the ground. His friend led him away from the scene.

After they had gone, she turned her attention back to Graham. "I can see we disagree on how to show compassion to our fellow man. I understood you to be a Christian, Mr. Lee."

"I hardly think this is the time or place to discuss such things." He nodded to his paymaster. "Carry on, Caleb."

Graham turned back to Clara and said, "Miss Stewart, let me get you settled in your cabin. The camp is not a place where women generally gather."

He leaned in and motioned with his head to the man who had reseated himself behind the desk and said, "He's my brother and not himself these days. Please forgive his behavior."

Exhausted and worn from traveling, Clara decided to end her pursuit of the paymaster's conduct or the doctor, who had clearly forgotten his mandate to serve. Perhaps Caleb was having a bad day. Heaven knew she had growled through many of those while living in Hamilton.

"It's a short distance to town—would you like to walk and stretch your legs?" Graham asked. Had he not heard her complain to the paymaster that she had already sufficiently stretched her legs?

"I left my cases by what I gather is the train depot still under construction."

"I will round up a wagon and team to lug over your belongings *after* I safely deposit you at your new home. If you don't mind my saying, it appears you need to find a chair and perhaps a pot of tea. Mrs. Tether—her husband is on the school board—was sent to your place to welcome you to Cranston. She's probably waiting for you now with tea steeped hot."

Clara's mother had always declared that a hot beverage cooled the insides better than the cold lemonade she presently craved to relieve her parched throat. At this point, she would have settled for anything as long as it included a chair to sit—as he'd accurately assumed—and rest her aching muscles. The opportunity to unwind from her long journey would put her thoughts aright.

"That is extremely kind of her. A refreshment would be nice."

Graham offered her his arm, giving Clara the hope that he had not forgone his practice of proper etiquette in coming West. He rarely commented on *her* social station in his letters, or much of his, for that matter, leaving her to wonder why he had abandoned his family estate to labor from dawn 'til dusk on the frontier. Perhaps, it was for the same reason as she'd left, with the hope that a true adventurer could surely make a go of it in this new land. Clara had prayed their influence as leaders in the community could serve to blend the diverse classifications that separated neighbors, but from what she had viewed, the settlement's populace remained as strangers. The mission that loomed in her imagination appeared unreachable. The residents came in many shapes, sizes, and nationalities. They were rich and poor, working at manual labor or as business tycoons. All of which would play a part when it came to adding a unique flavor to Cranston.

Perhaps the Lord had put her there at a time such as this, for a touch of humanity and etiquette would go a long way toward meeting the worker's dire needs, as she had witnessed. The thought took instant hold in her mind, and she sighed at the enormity of the task before her.

Day one in the small, fledging town of Cranston had defined her mission to children and a community that seemed more under construction than in operation. Preparing the train stop for the passengers who would ride the land from east to west upon the railroad's completion, seemed a daunting commission—both economically and emotionally—though it was sufficient motivation for all citizens concerned.

At the sight of her cabin, a true pioneer spirit swooped in upon Clara. It was quaint, made from logs with a covered porch stretching the entire width of the structure. It was precisely the image she'd conjured up in her mind of how a home in the Rocky Mountains should look. To its north sat the schoolhouse, built equally rustic but complete with a belfry. To her relief, a proud white stone structure with a wooden cross perched on the roof stood within view of her front door. Clara believed a community that welcomed God was a good place to call home.

The school bell atop her workplace left her spellbound, and she stopped to take it all in. To be the first teacher to pull the cord and call inside the children who were ripe for knowledge left her in awe. In Clara's humble opinion, a career as an educator held no greater honor.

She sensed the irritation mounting in the man standing next to her. Her arrival apparently served to waylay him from more pressing tasks. The emotion he stirred in Clara that day did not measure up to the reactions he had aroused while reading the gushing words he'd expressed in his love letters. For the first time in a long time, she wondered if agreeing to this mail-order escapade had been such a good idea.

Chapter Three

Graham knocked on the door of the cabin assigned to Clara. Mrs. Tether opened the door, a jolly looking sort, with a huge smile and eyes that radiated a hearty welcome for Cranston's newest resident, standing beside him.

Graham made the introductions.

"Of course, she's the new teacher," Mrs. Tether said, impatiently, after Graham included the newcomer's occupation with her name. "We haven't invited any other lady to live here or to drink my tea. Men," she said playfully while rolling her eyes at Clara. "Look at you, just as pretty as a picture. My grandson, Timothy, will fall in love with you on the first day of school." She reached for her arm before glancing back at Graham. "Have you finished work for the day? Would you like to sip tea with us ladies?"

"No. I just got back from the Groger site and have some catching up to do."

"Just as I thought," Mrs. Tether said. "With the long hours you keep, it's a good thing your fiancé has a career, or she'd be mighty lonely waiting for you to come calling."

"Never thought of her vocation in that light. I suppose a teacher would be kept busy with a classroom full of students." He touched the rim of his hat. "You two enjoy your visit, and I'll be back shortly with your cases, Miss Stewart."

"Thank you, Mr. Lee," Clara said. "We'll save you a cup of tea to give you some energy to tackle the rest of your day."

"I might even share a cookie with your fellow," Mrs. Tether said, laughing and tugging Clara into the house. "I love the name Clarissa. It's a shame you young folk shorten them up. I had me a grandma with a similar name, and she was the belle of the ball back in civilization." She slammed the door shut with her foot, and the new teacher shifted to peek through a nearby window to see if Graham still had his nose intact. By then, the man was halfway to the horse he'd tied at the hitching post. Graham swung his body over the saddle in one easy sweep and galloped away.

"Do you like the man you've come to marry?"

Clara hurried away from the window to join Mrs. Tether, who looked on with interest. "I hardly know him. Ask me in a month."

"A month? I suspect Graham will want the wedding over long before that."

"Then he is in for a surprise, isn't he?"

Mrs. Tether whistled. "My, oh, my. I wonder if you are of the gentile nature he assumed would show up as his mail-order bride."

"If Mr. Lee expected his woman to take on the role of a doormat or obediently follow his lead like a trained animal then I am definitely not what the man expected," Clara said with an air of independence she sincerely hoped would not be shunned in the West. "Now, how about that tea? My mouth has been watering ever since Mr. Lee mentioned it."

The wife of the schoolboard member was a boat load of information. She appeared to be the town busybody—Clara had her pegged upon their first twenty minutes—who knew the owners of every business and the latest gossip attached to their names and families. She also seemed to feel it her duty to furnish her unique spin on the town's officials and what they were doing wrong, but when she delved into the hypocritical behavior of one of the church members, Clara drew a halt to her rambling.

"Mrs. Tether, did your husband tell you when I was to meet with the schoolboard to discuss my new teaching position in your wonderful town?" Clara emphasized the word wonderful, hoping to dispel the woman's derogatory remarks from her mind.

"Tomorrow afternoon at two. I can come by and pick you up if you think you might get lost."

"I am usually capable of following instructions, and I possess a good sense of direction." When she saw the corners of the woman's smile drop, she reneged, "But I would appreciate your company if you have the time."

"Oh, I do, indeed." Mrs. Tether appeared revived. She peered out the kitchen window and sighed. "I should get home and start supper. Mr. Tether is a stickler for the evening meal being served at five-thirty sharp."

Clara stood. "I am beholden for the kindness you've shown me this day, ma'am. It's been—a definite ray of sunshine to end my weeks of traveling."

"When Mr. Lee gets here with your things, give him a cookie, and let him gulp his tea on the front porch. You don't want people talking your first day here."

Clara sighed. It seemed the proverbial grapevine thrived everywhere. "I'm not in the mood for a lengthy visit anyway. I want nothing more than to explore my new home and retire early."

"We ladies did our best to think of everything you might need. If we've missed anything just go to Al's Mercantile to pick it up. The schoolboard has an account there, and emergency items are given to you for the first week only, and then you are on your own." She headed for the door to leave, but she stopped, glanced back, and said, "But judging by your clothes and fine manners, I suspect you've brought some money of your own to set up housekeeping."

"I did, Mrs. Tether, but thank your husband and the board for their kind offer. I think I will love your little town. You have made me feel very welcome in your midst."

Clara closed the door behind her first guest, leaned against it for support, and expelled a sigh, long and deep. The woman's charity came with a price tag—the cost of Clara's patience. The lady's non-stop chatter was exhausting. Clara had never been one given to gossip and she had often silenced her peers when they attempted to pull her into their critical babble.

She pushed away from the door and took the time to study her surroundings. The kitchen, dining, and sitting area located to the left of the entrance made up the largest room, but the furniture placement served to separate the spaces, clearly defining the purpose of each section.

It was homey. An Oriental rug had been spread under a rocking chair and two arm chairs, should she have company other than her fiancé—woe be to her to have a man inside the house unchaperoned. Her father would be pleased to hear that etiquette was still alive and well in the Wild West. She chuckled and slid her fingers along the face of the leather

Bible lying on the small decorative table. The sitting area faced a rustic stone fireplace that reached the ceiling. It would serve to keep the home warm when winter arrived in all its fury.

The working kitchen had a long counter with a basin sitting under a hand pump in the center, a convenience when it came to bringing water from the outside source inside. How splendid that she would not have to fetch it from the nearby mountain stream, which had been predicted as a strong possibility in *Preparing the Pioneer* book that she had read many times over from cover to cover. Overhead shelves had been stocked with dishes, pots, pans, cutlery, and anything a hostess might need to set her table for guests. She would add many more once her chest arrived, including items received as gifts and personal favorites she had saved when envisioning setting up her own home someday. An ice box sat in the corner. Alongside it was a large pantry with doors to hide the generous supplies stored within. The cookstove was new, the shining blacktop still untouched. Clara did not have any experience when it came to food preparation. Her only knowledge had been gleaned as a child, watching as the hired cook provided meals for the family, but she would enjoy experimenting in the kitchen, learning the craft before her husband arrived on the scene.

In the dining room, six chairs sat around a rectangular wooden table, the top planed smooth to the touch and polished to a shine with a rich, oil finish. A vase filled with flowers adorned the center and the friendly gesture brought joyful tears to Clara's eyes. The padding quilted into the chair cushions would provide a comfortable spot for sitting, and the striking blue pattern complimented the curtains hanging from the two windows at the end of the room.

She made her way to a doorway on the far side of the main room and opened it to find a fair-sized bedroom, and the delight that filled her released an unexpected smile. Clara savored the woodsy smell of the four freshly-shaven logs serving as posts to support the frame under the double bed. A colorful quilt covered the mattress, giving the piece of furniture front stage in the room. The end tables were built of the same pine wood, and there was a lantern on one. The striped curtains hung down each side of the long, narrow windows, bringing a bright, feminine touch to the space. Although the fabric dropped heavily, she supposed the thick lining would serve to keep out the morning sun should she be given the opportunity to sleep in past daylight. An oversized wardrobe, a fully stocked desk, and a long, low dresser with an ornate pitcher and basin on top completed the remainder of the interior bedroom décor.

All in all, it was a very nice home for an educator in the back hills of nowhere. Clara was impressed, and at the end of touring her new space, she felt revived.

A knock sounded at the front door, and she hurried to answer the summons to see Graham standing there. "Sorry for the delay. My staff needed some reminders, and it waylaid my getting here with your belongings."

She dared hope the paymaster might have received a reprimand for his earlier behavior, regardless of being a relative or his state of mind. She'd been taught that a job instructing children was a sacred task and resolved never to take her personal frustrations out on her students. The same should go for any position of authority, including those lording over newcomers to the country.

"No trouble at all," Clara said. "Would you have time to sit on the porch with a cup of tea and one of Mrs. Tether's cookies before returning to work?"

"I would like that, Miss Stewart."

Graham dragged in all her cases along with the huge chest and left them parked by the front entrance. She took the opportunity to duck into the kitchen to prepare his snack, peeking intermittently to notice the way his muscles bulged under his shirt as he shifted the heavy load. She had packed for *the rest of her life*, leaving little in Hamilton that might entice her to return should the going become rough.

Clara motioned at the tray she had placed on the table outside, nestled between two chairs. He waited for her to sit. She poured the hot beverage from the tea pot into his cup first, then into hers, before passing him a serviette and offering him a cookie from the plate.

He took two and grinned. "Thank you. It's common knowledge that Mrs. Tether makes the best oatmeal raisin cookies in Cranston."

"They are extremely tasty. I must ask her for the recipe." She felt nervous in admitting it, but she wanted to be upfront with the man. "I have much to learn in the kitchen. You will need all the grace you can muster not to ridicule me in my attempts."

"I'm sure you will succeed at anything you put your mind to," he said as he bit into the cookie.

"What makes you so sure, Mr. Lee?" Clara sipped her tea, watching his expression over the rim of her cup as he searched to find the proper answer.

"You have spunk and intelligence. You notice things others do not, and you take charge. I see a strong frontier woman waiting to explode upon our tiny piece of God's majesty, and one equally capable of causing unease for anyone who dares stand in the way."

"All of that after one encounter? I shall have to work to save some surprises for another day."

"Don't forget the letters. I am very good at reading between the lines," Graham said. "Still, I have no doubt the good and the bad shall make an appearance, but I hope you will get acquainted with your surroundings before making too many judgment calls."

"I shall strive to keep an open mind, but as my father would tell you if he were here, I have strong convictions. Many have labeled me too black and white."

"You will confront a lot of gray areas here, Miss Stewart. Sometimes it is better to traverse the storm rather than oppose it, and watch for God's opportunities to serve a greater purpose."

"Wisely said, Mr. Lee. I shall attempt to keep the bigger picture in mind." Though she felt rebuked by the Lord, He had used her betrothed to refocus her energy on His plan for her in this society.

"I would appreciate that."

"Tell me about your job. It must be an overwhelming task to run the railroad lines through and around these massive mountains."

"It is a challenge, indeed. We sometimes wind back and forth unnecessarily to create a gentler climb for the future trains. Sometimes, it's easier to tunnel through rock and avoid a treacherous drop to the valley floor rather than hug the mountain."

"And you decide the path?"

"Yes. I hope you will excuse me when at times I go on scouting trips with the geographical team to document the next ten miles of track."

"Is that where you were today?"

"No, some trouble at the Groger site I had to deal with."

"Well then, when we're together, I will attempt to take your mind off of your problems and the enormous contract assigned to you."

"I will enjoy the distraction, Miss Stewart, especially from you." His infectious smile reached deep into her soul, and her heart confirmed that God had indeed come before her to prepare the way.

Clara began to dress for the meeting immediately after downing a ham sandwich, which agitated her nervous stomach. This would be her first interview anywhere, and she firmly believed that one could never take back a bad first impression. In reminisce, Graham had proven that theory wrong just yesterday by standing her up at the train station and then managing to redeem himself before nightfall.

She chose the most business-like outfit in her wardrobe. The teal bowtie around her neck matched the color of her skirt, and the white silk blouse under the snug, fitted jacket offset the entire look. She wore sturdy black shoes on her feet and a modest hat on her head to protect her dark tresses from the sun. Her scholarly appearance portrayed a serious commitment to teaching, one she hoped the board members would notice and appreciate.

The young educator stared at her figure in the mirror, seeing herself for the first time as an independent career woman and not just another girl lost in a pool of courting contenders from which suitors could have their pick. Her dream of living the frontier life had come to pass. Now she just had to convince the board that she was made of enough stamina to survive.

Clara selected a small drawstring purse from her collection and left the bedroom. In glancing out the front window, she spotted Mrs. Tether marching up the road. If anything, the woman proved punctual, arriving one half hour before the scheduled appointment. She opened the door and stepped onto the verandah to greet her neighbor.

"Good afternoon, Miss Stewart," Mrs. Tether's voice rang out as she waved heartily. She appeared to be in a jolly mood, and Clara smiled, glad her first encounter with the townsfolk had been a positive one.

"Hello, Mrs. Tether. It's a beautiful day to take a stroll."

"Yes," she said a little out of breath, "but in my worry that I might arrive late, I fear my pace was faster than these chubby legs can manage."

"We can take it slow from here on out. The town center doesn't appear to be far," Clara said, skipping down the porch steps to join her in the yard.

As they strolled down Cranston's main street, Mrs. Tether put faces and locations to the characters she had mentioned the previous day. By the time they reached the town hall, Clara's head buzzed with information overload.

"Now, don't you let any of them in there give you a hard time. Your position is finalized, and this get-together is a mere formality. They know it as well as I. Besides, they all like Mr. Lee, who has managed to build two distinct societies in one small area, so his courting you is in your favor."

"I wish to gain favor on my own merit and not because of the man I've come to marry,"

Clara said, "and although I have had little interaction with Mr. Lee's working community, I believe the Good Book does not discriminate against any of His creation. He wants us all to dwell in unity and love."

"The camp workers are not believers, so how can our situation apply to the Word?"

"We were all created in the image of God, and every knee that bows is a candidate for Christianity. If they have not heard the good news, perhaps we should take it upon ourselves to introduce them to our Creator God"

"That would be the Reverend's responsibility, not a woman under the protection of her husband."

"Then I am grateful I have no husband to dictate who I spend my time with as of yet."

Mrs. Tether grunted and pointed at the entrance. "Just inside that door, first room on your right is where the committee is meeting."

"What a grand building. It is beneficial that the town hall be fully constructed and active while the community grows. It gives the locals a sense of stability," Clara said.

"I agree. My sons did a lot of hammering on that place—one is a carpenter and the other a stonemason. It's excellent work, if I do say so myself," she said, her face beaming with pride. "Provides Cranston with a personal touch, and the services inside help to keep the riff-raff in order."

"It will, at that." Clara picked up the hem of her skirt and started up the steps. "Wish me luck, Mrs. Tether," she said as if her correspondence hadn't already secured her job. She hoped the members would not be rigid and controlling for her ideas when it came to conducting education bordered on the radical.

Graham glanced at his time piece and sighed. Clara's interview would finish shortly, and he was eager to hear how the old sticks-in-the-mud reacted to the spitfire of a new teacher. Not that they could be choosy—there certainly wasn't anyone lined up to challenge her for the position—but in his heart, he'd like the townsfolk to think highly of his bride and accept her as they had him.

He pushed the paperwork on his desk aside and stood. A man courting a girl needed to make time for her. He could catch up with work later, even if he had to burn the candle late. He left the railcar office and rode his horse into Cranston in time to see Clara exit the town hall.

She was a beauty, no doubt about that. Graham preferred dark haired women; grateful she was not like the flighty blonde he'd taken to dinner a few months back. He wanted confirmation that the lady with whom he was corresponding would hold his heart captive for the long-term, and that lone-date with the fair-haired chatterbox had proved his loyalty to the mail-order bride beyond a shadow of a doubt. Caleb had warned him that the mail order bride needed taming, but then the younger Lee favored a more obedient type—all beauty and no brains—that would not conflict with his plans. Graham much preferred a high-spirited woman, one who would keep his life interesting to some degree and not conduct herself as a puppet on a string.

Graham dismounted, removed his hat, and met Clara at the foot of the steps. "You are looking perfectly scholarly this afternoon, Miss Stewart."

"I hope the committee inside came to that conclusion."

"You appear uncertain—did you run into a brick wall with the bunch?"

"Not anything that I couldn't skirt around to pacify them," she said, that playful twinkle in her eyes returning to her face. "Are all schoolboards made up of elderly members with little vision for the future?"

"This one is, but I suspect that will change as new folks move into Cranston."

He offered her his free arm while holding onto the horse's bridle with his other hand. "May I interest you in an afternoon pastry and beverage at Francine's Diner?"

"Mrs. Tether gave her establishment a raving review, although hesitantly, I might add. She suspects the woman gets away with too much, and it gives her husband a bad name." Clara studied Graham. "I am pleased that you are not so old fashioned and restrictive. I daresay that I could not endure the weight of living beneath a man's boot."

"I suspected as much." Graham grinned. "Your letters were brimming with independence, but there was also a favorable dose of respect that I can live with."

"It is helpful that we got acquainted through the mail. It will make our courtship so much easier."

"Let's hope so." He lifted his brow, seeing first hand that the lady seemed capable of lobbing surprises his way as an everyday occurrence. It was something that might prove a bit tough to rein in should it become necessary. He prayed it would never come to that.

After they were seated and sipping the coffee the waitress had brought to the table, Clara withdrew the key from her purse and said, "I can't wait to see the schoolhouse. Opening day seems so far away but I am glad to be here early, to get established in the community."

"I am pretty sure the children do not share your urgency," Graham said, "though most busy adults putting down roots here will be happy when the youngsters have somewhere to go during the day and won't be underfoot."

"Likely so. Care to come with me to spy-out the school room before you are forced to return to your duties?"

"That would be nice. A man needs to know where to envision his sweetheart when they are parted."

"Sweetheart seems a bit forward, Mr. Lee."

"We *are* courting, and I think of you as my sweetie—do you mind?"

Her face flushed crimson. "No, I suppose that is a compliment, sir."

"Indeed." His fingers drummed on the table and finally he blurted out, "Are you going to drag this courtship out, or should we wed before the children begin classes?"

"I was hoping to be swept off my feet by your handsome demeanor."

"You were? Well, I expect I can manage that," he said in a teasing voice, as if wooing his betrothed were a game.

"I realize we have become acquainted through the letters, but do you not wonder if the face-to-face reality is more relevant in the final decision-making process?"

"I have already decided to marry. I thought you had, too."

"My father said I had the final choice should I arrive to find you as wild as the West is rumored to be."

Graham laughed. "We do have wild, but I shall treat you with the gentleness you deserve, my love. You need not concern yourself about that, my future Mrs. Lee."

"I could not help but notice that you and I have the same coincidence in first names as last names—Stewart and Lee."

"Good catch," Graham said

"And from my reading, I'd understood the name Lee to be of Chinese ancestry. Do you have connections in your lineage?"

"Now you are reading far too much into the name," Graham said. "It is purely coincidental. Although, I think the Good Lord is having a chuckle up there on account of placing me in the isolated Rocky Mountains working with immigrants of such descent. It has inspired me to become His mediator in this place."

"I am impressed, Mr. Lee." Clara lowered her gaze, wondering if he were up to having his character challenged. Clara plunged ahead, nevertheless. "I must admit that I did entertain some concerns as to your role as arbitrator between the workers and the townsfolk."

"How so?"

"I see you have not forced your physician, who was hired to care for your employees, to provide treatment for the men living in the camp. That gives me cause for concern."

"I cannot force the medical man to treat anyone. There are still hurdles left to jump before the two groups are integrated."

"You pay his wages, and I suspect that is reason enough to enforce his job description as you see fit," she said. "Do you not view it as your duty, to also be the bridge between the chasm separating your employees, not just the citizens in Cranston?"

"It is not that simple."

"It's as good an excuse as any, Mr. Lee," she said, wondering just how genuine his claim to mediator rang true. "I view our assignments in Cranston as God positioning—as you alluded to earlier—for this time and place, to instill a sense of harmony to the people under our care."

"Prejudice is a heavy burden in our midst, one you know little about."

"Perhaps, but I shall walk obediently in the shoes God gave me to wear in your town, Graham Lee, and do it without compromise."

"I love your mission, and together we might make a difference," he said. "And in case you are wondering, I am delighted with my mail order bride."

"I am glad to hear that."

"Compassionate Clara—I think that is the nickname the locals will give you."

"There is no crime in extending kindness toward all people."

"Your concerns are duly noted, Miss Stewart, and your humble servant will consider his deficiency in the matter." His voice came across as being a bit too jovial. Judging by the frown she cast him, Graham wondered if his flippant comment had put her off.

Clara wiped her gooey fingers on the napkin, stood, and smiled politely. "If you are finished, I am most eager to see the schoolhouse."

"Of course," he said, jumping to his feet. "Time sure flies when visiting with a pretty lady."

"Save your flattery. I judge character by actions, not fancy words on paper. You would do well to remember that."

He wiped his mouth with the corner of his napkin to allow him time to collect himself.

"You *are* a handful for sure, just like Caleb said."

"Your brother is a subject for another time. For now, I want to enjoy exploring my space with you, and move forward in our courting adventure."

"Sounds fine to me," Graham said, definitely interested in socializing with his mail-order bride.

Chapter Four

Clara watched from the window as Graham mounted his horse and headed back to work. He was a complex man, and she often felt confused about his principles. She realized character growth was an ongoing process and she would give him the benefit of the doubt as to his present inconsistencies.

An hour had slipped away in an excited rush of emotions. Graham had provided a few good suggestions, and it warmed her heart to think he liked children. He also carried all the boxes she'd packed for the students from the cabin to the schoolhouse. Those muscles had come in handy again.

She sighed and turned to study her classroom. At the center front was a large teacher's desk with a blackboard behind it, and in the left corner, a potbelly stove to keep them warm in the winter. There was one main aisle, and on each side, were bench seats big enough to accommodate three students set four deep, complete with a u-shaped desk and spots to store books out of sight. After counting the seats, she concluded the classroom would sit twenty-four children comfortably. She'd seen a few youngsters racing in the street earlier, but she supposed there were others, enough to warrant hiring a teacher.

Clara opened the first box and ran her fingers over the hard covers. She loved books of all kinds and had brought novels and readers from home, not knowing what the new schoolboard in the mountains would have available. A shelving unit to the front, right, of the room was spacious enough to house them all. When Clara finished her task, she stood back to view the full shelves, the presence of the written word bringing the teacher a sense of pride.

A movement at the back of the room startled Clara. She twirled around to see a clean-cut young boy standing there, with freckles and one front tooth missing. "Afternoon, Teacher. Granny said you was here, and I just had to see fer myself."

"Your name wouldn't happen to be Timothy, would it?" Clara asked.

"Now, how'd you know that?"

"I met your grandmother, and just made an educated guess."

"Well, I'll be. If education makes folks that smart, I reckon you'll find me here every time the door opens."

Clara smiled. "Come and see the books I brought. Do you like to read?"

He removed a full-length novel and glanced at the first page. "I can't read *that* good, Teacher. Maybe if you have something simpler?"

She passed him a first-grade reader, and he grinned at the sight of the easy words. "I might be able to read this one. Pa has me working pretty hard at the store, and I'm much better at arithmetic. We've been in Cranston six months now, and my lessons have fallen behind with the folks too busy to teach me."

"Well, I'm here now, and before you know it, you'll be reading that complicated novel or my name isn't Miss Clara Stewart."

"Miss Stewart—I like that name."

"So do I." She laughed, and mussed the top of his curly hair. "Can you tell me how many students will be joining us?"

"I reckon around fifteen, Miss Stewart. All different ages, but likely most stuck at the same learning spot."

"That should make my efforts easier," Clara said.

She watched him pick up a title written in Chinese, a book she'd included knowing there might be students who understood the language. "The words on this cover look like pictures," Timothy said.

"It's Chinese. How many children will come to school from the camp?"

The boy's face took on a surprised look. "Oh, none, miss. Those old buzzards who run the town would throw a hissy-fit—no offense intended since Grampy is one of them."

"I saw a great number of children in the camp when I arrived—do they have their own teacher?"

"Not that I know of. Even if they did, no one there can teach reading, writing, and arithmetic the Canadian way. They're smart enough, but got no education since coming here, miss."

Clara chuckled, thinking Timothy's speech could use some upgrading as well. "The immigrants are new to our country and deserve an opportunity to study the same as anyone else." Clara's mind worked frantically to figure out a way to get them inside her classroom without the townsfolk rebelling.

"I'm partial to your way of thinking, Miss Stewart. Ling Chuse is my friend. We sneak off sometimes to play." Timothy face clouded, and in a nervous voice he said, "You won't tell Granny, will you? You knowing her and all?"

"I won't tell." She went to her desk and picked up her purse. "Would you introduce me to Chuse?"

"Sure, but most woman folk from town don't go into the camp."

"Why—is there disease?"

"No, Miss." He seemed embarrassed, and Clara felt annoyed that one so young would be subject to prejudice of that magnitude.

"Then you and I shall sneak down and say hello to your friend—how about that?"

"Sounds like fun, Miss Stewart. It's not like sneaking when an adult comes with me."

She locked the door to the building and hurried to catch up to the eager boy. "You might have to slow down. This dress is rather cumbersome and folks hereabouts would think it odd to see me wearing pants like you."

"That'd be quite the spectacle, Miss Stewart," the boy said roaring with laughter. "But you do look mighty pretty in that dress. Pants wouldn't fit you the same."

"A boy with a silver tongue—shame on you for complimenting your teacher like that," she said playfully.

"Didn't mean no offense by it, Miss Stewart."

"None taken, Timothy."

They walked across the plush green grass of the valley floor, and as they neared the smoke billowing from the outside campfires, Clara stopped to take it all in. She'd read of cowboys camping out on the range for a short time as a part of their work. She could understand that, but families stuffing all of their possessions into a tent they called home seemed degrading to the girl who had never lacked one single thing her heart desired in her entire life. Mostly women and children milled about the encampment. Some of the ladies cooked over a fire while others chopped vegetables or pounded spices on a large flat rock, and some were seated on the ground, sewing. Groups of children carried armloads of wood while the lucky ones played a game with a stick in a patch of sand. The men were likely still off working on the railroad that time of day.

"This way," Timothy said, pulling her to the east side of the settlement. When he spotted a young lad, he called out, "Ling Chuse—come and meet my new teacher." He looked at Clara and explained, "His family are from the newest bunch of arrivals, and I've been helping him with his English. He's pretty smart."

"Really? You teach English?"

"I know I'm not an expert, but even slang is better than nothing."

"You're right, and that makes you a very creative and effective teacher, Timothy."

"Why, I plumb never thought of it that way, Miss Stewart. Granny would roll over laughing at the thought of me being a real teacher."

"You can be whatever you want to be, young Timothy. Follow your dreams and your heart." She inhaled deeply. "Now, how about some introductions?"

"Chuse, this here is Miss Stewart. She's going to be the new teacher in Cranston."

The boy's head lowered slightly. "Nice to meet you, miss." He looked around and added, "A fine lady like you shouldn't be here."

"Nonsense. I can go where I please. Unless you think *your* parents will be offended," Clara said.

"Not *my* parents," Chuse said.

"I was informed that you will not be joining us at the schoolhouse when classes start up."

A voice from behind answered, "That would be true, miss."

Clara turned to face a woman clad in a plain dusty skirt and a shirt tucked in at the waist. Her hair was jet black and wrapped in braids around her head like a crown.

She reached out her hand in greeting, "My name is Clara Stewart—Cranston's new schoolteacher."

"I am called Ling Aihan."

"That is a very pretty name. I hope we can become friends."

She seemed confused. "Are you Lee's new woman?"

"I am under his protection, and we are courting, so I suppose you could call me that."

"He won't like you being here." Her hands hung at her side, anxious fingers fidgeting at the folds of her skirt while her eyes scanned the area.

"Mr. Lee will get used to it. I understand your children have no teacher in the camp to help them learn English or secure an education."

"You would be right there, miss. There are many ill-it-er-ate persons in the camp," she stretched the word out and looked at Timothy for confirmation.

Her son's friend grinned and nodded his head. "You got the big word right, ma'am."

"I've been studying the lessons you leave for Chuse, Timothy, but I agree, we will need a better understanding of the language to settle into your country."

"*Our* country," Clara corrected the woman before turning to Timothy. "You *do* have a teacher's heart, young man."

"Yeah, but I keep the lessons pretty simple most times. Mrs. Ling is extra smart and picking the language up faster than I can provide new words," he said humbly.

"Simple is good for most at the beginning. People absorb information differently." Clara turned to Ling Aihan. "Would you organize a group and allow me to come out to teach you here, in your camp, so as not to ruffle any feathers in town by inviting you into the schoolhouse?"

Timothy squealed and added excitedly, "I could be your helper, Miss Stewart. I know a lot of folks."

"I don't want you to get into trouble," she said to Timothy.

"You are a newcomer and haven't—"

Clara cut off Aihan's line of reasoning.

"I am a teacher, pure and simple, and everyone needs to learn how to read and write if they wish to succeed in life. I took an educator's oath, and I am very serious to follow my mission. No one will take that from me, Ling Aihan."

"I can gather those who want to learn, if you will come."

"I will come. School hasn't started in town yet, so I have more free time now than I will in the fall, so we should get busy and learn the basics." Clara looked at Timothy. "If you are determined to help, can you slip away at nine in the morning?"

"I can, but this here venture won't stay secret for long, Miss Stewart."

"We shall get started and take each day as it comes, young Timothy." She turned back to the mother and boy, who stood nearby dumbfounded at the sudden turn of events.

"Our very own school at the Cranston Camp—no one will believe me." Aihan's eyes pooled with tears. She nudged her son to move aside as the two visitors scurried away.

"They seem pleased," Clara said to Timothy. "Now, we need to put our heads together and figure out how we will instruct them."

Teacher and apprentice chatted all the way back to town, planning the new classes as they walked.

"If you have some bills and coins, Miss Stewart, I can help coach them about money. I know lots about that from the store. Camp workers suspect the paymaster cheats them out of wages, his knowing most of them can't count the currency."

"Do you think so? If that is the case, Mr. Lee should be told."

"That would just make their lives more miserable, but if Mr. Caleb knew they could add up the bills, maybe it wouldn't be so easy to pull the wool over their eyes."

"Aren't we the rebellious duo today?" Clara scuffed the top of his head with her hand. "This won't get you into serious trouble, will it?"

"It might, miss, but when you got the itch to teach, no one can scratch the bug out, even when your head is full of it."

"Are you talking ticks or knowledge in your head?" Clara asked, chuckling at his twist on words. "You are a most delightful lad. I shall have to learn this picturesque language you speak."

"Aw…, Ma says I talk in riddles and need schooling to straighten out my mind, and sometimes I think Grampy is embarrassed, him being on the schoolboard and all."

"How old are you, Timothy?"

"Turned eight last month, Miss Stewart. We came West just when I was about to start school back in Saskatoon, so I sort of missed the chance. Lots of folks here put great stock in a teacher coming to educate the youngsters."

"I am glad to be of service," Clara said.

"Do you like Mr. Lee?" the boy asked.

"I don't think *that* is any business of yours, but yes, he seems to be a fine man."

"You come all this way to marry him, right?"

"I *came* all this way to marry Mr. Lee," Clara corrected him, "but I don't think this is a proper discussion to have with my new eight-year-old friend."

"I know about mushy stuff," he said. "I saw my parents kissing once."

"That discussion is definitely none of *my* business, young man. A gentleman in training needs to watch his tongue." She scanned the grand spectacle around her. "I have a secret."

The boy stopped and stared. "You can tell me. I won't utter a word even if they tie me to a post and whip it out of me."

"I doubt anyone is *that* interested in my musings," she said, enjoying the lad's spirit. "I came West primarily to teach and see the mountains. Mr. Lee was the security my father insisted upon, but he took third place in my reasons for coming. That said, I am growing fond of the man."

"He's all right, but I'm with you on the mountain views. Ain't nothing more spectacular in all of the Good Lord's creation."

"If you are going to be my assistant, you will need to speak correctly."

"Yeah, I know ain't ain't a real word—or so Granny tells me all the time."

"It's that slang you mentioned earlier, not proper English."

"Yes, miss. I'm really good at slang."

"Not under my watch, you hear? School is in early for you, Timothy Tether."

When they reached her cabin, Timothy removed his cap and beat it on his leg as she'd seen men do on occasion since her arrival. "Be saying so long for now, Miss Stewart—got chores waiting for me at home—but I'll see you back here first thing in the morning, and we'll troop to the camp together. Wouldn't do you well to go in there by yourself." He twirled the hat in his fingers as if to confirm his authority as her protector.

"Thank you. It was very nice meeting you, Timothy. I think we will have a long friendship, you and I."

The fragrance of the mountain air, the sweet valley wild flowers, and the grasses blowing in the breeze lulled her off to dreamland as soon as her head hit the pillow. In the morning, Clara could not recall having ever slept so soundly.

She already loved Cranston along with the people on both sides of the invisible social fence, and thought of it as her home. There was something noble to be said about being in the thick of a changing world. The railroad would link the East to the West, expanding and altering the landscape for countless travellers. Sure, there would be the greedy ones whose sole purpose was to turn a profit, but many would come for the adventure and to leave their imprint on the foothills of the magnificent mountains. Her name might never be written in the history books, but it would be engraved in hearts like the young Timothy's, and his Chinese friends, and hopefully many more before she finished her mission.

Today's school session in the camp would surely ruffle some self-righteous feathers, but her decision to help the immigrants adjust to their new country would not fail for her lack of trying.

Timothy arrived on schedule and seemed more excited than her, if that was at all possible. The young appeared able to express joy without reserve, which caused her to wonder at what point adults quenched such openness of spirit. That day, she hoped her students would see her heart and pride in their achievements.

The camp was a buzz with activity. Mostly women and children drifted toward the center ring Ling Aihan had organized for their classes to convene. Although, a quick count filled Clara's heart with excitement, she also realized she did not have nearly enough slates for the bunch.

Aihan smiled when they approached, her arm sweeping over the people seated on the ground. "I passed the word around last night, and everyone is eager to learn. Do you mind adults coming alongside the children, Miss Stewart?"

"Not at all. You will all need to update your education now that you've chosen to join our Western culture."

"Is written English close to Chinese?"

"Not at all. I am jealous of the picturesque way you print your letters."

The few adults nearby groaned when overhearing that school might be tough.

"But children learn quickly, and they will help the adults practice when I'm not here—just like Timothy and your son Chuse did to get you started." She opened the burlap case and withdrew slates and pieces of chalk. "Give one to each family—they will have to share."

The students mastered printing the first three letters of the alphabet and tested the soft and long sounds of the letters as they were found in familiar words. They shouted words they knew that started with the letter back at her. Apple seemed the favorite choice, which motivated the group break for a midmorning snack. During the second session, Timothy taught them how to count in English, and showed them bills that corresponded with the numbers. In closing, he demonstrated what twenty-five dollars would look like when their men brought home their week's wages.

Clara stayed to eat lunch with Aihan, but Timothy had to hurry home for a pant fitting. His grandmother was sewing him new trousers, and she expected him back for the noon meal. The older ladies had fried up some vegetables in a tasty sauce over the open fire and piled it atop a mound of white rice, a community offering in which everyone in the camp partook.

"This is very good. You shall have to tell me the ingredients in your secret sauce so I can feed it to Mr. Lee after we are married."

The group went quiet and one lady piped up, "Do you like Mr. Lee?"

"I do," Clara said. "He has a good heart, just a bit rough around the edges, but I can iron those out in time."

The women laughed, and the tension that had erupted seemed to break. Clara felt the need to support her betrothed. "Mr. Lee has a huge task ahead of him—many miles of track to lay before the contract is up. Your men are doing a splendid job in helping him meet his deadlines. He has said as much to me."

"He appreciates our men?"

"He does. Unfortunately, not all of the hired supervisors your men encounter daily do things the way he instructs, but he is one man, and he can only be in one place at a time."

"I understand that. Mr. Lee is always respectful when he talks to us ladies, and I caught him showing the youngsters an alley game once. His heart is good, just like you said, Miss Stewart."

"I am glad to hear you say that. We are trying our best to make you comfortable in your new land," Clara said.

"Mr. Lee said the very same thing. Being known for kindness is a noble attribute," Aihan said.

"Attribute—is that a new word?"

The woman blushed.

"And I shall always remember your kindness in sharing this meal with me. It was very good," Clara stood, "But I mustn't stay any longer."

"Will you be back tomorrow?" Aihan asked.

"I can come until regular classes begin in Cranston. The town has paid me to teach their children, so that must be my priority, but by then, the group here should have a good enough grasp of the alphabet to practice on their own, and I will come Saturdays on my own time."

"We appreciate whatever time you can give us."

One of the nearby ladies filled the canvas bag with the slates and chalk and handed it to Clara.

"Thank you. These are my personal supplies, so the town will not make a fuss about my sharing them outside the classroom.

"It's been a fruitful morning, but chores await us all." Clara waved as she left the camp, her spirits high, and her mind racing with ideas for the next day's lessons.

This routine continued for two weeks, and those who had guessed what was happening at the Cranston Camp, did not feel the need to throw it out for the vultures on the grapevine to dissect.

The second week proved to be the longest, with Graham being called away to map out the next stretch of rail line. The hours not spent at camp with her new friends and students stretched out, and at times, a deep loneliness overtook her. She had not realized she would miss Graham's companionship so intimately.

The afternoon before Graham's return, Clara noticed Mrs. Tether standing in front of her cabin as she approached after a camp session. To avoid having to supply an explanation, she ditched the bag of supplies behind a tree.

"Good afternoon, Mrs. Tether. A wonderful day for a long walk."

"Indeed. I got to thinking that you must be lonely with your man gone. The social committee is meeting at two to plan the back-to-school event, and we wondered if you had time to join us. You being the teacher, and all, might have some grand ideas to share."

"Since this is the *first* school year in Cranston, this event must also be a new venture," Clara said.

"Surely is, but it's one worthy of celebrating. Folks seem to lose themselves in getting all of the outside work done before winter sets in. Some keep their noses to the grindstone, attempting to outdo the competition. Regardless of the reason, I suspect our residents have forgotten that we need a touch of fun, maybe kick up our heels on the dance floor."

"And drink spiked fruit juice," Clara added, noting the shocked expression on Mrs. Tether's face. "That suggestion would have come from my father, or any man on a committee involving fun and dancing."

"Of course, but there will be no alcohol in an event involving families and children." Mrs. Tether sounded emphatic about that detail.

"As any honorable citizen would surely agree, Mrs. Tether," Clara said. "Let me go and clean up, and I will meet you there at two. Where is the meeting?"

"At Francine's Diner."

"Perfect. I have been there on occasion with Mr. Lee. I will be on time, bubbling with suggestions for the event. I am pleased to be included, thank you."

"I figured you coming from…well, fancy social circles, that you'd be full of good ideas."

Clara placed her foot on the first step leading onto her verandah. "See you soon, then." When she reached the front door, she turned to see Mrs. Tether's carriage riding off toward Cranston. Clara retraced her steps to the tree where she had dumped the slates and chalk—evidence of her sideline charge at the camp. She felt deliciously mischievous when retrieving them without notice. No sense igniting an unnecessary fire she couldn't put out in the hearts of the locals.

Chapter Five

"School starts in early September."

"So soon?" Clara asked. Time seemed to be flying by.

"This is not a big farming community yet. Only two homesteads presently operate outside of town in the fertile valley. They supply the meat and dairy products for us to purchase at the store and the butcher shop. The majority of parents and students are eager to get the program underway." Mr. Glenning cleared his throat and added in a haughty voice, "Time for us to see if the new teacher will make the difference we hired her for."

"The children and I will do our best, sir. And, of course, I am ready to begin anytime."

"It gets mighty cold up here. Tends to send tenderfoots back to civilization," he said, burying his demeaning attitude deeper into Clara's patience. She sensed his underlying doubt in her ability to succeed in her mission and perhaps even some tension derived from the possibility he'd heard rumors about her trips to the camp. She wondered if he was baiting her and decided not to fall prey to his intimidation.

"*This* tenderfoot has calloused feet, Mr. Glenning, and she is not afraid of nature's chill or those tendered by uninformed men," Clara said before reaching for the paper and pen she'd placed in her case. "Shall we get down to business? We have a celebration party to plan—one that will go down in Cranston's history books."

Mrs. Tether squealed with delight when she shook her finger in Mr. Glenning's direction. "Didn't I tell you inviting a socialite schoolteacher would be a good idea?"

"You did." The man appeared somewhat humbled and busied himself by shuffling papers.

"Welcome, Miss Stewart," Mrs. Hycrest said, grabbing her pen and opening a book that lay on the table in front of her. "I'm the official note-taker, so you won't need to bother."

"It's a habit of mine to document meetings, so I don't forget anything. Especially if a job is assigned to me."

Mrs. Tether, the president of the social committee, spoke first. "The date is our primary consideration. How does Saturday, August 22 sound? The weather is still favorable, and Miss Stewart will have ample time afterward to clean up and prepare to receive the children on September 8."

"The twenty-second is not in the far too distant future?" Clara asked, panic in her voice. Never had an event in Hamilton been planned in such a short time. "And will the children be ready to settle into lessons at the beginning of September?"

"The season is fast departing," Mr. Tether explained. "Surely, you came prepared with planned lessons for your students." He covered his mouth and coughed. "My concern here is primarily the children."

"Yes, and this being a school event is the *only* reason a board member was invited to join the social committee to plan the affair," Mr. Glenning stated, seemingly taking his solo male presence on Cranston's social committee seriously.

Clara nipped the awkwardness that interchange caused in the bud. "Of course. I can be ready whenever the board says, but I might as well say this out straight, right at the onset of our planning. As you are all aware, Mr. Lee and I are engaged to be married. I thought it might be nice to have my students and the townspeople he serves in attendance when we say our vows."

"A wedding? At a back-to-school event?" The idea undoubtedly surprised Mrs. Hycrest.

"I think it's a splendid idea," Mrs. Tether chimed in.

"Why am I not surprised?" her husband said. "You are forever the romantic."

"I haven't heard you complain all these years, Mr. Tether," his wife said, playfully pinching his reddened cheeks and chuckling.

"You are getting off-track, woman." He straightened in his chair and looked at Clara. "I suppose a wedding is more proper than dragging out the courtship. According to her job application, Miss Stewart will be twenty at Christmas—any decent woman should have nabbed a man by then."

"Twenty? I daresay. I already had two young'uns by then," Mrs. Hycrest said.

"Please, when I choose to marry is no one's concern." The reminder of her twentieth birthday brought Granny's inheritance to mind. It also served to seal her matrimonial date. She was eager to have the formalities over and done with, quite satisfied with the railroad manager she'd come West to wed.

The past year had flown by, filled with Clara's preparations to come to the Rocky Mountains, her travels, settling in Cranston, and courting the prestigious Graham Lee. Her parents in Hamilton would be pleased to hear that the date for the wedding had been set just under-the-wire of the financially significant twentieth year of her life. She wondered what Graham would think when she informed him that not only would he receive a gift of money from Charles Stewart to marry Clara, but his new wife would be very wealthy in her own right come the holidays.

"We shall plan the ceremony for the end of the day just before the dance, so we can send the couple off proper-like."

"Sounds perfect, Mrs. Tether. Thank you for your support," Clara said. "But for now, let's concentrate on the daytime events."

"Games for the children are a must," Mr. Tether said. "Get the fun out of their system so they can clamp down on their studies when the school bell rings and classes begin."

"You're just an old kill-joy," his wife said. "I swear you came out of your mama's womb full grown without an ounce of fun in those bones of yours."

"I know a lot of games we played at Sunday school picnics while I was growing up. I can organize those," Clara offered.

"Good. That was never my area of expertise," Mrs. Hycrest said. "We shall leave that in your capable hands, Miss Stewart."

"Food is mine," Mrs. Tether said, "and you know I can get the town's ladies to make their best recipes for an opening lunch event."

"My grown children say I have a knack for decorating," Mrs. Hycrest said, "and I still have that pretty archway we built for my daughter's nuptials in the early spring. I can set that up in the church for Miss Stewart's wedding later in the day."

"What do you want me to do?" Mr. Glenning asked.

"We will need some posters printed off to spread the news—not about the wedding, just about the school event. Remember that Mr. Lee and Miss Stewart want to surprise everyone."

"I know how to keep a secret," he grumbled. "If you need any help setting up games that morning, Miss Stewart, you feel free to summon us fellows. We'll be as close to you ladies as a shout if there's any manual work needing done."

"I am sure we will need your strong muscles when the set up begins," Clara said. She watched as the men shone in response. Seemed that a man offering to come to a woman's rescue always managed to put a shine on a fellow's ego. "Thank you for offering, gentlemen."

"Well, I reckon the party is planned," Mr. Tether said, standing and squeezing into his undersized suit jacket. "We have an order ready for pick up at the store, and my tummy is grumbling like a bear thinking about those steaks from the freshly slaughtered cow he's wrapped up for us."

"You're going to need new duds if you keep eating like you do, Mr. Tether." His wife stood, picked up her purse and headed for the door. "Well, hurry up, old man—the cooking won't get done by itself."

The group broke up, and Clara decided to go to the store and see if she couldn't pick up some little prizes for the students participating in her games on the twenty-second of August.

Clara scanned the horizon, every day and every night while Graham was out of town. There was trouble at the Groger site again. It seemed to have more disciplinary issues needing his attention than the Cranston location.

After a full morning teaching at the camp, Clara glanced up from her packing of the supplies away to see Graham headed her way. Her heart did that little flutter she'd come to expect whenever the man came near. Even the fine hairs on her arm stood up against her dress's long sleeves. She had told her father she wanted the goosebumps—well, here they were—and she marveled at the feelings that they stirred inside.

"I hear the teacher has been up to mischief while I've been away," Graham said as he took Clara's hand in his and kissed it.

"Depends on what one calls mischief."

"The locals aren't pleased that you are traipsing to the camp every day to teach the immigrants English."

"I knew the secret would leak out sooner or later, but it has been a fun ride, Graham Lee."

"I'm sure it's been that, my wild rebel of a woman."

"It is my calling to teach. Wherever I see a need," she said. "Surely, you don't consider that rebellious?"

"No, I understand completely and I'm all right with it, but the news breaking out into the open is making my life a mite miserable, and it may jeopardize your teaching position at the school when it opens."

"And who will take my place, might I ask?"

"Are you willing to gamble your future on these immigrants who are here today and likely gone tomorrow when the railroad company no longer requires their services?"

"They won't go far because they won't be able to afford it. Most will settle in larger towns and cities where they can find work. And how, pray tell, will that happen without a better understanding of our language so they can apply for a respectable position?"

"You can't take on the whole world, Clara."

"But I can take on the small corner the Lord has placed me into. It's my Christian duty and my privilege. Besides, I love it. They are fine people—polite, grateful, and brilliant students."

Graham fanned his fingers through his hair and sighed. "And what about us?"

"What does teaching immigrants have to do with us?"

"If the whites, who are set in their ways and not willing to change, shun you, Clara, it will also bring my reputation down as your fiancé, and perhaps even the railroad when visitors start coming."

"Is that what you're worried about? Does being accepted by the majority make ignoring the minority acceptable? This is not the man I've grown to care for," Clara said. "And a company who worries more about reputation than humankind is not anything I want my name attached to."

"I understand where you're coming from; and I do try my best to make life tolerable for the camp workers, but some things are out of my control. It's just the way of things."

Clara lifted her brow. "And *that* makes it right in God's eyes? The people are given wages in one hand, and then forced to give it to the men with the other, who bring supplies—and at top dollar, I might add—into the camp. You do know the shop owners of Cranston won't let the immigrants inside their places of business providing the decent prices we all enjoy. The workers are destitute. Have you observed their clothing? How do you expect them to survive out there in the coming winter?"

"They seem to manage in the tents and I showed some how to make igloos last year when the snows came. They are very resourceful."

"It's inhumane. Do *you* not enjoy a nice fire and a warm bed to sleep in when the storms rage outside?"

Twinges of annoyance crept into his face, and Clara knew she had crossed the line.

"It's too much, too fast, Clara. Can you not slow down with your humanitarian campaign? It's a war you cannot possibly expect to win overnight."

"Who says?"

"And this is the homecoming I receive from my beloved? I hoped for something a little less stressful," Graham said emphasizing a long sigh. "Talking to you sometimes is like beating my head against a brick wall."

"Do you do that often?" she said, hoping to sound amused. He did seem to appear fatigued after his time away.

A movement to his left caught his eye, and he called out, "Timothy—is that you hiding over there?"

The young boy crept out from behind the tent and moved to where the couple was arguing. "Yes, sir."

"If your parents knew you were in the camp, your backside would be tanned so hard you wouldn't be able to sit for a week."

"Yes, sir."

"Is that all you have to say for yourself?"

"When you got the itch to teach, Mr. Lee, there's no holding back the tide."

"Teach? You mean to say you are helping Miss Stewart educate these people?"

The lad's face brightened. "Yes, sir, and they're picking it up so fast pretty soon they'll be teaching me."

Graham cast Clara a stern warning. "You have gone too far involving Timothy in this endeavor."

"In that, you are probably correct. The boy seemed eager to introduce me to his friend, and the mission sort of mushroomed from there."

"Send him home before his folks discover his whereabouts. His grandfather is on the school board, and using a child in this manner will surely cost you your job."

She turned to Timothy. "Mr. Lee is right. I should have sent you home after the introduction to your friends." To Graham, she said, "And as for my job, is it not possible these people are my reason for coming here? Settling into a new land is difficult enough without being illiterate on top of it all. I might be far happier with them than holed up in a fancy school with narrow-minded supporters."

"Clara, please. Think about what you're saying."

She realized her words had escaped her mouth like excess steam, her comments not clearly thought through. Clara took a deep breath and backed off. "I've been known to race ahead with my convictions rather recklessly in the past, but you have shown me the value in moving at a slower pace here in the West. I shall work harder to guard my tongue, but I cannot guarantee I will come to any different conclusions concerning the matter."

"That's all I ask. Let me walk you both back to town."

Timothy skipped ahead of them.

"The people in the camp like you, Mr. Lee, although there are times, I am uncertain as to why." She hoped her grin gave her playfulness away. She hated arguing with Graham and strove to make amends.

"They've probably heard from other camps that I am the most tolerable of all managers on the railroad line."

"Heaven help them. Whatever will become of those who have placed their trust in the government believing that a better life was theirs on Canadian soil?"

"They have escaped from a country devasted by war, so who are we to judge which life is better? I for one do not know the answer to that. I am only one man with a huge job to do. I don't have time to campaign for human rights."

"But I do, and your supporting me will ensure my success, at least in our small corner of the world. We can help the families placed under your care, enable them to stand strong and move forward after the railroad work has been completed."

"You are like my conscience taking bodily form." The remark did not sound favorable. A man should never disregard his principles due to busyness.

"You are a good man, Graham. Did you ever consider that a true show of kindness might unleash a workforce willing to do anything for you, be it moving mountains or laying lines on time and with the same passion you possess? That is what I have discovered after simply teaching them the alphabet. The families love me and Timothy, and they show it in a hundred different ways every day."

"I suppose we both have some thinking to do tonight. Miss Clara Stewart—you are an angel in disguise."

"Don't be ridiculous. I am, however, confident that the Lord is leading me in this, and He has a wonderful outcome in store for us all."

Timothy waved goodbye as Graham and Clara stopped at the foot of the stairs to her cabin.

"Will you have lunch with me tomorrow at Francine's Diner?" Graham asked Clara.

"I shall be honored to dine with you."

"Do I sense a counterattack in that statement?"

"Not at all. I have not changed my mind about marrying you, Graham, if that is your concern." She wondered about telling him that she'd already taken the first step by setting the date with the committee members, but it could wait.

Graham laughed. "I'm not exactly worried about *us* making it, but our making it here, in the mountain town I have grown to love, might be a concern."

"I believe in both. Our future, along with the people who have settled here." Clara stood on her tippy-toes to kiss his cheek. "Ye of little faith. Sleep well tonight, and watch for the hand of God to reveal the way to brotherly kindness."

Chapter Six

When pay day arrived, Clara was curious to see how much her students had learned about the value of money and if they had the courage to question the amount allotted to them, should it not be the agreed upon wage. The rumor the paymaster pocketed some money designated for the employees who didn't know better had not been proven. Clara had not heard any public accusations against the man, but Timothy continued to insist on Caleb's guilt. Clara attempted to recall just how much cash she'd picked up off the ground the day she arrived, to no avail.

She took extra time with her grooming, hoping to see Graham in his office and get in a visit while she was at the train station. The paymaster was busy setting up his table to distribute the payroll, so Clara walked on to where five train cars sat motionless, the space presently being used for offices, dining, and bunkers for the single white workers who did not reside in town.

Upon her arrival, Clara was pleased to see that the depot had grown walls and a roof since her last visit there, and several men were busy putting in windows and doors.

"Howdy, Miss Stewart. Mr. Lee is in his office."

"Thank you. You men are doing a fine job constructing the Cranston Depot. It will be a welcome sight for the travelers coming West."

"It will, indeed. The name is Russ, and you can do me a favor by putting in a kind word with the boss, miss." He grinned and waved his hat. "You have a nice day."

Clara mounted the steel steps to the door marked "Graham Lee" and knocked. "Come in," a voice called from inside.

When she crossed the threshold, Graham looked up from his desk, grinned, and jumped to his feet. He hurried over and lifted her hand to his lips. "I swear, you grow lovelier each time I set eyes on you, my dear."

She blushed. "A woman never tires of hearing such praise."

"To what do I owe the pleasure of this surprise visit?"

"I'm just taking a stroll, enjoying some exercise on this splendid day. I found myself close by and thought I'd drop in. I just never know when you'll be off and running again."

"I'm back for a while now. The men at the next station have their instructions, and work will start there promptly. When the blasting is complete here, the men can start laying the line that will meet up with theirs."

"Running a railroad line is quite the process."

"Especially through the mountain ranges, but I love a challenge."

Clara noticed another desk in the corner. "Does your brother, the paymaster, work in this office with you?"

"He's likely in here more than me, but yes, we share the space."

"How is he doing? When I arrived, you suggested that he was going through a rough stretch."

"Seems to have gotten over the hurdle. Suppose he wasn't nearly as smitten with his expensive sugar tart as he claimed when he arrived in Cranston all broken and inebriated."

"Maybe he hides his broken heart well—the he-man type."

Graham laughed. "Yeah, we fellows do like to put on a strong front." He held her gaze and she saw the mischievous grin work its way to the surface. "Now, *you* don't have any plans for breaking my heart, do you?"

"Not at all, sir. I was thinking about what you suggested."

"What might that be? I am full of ideas."

"About us marrying before school starts up."

"That's a heap closer than the town can prepare for the new teacher to get married. They'd like to make it a grand affair."

"What about you? Are you up for shining those boots and smiling for all the folks in town while you trade away your bachelorhood?"

"It sounds rather unpleasant in that light."

"Marriage is a big commitment. We *could* wait until Thanksgiving. Give you more time to fully understand what you're getting into."

"We could. Either way, I am committed, Miss Stewart."

His gaze consumed her, and she smiled, feeling the warmth of his affection as it reached her soul. "Well, then, let's make it before school starts. I am rather eager to change my surname to Lee."

"Mrs. Lee—sounds right pleasing."

"To me, as well. I'd best let you get back to work. I have a wedding to plan," Clara said, knowing some of the details were already underway. "I wouldn't want your men to say you are shirking your responsibilities while wooing your woman during work hours."

"A man in love is given some grace."

"Will you be joining me at church for the Sunday service?"

"I'll be there. Clean dungarees and boots so shiny you'll see your image in the leather."

Graham made her happier than she'd ever been. When she was with him, she felt that special tingle she missed with the gentlemen callers back home, and when he kissed her fingers, she felt she would surely drown in its wake. That was a promising start on which to build a solid relationship with her railroad man out here in the Wild West.

"I am on the social committee planning a special back-to-school event, and I was brazen enough to suggest we might throw the teacher's wedding into the mix."

"You did?"

"I did, and they were all in agreement." Clara smiled, and he kissed her cheek, his delight reflecting in his gaze. "You are one snapper of a catch, Miss Stewart. Just let me know the time and the date, and I'll be there."

"Has my father paid you the full amount for your commitment?"

"He just needs to know the date, as well, but Clara, I think we've gone beyond that initial concept of the money being *mine*, haven't we? I'd like to think we've grown fond enough of one another that your father's wedding gift will be spent and enjoyed together."

"I recall hearing those same words coming from his lips as well. I have big dreams, and I can't wait to share them with you, Graham," Clara said light-heartedly, heading for the door. "Have a pleasant day."

Her pace quickened as she neared the outside station, which had already been set up, and the employees were lined up to receive their wages. This time, she stopped short before reaching the paymaster's desk and stood out of sight in the shadow of the bunker car to watch.

Only one man questioned the wages he received and immediately proceeded to count the bills aloud for all to hear clearly that Caleb had shorted him.

"Who taught you about money?"

"My son."

"Smart boy—didn't think you had any of those in the camp."

"My boy is very smart. Miss Stewart always praises him."

"Miss Stewart, you say?"

"I need four more dollars, Mr. Caleb." The man stood firm, waiting patiently while the paymaster slapped the money left owing him on the desk without apology.

Apparently, Graham had not told his brother about her teaching the camp children. Either that, or the man believed the sons would not pass along the information to their working fathers. Would Caleb create a bigger fuss now that his hand had been caught stealing from the railroad's cookie jar? Surely Graham possessed the scruples to prosecute such an act when it occurred within the company and under his leadership, even if his brother was the culprit, and it might tear out his heart to do it. Graham had called Clara his conscience. That might hold some weight when it came time for his brother to undermine her activity with the hope of covering up his abuse of the position with which Graham had entrusted him.

Would Graham support her or Caleb? That was the question eating at her heart.

Clara noticed Wong, the man with the sore leg she had met on her first day in Cranston making his way to the front desk next. She watched as he, too, counted out the amount handed to him. She noted the scowl on Caleb's face. It looked good on him, she thought without an ounce of regret in her mind.

She had not seen Wong on her many trips to teach at the camp, but his wife had told her that Mr. Lee had sent some medicine and bandages to help heal his leg. She had wanted to thank Graham, and she could have done so a few minutes ago during her visit to his office, but the incident had slipped her mind.

Clara had seen Graham's continual struggle when it came to maintaining equality for all. It took ingenuity to navigate orders from the higher-ups and divvy the jobs out to his hired men, all while accomplishing the tasks and balancing a clear conscience. It was a heavy responsibility for one man.

Her man.

She'd seen him hold fast to praiseworthy morals while making difficult decisions in the wild, ever-changing frontier. Yet, for him as boss to charge his own blood kin of thievery was a heavy accusation to make public. Or worse still, allowing his ethics to be swayed by the denial that would likely come from his brother, while his betrothed's actions in the camp would come under the scrutiny of a prejudicial system. It seemed a choice too large for any man to make. She felt Graham's heart break, as surely as if it cracked within her own chest.

Her lesson in learning to survive in the West while balancing adventures both good and bad, was well underway. Clara hoped that when it came down to the bottom line, Graham would opt to support her over Caleb in the fragile situation about to unfold in their midst. A mess certain to worsen before it got better.

Clara pulled the last batch of cookies from the oven, and at the same time, she heard a repeating thump on her door. "Miss Stewart—are you in there?"

Someone is impatient this morning, Clara thought, wiping her hands on her apron before slipping it off on her way to greet the early caller.

She opened the door to see a red-faced Mrs. Tether standing there, hands placed firmly on her hips, the young Timothy peeking out from behind her full skirt. Clara recognized a few of the others gathering outside her door as local businesspeople she'd met since her arrival.

"Miss Stewart, it has come to my attention that you have been educating people at the camp and dragging my grandson along with you."

Timothy shrugged his shoulders, and mumbled, "Sorry, Miss Stewart. I tried to explain, but—"

"You hush. The blame falls on the teacher's shoulders."

"You are right, Mrs. Tether. I knew some might object to my opening a class for the immigrants—that is on me—but I should never have allowed Timothy to stay without permission. I apologize for my poor judgement."

"I should say." The woman nodded to the group while tugging on her waist shirt, which fit too tightly and barely covered her protruding tummy.

"But I do not regret educating our country's new residents. School in Cranston has not officially opened for the town children, but I assure you, my service there will not suffer with what I choose to do for others in my spare time."

"That is far too many students for one lady to handle. Surely, *our* local youngsters will suffer from your divided attention," Mr. Tether said, moving in beside his wife. Judging from her supportive onlookers, Clara concluded they'd considered her conduct an unheard-of practice in the West. It turned out that all classes of people—not unlike the one she had escaped in Hamilton—segregated those who did not fit their definition of acceptable.

Clara noticed Graham galloping from town in their direction. Her betrothed to the rescue. She felt annoyed that she needed a man to save her from accusers after doing the right thing in the eyes of the Lord. But they were a team, and she wanted him by her side.

She attempted one final plea. "I saw a need in our community, and since I had the expertise, I thought it my Christian duty to share my knowledge. Writing and comprehending the English language is a challenge for all to learn."

"We didn't ask them here," someone shouted from the crowd.

"Miss Elise Grattish—is that you?" Clara shielded the sun from her eyes to scan the back of the crowd. "I beg to differ—the government has invited them to help build our country.

"And I do want to thank you for that bolt of material I purchased the other day. I've already begun to sew a new outfit. Did it cross your mind that by shunning a vast assembly of our neighbors, you are losing the opportunity to expand your clientele? There are many friendly women in the camp who would love to shop for clothes in your store."

The dress shop owner appeared embarrassed to have been called out. Clara rectified that just as Graham pulled up and slid out of his saddle. "As are the rest of you. I can teach English, but you have skills and services these folks need to flourish in our land and so do they, if you'd give them half a chance."

Graham took off his hat and bowed ever so respectfully to Clara. "Good morning, Miss Stewart. I see you have quite the gathering at your door this early hour of the day."

A voice from the crowd gained a false sense of courage by Graham's presence. "You need to keep your woman in her place, before we're forced to renege on her paid teaching position and cast her out. We're trying to grow an honorable town here, and she's breaking all the rules."

"Now don't be hasty, George. When you get to know our new schoolmarm, you will see that the Lord sent us the kindest woman in the entire country who has everyone's best interests at heart. They love her at the camp. Why, she and young Timothy have made great headway in their education."

"Without our permission," Mrs. Tether said as she hugged the squirming boy tightly to her leg.

"For which I have already apologized, ma'am. Timothy will not accompany me again."

"See?" Graham said as if her promise settled the matter. He leaned over and scuffed the top of Timothy's hair with his fist. "But we all know the Tether lad has a mind of his own, and this wouldn't be the first time he went against the flow of things."

A murmur came up from the crowd, and the air stilled…. momentarily.

A deep rumble shook the earth. As it traveled underfoot through the crowd, Clara reached for Graham's arm to balance herself.

"What's that?" a man from the crowd yelled.

"It sounds like blasting, though there isn't any assigned for this area. We're further on down the trail now," Graham said as he put his hat back on his head. "Now, break this up, folks, and let me tend to my railroad business."

A chorus of screams filled the air, and the crowd that assembled at the schoolteacher's cabin stared in disbelief as rocks plummeted from mountainous heights upon the unsuspecting camp dwellers.

Chapter Seven

Clara's heart raced as rapidly as her feet, as she joined the crowd leaving her doorstep and heading for the scene. The mountain wall, which usually protected the camp from the onslaught of nasty weather, had turned on the people, loosening rocks of all sizes to drop on anyone lingering too close to the foothills.

"A rockslide!" someone yelled above the roar as if the event needed clarification in anyone's mind.

Clara moved in alongside Mrs. Tether and rested a hand on her arm. "Perhaps you could go for the doctor. Someone might be hurt."

"I can do that," she said, and then sheepishly added, "About that back there—"

"That's not important right now. Please, just get the doctor."

The woman rushed back toward Cranston.

Clara hurried to catch up to Graham. When he noticed her beside him, he asked, "Can you organize the help here? I want to find out who is responsible for this disaster before the trail grows cold."

"Of course." She watched him speed away, before turning to survey the face of the mountain, currently silent, its resulting destruction staring her in the face. An avalanche of fallen rocks littered the ground where cook stations and tents had been occupied earlier.

As she entered the camp perimeter, Ling Aihan rushed over. "Clara—the children were playing there. They tried to run but some tripped, and the mothers tried to help, but the rocks kept falling." The woman's voice cracked with emotion as tears ran down her cheeks.

"I've brought help from the community. Ask the people to gather all the tools they can find: shovels, pry-bars... We will dig them out, and the doctor is on his way."

Many of the townsfolk who had raced to the scene now stood dumbfounded, looking at the camp they'd likely never stepped a foot in before.

"Men...ladies!" Clara called out. "Listen up. There may be children and adults buried under that rubble, and we need to get them out as swiftly as possible if there is any chance of saving their lives."

She noticed the pile of tools mounting under Aihan's instruction and pointed to it. "Grab something to dig with. Ladies, use your bare hands to move some of the smaller stones, and, call out if you see any sign of clothing or flesh so we can come to help clear it faster."

Clara recognized the man who owned Cranston's Hardware standing nearby. "Clayton, go to your store and put any tools that might help us in a wagon to bring back here. Please, hurry—lives are hanging in the balance."

The crowd that was initially embolized with fear now spread out and began the tiresome task of clearing the foothills of fallen rock in search of the bodies trapped underneath. Clara grabbed a blanket hanging from a line and tossed it on the ground close to a spot where she knew the children played alley. Other ladies joined her in throwing stones on it, and when it was full, they slid it over to the clearing to dump. Three dumps later, a voice squealed, "I see an arm!"

Many rushed to the mother's side, and a frenzy of removal began until Chu Tang's limp form had been exposed. Clara scanned the area in the hope that the doctor had arrived. She located a man carrying a black bag and hurried in his direction. "Over here," she yelled to him. When he saw her motioning, he rushed to fill in the gap between them."

"Thank you for coming so swiftly, Doctor. We have uncovered a wee one who needs your attention. What can I do to help?"

"Find us a tent where we can house the injured. I won't be doctoring out here in the open for everyone to gawk at."

She hated the tone of his voice, and her eyes must have displayed her distaste.

"Lee sent me, and I'm obeying orders—haven't changed my idea about being here one iota."

"Do your best, Doctor. A life is a life in God's eyes and a doctor's mission is to heal. It's really quite simple." She left him staring at the sight unfolding around him. Clara sensed a softening in his features, and she was sorry that it took a tragedy to bring out the best in some people.

Clara hurried to find Ling Aihan. "Who has the biggest dwelling, one that will house the injured as we find them so the doctor can be in out of the dust and the sun?"

The woman seized Clara's arm and pulled her over to a large canvass tent. "We eat here sometimes when it rains or gather to visit at night. We can spread blankets on the ground for the patients." Aihan saw one of her friends passing by and called out, "Fia, we need lots of blankets, basins, water jugs, and any medical supplies we have in the camp to be brought here. Find some ladies to help you, and hurry."

Hours later, Clara led a volunteer from town with a broken arm to the medical tent. She passed him off to the reception girl at the door and stood to scan the activity inside the make-shift hospital. Despite the suffering in the room, she saw something that had not existed in Cranston prior to the catastrophe. Chinese and whites working amiably together side by side. Dr. Sanford from Cranston was on one side of the room and Dr. Freeman, the railroad physician, tended to patients on the other side. Ten bodies were stretched out on the floor—six children and four adults—the latest patient suffering a minor injury was getting his arm in a sling, and made the count eleven.

There had only been one fatality of the day thus far.

An older man who had been playing with the children at the time of the rockslide, was pinned against the cliff, and had not been uncovered in time to save his life. Clara's heart broke while listening to the man's wife wail, the rocking chair squeaking a sad tune as she caressed his broken body in her arms upon his discovery. There would be deep mourning in the camp in the days to come. The rest of the victims would recover, and for those lives, Clara thanked the Lord. That and for the quick response to the community emergency, not to mention the ease with which the races had come together to combat it. Their unity spoke volumes for the admirable character exhibited and produced hope for a future that might eliminate prejudice altogether.

Graham climbed onto the saddle with less vigor than he should have exhibited when going to investigate an incident. He kicked Chet into motion. The explosions in their sector had been completed, the ammunition already slated for transporting to the next mountain that barred the line's progress. Still, the pathway for the tracks steered far to the right of Cranston. Its safety, along with other train stops along the way, had been established long ago in the planning phases of the project.

He tied Chet to the hitching post outside his office and raced inside, hoping to find someone who might know what was going on.

Russ leaned over the conference table, studying the railroad line map stretched out on it.

He looked up. "Boss, glad to see you. Can't find the source of the blasting. I thought that part of the job had moved out of the area."

"It has," Graham said, confirming the man's conclusions. He closed the door behind him and moved closer to his employee, one he considered worth his hire and slated for advancement the next time a position opened. "Where is everyone?"

"I pounded the last nail in the depot, and when I came to freshen up, I found the place deserted. I wondered about that, but then I figured that most had gone on to get the job started at the next station. When the blast splashed the water from my washbasin onto my pants, it sure changed my way of thinking quick, Mr. Lee."

"Get your horse, and let's ride. If there are any signs of activity left, we'll find it."

The two men set off on their horses, Graham leading to the spot where he'd initially seen the cloud of dust in the distance while still at Clara's place. He knew the area like the back of his hand and felt confident he'd recognize any changes since his last survey.

Russ pulled up alongside him and pointed to the ground. Someone stopped and dismounted—looks like a man from the boot prints. "Only one set of horse hoofs, sir, headed toward the mountain range that backs the town site."

"Good catch, Russ. This whole mess has my head in the clouds instead of on the ground watching for clues."

"Understood—wouldn't want to be wearing your shoes today, sir."

"Yeah," Graham murmured as he slid back into the saddle, ready to pursue the lead he hoped would end in discovering whoever had set off the charge. Whoever it was, he would pay dearly for this deed.

The tracks heading to the left—a no-powder zone—left easy-to-follow depressions in the soil and on the damp grasses. The mountain in question loomed ahead, and Graham pulled back on the horse's reins to survey the scene. "The explosion made quite a mess here. Easy to see where the ranges connect to the back and peaks of Cranston Mountain. It's the very reason we steered clear of this area."

"Safety first is what I respect about you, Mr. Lee."

"Today, I failed miserably." Graham sighed long, its weariness full of self-condemnation. "Some lunatic with a bee in his pants and explosives in his hand is on the loose. This will only serve to widen the division between the ranks. No doubt in my mind this is the source of the trouble. Blasting there would be enough to shake the foundations and cause a landslide of rock and dirt to fall on the Cranston camp."

"Is that what happened? Are the campers all right?"

"I left Clara Stewart in charge of the rescue efforts. She is more than capable of organizing the bedlam there. I left hoping to find the person responsible and end his rampage while the trail was still hot."

"Yes, sir, your lady has a kind heart. You sure got yourself a prize there," Russ said. "And don't you fret; we'll find our man."

"Agreed." Graham nodded at the mound of rubble stacked against the rock cliff's opening. "You didn't hire on for a manhunt, lad."

"Things happen out here none of us bargain for," Russ said. "I got my guns handy should that become necessary."

"I hope we can take him peaceably. I want to understand a man's reasons for this kind of behavior."

"Lots of fellows with their own bias agendas working the line," Russ said.

"Suppose I can't govern a man's mind, but I can his actions. I am the boss of this outfit, and he will answer to me and the law for this malicious attack on our community."

"Yes, sir. I'm behind you there."

"Good. Then let's get this investigation over with and hope his horse's getaway imprints weren't covered over by rocks."

It took an hour for the trackers to pick up the fleeing trail heading east, and following it took them on a merry chase. When the train cars came into sight, the men stopped.

"Guess it's one of us that has a burr under his saddle, Mr. Lee."

"It appears that way," Graham said, "but finding him among all the personnel hanging around here will be a difficult task."

"We can eliminate you and me," Russ said, attempting to sound chipper. "It's a good start."

Graham chuckled. "It is indeed." The man kept him grounded, and Graham appreciated his presence. "Let's start interrogating, shall we?"

"Me, sir? You want my help?"

"I do. Two heads are better than one, and you're a smart, young chap. I hope to keep you close by me until this job is finished."

"You can count on me."

"I know I can. Let's ride."

When they tethered their horses in front of the office, a small group of men lingering nearby gathered in front of the train car. Graham stood on the steel platform in the doorway and shouted, "Since you are not helping out with the crisis at the camp—which would have been my preference—I have questions for every one of you." The fact that the ten workers standing in front of him had not rushed to the campers' aid at the onset of the rockslide made Graham suspicious of their motives. Perhaps the guilty party he sought stood among them. It motivated the boss to begin the questioning right away.

"One in here at a time. When you're done with me, I hope you have the decency to hightail it over to the camp and help dig out the survivors. I can't believe that anyone needs me to tell him when one of his fellow men needs assistance. You all heard the explosion, but I suppose that is an issue for another day."

Graham beckoned to the closest man. "Come on, Bill. You can be first on the chopping block."

He ushered Russ and Bill into the office car ahead of him, surprised to see Caleb sitting calmly with his feet resting on his desk. "Who gave you the day off? Why aren't you out helping at the camp?"

"They have plenty of help without me. Besides, you hired me for office work, not manual labor."

"We do whatever happens to come our way. God expects us to extend a hand to our fellow man in need."

"Not too caring what your God expects. He doesn't know I exist, and I like it that way."

"Our mama would cringe if she heard you blaspheme like that."

"Are *you* going to tell her, brother?"

Graham shook the cobwebs from his head. His influence on Caleb was nil. His best efforts to straighten out his misguided life had gone by the wayside. "Go find somewhere else to sit until I call you in for questioning."

"Questioning? About what?"

"I got Bill in here now. Go and wait with the others outside," Graham said forcefully.

Caleb grumbled his annoyance all the way across the room, dawdling as if he had the entire day to reach the door.

"Sit down, Bill," Graham said as he settled on the chair behind his desk. Russ took up his position, leaning against a post close to the window to listen in on the interrogation.

"Where were you when the explosion happened?"

"In the bunk car, going through the medical kit for some medicine to quiet this powerful headache that won't let up."

"Sorry to hear you're feeling out of sorts. Was there anyone else with you?"

"Shane and Jasper were playing cards. We all worked night duty and hadn't been up long."

"Did you see anything suspicious before or after the explosion?"

"Not much activity around here with so many blokes heading off to the hills with buggies of materials needed to lay down the next few miles of tracks."

"Thank you, Bill. That narrows my search down some. You can be excused. Send in the next man."

When the entire group had been thoroughly questioned and all seemingly had an alibi as to their whereabouts, Graham and Russ were left no better off than before. Caleb strolled in as the two men huddled over the few notes Graham had made during the inquiries.

"Caleb—I almost forgot about you," Graham said. "Come—take the chair."

"You're going to drill me like you did the common riffraff out there?"

"Don't pull the poor relative act today. I'm not in the mood," Graham said. "You are a railroad employee, the same as everyone else here, and you will get the same treatment."

Caleb grunted as he plunked into the chair, took out his jack knife, and began cleaning under his nails.

"Pencil dust gathering under those nails?" Russ asked. Graham heard the light-hearted tone in the comment, but he noticed the snub he received from Caleb as if he were an annoying fly.

"You weren't here when I came from town immediately following the explosion. I checked the office, and found only Russ."

"I came in later. Went for a ride to the bluffs this morning to get away from work. This place has a way of closing in on a person."

"The great outdoors or the people?"

"Both. Starting to hate all those mountains."

"You can go back to Toronto and try your luck there again," Graham said.

"Might just do that."

"Did you ride to the bluffs alone?" Russ asked.

"I said I wanted to get away," he snarled. "Why would I bring company?"

"I just wondered if maybe you were sweet on one of our women-folk and took her riding."

"Naw, I leave the courting to my brother. Women and me don't get along—especially *your* woman." He aimed that remark at the boss.

Graham picked up on his same scorn and wondered what on earth he could have against his soon-to-be sister-in-law. "What did she ever do to you?"

"She's a busybody who doesn't know her place. You would do well to send her packing back to where she came from."

"That's not going to happen, Caleb. Clara and I are soon to be married. She is joining the Lee family, which, last I checked, included you."

"All the more reason for me to leave."

"I don't understand your attitude," Graham said, attempting to control his temper. "You come out here crying the blues about how the world did you wrong back home, you accept all the perks I give you to help the railroad's financial operation, and still, you carry a chip on your shoulder big enough to crush a man."

"I don't expect you to understand. You were always the frontiersman in the family. I would have been happy just to marry wealthy and let the old money fester in my bank account."

"Back to the issue at hand," Russ said, reining the two brothers in. "When did you get back from your ride?"

"None of *your* business. Graham, get rid of him."

When the boss started to object, Russ lifted his hand to stop him. "I think I'll step outside, fellows, and get some fresh air. Let you two iron out the family stuff."

Caleb continued to dig the dirt out from under his nails while Graham sighed and relaxed back in his chair.

The investigation was no further ahead, and his head throbbed from Caleb's attitude. A movement outside the window on the wall beside his desk distracted him, and he stared at Russ, who was rummaging through Caleb's saddlebags. Now, what was he up to? He'd noticed that the man's interest had gained vigor when his brother started talking. Their cynicism had weighed heavy in the air. Graham sincerely hoped that Russ's dislike of Caleb had not been the incentive to fuel his protégée out to nose through his brother's belongings.

When Caleb noticed Graham staring outside, he leaned forward in his seat and gazed out. "Why, that good for nothing…" Caleb jumped to his feet and raced toward the door with Graham on his heels.

Caleb soared clear of the two iron steps and landed with a thud on the ground before rushing to the hitching post where several animals were tied, including his. Without a word, he slammed his fist into Russ's jaw. The startled victim lost his balance and toppled to the ground, his assailant landing on his stomach and unleashing a succession of pummels to his face.

Graham stood on the spot, stunned for a few seconds. He had seen the stick of dynamite fly from Russ's hand upon Caleb's initial impact with his face. His heart denied what his eyes beheld while his mind screamed that they had uncovered the guilty party. Somehow, Graham found his feet and pulled his brother off the stricken man.

He nodded to a couple of bystanders. "Come and hold him." When his brother was sandwiched between two strong men, he offered a hand to help up Russ before walking to where the evidence lay on the ground. He brought it over and waved it under Caleb's nose.

"You don't have any use for dynamite—what was it doing in your saddlebag?"

"He planted it there," Caleb accused Russ, He spat on the ground close to where Russ stood, wiping blood from his face with a hankie.

Graham knew that could not be the case, although in all fairness, he hadn't searched the bags Russ had tied to *his* horse. Still, he had to be thorough, this new charge hurting as much as Caleb's betrayal. "Russ, how do you answer to that accusation?"

"There's more where that one piece came from."

Graham walked over to Caleb's open saddle bag and groaned at the sight of dynamite, matches, and rolled-up rope with singed edges.

"Check mine, too, boss," Russ said. "I got nothing to hide and won't have any suspicion cast my way in this matter."

Graham understood his reasoning and proceeded to Russ's mount. He opened the bag on the back to find nothing. He turned to study his brother, seemingly a stranger to him now. Perhaps he'd always been, seeing how the Lee brothers were as different as day and night.

"Why would you light a fuse over there? You had to know it would cause danger and havoc in the community we are trying to build here in Cranston."

"I don't care about the mixed-up bunch in your community. It's a fuse bound to be lit at some time or another."

"Not while under my watch," Graham said. He took a small, thin rope and tossed it at one of the men. "Tie him up good and tight and deliver him to the jailhouse in town. Tell the sheriff I'll be along shortly to press charges."

The men obliged the boss. The others who were still hanging around watched in silence as the three staggered off. Caleb turned back to badmouth Clara one final time. "Don't you go thinking you got yourself an angel to marry. That girl is just as guilty as me. She had no need to turn the workers against me."

"Get him out of here, boys," Graham yelled. After he'd calmed his rattled nerves, he spoke to Russ. "Go clean yourself up, and meet me at the camp. We'll head into the sheriff's office together after I see Clara."

"Your girl isn't to blame for any of this unless a compassionate heart is a crime now," one of the fellows nearby stated with confidence. "Showed this town what a sorry lot we are." A couple of others in the small crowd nodded their agreement, and it warmed Graham's heart.

"Never thought it our place to say before, but I'd be checking my books if I were you, Mr. Lee," another called out.

"Books?" Graham could not think straight. Duty and emotions were tearing him apart piece by piece. "Thanks for standing up for Miss Stewart and warning me about the books. You fellows might be called on as witnesses to Russ finding the evidence in Caleb's bag."

"We ain't going anywhere, boss," a few responded.

Graham flung the saddlebag full of evidence over his shoulder, mounted Chet, and rode toward the camp. If ever he needed to see Clara's face and hear her soothing voice, it was then, and before his knees buckled beneath him and his heart failed him for the deed he must execute against his family.

Chapter Eight

The sun hung low in the sky when Graham showed up at the medical tent. His distant and troubled expression concerned Clara as he braced himself against a tall cupboard inside the door.

Clara sat next to a boy on a matt spooning broth into his mouth. She wiped the patient's mouth and laid him back down, where he immediately closed his eyes. Bowl in hand, Clara rose, walked toward Graham, and dropped the dirty dish into a washbasin that had been designated for the supper dishes.

"Clara, you look exhausted."

"It has been a long day, but the volunteers and doctors saved all but one."

"That is a miracle," Graham said, his face showing a hint of relief by the outcome.

"Did you find the source of the trouble?" she asked.

Rather than answer he question directly, he said, "Will you walk with me?"

"Of course." She removed the soiled apron the ladies had provided her, took his arm, and exited the tent. Clara breathed in the fresh evening air and followed his lead to a deserted spot off in the distance. They sat side by side on a rock bench under the overhang of a shaded tree.

"I find myself at a difficult bypass." Graham hesitated, his eyes studying her. "My brother ignited the dynamite in a location that had long been blocked off and marked as unsafe. He caused the calamity here today."

"Your brother?" Clara gasped. "How horrid."

"I'm surprised he even knew how to set the stuff off," Graham said. "But it gets worse. He says he did it because *you* backed him into a corner. He claims you are as much to blame as him and should be called up for sighting the workers against his authority."

Clara let out a long sigh. "Caleb is angry with me because the workers can now count the money he gives them for wages, and he is no longer able to skim the top for his own profits."

"Caleb didn't mention that detail, but one of the men proposed that I check the books. Maybe he suspected my brother had pilfered from the railroad wages, too. I half-suspected something was amiss—the figures didn't add up in my head and I didn't take the time to study the records. Turns out I'm to blame for the mess in putting off the investigation. I should have followed my intuition and not blindly trust that Caleb had it all under control."

"My father always said that every man—especially in finances—should be accountable to someone else. It silences the temptation."

"Wise man. It boggles my mind to imagine that Caleb thinks others should pay for *his* shortcomings. Suppose it goes back to Toronto, when his woman's family rejected him, mainly because he had insufficient funds in his bank account, or so he'd claimed. When he first arrived, he cried the blues about his employer at the bank having accused him of padding his purse using stolen money to win her back again. I chose to believe that my brother would never go to such lengths to appease a woman or her family. I believed his woe-is-me love story of rejection to be the real source of his running, not even considering that fraud charges might have forced him to hide in the West. But it all makes sense now. Stealing has become a way of life for him, and I did Caleb a disservice by sticking my head in the sand and trusting him with company money."

"You thought the best of your brother," Clara said, feeling the depth of his grief and disappointment. "None of his actions are your fault."

"But I hired him to look after railroad funds, giving him a second opportunity to swindle folks. Most likely, he planned to prance back to Toronto and jam his newfound, ill-gotten money into the face of the girl's father all along. It seems he just wants to marry wealthy and be positioned to live off old money from empires built by the previous generations' sweat of their brow."

"I am so sorry. This must be painful for you."

"It's more painful not to see an inkling of remorse in the man. I'm embarrassed to call him kin."

Regret for her selfish concerns swarmed Clara's being, recalling how she had feared Graham might blame her for teaching numbers to the working immigrants. Instead, she now ached to see the alternative unfold. Caleb had broken his brother's confidence, and her betrothed had lost a piece of his lineage to crooked dealings.

"Where is he now?" she asked.

"I had to send him to Sheriff Langley for holding. He will be fired and no doubt brought to trial for his crimes."

Clara walked into his trembling arms and he clung to her, sobbing quietly on her shoulder.

Graham depleted his emotional outpouring and pushed away, smiling half-heartedly. "Sorry about that."

"It's been a rough day, and the people expect far too much from you. I hope you know my shoulder will always be available to you whenever you need it."

"And mine, yours," he offered in return, "although I suspect you are far stronger than I." He glanced around the camp. "You appear to have done a fine job unifying the rescue party."

"I was encouraged to see all of our neighbors working side by side, and I am hopeful that relationships will be different following this crisis. Compassion for the needy holds no boundaries where God is concerned."

"Amen. I need to marry you, Miss Stewart—yesterday."

She grinned. "Soon, my love. The next time we gather as a community shall be a pleasant one, I assure you. I shall be the first to call summer vacation to an end by ringing the brand-new bell to welcome the people inside for a grand back-to-school event *and* a secret wedding celebration to end the day."

"Good thing the schoolhouse and the church are so close. It'll be double the fun with that bell."

"And our future home is within easy walking distance, Mr. Lee," she said, feeling the heat rush to the back of her neck. "You shan't be cold this winter locked away in that steel car."

"And much more private for newlyweds, I daresay. I accept the invitation."

She cringed at the picture forming in her mind. "I had no intention of moving outside of my peaceful abode inside the Cranston town limits to become another body crammed into a train bunkie with a bunch of single men hovering nearby."

Graham smiled. "I do have my own quarters. Being boss comes with certain privileges."

"Not good enough. You will love my quiet cabin after having to listen to construction all day long."

"How many days again?" Graham said, glancing around before planting a stolen kiss on her red lips.

"Three weeks. That will allow you plenty of time to work ahead so we can enjoy five full days of vacation before classes begin."

"You appear to have this all mapped out quite nicely."

"I do try to accommodate."

"I see Russ riding up. He's accompanying me to the jailhouse to press charges against Caleb," Graham said, standing and reaching for her hand. "Let me walk you home. Tomorrow will be soon enough to plan the funeral."

"Do you think the townsfolk will come to support the grieving camp migrants or…"

"—Maybe this demonstration of kindness is just a one-time compromise?" he said, finishing her sentence. "Bite your tongue, woman. We will announce the service time in Cranston for all to hear. I suspect the folks whose hearts were born anew here today will win out over the belligerent ones of yesterday."

"I do pray so."

The men led their horses as the three traversed the short distance to Clara's home.

He left her with a lingering kiss on her cheek. The men mounted their horses and rode toward the town and the business they could not sweep under the rug, Clara put aside her exhaustion and prayed for all involved, especially for the poor soul of the misguided man behind bars that night.

The funeral was organized for the following day at three. A section of hilly land on the outskirts of town was fenced in and designated as Cranston's graveyard. When Graham nailed the posters with the location and time of the service around Cranston, he noticed it had raised a few eyebrows, but no one voiced their objection. It seemed a greater respect was allotted to the railroad manager, who had willingly placed his brother in the sheriff's care to render justice for the despicable act that had cost a man his life. The swindling remained under wraps, at least for that day, but it would no doubt be new juice for the grapevine once the railroad lawyers got hold of the case.

Graham was surprised he hadn't been raked over the coals for being a poor judge of character when it came to those he hired for such an important job but there was not one complaint from the local populace or any of his superiors. It seemed there existed plenty of shady activity surrounding the extension of the Pacific Railroad Line from the East to the West, and the men in charge of the enterprise hailed the integrity of the manager they'd chosen for the Rocky Mountain passes.

At three, the preacher led a congregation of Chinese people from the camp to the graveyard while several men on each side of an intricately crafted box carried the remains of their comrade.

What no griever expected was to see a similar throng of Cranston locals file through the town streets. Each of them provided a dose of encouragement for their fellow residents, who knew in their heart of hearts that attending the victim's final passage from this earth was the proper thing to do.

Clara dared to believe it was a sign of good things to come.

God was alive and thriving in the Rocky Mountains.

She was not so naïve to believe that all future incidents between the Cranston locals and the neighboring railroad worker's camp would tie up neatly. Creating a lasting harmony between the two different cultures would be an ongoing process, with the give and take of a false sense of supremacy often tipping the balance scales.

Although a deadly crisis and the devastating sentence of the guilty man would not have been the agent of Clara's choosing to encourage cooperation, she surrendered to its results. God intimately knew the hardness of everyone's heart and what it might take to nudge them in His direction. It took faith to believe He was still in control despite the heartache and injuries of that day, yet Clara had felt His peace weaving in and out through the crowd who stood to honor the man the camp had nicknamed the Children's Friend.

The hole was dug and it stood at the ready to receive the pine wood box that had been engraved with depictions of scenes from the man's life. The camp's woodworker was an elderly man who had honored the deceased with a carved legacy of the road he'd traveled.

The preacher read scripture, though most of his words went over the heads of the Chinese, who barely understood the English language let alone Old English from the King James Version of the Bible. Clara recalled that the Word never returned void, and she stood firm on the conviction that the Holy Spirit was at work in their midst.

The area cleared after the final Amen, but Clara lingered to watch the departure of the quiet procession. She felt a hand on her arm and looked up to see Graham beside her.

"What are you grinning about?"

She cast him a startled look, never imagining she wore a grin on her face at the conclusion of a funeral.

He raised a brow and said, "You are not hiding your thoughts well if that was your intention."

Clara relaxed and gave in, smiling openly. "Well, I see young Timothy walking beside his friend Ling Chuse, and Mrs. Tether is not pulling him away. I also see Ted Claussen, who considers himself a master craftsman chatting with old Shiue Ming, who has surpassed any piece the business tycoon might have presented as *his* best work. I also see—"

"I get the picture," Graham agreed, gazing at the dispersing crowd. "It's long overdue in these mountains, and all because of one fearless Easterner who never gave up."

"It's a small victory that, unfortunately, cost the people in our district plenty, but it's a start. This community will need to exhibit unity to those who come West after all the hard work you've put into building this magnificent railway line is completed." She did not try to hide the pride that swelled up inside her. "It is exciting to play any role in the advancement of our country. It only goes to show me just how small my world was before I came here."

Clara rubbed her tummy and hooked her arm through his. "I am hungry. Do you have time for an early supper at the diner?"

"I shouldn't, but who can deny that pretty face of yours anything?" Graham said as they started down the knoll toward town.

"My father couldn't, and that's why I am here." Clara laughed unreservedly, feeling all of her worry and fear dissolve into thin air. A victory in the wake of tragedy held its own delicious flavor, and in the aftermath of mourning, she felt a great joy for the future erupt in her spirit.

Chapter Nine

Life slowly returned to a new normal after that life-changing day, and although the camp population still generally kept to themselves, no one appeared shocked when their paths crossed, and most spoke cordially.

Everyone gathered outside the town hall to comfort Graham when the sentencing was passed on his brother for swindling the railroad and killing a man in the rockslide he had initiated. The Northwest Mounted Police escorted the condemned man out of town two days later. Railway guards had been assigned to cart Caleb on an outgoing train back to Toronto, where he would stand trial for crimes committed on that front as well. The foolish man's initial goal to strut his ill-gotten wealth in the face of his lost love's father would fall sadly by the wayside, replaced by embarrassment to the Lee family.

Graham was distant for a few days following his brother's removal from Cranston, opting to spend time alone and avoid friends whose only wish was to console him, though most found themselves at a loss for words.

Clara found Graham seated on a bench outside the newly constructed train depot and went to sit beside him.

He acknowledged her, wrapped an arm around her shoulders, and pulled her close. "You should have worn a heavier shawl. There is a chill in the air."

"Oh? I much prefer your arm," she said in a teasing manner.

"How are those wedding plans coming along?" he countered.

"Right on target. Of course, only the committee, the preacher, and his wife are aware of our surprise ceremony. Secrets can be such fun."

"Some are fun, yes."

"Are you still worried about your brother?"

"I don't think he will do well in prison. Caleb thinks himself rather tough, but I suspect he hasn't met the scum of the earth yet," Graham said. "I never should have left him in charge of company funds. The temptation was too great."

"You can't blame yourself for trying to help him flourish in the new land. A while back, you said that you believed his troubles in the East were only rumors. You had no way of knowing he was, indeed, guilty, not to mention running from the law."

"I should have guessed. He was always a gold digger at heart. Even when we were kids, and he had no real need for extra money, he would hang out at the store and waylay lads, bullying them for their pocket change."

"That is a sad memory."

"And I didn't do much to nip that behavior in the bud either. Just figured he'd grow out of it."

"We will trust that during his confinement, the Lord will deal with his heart and inspire a change in him that he won't be able to deny."

Graham stood and pulled her to her feet. "Have I told you lately how glad I am you came to Cranston and how blessed I feel that you are willing to become my wife?"

"Not in so many words, but you are a creative sort of gent. I got the picture."

"So, what do I need to do to make this wedding happen, sooner rather than later?"

"Show up in your finest Sunday go-to-meeting duds, find yourself a best man who knows how to keep a secret, and plan our short honeymoon. That's it in a nutshell."

"Who will you ask to stand with you?"

"I was debating on Ling Aihan,' she said nervously.

"Timothy's friend's mother from the camp?"

"She has been my right hand when it comes to helping me communicate with the students, and a sweet friendship has developed between us."

"That should create quite the splash at our wedding, but go for it, my miracle woman."

"I *could* ask Elise from the dress shop. She is toning down the rather extravagant gown my mother had fashioned for me before I left Hamilton."

"Not in the mood for extravagance?"

"Not entirely. Bringing the city to our small town here in the mountains is thwarting boundaries I don't want to cross. I think simple and regal is better than extravagant in our case."

"You, Miss Stewart, will look gorgeous in anything you choose to wear."

"I do want it to be the perfect day for us. And there shouldn't be any noses out of joint as the campers aren't actually a part of Cranston's official school-opening celebration."

"Agreed. We do want the event to run smoothly, but won't you miss your new friend at the ceremony?"

"I can ask the committee to see if she'd be welcome, but I won't risk some hot-head spoiling it for the children or for us."

"The two communities have shared a funeral. Interesting enough, I've heard it said by some disgruntled grooms that getting hitched is the first nail in a man's coffin," Graham chuckled. "Maybe there is not that much difference in the two events, after all."

Clara jumped up and slapped playfully at his arm.

He ducked, stood, wrapped an arm around her waist, and pulled her closer to him. "Don't expect that will be my assessment when it's all said and done."

When they were inches apart, she smiled. "You are absolutely incorrigible, Graham Lee."

"I do my best to oblige," he said, planting a kiss on the tip of her nose. "I realize you can muster up enough trouble on your own, but it's nothing compared to the spice I will add to your life."

In the days following, Clara doubled up on the sessions at camp, hoping to impart as much education into their eager minds as possible before the weather changed for the worse and her schedule filled up. Her invitation to join the social committee helped ease the occasional bouts of homesickness, allowing her to mix a bit of what she'd learned in the social circles back home with the growing Western community. It wasn't that she yearned to step back in time—she loved her new life in the Rocky Mountains and the mission God had entrusted her with for the people's future, but the Stewart family would forever occupy a special place in her heart.

The back-to-school celebration was the first social event she would help to organize in Cranston, and because of its involvement with the children, the memories created would mark the beginning of her career. Now that she understood the community's needs better, the new teacher found herself seated at her desk most evenings, preparing lessons that suited the local students best. And as if that wasn't enough to send Clara's mind into a frenzy, her wedding loomed on the horizon. Although it would not be the Victorian splash in society it might have been had she remained in Hamilton, it was *her* wedding, the event that had filled her dreams since adolescence, and nothing could be more life-defining than that.

Time seemed to fly, and soon August 22 loomed on the calendar. The back-to school celebration and her wedding day combined into one would signify the two milestone events that would change her life.

Clara spent the eve of the big day with her newest friend, Elise Grattish, bathing and pampering their bodies with tantalizing fragrances in preparations for the next day.

As they sipped tea on the front porch, clad in their night clothes and wrapped in blankets while staring at the stars, Clara broke the silence. "What brought you to Cranston?"

"I hated when people thought of me as a destitute old maid at age twenty-one, only fit to care for my aging parent. When my father dared to dream of spending his final days in the mountains, I decided to break free of their label. I love fashion and sewing, so I figured I would fare well in the dress industry. The railroad's expansion will tempt ladies with its invitation to come and see the beauty that lies within these mountains, and I shall be here waiting for them with unique clothing designed especially to add to their experience."

"Good choice, Elise. A lady always loves to feel new fabric and buy a new outfit."

"Even now, business is booming just serving the ones who have come along to build our town. Think of the ones still yet to come as our town grows—I can't imagine how much more frantic my schedule will be when the trains stop here to allow women passengers time to shop before moving on."

"More business will help pay for additional help in your shop, not to mention give one of our locals a job. There are young girls signed up for my classes who might fit that role when the time comes."

"It is rather exciting. I feel like a true frontier settler on the threshold of something big about to happen."

"I know the feeling," Clara said. "And I am pleased we will do this together. Your friendship means everything to me, Elise."

"And yours to me. I love that you were able to upset the applecart here with such grace. It needed to be done, and I am not nearly that outspoken or brave. The townsfolk were stuck in a rut, fearful to move forward, but it's a new time, and we need to embrace it. The majority feel the atmosphere has changed for the better since you've arrived.

"I am pleased to hear that. Sometimes I think I am a bull in a shop full of glassware."

Elise laughed. "I envy your daring spirit and hope to catch your infectious boldness. My siblings have scattered across the countryside with their spouses, and Mother passed away a couple of years ago. Father is sickly—though I suspect it's grief that has crippled his body. The move here made him smile, so we came, but I have to admit, making friends has not been easy. Everyone here is so focused on being the best and outdoing our business competition that we've put up walls to protect ourselves. I hope to inspire some attitude changes in that respect."

"My father in Hamilton, says competition is good. It keeps businesses up-to-date and on their toes. Customers are as unique as the marketplace, and there is room for diversity in every field. To serve the multitudes of people who will come West, it's in your best interest that local businesses work together, all of them bent on building a one-stop shopping paradise that will have the reputation as the best this side of the Rocky Mountains."

"You make it sound even more exciting than I imagined. I will try to be a spokesperson in my field of interest as you have been in yours, Clara Stewart."

"And that is all God expects of us, to be his hand of harmony extended to all." Clara stood. "I fear we must turn in. I have enjoyed this time with you, and we shall do it again, one day when my husband is away from home conducting railroad business."

Elise stood and hugged Clara. "I am tired, and we can't have the bride with black circles under her eyes tomorrow." The girls laughed and Elise started inside.

Clara was pleased that she had chosen Elise as one of the women to stand with her on the most important day of her life. As it turned out, her friend felt equally blessed, considering Clara's wedding a turning point in her life as well, both personally and professionally. Clara glanced back at the moonlit sky before closing the door. Stars filled the expanse, their glittering presence providing a romantic night's spectacle enough to fill a young woman's dreams.

It was late when they crawled under the covers, exhausted but fully elated, looking forward to the events of the next day.

The following morning, Clara spread the wedding gown flat on her freshly made bed, ready and waiting for the final event of the day. Alongside it lay two simple yet eloquent gowns for Elise and Aihan to wear for the ceremony. The party dresses she and Elise would wear for most of the day's activities lay on chairs, but the work dresses for the morning's chores took first picking.

"I don't recall the last time I changed outfits two times in one day. I daresay my life has become rather humdrum," Elise said pulling the work dress over her head—a suitable garment for the tasks that lay ahead of the committee planners.

"I have three changes," Clara said with a smile, "but adjusting my outfit to fit the occasion is not a new practice for me. At home, just showing up for the supper meal required a dinner dress, especially when Father entertained, which was almost always."

Clara wore a simple skirt and blouse, sturdy shoes, and a sunhat to accomplish the morning groundwork needed for the outside fun with the children.

Elise downed the last of her coffee and stood. "Shall we be off, Clara? There is much to do before the community arrives, and in droves, no doubt. Everyone is excited to forget about the future we are all laboring toward and simply stop to enjoy the moment. That will be a step in the right direction, I daresay."

"We will organize many more, especially in the winter, when folks might feel depressed from the cold and isolation."

"Agreed." Elise hugged Clara. "I am so glad you came to Cranston. I might have curled up and died of a lonely heart if you hadn't sparked some life back into these bones."

"I'll be watching for a fine gent worthy of your affection in the crowd today," Clara said as she walked to the door. "I might enjoy some matchmaking on the side. See if I can do as good a job as my father apparently has in sending me here to become Graham's wife."

"Don't you go pushing the envelope, Miss Clara Stewart. I can find my own man. I just haven't been interested before now."

The women laughed as they headed through the door. They picked up the supplies they'd piled on the porch, and headed for the school yard where they staged games and marked start and finish lines for the planned races. Mr. Tether and Mr. Glenning showed up midmorning to construct the long tables on which the guests would place their food contributions, and when the men were done, Mrs. Hycrest covered the rough wood with bright orange and turquoise linens.

With the outside preparations completed for the picnic and game portion of the day, the team of decorators moved inside the church. When Clara peeked inside to see their progress, she spilled uncontrollable tears at the sight of the colorful fresh flowers and evergreen branches woven into the archway that would be used for her wedding ceremony. Mrs. Glenning and the preacher's wife, had helped Mrs. Hycrest beforehand by crafting large bows, and now the ladies were fastening one on each pew down the middle aisle. A crystal vase filled with long-stemmed mountain blossoms had been placed on top of the organ to complete the décor.

After viewing their simple efforts, Clara slipped away as silently as she had arrived. She wiped the trail of tears from her cheeks, her heart full to overflowing. It could not be compared to the grandeur of the Hamilton Cathedral, but the venue felt comfortable, and it was the perfect fit for her Western setting.

Clara and Elise hurried home and changed into the outfits they would wear for the middle portion of the day. The festive green dress with ivory trimmings on the collar, wrists, and layered skirt, somehow emitted the party appearance but maintained a respectful air that would conform to her classroom scheduled activities.

The women split up after that, and Clara went directly to her classroom, hoping to enjoy a private moment before the back-to-school celebrations began. She fingered the braided bell chord she would pull to call her students and guests into the school after the late lunch and the fun time outside had concluded. Clara strolled down the aisles, imagining the children who would sit in them while under her tutelage and lifting each one to God in prayer.

A roll call was planned for that day, with the parents lining the side walls, proud as punch to hear their offsprings' names called out from the first page of Cranston's school registrar.

In her fanciest handwriting, Clara wrote her name, Miss Stewart, on the board, and beneath it in brackets, she wrote "soon to be, Mrs. Lee." At that point in the day, she would still be single, with the guests none the wiser that her surname was about to change.

Clara retrieved her favorite book of poems from the shelf and placed it on top of her desk, marking the page she would read to the assembly. Words were like magic, and she had sought out the perfect passage to hold her audience's attention with the melodic rhyme of a "Back to School" Shakespearian sonnet. The diversity of his work had inspired her from an early age, and she enjoyed the intensity of his approach to drama, tragedy, or even the humor he injected into his stories. She hoped, in turn, that this introductory narration to Cranston might serve to inspire the gift of learning in her students, and have them laughing at the antics the reading had to offer.

She heard horse hooves pulling wagons outside of the schoolhouse, and the immediate calls of greeting from neighbors who were eager to socialize. Clara experienced a rush of nervous jitters running rampant up her arms. The event was underway. She walked to the door and swung it open wide to behold the crowds that had already gathered, Women added their food contributions to the table and the moments their backs were turned, the meticulous Mrs. Tether rearranged the dishes to fit her fancy.

Five o'clock rolled around all too soon.

The success of the bountiful midday luncheon and the rambunctious games enjoyed by both children and adults were behind them now. The third segment of the day was underway as Clara rang the bell to summon the group together. The teacher reveled at the sight of the happy faces of her neighbors as they passed her by in the doorway. When the commotion in the room silenced, she took a deep breath and walked up the aisle to her desk. She focused intently on every word she said from the front of her tiny classroom. Their heartfelt emotions stirred in the air, and Clara supposed there could be no greater feeling than the unveiling of a community's dream come true.

At the close of the opening ceremony in the classroom, she led the group in the Lord's Prayer before inviting them to move to the church for what the committee had labeled as "a thanksgiving singalong.' The day had unfolded perfectly thus far, just as the planners had hoped, with each event being a running success leading to the highest point of the day, at least, from the bride's perspective. Following the singalong, the wedding march was due to play, and when she entered the church, her life would change forever. Clara dared to hope she had not unconsciously given away the upcoming secret ceremony, as her inability to keep her mounting distraction in check while waiting for the wedding had grown more difficult by the minute.

Clara Stewart dismissed the crowd, instructing them to move over to the church for the singalong to allow the dance crew the time to set up for the final event before the evening concluded and the crowd broke up for home. Mr. Glenning and Mr. Tether lingered behind to push the desks against the wall and rearrange the front platform for the musicians who had been asked to play some dance tunes for the couples and children to end the day's festivities.

Of course, none, not even the musicians, knew that when the crowd had returned in forty minutes, it would be to celebrate her after-wedding party. She would be Mrs. Lee at that point and she suspected her dancing feet would never be able to catch up to her rapid heartbeat.

Elise crept up behind her, as Clara stood at the door, watching the crowd casually chat as they shifted the short distance from the schoolhouse to the church. "You did a marvelous job keeping your secret intact all day long. If I didn't know better, I would never imagine you were about to repeat your vows before the congregation."

Clara grinned at her friend. "The most difficult times were when I saw Graham off in the distance eyeing me up with that silly grin he likes to wear."

"The citizens of our little town in the mountains will forever remember the unfolding of your best-kept secret, my friend, on the heels of the first back-to-school festivities in Cranston."

"We have drenched this event in prayer. I knew God would show up," Clara said seeing that the crowd was almost at their destination. The sun began its descent, and her gaze transferred as it lingered on the spectacle in the sky, its crimson and orange colors spreading like fingers to pierce the fluffy white clouds in the blue sky. It defined the horizon, and seemed to welcome the union of the two hearts who nestled under His newly anointed matrimonial umbrella.

Elise placed a hand on her shoulder. "Are you ready?"

"More than ready," the bride said, looping an arm around her friend's. Together they skipped down the school steps.

Clara and Elise's giddy laughter encircled them as they might two schoolgirls with a secret, while anticipating the local's response to the surprise she was about to break forth in front of them. They rushed into Clara's cabin, where the two women hugged Aihan who stood waiting for them and the final dress change of the day. Clara had been thrilled when the committee consented to allow her camp friend to stand at the front with her when she took her vows. Her husband, Ike, would stand next to Graham—a decision the groom made to solidify their united stand—along with Russ, his new payroll man. The blending of Chinese and white at the front of the meeting room would satisfy any lingering questions the community might have as to the Lee family's position concerning segregation. The newlyweds, Graham and Clara Lee, would open their hearts and declare their commitment that day to all residents of Cranston and the surrounding area.

Graham was all thumbs, requiring Russ to help him with his tie. He was able to wear his finery all day long and not raise suspicion, whereas Clara would have given it away if she marched around in white satin and delicate lace. He found it humorous to watch Clara squirm and flush pink when he winked or threw her a kiss, oblivious to anyone who might happen close by. The railroad manager could not be prouder of the woman who had maintained full control of her students in the classroom earlier. She held the entire adult audience captive during her recital, bringing listeners to spontaneous tears, and moments later, bursts of laughter, in awe of the changing storyline. She was a magician—better than he had ever seen in the Toronto theaters. He chuckled, wondering if that ability might come back to bite him in the butt in the years to follow.

Her love and compassion were the characteristics that rendered her as unforgettable, a gem in the making. Near as he could tell, the woman gained attention unknowingly as she went about her business, unaware that any friction she might have caused by her well-meaning efforts only served to shape another beautiful stone in her pile of redeemable traits.

From the entrance of the church, Graham noticed his groomsman arrive, and he hurried over to shake Ike's hand in the church yard. The man would join them for the singalong and be present when his wife, Aihan, Elise, and the bride showed up for the ceremony. He pushed the man inside the building ahead of him and chanced one final glance back toward the cabin. He caught a glimpse of Clara and Elise slipping into his soon-to-be home.

After that night, her dwelling would become his, free to come and go at will, the confines of their chaperoned courtship finally over. He would be forever grateful that Cranston was not as picky about hiring only single people to teach as was the case in some communities. He knew her heart quickened whenever an opportunity to instruct another came her way. The satisfaction lit up her features as much as the thought of marrying him did. Would she have chosen him over teaching had the schoolboard been a stickler and demanded unmarried candidates? The thought almost made him break out in a cold sweat, for he never would have asked her to make such a sacrifice.

God called folks to different missions. Hers was not only with the Cranston children, but also the adults and youngsters at the immigrants' camp. It was an unexpected mission she had taken on with a joyful spirit, with no questions as to its social acceptance swaying her decision.

He counted the songs and the minutes it took to sing them, sneaking glances at the organist, who stood on the alert, watching for the girls to arrive at the back of the room. When she signaled with a nod of her head, Graham nudged the arms of the men seated on either side of him and grinned.

"Blessings All Mine" ended in hearty volume, and the preacher stepped inside the archway from the back, holding his Bible. "Folks, we've had us a mighty fine day, with plenty of good food, fun, and exercise enough to awaken my old bones. We've been privileged to sit in the new teacher's classroom and listen to her tell a delightful story. I'd like to add that your singing here this evening has topped the cake, its sweet fragrance drifting upward to touch our Lord's heart."

The congregation shouted, "Amen," and a joyful murmur filled the room. Pastor Tremain Bilmire raised his hands to regain their attention. "I can feel the peace and thankfulness you have expressed for His blessings to us here in Cranston."

Mrs. Bilmire, seated behind the musical instrument off to the side, depressed and held her finger down on one of the organ keys. When she gained his attention, she cast the preacher a stern *get with the program*, warning.

He cleared his throat. "I've kept this secret long enough," he began, stopping the chuckles that filtered throughout the room. "You've all met Miss Clara Stewart earlier as the new schoolteacher, but now I want to introduce her to you as our very own Graham Lee's mail-order bride. There's been quite the romance budding under our noses here in our Rocky Mountain paradise, but tonight, these two fine young people will take their vows before God and man."

The crowd jumped to their feet and roared, the sound reverberating a jubilant echo throughout the building. Graham took that as his signal to go line up with Russ and Ike at the front. The time had finally arrived, and his mouth instantly dried up like prunes in the hot sun. He wondered if he'd have the ability to articulate the words, "I will" in response to the preacher's all-important question.

When the music started, Aihan came first, which, to his relief caused no surprise among the congregation. Elise followed, and the two women stood next to each other on the opposite side of the archway. Both ladies' cheeks were rosy with excitement, a prelude to the ultimate loveliness yet to enter. Graham held his breath.

Clara appeared. The setting sun spilled over her, its glow lighting her from behind through the open doorway, outlining her with a halo of perfection. She stood transfixed in the doorway, capturing and holding his gaze. His heart did a somersault, and the strain left it hammering in his chest. Was there a word in the English language that described such exquisiteness in bodily form? He would have to ask the teacher later, he mused, wondering about the crazy mix of emotions and thoughts navigating through his head. This woman was sure to outshine any others he'd seen in high society back in the cities they had both left behind. He wished her father could see her happiness, and know that his plan had been a good one from the start. Graham would have taken her even if she'd been a pauper. In fact, he might suggest they give her father's money to the poor and simply live on love. Graham figured he had enough stored up from that very moment to last a lifetime.

Strains from the wedding march started, and she began to walk too slowly for his liking. The impatient man would like nothing more than to lift her into his arms and feel the rush of the sleek fabric against his pant legs as he spun her around. Graham forced his mind to surrender to the order of the ceremony as the preacher had instructed yesterday, but at home, in the cabin later, he would spin her until she was as dizzy in love as he.

When the sweet, lilac fragrance reached his nostrils, he breathed in her presence. She stood close, hesitant to break contact with his intense gaze. Momentarily, she turned her attention toward the preacher. Perhaps she was as eager to get the deed done as he was. Even in total distraction, Graham vaguely heard the scriptures Pastor Tremain read from the Bible, his inner man surging in agreement to God's plan; "the two shall become one, under His umbrella of protection." The vows were repeated, and he found an adequate voice to declare his love and commitment to the woman by his side, "until death do us part," he promised. Graham hoped that would be a very long time in coming.

"I now pronounce you husband and wife," the preacher said, and the groom bent in to kiss his bride. He could not recall a more perfect moment in his entire life.

When the couple stepped outside to face the setting sun, the campers greeted them with a shower of rice, having listened and watched the ceremony from the open door. It was one more tiny step toward the merging of customs and friendships between the workers and locals.

Graham suspected that God smiled down upon the scene from the heavenlies, pleased at the outcome of not only their marital union but the coming together of his community.

The newlyweds were the first on the dance floor, wrapped together as if in a cocoon for a a slow waltz, oblivious to the onlookers. Cheers went up at the end, and Clara blushed when he stole a kiss. "I love you, Mrs. Lee," he said above the din.

Clara responded likewise. "I love you, too, Mr. Lee."

After an hour of learning new dance steps, which served to twirl her mind even more senseless, the couple cut the enormous cake and served a piece to each of their friends. When done, they prepared to leave. Clara tossed her bouquet, Elise caught it, and the girls giggled and hugged at the outcome.

When they closed the door of the schoolhouse behind them, someone rang the bell, and it echoed in the night wind all the way to their cabin. Graham picked her up into his arms and carried her inside. When he placed her feet on the floor, he helped himself to a very long kiss. She pushed him gently away, and he grinned when he noticed her breathless. "Did I tell you how gorgeous you are? I love white on you. It brings out those dark tresses and the wild intensity in your eyes." He proceeded to pull out the pins from her hair, loosening it so it would fall around her shoulders. His fingers entwined in the mass and he said, "Oh, my, you are a beauty."

"You are not so bad yourself, husband."

Graham did a quick scan around the room. "You've decorated the place to look really nice—cozy, warm, and inviting." He seemed tongued tied and was spouting anything that came to mind.

Clara laughed. "Glad our home meets with your approval, but if you don't want a nighttime beverage beforehand, I suggest we retire. It has been a very long day."

"Yes, ma'am—no drink necessary," he said eagerly. "We can do that."

They moved toward the bedroom and he kicked the door closed behind them. A very long and wonderful day, indeed.

Four months later, Clara received a birthday package from Hamilton. In it was the deed and the first installment of her grandmother's inheritance.

After her birthday supper and cake at Francine's Diner, a celebration with many of their friends, the couple returned home. Clara held his hand and led him to the box on the table.

"I got a package from home earlier."

"How wonderful. I am so sorry your parents are missing all of these events in your life. It must hurt both sides to be separated by such great distance."

"They knew I would be gone for life when they sent me West, but perhaps they will come to visit once the railway line is complete. I would love for them to see our mountains."

"We shall invite them, for sure, and maybe mine, as well. Family is important."

"Did I ever tell you about my grandparents?"

"I don't think so," he said, pouring each of them a cup of coffee from the pot simmering on the cookstove.

She took a long sip. "Grandfather has been gone for years now, and my dear Granny thought it wise to leave conditions on my inheritance."

"She did? Smart woman." He chuckled and ducked from her playful swat.

"I had to be married by my twentieth birthday, which was today, before receiving her treasures."

"Is that what's in the box?"

Clara opened it and brought out a ring. "Her wedding ring goes to the eldest granddaughter." Next came a notebook. "This is full of marital advice she was never able to give." Then came the envelope. She carefully withdrew a legal document from inside of it. "And this is to the bulk of her wealth. Some went to my younger siblings, but this was put in trust for me the day I was born."

"Money? You've inherited your grandmother's money?"

"Don't look so surprised. You knew my family was well-off when I came."

"Yeah, and I was perfectly happy with the amount your father gave us as a wedding present."

She laughed. "In a round about way."

"Why didn't you tell me before about this coming on your birthday?"

"I wanted to enjoy living on our wages for a while before my husband went crazy with these additional dollars at his fingertips."

"It's your money, not mine."

"It's our money, and I was hoping we could use some of it to build shelters for the campers. It's getting way too cold over there and my heart breaks for them."

"Not at all surprised that your compassion kicked in at about the same time as the box's arrival."

"Would it be all right? I don't want to step on any toes, and we'd have to hire people to construct the buildings."

"I can put Russ in charge of that. He helped with the depot and knows most of the fellows with carpentry skills." Graham took it one step further. "What will we do with the buildings after the railroad has been completed and the campers move off to find work elsewhere?"

"I am sure that when the time comes, a need will present itself."

He smiled and squeezed her hand. "Our friends at the camp will have a good Christmas this year."

Clara's excitement increased. "Christmas! We couldn't possibly have any buildings constructed in that short of time."

"The hope of things to come will be a welcomed gift," Graham said. "We'll start planning tomorrow and see how quickly we can make it happen."

"Oh, Graham—to be honest, back in Hamilton I was ready to throw this inheritance to the wind if I had to marry to receive it. Now, I am so thankful for the money *and* my husband. Granny would be so impressed."

Clara kissed Graham, the taste of coffee on his warm lips. When they pulled apart, she said, "To think I actually dreaded turning twenty. This is my best birthday ever."

The End.

Join Forces with the Author and Fans

Come join the fans at:
Dream Creations: Romance FB group to interact.
https://www.facebook.com/groups/1118008614903688

See all this author's titles on **Amazon Author Page**
https://www.amazon.com/-/e/B00J9RM116

Sign up for the weekly newsletter, where she chats about her life and books. You will find promotions, parties, sales, new releases, or discounted sweet/Christian romance books from other authors. Join now and download a FREE gift—The Orphan Flower.
http://eepurl.com/djNqjn

You can subscribe to her website **to stay updated and receive occasional blogs in your inbox: Heartwarming Romance: https://www.marlenebierworth.com**

Do you like Book Bub? **Follow me there!**
https://www.bookbub.com/profile/marlene-bierworth

Author's Bio

Dream Creations: bringing words of hope for the nations. Marlene writes sweet/Christian heartwarming romance books, both historical and contemporary, with a twist of mystery, adventure, suspense, and drama to set your pulse racing. She is a follower of Jesus, a wife, mother of two, grandmother of five, and great-grandmother of two. God's blessings are new every morning.

Marlene enjoys church activities, reading, hiking, oil painting, cruising, traveling, and socializing with family and friends. And she loves interacting with readers and fellow authors. "Retirement does not get much better than this."

Miss Spencer Meets Her Match

by Linore Rose Burkard

Can true love happen under false pretenses?

Millicent Spencer has no wish to attend the Cinderella Ball that the Dowager Countess of Beaufort is holding to force her son to choose a wife. Just returned from years in America, Millie despises the closed system of the British peerage. She attends the absurd ball only under protest—and in disguise as a companion to her simple cousin Sophina.

The dashing and powerful Earl of Beaufort is a longtime bachelor with no interest in wooing a wife. To escape the role of Prince Charming at his mother's ball, he trades places with an innocent vicar and attends the event as a man of the cloth.

Neither expects to meet the one they didn't know they were waiting for. And neither guesses that their clever disguises will imperil the deepest wish of their hearts!

"An honest answer is like a kiss on the lips."

Prov. 24:26 NIV

Chapter One

"Do you know, I think this may work," the Earl of Beaufort declared to Mr. Sandstone the vicar with an impish smile, as they stood in the earl's private dressing chamber. The earl, Allen Prescott Courtenay, thirty and handsome, wore an ensemble entirely of black from his shoes, stockings and breeches to a twin-cut tailcoat in broadcloth and a high, black-buttoned waistcoat. Only the small knot of a neckcloth and barely an inch of his stock peeked out in white to relieve the severity.

It was a fine outfit—for a clergyman. The earl was not, nor was he preparing for religious orders, but for a ball. Disguised as Mr. Sandstone, the vicar.

Mr. Sandstone eyed his lordship with consternation. The earl's dark, thick locks, accented handsomely in wavy lights from the sun streaming through a window, framed a strong-featured head, noble Roman nose, and a light sprinkling of premature grey at the edges of his hair which gave him a look of maturity beyond his years. He had prescient, penetrating azure eyes that beheld the vicar with authoritative confidence.

"Are you certain, my lord, that this er, deception, is necessary?" asked Mr. Sandstone, a mild-mannered gentleman in his mid-forties. He didn't wish to make himself odious to the son of his benefactress, the Dowager Countess of Beaufort, but to aid that son in subterfuge was a questionable business for a clergyman.

"As I explained yesterday," replied the earl patiently, "my dear mother is hosting the ball ostensibly in my honor but with the sole intention of forcing me to choose a wife. I will not play 'Prince Charming' to a 'Cinderella.'"

Lord Carlisle, standing by, spoke up. He was a decade older than the earl, and though loyal to him, had a soft spot for his winsome mama. "My lady only means to help you retain the title."

The earl sighed. "Blast that ancient custom!"

Lady Beaufort had plagued her son about the ultimatum—reminding him only recently (though he had come into the title after the sad demise of his elder brother, three years since)—that an ancient stipulation for the line of Beaufort dictated the earl must marry before his thirty-first year or retire the earldom upon his death.

When informing him of the "Cinderella Ball," (for so she had styled it), she'd said, "Surely, you cannot wish to cede everything this family owns—title, lands, holdings and honors—to the crown? Not when the sole requirement for you to keep it is to find a wife! Does not the Bible say, 'He who findeth a wife, findeth a good thing'?"

Allen understood the urgency of the situation, being on the cusp of his thirty-first year. The problem was, he hadn't had time to bother with marriage and had no real wish to marry.

It wasn't that he disapproved of marriage particularly, or even marriage for himself, not in theory. But since stepping into the title, every unmarried lady of his acquaintance seemed intent upon flattering him. Their behavior to him as a second son contrasted noticeably with their behavior now. In conversation, they were subservient and held to no strong opinions (lest they disagreed with his). In matters of taste, they were yielding and conformable so that he never knew their true preferences.

Aristocratic ladies were the worst offenders. Those with lesser titles aspired for greater ones. And daughters and sisters of peers, commoners themselves, longed to possess any title.

Moreover, he'd met the available misses from the ranks and families of the peerage and had not found himself enamored. To put it simply, he hadn't found a woman he wished to take home with him, to live with in sickness and in health.

Worse, his impression that most women were title-hungry had only been strengthened over time. By the end of last season, he'd decided if God were to provide him a wife, she could not come from the aristocracy.

He vowed that his wife—if wife there must be—would be an honest woman, not moved by his rank. The conundrum was how to find such a lady. He was coming of the reluctant opinion that she did not exist.

It was a chance encounter with the vicar Mr. Sandstone, who had arrived at the estate the day before, which gave the earl the brainchild of switching places. Mr. Sandstone was a favorite with Lady Beaufort, the earl's mama.

When he and Lord Carlisle saw the clergyman leaving his mother's apartments, the earl had the sober thought that a mere vicar was better off than he, in that the whole unmarried female sex did not hanker after *him* with socially ambitious hopes, fawning and flattering.

And then it hit him.

He must trade places with the clergyman for the ball.

He would attend his mother's frivolous Cinderella Ball, but not as the Earl of Beaufort. No, he would go as the vicar and mingle with the flock in such a way as to discover the true nature of ladies without their obsequious attitudes. It was fortunate he had stipulated that not a single lady of the peerage, nor the sisters or daughters of a peer, nor any female of his acquaintance could be invited. He had hoped that such an outrageous requirement would deter his mama from holding the ball.

It had not.

But the result was that thirty women of the gentry, invited from neighboring counties (after an assiduous search by her ladyship's man of business) did not know him by sight. Neither did they know Mr. Sandstone. This ensured his disguise was not only brilliant but fail-safe.

In clergyman's weeds, he'd be in an excellent position to sound out a lady's depth of character, even upon so short an acquaintance as a ball could provide.

The sole danger was that even when off her guard, no good woman to admire, to interest or excite him might be found. In which case he would have to broaden his search or be forced, if he were to save the family from disgrace and bankruptcy, to marry a woman that lacked his high regard. Casting the thought aside, a surprising sensation of freedom filled him now that he was prepared to face the ball as the vicar. It almost made him look forward to it.

Mr. Sandstone, dressed in the earl's ballroom finery, looked on worriedly. He cleared his throat. "My lord, as a man of God, can I persuade you to abandon this scheme? Honesty is the thing that best achieves happiness in life. Depend upon it, your future matrimonial harmony is at stake."

The earl replied, (not without compassion, for he could appreciate a minister's misgivings for such a thing), "My good man, the subterfuge is for the sake of honesty. The title has caused many a lady to abandon it, to forget her feelings and disposition to be agreeable to mine. With that obstacle removed, I shall assess a woman according to her true nature."

Mr. Sandstone replied (reasonably he thought), "People are apt to hide their true natures from clergymen too, my lord. They may wish to be seen as more pious than they are. I hardly think that dressed in my garb you will discover a young lady's true nature any more than if you were to appear as your noble self."

The earl smiled at the vicar's earnestness but felt not the least inclination to abandon his plan. "Piety in a wife would not impress me nearly so much as a woman who puts character above a title. If such exists," he added sardonically. "But I will take your words to heart, Sandstone."

"Does that mean, my lord, you are willing to drop the scheme?" asked the vicar with sudden hope. He often felt his sermonizing, even in polite conversation, fell on deaf ears. Could it be his little warnings had hit the mark?

"We shall exchange identities as planned," his lordship replied evenly with a curl to his lower lip.

Mr. Sandstone's hopes evaporated. A mere three years as the title holder had not been lost on this 14th Earl of Beaufort. There was no doubt but that the vicar must do precisely as he was bid.

Chapter Two

When a footman reported to Lady Spencer of Astor House, widow of the late Baron Spencer, that her daughter was nowhere to be found on the estate, she pursed her lips, dismissed the man, and, only stopping to summon the housekeeper, set off to search for the girl. She had a good idea, knowing Millicent, where to find her, and was already rehearsing the combing she would give her when she came upon her.

Sure enough, in ten minutes she found the "Honorable Miss Spencer," her eldest child, on her knees by the bedside of a maid in the servants' quarters. Just as she'd suspected! The footman hadn't thought to check there, for in many a household the servants' wing was rarely trespassed upon by the family if they could help it.

The maid had fallen ill, and Millie was in the act of administering a spoonful of Godfrey's Cordial, a healing tonic she had fetched herself from the apothecary when her mother appeared, surveying the scene with narrowed eyes.

"Mama!" she said with a sweet smile, turning sky-blue eyes to her mother.

Most people found Millicent's smile irresistible, for Millie had the type of beauty that exuded sweetness. But her iron-willed mama resisted it, continuing to frown mightily.

"It isn't the plague, I daresay," Millie continued, her thick black hair peeking out in curls from a frilled morning cap. "I only came to give her this physick. Mr. Addison vowed 'twill get anybody on their feet."

Her ladyship's frown deepened. "What shall I do with you? Do you wish to fall ill too? And pass it on to me and your brother the baron, no doubt?" Her glare took in the invalid.

"Ah told miss not to trouble herself, mum!" cried the young prostrate guiltily from the sickbed, trying to sit up in her agitation. Millie gently urged her back to a prone position with one hand on her shoulder.

Only two fortnights ago, Millie had returned from America. Lady Spencer, never an affectionate mother, had not minded that her late husband had gone off to America six years ago on business prospects and taken their only daughter with him. Their son, the heir, five years of age, had remained at home, which is what mattered to her.

Unfortunately, upon Millie's solo return from America—for the baron had died in Boston of influenza—Lady Spencer discovered she had brought back with her the wretched idea that all humans were created equal and must be treated that way regardless of rank or class. Not only this, but she now often quoted the Bible and could be found with her nose in the prayer book at any hour.

Lady Spencer's growing impatience with her daughter was exacerbated more by the fact that Sophina Allred, younger than Millie by three years, had come to visit to get acquainted with her long-absent cousin and had brought with her an invitation to an upcoming ball at Beaufort House. Millicent had not received one.

The ball was the chance of a lifetime. Lady Beaufort's sole purpose in holding it was so her son would choose a wife, even calling it a "Cinderella Ball." The premise, of course, to Lady Spencer's mind, was patently absurd. Not because a vibrant, handsome earl, only thirty years old, was expected to choose a bride like a man at a horse auction, but because her ladyship would allow no woman of title or from a direct line of the aristocracy to attend. It was utterly unpatriotic. It was absurd. It meant even a lowly baron's daughter was excluded.

The new earl was as much a stickler, it seemed, as her Millicent, with utterly peculiar anti-British ideas. Did not earls always wish to marry into another noble family? This 14th Earl Beaufort was an odd duck, to be sure.

Nevertheless, an earl was an earl, and the whole world knew this one was under compulsion to find a bride. The Cinderella Ball was his mama's solution to a stipulation of some sort that required the earls of Beaufort to marry before their thirty-first year.

Cousin Sophina was able to attend, to be one of the female hopefuls at the ball, as she was a relation on Lady Beaufort's side, not in a direct aristocratic line.

Sophina was pretty enough, bright-eyed, and whose sole flaw was to be rather addle-brained. When her ladyship had questioned the girl to see if she knew Millie's whereabouts that morning, she had responded gravely that she would not know, as she must remain abed until the sun, streaming in from a window, hit a certain spot on the floor. She must not stir until it hit that spot, she said, pointing at a particular area of the floor, or she'd have bad luck for the rest of the day. Already she was suffering from the headache, she explained, after attempting to rise too early.

Lady Spencer's wounded sensibilities were further tried because Millie wasn't the least bit sorry to be excluded from the ball!

The great shame of it was, though Millicent had peculiar ideas since her return, she was startlingly beautiful, with oval, expressive eyes, and a nose and mouth in perfect proportion to those eyes. Her hair curled without the aid of curling papers. Her cheeks held a light rose bloom that deepened when she felt strongly on a subject, and her lips were a shade of lush red any artist would delight to capture. People said she had the face of an angel.

Lady Spencer would have delighted to see her making a splash at Beaufort House after her long absence from the country. She could hardly wait to hear the praise her handsome daughter would garnish, even if she was older than the other young ladies. But to her dismay, when Millie had seen the invitation for her cousin the week before, she had sighed contentedly, declaring, "Thank goodness, I am not wanted! I have no wish, as you know, Mama, to marry into an ancient patriarchal and unfair institution such as the peerage."

Lady Spencer's eyes had bulged and sparked fire. "Your father was a peer, and your brother is now! Would you strip the title from them?"

Simple Sophina looked adoringly at her cousin. "Is it—pat—pat-riarchal?" she asked, innocently.

"Of course!" Millie answered. "Primogeniture and all that. My brother was heir, as you know, though I am the firstborn. That, my dear girl, is patriarchal. One hardly sees that in America."

"Would you prefer," Lady Spencer had asked, tight-lipped, "if you had become a baroness in your own right?"

Millie looked at her, startled. "Upon my word, no, that is not what I meant," she said, though what she did mean seemed suddenly vague. Something about once a commoner, always a commoner (except by marriage), whereas in America, good hard work could raise a man to the highest degree of income and respect.

Lady Spencer gritted her teeth and thought perhaps it was best Millie did *not* attend the ball. A month from her twenty-sixth year, her daughter might soon be considered "on the shelf," past the bloom of her youth despite her beauty, but she could make their whole family odious with her disgraceful ideas.

"Up, up, with you!" she ordered. "Mrs. Hansom shall administer the tonic, you foolish girl."

Mrs. Hansom, the housekeeper, stood behind the mistress with a concerned expression, and nodded vehemently. "That I shall, to be sure, miss!" she said.

Millie pursed her lips, replaced the cork on the bottle in her hands and put it aside. To the maid she said gently, "I'll see that you get the afternoon and evening doses if you're not improved by then."

"Thank you, mum," the maid answered gratefully and with a touch of veneration in her eyes. Her gaze darted nervously at Lady Beaufort who stood watching with a frown.

Millie rose and accompanied her mama from the room.

"I fear your time in America has quite eroded your sense," her mother lamented as they headed for the breakfast parlor.

"I should say it has enlarged it, Mama."

Her ladyship's lips pressed into a line while Millie's clear blue eyes surveyed her innocently. "Your life is here in England now, and you must comport yourself accordingly. Though you are barred from the earl's ball, seeking to wed into a noble family is wise. Playing nursemaid to a servant is not. One must be wise in life."

"Kindness is never unwise," returned Millie complacently, as they took seats at the breakfast table. She nodded her permission for a footman to fill her teacup.

Her mother looked shrewdly at her and quoted, "'A servant pampered from his youth will bring grief in the end.' From the book of Proverbs, is it not?"

"Ministering to the sick is hardly pampering, Mama."

"It is, depend upon it! Let servants take care of servants. You have more important things to do."

"What is more important than people? And all are created equal." Millie's complacency as she spoke was as maddening to her mother as her sentiment.

But if the girl expected that truism to silence her parent, she was disappointed, for the lady instantly replied, "In the womb, perhaps, but not after they come out of it. Then, it is birth and breeding that make a person. And pray, do not forget that, Millicent," she finished with an emphatic nod. "I will brook no more time wasted on the servants, mind you."

"But I have all the time in the world, as I am not going to the ball like Sophina," Millie replied unhelpfully. She looked around. "Where *is* my cousin? Still abed?"

Her mother rolled her eyes. "I expect the sun has moved sufficiently so that she shall appear shortly."

Millie nodded, knowing her cousin's strange ideas.

Sophina did not appear.

When, at half past one, her cousin had still not come down, Millie went to see her.

"Sophina dearest!" she exclaimed, after entering the room to find her cousin still abed. "Are you unwell?"

Sophina raised her head. Her eyes were only half-opened. "I fear—that is, I think—yes, yes, I am unwell. Whatever the maid has caught—I must have it too." She closed her eyes and turned over, facing away from Millie.

Going swiftly to the other side of the bed, Millie put out a slim hand to feel her cousin's cheek. "I am sorry, dear cos—but you do not feel hot, though you look fagged. I'll fetch you the cordial." She turned to leave but stopped and gave Sophina an earnest look. "If you remain unwell, at least you can now be honorably excused from the ball." Continuing to gaze at her she added, "Though I daresay you would have preferred to go?"

Sophina's eyes flew open. "No! Please say not a word to my aunt, but my heart quaked at the very thought. Me, meet an earl?" She blinked pitifully at Millie, who nodded and went to fetch the tonic from where she'd left it earlier in the servant's quarters. She was happy to have a chance to check up on Mary, the maid. Millie had given her a reading lesson only the day before. If the lower classes learned to read, she reasoned, they could more easily better their station in life.

When she'd looked in on Mary and returned to the invalid's bedside, the moment she approached it, Sophina's eyes opened wide and she sat up. Before Millie could remonstrate with her, she exclaimed, "YOU must go, Millie! While you were gone, it came to me. *You* must go! To the ball. In my place! The earl will fall in love with you at first sight, I have no doubt. You deserve to be a countess. Only think of all the good you could do as a countess."

The whole household knew Millie's highest aim since her return was to discover what good she could do for the world. Teaching a parlor maid to read was just the beginning, and even that had to be done secretly, for her mama would never countenance her doing it. Opening a school for girls, for those of the lower classes who could not afford to pay a farthing, was what she most wanted to accomplish. This, she felt, could redress at least one inequity of the English class system.

"You could open the school you talked about, I have no doubt!" Sophina cried as further ammunition to get Millie to take her place. "You see? You must go in my place!"

Sophina looked quite pretty in her nightdress and mob cap, and Millie saw she was utterly in earnest, but she sputtered a laugh. "You absurd child! I should like nothing less than that, I assure you. You know I have no wish to wed an earl, besides which, it would not be honest, dear cos."

"But think of the good you could do," the girl repeated. She lay back down, and her voice grew fainter but remained troubled. "As a countess, you could help hundreds of girls learn to read. You could send aid to poor families. Only think of the influence you would have! The resources. How else will you bring justice to this pat-patriar-chal system but by using it for good?"

Millie stared at her cousin. She had spoken with more sense than she usually displayed, but the idea was of course ridiculous. She could not pretend to be her cousin. Still, something in her stirred at the image of herself as a benefactress to the surrounding countryside, helping the sick, the weak, and the poor. She felt a warm, soothing glow inside as the idea filled her brain and heart. An image of a school for girls came to her, and herself, proudly inspecting the premises as the founder and underwriter. How proud she would be! She envisioned scads of servant girls with their noses in books, all dressed in simple frocks bespoke by the school. She would see that they had clean shifts as well, white caps, stockings and slippers, as well as books or slates, pencils, and… and suddenly her rosy vision vanished.

It took money to do that.

"Consider it!" cried Sophina again, desperation in her voice as if it were a life or death matter.

Millie said, "Why do you fret so? If you are unwell, my mother will not force you to go."

Sophina frowned. In a miserable voice she admitted, "I am not unwell. I am endeavoring to be unwell because I cannot face this ball!"

Millie sat on the bed, her lips pursed to hold back a grin. "Come, come, you need only appear and possibly submit to standing up once with the earl. You have had sufficient dance lessons, and my white-work evening gown with embroidered roses looks lovely on you."

Sophina only shook her head, her brow creased with worry. But suddenly she gasped and looked up. "Millie, I have it! If you'll go in my place, I'll go as your companion!"

"Did you include a companion on your reply to the invitation?"

Sophina's face blanched. "Papa sent the reply. I should have cried off had it been in my power."

Millie said, "I suppose they shan't mind. I will accompany you as *your* companion since you need someone to bolster you."

"No, no, no!" Sophina wailed pitiably. "You are ten times more graceful on the floor than I, and you have beautiful gowns from all the dinners and balls and soirees you attended in Boston!"

"They are last year's fashion," Millie put in. "It takes a dreadfully long time for the newest modes to reach America." Her mother had summoned a local seamstress to supply new gowns for her and refashion some of the old ones. The styles were taken directly from the latest issue of *La Belle Asembleé*, but the frocks weren't yet finished.

"Your gown with the French gauze is close enough and you will look *divine*. Please, consider it, Millie! And *quickly!*" Her eyes were pleading pools of brown. "You know I lack social graces! Papa kept me in the schoolroom with the girls and I attended precious few events, never a ball."

Millie said, "Your papa is an eccentric. But now we can begin to redress that. He denied you opportunity but as he plans on leaving you a small fortune since he has no male heirs, that 'tis worth, my dear girl, more social graces than any finishing school or experiences can provide."

"'Tis too late, cos. I am reconciled to becoming a spinster. My money shall be spent caring for my younger sisters and seeing *them* well married."

Millie made a scoffing sound. "Nonsense! You are at a perfect marrying age with your best years ahead of you. I am more near spinsterhood. I will think on your idea only if you rise this instant, take some nourishment, and prepare to go."

Millie had no intention of impersonating her cousin, but knew that to consent to considering it was the only way to manage Sophina.

Her cousin nodded unhappily. "Very well."

Chapter Three

Thinking more on it as she went her way, Millie had to shake her head at Sophina's idea. She could not appear at a ball as someone other than herself. As Sophina's companion, although she would have precious little chance to meet a clergyman, much less the one of her dreams (for who gave the least notice to a companion?) she might have the satisfaction of seeing Sophina meet a suitable match.

Millie herself did not expect to ever meet her match, for she wished to do a great deal of good, but whether to open a school or distribute food or medicine, it seemed she would need a small fortune. And most men did not relish having their fortunes spent on charity.

In Boston, she had been quite infatuated with Mr. Harlow, the minister who oversaw good works for the poor through the church. He was a generous man to the indigent. That's when she had begun to fancy herself a clergyman's wife, serving unfortunates beside such a husband.

But Mr. Harwell told her papa he could not think of asking a baron's daughter to wed him. This, despite the fact that Baron Spencer had assured him Millie was a commoner like himself. Only the baron was a peer of the realm, not his daughter.

But he failed to make an offer, even after giving the appearance of being smitten with Millie. She still had a small pile of polite missives he'd written her, including a love poem in which he'd styled her as "his angel." She planned on burning them. Was not this also a reason to despise the nobility? Having a titled father had robbed her of her hopes.

And then Papa had fallen ill and never recovered. Before the end, he had rasped out his regret about Mr. Harwell, adding, between laborious breaths, "Even here, class distinctions rule with some, my dear. Even here."

She had vowed that "class distinctions" would not rule with her, reminding herself that there were plenty of clergymen in the world whom she might marry and serve the poor with. She would find an English clergyman to admire as she had in Boston. She hoped he would not be purse-pinched. Her heart lifted at the thought.

But her spirits sank again as she reflected that most English clergymen could hardly do much for the poor, as they were not well-heeled themselves. It occurred to her, in fact, that most clergymen—at least the ones she had observed—were not overly zealous to help the poor, being overworked already. This was particularly true of curates and sometimes rectors who might have numerous parishes to oversee or conduct services for. Poor curates were a byword, weren't they?

Indeed, finding a wealthy man in the church was as like to happen as finding an ostrich feather on a pigeon. In all likelihood, she never would meet her ideal match.

Their parish rector was married, (she'd found out this past Sunday, her first day in church since her return) and the curate, Mr. Atkins, was a young man who preached with a weak voice occasioned by a chronic cold and cough (according to her mama and Sophina). Worse, he had hardly met her eyes during their introduction. She found that decidedly unappealing. And he fit the "poor curate" category perfectly.

And suddenly it hit her.

Earls had fortunes. Most of them, anyway. If Sophina were to marry the earl—and her modest fortune might be enough to tempt him—she would be in a position to help the poor, to aid the sick, to start a school! (With Millie's wise counsel and help, of course.) Sophina was right. Think of all the good a countess could do, and Millie would be there to ensure she did it. There was no guarantee Sophina would claim the earl's attention, much less his favor to elicit an offer, but what was there to lose?

Earl Beaufort must offer for someone. Sophina may as well be in the running.

And mayhap there could even be a clergyman in attendance.

Chapter Four

Mr. Sandstone was the former rector of the earl's parish and now vicar of Shrewbury. He owed his present appointment to Lady Beaufort, the dowager countess, for it was she who had vociferously put his name forward to the bishop when the vicarage became available. Indeed, she had been central to his rise to the rectory eight years earlier, after serving as a curate.

His income was slightly lower as a vicar, as his new living did not include rights to all tithes. Nevertheless, he enjoyed his rank in the church and the respect of his parishioners. He owed it to Lady Beaufort to help her son in any way possible.

When the earl and Lord Carlisle accosted him the day before, pulling him into a private chamber to put forth the scheme to trade identities for the ball, he felt himself in no position to refuse. Moreover, the earl wasn't asking, but insisting.

"For this one night, this wretched night," his lordship had explained. "My mother is trying to fashion me as Prince Charming and has summoned unmarried ladies from outside of this county—for I know of none in our vicinity to interest me—to Beaufort House for a ball. A *Cinderella* Ball," he'd added beneath his breath with a bitter curl of his lip.

He'd explained how he hoped to find ladies unguarded in their discourse and behavior, adding, "'tis the only means by which I can brook attending. Every hopeful female I have encountered since assuming the title has played up to me, sweet as treacle, or, equally disheartening, hardly spoke to me at all in fear of displeasing."

"But, sir, what if a lady's true nature is sweet?" he'd objected. "Do we not possess in England the sweetest young ladies in existence? Genteelly bred, delightful in disposition?"

The earl pursed his lips. "You have not married one yourself, sir," he observed. "I assure you, I know the difference between a sweet-natured girl and a syrup!" He shook his head. "I must be allowed to observe a lady off her guard."

The vicar's pulse quickened, for one did not like to disagree with an earl, especially the son of his benefactress. But summoning his courage he said, "I daresay, my example of not entering the married state must not be yours, my lord. I am not, er, at ease in the company of ladies. My solitary existence is due to my own unhappy reticence, not because I do not find women lovely and appealing." He shook his head. "The more lovely they are, the more awkward I become."

When the earl said nothing, he continued, "In any case, my lord, I must object to your scheme. I cannot like it."

Lord Beaufort's brows darkened. "If you wish to see me fulfill the dearest hopes of my mama and rescue the title from peril, then this, Mr. Sandstone, is what you must do, like it ever so little. Trade places with me for one night. If you refuse, I have no choice but to take myself off to London or some remote place where I am sure my carriage will suffer a broken wheel and I will fail to make it to the ball."

The vicar recognized defeat. With a quaking heart, and pursing his lips hard, he asked reluctantly, "Is her ladyship aware of the scheme?" He must never be at cross-points with his benefactress, the dear lady to which he owed his comfort and place. Neither did he like to be seen as doing anything wrong, even if it hadn't been his idea.

"She will be shortly," he was assured. "And because she wishes me to come to her hare-brained ball, she will accept it."

Lord Carlisle nodded his agreement. "Not happily, perhaps, but I have every confidence she will."

The earl turned to his friend. "And you must tell her, Carlisle. You know her best of all my acquaintance and have a singular rapport with the countess that others lack, even myself."

"The soon-to-be *dowager* countess," Lord Carlisle corrected him. "There will be a new Countess Beaufort, recall. Your wife," he added with a sly grin.

"My wife," the earl repeated faintly. "By some miracle, perhaps. Can there really exist a woman who is not swayed at the thought of being a countess?"

"Miracles never cease," Charles quipped.

"Indeed, my lord," put in the vicar rather miserably, for he felt it was nothing short of a miracle that he was agreeing to impersonate the earl. Yet could it be a miracle, a work of the Creator, when it meant he was to dissemble, to mislead? How could he call that a miracle?

Before he could add to his regrets, the earl turned to him with an ingratiating grin.

"Obliged, Sandstone. Much obliged."

Chapter Five

The vicar slept badly. A guest at Beaufort House, ensconced in as commodious a bed chamber as a man could wish with a mattress sprung with splendid cording, he should have enjoyed a superior night's rest, but had not.

The prospect of assuming the earl's identity that coming evening filled him with trepidation.

His brief encounter with her ladyship on his way to breakfast should have bolstered his spirits, for she came upon him with a smile and with gratitude for his part in the scheme.

The dowager was a handsome woman in her early fifties, her blonde hair still more blonde than grey, and her fine features still firm.

"Many thanks, sir," she said sincerely, "for agreeing to my son's havey-cavey scheme. I daresay, I dislike it, but my *dear* Carlisle assured me 'tis the only way to be certain of my son's attendance!"

The vicar had heard Lady Beaufort referring to Lord Carlisle in this manner before, so this did not surprise him. But her hurried manner of speaking gave him no opening to say, "I agree with you utterly, ma'am, 'tis an ill-conceived idea." Or even, "Not at all; anything I can do to help, of course."

The dowager continued as a spark of indignation in her eyes melted into amusement. "I warrant I am less concerned with *how* he chooses a wife, so long as he does! I am sure he explained to you the dire circumstance we find ourselves beneath."

"Indeed ma'am, or—" He was about to say, he would never agree to such a dire remedy but she went on, "Bless *dear* Carlisle! He explained it to me in such easy terms, and with such assurances that Allen will indeed find a woman to whom he can make an offer, that I could hardly cavil, now could I?" She gave the vicar a wide-eyed look, spreading her hands apart.

"Of course not, ma'am," he agreed.

"And is it not providential that not a single lady on the invitation list has met Lord Beaufort? Or you, I presume?"

His lordship had given the vicar the list to peruse, and it was true he knew not a soul on it.

Smiling, and with a nod of her head, she said, "I always took you for an understanding man, Mr. Sandstone. But I must not keep you from your breakfast. Please go and enjoy yourself."

With a benevolent smile she added, "I must confess, it comforts me to know you are in agreement with the scheme, sir." She raised her hands. "To have heaven's blessing on such an endeavor is precisely what it needed!"

She was off with a swish of her skirts before he could object. Mr. Sandstone did not wish her to believe his acquiescence in the plan meant that heaven agreed with it. It struck him afresh how the behavior of a clergyman was often viewed as a reflection of God himself. If people were injured or offended by a man of the cloth, they reacted as if God had failed them. It was a heavy burden, and an unfair one. He was only mortal, after all. A sinful being like the rest of mankind, in need of a Savior.

Never had that truth been borne in upon him more than when, later that day, a footman found him walking the grounds of the estate and summarily hurried him to the earl's private apartments, directly into his dressing rooms.

He'd not so much as exchanged greetings when my lord's valet began unceremoniously stripping him, without so much as a how d'ye do? It was unnerving.

And now, he was a stranger to his own eyes. He wore the earl's spectacular coat of blue superfine, a dazzling white shirt, cravat, finely embroidered gold-colored waistcoat, superior silk breeches, stockings and gleaming black shoes.

They say, "clothing makes the man," but he felt ill-suited to filling such clothes. He'd said as much to the earl. "I cannot bend Ulysses' bow, sir," knowing himself unequal to the task. He stood half an inch shorter than the earl, besides lacking his commanding air. The vicar was no slouch, but he walked lightly on his toes and had what seemed to others, a simpering air.

All of this, he felt, should have alarmed his lordship.

"Sir, may I again implore you to drop this scheme? Honesty from the start saves you later distress and reassures your acquaintance—a future bride most of all—of your integrity."

"Fret not yourself, my dear sir," the earl replied. "My mother, so Lord Carlisle tells me, is in perfect agreement with the plan."

The vicar replied, beneath his breath, "Your mother is not the only one I answer to, my lord." But he sighed and bowed his head, comforting himself with the thought that his deception was to last only a few hours, and it was for the good and worthy cause of helping his lordship choose a wife and retain a noble title.

Lord Carlisle, who had until this moment been lounging against the doorjamb of the dressing room in silent observation, said "Do not forget the ring," referring to the family jewel on the earl's right hand. In seconds it was transferred, and the parson held it up, scrutinizing it with a dazed glint in his eyes. It was a black diamond ring framed by a tier of white diamonds and then rubies, worth a fortune, he was sure. He felt no little apprehension to find it upon his person. He stifled his qualms, however, and waited to see what else would be required of him on this strangest of evenings.

"You'll not regret this, Sandstone," said Lord Beaufort with a nod of approval.

The vicar replied with his usual honesty, "I fear I do already, milord."

The earl chuckled. "I daresay I shall find a way to give you thanks. Only imagine, tonight you shall have the fawning admiration and longing glances of every unmarried lady present, and there will be many." He surveyed the minister, now dressed in his own fine evening clothes. "Do you know, sir, as you mingle with the softer sex tonight, you may even find one you favor?"

"If I favor one, it shall be for yourself, sir. I will recommend her to you."

"But the lady I can favor will not be the one you do," he returned. "Are we set, then?"

Mr. Sandstone's misgivings returned. "But if someone were to guess," he said in a complaining voice which he could not help. "I do not possess your air, sir."

The earl looked directly into his eyes. "No one will know you except my mother and her circle—and their lips shall be sealed as she will give them to understand (as Lord Carlisle gave her to understand yesterday) 'tis the only way I will choose a wife. You are safe from discovery and censure, I assure you."

Mr. Sandstone swallowed a growing lump in his throat. "As you wish, my lord."

Later, when the earl was alone with Lord Carlisle, he said, "You realize, Carlisle, 'tis hopeless. What on earth possessed her ladyship to think I could choose a woman to be my wife, my countess, to share my home with, based on a *dance*, of all things!"

"I have heard you say," Carlisle returned, in his usual calm manner, "you have not married because you have not found a woman you wish to take home with you."

The earl nodded. "Yes, I have said so."

His lordship said, "When you meet a pleasant lady, then, you need only ask yourself, 'Could I take her home? Do I wish to see her when I rise in the morning?'" His voice took on a wishful, faraway tone, and he spoke into the distance, as in a reverie. "'When I take my meals, should I enjoy looking up to see *her*? When I go to town, should I like her to be at my side? Does she fill my heart with joy? Do I adore the sound of her voice, the soft sparkle in her eyes?'"

The earl watched his friend in astonishment. "By Jove! Who is she? You have evidently given meditation to such questions. Who is the fortunate woman?"

Lord Carlisle shook his head and came back to the moment. "I speak only for you. I have no hopes with the one I admire. To her, I am a friend, only a friend; and society would frown upon an alliance between us, I assure you."

"Is she married?"

"A widow."

"What, then, is your obstacle?"

His lordship sighed. "Our ages do not suit."

The earl rubbed his chin. "Lord Markay married a girl of thirteen only last week. How young is she?"

Lord Carlisle gave a sad smile. "Let us not discuss it. For now, we must concentrate on finding *you* a wife."

Chapter Six

Earlier that day of the ball, Lady Spencer visited the invalid, her niece, with the sole purpose of convincing the foolish chit to rouse herself and attend the event. To her mind, the girl must needs be at death's door before she would countenance excusing her from it. It was her chance to marry an earl, for heaven's sake!

To her surprise, she found Sophina getting ready for the ball. Even better, Sophina gave her the happy news that Millicent would accompany her. But she planted in her ladyship's brain the idea that Millie should go in her place, not as her companion. Lady Spencer liked it at once. Millie was beautiful, graceful in comportment, and sure to garner the attention of the earl.

She summoned her to the parlor, and gave her to understand in no uncertain terms, as soon as Millie seated herself primly in a facing chair, that she was required to do as her cousin suggested. Her ladyship fully expected fierce opposition.

"Mama, I am willing to go," Millie replied, to her mother's astonishment. "I shall be Sophina's companion."

Her mother's eyes bulged. "Do not be absurd! You must go in her place. As Miss Allred."

Millie's heart skipped a beat, and her brow wrinkled in distress. "What good can that accomplish? Pray recall, I have no desire to go at all." Hoping to dissuade her stalwart mother, she added, "And if I were to gain the earl's favor, if I were to be chosen like Cinderella, the moment he learns I am a baron's daughter, he will want nothing to do with me. Recall, Mama, no woman in a direct line of a peer may attend."

"A man looks at a lady's appearance before anything else," replied her mother.

"And their second look is at her fortune."

"You have fortune," replied her mother, undaunted. "Five hundred pounds a year."

Millie made a scoffing sound. "That is hardly enough to interest an earl. Sophina shall have more. My best hope, my only wish, is to meet a clergyman. Lacking that, a God-fearing man of means. I shall go in my own name as Sophina's companion, which is perfectly respectable, and see if there is not a dashing clergyman present."

"Even a clergyman will hardly acknowledge a mere companion."

"Then I should not seek his acquaintance or desire his good opinion," she replied, undeterred. "A true gentleman would bestow his notice upon any respectable woman."

Smiling, and beginning to dream a little, she added, "Only think if there were to be a dashing, personable man, a rector perhaps, with multiple livings, and no regard to rank or class! With a number of livings at his disposal, he may be a wealthy man, as indeed he must be, to make charity a priority."

"Fustian and nonsense. A wealthy, dashing clergyman who disregards rank? You may as soon find the crown jewels beneath your pillow!"

Millie said, "I know 'tis unlikely."

"'Tis more than unlikely. Clergymen frown upon balls to begin with. They call them 'godless, vain affairs.'"

"Not all clergymen." Millie thought suddenly of Mr. Harlow who was dashing in his way and did attend society balls. He was not very wealthy, but she had been ready to accept him, had he offered for her. Now she knew better. She must find a man with a good heart *and* a good income. It was the only way to help the less fortunate in a meaningful manner.

Her dreamy smile vanished, but she said, "One never knows, Mama."

"I do know. Your idea is a fool's paradise. You would do better to seek an ordinary man of means or a title."

"Rail at me all you like, Mama, but I would choose a clergyman over a title. Recall, I am convinced our nobility has outlived its usefulness," she said, ignoring the fact that she had decided it would be useful indeed if Sophina were to become a countess. Going further, she said, "We should abolish class structure like the Americans!"

Her mother studied her in alarm. "They may not have aristocracy, but I can assure you they have upper and lower classes. Do not say you are so egalitarian that you could choose a poor man who might gain your fancy?" The very idea filled her with dread.

Millie frowned, pursing her lips. "I suppose I would, if I loved him. A wealthy man is preferable, however, as he can afford me the opportunity to be a benefactress to the less fortunate."

"So that's your game!" Lady Spencer's brows rose considerably.

Millie nodded stoically. "My heart's desire is to serve the poor. A wealthy man, ideally, a clergyman, shall wish to do so also." Her heart was beginning to pound, for she had not expected her mother to espouse Sophina's outrageous idea.

"Your heart's desire? Your heart's desire?" her mama repeated, as if unable to believe her ears. "What has the heart to do with marriage? It is a business transaction, my dear. And you must make the most of it." She frowned at her daughter. "Depend upon it, ladies who are dictated to by their 'heart' end up ruined and in the workhouse."

"That is not always the case, Mama," replied Millie, clutching a lace-edged handkerchief in her hand.

"But 'tis often the case. And here, providence is providing you an opportunity to secure your future comfort, to find a wealthy man, for Lord Beaufort is as rich as Croesus! Besides which, for all you know, you may *fancy* the earl!"

"I should have to fancy him very much indeed to join the patriarchal system as his bride!" Millie came swiftly to her feet and strode to the window to stare unseeingly at the street below. She fingered the lacy edge of her handkerchief. She was determined to stay true to her best hopes, but her mother was causing an alarming flutter in her stomach.

"Foolish gel. You are already part of it, being a baron's daughter. You are part of it by virtue of being English." She surveyed Millie, frowning, and an idea formed in her brain.

"Have you considered that the earl must be a liberal-minded man? Only think on it! What sort of man bans the upper class from his ball?"

Secretly, Lady Spencer thought he was either addle-brained or that it was all some kind of hum. But she pointed at Millie. "You of all people, who despise a class society, should rejoice in a man who does likewise. Earl Beaufort must be quite, er, American, in his ideas, for he bans the upper class in order to choose a bride from a lower one!"

Millie turned from viewing the street and nodded as if the point was well taken. She hadn't considered it in that light. Perhaps the earl was modern and liberal. She would like that, indeed.

"He may be exactly the sort of man you seek," her mother continued. "A man of new ideas, generous to the less fortunate, unmindful of rank."

But Millie said, "Now you're coming it too brown, Mama. The purpose of the ball is so he can retain his title; that is hardly being unmindful of rank."

"Ah, but he is willing to marry beneath him. Indeed, he insists upon it! That, Millicent, is liberality, and ought to please you."

Millie resumed her seat and surveyed her mother as calmly as she could. "If indeed he is willing, I do not dislike it, I grant you. But I should not be in the least surprised to find it is all a lark."

Even Lady Spencer wondered. The earl would be a laughingstock if he was seriously ruling out all ladies of rank. It simply was not done. But she said nothing.

Millie said, "If Earl Beaufort is as liberal-minded as you suggest, then even a lowly companion must be within his notice. I shall go as my cousin's companion." She said this without believing it might really be so, but in order to silence her mother's objections.

"You will attend as Miss Sophina Allred. Let Sophina attend as your companion. Or neither of you go."

"You would deny Sophina this opportunity?"

Her mother scoffed. "What earl in his right mind would consider her, my dear? She is too missish and—peculiar. You are much more likely to command the man's attention. You must go in her place."

Millie gave her mother an affronted look. "And dishonor myself and everyone I meet by deceiving them?"

"Is posing as a companion any less deceiving?" The critical eye of Lady Beaufort made Millie's heart skip a beat. She had not thought of it that way. She frowned.

Her mother, circling her thoughtfully, one chin on her hand, said, "Why, my dear, can you not think of it as your way of behaving like an American? Free of titles and the obligations associated with them. Think of it as taking a new name upon yourself to complement your feelings on the patriarchal system."

"Then, if the earl realizes he must have you—and if he has a brain in his head, he surely will—you will be free to disclose the truth of your identity. After you accept him, of course. When you confess all, he will wholeheartedly forgive you, being so far taken with you."

"You are assuming I would welcome his offer, were he to make one. And, I tell you again, Mama, I can only attend this ball as Sophina's *companion*. At least then I should be known by my own name." Millie felt heat rush to her face.

Lady Spencer's brows darkened and her lips were set in a line. Putting her hands firmly together on her lap, she said, "Millicent Spencer, hear me on this. You shall not step foot out of this house—neither you nor your cousin—unless you agree to go *as Miss Allred*! I will not have a daughter of mine appearing as a—a—servant!"

"But then my cousin must appear as one!"

"Better her than you! She is not a baron's daughter."

Millie was almost ready to give up the scheme entirely, but she thought of Sophina. Even though she disapproved of the institution of the peerage, its advantages could not be denied. The girl must not be blocked from her chance to join it.

And then it occurred to Millie that all she had to do was allow her mother to *think* she'd go as Miss Allred, when in reality, she would be presented as her companion. Sophina would have the chance of a lifetime and perhaps win the earl's hand. Millie would not allow her to miss it.

Saying a quick prayer for forgiveness for the necessity of a white lie, she said, "Very well, Mama," to that lady's intense satisfaction. "Only I shall come clean about my identity if I happen to meet a good-hearted clergyman."

Lady Spencer's brows rose. She considered the odds of that happening as slim as herself marrying the prince regent. But she admonished, "Only if you constrain him to the strictest confidence. The earl must not know."

Millie shrugged. "I care not if he knows." Stifling her conscience, she added, "I shall attend as Sophina Allred since it pleases you so well."

Lady Spencer was satisfied. What woman could be as charming and graceful as her own Millicent? Going by her cousin's name was not ideal, but what man could do anything other than forgive the sweet face of an angel?

The important thing was to get Millie there.

Chapter Seven

Standing outside the ballroom that evening just as the first carriages bearing guests were arriving, Mr. Sandstone could not help but try one last time to reason the earl into dropping his scheme.

"Your lordship, only consider—what if I become a marplot and ruin the scheme by my behavior? I daresay I shan't be very convincing at playing an earl, my lord."

The earl replied, "You must call me Sandstone, '*my lord*.'" And he smiled his most disarming grin.

Mr. Sandstone visibly withered.

Beside him, Lord Carlisle chuckled. "You will enjoy an evening of privilege, dancing with ladies who long to stand up with you. Speak freely, be yourself in Beaufort's clothing. Nothing will come of it for you, but for his lordship 'twill make all the difference. Think of it as a diversion, Sandstone."

"Perhaps it shall divert you, sir," Mr. Sandstone returned, his lips compressed at the prospect of being an object of mirth. "But for myself, it is distasteful. I must play-act a role I cannot fill, and I must mislead innocent young women."

"Innocent?" the earl spoke up, his brow raised. "They are hardly that. They are groveling for a title. You will discover this for yourself as you speak to them."

"My lord! Er, that is, my dear sir!" the vicar corrected. "Do you still maintain, all young women are covetous of a title? I am sure many have no wish to rise above their station."

His lordship replied smoothly, "If that is the case, they would not be coming tonight."

The vicar replied, "But perhaps a parent forces them to come."

"Whether forced or not," the earl replied cavalierly, "tonight they will be hopeful. Tonight they will grovel, depend upon it."

Even Charles, inured to the earl's cynicism concerning the opposite sex, grimaced. "Not all ladies are fortune hunters, Allen."

The earl sniffed. "Their mamas then. I assure you, all of the socially ambitious will be here."

"I warrant you," Sandstone said, holding up a finger. "I shall find you one who is not."

At that moment the men noticed the earl's mother, Lady Beaufort, at the far end of the corridor, giving last-minute orders to a cadre of footmen.

Lord Carlisle, watching her, straightened his waistcoat and jacket. He cleared his throat. "Remember, Sandstone. You're saving the title and an ancient family from ruin. Her ladyship depends upon it. She will be endlessly grateful to you and all you need do is endure one night's discomfort. Surely, in that light, it isn't too much to ask of you?"

The vicar swallowed, nodding. He agreed with Lord Carlisle that the cause was noble enough; it was the means of achieving the cause that unsettled him.

The earl added, "And 'tis no difficult thing for you to mingle among the feminine flock, dear sir, for, in truth, your profession suits you for it."

The minister gulped. "My temperament does not. Recall, I can hardly speak to a lady unless I am called upon in my ministerial capacity." He frowned but raised his head and straightened his shoulders. Taking a deep breath, he said, "Nevertheless, if I must mislead the young ladies—for a few hours—then I'm afraid I must." Secretly he thought, "God, forgive me!"

"You'll be doing the ladies a service," the earl replied. "They shan't have to suffer my sarcasm or skepticism. I shall be only a parson tonight, of no interest to fortune hunters and in no danger of getting shackled by one for life. And, if you do fail to impress in your role as me," he smiled charmingly, "the young ladies shan't go into declines for not having captured an earl."

He turned to Carlisle. "Miss Greyson, do you recall? Went into a decline and missed an entire season on my account, so they said!" Carlisle nodded, remembering.

"I suppose that is true," the vicar agreed, self-deprecatingly. "They will leave, rather, (if I behave in my usual manner) feeling they have escaped a snare!"

This was an utterly uncomplimentary view of Mr. Sandstone's appeal to the opposite sex, but alas, it was mostly true. Mr. Sandstone was a bumbler in the presence of ladies, save for when he was delivering a sermon or called upon for clerical advising. In his official capacities, when he donned spectacles and his church robes, he was as proficient as ever you please, but in a social setting, and among women, he grew awkward and gauche.

But this did put a new light on his role for the evening, and he felt his first inkling of confidence that perhaps he could handle the little game. This was a mercy, for he could never have been equal to impersonating the earl's manners, which were distinctly unlike his own. The earl was quick-witted, gentlemanly, and unruffled in anyone's company. The minister was slower of thought and speech, deferring conversation so others might take the lead.

Upon the whole, it made his mission seem almost Christian when he thought he would be saving young ladies from the humiliation of the earl's jaded attitude.

Lady Beaufort came abreast of them and looked quizzically at her son, and then at Mr. Sandstone. "So you are determined to maintain this charade?" she asked the earl, in a flat voice.

"Good evening, my lady," he replied with a smile, bending to kiss her on the cheek, but, catching himself, took her hand and kissed it instead. "As Mr. Sandstone, I must not presume to kiss the cheek of a countess," he explained. "You look stunning, as always. Does she not, Carlisle?" he asked, turning to see his friend's expression.

"She does indeed, as ever," His Lordship said, feasting his eyes upon her.

"*Dear* Carlisle," said her ladyship, holding out one hand to him with a smile, which he took, raised, and kissed softly. "Always the faithful friend."

Lord Carlisle's smile faltered, but he bowed. "Of course."

Lady Beaufort turned to Mr. Sandstone. "As the earl, sir, you will stand by me to greet our guests. You will stand after him, my lord," she said to Carlisle. "And you," she pointed to her son, "will stand after his lordship."

"Come," she said, and led the way into the ballroom. The earl raised a brow at Mr. Sandstone, who straightened his neckcloth nervously, cleared his throat and followed her ladyship into the room. Lord Carlisle and "Mr. Sandstone" joined them.

Chapter Eight

Earlier

When Millie told Sophina her plan, that she would agree to use her name for her mother's sake but would really go to the ball as her companion, Sophina looked sadly at Millie, bowed her head and said, "Very well, cos."

"This is for your benefit, dearest," Millie added, watching her forlorn reaction.

Sophina looked up tragically. "But I have no wish to marry an earl!"

Millie shook her head impatiently. "We seldom know what is best for us. Let Providence decide the matter."

"But I shall not know how to comport myself!"

"No matter, my love! I shall tutor you."

They spent the few remaining hours preparing for the night. They had to share Celine, the lady's maid, but Lady Spencer made up the difference by hovering and aiding, pulling stays tight, fussing with hair accoutrements, and sending Mrs. Belloc, their housekeeper, running for her ladyship's jewelry to adorn Millie's neck and ears. She ensured that Millie's hair was finished to perfection before Sophina's could be touched, reminding the ladies that a companion must not look too modish. Millie refused to wear any paint on her face, despite her mother's urging, for she had a dislike of cosmetics. But by the time the carriage was called, both ladies were gowned and coifed to her satisfaction.

But not to Millie's. Her gown was too rich for a companion, she knew. It was a round dress with short, puffed sleeves, low-necked, and with an elegant embossed French gauze over an Amaranthus silk slip. The net of the sleeves was interspersed with pearls laid on in waves, mirrored at the bust and hem. Her headdress was a tiara ornamented with flowers and pearls. Sweet ringlets framed her face on both sides, while pearls graced her neck and ears, and a fine gold chain supported a lorgnette. She wore white kid gloves, white corded silk shoes, and carried a fan.

Sophina's gown was of fine lawn in white-work, the bust ornamented in white silk embroidered roses. She too had kid gloves and silk slippers, and about her neck was a topaz cross. She wore a headdress of white flowers, and also carried a fan.

Millie planned on removing her earrings and the tiara (which Celine had painstakingly put in place "just so") during the carriage drive, and making Sophina wear them. Her own hair had curls and ringlets enough and did not require any headdress.

To her surprise and consternation, Sophina was not amenable to the idea. "Do not you touch your tiara!" she admonished, in as strong a tone as Millie had ever heard her use. "It looks perfect against your dark hair, and I should be very proud to have you as my companion."

"But surely, if I were your companion, I could not be dressed in this finery."

"A companion may dress as well as the family allows, and let us say, I allow it. Do not touch a thing. You look divine."

Millie was shocked at the change in her sweet cousin and could only meekly submit. She supposed she was being treated as a companion, which was fitting.

At sight of the great house, her pulse quickened and her stomach tightened. She felt almost breathless as they stepped down from the carriage. Despite all her airs and graces regarding American ideas of equality, Millie felt a strong tug at her heart when she and Sophina entered Beaufort House. The place was dazzling, and a heady sensation of unexpected pleasure filled her. Not only was the immense house well-lit outside with bright flambeaux, staffed with starched, liveried footmen, and the entrance hall circled with bright candelabrum and a chandelier, but an aroma of roses filled her nostrils.

As they were directed down a short, wide corridor to the ballroom, austere portraits of great beauty lined the walls. Elegant tables bore bouquets of red roses in ornate vases, and the carpet beneath felt plush right through her silk dancing slippers.

Of course an earl would have a sophisticated, richly appointed home. But she must not forget that earls had such privileges and money due to their birth, not their character, industry or intelligence. The aristocracy had its perks only for the privileged few, she reminded herself. It was an inequitable, outdated institution.

She could not deny, however, that Beaufort House was the epitome of taste, appointed with elegance to every last detail. But the ballroom was ahead, and meeting the family, and being presented as a companion. Her stomach churned.

They joined a line of ladies waiting to be announced, and Millicent prepared herself. "Do not forget," she whispered to Sophina. "You are yourself. I am your companion."

Sophina nodded unhappily. And then something unexpected happened. Millie had no idea of it coming. The servant, on Sophina's side, took her invitation, read it, and then bent his ear to hear Millie's name. Then, motioning Millie ahead of Sophina, announced, in clear, strident tones, *"Miss Allred."* And, a few seconds later as Sophina followed, "And Miss Allred's companion, Miss Spencer."

Chapter Nine

Millie was shocked, but there stood the Beaufort family in a line, her ladyship at the head, smiling and nodding regally at her. She had no choice but to keep moving and greet them.

Had there been a mistake? Had the man got their names wrong? But then in a second, she understood that Sophina—the sly goose!—had switched them. It was jarring. It produced a peculiar, discordant element that jangled at her nerves.

In one sense, she ought to be happy to be merely Miss Allred. Did it not fit her idea of a more just and equitable society? But she could have been merely Miss Spencer if Sophina had not made sixes and sevens of her plans!

She swallowed her qualms, smiled, and curtseyed prettily to greet the family. Lady Beaufort looked her over appraisingly and with seeming approval. She took Millie's hand and said, with a warm, endearing smile, "Miss Allred, is it? Welcome, my dear." She paused and then added, still eyeing Millie appreciatively, "You must be sure to meet our vicar—he's at the end of the line, you know," she added with a nod toward a tall man at the end.

"Your vicar?" Millie exclaimed, louder than she meant to. She could not have been more surprised—or delighted—had the countess offered to introduce her to King Solomon! How odd, and yet how strangely auspicious! She had come with the hope of meeting a clergyman. Was this not a sign from God? That he approved of her hope?

"I'd be honored, your ladyship," she replied sincerely, almost unable to believe her good fortune.

The 'earl,' next in line, had heard Millie's reaction and seen the unmistakable pleasure on her face, as had the real earl. Both men studied her with interest.

"Miss Allred," Lady Beaufort repeated, nodding as if to memorize her name. And then she looked thoughtfully at Sophina saying, "Miss *Spencer*. I feel I know that name, somehow."

Sophina stood speechless, and Her Ladyship said, "No matter, welcome, my child."

Millie swallowed. Her ladyship had heard of Baron Spencer of Astor House! But she shrugged it off. She had received an unexpectedly warm reception from the countess, and, more surprising, mention of a clergyman! But she was now before the earl and curtseyed again. She raised eyes that held a challenge in them to his, but his head was bowed and he said politely, "Miss Allred, a pleasure," looking up only to take a fleeting, nervous glance at her.

"My lord," she murmured, her challenging gaze melting into amusement. Why, the earl was a bumbler! Not the ladies' man she'd imagined.

"My lord," she murmured again to the placid eyes of Lord Carlisle, and then, giving yet another curtsey, was greeted handsomely by the vicar, a tall, distinguished-looking man. He took her hand, raised it while he bowed very nicely, and then lowered it, meeting her eyes all the while. His were clear, intelligent, and probing. Millie's heart took a flip.

"Miss Allred," he said, "an honor."

"The honor is mine, sir," she returned sincerely. She marveled that he was in the line of greeting, which meant he must have a high standing with the family. But she did not detect a trace of condescension in him, which she liked. But such a handsome man! Surely there was something she could say to him. "Are you truly a vicar?" she asked, before she knew what she was saying.

Mr. Sandstone stared at her for a moment. Lord Carlisle swiftly said, "Have you cause to doubt it, Miss Allred?"

Millie smiled and said, "Not at all. I hardly know why I asked. I beg your pardon," she said to the vicar with a winsome smile.

Mr. Sandstone's lips pursed as though stifling a smile but, just when she thought he would release her hand, said, "If I might be so bold, may I have your first dance?"

Millie's cheeks flushed. "You may. Thank you, kindly."

He said, loud enough for the earl to hear, "Unless the earl wishes to claim it?"

Earl Beaufort looked over with a look of alarm. "No, er, not at all, er, Mr. Sandstone." He gave Millie another fleeting, nervous glance and turned back to face the next guests.

Mr. Sandstone bowed again. "I thank you," and then released her hand. His eyes were strangely thoughtful. Millie swallowed and curtseyed again. She waited for him to greet Sophina, which he did politely and with a bow. But he did not take her hand.

They passed into the room. Her cheeks were rosier, her heart was aflutter, and the dancing had not even begun. Already she'd been asked to stand up, and by a dashing clergyman! Wait until she told Mama. Neither of them had truly expected such a man to attend!

But she looked with exasperation at her cousin, her eyes accusing. Sophina looked away uncomfortably and then back at her.

"I am sorry, Millie, but I could not help myself. I told you I could not *bear* to meet an earl."

"But you already have met him. And you can see he is nothing to fear. The man is shy, if not downright backward," she said reprovingly.

Sophina nodded. "How was I to know? Don't be cross, cos."

"I fear you have got us into a hobble," Millie said, "for trouble is sure to arise from this." But she realized what was done was done, and she nodded. "Let us find a bench for you so you can watch the ball. Companions are not asked to stand up. And there are precious few men here, it seems, in any case."

"Why should there be more?" Sophina uttered. "The only man the ladies care about this evening is the earl, is it not so?"

"Not to me," murmured Millie, searching about for the tall Mr. Sandstone.

Chapter Ten

Around them, other young ladies and their companions stopped speaking to study them, the looks on their faces not nearly as serene or welcoming as her ladyship's or Mr. Sandstone's.

Millie felt suddenly as though she were Daniel in the lion's den. She hadn't given a thought to the notion that there would be envy and competition filling the room like smoke from an oven.

She saw the band in one corner, discordant notes emanating out as they tested their instruments. The ballroom was huge, roomy enough to hold a crowd far larger than the present company, and much brighter than any she'd been in before.

"The stamped floor is exquisite, is it not?" murmured Sophina. Followed by, "Good! Beeswax candles," as she studied the ceiling with its numerous bright chandeliers. "I'm glad of it," she continued, "for our gowns shan't be dripped upon. Our housekeeper told me she worked for a lady who left a ball with two ruined spots on the back of her gown. She had the remnant made into a mere shift and a cap." She shook her head.

"How can you look at candles?" Millie murmured, too busy calming the jangling in her stomach to pay much heed. She had not expected a fit of nerves on account of a clergyman.

"I should rather study the room than the people," Sophina said. "Candles do not disturb my sensibilities."

After the band went into their opening flourish to announce that dancing would begin, she saw the tall figure of Mr. Sandstone approaching in easy strides. He walked with confidence. Heavens, but he was handsome! She noted broad shoulders, a slim waist, and fine, fine, calves. Her heart thumped. Married, no doubt, she thought, with a sinking feeling inside, but she had no time for further thoughts as he joined them and bowed very nicely, saying, "Miss Allred, I believe we are engaged for this dance."

Millie stood and curtseyed. "Yes, sir, I thank you."

No sooner did he take Millie's hand at the greeting line than Allen knew he must speak with Miss Allred. Her reaction to meeting him—a vicar, so she thought—was utterly intriguing. She seemed genuinely pleased. Other ladies greeted him stiffly, or merely with politeness, saving their deepest curtseys and demure "my lords" for whom they believed was the earl.

His disguise was proving valuable and the dance hadn't yet begun. He had, by virtue of their manner of greeting, already narrowed down the possibilities of ladies he might form an attachment to, to three. Out of thirty-five eligible ladies, this made his mission that night far easier than it might have been. If he stood up with each of the three once, or even twice with a woman who continued to interest him, he might find himself willing to court one.

The idea of his mother's that he would choose a wife tonight—upon his first meeting with a woman—was patently absurd. The matter held too much import to be settled so frivolously. He had no wish to find himself in a loveless marriage, which a hasty decision could easily lead to. Nor did he wish, like Lord Househall, to marry a wife who was lovely but who turned out to be a shameless flirt, spendthrift, and hoyden.

No, he must give the matter time enough to feel secure of the lady who would receive his offer, become his countess, and share his home—and bed. The most promising of the three, to his mind, was Miss Allred, which was why he asked for her first dance. Not only did she greet him with sincere warmth, but her questioning his identity afterward was thoroughly fascinating. He must know her better.

Moreover, her knowing demeanor after receiving the "earl's" timid greeting struck him as a sign of a bright mind. Other women merely looked disappointed, as if they thought the earl was capable of much warmer a greeting, only had not seen fit to give it to them. They took his manner as a personal affront. Miss Allred had not.

He gave a slight nod to Miss Spencer, the companion, and led Miss Allred to the floor.

Millie gave a quick look back at her cousin, whose face was pinched with apprehension. She flashed a smile to show she was happy to stand up with this man (despite her nerves). Why, Sophina ought to be happy for her, not worried. But she was a silly girl and, as she had lamented to Millie in the past, socially awkward.

Millie could not comprehend why Lady Beaufort had particularly directed her attention to the vicar, but it didn't matter, did it? Here he was, already introduced, refreshingly bold, nothing at all like their curate, Mr. Atkins.

As they crossed the floor, she again felt the eyes of the company upon them. The tension in the air, as though everyone waited to eat with knives raised, must ebb now, she thought, at least for her, as they saw she was standing up with the clergyman, not the earl.

"Your companion is young," he said, turning to look questioningly at her.

Millie swallowed. "Yes! A family friend."

He nodded thoughtfully. "Fortunate for you."

She would have liked to know what he meant by that but did not wish to question him. To their right, she saw Lady Beaufort leave Lord Carlisle's side and wait for the earl to join her on the floor, for they must open the dancing.

After a shortened quadrille, in which one could not say the earl danced with grace, though he managed the steps, Mr. Sandstone retained Millie's hand on the floor. He meant to dance with her again! Was this not unusual?

He said, as if reading her thoughts, "That was hardly a dance. Am I too bold to keep you for another?"

Millie, who loved dancing, shook her head. "Not at all."

Her ladyship then accepted Lord Carlisle's hand, and he led her to stand near Millie and her partner. Millie wondered if Lord Carlisle and her ladyship were more than acquaintances. He had stood in the greeting line with the family, and their smiles at each other, as they waited for the music, looked warm, almost intimate.

She glanced at Mr. Sandstone and found him studying her. He looked away, then frowned slightly at the earl, as he finally came forth leading a woman by the hand.

When the three couples were in place, the music started up for a waltz.

A waltz! Mama had insisted Millie have a dance master in Boston, so she was well familiar with the steps. Mr. Sandstone put an arm comfortably about her waist, not too tight, but just firmly enough. With their bodies close, Millie tried to concentrate on anything except his heady nearness.

But gasps and titters were coming from the onlookers. She saw then that the earl was behind time, his arm awkwardly about his partner, his steps fumbled and slow. He was not a proficient! An earl, of all things. The unhappy lady with him, looking at the reactions in the room, seemed to be holding back tears.

Mr. Sandstone frowned in the earl's direction. "It seems Beaufort does not enjoy a waltz."

"I am afraid not," Millie agreed, hiding a smile.

"I would that he had told me," he added with a touch of irritation, a remark Millie found inexplicable. As if realizing this, he smiled and changed the subject. "I am happy to find that you, Miss Allred, are at home on the floor."

"As are you, sir," she said, returning the smile. And he was, leading them about quite reassuringly.

Murmuring continued about the room, as the earl continued to flub the dance. Some ladies shook their heads, some covered their mouths so as not to laugh out loud.

But Millie's heart was light. This clergyman was delightful. His eyes, his voice, his manner, all so pleasing. She needed to know if he was married. Then, she would have only to discover whether he was a good man, a good minister, that is. One who loved God. Many a clergyman went into the church merely as a vocation, not as a religious calling. She wanted a man who cared for his parish, who might countenance having a charitable wife with grand plans for improving the lives of the lower class.

Help me to know, Lord, she prayed silently.

But Lady Beaufort, also frowning at the "earl," broke apart from Lord Carlisle and buzzed about directing footmen who began to snuff out some of the chandeliers. She spoke to the band, upon whence the dance abruptly ended.

Mr. Sandstone released his hold of her and bowed lightly. Millie was sorry to come apart from him, having enjoyed the dance very much. She felt like she had found a gold coin and picked it up, only to have it snatched from her fingers by a magpie. Not since her father was healthy, back in Boston, had she waltzed, and never with so exciting a figure as this vicar.

"Will her ladyship cancel the evening, do you think?" she asked in surprise.

"I think not. She is dimming the lights to spare the earl scrutiny, I should say. She has great hopes for her son this evening."

He held out his arm, which she took, feeling pleased. He led her to the side of the room and began promenading. Millie was glad. She wished to know more of this man.

She searched her brain for something witty to say but could only remember his earlier remark. "You enquired about my companion," she said.

"Yes, her youthfulness. She seems hardly qualified to chaperon."

Millie nodded, agreeing. "I daresay you are right. Though she has had to care for younger siblings most of her life."

He nodded. "Ah. But you are fortunate, for other young women must be on their best behavior with their battle-ax of a mama at their side, or grandmama, or aunt."

Millie giggled, and he flashed a charming smile at her. "Have you no mama, or grandmama or aunt to accompany you?" he asked.

"Oh, a proper battle-ax of a mama, I assure you," but then she blushed. "Though I should not say so."

"But she allowed your young family friend to accompany you, Miss er…"

"Miss Allred," Millie said promptly and then caught herself, "Oh, er, you mean my companion, of course, my cousin, Miss *Spencer*."

He noted the mistake, but said only, "Your cousin? More than a family friend, then."

"Yes," Millie acceded uncomfortably.

"Is there not a Baron Spencer?"

"Is there?" Millie's cheeks grew hot. "Oh, now you mention it, yes! I believe there is a distant connexion." Now she was compounding her deception with more of it! But she had no time to think how to recover herself. To move the conversation on, she added, "Mama had the headache, I'm afraid, which is why Miss Spencer is with me." *A third lie! She would need a great deal of time for prayers that evening, for confession alone.*

She felt his piercing eyes upon her, thinking. Slowly he said, "You are in an enviable case."

Millie had to smile, for many a clergyman might "tsk, tsk," her for coming with so young a companion, instead of seeing it as a boon. "You are very singular for a clergyman, sir," she said, smiling.

"You have no idea," he returned easily with a sideways glance, making the grin on her face broaden further. She wished to know what else he might say on it, but decided she must rescue poor Sophina's reputation.

"I can assure you, my cousin has carried much responsibility for her age. Her mother died in an accident years ago, and Sophina has raised the rest of the brood. She stays with us for a few months, ostensibly to grow reacquainted with me—for I am only just from back from a-an extended journey, you see—but really because her father wished her to attend this ball. It is a welcome respite for her, however, from her responsibilities."

"And where are you just back from?"

"My father had business in Boston," she answered. She went on to explain that she'd lived with him there for near six years and decided she liked Americans very much indeed. This included their ideas of a republic as opposed to a monarchy. She watched his face to see his reaction to that statement, but he merely raised a brow.

Glancing about, she saw the same stony visages of the ladies staring at them. If they were not glaring at Millie, they were looking enviously at the man whose arm she was upon.

As if reading her thoughts, he said, "We have an unhappy ball, I'm afraid."

"There is no dancing!" Millie exclaimed. "They are longing for attention." She had a thought. Trying to sound as nonchalant as possible, she asked, "Is *Mrs.* Sandstone among them?"

His lips curled slightly. "If I find her, I shall introduce you. Only there is no Mrs. Sandstone as yet. If there were, I suppose I would be quite the ogre to ignore her in favor of speaking with you—or any other woman."

Millie's cheeks flamed. She was being so obvious, inquiring as to his marital status! What had possessed her? Why could she not have remained on safer ground, meaningless chit-chat or pointless banter? A simple inquiry of anyone who knew him could have satisfied her curiosity on that head. But to hide her pleasure at his answer, she said, "In that case, I thank you, but may I ask, to what do I owe the favor of your speaking with *me*?"

He turned with a sparkle in his eye. "You made plain you were happy to make the acquaintance of a mere clergyman, rather than holding out for the earl's notice. That is enough to warrant my attention, for in this room I doubt I should find many of a like mind. But why is that?"

Millie studied him. Should she tell him how her time in Boston had acquainted her with how much good work could be done by the church for the less fortunate? That it had engendered in her a desire to be a minister's wife so she might serve side by side with a good man? In short, that she wished to marry a clergyman? She could not tell *him* that! She took her other option, which was to reveal her feelings about the aristocracy.

"Shall it offend you if I tell you I do not approve of the peerage?"

He sputtered a laugh. "But here you are, at the earl's Cinderella Ball, eager to meet the man."

"I never was!" she returned, honestly. "As I told my mother numerous times, I have no interest in being a part of the outdated aristocratic system."

His eyes sparkled. "Fascinating! Pray, continue."

Chapter Eleven

Millie said, "I fear you will think it quite shocking in me, but my time in Boston impressed me with views that are…different from most."

"Yes? How, precisely? Do you refer to favoring a republic?"

His eyes were warm, and he seemed just as agreeable as ever. Millie decided she would not be odious to him if she said more, so she launched into her views about the peerage.

"Outdated," he repeated, rubbing his chin with his free hand. "In what capacity do you see it so?"

Millie said, "As I see it, in the feudal days, lords were necessary to protect the king and the people. But they no longer serve either purpose. In fact, one could say they make life harder for the ordinary man. One need think only of enclosure, or the corn laws. The House of Lords," she paused to say, with an emphatic nod of her head, her curls bouncing, "you must admit, exists primarily so the lords can protect their interests. And is that not to go against the interests of the lower classes?"

Allen was delighted to find that she was a thoughtful woman, although he did not agree with her. Beauty and sense in one person, and one who neither coveted the earl's hand in marriage or, he could assume, his fortune—'twas more than he'd hoped for.

He said, "Speaking only for Beaufort House—for it is one I am most familiar with—I can say the family is generous, supporting many charities, holding a lavish Harvest Home year after year, a Christmas Hall, and Mayday festivities. In addition, I know for a fact that her ladyship, when apprised of a particular case of hardship, has often sent baskets of food and supplies and even her own medical man on occasion to the unfortunate household in need."

Millie smiled. "Now I understand why you were in the receiving line with the family; you are quite their defender. And such charity is all well and good, but only what they should do. And I daresay, if I were to guess, they are giving out of their bounty and hardly feel it."

"But the point is, Miss Allred, they have the bounty and can give. I would hazard a guess that many a charitable institution would go bankrupt without the upper class."

She gave him a bright-eyed look, "But what do you say about enclosure? Denying access to lands that were traditionally open to the people?"

As difficult as that may have made life for some, enclosure laws have ensured that much arable land is put to more efficient and profitable use. This is for the benefit of the country as a whole."

Millie made a scoffing sound. "It may add more production to the soil, but at the cost of many a livelihood, and the greatest profit, again, is for the landowner."

"Yet the people who formerly tilled the land are now employed in cities, in manufacturing, so that the fine lace and ribbons you ladies adore can be made at less cost. That is merely one example of the increase in manufacturing as a result of enclosure."

She said, "Nevertheless, it has forced whole families to pull up roots and leave the countryside they love."

He gave her a pointed look. "Has your family suffered from enclosure?"

She met his eyes. "No, not in the least."

"Have the corn laws caused a hardship for your home?"

"No. But you must know prices have gone up for everyone as a result of them and caused many a hardship for the poor. And to profit whom? The wealthy landowner, like Earl Beaufort!" She cast a reproving eye over to where the earl was standing in conversation with a lady. He looked uncomfortable, as if he wished to loosen his neckcloth.

Allen bit back a smile. He felt he'd stumbled upon a gold mine. Was not Miss Allred precisely what he had not dared, not hoped, to find? Her views were both a godsend—for it made her different from the socially ambitious seeking a title—but also unfortunate, as she had convictions that might affect his suit for her, were she to discover his rank. But views could be reasoned with…

"'Tis an unfortunate result," he replied, pulling her attention back, "but the point of the law was to strengthen British independence by keeping its landowners from ruin due to foreigners flooding the market with cheaper goods. Do you prefer that we enrich the coffers of foreign countries rather than our own?"

Millie had never thought about it in such a light. "Well, I suppose not, now you frame it in that manner, but if imported grain can be less costly, why cannot domestic grain?"

He grinned. "A complex question, more complicated than I can explain right now, but is that, and enclosure, your chief complaints with the aristocracy?"

"Primogeniture," she told him flatly, meeting his eyes with a look of victory, as if she had said, *There. Try and explain that one!* "It ought to be abolished," she added, as her eyes sparked with feeling like tiny flames lighting and then getting snuffed out.

The earl raised a brow. "Very American of you," he said placidly.

"Thank you." She eyed him uncertainly though, for she wasn't quite sure his remark was meant to be a compliment. When she felt fairly certain he wasn't quizzing her, she added, "In America, anyone can work their way up from humble beginnings to the heights of society. Here, only a privileged few may ever hope to attain it."

She looked adorable, he thought, when feeling smug. He had a sudden wish to dance with her again.

She continued, "In this country, one is 'born to the purple,' as they say. Men value themselves upon their ancestors' merits, not their own. And peers have unfair privileges. Look at Lord Byron, convicted of manslaughter, and he merely pays a penalty and is free. A poor man would have hanged."

"There I agree with you. Peers have privileges. Peers make the laws. But any man can find his way to a seat in Parliament."

She looked somewhat appeased but continued, "Here wealth is passed on to another man without the least effort, industry, or honor on his part, or—"

"Do not say in America wealth is not passed on? To one's heirs? Without the least effort or industry on their part?"

Millie's face blanched. "Well, it 'tis, of course. But a woman may inherit it."

"Surely you are familiar with jointure. A man can leave whatever he likes to a woman in England if he specifies it in his will."

"Except his title, and in many cases, his home and income."

He nodded. "Point taken. He must plan in advance for her care if he wishes to leave her well off, but it can be done, Miss Allred."

"Not in all cases."

Delightful! He thought. She maintains her convictions with no thought to mold them to my preferences. He said, "Do all cases in America work out for a woman's best interest, then?"

Millie made no reply, for she knew women in America without husbands to support them were no better off than in her home nation.

He said, "In either country, at least *for this present time*, the truth is, a woman does well to marry well, would not you agree?"

As he said the words, he had a sudden insight. The women who fawned up to him, the ones who pushed aside their tastes, preferences, and personalities trying to please him—they were only seeking to marry well because they considered it their best chance for happiness in life. And how could he blame them? *A woman does well to marry well*. He'd said it himself.

Yet some were already wealthy and striving for social advancement—these he would continue to avoid and dislike. But there were women, he was suddenly sure, who merely wished to rise out of need and uncertain futures by marrying well.

Millie, meanwhile, thought about her own life and her hopes of marrying a wealthy clergyman. She was living proof of the truth of his words! She was no different from the others here who hoped to marry the earl, not really. While she did not covet a title, she was every bit as hopeful of finding a man of means. It disheartened her.

"I do agree," she said at last, in a quiet tone. She looked up at him uncertainly. She ought to tell him the whole truth at once, that she was not Miss Allred, but Miss Spencer. She had not been invited to the ball, and that she too was seeking to marry well, even if she did not aspire to being a countess. Did she not tell Mama she would come clean to the man if she met a clergyman?

She wondered if he would be done with her if he knew.

"I should tell you—" she began. But she faltered, filled with confusion.

She looked so uncertain, so burdened, that he took both her hands in his. "Fear not, Miss Allred. My profession suits me for hearing confessions. And I can assure you of the strictest confidence."

She gave him a look of gratitude, though her heart felt like it had sunk into her slippers.

The earl congratulated himself. He felt he was playing the part of Sandstone to perfection. This intriguing beauty trusted him. And for some reason, he was very, very glad she did. He waited expectantly for her to start, sure she would confess she had come for the chance to marry the earl. He felt less inclined to take a disgust of her for it, having realized why women behaved that way. But in truth it was more than that. He did not wish to find anything at fault in Miss Allred. Had he ever felt thus about a woman before?

She pulled him from his thoughts. "The thing is, you see… I am…"

"Yes? You needn't fear surprising me. Do not all young women hope to meet an earl at his Cinderella Ball when he must choose a wife?"

"But I did not come on account of the earl," she objected, and her large eyes and tone assured him she meant it. "It astounded me when Lady Beaufort said I must meet you, a vicar."

"Did my lady say you must know me?" He shook his head, smiling. "My appreciation of the countess knows no end."

She lowered her eyes. "I had no idea of your being here, of course, but…" Her eyes rose slowly, and her cheeks flushed prettily, "but you see…it was my one hope in coming to meet a man of… your profession."

She waited to see if this would shock him.

Allen was surprised but not shocked because her easy manner to him all along spoke of her having a high regard for the clergy. Her manner upon meeting him at the first was in keeping with her declaration.

He said only, with a gentle smile, "As the sole representative tonight of such men, then, I hope I do not disappoint."

"Not at all," she said, beholding him afresh, admiring the azure eyes, the touch of grey at his temples and thick hair, the strong, well-proportioned features. There was nothing about him, either in appearance or manners, that Millie did not like. Realizing she was staring, she forced her eyes from his face. She could tell he believed her about wanting to meet a minister, so she continued, "In Boston I formed the idea in my head to help the less fortunate when I saw the church's committee doing much good there."

"Are you a Methodist?" he asked, with surprise in his voice.

"No. But I do hold to that belief of evangelical Anglicanism that I suppose most mirrors the Methodist view." When he received that information with equanimity she continued, "Even the parson, one Mr. Harwell, contributed many of his energies to the cause." *Oh, dear. Why had she mentioned Mr. Harwell?* She felt her cheeks blush afresh beneath Mr. Sandstone's keen gaze.

"Did you care for this Mr. Harwell, by chance?"

His sharp eyes missed nothing! "You are very observant." She shifted uneasily on her feet but realized she had nothing to hide about admitting that she'd considered the man for a husband. She told him about the lovelorn Mr. Harwell (only leaving out the part about her being a baron's daughter), ending with, "I should have married him had he offered for me."

Chapter Twelve

Allen could hardly believe his luck. Not only did Miss Allred seem like the sort of woman he had hardly dared hope to meet—one not grasping for the title—but she hoped to meet a clergyman, just when he had decided to be one! Of course he would have to reveal his hand were he to decide to pursue hers, but that could wait.

Lady Beaufort was suddenly upon them. "Er, Mr. *Sandstone*," she said carefully, "your presence is required elsewhere. You have not forgot your er, business, sir?" she asked. Despite her approval of the lovely Miss Allred, it seemed to Lady Beaufort her son was neglecting the other young ladies in favor of this one. She thought he must speak to all before making his choice. In addition, she wished to inform him of a concerning matter she had just been apprised of.

He bowed to Millie. "I beg your pardon. I must off. I hope we may resume our conversation later."

As Millie watched them walk off, she was disappointed at losing Mr. Sandstone's captivating attention. She felt warmth in his presence and beneath his gaze, as though an umbrella of something good, of comfort, had overshadowed them as they spoke.

Nevertheless, she also felt she had been at the point of execution and received a sudden reprieve. She had told Mama she would come clean at once if she met a clergyman, but, just when she was at the point of doing so, dreaded it. He could only despise her had she confessed to not being Miss Allred. And to being a baron's daughter. He was a man of God who surely valued honesty above all things, and she had been dishonest.

He was remarkably pleasant to speak with, however, and a very good listener. He made her feel as though no one else in the room mattered. Even more, his full attention, probing eyes and questions, made her feel no one else existed.

It was a rude awakening when Lady Beaufort called him away. But of course she must not expect to monopolize the man's attention. That would be rude of her.

She had not asked him a single question about his parish work, or whether he entered the church as a vocation only or as a calling. She hoped they would dance again, or at least speak; there must be more opportunity to talk.

Returning to Sophina, her heart was both light and dark. Mr. Sandstone had been unfazed by her anti-British sentiments regarding the peerage. But would he be so forgiving about a false identity?

Chapter Thirteen

Lady Beaufort spoke in a guarded tone to her son as she led him away from Miss Allred. "Allen, you must know, that Spencer girl can only be the daughter of the late Baron Spencer. Lord Carlisle informed me he had heard of the daughter's return to England after her father's sad demise. I recognize her not, therefore, I think 'tis she."

"Miss Allred's companion, you mean?"

Lady Beaufort nodded. "Posing as one, I should say. I think you must stand up with her. Or, at least, engage her in conversation." Her ladyship, far from being displeased that a baron's daughter had had the temerity to come to her ball though not invited, was glad to know of a girl from a respectable, noble family whom her son might consider for a wife. Even if the girl was pretending to be beneath their notice as a companion, peculiar as that was.

Before he could object, she added, "She may be in the line of a peer, but you have not met her nor taken a disgust of her. She must have an opportunity to make an impression upon you."

Allen received this information calmly, merely nodding his head, but his brows were gathered in thought. He was remembering Miss Allred had mentioned coming back recently from abroad, and that she had called her companion Miss Allred.

His mother continued, congratulating herself secretly for having forethought of any possible objection her son could make. "As you are in the appearance of a clergyman, it will make no stir if you approach a lady's companion for conversation. In this case, I am almost happy for your disguise, as it allows you to make her acquaintance."

"I shall do that, my lady."

Her eyes lit with surprise, for she had expected a much worse time of it. "Shall you?"

"This moment, if you shall allow it. As long as my *counterpart*," he said, looking about the room, "is doing his office with other young women."

Lady Beaufort's lips pursed as she glanced over at the "earl." He was nodding but looking completely ill-at-ease, wiping his brow with a handkerchief, as he spoke with a Miss Edwina and her matronly aunt, Mrs. Chesley. Lady Beaufort had heard something of the conversation, or, more accurately, a monologue, as Mrs. Chesley gave her detailed account of why her charge was exceedingly eligible to be the next countess. She was mistress of the finest accomplishments and the perfect temperament, she spoke French and Italian; she was a paragon of virtue; in short, she embodied everything that could be wished for in the earl's wife.

Mrs. Chesley had already given these indisputable facts (as she called them) to Lady Beaufort who must, she said, dispose her son to offer for Miss Edwina.

Lady Beaufort had a moment's sympathy for her vicar, knowing Allen would have been far more fit to put an instant stop to such pandering, but she also knew Mr. Sandstone would survive. He might even discover that most ladies were self-absorbed and less ready to be critical than to be grateful for a listening ear. The experience, in other words, might be to his future benefit. He might learn it was not impossible to speak with the opposite sex as he had long imagined.

Allen informed his mother of the two other women he would spend time with before making his choice. (With no intention of choosing a wife that same evening, but his anxious mother need not know it.)

She located the ladies in question, and then, looking about for Miss Spencer, saw Sophina on a seat beside the lovely Miss Allred, looking rather absent-minded. No matter. Allen wouldn't wish for a bluestocking.

"Sir, go see if the girl—Miss Spencer—is one you can admire."

Chapter Fourteen

It had not been lost on her ladyship that their guests were milling about looking disgruntled. They had expected a ball, not a dull waiting room. The "earl" could only speak to one lady at a time, leaving the others unoccupied and bored. There was a card room, but many ladies did not play.

As Allen made his way toward the intriguing Miss Allred and her companion, the band struck a musical flourish and then stopped. Lady Beaufort, coming out to the center of the floor cleared her throat. "We will resume dancing. There will be country dances now, starting with a Scottish reel."

There was an instant round of clapping and murmurs of approval.

While her ladyship could not supply a great deal of males to stand up with them, she could at least give them occupation. She continued, "The earl will choose a partner, and the rest of you must form pairs, ladies with ladies."

Mr. Sandstone came to his feet in relief. Miss Edwina smiled up at him, sure to receive his invitation to stand up. But he moved off, leaving her and Mrs. Chesley in great frowns.

He approached another young woman, bowed, and held out his hand. He had made his choice for the dance. Instantly following was the sudden swishing of skirts and shuffling of slippers and scuffling about as women found partners and took to the floor. They should have preferred being the earl's choice, even if he was a bumbler, to dancing with another female, but it was superior to sitting like wallflowers with the mamas, aunts, and dowagers.

Sophina was the first to see the vicar approaching, and his eye was upon *her*. She nudged Millie in alarm. "Millie! The vicar, the one you stood up with, he's coming! And he is looking at me in a most terrifying manner."

Millie tore her eyes from the dancers and saw it was indeed the interesting and pleasant Mr. Sandstone. She caught his gaze and smiled. "He is not terrifying, I assure you," she murmured, as he returned a very fine nod. Soon he stood before them and bowed.

"I notice you ladies do not dance?" he questioned.

Millie wished Sophina to say as little as possible, and not trusting her to do so, hurriedly replied, "We are happy to observe tonight, sir." She added, "Would you please to sit?"

He gave a quizzical look. "I daresay you'd prefer if Earl Beaufort were to join you instead?"

Millie smiled, "By no means, as you well know."

"But you must allow that your presence here ensures the earl will interview you."

Millie said, "My mama sent me for that purpose, I grant you. But I never did wish to be an earl's wife, as I told you earlier. Nor do I now." She took a breath, thinking. "The sole benefit, were I to consider it, would be that as a countess I could implement programs for the poor in the neighborhood."

His brows rose. "That, the sole benefit? You are narrow in your conception of what it would be like to be a countess." His eyes fell to the spot open to her left, for Sophina, sitting by and listening with every fiber of her being, but pretending to look about at the ballroom, was on her right.

Taking the empty seat, he met her eyes. "You told me I was singular for a clergyman, but I must say, you are singular also, Miss Allred. Every other female here, I am sure, would like nothing better than to elicit an offer from his lordship."

"*I* would not!" put in Sophina heartily. She colored then, realizing too late the conversation was not hers.

"You too would not?" Mr. Sandstone asked, admitting her to the dialogue, and happy to have it so. His brows were high. When Sophina just gave him an agonized look and then turned away, he said, gently, "Come, be plain with me, Miss Spencer. Why do you say two women in their prime have no ambition to marry an earl when the chance to do so is upon them?"

Millie dreaded Sophina's answer but could not think how to avert it. The girl was sure to say something too revealing, or worse, incriminating.

"I would not put myself above my station," Sophina explained, "or expect an *earl* to take an interest in *me*. But I told Millie *she* ought to marry the earl, being— "

"Being *what*?" Millie cried sharply, turning to Sophina with a look that fell somewhere between murderous and wishing to strangle her. Millie was sure her cousin had been about to reveal that she was a baron's daughter.

Sophina said, "I—I only mean, since you wish to be a-a benefactress."

"Sophina!" Millie could not bear a second more.

But Mr. Sandstone, smiling, said, "Nay, let her continue, Miss Allred. She is all honesty and no artifice. Her answer intrigues me and is no more than what you have already told me."

Millie looked at him with surprise for reading Sophina's character so well. "You are right about my cousin. But her lack of artifice is at my expense, if you please."

He said, enjoying himself, "If you have naught to hide, you have naught to fear."

Millie swallowed and tried to look innocent. *If you have naught to hide*…Oh, why, why, had Sophina not followed her plan? Then she would have naught to hide, for no one would have given her notice as the companion. No one except possibly Mr. Sandstone, that is. But if he had, she would have only to confess being a baron's daughter. Now she had to deal with using an alias. The two combined seemed to compound the weight of each.

To change the subject, she asked, "To what do we owe the honor of your attention, sir?"

"Merely to your being here," he replied, looking as if her question amused him. "Are you eager to be rid of me, Miss Allred?" The idea delighted him for some reason. Miss Allred was about as far from a simpering fortune-hunter as he could wish. But of course, she did not know him to be the earl.

"No," Sophina answered automatically, hearing her name. To her own surprise, she found the vicar's presence tolerable.

"No!" echoed Millie quickly, turning to give Sophina a wide-eyed look meant to be a warning.

Sophina, to Millie's horror, covered her mouth with one hand. "Ooops." Millie's eyes widened more, and she could not prevent a deep flush from creeping over her face and neck. Sophina was sure to give them away!

When she turned back, she found Mr. Sandstone looking on with a grin. But he quickly changed his expression and cleared his throat.

Millie hurriedly changed the subject. Watching the boisterous reel on the floor, the dancers making a happy pounding of feet, asked, "How is the earl to make his selection if not by talking while dancing?"

"He will speak with every woman in attendance," he replied. "I expect, when this dance ends, he shall decline any further dancing in favor of conversation."

Sophina went pale, but neither of the two noticed, not looking at her.

Millie said, "It cannot be agreeable to him to choose a wife in this fashion."

He nodded. "My feelings exactly, Miss Allred. How can he choose, knowing so little about a lady? It was an ill-conceived idea, I assure you."

Millie said. "I, for one, pity him." She saw the earl wiping his forehead with a handkerchief.

Sophina made a strangled sound in her throat, and their eyes turned to her.

"My dear!" Millie cried. "Are you unwell?"

Sophina swallowed. To Mr. Sandstone she said, "I daresay, sir, you do not mean the earl shall speak to *every* lady present but only the *eligible* ladies?"

He regarded her momentarily. He could not guess why they did it, but he was coming fast of the assurance that these ladies had switched identities. "Does the earl intimidate you, little one?" he asked, kindly.

"I think all gentlemen do," Sophina answered honestly.

"That must include me, then," he said as if he were sorry it was so.

Sophina caught the nuance in his tone. "But you, being a vicar, are far less intimidating, sir," she said, fully satisfied she was easing his mind.

Millie sat stiffly, waiting for something disastrous to come from her cousin's lips. But suddenly she could abide it no longer. "Mr. Sandstone," she said, turning to him. "Will you be so good as to accompany me to the refreshment table? I shall fetch Sophina a drink."

His eyes sparkled at her, as if he understood. She told herself, he cannot know, of course, he cannot know. But still, it niggled at her that he did. His prescient gaze, knowing manner—as if he saw right through her. Right through Sophina too. But if so, would he not have something of censure, of disapproval to say?

"I am happy to fetch you both a drink," he returned, coming to his feet. "No need for you to trouble yourself."

But Millie came to her feet as well. "Not at all. I should welcome the exercise."

He offered his arm, and going around the edges of the room, led them to the antechamber where tables were set up. A servant, with haste and an odd look at Mr. Standstone, quickly procured two glasses and waited to hear their preferences.

"Which do you prefer?" Mr. Sandstone asked Millie. "The house negus? Ratafia? Orgeat? Madeira?"

"They have all those?" she asked, amused.

"The Beauforts are well-heeled, Miss Allred. You should expect nothing but the best. Do you have a preference?"

He half-expected her to inquire about his preference so she could mold her taste to his—he'd experienced this many times in London—but Millie said, without hesitation, "The ratafia, thank you."

"Two," he told the servant.

The man nodded, "Yes, mil—"

"Sir!" Mr. Sandstone exclaimed.

"Yes, sir," the man said without a hint of emotion. The earl had well-trained servants.

Millie felt she'd missed something because it seemed Mr. Sandstone had spoken harshly, but she said nothing. In moments, Mr. Sandstone handed her a glass and then led her back to where Sophina sat waiting. He handed Sophina the second glass, to which she was so surprised she almost dropped it, exclaiming, "Oh! Thank you, sir!"

Millie expected he would take himself off then, but he lingered. He stood at an angle in front of her, so he could at once speak to her or look about at the room with little effort.

As soon as the music ended, the vicar looked at Sophina. "It occurs to me the earl would like to know you, Miss Spencer."

Sophina looked at him blankly until she remembered he was addressing *her*. "Oh, me?" She paled considerably. "Why is that, sir?"

Chapter Fifteen

Allen stifled a grin. "I have a hunch, you might say." He bowed for the benefit of both. "I shall bring him shortly, but rest easy, Miss Spencer. I assure you, speaking with him is as speaking to, er, to me, a vicar."

Sophina's hands gripped the edge of the bench, and she watched him walk away, horrified.

"You keep forgetting who you are!" Millie scolded. "Why did you switch things out? You should be here by your own name, and me, by mine."

"Millie! That matters not, now! He is bringing the-the *earl*! To meet ME. May we quit this place now, please?"

"Of course not," Millie returned. "Are you still afraid? You saw how timid he is."

"Yes, but I—I am more timid than he. Perhaps I can wait outside in the carriage."

"Don't be a goose."

"Let us leave together, then!"

Millie considered it. She had not wished to come to begin with. She had certainly not wished to come as "Miss Allred." But she had met a most interesting man, against all odds, a dashing clergyman! He was intelligent and gentlemanly. But he believed her to be someone else. Nothing good could come of an attachment begun on false footing, she was sure.

She cleared her throat. "I suppose we must…"

"Yes! Let's!" Sophina jumped to her feet in quite an unladylike manner.

Millie reluctantly rose. How she would have liked to speak longer to Mr. Sandstone. She would have liked to find out more about him, about his connexion to Beaufort House. Something inside her felt there was no more suitable man in existence, suddenly, than he. Even Mr. Harlow could not hold a candle to him.

Though all her hopes might be crushed when she told him the truth, she had to know. She had to take that risk. She touched Sophina's arm. "Let us stay a little longer."

Sophina groaned. "When the earl approaches me, I shall swoon, I warrant you!"

"Silly girl! You must not! Did you bring a vinaigrette?"

"No. I thought I'd be safe from the earl's notice as the companion."

Millie's lips pursed. "So you planned it from the start."

Sophina said, "I had to. You see why. I cannot abide meeting an earl!"

"He is only a man, my dear!"

"No, he is not! He is a peer of the realm!"

Millie searched the room and found that Mr. Sandstone was speaking to the earl but looking their way. The dancers were regrouping in a double line. In another moment she saw the two men coming toward them.

"This is extraordinary," Millie murmured. "How did *we* manage to get the attention of these two men?"

"'Tis you who did it," Sophina answered. "You are beautiful, Millie. You must accept that."

"And what are you? A pudding face? You have your own style of beauty and Mr. Sandstone must agree."

They could say no more as the men arrived, bowing politely. Millie felt she could perceive the bench shaking from Sophina's trembling.

"Miss Allred," Mr. Sandstone said, "Would you do me the honor?" He held out his arm. Millie was unsure what honor he was requesting, but she rose automatically.

Sophina gasped. She would have cried, "Do not leave me, Millie!" but could not due to the present company, and so merely sat there, feeling ready to have apoplexy if one so young as herself could be at risk for that.

"My lord," Mr. Sandstone said to the "earl," "Miss Spencer requires your *aid*."

The "earl," who had been nervously folding his hands together and apart, looked with sudden interest at Sophina and ceased his movement. "Does she, indeed?"

"She is quite ill at ease," Mr. Sandstone continued, to Millie's amazement. It was to Sophina's amazement too, but she nodded vehemently because he was exactly right.

A change came over the earl. Instead of the hesitant, awkward man he had seemed earlier, he took a breath as of a man who had just finished a rich, satisfying meal. "May I?" he asked, motioning to the seat Millie had just vacated.

Sophina nodded curtly. She could hardly say no. Nor could she speak, not trusting her voice not to shake.

He sat down with almost a contented sigh. With a mild, almost affectionate look, he turned to her and said, "Tell me what plagues, you, Miss Spencer. I assure you, I am well acquainted with hearing troubles and I daresay, I may be able to offer you some comfort. I am a God-fearing man, you see, and make Bible reading a daily discipline."

Sophina's eyes widened and lost some of their fear like an animal reaching safety after being chased by a predator. This man seemed comfortable and kind. She felt no haughtiness, no indifference, no expectations other than to be herself. "That is—that is heartening, sir."

And that was all Millie heard, as Mr. Sandstone had taken her hand and now put it upon his arm and walked them off.

Chapter Sixteen

Millie found herself speechless, looking up at Mr. Sandstone curiously. It astounded her that he had so adroitly assessed Sophina's character, and that, knowing it for what it was, thought her worthy of the earl's attention. It was almost as startling to have seen the bumbling earl, who could not do a waltz, speaking with such ease and an air of authority.

It was as if he had become a different person. But something inside her smiled at the thought, for he seemed exactly the kind of man, if such existed, who might be the perfect counterpart for sweet, foolish Sophina. She remembered her mother's words earlier. *No earl in his right mind would give notice to your cousin.* How very wrong you are, Mama, she thought!

Mr. Sandstone said, once again promenading with her about the room, "Am I too bold in securing your company for more conversation, Miss Allred?"

Millie shook her head. "Not at all." She hoped it was not evident that she was rippling with a mixture of excitement and trepidation. Now would come the conversation she needed as to his calling, his vision for his church and parish. Now she would discover his depth of faith—or lack of it. Then must come the inevitable revealing of her deceptions, but suddenly they did not appear too flagrant.

She had not meant to disguise herself as Miss Allred. That was truly Sophina's doing. And she had agreed to hide her lineage only so she could accompany Sophina to the ball and keep her from losing her opportunity for betterment. Surely that was not too wicked, was it?

He said, "You mentioned earlier, you hoped to meet a man of my profession."

She nodded.

He continued, "And that you were almost married to a man of the cloth."

She nodded again. "Yes, Mr. Harwell."

"Is that your only requirement in a man? That he be ordained in the church?" he asked, with a smile.

Millie smiled back. "I never thought of it that way. I only determined that my life must be useful; that I must help improve the world in some way. The Church seems the best means of doing it, first, for shining forth the light of the gospel of Christ, and second, because it does more good for humanity than any other institution save marriage and family, and it is largely concerned with those, too." She blushed lightly. "I gave too long a reply."

"'Twas a fine reply," he said, meeting her eyes briefly.

Allen realized he was almost anxious to hear her replies. He, who had never found a woman before who filled him with such solicitude.

"I begin to think you are almost a saint," he said, quite seriously. *Too good for him by far*, he thought. "Unlike the vast majority of women I have met, you are not seeking to raise your station in life through marriage. You are neither a fortune hunter nor a coquette—"

Millie's face blanched. He saw her expression and said, "Do I disturb you? I beg your pardon."

Millie said, lowering her eyes, "You do not disturb me. 'Tis just that I know myself, and how very mistaken you are." She gave him a look of regret, earnest and endearing.

Her eyes searched his, questioning, vulnerable, and he wanted to pull her close and reassure her that she could tell him anything, and it would be alright.

"I must tell you, Mr. Sandstone, how wicked I am!" She looked ready to cry. He stopped walking and led her to a nearby double bench against the wall. He suspected that she was muddled, perhaps, but not wicked. She and her cousin had concocted some scheme, but he felt in his heart it was anything but wicked.

Millie went on, "I fear I am a fortune hunter, no less self-seeking than these ladies hoping to wed his lordship." She gestured out at the roomful of hopefuls. "You see, I too came with hopes."

"You hoped to meet a clergyman," he said, recalling her words.

She nodded. "Yes, but I hoped to meet a-a-wealthy clergyman." She gave him a look which said, "I am sorry, but that is the truth."

He suppressed the urge to laugh and asked, "What on earth made you suppose you would find one here?"

"I hardly expected to! I cannot tell you my surprise to find *you* here." He seemed to expect more, so she continued, "I only agreed to come for Sophina's sake, for she was ready to cry off and miss this opportunity which could free her from her father's house and open the world to her!"

Ah, here was the point, the heart of the mix-up, whatever its origin. "Do you mean to say," he asked in a cool tone, "you came to give your *companion* the chance to win the hand of an earl?"

Millie colored, having forgot all about Sophina being her companion. It seemed now was the moment of truth. She hadn't meant for it to be, but did ever a man question a woman as much as Mr. Sandstone was questioning her? She had been enjoying his attentions, even his questions, for it showed interest. But now it was all likely to end.

She had said too much and must reveal everything. She prayed quickly that she wouldn't make a mull of it. "*I* was supposed to be the companion, not Sophina!" she blurted out, and she could not disguise the indignation she still felt at Sophina's trick. If it had not been for her foolish cousin, she would have been known as herself, Miss Spencer, even though her connexion to the barony would still have been hidden. That alone would not be so odious to confess, but having to admit she was not someone whom she had claimed to be, and having to admit she was someone other than what she had claimed to be, seemed beyond the pale, even for a minister's ears.

Before she could explain further and tell him her real name and lineage, Lady Beaufort came abreast of them and stopped. She looked at the clergyman. "How do you find the ball, sir?" she asked cautiously, noting that her son was once again with Miss Allred. She felt it must signify. This was the heart of her question.

"Quite to my liking, I thank you, your ladyship."

The countess's expression lightened. "Upon my word, I am glad to hear it!"

"This is Miss Allred," he reminded her.

"Yes, Miss Allred," she repeated, studying Millie and then giving Mr. Sandstone a wide-eyed stare. "How delightful." She asked, "Does this mean you have intelligence for me? Any news?"

Mr. Sandstone said, "I expect that the earl may."

Her brow rose. "The earl? *Only* the earl?"

He nodded, a small smile playing at the edges of his mouth.

"Are you certain?" she asked.

"I am." It had not escaped his notice that the clergyman, aka, the earl, had not risen from talking with Miss Spencer. If he did not mistake the matter, the man would find the young woman was everything he needed in a wife. It did not occur to him that Sandstone would make the decision that evening, or that he would announce it to the company.

But when Lady Beaufort approached the "earl" and asked him, "How do you do, sir?" he stood up excitedly.

"Your ladyship!" he exclaimed. "Allow me the honor of informing you"—and he turned to Miss Spencer with a beatific smile—"that I have done my office!" He looked back at her ladyship with countenance lit up as by a hundred candles. "The earl has chosen a wife!"

Lady Beaufort's features turned to astonishment and then delight. She inferred the man was speaking for her son. "Indeed? Is it Miss Allred?"

"Miss Allred? No, ma'am. Let it be known," and he cleared his voice and spoke in a loud tone, "that the Earl of Beaufort is to marry Miss Spencer, Miss Millicent Spencer!" His eyes were shining.

Three ladies nearby heard this and hurried off, their faces showing disappointment and anger. Her ladyship's expression froze momentarily. She looked over at Sophina, and her eyes widened. She was about to say, "Are you quite certain that is the *earl's* choice?" For she wondered if the man had forgot he was only play-acting. She'd been watching with eagle eyes to see Allen's progress with Miss Spencer but saw him abandon the chit to his counterpart and resume walking with Miss Allred.

She had fully expected to hear that he would choose Miss Allred.

However, Miss Spencer was the girl from a noble family and would have been her preference for her son. Only her vicar looked like a man in love with the lady, while her son did not. Further, Miss Spencer's eyes were like to pop out of her head. She looked mortified.

Sophina, in truth, was so mortified at what she'd heard that in another moment, she swooned in a crumpled heap.

"My dear!" cried her ladyship. "Help her, Sandstone!" she cried, forgetting he was supposed to be the earl. She looked about, wringing her hands. "Lord Carlisle! Smelling salts! Beaufort!" In the general mayhem that followed, including a sudden exit of the ladies, for they'd heard the sad news that the earl had made his choice and it wasn't *them*, Sophina was carried by a valiant Mr. Sandstone—the real one, to an antechamber off the main corridor.

On the other side of the ballroom, Millie watched a stream of women, all who, upon hearing news of some kind, began to leave. Mr. Sandstone motioned to a footman who came to him at once. "Instruct the ladies to the supper room. They mustn't leave without eating. Her Ladyship would be much vexed."

"What has happened?" Millie asked Mr. Sandstone. "Why are they leaving?"

A lady passing overheard her and stopped. "The earl has made his choice," she said flatly. "He is to wed a Miss Spencer."

Millie's eyes popped open and she gripped Mr. Sandstone's sleeve. He looked from his arm to her face.

"Does that distress you?" he asked, watching her. It seemed he was having trouble keeping his mouth straight.

"Miss-Miss Spencer? I daresay it must be a *fudge*! There is some mistake!" She plucked her fan open and fanned herself rapidly.

"What mistake is that?"

"Why, why—Miss Spencer cannot be the *earl's* choice!"

"And why cannot she be?"

Millie fumbled for words. She had never meant to deceive him about her identity, but the night had gone so fast and just when she would have explained, there were interruptions, and she never got to. In desperation, she cried, "The truth is, Miss Spencer is a baron's daughter!"

One brow on his handsome face rose. "And you would have me believe a baron's daughter is your companion?" He must force her to confess all, though he saw her evident distress. Oddly enough, and to his own surprise, it only made him want to embrace her and kiss away the confusion. In fact—and he realized this in an astounding moment of wanting her—he wanted to take her home. He wanted to…what had Carlisle said? Wake up with her beside him. See her across the table at meals. Have her upon his arm in town and at

Carlton House, at balls and assemblies and dinners.

The truth hit him like a cannonball to the gut.

He had found his future wife.

Chapter Seventeen

He had only to see if she would be honest with him about her identity. And then another truth hit him. He too would have to be honest about his. And what if his sweet Christian bride refused to wed him as he was no clergyman? Worse, he was an aristocrat, part of an "outdated, unfair institution" who had bamboozled her.

He had ever viewed his rank as an advantage in society, despite the difficulty it had raised for him in finding a wife. But with Miss Allred—really Miss Spencer, he was sure—it could be a fatal disadvantage.

She said defensively, "A baron's daughter may well be a companion, as any gentleman's daughter may, but she cannot marry the earl, for he banned anyone from a noble family to so much as appear at the ball!"

"I should say, he has changed his mind," he said, with a little smile. "Why do you not rejoice in her good fortune?"

Lady Beaufort was suddenly before them, looking vexed and disturbed. Just then, Millie saw the earl carrying an unconscious Sophina in his arms! She gasped and would have rushed to her side, but Mr. Sandstone quickly put his hand over hers, holding her in place.

Lady Beaufort said, her lips in a hard line, "What are you playing at, Allen? Or has Mr."—she looked at Millie, and amended, "I mean, er, has Beaufort forgot himself? I believe he is enamored of Miss *Spencer*," she said meaningfully. "What are you going to do about it?"

Millie found this exchange baffling, but she said, "Yes, what are you going to do about it?" for she hoped with all her heart that he would do *something*. She did not see what a vicar could do to deter an earl's wishes, but Sophina had not set the earl straight and something must be done. But she could contain herself no longer. She simply had to get to Sophina and ensure she was all right. "My dear sir, my lady!" She exclaimed. "I beg your pardon, er, your pardons, but I must see to poor Sophina!" She curtseyed and hurried off in the direction she'd seen the earl carrying poor Sophina.

Lady Beaufort's eyes narrowed. "Now tell me what you are about. It has been announced you are to marry Miss Spencer, not Miss Allred. I daresay, I do not object to Miss Spencer, but it seems you fancy Miss Allred."

He said, "Do not fret, ma'am. The earl will indeed marry Miss Spencer." He winked rakishly at his mama and went to follow after Millie.

His mother stood staring after him disconsolately. Lord Carlisle came up to her, and she turned to him with relief. "Oh, Carlisle! My *dear* Carlisle! I do not know what to think! Allen is beside himself, my clergyman has forgot he is not really the earl, and he has chosen a wife for my son in his place! What am I to do?"

Their eyes met. Hers were filled with worry, with fear, with distress. But as she gazed into the calm, light grey eyes of Lord Carlisle, her faithful friend and sometime counselor, friend to her son, too—she remembered that he was a decade younger than herself—but suddenly realized she wanted more than friendship with him. She gasped.

Lord Carlisle's countenance remained the same, steady, loyal, caring, and warm. He said, "I warrant Allen has a plan. He shan't marry where he is not disposed to, my lady, have no fear."

Lady Beaufort swallowed. What a terrible time to realize she cared more for Lord Carlisle than she'd realized. A man her junior by ten years! What would he think?

She must focus only on the current crisis. She cried, "Allen has spent an inordinate amount of time speaking to Miss Allred, did you note? And now agrees to marry Miss Spencer?" She gave him a wide-eyed look and gripped his arm. "He told me himself, 'the earl shall indeed marry Miss Spencer.' What do you make of *that*?" Her tone was as if she had held up the trump card in a high-stakes game of écarté.

Lord Carlisle chuckled. "There is always a method in Allen's madness, I assure you."

His calmness, in the face of this disturbing turn of events, began to calm her too. But she said, "Do you indeed think so? I cannot make heads nor tails of this muddle!"

"Depend upon it, Allen knows what he is about."

Lady Beaufort felt for the thousandth time how grateful she was for Carlisle. He was so—so—steadfast! Reassuring.

He added, "I know your son well enough to say that with utter confidence."

She released her grip on his arm. "I beg your pardon, sir," she said, somewhat embarrassed. "I have hung upon your sleeve like a-a-child."

"Not at all, my lady," he said softly, still meeting her gaze with his calm, sea-grey eyes. He took her gloved hand back and kissed it softly. "You may hang upon my sleeve whenever it pleases you."

Lady Beaufort looked up, saw the warmth in his gaze, and a smile curled her lips. Her heart warmed right through as if she'd held it out toward a blazing fireplace on a cold night. Lord Carlisle was the fire.

"Thank you, my lord," she said in a subdued tone, using the honorific she normally eschewed.

"I think I prefer Carlisle from you," he said, smiling. He raised her hand again, this time leaving a soft, lingering kiss upon her glove. He wished to turn it over and kiss the palm of her hand but did not dare, remembering they were in the ballroom and the public eye.

They stood there, smiling idiotically at each other as people in love do. Particularly people who had not realized they were in love until that moment. Lord Carlisle had known his feelings for a long time, but he had ever doubted her ladyship's. He had never been certain he held a place in her heart other than "friend."

He had bided his time, staying as close as he dared, being ever available. He'd come to her dinners, her suppers, her assemblies. As Allen's friend, he was easily included in smaller family affairs as well. For years now, he'd waited. Waited to see a sign in Lady Beaufort that she cared for him in return. As he smiled into her eyes and saw the deepening look in hers, he knew she was suddenly aware, not only of his feelings, but of her own.

Lord Carlisle felt his heart expanding with joy. Suddenly Lady Beaufort had discovered there was indeed a space for him. A space for his being more than a friend to her. He would offer for her only after speaking to Allen, out of respect. But soon, soon, they must marry.

Their smiles were genuine and mutual.

Chapter Eighteen

Millie was directed by a footman out to the corridor and then to a small side parlour. She stopped in the doorway, for her cousin, lying on a settee and surrounded by the earl and two housemaids, was just coming to as one maid passed a vinaigrette beneath her nose.

"Oh!" Sophina cried, sitting up violently. "Oh!"

The earl was on his knees by her side. "My dearest lady," he said pleadingly. "I beg your forgiveness. I never meant to alarm you so."

Millie rushed to her cousin's side. "Dearest!" she cried. "Are you all right?"

Sophina sniffed and held her head. "Heavens! I have the headache. And I—I may be violently ill."

"Please," Millie said, turning to the earl, "we must repair to our carriage." He nodded and then, after taking one last, adoring look at Sophina, hurried from the room.

The invalid looked tragically at Millie. "My stars! I never knew a man could offer for a woman so soon."

"But he had to make an offer tonight. Did he truly offer for you?" Millie asked, though she knew the answer. It had already been announced.

Sophina nodded. "I said yes, I said yes," she cried, "for he is the dearest man in the world! And then I remembered he is an earl!"

"But you forgot you are not Miss Spencer."

"Oh, dear me! It happened so quickly. But cos—" and here her face screwed up painfully. "I cannot become a countess—by your name or mine!"

"Nonsense," said Millie. "Of course you can."

The maids, one still holding the vinaigrette, stared at each other with expressions of puzzlement.

Sophina, quite overcome at the thought of being ennobled, lay back down upon the settee.

When the earl returned in a moment saying the carriage had been called for, Millie began to help her up. Mr. Sandstone entered then, and the atmosphere swiftly changed. The maids curtseyed, and the earl said, "Miss Spencer is distraught, sir. Merciful heavens, can we be done with our masquerade?"

"Silence!" said Mr. Sandstone rather severely.

Millie looked questioningly from one to the other. For a clergyman to speak in such a manner to the earl was astonishing. But then, she did not understand their relationship. Something was up, but she could not discern what it was. A masquerade? This ball was no masquerade, save for herself and Sophina, who had "masked" their true identities.

"I am glad you came," she said sincerely to Mr. Sandstone, "as we must be on our way. My cousin is not well, as you can see."

He gave her a dissatisfied look, putting his hands on his hips.

Millie's brows rose. She was mystified by his demeanor.

"And you are content to leave things at that?" he said, suddenly moving forward and grasping her hand. "Not so fast, Miss Allred. I believe we have unfinished business." He led her from the room, turning to look at her with an unreadable expression. He pulled her aside into an adjoining parlor, another small room.

After they entered, he released her hand and stood, looking at her with that same peculiar, dissatisfied expression. Millie stared back at him, her heart pounding in her chest.

"What shall I say to you?" she asked.

"You might tell me the truth before you leave."

"Oh." She drew out the word, "oooooh."

"Yes."

She looked at him sideways and clasped her hands together. "How long have you known?"

"Since you called your companion Miss Allred."

Millie nodded.

"I never meant to deceive you," she said, twisting her hands together and apart. "I never meant to sham anyone. Sophina was supposed to come as herself, and I as her companion."

"Because you are a baron's daughter?"

Millie nodded. "Right." Suddenly her eyes flashed. "'Twas an unfortunate restriction, and that is the kindest term I can use for it."

Allen's eyes twinkled. "What term would you use if you were not kind?" For some reason, he was eager to know.

Millie's gaze sparked like tinder into a flame. "Addle-brained. It was wholly addle-brained!"

He chuckled. "I didn't think so at the start, but having met you, I quite agree with you. Imagine not inviting Miss Spencer!"

Millie favored him with a little smile, but said, "Well, I did not care for myself, but to ban an entire class of women seemed excessively absurd."

He nodded. "Just so."

She peeked to see if he was humoring her but could not tell. She continued, "Well, when it came time to be announced, my cousin gave her name as belonging to me and told the servant she was the companion, using *my* name!"

"So you are Miss Spencer, and she is Miss Allred. As I deduced."

Millie nodded. "I only agreed to come so that *she* would."

"But you did come, and with hopes."

"To meet a clergyman like—like yourself," Millie said in a lower voice, shyness creeping into her tone. She looked at him with approval in her eyes. She had to smile. "I daresay, I did not expect to."

"Knowing your cousin's timidity, what made you think she ought to come?"

"It was her best chance to escape her father's household and his tight chains upon her.

Mama said the earl must pick a bride. Why should Sophina not be in the running, I thought. She had naught to lose."

She thought about it for a moment and then smiled again, her eyes shining. "And only look at the result! He offered for her! 'Tis nothing short of a miracle!" But her face sobered quickly, as she said, "We have only to settle the matter of her name with the earl. He must understand he is to marry Miss Allred, not Miss Spencer."

"I am sorry to disillusion, but the earl will indeed marry Miss Spencer. It has been announced and cannot be undone."

He came closer to her.

Millie's face froze in horror. "Oh, do not say so! *I* could never marry the earl!"

"But you wanted a wealthy man, and the earl is that in spades. You could do all the charities your pretty little heart desires. It is nothing more than what you said you wanted."

Millie thought frantically that somehow that conversation had gone all wrong. She had never meant what he suggested. She turned on him, wide-eyed. "I never said I did. I never said I would marry a man *only* for his wealth!"

She felt suddenly faint and made her way to a high-backed chair. Mr. Sandstone stopped her from sitting and led her instead to an adjacent settee, taking the seat beside her. "I only meant," she explained, her face a picture of woe, and holding a hand to her chest, "that it would be a good thing if he had an income, but I never meant I would marry a man for it!"

Mr. Sandstone bit his lip to prevent a laugh from escaping.

Millie fell back against the seat, placed a hand on her forehead and moaned again. Suddenly she sat up straight. "An announcement cannot be *binding*!" she said, in an agonized tone, looking at him as though Napoleon had just stormed the gates with a battalion.

"Oh, but it can be," said Mr. Sandstone calmly. "I have no doubt but that a servant is en route to the rector's house this moment, to announce the banns."

Millie turned to him in horror. "But he did not offer for *me*! He offered for Sophina! The earl will tell you himself!"

He took one of her hands. "He offered for Miss Spencer. But does it really distress you so? The prospect of becoming the next Countess Beaufort?"

Millie moaned. "Oh, do not even say such a thing! I could not bear it, I assure you!" Her heart was beating hard, her hands beginning to feel damp inside her gloves. How had she got herself into this awful predicament? She drew off her gloves and threw them on the side table, hardly knowing it. She took a cooling breath, and fanned herself. Mr. Sandstone took the fan from her and fanned her himself.

"Thank you," she said, glancing at him gratefully. That he was breathlessly handsome, so close, and yet so out of reach—for she was betrothed to the earl!—seemed only to worsen her plight. "You are a good, kind man."

"Not always," he said, very truthfully. "And, if it makes it any easier for you, though I regret to inform you, I am not the man you hoped to meet. I am not a wealthy clergyman."

She blinked at him, thinking quite the opposite, that he was everything she'd ever wanted in a man, no, *more* than she dared wish for or hoped to meet. That he was not wealthy seemed of the least importance. She said honestly, "I hardly expected to, sir."

"I am, unfortunately, of a middling income." He gazed keenly at her.

Millie blushed. He felt he needed to explain his living to her! She had been far too outspoken about matters of finance—a thing her mama would be ashamed of, did she know it—and now poor Mr. Sandstone felt he must admit his flaw.

"My dear sir!" she exclaimed. "I beg you, do not—!"

"But is that not what you wish to know? Whether you have met the man you desire and therefore can spurn the earl's suit?"

Millie was crimson now and shut her eyes in horror. "Oh, how wicked I am!" Opening them, she found him studying her. "I beg you to forgive me! 'Twas all just—a dream! A vain imagination. Who am I to be a benefactress to the poor?"

He smiled. He met her eyes in silence, then ran a finger gently down the side of her face, touched one hanging curl, then dropped his hand.

"I daresay you are exactly the type of woman who should be."

Millie was unsure of his meaning. Did he mean she should be a benefactress, therefore he was not the man for her? Or did he mean, she should be, only he himself could not provide her the opportunity, though he may be the man for her? Was he telling her of their suitability or unsuitability?

He said, "Only think. A countess can be a benefactress. And you cannot despise a title when your father was a baron, and your brother is now."

"'Tis the principle of the thing," she said, "not to mention *I can never marry the earl*!"

"The principle?" he asked. He moved a tad closer to her on the settee.

She nodded. "All men are created equal. In America they are. Here a man with a title feels superior to his fellow beings. Be he a reprobate, a scoundrel, what have you, he feels superior simply by virtue of birth! I own, I cannot abide it!"

He nodded, though a small smile formed around the edges of his mouth.

She looked up at him, suddenly aware of his nearness. To think that she might have continued an acquaintance with this beautiful man, a man of God, and that instead she was leg-shackled to the earl and all because of Sophina's deception! She stared into his azure eyes, thinking how deep they were, how she could get lost in them. Blinking, she said, "Cannot you, being a vicar, send to the rector and tell him to ignore those banns?"

Before he could reply, she gasped and cried, her features suddenly alight with hope. "What a ninny I am! I can myself object when the banns are read. I can explain the mix-up."

She looked at him and said in her shyer voice, "Or you could, sir, if it pleases you to do so?" Her cheeks flamed, but so did her heart. She felt almost breathless with those beautiful azure eyes upon her. This was a crucial moment, when he must show if he cared for her or not.

"I am sorry to disappoint, but I could never cross the earl's wishes."

She opened her mouth to speak, but not a word came forth. Disappointment crashed through her. It felt stronger than when she realized Mr. Harwell was not to offer for her. It felt utterly wrong, as though every hope in life had been dashed forever.

He stroked the side of her face, making her turn to him.

"However…what if I and the earl were to switch stations? What if I were the earl, and he the clergyman?" he asked. "Would that make your prospect as a countess endurable?"

Millie shook her head. "This is no time for useless speculation. If you were the earl, if it did not ruin your character, you would still be as agreeable, I daresay, but you are not!"

Ignoring that, he said, "Would it suit your hopes? Do you prefer me to the earl?"

Millie blinked back tears. "I should think you know the answer to that," she said rather heatedly. "You are more than I ever expected to find in a man! Now I think on it, I do not care a fig if you are of a low income. It signifies nothing!"

"Middling," he corrected her, wanting to take her in his arms right then.

"Whatever it is, I count it immaterial!" She looked up at him, feeling a wave of warmth and affection for him that was almost frightening. She loved him! Was it possible to love so soon?

In her shy voice, she said, "I suppose, even if you were an earl, I could forgive it in you. I am sure you would be agreeable, whatever your station in life."

Earlier this would have struck him as amusing, but now it was of grave importance. "I am glad to know you can forgive it in me."

But Millie tried to rise; she'd had enough. He did not love her enough to question the banns. There was no more reason to stay.

But he said, "One moment more, Miss Spencer. Millicent Spencer," he said slowly, as if playing the name upon his lips as one would try a new melody on a pianoforte. Millie shivered at the sound of her name on his breath. She loved his manner of speaking it. He gently made her resume her seat.

Her heart was pounding, her cheeks hot. Her insides felt shaky with disappointment, for she was in love, but he would not resist the earl's wishes.

"I must beg your forgiveness," he said, in a soft voice, his hand again stroking the side of her face. Millie loved his touch and could not reprimand him, though it seemed he was content that she should be another man's wife.

He turned her chin so she had to look at him, into his eyes. They held the first glimmer of vulnerability she'd seen in them.

"I am not a vicar," he said.

She blinked. "What?"

"I am not a vicar. My name is Allen Prescott Courtenay, 14th Earl Beaufort."

She stared at him, her eyes like an active volcano, pulsating from their depths.

"How dare you play games!" she cried, again trying to rise. "This is beyond the pale! Cannot you see, I am in earnest? That, if you were to be the earl, I should be entirely relieved at our betrothal? How can you torment me?"

He grasped her arms, managing again to gently return her to her seat.

"That is why I must beg your forgiveness. I am not trying to torment you but to put your fears to rest. I pray this is a *coup de grace*, if a blow, then a blow of mercy. I am indeed the earl."

Millie made a huffing sound. "You jest, sir!"

The earl lifted her hands into his, and then kissed each one, softly and lingeringly. He loved that she had removed her gloves. It astonished him how much he wanted to take and kiss not only Miss Spencer's hands, but her lovely, soft lips.

Looking into her eyes he said, "I am in earnest. I asked Mr. Sandstone, who is the vicar, to switch places with me for the ball, for, like yourself, I thought the premise absurd. He was quite averse to the idea and came around to it unwillingly."

The outrage in Millie's eyes began to fade. The first inkling that he was telling the truth dawned on her. She remembered what the earl—no, the vicar, if he was in earnest—said earlier, *Can we end this masquerade?*

He waited to see her reaction, adding, "I wished to know a woman's character without the hindrance of the title. Can you understand that?"

Millie nodded, but was still numb with the revelation, letting it sink in.

"So you see, the earl shall indeed marry Miss Spencer—if she will have him?"

Millie's heart seemed frozen with the shock of it. Mr. Sandstone was the earl! No, not Mr. Sandstone, but Lord Beaufort! My word! It seemed impossible…But she realized she hardly cared whether he was or was not titled. What cared she about anything except that he wanted her, he wished to marry her! Nothing else signified.

He grasped both her hands in his and turned to her, his eyes filled with concern. "I realize what a disappointment it must be to you that I am no clergyman."

A rush of heat filled her heart, her mind, her body. This wonderful man thought he was a disappointment!

"And I grilled you mercilessly, knowing you were not Miss Allred, even while I allowed you to believe I was Mr. Sandstone." His eyes implored her. "*Can* you marry me, Miss Spencer?" he asked softly.

Reining in her sensibilities, tamping down the sudden fire filling her being with light and joy, she smiled demurely. "The announcement has been made, my lord. 'Tis binding, you know. I have no doubt a servant is en route to the rector this instant to announce the banns."

He grinned and took her into his arms.

She threw her arms about his neck. Oh, how wonderful it felt to do it!

"My darling Millie." He kissed her lips, stopped and kissed them again, then her cheeks, and her nose. Then her mouth again. Millie felt the world moving beneath her feet.

She had come to the ball a different woman! A woman believing she should never find the match she desired. A woman entirely sure of herself, sure she would never join the aristocracy.

She had come, not as who she was, but as someone else. She would leave not as who she was, but a woman who could hardly stand to wait to be someone else, a countess! The wife of an earl, *this* earl, for he was a man who met her not as who he was, but as someone else. Neither had malicious intentions, but both had worn disguises. And both had discovered, through them, the one they could love forever.

Millie had truly—*magnificently*—met her match.

About the Author

Linore Rose Burkard loves to craft stories that fill a sweet spot for readers who savor the era of Jane Austen and happy endings. An award-winning author best known for Inspirational Regency Romance, her first book with Harvest House (*Before the Season Ends*) opened the genre for the CBA. Influenced by Georgette Heyer, Linore's historical romances are light-hearted but steeped in Regency authenticity. A *magna cum laude* English Lit. grad from CUNY, Linore now resides in Ohio with her husband and family, two cats, and a Shorkie. In addition to writing, Linore is a book coach, a publisher, and President of the Dayton Christian Scribes. She also writes contemporary love stories and, as L. R. Burkard, young adult apocalyptic suspense. Generally low-key, she is known to yell at the TV during Mets baseball games. (You can take the girl out of New York but…)

https://www.LinoreBurkard.com/newsletter

The FB group link is: https://www.facebook.com/groups/123347423926

THANKS SO MUCH FOR READING!

I really enjoyed writing Miss Spencer's story, and I hope you enjoyed it too.

But don't go yet! I'd love to send you my newsletter so I can keep in touch. I'll update you on my latest releases, book sales, bargains, and include amusing stories and inspiration. Sign up HERE: https://www.LinoreBurkard.com/newsletter. (You'll also get a free Inspirational Regency romance, *Before the Season Ends!*)

You can also join me at my Facebook reader's group to chat, share book thoughts and more. Hope to see you there!

Affectionately,
Linore

Lissa and the Spy

by Camille Elliot

In Regency-era London, Miss Lissa Gardinier enters her second Season seeking a marriage in order to escape her mother's constant criticism. So she represses her cheeky remarks behind a quiet, innocent facade.

The enigmatic Lord Jeremy Stoude is dismayed when a chance encounter with Miss Gardinier entangles her in his world of secrets and subterfuge. He cannot afford to be distracted by Lissa's charming smile and unflappable demeanor.

As danger stalks them and true feelings come to light, can Lissa and Jeremy navigate the labyrinth of society's expectations and their own insecurities to find love?

But the LORD said unto Samuel, Look not on his countenance, or on the height of his stature; because I have refused him: for the LORD seeth not as man seeth; for man looketh on the outward appearance, but the LORD looketh on the heart.

1 Samuel 16:7

But God commendeth his love toward us, in that, while we were yet sinners, Christ died for us.

Romans 5:8

Behold, what manner of love the Father hath bestowed upon us, that we should be called the sons of God: therefore the world knoweth us not, because it knew him not.

1 John 3:1

Chapter One

Spring, 1807
London

If only she were allowed to open her mouth.

Lissa reflected that in all fairness, she was not *prohibited* from opening her mouth. She was allowed to drink champagne and eat the delicacies offered by the host of the ball. She was allowed to discuss the weather, she was sure. And her mother likely wouldn't be disappointed if she discussed fashion with a young lady or gentleman. She might even be allowed to say something ignorant about Napoleon, as long as she accompanied her words with a smile and a giggle.

But she had been ordered—under threat of being sent back home even in the midst of the Season—to keep her tongue under control while in London. Lissa didn't think her tongue was particularly out of control. She had perfect control of her words. She had completely meant what she said when she compared Lady Adderly's hat to a molting chicken.

And to be perfectly honest, she had been extremely polite when she asked Mr. Peterson to take more lessons from his dancing instructor. There was nothing rude about a gentle suggestion such as that, surely?

Because she could have instead told him that he stomped on her foot like a bad-tempered donkey trying to maim its owner. She had exercised an iron grip on her tongue in that instance, and yet her mother had scolded her.

Mr. Collingworth came up to her, accompanied by Lady Cliffton, the hostess of the ball. As always, Lady Cliffton's jewelry—while in good taste—was as flamboyant as the matron. "Miss Gardinier, allow me to introduce Mr. Collingworth."

Lissa curtseyed, keeping a polite smile on her face, while Mr. Collingworth bowed. In truth, they had been introduced last year, in her first Season, but from the vacant look upon Mr. Collingworth's face, he had likely forgotten about it.

"Would you do me the honor of a dance, Miss Gardinier?" Mr. Collingworth asked, and Lissa assented.

He had danced with her the last time they met, as well. A perverse side of her wondered if he would speak of the same things as before.

She was not so obedient to her mother that she would subject herself to the torture of conversation topics such as the weather and the food at the ball, which she'd already discussed at length with her other dancing partners. So she asked a more unusual question. "Mr. Collingworth, shall you miss activities at your country estate while you are in town?"

His slack-jawed face abruptly became animated. "Yes indeed, Miss Gardinier. I breed hunting dogs, you see, and I've had particular luck this year with several pups …"

It was not that Lissa was interested in the pedigrees of his hunting dogs, who all seemed to have the most ridiculous names. It was that Mr. Collingworth became more interesting as he waxed eloquent about something that interested him, as opposed to the safe topics to which Lissa's mother had restricted her daughter.

Her dance with Mr. Collingworth last Season may have been the start of it all. At the beginning of the Season, she'd been overwhelmed by the number of people at each party compared to the small gatherings in her home village, and by the way they all seemed to know each other and converse so easily with each other. She had attempted to join in their conversations, but while every one of her peers knew about the latest fashion plates from France, no one was particularly interested in the latest discussion in the House of Lords, or at the very least, they didn't admit to doing so. And they visibly shied away from speaking about the war, as though it were a dirty topic that only the uncouth brought up in polite conversation.

She had ended up not saying much at all, which she belatedly realized made her uninteresting and boring compared to other young women. It hadn't helped that Lissa's face was rather plain, and her only beauty, her blonde hair, had been ruthlessly styled in a ridiculous—but *a la mode*—fashion that made her look like an egg had exploded.

But last year during that first dance with Mr. Collingworth, upon seeing him excitedly discuss his dog breeding, she had been encouraged to also speak without restraint. So she had voiced her exact thoughts rather than hiding behind a vapid facade. "Why in the world would you name a dog Lickspittle Furrybottom?"

At Mr. Collingworth's startled look, Lissa realized that she'd said that out loud *now*, in *this* dance with him.

"… Not that it's not a lovely name," she added lamely.

Mr. Collingworth didn't believe her, and his conversation faltered. She regretted that, for she hadn't intended to be rude to him.

"Er … did I speak of Lickspittle Furrybottom?" he asked.

Lissa did a mental shriek at her mistake. "We spoke briefly about her last year. You were worried about her compatibility with Snout Droolalot." To alleviate his embarrassment at not remembering her, she said, "I was relieved to hear that Lickspittle Furrybottom and Snout Droolalot had such a healthy litter. What are your plans for their puppies?" Talking about puppies was acceptable dance conversation, wasn't it?

It pleased Mr. Collingworth to continue discussing puppies for the remainder of the dance.

He delivered her to the same spot where she had been standing, but he seemed a bit anxious to be rid of her. Lissa sighed. She had not intended to do so, but perhaps she had intimidated him after all. Hopefully her mother wouldn't notice—

"Lissa!" Mrs. Gardinier hissed as she appeared at Lissa's side as if out of thin air. "What did you say to Mr. Collingworth to make him look as though he'd been flayed alive?"

"We only spoke of his hunting dogs," Lissa said.

"I didn't ask what *he* spoke of. I asked what *you* said."

Her mother knew her too well. "I might have let slip that we met last year."

Mrs. Gardinier gave a heavy sigh that emptied her entire lungs of air. "And he did not remember you?" she guessed. "Lissa, really! Can you not be polite for one second?"

"I was extremely polite." She doubted any other young woman in the room would have even bothered to ask about Lickspittle Furrybottom and Snout Droolalot's emotional conditions.

"Not polite enough to watch what you say," her mother snapped. "You may have thought I was merely bluffing, but I will send you straight back to the country if you offend anyone else this Season."

"I never *intend* to offend anyone," Lissa said. She simply said what was on her mind. Granted, she *had* intentionally insulted Miss Church-Pratton for her snide remark about Lissa's uncle's profession as a physician (as if saving lives was something the family ought to be ashamed about), but she had not intentionally set out to embarrass Mr. Collingworth (even if hunting dog pedigrees was not one of her favorite subjects).

"You are embarrassing *me*," Mrs. Gardinier said.

Mrs. Gardinier was not embarrassed simply by Lissa's lack of suitors. She was embarrassed because in her youth, she had easily formed an attachment with one of the most eligible bachelors in town. (Lissa had difficulty believing that the man who padded around his study in his stocking feet was one of the most eligible bachelors in his heyday, but perhaps there was no accounting for taste.)

"And it reflects poorly upon your sister," Mrs. Gardinier added.

"I am hardly hindering Miriam's success," Lissa said. Her younger sister, pretty and charming, had quickly become one of the belles of the Season. Even Lissa's status as a "disappointment" for not forming a match in her first Season and being forced into a second one hadn't cast a shadow on Miriam's popularity.

"You should learn to be more like Miriam," her mother said for the hundredth time.

Lissa tried, she truly *tried* to be pleasant and lively like her sister. But whenever she grew relaxed around a group of people, she inevitably said something that made everyone stop and stare at her. Such as speculation on Napoleon's next campaign or the frustrating tendency of Mrs. Radcliffe's milksop heroines to faint at the least hint of distress.

And so last Season, with her silence and plain face, the most anyone could say about her was that she was quiet and "unusual." Even Lissa felt she was heartily boring, especially when compared to the lively beauties, charming beauties, or cold beauties who had descended upon London.

Ironically, once surrounded by the crowds of London, Lissa had grown more conscious about herself—and her failings. This year, as soon as she had entered town again, the weight of not measuring up to her mother's—and society's—expectations settled upon her shoulders like an overstuffed peddler's pack, causing an ache in her neck and a constant headache at the base of her skull.

Her mother said she was merely slouching too much.

"You will not allow this Season to be a repeat of last year," her mother said. "Otherwise, I shall spend all of the winter *re-training* you in how to behave as a proper young lady."

Lissa shuddered. She did not fear the training, but it would mean her mother's criticisms would increase tenfold, and she wasn't certain if she could withstand that.

"I do not know what I shall do if any of my daughters requires more than two Seasons to make a match," Mrs. Gardinier muttered.

Lissa exerted herself to *not* retort that her younger sister Keriah was likely to disappoint her mother (assuming Lissa managed to somehow snag a husband).

"I shall be completely inoffensive to everyone," Lissa said.

Her mother gave her a baleful look. "As you were with Mr. Collingworth?"

She had already forgotten how she failed spectacularly with him. "I shall be completely inoffensive to everyone *from now on*."

Mrs. Gardinier snorted. She pulled Lissa with a grip like a vise on her elbow. "Come. Let us speak to Lady Wynwood. Perhaps she may find you an acceptable partner."

"Isn't she occupied with finding *Phoebe* an acceptable partner?" Keriah's best friend, Miss Phoebe Sauber, was debuting this year, sponsored by her aunt, Lady Wynwood.

Keriah had wanted her comeout at the same time, but the Gardiniers had a tradition of allowing their daughters to debut only once they turned nineteen. Lissa herself had turned twenty during last Season, which made her feel ancient next to the dewy seventeen- and eighteen-year-olds around her.

"Anyone of whom Lady Wynwood approves must be an excellent candidate, and Phoebe can only dance with one man at a time. I'm sure any of the other gentlemen will be happy to dance with you."

Lissa dearly wanted Phoebe to have a successful Season, but so far, it had looked like a repeat of Lissa's. In Phoebe's case, her great height made some gentlemen avoid her. Her nervousness hindered it, but her conversational skills were superior to Lissa's—unfortunately, she could not meet enough gentlemen to appreciate them.

When they neared Lady Wynwood, a young man was just leading Phoebe out to the dance forming. Unfortunately, there was no excess of gentlemen around for Lissa to pick up the dregs. Indeed, Phoebe's partner looked to be grudgingly doing so, since he was a good four inches shorter than she was.

Fortunately, Lady Wynwood took pity upon Lissa. After they exchanged greetings, she took Lissa's hand with a warm smile. "I know just the partner for you, my dear. Won't you join me?" To Lissa's mother, she said, "You may safely leave your daughter with me."

At that point, Lissa would have said anything to escape her mother.

Lady Wynwood guided her through the crowd in the ballroom. She chatted with Lissa, sharing some mild gossip, pointing out men to avoid at all costs, naming women who would certainly be scrutinizing her behavior.

While the Gardiniers were eminently respectable, Lady Wynwood's acquaintance was wider and perhaps possessed deeper pockets. She was also a fount of information.

Lady Wynwood was about to steer her toward Mr. Collingworth before Lissa indicated she had just danced with him, so she instead detoured toward another young man, Mr. Gillard, and ~~bullied~~ suggested that he ask Lissa to dance the next set.

They had not long to wait until it began, but the steps of the dance did not allow them to converse until the next figure, so Lissa had that much more time to think of an innocuous discussion topic. "Mr. Gillard, what have you enjoyed most this Season?"

"I am most interested in theater," he said with some fervor. "London has many wonderful playhouses."

"Indeed? What have been your favorite plays?"

"I saw Kemble playing *Hamlet* at the Drury Lane Theater. Simply marvelous." His eyes glowed as he recalled the performance. "He was so dignified and had such a magnificent presence on stage."

"I saw *Hamlet* a few weeks ago," Lissa said. "He was indeed quite wonderful." She privately felt that Kemble's performance was a trifle dull, lacking in the strong emotions of other actors, but she kept her opinions to herself. Her mother would be proud.

Or her mother would simply assert that Lissa should not need to be praised for simple common sense and tact.

"But I most enjoy comedies," Mr. Gillard continued. "I recently saw *She Stoops to Conquer* at Haymarket Theatre."

"That sounds delightful."

"And the other day, I saw a new production called *The Goose in the Bedroom* at the Kitten Theater. Quite amusing, I assure you."

"How lovely." Lissa had heard other young ladies whisper scandalously about places such as the Kitten Theater, where the entertainments were of a less cultured and more improper variety. She had to bite her tongue not to ask, *Was not the plot as thin as the actresses' costumes?*

She was certain Mr. Gillard did not bring up the place in order to scandalize her sensibilities, and so she smiled vapidly and nodded at his exuberance over his chance meeting with one of the persons employed at the theater to move scenery, and how they had raved about the performance together.

"Mr. Dunmark has said he would like to write a play of his own," Mr. Gillard said. "I look forward to seeing it performed."

At last, the dance concluded, and Mr. Gillard deposited her to stand alone in a corner of the ballroom. He made a quick escape so that yet another woman as frightening as Lady Wynwood would not force him to dance.

Lissa's vantage point gave her an unobstructed view of the small alcoves that dotted the walls, created by artfully placed potted palms and ferns. She should have been mortified to be alone and without a dance partner, but she found it refreshing to be allowed a few minutes to watch the proceedings without fear of censure from her mother or anyone else.

There was Lady Barbara, standing in silent adoration of Mr. Harwell, who only had eyes for Lady Annamaria, who was unfortunately recently engaged to Lord Spenceley, and as far as Lissa could tell, both parties cared not a whit for each other.

A little ways away from the romantic drama stood Lord Stoude, alone as usual. Lissa fancied herself to be the only person to notice him, for he tended to fade into the periphery of every entertainment. Many young women had insisted that he was cold and reserved, utterly disinterested in marriage. Lissa wondered if perhaps it was resentment over the fact that he gave frosty responses to any young woman attempting to flirt with him. But too many had received the same treatment at his hands, so it was not merely a disgruntled young miss spreading stories to assuage her pride.

But there was something about Lord Stoude's posture that made Lissa's eyes linger upon him. While outwardly he appeared to be watching the dancing, a very subtle tilt of his head, the slight leaning of his body, made her immediately wonder if he was trying to overhear someone's conversation.

He stood in an alcove, surrounded by leafy potted shrubs, and his vision would have been blocked as to the occupants of the alcoves to either side of him. Lissa, however, could see into the farther alcove, which contained the conversation that appeared to interest him.

Two gentlemen stood close to each other in a corner of the ballroom similar to where Lissa had hidden herself. One was tall, slender, and fair, and although they had not been introduced, Lissa had heard him referred to as Mr. Galland. The other man was unknown to her, slightly shorter but similarly fair.

They would have been unaware of anyone on the other side of the potted plants listening in on their conversation, which appeared to be quite serious.

Lissa took in the men's shifting eyes as they slowly roved the ballroom, the lips barely opening as they spoke to one another, the hunching of shoulders as if to shield themselves from any others. They were not speaking of sports or politics, but something they wished to remain private.

Lord Stoude could not have seen them, but Lissa spotted the moment the two men began turning toward the direction where he hid.

She did not know what propelled her feet forward, but suddenly she stood before Lord Stoude. Without even a curtsy, she said, as if the two of them were continuing a conversation, "Why, thank you, Lord Stoude, I am pleased you enjoyed my mother's card party last week. Might I hope to see you at the soirée tomorrow night?"

He had seemed indifferent when she first came up to him, then startled, and when she began speaking, a crease appeared between his dark brows for a moment. She could not tell if he was confused or affronted, but since he hesitated in showing his displeasure, it allowed the two gentlemen to walk past his hiding place.

Mr. Galland and his friend gave hardly a glance at Lissa and Lord Stoude, who looked for all the world like any other couple socializing in the room. If they had walked past and seen him alone, would they have been suspicious or equally as unruffled as they appeared to be now?

She looked up at Lord Stoude, wondering how he would react. His eyes narrowed as they fell upon her, and perhaps there was even a spark of amusement. Or was that admiration? Or was Lissa only seeing what she wished to see?

He did not respond as she had expected. She thought he might pretend indignation, or surprise, or confusion.

Instead, he simply bowed to her. "I bid you good evening, Miss Gardinier."

Lissa felt a rush of exhilaration that he remembered her name, but it was almost immediately doused as the meaning of his words sank in, and she realized that he had moved to walk away from her.

She had already done one highly unusual action with him—what was one more? She didn't bother to rein in her annoyance as she said, "How fortunate that my assistance requires no gratitude. I suppose my acting was so subtle, the emotions so believable, that you've quite forgotten whatever it was that I have done."

Lissa immediately regretted her words, expecting a blast of scorn from him and another scolding from her mother.

But Lord Stoude's infamously chilly expression thawed enough for the corners of his lips to deepen and curve upward a smidgen. Not quite a smile, but not a look of disdain, either.

"And what have you done, Miss Gardinier?" Lord Stoude looked almost … she would say *delighted*, but the word was incongruous with his reputation as being stand-offish and dispassionate toward everyone.

Lissa would have demanded why he was attempting to overhear Mr. Galland's conversation, but she had the suspicion that he would immediately stop almost-smiling at her and take his leave. "And really, you would be quite handsome if you smiled more often."

His eyebrows rose as she realized she'd spoken aloud.

If it were any other man, and if she weren't so exuberant about rescuing him from notice by Mr. Galland—and annoyed that he refused to acknowledge it—she might have added that he was quite handsome even when he didn't smile. But he might guess that was a bit of a lie, so perhaps it was just as well she didn't try to assuage his pride.

So instead, she said what she honestly wished to say to him. "The least you can do is dance with me, and I shall let you eavesdrop on other couples in the ballroom as you so desire."

He gave her a pained look. "I have no wish to eavesdrop on other couples, Miss Gardinier."

"That implies that Mr. Galland's conversation was of a more serious nature. You are a man of substance and have no need to rob him, and as far as I know, Mr. Galland has no daughters for you to kidnap, although he might have one or two by-blows—"

"Why do you immediately assume I intend to steal from him or deflower a virgin?" Lord Stoude looked slightly scandalized.

"It must be because I have recently read one of Mrs. Radcliffe's works," she said thoughtfully. "There are certainly enough dastardly noblemen in those novels to make one believe the entire aristocracy is degenerate."

"And it is inappropriate for you to mention by-blows," he added grumpily.

She brightened. "Then you should dance with me to distract me from such topics."

He sighed. "Won't you take a stroll about the room with me, Miss Gardinier?"

"I have not missed the fact that you disregarded my suggestion of a dance," she said as she placed her hand on his arm, blithely ignoring the fact that her mere suggestion was rather rude. "But it is better than standing in a corner or discussing hunting dog pedigrees."

"I beg your pardon?"

"Are you acquainted with Mr. Collingworth? He is a very amiable gentleman, and his passion for hunting dogs rivals none. He was regaling me with the courtship woes of his hound Lickspittle Furrybottom."

A choking sound erupted from Lord Stoude's throat, but aside from a stiffness of his jaw, his face remained polite and impassive. "Indeed?" His voice might have been a bit higher pitched than normal, but it was difficult to tell over the strains of the music and the murmur of voices.

"She was eventually made happy by a wonderful dog named Snout Droolalot."

This time, Lord Stoude sputtered sharply. He glared at her. "That is pure invention."

"It is not, I tell you the truth. We were just discussing their litter, and what can be more delightful conversation than the topic of puppies?"

She had not noticed it at first, but Lord Stoude was walking at a rather fast clip. He barely had time to nod at acquaintances as they passed by. Lissa hoped she was not offending a matron by her mere dip of the head at some of them, for she could not stop to curtsy.

"Perhaps you might know of a young lady as enthusiastic about hunting dogs as Mr. Collingworth? He really is a nice man, and it seems a shame that he has no one to share his interests."

"I am afraid that …" Lord Stoude suddenly broke off. "Truth be told, I have a cousin who is rather fanatical about the hunt."

She smiled up at him. "They sound perfect for each other. There, do you not feel the satisfaction of an opportunity to bring others joy?"

He eyed her. "You are assuming they will find each other pleasant company. They may loathe each other."

"I find it hard to believe that two hearts who are both enlivened by the thrill of the chase would not be compatible. I wonder if they will name a dog after us? Baying Stoudegarden, perhaps?"

Lord Stoude snorted with laughter, although he covered it up with a cough. "I dearly hope not." He turned to study her face with narrowed eyes. "Why are you so interested in others, Miss Gardinier?"

"Are people not fascinating?"

"You might do better to ignore your observations."

His words were faintly ominous, and therefore, Lissa laughed in his face. "So dramatic! Was that meant to sound threatening? Or perhaps you are concerned for me? Why *were* you eavesdropping on Mr. Galland?"

She had not been even attempting to curb her mouth, and so she regretted it as soon as she brought up the topic.

Lord Stoude's face was still polite, but became as smooth as marble. "I thank you for an entertaining diversion, Miss Gardinier." He stopped in front of a young man who looked to be barely old enough to attend the ball. "May I introduce you to my cousin, Mr. Calveston? Percy, this is Miss Gardinier."

She had barely risen from her curtsy when Lord Stoude began to turn away. "I bid you good evening, Miss Gardinier."

Lissa stared at his back a moment before Mr. Calveston stammered, "Would you care to dance, Miss Gardinier?"

She accepted graciously, determined to put Lord Stoude from her mind. Considering how she had blundered in her dealings with him, she was unlikely to see him again this Season.

Chapter Two

Lissa really did try to avoid Lord Stoude, but he kept turning up at all the events to which her mother dragged her. It was understandable since they seemed to possess similar social circles. But she resented the fact that it appeared as though she were following him around, when she had been earnestly trying to do the opposite.

Although once she determined they had happened to attend the same party, there was no harm in watching him for more suspicious behavior, surely?

She had learned from two matrons at the ball the other night that the name of the man to whom Mr. Galland had been speaking was Mr. Morfin. She did not see either of them at the next few gatherings, and at first she thought Lord Stoude would do nothing more interesting than drift about the room, silent and aloof except for the few occasions he would speak to this gentleman or that.

However, at each of the next three parties that Lord Stoude attended, he seemed to exhibit similar behavior as he had with Mr. Galland. In general, Lord Stoude would be quiet and unobtrusive, which allowed him to effortlessly choose a space half-hidden by plants or another group of people that afforded him an opportunity to eavesdrop on other guests.

It was not obvious that he was listening in. Lissa only noticed because she was watching him so closely. His eyes would glaze over slightly as he pretended to look out at the room but was secretly attentive to what he heard nearby.

Lord Stoude did not merely indulge in his prying behavior. At other times, he would interact quite charmingly with various gentlemen with whom he was acquainted. It was his behavior *before* he sought out those people that aroused Lissa's curiosity.

He would scan the room with a dispassionate expression, but his eyes keen and focused. Once he found his target, he would make his way toward them as naturally and quickly as he could.

Lord Stoude was doing that at the present moment, at Mrs. Twinsom's card party.

Lissa followed his gaze and thought he might be going to speak to Lord Russby. He was a gentleman of loud opinions, for she had overheard those herself at some point this evening, but she had noticed that earlier, Lord Russby had spoken quietly with another gentleman whom she did not know. It seemed slightly odd behavior for a man so professedly frank in his speech.

Lissa had been speaking with Phoebe and attempting to encourage the young woman. "I am certain Mr. Greer was not offended that you stepped upon his foot. After all, he was wearing shoes whilst you wore only satin slippers."

"He winced as though I'd jammed a nail through his ankle," Phoebe said morosely. Unlike when Lissa saw her in the country, she was hunching her shoulders, but instead, it only made her appear larger.

"Stand up straight. You look like a bull in a china shop attempting not to damage anything."

Phoebe only half-heartedly unbent her spine. With her head lowered, she looked insecure and unhappy.

Lord Stoude stationed himself near a card table, supposedly interested in watching the gameplay, with his back to Lord Russby. Lissa did not think he would overhear anything of import, for the room was crowded and Lord Russby could have been overheard by anyone. He would not discuss something like an illegally acquired art piece or a smuggling run.

That thought made her pause. Perhaps Lord Stoude was seeking out potential smugglers among the *ton*? But should he not leave that duty to the excise men?

At last, Lady Wynwood arrived to ~~drag~~ lead Phoebe to a card table. She invited Lissa also, but she disliked cards in general. In Whist, she could guess with some accuracy as to each person's hand based upon the cards that were discarded, which made her frustrated with her partner. Round games were too dependent upon chance rather than skill, which bored her.

She copied Lord Stoude and pretended to watch a table of matrons (whose play was rather ruthless) while keeping an eye on him. He surprised her by wandering around the table, still observing the game, but positioning himself near another gentleman also watching the players. He said something to the older man and was answered. After another moment of silence, he said something again, and the two began discussing something.

Lissa made her way to that corner of the room, and by the simple expedience of standing to watch a neighboring table, managed to listen in on the two men's conversations.

"Yes, I heard it from Mr. Jardine," Lord Stoude was saying. "How much did Mr. Tuller lose to you?"

"Nearly twenty thousand pounds," the other gentleman said.

Lord Stoude shook his head. "I'd heard rumors he was in tick. If he gave you his vowels, you might not see that amount anytime soon."

"On the contrary, he paid in full the next day."

Lord Stoude looked astonished, although there was some stiffness of his mouth that made Lissa think he was merely pretending. "Is that so?" he asked. "Perhaps he won at another table?"

"I had not heard it. But you can be sure I shall not sit down with him again," the man said. "I have no wish to beggar his wife and daughter further."

Lissa would have thought Lord Stoude was simply relaying harmless gossip, but the fact that he already knew about Mr. Tuller repaying his debt promptly made her suspicious. Why was he inquiring about another man's losses?

No, she corrected herself. Not his losses, but his sudden influx of funds he ought not to have had.

The game Lissa was watching ended, and the players rose to seek refreshment. She wandered away without looking at Lord Stoude.

Which was why she nearly jolted in surprise when he found her ~~hiding~~ enjoying a quiet moment on a chair shoved against the wall next to the empty pianoforte.

"I am surprised you did not join the round game," he said as he dropped into the chair next to hers.

"I did not even see you approaching," she said, holding a hand to her rapidly beating heart. "I suppose you have cultivated your ability to traverse unnoticed."

Ignoring her jab at him, he nodded to the nearest table, a large one with several young ladies and gentlemen in a rather rowdy game.

"They did not ask me to join them, and I disliked making an odd number at table," she said primly.

"You do not seem the sort to care about that," he retorted.

She tried to be offended, but could not because he had taken the time to discern her tendencies. "To be honest, I would likely say something offensive or scandalous, so I did not try to join them."

"Scandalous? Surely you would not say anything of which your mother would disapprove?"

"And what would you know of the sorts of things of which my mother would approve?" She sniffed. "If you must know, I would likely say something about Napoleon."

His gaze suddenly grew keen. "And what would you say?"

"Nothing unpatriotic, I assure you." Now she regretted not guarding her tongue. But it was too easy for her to remain uncensored with him, for he had already seen her at her most natural and unladylike.

"Such as?" he insisted, his gaze growing more austere.

She gave in, for she admitted that she was slightly intimidated by his handsome face looming over her. "I read that the Battle of Eylau last month was carnage on both sides. Napoleon may be a brilliant tactician, but his losses in Prussia are mounting. I wonder how long the French army can sustain such attrition."

Lissa steeled herself for his disapproval, ignoring the painful twisting of her stomach at the thought that he would be repulsed by her.

Instead, he looked rather stupefied at her words.

"May I ask you not to stare at me in astonishment as though I were a squirrel that has suddenly quoted Shakespeare?" she asked acidly.

He blinked. "I beg your pardon. As to your comment, what intrigues me is how the Prussians will respond ..."

The two of them remained unnoticed in the corner for nearly a quarter of an hour as they discussed the war. Lissa admitted she had not been so thoroughly entertained in all her life, for the gentlemen in her family were not as avid in their following of the battles, and she had no one else with whom to air her views.

They were interrupted when the round game concluded with loud exclamations of triumph and losses. Lord Stoude glanced in that direction as though abruptly woken from a dream.

Lissa tried to be straightforward in facing her fears and disappointments. "I know you did not seek me out to teach me military strategies," she said. "I suspect that you have an enigmatic reason for eavesdropping or pursuing conversations with others. It must be important, so why are you wasting time sitting with me?"

She knew why she was pushing him away—if she did it first, it would not hurt so much when he said his peace and left her. He was the most fascinating man she had met, but her dowry was modest and her face barely passable. She did not wish to think more fondly of him than she already did, or else the end of the Season might bring her more heartache than she had expected.

"I am at a loss as to why you think I have been eavesdropping," he said. "I hope you do not think me so rude as that."

Her eyes flattened. "What is rude is that you are continuing to treat me as though I were entirely ignorant. It is insulting."

She had the satisfaction of seeing guilt and contrition in his blue eyes. But he did not acknowledge her words. "I have noticed you watching me, Miss Gardinier, and I simply wished to know why."

Lissa herself did not know why he captivated her. His unusual actions brought anticipation to what had been a dull Season, but she did not know why she sought to understand his motivations. Or perhaps she was infatuated with the first man who witnessed her true self and did not back away from her as though she were a bad-tempered goat.

But she did not wish for him to know that. So she said, "I have been observing you because you are acting so suspiciously."

His brows drew down. "I have not been ... I have been entirely myself ..."

She affected a tiresome sigh. "You really must be a little more subtle, my lord."

"Subtle—?!" He frowned deeply as he stood. With a jerk, he gave a stiff bow. "Good evening, Miss Gardinier."

Lissa had the dubious satisfaction of watching the man walk away from her again, this time in a huff.

Chapter Three

Lissa was certain that she must have finally offended Lord Stoude and he would avoid her. So she nearly fell out of her chair when he sought her out at a ball the next day.

It might have been romantic if he'd come up to her while she was in the ballroom, but alas, she was sitting at a chair conveniently placed near the buffet table in the dining room of Lady Relford's townhouse, filling her plate every time it emptied without needing to stand up.

Two elderly women were leaving the room at the time, but Lord Stoude ignored their stares and whispers as he brushed past them. They had barely gone before he promptly sat down next to Lissa.

She paused in the act of putting a lobster patty in her mouth and stared at him incredulously before remembering to close her mouth and put down the patty. "Good evening, my lord."

He simply nodded without speaking, looking over the food she'd piled onto her plate, then abruptly stood up again and went to the buffet to collect some food for himself. She almost expected him to pick at a few things and then leave the dining room, but he selected a slice of veal pie and then sat back down next to her.

Lissa had finished her lobster patty and wanted more, but felt self-conscious about shoveling food onto her plate directly from her seat right in front of him. (It had also been rude to do it in front of the two elderly ladies, but Lissa hadn't cared half so much about their good opinion.) So she picked at the pineapple, which was sour.

She wasn't entirely certain if she ought to strike up a conversation or if he wished to eat in peace, so she opted for silence (her mother would approve). But if she had been eating, she might not have noticed when he took a bite of veal pie and his face contorted.

He shuddered and set his fork down. He looked as though he strongly wished to spit out his mouthful but was too genteel to do so.

"It is a bit heavy on the pepper today," Lissa said. She had found it quite refreshing, so his reaction surprised her.

After long moments of suffering, he managed to swallow. "Indeed," he said in a strangled voice.

"It was not to your liking, I take it?"

He wiped his mouth with a napkin. "I do not much care for spicy food."

Lissa hadn't thought it was quite *that* spicy, but her younger brother had a similar preference, so she both understood him and knew what to do. She plucked a fresh plate from the table next to her and took some of the lobster patties.

"Allow me," she said to him and stole his plate from his slackened fingers, replacing it with the lobster patties. At his nonplussed expression, she explained, "They are a bit more bland."

Perhaps she should not have treated him as though he were a fourteen-year-old boy, but he reminded her so much of her brother, Henry, and so she had responded automatically. He looked down at his new plate, then back at her.

Warmth climbed up her neck. She was about to take the plate back when he tasted the patty.

He nodded. "It is quite delicious."

His piece of pie had only a single bite taken—and with a clean fork—so Lissa began finishing it. She enjoyed the way the pepper made her tongue numb.

Only as his eyebrows rose did she realize that what she had done was likely quite uncouth.

But in the next moment, she was taking another bite. Lord Stoude had already seen some of her true nature, so there was no use trying to pretend in front of him.

"Did you read the newspapers yesterday, Miss Gardinier? There was a piece about the Royal Navy."

She had indeed read it and felt the writer was unjust in his assertions. She voiced what had come to her mind when reading the article. "The tone was so irritable that it sounded as though the writer were suffering from indigestion as he wrote."

Lord Stoude smiled, and her embarrassment vanished.

That night was the first of several with Lord Stoude. He would always find her when she had escaped to a quiet corner, and they would discuss the war, or Parliament, or any topic that Lissa cared to introduce.

She looked forward to those few minutes each evening when she could speak at length on the subjects about which she cared the most. She had no need to pretend to be quiet and proper, for Lord Stoude did not seem to mind. In fact, the way he continued to seek her out seemed to indicate that he might even value her opinions and conversation.

Of course, he always appeared when she was hidden from the rest of the party, so they were never interrupted or noticed by anyone. She found it remarkable that he always knew exactly when to find her and where she would be hiding.

Several nights later, Lissa limped to the pianoforte in the corner of the drawing room at the Church-Prattons' ball. She sat down heavily upon the seat in front of the instrument even though she had no intention of playing. She was partially obscured by a table laden with drinks, so she hoped to go unnoticed for a few minutes before her mother found her again.

She tried not to hope that Lord Stoude would come up to her, and also tried not to feel so pleased when he did.

He sat in a chair next to the instrument, his eyes raking over her.

"Good evening, my lord."

He nodded distractedly. "Were you limping?"

"It is a trifle."

"What happened?" he persisted.

She sighed. "I met Mr. Adderly, who was unfortunately in his cups. He attempted to guide me out of the drawing room, but when I resisted, he pulled at my wrist rather forcefully and I stumbled. He then stepped on my foot." She honestly did not know how *she* could be the one to stumble and yet *he* was the one who stepped on her. She did not think she was so remarkably clumsy, and yet Mr. Adderly was even clumsier still. He must have been far more drunk than he appeared.

Lord Stoude's face suddenly darkened. "Mr. Adderly, you say?"

Lissa shivered at the chill in his voice. "Are you acquainted with him?"

"Of a sort." He frowned, then added, "It might be best to avoid his company in future. He was recently sent down from university, and the rumors about him are … unsavory."

"Surely all young men drink and gamble when they first come to town?"

"Indeed, but it is said that his attentions toward young ladies have been … less than honorable."

The chill enveloped her body now. "Thank you, sir. I shall take great care in any further acquaintance with him."

There was an awkward silence between them. She was grateful for his concern—her mother had only cared that Mr. Adderly was from a wealthy family and was willing to dance with Lissa, and so she had not made more inquiries into him.

"Are you at all interested in fashion, Miss Gardinier?" he suddenly asked.

She frowned. "Are you implying my dress is displeasing?"

"Of course not." He looked genuinely appalled. "I beg your pardon. I meant in terms of fashion in general. Do you keep up with the ladies' magazines?"

"Oh." She should have known he would not deliberately insult her. But then again, despite their stimulating conversations, she knew very little of him. "Yes. My younger sister, Miriam, reads them several times over. I am not so fervent, but I do keep apprised of style and trends."

"I suppose most who arrive for the Season are the same." His eyes surveyed what he could see of the crowded drawing room from their corner of it. "Are there any young women in particular who are at the forefront?"

"What do you mean?"

"Oh, any woman whose mode of dress is more *au courant* than all others."

She sat back, and her eyes narrowed as she studied him. "I shall answer the question you did not ask. In general, I do not see women whose gowns might have been made by, say, a Parisian modiste within the last year, women who may have connections that enable them to keep abreast of the latest designs before they have even crossed the Channel to our shores."

His face had grown very still, which was more telling than if he had responded to her.

She had been watching the men with whom he interacted as well as those upon whom he seemed to eavesdrop. There was no discernable pattern at first, but then she started to see the threads binding them all together.

Men who suddenly received an influx of money, men who engaged in certain political salons, men involved in trade yet whose fortunes had not waned with the blockade of French ports, men who traveled outside of England.

Lord Stoude was a spy. And he was seeking out any who might sympathize with France.

It was understandable. Surely the Crown would need to keep watch over malcontents. She did not understand why Lord Stoude was tasked with this, but he was surely in an excellent position to speak to those of the *ton* who might wish to aid Napoleon.

"That is, in general," Lissa repeated. "However, the other week, I did notice that the gown Mrs. Whichard wore to a ball had superior drape compared to lesser silks, and while I am not as knowledgable about French damask patterns, the fabric had been woven in a design I've never seen before."

"Mrs. Whichard, you say?" He was intrigued but trying not to show it.

"Perhaps you may find yourself nearby when she is speaking to one of her friends," Lissa said.

She expected him to deny that he did anything so crass as eavesdropping, but instead, he bowed his head. A silent acknowledgment, but not a formal one.

She wanted to ask him about his doings and was surprised at herself that she did not. Ever since that first ball when she had artlessly asked him about Mr. Galland and he had closed himself off from her, she had not ventured into those murky waters.

It was perhaps because she assumed that what he was doing was important, and an ignorant girl like herself ought not to stick her nose into it.

He was watching her warily, uncertain how she would respond to his nod.

Lissa refrained from voicing the questions crowding her mind. "I have heard there is a very fine production of *Don Giovanni* playing at the King's Theatre. Have you seen it?"

The relief in his eyes, followed by a half-smile of gratitude, seemed to wrap around her like a gentle breeze. Or a sweet embrace.

"I have not, Miss Gardinier. Do you plan to attend?"

"I …" She suddenly spotted her mother, who seemed to be headed directly for her. "Good gracious! How did she find me so quickly this time?"

Instead of being confused at her words, he had mirth brimming from his eyes even as he tried to keep his mouth sober. "Your mother?"

"I suppose I do tend to favor musical instruments as places to hide. I shall need to add more variety." She stood and bobbed a curtsy to him. "I beg your pardon, but I must effect a hasty retreat."

She whisked away, shielded from her mother's keen eye by the drinks table and a group of men clustered around it.

Had that been a hint of disappointment in his expression as she left? Surely not. He was doing Important Work (she assumed his work required the capitalization) and was likely using her as a foil somehow to more effectively ferret out information.

Unfortunately, in her mad dash to escape her mother's notice, she had not been attentive enough about where she was headed. She found herself next to Miss Church-Pratton, the daughter of the hostess, and her friend Miss Amsden, in the midst of a conversation.

"He is an unfeeling wretch," Miss Church-Pratton complained, her eyes fixed upon a young man going through the lines of the dance.

"Now, Belinda, you must see that he could not dance more than twice with you. Of course he would dance with other ladies." Miss Amsden seemed to be trying to soothe her friend, but there was a gleeful light in her eye, as though she were entertained by her friend's misery.

"But he is my betrothed," Miss Church-Pratton said. "There is no harm in dancing more often with one's betrothed, surely?"

Lissa looked out at the dancers and saw a dark-haired young man with a rather stiff, upright bearing who was dancing with Miss Gillard. The young woman was barely fifteen, and yet her parents had brought her to London for her comeout this year.

Miss Church-Pratton's sulking face was nonetheless quite pretty, although her blue eyes coldly surveyed the crowd. The ball was to celebrate her engagement to Lieutenant Terralton, and while Lissa had not thought that the two had appeared very close, perhaps she was more attached to her swain than she let on.

"At the very least, he should not dance if he cannot dance with me," Miss Church-Pratton said. "Why am I left to stand here without a partner while he escorts every whey-faced miss in the ballroom?"

Ah, so the truth was that Miss Church-Pratton was unhappy that she had no dance partner. Lissa thought it was rather unreasonable of her to blame him for dancing with others.

Unfortunately, Miss Church-Pratton noticed Lissa at that moment, and her face turned an unpleasant shade of puce. She, the belle of the ball, was forced to stand and watch along with someone as unpopular as Lissa.

"Why, Miss Gardinier, I do beg your pardon. I did not even notice you were there. You do tend to *fade into the background*," Miss Church-Pratton said in a sweet voice.

Lissa's mouth tightened. She and Miss Church-Pratton had debuted last year, and so the two of them had seen each other quite often as the Season progressed without prospects for either of them. Miss Church-Pratton had seemed to think Lissa possessed a sort of bad luck that kept the men away from her.

"I have not seen you dance yet, Miss Gardinier," Miss Amsden said, tittering behind her fan. "Perhaps the gentlemen have forgotten you are there? Shall I venture forth to remind them?"

"Now, Cala, not every young woman can be *noticed*," Miss Church-Pratton said as if she herself had not been raging only moments before at being left alone for the dance. "After all, a lady must be *lively* to catch a gentleman's attention."

Lissa kept her face impassive, although Miss Church-Pratton's words cut rather deeply. Her mother had often lamented that she needed to be more *lively* in order to appeal to young men.

"And how is your sister enjoying her Season, Miss Gardinier?" Miss Amsden asked with false friendliness. "I was astonished to discover you were related. She is so very pretty and with such charming manners."

"Yes, Miriam is quite popular," Lissa managed to reply in a credibly calm voice. Her mother kept comparing the two sisters and lamenting as she compared Lissa to her own Season many years ago. Lissa had had quite enough of her mother's complaining that her eldest daughter was not as vivacious and endearing as the younger.

Their barbed comments pricked her like poisonous thorns, working their destruction deeper into her heart. She should not have been so affected by the careless words of those such as Miss Church-Pratton and Miss Amsden—she prided herself on her disinterest in the opinions of others, especially those for whom she held no regard.

And yet her spirits began to sink within her, like a leaking ship on turbulent waters. Apparently, she was not as immune to the humiliation of such comparisons as she had thought.

Like a wild predator that had caught the scent of blood, Miss Church-Pratton advanced. "Perhaps your sister might find a husband for you, Miss Gardinier, once she is married. Once I am Mrs. Terralton, I myself shall help all my friends to find respectable partners."

"Surely there can be someone who can appreciate your *unique* qualities, Miss Gardinier," Miss Amsden said, smiling and displaying her slightly crooked teeth.

"I am certain you are correct," Lissa forced herself to say in a slow, measured voice. This clenching in her heart, this twisting of her stomach, this feeling that she was alone …

She forced herself to remember the Bible verse the rector had read at church this past Sunday, for at the time it had felt like a balm upon her bruised soul. *For the Lord seeth not as man seeth; for man looketh on the outward appearance, but the Lord looketh on the heart.* God surely valued her more for her inner character than her outward appearance or social status.

But it was difficult for her to truly believe that anyone would want her enough to marry her. Of if they did, they would only see the silent and reclusive Miss Gardinier, who was spiritless and dull.

The dance ended, and Lieutenant Terralton escorted Miss Gillard to her mother, then returned to Miss Church-Pratton's side. She was giving him a whispered scolding for his inconsiderate behavior.

Lissa found herself pitying the young man. He was not handsome, with a rugged face, and his hair had already become disorderly, sticking out from his head and making him look surprised. He withstood the unreasonable scolding from his betrothed with a cool but polite expression, although Lissa caught the tightening of his jaw at certain choice words from Miss Church-Pratton.

If marriage would have as unhappy a future as theirs was likely to be, Lissa didn't wish it.

If only she could convince her mother of that desire.

But suddenly a familiar pair of shoes entered her vision, and she realized she'd been staring at the floor. She lifted her eyes to see Lord Stoude standing before her.

He greeted Lieutenant Terralton by name, even though the younger man would not have been in his social set, and he also bowed to Miss Church-Pratton and Miss Amsden. Miss Church-Pratton preened, likely expecting the infamously detached Lord Stoude to have unusually come to ask her to dance.

But then he shook up the entire group by turning to Lissa. "Would you do me the honor of dancing with me, Miss Gardinier?"

Chapter Four

Lissa tried not to gape, but she suspected her jaw dropped open.

Lord Stoude hardly ever danced. Occasionally he would be captured by a society matron and prodded to ask a certain young lady for a dance, but he had been known to deliberately disoblige some women, giving him a rather intimidating reputation. Women had stopped trying to force him to dance to their tune (rather literally).

And he never took the initiative to seek out anyone and ask her to dance. Except for right at this moment.

Lissa suddenly realized she hadn't yet answered him. "Are you ser—rather, I would be honored, my lord."

His face was a trifle stiff as he led her away from the stunned women. "For a moment, I had the mortifying fear that you would refuse me," he muttered in a low voice.

"I beg your pardon. Your question had the effect of a blow to the face, and I was attempting to regain my composure."

"Surely it was not so shocking."

"It was every bit as shocking! But I must thank you for doing so in front of Miss Church-Pratton and Miss Amsden. It could not have happened to more worthy witnesses."

His mouth had tightened as she spoke the young women's names. "I did not like how they spoke to you."

They reached the crowded ballroom floor and separated for the lines of the dance, so Lissa had a few moments to compose herself after such a revelation. Had he been eavesdropping upon them? She had not even known he was nearby. Perhaps she was not so perceptive as she had believed.

And he had cared enough to … what? Want to rescue her? Want to put them in their place? The thought of either made her feel a wonderful warmth within.

When the movements of the dance brought them together again, she said, "I thank you for your attention, my lord. You are very kind."

"For asking you to dance?" He tried to lessen the nobility of his action, but she would have none of it.

"For saving me from such harpies. If I had not promised my mother I would behave, I might have compared Miss Church-Pratton's hair to dirty Thames water."

"If you said it with a smile, I'm certain she would not even notice the insult."

She beamed at him. "Was that a joke, my lord? How astonishing!"

He frowned at her.

Lissa ignored his displeasure. "If you would but take snuff and wax eloquent about your tailor, you shall become like any other gentleman in London."

"I *am* like any other gentleman in London."

"*Now* you are, for you are dancing."

He scowled at her, and she saw a red glow about his square jaw. But when she laughed at him, he merely sighed and continued the dance.

When the set ended and he escorted her from the floor, she expected the whispers from the crowd. She would rather face them than her mother at the moment, so she requested that he deposit her near Phoebe and Lady Wynwood.

The two ladies cast curious glances at Lord Stoude after he bowed and walked away, but otherwise, they did not pester her about her dance partner. Lady Wynwood already knew why Lissa had joined them. "You cannot hide from your mother forever, my girl."

"I can hide until the first fever of excitement has passed." Lissa moved a bit further into Phoebe's shadow, grateful that the woman was so tall. "Then her interrogation shall be only one hour instead of two."

"I think you underestimate her enthusiasm," Lady Wynwood said dryly.

Tto Lissa's dismay, a young man approached to ask Phoebe to dance, and then Lady Wynwood's longtime friend, Mr. Drydale, came to claim his promised dance with that lady. However, he did ask for the next set with Lissa.

"How else may I quiz you about Lord Stoude's singular behavior?" he teased Lissa with a wink as he led Lady Wynwood away.

Lady Wynwood slapped him with her fan. "Behave, Sol." But then they moved too far away for Lissa to hear what else she said to him.

She had resigned herself to standing on the edges of the ballroom for yet another dance when a young woman approached her. Lissa immediately dropped into a curtsy. "Good evening, my lady."

Lady Charline Halberstam, daughter of the Earl of Rowsby, was in her third Season, and Lissa had been introduced last year. Unlike Lissa, Lady Charline's parents seemed perfectly content to allow their daughter to remain unmarried, and they had not attempted to arrange a match for her.

Of all the people Lissa might have expected would approach her for gossip about Lord Stoude, Lady Charline was rather far down the list.

The young lady smiled at Lissa, but she couldn't help feeling there was a slightly cold, calculating gilding to it. She had not been very friendly with Lissa last year, but she had not been unkind, either. In all respects, she was vastly superior to women like Miss Church-Pratton and Miss Amsden.

"You have caused quite a stir, have you not? Lord Stoude rarely surprises anyone, and yet his actions tonight might seem to be making a declaration."

"Surely not, my lady." Lissa struggled to keep her expression innocent, not wishing to appear too pleased or flustered. Her mind swirled madly in panic at the thought of salacious gossip that might paint Lord Stoude in an unfavorable light as the swain of someone so unremarkable as herself, and she attempted to nip that in the bud. "I assure you, there is nothing between Lord Stoude and myself. It was merely an act of politeness. At best, we are friends."

"Oh? And yet Miss Church-Pratton and Miss Amsden seem thoroughly perturbed."

"From what I have heard of him, Lord Stoude regards the dance floor as warily as though it were a battlefield. He likely believed it was a strategic action."

Lady Charline glanced in the direction of the two aforementioned ladies with a hint of … was it exultation? "That may be so. Or perhaps you are simply too modest. I had thought there might be more to the matter than a single dance."

Lady Charline was not the type to enjoy amorous tales, and yet Lissa found it strange that she circled back to the topic. It was as if she wanted to see if she would trick Lissa into revealing any emotional entanglements.

And while Lissa couldn't say she wasn't attracted to Lord Stoude's strong, stoic figure, she certainly would not reveal that here. She straightened her back and looked Lady Charline in the eye, adopting a cool expression. "No, my lady. There is no romantic connection between us."

Now Lady Charline's smile had that slow, satisfied quality of a cat that had got into the cream. "Well, if that is the case, who am I to question you?"

It had been the right thing to say, for Lord Stoude's sake. And yet Lissa felt her heartbeat echo in the empty cavity in her chest.

"How are you enjoying this Season so far, Miss Gardinier?" Lady Charline asked in a lazy, cultured tone, but there was an impatient expectation to her gaze that made it clear she had some other motivation for her question. "I venture to guess that you are finding it more comfortable than your debut last year."

"Yes, the Season has been quite lovely," Lissa said automatically.

"Seeing as we are old friends, perhaps you might join me for an evening at the opera this week?"

Lissa continued to vapidly smile at Lady Charline as she attempted to regain her wits. What could she mean by the sudden invitation? But as she thought back to their conversation, she suddenly understood.

"I am honored, my lady, that you would think so highly of me." Lissa kept her voice pleasant and appropriately humble, but behind her mask, her temper began to simmer.

"Of course. Why should I not wish your company, when you are so charming and we have known each other since last year?"

"You flatter me, my lady. But surely one of your closer friends might desire to accompany you to the theater? I would not wish to take their place." Lissa's mother would be delighted at her sudden bout of deference—or perhaps vexed that Lissa did not take advantage of Lady Charline's generous offer.

Lady Charline ran roughshod over Lissa's hesitation. "Nonsense. It will be a pleasurable evening, for I shall invite Miss Templeton and Miss Farrimond, as well. My brother and his friend Mr. Cirling will be attending, as well as my cousin, Mr. Fitchette. I daresay you will enjoy the company."

"I am afraid I am not well acquainted with any of them. Perhaps they would resent an interloper amongst such an intimate party." Lissa was doing her best, but Lady Charline simply wasn't taking the hint. She was not very skilled at subtlety. It would be much easier if she could simply say, *I would rather prefer to eat mulch than join you and your friends at the opera.*

Lady Charline seemed incredulous that Lissa did not immediately jump at the opportunity to bask in her friends' congenial company. "You undervalue yourself, Miss Gardinier. They all find you quite agreeable, I assure you."

Lissa resigned herself to the inevitable.

"You must invite Lord Stoude, of course," Lady Charline said. "You mentioned that you are friends, did you not?"

There it was. "I do not know that he would accept my invitation."

"And why not? He has danced with you, which indicates he favors you more than other young women. Who better to entice him to an evening's entertainment? I imagine he would be pleased to join us."

"I shall certainly ask him, but I cannot promise that he shall agree." Lissa didn't want to ask him—perhaps she could artlessly mention it in passing: *You wouldn't wish to attend the opera with a woman who might have designs upon you, would you? And I'm certain her friends are quite tiresome.*

"I am certain he would not deny you such a request." Lady Charline looked positively gleeful. "I am looking forward to our evening together already."

Before Lissa could think of a way to tactfully voice her doubtfulness that Lord Stoude would do anything more than immediately shoot her down like a partridge, Lady Charline began chattering about the details of the evening.

Lissa had guessed she would be enlisted to persuade Lord Stoude to make up one of the party, but she still felt indignation at being so ill-used. And how would Lord Stoude react once she had taken advantage of their acquaintance?

Or even worse—what if he found the other company more amusing than her own?

Her evenings of rousing conversation were coming to an end, she feared. She should not be so disheartened, for she knew it was certain to happen eventually, although she had been hoping it would not have come so soon.

But more than her disappointment and the dread of her task to invite Lord Stoude, she felt burning resentment. For Lady Charline had swept her up into a current which was far beyond her control.

She didn't like it. But she also had no idea what to do about it.

Chapter Five

Lissa's younger sister, Miriam, had not been well-pleased when she heard about the invitation to the opera. If she could have transferred the invitation to her sister, she would have done so in a trice, for she had the sinking feeling that Lady Charline simply wanted to use Lissa for her own ends. She had no wish to spend the evening in the company of a woman whose motivations were so layered.

Although … was that entirely accurate? If Lord Stoude also attended the opera …

But every time the thought entered her mind, Lissa shooed it away like shooing away the hens back at home. He was unlikely to accept her invitation. In fact, her forwardness in presuming upon their tenuous friendship and dragging him into a party of individuals with whom she had little connection might give him a disgust of her.

But she did not voice any of these things to her sister, who only saw Lissa's silence as some sort of triumph over her. She complained to her mother, who nagged Lissa to ask Lady Charline to extend the invitation to Miriam, as well.

"I know not the size of the Halberstams' box," Lissa said. "It may not fit more, and Miriam would make it an odd number." Not that she particularly cared about the practice of making up even numbers, but she had the feeling Lady Charline certainly would.

"You see, Mama? Lissa is being deliberately disobliging." Miriam sulked in the corner of the coach as they rode toward the Farrimonds' party.

"Lissa, how can you be so uncharitable?" Her mother tried to glare at her, but the carriage happened to hit a large rut in the road at that moment, causing all of them to jump in their seats, and it took another minute for them to put themselves back to rights.

Lissa was about to relent and offer to ask Lady Charline if she might switch with her sister, but what if Lord Stoude accepted? In that situation, the thought of Miriam sitting next to him at the opera stayed her tongue. She had no reason to believe he would find her sister to be better company than herself, but she quailed at the thought of putting it to the test.

"You must ask Lady Charline to include me," Miriam demanded. "Mama, tell her she must."

"Yes, I do not see why you should not wish for your sister to enjoy the same entertainments," Mrs. Gardinier said.

Lissa winced, grimaced, and finally toppled like a fragile tree to the violent storm that was her mother and sister.

Due to the congestion of other vehicles discharging the guests, the Gardiniers' carriage inched forward at a crawl, but they finally alighted before the Farrimonds' townhouse. Miriam flounced ahead, impatient to meet up with her friends and the beaus she had gathered around her in the few short weeks of the Season. Tonight, she wore an especially lavish gown of pale orange with gold thread, and on any other young woman, it might have looked garish. But on Miriam, the shimmer of the gold brought out the shine of her blonde curls, and the orange color gave her pale skin a slight blush.

Lissa had also dressed with care. In fact, she had paid more attention to her *toilette* in recent weeks, ever since Lord Stoude had started speaking to her at evening engagements. She couldn't do anything about her plain face, but the faintest shadow of kohl to her eyelashes and brows made her features stand out and her skin not so sallow, and her maid had added a touch of oil to her golden hair to make it glossy.

Her gown also was new, made of palest blue-green silk that felt cool against her skin. She liked how the color gave a tint of green to her gray eyes.

At the head of the receiving line, Miss Farrimond smiled at Lissa. "I am looking forward to our night at the opera, Miss Gardinier. Will Lord Stoude be joining us, as well?"

"I am afraid I have yet to meet him again to inquire," Lissa said.

"We invited him tonight, so please do induce him to join us."

The mention of the opera made Miriam's face turn stormy, but when she reached Miss Farrimond, she had erased any hint of her vexation.

Miss Farrimond gave Miriam a sour look before greeting her with an insincere smile. Miriam was polite, but there was a touch of satisfaction in her gaze that made Lissa pull her aside as they departed from their hosts. "What has occurred between you and Miss Farrimond?" Lissa hissed.

Miriam tried to pull her arm away, but Lissa was a great deal stronger. "It is not my fault that she fancies a young man who is utterly fascinated with me instead."

"You have more than enough beaus," Lissa snapped. "It isn't as if you can marry them all. Can you not leave him alone?"

"He will not leave *me* alone," Miriam insisted, although Lissa caught the hint of pride in her voice at her conquest.

"At the very least, stop misleading him. You would do well not to antagonize every young miss debuting this Season."

Miriam tore her arm away from Lissa's grip at last and marched away.

"What did you say to her?" Mrs. Gardinier demanded but did not remain for an answer and followed after her younger daughter.

The ball was crowded since there were a great many couples on the dance floor, and the rest of the guests were compacted against the walls. Lissa disliked such crushes, but this year was the debut of the Farrimonds' only daughter, so they had invited all the world to her party.

With her mother tending to Miriam's wounded sensibilities, Lissa wondered if she would dance at all tonight. But Mrs. Fairbanks, who was bosom bows with Lissa's Aunt Ellen, approached her with a gentleman.

"Lissa, my dear, I would like to introduce to you Mr. Morfin," Mrs. Fairbanks said with a genial smile.

Lissa's body instantly froze, and she found she couldn't move. She tried to act normally and hoped her smile wasn't as stiff as it felt. "How do you do, Mr. Morfin?"

The last time she had seen this man, he had been having a serious conversation with Mr. Galland, the first time she caught Lord Stoude eavesdropping. He and Mr. Galland had walked past her and Lord Stoude, but he appeared not to have remembered her. "It is a pleasure to meet you, Miss Gardinier. May I have the honor of this dance?"

She numbly accepted, although her feet felt like blocks of ice as he escorted her to the lines of the dance. Lord Stoude had not admitted that he was seeking out dissenters, so she had no reason to believe Mr. Morfin was involved in anything untoward. There was no need for her to be nervous.

And yet her knees trembled.

She tried to discreetly look about the ballroom for Lord Stoude, but she could not see him. In the next moment, she scolded herself. She had no need for rescue at the moment—Mr. Morfin was all that was amiable. In fact, for a potential traitor, he was remarkably pleasant.

"And so while I wholeheartedly recommend the countryside around Bath, at all costs, you must avoid drinking the waters." He gave a mock shudder and then smiled at Lissa.

"I shall certainly take your advice, sir." Lissa grew less anxious as the dance progressed. If she weren't still a bit wary of him because of Lord Stoude, she would be rather bored.

Or perhaps it was that every man was boring compared to Lord Stoude, with the air of mystery about him from the secrets he was keeping and the probing questions he asked when he discussed more traditionally masculine topics with her.

After the dance, as he was escorting her from the floor, he guided her around two gentlemen having an argument about Napoleon.

Mr. Morfin then asked one question that made Lissa a bit uncomfortable. "These are such uncertain times with France. A wise man must always consider the best course of action for himself and his country, don't you think?"

Lissa adopted a more vapid expression. Inwardly she wanted to grab him and shake him until his teeth rattled, demanding, *Why would you ruin a perfectly nice dance with your dubious political leanings?!*

Should she probe him in order to attempt to aid Lord Stoude? But she was not aware of what he wanted to know about Mr. Morfin. In not understanding the fullness of the web of information Lord Stoude was weaving, she would only blunder like a fly begging to be eaten, and she didn't wish to inadvertently arouse Mr. Morfin's suspicions about her.

"Cannot we believe in the strength of our military and government leaders?" she asked, hoping that was vague enough. "I have no wish to be ruled by the Corsican. It would be quite horrid to be forced to speak French."

Mr. Morfin gave a pained smile, looking genuinely embarrassed for her, and his gaze shifted away from her.

Her mother would be outraged that she would deliberately wish a man to disregard her, but she could not release the knot of tension within her while she was in his company.

Was she unjust in her suspicions of him because of Lord Stoude? Should she try to knock down her walls of caution? He had not the look of a cruel man, and he had not told her Banbury tales about her beauty and grace, as other men had done. He was a bit plump about the waist, and he was only an inch or two taller than she was, but his face was amiable, surely?

She was still undecided when he deposited her near her mother, who was waiting for both

Lissa and Miriam to return from the set. Mrs. Gardinier was introduced to Mr. Morfin and seemed quite pleased that Lissa had managed to *not* offend an eligible gentleman.

A shadow suddenly fell over her, and she looked up in surprise to see Lord Stoude's stern countenance.

Chapter Six

He seemed even more forbidding than usual, and she was about to demand why when she remembered that they were not alone, but in the presence of her mother.

"Lord Stoude." Lissa curtsied, but she was wracking her brain to try to guess why he had approached her here, of all places. Why not wait until she'd found a quiet corner? His very presence was putting her mother into palpitations, and Miriam had also arrived, escorted by her dance partner, with both of them staring with wide eyes at him.

"Miss Gardinier, would you do me the honor of this next dance?" Lord Stoude held out his hand.

She did not react quite as badly as she had the first time—perhaps practice does make perfect—but those were still words she would have never expected to fall from his mouth. Astonishment made her freeze for a second or two, but then she forced herself to place her hand in his and mumble her assent before she shamed herself entirely.

"Is it so distressing to dance with me that you must hesitate each time?" he asked as he led her away. He scowled at her, but she could somehow tell that he was not as unhappy as he pretended to be.

"I believe I told you last time that it was like a punch to the face," she said tartly. "This time was merely a knock to the head."

"Asking a woman to dance is not a bout of fisticuffs," he groused.

"*You* asking a woman to dance makes me rather feel like I've been knocked about," she groused back. "Perhaps if you did it more often, it would not feel like being run over by a pig."

He narrowed his eyes at her. "That was oddly specific. Have you been run over by a pig?"

She put her nose in the air. "That may or may not have happened when I was nine."

Lord Stoude's mouth deepened into a straight line, but she could tell he was trying not to laugh. And that made the knot in her stomach ease.

However, as the movements of the dance brought them closer together, he said in a low voice, "I would ask that you attempt to avoid dancing with Mr. Morfin in future."

She blinked at him in confusion. "Good gracious, does he indeed have nefarious business you are investigating?"

He frowned at her, even though Lissa had kept her voice equally quiet. "I am not investigating anything," he insisted.

"No, indeed," she agreed quickly.

She could only describe Lord Stoude's expression as a pout.

"I shall do my best, but my mother is quite taken with him." She suddenly stared at him. "Is that why you asked me to dance? So that my mother's attention—and her hopes—might be transferred to you instead? It is deplorable of you to encourage flights of fancy in her, my lord."

"I was doing no such thing. Can I not simply wish to dance with you?"

Rather than being flattered (well, she might have felt a tiny spark of flattery somewhere in her chest), she gave him a level look. He would be powerless against the stabbing disbelief in her gaze!

In actuality, he was quite resistant to her gaze and merely changed the topic. "Your gown is quite fetching, Miss Gardinier."

She stumbled on her next step and nearly knocked into the woman next to her. When the dance drew her close to Lord Stoude again, she demanded, "Do you wish something from me?"

"Of course not. Why would you think that?"

"You have never complimented me. I can only assume you are hoping to win my favor in order to ask me to do something for you."

He sighed. "I wish no such thing, I assure you."

She brightened. "Excellent. For I wish to ask something of you."

"What is it?" Lord Stoude's expression grew instantly wary, and she hoped she was not repelling him by what she would say next.

But she was honest enough with herself to admit that she dearly wished to go to the opera with him, even if it must be in the company of Lady Charline and her friends. He would never invite her himself, and being in a large party would allay any gossip about him that the evening might otherwise engender.

"Lady Charline has invited me to the opera with her and some friends. If it pleases you, you are invited to join us."

A crease appeared between his brows. "I had not realized you were so close with Lady Charline."

"Neither had I," she muttered.

His mouth quirked, and he almost-smiled again.

"If you must know, it is entirely your fault," Lissa said. "Lady Charline saw us dancing last and assumed we were good enough friends that inviting me would bring you along like a matched pair."

The dance separated them, and when they came together again, he said, "I am not a teacup."

"You needn't accept if you wish." If he didn't, Lissa would plead with Lady Charline to take Miriam in her place, if only for the sake of peace in the Gardinier household. Because Lord Stoude would surely say no.

"I would be delighted to attend the opera with you."

She almost stumbled again, but Lord Stoude put a fleeting hand on the small of her back to help her regain her balance.

"You will go?" she asked, dumbfounded.

"Of course. Did you not invite me?"

"Well, yes I did, but …"

He looked closely at her. "Do you not wish me to accept?"

"On the contrary, I wish to go to the opera with you." She nearly blurted, *Quite a bit*, but thought she had flattered him enough.

"Perhaps you might accept my invitation, as well," he said.

"I *knew* you asked me to dance in order to request that I do something for you. What is it?"

He gave her an exasperated look, but continued, "Would you do me the honor of joining me for a walk in Green Park tomorrow afternoon?"

She was so astounded (yet again) that only a single "Oh" popped out of her mouth.

"'Oh?'" he asked. "Is that a yes or a no?"

"Yes, that is a … er, yes." Something was bubbling up in her stomach, or perhaps it was her chest. It felt quite warm. She hoped it was not the salmon she had eaten earlier.

The corners of his mouth curled up just a little. Really, those almost-smiles of his seemed to make her heart beat irregularly. It was most distressing.

She couldn't spot her mother, so he escorted her to a quiet corner of the ballroom. As soon as he had left her, Lady Charline pounced upon her. "Good evening, Miss Gardinier. I see you danced with Lord Stoude. I hope you enjoyed your dance. Did you by any chance ask him about the opera?" Lissa wasn't certain she even breathed once as she spoke.

"He has graciously agreed to join us."

Lady Charline smiled widely, and it made her look quite stunning. "I am ever so relieved. It would have been quite disappointing if he had refused."

"May I ask a favor, my lady?" Lissa asked hesitantly.

Lady Charline was still flush with the happy anticipation of Lord Stoude's presence, and she had a smile on her face as she answered, "Of course."

"My sister Miriam has expressed an interest in the opera. Might it be possible for her to join us, as well?" Lissa didn't want to ask this, but she also couldn't go back to her mother and admit she had not even attempted to include Miriam.

Lady Charline's face grew more cool, but she still held a polite smile. "I beg your pardon, Miss Gardinier, but I am afraid our family's box cannot hold more than the number in our party. I do so hate to disappoint your sister."

"I thank you for your consideration, my lady. I apologize for my boldness."

"What is a request among friends? You need not be dismayed. I look forward to our evening this week."

She left Lissa just as Miriam came up to her, demanding to know what had been said. Her sister's countenance grew tempestuous, but she pasted on a smile as another young man approached to claim the next dance.

The storm broke as soon as the ladies returned to their townhouse.

"Lissa, what did you say to Lady Charline?" Miriam demanded before they had even closed the front door.

Lissa refused to answer in front of the servants and simply walked up the stairs to her bedroom.

Miriam followed at her heels. "Well?" she asked.

"Yes, Lissa, whatever happened?" Mrs. Gardinier had trailed after her daughters and now closed the door to Lissa's bedchamber. "It was a simple enough request."

Without the servants, without a ballroom of people, Lissa felt no need to be the quiet, plain woman with whom the rest of the *ton* was familiar. She glared at Miriam. "I asked Lady Charline, and she refused. It was a rude request in the first place since she is the host of the outing."

"How can it be rude to show your affection for your sister?" her mother asked.

"How is it *not* rude to wish to invite herself to Lady Charline's entertainment?" Lissa countered.

"You simply don't wish for me to be there," Miriam accused. "You never want anything pleasant for me."

"That is patently untrue."

"Why can you not speak to Lady Charline about Miriam attending instead of yourself?" Mrs. Gardinier asked. "Surely such an outing would not appeal to you."

"Such an outing would appeal to me greatly," Lissa said through gritted teeth.

"But you have been to the opera before. This would be a wonderful opportunity for your sister."

"Lady Charline asked me to invite Lord Stoude, and he has already accepted. It would be extraordinarily rude for me to bow out now when I was the one who asked him to join us."

"You only wish to go because of Lord Stoude," Miriam said.

Unfortunately, that struck too true a note within her. Lissa's lips pressed together.

But Miriam didn't notice her reaction, didn't even wait for her to reply. "You know that you were only invited because of Lord Stoude. Lady Charline would hardly notice if we switched places."

Lissa breathed slowly to try to control her temper. "There is no point in bemoaning the issue, for she has already said no."

Miriam wasn't listening to her. "And why is Lord Stoude paying any attention to you at all this Season? He is wealthy, has a title, and is a very eligible bachelor, but according to the gossip, he has been so aloof in years past that women have given up on him."

"Well, it is no wonder, for the man has often enough refused to ask a woman to dance, no matter to whom he might be introduced," her mother said. "They say that he is heartless and rude."

"Lissa, are you hoping to catch his attention?" Miriam asked in a scoffing tone.

"He has danced with me only to be kind." Lissa would have liked to insist that Lord Stoude preferred her company to other women, but what was the point in misleading her sister? Miriam might be so jealous that she would do all she could to find the truth of the matter.

"But he *danced* with you," Mrs. Gardinier said.

"He has not behaved in any way to indicate he wishes to court me." But then she remembered his invitation for the morrow. Would not that constitute an interest in her?

The problem was that Lissa found it hard to believe he might favor her when there had been scores of women more beautiful and accomplished over the years who had tried and failed to bring him up scratch. And certainly none as odd as herself.

Miriam sniffed. "He probably danced with you to escape dancing with someone else."

Or perhaps because he knew, after speaking to her so often, that out of all the other young ladies, Lissa would not assume he was interested in her. He would have known that he could dance with her without the fear of giving her false romantic hopes.

"He is not ugly," Miriam said consideringly. "I would not mind marrying him."

Such mercenary words spoken about Lord Stoude were the final straw. "If you are quite done, I would like to go to bed," she said acidly.

"You needn't be so peevish," Miriam said, although she headed toward the door. "It isn't as if he would choose to marry you."

With those heartless words, Lissa shut the door behind her sister and her mother.

She didn't immediately call for a maid to help her out of her dress. She sank onto a stool in front of the fireplace, which had a small fire burning to ward off the chill of the spring evening.

Miriam was simply being spiteful, she knew. Or she was merely too self-centered to think of how her words might hurt her sister's feelings.

But her words were also *true*, and they cut more viciously because of it.

Lissa could never attract Lord Stoude in a more romantic way. He would surely need a proper woman who would be a proper hostess and a proper mother for his children. Or else he might marry someone who could share the danger of his investigations—for he was investigating, no matter what he might say in protest.

Why could Lissa not share that danger? Except she was not a soldier. She was a young miss with hardly any accomplishments and a slightly unhealthy interest in the war and Parliament.

Why was she not a woman who could make a brilliant match in her first Season? Why could she not be vivacious and popular? Why must she be such an oddity?

What was wrong with her?

Chapter Seven

Lissa deliberately did not tell her mother and sister about Lord Stoude's invitation to the park the next day, and when they left after luncheon to shop for some ribbons to match her sister's new dress, she thought she might be able to sneak out of the house (if it could be called sneaking when Lord Stoude arrived and she simply left with him). The servants would tell her mother later, but she could avoid the inevitable questions when he came.

He arrived promptly at five o'clock. She could have predicted his punctuality based upon what she knew of him, and for once, she was glad he was rather rigid in his discipline. She had been dressed in a walking dress and (rather dashing) bonnet for a quarter of an hour beforehand, so when she heard the carriage wheels stop outside the townhouse, she was already hurrying down the stairs. Other women may insist upon not appearing too eager, but since she suspected Lord Stoude had some other reason for this invitation, she felt no need to impress him.

As she entered the entry hall, the butler was just opening the door to Lord Stoude. He seemed a mite surprised to see her—he had perhaps been victim to too many ladies who thought it necessary to keep their escorts waiting.

He was even more surprised when she said briskly, "Good afternoon, my lord. Shall we be going?"

"Your promptness is commendable," he said, although his eyes were roving around the entry hall and glancing up the stairs.

Had he been hoping to see Miriam? Had she completely misunderstood his invitation? Had he asked her so that her sister might be more readily induced to accompany them?

Before she could ask, she suddenly heard the door knocker yet again, and the butler opened it for her mother and sister, just returned from shopping. What an abominable time for them to return! She must have missed hearing the carriage when she was descending the stairs.

"Lord Stoude!" Her mother was more shocked than pleased by the visitor at first. But then her eye darted between him and Miriam, who looked equally confused, and she smiled widely. "I was wondering whose fine phaeton had pulled up in front. How lucky that we returned early. Won't you come up to the drawing room for some tea?"

"Good afternoon, Mrs. Gardinier, Miss Miriam." He glanced at Lissa.

She was profoundly glad he was such an intelligent man. He had already guessed she hadn't told her family about the outing, but he also saw the consternation on her face and seemed to know exactly what she wanted him to say. "I beg your pardon, but I had arrived to ask if Miss Gardinier would go walking in Green Park with me. We were just about to leave."

"Lissa?" Mrs. Gardinier then noticed her eldest daughter waiting at the foot of the stairs. "If you would care to wait but a moment, my lord, I'm sure my daughter Miriam would be ready in a trice and able to join you."

He had too firm a control over his features to react to this suggestion, or even to indicate if he desired it or not. But if he had wanted Miriam's company, he would have extended the invitation when he explained why he was there, so Lissa could only assume he wanted her assistance alone in order to accomplish some sort of spying.

"We mustn't allow Lord Stoude's horses to stand any longer, Mama," Lissa said as she strode forward. "Thank you for waiting, my lord."

She guessed correctly, for he offered his arm with alacrity and led her toward the door, which the butler opened for them.

He said nothing on the drive to the park. Once there, he left the vehicle with the groom and led her down a shady path, trailed at a discreet distance by her maid.

It was a cloudy day with a soft breeze that felt colder for lack of sunlight, but Lissa had worn a thick spencer. There were fewer people in Green Park than she expected, even though it was the fashionable hour. She knew that many of her acquaintance preferred to ride their horses or vehicles in Hyde Park.

"I hope you were not disappointed, my lord," she said. "Or had you hoped that my sister would join us?"

At first, he looked puzzled by her words, but then he shook his head. "I am delighted by your company, Miss Gardinier."

"That is such a terribly vague answer. Did you do that on purpose to annoy me?"

He gave her that ~~adorable~~ mysterious almost-smile. "I would never dare."

"Well then, I am certain you had a reason to invite me. There are too few people for you to eavesdrop upon, so perhaps you wish me to engage with a gentleman's companion as you wring state secrets from him?"

Strangely, his eyes seemed rather intent as they rested upon her. "Could I not simply wish to enjoy your company, Miss Gardinier?"

Her heart stuttered, but she gave a little laugh. "You almost sounded sincere when you said that, my lord. Very well, I had not really expected you to tell me, but I thought I should make an effort to ask."

Why did he seem troubled by her answer? Well, it was likely that he did not wish for her to mention his clandestine activities.

"Come, my lord. None can hear us, so tell me your thoughts on the reactions of others now that the bill to abolish the slave trade has passed through Parliament."

He hesitated, but finally answered her. They became so caught up in the discussion that the world fell away, and she quite forgot she was in the middle of Green Park. She almost forgot he was handsome, and rich, and smart, and that she was a secret bluestocking.

They only stopped their conversation when someone ahead of them and quite close cleared his throat.

Lissa paused, spotting an older gentleman with a barrel-shaped torso standing in the path directly in front of Lord Stoude. It was very curious, for there was room on the path for him to have avoided the preoccupied couple entirely, and yet he was nearly upon them.

Lord Stoude jerked abruptly, which astonished Lissa. Even when he found her hidden away and entered into lengthy debates with her, his eyes were always flicking around them, observant of everyone nearby.

"I beg your pardon, sir. I was not attentive to my surroundings." Lord Stoude bowed as though he had been the one to nearly run into the man.

"Do not concern yourself," the man said. His large eyes settled speculatively upon Lissa for a moment, which made her straighten her spine and stare right back. He might have smiled slightly at her reaction, but she couldn't be certain because he quickly held out his hand. "It is good to see you again, my lord."

"The same to you, sir." Lord Stoude shook his hand.

It might have slipped her notice if she hadn't already been wary of the man. But he had seemed to deliberately attempt to collide with Lord Stoude, and so she was cautious of him.

And so she caught the tiniest glimpse of a corner of a folded note in Lord Stoude's palm as he shook the other man's hand.

Neither acknowledged the exchange. They simply nodded and then continued on.

When they were far enough away that the man couldn't hear them, she said, "How strange that you did not introduce us."

"To be honest, Miss Gardinier, I couldn't recall his name. Rather than cause us both embarrassment, I thought it best to simply make my escape."

But he had not the uncomfortable countenance of a man admitting to such a grievous social *faux pas*. He seemed altogether composed and maybe even a little relieved now that the encounter was past.

Lord Stoude quickly continued, "We were speaking of Spain, were we not? I fear the wealth of the West Indies is too great a temptation. Their economy is so bound to the slave trade that I cannot imagine them following our example anytime soon."

She suspected he wished to divert her from thinking about the man, and while it annoyed her, she had already resolved herself not to pry. He had the right to his secrets, and it wasn't as if *she* had the right to demand he reveal them. So she reluctantly allowed him to guide her back to their previous topic. "And yet their colonies in South America are already pushing for independence …"

Now that he had apparently accomplished his goal in Green Park, Lissa thought he would immediately escort her home, but to her surprise, they spoke at length on topics aside from the slave trade bill. They remained in the park rather longer than most would consider proper, but she didn't protest. She loved the timbre of his voice, the passion behind his strong opinions, the way his blue eyes looked deeply into hers as he listened to her. She could almost believe that he might fancy her.

But that was undeniably ridiculous.

He had invited her to the park in order to meet with the man in a way that seemed coincidental. And from the way she had continued to keep silent about his more questionable actions, he likely knew she would not inquire about it. Or if she did ask, that she would not be offended if he avoided answering.

Lissa's heart sank as they returned to the phaeton and drove back to her home. Her mother and sister might be so upset that they would even do their impersonation of dying cats. The screeching was the worst—she could swear she heard the china tremble.

As Lord Stoude left her on the family's doorstep, the door held open by the butler behind her, she paused in bidding him farewell. The servants were far enough away that they would not hear the words she sweetly but quietly murmured to him.

"My lord, do call upon me anytime you need to once again accidentally run into Sir Derrick Bayberry."

His eyebrows might have risen at the revelation that she had known the man (although it was only because he'd been pointed out to Lissa by Lady Relford at a ball two weeks ago).

But he did not reply. Instead, he simply smiled at her—not a full grin, but more than the almost-smiles he'd been giving to her.

Lissa nearly swooned at the sight—and she *never* swooned, but Lord Stoude's smile simply had that effect on her.

Then he was bowing to her, and before she knew it, he was driving away.

Chapter Eight

The crash of the door knocker interrupted Lissa's family at breakfast. The early hour was unusual enough, but Lissa's parents shot each other startled looks to silently ask if either of them were expecting a visitor. This lack of coordination was curious since her mother commanded their social schedule like a general.

The fact her parents had not expected anyone gave Lissa a sense of foreboding, but she was also nearly finished with her meal. She would have liked to linger over her tea, but Miriam's incessant barbs such as, "I daresay Lady Charline must be desperate for entertainment for them to invite one such as you," and "I am astonished that you would not wish to broaden my horizons with a visit to the opera, but you have always wished to confine me to our humble little life out of jealousy that I will fly higher in society than yourself," and "I should hope you will not be so clumsy at the opera, Lissa. It would be such a pity if your appearance became memorable for the wrong reasons."

That last was when Lissa had become so irritated she made the cup rattle when she replaced it in the saucer. Her father finally silenced his daughter with a firm, "Enough, Miriam."

Thus the family table had been quiet when the visitor arrived.

Eager to escape the table, and suspecting that so early a call would not be formal or social, Lissa asked, "May I be excused? I shall see who it is, shall I?"

"How uncivilized!" her mother said. "There is no need, for the butler shall inform us shortly."

"I rather suspect it might be better for someone to greet the visitor first," Lissa said.

Not a moment later, the sounds of a strident woman's voice washed up the stairs and through the walls like a crashing ocean wave. The family recognized it immediately, and her mother jumped to her feet and rushed out of the room. Lissa followed a bit more slowly, but Miriam remained sulking at her seat until her father prodded her to join them all.

In the entry hall, Mrs. Gardinier embraced the newcomer whilst jabbering, "so unexpected," and "arrived early." Her words were difficult to hear because the woman demanded, "Am I so insignificant that my own sister must keep me waiting in the entrance hall for nearly a minute before greeting me?"

It had not been so long, but no one remarked upon that fact.

"Good morning, Aunt Ellen," Lissa said as she descended the stairs. "I had not known you would be joining us in town."

The towering matron looked down at her diminutive sister. "Did you not tell them, Hortensia? I informed you by letter last week!"

Reduced to incoherent phrases as she always was by her sibling, Mrs. Gardinier mumbled about "no day indicated" and "busy social schedule."

Aunt Ellen presented her cheek to be kissed by Lissa, and Miriam and her father joined them at last. After another round of greetings, Aunt Ellen declared she was famished, and she linked her arm with Miriam's to be led to the breakfast room.

Lissa's mother held her back in order to hiss in her ear, "You must give your regrets for tonight and let Miriam go in your stead."

"Whatever for?"

"Tonight, your father has a meeting with the owner of the land he is hoping to purchase, and I have been invited by Lady Jersey to a party from which I cannot bow out."

"I can understand not wishing to upset Lady Jersey, for she would be unpleasant were you to disappoint her, but Miriam will be home with Aunt Ellen."

"She interacts much better with you than with Miriam."

"Then Miriam should learn to mind her manners more with Aunt Ellen," Lissa said with exasperation. "She reaps the fruits of her own impatience."

"Ellen wrote that she was thinking of inviting you to Bath with her at the end of the Season," her mother said. "Would you wish to jeopardize that invitation by leaving her to Miriam's whims?"

Unfortunately, Lissa could see Aunt Ellen being so affronted by something Miriam said that she would leave London in high dudgeon.

And while Lissa loved her family's home by the sea, she loved the city far more, with its newspapers and lectures for many different interests. Why, just the other day she had discovered the existence of a botanical association and given Phoebe, who had a miraculous skill in growing roses, the information for the next meeting so that she could attend.

Lissa would enjoy London far more if she weren't being paraded in front of eligible partis like a horse for sale at Tattersalls. Bath with Aunt Ellen would be a relief from her mother's schemes and a round of stimulating lectures and salons.

The face of Lord Stoude arose in Lissa's mind as she had seen him last, that smile turning his eyes into the glittering blue of the sea and playing havoc with her equanimity. She was torn between wanting to go to the opera with him and the sensible notion of distancing herself so that the end of the Season would not leave her heart pricked and bleeding.

Added to her desire to protect herself was the allure of the Bath libraries and literary gatherings.

"I shall send a note to Lady Charline."

Lissa knew she was not as emotional as Miriam, but until that moment, she had not realized that she was fully as selfish.

Or perhaps not. Miriam was to leave the house early for a lavish dinner that Lady Charline had arranged before the opera. In the entry hall, Miriam told Lissa, "I intend to take this opportunity to monopolize Lord Stoude's attention."

"Whatever for?" Lissa paused in the act of handing her sister her evening cloak. She was serving as a maid since their mother's lady's maid was attending to her mistress at the moment, and Lissa was only dressed for an evening at home.

Miriam snatched the cloak from her lax fingers. "Did you think you were the only one to harbor a *tendre* for him? He is most handsome. I have had a romantic interest in him for an age."

Just the other week, Miriam had professed she would die if Mr. Harwell did not return her affections, and so Lissa held her tongue.

"And once Lord Stoude realizes how superior I am to any other woman of his acquaintance"—she gave Lissa a pointed glance—"I will capture his heart and leave my competition behind."

"Yes, I daresay you shall," Lissa replied, affecting a bored tone. Inwardly, she seethed and raged that her sister would toy with the emotions of a man as sensitive and awkward as Lord Stoude.

True, he did not appear sensitive or awkward at all, but Lissa had seen beneath his cool facade. He had been so easily offended when she criticized his subtlety, and he'd been surprisingly insecure when asking her to dance, even though he hadn't shown it.

For a moment, she regretted writing to Lady Charline to ask for Miriam to be allowed to be her replacement for the evening (well, regretted a bit more than the hundred other times she had regretted it throughout today). Unleashing Miriam upon Lord Stoude seemed cruel and merciless.

But Miriam's gloating face forced Lissa to swallow her ire and paste a placid mask upon her own. She reminded herself that this was for the best—for her heart, at least. And in a few weeks, she would be off to Bath and would never see Lord Stoude again, especially if she managed to seduce some hapless scholar in a literary salon and be married.

However, after dinner, Aunt Ellen announced, "I shall retire early tonight. The day's travel has wearied me excessively."

Which was a strange statement considering she had stopped last night at an inn just outside of London and had traveled barely an hour this morning. But Lissa only felt a burgeoning rage weighted down by clumps of disappointment. She had missed the opera for nothing.

Had her mother known this? She glanced at Mrs. Gardinier, but there was only a flustered solicitude for her sister's health and rest. Lissa's father cast her a sympathetic look, which only made her mood sink lower.

Perhaps her mother had not known, or perhaps she had, but her determination to marry Lissa off this Season was overriding any sense of guilt. Regardless, she turned to her daughter. "Lissa, you will attend Lady Jersey's soirée tonight with me."

"But I am not dressed."

"Oh, do not tell me it will not take you more than a half-hour. You are not Miriam, after all."

In point of fact, it took her forty-five minutes, but they would not arrive too late at the party. In the carriage, her mother harangued her, "For goodness' sake, you look as though you are attending your dog's funeral. At least try to smile."

"I would rather go to my dog's funeral," Lissa shot back. She wanted to ask if her mother had guessed that Aunt Ellen would go to bed early but knew it was useless. Mrs. Gardinier would insist she did not, even if she had suspected, since it all worked out well for her favorite daughter.

They were silent as they drove through the darkened London streets. An overturned cart forced them to detour, and lights and laughter caught Lissa's attention out the carriage window.

They were passing the theater. Vehicles crowded the street, slowing them to a crawl and showing clearly the attendees entering the building.

Which was how she saw Lady Charline standing beside a carriage from which she had just alighted. She was joined by Miss Farrimond and Miss Templeton, who were chatting with Lady Charline's brother, Mr. Halberstam, and a young man Lissa recognized as Mr. Fitchette. She guessed that the other young man was Mr. Halberstam's friend, Mr. Cirling.

Lord Stoude was at the moment helping Miriam descend from Lady Charline's carriage. Lissa expected her sister to be smiling brightly and exerting all her charms upon the company, but instead, there was a rather sulky cast to her lower lip.

Then Miriam looked up at Lord Stoude, and her sullen mood vanished, driven away by the sunbeam of her smile.

Lissa's carriage continued on its way, leaving her with that brief scene lingering in her mind's eye.

She stared unseeing out the window, keeping her face composed. But somewhere in the depths of her chest, she felt a large, hollow space open up. The silence in the carriage only emphasized her sense of isolation.

She tried to shake off her mood, but it persisted until she arrived at Lady Jersey's soirée and all throughout the frightfully elegant evening.

Lissa felt she had lost something very precious, something which she couldn't regain again.

Chapter Nine

Two days later, Lissa had an ominous premonition the moment she entered the front doors of Mrs. Fairbanks's home.

She didn't know what exactly caused her to feel that way, nor did she know what sort of danger she feared. And after a moment, she tried to brush it away from her mind. It was ridiculous to think something terrible would happen here, at a highly anticipated ball given by one of the wealthiest families in London.

Besides, it could be that she was simply out of sorts. She had awoken with a headache that persisted all through the day, and although she tried to beg leave to absent herself from the party tonight, her mother had firmly refused. Aunt Ellen had added her protests, insisting that she desired Lissa's attendance upon her at the event, for a note sent 'round that morning to her good friend Mrs. Fairbanks had secured the additional invitation to the ball.

Lissa smiled through the pounding of her head as she curtsied to Mrs. Fairbanks and her granddaughter, whose debut was being celebrated with the ball tonight. She then gratefully left the receiving line to head into the ballroom. Mrs. Fairbanks's home was quite large, and she had invited enough people to fill the space to bursting. Lissa wondered if there would be enough room for dancing at all.

Once the ball officially opened, space was cleared and lines formed. Lissa's father had joined the ladies this evening, and as soon as the family had entered, he had met with a friend, Mr. Imbert, accompanied by his son, Mr. Dolphus Imbert.

The young man only had eyes for Miriam, but he very properly asked for Lissa's hand in the first dance. He would have been disappointed anyway, for Miriam had promised the first dance to another young man in her entourage, who appeared almost immediately to claim it once the first strains of the string ensemble were heard.

After the dance, she was fearing another evening where she stood, unwanted, along the wall, when Lissa was surprised by Lord Stoude's young cousin, Mr. Percy Calveston, who asked her to dance, followed by Mr. Collingworth.

Mr. Calveston's conversation was all that was proper (if heartily boring), and at first, Mr. Collingworth repeated inane pleasantries. It took only a gentle prodding from Lissa to steer him toward his beloved dogs, and she was thankfully able to suggest some rather more conventional names for the puppies of his new litter. She did not know if he would take her suggestions, but it was surely better than the names he had been considering, such as "Whiskerwiff Thunderbark" and "Howlsbury Squirrelbane."

Unfortunately, her headache did not abate. She found herself ducking her mother's notice and making her way toward the other end of the ballroom, intent upon the door to the hallway outside.

She found her journey blocked by clumps of people, which she skirted except for one particular group laughing with each other. It consisted of Lady Charline and everyone who had joined her party at the opera the other night, including Miriam and Lord Stoude.

They were far enough away, and there were enough of the other guests in between, that they would not notice her. Lissa stood perfectly still, a frozen figure, as she watched Lady Charline lean close to Lord Stoude, smiling as she said something. Lord Stoude had that almost-smile on his face as he looked down upon her, while others in the group chortled at the story she was telling, Miriam alone held a stiff smile, outwardly amused but with peevishness in her green-gray eyes as she stood on the other side of Lord Stoude.

It might have been amusing, perhaps a scene from a farcical play, if Lissa hadn't felt as though winter winds swirled all around her, removing her from the ballroom and all the people within, a statue of ice. With a raging headache.

She turned and moved away.

Lissa didn't know at first where she was going, but she happened to glance up and spot her mother speaking to Lady Wynwood. While that was a great deal better than if her mother were alone, Lissa knew she wouldn't be able to hide her distress from Lady Wynwood, and she didn't wish for anyone to know. To everyone, she was already a figure of pity—quiet and plain, sharp-tongued to her friends and family, and heaven help the man who was tricked into marrying her.

The next moment, she admonished herself. She was being unreasonable—not everyone felt that way about her. And yet she did not want to add to their sympathy by revealing her pain. She couldn't bear it.

She turned around again. There was surely another exit from this infernal ballroom.

At last, she found a small servants' door next to a table set against the wall. She needed to squeeze her way past a group of older men discussing a horse race, but she managed her escape.

Once outside in the hallway, she headed up one of the two wings of the stairs. On the open gallery on the next floor, numerous paintings adorned one wide wall, with the railing overlooking the lower level and the staircase.

On this floor, hallways led to other wings of the house. Only a few people strolled in front of the paintings, and Lissa joined them, pretending to admire the landscapes, some wider than she was tall.

The empty space inside of her had begun to thaw, and while she preferred to be alone at the moment, she also felt lonely. She was such a hypocrite. Hadn't she chosen to remain at home in order to focus upon the more distant goal of Bath? Hadn't she desired to rid herself of any warmer feelings for Lord Stoude in order to build walls around the equanimity of her mind?

The sight of Lord Stoude enjoying Lady Charline's company—and in the midst of others—should not have distressed her. The regret at missing the opera was not hers to feel, for she had handed the opportunity to her sister of her own free will.

She sat on a chaise lounge that had been placed along the railing and looked down at the wide landing below, where the two wings of the stairs ended. Occasionally the ballroom door would open, sending a roar of sound before it was cut off by the closing door. Then a servant would cross the space, bearing a tray, or a guest would appear and climb the stairs to head to the retiring room that lay along one of the hallways.

Lissa knew her mother was likely looking for her, but she couldn't force herself to leave her place of rest. Just a few more moments, and then she would return to the ballroom and the torturous prospect of waiting to be asked to dance.

The door opened and Lady Charline's cousin, Mr. Fitchette, appeared in her line of sight. He strolled very slowly toward the stairs ... almost as if waiting for someone.

And only a few seconds later, the ballroom door opened again, and another guest emerged. But Lissa instinctively shrank down slightly as she spotted the tall figure of Mr. Galland, the first man she'd seen Lord Stoude eavesdropping upon.

"Mr. Fitchette, what a pleasure to meet you here," Mr. Galland said.

Mr. Fitchette's reply was too indistinct for Lissa to hear, but then the two men headed down the narrow hallway that ran alongside the ballroom, out of her sight.

She had no reason to be wary of Mr. Galland, for Lord Stoude had not confessed to her what exactly he had been doing or why he had been interested in the conversation between Mr. Galland and Mr. Morfin. But she remembered Lord Stoude's reaction when she had danced with Mr. Morfin, the way he had quickly approached her to (astoundingly) ask her to dance, as if stealing her away from him. Would he have done the same if it had been Mr. Galland who asked her to dance? Or was she mistaken in her presumption about Lord Stoude's purpose in listening to these men?

Still, she found herself rising and hurrying down the stairs, turning sharply to peer down the hallway where the two men had gone. They were at the far end, discussing something, although their expressions were as neutral as if they merely debated the quality of the champagne. After a moment, they opened the door to the dining room at the end of the hallway, where the buffet had been laid out.

She wondered if she should follow them. But in the wide-open dining room, if she crept close enough to overhear their conversation, they would surely notice her and not discuss anything of import.

And really, was she fancying herself a spy? How ridiculous. She didn't even know what tidbits of information she ought to listen for.

With a deep breath, she squared her shoulders, preparing to enter the ballroom again, when the door ahead of her opened and Lady Charline appeared, followed by Lord Stoude.

"Why, Miss Gardinier," Lady Charline said, her eyebrows raised.

Ignoring the tightening sensation in her chest upon seeing them, Lissa curtsied. "Good evening."

"Perhaps you might assist us," Lady Charline said. "Have you seen my cousin, Mr. Fitchette?"

Lissa glanced at Lord Stoude. "He and Mr. Galland just entered the dining room a few moments ago."

Something flashed in his eyes, and he gave the barest of nods to her.

"Thank you." Lady Charline turned down the hallway but stopped when she realized Lord Stoude was not following her.

He had instead stepped closer to Lissa. "I was surprised to see your sister join us for the opera instead of yourself, Miss Gardinier."

"My aunt required my assistance," she said meekly. *It was what you chose,* she reminded herself. She had no reason to feel such bitterness when telling him.

"Oh, Miss Miriam explained that Miss Gardinier is not inclined toward the opera," Lady Charline interjected.

That little wretch! Lissa wanted to argue but knew her best course of action would be to avoid further conversation as quickly as possible. "Yes, that is true," she said in that same meek voice. "I beg you will excuse me." She curtsied again and turned, heading upstairs once more. This time she went into the ladies' retiring room.

The maid stationed within was quite solicitous, and within moments Lissa was reclining upon a sumptuous chaise lounge with lavender water dabbed upon her temples. However, her time alone only made her remember Lord Stoude's confused eyes as she made her excuses and left him. She might have mistaken the confusion for concern, but that would have simply been indulging her imagination.

A few minutes later, an older woman entered, requiring the maid's help with a falling headdress. The lady may not have even noticed Lissa in the far corner.

Unluckily, Lady Charline saw her as soon as she entered the retiring room, a few minutes after the lady had left with her repaired hairdressing. Lady Charline waved away the maid's inquiry and instead sat next to Lissa.

"I was worried for you, Miss Gardinier. You looked terribly pale when you left us."

"Merely a slight headache." Wishing to turn the subject, she asked, "Did you find your cousin?"

"Oh, indeed. Mr. Fitchette was stuffing his face with almond cakes and had entirely forgotten about his dance with Miss Farrimond. She was quite incensed, but forgave him when he insisted upon the next dance."

"Are they good friends?"

"Yes, they have known each other since they were children, although they had not seen each other for several years before this Season, when Miss Farrimond made her debut."

Lissa almost said something like, *I would have liked to have become more acquainted with him and your other friends at the opera,* as if hinting to Lady Charline that she would like to be invited to join her for another outing. But she refrained, for Lady Charline had no more use for her—Lissa had done her part by inviting Lord Stoude—and she'd be unlikely to invite her to any other gathering.

Instead, she said, "Miss Farrimond seems to have had a very successful debut Season so far."

"Indeed, she has met many interesting people." Lady Charline smiled at Lissa. "Whereas *I* am most pleased to have met Lord Stoude. It was thanks to your invitation that he joined us at the theater. We instantly became good friends."

Her throat felt tight, but she returned the smile—if a bit weakly—and said, "How wonderful for you."

Lady Charline leaned in, although there was no one in the room to hear except for the maid, who had moved a discreet distance away. "In fact, may I beg for your assistance again? I am torn as to a suitable venue for an outing with Lord Stoude. May I ask your opinion?"

Lissa swallowed. "When will your outing be?"

"Oh, I have not yet asked him, but when we parted that evening, he had indicated *great* interest in another entertainment with me. I thought to ask him to accompany me to Lady Wynwood's concert next week, or perhaps to a private art exhibition. What do you think I should select?"

Lissa's first thought was, *Where would Lord Stoude be most bored?* But then she smothered her uncharitable feelings. "Has Lord Stoude indicated he is most fond of music or art?"

Lady Charline's delicate eyebrows arched in surprise. "Why, I thought you might know, since you are friends with him."

They had mostly discussed subjects that Lissa couldn't repeat to Lady Charline for fear of being labeled a bluestocking or a woman meddling in men's affairs. When a string quartet was especially loud and a bit discordant, he had remarked that the violinist was certainly playing with much fervor. "The concert, perhaps? Lord Stoude once expressed appreciation for the musicians at a ball."

Lady Charline glowed as she thanked Lissa. "I shall extend him an invitation." She laid a hand upon Lissa's. "I am most grateful to you, Miss Gardinier, for your help. I hope that as we spend more time together, Lord Stoude's preference for me might grow into something deeper. And it is all thanks to you."

She gave Lissa a significant look, then rose and left the retiring room.

Lissa felt more drained than when she'd first arrived. She resisted the childish urge to fling herself back upon the lounge in exhaustion.

Yes, she had understood the message quite well—it was a warning for Lissa to stay out of Lady Charline's way.

Chapter Ten

On the evening of Lady Wynwood's concert, Lissa greeted her hostess and Phoebe and entered the ballroom, trying not to be obvious she was searching for a particular couple, and also trying not to feel guilty. She had given her honest opinion to Lady Charline, and it was hardly her fault that the Gardiniers were always intending to go to the concert, since they were good friends with Lady Wynwood's niece.

However, the event was such a sad crush that Lissa saw only the press of bodies. She wove her way amongst the crowd but had only maneuvered through barely a quarter of the room before the signal was given for the concert to start.

Lissa hastily found her mother and sat beside her, with Miriam on the other side. Aunt Ellen was out with her other friends. Her father had refused with a shudder, which was just as well, for the one time he had accompanied them to a concert performance, her mother had been nudging him the entire evening to keep him from dozing and snoring.

And if Lissa looked around a bit while the musicians played, surely no one noticed. In fact, half the audience murmured among themselves during the performances.

It was most likely due to the melancholy tones of the pieces being performed that explained her low spirits as the evening went on, and not the fact that she did not spot Lady

Charline or Lord Stoude.

Why had she expected them to be here? Lady Charline would likely have taken the opposite of Lissa's suggestion. After all, she saw Lissa as enough of a threat—or at least a distraction—to warn her off. She wouldn't be able to trust a word Lissa said in regard to Lord Stoude.

Lissa wondered if she ought to be flattered that Lady Charline thought enough of her to make clear her claim over Lord Stoude's attention. She could have disregarded Lissa entirely as a harmless acquaintance who would have no effect upon her own plans.

At the intermission, Lissa's mother and sister rose to greet friends, but she remained seated. She had had quite enough of pushing through the crowds.

Lady Charline had likely invited Lord Stoude to the art exhibit, knowing the Gardiniers would be at Lady Wynwood's concert. Lissa repeated to herself that she had no reason to feel guilty that she came, for Lady Charline and Lord Stoude were likely not even here.

And in coming to the concern, what had she been hoping? The torture of seeing Lord Stoude laughing with beautiful, rich Lady Charline? (Never mind that Lissa hadn't seen Lord Stoude laugh even once.)

It was only by sheer chance that she glanced around and was knocked out of her maudlin thoughts by the sight of Mr. Galland and Mr. Morfin.

They stood in a corner near the stage where the musicians had played. They were not isolated, for too many people pressed around them for that, and their expressions were congenial as they chatted with each other.

Really, what had Lissa been thinking? It was ridiculous that Lord Stoude had been listening in on their conversation. She was seeing traitors and spies everywhere simply because her own life was so uneventful.

But she couldn't take her eyes from the two men. Which was why she saw the exchange, even though it was but a mere moment.

Mr. Fichette made his way toward them—no, he merely nodded to the two men as he passed by them. He was with another gentleman who also nodded and then shook Mr. Galland's hand.

Words were exchanged, but the men's expressions were rather somber, like mourners at a funeral rather than a brief greeting at a party.

Then Mr. Fitchette and his companion had moved on, and Mr. Galland and Mr. Morfin continued standing together.

But Lissa had seen a handshake like that before—the strange curl of the fingers rather than a full, open palm just before engulfing the other hand. Lord Stoude's handshake with Sir Derrick Bayberry at Green Park had been just like it.

She found Mr. Fitchette and studied the man with him—no, the two had already parted. If she hadn't seen them pass in front of Mr. Galland and Mr. Morfin, she wouldn't have even known Mr. Fitchette was acquainted with him.

The man was tall, with a full head of black hair, a bit longer than was fashionable, and with a slightly wild air. He was handsome, but not enough to set hearts fluttering and bring him more widespread popularity. A sharp nose rose above a wide, mobile mouth that smiled at the woman whom he had just greeted.

What a curious interaction. Should she tell Lord Stoude? But she didn't know the name of the other man, so she would need to describe him. Would that be enough to identify him, or would it only cause Lord Stoude more work to try to find him?

If only Lady Charline had dragged Lord Stoude to the concert. But even if Lord Stoude were here, she was unlikely to find him—

"Good evening, Miss Gardinier."

She was startled out of her thoughts by a deep voice quite nearby, and she saw Lord Stoude walking between the row of seats directly toward her.

"My lord." Lissa hastily rose and curtsied. Now that she saw him, she was utterly mortified. Thank goodness Lady Charline was not with him to see Lissa attending the concert like a lovesick fool hoping for a glimpse of the object of her affection.

"Are you here with your mother?" he asked, looking around.

"She is speaking with friends, as is my sister." Lissa automatically assumed he had meant to ask after Miriam, since that was what most young men did if they came up to speak to Lissa. But as soon as she spoke, she wondered if Lord Stoude had indeed ~~descended to that low level of intelligence~~ become so fond of her sister after that one night at the opera. After all, he had not visited the house as other young men had done.

He gave one of those almost-smiles she knew so well, and her breath rose in her throat at how handsome it made him.

"If your mother is accompanied by your sister, then perhaps you might care to join us? We are sitting very near the stage."

Lissa had to stiffen so that she wouldn't physically recoil at the thought of sitting with him and Lady Charline. Granted, there were probably others with them, but she had no wish to expose herself to Lady Charline's icy smile when she saw Lissa interrupt her cozy party of friends. And Lady Charline would be entirely correct to assume Lissa was haunting them.

"I thank you, my lord, but I must remain with my mother," she said in a cool voice to hide her agitation.

His expression of disappointment looked almost real. Well, he was a spy amongst the *ton*, so naturally he must be an excellent actor.

A reminder of his activities only depressed her mood even further. She was a silly girl while he had more important things to accomplish. He was likely merely using her to do his job since she conveniently wouldn't ask questions or interfere. At best, he thought of her as a friend with whom he had mildly entertaining conversations.

At that moment, there was the signal for the end of intermission. Lord Stoude bowed to her. "Do enjoy the rest of the concert, Miss Gardinier." He turned to leave.

Her mouth moved before she could think. "Lord Stoude."

He turned back to her with alacrity. "Yes, Miss Gardinier?"

She moved closer to him, enough to smell the spice of ginger and the sweet grass scent of chamomile and linen, overlaid by his natural musk. It was an unusual cologne, but she realized it matched the hard, indifferent Lord Stoude, reminding her of river stones in summer.

He had stiffened slightly as she drew near, but he bent his head close to hear her words.

"I saw a strange, brief exchange." She described the four men greeting each other, and the handshake, and also the curious way Mr. Fitchette and his friend had parted so quickly afterward.

"Point out the man," he murmured to her.

She feared at first that she would not be able to do so, with the guests all returning to their seats, but she found him near where she'd last seen him. She pointed toward Mrs. Whichard, who was just sitting down next to him. "The man sitting to Mrs. Whichard's right."

Lord Stoude grew very still as he spotted him. "Are you certain?"

"Yes."

His jaw clenched briefly, then his face relaxed once again into his normal distant mask, although now it held a slight chill. "I thank you, Miss Gardinier. More than you could ever know."

"Was it useful, then? I wondered if I were being foolish."

Instead of answering her, his blue eyes bore into hers. His voice was so low she barely heard him. "You must not become more involved. Stay away from any of those men if at all possible."

"But why?"

He hesitated, and she instantly knew that he was contemplating lying to her.

"Tell me the truth," she said firmly. "I am not missish. I would rather know."

Reluctantly, he said, "It may be dangerous. *They* may be dangerous."

She swallowed, then said, "Thank you for telling me. I shall be careful."

The look in his eyes was concerned, but there was a gleam of something almost … admiring. "Won't you change your mind and join us?"

"Thank you for the offer, but I must decline." She was abruptly reminded of Lady Charline, and while she had just informed him she was not missish, the thought of watching him enjoying Lady Charline's company filled her with dread. She could not face that. Not yet.

At that moment, her mother and Miriam made their way down the row toward their seats. "My lord, how delightful to see you." Miriam's charm blasted at him like a rush of floodwater.

He merely bowed to them both. "I wish you both a pleasant evening. I must return to my party."

After he left, her mother asked, "Why was Lord Stoude speaking to you?"

"I called him over to greet him," Lissa said. They would think she had tried to assert herself and Lord Stoude had simply been polite to walk toward her to respond to her.

Lissa watched his figure make his way to the front of the room. She suddenly realized she had assumed he was with Lady Charline, but was he with another group of his friends instead? (Never mind that she hadn't noticed if he even *had* friends at any of the gatherings they had attended.)

But no, she saw Lady Charline's bright hair, bedecked with diamonds and ribbons, and saw her profile as she greeted Lord Stoude back at his seat. Standing next to her was her brother. Then they all sat down and were lost from sight.

Lissa turned to her mother. "Mama, could we leave?"

"Whatever do you mean? Of course we cannot leave."

"Why would you wish to leave?" Miriam asked. "The tenor who is to sing next is purported to be monstrously handsome."

It had been a futile attempt to escape. She simply hadn't wished to run into Lady Charline at the concert's end. It was cowardly, but she simply couldn't bear to see them.

She had asserted her courage to him, and yet she cowered in her seat throughout the rest of the concert.

Surrounded by guests all around, she nonetheless felt terribly alone. Who would possibly understand her? Who would like her enough to want her?

No one. Lord Stoude had seen her as she was, and while he did not seem to mind her oddities, he had no interest in her, for he had enjoyed Lady Charline's company far more.

At that moment, she felt that she would always be lonely.

Chapter Eleven

Lissa never understood why a Venetian Breakfast was always held at noon, and sometimes later. Why not simply call it a Venetian Luncheon? Or would it no longer be "Venetian" if it were a luncheon?

The food was also un-breakfastlike, which always saddened her since breakfast was by far her favorite meal. She only picked at the boiled pigeons in rice and sipped some almond soup.

Her dissatisfaction with the Venetian Breakfast had *nothing* to do with the fact that Lord Stoude was not in attendance.

The party was hosted by the Gillards', who had lavishly hired out Lovers' Walk, a secluded area in Vauxhall Gardens. Lissa had been invited to a large party at Vauxhall last Season, experiencing the thrill of sitting in the supper-boxes and viewing the Rotunda under the colored lights, but it would have been too scandalous to venture into the dark Lovers' Walk. During the day, the Lovers' Walk was picturesque with wooden arches and trellises covered in climbing plants, rustic benches, discreet pieces of classical statues, and small landscaped garden plots.

After eating, Lissa's mother threatened her with banishment to the country if she did attend to Aunt Ellen, who had been graciously included in the invitation, and so she accompanied her aunt in speaking to old acquaintances. She smiled blandly when her aunt's friends teased her about "waiting too long to capture a young man" and admonishments not to turn her nose up at a potential suitor for insignificant reasons.

She was rescued by, of all people, Miriam.

"Lissa," her sister said as she came up to them, "I wish to walk down the path. Will you accompany me?"

She looked around for her sister's entourage. "You have no one to escort you?"

Miriam's lips pursed for a moment before she gave her a smile that would be truly angelic if it weren't so obviously false. "But I wish to enjoy the views with my sister, not with anyone else."

Aunt Ellen's friends smiled broadly at the two women.

"By all means, take your sister," one said.

"We shall have a good long coze, Ellen, shan't we?" the other asked.

Well, Lissa wasn't about to refuse this opportunity to escape the conversation, which had turned to various aches in bodily parts that would horrify her mother if Lissa mentioned them. She rose and curtsied, then followed Miriam down the Lovers' Walk.

"If you are intending to meet with a young man, I will *not* conveniently disappear," she hissed at Miriam.

Her sister attempted to look offended, but there was color bringing a lovely glow to her round cheeks. "As if I would do anything so improper." She sniffed.

"But you *are* hoping to meet a young man, otherwise you would have asked one of your swains or your friends to come with you." Lissa's mouth flattened. She apparently did not pose much of a threat of stealing the young man's attention from Miriam, which was why she'd been chosen.

"If you must know, I am hoping to find Lord Stoude."

Lissa stumbled slightly. "He is not here," she said.

"I have it on good authority that he was especially invited, and he sent in his acceptance."

"That doesn't explain why you needed me rather than one of your other female friends."

Miriam pouted, reluctant to answer.

Lissa abruptly turned and tugged at Miriam's arm. "We're heading back." The last thing she wanted was to allow Miriam to accomplish whatever selfish purpose she had regarding Lord Stoude.

"Wait! Oh, very well, I shall tell you." Her pout turned into a scowl. "Lord Stoude mentioned you were pleasant to converse with, and I thought he might be more willing to stay and chat with me if you were here."

The delighted warmth in her chest blossomed, but just as quickly shriveled and died as she remembered the concert the night before. "Since when do you require my help to converse with a young man?"

"I don't!" Miriam hotly retorted, but her anger cooled at Lissa's suspicious gaze. "Good gracious, haven't you even noticed? I did not think you were quite so obtuse."

Lissa's response was to tug her back toward the tables.

Miriam dug her heels in. "Lord Stoude enjoys your company!" she said quickly. "Although why, I have no idea. At the very least, he is not repelled by you."

"I'm sure the same could be said of you or any other young lady," Lissa said coolly, although the feelings churned in a whirlpool in her chest.

"Of course not! At the very least, he never looks bored when he dances with you, so perhaps your oddity is amusing to him. He likely doesn't see you as a woman, which is why he seems a bit more friendly with you than with others."

Lissa ignored the jab. Like a firework, the joy blazed in her and then died just as rapidly. "You would have done better to ask Lady Charline for her company instead of mine. He was at the concert with her last night."

Miriam's mouth cracked open in bewilderment, but she was too refined to let her jaw drop. Instead, her surprise made her seem more delicate and lovely. Lissa buried a note of jealousy —she always looked ridiculous when she was startled by something.

"Then let us find Lady Charline." Now it was Miriam who tugged at Lissa's arm.

She couldn't admit that she'd been trying to avoid Lady Charline. Had Lord Stoude told her about seeing Lissa at the concert last night? He must have done so. How would the lady feel to hear that Lissa had not heeded her warning?

Well, but Lissa had tried to avoid Lord Stoude at the concert. Surely that counted for something?

Lady Charline was easy to find, for she had surrounded herself with her finely dressed friends, and they were laughing at some story she had told.

Miriam appeared at her side and curtsied. "My lady, how lovely to see you."

Lissa also hastened to curtsy politely, but she kept her eyes lowered. Lady Charline's expression had soured upon seeing the two sisters. She must have indeed heard about Lissa's attendance at the concert and the fact that Lord Stoude had gone to find her. It was hardly Lissa's fault, for the family had always intended to go to Lady Wynwood's affair, but she still felt Lady Charline's cold gaze upon her.

Miriam was many things, but saying a great deal of nonsense in the politest way possible was a particular skill. So was maneuvering the conversation toward the topic she most desired to speak about.

"Why, we are almost all those who attended the opera with you, my lady," Miriam said with charming artlessness as she gestured to the people in Lady Charline's circle. "We are only missing Mr. Fitchette and Lord Stoude. Did they send their regrets?"

"When I spoke to Lord Stoude last night, he indicated that today he would be forced to excuse himself unexpectedly," Lady Charline said with another sour look. Perhaps she was upset not so much at Lissa but at the absence of her beau.

"How disappointing," Miss Farrimond said. "What of Mr. Fitchette? I had thought he was to have escorted you, my lady."

"Yes, I am quite vexed with him." Lady Charline's pale blue eyes sparked with temper, and Lissa almost expected her to stamp her foot. "He did not even send a note to warn me that he could not attend. I was left waiting nearly half an hour before my brother agreed to come with me."

"I only came because you bullied me," Mr. Halberstam said sulkily.

"Do hold your tongue," his sister snapped at him.

Miriam hid her disappointment well, and she engaged them in a few more minutes of light conversation before taking their leave of the group. Her face dissolved into an aggrieved expression as they walked away. "How vexing! At the opera, he specifically said he would be at the Gillards' Venetian Breakfast."

Lissa ignored her sister's grumblings. Both Lord Stoude and Mr. Fitchette were suddenly absent? Did it have anything to do with what Lissa had told him at the concert?

At the next four social gatherings, Lissa searched in vain for Lord Stoude.

Perhaps he had left town? He had no reason to tell her if he had done so, but why had it been so sudden?

Also absent was Mr. Fitchette, although it was more difficult to tell if there was anything unusual in that. He did not always accompany his cousin, and he had many other friends of his own, so he might have been spending time with them.

Lissa didn't wish to do it, but she finally girded her loins and hardened her heart, and at Mrs. Jardine's soirée, Lissa went up to Mr. Percy Calveston, Lord Stoude's young cousin. She would normally be appalled to be using the young man for her own ends, but squeezing him for gossip was *mostly* harmless, wasn't it?

After a short concert that opened up the evening, the guests parted to open up a space on the floor for dancing, while on the other side of the room, a few card tables were set up.

Lissa managed to sidle up and "accidentally" bump into Mr. Calveston as he stood on the edges of the room. "Oh! I do beg your pardon, Mr. Calveston."

She might have hit him rather harder than she intended, for he was trying to rub his side discreetly. "It is nothing, Miss Gardinier."

"Are you not dancing, Mr. Calveston?" Lissa nodded to the lines of dancers in a horrendously blatant bid for an invitation.

Mr. Calveston was always imminently polite. "Would you do me the honor of the next dance, Miss Gardinier?"

"I would love to." They were still in the middle of the set, so she smiled at him. "I believe that the last time we danced was at Mrs. Fairbanks's ball for her granddaughter's debut. It seems ages ago."

"I am afraid I have not attended many events lately, else I would have asked you to dance before this." His words were polite, but his cheeks were a trifle pink, perhaps out of embarrassment.

Lissa bit her lip. She had only wanted to make him feel more comfortable with her. "I beg your pardon, I meant no criticism. I merely wondered that I had not seen you or your cousin, Lord Stoude, at the events I attended this past week."

"Some friends from university invited me to some of their engagements," he said, his cheeks turning even redder.

She was as clumsy as an ox on ice skates! She'd forced him to admit, if vaguely, that he'd been carousing with other wild young men. He would not open up to her if she kept flustering him.

Lissa decided to simply be honest with him—she was not as skilled at nuanced conversation as her sister, and it wasn't her character, in any case. "I am glad to see you here tonight. I do apologize, but I wondered if you might know where Lord Stoude might be? He promised a dance the next time we met, but I have not seen him lately." God forgive her for the lie, but she needed some reason to ask about his whereabouts aside from admitting her burning desire to run him to ground like a hound on a fox.

"Oh, Cousin Jeremy has had to make excuses for the last four evenings, but he said he would attend the soirée later tonight."

The thought of seeing him again made her heart beat faster, but she hid it with (what she hoped was) a sweet smile. "Thank you for the information, sir."

During the set, she recalled what they had discussed the last time they had danced together. "Mr. Calveston, you mentioned that your father might purchase a commission for your younger brother. Has he decided to do so?"

"No, my brother has mentioned he does not wish to join the army." There was a strange bitterness in his tone that Lissa immediately noticed.

"By any chance, do *you* wish to purchase a commission?" she asked.

His startled gaze was all the answer she needed. But then he frowned again, looking remarkably like his older cousin. "It would be quite impossible. I am my father's heir, and he has no wish to send me to war."

She wanted to say that his father had a perfectly acceptable heir in his younger brother, and to assume that Mr. Calveston would die in battle was terribly pessimistic. But it was not her place to speak of his family situation. "I apologize if I have made you uncomfortable. Perhaps you might find work in the Home Office? I have read that Napoleon made overtures for peace with Russia."

"I doubt his sincerity," Mr. Calveston said. "He is the sort of man who thrives on conquest."

They had an enjoyable discussion about the war for the rest of the dance. It was not as intellectually stimulating as her conversations with Lord Stoude, but it seemed to cheer Mr. Calveston from his frustration over not being allowed to purchase a commission.

She was not surprised when Lady Charline found her about half an hour later. "Miss Gardinier, how delightful you look tonight." Lady Charline's smile was all that was amiable, but the friendliness did not quite reach her eyes. "I wonder if perhaps you have heard of Lord Stoude's whereabouts? He promised a dance to me the next time we should meet."

Lissa had just told the same lie herself, and yet Lady Charline's words stabbed her like a poker to the stomach. She didn't wish to tell her the truth, but Mr. Calveston had released the information so casually, she knew she could not keep it to herself. "He is expected later this evening, I believe."

Lady Charline's eyes became glittering blue diamonds. "Is he? How wonderful. I hope he will not arrive too late."

Lissa remembered the concert, and nonchalantly asked, "Is Mr. Fitchette not here tonight? I have not seen him since Lady Wynwood's musical evening."

Lady Charline's expression morphed to one of supreme annoyance. "He has disappeared quite suddenly. It is most vexing, for I had been counting upon him to escort me to several events."

Did that have anything to do with what Lissa had told Lord Stoude about him? She wasn't certain how to feel about that.

"I am sure he will return soon," Lissa said insincerely. "From what I have seen of him, he would not willingly leave his beloved cousin for too long."

Lady Charline was only partially encouraged by her words, and after a bit of stilted conversation, the ladies took their leave of each other.

Lissa was quite proud of herself that she didn't haunt the entrance hall of the home in hopes of seeing Lord Stoude when he arrived. She might have lingered a bit too long in the dining room in hopes a certain nobleman might find her hiding there, but soon her mother discovered her and dragged her out to the saloon for more dancing.

Several more guests arrived later in the evening, but look as she might, Lissa didn't see Lord Stoude among them. Then in the next moment, she was mentally flogging herself for being so anxious about seeing him again. She had deliberately chosen not to attend the opera in order to set her sights on Bath rather than letting him continue to arouse hopes in her heart. She determined to think no more of him.

Lissa had been standing next to her mother and listening to her make desultory complaints about the heat of the room and the fact that she believed one of the ladies at her card table earlier in the evening had cheated. It was the reason she'd quit the game and come to find Lissa, and the reason why she was here now, searching the crowd for a new dance partner for her.

It was nearly impossible for Lissa to pretend to be listening, and she found herself staring at her feet. She lifted her head and saw Lord Stoude almost directly across the room from her.

When had he arrived? How had she not noticed when he entered the room?

Then the heat from the press of bodies became as nothing to her, because ice was frosting over her heart and lungs. He was speaking earnestly with Lady Charline—not quite a serious conversation, but he had no attention for anyone else around them.

At that moment, a light supper was announced, and the guests headed toward the dining room. Lady Charline took Lord Stoude's arm. They were walking directly toward Lissa.

They both saw her. Lady Charline sent a triumphant smile at her.

But Lord Stoude simply looked at her, as though seeing right through her. He did not even acknowledge her—instead, he gave a brief nod to her mother, then turned to Lady Charline with that almost-smile on his face and said something that made her laugh.

Then they walked past Lissa without another glance.

Chapter Twelve

"What did you do to Lord Stoude?" Lissa's mother hissed.

"Why do you assume I did something? I have not spoken to him since the concert."

"Then why did he seem so cold? He was so friendly when I spoke at length with him at Mrs. Fairbanks's ball."

"Perhaps you should ask if Miriam said something to him."

To her surprise, her mother didn't immediately defend her younger daughter. "She has been rather irritable lately. She might have said something rude to him when he arrived tonight."

Lissa found a table for her mother and sat her down next to one of her friends. After collecting food onto plates for the two ladies, she served them and left the dining room while they chatted and ate, unaware that she was not serving herself.

There was an older woman in the ladies' retiring room, haranguing a maid to urge her to hurry up and fix a seam of her bodice that had torn. Lissa closed the door and wandered the house, finally finding an open door leading into the library.

It was a rather small library, but tall, with a narrow walkway around three of the four walls, although the second story did not look tall enough for a person to stand upright without hitting his head on the molded ceiling. There was only one chair in front of the tiny fireplace and on the outside wall, a window seat. An old, elaborately carved wooden pedestal took the place of pride in the center of the room, upon which rested an old family Bible. Only one glass-fronted bookcase stood in the corner with old leather-bound books locked away within, but the majority of the books were on shelves on the second story, packed tightly next to one another. The entire room smelled of old leather and parchment, and the small space made the air seem a bit suffocating.

Lissa sat in the window seat and looked out at the dark night, unable to see anything beyond the glass due to the candles on the mantlepiece.

She kept seeing the moment his eyes passed over her, feeling the pain prick her again and again.

"I love him," she realized.

She had tried not to do so—how she had tried! She would be a fool to have any hope that wealthy, handsome Lord Stoude would see her as anything more than a slightly entertaining peculiarity.

Maybe if she had hidden her true self from him, he might have seen her as a woman and not simply a foolish girl.

Or maybe he would not have spoken to her at all, because with her plain face, she would have simply been an insipid young miss in her second Season.

The sound of footsteps made her tense, but then she realized they were from a woman's slippers and not a man's shoes. She didn't relish her solitude being interrupted, but she shouldn't have hoped for a quiet moment in the middle of a party.

She could go home later and feel all the biting cuts of the despair eating away at her insides.

To her surprise, Lady Wynwood entered the room and smiled as she saw her. "There you are, my dear."

"How did you know I was here?"

"I didn't." Lady Wynwood cocked her head. "I felt God guiding me here, to you." She sat down on the window seat with her.

Lady Wynwood always spoke as though God were a houseguest in her heart. Perhaps He was. She had a confidence given to her by her faith, an inner strength that was unlike anything Lissa had known.

"What is troubling you, my dear?" The light brown eyes caught some of the candlelight and seemed to flicker golden with the flames.

Lissa didn't know what to say. She was terribly unhappy, but she also knew it was of her own making—no one had tricked her or misled her. And yet it made her feel so frustrated with herself.

She said the first thing that came to mind. "Have you ever been in love?"

Lady Wynwood ran a hand over her hair, smoothing the blonde strands, including the one white streak over her left temple. But when she looked into Lissa's eyes, there was a slight smile upon her face, and her gaze was warm like liquid sunlight. "Yes," she said simply.

She looked like a woman *still* in love. Had she loved Lord Wynwood so much? Lissa hadn't realized Lady Wynwood's marriage had been so strong.

"Well, love is dreadful," Lissa said flatly.

Lady Wynwood bit back a smile. "Yes, it certainly is."

She had used the present tense. Had Lissa been mistaken? Was she in love with someone now? It wasn't so unusual—she had been a widow for seven years now.

"But not all love is so terrible," Lady Wynwood said.

"It is when it makes me feel ..." Lissa sighed. "So undesirable."

"I can say nothing for the gentleman's poor taste in not seeing the rare jewel in front of him." Lady Wynwood laid a hand over Lissa's. "But let me tell you that you are not undesirable. You are very much loved."

Lissa thought of her family—even her mother, for all her complaining, only wanted the best for her. "I suppose so."

"The way you see yourself is reflected from the eyes of the person you esteem the most."

"Yes, it seems obvious when you say that. But it also makes me aware of how much I've elevated him into that person, and that's just depressing."

"There is one Person whose love for you is vast and deep." Lady Wynwood smiled, and it was as if there was a light shining from within her eyes rather than simply from the glow of the candles. "And when you can esteem Him the most, His love for you makes you *beautiful*."

The word took Lissa's breath away. She wanted to be beautiful to someone. And she realized she was not even beautiful to *herself*.

Tears welled in her eyes and in her nose, but she had not even consciously realized she was so upset. "I feel so … unlovable." Her voice was a rasping tree branch against a window in winter.

"Oh, my dear girl." Lady Wynwood gathered her in her arms. "You are very loved. God loves you so much that He sent his Son to die for you, to sacrifice for your sins. 'But God commendeth His love toward us, in that, while we were yet sinners, Christ died for us.' What is greater love than that?"

She had heard the verse in church on Sunday, but it had not impacted her as it did now. To love someone enough to die for them. Now that she knew she loved Lord Stoude, she could take that emotion one step further and imagine a love deep enough to die for someone.

It was as if she could hear the Lord Jesus Christ whispering to her, *I loved you enough to die for you.*

Yes, that kind of love was beautiful. It was enough to make a person beautiful.

"It will seem difficult now," Lady Wynwood continued, "but remember that your Heavenly Father is with you always. You are not alone because you belong to Him. 'Behold, what manner of love the Father hath bestowed upon us, that we should be called the sons of God.'"

Lissa was a child of the Lord God, even more than she was a child of her parents. And He loved her. And she was His.

Her tears had dried up, but she didn't remember when that had happened. She rubbed her gloved hands against her face, but then Lady Wynwood shoved a handkerchief at her.

Lissa held it up. It was quite large—larger even than a man's handkerchief—and while it was edged with lace, it was also very … blue.

Lady Wynwood interpreted her look and sighed. "My maid, Aya, made it for me when I complained that my regular handkerchiefs couldn't be used for more than one piddling sneeze. It is blue because she made it from leftover dress fabric."

Lissa definitely used it for more than one piddling sneeze. She blew her nose loudly.

"There now." Lady Wynwood stood. "When you are ready, go to the retiring room and ask for some cool water for your eyes. Don't remain here for too long, lest your mind spiral down toward more maudlin inclinations again." With a smile and a pat on her shoulder, she left Lissa to her thoughts.

It seemed as though she had only been here for a moment, but a look at the clock indicated that supper had ended long since. Lissa's mother would be looking for her soon.

But she did not wish to leave the sanctuary of the library at the moment. She had learned something important about God, and about herself. And even about her feelings for Lord Stoude.

She had found no answers or balm for her heartache. And yet she felt a vast sea of peace inside of her, a calm that stretched on and on. She could not explain it, although she knew why it was there—she knew God had placed it there, just for her.

At last, she knew she should return to the party. There would be a little more dancing and cards after the supper, but soon she could persuade her mother to leave, assuming they could drag Miriam away from her many admirers.

Lissa had been too distraught to pay attention to her surroundings, so she didn't notice until she heard the click of the door as it closed.

Mr. Cirling stood there. He had gone to the opera with Lady Charline and Lord Stoude. Lissa had been introduced to him—may have even danced with him once—but they had not spoken at length. She only knew his name when Lady Charline mentioned that he was a friend of her brother.

Now, his wide, round face was set in grim lines as he advanced toward her. Lissa instinctively rose to her feet, her heartbeat quickening. She didn't like the hard look in his eyes, the slight sneer on his lips.

Nor did she like the length of cloth in one of his hands, and the coil of rope in the other.

Chapter Thirteen

"You're coming with me," Mr. Cirling said.

"No, I am not," Lissa said.

He blinked at her. He had probably expected her to shriek or swoon or cower. But that was the mask she donned for society, and right now, she certainly wasn't going to be *polite* to him.

After a moment's hesitation, he took a step toward her.

She backed away. "I shall scream."

He smirked. "I paid a servant to keep everyone away from this portion of the house for a few minutes. No one will hear or save you."

Lissa was already afraid, but now she began to panic. She had been counting on her amazing ability to make a nuisance of herself and arouse murderous emotions in others (never before had she taken such pride in it), but she had been assuming that if she engendered enough frustration, she could rouse the servants or a guest to come to her aid. But no help would come.

He took another step, but she swiftly moved to the side, trying to circle back to the library's only door. "Why are you doing this? Even my mother will admit that my dowry is hardly worth the torture of dealing with me."

Mr. Cirling had been stalking toward her, but now he hesitated, his expression incredulous. "Dowry? Did you really think I'd be remotely interested in marriage to someone like you, plain as a pikestaff?"

The insult might have dejected her if it had been flung from someone else, but coming from his frog-like mouth while he scorned her with his bulbous, frog-like eyes, it made Lissa's ire blaze. "I see you are a person who cannot speak without unleashing your frustration over your unpretentiousness through denigration of others."

He had to pause to unravel her words and realize she had slighted him. It gave her time to move closer to the door.

But he was not distracted for long. He reached out a long arm and grasped her shoulder even as she darted toward escape.

His grip was painful, but she thrashed and fought and screamed. She held nothing back, tearing the restrictive seams of her gown at her back and arms. She managed to slap him a few times, grateful she'd worn a bracelet that left a small cut over his eye.

She paused only to demand, "Why are you doing this?" Lissa had considered asking earlier, but he had no reason to answer her. However, he had motivation now—she had stopped fighting him for a moment. He might be induced to speak while he caught his breath.

He glared at her with one eye while his hand dabbed at the blood dribbling from the other. "Do not try to convince me that you do not know."

"Know what?" she asked in exasperation. Really, how could she get Mr. Collingworth to blather on about ridiculous dog names with such ease, and yet she couldn't induce this man to explain something as simple as why he wanted to capture her?

He ignored her and tried to reach for her again, but she slapped him away in a wild whirlwind of hands and a few kicks with her slippered feet, aimed at his unprotected shins. He hissed and limped backward a step.

Unfortunately, it was possible that her toes hurt as much as his shins. "Why are you doing this?" she repeated.

"I saw you speaking to Lord Stoude at the concert."

Lissa resisted the urge to roll her eyes. "So did everyone else seated around me."

His face darkened. "I saw you point to Mr. Lades."

She blinked at him. "Who?"

Mr. Cirling's face now turned an alarming shade of puce. "Mr. Lades!" he said unhelpfully.

Lissa thought about her conversation with Lord Stoude, short as it had been. She had only pointed to one person—Mrs. Whichard. She had done so to bring his attention to the man sitting next to the woman.

"I didn't point to any man," she insisted, since it was true. "I merely pointed out Mrs. Whichard."

"I know everything was your doing! Mr. Lades was snatched away by Lord Stoude and two other men directly after the concert. No one knew about his involvement."

He could hardly say that, since Mr. Lades had met with Mr. Fitchette, Mr. Galland, and Mr. Morfin in sight of everyone at the venue, and they had already been under investigation.

"I haven't the faintest idea what you are talking about," she said. "Why would Lord Stoude do something so wicked? And why would you do this to me? I can hardly tell you where your friend has gone."

But her words seemed to harden his resolve, as his eyes focused upon her. "You will be my hostage. I shall *make* Lord Stoude release Mr. Lades or you will die."

She resisted the urge to swallow. "Why do you think Lord Stoude would care in the least what happens to me?" It still stabbed at her, the memory of his cold glance before turning away.

He didn't answer. He grasped at her, pulling at the top of her long evening glove. She straightened her arm to slide it off of her, but the kid leather bunched at her wrist and caught.

Lissa flailed and fought, shrieking with all her might, but then he managed to land a solid blow to her temple.

Pain exploded in her head. She almost felt as though she could see her agony as it raced across her vision in sparks.

While she was dazed, Mr. Cirling managed to trap her hands and tie them with the rope. He stopped her cries with the cloth stuffed into her mouth and tied tightly around her head.

She still dug her heels in as he dragged her to the door, but her head was pounding, and she couldn't fight as hard as she had before.

Once outside the library, the hallway was empty, as he had said it would be. He yanked her toward the servants' stairs at the other end.

No one would come for her. Lady Wynwood had deliberately left her alone to tend to her swollen face, so she would not expect Lissa back to the saloon very soon.

And Lord Stoude ... he didn't care for her in the least. She had been useful perhaps, for a time. She began to wonder if their conversations had all been a dream or a delusion.

But she remembered Lady Wynwood's words: "... *Remember that your Heavenly Father is with you always. You are not alone because you belong to Him. 'Behold, what manner of love the Father hath bestowed upon us, that we should be called the sons of God.'*"

God was with her, even now. She had to believe that.

Lord, please help me. Please let him find me.

Jeremy pretended to be fascinated by every word uttered by Lady Charline and kept a smile on his face. His friends insisted it was *not* a smile, but he had it on good authority that it *must* be a smile, for his lips curved up ever so slightly, and more importantly, when he smiled, Miss Gardinier smiled back at him.

At the moment, Lady Charline was being even more tiresome than usual, but he needed to ascertain if she knew anything about her cousin's business. He did not think she did, for he had already had a long conversation with her brother earlier this evening before arriving at the Jardines' soirée. As far as he could tell, the man hadn't known anything about Mr. Fitchette's darker activities. He had been aware of Mr. Fitchette's admiration of Napoleon, although not his deeper infatuation.

And so Jeremy fulfilled the extent of his duty and subtly probed Lady Charline, testing her, observing closely to catch her in incriminating responses. The woman had the intelligence of a goose.

He couldn't help but compare her with another woman, one whose hair was a darker blonde and with greenish-gray eyes sparkling with complex ideas and the insight to see the foibles of society.

The thought of Miss Gardinier made him realize she hadn't yet returned to the party.

Jeremy had been watching her rather more closely than usual because of what had happened after the concert a week ago, and because of his intentions tonight to interrogate Lady Charline and Mr. Cirling. He did not think Miss Gardinier would be in danger, and he could not remain as close to her as he would like, but he still found his eyes seeking her out wherever she was.

Except that she'd left the dining room during supper and hadn't returned. Lady Wynwood had also noticed her departure, and after a few minutes, she spoke to her escort, Mr. Drydale, and then left the room, as well. He thought she might have gone after Miss Gardinier.

But after supper, Lady Wynwood returned to the saloon without Miss Gardinier. She did not look concerned, but Jeremy wondered what had occurred.

Had another group of women treated her with disdain? He understood why she hid her true, irreverent thoughts behind a silent, dull façade, but it also invited the attention of others dissatisfied with themselves and desiring a target.

Or perhaps her mother had made yet another comparison between Miss Gardinier and the younger, more favored sister? Jeremy found Miss Miriam Gardinier utterly unlike her older sister, but he could see how she was very similar to their mother.

As the minutes ticked by, he grew more impatient with Lady Charline, more impatient to see Miss Gardinier again. But he still needed to speak to Mr. Cirling.

Now that he realized it, Mr. Cirling had left the saloon directly after supper and had not yet returned.

The unease began to foam inside of him—a feeling utterly without logic or reason, and yet he could not ignore it.

His work was not often of an urgent variety. He collected information, organizing it and drawing conclusions. He was not like the others, who placed their lives in danger battling more aggressive foes. His tasks did not involve combat or rescue.

But now, something inside him was urging him to take action. Some instinct was telling him that time was of the essence.

He bowed to Lady Charline, even though she had been mid-sentence. "I beg your pardon, my lady, but I recalled an urgent matter I must conclude with a guest at the party. I will take my leave of you now."

Lady Charline's face reddened at his rudeness, but she was too well-bred to do more than frown and nod disdainfully. "Very well, Lord Stoude. I do hope to see you again soon."

She likely expected him to call upon her at home, and he felt faintly guilty for raising her expectations with his time spent in her company. But he had made no promises, nor had he flirted with her outright.

He didn't even know if he knew *how* to flirt.

But he would like to try flirting with Miss Gardinier.

And so he began searching the house for her.

Lissa stopped struggling while they were on the servants' stairs, not relishing the thought of accidentally falling down the steep steps in the darkness.

She also used the darkness of the stairwell to reach up to her bodice and remove the brooch pinned there. The torn seams from her earlier struggles had also bent the pin of the brooch, making it easy to tear it free from the fabric. Mr. Cirling followed behind her and didn't notice.

He grabbed her arm and pulled her through one of the back doors of the mansion, which led into a paved back area holding the privy and a small laundry building. They headed in the direction of the mews.

Lissa waited until they passed the door to the half-basement, then struck at the largest area of skin showing—his face. She did not hesitate and attacked viciously, and the brooch pin tore deeply into his cheek. His cries echoed against the wall of the house, and his grip on her arm was released.

She ran with all her might down a short flight of stairs toward the half-basement door. She had seen that it was cracked open, so she knew it wasn't locked. Her hands scrabbled at the latch, then pulled it open.

Mr. Cirling's hand whistled past her ear and slapped the door, slamming it shut with a loud *bang!*

Lissa had chosen to try to escape rather than remove the gag, which was tied tightly around her head, but now she scrabbled at the cloth. If she could but scream …

She tugged at the cloth in vain. He grabbed both her arms.

Lissa kicked and struggled with all her might. The sides of the stairs, made of stone, allowed her to place both feet against the wall and push, throwing Mr. Cirling off balance. He fell, but he did not release his hold on her, and Lissa fell with him.

It was a race to see who could scramble to their feet first. Lissa was hampered by her wrists, still tied together in front of her, and she found it hard to breathe through the gag in her mouth. She stepped on his leg and slipped to her knees. He rose above her and grabbed at her, but she merely kicked and twisted until they went down again.

But the third time they fell, Mr. Cirling finally realized an easier way to capture her—he slapped her across the face.

For the second time that night, stars flew across her vision. He took advantage of her weakened limbs and dragged her up the steps, continuing his march toward the mews.

The slap was considerably less painful than when he'd hit her temple. Lissa recovered before they moved more than two-thirds of the way across the courtyard, and she began screaming ineffectually into the gag and bucking against his hold of her arms.

While the courtyard was dark, it was not entirely black, for lights shone from the upper floors of the Jardines' house and from the neighboring townhouses. So Lissa saw the large shadow looming over them only a moment before a fist smashed into Mr. Cirling's face.

His head jerked back and his hands loosened on her. Lissa stepped back quickly, out of the way of Lord Stoude's broad shoulders as he attacked Mr. Cirling.

Her abductor was not dazed for long, however, and wild blows flew between the two men.

She continued trying to untie the gag, which had been pulled into a hard knot. She pressed her back against the laundry building, but she couldn't move farther away because the fight ranged over the wide area directly in front of her, blocking her path either back to the house or toward the mews.

The two men had grabbed fistfuls of each other's collars, and Lord Stoude had pushed them more toward the mews. Lissa took advantage of the brief opening and darted back toward the house.

But too quickly, Mr. Cirling spun Lord Stoude in a circle and they crashed into Lissa. She was sent sprawling to the ground.

She tried to crawl away as quickly as she could, but the only warning she had was the scuffle of heels against the ground before a foot landed a glancing blow to the back of her head.

"Lissa!"

She didn't realize she'd been knocked unconscious until she woke up. While she was still on the ground, strangely, she was no longer gagged or tied. And she was staring up into Lord Stoude's face.

Had he called her Christian name? She couldn't quite recall. But the concern on his face instantly melted into relief as she looked at him.

Lissa finally realized she was held in his arms when he drew her closer to bury his face in her shoulder. His strong, solid chest pressed against her, and she was surrounded by the scent of ginger, and chamomile, and river rocks.

She breathed deep, feeling his heartbeat gradually slow.

He pulled away from the embrace, looking into her face. In the darkness, she only saw the occasional glint of candlelight in his eyes.

"You were injured for my sake," he said hoarsely.

"I was injured because I was not about to meekly be abducted," she said. Her throat felt raw from her screaming, and she swallowed. "I am afraid I annoyed him. Where is he?"

He cast a glare to the side. She followed his look and saw the shoes of a prone figure, the ankles tied with a rope that looked familiar. Mr. Cirling was not moving, so she assumed Lord Stoude landed a blow to render him senseless.

"Well, he looks quite comfortable." Her own limbs felt like jelly, and she was content to lie there with Lord Stoude's arms around her. "Are you injured, my lord?"

The line of his left cheek made her think it was swollen. Was his face getting closer?

His head blotted out what little light there was, and then his lips were on hers.

They were warm and soft, and she tasted the wine he had drunk at supper. And then she forgot about that as he kissed her again, more deeply, tightening his arms around her to hold her tightly against him.

It was marvelous. It might be more marvelous if her head wasn't spinning quite so much.

When he pulled his head back, she opened her eyes to look into his. He was so close, and so dear to her. "How did you find me?"

"I noticed you hadn't returned to the party."

"You noticed when I left?"

"Of course." He kissed her again, tenderly, and she almost forgot what she had asked him. "I might not have found you if I hadn't heard a door slam."

"I tried to escape, but Mr. Cirling slammed it shut. He owes me a new brooch," she grumbled.

"Was that what caused the nasty cut across his face? Well done." She heard the smile in his voice and wished she could see his face more clearly.

"Really, it's quite nice to lie here with your arms about me, but the ground is a trifle cold and I cannot seem to ignore the unconscious man nearby."

He might have snorted in laughter, but then he kissed her again briefly. "Can you sit up?"

She nodded and he helped her to sit against the wall of the laundry building. "I am sorry, but I must leave you for a few minutes while I find someone to help me."

"Go, go." She tried to wave her arm, but it felt like limp, damp rags.

It was a rather frightening few minutes to sit there in the courtyard next to Mr. Cirling's unmoving form. She might have slid closer to him in order to deliver a few solid kicks to his backside, but she would never admit to it, and he did not notice.

The identity of the man who returned with Lord Stoude made Lissa tilt her head in surprise. "Does my lady know what you do?" she asked Mr. Drydale.

"I'm fairly certain she does," he murmured.

"May I leave this to you, sir?" Lord Stoude asked the older gentleman. At his nod, Lord Stoude bent and picked Lissa up.

She knew she was considerably heavier than a feather, and Lord Stoude did grunt a little as he rose to his feet, but he held her tightly. She rested her head against his shoulder. Yes, it was quite nice being pressed so close to his chest.

They encountered a maid as he was climbing the stairs, and she quickly led them to a guest bedroom. He sent her for a doctor, and she was so flustered that she rushed away, leaving them alone in the room.

Lord Stoude panted slightly because of the stairs, but he laid her gently upon the bed.

She reached out to touch his cheek (the one not swollen), glad that she now had feeling back in her arms. "I am certain there are many things you must do. You should go and attend to them."

He frowned down at her.

"I shall be resting here," she told him. "There is no cause for worry."

He put his hand over hers, pressing her palm into his face. Then he released her, bowed, and left the room.

That was the last she saw of him for the next week.

Chapter Fourteen

Lissa's dizziness and headaches plagued her for four days. Her weakness continued for a few days longer. During that time, she saw nothing of Lord Stoude during the day.

And at night, she replayed their kiss(es).

She would have thought it all a dream but for one amazing occurrence. *Seven* occurrences, to be exact.

Every morning, flowers arrived for her. Expensive hothouse roses in shades of red and pink, orchids of purple and creamy white, and also less exotic offerings—violets and hyacinths. But then he must have learned that her favorite flower was the camellia, for the last two days, he'd sent camellias in white, pink, and red.

She assumed the offerings were from Lord Stoude—the card was frustratingly signed merely "J. S." Lissa glared at the small card in her hand as her mother's lady's maid arranged the camellias from yesterday morning in a vase in the drawing room.

"I'm certain he'll come to visit you soon, miss," Mrs. Peyton said.

Lissa dropped the card into her lap, embarrassed that her thoughts were so easily read. But those dratted flowers were the reason she had insisted upon sitting in the drawing room this morning rather than remaining in the privacy and comfort of her bed to secretly read a gentleman's magazine. She sighed and picked up the novel she had borrowed from her sister.

"Don't you look a treat, miss?" Mrs. Peyton asked with the familiarity of a long-time retainer. "Your shawl matches your lovely flowers."

Mrs. Peyton had insisted upon wrapping her in her warmest shawl, a favorite that had been knit in shades of red, pink, and white, despite the fact it was a bit too informal for the drawing room. But Lissa could not gainsay the concern of the servant who had been the first to braid her hair.

"I'll bring you some tea, shall I?" Mrs. Peyton bustled from the drawing room.

The novel was incredibly boring, involving the heroine shrieking and swooning at every little thing. Lissa felt she had the right to criticize since she had only swooned when her head had been knocked about. She had even managed to draw blood with a broken brooch. She felt more like the hero than the heroine.

She was about to toss the novel aside and ask her maid to fetch the newspaper when the knocker sounded.

It was early for visitors, surely? Her family rose later in town than in the country, but her mother and sister had left for shopping directly after breakfast. Her father was holed up in his study, so perhaps he expected someone on business.

But then she heard the firm tread on the stairs, and suddenly she didn't know what to do with her hands. She picked up the novel, put it down, wrapped her shawl more tightly about her, then loosened it to attempt to make it fall more gracefully and not look like the fleecy, informal garment that it was. Then she noticed her gloves, discarded beside her, and hastily drew them on.

The drawing room door opened. "Lord Stoude," the butler announced.

He stood tall and seemed to fill the space so that the room felt smaller. His eyes were very blue in the sunlight streaming through the windows, and they searched her face, his brow furrowed.

"Forgive me for not rising, my lord," Lissa said. She did not think her legs could support her even if she tried. Now that he was here, after she'd spent seven days cursing him for not even properly signing his name on his card, she didn't know what to say to him.

Her mundane words seemed to relieve him, for his brow cleared and he almost-smiled.

Lissa couldn't seem to stop herself from responding to that smile like a flower bud unfurling. Too late, she put her hand to her mouth to try to hide her answering smile. "Won't you sit down?"

Mrs. Peyton had risen, and she now bobbed a curtsy. "I'll fetch more tea," she said, even though the teapot was surely still hot from when she'd brought it only a few minutes ago. She gathered up the tray and left the two of them in the room with the door open.

Rather than sitting in the chair across from her, Lord Stoude took the seat next to her on the sofa. "I am glad to see you looking well today, Miss Gardinier."

"Your timing is quite favorable, for yesterday I looked 'like death,' according to my sister. How did you know I would be downstairs today?"

"I have been delivering the flowers in person every morning," he said. "The maid who relieved me of them in the entrance hall told me that you were in the drawing room."

Now that she thought of it, Mrs. Peyton had been the one who suggested she come downstairs. "But my mother told me nothing of your visits."

His eyes slid to the side. "I have only left my card on the other days."

She could hardly blame him for not wishing to spend a quarter-hour with her mother and Miriam, and at such an unusual time of the day. Miriam, as self-centered as she was, might have begun to hold expectations of the gentleman toward her own lovely person, no matter what he professed was the reason for his visit.

"I am glad you have come," she said. "I wish to thank you for the flowers, and for saving my life."

He turned his eyes intently upon her face. "I am overjoyed that you are looking well. I can only be glad I arrived in time."

Lissa drank in his gaze, the beautiful blue of his eyes, like glittering beryls of the finest hue. "I prayed for you to find me, and you did."

For a moment, he looked unsure and hesitant, but then he said, "I felt something urging me toward that side of the house. Then I heard the door slam, and that is where I found you."

"God guided you to me. Despite my fear, I felt He was with me."

Lord Stoude reached over to take her hand. "I apologize for putting you in danger."

She squeezed his hand. "I chose my own actions. Did we accomplish something good?"

"Yes," he said, his expression firm. "We protected England."

Warmth flooded her chest, and she smiled at him. "I have always felt particularly useless as a society miss. I quite liked helping you, even if only in small ways."

"Putting yourself in danger is not a small way," he said sternly. "You should have been able to enjoy your Season."

"I doubt I could have. My mother was always telling me that I wasn't fulfilling my role as a good daughter, since I was not taking the *ton* by storm."

"I am grateful you did not take the *ton* by storm."

She realized he still held her hand, and she tried to pull it back. "Are you, indeed?" she asked in her chilliest voice.

He almost-smiled again. "Otherwise, I might not have become better acquainted with you." He kissed the back of her gloved hand.

She felt the warmth of his breath through the thin silk, and the sensation made her own breath catch. But then her heart began pounding rapidly when he removed her glove and pressed his lips to her palm. The feel of his mouth on her skin made her tremble.

He looked directly at her, capturing her with a look of tenderness and a hint of pleading in his eyes. "When I saw you injured on the ground, I went wild. It made me realize how much I care for you." His hand, still holding hers, tightened. "I could not bear it if something happened to you. I wish to always be with you so that I may protect you. Say you will marry me, Lissa."

His words thrilled her (to be honest, his words made a voice inside of her shriek and jump around in circles), but she swallowed and forced herself to ask, "What of Lady Charline? You were eager to go to the opera and Lady Wynwood's concert with her."

Lord Stoude grimaced. "I went to the opera because I wished to grow closer to her cousin, Mr. Fitchette, who was suspected of selling arms to the French. And as for the concert …" Now he frowned. "I did not attend the concert with Lady Charline. I went with Mr. Drydale, whom you met briefly."

"But I saw her sitting with you."

"She arrived with her brother, but she noticed me and came to sit next to us. Lud, did you think I had asked you to sit with her?"

Had it all been a misunderstanding? Lissa remembered feeling so downcast at the sight of Lady Charline speaking to Lord Stoude.

No, it could not have been simply a misunderstanding. "What else was I to think when you spoke at length with her at the soirée?"

"I assure you, I did not enjoy it in the least." He looked as though he'd bitten into an exceptionally sour lemon tart. "After the concert, I and my compatriots arrested Mr. Fitchette, Mr. Galland, Mr. Morfin, and the man you pointed out to me, Mr. Lades. At the soirée, I needed to speak at length with Lady Charline, her brother, and Mr. Cirling that night to determine if they knew anything of their cousin's activities."

Lissa pouted at him. "You should have spoken to Mr. Cirling first."

He kissed her palm again, making her heart leap. "I apologize, my darling. I regret that I did not."

She decided she liked it when he called her "darling."

"Lissa, I have cherished you since our first encounter, when you prevented me from notice by Mr. Galland and Mr. Morfin. I was continually drawn to you wherever you hid yourself, and our conversations made me feel relaxed and content." He folded her hand in both of his, looking grave. "The nature of my … work is not usually as violent as several days ago, but it does demand secrecy and deception. I believed that involving a wife in my web of lies would be unfair to her. But then I met you, who saw through my actions and moved to aid me, and I fell in love with you."

His affectionate words made it hard for her to breathe. "A woman who loves you will support you as you work to protect England."

"Does that mean that you care for me?" An almost-smile hovered around his mouth, but his eyes were strangely vulnerable.

"I have loved you for a long time, but I thought you could not possibly be interested in a woman like me, plain and with an impertinent mouth."

He suddenly smiled, and then Lissa really did think she would swoon at the magnificence of that smile. Perhaps the heroine in the novel was not *quite* so silly.

"I happen to adore your impertinent mouth," he said.

And then he kissed her to prove it.

Connect with Camy

Thank you for reading *Lissa and the Spy*! Lissa appears again in *Lady Wynwood's Spies, volume 1: Archer*, which takes place in the spring of 1811. I hope this story explains the deeper meaning behind the words Lissa speaks to Lady Wynwood in that book.

Lady Wynwood and Mr. Drydale go on to have their own adventures in the Lady Wynwood's Spies series.

Miss Church-Pratton is my favorite villainess, for she has appeared not only in this book but also in *The Spinster's Christmas* and *Prelude for a Lord*. You can find out what happened to her betrothed, Mr. Bayard Terralton, in *Prelude for a Lord*, which takes place in the winter of 1811.

Get the Lady Wynwood's Spies prequel *The Gentleman Thief* FREE when you sign up for my newsletter (https://dl.bookfunnel.com/n0dnatyhqw). After a few welcome emails, I send out newsletters about once a month with a sale on one of my books, a freebie, or news about when my latest release is available.

Camy

Author bio:

Camy writes Christian Regency romantic suspense as *USA Today* bestselling author Camille Elliot and Christian contemporary romantic suspense as *USA Today* bestselling author Camy Tang. She grew up in Hawaii, where she started reading Regency romances when she was thirteen years old. Now she lives in northern California with her engineer husband.

She graduated from Stanford University in psychology with a focus on biology, and for nine years she worked as a biologist researcher. Then God guided her path in a completely different direction and now she's writing full time, using her original psychology degree as she creates the characters in her novels.

She was a staff worker for her church youth group for over 20 years and used to lead one of the Sunday worship teams. She loves to knit antique knitting patterns and is learning Japanese.

Visit her website at https://camilleelliot.com/

Abiding Faith – Freedom's Call

A Novella of the American Revolution
by Louise M. Gouge

Is it a noble thing for a man to fight for freedom? Or should he let God fight for him? When does a man ... or a woman ... take up arms and join the battle? A pacifist Quaker widow and a prisoner of war Patriot risk their hearts ... and their lives ... to find God's will. But will the gap between her peace-loving faith and his determination to return to fight in the American Revolution be a chasm too wide to cross?

Acknowledgments

As with all of my stories, my late husband, David, was the original inspiration for *Abiding Faith – Freedom's Call*. While I miss David, I rejoice that he is celebrating in Heaven with our Lord and Savior Jesus Christ. We who trust the Lord for His free gift of salvation do not grieve as others who have no hope. One day I will see my Jesus face to face and be reunited with David and all my family and friends who have gone to heaven before me.

Scripture Verse: "But they that wait upon the LORD shall renew *their* strength; they shall mount up with wings as eagles; they shall run, and not be weary; *and* they shall walk, and not faint" (Isaiah 40:29, KJV).

Chapter One

St. Augustine, East Florida Colony
January 1781

"Married?" Anne tried to keep the surprise from her voice. But her dear elderly cook seemed an unlikely choice for any unattached man, even in a military town where men greatly outnumbered women. Guilt stung Anne's heart over such an uncharitable thought, even as she battled dismay. Without Cook, how could she manage? She settled into a drawing room chair and invited Cook to sit beside her.

"Yes, ma'am." The wiry little woman sat on a chair's edge, and her pale blue eyes twinkled in her thin, well-worn face. "Sergeant Martin ain't much to look at, but he's a kind, jolly soul." She chuckled, sounding like a crone's cackle. "And he likes my cookin'."

Now Anne understood. "I know you'll feed him well, but will he take good care of you?"

"Yes, ma'am. He's a fine Christian, and he's already found rooms for us over on Charlotte Street." Her bushy gray eyebrows bunched. "I hope you don't mind, Mrs. Hussey."

"Not at all." Anne patted Cook's hand. "I would see thee happy." She lapsed into plain speech, as she did when her emotions rose to the surface. "We'll talk more later. Is the cart ready?"

"Yes, ma'am." Cook stood. "D'you want me to help you push it over to the Parade?"

"No, thank you. I can manage." When Anne rose, weariness swept through her body, belying her words. She straightened, refusing to succumb to the aching, exhausting grief that had been her companion these past months. God would provide whatever she needed, as He had since Artemis's death last September. Although her husband had grown abusive, she still missed him, or at least missed the fine young man she'd married seven years ago.

She shook off such thoughts and turned her mind to the day ahead. Outside in the crisp early morning air, she gripped the handles of her low, boxlike cart and pushed it through the wooden gate and into the street.

Despite the exertion required to convey her produce to the Parade, she enjoyed early mornings. The aroma of the freshly picked oranges and the abundance of squash, green beans, and other vegetables from her garden reminded her of God's provision. She had her health and her house and two ladies as tenants. Of course, one woman would soon marry her beau, just as Cook would do. No woman remained unattached for long in St. Augustine. Although newly widowed, Anne had received proposals, too. But she would never marry again. Even the kindest man might become cruel if he failed to rely upon the Lord when trials came.

It did no good to think about Artemis's failures rather than his good qualities. He'd worked hard and had become Governor Tonyn's close confidant, which showed his dependability. But he'd pinched every penny except when it came to dressing in colorful finery. Pride and ambition had truly been his downfall. But remembering his faults was useless. On this mild winter day, she must turn her thoughts to God, who never failed His children.

The scents emanating from the Parade reached her nostrils long before she pushed her cart into the broad plaza extending eastward from the governor's house to Matanzas Bay. The butchers had killed their day's livestock quota, and the stench wafted on the wind. Anne prayed they would sell all the meat, for by law they couldn't sell it on the second day. Her cart was usually empty before the noon church bells rang.

"Good morning, Mrs. Hussey." The governor's middle-aged black cook waited for her under a spreading magnolia tree.

Anne's heart warmed. "Good morning, Friend Maude." As she shoved her cart into her usual spot, she prayed silently that God end the evil slavery binding the cook to the governor while her children had been sold to a nearby plantation owner.

In contrast, the Lord had given Anne freedom, but what should she do with it? On these pleasant winter days in East Florida, she often longed for the snows of Nantucket. Since Artemis's death, she sometimes dreamed about the island of her birth and the Friends meeting where she could worship the Lord with likeminded believers. But until the dreadful war in the northern colonies ended, she must remain in St. Augustine. Still, she could pray for the souls who crossed her path and try to minister to those in need. Most important, she would seek God's will, not her own, for that was the foundation of her faith.

Patrick Blakemore shielded his eyes against the bright morning sun glistening off Matanzas Bay. In the past four days, he hadn't recovered normal sight after five months in Fort St. Marks' windowless prison. Now that Governor Tonyn had released him and his fellow Patriots to wander St. Augustine at will, Patrick would have no trouble keeping his carefully worded promise not to escape the walled city. His former strength was nearly gone, and his uniform hung on him as if on a peg. Further, the anger that had kept him alive in the dank prison long ago dissipated in the reality of his mortal body's weakness. Now he simply wanted to live.

No, that wasn't true. These past few nights as he lay abed in his rented room above a tavern, stirrings deep in his mind reminded him of the dreams to which he'd once aspired. Such thoughts were healing. He wanted to regain his stolen strength and return to Virginia to fight another day for the Glorious Cause. And he wanted to regain the passion that had taken him from his father's manor house in England to the American colony where he at last had found his life's work and a cause in which he could believe—freedom.

But before he could escape an untenable situation, he must rebuild the strength he'd known as a carpenter and later as a major in Washington's infantry. Here on the wide St. Augustine common, which they called the Parade, he could purchase food and pay the tavern owner to prepare it. His captors had permitted their prisoners to retain their dignity in one vital way. They seized weapons but not personal belongings or money. Patrick wore his uniform as required by his captors lest he be considered a spy and which he'd scrubbed almost threadbare after his release to remove the stench of prison. His modest stash of silver and copper coins were tucked in a leather bag and clinked against his bony thigh as he walked onto the sandy lawn to search among the vendors for the right items to feed an appetite long denied.

Seeing a cart of oranges under a magnolia tree, he felt a sudden urge for the tangy fruit. In England, his father maintained a hothouse that provided a variety of citrus, and Patrick's mouth watered at the memory of their French chef's many delicious fruit creations.

He surveyed the various other vendors, but his eyes kept returning to that one proprietress in particular. The slender, dowdy-looking woman in widow's weeds bent over her low cart arranging her modest inventory to its best advantage. Poor thing. Yes, he would rather help this needy soul than the proud Loyalists who flew Union Jacks above their carts and shops. No such ensign marred her display.

He approached just as she lifted her head and gave him a gentle smile. Patrick withheld a gasp. Why had he thought her dowdy? She wasn't even plain. Her dark brown eyes seemed all the darker contrasted with her porcelain complexion, and her rosy lips were smooth and plump. Neither tall nor short, perhaps five feet three inches, she appeared to be in her mid-twenties. Her light brown eyebrows suggested her hair was brown, but she wore a black mobcap and a wide-brimmed straw hat, so he couldn't know for sure. Her black, unadorned gown was fastened high at the neck, and she wore a light woolen cape over her slender shoulders. Even her lavender fragrance carried on the breeze and crowded out the less pleasant scents on the Parade.

"May I help thee, friend?" Her musical voice swept through him like a long-forgotten song, and emotion rose in his chest. A Quaker lady. Like his mother.

He coughed into his fist. "Yes, ma'am. I saw your oranges." But now he could see only her.

Her warm gaze exuded kindness, even pity, and suddenly Patrick felt the weight of his thinness. He might find her beautiful, but she would see only a scarecrow. The other day as he'd shaved away his four-month beard growth, he'd been shocked by the sunken eyes and cheeks reflected back at him in the looking glass. What woman would look beyond that and perceive the well-formed, sought-after, and far-too-proud youth he once had been?

While he stood silent as the scarecrow he resembled, she grasped a paring knife, cut open a plump orange globe, and held half out to him. He stared at it as if it were some foreign object. With juice dripping over her hand, she gave him a kind smile.

"No charge." She whispered the two words, perhaps assuming he couldn't afford the purchase.

"No. Thank you." What was the matter with him? Too much time had passed since he'd been in the company of ladies. "I mean, I can pay." He dug out a copper penny and offered it. Their hands did a ridiculous dance in the exchange of money for fruit, with juice dripping over everything. He finally stopped the stream by slurping the sweet liquid in a most uncivilized manner. He then plunged his teeth into the succulent pulp and felt his body infused with the promise of strength. "Umm. Delicious." He grinned and shrugged sheepishly. She must think him an oaf.

Or maybe not. Compassion shone from her brown eyes. "Very good, sir." She watched him briefly, then gazed beyond him as if searching for other customers.

The gesture reminded him that he was staring at her, yet somehow he couldn't move.

What madness compelled him to stay? Even if she was a Quaker, no doubt she felt some allegiance to the British Crown or she wouldn't be living in this Loyalist haven. Perhaps the best way to break this absurd mystical hold she had on him would be to insult the king. In a decent way. Of course. And with humor. Of course.

"You may be interested to know, madam, that I have just arrived in the city after a long stay in the palace at St. Marks." He waved his hand toward the fort beyond the town's edge. "Courtesy of Old George III. Can't say much for the bill of fare." He patted his sunken belly. "But the accommodations, well, what can one say about a small, damp, windowless bedchamber shared with thirty other men?" That didn't sound at all funny, but he stared at her to gauge her reaction.

To his horror, her eyes reddened. He was a boor to speak of such things, especially to a lady.

"I can see you have suffered greatly, sir. May God grant that your health returns soon."

He couldn't bear her compassion any longer. "Well, yes, of course." Though he tried to sound jovial, he heard the croak in his voice. "Now, may I purchase four of these fine oranges and perhaps a squash or two?"

He dug out another coin, and his stomach lurched over how few were left. Hunger must not drive him to foolishness, and he was already spending his money too rapidly, with no hope of replenishing. The British forbade prisoners to receive pay from the American military. They did permit private citizens in the northern colonies or abroad to send money, but Patrick had no one to write to and ask for help. Certainly not his family, Loyalists, all of them.

Still, he must pay the lady and solve these problems later. "Here you go." He handed her two sticky coins, shrugging an apology.

"Thank you, sir." She counted oranges into his arms, only to have two bounce to the ground and roll away, gathering sand as they went. "Oh, dear."

She came around the cart just as Patrick bent to retrieve them. With both intent on the same purpose, her hat fell off and they bumped heads, and the entire armload scattered across the sandy lawn.

"Oh." Her mild exclamation didn't quite express Patrick's pain from the hard collision, but he bit back a harsher word.

"Are you all right?" He took her elbow and studied her face.

She wobbled her head and rolled her eyes in a comical way, and an attractive grin broke over her lips. "I am well, I assure you."

Patrick laughed heartily. The lady did have a merry disposition.

"Now, about those oranges." She restored her hat to her head, then dipped down and began to gather the fruit in her apron. "My patrons usually bring a bag…"

"Ah." Patrick untucked his linen shirt to fill it. "Alas, I left my silk purse in my room."

The lady rose gracefully and retrieved a small burlap bag from the side of the cart. "This will help, I believe."

Patrick grinned his gratitude. "You're too kind, Mrs.—"

She hesitated, and he realized his error.

"Forgive me. When I return your bag, I shall find someone who can speak for me and introduce us properly."

He thought her cheeks took on a pink blush, but in the tree's shade and with his weakened vision, he couldn't be certain.

With the oranges and squash filling the sack to the brim, there was nothing left for him to say or do. He dared not ask when she would return to the Parade, for that would be ill-mannered indeed. And for some reason, he wanted this pretty vegetable vendor to like him. But, as with many battles he'd fought, perhaps the best strategy was to withdraw, recoup, and return to fight another day.

Ah, what a poor analogy when considering friendship with a peaceful Quaker lady. But if his aim was to escape this city and return to the war, perhaps a pacifist could be the one person who would help him.

Chapter Two

Anne didn't quite know what to think about the tall young man who had bought so much of her produce. The oranges would keep, but she should have told him to eat the vegetables soon or they would spoil. And he certainly did need to eat. Although he wore a clean if tattered uniform and had shaved recently, his sallow skin and dull brown hair revealed a lengthy abstinence from nourishing food. Lines around his eyes suggested fatigue rather than age, and she guessed he might be younger than thirty. In addition to the unremarkable soap smell, she also detected a hint of delousing solution.

Indignation flared within her over the cruel conditions the prisoners suffered at the fort. But her resentment would make little difference in men's affairs, so she surrendered the emotion to the Lord and resolved to pray for the soldier. A strange intuition directed her gaze toward the path he had taken after leaving her. To her surprise, he stood at the Parade's edge with Friend Kennedy, pastor of St. Peter's Church. Perhaps he was a Christian.

Not that she doubted it. His gray eyes held an appealing gentleness that stirred her heart. If the Lord should send him her way again, perhaps she could minister to him somehow. At the least, she could offer to mend his shabby clothes and invite him to supper, if the pastor and his wife would accompany him for propriety's sake. With Cook's forthcoming departure, the supper would have to be soon, for Anne needed to regain her neglected cooking skills before serving company.

As did most other Parade vendors, she'd sold much of her inventory by late morning, but she lingered another half hour, hoping to sell it all. But as noon neared, she saw another soldier approaching and wished she'd gone home.

"Good morning, Mrs. Hussey." British officer Ares Lyttle strode toward her wearing his usual broad smile. With his long blond hair pulled back in a queue and his crimson and white uniform perfectly pressed, the man was pleasant enough to look at. But he was somewhat overbearing. Like Artemis. "How are you faring this fine day, madam?" He removed his cocked hat and bowed low. When he stood upright again, his blue eyes gleamed with a disconcerting intensity, unlike the mildness in the prisoner's eyes.

"I am well, friend." Anne busied herself organizing her remaining lettuce, squash, and green beans into a pleasing arrangement. "And you?"

"Very well now that I am in your lovely presence." He leaned one hand against the magnolia tree. "I came to escort you home. This cart's entirely too heavy for a delicate lady to maneuver over our rough streets."

"I thank you, sir." She surveyed the Parade, hoping another customer would come. "But as I have told you, this is my exercise. I enjoy it."

"Ah, me." He leaned his back against the tree and crossed his arms. "Would that I were a wealthy man. I would lavish every luxury upon you so you would never have to labor so strenuously again."

"Hmm."

He deserved no further answer. They'd already discussed the matter, yet he refused to comprehend the satisfaction she received from planting and harvesting food for her neighbors.

He moved closer to her cart, and she inched around to the opposite side.

"Dear lady—" He chuckled softly. "—your late husband, my good friend, will rise from his grave and haunt me if I do not make certain you are taken care of."

Anne stared at him. "Have you never read the Scriptures, sir? For the Christian, to be absent from the body is to be present with the Lord, and therefore you'll not be troubled by such a specter." At least she hoped Artemis had made his peace with God during his fatal illness.

"Well, now..." Ares Lyttle coughed and blustered. "Of course I was speaking figuratively."

"Hmm." *Lord, please deliver me from this man.* She surveyed the area, hoping for reprieve.

A red-coated private rushed toward them, his eyes focused on her unwanted companion. "Lieutenant Lyttle, sir, Colonel Luger requests your presence immediately. Seems that French fella has escaped again."

Ares Lyttle uttered a mild oath, then gasped. "Forgive me, Mrs. Hussey. That prisoner will be the death of me." He bowed and hastened away, grasping his sword's hilt as he ran.

Anne released a sigh and then a laugh. Poor Ares Lyttle. He'd begun his suit the day after Artemis died, sealing her heart against him. Nothing he had done in the past months changed her feelings. The one time she relented and invited him to dinner, he seemed more interested in the architecture and furnishings of her house than in her. Very strange.

A tavern keeper purchased her last wares, and she tucked the coins into the small bag at her waist. Gripping the handle of her cart, she lifted the back end to rest on the two front wheels and turned toward King George Street. Before she could give it a good shove, Friend Kennedy approached with the American prisoner in his wake. The kindly minister gripped the younger man's arm to urge him forward.

"Mrs. Hussey, do you have a moment?"

As always when the Lord's prompting was evident, Anne's heart warmed, and peace swept through her. "Yes, Friend Kennedy. Always for you." She set the cart down.

"Mrs. Anne Hussey, may I present Major—" He coughed lightly. "—Patrick Blakemore, lately of Virginia."

"Friend Blakemore." Anne offered her hand to the man to shake.

Instead, he kissed it, a touch so gentle she barely felt it as soft warmth swept up her arm. "Mrs. Hussey, I am honored." He gazed briefly into her eyes, but didn't stare.

Reverend Kennedy again coughed. Anne prayed he had not contracted an illness.

"Mrs. Hussey, Major Blakemore is a fine Christian. He asked me not to say this, but I know of his family in England." He cast a scolding glance at the man. "They are good people, and so is he, despite this nonsense about fighting for the rebels." The minister nodded to them. "Consider yourselves properly introduced." He walked a few feet away, then turned back. "Madam, perhaps you can persuade this gentleman that it is wicked to fight against the Crown, God's chosen authority." He spun on his heel and strode away.

Friend Blakemore gave Anne a sheepish grin, and she laughed.

"You'll forgive me, sir, if I excuse myself." She gripped her cart handle and lifted. "I am expected at home."

Before she could move the conveyance, the gentleman placed one hand on the bar. "Permit me, Mrs. Hussey."

"But—" She tried not to look at his gaunt frame, but her eyes betrayed her. His blue woolen coat hung on him as though made for a far more robust man.

"I'm stronger than I appear." Remarkably, no pride or even embarrassment tainted his tone. And, as if to prove his words, he placed his bag into the cart, then leaned into the task, moving it forward with obvious effort.

"Very well. Thank you." She fell into step beside him. "In return you must stay for our midday meal. I have several boarders who will also partake with us."

His eyebrows arched. "You won't have to ask me twice." A grunted chuckle escaped him. "In fact, this is answered prayer."

"You are a praying man?" She noticed the strain in his posture as they continued down the narrow street and entreated the Lord that he would not collapse.

"Yes."

He huffed out the word, and Anne's concern grew. But she wouldn't help him unless he completely gave out. Despite the cool breeze, sweat formed on his forehead. They reached a cross street and paused while several soldiers ambled past. The men laughed rudely and called Friend Blakemore a dimwitted American and worse. She noticed his clenched jaw and a fiery glint in his gray eyes. Would he retaliate in kind? But when he said nothing, her concern shifted to whether he could begin to push the cart again now that he had lost his momentum. Yet the brief respite seemed to have revived his strength, for he plunged himself into the task with renewed vigor.

Anne refrained from any further conversation so her companion could concentrate on his endeavor. She would behave as if they were out for a stroll, as if nothing were amiss, yet every step brought a prayer to her lips for his strength.

None too soon they reached the coquina wall surrounding her property, and she swung open the rough wooden gate. The soldier shoved the cart through and across the yard, then set down the back legs. He exhaled a long, shuddering breath and wiped his forehead with a clean linen handkerchief that was gray with age. "There." His attempt at a smile appeared more like a grimace.

"I thank you, Friend Blakemore." Anne ached to help him to a chair inside, but again knew she must act as if nothing were amiss. "If you walk around to the back, you'll find a washstand by the kitchen house."

He gave her a curt nod, but she took no offense. Instead, she went inside and freshened herself in her bedchamber, then met her two boarders and Cook in the dining room.

"We have a guest, ladies." She briefly explained the situation.

As expected, Mrs. Cameron wasn't pleased to anticipate sitting at table with a rebel soldier because her late husband, a British officer, had been killed in the war. But she promised not to cause a scene. Mrs. Wills would soon marry an overseer from a nearby plantation, and she felt only generosity toward others these days. Likewise, Cook promised to serve the man a hearty portion of ham and greens. When Friend Blakemore entered the dining room, they all turned to greet him.

Anne made introductions and waved him to the captain's chair. "Please sit here."

He hesitated, then sat. "Thank you." Hunger and weariness shone from his eyes, and even Mrs. Cameron cast a compassionate glance his way.

"Friend Blakemore," Anne said. "We rarely have a gentleman with us. Will you ask the Lord's blessing on our meal?"

"Gladly, ma'am." He bent over his plate and released a soft sigh. "Lord, for what we are about to receive, we are truly grateful. Use it to strengthen our minds and bodies so that we may better serve you. Amen."

The ladies chorused "amen," and Cook began to pass the bowls and platters.

"Gracious, boy," the elderly woman said. "You're skinnier than me." She emitted a brief cackle, then saw Anne's frown.

Yet Friend Blakemore laughed as well. "Yes, ma'am. Let's see what we can do to remedy that." His manners couldn't be criticized, but he did devour several bowlfuls, all the while making polite conversation with his dinner companions about matters both spiritual and mundane. To Anne's relief, he seemed to have recovered from his hard work on her behalf.

As the meal progressed to dessert—scones covered with a rich, creamy lemon sauce, Anne decided she had never met such a fine Christian gentleman. In fact, she would like to continue her acquaintance with him. Somehow she must devise a reason, within the boundaries of propriety, to invite him back to her home.

Patrick hoped the ladies didn't notice how hard it was for him to restrain himself. If alone, he would probably put his face in the plate and gobble up the food like a pig, just as he had in prison. But then, the guards hadn't provided utensils, and the food was swill, so he'd had no choice. Since his release, he had eaten his meals at the tavern, where he'd struggled to remember he was a civilized man, one who'd been raised with aristocratic manners. But now, as he consumed the mouth-watering fare, voracious hunger nearly overpowered him, as if his entire body ached to be filled. Even now, he forced his hand to lift the spoon slowly and eat a modest bite of lemon scone. The rich creamy topping brought a rush of saliva, which he caught with his napkin. No wonder one of the British soldiers wanted to marry Mrs. Hussey's cook. Patrick would marry her himself for such cooking.

Such thinking was absurd. But never in his life had he faced such all-consuming hunger. He needed to master it immediately, or he would shame himself in front of these gentle ladies. His attempts at polite conversation had thus far met with their approval. Even the redcoat officer's widow, Mrs. Cameron, looked at him with kindness as he tried not to shovel food into his mouth.

What did the Proverbs say about gluttony? *For the drunkard and the glutton shall come to poverty: and drowsiness shall clothe a man with rags.* Patrick was already in near rags. If he continued to eat like this, he would soon spend all his money, with no hope of replenishing it. Poverty and starvation would be his lot, a shameful end for a proud British earl's third son. But Patrick was no wastrel, no prodigal son. He knew why God had brought him to these shores, why he had fought so furiously in the Revolution. And the sooner he regained his strength, the sooner he could return to that valiant cause.

While the ladies chatted, he glanced around the room. The dark oak woodwork and finely papered walls resembled those of an English country home. The room boasted few adornments other than strong, serviceable furniture. The unlit hearth served both the dining room and parlor. The mahogany mantel held only flint, a steel striker, and tightly wound pieces of char cloth. Drawings of St. Augustine scenery hung in simple frames over the sideboard.

Lines in the plastered ceiling and a warp in the door frames drew his carpenter's eye. No doubt this old building required repairs. Perhaps he could offer his services to Mrs. Hussey. Before the Revolution began, he had apprenticed himself to a carpenter in Virginia, and should the United States succeed in throwing off the British yoke, he would return to that occupation. It was none too soon to regain his skills. The work would fill his days and help him regain lost strength.

"Mrs. Hussey." All the women snapped their attention his way, and he withheld a chuckle. He hadn't received such attention from ladies—and for so little reason—since he'd left his father's manor and sailed to Virginia at eighteen. "Forgive me if this seems rude. However, I see that your house needs repairs, which I would be happy to do."

Mrs. Hussey's dark brown eyes caught a bit of winter sunshine through the window and gave off an amber flash. The shards struck his heart in a most pleasant way. She tilted her head. "That would please me, sir, but only if I may pay you."

Now Patrick took a turn pondering her words. "This meal is payment enough, ma'am."

The other ladies tittered like a flock of birds, but Mrs. Hussey emitted a soft, melodious laugh.

"You have named your price, friend. I shall provide two meals a day to you until the work is completed."

Patrick swallowed hard, then bowed his head to her. "We have a contract, dear lady." Surely the Lord would use this situation to rebuild his lost strength and give him the satisfaction of helping a kind, generous woman. He bowed over his plate again, but this time to offer a silent prayer of thanks.

Anne stared down at her plate to hide her tears. She'd prayed last night for some means to fix the house's disrepair and now saw the Lord's answer.

"Ma'am?" Cook stood and picked up her plate. "Shall I clear?"

"Yes." Anne lifted her own plate. "We'll all help. Except for you, Friend Blakemore. You may rest in the large chair in the parlor. At your leisure, you may inspect the house to see what needs to be done." She wouldn't insist if he wanted to begin his inspection now, but she hoped he would choose a healing respite.

"Yes, ma'am." Gratitude shone from his gray eyes, and his sallow skin had already begun to take on a healthier hue. Still he moved toward the parlor with a stiff bearing, as though walking pained him, and sat in Artemis's leather chair. The quiet sigh he released broke her heart, for it seemed to give vent to a host of emotions.

He glanced up at her, and his eyebrows arched in a question.

Her cheeks warmed. "Are you well, friend?"

His gaze softened, and his lips curved to one side in a charming smile. "Getting better every minute."

Anne forced herself to look down at the table, but hardly a thing remained for her to remove. How had the other three ladies worked so fast around her?

Cook returned and took the plate from Anne's hands, then bent her head toward the parlor. "Go on, dearie."

"W-what?" Alarm shot through her. Then she understood. Dear little Cook, so newly fallen in love herself, must be pushing her toward this man. What romantic nonsense. One marriage was enough for Anne. And this man was a soldier. If her once peace-loving husband could become violent for no good reason, how would a soldier treat his wife?

Cook nudged her with a bony elbow, a gesture she never would have employed when Artemis was alive. "You deserve to sit, Mrs. Hussey. You were on your feet all morning." She winked to punctuate her words.

Anne shot a glare her way, then relented. "Very well." After all, her feet did ache.

As she walked toward the settee, she heard Cook's merry cackle trailing out the back door toward the kitchen house. Mrs. Cameron and Mrs. Wills excused themselves and retired to their respective bedchambers.

Friend Blakemore had rested his head against the chair back and closed his eyes. At her approach, he jolted, then stood and teetered a bit, blinking his eyes as if to clear his vision. "Forgive me." The rasp in his deep voice seemed to startle him, but he coughed it away and chuckled. "I'm awake now."

His good humor lightened her heart. Here was a man who faced his weakness with wit and courage. That would no doubt help in his healing.

"Please sit down." She settled in a chair and took up her knitting from the tapestry bag beside her. "You must tell me more about yourself. Tell me about your family in England and why you have set yourself to fight against them." His eyes widened, and she realized how rude the question must seem. "Forgive me. I have no right to inquire about such things."

He studied her for a moment, yet she felt no apprehension. His gaze was as gentle as of one speaking to a child. "I am not offended. You have made me feel very much at home." He glanced down at his hands. "I come from a good family, as Reverend Kennedy said. When I was eighteen, my father sent me to Virginia to invest in a business." He cleared his throat again and stared above her head. "On the voyage over, I fell in with some charming scoundrels and gambled away all the money he'd entrusted to me."

"Oh, my." Anne's heart ached for the foolish boy he had been, for the hard-won lesson was written in his eyes.

He grunted, not impolitely, merely acknowledging her response. "Indeed. When I appealed to my father to rescue me, he said I must rescue myself. So to shame him, I apprenticed myself to a carpenter, a Christian man who taught me to use my hands, unacceptable for a son of—" He cleared his throat "—a man in his position. But I found great satisfaction in it. Found I had a gift for making and repairing wooden things. But my master taught me something far more important, and that is the way to peace with God." A long sigh. "But alas, peace within a man's heart is difficult to maintain when all around him is talk of war. I found myself in agreement with the rebels."

Anne's emotions rose and fell at each turn of his story. Why did men always resort to war?

"I see the question in your eyes," he said. "Like my mother, you are a woman of peace. But there comes a time when a man must stand up and fight for what is right." Despite the strength of their meaning, his words came out in a whisper. "He must defend those principles and beliefs most precious to him."

She inclined her head slightly. Not too long ago, she had protected a loved one from Artemis's fists and received the blows herself. Yet she hadn't raised her hand against her husband. And after that, whenever he turned his full abuse on her, she had often considered fleeing, but never retribution. God had fought for her and ended Artemis's cruelty…and his life. Which was both a relief and a grief.

But how well she knew God didn't always deliver his children from evil forces. Would He protect her from Ares Lyttle, or would Governor Tonyn insist that she marry the British officer, a man whose forceful, intrusive manners did not inspire confidence, much less affection.

Lord, please rescue me again. I cannot bear the thought of marrying any man, especially Ares Lyttle.

Even as she silently prayed, Friend Blakemore's gaunt face came to mind, and particularly his gentle eyes. Mercy! What was she thinking? She reconfirmed to herself that she would never marry again, and certainly never marry a soldier.

Chapter Three

Early the next morning, Patrick sorted through the rusted tools in the shed beside Mrs. Hussey's kitchen house. Spiders and palmetto bugs skittered away, with several large lizards chasing after them. Patrick barely registered the movements, so used to these small creatures as he was.

Mrs. Hussey had provided ashes, vinegar, salt, and rags so he could clean soil and rust from the long-unused implements. Sand was also plentiful to use as an abrasive for stubborn corrosion crusts on hammers, saws, awls, augurs, chisels, squares, bevels, and planes. The late Mr. Hussey had a fine tool collection, but obviously hadn't used it. Patrick considered which ones could be used as weapons when he made his move to escape St.

Augustine.

A woodpile lay outside the shed where he hoped to find boards large enough for his repairs. When he moved the first plank, a three-foot-long black, red, and yellow snake slithered away. Patrick shuddered. While the coral snake's short fangs usually prevented bites through normal clothing, Patrick's threadbare trousers might be insufficient protection if he encountered another one or, worse, a rattlesnake. One of his fellow prisoners had attempted to escape, only to be brought back to the prison suffering from a viper's fatal bite. Patrick had nursed him as best he could to no avail. The memory set his nerves on edge.

"Friend Blakemore."

Patrick gasped, and he dropped the plank back onto the woodpile. Turning to see Mrs. Hussey holding a pewter tankard, he felt heat rush to his face. He'd never startled easily before his imprisonment. But unexpected lashings happened all too often. He struggled to regain his composure.

"Mrs. Hussey." His voice was still raspy, his posture still bowed with weakness. No one who had known him either in England or Virginia would recognize the shell of a man he'd become. Worse, the sympathy…pity? in this kind lady's gaze ate into his soul. None of the young ladies who had flirted with him in Father's London drawing room would now give him a first glance, much less a second one.

"Would you like some lemonade?" She gave him a bright smile and held out the tankard. Her gracious way of ignoring his discomfort soothed his soul.

"Thank you, ma'am." Patrick took the tankard and sipped carefully, somehow managing not to gulp the contents. With each sip, the tangy, sweet liquid seemed to flow to his limbs and give them strength. As he drained the last drop, he couldn't withhold a satisfied sigh.

"Thank you," he repeated and returned the tankard to her.

"You're welcome, Friend Blakemore." She continued to stare at him.

Did he have something on his face? He'd washed and carefully shaved this morning before leaving his room above the tavern. "Do you have a question?"

She blinked. "Oh, yes." Color appeared on her smooth cheeks. "Have you found the tools you'll need to do the work?"

Heat also filled Patrick's face. Surely they would soon get past these foolish reactions to each other. It would do no good to form an attachment to this beautiful lady, then leave her behind when he escaped the walled city.

"Yes, ma'am. Mr. Hussey's toolbox is quite well stocked. The tools just need to be cleaned and sharpened." He forced his eyes away from her and toward the woodpile. "As for the wood, some boards are too weathered and warped to be useful for anything but the fireplace or the kitchen house oven. But some can be used." His eyes turned back to her of their own accord.

"That is good news." She looked away. "As you can see, we still have many oranges on the trees. Please help yourself."

"You're very kind." Why couldn't he look away from her? Perhaps those many months in prison had addled his brain and caused him to forget his manners.

"Well then." She turned. "I shall leave you to it, Friend Blakemore."

Light fragrance trailed after her as she walked toward the main house. Gardenia, if he wasn't mistaken. Patrick's new favorite perfume.

What are you thinking? You cannot let yourself become attached to this woman, no matter how appealing she is.

Anne mentally shook herself. What was the matter with her, staring at poor Friend Blakemore that way? She could excuse herself by saying she only wished to ascertain his health and ability to do the work, but that would be a lie. Something else drew her to the American soldier, but she couldn't yet identify it. Perhaps it was the integrity that beamed from his gray eyes despite his weakness. Ares Lyttle stared at her with a possessive look, as if she belonged to him. She shuddered at the thought.

She mustn't waste more time on such foolishness. It was time to pick vegetables and fruit. Now, where was her basket? Still in the kitchen house, of course. She'd gone there to fetch it when the idea came to offer Patrick some lemonade. After all, he'd been at work since before sunup. She'd hastily squeezed the lemons, stirred in some honey, and added water before taking it out to him. Hurrying out again, she wondered if he would think her silly as she made this second trip to fetch her basket. To her relief, he was too busy to notice as she walked by.

Basket and knife in hand, she crossed the wide yard to the garden and selected ripe squashes, beans, tomatoes, okra, and beets, then picked oranges and lemons from the trees. She loaded her cart and checked her pocket to be sure she hadn't forgotten the coins she might need to make change. Pushing the heavy cart toward the front gate, she was startled to find Friend Blakemore walking beside her.

"Please permit me to see you to the Parade, Mrs. Hussey." Determination shone from his eyes as he put his hands on the bar.

"Oh." Anne bit her lip to stop a refusal, which would only insult him. "You're very kind, but I'm used to it, and—"

"Please." He gave her a gentle smile, which softened the harsh planes of his gaunt face. "Exercise helps my recovery."

What a gentleman to make it sound like she would be doing him a favor.

"Then, yes, of course you may help me." Should she offer to pay him? Or would that insult him?

They walked in silence along the gravel street, with his labored breathing the only sound she could hear, though the city was waking up and many other noises surrounded them. At the Parade, he parked her cart under the spreading magnolia tree.

"Will this do?" He wiped perspiration from his forehead with a dingy handkerchief.

Anne wondered whether it would be improper to offer him Artemis's fine linen handkerchiefs? "Yes. Just so. Thank you."

"My pleasure, Mrs. Hussey." He offered a slight bow and a smile. "Is there anything else I can do?"

The gentle look in his eyes captured her gaze longer than she intended.

"Ma'am?" That soft smile broadened.

"Yes. No. That is all." Now she needed her handkerchief to dab away sudden moisture on her face.

"Very good, ma'am. I'll return to my repairs." He doffed his tricorn hat and turned away, trudging back toward the street.

"Who's that poor soul, Miz Hussey?" Maude, the governor's cook, approached, her canvas shopping bag slung over her arm.

"He's—" Anne's voice came out a raspy whisper. She cleared her throat. "He's one of the American prisoners. He's agreed to make some repairs to my house in exchange for food."

"Hm." Maude watched the major for several seconds. "Mighty kind of the gov'ner to let them roam free that way."

The wistful look in the cook's eyes touched Anne's heart. Growing up in the Society of Friends, she'd always abhorred slavery. Perhaps when this war was over and she returned home, she could join the abolitionists' work against the evil institution.

"Yes, I suppose so. Now, what do you think of these fine green beans?"

"Very fine indeed," Maude said. "I'll take some of those onions and potatoes and cook 'em all up with fatback." She grinned. "Gov'ner Tonyn does like 'em cooked that way."

"Very good." Anne helped her make a selection and put them in her bag.

Maude held out her payment, which Anne never counted.

"Thank you, Maude. Have a good day."

Her next customer was Joanna Wellsey, the military doctor's wife and Anne's good friend. "What do you have today?" The daughter of a Cherokee woman and Scottish innkeeper, she spared Anne a rare smile.

Anne waved a hand over her cart. "Many choices, as you can see."

Joanna selected several items. "My own garden plot is miserly this year." She touched her rounded belly. "These will be good for our son."

Anne's heart dipped unexpectedly. No, that was wrong. She must rejoice with her friend, not envy her because her own womb must forever lie barren. She could take comfort in helping her friend because her garden flourished in this temperate climate.

After Joanna left, a shadow fell across the cart. She looked up to see Ares Lyttle staring at her, a smirk twisting his lips to the side.

"Good morning, my dear." He stepped too close for her comfort. "I'll be happy to assist you by taking your cart home." He nudged up against her shoulder and gripped the bar. "Shall we go?"

"Mrs. Hussey, ma'am." Friend Blakemore trotted toward her across the lawn. "Forgive me for being late."

Late?

"If I may be so bold, Lieutenant Lyttle, sir, please don't trouble yourself." Friend Blakemore moved up beside the British officer and also placed his hands on the bar. "Mrs. Hussey has engaged my services to assist her." He gave the lieutenant a grin Anne could only call boyish. "As you know, sir, the commandant gave us poor prisoners a way to provide for ourselves, lacking payment from our army as we are. Mrs. Hussey has been so kind to hire me, and I know you wouldn't wish to go against the commandant by depriving me of honest, much needed wages." To emphasize his plea, he tugged at a lock of hair, an obsequious gesture Anne had seen servants offer their employers.

"Well, I…"

"Yes, you must permit my servant to do what he's paid for." Heat rushed to her cheeks.

Had she just told a lie?

Ares Lyttle huffed. "Very well. But I shall accompany you to be sure he doesn't falter in his duties." He snorted out a laugh. "Or simply falters, scarecrow that he is."

It appeared the lieutenant's cruel remark bounced off Friend Blakemore without injury, for which Anne was thankful. He even sent her a mischievous wink the other man couldn't see. But now as they walked down King George Street toward her home, some townspeople stared. What were they thinking? As a widow, she was vulnerable to men like Ares Lyttle, who thought they could pressure her into marriage. Others had done the same to Anne's foster sister, Dinah Templeton, until she had been swept off her feet by the dashing English naval Captain Moberly. When Anne had been protected by her married status, she'd not fully understood Dinah's dilemma. Due to Artemis's influence with the governor, no one had dared to disrespect her. Now she understood what Dinah had gone through, so she must continue to exhibit behavior above reproach.

"Mrs. Hussey." Friend Kennedy hailed her. "I had hoped to purchase some oranges from you, but I see your cart is empty."

"Don't be dismayed, sir." She grabbed this opportunity as from the Lord. "There are more on the tree. Will you come with us?"

The minister's presence would protect her from unkind speculation by her neighbors.

I thank Thee, Lord.

Inhaling slow, deep breaths and quietly exhaling, Patrick endeavored to conceal how hard it was to push Mrs. Hussey's cart. True, it was lighter than when he'd brought it to the Parade that morning. But at that early hour, the day had been cooler, and he'd felt rested from a good night's sleep. He'd also not spent four hours laboring in the sun to work on the lady's house. Despite the temptation to surrender to his fatigue, a quick glance at Lieutenant Lyttle infused him with renewed strength.

Patrick would pretend deference to this man, but he wouldn't let him crush his soul, as most British soldiers seemed bent on doing. For some reason, Lyttle watched him with particular interest. And now Patrick would return the favor. Clearly, the lieutenant had an eye for Mrs. Hussey. Just as clearly, she did not wish to receive his attentions. Perhaps she could see the man had no scruples, despite his outward show of proper manners. How glad Patrick felt that he'd listened to the Lord's prompting to return to the Parade to escort her home. Of course, Reverend Kennedy was above reproach, never mind his belief that King George had the right to oppress the English citizens living in the colonies. The good pastor seemed aware that the lovely widow needed protection.

They reached the white coquina wall of her property, and Lyttle rushed forward to open the wooden gate.

"Take care, man," the lieutenant barked, as though he'd been forcing Patrick to do his work. "Don't scratch the cart sides."

Patrick grunted out a compliant "aye, sir," even as heat rushed up to his face. *Lord, help me not to respond to this man.* Defiance would do him no good, but only further alienate the soldiers for whom he held no respect. Billeted here in St. Augustine, far from the war, most had never seen a battlefield, yet they behaved as conquerors. What foolishness. Growing up an English aristocrat, Patrick had also felt himself above other men. A few years in Virginia helped him to understand the colonists' complaints and to join their cause.

"Now, Mrs. Hussey, what else can I do for you?" Lyttle's words suggested he'd done her some great service.

As Patrick pushed the cart toward the kitchen, he glanced at the lady, who stared at Lyttle soberly.

"Why, nothing at all, Ares Lyttle. I must see to my boarders." She waved her hand dismissively, then gave the pastor a soft smile. "I thank you for your company, Friend Kennedy. Please stay a moment, if you will. I believe Mrs. Wills wishes to discuss with you her upcoming marriage. And do not forget to pick your oranges."

"Of course, Mrs. Hussey. Thank you." A twinkle in the reverend's eyes revealed his understanding of her request. "Good day, Ares Lyttle. You'd best hasten back to the fort, or you'll miss your noon meal."

Patrick ducked his head to hide a smile, but still managed to see the fury on Lyttle's face. Without the pastor's dismissal, the lieutenant might have found a way to prolong his stay. Patrick vowed to himself that he wouldn't permit the officer to bully the lady, but he had little strength to back such a promise. At least not yet.

Could that be why the Lord had allowed his carefully planned escape to be foiled? That he should stay and protect Mrs. Hussey while he regained his health and strength? The idea both rankled and soothed him. He *must* escape and return to the war. Yet how many times in his life had God diverted his plans only to bring about some different, perhaps even better, thing Patrick hadn't foreseen?

Trust in the Lord with all thine heart, and lean not to thine own understanding. In all thy ways acknowledge Him, and He shall direct thy path.

The Scripture verse he'd learned at Mama's knee came to mind and settled his heart. He would continue to watch for chances to escape, but he wouldn't leave Mrs. Hussey unprotected. After all, wasn't it the soldier's duty to protect the innocent from oppression, no matter what it cost him? As the great patriot Patrick Henry had boldly declared, "Give me liberty or give me death."

On the battlefield, Patrick had seen enough death to dread it. Had seen more than one fellow soldier flee in fear when the tide turned against the Patriots. To his honor—or his folly, Patrick had stood his ground until a redcoat knocked him unconscious and he'd been dragged away into captivity. No, not folly. He would do it all again for the Patriot's Glorious Cause, no matter what it cost him.

Chapter Four

While Friend Kennedy chatted with Mrs. Cameron and Mrs. Wills in the drawing room, Anne helped Cook carry the plates and utensils from the kitchen house, grateful the woman would be with her for another few days. Once Cook married her soldier, how could Anne manage to sell her vegetables at the Parade every day and have the expected noon meal prepared for her boarders? Mrs. Cameron was already complaining that she couldn't stay long in a boarding house that didn't meet its commitment to feed her sufficiently.

Anne left Cook to set the table and made her way back outside, eager to inspect the work Friend Blakemore had done this morning. That wasn't exactly true. She wanted to be in his company again, and not over a meal. Just to be sure his health was improving, of course. After they ate the noon meal, perhaps his color would improve. He'd seemed a bit peaked after so gallantly pushing her cart back home. She was so grateful he had cut short Ares Lyttle's attempt to force his help upon her. She'd silently thanked the Lord that both Friend Blakemore and Friend Kennedy had understood her dilemma and protected her from the British soldier's intrusiveness. They hadn't spoken an untruth. If not her servant, Friend Blakemore was her employee, of sorts, for he was repairing her house. If he saw other chores that required his strength, however limited, she wouldn't forbid him to do them. And Friend Kennedy had indeed wanted to purchase her oranges and had been grateful that some were still available on her tree. She did feel a bit curious as to why he, rather than his cook, came to make the purchase, but she would accept his actions as the Lord's providence. And it was true Mrs. Wills had mentioned she wished to seek the minister's advice, so Anne hadn't misspoken about that either.

Eager to discuss the repairs on her home and just as eager to be in Friend Blakemore's company, she found him waiting for her outside the kitchen house.

"Ma'am, I inspected the roof, and it's in good condition for the most part." Hands fisted at his waist, he stared up at the roof with a probing look. "That coquina the builders used —" he waved a hand upward "—is unlike anything I've encountered in Virginia. It has protected your house from the ravages of time and weather. Only one small spot was damaged, and it should be easy to repair."

Trust swept through Anne's chest. He obviously knew what he was doing.

"And the inside, Friend Blakemore?"

He chuckled. "Ma'am, you may call me Patrick, if you like."

Heat rushed to her cheeks. "Well…"

"Unless your religion forbids it." His smile turned into a teasing grin.

Once again, something stirred in her chest. She quickly quashed it. "Not at all. Our plain form of address is meant to show both equality and respect." She didn't intend severity, but somehow her words sounded cross in her own ears.

He winced. "Of course." He gave her a little bow. "My apologies."

She bit her lip. In truth, addressing a man with both Friend and his surname, a woman could keep him from becoming too familiar with her. Yet somehow she didn't feel the need to do so with this man. "As you requested, I shall call you Patrick."

His smile returned. "Thank you, ma'am."

No matter how much Patrick wanted to address his employer as Anne, he would wait for her to invite him to do so. Unlike the Quaker custom of showing equality, the form of address used in Virginia, in the aristocratic circles in which he'd grown up in England, and as a soldier, had little to do with equality. Instead, it indicated the relationship one had with the other person. And, of course, in each of those places respect was doled out sparingly to honor men of higher rank and to keep the lower classes in their place. After many months in prison, he'd had time to reconsider such matters. Could he truly honor the British officers who'd treated him so cruelly and reinforced his belief in the Revolution? Could he fail to honor the Patriot privates imprisoned with him or the slaves who showed kindness to him as they brought the meager allotment of bad food each day? Indeed, prison had brought about equality among those who had no power. Maybe the Quaker custom had much merit.

Still, if he took too much liberty in addressing this lady, it could damage her reputation. And above all else, he was determined to protect Mrs. Hussey from every threat.

"Shall we go inside, ma'am?" Patrick waved a hand toward the back entrance to the house. "While the roof can be quickly repaired, the interior ceiling and walls appear to need considerable work."

"Very well." A slight frown appeared. "Do you expect it to cost much?"

"I won't know for certain until I tear out the damaged and rotten parts." Patrick opened the door for her. "But I think the wood I've salvaged from the woodpile will suffice in most cases."

Nodding her appreciation, she walked into the back hallway. "I know you'll do your best."

In the dining room where Patrick had first noticed damage, he showed Anne where he had pulled out the cracked plaster to reveal the narrow lath boards underneath. "This doesn't seem to be the usual interior construction here in St. Augustine."

"No, it isn't. Artemis made some changes after he purchased the property." She sighed. "He sent me to stay with Dr. Wellsey and his wife while he worked on it, so I had no idea what he was doing. I'm certain he meant it to be a nice surprise for me to have walls like those in our home in Nantucket, but—" She bit her lip as though stopping herself from saying more.

He wouldn't pry. Marriage was sacred between husband and wife, and her loyalty to her scoundrel spouse even after his death gave Patrick more cause to appreciate the lady. As the Proverb said, the heart of her husband could safely trust in her. Too bad the same kind opinion couldn't be held for Artemis. Even in the darkened prison where he'd spent these last months, gossip had filtered in of the overly-ambitious former Quaker government official with a particular hostility toward Patriots. While Mrs. Hussey certainly must have challenges as a widow, Patrick couldn't tamp down the thought that she was better off without Artemis Hussey.

"That small opening in the roof allowed rainwater to seep in and ruin the plaster and rot the wood over time. With your permission, I'll rip out the rotten parts and rebuild them following Mr. Hussey's Nantucket design."

"Do you not think it should be rebuilt according to the St. Augustine architecture?"

He hesitated for a moment. "I…" Looking away, he considered his response. If she wanted her home to conform to the local style, he might not be able to do the improvements to her satisfaction because he would be learning as he worked.

"No, I agree." She gave a decisive nod. "Make the repairs as you see fit. Now, if you'll excuse me, I must help Cook bring in our noon meal."

Her words seemed to summon Patrick's appetite, for his stomach rumbled in anticipation. As heat rushed up his neck, she gave him a merry smile.

"And apparently not a moment too soon."

"Yes, ma'am."

Patrick had eaten mostly mushy beans as a soldier, but they'd never tasted like the bean stew the cook had prepared. Small bits of salt pork and herbs enriched the flavor, making the meal a pleasure rather than a chore necessary for survival.

Mrs. Hussey had invited Reverend Kennedy to join them, and his presence brought a sober mood to the meal. The two boarders, Mrs. Cameron and Mrs. Wills, simpered as they chatted with the minister. Cook also sat at table with them due to Mrs. Hussey's insistence upon equality among employer and employee, a view Patrick also benefited from. His aristocratic blood notwithstanding, as an apprentice in Virginia, he hadn't been afforded that courtesy but had eaten in the kitchen house with the servants.

This was more food for thought as Patrick considered his views. But what did God think? Despite Mama's Quaker influence, his father and tutors had taught him that the Great Chain of Being was God's plan for the Universe, with bishops, kings, and the nobility seated far above ordinary men. But in Virginia, as the Revolution was fomented among aristocrat and servant alike, Patrick's views had begun to change. Perhaps working for Mrs. Hussey would change him further. He had no objection to that.

With her table surrounded by good friends engaged in pleasant conversation, Anne felt unexpected joy sweep through her soul. She hadn't planned this gathering, but rather had been dreading the coming days when she would be alone in this house and responsible only for herself and Mrs. Cameron, if the lady deigned to stay here. As Anne listened to her guests' conversation, she shook off self-pity. The Lord had given her this day, for which she thanked Him. And also for Patrick's careful assessment of the repairs needed for her house. The Lord promised His care for widows, and He truly was keeping His promise.

Another cause for joy was her decision to address Patrick by his Christian name. That it excited her so much should cause her concern, as she knew so little about him. But something genuine and trustworthy shone from his gray eyes, and her inner light indicated it was safe to know him better, even though they had only met yesterday. She had known Artemis since early childhood and had trusted him above several young men who had asked to court her. Yet the length of their acquaintance gave her no hint that he would turn into an angry, avaricious, and abusive man. But perhaps that should be a caution to her in regard to Patrick.

If they lived in Nantucket, she would have no difficulty keeping her acquaintance with him more formal, for such friendships were frowned upon by her Friends meeting, perhaps even leading to the elders putting a person out of the meeting. Had she become too liberal in her thinking here in St. Augustine, where she had no religious elders and had to rely on her own Scripture studies and inner light for direction?

Lord, only Thou knowest what I should do. I am trusting in Thee. Please direct my path that I might not sin against Thee.

Warmth and peace flooded her heart. While she didn't yet have clear direction, she would go forward with her friendship with Patrick. In the depths of her being, she hoped the Lord would approve.

Chapter Five

The following week, Patrick watched as the workmen repaired the coquina roof, hoping to learn from their skillful manipulation of the unusual building material. If he couldn't escape St. Augustine, he would need more work to survive after he completed Mrs. Hussey's repairs. Every skill he added to his carpentry toolbox would provide more opportunities for employment.

As it was, he eagerly anticipated the roof's repair. Until no rainwater could seep into the interior, he couldn't begin rebuilding the damaged walls. In the meantime, he spent his days cleaning Artemis Hussey's rusted tools and preparing the wood he would use inside. In the damaged area of the dining room, he had salvaged most of the wallpaper with the help of Mrs. Cameron, who'd once owned a fine house in Boston. The lady, probably in her mid-forties, had apparently been inspired by her landlady's renovations to reclaim her dormant decorating skills. Together, they made a plan to reconfigure the sturdy floral paper to recover the plaster wall once it was repaired.

Over the next few weeks, deeply involved in his improvement work for Mrs. Hussey, Patrick paid little heed to the improvements to his own health and body until one morning when his well-worn shirt tore across the back. His first response was dismay. He had washed it nightly to keep it from stinking as he worked around the ladies, which only added to the fabric's deterioration. With no other clothing to replace the ruined shirt, he would have to suffer his woolen jacket's warmth in the rapidly warming spring. His worried thought was quickly replaced by the realization that he had regained muscle and strength, a blessing and a promise of more improvements to come. Perhaps Mrs. Cameron would help him mend the shirt. With that thought in mind, he donned his jacket over the torn shirt and hurried from his tavern lodgings to Mrs. Hussey's home just in time to push her cart to the Parade.

"I notice you always wear your uniform jacket." She walked along beside him as he pushed the cart with ease. "As the day grows warmer, won't you be too hot?" A hint of color touched her cheeks, as though she feared her question too intrusive.

"Yes, ma'am." He shot her a grin. Might as well tell her his dilemma. "Seems the back of my shirt has given out."

"Oh, that won't do." Her pretty face took on a maternal look. "You must try one of Artemis's shirts. If it fits, well and good. If it doesn't, I'll refit it for you."

Patrick hesitated. "You're very kind, Mrs. Hussey. But I would be considered a spy if not in uniform, however ragged it is."

"Humph." She sniffed with apparent indignation. "Do they expect you to walk around in rags?"

He wouldn't remind her that was exactly what the enemy soldiers expected. Instead, they continued in silence for another block.

"I shall speak to Friend Kennedy and ask him to speak to Governor Tonyn."

Patrick stopped. "Pray do not, Mrs. Hussey." The last thing he needed was to bring the governor's attention to himself. "I can wear my jacket—"

"Over a new shirt?" She gave him a teasing smile.

He chuckled as he moved the cart forward again. "Yes, Mrs. Hussey. Over a new shirt."

She inclined her head toward him and whispered, "And you must now address me by my Christian name."

He stopped again. "Perhaps when we're at your house." It wouldn't do for soldiers or townspeople to overhear him. These past weeks, he'd been around them enough to know they thought him barely above a slave. His earlier wish to have her permission to call her Anne no longer mattered when such behavior could harm her reputation. He would defend her good name at all costs to himself.

She nodded. "Yes. When we're at my house. Now, would you please hurry along. My customers are expecting me."

"Yes, ma'am." He shoved the cart forward again. If she was eager to sell her daily produce, he was just as eager to get back to her house and finish framing the wall's damaged section.

His fondest desire these past weeks had been to delight her heart. If they resided in Virginia, he would bring her fresh spring flowers every day. As it was, he felt his own heart tugging him toward her more and more. Her thoughtful care of her boarders…and him, and her generosity to her cook and to Mrs. Wills as each woman had married her soldier, revealed Anne's goodness and selflessness, further ensnaring his heart.

For the first time in many years, he felt a longing to have some position or wealth with which to win a lady's hand. Anne, humble as she was, did not seem to consider such things important. Like his mother, she preferred plain living, much to Father's annoyance. But Patrick had found the wealth's trappings brought no satisfaction unless accompanied by freedom to follow God's call upon his life. While Mama would understand, Father and Patrick's two older brothers would not. Before the Revolution began, when he was still communicating with them, they had been appalled to learn he was working with his hands. Somehow their stinging disapproval faded into oblivion when he saw the gratitude and happiness in Anne's eyes over his simplest completed tasks. He could bask in her approving gaze the rest of his life.

Did that mean he loved her? He might as well admit that it did. In fact, he had begun to love her the first moment he saw her that day in January when they met on the Parade. Yet even if she loved him in return, what future would they have here in his enemy's walled city?

No, the only path to a future with Anne was for Patrick to return to the war and fight it to victory. Then he could offer her a home in Virginia, where they could build a life together.

Patrick emitted a quiet, humorless chuckle. If the British soldiers even now tossing at him insults of "traitor," "dog," and worse knew his lofty thoughts toward the lady, they would probably beat him senseless. Unless, of course, he revealed to them he was Lord

Grandstone's son. That would only prove him to be a hypocrite, for he had cast off his aristocratic heritage the moment he joined the Revolution. Thus he must keep his identity hidden from them.

They reached the Parade, and he moved the cart into its usual spot.

A soft gasp from Mrs. Hussey, Anne, refocused his thoughts. He followed her gaze toward Matanzas Bay and stifled his own gasp. A British frigate bobbed in the water, a new arrival since yesterday afternoon. Did its arrival mean the governor planned to move the Patriot prisoners to another location? Perhaps the prison fort at Puerto Rico or, worse, a prison ship.

Patrick and his fellow Patriots had been forbidden to write notes or even to have private conversations with each other as a condition of their freedom to roam the city. They'd managed a few hand signals and the rare, whispered comment, but in this walled city so far from the Revolution, good news never reached them. Their British jailers would never want them to be encouraged.

Seeing several blue-coated naval officers headed across the Parade, Patrick gripped his emotions as he had always done before a battle and prayed. *Lord, help me.*

Anne noticed Patrick's stiffened posture and furtive glances toward the uniformed sailors walking toward them. As they came within a half dozen yards, she let her small purse fall to the sand. Her coins spilled out in a heap.

"Oh, my." She clicked her tongue. "Patrick, would you be so kind?" She waved a hand over the coins.

Surprise filled his eyes, then understanding. He bent behind the cart and began picking up the coins one at a time, brushing off the sand, and placing them back in her leather bag. The officers came closer and smiled. The captain tipped his bicorn hat in her direction.

At that moment, Maude stepped up to the cart and placed her slender body in front of Patrick's kneeling form. "Miz Hussey, I don't know how you manage to have such fresh vegetables every day." Sliding a glance at the now-passing men, she spoke in her rich, soft, alto tones that always reminded Anne of thick maple syrup.

"The Lord has blessed my humble little garden." Anne gave her an understanding smile. "And through it, I am so pleased to serve you, Maude." She helped her make some selections for the governor's table.

Anne prayed the sailors would pass by without noticing Patrick. She completed her transaction with Maude just as Patrick retrieved the last coin and stood. He glanced toward the retreating men, whose destination appeared to be the very tavern where Patrick rented his room. Would that create a dilemma for him?

As though someone had called out to the men, one turned back, stared toward Anne's little trio, then urged his friends to go on without him. He walked slowly back toward the cart. While Anne's heart jumped, Patrick's face paled.

The officer stared at him, his eyes reddening. "Tricky." He seemed to choke out the word.

Patrick heaved out a deep sigh. "Hello, Dash."

Chapter Six

After a half-second hesitation, Patrick lunged into his next older brother's open arms and held on as if to a lifeline. As hard as he tried to keep in mind that Dash served the enemy, he couldn't stop his tears. He also couldn't mistake the fierce hug his brother returned, confirming his returned affection. After several moments, they stepped back as if by agreement, still holding each other's arms.

"Great heavens, Tricky, look at you." Dash laughed, his voice breaking with emotion. "You look so battered, I would hardly know you. What have those colonials done to you?"

His words caused a double check in Patrick's spirit he dared not ignore. They were enemies, yet they were also the same blood. Barely a year apart in age, they had grown up causing mischief together. Had shared boyhood foolishness while their older brother, Gregory, Viscount Ashford, was often required to spend his days learning to be their father's heir. Patrick was loath to destroy the fragile bond this meeting might engender, but truth must be spoken.

He let out an ironic laugh to answer Dash's question. "It isn't my compatriots who have battered me, brother, but yours." At Dash's frown, he added, "But let us not discuss such things. How is our mother?"

Dash gave him a chiding frown, then softened. "She was well when I sailed from Portsmouth six weeks ago. Still grieving for you." He grunted. "To her, you're still a lad of eighteen sent from home too soon by our father." Now a grin. "She would be appalled at your untidy appearance. Mama may not care for fashion, but as you know, fastidiousness is absolutely essential to her."

Patrick chuckled, his breaking voice echoing Dash's. As they'd grown up, few people could tell them apart. "I miss her as well. It is her faith, and I'm sure her prayers, that have sustained me." At least she wouldn't condemn his choices, though they might grieve her. "And our sisters?" The charming little twins had been a late addition to the family and only five or six when Patrick last saw them ten years ago.

"Quite the beauties and due to make their introduction to Queen Charlotte next spring." Dash glanced over Patrick's shoulder. "Perhaps we should move our chat to the tavern."

Patrick turned to see the quizzical look in Anne's eyes. What must this dear lady be thinking? "Mrs. Hussey, may I present my next older brother—" he glanced at Dash's indigo blue jacket, with its single gold stripe and white cuffs, "—Captain Dashiell Blakemore? Dash, this is Mrs. Hussey, my employer."

"Your..." Dash's eyes widened. "What?"

"I am pleased to meet you, Friend Blakemore." Anne gave him a warm but businesslike smile. "Thy brother has been a valued employee these past weeks. Perhaps you would like to join us for our noon meal to observe his improvements to my house."

"I, uh...well, Tricky, I never would have envisioned you employed by a Quaker lady, much less such a lovely one." Dash removed his bicorn hat and swept an elegant bow toward Anne. "Mrs. Hussey, it is an honor to meet you. I do hope you'll forgive me if I must decline your invitation. My officers are expecting me. Another time?"

"It will be a pleasure, Friend Blakemore."

"We are not done yet, *little* brother." Dash stood equal to Patrick's almost six-foot height, but he had always used his eleven month age advantage to lord it over Patrick…when it seemed convenient. "Mrs. Hussey." He bowed again, donned his bicorn hat, then strode toward the tavern.

And with him went a piece of Patrick's heart.

"May I assume you weren't expecting your brother, Patrick?" Anne's softly spoken question reminded him of where his heart truly dwelt.

He grunted softly. "I was not. Yet I cannot help but think my father arranged for him to be sent to St. Augustine rather than farther north, where sea battles are raging. I doubt Father would wish for his spare heir to be endangered any more than necessary."

"Or perhaps he learned of your imprisonment and sent your brother to free you and fetch you home." Sadness colored her tone.

Patrick winced. "You always see the gentler side of a matter, don't you?" He shook off the depression that had tried to engulf him since the moment he first saw Dash. "Ma'am, that wall won't build itself. If you'll excuse me, I'll return around the noon hour to assist you with the cart."

"Very well." She nodded, her smile sympathetic as she turned to greet her next customer.

Oddly, as Patrick began his trek to her house, he felt invigorated. If not for fear of drawing the usual taunts from the passing redcoats and street boys who often cast stones at him, he would jog up King George Street for some much needed exercise. But running would only call attention to himself, which he'd endeavored to avoid at all costs these past months of relative freedom. If the soldiers grew used to him so much that they failed to notice whether he was present or absent, he wouldn't be missed after his eventual escape.

He grunted at such a foolish thought. Now that Dash had acknowledged him, he had lost all hope for anonymity. His gregarious brother hadn't tried to hide their relationship in the Parade's open expanse. Several passing soldiers had glanced their way, curiosity lighting their eyes. And even now, Dash was probably regaling his junior officers with tales of their boyhood escapades around Grandstone Abbey, then shaking his head with sorrowful regret over Patrick's supposed madness in joining the Patriot cause. Perhaps he shouldn't be so hard on his brother. Surely their familial bond would keep him from disparaging Patrick. Too much.

By the time he reached Anne's house, sweat and tears mingled on his cheeks. His family would never understand why he had joined the Revolution, but that didn't stop him from loving them, even his autocratic father. And his adorable little twin sisters, nearly old enough to be presented to Queen Charlotte and enter the London marriage market! It cut into his heart almost as sharply as thinking of Mama's grief for him. It wasn't his loved ones he had broken with, but King George, who refused to acquiesce to the justifiable complaints of his thirteen former colonies, who in turn had united and declared themselves independent states. Had Father or Ashford or even Dash ever read their *Declaration of Independence*? If so, how could they not see that any man of faith and good sense would cry out and revolt against the king's injustices? If they hadn't read it, how could Patrick ever persuade them of his reasoning?

He'd completed framing in the dining room wall's new section, and now, as he added lath strips to the studs, a new thought consumed him. What if he could persuade Dash to read the *Declaration*? Surely he would see reason. Patrick must find a copy of the document, but would anyone in St. Augustine defy Governor Tonyn's ban and own one? If not, perhaps he himself could remember enough to write down. Then he must get Dash away from his fellow officers and force him to read it and listen to reason. A mad plan but one he must execute without delay.

Even before her stomach rumbled with hunger for her midday meal, Anne looked down King George Street in anticipation of Patrick's return. In truth, she could manage the cart herself. But during these past weeks, his company had become so dear to her that she wouldn't leave the Parade until he arrived. With only a wilted bunch of lettuce remaining on the cart, she'd done well today. Her coin-filled leather pouch weighed heavily from her belt…and on her mind. Perhaps not all the sailors who had disembarked from the newly arrived ship were gentlemen like Patrick's brother. She had never been robbed or even accosted by the red-coated soldiers, but would the sailors treat her with the same respect? While she preferred to think the best of her fellow man, her marriage's reality had taught her some men, like Artemis, chose bad behavior if it brought them monetary gain.

"Ready, Mrs. Hussey?" Patrick approached, and warmth flooded Anne's heart. As usual, sawdust clung to his woolen jacket, but she wouldn't call his attention to it. When Dashiell Blakemore mentioned their mother's preference for fastidiousness, Anne had fully understood. Artemis had been careful, even prideful about his appearance. Yet she could only look upon Patrick with approval, no matter his rags or worn-out shoes or plaster bits splattered across his jacket front. From the gentle smile on his lips, one would never know he'd had such a dramatic reunion with his brother only four hours ago.

"Mrs. Hussey!" Ares Lyttle, as he did almost every day, hastened toward them before they could leave the Parade. "Mrs. Hussey, you truly must permit me to accompany you home." He cast a dark frown toward Patrick. "I wouldn't have you accosted on your way."

His insult to Patrick caused heat to rush up Anne's neck like a fire. She took a cooling breath before daring to speak, lest she lash out at this man. "Thy concern is unwarranted, Ares Lyttle. My employee is more than sufficient protection for me."

She glanced at Patrick, whose jaw was clenched. Dear man, how Ares Lyttle must annoy him, and yet he dared not speak up for himself or risk being returned to the prison.

"Truly, madam—" Ares Lyttle gave Patrick a withering stare, almost like a challenge "—if Blakemore has no better sense than to rebel against his God-given authority, His Majesty King George, then how can we trust him for a simple walk across town?"

Anne lifted her chin and frowned. "You speak thus every day. My answer is unchanged. Now, if you'll excuse me, I have an errand to attend to, and you are hindering me. Good day." She spun around and marched toward King George Street. The cartwheels' rumble on the sandy ground assured her that Patrick followed her. A backward glance revealed, to her relief, that Ares Lyttle did not.

Instead, he called out, "I shall call upon you later today, madam."

She didn't dignify his unwelcome promise with a response. Marching down a side street, she realized Patrick would follow and regretted he would have extra steps with the cart. After turning a corner, she waited for him.

"If you wish to go back to the house…"

He gave her a smile she felt down to her toes. Oh, dear!

"Mrs. Hussey…Anne…" He whispered her Christian name. "How can I see to your safety if I'm not with you?" A twinkle lit his gray eyes, and a teasing grin quirked his lips to the side.

She tried to smother her own grin but failed. "Very well. Follow me." Again she set out for her destination. Halfway down the block, she stopped at a two-story wooden building with a sign over the door announcing Patton & Forbes. "Here we are. I shall be only a moment." She stepped toward the open door and was greeted by the heavy aromas of cigar smoke and pickled herring.

"I shall await you here." Patrick's whispered promise caused her heart to skip.

Before she could chide herself for her foolish reaction to him, Mr. Patton emerged from the back office.

"Mrs. Hussey, how good to see you." The graying, fiftyish gentleman removed his spectacles and gave her a little bow. "What may I do for you today?"

"If you would be so good, sir, I am thankful to the Lord for my success, but it weighs heavily in my purse. Please add it to my funds in your vault."

"Of course, dear lady." He took her leather purse and poured the contents onto the wooden display counter. "Shall we count it together?"

"Yes, please." She trusted him without hesitation and would accept his careful accounting, but he insisted it all must be counted and recorded in his ledger under her watchful eye. In addition, he always gave her a receipt.

After the chore was completed, she bade him good day and started for the door.

"Ah. I almost forgot," he said. "You have two letters. Wait one moment." He made a quick trip to his back room and emerged carrying the two missives.

Her heart pounding, she thanked him, tucked the vellum letters into her pocket along with her receipt, and walked out into the sunshine. Two letters! But from whom? She hadn't dared to look at the return addresses, for that would tempt her to read them right here on the street. Instead, she hurried home, with Patrick close behind her.

Leaving him to manage the cart, she made her way to the kitchen, then took the meal into the house. Mrs. Cameron stood in the dining room, arms crossed, and tapped her toes as Anne scurried to carry the food to the table. She had left the cast iron pot simmering over a banked fire in the kitchen house, and the beans should be ready to eat. Last evening, she had prepared the cornbread and cut the greens to accompany the meal. With her former cook married and living elsewhere, Anne now needed to manage every chore, including meal preparation. She had scrambled to remember how to cook, and slowly her abilities were returning, but sometimes disaster struck. As it did today.

"These beans are hard as pebbles." Mrs. Cameron dropped her spoon back into her china bowl. "The cornbread is dry, and the greens are gritty with sand." She scowled at Anne, then looked at Patrick. "Do you not agree, Mr. Blakemore?"

Patrick swallowed the bite in his mouth before answering. "You must forgive me, Mrs.

Cameron. It's my fault." He glanced at Anne before continuing. "You see, I failed to check the fire to ensure the beans were boiling, and the greens were washed only once before going into the pot."

How like this kind man to take the blame for her failed meal, all without telling a lie, and all for the sake of helping Anne. In that moment, she knew she loved Patrick Blakemore. From his dear smile at her now, she believed he loved her in return. Would that they were free to live as they pleased far from soldiers and sailors and prisons. Oh, for the peace of Nantucket! Perhaps she should offer to sell this house to Ares Lyttle. After all, he proposed marriage to her every other day, and she had no delusion it was because he loved her. No, he merely wanted to own the house. If he kept his vow to call on her this afternoon, perhaps she could suggest that he buy it.

The idea both frightened and excited her. By owning her own home, she had a measure of security. Dare she surrender that when she had no other place to live? Yet the idea of being free from the anchor holding her here in St. Augustine sent an unexpected thrill through her chest. Even so, she had learned through her unhappy marriage that she couldn't depend upon her feelings in making decisions large or small. As in all things, she must pray.

Lord, what would Thee have me do?

Peace settled in her heart. In God's time, He would show her.

Chapter Seven

Patrick scolded himself for his failure to stir the fire under the beanpot, a small task he had done without telling Anne ever since her cook left a month ago. Today he'd been too caught up in a discovery. Days ago, when he tore out the wall's damaged parts, he hadn't noticed the brown leather satchel lying hidden on the tabby floor, partly because of his still recovering eyesight. If not for a glimmer of light on the brass buckle, he would have closed the wall, and no one would ever know it was there.

A quick look at the satchel's contents made clear Artemis Hussey had been involved in unsavory activities that belied his claims of loyalty to Governor Tonyn and the British Crown. Names and dates implicated both Hussey and that obnoxious Lieutenant Lyttle in the theft and smuggling of exports from local plantations, as well as the names of British privateers and pirates who were their partners. From Anne's refusal to accept Lyttle's courting, Patrick doubted she knew about her husband's illegal activities. If she had known, she would have either made a deal with Lyttle or, wanting to stop his persistent suit for good, would have taken the information to the governor to see the lieutenant punished. But if these papers came to light, would anyone believe in her innocence? They might charge her with complicity with Artemis's activities, perhaps even treason. They had the power to claim her house and possibly put her in prison. Patrick resolved to protect Anne from more than a bothersome suitor.

After a quick perusal, he tucked the papers back into their oilskin sheath. But what to do with them? If they were found in his possession, he could be shot or hanged. Both thoughts turned his stomach. If he were to die in this Revolution, let it be for his honest fight against the British, not for the sins of a traitor to both the Patriot cause and the British he claimed were his friends.

In his search for building materials around the property, he had found a hidden door behind the hearth in the kitchen house. While it wasn't the best hiding place, it would have to do until Patrick could decide how to use the papers to Anne's advantage…or not use them at all. *Lord, You must help me protect Anne.*

For, as he had learned all those many months in prison at Fort St. Marks, without God's help, he would surely fail.

After Mrs. Cameron retired to her bedchamber for her afternoon nap, Anne cleared the dining room table and, with Patrick's help, carried the dishes and leftovers to the kitchen house.

"Patrick, may I assume you have been stirring the fire under my cooking pot?"

He shrugged in his charming way. "Well, except for today."

She laughed softly as she placed the used dishes into a metal pan, sprinkled a spoonful of salt over them, and measured in some lye soap. "Yes, well. I thank you for your kind assistance, which falls far outside carpentry work." Water simmered in a pot set over the rekindled fire, and she ladled several scoops over the dishes. Lazy suds appeared on the water's surface.

"Anything I can do to help you." He lingered by the door, his gray eyes focused on her. "We haven't had a chance to speak about my brother."

Swishing a bowl in the hot, soapy suds, she nodded. "I must admit I'm curious. I assume he serves the English king, yet I saw great affection in the way he regarded you."

He huffed softly. "We were inseparable as children, along with our older brother, Ashford. As we grew older, Ash was required to, uhm—" He bit his lower lip. "—to learn the family business from our father."

"Patrick." Anne gave him a chiding look. "I may not regard one man above another in rank, but I do recognize English aristocracy when I see it." She shrugged. "You come from an aristocratic family."

He leaned a shoulder against the door jamb. "You're quite perceptive. Yes, my father is Lord Grandstone, an earl, and he owns Grandstone Abbey. My eldest brother is his heir, and Dash is the spare heir until Ashford marries and produces sons."

She read sorrow in his eyes, perhaps over their current enmity. "And yet you feel called to fight against them?"

He frowned. "Not against my family, only their king's oppression against his former American colonies. Only on that do we disagree."

He appeared to be considering his next words, so Anne waited.

At last, he said, "My mother is a Quaker, like you. I am certain she is heartbroken about the division in the family. I would do anything to alleviate her pain."

"Except to cease your rebellion."

He emitted a harsh laugh. "Some ideals transcend familial ties. Freedom calls to me as surely as God's Spirit called me to Jesus Christ."

Anne turned back to her dishes, hiding a gasp. "Would you equate your cause for freedom to our Lord's salvation of sinners?"

Patrick walked over, stood close to her shoulder, and spoke in solemn tones. "We believe God is with us in our righteous cause." He heaved out a great sigh. "Of course, my family believes their stance is the righteous one."

Despite his closeness, she felt no threat. In truth, she would gladly lay her head on that broad shoulder after her wearying morning. *Anne, you are a foolish woman!* She mentally shook herself as she placed a dish beside the pan and reached for the tea towel. To her surprise, Patrick reached it first and began drying the washed dishes. It seemed such a natural gesture that she made no objection. How could she feel so comfortable speaking with him when they had known each other just short of two months?

Before she did something to embarrass herself, she said, "Sadly, many families are thus divided, and not only about matters of human governance."

"You and your husband?" He winced. "Forgive me. I don't mean to offend."

"I'm not offended. Artemis was who he was. If the war had not happened and we had remained in Nantucket, he would have continued as a businessman, well-liked and successful. But his allegiance to the king caused his friends to turn against him. Their disagreement grew so sharp that they threatened to tar and feather him." She sighed. "We fled to St. Augustine with only a few possessions. The Lord provided a friendly merchant ship's captain, my foster sister's brother, who sailed us here."

Remembering Dinah brought another memory. As soon as she finished cleaning up the kitchen, she would have two letters to read, one no doubt from the beloved foster sister with whom she had grown up after they both were orphaned.

"A merchant captain?" A light flickered in Patrick's eyes. "Was he…?" He frowned. "No, that wouldn't be possible."

Anne struggled with her conscience for several moments. Just how much should she tell Patrick? Perhaps it would encourage him to know what had happened here. "Because this captain no longer sails these waters, I'll tell you what I didn't learn until later. He was robbing British merchant ships to supply the colonials."

"A privateer?" Patrick's eyes widened with understanding, and he chuckled. "Do you speak of Nighthawk? We heard of him in prison and cheered his endeavors."

"The British say he is a pirate." Anne's heart sank as another memory surface. "After Artemis learned he was Dinah's brother, Jamie Templeton, he threatened to expose him to the authorities unless she agreed to marry his wealthy friend, Mr. Richland. He even imprisoned her in her room." Her eyes stung at the memory. "She and Captain Moberly had exchanged promises, but Artemis…" Her voice caught at the memory of her husband's growing rage. "I couldn't permit her to be forced into a marriage she didn't want, so I appealed to the captain, and he quickly came to Dinah's rescue. Artemis did not appreciate it."

As foolish tears rolled down her cheeks, she pulled a handkerchief from her sleeve and dabbed at them.

Patrick touched her shoulder, a touch so gentle it only increased her sorrow. Artemis had once been that gentle, that tender.

"Did your husband mistreat you?"

She could only nod in response.

"Ah, dearest Anne." Patrick gently tugged her into his arms and kissed her forehead. "How could any man…?" He paused. "Forgive me. I have no right." But he still held her in a gentle embrace.

Anne sighed as she rested her head against his chest.

The creak of the main house's back door startled them both. As if by agreement, they jumped apart and busied themselves with completing the cleanup from the noon meal. As footsteps neared, Patrick grinned and winked at Anne. She had difficulty hiding a smile in response. Something had shifted in their relationship, and all for the better.

"Well, there you are." Mrs. Cameron bustled into the kitchen house, huffing in annoyance. "Am I to be your housemaid, Mrs. Hussey? You have a caller." She walked toward the front gate. "I am going shopping. I do hope you will have a better meal for supper this evening."

Patrick's heart hadn't been this full since he decided to join the Revolution. He loved Anne, and from her response, he believed she loved him in return. And to think she knew Nighthawk! Surely somehow the Lord would use this connection to provide Patrick's escape from St. Augustine. Despite her claim to the contrary, did the privateer still sail these waters? And if so, would Anne agree to leave with him? Too many questions, too many uncertainties. But learning her husband had mistreated her settled a deep resolve in Patrick's heart. He wouldn't leave her to be forced into another unhappy marriage.

He waited until she and Mrs. Cameron returned to the house, then followed, tools in hand as an excuse to learn who had come to visit her. From his workplace in the dining room, he could see into the drawing room, where that obnoxious Lieutenant Lyttle sat possessively in the late Artemis's chair, legs crossed and a pipe between his lips, as though he were lord of the manor. On the adjacent settee sat a woman Patrick recognized from the tavern.

"My dear Mrs. Hussey, I am certain you will have no objections to Mrs. Steele staying in your recently vacated guest room." Lyttle waved a careless hand in the air as though the matter were settled. "You'll be pleased to know she can cook and clean in exchange for her room."

Patrick turned a casual glance toward Mrs. Steele, who lounged on the settee, hardly a posture for someone seeking a position as a servant. To his dismay, Anne's fair face grew even paler than usual.

"Why do you make such assumptions, Ares Lyttle? I am not seeking a servant at present."

The word "servant" appeared to offend the woman in question. She glared at Lyttle, who returned a warning glare through narrowed eyes. He turned an oily smile toward Anne.

"But when we marry, my dear lady, we will require at least one servant." He spared Patrick a brief, withering stare.

Anne seemed to wilt a little, then straightened. "Another assumption, sir, that you must not make. I will not marry you."

He laughed, a wicked sound. "Ah, well. You know how Governor Tonyn doesn't want single women in St. Augustine left without a husband to protect them. He has approved our marriage, and that will be the final word on the matter."

Patrick ground his teeth. What he wouldn't give to pound this man into the ground. Before he could give vent to his anger, Anne spoke with quiet firmness.

"Indeed it is not the final word, Ares Lyttle. You cannot force me—"

"But I can arrange a proxy to speak the vows for you." Lyttle glanced again toward Patrick, who had kept his face toward his work, but watched the scene from the corner of his eye. Lyttle stood and strode toward him. "Here now, traitor, mind your business." He studied the replastered wall. "Tear this out, man. Who gave you leave to do this work?"

Anne was beside him in an instant, moving between Patrick and the lieutenant. "Ares Lyttle, you must stop straightaway. You have no authority in my house. You must leave now—"

At the anger mounting on Lyttle's face, Patrick gripped his own anger. "Ma'am, I believe I can help." He looked over her shoulder at the other man. "Sir, having heard of your friendship with Mr. Hussey, I can only surmise you're looking for a satchel he left behind at his untimely death." He gave Anne a deferential grimace. "Forgive me, ma'am. I shouldn't remind you of your loss—"

"Never mind that, you oaf!" Lyttle moved Anne aside and stood nose to nose with Patrick, nostrils flaring. "Where's that satchel?"

With some difficulty, Patrick swallowed his own rage. "Sir, it was not my business, so I placed it in the lady's extra bedchamber, planning to tell her at the first opportunity—"

Lyttle didn't permit him to finish but strode down the small hallway toward the back bedchamber. To Patrick, it seemed odd the man knew exactly what room he had referred to. Hussey must have entertained him here at some point.

In moments, the lieutenant returned waving the open satchel in the air, his eyes dangerously wild. "What have you done with the papers, traitor? Where are they?"

"Papers?" Having perfected the innocent act from early childhood, Patrick blinked and tilted his head. "Sir, I know nothing of papers—"

"You're lying." Lyttle grabbed Patrick's shirt front and jerked him closer. "What did you do with them?"

"Stop it!" Anne grabbed the lieutenant's arm. "I forbid you to abuse my employee this way!"

"Stay out of this, Mrs. Hussey," Lyttle growled as he shook off her hand. "Blakemore, so help me—"

Patrick trembled with rage, and his right hand fisted. Before he could break free from Lyttle and strike him, knocking sounded on the front door.

Confusion flooded Lyttle's face, and he released Patrick and glared at Anne. "Who's that?"

The sweet lady lifted her chin, and her usually peaceful eyes blazed. "How could I possibly know?" She spun on her heels and strode through the archway toward the front hall with Lyttle on her heels. Patrick shook off his indignation over being treated so roughly by a man who was a junior officer to his own rank, and angry at himself that he hadn't dared to beat Lyttle to a pulp. Yet what protection could he provide for Anne if he were thrown back into the prison?

Unable to see the entrance, he followed Lyttle, resolving to help her, no matter the consequences.

"Mrs. Hussey." Dash's cheerful voice wafted through the rooms, and Patrick's heart lifted, then plunged to his stomach. What could his brother possibly want?

Chapter Eight

Anne's eyes stung with sudden tears, but she managed to smile at Patrick's brother. "Friend Blakemore, welcome. Please do come in." She stepped back and waved toward the drawing room. Behind her, she heard a ragged gasp from Ares Lyttle. Surely the Lord had sent the captain to help with this intolerable situation. "Sir, have you met Ares Lyttle?"

The captain removed his hat and reached out to his fellow British officer. "Lieutenant Lyttle, I have heard your name mentioned."

"Captain Blakemore!" Suddenly all smiles and affability, the lieutenant shook the captain's hand perhaps a little too forcefully. He blinked his eyes, and his smile faded. "Blakemore. I, uh, are you...?"

"Tricky!" The captain broke away and strode into the drawing room, where Patrick now stood. He clasped Patrick's upper arms in a fond gesture. "Brother dear, how good to see you again. I suppose the lieutenant here is charged with making sure you don't escape." He laughed at his own words, but poor Patrick blanched.

Oh, dear.

"Um, I, uh..." Patrick glanced at Anne, and she sent him a reassuring smile.

Ares Lyttle appeared a bit pale. Clearly, he was shocked to learn of Patrick's relationship to this officer. Relief flooded Anne, and she tried not to feel a modicum of victory over her unwanted suitor.

While Patrick showed his brother his work on the dining room wall, Ares Lyttle followed along, seeking for all his worth to appear like Patrick's friend. As for the soldier's woman companion, she had disappeared.

Anne heard unexpected sounds and walked down the hall. In the spare bedchamber, once Dinah's room, the woman was rummaging through the clothespress, tossing aside the few clothes Dinah had left behind.

"What are you doing, Mrs. Steele?"

"You and that American soldier have the papers the lieutenant wants. Where have you hidden them?"

"I know nothing of any papers, but I will thank you to leave this room *and* my house."

"Not 'til I find those papers—Ah! Lieutenant Lyttle. I haven't found them yet."

Anne turned to find the man himself standing in the doorway, his eyes wary.

"Never mind, Nancy. Come with me." He beckoned to her. As they moved past Anne, he whispered, "You won't escape my plan, Anne. I shall have you as my wife no matter how much you protest."

Her legs shaking, Anne collapsed onto the bed and struggled against tears. Was it true that Ares Lyttle could force her to marry him? Could she appeal to Governor Tonyn, who hadn't spoken to her since Artemis's funeral? Did he regard her as a useless female who must be relegated to obscurity so he need not concern himself with her?

Lord, help me. Thou knowest what my future should be. Perhaps it is Thy will for me to marry Ares Lyttle that he may come to know Thy grace and love. If so, be it done unto me according to Thy will.

Instead of the warm peace that often followed her prayers of surrender, Anne felt only nausea. Marriage to that horrid man would surely cause her death.

"Now, little brother, what are we going to do with you?" Seated on the drawing room settee, Dash regarded Patrick with concern, his gentle voice reaffirming their fraternal bond. "We cannot have a son of Lord Grandstone back in prison or, worse, on a prison ship."

Patrick pulled in a deep breath, still feeling Lyttle's noose-like grip on his shirt, still feeling shame over not having the freedom to strike his adversary. Unlike the Patriot cause for which he fought, he couldn't fight back against Lyttle *or* his own brother.

Lord, help me. I cannot bear to lose Dash's love and regard, but I refuse to become a traitor to the Patriot cause.

"Captain Blakemore." Lyttle appeared in the doorway, his strumpet at his shoulder. "I hope you will excuse me, but I must attend to the governor's business." He reached out to Dash.

Dash stood and accepted Lyttle's outstretched hand. "Good day, lieutenant. I am certain we shall meet again."

Despite his brother's genial words, Patrick knew him well enough to see his posture and the slight smirk on his lips that revealed his true perception of the other officer. Nor did he acknowledge the woman, clearly comprehending her disreputable character. Dare Patrick hope he could enlist Dash's help in protecting Anne?

As the unwelcome couple left the house, Anne emerged from the back room. Patrick could see she was struggling not to weep. Then, brave lady that she was, she inhaled a bracing breath and gave Dash a gracious smile.

"Will you stay for supper, Friend Blakemore? Our fare will be simple. Bread, cheese, and fruit."

Dash gave her a bow that would make their parents proud. "Dear lady, after my many weeks at sea, that sounds like a veritable feast. I would be honored."

"Then you must excuse me to make the bread." Anne's sweet gaze took in Patrick as well as Dash.

"Of course." Dash's gentle returning gaze revealed only respect, so different from Lyttle's possessive stares. "In the meantime, Tricky and I will tour this fair city. Come along, little brother." He threw an arm around Patrick's shoulder, making clear he had no choice in the matter. He dared not squirm from Dash's firm grasp, but why must he parade him around town where everyone could observe their twin-like resemblance and discern their relationship. Wouldn't that harm Dash's reputation? Perhaps cast aspersions on his loyalty to the Crown?

Another thought quickly replaced his concern. If the captain of the newly arrived British frigate protecting St. Augustine was observed with him, this might suggest his protection of his "errant" brother. Surely this was the Lord's doing, for which Patrick lifted a silent prayer of thanks.

Anne covered the kneaded dough with a damp tea towel and breathed out a prayer that it would rise, then sat to rest for a moment before gathering fruit for tonight's supper. A soft crackle in her skirt reminded her of the two letters, and her heart skipped. Would this day turn to something pleasant rather than threatening?

To her delight, one letter was from Dinah, so far away in England now. The other came from Rachel Moberly, Dinah's sister-in-law, whose husband, Frederick, was the king's magistrate in St. Johns Towne, a day's journey from St. Augustine. Which to read first? With hands shaking with giddy joy, she snapped the wax seal on Dinah's missive and unfolded the vellum page.

Dearest sister of my heart,

I pray this letter finds you well. Thomas and I received the news of Artemis's death with a mixture of relief and grief. In these past few years, he was not kind to you, but I force myself to remember his younger days, when he courted you so sincerely. May God forgive him for his later sins.

I am distressed to think of you living alone in St. Augustine. How well I remember the pressure to marry an unwanted suitor, so I hope you are not suffering the same unpleasantness I endured and from which you helped to save me.

To ensure your safety, you must come to live with us here at Thomas's roomy estate. My invitation is more selfish than kind. As the only American in the English branch of the Moberly family, I am sometimes only tolerated, and that because Thomas is a great naval hero. Thomas assures me things will change when we welcome our first child in a few months, for this vast clan values motherhood above all womanly virtues. Most of all, your company would be a great consolation to me.

We have written to Mr. Patton and asked him to arrange safe passage for you. Do come, dearest Anne. No need to write ahead. We have a place for you.

Fondly,

Your sister Dinah

Tears streaming down her cheeks, Anne clutched the missive to her chest. Truly this was answered prayer. And Dinah was expecting a baby. What joyful news! Yes, she must sell her house and go to England.

As quickly as her heart lifted in hope, she felt a check in her spirit. What about Patrick? Did his kind regard for her extend to a deeper feeling of which he had not yet spoken? Did they have a future together? Did he even want that? Or was his longing to return to that horrid war stronger than his thoughts of her?

Foolish woman! She would never ask him to turn his back on the cause in which he believed with all his being, any more than he would ask her to abandon her faith. And he certainly wouldn't wish to go to England with her.

She heaved out a sigh and refolded the letter, only then remembering the one from Rachel. Her husband, Thomas's younger brother, had always been friendly to her. She broke the seal and unfolded the missive.

Dear Anne,

I hope this letter finds you well. Frederick and I have been very concerned about you since hearing of Artemis's passing last September. Further, we are alarmed by recent information from Mr. Patton concerning a certain British soldier who is pursuing your hand in marriage against your wishes. We will be sending our plantation foreman to St. Augustine for supplies and would be honored if you would consider returning with him to St. Johns Towne to live with us. If you decide this would be best for you, we will assist you in finding a buyer for your house.

Our foreman will deliver this message to Mr. Patton for you.

Your dear friend,

Rachel Moberly

More tears streamed down Anne's face. Until this moment, she hadn't realized how alone she'd felt for so long, even before Artemis died. Now she had two dear friends who wanted to take her under their wings. The warmth of their invitations swept through her like a calming balm.

I thank Thee, Lord. Now please give me guidance as to what Thou would have me do.

"Of course I have heard of the colonials' so-called independence declaration, but no, I have not read it." Dash ambled alongside Patrick on the sandy shoreline of Matanzas Bay. "To do so would be akin to treason. Is it any wonder Governor Tonyn hasn't permitted the local planters to form a general assembly until recently? Uneducated men without understanding of God's natural order cannot be trusted to govern, nor even to gather in large numbers where unwarranted rebellion can be provoked."

Before answering, Patrick reminded himself that Dash had never lived in the former colonies, had never seen for himself nor been a victim of the injustices forced upon honest English citizens by King George and his minions. Most important, he didn't realize that intelligent, highly educated men had written the *Declaration* and based it upon reason and logic and mankind's basic God-given rights. Perhaps those deficits in his understanding were the clue to winning him to the Patriot cause. Patrick must plan his argument well. But another matter sat heavy on his mind.

"Brother, tell me truthfully. Did Father arrange for your assignment to St. Augustine?" He gave Dash a knowing smirk. "Perhaps with Mama's encouragement?"

Dash shrugged, but his ruddy cheeks reddened, a sure sign Patrick had hit the mark.

After several moments, he huffed out a sigh.

"I should very much prefer to be in the thick of battle near New York or invading the Virginia and Carolina coasts. Our navy is the most powerful in the world, and we'll soon quash the rebels—" He grimaced. "I have said too much. We agreed not to discuss the war."

Patrick let Dash's remarks pass, although his brother's assertion made him sick to his stomach. Perhaps it was true that the newly formed United States couldn't win the war at sea. That was, unless the French navy answered Washington's plea for help. But an argument with Dash wouldn't bring victory.

"Tell me about the lovely lady who has employed you." Dash raised one eyebrow. "If I'm not mistaken, that bothersome Lieutenant Lyttle has his eye on her." He emitted a phony cough. "As do you, I suspect."

At last a subject about which Patrick could speak freely. "Dash, I love her." He blinked, surprised by his own words. Might as well say it all. "I would do anything to protect her from that monster, but if I take action, I'll only end up back in the hellhole at Fort St. Marks."

Dash nodded soberly. "Well, that's not going to happen. Father did arrange my deployment to the East Florida coast, but he did so knowing you had been imprisoned here. He sent me with orders to bring you home."

"What?" Patrick halted in his tracks. "Surely you don't think I can return to England. I'd be hanged as a traitor."

"Indeed you will not. At considerable cost and at great peril to his political career, Father has obtained a pardon for you directly from His Majesty. All you need to do is—"

"Stop!" His stomach threatening revolt, Patrick crossed his arms and stared out beyond the bay toward Anastasia Island. "Nothing you say will persuade me to give up my commitment to the cause of freedom."

Dash remained silent for several minutes. Above them, seagulls called to each other. From beyond the mouth of the inlet came the distant ocean's roar. The scent of fish mingled with the fragrance of magnolia blossoms on the trees that dotted the city.

"Consider this. If Mrs. Hussey returns your affection, you can marry here in St. Augustine and she can go with us. She and Mama will enjoy the fellowship of their Friends meetings."

"I would be ashamed to propose to her under such circumstances." Patrick blew out a cross breath. "Even with her Quaker beliefs, she would lose respect for me if I so easily betrayed a cause I believe in and am willing to die for."

Again, Dash stood silent, this time hanging his head. "I fear you do not understand what I am attempting to tell you in the kindest possible terms."

Patrick slid him a wary look, his heart racing with trepidation. "Why dissemble, brother? Haven't we always been honest with each other? Spit it out."

"Very well." Dash ran a hand down his cheek, massaged the back of his neck, and ground the toe of his black shoe into the sand. Then he faced Patrick. "I have letters to Governor Tonyn and the commandant of Fort St. Marks ordering me to take you back home whether you want to go or not."

Patrick felt the blood drain from his face, felt his heart land sickeningly in his belly. "You mean—"

"Yes, dearest little brother." His eyes reddening with unshed tears, Dash gently gripped Patrick's shoulder. "By order of His Majesty King George, I am here to arrest you and take you back home to England."

Chapter Nine

"Well, I must say, Mrs. Hussey—" Seated across the table from Anne, Mrs. Cameron spoke with uncharacteristic friendliness. "—this bread is delicious. Don't you agree, Captain Blakemore?" She batted her eyes at the captain, no doubt charmed by what she considered his august presence.

"Indeed, it is tasty, madam." Patrick's brother appeared unfazed by the woman's simpering. Perhaps he was accustomed to women fawning over him. "And these raisins, dried apples, and goat's cheese are fine fare indeed after my many weeks at sea. My compliments, Mrs. Hussey."

"I thank you both. It is my pleasure to set the Lord's provision before you." Anne turned to Patrick, who had barely touched his supper and whose face seemed strangely haggard. "Isn't it to your liking?"

He smiled at her. In truth, it was a grimace. "The heat has stolen my appetite, ma'am." Despite his assertion, he nibbled a dried apple slice.

Mrs. Cameron continued to monopolize the captain's attention, so Anne felt no need to say more. At least not yet. She must find a way to speak to Patrick alone before he left this evening for his lodgings at the tavern. Dared she hope that he would care about her two invitations? That he could offer advice or suggestions as to which she should accept? Or should she accept neither?

The meal completed, Patrick helped her clear the table and carry the dishes to the kitchen house. The captain followed them as they walked out the back door, then leaned against the door jamb with arms crossed and eyes focused on his brother. Was he keeping an eye on them for propriety's sake? After Ares Lyttle's horrid threats, she welcomed his gentlemanly behavior, not to mention his apparent power over her adversary.

"Did you quarrel with your brother, Patrick," Anne whispered. "Forgive me. I shouldn't intrude—"

"No intrusion, I assure you, dear Anne." He gave her a sad smile. "It wasn't a quarrel exactly. He was sent here by our father to forcibly take me back to England."

Anne inhaled a sharp breath. "But…oh, dear."

As though it were his chore, not hers, he dipped water from the cauldron hanging over the hearth's smoldering coals and poured it into her wash basin, then added salt and lye soap. "I'll wash. You dry." He winked at her.

"Oh, dear Patrick." Her eyes stung with unshed tears. "What will you do?"

Plunging his hands into the basin and lifting a plate, he shrugged. "What choice do I have? At great political risk to himself, my father obtained a pardon for me from King George. While I suppose I should be grateful, I fear it only reveals Father still thinks me a foolish boy, not a man who can make his own decisions." Using a sponge, he scrubbed the plate more forcefully than it required. "I…" He looked at her and blinked, as though changing the subject. "Anne, I care for you more than my own life. Tell me now whether we can have a future together. If not, I must go with Dash—"

Without hesitation, she gripped his arm. "Yes, dear Patrick. I can think of no future without you."

Hands dripping, he pulled her into his arms and nestled her head against his shoulder. "Dearest Anne, what shall we do? I confessed my feelings for you to Dash, and he said we could marry here, and he'll take us to England."

Did she truly have a third option? "Oh, Patrick, could we…*no!* your heart is in the Patriot cause. You mustn't abandon your most dearly held beliefs."

He leaned back to gaze into her eyes for several moments. "You would support me in this matter?" At her nod, he laughed softly, joyfully. "Oh, Anne, my dearest Annie. You give me hope and strength." He bit his lower lip. "But what choice do we have to do otherwise?"

She stepped from his all-too-comfortable embrace. "We do have choices. Just today I received letters from my sister Dinah in England and my friend Rachel in St. Johns Towne, both inviting me to come live with them. Perhaps your brother would agree to placing you in Frederick Moberly's custody. He is the king's magistrate in St. Johns Towne. Surely Dash will agree to the plan."

Patrick's face brightened, and he seemed to ponder the idea for a moment. "Only one way to find out." He stepped over to the kitchen house door and beckoned to his brother.

Dash, whose resemblance to Patrick was striking, strode across the yard. "What is it, little brother?" He chuckled. "I thought to give you two more time together."

Patrick gave him a broad grin. "She said yes."

"Well done, little brother!" Dash laughed and slapped Patrick on the back, then turned his smile toward her and, with a bow, took her hand. "Mrs. Hussey, as you are to join our family, may I have the privilege of addressing you as Anne?"

Heat rushed up Anne's neck. "Yes, you may." She shared a fond look with Patrick. This almost seemed beyond her fondest dreams. Almost. "Captain Blakemore—"

"Dash, please."

She nodded. "Very well. Dash, are you certain your family will agree to our marriage? I am not an aristocrat, but an orphan from an early age. My people weren't wealthy. While Scripture teaches us the Lord sees no class difference, perhaps your family and friends would view the matter differently."

Now the brothers traded a look. Both grinned as if in conspiracy.

Patrick pulled Anne to his side. "Dearest, our father can make no complaints. He married Mama, whom many of his peers considered beneath him."

"True," Dash said, "she is the daughter of a minor baron and had a small inheritance. But no matter. Father married for love, and he can expect nothing different from his sons." He chuckled. "Now, as to his daughters, I cannot guarantee his choices. Our darling sisters will surely be sold off to the highest-ranking peers."

"With appropriate fortunes, of course." Patrick smirked at Dash, and they both laughed.

Anne stared from one to the other, her jaw dropping. Then Patrick winked at her. She slapped his arm.

"Oh, you're making a jest. Your father won't sell his daughters."

"No, of course not." Dash's kindly expression dispelled Anne's last concern for those unknown young ladies, perhaps soon to be her sisters. "Now, on another topic. What must we do to arrange your marriage and your journey to England? I am assigned to the East Florida coast for another thirty days. We can sail for England after that."

Patrick gazed down at Anne. "Shall we ask Reverend Kennedy to cry the banns for the next three weeks?"

Anne thought for a moment. What would the elders of her Nantucket Friends meeting think of her embracing this Church of England ritual? More important, what did her own inner light tell her? Was she being led by God's Holy Spirit or by her own heart's romantic longing?

"Will you grant me time to think about it?"

His gaze softened. "Of course." He glanced at his brother. "She sounds like Mama, doesn't she?"

"I am delighted to agree." Dash glanced around the kitchen. "Well, I shall leave you to your dishwashing." He smirked at Patrick. "Never thought to see you doing such chores, but, oh well."

Patrick grinned. "Wait until you fall in love, brother. You'll find yourself doing chores you never imagined."

A faint shadow seemed to cross Dash's eyes, and he shrugged. "I have no doubt you speak the truth."

Anne's heart went out to him. Had he been disappointed in love? If so, she supposed she would learn about it soon enough.

Patrick barely felt the hard gravel beneath his thin-soled shoes as he walked down King George Street beside Dash. To think that Anne loved him and was willing to spend the rest of her life with him! He had never known such happiness, nor such hope for the future. Yet thoughts of the future almost halted him in his steps as he considered the vague agreement they had reached with Dash. King's pardon notwithstanding, he couldn't bear to go to England, not as long as the war continued. Considering the king's refusal to remove the heavy taxes levied against his colonists, Patrick hated that Father had been required to pay a heavy ransom to obtain that pardon. Perhaps he should feel guilty. But he hadn't asked to be pardoned and wouldn't accept it because he had done nothing wrong. How would his refusal affect his return to his father's estate? Or the restoration of their familial bond, if that could ever happen?

As they neared the tavern, a new idea came to mind, bringing with it great hope. Of course, he would need to talk privately with Anne to be sure she agreed with his plan. Instead of traveling to England, he must urge her to accept the invitation from Rachel and Frederick Moberly. Whispers among the prisoners had suggested that Moberly secretly supported the Revolution and was in league with the privateer Nighthawk. No one would speak of it within the hearing of the guards, for that would betray a fellow Patriot. But the men used any means possible to encourage each other that the war continued despite their imprisonment.

They entered the tavern and took seats at a small table. Dash nodded to the strumpet who kept company with Lyttle. She sidled up to him suggestively and bristled when he leaned away from her. Waving dismissively, he ordered, "Rum."

"As you wish, my pretty captain." She sauntered off, in no hurry to serve them.

Dash shook his head in disgust, then eyed Patrick. "You will be interested to know that Father has joined the Charles Fox coalition in Parliament who no longer support the war against the colonies. While I cannot agree with his urging His Majesty to immediately withdraw from the conflict, I do hope and pray for peace. We have already lost too many good men."

"On both sides." Patrick's heart still ached at the memory of his good friend, Abel Woodsmith, who had taught him everything he knew about carpentry…and who'd been struck down beside him in battle.

After a moment, Dash's disclosure came into focus, and Patrick said, "I am glad to hear about Father's new position. No doubt he was influenced by Mama's gentle persuasion. I would wager she didn't keep quiet about her disapproval of the war."

Dash chuckled. "How well you know her." A fond look filled his eyes. "She'll be more than pleased to see you, as will our brother and sisters."

Nostalgia stung Patrick's heart. He'd had an idyllic childhood on Father's estate, only comprehending how little true freedom he'd had after he began his apprenticeship with Abel in Virginia and learned the true nature of what was happening in the colonies.

The serving woman plopped two full tankards on the table, causing rum to splash out. She didn't bother to wipe up the mess. "Need anything else, my lovelies?" As she had since Patrick began renting his lodgings, she stared into his eyes as though trying to impart some meaning on which he refused to speculate.

"No." Again, Dash waved her away without looking at her. He sipped his rum and eyed Patrick's untouched tankard. "Not thirsty?"

Patrick shrugged. "I took a vow not to drink spirits until our freedom is won."

"What?" Dash blinked and peered over his raised tankard, chuckling. "Then I fear you have relegated yourself to a life of abstinence, brother."

Patrick leaned back in his chair and crossed his arms. "We shall see."

Another chuckle. "Perhaps we should order you some tea."

Patrick snorted. "I think we made our opinion of British tea quite obvious back in '73."

"We?" Dash set down his drink and leaned toward Patrick, eyebrows arched in horror. "I beg you, brother, you must assure me you didn't take part in that dastardly destruction of an honest tradesmen's property, whose worth was ninety thousand pounds, and, I hasten to add, was under His Majesty's protection. I beg you—" His tone turned to pleading. "—you *must* tell me you did not participate."

Patrick rolled his eyes. Why did this harmless yet rebellious event bother Dash more than the countless Redcoats Patrick had faced in mortal combat? "Obviously you know nothing of our American geography. Boston is hundreds of miles from Virginia where I resided. But the courage of those Patriots in refusing to pay ridiculous taxes on such imports was a catalyst to my joining the Revolution."

Dash stared off, his jaw tightening, his hand fiercely gripping the handle of his tankard. For a moment, Patrick feared his brother would toss the contents on him. Instead, his expression softened.

"We truly must not discuss the colonists' useless conflict, Tricky. Foremost in all my thoughts must be to deliver you safely to our parents." He stood and tossed a coin on the table. "I am billeted at the military barracks until I sail out on patrol. If you or your Mrs. Hussey require my assistance with that pesky lieutenant, send word—"

"With my manservant?" Patrick gave his brother a teasing smirk.

Dash rolled his eyes. "Surely you can find a lad in the streets willing to earn a half pence."

"Yes, they're all eager to help a Patriot, especially when such *lads* take great pleasure in hurling rocks at me."

Dash winced and briefly glanced down at his feet, clearly troubled by Patrick's claim. Was he recalling the respect village boys heaped upon them on Father's estate? With their families' livelihoods at stake, no one had ever dared to raise a hand against the earl's sons, Ash, Dash, and Tricky.

Dash straightened. "Nonetheless, I am willing to help you. Surely that means something to you." He spun away and strode from the building.

His heart aching, Patrick trudged up the stairs to his tiny room. In truth, Dash's fraternal devotion deeply stirred his soul. What career advancement did his brother risk by helping him? Just as important, what did Patrick risk by placing himself in Dash's hands?

Chapter Ten

Anne gathered ripe squashes, string beans, and two dozen carrots. Her spring harvest was thinning, so she would have to plant more this afternoon. With her last oranges and lemons already on her cart, she would probably have a short morning at the Parade. She was glad she still had dried grapes, plums, and apples to add to today's produce.

The creak of her front gate drew her attention, and she peered around the kitchen house corner. Seeing Patrick enter, she released a sigh of relief. She'd awakened before dawn with an odd, foreboding feeling, though she couldn't discern why. As always, before beginning her day, she read a Psalm and prayed, seeking the Lord's peace and direction for the day. Today, she had added a special petition for wisdom about Dash's invitation to accompany him and Patrick to England. Perhaps that was the cause for her unease.

"Good morning, dear heart." Patrick strode across the sandy yard. "Are you ready to go?"

"To England?"

He grimaced comically. "Um, no. I meant to the Parade."

His easy manner made her laugh. "Oh. Oh, yes. Of course. And good morning to you, dear Patrick."

He moved closer to her and, instead of taking hold of the cart, gazed down at her, a hint of a smile on his lips, a hint of a question in his eyes. She returned a consenting smile. To her foolish disappointment, he leaned forward and placed a sweet kiss on her cheek instead of her all-too-willing lips. Without meaning to, she frowned in disappointment.

He gave her a teasing smile. "Shall we go?" He grasped the bar and pushed the cart toward the gate. She walked beside him, wishing they were out for a stroll rather than on their way to her place of business.

"Have you made up your mind about going to England with Dash?"

"I have another plan," he whispered as he nodded toward the red-coated soldiers coming their way. "We can talk about it later."

"Yes, of course." Her heart skipped at the idea of making plans with him. "Should I speak to the land agent, Jesse Fish, about selling my house?"

He appeared to consider her question, then nodded. "It won't hurt to have him start searching for a buyer, but be sure he knows we aren't leaving yet, and you'll need a place to live until we do." He winked at her. "Don't start packing yet."

To her horror, the laugh she intended came out as a giggle. Heat rushed up her neck and filled her cheeks. Patrick didn't appear to notice her girlish lapse or her blush.

He settled the cart in its usual spot under the magnolia tree. "I'll return at midday." He took a step toward her, then glanced around at the soldiers and various citizens filling the Parade. With an apologetic smile, he tipped his battered tricorn hat and strode away.

As usual, Ares Lyttle approached her with a possessive air. "Ah, my little fiancée, have you planned our wedding yet? Perhaps if you sell enough—" He waved a hand over her cart as though her carefully grown produce had no value. "—perhaps you can purchase a new gown. Something bright to get you out of those dreadful widow's weeds."

Anne glanced toward the street where Patrick had just disappeared around the corner, then swallowed hard. What could she possibly say that she hadn't already said to this odious man?

"Why, Mrs. Hussey." Maude appeared from the direction of the governor's palace. "Are you to be married?" She stared at Ares Lyttle up and down, a doubtful look in her dark eyes. "To this man?" Her tone made clear her disapproval.

"Silence, you stupid cow." Ares Lyttle glared at Maude and took a threatening step toward her. "This is none of your concern."

Maude moved closer to Anne, no fear in her face. "Ma'am, do you plan to marry this man?"

"No." Anne shook her head. "I have told him repeatedly I won't marry him, yet he insists —" Her voice broke.

"It's all right, ma'am." Maude placed an arm around Anne's waist.

Bolstered by her help, Anne stiffened her spine. "He has threatened to force marriage upon me through proxy, claiming he has Governor Tonyn's approval."

Ares Lyttle reached out to grab Anne's arm, but Maude stepped in front of her and blocked his hand.

"You keep your hands off her."

Instead, the evil man shoved Maude away from Anne. "Get out of here, you useless—"

Maude regained her balance and stood tall. "I ain't gonna leave till I have the gov'nor's breakfast fruit."

Shock filled his face. Hadn't he realized Maude was the governor's cook?

"Very well. Get your fruit." He stepped back. "And be quick about it."

"Mrs. Hussey, ma'am," Maude whispered, taking her time to make her choice. "Don't you worry. I'll be telling the governor about this."

"I thank you, dear friend."

Maude paid Anne and collected her purchases. "I'll see you tomorrow, ma'am." She glared at Ares Lyttle. "Humph." She walked toward the governor's mansion humming.

Ares Lyttle ground his teeth. "This is not over, my dear. If you think a slave has more influence over the governor than a decorated soldier, you are sadly mistaken." Shoulders stiffened, he marched away.

For the rest of the morning, only a few customers approached Anne's cart. Thus, the morning passed slowly. At last, Patrick came striding around the corner of King George Street and across the Parade. Her heart lifted and settled an important matter in her mind.

"Dearest Patrick." She dared to address him fondly and was rewarded with a broad smile.

"Dearest Anne. Did you have a good morning?" He eyed the few remaining items on her cart.

"Good enough." She stepped aside so he could grip the bar. "If you will accompany me to Friend Kennedy's residence, I should like to inquire if he'll cry the banns for us beginning this Lord's Day."

Patrick's face brightened even more. "Oh, my dear…" He moved closer to her, but glanced around the Parade at the crowds going about their business, and paused. "You've made me the happiest man." Rich emotion filled his voice, and his eyes shone with moisture. "You do understand that life will be difficult in England? I have no assurance of —"

"Shh." She touched his lips to silence his protest, then brushed away her own tears. "The Lord will see to all of that." She took a step back. "Now, let us hurry to Friend Kennedy and tend to our business with him. I mustn't serve dinner late, or Mrs. Cameron will scold us."

Patrick shuddered in his comical way. "Indeed, we must avoid that at all costs."

The minister showed no surprise at their request. "I have long noticed your fondness for each other." He peered over the top of his spectacles at Anne, then Patrick. "I always insist upon a counseling session for my prospective couples. If you agree to this, I will agree to marry you."

After giving him their assurances and making their first appointment for the next afternoon, Patrick and Anne returned to her house. While Patrick tended the cart, Anne checked the beans and ham. She could tell Patrick had stirred the pot and stoked the fire. He also had made the cornbread, which she had forgotten this morning. And all without boasting or demanding a returned favor, as Artemis did for every small thing he did for her. Such a dear, humble man was Patrick. But she must cease this comparison between them.

Perhaps it was the joy overflowing her heart, but to Anne, even Mrs. Cameron seemed more pleasant during their midday meal, no doubt because the food was edible, even delicious. What would the lady do after Anne sold the house? Rooms were hard to come by here in St. Augustine, especially with the newly arrived sailors requiring a place to live between voyages. Feeling a strong sense of responsibility for her tenant, Anne would pray that the Lord would provide for her.

While Patrick continued his work repairing the dining room wall, Anne spent the afternoon preparing her garden soil for a new planting. Using her pitchfork, she mixed into the sandy soil the compost saved from her vegetables and manure purchased from the city's stable owner. As the afternoon wore on, she noticed a tall man in brightly colored Minorcan garb beckoning to her from outside her front fence. Despite the wide-brimmed straw hat shielding his face, she knew him straightaway. Dropping her pitchfork, she dashed across the yard to the gate, quickly unlatching it.

"Come in, Jamie Templeton." She spoke softly, urgently, glancing down the street to be sure no one was watching them, then grabbed him by the arm and tugged him inside. "How can you be here? Have you no fear of the danger?" She locked the gate behind him and led him to the kitchen house.

When they were safely inside, he gazed down at her, a gentle smile on his lips. "Didn't you receive my cousin's letter? I've come to take you to Bennington Plantation."

Anne gasped. "You are the foreman?"

He chuckled. "No. Cousin Rachel sent me instead."

Anne stared at him for a moment, trying to sort out the complications his words provoked. Hadn't she just today decided to go to England with Patrick? Yet here was Jamie Templeton risking his life to assure her safe travel to an entirely different destination.

Lord, what shall I do? What is Thy will? How can I leave Patrick when we have only just agreed to marry?

"Mrs. Hussey." Jamie Templeton gazed at her with concern. "Are you well?"

The kindness in his voice severed her tenuous hold on her emotions, and she broke down in tears.

Still basking in the joy of Anne's agreement to cry the banns for their marriage, Patrick stirred fresh lime plaster to apply to the lath strips. Her trust in God's control of their future heartened his own faith. Surely Father wouldn't have sent Dash to fetch him if he had no plan for his future. Given Father's disapproval of King George's continuing the war, perhaps Patrick could find a way to advance the Revolution from Father's estate. Once there, he would pray and watch for every opportunity.

Hearing the iron gate squeak, he felt a spike of alarm. He should go now to discover who had entered, perhaps that cur, Lyttle. But if he left this fresh plaster, it would dry out and become unusable. He could neither waste it nor rush the job and do it poorly. Anxiety grew in his chest that the newcomer might be the lieutenant. He quickly smoothed the mixture across the lath, then wiped his hands on a rag and made his way out the back door.

Through the open kitchen door, he saw a large man hovering over Anne, who was sobbing. Heart in his throat, he dashed across the yard.

"Anne!"

The man turned, his posture defensive. Patrick glanced at the woodpile. Could he reach the ax before this intruder realized his plan to protect Anne?

"Patrick!" Anne bolted toward him, but instead of rushing into his open arms, she grabbed his hand and dragged him past the man and into the kitchen house. Once there, she closed the door, then took a handkerchief from her sleeve and dabbed at her tears. Patrick tugged her into his protective embrace.

The tall, broad-shouldered stranger stood back, arms folded, a frown visible under the brim of his broad straw hat.

"Who are you?" Patrick demanded. If every other defense failed, he could grab the poker from beside the oven…

"Who are *you*!" the man returned.

"Oh, stop it!" Anne stamped her foot in the first display of pique Patrick had ever observed. Her strength cooled his raging emotions. Somewhat.

"Patrick—" She softened her voice. "—this is Jamie Templeton. He has offered to take me to Bennington Plantation." She looked at the other man. "Jamie Templeton, this is Patrick Blakemore." She gazed up at him, her eyes exuding love. "My fiancé."

"Your—?" The man chuckled. "Well, perhaps my trip has been unnecessary." He stuck out his hand toward Patrick. "Honored to meet you, sir. Your uniform, ragged as it is, tells me much about you."

Jaw dropping, Patrick stared unmoving as he realized this was the legendary hero, Nighthawk, until Anne elbowed him in the ribs.

"Oh. Yes." He grasped Templeton's hand and shook it, perhaps a bit too enthusiastically. "I am honored to meet you as well, sir." He glanced out the window to be sure no one lurked nearby. "Your reputation precedes you, Captain."

Templeton ran a hand down the blond stubble on his jaw. "That's always a concern in my, um, occupation."

"But I would never—"

"Of course not." Templeton turned to Anne. "I would not wish to rush you, ma'am, but you understand I cannot stay long. If you decide not to go with me, what shall I tell Rachel?"

"Oh, dear." Anne gave Patrick a pleading look. "What shall we do?"

Her sweet dependence on him sent warmth flooding his chest, but a cautionary instinct asserted itself. "We have much to consider, my love." He eyed Templeton. "My brother serves in the British navy. He was sent by our father to take me home to England." He placed an arm around Anne's waist. "Several days ago, this beautiful lady agreed to be my wife, and today, she agreed to go with me to my former homeland."

"But now we have another option." Anne leaned into his side. "Oh, Patrick, would your brother permit you to go to Bennington Plantation?"

"Blakemore." Templeton frowned. "Is Captain Dashiell Blakemore your brother?"

Patrick nodded. "He is."

"Huh." Templeton huffed out a breath. "I know him. Or rather, I did. We were on friendly terms. I even received his occasional protection for my merchant ship. However, once Captain Moberly discovered my identity over a year ago, I could no longer ply my import trade here for fear the Brits would uncover my privateering."

"Dear Captain Moberly." Anne sighed. "He was so good to me and of course to your sister. Did you know Dinah has also written, inviting me to live with her and the captain?"

"No, I didn't." Templeton chuckled. "You have many choices, dear lady. What will you do?"

Again, Anne gazed up at Patrick, expectation beaming from her eyes. "What shall we do?"

His heart once again near to bursting at her trust in him, Patrick gladly embraced his responsibility for her safety and care. He turned to Templeton. "Captain, what do you advise?"

The captain furrowed his brow for a moment. "My uncle, who reared me, always said no wise decision was ever made in haste. We must pray. I know my cousin and her husband will welcome you, too."

Patrick considered this welcome invitation. Taking Anne there would be the better plan. She would be safe with her friend Rachel, and he could escape, travel north, and rejoin his regiment.

"I'll ask Dash if the plantation is an acceptable option." Another thought. "Are you certain your identity has been exposed? Among our Patriot prisoners at Fort St. Marks, no one connected your name to Nighthawk. And no soldiers boasted of discovering who you are."

"Ah." Templeton scratched his chin again. "That would be good news. It would give me the freedom to sail the *Fair Winds* into the harbor with its cargo." After a moment, he leaned toward Patrick. "Can you uncover the truth?"

"I'll find out what my brother knows."

"Um, maybe—"

Patrick chuckled. "Never fear, Captain. I know exactly what to say. In the meantime, do you have a place to stay here in St. Augustine?"

"I know a place," Anne said. "Come with me, Jamie."

As they exited the property, Patrick returned to the house to check his work. When the plaster dried, he would need to sand out the ridges left by his trowel's edge, but the wall would soon be ready for the wallpaper Mrs. Cameron had spent many hours repairing. He found her involvement in this improvement interesting, considering her many unwarranted complaints against Anne as her landlady. Perhaps she was merely bored, perhaps a little bitter over the course her life had taken.

He cleaned up the floor and his tools, then went outside to see if Anne had returned. He found her turning the garden soil with a pitchfork.

"Allow me." He reached for the tool, but she shook her head.

"*My* job." She gave him a merry smile.

"Very well. But when we have our own home, I'll do the heavy work."

She stopped and leaned an arm on the pitchfork handle. "Your words give me such hope."

He could easily fall into her beautiful brown eyes. "How could we live without hope?" He shifted his stance to keep from kissing her. "For instance, you plant because you hope for a harvest, but—" He winked at her. "—perhaps someone else will reap that harvest."

She smiled as she bent to her work. "Don't you have something to do? As in finding your brother?"

He chuckled as he walked toward the front gate. "Yes, ma'am."

Chapter Eleven

"Reverend Kennedy will cry the banns the first time tomorrow after his sermon." Patrick sat in Dash's sparsely furnished room at the military barracks, while his steward, Jolly, went about his work freshening Dash's extra uniform. Patrick had long forgotten what it was like to have a perfect servant tend his duties so discreetly. But the man had ears, so any words spoken in his presence could create danger for Templeton. He would stick to safe subjects when Jolly was in the room. "With two more weeks required before our marriage, will that work with your orders to return to England?"

"It will." Dash was all affability, clearly pleased over Patrick's plans. "I know Father and Mama will welcome your sweet Anne into the family. And of course, they'll be more than happy to see the prodigal return home." He quirked his lips to one side in his familiar teasing grin.

The word "prodigal" needled Patrick, but he wouldn't comment now. Instead, he exhaled a long sigh, hoping to inject just the right amount of drama into his tone. "My dear sweet Anne. She won't resist our plans, but her heart's desire is to accept her friends Rachel and Frederick Moberly's invitation to live at Bennington Plantation."

"Ah." Dash's posture slumped. "I'm sorry to hear that."

After a few quiet moments, Patrick added, "And *my* heart's desire is to please my beloved." He gave his brother a pleading look. "Couldn't you permit me to take her there? I wouldn't resist being in Frederick Moberly's custody. He's the younger brother of Lord Bennington and Captain Thomas Moberly. As magistrate, he's proven his loyalty." Not to King George, but Patrick wouldn't say that.

"I understand." Dash nodded. "However…" He leaned toward Patrick. "*You* must understand that when Father learned of your capture and His Majesty's plan to send you and all such rebels to a prison ship, Father paid a hefty sum to secure your pardon. With the war costing everyone almost beyond their means, I cannot in good conscience fail to return you home. I didn't intend to tell you this, but Father has a plan for you to repay him."

Guilt slammed into Patrick's chest. "Yes, of course." He'd already cost Father too much, both as a foolish youth and now with this ransom, for his payment to the king couldn't be called anything else. Though he never would have asked to be ransomed, honor demanded that he at least try to repay Father, or at the very least, try to repay him in part. *What now, Lord?*

"Perhaps we can arrange for Anne to see her friends before we sail." Dash offered a conciliatory smile. "I am acquainted with Rachel Moberly's cousin, Jamie Templeton, a Loyalist merchant captain." He frowned. "I should say, I did know him. None of our friends in the admiralty have heard from him almost a year. We fear he may have met with disaster, perhaps his ship being sunk by that fiend Nighthawk who continues to bedevil our supply ships."

"How interesting." Patrick barely managed to conceal his shock. He hadn't needed to mention Templeton, yet had learned all that was required to reassure him. Surely the Lord was watching over the privateer's endeavors for the Revolution. Nor could Patrick deny the Lord's hand on him, as well. He hadn't been forced to lie to Dash. Yet now he must resign himself to returning to England. "I'll ask Anne if a short visit to the plantation will please her."

Entering the large church at Patrick's side, with Dash leading the way, Anne ignored the glances from numerous parishioners. Not that they were unfriendly, merely curious about seeing her here, she supposed, for some were her frequent customers and knew of her Quaker faith. With Dash ushering Patrick and her into the pew and taking the aisle seat for himself, she sat between the brothers.

The disparity between Dash's pristine uniform and Patrick's clean but tattered one did nothing to diminish the brothers' warm friendship. Anne was thankful she had given Patrick one of Artemis's finer white linen shirts. Mostly hidden under his blue woolen jacket, it nonetheless improved his overall appearance. While it mattered little to her, she knew some parishioners held strong prejudices. For her part, she could only feel a modest pride in being in his company, rags and all, in this public place.

Across the way, Mr. and Mrs. Markham and their daughter, Elizabeth Wayland, smiled and nodded to their little group. Mr. Markham was a wealthy and influential St. Augustine merchant, Mrs. Markham ruled the ladies' social scene, and Mrs. Wayland had married a British naval officer a year ago and now awaited their first child at her parents' home while her husband tended his duties at sea. Anne lifted a silent prayer for his safety.

Unaccustomed to the Church of England liturgy, she followed along as Dash pointed out the appropriate passages in his well-worn *Book of Common Prayer*. She particularly enjoyed Friend Kennedy's homily, which referenced the story of the wastrel son from Luke's gospel. How she wished for paper and pen to write down his points. As it was, she could only feel grief that Artemis had never run home to his Heavenly Father, at least not to her knowledge. Perhaps as he lay feverish and dying, he had repented but had been unable to tell her. In the service, nothing contradicted her own biblical beliefs. And she found that kneeling on the bench before the pew was much like her own customary posture for prayer.

At the end of the service, the minister stepped down from the dais. "And now, before my final prayer, permit me to call your attention to this happy news. I have the honor and joy to publish the banns of marriage between the widow Mrs. Anne Hussey of St. Augustine and the Honorable Patrick Blakemore, youngest son of Lord Grandstone. This is the first time of asking. If any of you know cause or just impediment why these two persons should not be joined together in Holy Matrimony, ye are to declare it."

"I do declare a just impediment!" Ares Lyttle, in full dress uniform, including a sword, stood up near the sanctuary front and stared angrily at her.

Gasps arose from the congregation, including from Anne.

"Mrs. Hussey is betrothed to me. Both Governor Tonyn and the lady's late husband have promised me her hand."

Anne's stomach rebelled, and she barely managed not to lose her breakfast. Beside her,

Patrick lurched forward with a growl, but Dash reached across her to pull him back and whispered, "You must let the lady respond."

"My dear Mrs. Hussey, what have you to say?" asked Friend Kennedy, a frown conveying his annoyance. Was he displeased with her or Ares Lyttle?

The whole congregation seemed to stare at her, and Anne couldn't control the tremors shaking her entire body. Before she could rise, Mrs. Markham jumped to her feet.

"What utter nonsense." She shook a finger at Ares Lyttle. "What gives either a governor or a dying husband the right to force a woman to marry a man when her heart is clearly set on another?"

A second woman stood. "No right at all." She poked her husband, who sat beside her. "Speak up, Henry." As he winced and lowered his head, she added, "You fought a duel for my hand."

Laughter spread through the room.

"Ladies and gentlemen, this uproar must cease!" His tone commanding, Reverend Kennedy held up a hand to halt the disruption. "We will take this matter into consideration *privately*. Now, let us pray."

Tears clouding her eyes, Anne sank down on the kneeling bench beside Patrick, who put a reassuring arm around her waist, then helped her stand after the final "amen."

"This will not go unanswered," Dash said. "Dear Anne, what would you have me do?"

"I…I don't know." She looked up at Patrick, whose scowl resembled his brother's. "I fear if we resist him too boldly, he'll imprison Patrick."

"No, that will not happen." Dash patted her shoulder and gave Patrick a firm nod.

As people filed from the pews, several glanced their way, and a few gave her encouraging smiles. Mrs. Markham, followed by her husband and daughter, approached, sympathy written across her face.

"My dear Mrs. Hussey, I well recall the day last year when your foster sister, our dear friend Dinah, endured a similar situation, with your husband trying to force her into marriage to that dreadful Mr. Richland." She huffed with indignation. "We won't permit you to be bullied into marrying that man, decorated soldier or not."

"If you require a place of refuge, Mrs. Hussey," Mr. Markham said, "you're welcome to stay with us until the matter's settled."

"I thank you, good friends." Anne blinked back tears. "But I must prepare my house for sale."

"Very well." Mrs. Markham squeezed Anne's hand. "You must let us know if we can help you."

As the family walked away, Friend Kennedy approached and spoke in a confiding tone. "Mrs. Hussey, we know there is nothing to this matter. Still, I must speak to Governor Tonyn and make certain all things are done in order." He glanced beyond her. "Ah, I see he hasn't left yet. Please excuse me." He walked toward the back of the church, where numerous people surrounded the governor, perhaps with their own petitions.

Anne could only wonder why the governor hadn't spoken up to answer Ares Lyttle's objection to the banns. Did that mean he supported the lieutenant's claim?

Before she and her protectors could move into the aisle, her adversary came striding toward them. "Well, now, Captain Blakemore, you can see what a sham this is. Why, Anne barely knows this traitor. You will forgive me, but of course that is what your brother is. I, on the other hand, was her late husband's close friend and business associate, and he did indeed ask me to care for her—"

"Lieutenant—" His voice strangely affable, Dash held up a hand to stop him. "—if you please, I doubt Mrs. Hussey has granted you permission to use her Christian name, so do *not* do that again." His tone still cordial, he frowned. "And, as Mrs. Markham said, no one can force her to marry someone not of her choosing." He stepped closer to the lieutenant, who moved back a pace. "Now, if you will excuse us, we have a picnic to attend."

Anne knew nothing about a picnic, but she gladly took Patrick's offered arm and left the church as she had entered it, with the two brothers. Yet, despite their protective presence, she struggled to keep fear from overwhelming her.

Patrick's soul had been nourished by the familiar worship liturgy from Dash's prayer book. His own had been lost somewhere on the battlefield where he lay wounded and unconscious for unknown hours. But while he had felt the Lord's closeness during the service, Lyttle had destroyed that peace. It chafed almost more than he could bear that he couldn't pound the lieutenant into the ground. Or at least challenge him to a duel, as that outspoken woman's husband had done.

How hard it was for him to hide behind Dash's authority and protection. Perhaps the Lord desired to further humble him, as if spending five months in Fort St. Marks' dark, dank prison wasn't sufficient for him to comprehend his own mortality and dependence upon the Almighty.

As they walked back toward Anne's house, Dash's last words sifted into his thoughts. "What's this about a picnic?"

Anne shook her head. "I fear the only picnic I can piece together will be quite meager."

"Never you mind, my dear." Dash chuckled. "I took the liberty of having my ship's cook prepare a small feast and deliver it to your house."

"Oh, Dash." Anne's eyes again shone with tears, this time appearing to be the happy sort. "How very kind."

"I had a purpose for it." Dash eyed Patrick and grinned. "I wanted you to experience for the first time one of our family's customs. On Sunday, our servants are granted a half day off, so the night before, our chef prepares a cold feast for the family to eat after church."

Pleasant memories of those repasts flooded Patrick's mind, causing his mouth to water. Cold meats, cheeses, pastries, fruit, and even confections. If he were a gluttonous man, he would be glad to move back to his father's manor house just for the food. But as a carpenter's apprentice who ate with the servants, he had learned to manage his appetite, which stood him well as a soldier who often experienced hunger. Still, today, once they sat down in Anne's dining room, he ate Dash's feast heartily for his health's sake, for he must present a robust physique to his parents.

Even though Dash continued to reassure her, Anne spoke little during their meal. Mrs. Cameron made up for their hostess's lack, extolling the meal, praising Reverend Kennedy's sermon, and even offering to help Patrick reapply the repaired wallpaper on the morrow.

"How lovely it will be when the wall is fully restored, Mrs. Hussey." The lady gazed at the wall with apparent affection. "I am so pleased that Mr. Blakemore found the unused remnants of the original. That should make our task much easier to complete."

Anne blinked, seeming to wake up from her depression. "Why, Mrs. Cameron, how can I ever thank you for your help in this endeavor?"

"Well…" Mrs. Cameron laughed. "I have an ulterior motive." She dabbed her lips with her serviette. "Dear Mrs. Hussey, I have only just received my late husband's pension for his service to His Majesty, and I should like to purchase your house."

Patrick's jaw dropped in surprise. Dash laughed heartily. Anne burst into tears.

With some difficulty, Anne dabbed at her tears as she tried to subdue her shock over Mrs. Cameron's unexpected announcement. "I thank you, dear lady, and I shall be delighted to sell you the house." No matter how little she offered, Anne would accept, for it was a sure sign that the Lord approved her plan to go to England with Patrick. "I believe it is time to retire from my produce business. Do you wish to continue it? I do have a new crop planted that will be ready to sell by June."

"Hm." Mrs. Cameron furrowed her brow. "I hadn't thought that far ahead, but, yes, I think that would be a fine occupation to take up. You must teach me all your secrets for growing such fine vegetables."

"I'll be happy to do so." To Anne's annoyance, her eyes continued to water, and her voice was garbled.

"Well, now." Dash took another sugary confection from the serving platter. "That is a fine development. It seems everything is falling into place for your marriage and your new life in England."

Patrick snorted. "Everything but dealing with Lyttle. You can be sure he won't be pleased to see someone else purchase the house, for I am convinced his only purpose in wanting to marry Anne is not that he loves her, but that he is determined to obtain this property without having to pay for it." He grasped Anne's hand. "I don't trust him, Dash. He's threatened Anne and—"

"And you, my love," Anne added.

He shrugged. "Never mind me. He isn't an honorable man. He comes here without invitation, bringing his strumpet—" He gave Anne and Mrs. Cameron an apologetic shrug. "Forgive me. I shouldn't mention such a person in your hearing." He exhaled a long breath. "Who knows what he'll do to try to stop this sale and force Anne to marry him."

"Brother, where is your faith?" Dash winked at Anne. "Tell you what. I shall order two of my marines to stand guard day and night to keep him out." He ate another confection, then sipped his coffee. "Now, brother, I should like to walk off this meal. Come with me to the military barracks to recruit those guards."

Patrick hesitated. "Anne, will you be all right?"

She gave him a shaky smile. "Yes, of course. Mrs. Cameron and I have much to discuss."

"Well, actually—" Mrs. Cameron rose and smoothed her skirt. "Church always makes me sleepy, so if you'll excuse me, I shall retire. After my rest, I'll visit my friend, the former Mrs. Wills, and her new husband."

"Dash, I shouldn't leave Anne to clean up alone." Patrick stood and began to clear the table. "Or even to be alone."

"Never mind, Patrick. I'll be all right," she said. "There's little to clean up from Dash's picnic. And surely, after this morning's public rebuke, Ares Lyttle wouldn't dare to come here."

After securing the doors and front gate, Patrick reluctantly followed his brother into the street. "We should hurry, Dash. A man without honor will think nothing of breaking into Anne's home."

"To what purpose, Tricky? I have warned him. The entire city seems quite protective of our Anne. That should be sufficient for a few hours." He patted Patrick's shoulder. "Fear not, brother."

Despite his words, Patrick did fear. Would the day ever come when he could make a decision on his own, when he would have the right to protect his loved one? Perhaps on the voyage to England, he would have the chance to explain to Dash that this was only one reason the former colonies rebelled against the king. British law permitted soldiers to be billeted in private homes, whether or not the owners wanted it. And not every soldier was a gentleman, hence many young women and girls had suffered for it.

"What did you think of the reverend's homily?"

Dash's question startled Patrick from his thoughts. Father had always encouraged discussions of their vicar's Sunday homily. Was Dash attempting to further draw Patrick back to family customs? He sighed. Might as well get used to it.

"It's always heartwarming to be reminded of our Heavenly Father's love."

"Yes." Dash glanced at him. "To know that God has compassion on His errant children, that He is always watching for us to return to Him, that He runs to meet us and restores us to full fellowship with Him. Our hearts and souls and minds should always be filled with gratitude."

Something in Dash's voice put Patrick on the alert. In the ten years since they had last seen each other, his brother had matured in spiritual matters, as had Patrick. No doubt Dash's responsibilities as a ship's captain had taught him much, just as Patrick had grown wiser through leading his own soldiers.

"Tricky, I cannot state it any more clearly. Like the father in today's homily, our father is eagerly anticipating your return." Patrick stopped in his tracks as Dash continued speaking. "He has compassion on your failures, but be assured he'll restore you fully as his son. No accusations. No recriminations. Only paternal love." Eyeing Patrick's clothing up and down, he chuckled. "Maybe even put a ring on your finger and a new robe around your shoulders."

When Patrick could find his voice, he stammered, "D-do...do you mean to say you and Father consider me a prodigal?" If a man's head could explode with outrage, his would do so right now.

Dash stepped closer and clamped a hand on Patrick's shoulder. "Dear brother, can you call yourself anything else?"

Patrick jerked away. "Indeed I can. I am an American Patriot. A soldier and an officer defending my country. I fight...fought for freedom. To be regarded as anything else is an insult." He posted his fists at his waist. "Do you really expect me to go with you and grovel to Father, as if I have done something wrong?"

Dash's face exuded sorrow, plus a generous, unwelcome dose of sympathy. "Grovel or not, dear brother, I am certain you understand that you have no choice."

Chapter Twelve

Anne cleared the table and carried the dishes to the kitchen house on a tray. Despite her dismissive words to Patrick, she doubted neither the public rebuke nor the locked doors and gate would keep Ares Lyttle out. But worry wouldn't keep her safe, so she finished washing the dishes, then returned to the house. She had always kept the Sabbath, only doing the most necessary chores, which gave her time to read her Bible while Mrs. Cameron rested.

Seated in the drawing room, she opened to Isaiah's twenty-sixth chapter, verse three, to read the comforting words. "Thou wilt keep him in perfect peace whose mind is stayed on Thee, because he trusts in Thee."

She rested her head against the chair back, letting that perfect peace wash over and through her as she drifted off to sleep. She awoke at the sound of the front door creaking open. She shook off her sleep, expecting to see Mrs. Cameron returning from her visiting. Instead, she stood and found herself face to face with Ares Lyttle.

"W-what are you doing here?" Her knees threatened to bend beneath her, so she grasped her chair arm. "You are not welcome." Her words came out in a whisper.

He took a step toward her, and she held up her Bible with both hands.

"The Lord rebuke thee for thine impertinence."

"Never mind that, you little minx." He grabbed the Bible and flung it across the room. "I've had enough of *your* impertinence. Where are the papers and the money Artemis left for me?" He grabbed her arm and shook her. "Tell me now or—"

"Mrs. Hussey!" Jamie Templeton stepped through the open front door. "May I be of assistance?"

Ares Lyttle released her and turned to face the captain. "Who are you? What business do you have with this woman?"

Jamie stepped over to Ares Lyttle, towering over him. Ares Lyttle shrank back. "This *lady* is a dear friend of my family, and therefore very much my business if she needs my protection. What business do *you* have with her?"

"How dare you question me? I have His Majesty King George's authority to guard St. Augustine." Voice wobbling, Ares Lyttle gripped his sword's hilt. "Friend or not, get out!"

"Sir, it is you who must get out." Jamie snickered. "Now."

Shaking with anger, his face filled with rage, Ares Lyttle began to draw his sword. "How dare you order me—?"

"What's going on here?" Dash walked in, followed by Patrick.

Anne rushed to her beloved's open arms. "Oh, Patrick—"

"Captain Blakemore!" Ares Lyttle shoved his sword back into its scabbard. "Why…why I am protecting Mrs. Hussey from this ragtag—"

"From my good friend, Captain Templeton?" Dash reached out to Jamie. "Good to see you, my friend. What brings you to St. Augustine?"

Dear Jamie hesitated briefly, then accepted Dash's hand. "Good to see you as well, Captain Blakemore." He shifted his stance, and Anne could see his clenched jaw.

Fear for him rose up like bile in her throat as she recalled the last time Ares Lyttle visited Artemis as he lay dying. Artemis had discovered Jamie's privateering for the Patriot cause and threatened to expose him. Had he revealed that information to Ares Lyttle? If so and he told Dash, Jamie would surely be captured and hanged. *Lord, please do not permit Dash to discover Jamie's secret identity.*

"Captain Blakemore—" Ares Lyttle's eyes blazed. "I must protest. Who is this man? He certainly has no right to—"

"Ah, but there you are mistaken, lieutenant." Dash chuckled. "I have learned from Governor Tonyn that this good man imports valuable merchandise into this fair city while many of our other merchant friends lose their cargoes to privateers." He lifted one eyebrow. "So, Templeton, what did you bring on this voyage?"

Although Jamie shrugged modestly, Anne could see wariness in his eyes. "Oh, just the usual. Rum from Jamaica. Silk fans and lacquered jewel boxes from China."

While the two captains chatted about their common seafaring adventures, Ares Lyttle tried to insert himself into the conversation, but they ignored him.

"Well!" Indignation pouring from him, he stepped toward the door. "Mrs. Hussey, you have not seen the last of me." He left, slamming the door behind him.

Safe in Patrick's arms, Anne released a long sigh, as did he. Only then did she realize how quiet he was, how sad his expression.

"Is everything all right?" she whispered.

He shook his head. "We can talk about it later."

"Very well. I—"

Laughter from the two other men interrupted her.

"What's so funny?" Patrick sounded quite irritable. What could have gone wrong while he and Dash were out walking?

"Poor man, Templeton," Dash said through his laughter. "I don't blame you. I would do the same."

"Why are you two laughing?" Anne felt some of Patrick's annoyance herself.

"Forgive me, Anne." Jamie gave her a sheepish grin. "I have been enjoying the hospitality of our mutual friends, Dr. and Mrs. Wellsey, but today, they're occupied with welcoming their first child. Being no help in such matters, I thought to impose upon *your* hospitality—"

Anne gasped. "Joanna is giving birth already? Oh, dear. Does she require my help?"

"I don't believe so. Her sister and her aunt are in attendance. And of course, her doctor husband."

Joy for her friend's happy occasion swept away Anne's anxiety. Perhaps one day, she and Patrick would be likewise blessed.

Patrick's concern for his own troubling affairs and safety dimmed in the light of Templeton's precarious situation. His own life wasn't at stake, but if the privateer's identity was discovered, he would be summarily hanged as a pirate. Yet Dash didn't seem aware that he was chatting with the notorious Nighthawk as he would with an old friend.

"So tell me, Templeton," Dash said, "when will you unload your cargo? I've not seen your ship in the harbor."

Templeton's posture appeared relaxed…except for a tic in his jaw. "*Fair Winds* is moored near Fort Matanzas awaiting permission to bring her into port." He shrugged. "It's been over a year since I last brought in a cargo, and I wasn't sure of my welcome."

Dash chuckled. "Nothing to worry about, my friend. Having wares from China, you can be certain the ladies of this fair city will be more than happy to welcome you." He turned to Anne. "Dear lady, I trust you'll feel safe with my marines, Samuels and Peters, outside your gate." He tilted his head in that direction. "Now, if you'll excuse me, I must return to duty. Tricky, shall I accompany you back to your room?"

Patrick didn't sense any hidden meaning in his brother's tone. "Thank you, but no. Anne and I have many things to plan before our wedding." He pulled Anne closer. "Will we see you tomorrow?"

"Alas, not tomorrow nor the days after. For the next week or so, I'll be patrolling the East Florida coast." He took Anne's hand and bent over it. "My dear sister-to-be, have no fear. I shall speak to Governor Tonyn before I depart regarding that odious lieutenant. After the banns are cried the third time, we'll see you and my brother happily married before we sail for England…and home." He reached out to Patrick.

As Patrick grasped his hand, an odd premonition nibbled at his mind. Despite the plans Dash had laid out for them, Patrick somehow doubted he would ever see his brother again.

While Anne put together a modest supper, Patrick helped Jamie settle in the crawl space above the kitchen house. After Dash's assurances, her earlier anxieties had faded but not entirely disappeared, and the conversations of her present companions only stirred up further concerns.

"My friend," Jamie said, "I know you're close to your brother, but I urge you to use caution when speaking with him."

"I agree." Patrick's eyes revealed his deep sadness. "As lads, no brothers could be closer to me than Dash and Ash, our older brother. But ten years can do much to change a man's perspective. I know Dash is an honorable man, but he is loyal unto death to King George. He sees me as a prodigal brother whom he needs to guide homeward to our father."

"Oh, my." Anne stopped kneading her biscuit dough. "Did he refer to this morning's sermon?" She shook her head. "How unkind. And untrue. You're not a wastrel but a diligent, hardworking man."

Patrick gave her a gentle smile. "Thank you, dearest." He glanced at Jamie, then moved to the hearth and reached into the hidden cabinet behind it. "On another topic, let me show you what was in that satchel Lyttle was so desperate to obtain." He drew out an oilskin sheath.

"Why, that must be Artemis's lost financial logs." Anne dusted flour from her hands and reached for the papers.

Patrick held them back and chuckled. "Let's not damage the evidence with flour."

"Oh." Anne felt a flash of annoyance, then laughed. "Very well, then. Read it to me."

Jamie peered over Patrick's shoulder. "Huh. Just as I thought. That scallywag was using his position in the governor's employ to embezzle gold."

"Look." Patrick pointed to a signature. "His partner in crime was indeed our adversary, Ares Lyttle."

"Why, the very idea!" Anne huffed. She'd never seen any gold. "I understood that he wanted to marry me only to gain my property, but he must have known Artemis had documented their activities, and he was desperate to hide his thievery."

"And now we have a weapon to put an end to his threats against you." Patrick pushed the papers back into the sheath, then returned them to the hidden cabinet behind the oven. "But not you, Templeton. You should leave St. Augustine now."

Jamie chewed his lip. "You may be right. But I vowed to my cousin Rachel that I wouldn't abandon Anne. I cannot leave until I know she'll be safe."

"You can be sure she'll be well taken care of, my friend."

"By going to England?" Jamie touched Anne's shoulder. "Is that what you want?"

Anne gazed at Patrick fondly. "I'll go wherever you think is best."

Jamie looked out the window for a moment. "You can both come with me. I'll take you to a safe place, perhaps an island held by the French in the Caribbean."

"Oh, Patrick, that would be so…"

"Dearest, I cannot run and hide. My father paid the king a large ransom for my pardon, and I am honor bound to repay him as much as possible." Patrick brushed a hand down her cheek. "Besides, even if I could accept, I would return to my regiment, wherever they may be."

Anne broke away from him and returned to her bread dough, now puffing up too soon before she could shape it into a loaf. As she moved the lump into her baking pan, she prayed for another solution to their dilemma. She could accept Patrick going back to his regiment but not returning to England in disgrace. Only one thing came to mind. "When Mrs. Cameron pays me for the house, we'll have her fifty-six pounds. You must use that to repay your father." She stirred the hearth fire and placed the bread pan in the small oven at its side. When she turned back to the men, Patrick tugged her into his arms while Jamie coughed into his fist.

"Dearest Anne," Patrick said, "my debt to my father is five thousand pounds and—"

"Five thousand…" Anne's knees buckled, and he caught her before she could fall.

In this moment, Patrick's heart swelled with more love for Anne than he could measure. She'd never have her own money, and Artemis had obviously been miserly in providing for her. Yet she would give him what was surely a fortune to her to save him from a future he dreaded more than dying on a battlefield.

"Well, then." She straightened her shoulders and shrugged him off. "'Tis off to England we go." She gave him a pert little smile before addressing Templeton. "So now, Jamie, you must leave before Dash returns. Please. If you are apprehended because you remained here on my account, I won't be able to face your sister."

Despite Anne's wishes, Templeton remained in his hiding place through the next week. The two burly marines who guarded the house seemed unaware of his presence as they greeted Patrick during his comings and goings.

With Mrs. Cameron's help, and to her satisfaction, the wallpaper was hung against the lime-plastered dining room wall. On Thursday, land agent Jesse Fish arrived with his legal papers. Following his instructions, Anne signed the house over to Mrs. Cameron and received her fifty-six pounds. The marines followed her and Patrick to ensure the money and a few other valuables made it safely to Mr. Patton's vault to be stored until their departure.

On Sunday, Patrick cleaned his tattered uniform as well as he could and donned the news shoes and stockings Dash had insisted upon giving him, then escorted Anne to church. To their surprise, Lyttle did not attend. At the service's end, Reverend Kennedy once again read the banns. The congregation seemed to hold their collective breath, but no further objection was made to Anne and Patrick's upcoming marriage.

After the service, Mr. and Mrs. Markham approached them.

"Dear Mrs. Hussey," Mrs. Markham said, "only one more week and you'll be free to marry. Will you permit me to help with your wedding? Perhaps prepare your wedding breakfast?"

"Oh, yes," gushed her daughter, Elizabeth. "How we do love a wedding, and it would be such a delight to arrange everything for you."

Anne gratefully accepted their offer, and the ladies began their planning. Even though they asked his opinion about several ideas, he deferred to their feminine wisdom. After all, weddings were the domain of the ladies. The groom had only to show up with a ring. It chafed almost more than he could bear that he couldn't purchase one for Anne. Perhaps Dash…no, he must not ask his brother for a single farthing. He owed him and the rest of the family far too much already.

As they left the church, he did his best to hide his crossness. Would he ever be able to provide for Anne as she deserved?

As younger sons whose eldest brother would inherit everything their father owned, Patrick and Dash had always been advised to marry heiresses, not an easy task among the English aristocracy in which titles, wealth, and political power were treasured above all else. While young ladies might flirt with those younger sons, they quickly dismissed them as unworthy suitors. Dash had made a fortune serving in the king's navy through capturing enemy ships and claiming their wealth, much like a privateer. When Patrick showed no interest in following his steps, Father had done his best to provide a future for him by sending him to Virginia to invest in a tobacco plantation, but Patrick had wasted the opportunity by gambling away the money.

No wonder Father considered him a prodigal. For that was exactly what he had been. But then, as a carpenter and later as a soldier, he had felt the modest pride that came with earning his own living. Now all that was lost, and he had nothing to claim as his own except the sweet lady walking beside him, her arm looped around his. Even Dash's two marines following them reminded him of how far he had fallen and how little power he had to lift himself up.

Anne glanced up at him. "Mrs. Cameron is so kind to permit me to stay in her house until we leave." Her lovely brown eyes seemed to see into his heart. "And so kind of Mrs. Markham and Elizabeth to offer to prepare our wedding breakfast."

"Yes, very kind."

Anne stopped. "My darling, what is it? Is something amiss." She laughed softly. "Other than our upcoming voyage upon which neither of us wishes to embark?"

Glancing back at their bodyguards, he chuckled and urged her to walk again. "Isn't that enough to discourage me?"

"We'll be all right, Patrick. Our Heavenly Father hasn't abandoned us. He'll show us the way."

"Your faith encourages me—"

A scream emanating from Anne's former property interrupted him. Mrs. Cameron ran into the street, arms waving. "Help! Help! They destroyed everything! Everything!"

Chapter Thirteen

"Please, Mrs. Cameron, you must calm down." Anne pulled the hysterical older woman into a firm embrace. "You'll make yourself ill."

Seeing her former home's destruction, she felt quite sick herself. The newly repaired wall was torn apart, with broken lath strips and torn flowered wallpaper scattered across the tabby floor. Anne's bedchamber suffered a similar fate. Even the bedding and upholstered furniture had been ripped apart.

"We don't have to wonder who did this." His face contorted with anger, Patrick began to pick through the rubble. "If I could get my hands on—" He glanced at Dash's two men, who stood by the dining room door. "A little help here?"

Peters, the one who appeared in charge, gave Anne an apologetic grimace. "Ma'am, I'm sorry for all this. Maybe one of us shoulda stayed here while you and the American went to church."

"Can't see why we woulda done that." Samuels gave his companion an oddly meaningful glare. "Cap'n Blakemore said to protect the lady, not the house."

"Yeah, but—"

"Gentlemen, please." Anne could see their dispute was further upsetting Mrs. Cameron. "If you would be so kind, please help Major Blakemore while I fetch our meal." She took Mrs. Cameron's hand. "Come, dear. Let's go to the kitchen house." Would the outbuilding also be destroyed? And where was Jamie?

The room appeared untouched except for her earlier preparations for the noon meal, but a brief shuffling above them put her on alert. It wouldn't do for Mrs. Cameron to learn of Jamie's presence. To her relief, the muffins and cheese slices still sat on the table underneath cloths. Only the plate she always set out for Jamie was missing.

"The vandals must not have come out here. We can be thankful for that. Can you take these to the gentlemen?"

Mrs. Cameron heaved out a deep sigh. "Yes, I suppose so." She picked up one platter. "Oh, Mrs. Hussey, how can I ever recover from this loss?"

Anne gave her a side hug. "With God's help, you can do all things. And I'm still here for two more weeks at least, so we'll help you." Her first impulse was to return the fifty-six pounds to Mrs. Cameron to pay for repairs. But she must ask Patrick first.

Mrs. Cameron gave her a watery smile. "You're always so good, my dear, even when I'm disagreeable."

The moment she left, Anne called softly, "Jamie?"

"I'm here." His face appeared in the small opening above her. "I heard the noises from the house and went to investigate. Lieutenant Lyttle and his female companion must have heard me enter the back door, because they fled out the front. Forgive me. I couldn't stop their destruction."

"You mustn't apologize. Every time you're seen, you're in danger. I do wish you would leave St. Augustine."

"Perhaps you're right. But I am dead set against Patrick's return to England. He must stay here and rejoin the Revolution. So until I am certain of that future for him and for you, I cannot in good conscience leave."

"But your wife and children? Your cousin Rachel—?"

"Shh!" He disappeared into the attic just as Mrs. Cameron returned.

"Are you coming, Mrs. Hussey?" She picked up the second platter. "The men are hungry."

"Yes." Anne grabbed a small pickle crock and a bowl of raisins and followed her friend out the door.

They all worked while they ate, attempting to bring some order to the chaos. By day's end, broken wood and glass were swept from the floors, the men had patched together beds for Anne and Mrs. Cameron, and the two guards had pallets to sleep on, one by the front door, the other by the back.

Patrick took Anne into his arms. "My darling, I don't want to leave you, but if I don't check in with the guards soon, they'll come looking for me."

"I understand. We'll be all right. Ares Lyttle wouldn't dare to come back with Dash's men here."

"Mrs. Cameron—" Patrick turned to her. "—tomorrow, we will protest this outrage to the governor. I'll go with you."

The lady had been weepy all day, but she rallied at his words. "Oh, yes, that would be so kind. Thank you, Major." Her addressing Patrick by his rank showed the lady's growing respect for him, for which Anne was grateful.

After Patrick left for the night and an exhausted Mrs. Cameron fell asleep, Anne continued to work by candlelight to restore a semblance of order to her bedchamber. The contents of her clothespress were strewn across the floor, so she sorted through them to decide what to take to England and what to leave to the city's poor. Only one woolen shawl remained on its shelf. Not the warmest nor a favorite, it would be left behind. But as she tried to lift it, it snagged on something at the back of the press. In the dim light, she could only feel her way to try to dislodge the shawl without tearing it. To her shock, the back wall slid aside, revealing a small nook. She brought her candle closer, and its light shone on a dark bag that felt like leather. Her pulse quickened as she pulled it out and the unmistakable clink coins met her ears. Artemis's embezzled money!

With shaking hands, she checked the space for more hidden treasures and was rewarded with a second bag. She wrapped both in the shawl to keep the coins from making noise and hid them in the travel satchel filled with clothes she planned to take to England. But what should she do with the money? While she doubted the sum was anywhere near the five-thousand-pound ransom Patrick's father had paid the king, perhaps it would pay part. Or must she return it to Governor Tonyn? Sleep eluded her as she shivered with excitement in anticipation of telling her beloved of her discovery and asking his advice on what to do with it.

Before dawn, outside her window, she heard the two guards talking as they made their rounds about the property. In one way, their presence gave her comfort, in another, fear. What if they insisted upon examining her belongings before she and Patrick left? *Lord, protect us. Protect Jamie.*

"He must think we're fools not to know he's there." Peters's gravelly voice was easy to recognize.

Samuels laughed. "Cap'n Blakemore should have his ship by now. The pirate's done for, that's for sure."

Anne's shivers turned from excitement to fear and dread. They knew Jamie was there! Even Dash knew it. *Oh, Lord, Thou must protect our good friend. Please do not let Dash find the ship or Jamie. Please...*

In the few months since meeting Anne, Patrick had never seen her frightened. His own faith had been bolstered by her calm spirit and trust in Almighty God. But in the early morning hours as they sat on the cast iron bench in the garden, she shook like a leaf in the wind, and her face bore evidence of a sleepless night. Tugging her into his arms, he tried to soothe her. "Shh. Don't be afraid, my love. Everything will work out."

"Oh, Patrick, I cannot help it." Resting her head against his chest, she heaved out a great sigh, then whispered both her good news and the bad. "I fear Dash knew Jamie's identity all along. We must warn him, but I haven't been able to speak to him without Mrs. Cameron or one of the marines hovering close by." Tears ran down her smooth cheeks.

Despite his shock, Patrick gently brushed them away. "And yet the Lord arranged for you to overhear the guards, thus providing a warning." He thought for a moment. "What will you do with the money?"

"What should we do?" She gave him a tearful smile. "Perhaps take it to your father?" She frowned. "Or must we give it to the governor?"

"No, it's your money. There's no need to return it to the governor's coffers. The British had taken far too much from us. But I won't take it to repay my debt."

"As soon as we marry, it will be *our* money. Many men enrich themselves by marrying heiresses." She gave him a teasing smile. "Consider me an heiress."

"I don't deserve you, my darling." Patrick kissed her forehead. "As to marrying you for your money, well, since having to earn my own way in the world, I have gained more self-respect through the work of my hands than the pride money gained by marriage could bring."

She gazed up at him. "But you will accept the money as the Lord's provision and give it to Dash for your father?"

After a moment, he nodded. "I will. Artemis took it from the king's coffers, and the king demanded a ridiculous, unheard of, and excessive ransom from my father for me, so this gold should go to my father. Does this sound reasonable?"

"Very much so. Now I can be at peace that we had done nothing amiss." The reassurance in her eyes earned her another quick kiss.

"Good." He glanced toward the kitchen house. "We must tell Jamie what the guards said."

"Should we write him a note?"

"No. Anything written can be used as evidence against him…and us." He grinned. "But speaking of written matter, you give me an idea. Do you trust me?"

"Always." She gave him that adorable smile that always turned his insides to mush.

How he longed to kiss her, deeper this time, and to sweep her away from all conflict and misery. With some effort, he managed to whisper, "This is what I'm thinking. We'll use Artemis's papers to force Lyttle to help us all get safely out of St. Augustine before Dash returns."

Her eyes widened. "But is that even possible? Won't he also demand that we give him the money?"

"No. While I have no doubt he's desperate to get his hands on it, he needn't know we found it. It's the papers that threaten him."

"If we leave the city, how will we make sure Dash gets the money?" She blinked. "I know. We can put it in Artemis's jewel box, then ask Mr. Patton to hold it for us in his vault."

"Won't he question you about having so much money?"

"I can wrap the coins to keep them quiet and seal the box. I can explain its weight by telling him it contains a special keepsake I inherited from my husband." She bit her lip. "That isn't a lie, is it?"

"Not at all. It is a keepsake, and as you said, you're an heiress." He touched her cheek. "When Dash returns and finds us gone—" His heart ached over deceiving his brother, but they had no other recourse. "—he'll assume we made our trip to St. Johns Towne. I can leave a message with Mr. Patton to give him the box if we haven't returned."

"Then you must write a letter to Dash explaining it's for your father."

"I will." He held her close and kissed her forehead. "We must tell Jamie our plans."

"If you can keep everyone occupied in the house while I prepare our breakfast, I'll tell him."

"Are you sure I can't help you?" Mrs. Cameron stood beside the kitchen worktable while Anne kneaded the bread dough for their noon meal.

Why, of all days, did she choose today to offer to help? Perhaps she was encouraged by their visit to the governor's mansion after breakfast this morning, during which an official took their report of the vandalism and promised to investigate the matter. They hadn't dared to accuse Ares Lyttle directly. It seemed these British soldiers did as they pleased with impunity.

"I thank you, but no. You must go supervise the men as they work on the repairs to your house or they'll surely do something amiss."

"Oh, my. I hadn't thought of that." Mrs. Cameron scurried away.

As soon as she crossed the yard and entered the house, Anne stood under the door in the ceiling and whispered, "Jamie."

No response. Was he sleeping?

"Jamie," she repeated, trying to keep the urgency from her voice.

Again, no response. Had he left? If so, how had he escaped the notice of the all-too-vigilant guards? No matter. As long as he was safe. But was he? And what did his disappearance mean to their plans to all leave together?

At the first opportunity, she whispered the news to Patrick. He checked the hiding place, only to confirm what Anne had suspected.

"Don't worry, my love," Patrick said. "We'll proceed with our plan. If he returns, all is well. If not, we'll sail to England with Dash whether we want to or not."

That evening after Patrick left for his room at the tavern and Mrs. Cameron retired for the night, Anne made sure the guards were at their posts. She quietly bolted her bedchamber door, then retrieved the money from its hiding place in the travel case.

As she counted the gold coins, she was astounded by how much wealth Artemis had accumulated in the seven years they had been in St. Augustine. Again, she grieved for the honest, kind man he had been before all his friends in Nantucket turned against him. But this grief would do nothing to help her or Patrick in the present.

She sewed each of the ninety-two gold pieces into strips of cloth so they would make no sound when moved, then bound them tightly with ribbon and placed them in Artemis's jewel box. Growing up in the Society of Friends, both she and her husband had believed that wearing any form of jewelry was prideful. After they fled their home island for the safety of Loyalist St. Augustine, Artemis began to admire and emulate the wealthy leaders of the city, wearing stylish and colorful clothing adorned with jeweled pins and silver buttons. Even his shoes boasted shiny silver buckles, which he shined every day to remove any dust or tarnish they'd collected in his walks through town. And of course elegant jewelry deserved to be stored in an equally elegant carved mahogany box, hence this sturdy container. Recalling Patrick's reassurance that Artemis's belongings were now rightfully hers, she decided to keep the jeweled pins and buckles. Perhaps they could be sold for a few pounds to help support them.

Her labors took most of the night, but she managed to sleep for a few hours before rising to prepare breakfast. She didn't look forward to this day. With Jamie gone, even though she was glad he'd escaped the guards, her only expectation for the future was the dreaded voyage to England.

When Patrick arrived to continue his repair work on what was now Mrs. Cameron's home, he found Peters and Samuels arguing inside the front gate.

"Ye dimwitted monkey," Peters shouted at the smaller marine. "It were yer job to keep watch. Now what'll we tell Cap'n Blakemore?"

Patrick opened the gate noisily to announce his presence. "Good morning, gentlemen. What seems to be the trouble? What's this about my brother, your good captain?"

"Nothin' ye need to know about." Peters scowled at him.

"Very well, then." He sniffed the air. "Ah, the aroma of fresh baked muffins." He patted his belly. "Just the thing to start the day off right." He sauntered across the yard toward the kitchen house.

Behind him the two marines continued to argue. Good. Their disagreement might provide a distraction as he and Anne made their escape from the city. Dash might have intended for the two men to guard Anne from Lyttle, but it was clear they also were expected to keep an eye on Patrick *and* Jamie.

Finding Anne alone as she made breakfast, he retrieved the oilskin from the hidden cupboard, then folded it and placed it at the bottom of Anne's mahogany jewel box. Next came the cushioned coins. At last he laid his letter to Dash on top of the coins, locked the box, and sealed it with wax. Once the wax cooled, he wrapped the box in a dusty burlap bag that smelled of moldy vegetables.

"That should keep our jailors from inspecting it," Patrick quipped. "Maybe they'll even let us make the trip to town without their company."

Anne grimaced. "And what will Mr. Patton think?"

Indeed, when presented with the odiferous bag, the gentleman did hold an embroidered linen handkerchief over his nose after Patrick set it on his table.

"Good gracious, my dear Mrs. Hussey. What have you brought me?"

"Please forgive me, Mr. Patton." Anne removed the bag and dropped it to the floor. "As you can see, this lovely box could prove tempting to the man who broke into my house… that is, Mrs. Cameron's house. It contains an heirloom from my late husband. I fear whoever that man was will return. May I impose upon your good will and place it in your vault?"

"Ah, yes, my dear. You may count on me." Patton examined the seal. "Very good. I'll put it with your money from the sale of your house, as well as your other savings."

Anne looked up at Patrick, and he nodded.

"Sir, I am so dismayed over the damage to the house," she said. "Patrick had just completed his repairs, and the vandals destroyed everything." She took a deep breath. "I believe I should return part of Mrs. Cameron's purchase price so she can buy supplies for him to repair it all again." Her voice wavered, and Patrick could see she hated what she considered lying. "So now I must withdraw all my savings to fund our visit to our mutual friends, Mr. and Mrs. Moberly, and to help Mrs. Cameron."

"Why, Mrs. Hussey, I have never heard of such charity." Mr. Patton's businesslike expression changed into admiration. "And both of you widows." He coughed into his fist, as though trying to reclaim a more severe demeanor. "Of course, you'll soon be wed. Congratulations, Mr. Blakemore." He reached out to Patrick. "I know you will take care of our Mrs. Hussey now that you're returning home to England. And do enjoy your trip to St.

Johns Towne."

Patrick shook his hand. "Thank you, sir." Never mind that the man hadn't acknowledged his military rank. But what could one expect from a Loyalist, even a kind one like Mr. Patton?

Everything was falling into place. Now he had only to confront Lyttle and threaten to expose his complicity in Artemis's embezzling and smuggling. If the lieutenant could be persuaded to divert the two guards, perhaps even grant passage out of the city gate, Patrick and Anne could flee St. Augustine for good before Dash returned.

"You needn't worry, lieutenant." Arms crossed, Patrick smirked at Lyttle, who paced nervously back and forth across the lawn. "My brother already granted permission for Mrs. Hussey to visit her cousin Rachel in St. Johns Towne. And when we return safely, you can have your papers."

Lyttle stopped pacing and jabbed an accusing finger against Patrick's chest. "How do I know you'll keep your word?" He held up one hand. "Don't answer that. How can a man who fought against his king be trusted?"

Patrick emitted an ironic laugh. "Considering the evidence I read, how can a man who fought *for* his king be trusted?"

Lyttle scowled and ground his teeth but didn't answer.

"Look at it this way." Patrick grinned. "Now that Anne has accepted my proposal and another widow owns the property, perhaps you can court her." He glanced toward the house. "As far as what may be hidden on these grounds, I haven't found anything of value." But Anne had. "If you marry Mrs. Cameron, though I pray you'll spare her that misery, you would be free to search at your leisure for buried treasure."

"One week." Lyttle glared at Patrick. "I will give you one week for your trip."

"And you'll write a letter of passage for both of us."

"Very well. But I have no control over Captain Blakemore's marines. They're ordered to keep watch over Anne…Mrs. Hussey and see to her safety. They must travel with you."

Patrick blinked, then laughed. "But, Lieutenant Lyttle, it was from you they were ordered to guard her."

Fisting one hand, Lyttle stepped back as though preparing to strike. Patrick tensed. If the man wanted a fight, he would not deny him the pleasure.

"Patrick!" Anne called as she walked toward them. "There you are, my darling. Why, Ares Lyttle, I didn't notice you. What brings you here?"

"Good day, Mrs. Hussey." The man had the decency to sketch a clumsy bow. "You will excuse me. I have my duties."

As he turned away, Patrick gripped his upper arm. "Passage for us and blocking the guards from following." He smirked. "Take them to the tavern and keep them occupied."

"You don't know the way to St. Johns Towne."

"This is true. But we have a Minorcan guide who's familiar with the route. He'll be our guide."

"Minorcan?" Lyttle spat on the ground. "A bothersome breed." He stormed off, not bothering to secure the gate behind him.

"What's this about a Minorcan friend?" Anne's sly grin suggested she already knew the answer.

Patrick wrapped his arms around her and gave her the kind of kiss he'd been longing to for weeks. To his delight, she melted into his embrace and returned the kiss with equal fervor.

Chapter Fourteen

Dash made the required rounds of the East Florida and Georgia coasts, searching the inlets and barrier islands for American vessels before heading south to Fort Matanzas, a small fort built by the Spanish to protect St. Augustine from southern attacks via the Matanzas River. Approached without warning, Templeton's *Fair Winds* should be easy pickings. But all he and his crew saw were Minorcan fishing vessels, probably from the Turnbull plantation. While he had no respect for Turnbull due to his duplicity and cruelty to his workers, the man had done a fair job of civilizing this wild area of East Florida. For that alone, he deserved some regard.

"Looks like we missed him, Captain." Midshipman Cummings stood at the ship's rail scanning the marshy landscape. "That Nighthawk is a slippery fella. I'll never forget the way he blasted one of our merchant ships to smithereens just so's he could get away from my Captain Moberly. And them being friends and all. 'Twas a pure shame. Pure evil."

"So you've said, Cummings." Dash closed his telescope. "It may be that Templeton has already made his way back to St. Augustine. Make all sail."

But the merchant ship wasn't in port, nor was Tricky anywhere to be found in the city. Even Anne had disappeared. His two useless marines were too drunk to remember their names, and when Dash questioned Mrs. Cameron, the poor woman could only answer with nearly incoherent sobs…something about "good, dearest Anne" returning the house's purchase price to her.

While Dash could only admire Anne for her generosity, his feelings toward Tricky were not so kind. What an apt byname he and Ash had given their younger brother. Tricky he was called. Tricky he was. For Dash had no doubt Tricky had helped Templeton escape, but it was Dash's own fault. He'd tried to be too clever in the whole affair. Had trusted his brother too much. Had thought his treating Templeton like an old friend would fool him into complacency so he could capture his ship and seize its cargo for a valuable prize. This was the last time he would underestimate his enemy.

Yet no matter what he told himself, he could never consider Tricky an enemy. Foolish, perhaps, but a good man in the depths of his soul. Dash prayed he would be happy with sweet Anne.

Resigned to returning home without his brother, he took his leave of the governor while Jolly packed his belongings. As he crossed the Parade back toward the military barracks, a well-dressed gentleman hailed him.

"Captain Blakemore, sir." The man strode toward him, a box under his arm. "I'm delighted to have caught you. I am William Patton. You may have heard of me? As you will be seeing your brother and his bride upon their return from St. Johns Towne, perhaps you can return this to them." He handed Dash a carved mahogany cask. "They left it in my safekeeping, but I am traveling myself for the next few weeks and would feel better if you took charge of it."

Relieved to learn Patrick had not absconded after all, Dash took the box in hand. "I thank you, sir." After a few necessary pleasantries, they took their leave, and Dash continued on to the barracks.

"Ready to sail, sir?" Jolly, the perfect steward, had everything in good order.

"Yes." As Dash set the box on a side table, curiosity gripped him. "No." He took out his folding knife and extended the blade, then sliced through the wax seal.

On top of the other contents lay a folded vellum page. He unfolded it to find a letter from Tricky explaining all…all except a promise to return to St. Augustine, a return to England and family. Sorrow gripped Dash's heart. In all his years in His Majesty's navy, he'd never found a closer friend than Tricky. Even Ash had held himself somewhat apart due to his responsibilities to the estate and his eventual elevation. Although they hadn't seen each other for ten years, he and Tricky had bonded again as only brothers could. Now, until this infernal war ended and the colonies were back under British control, he could only grieve over the loss of his brother, for he would not pursue him. His first duty was to return to the war. Going back to England without Tricky would serve no purpose.

What could have caused Tricky to turn traitor? To follow the leaders of a useless rebellion? Perhaps the only way to understand would be to read his contraband copy of the infernal declaration by which these Americans had severed their ties to England.

"I now pronounce you man and wife." Frederick Moberly closed his *Book of Common Prayer* and shook Patrick's hand while his wife, Rachel, kissed Anne's cheek.

"Are you certain you won't stay here with us, Major Blakemore," Moberly asked. "We have plenty of room, and if you can endure the noise of the eight children—"

"Frederick!" Rachel glared at him indignantly. "If you are referring to the music of our darling children's voices—" She sent a maternal smile in the direction of her five children and their nursemaid.

Standing beside his wife, Marianne, and their three children, Jamie chuckled. "Only my cousin would call it music."

"Thank you, Moberly," Patrick said. "But you know what I must do. Templeton has offered to take me to Virginia, where I hope to rejoin my regiment." He held Anne close. "But if you will care for my wife, I'll be eternally grateful."

His new friends were entirely accommodating. While Templeton prepared his ship for their voyage, Patrick and Anne had three days to enjoy the bliss of married life before their separation began. With God's help, perhaps the Revolution would be won before the year was out and they could settle in Virginia to begin their new life in freedom.

January 1782
St. Johns Towne, East Florida Colony

With her newborn daughter in the cart beside her, Anne held her newborn son and watched the *Fair Winds* sail up the St. Johns River, waiting among the families of the ship's crew. Would Patrick be among those returning on Jamie Templeton's ship? Or would he be coming home at all? She hadn't heard from him since August, when he wrote of finding his regiment near Yorktown, Virginia.

In December, news that war had ended in October at last reached St. Johns Towne, signaling many changes to come. To Marianne's great relief, Jamie would no longer be hunted as a pirate by the British, who would soon be scrambling back to England. With East Florida Colony still under British control, Frederick and Rachel had never been suspected by authorities of helping the Revolution, but what would they do now? Continue to manage Lord Bennington's indigo plantation? Sail back to England? Or move north to the United States?

The ship anchored in the deeper part of the shallow St. Johns River, and several small boats were lowered, filling quickly with crewmen, their eagerness to reach land apparent by their energy as they rowed toward shore. Three boats moored in the slips, and Anne's heart dropped. She walked to Marianne Templeton, who also held a new infant.

"I don't see our husbands among these men."

Marianne kept her gaze on the ship. "The captain is always the last to disembark." She gave Anne a sympathetic smile. "Perhaps Patrick is—"

"There's Papa!" Young Jamie Templeton jumped up and down in excitement, and two of his younger siblings copied his joy.

Another small boat crossed the water, Jamie's large frame visible among the rowers. As they neared the slips, the men leapt out into the shallows and splashed toward their loved ones. Jamie hurried to his family and was quickly surrounded, all the children clamoring for his attention. Anne watched with a bittersweet ache in her heart. Was she to be widowed again? This time there would be no feeling of relief, only crushing grief.

"Mrs. Blakemore—" An almost forgotten voice spoke behind her. "—have you no greeting for your husband?"

She clutched her infant tighter and swung around to find herself in the arms of her beloved. "Patrick! You *have* returned."

He gave her a hearty kiss and, despite her armload, she returned it as best she could.

"And whom have we here?" His gray eyes shone with joy and love.

Her voice choked with emotion, she managed, "Your son." She nodded toward the infant in the cart. "And this is your daughter."

"Twins? God is good." Patrick's eyes filled with tears. "What names did you give them?"

"I waited for you." Anne placed one precious bundle into his father's arms and lifted the other into her own.

After several moments, he said, "I can think of no better name for my son than Freedom."

Anne laughed softly. How like him to choose that name. "Then I shall call our daughter Faith."

Careful of his full arms, Patrick bent to kiss her again. "Perfect. Our faith has led us to freedom through the power of the Almighty. Thanks be to God."

Only then did Anne let her tears of joy flow. Truly God had done something wonderful, not only for their little family, but for the United States of America as well.

"Yes, thanks be to God, for He has done marvelous things."

Not the end, only the beginning!

About the Author

Anne and Patrick's story began with Anne's friends in my previous American Revolution novels: Frederick and Rachel Moberly (***Love Thine Enemy***), Jamie and Marianne Templeton (***The Captain's Lady***), and Thomas and Dinah Moberly (***A the Captain's Command***). In addition, you can learn more about Thomas and Dinah Moberly's next generation in ***The Gentleman's Proposal***. Hopefully in the future, we can learn more about the dashing Dashiell Blakemore as he returns home to England at the end of the American Revolution.

Award-winning South Carolina author Louise M. Gouge writes contemporary and historical romance fiction. A former college English and humanities professor, Louise is a member of the Christian PEN and has been copyediting for well-known authors for fifteen years. Married for fifty-four happy years to her husband, David, Louise is now widowed and spends her days researching and writing her next novel.

Web site at **https://louisemgougeauthor.blogspot.com/**
Facebook: https://www.facebook.com/LouiseMGougeAuthor
Follow me on BookBub: **https://www.bookbub.com/profile/louise-m-gouge**

Grace in the Storm

by Tricia Goyer

In Key West, where the mosquitoes are as strong as the rum, and the pirates are as shady as the palm trees, Grace Richardson firmly believes there's no such thing as a respectable pirate. Imagine her surprise when Captain Noble, more battered than a well-used treasure map, shows up at her doorstep, barely clinging to life. Despite her reservations, Grace can't bring herself to turn him away. She's been toiling away at transforming her late uncle's tavern into a cozy sanctuary for the town's down-and-outers. But when a hurricane strikes, upturning everything, Grace is forced to band together with Captain Noble to save those she's sworn to care for. Grace learns to trust Noble with their very lives as they navigate the chaos and danger, but can she risk her heart? Will she discover that even the shadiest of pirates can change, or will her doubts tear them apart?

He stilled the storm to a whisper; the waves of the sea were hushed.

Psalm 107:27 NIV

Prologue

1847 Key West, Florida

Dearest Mrs. Parker,

I hope this letter finds you in good health and spirits. I am writing to express my deepest gratitude for holding the teaching position for me. Your kindness and understanding mean the world during this tumultuous time. As I sit down to explain the events that have transpired, I need to journey back to paint a complete picture of the path that has led me to where I am today.

My story begins with my beloved Uncle Stob. He was more than just an uncle. He was the father figure who raised me with unwavering kindness and a keen determination to provide me with the best life possible. When he decided to leave Homestead, Florida, and set his sights on Key West to establish a tavern, I was eager to join him on this new adventure. That is until the day a letter arrived revealing that Uncle Stob had found the man I was to marry.

I was torn. My heart yearned for a family and the love of a husband, but my instincts screamed warnings about this arranged match. Yet, as letters began to arrive from William, I found myself drawn to him. He affectionately called me Cricket, just as my uncle had. But more than that, his words painted a vivid picture of Key West, a town overflowing with need. He wrote of the abandoned slaves seeking freedom, the orphaned children left behind by the dangerous maritime industry, the sickly sailors recovering from their voyages, the widows struggling to make ends meet, and the impoverished immigrants from the Bahamas and Cuba seeking better opportunities. Through his letters, I felt a stirring in my soul, a sense that perhaps our correspondence was not just about finding love but about discovering a greater purpose of caring for those in need.

Could I genuinely commit my life to a man I had never met? Just as I was grappling with these questions, a friend of my uncle arrived, claiming that William was a pirate, of all things! His words struck fear into my heart. I felt betrayed by my uncle's deception. With a heavy heart, I made the difficult decision to break off the engagement, leaving William bewildered and heartbroken.

In the aftermath, I learned of my uncle's passing. He had left me his tavern, and I felt a call from God, a sense of purpose I had never known before. I would transform the tavern into a haven for the abandoned slaves, orphaned children, sickly sailors, widows, and impoverished immigrants that filled the streets of Key West. William's letters had planted a seed, and now I could nurture it. As you know, I traveled to Key

West, ready to embark on this new journey.

But as I settled into my new life, pouring my heart and soul into the tavern, I couldn't help but wonder … what had become of the pirate who once called me Cricket. Our story is on the pages to follow. After reading it, you'll fully understand my answer as to whether or not I will return to this teaching position.

With tears and appreciation,

Grace

Chapter One

William Noble—Capt'n William Noble—hunched over the oars, his back screaming in protest with each labored stroke. Sweat dripped from the tip of his nose, mixing with the spray of the choppy sea. His shirt clung to his back, heavy with saltwater and his own blood. A crimson stain spread from his side, a constant reminder of the fight that had cost him his ship, crew … and maybe his life.

He squinted through the glare of the tropical sun, his eyes burning from the salt spray. The shore was a hazy smudge on the horizon, growing larger with agonizing slowness. Noble grunted, heaving at the oars. His hands, raw and blistered, slipped on the wooden handles. He clenched his teeth, fighting a wave of dizziness. He couldn't afford to pass out. Not yet.

The small boat lurched, taking on water. Noble's side throbbed where the knife had pierced him—a sharp, burning pain that pulsed with every breath. Blood had soaked through his shirt, drying in a sticky crust. His vision dimmed, black spots dancing in the periphery, yet he gripped the oars. His mouth was parched, lips cracked and peeling, the taste of salt clinging to his tongue. He had been on the sea for a day and a night, and the dehydration gnawed at him, sapping what little strength he had left. But he was running out of time.

With a Herculean effort, he dug the oars into the sea, throwing his weight against them, his muscles screaming in protest. Finally, the boat scraped against the sandy bottom, jolting him. Noble let out a shaky breath, sagging forward. He'd made it. Barely. His wound flared with pain, a reminder of how close he'd come to losing everything.

He stumbled out of the boat, knee-deep in the warm surf. The water swirled around his legs, tinting pink where his blood seeped into the sea. Each step was a battle, his legs trembling, threatening to give way beneath him. Noble staggered up the beach, his boots heavy with seawater and exhaustion. The sand clung to his soaked clothes as he collapsed, the grains pressing into his wounds. He rolled onto his back, staring up at the sky—a brilliant blue, deceptively peaceful, as if mocking his suffering.

Noble let out a hoarse laugh, the sound more like a rasping cough, gritting his teeth against the searing pain that radiated from his side. He'd survived the sea, yet another merciless adversary, only to become easy prey for whoever might find him next—whether it be a passing stranger or death itself.

"Grace ..." The name was a whisper on his lips, more a prayer than a plea to a woman he'd never met. Rumors'd drifted in like the tide of an unexpected angel buying Ole' Stob's tavern. Some said she was a do-gooder from New York, all prim and proper, who'd bolt once the first storm hit. Others whispered she'd lost someone to the sea and made a vow.

Before he'd heard this woman Grace had arrived, Noble'd wondered if Stob's niece Cricket would come. But that was a fool's hope. He smirked at the sea, remembering the fool he'd been five years ago. He'd agreed to marry Cricket, pouring his heart into letters for months. But she'd stopped writing, left him with nothing.

Cricket wouldn't be found in Key West now, among the soldiers, the runaways, the orphans, and the pirates. Noble did not doubt that this new woman, Grace, would leave, too. But he might make it through if he could get her to tend his wounds. He could imagine this Grace—a woman with kind eyes and hands that healed. She was his last hope.

Noble remembered the cook's words, spoken in hushed tones over a bowl of sea stew, the firelight casting shadows on the older man's weathered face. "She's an angel, that one," the old man had said, his voice filled with reverence that belied his rough exterior. "Took in the likes of me, and I ain't no prize. Runs a tavern, but not just any tavern. A place for them that's been broken, like herself."

Noble clung to those words, a lifeline in the storm of his thoughts. He knew he had to find her. Suppose he could hold on just a little longer. The pain in his side flared, but he pushed it down. He focused instead on the distant image of Grace and the hope that she might be—as the old cook described—an angel for the broken.

Grace. The word was a name. But it was more than a name. It was also from a song that had slipped from his mother's lips.

His mother had been an angel. A captain's wife with a fierce love for her husband and son. She'd read from the Good Book morning and night. But when word came that her husband had gone down with his ship... Noble wondered if it was a broken heart that killed her, not pneumonia.

He'd been a young man, old enough to sign on with merchant vessels. He'd saved his pay and dreamed of a future. He'd even survived a wreck himself. But his victory was short-lived. A letter from Cricket waited in Key West, breaking their engagement. She called him a pirate.

His replies came back unopened. So Noble decided, what's the use in being good? He'd become a pirate captain but vowed never to harm women. They called him Captain Noble, a pirate with a code.

Amazing grace. Noble could still hear the haunting and sweet melody echoing in his mind like the ghost of a long-forgotten lullaby. But he pushed that thought out of his mind. Sentiment was a luxury he couldn't afford, not now.

Noble hadn't been the worst pirate but hadn't been all good either. Good enough? The pain radiated in his heart at the thought. It wasn't just the wound in his side that ached, but the weight of his past deeds. He'd walked a thin line, adhering to his code of honor in a profession with little use. Had it been enough to balance the scales, or was he forever damned by the lives he'd taken?

"Grace ..." He whispered once more. In his desperation, she was the one who came to mind. Noble refused to think of Cricket, who'd broken his heart. He'd given up on love. Instead, he wished only for a spark of kindness.

Perhaps, just perhaps, Grace would find it in her heart to help a broken man, no matter his past. She was his only hope. And so, with her name on his lips, he let the darkness take him, praying he'd find mercy when he woke.

Chapter Two

The warm sunlight streamed through the window, casting dappled patches of light and shadow across the worn wooden floor. Dust motes danced lazily in the air, highlighted by the golden rays, while the scent of saltwater mingled with the musty smell of old ropes and sun-bleached driftwood that adorned the walls. The tavern, once proud, had seen better days. Its faded curtains fluttered weakly in the sea breeze. Treasures from the sea—bottles pulled from the depths, barnacle-encrusted trinkets, and pieces of driftwood—were scattered haphazardly around the room, each telling its own tale.

Grace stood amid it all, feeling the sun's relentless heat beating down on her, a trickle of sweat creeping from her brow to the tip of her nose. She wiped it away with the back of her hand, hearing Mrs. Parker's voice in her mind. "That's not very ladylike, Miss Richardson."

Grace smirked, her eyes narrowing as she surveyed the tavern. "Well, I'd like to see how you'd do better trying to run a tavern with more loose boards than fixed ones," she muttered, imagining Mrs. Parker's scandalized expression. Of course, Mrs. Parker wouldn't have answered. Instead, she would have fainted immediately after hearing "tavern." The thought brought a brief smile to Grace's lips.

Birds sang outside, their cheerful tunes at odds with the worn-down state of *The Gator and Galleon Tavern*. Grace had wrestled with whether or not to keep the name after she'd claimed her inheritance. The place had a history, much like the treasures that filled it, but it was a history as battered as the tavern itself. She felt the rough wood of the bar beneath her fingertips, the surface pitted and scarred from years of use, and sighed. The tavern was hers now, for better or worse, and she would see it through.

Mrs. Parker would be pleased to discover that Grace had only kept the name to woo the sailors who stopped in Key West, hoping for a meal and a song or two. In Grace's plan, the food would satisfy them, the song would hold them, and kindness would do its own good work.

Grace hadn't tested her plan with wooing sailors. There hadn't been time. The moment she set foot on Key West, the news of her uncle's death met her like the heavy, humid air that clung to her skin. The tavern stood as a battered remnant of the storm that had ravaged the island the year before—shattered windows, a sagging roof, and walls that groaned with the weight of time and the relentless wind. But the kitchen, by some stroke of luck, had held together. That was enough for her to start.

Grace lit the fire beneath the pot as she had over the previous months. Soon, the smell of clam and potato stew drifted out into the midday activity, carried by the salty wind. It wasn't long before her customers, whom she now considered dear friends, arrived. The aroma drew them. And also the promise of something warm and familiar in a world that had turned so harsh.

They weren't the paying kind. Old sailors, who'd once made a living in the deep waters, were now left stranded by the sea's cruelty, gathered in the shadows. A few former slaves, free in name but still shackled by poverty, hovered near the entrance. Two women with children clutched close, their faces lined with the weariness of constant struggle. Grace offered a smile as they watched her with eyes that spoke of hunger and hope in equal measure.

Once a thriving hub of wealth from the wrecking industry, the island now bore the scars of the storm and the economic shifts that followed. The harbor, one of the finest in the Gulf, still saw ships come and go, but the wealth that had once flowed so freely had ebbed, leaving behind only those too stubborn or too poor to leave. Grace knew she couldn't turn them away. Not now, not while they needed her, and not while she waited for the ship with the building materials her uncle's last inheritance had bought. The ship that would bring the hope of rebuilding, of making the tavern something more than a crumbling relic of better days.

Until then, she would feed them one bowl at a time. The stew might be thin, and the bread might be stale, but it was something to fill the belly and warm the soul.

Jonah, still a boy in many ways, settled near the hearth. He had been pulled from the sea's grip a few years back, saved from the treacherous waters that had claimed so many others. Now, he watched Grace with eyes that had seen too much for his years, eyes that spoke of the island's harsh realities. His fingers tapped a rhythm against the worn table, a rhythm that matched the beat of the waves outside and the distant sounds of the town. In Key West, the past and the present collided daily, where the old Spanish architecture mingled with the rough wooden buildings, where the streets were filled with the languages and customs of the many who had made this island their home.

And then there was the singing. It had started softly, just a hum under her breath as she worked. But now, they joined her, their voices rising and falling like the tide, a song that echoed the rhythm of the sea and the heartbeat of the island itself. It was a song of survival, of holding on, of finding a way to live through the storms and the changes that swept through their lives like the hurricanes that battered their shores.

Grace didn't know if the ship would come or if the tavern would ever be more than a refuge for those lost at sea and lost in life. But for now, she had the kitchen, the stew, and the songs that carried through the night. And on this island, where the past was never far away and the future always uncertain, that might just be enough.

As she sliced up the last of the bread and prepared to hand it out, Grace's mind drifted to darker thoughts, the stories she had heard about slavers and pirates, men who dealt in human misery with less regard for those they captured than the treasure they plundered. Though the slave trade had been outlawed, she knew all too well that it still lurked in the shadows, just as dangerous and vile as ever. She felt a surge of anger, her distaste for those men a bitter taste at the back of her throat. The thought of them made her skin crawl, and she couldn't help but clench her fists at the memory of what they'd done to Jonah and countless others like him.

"Miss Grace?" the boy's voice broke into her thoughts, snapping her back to the present. She turned to see Jonah standing at the door. Although only ten, the dark-skinned boy, as thin as a rail, had already reached her height. Of course, that wasn't saying much.

"Yes, Jonah, what is it? I'm so sorry. My mind was wandering." Her voice softened, though the anger still simmered beneath the surface.

"I was sent to tell you, ma'am, that one of the privateer ships has come in. They're a rowdy bunch, and—"

"And?" Grace paused from stirring the stew, the savory aroma of the simmering broth filling her senses, a stark contrast to the bitterness in her heart.

"They're extra rowdy today. News is they came upon some men floating in the sea and plucked them from the depths. And … then found another on the shore." Jonah rubbed his brow and squinted, the boy's voice wavering as if trying to piece together the story he'd been told to relay.

Grace's stomach churned, not just from the stew's pungent scent but from the news Jonah had brought. She could almost hear the rowdy shouts of the privateers, the clinking of bottles, and the heavy thud of boots against the wooden floorboards as they reveled in whatever grim find they'd made. Her knuckles whitened as she gripped the wooden spoon, her thoughts racing. Those men, whether slavers, pirates, or both, were the kind she despised with every fiber of her being. And soon, they'd be here in her tavern.

With a quick motion, Jonah rose, hurried to the door, and pointed. "That's the one—the troublemaker from the shore—they're bringing up to *The Gator and Galleon*."

Grace's jaw dropped the same moment the wooden spoon she'd used to stir with was released from her hand. It plopped into the bubbling stew and sank under the golden chowder before she could snatch it up. "Here?" Grace placed a hand over her head and tried to still its wild beating. "Why would they bring a troublemaker here?"

Grace's heart quickened as she hurried to the window. An officer marched down the sidewalk, a prisoner at his side. The man's hands were shackled behind him, his dark hair mussed, his beard trimmed. He was a pirate, no question. Yet, something about him stirred an unexpected warmth in her chest.

Grace chided herself. She couldn't have a pirate in her rehabilitation center. But her racing heart, the flush rising to her cheeks, told a different story. She pressed a hand to her forehead. "He can't stay," she muttered. "What are they thinking? He's the last thing I need."

Jonah shrugged but answered all the same. " 'Cause he's injured and needs some tending to."

And as she looked at the man struggling forward with labored steps, really looked, she saw something else. A spark in his eyes, a determination in his jaw. Maybe, just maybe, he wasn't beyond redemption. Then again, who was she to think such things? Grace quickly pushed that thought away.

Placing a hand on her hip, Grace jutted out her chin. "I'm not a doctor, not even a nurse. Why would they think—" Yet the coughing of an older man interrupted her thoughts. He sat on a reed mat next to a woman who'd been battling a fever for days. They'd come for food, and Grace couldn't turn them away.

"Yes, well, I have been tending to many folks lately, but I have all the work I need. And I especially do not want a troublemaker under my roof."

"But the pirate needs—"

"Pirate! Absolutely not. An injured, troublemaking pirate is the last thing I need under my roof. Just think of my *reputation*."

Even as the words spouted from her lips, familiar Scripture filled her mind. "When I was hungry, you fed me. When I was thirsty, you gave me something to drink. When I was in prison—" Grace shook her head as if doing so would silence the familiar words. Of all the times for God's Word to fill her thoughts.

This is different. This is unwise. Mrs. Parker's face filled her mind again. If the older woman would faint immediately to hear that Grace now owned a tavern, she'd fall dead to hear that she'd invited an injured, troublemaking pirate in to be cared for. And without a chaperone! No, it wouldn't do at all. "Please tell them not to bother coming." She crossed her arms over her chest. "I cannot provide assistance at this time."

Instead of arguing, Jonah's eyes grew wide, and he stepped back out the door, looking down the dirt path toward the docks. And that's when she heard it—shouting. No, more like hollering and yelping. But as the voice rose in volume, Grace knew two things. The injured, troublemaking pirate was headed in her direction, and if he were as stubborn as he was loud, there would be no way to kick him out.

Chapter Three

Captain William Noble shrugged his shoulders and twisted his neck, trying to stretch out the knotted muscles that sent fiery pain down both arms. The chains clinked with each movement, a harsh reminder of his captivity.

"Listen, Cookie, just unlock these irons, will ya? My arms have been locked back for days, and it's an uncivilized way to treat any man, especially your former Captain." His voice was rough, his throat dry from days without proper water. The words tasted like dust in his mouth.

Noble had woken up on a sagging cot in one of the jail cells, his arms shackled painfully behind him. The rough iron bit into his wrists, the pressure a constant throb. The air reeked of saltwater and sweat, mingling with the musty scent of old wood and tar. He'd still be lying there if it hadn't been for his injury. The throbbing gash on his side had kept him from drifting back into unconsciousness, a burning reminder of his failure. Cookie claimed he'd heard shouts from fevered dreams and recognized Noble's voice, insisting he be taken to be tended to. The weight of being locked up pressed on him just as heavily as the ache in his side, a grim reminder of how far he'd fallen.

Noble gritted his teeth, the memory of his choices gnawing at him. He had stolen from robbers but never harmed a soul. He'd made sure to protect any womenfolk they'd come upon, insisted his crew stay sober and never curse. He'd tried to maintain some semblance of honor, even as he danced on the edge of piracy. But things turned south quickly when his crew had grown tired of his rules and rose against him in mutiny. Noble wouldn't be booted from his ship so easily, but what was one man against three? When one of the knife jabs struck his side, he'd relented, climbing into the rowboat with the bitter taste of defeat in his mouth. But it may have been a blessing. Grace from the Divine?

His thoughts turned to the wreckage. The crew must have hidden away drink and had quite the party after disposing of their noble captain because he'd woken up to see debris drifting around him—proof they hadn't heeded the lighthouse. Sometime in the night, his ship, *The Pretender*, had crashed upon the rocks, a fitting end to their treachery.

The smell of saltwater and tar filled his nostrils, mingling with the distant scent of fresh bread and fish being fried somewhere in town. Through blurry vision, he could see the masts of ships bobbing gently in the turquoise water of the harbor. The cries of gulls wheeling overhead punctuated the steady hum of activity from the docks. His feet shuffled down the sandy roadway from the docks to the cluster of wooden buildings radiating from the harbor like sunbeams, a far cry from the bustling ports he once knew.

"Ain't my captain no more," Cookie said with a slow drawl, his words moving as sluggishly as his plodding steps. The old sailor's face was weathered, skin darkened by the relentless Florida sun, his eyes shadowed under a wide-brimmed hat that had seen better days. "Ain't been my captain for two plus years since you decided to go the way of pirates." Cookie clicked his tongue, the sound sharp in the still air. "I told you then it wouldn't work any better for you. Bet you wish you would've listened now, don't you?"

Noble said nothing, his gaze drifting over the familiar yet distant sight of Key West. The town had a rough, untamed beauty, with its wooden structures and sandy streets. The heat pressed down like a heavy blanket, the sun baking the earth beneath their feet. In the distance, the tall palms swayed gently in the breeze, their fronds whispering secrets of a life that seemed forever out of reach.

But it wasn't just the heat that weighed on him—it was the knowledge that he'd lost everything he once held dear. His ship, his crew, his honor.

Perhaps, he thought now, it had been mercy. A chance to escape the man he'd become. The thought burned, as corrosive as the sea air. Noble closed his eyes, the weight of his chains pulling him down. He was a pirate, fallen and failed. But as he took in a breath, heavy with the scent of salt and old wood, he felt a spark within him. A spark that, even now, refused to be extinguished.

"Cookie," he rasped, forcing his gaze to meet the old man's. "You ever hear stories about me? About how I ran things?"

Cookie's weathered face creased in a frown. "Aye, Captain. Heard you only took from them what had more than they knew what to do with. Heard you looked out for the widows, too."

Noble's laugh was rough. It scraped at his throat. "Aye, well, I reckon that's true. But it doesn't change what I am. What I've done."

"You may call yourself a pirate," Cookie said, his voice low and steady, "but no one believes it. Not really."

A memory flared in Noble's mind then, sharp as a cutlass. "You remember that time off Havana? When the Spanish man-o'-war ran us down?"

Cookie's expression shifted. A flicker of surprise lit in his eyes. "Aye, Captain. You got me out of the drink and hid me in the cargo hold. Saved my life."

Noble's gaze fell away, the memory a bitter mix of pride and regret. "I've done some things right, I suppose. But it don't erase the wrong."

Cookie's gnarled hand settled on his shoulder. "Maybe not, Captain. But it counts for something. Means you ain't lost yet."

Noble's throat worked, but he couldn't manage words. It was a small comfort, but he felt a spark of hope with Cookie by his side. A chance to find his way again, to leave the pirate behind.

The weight of his chains seemed a little lighter then, the pain in his side a little more bearable. He breathed in, the air a little sweeter with the scent of salt and maybe … possibility. He was a long way from redemption, but with Cookie's help, he might find a way to survive.

An ache filled Noble's chest with Cookie's words. The large man used to look at him with respect—they all did. Not that it mattered. Their respect for him hadn't meant a thing when the woman he loved accused him of being a pirate. For over a year, he'd spent every moment of his free time writing to Cricket, sharing his heart and dreams.

Yet, instead of drawing them closer, each new response from her had brought distance. Then, he received the letter that declared that she was ending their courtship and she did not wish to receive any more correspondence. Noble had lost his mind—or at least his good sense. He sold his small ship that he'd been using to transport supplies from Key West to the Bahamas, and he joined up with the next crew that had come into port. Sure, it had been a pirate crew, but what did it matter? He had no one to impress. Besides, he could at least have some riches if he couldn't have the girl. The only problem was, no matter how much he'd claimed for himself, it had never been enough to ease the ache in his heart.

"Do I ever listen?" Noble mumbled, more to himself than to Cookie. His words were slurred, and his mind fogged with pain. Suddenly, he gasped and cried out as another lightning bolt of pain shot through his neck, searing like fire. "Listen, I still have an 8-piece hidden in my shoe. I promise to buy you a hot meal and a cup of warm rum when we get to *The Gator*. Just unlock me, will you?"

Noble staggered. The pain in his temple flared, overwhelming the ache in his neck. The world around him seemed to turn a shade of dark gray, the edges blurring as his knees buckled beneath him.

"Hold it steady there, Noble," Cookie said, his voice gruff but tinged with concern as he grasped Noble's arm to keep him upright. "Don't have to get dramatic."

With the jingle of keys, Noble heard the click of the lock releasing the irons. His arms flopped forward instantly, the sudden freedom almost alien after days of confinement. His limbs, weak and unsure, floated as if they didn't quite belong to him. Or maybe Noble himself was floating, his body teetering on the edge of consciousness. He hit the sandy path with a thud, the impact jarring but distant, as if it belonged to someone else.

The world around him darkened, the sounds of Key West fading into a dull roar. Noble tried to focus on Cookie's words, something about *The Gator* no longer selling rum, but it was a losing battle. His mind felt fogged, his thoughts slipping through his grasp like fish in the water. But then, a name cut through the haze. *Grace.*

Grace, with her hands gentle as a summer breeze, her voice a soothing balm. Grace, who'd bought up Stob's Tavern and turned it into a haven for the battered and bruised. They'd called her the ministering angel, and it fit.

Maybe she could stitch up his side. Pour some of that cool calm into his soul. Maybe, just maybe, she could show him how to earn back what he'd lost. Cricket's love, Cricket's trust...he could still taste the loss of it, bitter as betrayal.

The thought of Cricket hit him like a blow, a fresh wave of pain crashing over him. He'd thrown her away in his stupidity and pride. But Grace … Grace might know how to fix it.

A spark of determination flared in his chest, burning away some of the fog. He needed to get to Grace. He needed her help, her guidance. And he needed it before it was too late. Before Cricket was lost to him forever.

He wasn't sure what type of joke Cookie was trying to play now, but it had to be something good. Just before the blackness completely overtook him, Noble was sure he heard a woman's voice—soft, yet commanding—calling to Cookie, asking what she could do to help. The sound was like a lifeline, pulling him toward something familiar and safe, even as the darkness closed in again. *Grace.* His ministering angel had come.

Chapter Four

Grace had been staring at the top button of the man's shirt for at least five minutes, her fingers hovering hesitantly above it. It made no sense. She'd been feeding and caring for anyone who came to the tavern seeking help. She'd bandaged wounds, nursed fevers, and even stitched up gashes without a second thought. So why couldn't she do what needed to be done now?

Come on, unbutton the man's shirt, Grace, and check his wound. Easier said than done.

Maybe it was because the man lying before her was the most handsome she'd ever seen, with dark, rumpled hair that begged to be touched, a straight nose, and high cheekbones that spoke of strength and nobility. The dimple in his chin had caused her heart to skip a beat, or perhaps the rippling muscles of his chest, partially revealed by his torn and bloodied shirt, made her pulse quicken.

Cookie had helped her set the man up on a mat in a quiet room of the tavern, away from prying eyes. The waning sunlight filtered through the open doorway, casting dappled shadows across the room. The smell of saltwater and stale ale lingered in the air, mingling with the scent of the herbs she'd prepared for healing.

"His name is Noble. Captain Noble," Cookie had said, his grizzled face softening as he spoke. "He's a good man, even though he tries to pretend he's a rogue. Folk say his name fits. Some call 'em the Gentlemanly Pirate. Even though he's been known to rob ships of their valuables, he insists his crew never touch the women. He leaves enough wealth for the men to care for their wives and kin back home. Not really like any other pirate I know."

Grace pictured Mrs. Parker's white face, nearly overcome with death, as Cookie walked out, leaving the man in her charge. Yes, the sight of Grace unbuttoning this handsome man's shirt would be Mrs. Parker's end. Yet Grace's former matron wasn't here, and still she sat. Grace had seen too much suffering and loss, yet now she was frozen in place by the mere sight of a man who needed her help.

With a deep breath, Grace forced herself to focus. She couldn't be distracted by his looks or the rumors surrounding him. This man, Captain Noble, was injured and needed her care, just like everyone else who had come through her doors. She reached out, her fingers trembling as they touched the fabric of his shirt. The material was rough, stained with blood and dirt, under her fingertips. Gently, she began to unbutton the shirt, her breath catching in her throat as she exposed more of his chest, the warmth of his skin radiating beneath her touch.

Her thoughts wandered to the stories she'd heard about him. A pirate, but with a code of honor—a man who robbed the rich but spared the helpless. A man who protected women and made sure his crew didn't fall into the usual debauchery that plagued other pirates. It was almost too good to be true. And yet, here he was, lying vulnerable and wounded before her, the weight of his reputation resting heavily on his broad shoulders.

Grace's resolve hardened. She would do what was needed, regardless of the man's past or striking looks. She would tend to his wounds as she had done for so many others. But as she carefully examined the gash on his side, she couldn't help but wonder what kind of man Captain Noble really was—and what fate had in store for him and perhaps for her.

"Mrs. Parker, I do understand the reasons for needing a chaperone," Grace murmured, almost as if the older woman were standing beside her, ready to scold. "But should this injured man be faulted for my not having one and be left to die from lack of care? And honestly, you were young once. Look at him, Mrs. Parker! Oh, just look at him."

With her heart pounding so hard she thought it might leap out of her chest, Grace jutted out her chin, steeling herself for what she knew she must do. She continued unfastening the man's shirt, one button at a time, her fingers trembling. A hot sensation filled her core, a mixture of anxiety and something else she dared not name. She blew out a heavy breath, trying to steady herself as she pushed aside the unbuttoned shirt, completely revealing the man's chest.

The stitched-up wound ran along his side, the surrounding skin swollen but not inflamed. Whoever had tended to him had done a fine enough job. She saw no signs of infection. Grace's brow furrowed as she examined the wound more closely. It was puzzling—if the injury had been properly treated, what had caused him to pass out cold? Were there internal injuries she couldn't see? Or perhaps he had been stricken with a tropical fever, a silent threat lurking beneath his rugged exterior.

Her gaze traveled up to his face, noting the knot on his forehead and the bruise above his left eye. A hard hit on the head could certainly cause unconsciousness, she reasoned. But as for the rest of him ... well, there didn't seem to be anything wrong. Not one little thing. His shirtless chest revealed rippling muscles beneath his sun-kissed skin, marred only by a single wound. His breathing was steady, his pulse strong beneath her fingertips.

Grace's thoughts returned to her imagining of Mrs. Parker's disapproval, but she shook it off. The man's well-being was her responsibility now, and she couldn't allow propriety to stand in the way of doing what was right. Yet, as she gently placed her hand on his chest to feel his heartbeat, she couldn't deny the warmth that spread through her, the undeniable pull of attraction that made her feel both guilty and exhilarated.

His skin was clammy, beads of sweat dotting his brow, a clear sign of the fever burning through him. As Grace gently wiped the sweat away, his eyes fluttered open, but he didn't see her. Instead, he looked off in a distant, unfocused gaze.

"Tropical fever," she murmured to herself, her mind racing. She needed to get his fever down and rehydrate him. Grace rose, her movements quick and purposeful. She mixed a draught of willow bark and mint, forcing the bitter medicine between his lips. He sputtered, but she held him steady until he swallowed. Next, she bathed his brow with cool, salted water, trying to leech out the heat. Grace couldn't shake the feeling that she was fighting against time as she worked.

The fever gripped him like a vice. His body was drenched in sweat, and his words were reduced to garbled nonsense. Grace sat beside him, her breath shallow, every instinct on high alert. She couldn't tear her eyes away from him, even though he never really saw her. How had he ended up like this? Had he been wounded in a noble cause, defending some helpless woman? Or had his life of teetering on the edge of law and crime finally caught up to him? Was he betrayed by those who wanted the spoils he carried, the treasure that made him both admired and despised?

Chapter Five

Hours ticked by, each one a tiny eternity. Grace knelt, her hands trembling like leaves as she bathed the man's forehead. His skin was fevered, radiating heat. It was supper time. The sun still clung to the horizon, casting a warm orange glow through the cracks in the walls. But in this windowless room, the only true light came from a candle's gentle flicker. It cast a warm, golden glow on the wooden table, the flame dancing and shimmering in the stillness.

A bead of sweat trickled down Grace's temple, but she didn't brush it away. She couldn't tear her gaze from the man's face, his features drawn in pain. Would he be okay? Her heart flip-flopped in her chest, a counterpoint to the ragged rhythm of his breathing.

She could hear the murmurs of the others gathering outside, their voices low and familiar, like the hum of bees in the summer air. These people, her people. United not by blood but by the trials they'd weathered. United in survival, in loss, in the bitter aftertaste of hardship. A family not of blood but of heart.

The scent of old wood and melting wax hung heavy, a comforting perfume. Grace's stomach growled, reminding her of supper waiting. They would get through this newest obstacle. They would face whatever came next together as a family. As long as they had each other, they could endure anything.

Finally seeing the man settle, Grace rose with a sigh. Tucking a strand of hair behind her ear, she walked to the tavern doorway, leaning against the weathered frame as she watched the others prepare for the evening meal. The long wooden tables, worn smooth from years of use, stretched out under the open sky, illuminated by the warm, golden light of oil lamps hanging from the beams above. The scent of freshly baked bread mingled with the aroma of roasting fish drifted through the air, carried by the salty breeze that whispered in from the nearby ocean. The rhythmic sound of the waves lapping against the shore provided a soothing backdrop, a constant reminder of the sea's presence in their lives.

Grace took a deep breath, savoring the mix of smells—the yeast from the bread baked that morning, the tang of the salt air, and the rich, earthy scent of the wooden planks beneath her feet. She could hear the clatter of bowls and cups as the children set the table, their voices a blend of excited chatter and hushed whispers. Miss Hattie, the oldest among them, was directing the younger ones with a firm but gentle hand, her wrinkled face softening into a smile as she caught Grace's eye.

"Miss Grace, the bread smells wonderful," Miss Hattie called out, her voice rising above the bustle of activity.

Grace smiled, pushing herself away from the doorway and walking toward the table. "Thank you, Miss Hattie. I made enough for everyone to have a good piece tonight."

Eli, a tall man with broad shoulders and hands rough from years of hard labor, was busy turning a spit over the fire at the edge of the porch. The crackling flames mingled with his deep, rolling laughter as he shared stories with Mary, a young widow who had lost her husband to the treacherous waters off the coast. Mary's eyes lit up as she listened, her face momentarily free from the shadows of grief that so often clouded it.

Grace stepped into the kitchen, where the scent of warm bread mingled with the salty air seeping through the cracks in the wooden walls. The room was dim, lit only by a single lantern hanging from a beam, casting long shadows on the rough-hewn table. She reached for the basket of bread, a small comfort, a brief moment of normalcy amidst her worries about the ailing pirate she tended.

She walked outside, the weight of the bread grounding her, if only for a moment. The rough texture of the crust brushed against her fingers as she tore each loaf into pieces, the crumbs scattering like dust onto the sandy ground. She moved purposefully, her actions steady, though her mind was full of thoughts and fears. Would Captain Noble be alright? Would he make it through the night?

Grace couldn't help but think of William. Even though they'd never met in person, care for this pirate stirred memories of another she had cared for. William's letters had come steadily, and they had planned to marry before she discovered his true nature.

"He's a pirate, ma'am," she'd heard from a trusted friend of Uncle Stob, who had come to visit Grace at *Mrs. Parker's Academy for Refined Ladies*. "Saw him climbing off a pirate ship with my own eyes."

That had been enough to break off their engagement, yet had she acted too hastily? She'd grown to care for William as he shared his dreams with her.

Yet maybe it had been easy to cast him away because William had only been words on a page. Now, she was faced with the reality of a true pirate—one of flesh and blood who stirred her senses and made her feel things she hadn't felt before. Lord, is this a test of my faith? Is it punishment for my pride and sin? Should I have asked William myself for the truth? The questions were endless and without answers. She attempted to push them out of her mind and focus on the task at hand. To feed those God had brought to her.

"Here you go, Sam," she said softly, offering a piece to the small boy who sat at the edge of the table, his eyes wide with hunger. His face was streaked with dirt, evidence of a long day spent playing outside.

"Thank you, Miss Grace," he mumbled, his voice muffled as he crammed the bread into his mouth with eager hands.

"Slow down," Grace said gently, a faint smile tugging at her lips as she ruffled his hair. The boy's innocence tugged at her heart. "There's plenty for everyone."

As she moved down the line, Grace's thoughts wandered back to the man lying in the small room at the back of the tavern. "Captain Noble," she whispered to herself. The name still felt foreign on her tongue, like a puzzle she hadn't yet solved. His presence stirred something within her, a mixture of curiosity and unease that she couldn't quite shake. What kind of man was he? And what would happen when he woke?

"Grace, are you all right?" Mary's voice pulled her from her thoughts.

Grace blinked, realizing she had been standing still, lost in her thoughts. She turned to Mary, offering a reassuring smile. "I'm fine, just thinking."

"About the captain?" Mary asked, her voice low, her gaze concerned.

Grace nodded, her fingers tightening around the handle of the basket. "I just don't know what to expect. I mean, he is …" *A pirate. So handsome. So … alluring.* "He is so … ill," she finally stated.

Mary placed a hand on Grace's arm, her touch gentle. "You've done all you can for him. Whatever happens, it's out of your hands now."

Grace nodded, but the weight of uncertainty still pressed on her chest. She had taken care of him, but what if he turned out to be a danger to them all? And yet, there was a part of her—small but persistent—who wanted to believe he was more than just a name whispered in fear.

The porch had fallen quiet as everyone settled in for the meal, the clatter of dishes and the murmur of voices creating a soft, harmonious hum. The night air was cool against Grace's skin, carrying the distant cry of a seabird. She looked over the gathering, these people who had become her family, and felt a deep, abiding sense of responsibility. They looked to her for guidance, for strength. She would not let them down.

She handed out the last of the bread and sat at the head of the table, the place reserved for her by unspoken agreement. The bread she had baked that morning was soft and warm in her hands, the taste of home and hard work.

The laughter and conversation around the table flowed like the tide, filling the night with a sense of peace and belonging. Grace's heart ached with a familiar longing as she watched them. She had been so young when the fever took her parents. Her memories of them were like fragments of a dream—her mother's gentle hands braiding her hair, her father's deep voice reading stories by the hearth.

These images had grown dim with time, but being with these people—her new family—allowed her to imagine what it might have been like to grow up surrounded by love and warmth. The ache in her heart was both painful and comforting, a reminder that she had found a place where she belonged, even if the road to get there had been hard.

Her thoughts returned to the man on the mat, drifting again to his uncertain fate. The sea had brought him to their shores, and it was up to her to nurse him back to health.

Captain Noble. Was he truly a man of honor, a gentleman who only took from those who could afford to lose? She shook her head, pushing the thoughts aside. It didn't matter what he was, not right now. What mattered was that he was in her care, and she would do everything she could to see him through this.

Grace excused herself from the table and headed back into the tavern. She walked over to the mat again, checking on Captain Noble and offering a silent prayer for his recovery. The night was falling, and soon, the others would call her to join them as they sang hymns by starlight. But for now, her place was here, by his side.

She sighed, looking at this handsome man and then realizing her heart was with William, too. Grace felt a tug of longing that surprised her. She had broken off their courtship because she'd heard he was a pirate, and now her heart was drawn toward the same type of man. Would she ever learn?

Chapter Six

A knock echoed through the dimly lit room. Grace sat up and brushed her hair from her face. Noble still slept before her. She must have drifted off, laying with her head near his on the blanket she'd rolled up to use as a pillow. The knock sounded again, strong and urgent. It had to be Eli. The older man had been a former slave, but she'd never asked how he'd found his freedom. Had he gone down with a ship yet survived? Had he escaped? Or had a kind master granted his freedom? None of that mattered now. Grace rose to her feet, pausing to steady herself before rushing forward.

Grace opened the door just enough to see Eli's weathered face in the moonlight, framed by the shadows of the porch area that stretched between the sleep quarters and the tavern. "Evenin' Miss Grace," he said, his steady voice tinged with an urgency that sent a shiver down her spine. "I've asked everyone to sleep in the tavern tonight. Jest wanted you to know."

She rubbed her brow, trying to make sense of his words. "Everyone's in the tavern?" Grace dropped a hand to her chest. "Well, I suppose Mrs. Parker doesn't have to worry about me having a chaperone."

Eli's brow furrowed. He tilted his head forward, cocking his ear toward her as if he hadn't heard correctly. "Excuse me, Ma'am?"

"I'm sorry, Eli. Sometimes I talk to, uh, myself." She rubbed sleep from her eyes. "Why is everyone staying here? For propriety? Protection?" She glanced over her shoulder at the sleeping pirate. "I doubt he'll do me any harm." Then she turned back to Eli.

"No, I suppose he won't, although that's not the big worry," Eli chuckled. "There's a storm brewin'."

318

Grace stepped outside. The cool night air brushed against her skin like the ghost of a long-forgotten memory. She squinted into the dark sky, searching for signs of the tempest he spoke of. "But it's not even raining," she replied, her brow furrowing.

Eli tilted his head back, eyes narrowing as he scanned the sky. "Aye, but I've worked on many ships, and there's a feelin' in the air. The wind's whisperin' secrets, and it don't take much to know when trouble's comin'." Eli's voice was firm, though there was an edge to it now.

Grace nodded, and a lump formed in her throat. She turned back to the room where Noble lay. Then, as if feeling her gaze upon him, Noble's eyelids fluttered like the wings of a dying bird. Was he waking? Panic seized her—when had he last eaten? Had she done enough to help the fever? Which should she be more concerned about, the man or the storm? The thoughts clawed at her.

"Eli, you know about the weather. Do you know much about doctoring?"

"Grace, the storm'll hit full force by tomorrow afternoon, mark my words. You need to keep him warm and his head elevated. If he wakes, try to get some broth in him, but don't force it. The fever's the real enemy now."

"That's what I thought."

"If you're planning to sit with him for a while, I'd suggest getting the most important things from your room now. Might be helpful to gather up any important items. You know, with the storm comin' and all."

Grace nodded, and for the first time, Eli's urgency started to sink in. The storm must be big for Eli to have gathered everyone up.

Eli lingered at the doorway, his hand gripping the worn handle, his face etched with a worry he couldn't hide. "If it gets bad ..." he said, his voice almost lost to an unexpected howl of the wind—at least unexpected for her. Goosebumps rose on Grace's arms. "If it gets bad, you get yourself to the safest place you can find. Don't wait for it to pass. These storms are like beasts—they tear at you until there's nothing left."

Grace swallowed hard, nodding again. "Yes, of course."

Yet even as she agreed, Grace knew she'd never be able to find safety and leave her patient alone. That didn't seem right. Still, she wouldn't argue.

As Eli turned to walk back to the tavern, he took another look at the dark sky. The storm was coming, and with it, a test of everything she had within her. Or so she guessed.

Noble had returned to a content sleep, and Grace took Eli's advice. She lit a hand lantern, and the flame flickered in the rising draft coming through the open door. It cast long shadows that danced across the walls.

With lantern in hand, Grace hurried to the next door, to her private sleeping quarters. It took just a moment to gather her most important belongings and carry them back to where Noble lay. Her Bible, the only photograph she had of her mother and father, and a small cloth bag where she'd tucked all of William's letters. Why had she kept the letters? Deep down, she knew. Willian had genuinely cared for her. He'd also shared so much of his heart within those pages. And maybe that was why the news that he was a pirate had brought so much pain.

Then, a new thought hit her. Maybe it had been *her* fears that had also contributed to her breaking off the courtship. She'd lived with Mrs. Parker and other young women most of her life. What did she know about relationships? Or marriage? Love? Grace sighed and placed a hand over her heart, wishing she could rub away the ache there. Maybe she knew more than she'd realized.

Grace settled next to sleeping William and pulled out the letters. One of the envelopes was still sealed. She smiled, seeing her nickname—the one only William and Uncle Stob used: *Cricket*.

My Dearest Cricket,

I hope this letter finds you in a moment of peace, though I know that peace has been scarce for you these days. My heart aches at the thought of you alone, struggling to mend the pieces that broke between us. There is so much I wish to say, so much I wish I could undo, but the one thing I cannot let go of is the truth of how I feel about you.

Cricket, you have been the light in my life, the one who made everything worth striving for. When I think of the future, I imagine your face and your smile—which takes quite the imagination since I have yet to see a photo of you.

For so long, I imagined how you would look at me—as if I could conquer the world. I dreamed of us standing together, our hands intertwined, watching the sunset on a life we've built side by side. I dreamed of a home filled with warmth and laughter, of children with your eyes and your spirit, of nights spent by the fire with you close, where nothing else mattered but that moment.

I know I failed you, Cricket. I should have journeyed up to meet you sooner. I should have helped you to understand the man I am. In your letter you said you've discovered things about me that I have hidden. I've searched my mind for what those things could be.

If I could turn back time, I would choose differently. I would go to you, Cricket. I would fight for us, for the love we shared, because it was real, and it was worth every challenge, every storm. I see that now, too late, perhaps, but I see it with a clarity that cuts deep.

I don't know if you will ever forgive me for not coming to you or if we could ever find our way back to each other. But I want you to know that I will never stop loving you. Not for a moment. Even now, as I write this, my heart is full of you—your kindness, your strength, the way you see beauty in the world even when it seems so dark.

If there is still a chance, if your heart hasn't closed to me entirely, I want you to know I am here, waiting. I will wait for as long as it takes. You are worth it. You are worth everything.

Take care of yourself, my love. I hope that wherever life leads you, it brings you happiness and peace. And if it leads you back to me, know I will be here, ready to start again, to build that future we once dreamed of.

With all my love,

William

Chapter Seven

Grace sat in the dimly lit room next to Captain Noble. Her hands trembled as she cradled her head. How could she have been so blind? She'd allowed herself to be swept away by the rumors and fear of the unknown. Then, in doing so, she had turned her back on the one man who had shown her nothing but kindness and sincerity. And love. Yes, William had loved her. She saw that now.

The truth cut deep—she had rejected William, not because of any fault of his, but because she'd let her own insecurities and the whispers of others cloud her judgment.

Worse yet, when her defenses were weak, she'd found herself attracted to a pirate. She'd been captivated by a rugged appearance that belied a dangerous life—one she could never truly understand. Grace's cheeks flushed with shame. She had been so easily distracted by superficial allure, allowing herself to forget what truly mattered—a man's heart and character.

She needed to make things right. She would ask the Key West postmaster about William as soon as she could. There may still be time to send a letter to plead for his forgiveness. But even as she resolved to do this, another weight pressed on her heart. This pirate, feverish and weak, needed care. She couldn't abandon him now, not when he was so vulnerable. There would be time to write a letter in the morning. For now, she had to focus on the task at hand.

Grace's gaze fell on the empty bowl that had held broth just hours ago. She needed to get more food for the pirate, something to keep up his strength. The tavern's kitchen was off-limits at this hour. If she started cooking now, she'd wake everyone bedded down for the night.

Thinking through her options, Grace remembered a root cellar she'd discovered a few days ago, tucked away behind the tavern. Quickly, she rose to her feet, determination setting her pace.

Grace stepped onto the back porch. The wood creaked under her weight. The night was dark, the air thick with the scent of salt and decay, as if the sea was warning her of the dangers. The lantern she held flickered weakly, casting just enough light to illuminate the path to the root cellar.

As she descended the steps, a shiver ran down her spine. The world around her felt charged, alive. The tension in the air was almost palpable. The storm wasn't just a distant rumble on the horizon—it was almost here.

Grace reached the small dugout near the trees, her uncle's storm shelter. The door groaned as she pushed it open, revealing the earthen walls and the shelf where he had stored a few supplies. Her eyes fell on the jars labeled "Meat Broth." The murky liquid shimmered in the dim light, and she hesitated. What kind of meat was it? The thought turned her stomach, but desperation overruled her fear. It might be all that stood between life and death for Captain Noble.

She grabbed a jar, its cool surface damp against her fingers. Grace also hurried to gather what else she could—a few potatoes and onions, a jar of pickled vegetables. Her heart raced, not just from the haste of her actions but from mounting anxiety. She could feel the storm building outside. The wind began to howl through the open cellar door. Its chill seeped into her bones.

Once this night was over, Grace knew she'd look at life differently. She'd stop allowing her fears to drive her. The storm would pass, as all storms do, and afterward, she'd find a way to make amends with William.

As she returned to the side room, arms laden with supplies, Grace couldn't help but glance up at the sky, now obscured by dark, swirling clouds. The storm was gathering strength. In the morning, she'd face the consequences of her mistakes and write a letter to William. For now, though, she had a pirate to care for and a heart full of regret to soothe.

Grace settled down beside Noble, and the man shifted. She stirred the cold broth, her hands steady despite the growing tension in the air. Outside, the wind had picked up, rattling the tavern's shutters.

Captain Noble's body burned, slick with sweat, his words whispers of delirium. Yet Grace stayed by his side, spooning bits of broth into his mouth.

Minutes passed, and thankfully, Noble sipped a few spoonfuls of soup. Time dragged, each minute pulling them deeper into the heart of the coming storm. Outside, the wind began to growl, low and menacing. It slipped through the cracks in the walls with an eerie whistle. Grace felt its chill in her bones.

Grace set the bowl to the side and moved to peer outside. She dared to open the door to get a better look. As the sun rose, the horizon was a murky line. Clouds swelled and darkened, pressing closer to the earth as if the sky was about to descend.

Two men walked past the open door, their voices low but clear. "The weather's turning, ain't it?" one said, his tone edged with unease.

"Like the calm before the storm, although it ain't much calm," the other replied, a note of foreboding in his voice.

As she moved back inside, the first raindrops pelted against the door, sharp as needles. The wind picked up, too, and the walls creaked under the strain.

Noble had to feel better soon. He just had to. She held the broth to his lips and felt a spark of triumph when he drank. He was a pirate, a man of violence and vice. But as she looked into his face, flushed with fever, something in her shifted. Perhaps, she thought, perhaps there was more to him than met the eye. And perhaps, just perhaps, Grace had a chance to heal more than just his body. She'd already paid the price once before for jumping to conclusions. William held her heart, but maybe Captain Noble needed a friend.

"What am I going to do with you, Captain Noble?" Grace whispered, her voice barely a breath. His closeness, the intimacy of her hands against his fevered skin, made her cheeks flush. But she pushed the feeling aside, focusing on the task at hand. This man's life depended on her, and she had no room for anything but her duty.

He groaned, the sound low and rough, like gravel shifting underfoot. She attempted to offer another spoonful of broth, but he turned his head away.

"Not now, Grace," he muttered, his voice hoarse, stripped of the command she assumed it usually held. The way he said her name startled her and made her pause. How did he know her name?

Grace's heart skipped, a flutter of unease mixed with something she couldn't quite name. Had she made a mistake getting this close? She had tended to men broken by the sea or their own vices before, but none of them had spoken her name like this, as if it were something familiar.

She set the bowl aside, carefully moving her fingers to rebutton his shirt. As she did, Grace ignored the sensation of his skin beneath her fingertips, the way his breath hitched when she touched him. Her hands were steady, but inside, doubt gnawed at her. The wind outside had picked up. The shutters clattered against the walls in a rhythm that set her nerves on edge. The storm was coming, and with it, a sense of dread she couldn't shake.

Captain Noble's lips moved again, softer this time, almost inaudible. She leaned in closer, her breath catching in her throat as she strained to hear.

"...a rose...so fair...the sea cannot compare..."

Her heart skipped a beat as the fevered words spilled from his lips, sounding like fragments of a poem. Was he declaring his love? But for whom? She couldn't be sure. Her mind raced with possibilities—what if he never woke up? What if he did? Despite the rumors, she had no idea what kind of man Captain Noble truly was. All she knew was that something about him stirred a feeling deep inside. And that couldn't be. She loved William.

With a final glance at the man lying before her, Grace rose from the mat. Then, her resolve hardened again. Whatever happened, she would see this through. Whether Captain Noble was a gentleman or a pirate—or something in between—he was under her care now. And Grace could not abandon a soul in need, no matter the consequences.

Chapter Eight

Noble lay still, the rough linen of the mat beneath him, the ache in his side a dull reminder that he was still breathing. The room was dim, with the morning light slipping through the door that had been cracked open. Outside, the wind howled like a beast, its breath rattling the shutters with a promise of fury yet to come. But in the room, the air was thick, pressing down on him harder than the pain in his side.

He blinked, eyes gritty and unfocused, struggling to distinguish the shadowed shapes around him. The world spun slowly, a ship caught in the undertow, as he fought to pull himself from the depths of fever. Sweat clung to his skin, cold now, the fire in his blood having ebbed to a simmer. His throat was dry, rough as sandpaper, and he could taste the sour remnants of sickness at the back of his mouth.

The sound of the storm was growing—distant thunder rolling closer, the first patter of rain like fingers tapping on the roof above. He could smell the rain, sharp and clean, cutting through the musty air of the room. It called to him, a warning and a challenge, and he knew that the tempest outside was nothing compared to the battle he'd waged within.

His limbs were leaden, the weight of his own body unfamiliar, as if he were wearing it for the first time. The pain in his side throbbed with each shallow breath, but he welcomed it, clinging to the hurt as proof that he was alive. He closed his eyes, just for a moment, gathering what strength remained in him. He felt the weariness deep in his bones, a heaviness that made it tempting to surrender, to let go and drift back into darkness.

But he couldn't. Not yet. He'd survived the fever, by some miracle or curse, and he wasn't about to let a storm take him now. He closed his eyes again and whispered a prayer, lips barely moving, asking for strength from the God he hadn't spoken to in years. He needed it, and he needed it now. The storm was coming, and he could feel it in his very soul—wild and merciless, like the sea he'd spent his life conquering.

He thought of Cricket then, the woman who had haunted his fevered dreams, the one he needed to find. The thought of her brought a flicker of warmth to the cold hollows of his chest, a spark of determination that chased away the fog. He would survive this, he vowed. He would survive the fever, the storm, and whatever awaited on the other side. Cricket was out there somewhere—he had to find her and declare his love and commitment to give up his waywardness, to become the man she needed him to be. But even more than that, the man God had created him to be.

With a grunt, Noble shifted. He winced as pain lanced through his side. His muscles protested, stiff and unyielding, but he ignored them. He had faced worse, and he'd probably face worse again. The storm was calling him, and he would meet it head-on. He was Captain Noble, and he wasn't done fighting.

He opened his eyes again and scanned the small space, his vision clearer now. His gaze found the woman beside him—Grace. She sat close, her hand resting on his arm. Her touch was warm and gentle, a kindness he'd almost forgotten. But there was something in her eyes, something far off, as if she held a part of herself back, locked away where no one could reach.

Noble opened his mouth, trying to speak, but the words caught in his throat. Instead, he watched her, the way her eyes fluttered closed. A storm was building, but her thoughts were in another place. She looked so peaceful, so sure of herself, and it stirred something deep within him.

The sea breeze drifted through the open window, bringing the salty scent of the ocean and the faintest hint of something darker, something ominous. Noble's instincts, honed by years on the sea, prickled with unease. He had seen storms brew and had felt the shift in the air that signaled danger was near. And now, that same feeling crept over him, a warning he couldn't ignore.

Grace stirred beside him, her hand slipping from his arm as she rose from the chair. She moved with quiet gentleness, deliberate and calm, but he could sense the tension in her shoulders. She kept her distance from him as if she feared what might happen if she came too close.

"Grace," he called out, his voice rough. She paused, turning to look at him, her eyes searching his face for something she didn't find.

Gritting his teeth, he pushed himself to sit upright, the room tilting dangerously as he did.

"You should rest," she said softly, her tone polite but distant. "You need to heal."

Noble took another deep breath, the cool air filling his lungs and, with it, a sense of purpose. Noble lay back on the cot, his body tense, his mind racing. Then, as if attempting a ruse, the wind quieted. The air was too still, the silence too heavy. He knew what was coming, and it wasn't just the storm that concerned him. It was the feeling that had settled in his chest, a sense of foreboding that went beyond the weather. There was something more at play, something he couldn't yet see, but he knew it was lurking beyond the horizon.

He stared at the ceiling. He had faced many storms in his life, both at sea and on land, but this one felt different. This one felt personal as if it was aimed directly at him.

He closed his eyes, letting his thoughts wander back over the last few years. Choices made, paths taken, all leading him to this moment. He had spent the last few years chasing after treasure, amassing wealth, only to see it sink with his ship, swallowed by the unforgiving sea. Everything he had worked for felt as fleeting as shifting sand, slipping through his fingers no matter how tightly he tried to hold on.

There had been a time when he felt strong, a time when his life had meaning beyond gold and glory. He remembered the letters he had written to Cricket, the way they had shared something deeper—a foundation of faith like the one his mother had instilled in him. Mother had built her life on Christ, a solid rock in a world of uncertainty. But that strength had deserted him long ago, leaving him adrift in a sea of heartache and regret.

He opened his eyes and stared at the ceiling, feeling the weight of his choices pressing down on him like the low, heavy clouds outside. The storm was approaching, fierce and unrelenting, much like the tempest brewing within him. Whatever was coming, he knew he couldn't face it alone. He needed her help, whether she realized it or not.

Grace—something about her that called to him, even in his weakened state, something deeper than the physical attraction that simmered between them. But no matter the pull he felt, he would not let it sway him. Cricket had his heart, and he was determined to find her again, no matter the cost.

Yet, as he lay there, the doubts crept in like the wind seeping through the cracks in the walls. Had his foolishness led him to lose everything? What had he even been chasing after all these years?

He had gained wealth only to see it slip through his fingers. He'd made a name for himself as a pirate—a good pirate if ever there was such a thing—but what did that matter now? The emptiness of it all echoed within him, much like the wind that howled outside, rattling the shutters and sending a chill through the room.

His thoughts drifted to the grand tombs and monuments he had seen in his travels, those pretentious tributes meant to gratify the vanity of the living rather than honor the dead. But the dead didn't need such things—what mattered were the memories they left behind, the lives they had touched. He thought of his mother's poem, the one he had found after her death. He couldn't remember it all, but a few stanzas had stayed with him, echoing in his mind.

The stars went down only to rise again on some fairer shore.

As the light of a star shined far through the night,

so, too, did the souls of those bravely gone,

living on in some eternal way.

On shifting sands, where time does wane,
Our steps may falter, yet they are not in vain.
For though the tides may wash them away,
the echoes of our journey stay,
engraved in hearts, like stars in the sky,
a guiding light that will never die.

The term "shifting sands" applied to every beach in Key West, just as it did to each of their lives. The sands shifted with every storm, revealing what lay beneath. Only after the storm, when the sand is blown away, could one see their true foundation.

Noble listened to the wind as it picked up, howling like a banshee, rattling the shutters and sending a deep, penetrating chill through the room. The storm was here, and with it, the chance to see what lay beneath the surface of it all.

He had to be ready. He had to find his strength again, the strength that had carried him through battles and storms before. But this time was different; he was fighting not just for himself but for Grace, for Cricket, and for whatever destiny God had designed for each of them.

The wind screamed through the cracks, the building creaking and groaning under the strain, but Noble didn't flinch. They would survive this storm. He would uncover the foundation of his life, the purpose that had eluded him for so long. And maybe, just maybe, Grace would find her strength, too.

Chapter Nine

Captain Noble lay still for a moment, straining to hear the murmur of voices from the tavern. The sounds of people waking, the clatter of dishes, and the rhythmic crash of the waves against the shore. But amidst all the familiar sounds, something felt off. The wind was picking up, whistling through the cracks in the walls, and the usual hum of the tavern felt quieter, as if the storm outside was already casting its shadow within.

Grace tucked a small bag behind a Bible on the table. Then she rose and hurried to the door. "I'm going to go make some food and help the others get ready. We need to be prepared, and you need to eat something. We'll all need our strength if this storm is as bad as it seems."

Pushing himself up on one elbow, he called out, his voice firm. "Grace, wait."

She paused in the doorway, turning back to face him, concern mingling with a touch of irritation in her expression. "What is it, Noble?" she asked, her tone gentle but edged with urgency.

Noble's gaze drifted to the window, his thoughts racing. "The lighthouse on Whitehead's Point," he began, his tone serious and steady, "you can see it from here, can't you?"

Grace nodded, stepping back into the room. "Yes, on a clear day, you can," she replied, her voice softer now, catching the gravity in his words. "But with this weather, it's hard to see much of anything."

He watched her as she lingered for a moment, her eyes scanning the darkening sky through the window as if searching for some sign, some hope that the storm might relent. But the clouds were thick and unforgiving, and Noble knew what they were up against. He could feel the weight of it pressing down on them, a force of nature that was relentless, and they were just small figures in its path.

He hesitated, searching for the right words. "This storm... I don't like the way it's creeping in."

Grace nodded, her own worry reflected in her eyes. "I know. I can feel it, too." She took a deep breath as if gathering her resolve.

Noble frowned, not liking her leaving his sight, but he knew she was right. She needed to check on those in the tavern.

"Be careful," he said, the words heavier than he intended.

Grace gave him a reassuring smile, though the worry in her eyes remained. "I will," she promised. Grace turned and left the room. Noble could hear the distant clatter of dishes from the kitchen as she worked quickly, preparing something to eat. He knew she was right—they needed their strength for whatever was coming, but his mind was too preoccupied with the storm to think about food.

With Grace gone, Noble felt the emptiness settle around him like a shroud. The sounds of the storm outside grew louder, the wind howled through the cracks, and the walls creaked under the strain. He could hear the distant murmurs of the others, their voices carrying an edge of fear, and he knew he needed to pull himself together. There was no time to waste—he had to be ready for Grace, for the others, and for whatever the storm would bring.

When she returned fifteen minutes later, carrying a plate of steaming stew, the storm had grown even closer, the tavern creaking under the mounting pressure. She set the plate down beside him, the warm aroma of the stew rising to meet him, mingling with the damp, salty scent of the sea that had begun to seep into every corner of the tavern. Noble glanced at the food, his stomach growling in response, but the urgency of the situation overshadowed his hunger.

"Eat," Grace urged softly, her voice firm yet gentle, carrying a tone of care that he hadn't expected.

Noble gave her a brief nod of thanks, but his mind was elsewhere. He could feel the tension in the air, thick and oppressive, pressing down on him like the humidity that clung to his skin.

Grace watched him for a moment, concern etched on her face, but she didn't push him. He watched as she moved to the window, peering out into the darkening sky. The wind howled louder now, rattling the glass in the panes, and the first raindrops began to splatter against the wood. "They're starting to board up the windows," she said, her voice tight. "We're doing what we can, but…" Her words trailed off, the unspoken fear hanging in the air between them.

Noble knew she was right. Boarding up the windows might slow the storm, but it wouldn't stop it. The tavern, sturdy as it was, would not withstand the full force of a hurricane. He had to get up and help, no matter how weak he felt. Lives would be lost if they didn't do everything they could to prepare.

His body protested as he pushed himself up, every muscle screaming in defiance. The pain in his side was sharp, but he gritted his teeth and pushed through it. He couldn't afford to be weak now. The tavern was more than just a building—it was a shelter, a last line of defense against the storm that was bearing down on them. And Grace, along with everyone else inside, was depending on him.

"I have to get up," Noble said, determination hardening his voice. "I have to help."

Grace turned to him, her eyes wide with concern. "You're still recovering, you shouldn't—"

"I don't have a choice," he cut her off, his tone leaving no room for argument. "We don't have much time, and this storm isn't going to show mercy. If I don't get up and help, we might not make it."

He could see the conflict in her eyes, the fear for his well-being battling with the reality of their situation. But she didn't argue further. She gave him a quick nod and helped him to his feet.

Noble stood slowly, swaying slightly as the room tilted around him. The storm outside roared, the wind tearing at the wooden walls of the tavern with a fury that seemed almost personal. He steadied himself, one hand braced against the wall, the other clenching into a fist at his side. He could feel the strength returning to his limbs, the resolve to survive, to protect Grace and the others, driving him forward.

"Let's go," he said, his voice grim but steady. "We have work to do."

What surprised him was the power he felt returning, slow but steady, surging through his veins like the rising tide. Once weak and trembling, his muscles regained their firmness, responding to his will as if awakening from a deep sleep. The ache in his body lingered, but it was overshadowed by the growing sense of strength in his limbs. He flexed his fingers, feeling the roughness of his calloused palms, the strength in his grip that had been absent since his injury. It felt good—like reclaiming a part of himself he thought was lost forever.

Chapter Ten

Walking was a struggle, but Noble pushed through it. The ground was cool under his bare feet, grounding him further and giving him the resolve he needed. The wooden planks creaked under his weight, groaning as the building strained against the relentless wind. The storm's roar grew louder, a constant, deafening sound, broken only by the sharp crack of branches snapping outside and the occasional thud of debris hitting the walls.

Noble reached out, steadying himself against the wall. The wood felt solid, but not unyielding, trembling under the storm's pressure. His vision cleared, the fog of illness finally lifted, and he focused on Grace.

"Get ready," he said, his voice firmer now, the authority of a captain returning to him. The wind whistled through the cracks, a high-pitched keening that set his nerves on edge. "We need to move. Now."

Grace nodded, the skepticism gone from her eyes, replaced by something else—trust, perhaps, or maybe fear. It didn't matter–they had to go, and they had to go now. The storm was a living thing, angry and relentless, and the building shuddered under its onslaught. The roof creaked and groaned ominously as if the nails were being slowly pulled from the wood. Every sound, creak, and groan reminded him that time was running out.

As they moved, the floorboards beneath them seemed to shift, the entire structure swaying with the force of the wind. The walls creaked and popped as if the very bones of the building were struggling to hold together. But Noble was steady now, his resolve hardening like steel. He wasn't going to let the storm take them. Not today. He took Grace's hand, her fingers cold in his, and led her toward the door, determined to face whatever was coming head-on.

They hurried to the main tavern, the urgency of the approaching storm driving them forward. As they entered, Noble's heart sank at the sight. Everyone was huddled together, their faces etched with fear. An older dark-skinned man stood over them, a long stick in hand, his posture reminiscent of a shepherd protecting his flock.

The image struck him—a scene straight out of the Bible, where a shepherd defends his sheep against the dangers of the wild. The picture couldn't be more fitting. These weren't sailors or strong men who could help fend off the storm. The room was filled with freed slaves, widows, and orphans, all so weak and defenseless.

Grace grasped Noble's arm, her voice low but urgent. "We need to get them to the root cellar. It's our best chance. They can't stay up here."

Noble nodded, his gaze sweeping over the frightened faces in the room. The wind outside had picked up, a low, mournful howl that cut through the humid air like a knife. He slowly returned to the porch, wincing with each step, and scanned the horizon. The sky had taken on a strange, ominous hue, a sickly yellow-green that sent a chill down his spine despite the oppressive heat. He had seen skies like this before, just before the world seemed to crack open and the sea unleashed its fury. The hurricane was coming, and it was coming fast.

"Yes, let's get to the cellar," he said, turning back to Grace, his voice steady despite the fear gnawing at him. "We need to get down there. Let's go get the others."

Noble took a deep breath, the air filling his lungs with a new vitality. The weakness that had plagued him was fading, replaced by a determination that burned within him. He wasn't fully healed, but he was stronger now, strong enough to face whatever lay ahead.

He breathed in deeply again, the air thick with the scent of rain and sea salt, the storm outside pushing its way into the room.

Noble's lungs expanded, filling with the dampness of the coming tempest and the life he had fought so hard to keep. Was it an answered prayer? He wasn't sure, but he wasn't about to question it. His pulse quickened, matching the rhythm of the storm, and with it came a clarity he hadn't felt in years.

The storm raged, and Noble, who had seemingly regained his strength, looked at her with alarm, his brow furrowed in concern. "Grace, we need to move quickly," he said, his voice taut with urgency. She could see the tension etched in the lines of his face, the way his jaw clenched as he spoke.

"Eli, help us get everyone to the cellar," she said. "Mary, make sure the children are safe."

"Keep them all together as we go," Noble cut in. His words were a command, but they also felt like a lifeline, grounding her in the moment.

Her heart raced. The children—their laughter and innocence echoed in her mind. She could almost hear their little feet pattering around the tavern, their bright eyes filled with trust. She couldn't let them down. She couldn't let anyone down.

But still, she felt the pull of the items she'd left in the other room. She couldn't leave those things. The thought of facing the storm without her Bible, the photo of her parents, and William's letters felt like a betrayal of everything she held dear.

"Just a moment," she said, her voice softer now, laced with an undercurrent of urgency. She could feel the weight of Noble's gaze on her, a mixture of concern and frustration, but she had to do this. The tavern walls felt like they were closing in, and she needed a piece of her past to carry into the uncertainty of the future.

As she turned to rush back through the weather to the nearby room, the sound of the storm outside intensified, a reminder of the chaos awaited. The wind rattled the windows, sending a shiver down her spine. But with each step, she felt a flicker of resolve ignite within her. She would return quickly, and she would keep those children safe. She had to.

"I will," she replied, but her resolve remained unshaken. "I'll be right back. Just give me a moment."

In the small room, she quickly grabbed her Bible, its worn leather cover comforting under her fingers. It had been her anchor through so many storms in life, and she wasn't about to face this one without it. Next, she reached for the small, weathered photo of her parents, the edges soft from years of being held. Their faces smiled back at her, a reminder of the love that had shaped her, the love that still gave her strength. Lastly, she hesitated for a moment before picking up the letters from the man she loved, the words etched into her heart.

With the precious items clutched to her chest, determination surged through her. Grace hurried back to the main room, her heart heavy with the weight of the memories they carried. She knew she couldn't protect everyone from what was coming, but she could at least hold onto these pieces of her past, these reminders of who she was and what she was fighting for.

"Noble," she called as she rejoined him, her voice steady despite the fear swirling inside her, "I've got what I need. Let's get everyone to safety."

He looked at her and quickly nodded toward the Bible she carried. "Good. We'll need that strength where we're going."

Grace held tight to her Bible, the photo, and the letters, feeling their familiar weight against her heart. With Captian Noble by her side and the strength of those who had come before her in her heart, she knew they could weather it.

Chapter Eleven

"Everyone to the cellar!" Noble's voice boomed over the storm, sharp and commanding. They looked to Grace, their eyes wide with fear and confusion, searching for reassurance.

The urgency in his tone matched the growing ferocity of the storm. She could feel the building shaking under the relentless assault of the wind, the floor trembling beneath her feet. The others in the room looked at her, their faces pale and anxious, waiting for direction.

"You heard him!" she called out, her voice rising above the howling wind. "Run to the cellar. Get inside quickly! Eli help Miss Hattie with the children. Mary, can you round up as much food as you can carry and bring it? We need to move fast."

Inside the tavern, the air was thick with fear. The group huddled together in the center of the main room, their faces pale and drawn in the flickering light of the oil lamps. Noble stood among them, his senses sharp, his mind focused. He had faced storms before and braved the sea's wrath, but this was different. Dozens of lives were at stake, and he knew one wrong move could mean disaster.

A sudden, sharp crack split the air, louder than the thunder, followed by a scream that cut through the noise like a knife. Noble's heart leaped into his throat as he spun toward the source of the sound.

"Jonah!" It was Grace's voice, high with terror. She bolted from the group, her skirts whipping around her as she ran toward the far side of the room.

Noble's eyes followed her, and he saw the boy—Jonah—trapped by the fallen beam. The roof had given way, the heavy timber crashing down in the corner of the room. Jonah was pinned, his small body half-hidden beneath the debris, his face contorted in pain and fear.

"Stay back!" Noble shouted, his voice cutting through the roar of the storm. He sprinted across the room, his feet slipping on the wet floor as he reached Jonah's side.

Grace was already there, her hands scrabbling at the beam, her face streaked with tears. "Help me! Please, help me!" she cried, her voice raw with desperation.

Noble dropped to his knees beside her, the rain pouring in through the gaping hole in the roof, drenching them both. He grabbed the beam, feeling the rough wood bite into his palms, and strained with all his strength.

The beam shifted slightly, but it was too heavy, too solid. Noble gritted his teeth, his muscles screaming in protest as he pushed harder. "Jonah, hold on," he gasped, his breath coming in ragged bursts.

The boy whimpered, his eyes wide with pain and terror. "I—I can't move," he whispered, his voice trembling.

"Don't you worry, lad," Noble said, forcing a calmness into his voice that he didn't feel. "You're going to be just fine."

Grace was beside him, her hands on the beam, her face a mask of determination. "We have to lift it," she said, "We have to get him out."

Noble nodded, feeling the weight of the moment settle around them. He positioned himself beside Grace, their shoulders brushing as they prepared to lift the beam together. "On three," he said, meeting her gaze. "One… two… three!"

With a grunt, they pushed upward, the strain coursing through their muscles as they struggled against the beam's weight. The boy's whimpers spurred them on, and they gritted their teeth, focusing on the task at hand.

Grace's face flushed with effort, but her resolve shone brighter than her fear. "Just a little more!" she urged, her voice fierce and unwavering.

Noble felt a surge of adrenaline as he caught her eye. In that singular moment, something profound passed between them—a shared understanding of the gravity of their task.

With a final, unified effort, they heaved the beam upward, and Jonah's body shifted free. The boy gasped, relief flooding his features as he scrambled from beneath the weight. It was a miracle. It appeared he had been unharmed.

Grace and Noble lowered the beam, panting from exertion, but a rush of triumph coursed through them.

Noble's gaze found Grace's. Grace's honey-blonde hair had come loose from its pins, and a tendril clung damply to her flushed cheek. Noble's fingers itched to brush it away, to feel the silk of her skin. Instead, he clenched his fist at his side, his heart thundering louder than the gale that battered the tavern walls.

"We did it," Grace whispered, her voice barely audible above the storm's rage. Her eyes, the warm brown of autumn leaves, shone with a mixture of exhaustion and exhilaration.

Noble nodded, a half-smile tugging at his lips. "We're not out of the woods yet," he cautioned. But his voice had a new timbre, a warmth that belied his gruff exterior.

The storm was upon them. The windows shook violently as the gale outside reached a fever pitch. Grace could feel the raw power of the storm pressing against the tavern, testing its strength. She knew they had little time before it would fully break upon them.

As the others scrambled to follow her orders, Noble pulled her close, his hand warm and steady against her back. "Listen to me," he whispered, his voice almost lost in the howling wind. "We'll get through this, I promise."

She nodded.

"And Grace."

"Yes?"

He wrapped a shawl around her shoulders. "You're doing a wonderful job. Now go!"

Chapter Twelve

She didn't have to be told twice. But even as she hurried outside, Grace could feel the storm closing in, relentless and unforgiving. It was a force of nature that would not be denied. The tree branches creaked ominously, the sound of the wind a constant, bone-chilling wail. And yet, with Noble by her side, she felt a spark of hope, a determination to survive that burned as fiercely as the storm itself.

As they hurried through the storm, rain pelted them with a relentless fury. Grace could feel the cold droplets stinging her skin and soaking through her clothes, but she barely noticed them over the roar of the wind.

Noble was beside her, his presence a solid, grounding force in the storm's chaos. She could see the determination etched in his features, the urgency in his movements. He was fighting not just the storm but something deeper within himself. She didn't know what demons he was battling, but she could feel their weight in the way he carried himself, the way he shouted orders over the wind, his voice a beacon in the darkness.

Grace nodded, urging everyone forward. "Follow us! We need to get to the root cellar now!" Her voice trembled, but she forced it to stay steady, to be strong for them.

The rain lashed at them as they moved, each step a battle against the wind that tried to push them back. The sound of the storm was deafening, a constant roar that drowned out everything else.

The ground was slick beneath their feet, turning into mud that threatened to pull them down with every step. Grace's heart pounded in her chest, a frantic rhythm that matched the storm's fury. She could hear the cries of the others, the children clinging to the women, older people struggling to keep up, but there was no time to stop, no time to look back.

Noble led the way, his broad shoulders cutting through the wind, his hand firm on Grace's arm as he guided her. She could feel the strength in his grip, the resolve that kept him moving forward despite the odds.

He was a man on a mission, driven by something more than just the need to survive. Grace could see it in his eyes—the determination to protect, save these people and save her. And something else, something deeper that she couldn't quite name. He seemed very unlike a pirate to her. Had she gotten him all wrong, too?

They reached the entrance to the root cellar—a small, weathered door set into the ground. Noble wrenched it open, his muscles straining against the wind that threatened to slam it shut. "Get inside!" he shouted, his voice barely audible over the storm.

Grace helped guide the others down the narrow steps, her heart aching at the sight of their fear-stricken faces. The storm raged on, the wind howling like a banshee, but the cellar was a refuge, a small pocket of safety amidst the chaos. As the last of them descended, Grace paused, the reality of their situation finally hitting her, and her breath came in ragged gasps. She looked up at Noble, their eyes meeting in the dim light, and at that moment, she saw something in him that made her heart skip—a flicker of vulnerability, a glimpse of the man beneath the stoic exterior.

Inside the root cellar, the air was thick with tension, every breath filled with the scent of salt and damp earth, as if the storm had taken hold of the atmosphere they breathed. The wind howled like a wild beast, shaking the cellar's wooden door and rattling the windows ferocity, making her heart race. It felt like the storm was alive, clawing at them, trying to break through.

"Grace," he called, pulling her back as she followed the others inside. She turned to him, her eyes questioning.

"What is it?"

"Thank you for caring for me." Noble closed the door and secured it. Then, like a marionette removed from its strings, he crumbled to the floor. Grace sat beside him, leaning her back against the wall.

She clutched the shawl tighter around her shoulders, but it did little to ward off the chill that had settled deep in her bones. The fear in her chest was a living thing.

"Noble," she whispered, her voice trembling with emotion.

He reached out, his hand warm and solid as it closed around hers. "We'll be all right," he said, his voice low but steady. "We'll get through this, Grace. Together."

She nodded, squeezing his hand, drawing strength from his resolve. The storm outside was fierce, but here, at this moment, she felt a spark of hope.

Chapter Thirteen

Inside the root cellar, the atmosphere was heavy with tension and the scent of damp earth. Grace swallowed hard, her eyes flickering with fear as she surveyed the room. Most of her friends were clustered together, some huddled for warmth while others had fallen asleep. Their faces pale in the dim light. The storm's fury was evident in every gust of wind that rattled the heavy wooden door and every creak of the timbers under pressure.

As the wind howled outside, Noble began to open up in ways Grace hadn't expected. He spoke of his past engagement, his voice low and confessional, and she felt a rush of surprise wash over her. "I thought I had it all figured out," he admitted, his gaze distant as if he were peering into a past that still haunted him. "We were supposed to build a life together, but it all fell apart. Sometimes, it feels like everything I desire is just beyond my reach."

A flicker of fear danced across Grace's heart as thunder boomed and crackled above them, the sound deafening, like the heavens were tearing themselves apart. His words hung heavy in the air, and she could see the hopelessness in his eyes, a vulnerability that scared her. It was as if he were bearing a piece of his soul, and she felt a deep connection to him as if she had known him forever, even though their time together had been so brief.

Sensing her unease, Noble reached for her hand, his fingers intertwining with hers in a comforting squeeze. "I'm sorry," he said, his voice filled with regret. "I didn't mean to worry you."

"No, it's… it's okay," Grace replied, her heart racing. She looked into his eyes, searching for the strength she knew he had. "We're in this together, remember? You're not alone."

He nodded slowly, but the shadow of doubt lingered in his expression. "Sometimes it feels like the weight of the world is on my shoulders," he confessed, his voice barely above a whisper. "I just… I don't want to let anyone down again."

Grace felt a surge of empathy. "You won't," she assured him, squeezing his hand tighter. "You're doing everything you can. We're all fighting this storm together. And I believe in you, Noble."

His gaze softened, and the storm outside felt a little less threatening for a moment.

Grace squeezed his hand back, her gaze locked on his. She could see the sincerity in his eyes, and despite the storm raging outside, a strange sense of calm washed over her with him beside her.

Noble began to describe a house he once dreamed of building—a charming little place, just like the ones on Fletcher Street, complete with a white picket fence and a sprawling garden. As he painted the picture with his words, Grace could almost see it in her mind, the image bringing a soft smile to her lips. For a fleeting moment, she allowed herself to imagine life far removed from the dangers they now faced.

"I used to dream of a life like that," she admitted, her voice barely above a whisper. "I thought I was in love once...until I discovered he wasn't the man he claimed to be." Her heart ached at the memory, but no bitterness was left—only a lingering sadness that settled in her chest. And a determination to find William and discover the truth.

Noble squeezed her hand again, grounding her in the present. "Well, what did he turn out to be?"

"A pirate, of all things," she added, a wry laugh escaping her lips as she tried to lighten the mood.

Noble chuckled, his voice warm despite the storm's rage. "Well, I suppose there are worse things than being a pirate's love interest." He winked at her, his playful demeanor a balm against the chaos outside. "At least I'm not hiding a ship and a stash of gold."

Grace rolled her eyes, but a smile tugged at the corner of her mouth. "I suppose that's true." The spark of attraction between them was undeniable, but as she looked at him, she knew there was something more—a connection that went beyond the fleeting moment. But what about William?

The wind outside roared louder. Grace must have fallen asleep. When she awoke, the storm had stopped, yet everyone decided to stay put—at least for a while.

"Noble," she said, her voice barely audible over the wind. "What's wrong?"

He turned to her, his eyes haunted. "I'm heartbroken, Grace," he admitted, his voice raw. "I've given my heart to a woman, and I don't think I'll ever get it back."

Shock rippled through her. "Who is she?" she asked, her curiosity piqued despite herself.

He hesitated, his gaze dropping. "I...I've never met her," he admitted. "We've only corresponded through letters."

Grace's eyebrows shot up. "You've fallen in love with a woman you've never met?"

He nodded, a wry smile twisting his lips. "I know it sounds mad. But her words...they touched something in me. She's kind, brave, and strong...and I feel a connection to her deeper than anything I've ever known."

Grace was taken aback. She had never imagined Noble as the romantic type, yet here he was, his heart laid bare. "What's she like?" she asked, her curiosity getting better.

He closed his eyes, a soft smile on his face. "She's... amazing. Her letters are full of life and laughter. She has a way of seeing the world that makes me want to be a better man. And her spirit... it shines through in every word she writes." Noble smiled. "She wrote about when she tried to plant carrots but ended up with weeds. She said the weeds were better at growing, so she let them grow abundantly." He chuckled, the sound rich and warm. "She had a way of making even the failures seem beautiful."

Grace felt a pang, a mix of joy and shock. The letters he spoke of were familiar to her, echoing memories from long ago. "Are you William?" she asked, barely recognizing her own voice, the words spilling out before she could fully comprehend their weight.

His eyes snapped open, confusion written across his face. "What do you mean?"

"I'm the one you've been writing to," she admitted, her heart racing. "I'm the one you've fallen in love with."

Shock rippled across his face, followed by a dawning realization. And then, a smile, wide and blinding. "Grace," he breathed, his voice full of wonder. "Cricket."

She felt the world shift around them. Memories flooded back—letters exchanged under the dim glow of her oil lamp, filled with dreams of gardens she wanted to plant. She remembered her words about the roses she longed to grow. She had described how the sun would catch the petals in the morning light, how they would dance in the breeze. "I wrote about the garden," she said, her voice softening. "The one with the marigolds and the daisies. I wanted it to be a place where laughter could grow."

"Yes," his fingers softly caressed her cheek. "I remember that."

Grace smiled at the memory. "And I told you about the neighbor's goat that got loose and ate half my marigolds. I thought I'd never see the end of it." She laughed softly, the sound mingling with the distant rumble of thunder. "You always found a way to make me feel like those stories mattered."

"Every word mattered," he replied, his voice steady. "You wrote about your dreams, your fears, and the small joys that made life worth living. I felt like I was there with you, planting those gardens, laughing at the goat, sharing the weight of your heart."

She looked into his eyes, and in that moment, she saw the truth of his words reflected back at her. "I wrote about the little things," she said, her voice barely above a whisper. "But I never thought it would lead me to you. I never imagined the man I poured my heart into would be standing here."

Captain William Noble moved closer, the air thick with unspoken emotions. "It's as if God's good and harsh plans conspired to bring us together," he said, his voice low and earnest.

Outside, the wind howled, but inside the cellar, they stood in a quiet understanding. Two hearts had found each other across time and space, bound by their exchanged words.

The storm lost its power at that moment, and the world outside faded away. The promise of a shared life remained a future where laughter and love could blossom like the flowers in a well-tended garden.

Epilogue

October 1846
Key West, Florida

*M*rs. Parker,

I write to you with a heart full of tumult, reflecting on the storms that have both raged outside and within. In the aftermath of the hurricane ravaging Key West, I have discovered something extraordinary—a love that has blossomed amidst the wreckage.

An injured pirate was brought to my door, and I tended to him best. Then, as the days passed, he spoke of the woman he'd fallen in love with. Amazingly, it sounded like me!

At that moment, joy and shock intertwined in my chest. "Are you William?" I asked, my voice trembling, the weight of my words spilling out before I could fully comprehend their significance. His eyes snapped open, confusion etched across his face. "What do you mean?"

Taking a deep breath, I steadied myself. "I'm the one you've been writing to," I admitted, my gaze locked on his, searching for understanding. "I'm the one you've fallen in love with."

Shock rippled across his features, quickly followed by a dawning realization. Then, a smile—wide and blinding. "Grace," he breathed, his voice rich with wonder. "Cricket."

Memories surged within me—letters exchanged, filled with dreams and hopes. I could almost feel the weight of the paper in my hands, the ink still fresh with my longing. I had poured my heart into those letters, detailing my days, fears, and aspirations, painting a picture of a life I yearned for but felt was just out of reach. "I remember writing about the garden I wanted to plant," I said, my voice softening. "And how I dreamed of a little house filled with laughter. I never thought…" My words trailed off, the weight of the moment settling around us. "I never thought it would be you."

His expression shifted, a mix of disbelief and joy. "You're the one who saw the beauty in the mundane, who found joy in the simplest things. I thought I was writing to someone who understood me, but I never imagined it would be you."

My heart swelled at his words, the connection between us deepening. "Those letters were my escape," I confessed, my eyes glistening. "I poured everything into them, hoping William, you, would understand my heart. And now, here you are, standing before me."

He leaned closer, the air between us charged with unspoken emotions. "It's like God brought us together," he said, his voice low and earnest. "All this time …"

In that moment, the storm outside faded into the background, our shared history enveloping us in warmth and possibility. We were no longer just two souls caught in a storm; we were two hearts that had found each other across time and space, bound by the words we had exchanged and the dreams we had dared to share.

I felt a laugh bubble up in my chest, a mix of joy and amazement. I had fallen in love with a pirate, and here I was, doing it again. But this time, it was different. This time, I fell in love with a man who cherished my words and stood by my side during my darkest night.

As the winds howled and the rain lashed down, I knew I would weather any storm as long as Noble was by my side.

After two full days in the cellar, we finally ventured out into a world transformed. The sun beat down relentlessly, sucking the moisture from the air. I squinted, my eyes scanning the devastation. Noble stood silent beside me, his face a mask of stone.

Before us, the sea had vomited up its dead. Splintered masts stabbed towards the sky like skeletal fingers. A ship lay on its beam ends, its hull shattered, gaping open like a festering wound. Brigs and schooners, their masts snapped like twigs, wallowed in the calm waters. In the shallow channel, three vessels had been swallowed whole, only their splintered decks visible. Four more floated belly up, their copper bottoms flashing like scattered pennies.

The air reeked of salt and death. I could taste the acrid tang of splintered wood and the coppery hint of blood. My stomach churned, threatening to empty itself onto the sand.

A lone gull wheeled overhead, its raucous cry echoing across the water. The only other sound was the gentle lapping of the waves against the shore. An obscene calm had fallen as if the storm had never been.

My boots sank into the warm sand as I walked the beach. It was a different color now, a blinding white that hurt my eyes. The lighthouse that had once stood proud was gone, washed away like a child's sandcastle. Waves rolled in, crashing against the empty shore. I felt a pang as if something within me had been torn asunder.

Noble's hand found mine, his fingers wrapping around me like a manacle. I didn't pull away. We stood there, two figures against the devastation, united in our loss.

The lightship at the N.W. The pass was gone, either sunk or torn from her mooring. My mind recoiled from the thought of the bodies trapped below. The screams choked off by the rising water. I knew the young man we'd pulled from the wreckage—recognized the shock of blue eyes frozen in death. How many more lay out there, their bodies unrecovered?

Key West itself was a ruin. Buildings stood with roofs torn off and walls collapsed. Debris choked the streets—splintered wood, shattered glass, the flotsam of lives destroyed. The only sound was the crunch of rubble beneath our boots.

The storm had raged around us, the winds howling like a beast. Noble's face was set in a grim line, his eyes fixed on some point beyond the horizon. I could feel the tension emanating from him, a palpable thing that seemed to crackle in the air.

I felt numb, my senses overwhelmed. The storm had left nothing untouched. I glanced at Noble, seeing my own shock mirrored in his eyes. We were survivors, left to pick through the wreckage.

The sun beat down, uncaring. I closed my eyes, letting its heat soak into my skin. I could feel the island's pulse beneath my feet, a steady heartbeat amidst the devastation. We would rebuild, I knew.

Together, we would help restore this island, caring for others as we tended to our own hearts.

We would gather the broken pieces and forge a new life from them, side by side, as partners in every sense. And as the sun began to set, casting a warm golden light over the ruins, I turned to Noble.

"We will celebrate this love," I said, my voice steady with conviction. "In the face of all this loss, we will find joy again. We will honor those we've lost by building a future filled with laughter and hope."

Noble smiled, his expression softening. "Yes, Grace. We will celebrate love, for it is what will guide us through the darkness."

And as we stood together, hand in hand, I knew that our love would be the foundation upon which we rebuilt—not just the island, but our lives. We would gather in the community, share stories, and find solace in each other. We would dance under the stars, laugh amidst the rubble, and let our love shine as a beacon of hope for all who remained.

Yours sincerely,

Grace

Courting Miss Darling

by Chautona Havig

A sister novella to *Jack: a lot of hullaballoo on the prairie*

Courting Miss Darling is a sequel to *Jack: a* Lot of Hullabaloo on the Prairie. Part of the Ballads from the Hearth series. Muriel Darling thought her heart rode off with a cowboy when he left town, but when that cowboy's boss starts writing her letters, it looks like maybe romance is in Miss Darling's future after all.

Chapter One

September 1885—

The echo of the silent classroom reverberated in Muriel Darling's head until it pounded with the persistence of someone demanding to be let out. *How can silence be so loud, so ever-present? I should be grateful for the lack of noise after today's wasted day.*

She stacked her books, and the sound made her wince. Her hat, fashioned in the style of a poke bonnet, she plopped on her head without bothering with the ribbons. After one last look around the room, her gaze examining each window to ensure they were closed, Muriel grabbed the books and strolled from the building.

The sweet afternoon air filled her nose and lungs, blowing away a bit of the pain of her headache. Roads that reminded her of their desperate need for rain dusted the hem of her skirt until she gave up hope of keeping it clean. *Women out here should wear nothing but brown skirts. It would save hours in laundering.*

As she passed the post office, Lew Fuller stepped out and waved. "You have a couple of letters, Miss Darling." He waved them as if to prove his assertions, and Muriel hurried to retrieve them. Lew passed them to her with some reluctance. "Didn't your mother write just last week? I hope it's not bad news. But I was happy to see Jack Clausen's name on the other one. I always thought that fella was sweet on you."

Despite her best efforts to remain calm, Muriel's heart fluttered, and her stomach flopped at the sight of Jack Clausen's beautiful penmanship. "Thank you, Mr. Fuller. I expect my mother has finally remembered that she was supposed to send me her receipt for pound cake. I don't imagine there is anything too alarming, but thank you for your concern."

Muriel smiled at him, waved, and with slow, deliberate strides, strolled through town to the little cabin the hastily assembled board of education had provided for her just on the outskirts. Her cat met her at the door, meowing for a bit of milk, but she ignored it. Instead, she went about her afternoon chores—a bucket of water for washing, stirring up the coals to ensure her dinner finished stewing, and pulling in the clothes from the clothesline.

She set up the ironing board, placed a couple of irons on the stove, poured a glass of water, and sat down with her letters. The first letter proved to be the receipt she expected and word that a cousin—only seventeen—would be married by Thanksgiving. *Lord, why have You chosen not to give me a family of my own?*

Her fingers slid the second, thicker letter closer. The way her name swirled across the front—*Miss Muriel Darling*—thrilled her to the very fingertips that slowly unfolded the letter. Another folded, sealed letter fell from the packet. The penmanship on that one, however, was unfamiliar.

Mittens hopped to her lap and rubbed his jaw on her chest as she unfolded the letter. "It's from Jack. What do you think it could be? Maybe…" Her words trailed off in a sigh of disappointment as she saw the signatures—Jack and Hazel Clausen. "He married her. I suspected he would, but is it wrong to admit I hoped one of them wouldn't forgive the other?"

But the cat's tail just twitched as he watched her sit back in the chair, letter in her hands, and begin reading.

September 1885

Jordan Creek, Nebraska

Dear Miss Darling,

Are you surprised to receive this letter? I write for several reasons, and foremost is to offer my gratitude once more for your help with my lessons and correspondence while I lived in Casper. The hours you spent trying to teach me things your youngest students know is a treasured gift.

I returned home to learn that my Hazel had been proven innocent (something I should never have doubted), and we married at the end of June. My employer has set me up operating a ranch near Omaha. Hazel wishes me to correct that statement to include her. We operate the ranch together, as she likes to remind me on a semi-regular basis. Her threat of no pies for a month had nothing to do with my correction of the facts.

Muriel's lips twitched. As disappointed as she'd been to see Hazel's name with his on the signature, she couldn't help but smile at seeing the Jack she'd known shining on the pages of the letter. *It's much less formal than the one I helped him write...* She stroked Mittens' fur and continued reading.

I told Hazel and my employer about you. They both wanted me to share their appreciation for the friendship you showed me, and this brings me to our purpose for writing. Please accept our introduction to a fine man who is interested in getting to know you.

My employer, Peter Donaldson, has written to you in the enclosed letter.

Cat forgotten, she toyed with the corners of the second letter as she read, backing up to reread that last sentence.

My employer, Peter Donaldson, has written to you in the enclosed letter. Hazel and I presented him with the idea of a correspondence with you, and after much consideration and prayer (during which time, Hazel drove me half-crazy with her impatience to know his decision), Pete wrote to you and has requested I forward that letter. Should, after reading it, you decide you might like to get to know him better, you may write to him in the care of the Riverton, Dakota Territory post office.

Pete is a godly man, well respected in Riverton, Abilene, Kansas City, and among cattle ranchers in general. He owns a fine spread in Dakota Territory—one of the largest in the nation. Hazel's father, a banker, has agreed to provide a personal reference. Additionally, you may write to (and possibly hear from) Mr. Franklin, the local minister, for further character and spiritual references.

If we have overstepped ourselves, Hazel and I offer our deepest regret and our apologies. The many times I have said something about Pete and mentioned in passing just how much I thought you would agree with something he'd said, or you had recommended a book he liked have turned Hazel's heart to matchmaking again. I fear our first success may have gone to our heads, but we hope you will pray about it. What better show of friendship than to make friends of our friends?

With sincerest admiration and hopes of your health and happiness,

Jack and Hazel Clausen

"Well, Mittens. That was… different. Whatever made him think I would consider correspondence with a stranger?" She pulled the cat into her arms and stroked his fur as her eyes tried to bore through the paper to see what was inside. "I suppose with men posting advertisements looking for a wife, this is an improvement. At least someone who knows both of us is involved. It's *almost* an appropriate introduction."

Despite her lofty words, Muriel knew she'd read the letter. She knew she'd likely respond. A woman of nearly twenty-eight didn't have the luxury of ignoring a potential prospect unless she wished to remain single indefinitely. "It's the modern age, I suppose. Conventional introductions have given way to mail." A slow smile spread across her face. "Just think, Mittens. In a year or two, a woman in California may receive an introduction by telegram as follows: EXPECT TELEGRAM FROM A MR. JOHN SMITH OF CHARLESTON STOP HE IS A MAN OF GOOD CHARACTER STOP PLEASE CONSIDER AS A MATRIMONIAL PROSPECT STOP CORDIALLY, ALICE."

As if disgusted by her repeated admonitions to stop doing something offensive, Mittens hopped down from her lap and disappeared out the door. Muriel reread the letter, pausing with a catch in her throat and a squeeze of her heart at the joke about no pies, and set it aside.

The thick, creamy paper of the second letter bespoke quality. Bold penmanship—legible, but without the flourishes that characterized Jack's—stared back at her, challenging her. She could almost rearrange the letters to say, "Open me."

Four pages of small handwriting—front and back on three. The man was either serious about the prospect, determined to drive her off, or desperate. Muriel tried to pray for wisdom. The words fizzled. She attempted to stifle the rising panic, and if she were honest with herself, hope. Instead, each second that passed increased her anxiety until her hands shook as she unfolded the papers and began reading.

Riverton, Dakota Territory

Dear Miss Darling,

I pray this letter finds you well and enjoying the new school year. Jack says you are an excellent teacher with a talent for inspiring the best in your students. I expect that Jack's letter came as a surprise, though I hope not an unwelcome one. When Hazel first presented her idea, I feared it might be uncomfortable for both of us.

Nevertheless, I agreed to write you. Rereading that hints that my agreement was extorted by force. This is not so. I confess to interrogating Jack about you. Jack spoke so highly of you that I think

Hazel grew a little green with jealousy. She insists it was merely the discomfort common to women in her delicate condition.

After our conversations, I consulted with our local minister and prayed with him. I then returned home for another week of prayer and searching of my own heart. I can truthfully say that I sincerely hope that if we find we enjoy each other's correspondence, we may find mutual respect, and eventually, affection.

To share a bit about me, my father began the ranch just after the War Between the States. He wanted away from the unpleasantness and the petty bickering between those who should have left their grievances on the battlefield after the South surrendered. He found it here in Dakota territory—first as a homesteader and later as a rancher. Before the war, though, he went to California during the gold rush, and spent just enough to buy a good claim that gave him a significant return on his investment. His success meant he needn't have worked again, but with first one son and then another, he believed it to be a wise thing to provide an example of diligence and industry for his children.

My brother, unfortunately, has proven to be a disappointment. I am grateful that my father is not alive to witness John's disgrace. John is the reason Jack had the good fortune to meet you. He concocted the scheme to injure Hazel's reputation and separate them. As you know, it worked. I tell you this only because I think it right that you should know the less savory bits of my family's reputation as well as the good ones.

Life in Riverton is pleasant. I have a large home a few miles outside of town, built in the style of the Californian rancheros, and a large herd of cattle. The town is small—only a few stores, a church, bank, school, livery, and of course, a saloon. The people are friendly, and we arrange as many social events as possible.

I'm a moderately educated man. My mother had been a schoolteacher before marrying my father, and her father had been a Harvard educated man—a lawyer. I could have attended a university had I not fallen in love with the wide-open prairies as a boy. I don't regret it, but as a concession to my mother, I spend many of my free hours reading.

My housekeeper would like me to tell you that she finds me not unattractive, a kind employer, and good with children. I do not quite know what to make of "not unattractive." Does that mean I am homely but not horrifying? Does it mean I have some handsome features and others that are repulsive? At least I think it means you shouldn't find me too repugnant. She has entered again and insists that I assure you that I do not have any profane or uncouth habits.

I suspect that she is eager to leave my service in someone else's capable hands. I should say something about that. I am not looking for a new housekeeper/servant. There are plenty of men and women who can do the job of running my household. Should Jack and Hazel's scheme prove successful, I would hope to have a companion for life. Better yet, I would hope to have someone as dear to me as Hazel is to Jack. If I wish for a new employee, I will place an advertisement.

Muriel rose as she read and carried her glass to the pitcher on the shelf above her window. She removed the napkin covering it and poured a new glass all without looking away from her letter for more than a second or two. Peter's mention of placing an advertisement amused her enough that she choked on her water as her eyes skimmed the words.

She coughed, sputtered, and gasped for air as the water worked its way from her windpipe. With another sip or two soothing her throat and chest, Muriel turned to the last page and read on, sorry to see the letter end so soon.

Though I have tried to share a bit of myself, I suspect my letter tells too little. I've given facts, but Hazel assures me that you will want to hear my heart between my words. She says you will want to know what I love most about the prairie, how it makes me feel, and what my hopes and dreams include. Those ideas are uncomfortable to convey at any time but especially so in an introductory letter.

I would like to learn more about you. Jack said you were originally from Ohio? What brought you to Casper? Have you family still in Ohio? I went through Ohio once with my father. The green farmlands beckoned to me. I was certain I would become a farmer.

Do you have brothers or sisters? Both? Have you met someone who has become dear to you in the intervening months since Jack's return home?

As a teacher, I imagine you have your favorite subjects and your least favorites to teach. Which are they? Jack described some of your students to me, and now I feel invested in them. Mary's lisp, Sarah's aptitude for spelling (and dare I add, her admiration for the winner of your spelling bee?), the unlikely winner (in Jack's opinion), John? Who gives you the most heartache? Who do you despair of influencing for the better?

This letter is already longer than I intended. Please take your time deciding if you wish to respond. If I don't hear from you for a year, it won't mean your letter then is any less welcome. If you choose not to respond at all, I wish you the best in all that you do.

Most respectfully,

Peter Donaldson

Donaldson Ranch

Chapter Two

November 1885

Rain pattered against Pete's window, the steady drum an unexpected blessing on a November afternoon. His ledgers lay open before him, but the numbers blurred. His housekeeper's daughter sat on the floor before the small fireplace that crackled and sparked and played with the little dolly Tilly had given her for her birthday. As she told the dolly stories of princes who arrived to sweep pretty girls away to castles in forests, Pete rested his chin on his knuckles and watched.

Though had only been two months since he'd written to Muriel Darling, being sent by way of Jack and Hazel meant he didn't know when it had been mailed. He might have reassured her that he wouldn't expect a swift reply, but it didn't mean that he didn't hope.

"Mr. Pete?"

Pete blinked and the blur that had been a turkey-red dress and blonde curls focused into Missy's wide-eyed face. "Hmm?"

"Why don't you get a little girl? I could play with her."

"I think your dolly would get lonely if you spent all your time playing with my imaginary daughter."

The child's curls tossed as she gave them a vigorous shake. "No... our dollies could play together. And we could pick flowers, and practice riding our horsies. I think you should get a little girl."

"I wish I could do that for you, sweetheart, but I can't order one from the Montgomery Ward catalog, so until the Lord brings me a wife and then a child, I must be content with you as my favorite little girl."

Missy gave him an odd look, hopped up, and skipped from the room. A few seconds later, her plaintive, "Mama!" rang through the house.

That had failed, and he didn't know how. A horse raced into the yard, never a good sign. Men didn't ride horses hard after a long day of work, and especially not in the rain. Pete jumped from his chair and went to put on his coat and hat. Cold air and rain assaulted him as he hurried out onto the porch and out into the yard.

Bob Graves swung off the horse before it had come to a full stop. At Pete's shout, he pointed to the mare. "Will you rub her down? Wes got kicked and cracked his head on a rock. It's bad. Gotta get the wagon. Abe's gone for the doc, but he ain't pro'bly gonna make it."

Grabbing the harness and traces, Pete began the process of hitching the horses to the wagon. Bob worked on the opposite side. As he worked, Pete requested details about accident, and as they finished, he steadied himself before asking, "Would you like to rub down Gertie while I drive out?"

Bob's answer came as he climbed up onto the box and into the seat, springs creaking as he settled in. His feet were hardly on the toe board before he clicked his tongue and barked, "Git." Bob possessed an excellent economy with words.

Meanwhile, Pete grabbed a large cloth and began the process of rubbing down the overheated and soon to be chilled horse. As he worked, he prayed for speed for the doctor, gentleness from his men, and a miracle for Wes.

The wait for news proved interminable. Pete paced before the open barn doors, ran in to give his housekeeper the news and ask her to cook up some broth, and returned to the barn to pace some more.

A rider finally appeared through the drizzle. Another followed. The wagon rumbled in, with a few other men and finally the doctor. Pete met the doc at the barn door and held his horse. "Should we carry him inside? We can put him in John's room if the house would be better."

"Let me get a look at him, but that may be best."

Since he couldn't get near enough to see Wes, Pete bolted across the yard for the house. Tilly met him at the door. "I've fixed up John's old room—fresh sheets, a fresh basin of water, bandages, blankets. I've got jerky stewing to make broth, but we might need to kill a chicken." She'd have continued babbling, but Pete stopped her.

"You've done well. We'll do our part, the Lord will do His, and we'll know what that means soon enough."

Missy tore through and wrapped herself around his legs. "Mama says Mr. Wes is hurt." She produced her dolly and shoved it at him. "He can have Bethy to make him feel better."

Refusing her gift would be cruel, but Pete knew he must. Tilly came to the rescue. "We'll just wait until the doc says he can have visitors. Bethy can't go in until then." The woman's voice grew stern. "And neither can you. No sneaking in when I'm not looking."

The child's face crumpled. One moment she'd been a picture of hope and concern and the next, she'd withered before burying her face in her mama's apron. Tilly picked her up and carried her off to the kitchen to help make nourishing broth for their friend. Frustrated and wanting to pound something, Pete took off for the chicken coop. He'd might as well take that frustration out on chores rather than let it fester.

Hours later, with Wes slipping further away with each passing minute, Pete sat at his desk pouring out his thoughts in a letter to Miss Darling—one he might never send.

Riverton

Dakota Territory

Dear Miss Darling,

Today, one of my men had a terrible accident, and we now take turns sitting with him until he dies. The doc tells us it could be a long, terrible passing. He's given Wes laudanum for the pain, but there is no laudanum for our pain.

Or is there?

I've spent the night pouring over the psalms, searching for hope and comfort in what seems such a senseless loss. I have found comfort, although it isn't the comfort I sought. Like the best advice from a friend, sometimes the Lord answers with what we need rather than what we seek.

Little Missy doesn't understand why she can't sit with "Mr. Wes" and hold his hand. She doesn't understand why we won't allow her dolly to cuddle up in bed with him and make his "ouchie" all better. I learned something about myself as I watched Tilly patiently but firmly deal with the child's demands and pleas. I fear I will be an indulgent father. Without Tilly's firm support, I would have given way to the child.

I mentioned it to Tilly a while ago and asked what it would harm Wes to allow the child that comfort. Tilly said it likely wouldn't hurt Wes at all now. I suspect you know what she said next. A teacher would be wise to being forethoughtful about children's characters. Tilly said, "But it will harm Missy to expect to be allowed free rein with her wishes. She needs to learn that even selfless desires become selfish if demanded."

Those words keep repeating themselves in my mind. They're wise, and they exposed a flaw in my own character. I don't think I expect my own desires to be gratified at any turn, but I still suspect that I would find it impossible to deny Missy's.

Would I be able to remain firm with my own child? I do not know. This situation has made me realize that I must choose a wife who will help me in this area. If I chose a woman as indulgent with our children as I might be, we would be overrun by our own offspring.

Pete cleaned his pen as the words dried on the paper. He blotted the pages, folded them, and slipped them into his drawer. He wasn't likely to mail that one. But perhaps if things did develop with Miss Darling or some other woman, he could refer to it before bringing up the topic in conversation.

December 1885

The frigid air bit hard but without the promise of snow behind it as Muriel closed and locked the schoolhouse door behind her. Though she'd decided against stopping in at Fuller's General Store, knowing there wasn't enough coffee to have a cup in the morning sent her feet in that direction after all. The door resisted opening, but Muriel jerked it hard and managed to squeeze through before it slammed shut again. A glance back showed her skirt free and clear. More than once, she'd entered on a windy day, taken a step forward, and found herself trapped until she freed her skirt from the door's clutches.

"Afternoon, Miss Darling." Mr. Fuller hurried down a ladder, a cloth in hand. "How may I help you?" The man could be domineering at times, but he was a good man and a conscientious businessman. Perhaps domineering wasn't the correct word. *Commanding* might describe him better.

"I need coffee, a bit of cheese, and a dozen or so of the boiled candies." She gave a little cough and added, "They save my voice some days."

Perhaps they did, but water might do just as well, and she knew it.

"Of course." As he began working, the man chattered. "That copy of *St. Nicholas Magazine* you asked for arrived just this morning." He crossed to the counter, reached beneath it, and produced the book.

Could anything be a better remedy for the melancholy that persisted in hounding her than a new story? Her mother had begun the serial in *St. Nicholas Magazine* last month and had insisted Muriel would enjoy it as a fine story to read aloud to her students. She'd even cut out the first pages from the magazine and mailed them to her so Muriel wouldn't be forced to summarize the story for the children.

Hattie and Daisy Bernard entered the store, chattering and giggling, but about what, no one could say. The wind whisked their girlish prattle off onto the prairie to entertain prairie dogs. Muriel smiled at them and scolded herself. *Becoming fanciful isn't the solution to loneliness. You'll begin collecting cats next.*

With her packages weighing down one arm and her purse much lighter, Muriel steeled herself against the wind and made for home. Lew Fuller chased her down. "I almost forgot. There was a letter for you today. All the way from New Orleans!"

Though he sounded surprised, Muriel could see that he'd begun to put pieces of a postal puzzle together. "Thank you. This is a confidential letter, so I appreciate you giving it to me privately." Perhaps that would keep his thoughts to himself.

Storm clouds darkened the sky. She had been so certain there wouldn't be snow yet, but now she could smell it. People had predicted cold, bitter winters for the past three years, and yet they'd been mild enough, considering.

By the time she reached home, even Muriel's eyelashes ached from the cold. Mittens yowled his indignation at her being late with his treat. With her parcels unloaded onto the table, and the cat circling her as if trying to trip her, Muriel hurried down into the cellar to retrieve a sardine from the tin. Mittens took off with it with only a tail flick of indignation now.

Her two-room cabin, was moderately temperate, but the cold had begun to seep in. The first thing she needed to do was to stoke her stove and set the last of the stew on to heat.

Pounding on her door nearly made her drop the coal scuttle on her toe. She set it back down and rushed to answer it. Henry Wimpole stood there, his scraggly beard stained with tobacco juice. "Mr. Fuller axed me ta come tell ya—no school tamorra. They's sayin' the storm's gonna be bad. Kids'll stay home till Mondee."

"Thank you, Mr. Wimpole." The man always made her uncomfortable, and not for the first time, Muriel thanked the Lord that she couldn't offer to share her supper with him. "You'd best hurry home before this gets any worse. I have a couple of rolls I could send with you—if you'd like?" When he nodded, she pushed the door shut and raced to retrieve two of her last three rolls. Oh, well. She could make more tomorrow.

When she opened the door again, Mr. Wimpole still stood there, back to the wind, hands tucked under his arms, looking as if Jack Frost had begun a new sculpture. "Here you go. Hurry home. So sorry I can't invite you in—the rules, you know."

Her conscience rebuked her as Muriel went about stoking the fire, reloading the stove, setting the table, and eating her stew. It had been a lie. She wasn't sorry at all. At times like these, she was grateful for the rules that didn't allow men in her home.

"Courtesy" allowed those disingenuous statements to appease the gods of society, but God Almighty said He hated a lying tongue. Muriel didn't know how to bridge the gap of kindness and honesty when honesty didn't feel kind. *Teach me, Father.*

After the dishes had been washed, she emptied the cat's box and refilled it with sandy soil she collected from the North Platte River's edge and put her bed stones on the stove. Muriel donned her nightdress, dressing gown, and two shawls, pulled on her thickest socks, and seated herself near the stove, ready to read her magazine.

By the middle of the chapter, she'd grown disheartened. Reading this book to her class might be a mistake. Her students lived hard lives. They woke, often before dawn, to chores in tiny homes with few necessities, much less extras. Discovering they would inherit a large fortune would mean dreams of full bellies, warm homes, and likely new shoes. They wouldn't be thinking of boot boys or apple sellers. They likely didn't know those people existed. As poor as Cedric and his mother might be, they were rich by comparison.

"Goody two-shoes." That's how they'd see Cedric. John Camden might understand and appreciate how a boy so young could be generous if he never realized he suffered want, but most of the children weren't that astute.

Muriel set the magazine aside and added coal to the stove before wrapping her rocks in the old horse blankets she used to protect her linens and carried them to her bed. She pulled her writing desk out, propped herself up against the headboard, and retrieved her letter opener from within the walnut desk. A quick slit offered the possibility of a world of change. As she skimmed the words within, Muriel's heart and mind tumbled about like a toddler running down a hill.

She pulled out her prized fountain pen. Her father had given her five dollars to buy herself Christmas and birthday gifts when she'd left Ohio, and she'd spent it *all* on paper, envelopes, stamps, a large bottle of ink, and a fountain pen. Being so far away from friends and family meant the need for correspondence, and she had no intention of allowing herself any excuse to avoid it—excuses like tonight.

Casper, Wyoming

December 9, 1885

Dear Mama and Papa,

I received your last letter the other day. A new baby for Jonathan and Becca! That is wonderful news. Are Annie and George as excited as the rest of us? Are they old enough to argue over whether a boy or a girl is preferable? I suppose Jonathan hopes for another pair of helping hands, but I can't help but think that after Herbert's three boys, we Darlings need a bit more feminine influence in the family.

It is cold here, bitter cold after such a mild summer. A snowstorm is coming and has closed school until Monday. Some predict we'll have record snowfall, but I doubt it will be that severe.

I have news and a request for advice. Della Dreyfus sent me news of an opportunity in New Orleans. After prayer and consideration, I wrote to inquire about it and received a reply today.

I love my position here, love the children, and am invested in in their welfare. John, Sarah, and Betsy in particular are excellent scholars, but the girls will marry, and John will likely serve whisky till his dying day.

Would waiting until I knew I was ready for a change be unwise? If one letter to one school provided such a quick and favorable response, would it be unrealistic to assume that there might be other opportunities if I went looking for them at the needful time? I'd prefer to head west than south. San Francisco appeals to me. I've spoken to a couple of women from there, and it sounds lovely.

Yawns punctuated each sentence until Muriel thought she'd fall asleep right then and there, but she needed to end with something else for her mother to stew on than her daughter's further travels from Ohio. Perhaps just a few words about the book…

St. Nicholas Magazine arrived today. I read through most of chapter two before I decided it was time for a quick letter and bed. Cedric is a dear child, isn't he? And what a wise mother! I won't have classes until Monday at the earliest, so I will have plenty of time to read the rest of the story… <u>after</u> I replenish my roll stores. Mr. Wimpole came to tell me about school closing, and I gave him my last two (aside from one reserved for my supper) rolls as a thank you.

Much love always,

Your Muriel

How she'd always wanted to write those words to a man who had truly claimed her as his own. At twenty-seven, the chance of that sort of love felt too far away to grasp. Her best options now were widowers needing someone to help raise their children and a hope for an affectionate companionship as time went on.

Chapter Three

Outside, snow swirled and danced, but Pete Donaldson sat in his study, his feet propped up on the desk, a fire blazing in his fireplace, and a letter—*at last*—in his hands.

December 29, 1885

Casper, Wyoming

Dear Mr. Donaldson,

You said you had no expectations of a reply from me, but I imagine after Christmas came and went, you didn't think I would respond. You would have been correct. I had no intention of corresponding with you. I didn't realize until I received Mr. Clausen's letter just how much I appreciate traditional courtship. I had an ideal I'd treasured deep within my heart. I simply didn't know that until the end of September.

Every year, the week between Christmas and the New Year, I review my choices, my dreams, what I had planned to do and what I didn't do. And here I am at the end of yet another year. I did many of the things I'd planned to this year. It has been the first one that I left almost nothing unachieved.

However, as I reviewed my diary and looked at the list of things I hoped to accomplish, I saw something I hadn't noticed when I made them. When I reviewed those from previous years, it confirmed my suspicions. For the first time, last year I limited my goals. Instead of dreaming of writing a novel or improving my social skills in order to be less invisible to a good man, I said I would write weekly in my diary, keep up with my correspondence, and plan the school exhibition (like the one where I met Mr. Clausen).

They were easy things. One might call them safe.

But as I look to 1885, I find myself discouraged. I'd like the <u>hope</u> of something deeper than writing home more often or choosing to set my hopes for a family aside. I have the opportunity at a school for girls in New Orleans. I hesitate to take it, but I can't help but wonder if perhaps it may be the Lord's will for me.

I likely still wouldn't have penned this letter had I not run across yours again while sorting this year's correspondence. I reread it and recalled how much I enjoyed it the first time. If you are curious, yes. I enjoyed it just as much the second.

You asked for more about me. Yes, I am from Ohio. My father and two of his brothers are farmers. The other brother is in the railroad, and another is a shopkeeper in our little valley. I am the only one from our entire extended family who has moved out of the state. It's difficult to be so far away from people who love me, but teachers abound in Ohio and are scarce west of the Mississippi.

Pete rose from his chair, letter in hand, and strolled out to the kitchen. "Hey, Tilly. Can I talk you into a piece of last night's cake and some coffee?"

"I'll have it right there." Her voice followed him as he wandered through the room and back out again. "Is that from Jack's teacher?"

"Mmm hmm…"

Not until he'd seated himself did Pete catch her next words. "Took her long enough."

A slow smile formed, but Pete just kept reading.

I do have siblings. My two older brothers both work with Father on the farm. Jonathan is expanding our dairy operation, but Herbert is much like our father—always about the earth and what to grow in it. I would never admit it to them, but their over-protection of my "virtue" directly contributed to my decision to come west. You see, Mr. Donaldson, when a young man says "Hello," it really is an insult to a young woman. Perhaps I should clarify. If a man says "Hello" to <u>me</u>, it is definitely untoward.

I almost chose to ignore your question about the condition of my heart. After all, if I had met someone in the intervening months, I wouldn't likely be writing you, would I? But then I realized that in your position, I might prefer a definite answer to that question—something to remove all doubt. So, I will tell you. No. I write to you heart-whole and willing for that to change. However, I should also tell you that I do not have much hope for this to be more than a pleasant way to pass a cold, lonely winter. I will understand if you choose not to write again.

My students are eager learners. Well, I should clarify that <u>most</u> of my students are eager to learn and grow as individuals. The young man you wrote of, John? His father owns a saloon and thinks his son should follow in his footsteps. I understand that kind of commitment to a family business. My father was much the same with my brothers. But John is truly the most intelligent person I've ever met. He should study at the best universities in the world. He should be an academic. But his father will use the lack of money as an excuse to keep John serving whiskey to undereducated cowboys for the rest of his life. I fear he will wither. Already, when work crowds out opportunities for John to study, I see the darkening clouds of melancholy settle over him. It infuriates me. I've considered asking Mr. Saloon Keeper (name withdrawn to prevent the charge of gossip) how he would enjoy mucking cow dung all day long, but I doubt he could grasp the analogy.

Pete's lip twitched. He'd never met the woman and had little idea of her personality, but he suspected she might just be a bit more feisty than he'd originally imagined. "That could make things ahh… interesting…"

"What's that, Pete?" Tilly stepped into the room with a round tray and set his plate and cup on the desk.

"I think Jack may have underestimated Miss Darling's pluck. He described her as gentle and a bit quiet, though he said she seemed to enjoy a good sense of humor, but I'm seeing... more."

Tilly paused at the door, waited for him to look up at her, and smiled. "I really hope she's the one for you. I hate seeing you so alone."

"Some would say I should have courted you or—"

Laughter filled the room—first Tilly's, then Pete's. She spoke first. "My, oh, my. That would be something. Please. Convince this woman to marry you before someone else gets that idea."

"I feel as though I should be insulted... but I can't. It's just too funny. I think your husband might just return to haunt me or something."

She left him alone, her chuckles reaching him now and then as she worked about the house. Pete closed his eyes, relaxed, and thanked the Lord that he'd read their relationship well. *I just can't imagine me and Tilly. We'd be miserable. And we both know it.*

The letter beckoned.

One thing in your letter did spark hope that we might be congenial. You asked about the students by name. You remembered their personalities. A man who does that is the sort of man who would interest me.

I am curious about something. You know why I haven't married. I don't believe I am repulsive to look at. I'm average featured, average sized, and of average or slightly above intelligence. But with brothers such as mine, there was little hope at home. And here, I am afraid, I meet few with whom I can have an intelligent conversation. None of this will surprise you, I'm sure.

But why have you not married? Did you choose bachelorhood and change your mind, or are there other reasons? At the risk of seeming disingenuous and fishing for compliments, if you have chosen to wait for just the right woman, I wouldn't want you to expect more from this correspondence than I could offer. I am not remarkable enough of a person, in my own estimation anyway, to be the fulfillment of some man's long-awaited dream.

In conclusion, this is what I have to offer in this endeavor of ours. Through our correspondence, I hope to make a friend. If we remain merely correspondents for the rest of our lives, I would be content with that. If something deeper develops, that would be welcome, of course. It feels unseemly to write of such things with someone of whom I've never met. However, it would be ridiculous to pretend that Mrs. Clausen's matchmaking scheme may not reach its intended goal. And now I fear I write in circles. Please do not tell my students that I have begun a sentence with a conjunction. Trust me when I write that I would never hear the end of their teasing, that it is so.

Perhaps I should summarize. I have no expectations and few hopes for this correspondence save the forming of a treasured friendship. More will be a gift from the Lord. Less will be disappointing but not devastating.

Speaking of the Lord, what have you learned in your Bible study of late? I was just reading Ecclesiastes chapter three this morning. These verses always feel as though they were written to soothe my order-loving spirit. I enjoy a place for everything and everything in that specified place. Whether it be my daily prayer time with the Lord, my evening meal (which, in a twist of irony, I am now late to begin to prepare), or a specific place on a shelf where I always know I can find my key to the school building, I am invigorated and soothed by the routine. So much of the Bible encourages us to trust the

Lord for His timing regardless of our knowledge of it. Alas, these verses remind me that the Lord has set these rhythms into being, and the Lord blessed me with them.

Yours most cordially,

Muriel Darling

Pete read the last paragraph three times before he pulled out a sheet of his best letter paper, prepared a clean nib, and began writing.

Perhaps immediately composing a reply, rereading it, rewriting it, and finally riding to town despite the threat of another snowstorm to mail it might be considered imprudent. At the least, one could lay a charge of impetuous, but Pete did not care. After two weeks of being trapped in the house with an injured man, he needed an occupation. Tilly had teased him all the way out the door, insisting that he'd already lost his heart to the Wyoming schoolteacher. He disagreed. He'd lost his heart to the idea of romance, though he'd never admit that, either.

Wisdom turned her steady gaze on him, looked him in the eye, and encouraged discretion and prayer. Loneliness (yes, he could confess to being lonely—if only to himself) begged him to write again. Pleaded with him to add all the thoughts and questions he'd only remembered after surrendering the letter to Thomas Greigson at the mercantile.

Pete's horse, Squanto, plodded through over a foot of snow as they made their way back from Riverton. Smoke rose from chimneys and his rancho-style home, one he'd always suspected might actually be more like a hacienda. He didn't know. He didn't remember California, although of all places, California had always had the greatest pull on him. Despite promising himself that he'd go back someday, he never had.

Did Miss Darling dream of traveling? Is it why she'd come all the way from Ohio to teach children in a rough town in the wilds of Wyoming? Would she like to see the East Coast, or maybe Chicago? Had she stopped in Kansas City on her way west?

California, though. Pete's father had described deserts, beaches, and everything in between. He still remembered the detailed descriptions of the trip around Cape Horn and up to San Francisco.

"When I arrived in '49, only a few hundred people lived there. By the time I sold out and moved here in '59, it had become a proper city—well over fifty thousand."

Pete ached to see the gold fields where his father had panned as hardly more than a boy and finally bought a partial share in a mine with a deep vein. They'd used hydraulics, a wonder of the time. To stand at the bay and look out over water his father had traveled all those years ago…

Then again, he had seen it, hadn't he? Mother and Father had left San Francisco and the gold mine in the Sierras when he was four, but Peter's first memory was of the trek across the Black Hills of the Dakotas. The Indians he'd seen.

As he rode into the yard, Pete took in the long, low house with its beams and archways. He smiled at the memory of his mother's joy when the wrought iron gates had been hung. Donaldson Ranch boasted a large, roomy—yes, he *would* call it a hacienda. It might not be the right word, but "rancho" had always felt redundant. A rancho on his ranch?

Smoke rose from the bunkhouse, and Pete considered joining the men in there. They probably played cards and would feel constrained by his presence, though. Instead, he rode Squanto into the barn, rubbed down the old horse, gave him a few oats in the feedbox, and made his way back to the house.

I could sell out. Move west. I have the funds. Contrition smote him. He lifted his gaze heavenward and scanned the sky for signs of impending snow as he prayed. "Lord, I'm becoming too hopeful and self-assured. Remind me that this is only a possibility. Please protect me from foolish decisions. The only thing worse than the loneliness that comes with this life would be the ever-present companionship of regret."

Missy flung open the door as he reached the step. "Mama made cookies. Come on!"

Pete promised to be in the kitchen in just a moment. "I need to wash up, sweetheart. I've been handling a smelly horse."

The girl skipped off, both excited to share her bounty and indignant that he would call Squanto, "smelly."

Alone in his room, Pete continued his prayer in his heart. *If I'm not the right man for Miss Darling, I pray You will make her decide against me right off. Please teach me what I need to learn to prepare to be a good husband to the wife that You might have for me.* After staring at himself in the small looking glass above the washstand for a moment, Pete continued. *Meanwhile, I pray for Miss Darling's John…*

Chapter Four

January 27, 1886

As irrational as it was, Muriel began anticipating a reply just two weeks after her letter left Wyoming and made its way to Riverton. By week three, her impatience grew to concern. Would she receive a reply, or had he changed *his* mind? By the fourth week, her eagerness fizzled into resignation.

Mr. Donaldson had given up on her, despite his fine words promising to give her time to consider. And it was only reasonable. She had waited over three months to respond.

So, with resoluteness all too familiar to her, Muriel set aside all hopes of a new friend and focused her time and attention on her work, her cat, and a new quilt she desperately needed before yet another winter in that freezing place known as Casper, Wyoming.

On an afternoon in late January, Muriel's students studied their spelling words, quiet whispers and murmurs filling the room as they worked on each word, spelling to themselves or quizzing one another from time to time. Some of the boys grew antsy after having been cooped up all day, and the younger children looked a little blue around the lips. Muriel made a decision.

"Class? Attention, please." All eyes turned her way. "It's cold in here, and we've had little time outdoors. Let's try something new. First, John, would you please add a log to the fire? It's growing colder every hour."

From somewhere near, a couple of the older girls murmured their opinions between themselves, "She probably misses that cowboy chopping wood for her. My mother says if she had exerted herself a little, she might have caught him."

What your mother doesn't know would fill more than a book of her suppositions. A gasp—was it hers?—filled her ears. The two girls' faces reddened, and Muriel struggled to find a way to cover her gaffe. *Please, Lord. Don't let me have spoken that aloud. It would be cruel enough if the girls knew I'd overheard them.*

She moved to the front of her desk, rubbing her hands together. "I may have a solution to our cramped quarters. We will quiz one another on our words and definitions, but we will each line up in the aisle like this…" Miss Darling walked up and down the center aisle, facing partners opposite one another. "Be sure you can hold your arms all the way out to your sides, so you don't touch one another. Can you?" She moved one boy over. "No, Bobby. Like this, see? We wouldn't want to hurt anyone. Now… just one slate per team… I'll collect the others and set them at your places. Now you older students, why don't you set yourselves up in the back…"

Once everyone stood ready for further instruction, Miss Darling explained. "There. Now, what you need to do is give your partner his word. For example: Joanna would tell Bobby to spell 'sat.' Bobby will do one jumping jack per letter. Like this." And there, at the front of the room, Miss Darling set aside all the primness she was known for and spelled "sat" with a full jumping jack for each letter. "S—" her arms and legs flew out and back. "A—" Again, she jumped. "T—." With arms at her sides again, she smiled. "We'll get a little exercise *and* exercise our minds at the same time. Now go!"

The experiment boasted immediate success. Within just a couple of minutes, the restlessness dissipated, and the room felt a tad warmer. Muriel walked up and down the rows, listening, correcting, encouraging, praising. So, when the schoolhouse door opened and Mr. Fuller appeared, her heart sank. *Surely, you do not think it is best for young children to stay cooped up in one room and strapped to their seats all day? I cannot let them out in this wind. It's much too cold.*

But even as her mind protested, Mr. Fuller began ordering the children to bundle up. "There's a blizzard comin', Miss Darling. You best get home quickly. I've got the wagon. I'll take the children who live farther out home myself." He pulled a letter from his pocket. "You've got mail from Dakota Territory."

She couldn't help it. Her heart leapt, her face flushed, and a smile formed before she could hope to prevent it. "Thank you, Mr. Fuller. Do you need help with the children? Perhaps I should—"

"Just get on home. I'll take care of the rest of 'em."

"But I can't—" Her words died as he threw her a look clearly meant to silence her. She swallowed her protest. *This is serious. It's more than the blizzard, isn't it? A gunfight?* Her throat went dry, and she began stacking her books in the little satchel she used in inclement weather.

"Now, everyone listen closely. You heard Mr. Fuller. We need to go home and quickly. Those who live on my way home may walk with me, but the rest of you pile in Mr. Fuller's wagon. And since we're likely to be snowed in anyway, there will be no school tomorrow. We'll meet again on Monday unless you have snow above your windowsills. Be safe and keep warm!"

John and Sarah helped her lead six of the youngest children through town to their respective homes. Miss Darling explained what little she knew and suggested darkening the windows. One woman protested, but she insisted. "I don't know what's happening, but Mr. Fuller made it clear it's more than just a coming storm."

At home, Muriel brought in as much coal as she could pile in the cellar, pumped as much water as her pails would fill, and cleared a path to an outhouse she suspected she'd never be able to use. She checked the rope that would lead her to the outhouse and smiled with satisfaction when it held fast. "I can hope, Mittens. I despise slop buckets."

All set for the blast, she moved her beans to the front of the stove, stirred them, and fried a Johnnycake to eat with them. The milk tempted her, but she'd never have enough for Mittens to last through the storm if she used more than just a little for cooking. "I'll have to content myself with coffee."

The letter, she propped up on the mantel—unopened.

By Saturday morning, Muriel had exhausted the limits of her self-control. She stumbled out of bed, stoked the fire, heaping extra coal in it, and began a fresh pot of coffee. Peering out the curtains showed the snow halfway up the front window. "I'll have to start digging us out this morning while the wind has calmed," she informed the cat. He just lolled about the fireplace content in a good blaze and the scent of coffee.

But as she poured a cup, Muriel found herself staring up at the letter. "I think it's been long enough, Mittens. After all, once I've opened it, I'll be able to read it a few times. That should also help drive away the doldrums."

So, with her long braid over one shoulder, her housecoat wrapped around her, and her feet still ensconced in three pairs of thick, wool stockings and her winter boots, Muriel sat at her table, slid the letter from its envelope, and began reading.

January 13, 1886

Riverton, Dakota Territory

Dear Miss Darling,

I hope this letter finds you well and warm. I received your letter on the sixth of January—unprecedented, don't you think? The speed at which things fly these days! I recall my father saying it took six months or more to get a letter to or from California when he lived there. And now, in just over a week, your letter arrived here in Riverton. Unfortunately, one of my men was fatally injured, and I have spent the last two weeks sitting with him until he died.

We're losing too many cattle. This winter has been strange. It isn't consistently colder than other years, but storms come up and catch us unaware. Two of my men have lost toes and one a piece of his ear. Abe says maybe with such an interesting conversational piece, people may not notice his diminutive stature. I've never met a more affable man nor one so alone. I think he would love nothing more than to find a woman to marry and raise a family with. It's a hard life for these men. But, for a man like Abe, I imagine it must be even lonelier.

Perhaps you can explain. Why would a man's height, or lack thereof, be such a disappointment to women? I tried to compare it to many men's preference for a pretty face or good teeth, but is that a parallel comparison?

Muriel smiled at the words. "Ah, but I think you've missed the most important thing. He is likely so conscious of his own height that others can't help but notice it. If he is dissatisfied with it, why should anyone else hold a differing opinion?" A thought occurred to her, and she jumped up to retrieve her slate. In her careful script, she wrote, "Tall women parallel, of course."

May I begin with my gratitude? Not only for your willingness to correspond but also for your forthrightness. My greatest concern over this unusual introduction was that polite conventions might prevent one or both of us from writing with frank honesty. I fear that would lead to disappointments. Sometimes we read more into someone's silence than we do into their words.

As to why I have not married, it isn't from lack of desire. Business and busyness are the primary culprits. When you add to that the dearth of unattached females in Riverton, it just never happened.

What kind of place is Casper? Is it wild like Abilene, Kansas or more civilized like Kansas City? And do you know enough of either of those places to answer? It's hard to remember how little people <u>not</u> in the cattle business know of places that are so essential to my livelihood.

What do you love best about Casper? Is the minister an excellent "divider of truth," or do the spring flowers turn the barren landscape into a riot of colors? Is it the barren landscape I've heard described? Perhaps it's an older woman full of wisdom or a small little boy at church with wide brown eyes and a smirk that melts your heart?

Also, what do you miss most of home? You spoke of your father and brothers. Is your mother still with us? Did you learn to love Jesus at her knee, or did you seek Him after moving to Casper?

Muriel's heart constricted to read the questions. Peter Donaldson showed intelligence, sensitivity, kindness. But were they genuine or shared to impress? Jack's earnest eyes, his quiet manner, the sincerity of his letter argued against such an idea. "Lord, I purposed not to allow my heart to become too hopeful, but I may need Your strength to accomplish that. I already catch myself hoping.... Dreaming..."

Mittens must have found her words concerning. He jumped into her lap, purred with all his might, and rubbed his head against her arm as if to reassure her. "Thank you, darling." Her gaze dropped back to the next page.

Life here in Riverton is hard on some. Winter is cold. It's bleak. But we have a large, comfortable home, a full larder, and close enough proximity to town to enjoy our local sociables. Our school has never held an exhibition such as Jack and you describe. However, I imagine our teacher, Mr. Rooksmark, might enjoy holding one. I will make a point of suggesting it next time we speak.

I've been reading Emerson's Essay on Friendship this week and recall his words about "troops of gentle thoughts emerging as we engage in personal correspondence. That well describes my feelings as I try to share enough that you may get a sense of who I am while ensuring I ask as much of you as courtesy allows. I find myself resisting the temptation to interrogate rather than question.

You asked about my study of the Bible. I have been reading Romans and James and comparing and contrasting them. If one did not believe that the Bible—the <u>whole</u> Bible—was the inspired Word of God, those two books would be enough to convince one that the Bible contradicts itself, and therefore, the Lord does. This, I do not believe, so I'm reading through them both, side by side. I have my mother's Bible open to James and my father's to Romans. It has been an enlightening study. I believe that the Lord must have put both books into the canon of Scripture to ensure that we balanced our inward faith and the outworking of that faith. Without both, one might easily be drawn into false teachings that eschew any demonstration of faith at all. Or one might find oneself entrapped in the idea that one must work diligently to ensure salvation. A ridiculous idea. As if anything or anyone but the Lord's blood alone could cleanse us from our sins. Once you find that precarious balance, you then are reminded by Paul—the reference escapes me, and I write from the barn for peace from Tilly's little daughter's playful shrieks. Paul says we are to "work out our own salvation with fear and trembling." (was that Timothy?)

Still, the spirit of the words comes through. We must bear fruit (which is, in a sense, a work) as evidence of our salvation, or we must question whether we have been regenerated.

My paper is almost gone, and I am disinclined to go inside again. Tilly might like a break from trying to amuse a little girl who cannot play outdoors in this wind. So, I'll hitch up the sleigh and see if Missy would like to come to town with me to mail this. Some wonder why I don't marry Tilly. We had a laugh about that the other day when your letter came. We would <u>not</u> be congenial. Still, when little Missy looks up at me with those big eyes and trusting face… I think it's a good thing her mother and I know we would not suit, or I might be tempted for the sake of the daughter. She is a dear child.

I pray this letter finds you well. If I did not thank you already for your reply, I thank you now. I feel as if you've granted me a great trust. I hope I do not fail you.

Most cordially,

Peter Donaldson

Ignoring her cherished routines, Muriel pulled out her writing paper and pen almost before she finished the last word. Her replies came swiftly as she described the close relationship with her mother, the guilt she felt at leaving just as her brothers had also married and moved out of the house, and the confidence in knowing that despite occasional complaints that she should return, Mrs. Darling was proud of her daughter's accomplishments.

She wrote of Thursday afternoon's class session, the blizzard that while severe enough, didn't come until many hours after she had arrived home, and her concern as to what had truly prompted Mr. Fuller to send everyone out of the center of town.

A better-situated building is my deepest desire. Our current one was a gift from a man who tried to

> *start a store and failed. It's an optimal place for a mercantile of any kind, but one cannot hope to survive in business if one allows customers to pay "next time I'm in town." Once word spread that he'd extend credit to anyone who asked, and that he never submitted requests for payment, the man was overrun with unscrupulous people who bankrupted him before the year was out.*
>
> *I would like to see the town sell the building and use the funds to build a school on one end of town or the other. My end would be preferable, of course. With plenty of fresh air and room to play, I think the children would enjoy an excellent and well-rounded educational experience. Spring and summer Sunday picnics would be more convenient as well. We could use the building to protect the food against flies.*

Hunger drove her to make a bowl of porridge, but as it stewed, she wrote. She described her classes, the copy of *Ivanhoe* that her mother had sent her for Christmas, and her appreciation for him sharing his study of Romans and James.

> *I too have wondered at the seeming contradictions. I assumed a reason such as you have found but am ashamed to admit that I never took the time to confirm those suppositions as you did. Additionally, is strange that you should mention Emerson. John and I were talking the other day, and he mentioned that he thought the inquisitiveness of children to be an indicator of their innate intelligence and cited a few examples from the classroom. Mr. Donaldson, my heart broke. He is so insightful! I gave him my copy of Emerson's first series and suggested he read Intellect. If you haven't read it lately, you might be amused to compare it to John's words.*
>
> *This brings me to one of my greatest faults, of which you may need to know. I've already begun writing letters to every college and university or person connected with one that I can recall. I am determined to find him a scholarship somewhere. It isn't any of my business. I should not interfere. Yet, I know I will not cease until someone has offered, he has refused, and he is wedded to that bar tap of his.*

Her hand reached for the page, ready to crumple it up again. *Muriel, Darling. If you tell him something like that, you'll scare him off for good!* But despite her self-recriminations, Muriel set the page aside, and kept writing. Part of her grew tempted to write crosswise as her grandmother had always done, but not knowing if Pete Donaldson knew how to read like that, she eventually signed her name, folded the pages, and settled for praying that somehow the mail would remain swift, even in the coldest, snowiest part of winter.

And then she picked up his letter and read it again.

Chapter Five

February 13, 1886

The first two weeks of February had been unseasonably warm—windy but without snow and moderate winter temperatures. That had all changed around ten o'clock. The sky darkened, and wind began to howl. Someone sighed, probably LuAnn Mercer. The girl had legendary sighs, but this time Muriel couldn't help but agree.

The children ate their lunches at their desks, swept the room afterward, and took turns running to the outhouse and back. Muriel took pity on them and suggested that the boys set up marble rings at the back of the room and in the cloakroom and that the girls laid out strips of paper to denote hopscotch squares. "You must be extra careful to stay off the lines. You'll skip the stone toss, however. You lose your turn if you forget to skip the next square each time." A second survey of the room showed she could create a second hopscotch course in the front if she moved her desk out of the way.

"Mix up the skill levels of your players, children. I will adjust class time to allow for everyone to have a turn, but we still have our history lesson."

Children jostled for position, and her youngest girl cried as she found herself almost last. Muriel hurried over and knelt beside her. "Watch how they do it. See what they do well and where they make their mistakes. The more prepared you are, the more time you'll have for jumping."

Emmy took the words to heart and focused so intently on each move made, that Muriel found it difficult not to laugh. She and Sarah Lunde exchanged amused glances, but a moment later, Muriel's heart sank as Sarah sent John a meaningful look.

Don't be so eager to grow up. Babies and children are blessings that I wouldn't begrudge any woman, but wait until you're fully grown before you take on what is also a responsibility.

Though she ought to have spent her time preparing for her lesson or reading through the essays she'd assigned to the three oldest students, Muriel sat squished against the back wall, her "desk" (a table, really) hemming her in, and allowed herself the joy of watching the children play, squabble, make up, and laugh. Eventually, the groups mingled. Felicity Monroe sprawled out on the floor to ensure the best shot for her marble, while Henry Clinton skipped through the entire hopscotch course in one turn before stepping aside for the next girl.

A thump against the side of the building prompted a few shrieks and several boys to crowd at the window. John turned to her, asking silent permission to investigate. Muriel nodded. A glance at the clock warned her she ought to hurry the children through their paces. "Has everyone had a turn? If not, remember where you were in the game and allow someone else to take a turn."

In her peripheral vision, she saw the pasteboard box of supplies and the large sheets of paper Mr. Fuller had donated to her project. She'd planned it for tomorrow, but if the wind should happen to drive in a storm…

A rap at the window showed John there, holding a branch from the cottonwood that grew a few yards from the corner of the building. He grinned, dropped it, and disappeared, only to burst in through the door a moment later. "It's howling out there," he announced to the room. You fellas'll have to hold onto your hats on the way home."

A low murmur began that swelled into an argument for and against the probability of a storm. That decided for her. Sometimes, one must adapt one's plans to the situation, no matter how much one felt discombobulated without structure and routine. Then a new idea prompted her to amend the amended plan all over again.

"All right. I need help with my desk, and then we have a project to do."

All eyes turned toward the shelf where she'd stored the box and the paper. "Yes, that is exactly right. I've collected quite a few supplies, including several pairs of scissors, so we're going to create Valentines." Murmurs and a few excited whispers filled the classroom at this. "Each student may only make two cards. You're free to give one to a best friend, but I recommend that you give the other to your mother, grandmother, or someone special to you at home. For all that is lovely in recognizing friendship, we mustn't neglect our family on special occasions."

There. Perhaps that would keep disappointments at bay. Inevitably, situations like this ensured one child or another felt left out. A stroke of genius swiped through her mind just as Muriel asked Sarah and Betsy to come forward and cut the paper into card-sized pieces.

"If you have a card for one of your classmates, leave it on your desk when you leave. I'll distribute them all to the correct desks after everyone goes home and there will be a treat in the morning." *May we all be able to come tomorrow!*

While the girls cut and passed out the sheets of paper, Henry and John carried scissors and the box of adornments she'd collected and moved among the students, allowing each one to pick out a few things to put on their cards. It was mostly scraps—ribbon bits that had frayed too much to be of use as hair ribbons or the remnants left over from a dress. A few buttons with the shank broken off, donated by parents who were happy to see them used. Beads from a broken necklace that had lost too many to be restrung, paper flowers she'd made of the tissue paper her mother had wrapped her Christmas gift in, and other bits of what otherwise would be trash. She'd even sacrificed a few pages from the Montgomery Ward catalog.

"If you are careful, you could cut a lacy border around a heart much like a snowflake. I tried it at home and found it worked well." Muriel pulled out her attempt and showed how folding a heart into pieces left it possible to create a cutwork design. "Feel free to draw or paste bits of floss to create designs. Be creative. If you need help, ask an older student, and older students must needs be willing to assist or we will be forced to put the projects away."

The hints of complaints that had begun ceased at that warning. "While you work, I'll read aloud about how Bonnie Prince Charlie escaped capture by the British."

Only two small squabbles marred what was otherwise a lovely and creative afternoon. Muriel didn't doubt that the children only half heard anything about Charles III. In fact, she read the entire lesson twice without a pause and not one of her students glanced her way to question it.

By the time the children had gone, and she had distributed the valentines, Muriel was relieved to find that only four of the students didn't have one. That meant, of course, that three of the children had more than one card. One of the boys had taken both valentines with him.

She cut out half a dozen cards from the paper that had been provided and carefully rolled up the remaining sheets. She'd leave them with Mr. Fuller on the way home. She'd also ask to buy a yard of ribbon to use on her cards. Well, she'd use it for her hair and use her old ribbon for the cards, but the effect would be the same. Her rose ribbon looked a little limp and frayed these days.

Outside, the wind tried to rip the papers right from under her arm, but Muriel squished it against her body and sighed over its now wrinkled state. She scurried across the street and down a bit, wrestling with the door until a cowboy who desperately needed a bath came to her aid.

"Thank you," she gasped. Prayerfully, he'd assume her breathlessness came from the fight with the door rather than her reaction to his stench or worse—to his attention!

"Always a pleasure, Miss Darling. If I might—"

She hurried inside and let the door slam shut behind her. Disingenuous as it might be, she offered him an apologetic smile and hurried to the counter. "I brought back the leftover paper and the two pairs of scissors you loaned us. The children had a wonderful time."

"Bringing back that paper wasn't necessary, Miss Darling, but I thank you just the same." He smoothed out the sheets and complimented her on how well preserved they were after being manhandled by student and wind alike. The scissors he put under the counter. "I have a letter for you. *Another* from Riverton in Dakota Territory."

Compared to her last letter, this had arrived in record time. "Excellent. I'd also like a pound of your boiled candy, a yard of pink ribbon, and two tins of sardines."

In the Lord's goodness, she managed to ask for everything without even looking at the envelope. She did, however, slide it toward her and judge its thickness…

She'd made beans with the ham hock one of the parents had given her, and it sat reheating on the stove. Cornbread baked in the oven as Muriel began assembling her Valentines. Two of the students would be pleased to receive a card from her, but Lester Simmons would be furious that none of the students had left him one. "Mittens, how does one convince a bully that his nasty attitude and behavior does not inspire friendship?"

Her cat curled about her feet and slept. "At least you keep me warm, my lovely."

Once more, Pete's letter sat propped on her mantel unopened. She'd promised herself she wouldn't touch it until she'd made the four cards, had eaten her supper, and had done the dishes. Muriel trimmed the ragged ends of her rose-colored ribbon, divided it into four pieces, and pasted it onto a small heart cut out of a larger one.

The cornbread nearly burned before she remembered to take it out. It required extra bacon grease to make it slide down (oh, how she wished she had butter), and to reward her diligence with her project, Muriel added honey to it. Between bites, she worked to finish all four cards, satisfied but not impressed with the results. They looked as good as most of the ones made by her students, and with a boiled candy on every desk, the children might not even care about her offering. She signed them, "your friend" and rewarded herself with one of the candies and her letter.

Four sheets of paper filled the thick envelope. *Four!* Additionally, a small valentine card dropped to the table as Muriel unfolded them. She set aside the pages and snatched it up. Her first actual valentine. It didn't have a sentimental "To the one I love" or "Be Mine" message. Amid sprays of lilacs behind a red heart, a dove carried a little envelope sealed with another red heart in its beak. The card simply read: *Valentine Greetings*. On the back, Pete had written, *My best wishes for a lovely day. Pete Donaldson.*

"Mittens… it's perfect. Personal enough to know he wanted it to mean something but cautious, too."

Mittens yawned, stretched, and stalked off to his basket, apparently offended at the lack of card for him.

Rising, Muriel propped the card up on the mantel where she could see it from anywhere in the front room and returned to the table to read her letter. A minute later, she, the letter, and Mittens (along with another of her candies) sat curled up against her headboard, the lamp burning bright on her bedside table. She read.

February 6, 1886

Riverton, Dakota Territory

Dear Miss Darling,

Your letter arrived this morning—all the way from Wyoming in just a week! I credit the mild winter for such speed and efficiency, and the Lord for giving us such weather. The trains and stages have little to impede their progress right now.

Though I ached to begin writing this letter the moment I finished reading yours, I forced myself to put away my pen (after setting down the date) and pick up Emerson's Essays. Intellect is an excellent one, and I see why you found a parallel with Emerson in John's observation.

You also had an interesting observation. I have not yet seen Abe, but I look forward to sharing your insights on self-confidence being the primary attraction in a man (when compared to height, at least). I wonder if a similar lesson lies nestled into almost any insecurity. My mother would say yes. I distinctly remember her telling me when I was quite small, "Peter, you are a son of the King of Kings. That means you are to be humble, for you are not the King Himself, and confident because your Father is the King and will protect you against all manner of things."

Mittens kneaded her shin as she flipped pages and continued reading. Stories of a card game gone wrong and the busted lips and black eyes that followed. At least Pete wasn't a part of that. Since another boiled candy in one night would be excessive, when her stomach growled, not happy that she hadn't had a second bowl of beans, Muriel crawled from bed, made herself another honeyed square of cornbread, and carried the whole thing back to bed. Her mother would be scandalized.

"If you're well enough to sit up and take sustenance, you're well enough to do it at the table."

According to Tilly, many women enjoy political discussions, although she admits that most of her acquaintance do not. Around here and down in Nebraska, President Cleveland's continual attempts to limit citizens' encroachment on native lands is a topic guaranteed to spark heated discussions among men and women alike. Even those sympathetic to the Indians and all they have endured realize the devastation it will cause to the beef industry if cattlemen are not allowed to graze their herds in Indian occupied territory.

Is this a subject of concern in Casper? Is it something of which you have an opinion? My ledgers hold opinions vastly different from my sense of "what I would that others do to me." Both war for and against the argument that mankind has conquered lands from the beginning of time, and even under God's directions sometimes. What would you say to that argument? If Wyoming were a state, would you vote for or against our president's policies. (I am correct that Wyoming gave women suffrage some years ago, am I not?)

And on that subject of suffrage, where do you stand? There is one woman in Riverton who is a keen supporter of the Women's Christian Temperance Union because she sees it as the first step toward universal women's suffrage in the United States. Her husband would be terrified if he thought her ideas worth a second thought. I don't doubt that she might be correct. As the temperance movement seems to have sprung from the abolitionist movement, it seems a natural progression.

Tilly just brought me a cup of coffee and a slice of pie—some sort of squash that still tastes like a pumpkin pie. She asked what I wrote about, and when I told her, she suggested that I should also give you my opinions on the subject.

I am of the opinion that when it comes to branches of the government that might restrict or preserve personal freedoms, anyone should have a vote. But when it comes to laws affecting real property only landowners should be allowed those votes. The unchecked taxation of property by vote of those who will only benefit from the revenue seems a dangerous route. Some might say it is easy for me to have this opinion in my position, but I can only defend myself thusly. My father taught me to despise the idea of property taxation before he ever owned an acre of his own. He opined that if a man is taxed on the money he earns and then on what he spent that money on, it is a double taxation. That one could be taxed on an annual basis for something meant only that the man did not own that property—he rented it from the government.

I agree with him in many ways, but I recognize that there are things that are easiest when funded by property taxes such as city improvements, police, sheriff, and fire brigades. If a town needs a mayor, it must have a way to pay for one (in the case of it being a full-time position, anyway). But for someone who has nothing to lose to determine how much I or any landowner should have to pay, that is something I cannot agree with.

Now, I have taken up much of my paper with politics. No matter how small I write, there is not much room left. I think I'll end on a less divisive note. Out the window, enormous storm clouds gather off to the west. I don't expect much to come of them. Many times this winter, we've seen fearsome-looking storms appear and disappear almost as quickly. Tilly says they must be female clouds because they can't make up their minds. If they were men, they'd bluster and roar and make nuisances of themselves.

Missy has stepped into the room to beg a bite of my pie. I think her mother has forbidden her a second piece. I gave her the smallest bite possible and sent her off again. But I wonder if I did the right thing. What do you think? If she were your daughter, would you feel undermined? Would the fact that I didn't know for certain that this is the case make a difference?

And what are your thoughts on children? I'd love a house overrun with them, but I'm not sure I'd wish that on a wife. What is the balance there? My best wishes for what I hope was a lovely Valentine's Day. I am off to town to see if Thom Greigson still has cards for sale. If there isn't one in this envelope, it is because I failed in my quest. Please accept my thoughts and prayers in lieu of pretty cards in that instance.

Yours most cordially,

Pete

Amazement, fury, agreement, confusion all roiled within her. Had she opinions on politics? Most certainly. On suffrage? Indeed! On taxes, the displacement of Indians, and even temperance she could pontificate for weeks.

Despite that, she held the pages clutched to her chest, closed her eyes, and tried to breathe in some scent of Pete's home. All she smelled was paper and the lingering scent of honey, likely on her fingertip somewhere.

Mittens hopped up, sat down and stared at her. "I wish I had time to send him a card, but tomorrow is Valentine's Day. Too late, I suppose."

Mittens licked his paw in a show of utter indifference.

"Then again, late, as Chaucer informs us, is better than never."

With that, she hopped up and went to stoke the fire in the other room. She had another card to make—something a little more special this time.

Chapter Six

February 18, 1886

Pete Donaldson needed a bath. Lying in bed might not usually create a desperate need for bathing but doing so with a raging fever for several days... did. Weak as the proverbial kitten, he'd promised Tilly that if she got the men to carry the water, he'd bathe. The thought sent shivers through him. And with the ruckus the men were making hauling those buckets into the washroom, he suspected he had only one or two passes before she knocked on his door.

The knock sounded before he'd finished that thought. Tilly stuck her nose in the door but kept her eyes averted. "Are you ready to shuffle down to the bath?"

"After the men have gone. It's bad enough I must sacrifice my pride before you."

"They've just gone out."

That didn't sound right. Hadn't he heard them go *toward* the bathroom? If she had something up her sleeve…

The door pushed open wider, and Tilly stepped in. "Let's go. You lean on me if you need help."

He would *not* need help. No, no he would most certainly not. Pete stood on wobbly legs and tried to pull on a dressing gown. Instead, he got one arm in and used his other hand to hold it close around him. His right arm shot out to hold onto the post at the foot of the bed as the room spun in lazy circles.

Tilly stepped close and draped his other arm around her shoulder. All hope of semi-modesty vanished, but at least she could keep her eyes forward. A nightshirt didn't offer enough coverage for his comfort. "All right. Let's shuffle you down to the tub."

At the bathroom door, Tilly slipped out from under his arm and pulled a packet from her pocket. "What's that?"

"Epsom salts. Doc said it was good for soaking the cloths we used to try to bring down Wes' fever, so I thought soaking *you* in it might be a good way to help keep your fever down."

He eyed her. "Have you been soaking cloths in it for me?"

Into the tub went the salts and out of the bathroom went Tilly. "I'll assume yes to be the appropriate answer, then."

Undressing took far more effort than it should have, but the water was still nice and hot when Pete slipped into it. He reached up onto the shelf beside the large, metal tub and pulled down one of Tilly's knitted cloths and a cake of soap. Growing up, they'd had flannel cloths—two pieces stitched together with embroidery of some kind. But Tilly's knitted cloths had enough texture to work loose the dirt from a long day's ride. *Or a week's illness.*

Just as the water began to cool enough to urge him out of it, a knock jolted him from thoughts of how he could make his illness a semi-entertaining story for Miss Darling. Abe's voice called out to him. "Need more hot water? Tilly sent me with another bucket for you."

Pete scooted as far back against the slanted end of the tub as he could and draped his towel over the top. "Come in."

A shuffle, a rattle, and finally Abe entered, a bit of cooler air following him. The house must need fuel in the stoves. He'd ask Abe to see to them.

"Feelin' better?"

Pete nodded and tried to keep his towel covering what he could without it dipping into the water. "Some. Weak, though. Probably couldn't mount Squanto if I tried."

As Abe pulled a plug from the bottom of the tub, he shook his head. "We need to set something like this up in the bunk house—would save hours of haulin' back and forth. We could even run the pipe off to the garden."

"That's where this one goes. I hope to put a pump in here, so we only need bring in hot water to keep us from freezing."

Abe glanced around the room. "There's space for a small stove. You could heat water there and it wouldn't be much work at all. Could double for wash day, too."

That did it. He'd order a stove and start work the minute the weather allowed for him to cut a hole in the roof. "Good suggestion. I'll rig lines she can hook up back and forth across the walls as well. It'll save having them in the kitchen and my shirts smelling like bacon."

Abe shrugged, plugged up the tub, and poured the hot water in. Peter squirmed a bit as it grew almost uncomfortable, but it would cool soon enough. "Thanks, Abe. Can you do one more favor?"

"Come help you out again?"

"I hope not, but if you'd be around in case, I'd appreciate that, too. No, would you stoke some fires in the house. It felt a bit cool when you came in."

"Might just be you. Feels fine to me. Your fever back?" The short man eyed him. "Should we call Doc out again?"

"Could just be that this room is that much warmer with all the hot water. I'll see when I get out. Thanks."

This time, Pete took the time to scrub up well, waited only until the water started to turn lukewarm, and hauled himself out again. It took all his strength, but he managed to wrap his dressing gown around himself and tie it. Dressing again? Well, that might have to wait until he'd had a nap.

Think I'll leave that part out of my letter to Miss Darling, but describing our new bathroom and laundry room might be of interest. Did I assure her that I wasn't looking for a replacement for Tilly? I should ask. He'd meant to, and perhaps when he wasn't so exhausted he'd know the answer, but in that moment…

February 27th

The frigid air of an oncoming storm buffeted Pete and Squanto as they rode into Riverton. He'd attempted church on Sunday and had nearly regretted it on the ride home, but Monday he'd awakened feeling like his old self. So, when he awoke that morning feeling finer than a frog's hair again, he'd eaten, taken a short ride around the ranch just to be sure he didn't tire more than he thought he would, and then took off for Riverton. He could chat with Dirk at the bank for an hour or two if that extra ride wore him out early.

Nothing would keep him from Riverton, though. He'd stay with Dirk and Deborah and sleep on their parlor floor before he'd miss the ride, much less the possibility of another letter from Miss Darling.

Had the valentine been too much? Would she tell him if it had? Should he ask? That thought prompted him to shake his head. No, he might ask if she wrote something that indicated discomfort, but borrowing trouble only put you in debt to a ruthless lender.

Squanto tried to work up to a canter now and then, but Pete kept him back to a trot. Walking would be best, but after so little exercise lately, he didn't blame the animal. "You can gallop when we near home—just for a short bit. I'll get Kurt to take you out tomorrow."

The fact that the roads weren't packed with snow made the trip take half the time it usually did. Though the wind tried to fight them every step of the way, the ground cooperated. Squanto picked up pace just as they entered the outskirts of town, and Pete didn't stop him. He wanted to get to Greigson's, too.

A wagon stood out front of the mercantile, its bed half-full of various supplies. James Gutermann must be gearing up for the drive. That man had waited too long one year and had paid nearly double what he should have. Since then, he went overboard in the other direction.

Pete hadn't tethered his horse before James and Tom Greigson came out, arms loaded with bags and boxes. Tom nodded his hello and called out, "Good to see you in town on Sunday. Heard you were at death's door."

"No one answered, so I came home."

Under cover of the men's laughter, Pete allowed them to load the wagon as he regaled them with the lesser of his embarrassing illness stories. From his delirious moment when he thought Missy was a calf in his room to how Tilly had played a trick on him. "I took two bites of that soup and was stuffed. She didn't admit that I'd fallen asleep for just a few minutes after finishing a full bowl until I wondered aloud if I should force myself to eat more so I'd get my strength back."

"Well, I've had another one of those letters from Casper here for a few days now. No one's been in to get it. Saw you at church and tried to hurry over to get it, but you were gone before I got back."

James looked mildly interested. Few bachelors in those parts received much personal correspondence. Still, he hoisted himself up onto the seat and waved before setting off again. "Glad to see you out and about, Donaldson."

Pete followed Tom inside and requested a few boiled candies while he waited for Tom to retrieve the letter. Would it be disingenuous to suggest he should get home before he taxed his strength? After a few seconds of pondering, he decided it wouldn't. Sunday had proven that he could be wrong about how well he truly was. Of course, the most important thing was the sooner he got home, the sooner he could read her letter.

"Here you go…" Tom pushed the letter across the counter before asking, "And how many candies did you think you wanted?"

"Just a handful. Something to suck on until I get home and a couple for Missy."

As he dug a small scoop into the jar and settled the candies on paper, wrapping them into a resealable packet, Tom rambled about various happenings around town. Pete counted out three cents for the sweets. Three for a penny.

"I added an extra for Tilly." Tom shook his head. "Amazing how her girl has grown. Seems like Benjamin died only last month, and now his girl is what… four?"

"Nearly five I think." Pete popped a candy into his mouth and tucked the flap back into the improvised bag.

"Some thought you'd marry Tilly after a spell."

That candy tried to escape into his lungs. Coughing and sputtering, and then coughing enough to mean business, Pete begged for a cup of water and shoved that candy into his cheek before speaking. "I…" He coughed again. "I hope you'll put a stop to that kind of talk if you hear it. Don't want to lose my housekeeper in a bid to ward off gossip."

Desperate to go before things got more awkward, Pete tucked the letter into his pocket and grabbed his hat. "Better head out. That coughing about did me in, and I've got a ride to go. Thanks for the water."

"Come back when you can stay for a while. We've missed you around town."

That made no sense at all. Pete rarely spent time in town. He'd made it halfway home before the desire to tear open that envelope and the reason for Tom's words blended into understanding. "He's suspicious, Squanto."

The horse flicked his tail in acknowledgment but continued his steady pace toward home. That seemed like reason enough for Pete to pull out the letter and pry it open. A gust of wind suggested that might not be such a good idea after all.

But the moment he arrived back at the ranch, Pete sent Squanto into the barn and asked Bob to unsaddle him. "Need to rest."

"You look better'n you did after church on Sunday."

Escaping Bob's observations took nearly as long as evading Tilly's insistence that he eat something, sit by the fire, and a host of other things he couldn't remember. Pete shook his head until she stopped jabbering and then said, "I need to lie down. Can you keep Missy at bay for about thirty minutes."

"Sure, sure. I thought you looked better than on Sunday but…"

"I am. Just trying to be sure I don't overdo it." Truth nudged his conscience and he added, "And I have a letter to read."

"From your darling?" Anyone who didn't know Tilly well wouldn't see the hint of a twist of her lip at that one, but Pete did.

"From *Miss* Darling." But it worked. Tilly called for Missy to help her dry dishes, leaving Pete free to snatch up a cookie and head back to his room. His study called to him, but despite not feeling sapped of all strength, he suspected he'd want a nap.

The old blue quilt had been removed from the bed and his mother's Indian Wedding Ring quilt lay across it. A subtle hint? Of that, Pete had no doubt. He flicked back the covers and found fresh sheets, too.

Propped up with every spare goose feather pillow they had, Pete worked open the envelope, pulled a thick sheaf of papers from it, and flipped through quickly. Five sheets! The date stumped him. February thirteenth *and* fourteenth.

As he unfolded them and smoothed them, a small card slipped from between two sheets. Pete set aside the letter and examined the card. Two layers of paper—one creamy and thick like her writing paper, the other thinner and mottled. They'd been stitched together with a purplish-red thread. Swirls of more purplish-red created leaves and vines around the corners, and in black ink he read: *And now abideth faith, hope, charity, these three; but the greatest of these is charity. I Corinthians 13:13.*

"I suppose that answers my question about the appropriateness of that valentine…"

With the card lying against his mother's quilt, he relaxed against the pillows and began reading.

Casper, Wyoming

February 13th and 14th

That "and 14th" had been squeezed into the margin and trailed up the side a bit.

Dear Mr. Donaldson,

> *Your letter arrived today and is proof of the marvel of modern speed and efficiency. When your valentine slipped out and onto the table, I couldn't have been more surprised or delighted. This is the first valentine I have ever received, and it came after a long afternoon of cardmaking with my classroom and an even longer evening making four more cards for students who wouldn't be receiving any if I didn't. In fact, I did not allow myself to open your letter until I had made those four cards and the cornbread for my dinner. Alas, that cornbread was nearly charred and required a significant amount of bacon grease and honey to choke down. Both times, but I'll get to the second piece in a moment. I forgot all about it in my eagerness to finish those cards and read your letter.*
>
> *By the time I'd finished your letter, I knew I wanted to send a card as well, belated though it may be. Alas, a schoolteacher cannot walk into a store and purchase a single valentine. You can imagine the gossip and/or rumors that would follow. I decided at once to make one. This is where I now endeavor to forgive you the fallout of your gift. Are you prepared to learn what you did to me?*
>
> *I made your card first. Please take note of that adjective. It set me up for a world of work and worry. I had my usual paper and scraps from the cards I made. Thanks to spilling my tea, I discovered that tea-dyed paper looked nice, so I soaked the whole thing and let it dry to give it color. Meanwhile, I went down into my cellar and pulled out a jar of pickled beets. I've been craving them for weeks, and using the purple from the beet to draw onto the papers worked well. I ended up using my old dip pen for this. I suspect that card smells of vinegar. Perhaps it will protect you from accusations of receiving perfumed letters from women?*

Pete couldn't resist sniffing. It might have been his imagination, but he did think he caught the faintest trace of vinegar. *I wouldn't have minded perfume, but…*

The letter continued describing the way she'd marked stitching holes with a ruler and pencil, stitched around the card with a running stitch and then back again to create a solid border. He examined it closer and saw she'd also added a couple of leaves to one corner. "Hmm… missed that at first. To be fair, they did blend with the thread and the vines she'd drawn on the brown "tea paper." That had been clever.

When he turned over the second sheet, he choked on a bite of cookie.

> *This is where I scold you. How could you do this to me? Because, of course, once I'd made yours, I felt compelled to make sixteen more. Yes, sixteen. It is just twenty minutes to midnight, and if I have any hope of getting this letter to you in the month of February, I must write tonight, but I now have tea-stained paper drying. For my students, I've chosen I John 4:8. God is love. This will take less time than a longer verse. I have also chosen to do a simple running stitch and tie the bottom corner in a bow. The threads for those are drying as I write.*
>
> *One good thing has come from this, however. It is possible that now those four students won't realize that I am the one who gave them the other card. I created block-like letters for it, in case disguising my penmanship would help, though I didn't think it would. I now have some hope of success.*

Tilly interrupted with a sandwich. "Are you hungry? I made a sandwich just in case." *You want to know what is in my letter.* Pete thanked her and asked if there was any milk. "My, yes. We're still getting plenty from Dolly and Henny both. I'll get you some."

She'd gone and returned in less than a minute. "Anything interesting in your letter?"

"Speaking of milk, it sounds like Miss Darling doesn't have access to good milk and butter. She mentioned using bacon grease to soften her cornbread." He found the passage and handed it over. "Blames me for overcooked cornbread, too."

A slow smile grew about Tilly's lips. "I don't get the notion that she's usually a distractable person." After a thoughtful pause, she read something again, let that smile grow, and passed back the letter. "If my son or brother got a letter like that, I'd say the lady was sweet on him."

Something about Tilly's words didn't quite ring true, but it wasn't until he'd read the entire thing three times, polished off his sandwich and milk, and gazed at the little "valentine" for far too long that he realized what it was. *Most folks don't write this much when they hardly know one another. The situations aren't parallel.*

He fingered the card. *But I'll concede things could be… hopeful. I wonder if she likes music.*

Chapter Seven

May 1886

Letters chugged their way across the prairies, pounded their way from station to town, and then back again through the long, winter months. Several times, Pete considered trying to make the trip to Casper to meet Miss Darling, but each time he dismissed it. Tilly hinted that if Jack could make it, surely, he could, but he merely teased her about wishing to marry him off before someone tricked them into matrimony and ignored the temptation with remonstrances to himself of, "You don't know her well" or "It's much too soon."

But despite those thoughts, he wondered just when he'd know he should meet her. *Once we meet, anything could change. We may find ourselves repulsed by each other, or perhaps only one of us might be. We may find that we converse better on paper than in person. Initial awkwardness is to be expected, but…*

So, each time he began a letter, he considered saying something, and each time he didn't. The Lord would show him—somehow. Someway. Someday.

Two weeks before the men began the big roundup and branding, while Pete loaded the chuck wagon and saw to chores around the ranch, Tilly went to town to retrieve the last of his supplies as well as enough to keep those staying behind well fed. She pulled into the yard waving an envelope like a banshee trying to scare off some innocent in the forest.

"It's here! I think that's the fastest one yet!"

Pete strode out and accepted it with as much nonchalance as he could muster. "Only stands to reason that they could come faster when the railroad crew has repaired the winter damage to rails and doesn't have any shoveling to do."

"Well, I'll get the guys to help. You go read and write that response. You might still be gone when the next one comes through."

The words stung more than he would have imagined. Perhaps he should have protested. But he didn't. Instead, he strolled inside and set himself up in his study with a refreshing glass of ginger water and a few cookies. There were times he could swear he smelled flowers when he opened her letters, but a second whiff always came up short.

She wrote of the beautiful prairies, the farmer's children who stayed home to help their parents and the town children who would only get ahead.

> *Sarah's family returns to their farm as soon as the snow melts enough to plow. But she walks into town two afternoons a week to go over her lessons with me. John finds things to do around the classroom on those days. They think they are subtle, but young love and subtlety are not friends.*
>
> *At eighteen, I would have thought it romantic to see a girl of fourteen so deeply attached to her young man. I would have cheered for them and prayed that they could be together always. It's strange how I'd forgotten what a silly romantic little thing I was. But I'm past twenty-eight now. Fourteen years her senior. She seems so incredibly young, and he has such a promising academic future ahead of him. Is it wrong to try to keep him from realizing that if he went to Yale or Harvard, he would have to leave her behind? Why do I fear he would choose her, instead?*

Pete reread the paragraphs twice, his eyes searching to see if his first impression were true and accurate. A smile formed. "Dear, Miss Darling... I hear it in your tone. You are still a romantic at heart. Your age and position have taught you prudence in how you express it, but...."

The next paragraphs spoke of a series of sermons their minister had begun, a picnic where a cowpuncher had proposed to her in front of everyone and then pleaded with her to refuse.

> *It was a dare! Can you imagine anything so ridiculous and uncouth? If it hadn't been so funny, I would have been mortified. Oh, the relief in that man's eyes when I assured him that I had no intention of accepting such a proposal! One of the other women there said that she would have expected I'd jump at the chance while it was offered. And that's when suspicions I've had were confirmed. This town really does assume that if a woman is unmarried, it is because she has never had the opportunity of marriage. And that, of course, made me think of you.*
>
> *That does not read well! Let me explain. I realized that you might be under the same misapprehension that because I have not yet found a man to marry, no man has ever offered. I now have had three offers. The first was by proxy when I was sixteen. My brothers gave him a sound thrashing, but I do believe Earnest was in... well, earnest. And on the train to Cheyene, we were stranded just west of Chicago for a whole week. In that time, a seminary student decided that since a wife is a beneficial commodity to ministers, and since we had managed to remain pleasant through such an ordeal as camping out beside a railway for the better part of a week, I would be a suitable choice. I told him I was a Quaker.*
>
> *I am not proud of that lie. It was immature and unkind of me, but he was quite sincere, even going so far as to assure me that he felt certain he would learn to love me... someday. I will never forget his words. "Muriel, darling—" (yes, he did that. Can you imagine? I didn't know if he was being tender*

or formal!) "You're not unattractive; you are intelligent and kind. We may serve the Lord together while we pray He will knit our hearts as one." How could I have refused such a sincere, endearing offer? So, in my cowardice, I concocted the Quaker story and told him I would be speaking at a meeting in Omaha. That solved my dilemma, for he had already waxed quite eloquent on the evils of women usurping the roles of men in the churches.

By this time, Pete's laughter filled most of the house. Great tears rolled down his cheeks as he imagined a woman with sparkling eyes and an impish smile hidden behind demure lips that refused to mock a man's sincere faith. "But you wanted to, Miss Muriel Darling… you most certainly wanted to."

Even before finishing the letter, Pete pulled out a piece of paper and began writing as if in the middle of the forthcoming missive. *I believe you may be the woman for me. Time will tell…* He chose his words with care, but a new determination filled him as he wrote.

As for your seminary student, I am confident that he was being formal. I can say this with great assurance, because in his position, I would never allow a woman to doubt my meaning. A simple two-letter word is all it would take to ensure that you could not mistake his meaning. But since he did not say, "Muriel, my darling," I am confident in his being formal and correct rather than affectionate. I do not believe you left a broken heart that would later be crushed by railway wheels.

With that waiting for him, Pete returned to Miss Darling's letter with an eager eye and anticipation filling him.

I may have also put myself in some small amount of danger. Some of the men of the town have taken to circling my house a few times before going home at night. Here is how it happened:

One of my sweetest little girls, Rosie, came to school on Monday morning favoring her arm and sporting a bruised cheek. I was tempted, I assure you, to march to her home and give her father a piece of my mind. However, I also knew that it would likely mean he took a piece. That man is a brute. So, instead I helped her fashion a sling and stepped out to go see what the sheriff might be able to do about it. In case you are curious, the answer is nothing. They cannot interfere with the discipline of a child. I agree with them. They can't and shouldn't. But this isn't discipline. It's brutality!

All went well until he stumbled into my classroom shouting and jerking at her sore—likely broken—arm. Apparently, she hadn't done some chore of hers well enough to suit his drunken inspection. How she could be expected to do much at all, I can't imagine. One of our other girls had been writing her lessons for her all morning.

Well, I stood up to him. I shook every second of it, I assure you, but I put myself between Rosie and her father and ordered him from my classroom. John must have decided things were going to get particularly nasty, because he dashed out the side door and returned with the sheriff. In the interim, I informed Mr. Kapinski that I did not allow disruptions in my classroom and that if he had issues with his children, he could deal with them at home.

This is a perfect example of my being more intelligent than some in my family might give me credit for. You see, he had shifted his anger from Rosie to me until I mentioned her again. Then his original anger at her flared once more. I took that as evidence of his distractibility and gave him a dressing down that I still can't remember. Sarah said I hardly took a breath from beginning to end. He shouted, railed, stormed—you've never seen anything like it. But when Rosie bumped her arm on my desk and whimpered, his attention was diverted once more. He reached around me to grab her again, and I slapped him. Just then, the sheriff came in and I accused him of taking liberties in my classroom in front of all the children. Every one of them corroborated my story. The sheriff hauled Mr. Kapinski out of there and with his anger fully settled on me, Rosie hasn't suffered any further abuse that I know of.

So far, he hasn't physically assaulted <u>me</u>, but my cat is missing. I suspect foul Kapinski play. And my outhouse was destroyed. The men are making me a new one now and patrol the area each evening. We can't prove anything, but…

Pete clutched the paper so tightly that it wrinkled. His eyes flashed, and his teeth clenched. "This kind of nonsense is unacceptable!" His voice reverberated through the empty house. After a deep breath, a long drink of ginger water, and a prayer for wisdom, Pete finished the letter. His reply formed with swift fingers and sloppier-than-usual handwriting.

May 1886

Riverton, Dakota Territory

My Dear Miss Darling,

Will it amuse you to learn that the entire ranch has ridden to town once or twice a day for a week—even knowing the likelihood of a letter before yesterday was highly unlikely? My employees enjoy it immensely when a new letter of yours arrives. They say I am distracted, and they can get away with neglecting their duties in favor of a card game or two.

This time I was particularly eager to receive it because the roundup starts in a couple of days, and I may spend some weeks in the saddle. It was a mild winter, though, so one hopes not.

Afterward, I make for my ranch in Nebraska to see how the cattle fared there as well as to see Jack and Hazel. Her time should be here any day now, so I hope to meet the baby, too.

His letter rambled, describing his preparations for the trip, what they did all day and how the branding would go. He even shared the things he thought Tilly might do while he was gone. He described his ride across the prairie, his swim in the river. But with every word, his concern grew until he could resist no longer.

I am aware that I have no claim on you or any right to make requests, but I cannot help myself. Please be careful. I admire your willingness to protect your student. It speaks well of you as a person and as a Christian woman. But injury to you will not likely prevent future injury to her. I wouldn't like to think of losing the chance to meet you someday.

Pete stared at his words, reconsidering each one until he decided not to second-guess himself. "It's time to hint at my hopes for the future." His pen scrawled across the page again until he reined it in to create smaller words that took up fewer sheets. He told her of Missy's cleverness—how the girl had almost taught herself how to read and of Abe's new sweetheart.

Mary is a lovely young woman who couldn't possibly be five-feet tall. She loves him <u>and</u> his stature. He credits you and your advice with making the difference. Learning to accept himself as having been made exactly how the Lord wanted him and exactly as the woman the Lord had in mind—presuming that the Lord wanted that for him—would want him changed his entire attitude. He has slowly developed a genuine confidence and comfortableness. I believe that is what Miss Mary finds most attractive. However, I also believe she finds someone who doesn't tower over her to be pleasant as well.

Alas, I must go now. Is it too much to admit that I find it harder and harder to end each letter? And why do your letters to me feel shorter and shorter when the page count clearly indicates that they are longer? I packed several sheets of paper and pencils. I thought I might have stories I wanted to share. Fatigue each day ensures that by the time we return to the ranch, we forget half what occurred. I'll mail a letter the moment I return.

Yours truly,

Pete Donaldson

Chapter Eight

May 29, 1886

The stack of essays on "kindness" seemed to grow rather than shrink with each one she read. Miss Darling pulled John's from the pile with less enthusiasm than usual and propped her head in her hands as she read it. Somewhere in the middle, a sound jerked her from her budding dreams of him mentioning her in his valedictorian speech at Harvard, Princeton, even *Oxford*.

Her eyes rose and her hands dropped to her lap. "Hello. How may I help you, Mr.…?"

"Donaldson. Peter Donaldson."

Her throat went dry, and her eyes widened. "You came?" The words came out strangled and hoarse. "Did I miss a letter?"

Peter Donaldson stood before her, hat in hand, a smile on his lips, and much more handsome than she'd ever allowed her to imagine. "You didn't. I was in Omaha ready to get on the train to Fargo and found myself purchasing coach fare to Casper instead." He set his hat down leaned against the desk, his face only a couple of feet from hers. "You see, there's this schoolmarm here in town who has been keeping me awake at night."

As much as she tried, Miss Darling couldn't lower her gaze. "And why would that be?"

His eyes darkened with intensity she hadn't expected. "That's what I'm here to find out." When she didn't reply, he stood and retrieved his hat again. "Will you be done soon? I thought I'd ask if I could escort you home."

"I can leave now. I was avoiding leaving and—" She swallowed hard and tried again. "I was finishing this here, but I can do it later this evening." Miss Darling fumbled as she tried to shove everything into a neat pile, but it only made everything a mess. With strict orders to gather herself together, Miss Darling reordered her stack of books, slid the papers into her portfolio, and reached for the pile. But Pete Donaldson had them in his arms before she could hope to.

"Which way, Miss Darling?"

She led him outside, locked the door, and pulled her poke bonnet on before turning. "We must walk through town. *All the way through town*," she added with emphasis.

"I enjoy a walk, don't you?"

"Yes…" She struggled with each step, wondering how to explain that he couldn't stay without sounding as if she made more of the visit than she did. *Then again, what is he doing here?*

"Mr. Donaldson?"

"I'd prefer Pete—even Peter—but yes?"

She nodded. "I can do that." She tried the name on for size. "*Peter.* I think you should know. I am not allowed to have gentleman callers in my home." She swallowed hard and gave him an awkward smile. "I hope you understand."

"I'm pleased they're careful of your reputation, but it must be inconvenient for you."

Whatever is that supposed to mean? Before she could formulate some other response, John crossed the street. "Miss Darling! I—" He frowned at the sight of Peter. "I'm sorry. I didn't know you had company."

"This is Mr. Donaldson—a friend of Mr. Clausen's. You remember him, don't you?"

"Yeah. Nice fellow. We all thought…" John turned almost as red as Miss Darling and almost shook himself. "Anyway, that geometry problem. I got it. You see…"

It took more effort to pay attention to John's careful explanation of how he'd made an error at the x-intercept. Before she could admit she hadn't followed it, Peter asked a question—one that showed he understood enough of geometry to follow it backwards from the explanation and have a sense of what the boy was doing. Miss Darling just listened until John waved off and hurried down the street to the saloon.

"I've never seen him confide in anyone like that. It took months before he would answer questions in class."

"Well, you're right about him. He's a bright young man."

She sighed before she could stop herself. "And his father has kept him out of school twice as much as last year. I haven't had a single reply to any of my letters."

"They probably have benefactors they must contact—things like that." As they neared the edge of town, Peter crossed the street, knelt, and picked a few yellow columbines. As he passed them to her, he gave her an enigmatic smile. "A pretty woman should have flowers when they oblige."

Is that your way of telling me you don't find me repugnant or an overt way of trying to compliment me? The question reverberated in her heart, but Miss Darling managed only to thank him and ask about his trip.

"Roads are atrocious, but that's to be expected, I suppose." As they neared her house he added, "Are you allowed dinner in town? The hotel…"

"If I stay on the first floor, There can be no objection." She giggled before she could stop herself.

Pete held her books close to him and waited. "I'm not passing these to you until you tell me what amuses you."

"The man who owns the hotel has a spinster sister—in her forties, I believe. He wants her to have my position, but the parents won't hear of it. He'll probably begin a campaign to convince me that I wouldn't want to let a fine man like you go—before tomorrow!" Another giggle escaped despite herself. "You should have seen how angry he was when Jack took off and never came back. He glared at me for weeks!"

At her doorstep, Pete waited as she bustled around the little cabin, filling a syrup pitcher with the flowers, and retrieving her books. His eyes met hers and held. "I'll call for you at… six o'clock? Six-thirty?"

Miss Darling smiled and nodded. "I'll be ready by six. Thank you." When he didn't respond, she caught his eyes. "Yes?"

"No… thank *you*."

Once Peter left, Muriel stood in the middle of the room, her eyes on the flowers and prayed.

Pete strolled down the main street of Casper, heart light and soaring. *She's more than I hoped for, Lord. If Jack hadn't met Hazel first…* He crossed the street to his hotel and took the steps with a lilt to his feet and a smile in his heart. The proprietor met him at the desk.

"What can I do for you, Mr. Donaldson?"

"I wondered if I could reserve a quiet table for two. Miss Darling has agreed to join me for dinner."

"Miss—you don't mean. That is, I wasn't aware you knew our fine schoolteacher!"

Though tempted to toy with the man's expectations Pete simply nodded and took off for a stroll around town. His watch ticked past the minutes, but he didn't trust them. Surely, it had to be well after six! But the tiny clock's hands said twenty-past five. Still, he walked. Walked and prayed.

When will I know? I could stay a week or two or go home Monday as planned. We could write with greater understanding of one another. Or, if in a week, I find myself still inclined to think well of her, would it be foolish to take a risk and…

His rational mind drove away impatience. "Don't be rash. Marry in haste and all that goes with it."

The saloon beckoned. While whiskey held little interest for him aside from occasional drinks with his men, the music was lively and there would be sure to be a card game in progress—a fine way to pass the time while he waited to walk to Miss Darling's house. *She didn't offer for me to call her Muriel. Wonder why…*

But before he could settle himself against the wall behind a poker table, John waved at him—beckoned him to the bar. "Mr.... Donaldson?"

"You have a knack for names."

"I've always remembered things if I heard 'em or saw 'em. Just lucky, I expect."

Pete listened as John rambled. He finally understood what Jack meant about the boy's apparent dullness. Never had he seen someone give off such an appearance of being dull-witted while carrying on an intelligent conversation. *You'd be a force to be reckoned with at a university. The "country boy from the sticks" would take Yale by storm.*

That thought prompted Pete to ask, "What would you study if you could study anything?"

"Hmmm... I don't know" John picked up a glass and polished it. "Maybe law—no. Medicine would be good. The doc here is getting old. But theology... that would be a fine thing to learn, wouldn't it? To learn the Bible in the original languages." Before Pete could formulate a response, John kept talking. "Miss Darling was telling us about archaeologists who dig up entire civilizations and learn about the past. And she told us about people who study chemicals and new ways to use them. She thinks that in our lifetime people won't rely on animals for transportation. She says they'll have engines like a train but that run on roads like carriages—steam powered maybe. And flying—she thinks people will create flying machines. To learn to do things like that..."

The boy's insatiable thirst for knowledge—he'd never seen anything like it. *I never cared to learn that much. I learned for Mother's sake. Well, and because it's a wise use of one's time. John certainly never had a desire...*

That thought sparked a new one, and another. He checked his watch, talked some more, and then pushed himself away from the bar. "I've really enjoyed our conversation, but I'm expected at Miss Darling's in ten minutes, so I should go. I'd love to talk again if you have time."

John nodded and turned back to his work, but something caused him to hesitate. "Mr. Donaldson?"

"Yes?"

"Miss Darling. She's a fine woman—a kind and good person." He ducked his head a little before correcting himself. "That's because of Jesus, of course. I know that. But..." The boy lost all timidity and squared his shoulders. His eyes caught Pete's and held them fast. "I wouldn't want to see her hurt." When Pete didn't respond, he continued, faltering again. "When Mr. Clausen left..."

Indecision wracked him. Speaking to a boy before Miss Darling—impossible. But not reassuring him—inconceivable. He tried for a compromise. "All I can assure you of is that I came heart whole, and if I leave otherwise, I hope it is because I've lost it to her."

That compromise lacked substance, but it would have to do.

Candlelight, lovely china—finer than anything Muriel had ever seen in Casper—and Mrs. Thomlin on the piano in the corner playing Beethoven. *Mr. Thomlin has spared no inconvenience to create the perfect setting, and I sit here feeling utterly ridiculous.*

"—find myself in an awkward position, Miss Darling."

After a steadying sip of water, Muriel met his gaze and offered a slight smile. "Why is that?"

"Well, I am here for obvious reasons, but someone else has captivated my attention."

I should have known better than to hope. Her smile faltered, but she began nodding with slow, deliberate movements in a poor attempt to give her mind something to do.

"I blame you for it, of course."

"Me!" Muriel's eyes flashed and her lips pursed. "What could I possibly—?"

Peter's slow smile arrested her protest. It could have done dangerous things to her heart, that smile. "You introduced us."

She blinked. His words did little to enlighten her. After dabbing at her lips for something to do, she managed to murmur, "I'm sorry, but I didn't realize I had introduced you to anyone but—" This time, her eyes widened. "John." Her lips twisted before she could prevent it. "That was unkind, Mr. Dona—Peter."

"Was it? I thought you would be pleased to know of my interest in your favorite."

"I am, of course, but the way you worded it—captivated your attention, I believe you said. It was…"

Peter's ears flamed just seconds before his neck and face reddened. "I can see how that might sound a bit… *intimate.* Then again," His eyes met and held hers in his gaze. "I can't help but be encouraged that you found it a little… *disheartening?* Perhaps?"

She felt her own cheeks warm. "Perhaps…" Muriel gave a small cough and returned the conversation to its prior topic. "What about John has captivated you? Is he not a remarkable young man?"

"He is. And I've been praying about this for such a brief time that I cannot make promises…" Peter closed his eyes and paused as if in a brief moment of prayer. "But I also cannot imagine the Lord wanting anything else from me."

A dozen possibilities raced through her mind, all more exciting than the last. *Just how wealthy* are *you? I know you're successful, but… surely, you couldn't afford…*

"My father left money for my brother's education, should he decide he wished it. Unfortunately, John had no interest in anything but drinking, gambling, and unfortunate women."

She couldn't help but sigh. "How is it that so often brothers are such very different people? I've seen it many times."

Peter nodded. "As have I. As I said, Father left money for John's education, should he choose it. But since he is no longer with us—"

"You mentioned he'd run afoul of the law—conspiracy to kill you, wasn't it?"

"Yes." The pain in Peter's eyes showed a love for his brother that must speak well of the condition of his heart. "But he tried to escape. He was shot."

"I am sorry." No other words were necessary or appropriate. Muriel ached to reach across the table and squeeze his hand. But it would never do.

Several long seconds passed before he spoke again. "It may have been foolish." Peter shook his head with a decided snap. "That is untrue it *was* foolish, but I never lost hope that we could be the kind of friends that brothers *should* be. I never lost hope that the Lord would regenerate John's heart and make him into the kind of man I knew he could have been." Before she could find words that wouldn't cause deeper pain, Peter smiled up at her.

"I sound so morose. John made his choices. I must accept them for what they were. But now I have an educational fund that my father left for John that will never be used as it was intended unless…" The excitement in his eyes—Peter looked like a child incapable of keeping a secret. "We offered it to *another* John…"

She hadn't allowed herself to hope. It seemed unlikely that his cryptic words could have meant anything else, but until the moment Peter actually *said* he wished to help her John, Muriel hadn't genuinely believed it possible. "Are you aware of how expensive—?"

"I am."

"And," she couldn't help but add, "would you not rather use the money for your own children's educations?"

Peter seemed to consider her words more thoughtfully than she'd expected. For one wild, rash moment, she nearly pleaded with him to ignore her cautions and help John before he could change his mind. But he spoke first. "Miss Darling—"

"I would be pleased to have you call me by my given name, Peter."

"Would it hurt or offend you if I didn't?"

Muriel felt her eyes grow wide and relaxed them again. Though she shook her head, she found herself asking, "Why?"

"It's… personal. For now. It is out of no lack of desire for a continued and…*deeper* friendship, I assure you." As she tried to find a way to respond without showing her curiosity and disappointment, Peter spoke as if the conversation hadn't been derailed for a moment. "Miss Darling, I am not an extremely wealthy man. Though I suppose compared to some, I am. However, barring bank failure, I should be more than able to provide whatever educations my own children desire."

Her throat went so dry even a few sips of water did little to soothe it. *I can't help but hear more in his words than he says, Lord. What does it mean?*

Peter stood and offered his hand. "Shall we take a walk around town before I escort you home?"

Unable to eat another bite, she nodded and tried not to allow her disappointment to show. She failed. Peter's face fell. "If you would rather go home right off…" His ears reddened again. "I should say, I am in no rush to return to a lonely hotel room, but you have had a long day, so if you'd prefer me to take you straight home…"

"The moon is only at a crescent, or I'd suggest we walk to the river. It's a lovely walk in full moonlight, but…" Thankfully, he'd turned to ask Mr. Thomlin to put their supper on his bill and missed her flaming cheeks. *You've lost your mind!*

Chapter Nine

June 5, 1886

Two days—it was all Pete had left. He rose that Saturday morning still undecided as to what to do. Many options lay before him—two with promise. However, those two were so opposite that he found them difficult to decide which was best.

But by the time he drove through town in the buggy he'd hired, Pete had all but forgotten his dilemma. The bright, fresh day with its gentle breezes and the sun shining down on him seemed to shout, "Rejoice and embrace this day the Lord has given you." And Pete determined to do just that.

Muriel opened the door wearing a dress of pale pink—such a color as few women in Pete's experience wore well—her eyes shining with excitement and, he hoped, eagerness. She offered him a picnic basket and stepped inside to retrieve her bonnet and shawl. Her voice called out to him. "Isn't today lovely? I had expected our ever-inconvenient wind to blast through in the middle of the night, but this breeze is just refreshing."

He helped her to the buggy, settled the basket at their feet, and climbed up beside her. "Where shall we go?"

When she didn't answer quickly, his heart sank. *I should have scouted for a nice place while she worked.*

"I think perhaps the river would be nicest, don't you? We may find it difficult to find a place where half my students aren't trying to fish, but…"

Is the hesitation then because you didn't wish to have them intrude on our time? That could be promising…

"Perhaps the other side of the river?" She gazed at him with eyes that increasingly did unfamiliar but not unwelcome things to his heart. "If you didn't mind a drive, we could just travel upstream until we're well past any of the homes of my students…"

He clicked his tongue against his cheek and the horse shot forward. "Upstream it is!"

With such a long drive, he would have imagined ample opportunity to lay out his thoughts about their correspondence, but sitting in such close proximity, her hair occasionally blowing over his shoulder, all rational thought left him. Muriel seemed content to ride and enjoy the fine weather. Was she as intensely aware of him as he was of her?

A lovely, oversized cottonwood ahead sent him down the embankment and as close to the water's edge as he felt safe. "I'll check the bank."

"It should be fine here. I think they water the cattle nearby during roundups," she assured him. Her eyes widened in dismay. "I forgot the blanket!"

Pete pulled one from beneath the seat. "I asked for one at the hotel."

They ate fried chicken and apple tarts by the side of the river, and their former quiet disappeared in a round of stories of their childhoods, their daily lives, their hopes—dreams.

Twice Pete tried to speak. Both times his voice failed him. But as the sun settled lower and lower in the sky, and stomachs began to rumble for supper, Pete knew he needed to speak then.

"I have a—" His lip curled with distaste at his unfortunate beginning. "That is…"

"And here I thought we'd gotten past those awkward moments at last."

Her words had the intended effect. Pete nodded and tried again. This time, he didn't allow himself to over-think his words. "I leave on Monday when the stage arrives."

"Now you've spoiled everything." If she hadn't had a hint of a smile at one corner of her lips, Pete might have believed her.

"Oh?"

"I'd almost forgotten that you don't live here. I'd rather not be reminded of your absence."

It was as much encouragement as a woman could offer him, and it was exactly what Pete needed. "I can't hope that you've grown as fond of me as a woman should be for—that is —" He growled in frustration. "Miss Darling, I am asking you to marry me." As her eyes Pete realized she hadn't guessed his plans. "I know it's premature, but I won't be *able* to return until after we take the cattle to market in September."

The woman fidgeted, unwilling to look at him now. "I—"

But Pete reached to cover her hand to stop her and pulled back again. "I'm not asking if you care for me. I couldn't expect that so soon. I probably don't care for you as much as I should before proposing such a change in our lives, but I think I will. I see no reason that I wouldn't love you very dearly and in probably much less time than might be expected."

Once more, she tried to speak. And again, he stopped her. "Miss Darling, I'm offering an unconventional marriage. I'm offering to bring you home as my bride but not as my…" He struggled to find a word that would fully convey his meaning without the need for excessive and embarrassing explanations. "Wife?"

She had formed a reply. Pete saw it in her eyes. Instead, her forehead furrowed, her eyebrows drew together, and her lips parted and hung there for a moment. "I don't understand."

How could you? I hardly do. But Pete tried to find a delicate way to explain. "I thought perhaps we could marry and finish our courting as husband and wife. In my home. If it takes a month—six—a year. I would…"

Her cheeks flushed pink. Her eyelids dropped, and Muriel cleared her throat. "And you find that preferable to returning in that year's time?"

She isn't keen on the idea. I shouldn't be surprised. If she didn't grow to love me, I would have trapped her in an unwelcome marriage. Then again, she was considering that all girl's school. Marriage might not have been in her plans if things between us never formed into an attachment.

With that thought in mind, Pete tried again. "For me, yes. I wouldn't ask it of you if I didn't think it the most likely way for us to truly know each other. And…" He couldn't do it. It might be the argument that convinced or repelled her. Pete couldn't decide which.

"And?"

He shrugged. "It seemed the best solution."

Her lengthy silence hinted at a negative response, but her head began to nod slowly as she pondered his words. "We have proven ourselves congenial—friendly, even. It isn't likely that we would find ourselves unhappy, even if we never did develop something… *deeper.*"

"That was my thought!" His voice boomed over the water, and Pete flushed as he lowered his tone. "I didn't like to suggest that you should settle, however."

"No one could ever consider themselves 'settling' for you, Peter."

It sounded like a "yes." Pete held his breath as he waited to hear a definitive answer. After several long, agonizing seconds, Muriel frowned. "I need to pray about this. I…" She hesitated before asking, "If I said no, would you still write?"

His heart plummeted at no and bounced up into his throat at the catch in hers when she asked if he'd write."

"Miss Darling, I'll write until you say you'll be my wife, or you tell me never to write again."

Muriel paced her little cabin. From the front door to the stove, to her bed and back to the door. With each footfall she prayed. With each turn she changed her mind. Of course, she should marry him. She'd spent every afternoon and evening with him that week, often sitting right there in the schoolhouse until nearly bedtime before he drove her home and back making enough noise to ensure the town knew exactly when they had gone and when he'd returned. She'd enjoyed every moment with him and had regretted every, "Good night." That each one had lingered longer than the last hinted at true congeniality.

"But that doesn't help me now, Father. Please. What do I do? He's leaving in two days!"

Without knowing what else to do, Muriel pulled out pen and paper and began writing. She would ask Mother's advice. No, the letter wouldn't be posted before Muriel had to give her answer, but perhaps writing it would settle some of her questions.

June 6, 1886

Casper, Wyoming

Dear Mother,

I have a confession to make. For the past six months, I have been corresponding with a man in Dakota Territory. This week, he came to Casper to meet me, and he has proposed.

That is the short story. The long story will take too long for the purpose of this letter, but suffice it to say, we have discussed many things in our correspondence. Topics have ranged from faith (his is genuine and his doctrine sound), politics (I think I agree with much of his, though I do not know if he agrees with all of mine), education (he values it and is even willing to pay for John Camden's college training if we can secure Mr. Camden's agreement), and even books. He loves music, which surprises me for reasons I cannot explain.

I believe he is as fond of me as is reasonable in such a limited acquaintance. While we have written many long letters back and forth (I have a rather large stack tied with a ribbon, no less), and have spent every waking moment possible in deep conversation. Yet…

I do not know what answer to give him. If he lived nearby, I don't know that I could have known him better in these months. He would have come to town once a week for church. I might have seen him more often than that or perhaps not. I do not know. But I think there would have been more time to see him at his worst if he were nearby. Does that make sense?

His introduction came with excellent references from a cowboy I helped tutor last year. It was Jack who made the introduction. I have great respect for Jack Clausen, so if Jack says Peter Donaldson is a fine man, I believe him. My question is more regarding whether he is the right man for me.

When he first asked, I had every intention of saying no. I did not know him well enough to risk the sort of vulnerability that comes with marriage. However, he has offered an unconventional (as he put it) marriage in which we marry now, and he will court me until we're both ready to embrace more traditional roles as husband and wife.

Yes, Mother, my cheeks burn hot enough to fry eggs just writing those words. But I believe I can trust him to honor that, though I have no idea how it would work in practicality.

Please, Mother. Tell me what to do. Or failing that, give me reasons to consider or refuse the offer. Peter says he will continue to write, even if I should say no, until I tell him not to write any more. He did not say he loves me, but I am certain of his regard and affection at least. Not all women are so blessed.

Muriel ended the letter as she sipped chamomile tea and shared one of Peter's stories about how a dog chased a cat through the church and out again just as the preacher had commented about the world going to the dogs and how that phrase fit with the Jewish opinion of dogs.

She folded the letter and addressed the envelope but left a stamp off. If she decided in favor of marriage, she'd burn the letter and write a different one.

It took ages to settle into bed before she turned out her lamp and rolled onto her side. Muriel whispered, "What do I do, Father?" once more as she closed her eyes and tried to imagine packing up her little cabin and heading north to Dakota territory. She made her decision moments before sleep claimed her.

Chapter Ten

June 7, 1886

Miss Darling didn't give him an answer until Sunday night. They'd spent the day talking, laughing, and pretending a weight didn't hang over them. Pete tried to show her how to skip a rock. She beat him in a contest five to three. He'd protested, arguing that she'd deceived him, but the smile she tried to hide hinted that she hadn't minded his arm around her shoulder as he showed her the best way to hold the stone.

"And besides," she'd said by way of encouragement, "*my brothers have always insisted that I skip so well because I am much shorter than they are. I have an advantage.*"

He'd insisted she had skill, and her brothers were sore losers. That had earned him a squeezed arm and a stroll along the riverbank. If he were honest with himself, and Pete had no intention of that, he'd admit that he'd nearly lost his head and kissed her. But with a proposal hanging like the sword of Damocles between them, he'd managed to resist, a testament to God's work in his life for certain.

Everything pointed to a yes to his proposal, so when he'd seen her to her door on Sunday night, and her eyes had glistened in what little moonlight there was, he'd been stunned. She'd said no. *"Not yet, Peter. I cannot. It's a lifetime commitment to love, honor, and obey. I can honor and even obey, but I need more time to consider what a vow to love means. Can you understand that?"*

The melancholy that stole over him on his way back to the hotel pervaded his dreams and woke him at dawn. Of course, he understood her. Who could not? Nevertheless, the disappointment still held him in a strangle hold.

Pete's carpetbag sat ready for him to put in his nightshirt, brush, and other toilet articles. He pulled on his boots and coat, checked the mirror once more, and left the room. Another mirror in the hallway just before the stairs arrested his attention, however. He looked as though headed to a funeral. As much as he wanted to enjoy his disappointment, silly though that may be, Pete forced his features to relax and descended the stairs at a moderate pace.

Mr. Thomlin met him at the counter and accepted his key. "Leaving us so soon?" The question couldn't have been more ridiculous, and the man's flushed neck hinted that he'd realized it too late.

"I have a ranch to run, and if it doesn't rain soon, we'll be scrounging for water for our cattle."

"I've heard local men complaining as well as our farmers. My wife insists we pump to keep our garden growing, but I don't know…"

Though Pete wanted to remind the man that having water to drink wouldn't do them any good if they'd starved to death, he suspected it would only irritate. Instead, he asked for breakfast in the dining room and slid his hand across the highly-polished counter. "It's been a pleasure, Mr. Thomlin."

"You come back as soon as you can."

The words, "I doubt I can return before autumn," slipped out before he could stop them. And when the man's smile brightened a little, he allowed himself to admit that he expected he would then, though.

"Our Miss Darling is a fine woman. A man won't find better anywhere around these parts." A harumph from the room behind the counter hinted that Mrs. Thomlin didn't appreciate the inference that her husband's statement inspired. "An *unmarried* man that is."

Don't do it. You'll only make things worse. When Mr. Thomlin appeared to expect a response, Pete mumbled something about not disagreeing in the least and turned away before he gave away thoughts best kept private.

The stage wouldn't arrive until ten thirty-five, if one could expect it on time. That gave him a little more than an hour once he'd finished his breakfast and stepped out of the hotel. Despite doing everything he could to draw out the time, he could now sit on a bench outside the Sheriff's office, or he could take a walk. Think.

Decision made, Pete strode back into the hotel and requested to leave his carpetbag behind the counter. "I'll be back before the stage arrives. I need a walk before sitting cramped in that thing."

"Certainly, certainly. It being Monday, most of the womenfolk are outdoors doing the washing…"

As if he didn't know it. Pete managed to give the man as confused an expression as he could muster before exiting the building once more. What he'd intended as a leisurely stroll became a near jog by the time he reached the edge of town. In just minutes, he rounded the corner of her little cabin and found her stoking a fire under a large kettle. Two wash tubs stood on sawhorses, and a washboard leaned up against one.

Miss Darling exited with a bundle of sheets in her arms and began stuffing one in the first wash tub. Before she could retrieve the kettle, Pete had grabbed a potholder and hefted it. "Morning, Miss Darling."

"Peter!"

Her delight in seeing him soothed the chapped places of his dreams. She'd been truthful. Time had made her decision, not lack of interest. "I had an hour to squander, and my father taught me never to squander but to invest."

Laughter he hadn't heard enough of bubbled over as she eyed him. "And what are you investing in? Laundry tubs? Washboards?"

"I hope my future."

A blush stole over her cheeks, but rather than drop her gaze, she met his. Pete couldn't help smiling back at her. He probably looked a fool, but if a man wasn't willing to be a little foolish over a good woman, he should walk away. Shouldn't he?

After a few agonizing seconds, Miss Darling turned back to her work. She grated soap flakes into the tub and grabbed her washing pole. Peter almost missed her whispered, "I wanted to say yes."

It took everything he thought he had left in him to pick up the large kettle and carry it to the pump. He was wrong. After a few pumps, he managed to call over his shoulder, "You did the right thing. It's a serious commitment. You shouldn't have doubts."

That caught her attention. He knew it because when he turned back with the kettle, she stood there, pole in one hand and a bundle of sheets in the other. "You have no doubts?"

Pete sloshed water onto his boot as the realization came that he did have some doubts—minor, but they existed. "None that override my certainty—they're doubts about me rather than you."

Once more, Miss Darling began stirring and kneading the pot, this time with more effort. In seconds, she wiped perspiration from her forehead before plunging that pole deeper again. "About you?" Were the words whispered or gasped?

What Pete *wanted* to say was that if she married him, she wouldn't have to do this sort of back-breaking labor. However, even more than the manipulation behind such a comment, the truth that it meant Tilly would have to do the work for one more person stopped him. So, he poked another small branch under the spider and nudged it until it caught flame. Then he rose, dusted off his hands, and turned back to her. "Will I learn how to be a good husband before I disappoint you? What faults of mine need addressing first before you weary of me? Will years of bachelorhood make me unfit to share a life, and if so, what do I do to remedy it?"

This time, she dropped the pole altogether and stared. "Those are—but how did--?" She shook herself a little and poked at the washtub again. "I've mused over my equivalent to those same questions." She shot him a quick look before returning to her work. "Why did we have such different reactions then? You forged ahead. I withdrew."

Answer after answer pleaded for an audience with Miss Darling, but Pete shoved most aside. Only one was both honest *and* supportive of her decision, and he *must* support her if he ever hoped to win the trust he craved. He moved to her side and took the pole from her hand. "I'll stir. You rest. I only have a few more minutes before I should return."

"You don't have—"

"No, but I want to. As to your question, I think the answer lies in our positions. I entered our correspondence with a hope—a desire to know you and love you." Emboldened by how easy it had been to admit that, Pete smiled at her burning cheeks and continued. "As I wrote, I prayed for us to forge a sincere connection that would lead to that love. I pursued marriage from that first letter. It seems only right that any doubts I have about it would come from an acknowledgement of my faults—the knowledge that you would have reason for uncertainty."

The marriage vows whispered themselves in his heart, urging him to confess that he understood women to give up so much more than their hearts in marriage, but should he remind her of that? Wouldn't it give her more reason to resist?

Her hand closed over his and she pulled the pole away with the other. "Thank you for telling me that. I needed to know you'd prayed about us—about it being more than a convenience."

That confession loosened his tongue. With a warbler calling for a mate in the branches of a nearby cottonwood, Pete caught her elbow and allowed his thumb to smooth a wrinkle from her rolled-up sleeve. He dropped his hand and cleared his throat. "Miss Darling, when a woman marries, she vows to love, honor, and obey. Those vows ask a lot of women, and our laws give them little in return. I am quite aware that if you married me, you'd give up much of your legal independence."

As he spoke, Miss Darling's eyes went wide. "That's almost what I said in my letter to Mother." She dashed into the house and returned with a few sheets of folded paper. "Read it. You'll see. And maybe you'll understand."

Was it his imagination, or did she whisper, "Better than I do," under her breath?

Peter hadn't been gone for more than three minutes before Muriel knew what she had to do. She snatched up the kettle and poured the water onto her fire before dashing around the house. Picking up her skirts, she raced up the road, gaining on Peter's retreating figure but not fast enough. Calling out to a man in the middle of the street? Not seemly. Allowing him to ride off without… what? What would she do when she reached him?

At the hotel, she saw him climb the steps and disappear inside. That slowed her. The stage always stopped by the livery stable. Why would--? *No… is he staying?* Hope and dismay tumbled about in an internal brawl until Muriel couldn't imagine who would emerge triumphant.

Just as she decided to turn back before anyone else saw her (she had enough witnesses already, thank-you-very-much), Peter emerged and looked right at her. Muriel's run had become little more than a shuffle by that point, and she began rolling her sleeves back down her arms in a desperate attempt at some semblance of respectability.

His smile grew with every step, and he moved as if dust clouds didn't announce the stagecoach barreling down the road about a mile back. Instead, he strolled straight down the middle of the street and met her there.

We must look like the unlikeliest of combatants in a showdown.

"Careful, Miss Darling. If you tell me you've changed your mind, I might just kiss you right here in the middle of the street."

All breath rushed from her, and the buildings began to sway. Muriel shook herself. *No need to fall to pieces. It was just a saying.* The man's eyes, however, decried that assertion.

"I—" She what? That was the problem. Muriel didn't know why she'd been compelled to come. Her heart and just insisted and she'd obeyed. *Which is why one should never listen to one's heart without good reason.*

Hope. She'd come because she wanted them to hold onto hope once he'd gone. She swallowed, ordered those swaying buildings to cease their movement, and threw all caution to the wind. Right there in the middle of town for all the world to see, Muriel Darling rested her hand on Peter's chest and kissed his cheek. Mortified, she backed away and prepared to flee.

He caught that hand. Held it. The stage must have been much closer than she'd realized, because they heard the rumble of horses' hooves as it approached. Her mind filled in the slowing, the jangle of the coach and its moving parts, and even the dust that swirled toward them, but her eyes fixed on Peter.

One step and then another brought them close enough for her to see amber and even a little gold in the man's eyes. His thumb brushed her cheek just as it had her arm not twenty minutes ago. He bent, pressed his lips to her forehead, and lingered. Her breath caught and only released when he finally stepped back again. "I'll write, Miss Darling. Just you wait and see. I'm not one to give up easily. And when I'm not writing, I'll be praying."

Chapter Eleven

June 18th

A letter arrived for Pete the day after he returned home. Miss Darling must have posted it within hours of him leaving, though he doubted if it went out before the next day. That letter had tracked him all the way up from Casper, only a day's ride behind him, too.

Tilly still sulked around the house, muttering comments about "silly, silly women without any sense" whenever he happened to be in hearing. Pete hadn't decided if she said worse when he wasn't around or if she spoke mostly to soothe his pride.

A man shouldn't let his pride come before love, and that's what I want, Lord. I want to love her more than myself.

While Tilly scolded little Missy for being reckless in her "dancing" with her dolly, Pete slipped into his study and closed the door. Instead of his desk, he moved to the chair by the window and cranked that window open as wide he could manage. *And thank You Lord for showing me these windows. I need to install those last two in the front room.*

The hot, dry air baked him a little as Pete pulled two sheets of paper from the envelope.

Casper, Wyoming

June 7, 1886

Dear Peter,

He couldn't deny seeing that "dear *Peter*" felt good. He read it again. And maybe once more, but he'd never admit it.

Dear Peter,

You have just ridden off on the stage, and I've spent the last hour crying. Did I make the wrong decision? I do not know. I added another sheet to Mother's letter and filled it with, "What do I do?" written every way possible.

The reckless, impulsive side of me says to fill my valise with whatever it can hold and climb onto the next stagecoach. I have saved enough for fare. The rational part of me insists that I haven't prayed about it enough. I haven't considered. It reminds me that I must live with the decision for the rest of one of our lives, and I'm likely to ensure mine is short if I rush in without careful consideration.

If you do not follow my meaning, I hint that you would be driven to throttle me.

However, I regret one thing so much that I write now, even before you have had a chance to consider if you escaped a foolish decision. Peter, I meant it when I told you I wanted to say yes. What I didn't tell you is that if you had told me that my decision that day was irrevocable, I know I would have said yes. You were wise not to do that, though. Later, if you had not given me time to think, to ponder, to pray, I would have resented you for it.

I miss you already, and I only had three men tease me and two women tsk at me. I consider that near to miraculous.

From there, the letter described how she needed to finish her washing, how someone had stopped by to warn her that Mr. Kipinksi had returned, *"from where, I do not know,"* and that someone had heard him vow to get his "revenge" on her. The men would resume their patrols (and now she knew why those had ceased), and she was not to go outside after dark. Her grumbling about a slop bucket soothed a bit.

He'd stayed in a hotel in Chicago once—one with lavatories that had pull chain toilets. Pete had a mad desire to see what it would take to put one in the house for her. But the drought. They couldn't afford to use water to wash away waste when they had a perfectly good outhouse.

Instead, he rose from his chair, stowed the letter in the desk, and nearly ran for the barn.

He'd seen a music box in Omaha—a "Symphonion" with disks that played beautiful tunes. Instead of one song from the box, it could play a dozen different songs if you had a dozen disks. He'd get Greigson to buy one for him and have it waiting for her.

If she came—and she *must* come eventually, surely—perhaps she'd dance with him some evenings. Just the two of them after Tilly and Missy went to bed. That would be one advantage to courting your own wife. Proprieties weren't necessary.

July 3, 1886

Peter's letter had sat on the mantel for two days. Muriel patted it as she passed, and had taken it down a dozen times already, but each time she'd managed to convince herself that while the contents would be lovely, she'd enjoy them more if she waited. That first day had been such torture that she'd gone to help Mrs. Lunde carry water from the river to their garden all day the next as a deterrent. On an endless repeat, she told herself it was like Christmas. She'd increase the enjoyment by intensifying the anticipation.

Her truthful self feared that Peter would scold her for being selfish or fearful. Worse than that, she feared he might tell her he needed a woman with more pluck and backbone. A wishy-washy woman wasn't much use to a man out here on the prairies.

However, Mr. Fuller stopped her on her way back through town as she walked home from the Lunde homestead and handed her a letter from her mother. She almost forgot to thank him before tearing it open and reading as she made her way back to her cabin.

Fowler's Mills, Ohio

June 24, 1886

Dearest Muriel,

How I wish I could hug you, kiss your cheek, and set you to work while we discussed your dilemma. You always resented that, didn't you? What I never could make you understand was how effective it was at pushing out all the extraneous that clamored for your attention and helped you focus on the true issue. Your father always became impatient with it, too. He'd hiss at me as he passed, "Just answer her question!" but I think now you understand why I did what I did.

I taught you to think. However, this back and forth taking weeks sometimes means that I cannot play at being "Socretesia" as your father calls me when he thinks I am not listening. This time I must simply tell you.

I believe you hesitated not because you don't know your own mind and heart, nor because you have an instinctive reserve against Mr. Donaldson that will likely show some great defect in his character sometime in the future. I do not you doubt it being the Lord's will for you. The answer, my dear, is far simpler. You hesitated because when you took the question to the Lord, you didn't do it to seek <u>His</u> will but rather expecting Him to confirm yours.

If you tell me this is not so, I will believe you. My dear, Muriel. I know you too well not to know how you react and think in these things. Do you recall how you agonized over your decision to move to

Casper? It wasn't a lack of interest on your part or any obvious reason the Lord would oppose it. He did not. You simply refused to ask His guidance without pushing your own will into the conversation. Is this not a comparable situation?

Becca has nearly doubled in size in just a month. Her mother and I suspect twins, but we aren't willing to say anything about them as yet. She's so busy that it doesn't seem to have made an impact on her, although I see Jonathan giving her odd looks from time to time. We will see, I suppose. It isn't as if one will simply run away from home to the wilds of Wyoming if she decides to.

The family news heartened and delighted her, but her mother's words still hovered behind every line. Had she prayed with a desire for God's will or for confirmation of her own? The answer niggled at her right up to the last line. Muriel read it twice to herself before reading it aloud one last time. "'Saying no until you could say yes with a conscience fully yielded to the Father's will was wise, even if unintentional.'"

Of course, Mother had teased that Father would expect Peter to visit and ask permission to marry her. She had also conceded that such an expectation was unrealistic and should never be considered. *"Such a waste of money, but if he brought you with him, it would be a treat, wouldn't it?"*

Muriel hadn't felt such a surge of homesickness since her first months in Casper, but a tiny part of her felt homesick for a place she'd never been—homesick for a strange house built like the haciendas of California.

That thought removed all ability to resist. The moment she walked into the cabin, she snatched up Peter's letter and went to sit beneath the cottonwood and read it there where the warbler had pleaded for a mate. Had he heard it that day? They'd been talking, so perhaps not, but she had. It had seemed fitting for the moment.

Riverton

June 19, 1886

My dear Miss Darling,

I arrived home on the seventeenth, and your letter arrived yesterday. What an unexpected treat. If there hadn't been trouble on the train, it might have beaten me here. We heard of a breakdown near Omaha, and I was grateful to have been in the stagecoach. We enjoyed a mud wagon from about thirty miles north of you. I much prefer those to the Concords in warmer weather. It might be dusty, but it is much cooler. The train is faster but only if one isn't camped beside the tracks with earnest young preachers trying to convert one to or from Quakerism. If I were there, I would wink right about then. I never did learn the art of a subtle joke. I tend to emphasize them before I know I have done it.

My first reaction to your letter was to learn how one installs one of those pull-chain, indoor toilets you see at fine hotels. Perhaps with the promise of never being forced to use a slop bucket or chamber pot again, you might be induced to join me in the wilds of the Dakotas. However, sense overrode sentiment, and I reflected that something that uses so much water might not be a wise choice during such a severe drought. And Miss Darling (I apologize for the conjunction), the drought becomes more serious by the day.

To relieve me of temptation and to take my mind off the potential loss of a small fortune in cattle this autumn, I rode into town and purchased a gift for you. It won't be here for a couple of weeks at least, but even if you left for Riverton upon the receipt of this letter, it should be waiting when you arrived. That pleased me. I think you may enjoy your gift, and I am certain you will enjoy the new curtains Tilly is making for what I now think of as "your room." I have always hated the drab, brown curtains in there, so soon there will be blue ones the color of a summer sky. They have tiny pink flowers scattered all over them but not close together. Each one is three or four inches apart from the next. If Tilly ever asks you if I described the cloth to you, you must tell her that I did.

Abe and Mary married while I was gone. He was certain he would lose his job over it, but he decided that she was more important than the job. I told them to build a room off the bunkhouse if they wanted, or he could try to build a dugout on the rise. It's not much of a rise, but it's enough that a low house would fit in it neatly. Especially with their heights. They decided to add onto the bunkhouse, though, and I am glad of it. I think Mary will be a steadying influence on the men. I do not hold with coarse language and such things, but not all of my men belong to the Father, and that shows sometimes.

Have you had a moment to speak to John and Mr. Chambers? I wonder if a letter from me might not go further. Not that you aren't a respected and wise woman, but sometimes men who do not value education listen more to another man who works with his hands than they would to an academic or a woman. It may not be right, but it is true.

Since we are to build an addition, I must keep this letter shorter than I care to. We have only until the end of the month or so before it will be time to round up the cattle again and begin the drive toward Abilene. While I make no promises, I admit to considering taking a train to Cheyenne and a stage from there to Casper once the cattle have been sent east. Please pray, dear Muriel. I may not be wealthy enough not to feel the loss that will come on the trail and at market, but I can bear it. There are many who, I fear, will be ruined this year. Those in Casper will also feel it, and you may find you have a smaller classroom this coming or the following term.

Is it silly for me to admit that I think I left part of my heart in Casper?

Yours in waiting,

Peter

Chapter Twelve

As the dry, miserable days of July and August dragged toward September, Muriel sorted her things, prayed, planned for the new school year, prayed, and avoided being outside as much as possible. Her garden had died almost before it had sprung up. She'd begun watering from the well, but as week passed into week with no rain, she couldn't justify it. As long as there were beans, flour, and salt pork at the general store, she wouldn't starve.

Her heart taunted her that Pete probably had beef nearly every week. She hadn't had beef since his visit. The chickens had quit laying eggs two weeks ago, so as soon as she had polished off one, she butchered another. Four chickens didn't last forever, though, and she was down to her last piece of breast meat. She'd put it in a pot with a few potatoes she'd purchased from Mr. Fuller and a carrot and turnip one of her students had brought her. The Applegates lived near the river where the soil wasn't nearly as dry, and it was easy to carry water up to their garden.

Peter's letters came nearly every week now. He no longer waited for her next letter before writing again, and Muriel found it difficult not to imitate him. She'd already done it once, but would again be too much? She felt certain her father would say so, but what would Mother think? The only way to know would be to ask, but Muriel feared that. What if she were wrong?

Without a garden to tend and with the need to conserve whatever water she could (one family had already left after their well dried up), Muriel found the days long and tedious. Each night, just as the sun went down, she hurried out to the outhouse and avoided drinking anything until after a trip at daybreak. Only once did she have to empty the "thunder bucket," as John called her slop bucket.

August 23, 1886

At the first streak of dawn, Muriel flung back the covers and bolted from her room. By the time she reached the outhouse, she'd finally managed to tie her dressing gown. Flinging open the door, she started inside and froze. Her scream pierced her own ears, and she backed away as Mr. Kapinski stepped from inside and grabbed at her.

"Took liberties with you, did I?"

Though it wasn't a rational time to do it, Muriel berated herself for not thinking through the consequences of her lie and then for not repenting. But on the heels of that lack of repentance, she choked out, "You most certainly did—with your child. You abused her and threatened me in my classroom. Inexcusable. Now leave."

If only her voice hadn't wobbled on that last word.

"I'll leave when I've finished with you."

He shook her as if to make a point, but what that point was, Muriel couldn't fathom. The moment he released her, Mr. Kapinski slapped her with force enough to throw her to the ground. She struggled to find her footing and failed. Mr. Kapinski reached for her, grabbing her wrist before she could brush the dirt from it. Her eye throbbed, her hands stung where dirt and gravel scraped skin away, and fear stole her breath, making it impossible to order him to let her go.

"You'll regret interfering, you…"

The words slurred, confirming her suspicions of his drunkenness, but she thought he called her a "*stara panna.*" It sounded lovely, whatever it was, but Muriel doubted it was complimentary.

Again, she screamed as he lunged for her and jerked her to her feet. Muriel nearly stumbled directly into him but managed to swing wide at the last second. It broke his hold on her and she fell to the ground once more. This time, the man grabbed her by the neck and hauled her to her feet.

With each second, he squeezed harder until she choked and clawed at his hand.

"Let her go."

Kapinski turned, slowly and without releasing her to stare behind him. Muriel tried to see who spoke, but the world had gone a strange reddish-brown color and black pushed inward from the edges of her vision. She felt herself drop, but her lungs refused to fill with air.

Wrinkled hands with rope-like veins held her wrist. Muriel knew because she couldn't see anything else. A cold cloth covered the right side of her face, and it felt so good against the throbbing that she wouldn't have moved it if she could. The man's head hung but why? Asleep? Bowed in prayer? It looked somewhat familiar, but she couldn't be sure why. And why was she in bed? That she was, she didn't doubt.

"What—?" She stopped herself. First, speaking made the throbbing in her face and head intensify beyond what she thought she could endure. And second, she knew the answer to the question. *Mr. Kapinski.*

The man raised his head and frowned at her. "You're back with us. Good. How does the head feel?"

"Doctor Sidney?" Asking hurt, but while it looked like the man, he usually wore a smile. This man looked... anything but friendly.

He yawned. "Young John caught me on my way home. The Waller woman had her baby last night. Called me in at ten o'clock, but she didn't give birth until near sunup."

"Is everything well with her?" The question hurt, but if it kept him talking... Dr. Sidney was known for being a talker once you got him going.

Unfortunately, it worked too well. The man rambled on and on about Mrs. Waller and half a dozen other births he'd attended that year. It was enough to make her reconsider her lifelong dream of having children.

Without any idea of what else to do, she pretended to fall asleep, and when she opened her eyes again, only the sounds of someone moving around the front room told Muriel she wasn't alone. At first, she thought she'd call out, but her throat felt sore. The last thing she needed was a summer cold, but then the memory of Mr. Kapinski's hands about her throat, the wild, black eyes, and the utter hatred spewing from him rushed at her and might have knocked her flat if she hadn't been already.

A glance at her sleeve confused her. Hadn't she been wearing her dressing gown? This time she did call out as she forced herself into a sitting position. "Hello?"

Mrs. Chambers stepped in. "Are you feeling all right, Miss Darling?"

"A bit sore, in need of the outhouse, and a bit confused." She picked at the pink sleeve of her dress—the one Peter had complimented the day they'd had their picnic. "Wasn't I still in my dressing gown?"

The woman hurried to help Muriel stand, something she felt unnecessary, and explained about having to change her. "Don't know if it was the long wait overnight or fright or both, but we had to get you out of your clothes before we put you in your nice, clean bed."

Had she been alone, Muriel would have allowed herself the luxury of a long, deep groan. Instead, she apologized and tried to decide if sharing such a mortifying story would be worth the indelicacy if it took Peter's mind off the unpleasantness with Mr. Kapinski. He'd said he came because she kept him awake at night, and he wanted to know why. But Muriel had figured that out the first time he'd asked about Mr. Kapinski.

First, the necessary. Then I learn what has happened while I was resting. Then, *I write. Perhaps learning that I am safe will change his mind about marriage.* She didn't think that likely, but if it could happen, Muriel wanted to know. *And if that sheriff hasn't done something about Mr. Kapinski, maybe I will choose a ranch in Riverton to a Casper classroom.*

That prompted a snort that earned her a curious look from Mrs. Chambers.

Chapter Thirteen

September 2, 1886

Three of Pete's men worked at the ranch to prepare for the drive southeast to Abilene, one went to town for last minute requests from everyone, and the rest worked to keep the herd together. Usually, they wouldn't leave before the fifteenth, but the cattle weren't as well-fed as they ought to be. They'd lose many on the trail.

Hundredweight will be low, too.

Profits would be minimal if not nonexistent this year, but if he could get the meat to market, he could make up for it next year. Surely, the drought would be over by spring. They just had to keep the calves and the yearlings alive until then.

Tilly popped her head in the door. "A couple of the fellas have come in looking peaky. I'm going to take more water out to everyone."

"You can leave it. I'm going in a few minutes."

At that moment, Dale rode in, waving a letter. That could only mean one thing, and Tilly pounced before he could put thoughts into some semblance of order. "Looks like your little lady didn't wait for your last letter. The mail's slowing right now with the weather. Everyone's talking about it. You read that letter and write one back before you head out in the mornin'. I'll take the water and take Missy, so she doesn't bother you."

He started to suggest she leave the girl, but Tilly had already gone. Dale came up to the window and poked the letter through, and Pete rose to take it. "Thank you. Get everything?"

The man nodded and then pointed to the window. "You oughtta get some screening like for doors and make some for the windows here. Keep the flies out."

Pete had meant to do it for three years running and he still hadn't. Muriel would appreciate it, though. "I'll get some in Abilene. Thanks."

Since he was up, Pete went to fill a cup with water and grab a couple of Tilly's cookies. He'd miss those. The sight of Tilly driving off across the prairie, a wagonful of water buckets bouncing over the dry, rutted soil, pricked his conscience. He should be doing that. It wasn't her job.

And she wanted you to write. She's probably terrified you'll decide she's more convenient.

He'd downed half his water and a cookie by the time he reached his desk—and by the time conscience overrode desire. He had men down. That meant the others had to work twice as hard. A letter from Miss Darling would be a treat after a long, grueling day. It was a thinner one. All the more reason to savor it. Hadn't she said she'd waited two days before opening one of his. She'd enjoy hearing about the tortures he'd endured not to be outdone by her.

Less than fifteen minutes after he received that letter, Pete took off across the prairie toward the hint of a valley that surrounded their river. The water had gotten so low that it stirred up the bottom when the animals drank. Men couldn't drink that if they wanted to. As the sun beat down on him, he knew just how things must have gone. He'd have to remind them to take care on the trail.

At the little rise just before the land sloped ever so gently toward the river, Pete pulled Squanto to a halt and surveyed the scene. They'd lost more cattle than he'd realized, or they hadn't found some. The herd smaller by at least ten percent—maybe fifteen.

He'd just turned to go fill in where George should be when Pete saw it. His heart slammed into his chest and jumped up into his throat. A croaked, *"Nooo…"* escaped just as he urged Squanto into a run.

September 27, 1886

September 12, 1886

Riverton, Dakota Territory

My dearest Miss Darling,

My heart is broken. I write from Tilly and Missy's bedroom, seated on the corner of the bed. If my words become indecipherable, you'll understand why. Missy fell asleep only half an hour ago, and I may think again. Think and grieve.

Tilly is dead, and it's my fault. I killed that poor child's mother with my selfish thoughtlessness. How can a body endure that sort of guilt and shame?

Muriel had stopped breathing at seeing "my dearest," and kept on holding her breath at the first sentence. Now her lungs burst in an explosive exhale, and she sucked in a sob for a woman she'd never met (and might confess to being a might jealous of, but only to her mother). "Dear, Lord, be with them," she whispered and continued reading. That Peter was wrong about his guilt, she had no doubt.

How can a body endure that sort of guilt and shame? Here is how it happened, because I think it important that you should know. The drought and heat combined to make a few of my men ill just before heading south with the cattle. Tilly took the wagon to bring more water to the others. I should have gone, but your letter had just arrived, and she insisted I read it and reply since I wouldn't receive anything from you for so long. Tilly Bolton was that sort of woman.

She hadn't been gone but a few minutes when I remembered how you'd put off reading a letter to increase anticipation. I knew it was what I should do. If men were ill, I needed to be out helping. I'd enjoy it more without the guilt of selfishness hanging over me. If only I had been swifter to a good conscience.

There's a slight rise at the back of the ranch. On the other side, it gently slopes down to the river, and that's where we keep the cattle before we head out. I rode to the top, surveyed everything, and was just about to fill in a gap when the unthinkable happened. Missy had a little dolly chain that Abe cut for her last night—one of those with five or six little dollies cut and connected at the hands. The wind snatched it from her hand, and she chased after it.

I can hardly stand to write it. Whether the flutter of the dollies, the flapping of her little dress, the fact that her dress is red... I do not know. But while everyone was distracted by good drink of water, that child took off after her toy. It spooked a steer. You can imagine the rest.

My men were brave, Miss Darling. They managed to get between the herd and those few cattle who had begun to run. Whether the blockade hid their view, or they felt hemmed in, I don't know. But it likely saved lives even as it risked theirs. Tilly saw almost at the moment that steer stamped and took off after her daughter. I think that made it worse. Her skirts flapped more than Missy's by far.

Sobs wracked Muriel as she tried to read through tears. That poor mother. The terror for her child. And Missy was there in bed, so... had she been injured? Muriel couldn't see the words anymore. She sobbed out her pain, fear, distress, and prayers until the heaving stopped and she could see again.

Her skirts flapped more than Missy's by far. You will understand, I think, how beautiful and horrible what happened next was. Tilly reached Missy just a moment before the cattle reached her. She scooped up that child and flung poor Missy as far away from the path of the cattle as she could. Little Missy flopped against a rock like a rag doll. They both hit ground at the same time.

I tried to make it to her, Miss Darling. I promise I did. The moment I saw that paper flutter from Missy's hands, I rode hard, but it was too far. And now Missy has no mama—no daddy. I'll keep her, of course. I'll raise her as my daughter. She'll have an equal share to any inheritance I leave my children, should I have any.

But my selfishness killed her mother. How can I bear that? How can she forgive it? And how, the question that seems most horrible to me right now (and further proof of my selfishness), would you ever consider marrying me after this?

What else the letter said, Muriel didn't know. She couldn't read more. She needed to write. To confront. To decide.

October 9, 1886

Never had Riverton been so empty. People didn't come to town unless forced to. The extra water needed for their horses couldn't be spared. Several had left already, remembering the mild winter with nowhere near enough snow. If another dry winter came on the heels of this drought, they wouldn't make it if wells began to dry up.

But a letter might have arrived by now, if the mail had become swift again that is. Also, the Symphonion he'd purchased had arrived long ago. Thom Greigson shouldn't have to wait for his money at a time like this. So, Pete had saddled up Squanto and set Missy in the saddle with him. The change would do her good.

She'd been so quiet since the funeral. The chatterbox who filled his days with ideas about everything from prairie dogs to storybooks had lost her voice almost completely during the day. Nighttime brought memories. The child woke screaming, weeping for her mama. Why shouldn't she? He'd kept her in the same room, hoping familiarity would be a comfort, but Pete wondered if a change might do her good.

Abe's Mary said no, but she wasn't a mother. How could he be sure she knew what was best? As they rode into town, Pete patted his vest pocket. He'd written to Miss Darling to ask her opinion. She hadn't said not to write anymore, and so he would.

Lord, please help her see I've learned my lesson, and stir compassion for us in her heart.

A few hands waved as they rode in, and Missy seemed to perk up a bit. At the mercantile, he swung down from Squanto, tied the reins, and held up his arms to Missy. She clung to him, so rather than set her down, he carried her into the store. One of the local children ran up to greet her, and to Pete's relief, she squirmed to be let down. A little boy joined them, and the three children went scampering off to do whatever it was children played at these days.

Pete met Thomas at the counter and passed over twelve dollars. "Thought I'd check the mail and pay for that Symphonion."

"Didn't come in until Friday. I thought about driving it out." The man's gaze shifted to where the children had disappeared through a door and back again. "Thought it might distract little Missy, but I've been keeping deliveries to a minimum."

Pete nodded. "Wise decision." After the men exchanged a few comments on the dryness, Pete sighed. "Concerned for my men. I should be there." His own gaze strayed toward the door. "But no, right now this is the place for me."

"Folks admire what you're doing, Pete, but that girl needs a mother."

When Thomas didn't offer a letter, Pete tried not to let discouragement take hold. "It's only right, and it's what Tilly would've wanted."

"Well, if you don't mind my sayin' so, I think you oughtta marry this Miss Darling of yours."

Why he did it, Pete didn't know, but he found himself blurting out, "I told her about the accident. It may be that she won't want to correspond anymore. We'll have to see. Mary's around, though. She gets a woman's influence there at least."

This time Thomas leaned forward, his voice low. "Think you ought to stick around town for a bit. I expect the stage any time now. Maybe there'll be a letter on it. Taking longer these days, the mail is."

"Might do that, if you don't mind Missy playing for a bit. That's the most like herself I've seen her since the accident." Accident. He said it like Tilly had suffered a fall or a broken bone rather than nearly crushed beyond recognition. At least Missy had been unconscious when they carried her away from the scene.

The three children came tearing into the store, excitement glowing. "Stage's come! We see the dust blowing in." Little Henry Boxer nearly screamed the words into Pete's knees before dashing back outside with the girls on his heels. Pete rushed after them and caught up just as a mud wagon pulled up to the livery. He held the children back. "Don't get too close."

"Naw, the horses is tired. They won't hurt us."

Missy looked up at him as if to decide who to listen to and, much to Pete's relief, took a step back. "I like the red one."

A second look at the team did show one horse whose coat had a ginger tint to it. "Me, too."

The driver hopped down, and another rider helped open the coach door. They didn't get many travelers coming *to* Riverton, but the stage often carried passengers on their way to other places, so Pete wasn't surprised when a gray skirt appeared.

He'd decided to go back inside with just one more admonition to stay back from the horses, when the woman stepped away from the coach, a valise in hand. Pete gaped. "Miss Darling?"

Her face, already flushed by travel, turned an even deeper pink at the sight of him. "Peter? You got my letter! I hoped you would!" She hosted up the valise and staggered toward him.

Henry Boxer, the little scamp, tried to take her bag, and only then did Pete remember his manners. It took half a dozen steps to reach her, take the valise from her hands, and throw caution to the dry, dust-filled wind. He pulled her into his arms and held her. "I didn't hope…"

"You sounded so discouraged," she whispered. Then she stepped back and dusted herself off. "I must be a sight."

"As Mr. Swift put it, you'd be one for sore eyes, then."

Was the smile due to the reference to the author or for him? Before he could ask, she had a question of her own. "Is there a hotel?"

His heart sank. He'd assumed…

One by one, Riverton residents stepped out of doors and inched closer to the livery. How word traveled in less than a minute, he couldn't imagine. Well, maybe just over a minute. Mrs. Franklin came out, drying her hands on an apron that she then untied and rolled into a ball. She met them at the corner of the livery and smiled. "Peter, is this your schoolteacher from Casper?"

How had—oh, yes. He'd spoken to the minister about it. She'd been in the other room and probably heard every word, and the whole town probably knew he'd written her for the past year. That brought him up short. Had it truly been a year?

"I'm Muriel Darling," his… could she be his bride to be? Why else would she have come? "I think I've startled him. I thought with him here, he must have gotten my letter, but he looks more confused than expectant, don't you think?" Muriel held out a hand and smiled. "Your husband wrote me the loveliest letter. I assume you had a part in it?"

They wrote to Miss Darling? My Miss Darling?

He found himself shooed toward the parsonage, and Missy abandoned her friends to follow. They'd almost reached the door when the girl tugged on Miss Darling's skirt and asked, "Are you Mr. Pete's darling?"

While Pete tugged at his collar, the women laughed. Miss Darling knelt down to Missy's level and asked, "What makes you ask that?"

"Mama prayed for Mr. Pete's darling, and you said you are a darling."

"Well, that's my name. Muriel Grace Darling. What is yours?"

The shyness he expected to overcome her didn't appear. Missy stared for a moment before saying, "Matilda Bolton."

"I think your middle name is Ann, Missy."

"Oh."

Miss Darling wove a loose strand of hair back into Missy's braid and said, "So... Matilda Ann Bolton. Were you named for your mama?"

Pete winced, but the girl bobbed her head, not seeming to be bothered by the reference to her mother. Miss Darling rose and took the child's hand. "That'll be a comfort for you, won't it?"

Though Missy didn't seem to understand, she did lean against Miss Darling's knee once they'd all seated themselves in the parlor. Miss Darling apologized for how dusty she was and had suggested she might want to brush off her skirts before coming inside, but Mrs. Franklin had assured her that furniture could be brushed if the prairie winds hadn't blown off enough on the walk over.

"Why don't you come help me fix some drinks and something to eat, Missy? I'm sure Mr. Donaldson would like to say hello to his friend without an audience."

Missy shot him a quick look, and at his nod, turned to drag herself away in Mrs. Franklin's wake. Pete moved from the chair he'd been offered to Miss Darling's side. "You wrote?"

"I did." She smiled as he took her hand in both of his. "I told you that you weren't to blame yourself, that you were misplacing your grief, and that you were an arrogant fool if you thought you could make a mistake that would add or take away one day of Tilly's life."

It wasn't a declaration of her wholehearted affections or even a modest hint at them, but it did soothe after the initial sting. "You're right, of course. My mind can see that, but my heart is broken."

If she hadn't squeezed his hand before speaking, Miss Darling's next words would have stung again. "Did you perhaps love her more than you thought you did?"

If someone asked me that about you, I might be forced to say yes. With his thoughts occupied thus, Pete just shook his head. "We were neither of us interested in a more personal relationship. She because I would never suit her, and I because I'd found someone who suited me much more." He swallowed. "You came... to stay?"

Miss Darling nodded. "I spoke to Mr. Thomlin and his sister and gave my notice to the board. I forfeited my salary by leaving, but a female teacher isn't allowed to be married, and

I said I would be before the middle of the month."

"You will be as soon as I can find Mr. Franklin—"

There Miss Darling shook her head. "No, Peter. I need a bath and a clean dress. I am filthy, I smell horrible, and my hair has enough dirt in it that it may sprout something when I wash. I have a clean dress in my valise, and I intend to be presentable when I marry you."

"But you will," Pete said again. He allowed himself to lift her hand to his lips. "Today? I can take you home as my wife today?"

"Yes."

Chapter Fourteen

They stood before Reverend Franklin in the parlor. Pete wore his best suit, procured from the ranch while Muriel bathed and readied herself. He'd also made a trip to the mercantile to purchase a thin gold band for her. Muriel had come down the Franklin's stairs in a blossom pink dress that suited her well but wasn't the one he recalled. Instead of a bouquet, she held a bundle of letters tied with a rose ribbon. And she held Missy's hand, listening with solemn attention to the words the minister read from the Bible. Pete tried to pay attention, but the sun shone through the parlor windows at such a perfect angle as to give Miss Darling an almost ethereal quality. A painter somewhere might do it justice, but he'd never seen a photograph like it. Still, he wished he had one.

A glance at Mrs. Franklin showed her smiling at him. She gave him a nod that conveyed all the love and approval he craved. A glance down at Missy showed the child staring up at Miss Darling with all the hero worship he'd seen in many of her students. How quickly she'd engendered the girl's affection. *Then again, she captured mine easily enough.*

Never had he felt more responsibility than when the minister asked him to recite vows to love and cherish her—to keep her safe. Those words weren't in any marriage ceremony he'd ever heard, but Pete added them at the end just the same. It was the least he could do after failing Tilly.

Muriel found it difficult to look at him, but when she finally nodded and said, "I do," her gaze met his and held fast. Unshed tears glistened in her eyes, and Pete wondered if they were for a life she'd given up or for the one she'd accepted. His prayer that he'd never disappoint her pressed in his heart until he felt it would burst.

"You may kiss your bride, Peter."

The amusement in the minister's voice hinted that it might not be the first time he'd suggested it. Pete flushed, gave Muriel an apologetic smile, and kissed her cheek before whispering, "Sorry. I didn't think of that."

But his concerns seemed for naught. Muriel just laughed, joked about him already regretting his vows, and hugged the minister and his wife. "I look forward to knowing you both better."

Mrs. Franklin served up supper, insisting they stay and urged Pete to let her keep Missy for a few days, but Miss Dar—that is his *wife* assured them it wasn't necessary. "I want to get to know her." She beamed at the little girl. "I know we're going to be great friends."

"I can show you the pony I get to ride. And I have a dolly and…" Missy's prattle. Pete's heart squeezed and a tear ran down his face and to his jaw before he felt it and brushed it away. Under the table, Mu—he couldn't think of her as Muriel yet. She'd be his Miss Darling until… someday. But his wife squeezed his hand under the table as if she knew and understood.

Thank you, Lord. What else could a man say or do when given a gift like her but to thank the Lord for it?

The strange house had an appeal Muriel wouldn't have imagined based on Pete's descriptions. The odd, rough outside walls, the wide archways along two sides, the way it sprawled across in one level rather than two—she'd never seen anything like it. It lacked a feminine touch, something she suspected had gotten lost in years without a mother or a wife. Had Tilly not felt free to create a homier environment, or had the work been more than she could keep up with?

Pete came in from the barn and washed up in the kitchen, his eyes never leaving her. He broke the silence first. "Read your letter while you told Missy that story." He nodded at her dress. "I'm sorry you spilled ink on your old one, but that's a pretty replacement."

"It gave me something to do in the last weeks before school started again." Muriel ran her hand along the back of a rocking chair. "This is lovely…"

And you are being silly. There's no cause for nervousness. You have your own room. He has his. And there are no expectations here.

"My father made it years ago. It got rickety being stored in the attic, so I took it down and worked it over a couple of winters ago." Pete came sat on the sofa. He didn't exactly pat the seat beside him, but the invitation was clear.

After hesitating too long, Muriel moved his way with a silly excuse. "I'm sorry for being so distracted. I've spent so much time sitting and being jostled about, it feels good to stand."

"We could walk. I didn't show you the barn or…"

They hadn't had such awkwardness since that very first day and it had dissipated quickly. Somewhere outside, a coyote howled, and others picked up the song, drowning out the birds calling and a cricket or two. Perhaps a walk would be wise, but weariness kept her rooted to her place. A thought prompted her to propose a compromise. "Would you take me on that walk tomorrow night? I'm just so tired. It's been a long ten days."

"Of course, I'm sorry. Can I get you anything? Coffee? Tea? Water?"

The poor man. His desperation to ensure she didn't regret those vows had followed them all the way from Riverton, all through the evening with Missy, and now… She must say *something*, but Muriel didn't know what would comfort him most. And then she did.

"Did I thank you?" At his questioning look, Muriel shook her head. "No, I'm certain that I didn't. You came to Casper—spent all that time and money. You asked me to be your wife, and I told you no. But you kept writing and kept opening your heart to me. And I'm so grateful. I wouldn't be here now if you hadn't." She swallowed a lump that had risen in her throat, considered her next words and examined them for truthfulness before adding, "And

Peter?"

His gaze never shifted from her face. In fact, she might swear they never wavered from her lips! "Yes?"

"There's nowhere else I'd rather be right now than here with you." She'd almost added, "and Missy," and changed her mind. It wouldn't do for him to think she'd *only* come to help him raise what some would see as "a servant's child."

Just as he'd done in the Franklin's parlor, Peter took her hand in both of his and held it. "I needed to hear that. Thank you."

"I know."

"I should let you go to bed, but I selfishly want to keep you close for a bit longer. Is that all right?"

Muriel nodded and arranged her features into what she hoped was a mask of alertness. "Tell me about your days. What do they look like? What should I expect to do? I was concerned about stepping on Tilly's toes before, but now I wonder about Mary…" She giggled. "You weren't teasing about her diminutive stature!"

"We used to call Abe, 'Demi,' but not since he married her. She'd probably pound every one of us." Peter leaned back against the sofa, allowing his shoulders to relax. One rested lightly against hers, and Muriel allowed herself to enjoy that closeness. She'd been so alone in Casper—an integral part of the community but separate from it as well. Every summer, she'd wandered from family to family, helping out and drawing that need for physical contact from students as she worked alongside them. This year, that hadn't been possible—not with the water shortage.

"—with Missy." Pete's words broke into her thoughts, and Muriel struggled to put them into some sort of context. He shot her a pained look. "I told you I wasn't looking for a housekeeper, and I'm not. I can hire someone else if Mary doesn't choose to stay on, and it isn't fair to you, but I need help with Missy. In an hour or so, the nightmares will begin, and I try, but…"

A child—that was something she knew a thing or two about. She asked questions, told funny stories, and listened to his. As the hours passed, she found herself leaning against him, needing to rest her head on his shoulder and unwilling to do it.

A little mantel clock struck eleven o'clock before Peter stopped in the middle of a story of a stubborn calf and stared at it. "She's not wakened yet."

Muriel yawned. "Maybe she wore herself out today."

After musing about that for a moment, Peter really looked at her and smiled. "If I didn't say it before I'll say it now. I'm so glad you're here." He reached for her cheek and stopped shy of touching it. "But you should sleep. I'll see to Missy if she cries."

At the door to her room, she turned to call out goodnight and found him right behind her. This time, Peter did touch her cheek. He leaned forward, kissed her forehead, and whispered, "Goodnight, Miss Darling."

It took little time for Muriel to change into a clean nightdress and braid her hair. Something Peter had said niggled at her right up to the moment her head settled into the pillow, and then she knew. "So… I'm still Miss Darling, am I?"

Chapter Fifteen

October 15, 1886

With Missy settled into bed, worn out after a day of working and playing, Pete met his wife at the door, and they started off toward the tiny creek that trickled past the pasture. The moon still shone bright in the night sky, though its brightest night had been three days past. A week. Miss Darling been there nearly a week, and he couldn't imagine life without her. How had he survived?

How had he fallen in love so quickly? Or had he? Had he loved her while in Casper? Books seemed to hint at a defined moment when a man or woman *knew*. He didn't have that, but the more he thought of it as they picked their way up the path, the more certain he became. *Tell her.*

The thought seemed to come from somewhere outside himself. Pete might have blamed it on God if he thought he could get away with it. But it wasn't God, and he knew it. It was the heart of a man eager to win the love of his wife. *A strange thought if ever I've had one.*

At the fencepost near the pasture, Miss Darling stopped and pointed at the sky. "A falling star."

"My mother used to tell me to make a wish."

Instead of making that wish, Miss Darling turned to him. "And what would you wish?"

Before he could talk himself out of it, Pete blurted out, "I wish you'd let me hold you."

She turned away, gazing out over the darkened landscape. Pete's hopes plummeted. It was too soon. Of course, it was. Not even a week and—

"Wish granted."

The words came whispered on the night breeze, but he caught them and held them fast. "Are you sure?"

"Yes." This sounded a bit stronger—bolder.

The moment his arms encircled her, that maverick tongue of his took off at a gallop. "I think I love you."

Miss Darling had started to relax, but something shifted. She didn't stiffen, but that moment of settling disappeared. A second, two, three... Not more than ten seconds could have passed before she tried to speak. "Sometimes I think—"

Pete cut her off. Stepped away. Folded his arms over his chest. "I promised you. I said I'd find a way for us that wouldn't put you in an awkward position, and I have."

Her cheeks flamed, even in the moonlight he saw it. Did she know that these discussions could be difficult for men, too? He allowed himself to touch her face. He did it too often he knew. But her cheek was so soft... so lovely.

"I—"

"Don't rush yourself, Miss Darling. Wait until you're certain. But if you change how you feel about me—about us—just leave your door open at night. I always walk the house before I turn in. I'll see it. I'll understand."

And I'll pray for it every night.

<hr>

November 1, 1886

Three weeks, Muriel mused as she stared at her bedroom door. *I've been in Riverton only three weeks. How could I love this man so much so quickly?*

All it would take to hint at the feelings swirling in her heart would be a few footsteps and the twist of a knob. Pete's solution had been so simple, so discreet.

Again, Muriel stared at the door and twisted her hands in her lap as she debated. Would he believe her? Would he understand?

She prayed for wisdom and then for courage before she rose from the bed, unlatched the door, and opened it a good foot. Shyness and unexpected anticipation flooded her. Muriel dove for the bed, pulled the covers up to her chin, closed her eyes, and waited.

<hr>

Sunlight streamed across the bed and into her eyes. Not for the first time, Muriel considered insisting that Peter move the bed to wall to the right of that window. *It's so stark—so harsh and glaring!*

But the thought of Peter sent her upright. She stared at the door and frowned. *I was certain I opened it.*

The firmly latched door mocked that thought. Chagrined, Muriel rose, dressed, and hurried out to the kitchen to offer, once more, to help Mary with the morning work. Mary would refuse. She always did. Peter would come in, lead her outside, and delight her with stories or inspire her with what he'd learned from his Bible reading that morning. He prayed with her, this husband of hers. He even found little ways to show affection without presuming too much.

Without presuming enough, sometimes.

That thought is all it took. As Mary drove her from the kitchen, and Peter appeared by her side, Muriel decided to allow herself a bit of flirtation. After all, Peter was her husband. He cared about her—loved her, in some fashion, anyway.

So, as they wandered toward the near-dry creek, Muriel allowed her eyes to linger on his face—just a little longer than usual. She touched his sleeve. She even squeezed his hand when he asked forgiveness for snapping at her interruption the previous afternoon. "I didn't even notice, Peter. Truly."

"Nonetheless, I did. I resisted apologizing for so much of the day, and then you were in bed."

"Well, of course, I forgive you—if you were wrong."

He didn't take her hand. The kiss she'd begun to dream of never materialized. Instead, he looped her arm through his and led her back to the house as he did every morning. Her disappointment grew keener by the step. So, just outside the back step, Muriel stopped him.

"You once said you preferred not to call me by my given name—you preferred 'Miss Darling.' But since we've been married, I don't believe you've changed that. Why?"

"I chose to continue with 'Miss Darling' because it gave me the opportunity to imagine what it would be like to call you something so dear—darling. Now… now you're still 'Miss Darling' in all but name. I'd rather save Muriel for when we are married in every sense."

Her throat swelled as he spoke, making it impossible for her to speak. Muriel just nodded and stepped inside without a word. His sigh—he tried to hide it, but he couldn't. *And you won't have to add "Miss" to darling for long, if you don't want to. How would you feel if you knew that?*

Four nights—four confusing, anxiety-riddled nights. Muriel waited as long as her eyes would stay open and fell asleep each time watching for an inky shadow in the darkness that seeped in from the hallway. Each morning, she awoke to find the door closed and even more determined to get the bed moved away from that wall.

But on the fourth morning, as she sat at the table with Peter, Mary chattered about being up several times in the night. "Oh, that reminds me, Muriel. I've found your door open all week. I closed it for you. You shouldn't do that, you know. It's safer in fire. It could block the smoke and flames so you could get out through a window. My mother was always…"

Whatever else Tilly said faded as Peter's head snapped up, and his eyes met hers. A silent question followed. It took more effort than she might have expected, but Muriel made the slightest nod. His fork dropped to his plate as Peter stood. His eyes never left her. "There's something I need to speak with you about. Would you come to my study as soon as you've finished?"

She didn't wait at all. The moment he stepped into the hallway, Muriel apologized to Mary, suggested that she leave their plates, and hurried after Peter. "I'm sure we'll be back in a moment."

Arms encircled her the moment she stepped into the study, and the door closed with just a kick of his boot. Peter held her close, buried his face in her hair, and she could feel him try to steady himself. "Did you really? All week?"

"Since… Tuesday?"

His lips found hers before she could confirm her befuddled thoughts. Her heart swirled in a vortex of emotions that fluttered to the floor and lay there. When he released her, she didn't know. But she heard words she'd waited to hear all her adult life—and for many years before as well. "I love you." No hesitation, no qualifier. Just confident, earnest assurance of his love.

"I think—" She cut herself off and rephrased. "That isn't true—it's not. I *know* I love you, too."

Their plates had been cleared by the time they left his study. Pete cut them each a piece of Mary's apple pie (vastly inferior to Tilly's, according to him) and didn't even try to keep his hand from touching her cheek, her arm, her hand. The day followed that pattern. Had Missy not been ever-present, Muriel suspected Peter might not have been as circumspect as he attempted to be.

But as they returned from their usual walk, Peter stopped her outside her door and stared at the knob. "If it should be closed, later?"

Muriel allowed a slow smile to form. She'd learned that he liked it especially when she did that. Bringing his face close, Muriel kissed him briefly, and whispered, "It's never closed to *you*."

Sunlight broke across her bed and blinded her into consciousness. A growl beside her preceded a protest. "How can you stand that, Muriel? This bed needs to move!"

Snuggled up against Peter's chest, she plotted. *Just how can I get him to say that again?*

"Muriel?"

That'll do.

The End

Author's Note

I hope you enjoyed this little glimpse into Pete and Muriel's lives. I had once considered making the second ballad, *Blind Child's Prayer*, be about Pete and Mary, but I couldn't do it. It would be forcing things rather than writing the best story I can. So, instead, I chose to continue Jack's tale from a different direction.

A few things. When I began writing *Jack*, I'd set it in 1888, and as such, all timing was perfect. Alas, by the time I got done editing (several years later), I'd forgotten *why* I chose that year and… I changed it to *before* the "hard winter" of 1886/1887, since that had such a devastating effect on cattle, and I didn't want prairies full of rotting cattle flesh in the spring and summer of 1887 in my story.

I chose 1888 originally because that was the year Casper, Wyoming was first inhabited (as Casper, not Fort Caspar). Then I promptly forgot about that when I changed the dates in *Jack*. The rediscovery in this story meant that I was stuck with a terrible mistake. Sorry, I moved habitation back to 1884 for the purposes of this story, and I pray the current inhabitants of Casper will forgive me.

And finally, I put a nod to the song "Utah Carl" (known as "Utah Carol" by Marty Robbins) in the scene with Tilly and Missy. I thought it might give Miss Darling an impetus to take a leap of faith. 😊 If you've never heard the song, I recommend it anytime you need a good cry. Otherwise…

Author Bio

USA Today Bestselling author Chautona Havig lives in an oxymoron, escapes into imaginary worlds that look startlingly similar to ours, and writes the stories that emerge. An irrepressible optimist, Chautona sees everything through a kaleidoscope of *It's a Wonderful Life* sprinkled with fairy tales. Find her at chautona.com and say howdy—if you can remember how to spell her name.

Connect with me online:
Twitter: **https://twitter.com/ChautonaHavig**
Facebook: **https://www.facebook.com/chautonahavig**
My blog: **http://chautona.com/blog/**
Instagram: **http://instagram.com/ChautonaHavig**
Goodreads: **https://www.goodreads.com/chautonahavig**
BookBub: **https://www.bookbub.com/authors/chautona-havig**
Amazon Author Page: **https://amazon.com/author/chautonahavig**
YouTube: **https://www.youtube.com/@chautonahavig**
My newsletter (sign up for news of FREE eBook offers): **https://chautona.com/news**

Learn more about the novel that inspired this book, *Jack: a lot of hullabaloo on the prairie* by scanning the QR Code below:

Jory's Story

by Lisa M. Prysock

Miss Marjorie Pritchard, known as 'Jory' in the village of Glad Crown, was once caught poaching as a young girl. Now, she is the protégée of a duchess, the wealthy Lady Kingston in Northampton. Lady Kingston, the vicar's daughter who married Xander, the Duke of Gladdington, believes it is her duty as a duchess to lift up those around her.

When the widowed Duke of Pensford is in desperate need of peace in his household and a governess, Lady Kingston recommends Jory for the position. She sees potential for Jory to rise above her circumstances and even marry the handsome duke. But with local adversaries, a spy underfoot, and a visit from the notorious Prince Regent, Jory's new role as governess becomes more dangerous than expected. When a country house party commences and scandalous rumors swirl in society columns, will love have a chance to blossom amidst such chaos?

Dear Reader,

Jory's Story, Book 1 in the *Mulberry House* series, begins when she first appears as a young teen girl in my book, *The Shoemaker*. Readers do not need to read that book to enjoy this one, but it has been on my heart to write the rest of Jory's journey for a long while. How good it feels to be here, finally writing it. Her story has sparked a new Regency Era series that will center around the characters and settings you'll encounter in this book…and likely, some new characters and settings too. I hope you enjoy it as the series unfolds.

Warmest Regards,
Lisa

For my dearest childhood friends,
Paula, Kim, Valerie, and Starla.
May you always know how
fondly I have treasured our youth,
memories of yesteryear,
and though we each bloom
where planted,
I look forward to an eternity
together in Heaven one day,
where we'll dance together
on streets of gold
with our Savior who
taught us to forgive,
love, believe, bloom, and grow.

Turn away from evil and do good; seek peace and pursue it.
Psalm 34:14, ESV

Prologue

December 3rd, 1818
The Annual Kingston Christmas Ball, Hillbrook Hall, Northampton

The Duchess of Gladdington, seated along the perimeter of the dance floor between two dukes, leaned closer to her husband and snapped her fan open, covering her mouth so the other duke, seated on her left, could not overhear her intentions. "Darling, I am in dire need of a favor," she whispered, refraining from fluttering her eyelashes.

He smiled at her, his brows arching. "What kind of a favor…and why do I have the distinct feeling that you are up to something?"

"I am not up to something, as you put it." She hid a smirk, knowing full well she was indeed up to something and turned her gaze toward the couples dancing in their ballroom. Keeping her voice low, she continued. "I am only hoping to distract the Duke of Pensford from you for long enough to prevail upon him to request a dance with Jory."

"Dance with Jory?" Xander rolled his eyes. Shaking his head, he lowered his tone to match her whisper. "We should not proffer the assistant of our governess toward Lord Thornberry. He is a duke, after all. Why dash her hopes when nothing could possibly come of it?"

She tilted her chin. "And that is precisely where you and I differ in opinion, my lord."

His eyes widened. "Do you believe that even if he were to fall madly in love with our employee—our Jory—that he would break the expectations of his family and the customs of society to marry a governess? And if I may remind you, one who was caught poaching from our land at the age of thirteen?"

She waved her fan a little faster. "I am not in need of reminding. I remember well the day your estate manager dragged her into your study. She was disguised as a boy until her hat fell off, revealing that mass of beautiful brunette locks. One of her most winning features, I think. In fact, I think her father's shotgun weighed as much as she at the time. But I think my protégée is ready for something more than teaching our daughters French, history, mathematics, art, and etiquette. While she does admirably in the absence of Mrs. Winthrop, who will not retire for a great many years, I think she deserves a chance at happiness. Do you not agree?"

Xander smiled and nodded at a friend passing by their seats before clearing his throat. "I cannot deny that you have spent a great deal of time and funds in providing Miss Marjorie Pritchard with art lessons, dancing lessons with the local dance master, pianoforte and violin lessons, mastery of the French language, etiquette, and much more. As much as we would provide for any of our daughters, in fact." He waved a hand about. "And I also cannot deny the fact she has likely read more than half of the volumes in our library, but I thought you wanted someone qualified to step in as our governess when Mrs. Winthrop visits her family or takes her leave for the seaside, and when she ultimately retires. And someone to assist Mrs. Winthrop with chasing after our daughters all day."

"That was my original intent, until I realized what a gem we have in Jory. She has flourished here in Northampton under our tutelage and watchful guidance, do you not agree?" Winnie held her fan still, waiting for her husband's answer.

"I suppose I do, and she means a great deal to our family. In truth, I would hate to lose her to Somerset. But still, 'tis an unlikely match, my lady." Xander patted her hand.

He couldn't dismiss her plans with a simple pat of the hand. She waved her fan aside as if to dismiss his dismissal of her plan, returning it in time to hide her mouth. Then she fixed her eyes straight ahead at the couples dancing to a country reel. "I know she is merely the daughter of a tenant farmer, but it is you, my darling husband, who has inspired me to lift all in society that I can above their plights…to relieve them of heavy burdens and place opportunity before them. To do good whenever I may find it in my power to do so. And if I cannot prevail upon Cambridge and other fine universities to open their doors to educate our nation's finest female minds, then I shall do what I can with whomever the good Lord in heaven above places directly under my nose." She nodded toward a lady friend seated across the room, who smiled in return.

Xander cocked his head to one side. "I do believe I see a gleam in your eyes."

"Despite that glimmer of hope you call a gleam, may I be so bold as to remind you, my lord, that I was merely a companion and a humble parson's youngest daughter when we married? And when you decided to raise Jory above her plight by not turning her over to the authorities and offering her the use of our library, not only was it a fine example and an act of great mercy, but a pivotal moment in my decision to marry you." She looked up at the ceiling where a chandelier sparkled, suspended in the center of the room above everyone. After admiring it for a moment, she stole a glance at her husband and smiled at him, their eyes connecting.

"Yes, well, *you*, my darling, were the exception to the rule." He grinned, his eyes dancing as his eyes traveled the entire length of her gown, causing her to blush and turn away with a smile.

Wouldn't Lord Archer Thornberry and Miss Marjorie Pritchard make as great a love match as her own with Lord Alexander Kingston, despite her impoverished upbringing? Did she not find similarities with Jory's circumstance? Certainly, she'd had it better than Miss Pritchard in many respects, but in truth, her situation had only been moderately better because her father had a modest living bestowed upon him by a member of the peerage in her childhood parish. She had been reared inside the comforts of a parsonage with a number of bedrooms and a smattering of elegant furnishings rather than the two-room, thatch-roofed dwelling where Jory's crowded family resided.

This fact was one of the reasons she'd ultimately offered Miss Pritchard a position, making her one less mouth to feed amongst Jory's widowed mother's brood. Rose Pritchard had her hands full, even without Jory, even though one or two of the Pritchard daughters had managed to marry soldiers. In any case, she aimed to help Marjorie Pritchard's plight by sparing her from spinsterhood. All she required was a suitable prospect as a husband for her protégée. And one happened to sit on her left at this very moment.

Xander Kingston leaned closer, drawing a circle around her wedding ring with his index finger. "Perhaps I fell instantly in love with you and have, as usual, underestimated your intentions and abilities. Once again, you astonish me. Who am I to stand in your way?"

"And there is more…" Winifred Kingston fluttered her fan, sure that she flushed two shades deeper than one of the pink roses in their summer gardens.

"Why did I not see that coming?" Her husband's mouth twisted into an amused smirk with his lips pressed together. "Of course, there is more, and I know you are about to inform me."

Winnie suppressed a giggle of delight at her husband's reactions and kept her voice low. "Xander, our dear friend and peer, the Duke of Pensford, is quickly approaching two full years of mourning the loss of his dearly departed wife. He has four motherless children at home. It is our duty to help him move forward in society, and yet he has not danced with a single lady from amongst all of our guests. And Mrs. Winthrop is presently occupied across the room in conversation, leaving Jory free to dance. It is the perfect moment. With your blessing, darling, I intend to ask him to dance with her."

"And the favor you require from me since I cannot disagree that this might be good for Archer, despite my doubts that anything will come from it…?" His brows furrowed as a puzzled look spread across his face.

"Simply put, if I must spell it out, please do not make yourself an excuse for conversation with him, but perhaps make yourself scarce and entangled in another matter altogether." Winnie fluttered her fan more rapidly, biting her lower lip. Would her husband oblige her request so the duke on her other side could not leave off dancing to converse with his friend?

Her husband nodded. "Ah, I think I understand now. I shall go and busy myself by speaking to some of our guests and leave you to your matchmaking efforts, but do not say that I didn't warn you it may not go as planned. If you, God forbid, passed away to heaven tomorrow, my lovely, I daresay it might take the rest of my life to look upon another with even half of the affection and adoration I have for you. It cannot be easy for him to be thrust into the idea of forming a new attachment. And even harder to consider it with someone outside of the peerage."

Winnie smiled and lowered her fan, more heat rising to her cheeks. "That is the sweetest thing you have ever said." Of course, it wasn't true. He'd said a great many pleasing sentiments to her over the years of their happy marriage. But his statements were sweet indeed, considering how often he opened his mouth and stuck his foot straightaway into it. Tonight, he was in a celebratory mood, and so was she. Even the Prince Regent had shown up for their ball, and many members of the Ton had traveled from London to be at their annual ball. They had a packed house full of guests and the evening had already proven itself a success by the sheer volume of attendees.

Xander rose from his seat, bowed to her, and made a beeline for some other friends, leaving her free to speak to Archer, seated on her other side—if he did not rise from his seat to follow her husband. She prayed he did not, and the Lord above granted that which she had requested, at least for the moment. Jory was perfectly suited to him, if only she could pique his interest, though she could not say for certain beyond a love for literature he and Jory shared as to why she felt that way. Only a particularly strong conviction she held.

A few seconds later, she leaned toward Lord Archer Thornberry before he thought to make his escape. He was certainly too handsome to stay in mourning forever, and at least the other unmarried ladies and their mothers did not hover about him presently. "Are you enjoying the evening's festivities, Lord Thornberry?"

He drew in a deep breath as if to draw himself up from his silent grief and released a long but contented sigh. "I am. And you?"

"Indeed, I am enjoying the ball…" Only, did she detect he harbored loneliness and was a tad bored in his mannerisms? Perhaps he was weary of being in grief and alone. Maybe he did not know how to achieve the act of mingling in society again. "But my Christmas happiness would be far more complete if you would do me the great favor of requesting a dance with our dear friend Jory, Miss Pritchard." She nodded toward the young lady seated on his other side. "She hasn't been asked to dance yet this evening, and it pains me to admit she is far too shy to approach our master of ceremonies to ensure she has dance partners. In truth, it also fills my heart with pangs of dread to see you not take in a single dance after coming all this way to Northampton to celebrate with us, now that we've pestered you out of London to accept our invitation." She'd almost said like old times, but thankfully had not. It would have brought his dearly departed wife to mind since they used to attend this very ball together.

Lord Thornberry stole a glance toward the beautiful governess assistant seated on his other side. Winnie now detected a bit of interest in the way he seemed to perk up at her request. He sat up straighter and his shoulders no longer sagged. She'd seen to it that Jory had worn one of her finest ballgowns from those she no longer needed, and she'd sent a maid to style her hair in a most attractive manner. Only a blind man would disregard Jory's fine features. And in truth, she bore some resemblance to his first wife. Would it count in her favor?

He turned back to Winnie. "Well, we cannot have you suffering from pangs of dread. And do forgive me for my inattentive manners, my lady. Perhaps I have been reclusive for far too long. I shall see to it that she has a fine spin about the ballroom."

Her mission accomplished, Lady Winifred Kingston smiled and relaxed in her seat, her eyes sparkling with evident enjoyment as the handsome couple took to the dance floor. In short order, she silently reveled in triumph when her husband returned to her side while the Duke of Pensford danced with Jory to a Scottish reel with a number of other couples in the grand ballroom at Hillbrook Hall.

The reel ended, but Winnie and Xander exchanged glances when Archer surprised them —and Jory too, judging by the look on her face—by asking her for the honor of the next dance as well.

Did he truly mean he wanted to get to know Jory a little more? Winnie's heart soared for her protégée. She intended to ensure that Archer was seated near Jory at tonight's dinner and some of the other meals before his return to Somerset. There, he planned to spend Christmas with his children, away from London and the scrutiny of the Ton, where all eyes could behold the inclinations and movements of the most eligible widower in all of England.

Only time would tell, but maybe the future would finally brighten for the lovely wallflower rapidly approaching spinsterhood. It would be a terrible shame to waste Jory's talents, beauty, and grace on a classroom—even if it did consist of her three precious daughters as pupils. Perhaps, with a great deal of prayer, circumstance might turn the tide for Miss Marjorie Pritchard after all...

Chapter One

Casting all your anxieties on Him, because He cares for you.

I Peter 5:7, ESV

August 25th, 1819
The Rose Garden at Hillbrook Hall, Northampton

Miss Marjorie Pritchard strolled at a leisurely pace, pausing to admire the vibrant blooms in the duke's well-tended garden. A monarch butterfly flitted about, catching her attention before landing on the petals of a bright pink rose. She adjusted her parasol to block the sun, enjoying the sound of laughter coming from the duke's three young daughters.

They squealed and bounded ahead of her with glee upon spying King Henry, their beloved black cat, having escaped the manor house. Well, he was almost all black, except for his white paws, chest, and the ring around his neck, making him look as though he wore boots, a waistcoat, and a cravat. Governess Winthrop busied herself some distance ahead of the girls, filling a basket of fresh clippings to create another bouquet for the schoolroom.

"King Henry! Come back..." Lady Celia—the eldest at eight years of age—called after their furry friend as he skittered away.

"How did you escape, Henry?" Lady Marcella, seven, put her hands on her hips before continuing with the chase.

Lady Rosina, five, hurried along lest she be left behind, holding the hemline of her dress far above her ruffled pantalettes trimmed with French lace. "Here kitty..." Since Bonaparte's defeat, at least they no longer had to resort to unusual methods to purchase imported French lace.

Jory couldn't help but smile at the scene. One could not deny the joy her charges brought her each day, and thankfully, she got along well with Mrs. Winthrop. When the governess had no need of her assistance, she could spend her free time reading or sketching. Or she might join the duchess with an embroidery project or some other ladylike pursuit.

Sometimes she spent weekends with her mother and siblings at home in their humble cottage dwelling, especially now that two of her younger sisters had married handsome militia soldiers after the war. But at Hillbrook Hall, she enjoyed a bedroom to herself, albeit simple amenities compared to the rest of the manor house, and albeit one door away from Mrs. Winthrop, who ran a tight ship.

Footsteps approaching from behind, and heavy ones at that, followed by a man clearing his throat, caused Jory to spin around in time to discover Farmer Owens cutting across one of the garden paths from the direction of the land he farmed for His Grace, the Duke of Gladdington, Lord Kingston. She usually saw Mr. Zachary Owens on Sundays when attending church in the village with her family or the duke's. And lately, she seemed to encounter him more than she cared to admit.

In recent weeks, he'd begun a campaign of sorts to bathe her in a plethora of unwanted attention and admiration, giving her bouquets of wildflowers, calling upon her at her mother's home, stopping to speak with her in the village of Glad Crown or after church—all when she least expected him to appear. She had done her best to remain polite without encouraging him, but upon seeing him in the duke's garden, perhaps she should discourage him. Now that he had nearly closed the space between them, her head tilted to one side and her eyes widened.

Clearly, the situation had gone beyond the pale. Napoleon may have been banished from throttling Europe, but a battle quest of her own might be in order, demanding some course of action. Because she had few suitors—in truth, no suitors—had she subconsciously allowed his pursuit of her to continue? Considering his frequently disheveled appearance, maybe it was time to find a way to insist he cease and desist his campaign. But presently, Farmer Owens bowed before her. And somehow, she did not think the duchess would approve.

"Mr. Owens…" She stiffened as heat rose to her cheeks. Had he dared to pursue her in the duke's garden then? A bold move, to be sure. What conclusions might her employer draw? And what would Mrs. Winthrop say? And what impression might he make upon her three little charges? At least he had worn his Sunday best, trading suspenders and soiled, worn work clothing for a cravat, a waistcoat under his slightly frayed Sunday best frock coat, a clean white shirt, and faded breeches. Most unusual for a weekday.

"Jory. Miss Pritchard, if I may only have but a moment of your time, I shall then return to my home and await your answer." He dropped onto bended knee before she could utter a word to deny his request for an audience of one, except for the fact they were not alone. She was surrounded by observers. Had Mrs. Winthrop gasped just then? It wouldn't surprise her in the least if one of her charges yanked on his frock coat to ask an impertinent question. Surely the duchess, likely sipping her customary warm chocolate from a china cup inside the morning room facing the garden, could see him trespassing into their private domain.

Caught off guard, her mouth gaped. He took her gloved hand in his before she could find her tongue. She tugged, but to her further amazement, he held her hand quite firmly, preventing her from withdrawing it.

"Miss Pritchard, I can no longer deny my feelings which have grown by leaps and bounds for you in recent weeks."

Leaps and bounds indeed, but she had yet to find her tongue, for he was a very stern man who seldom smiled. Who knew what reaction he might have if she found her voice?

"I come with my heart in hand to ask if you will do me the pleasure of becoming my wife. I realize ours would be a simple life together, not so grand as all of this." He looked around at their surroundings and cleared his throat. Then he smiled, adding to her astonished gaze. "But it will be a loving and affectionate situation. I would look after you and do my best to serve you for the rest of my life."

Seeing the hope in his eyes, she stammered. "M-mister Owens, I cannot…" How could she decline Zachary Owens without offending him?

The terrace doors burst open, and the duchess came running outside, the train of her gown rustling over the stones after her, a letter fluttering in her hands as she waved it, calling out, "Jory, I have the most wonderful news! You will never believe who has…" The duchess stopped a few feet away from them, breathless. "Oh, pardon me. I didn't know you had a guest."

Mr. Owens rose. Removing his top hat, he bowed to the duchess. "I beg your pardon for intruding, my lady. Miss Pritchard and I can continue our discussion later."

Jory's eyes widened. Or maybe not ever.

He cast a longing glance at her one last time before turning on his heel and dashing away, leaving her more speechless than his arrival had. The duchess paused at her side, and together, they stared after him.

"Was Farmer Owens proposing an offer of matrimony, or did my eyes deceive me?"

Jory turned to face the duchess, as curious about the letter in her hands as what had prompted the farmer to believe she shared his sentiments. "Your eyes did not deceive you, and I am as shocked as you. I had no idea. Only that he has recently begun to call upon me whenever I am at home with my mother. He has taken to attempting to speak with me if I encounter him in church or the village. A most disturbing situation. I fear I do not know how to decline him."

"Indeed." The duchess tucked her arm in Jory's elbow and turned her toward the manor house. "Well then, we shall have to see to it that you are not at home with your mother, because something most wonderful has happened. The governess for the Duke of Pensford has abandoned her post."

"Oh." Perhaps the dastardly Duke of Pensford deserved it. She didn't see how it was wonderful. He had danced with her twice at last year's Christmas ball, indicating an interest in her before all of the fashionable guests, and with the Prince Regent present among them. He'd spoken at length with her at several dinners during the week of celebration at Hillbrook Hall, telling her about each of his four children and his estate near the village of Pensford in Somerset.

He'd strolled through the conservatory with her, laughing heartily when she told him how she'd been caught poaching as a youngster on Lord Kingston's land. He had encountered her twice in the library, greeting her warmly, eager to discuss his selections with her and hear about her literary selections. And then he'd disappeared entirely. Dropped off the face of the earth. Dashing her hopes, not so much as one letter arriving since last December.

"He writes to ask for you specifically, wondering how soon you can arrive as a replacement. He is in dire need of your assistance, Jory." The duchess smiled.

"*My* assistance?" Jory's brows rose. Would her employer send her away to become his governess? Surely, he had found some other romantic interest after all of this time—the only reasonable explanation for his lack of communication. He had obviously decided she was too far beneath him since she wasn't a member of the peerage. Could her heart bear becoming employed as his governess, relegated to observe him in a new romantic relationship? It all sounded like a cruel joke. Surely the duchess did not intend to cast her off upon the Duke of Pensford as one of his employees after his disappointing behavior.

"Yes. He inquires specifically about you. I knew he eventually would come to his senses. He and his sisters and the children are in London after enjoying a few weeks at the seaside in Brighton, but he would like you to join him in Mayfair before they retreat to Mulberry House. Well, I assume he will soon depart for the countryside of Somerset until November, when the season begins."

"I see…" But how could she tell her benefactress she had no desire to leave Hillbrook Hall? She was happy with her life near Glad Crown Village, except for the fact she found offers of marriage limited to farmers who were very stern, and she could not picture herself married to someone who seldom smiled. Possibilities were especially limited now that the war had ended, and no new regiments of soldiers flocked to the area.

While she had enjoyed her two dances with the Duke of Pensford last Christmas, much time had passed since then. Surely, His Grace would never consider her anything more than a governess, though the way the duchess had often spoken of him since the ball indicated she harbored higher hopes for them.

By all indications, her plans for Jory went far beyond the role of a governess. Hadn't Jory learned after the long-ago dances with the Earl of Dunmore, Lord Cunningham, who had danced with her at a different Christmas ball, that she should never hold onto notions of anything more when it came to the upper classes? *That* situation had only left her with something akin to a broken heart. No, not akin. Most definitely a broken heart.

But he at least *had* corresponded with her. And not merely twice, but thrice. Nonetheless, she had recovered, and despite far more attention lavished upon her from Lord Archer Thornberry who had stayed longer than merely for the day of the ball as Lord Cunningham had done, she had managed to keep her heart in check and her hopes low. Though it had required a great deal of effort on her part after he'd danced with her twice, as the Earl had done.

She had seen Lord Josephus Cunningham, the earl, a few times since that ball, held two years previous. And though she did hold a certain fondness for him because of his humor and lighthearted personality, she'd found him somewhat fickle when it came to women. He danced and mingled with other ladies too when he'd left Nottingham to make his way to Northampton for other parties held at the estate of her benefactors. But alas, he spent most of his time in London, where the duchess had insisted she attend as her companion alongside her and the Duke of Gladdington for several evenings of dancing and dinner parties last year.

The duchess chatted on, seemingly oblivious to Jory's reservations. "Now, we must see that you are properly packed for the journey. You shall take one of my lady's maids and since it is a long journey of three days to London, you shall ride in my chariot with postilion drivers. You will need your best frocks, for everyone knows the duke and I think of you like one of our very own daughters."

For this, Jory was most grateful, though it did little to endear her to her sisters, who somewhat despised her for it. But several of her sisters had found husbands, and she had not, so it was they who seemed content with their newfound marriages. Would she ever find such happiness?

Her Grace paused near some of the garden's finest rose shrubs, but she didn't take time to notice them as her eyes grew wide. "You shall tuck a blunderbuss under your seat for extra safety measures. Of course, the drivers will be armed, but all the same, I know *you* of all my lady acquaintances and dearest friends can handle a blunderbuss. Keep it with you for as long as you are separated from us. I want you to have a means of protection, but do not mention it to anyone. I shall have a word with Alton about the preparations."

Alton, the butler, could be counted upon for discretion. Resuming their walk toward the house, Jory couldn't help but raise an eyebrow and smile at these remarks. A governess with a lady's maid? How ever would she explain *that* to Lord Thornberry's staff? They would despise her from the start, but taking someone along to style her hair and look after her wardrobe did please her. She would be too busy tending to the children to give much consideration to those matters. And a journey in the stylish Kingston private traveling chariot? With her own firearm too! How could she say no when a chance to see more of England presented itself? It all sounded rather exciting, except for her dreaded destination, for she had no desire to see the duke again and had given up any ambitions with him.

"We must make haste. I'll have one of the maids come and help us fill your trunk with the very best gowns. You'll need to pen a letter of explanation to your mother instead of going home to say your farewells lest you run into Mr. Owens again. I'll ask Alton to have one of the footmen deliver the letter for you."

The duchess opened the terrace doors wide, and Jory dutifully followed her inside, but things were moving rapidly. Her Grace left little opportunity to utter more than a few words of reply. Just as it had been with Farmer Owens, when she couldn't find her tongue. Goodness, what a day she was having! Things were happening so fast—too fast.

"Now Jory, if it were me, I wouldn't pen a reply to Farmer Owens yet. Next time I see him, I will take him aside and explain that you were needed elsewhere on a most urgent matter. I shan't tell him where you have gone, no matter how hard he presses me. I advise you to ask your mother and siblings not to mention it either. Perhaps you should pray about his offer whilst you are getting to know Archer. It is good to have options when it comes to marriage, but there is no time to answer him now, not when the world is about to open before you with opportunity. You must leave at once, before this very day is out. I shall send a reply to the duke in today's post so he will be expecting your arrival three days hence. The mail coach always travels faster than anything else."

"I do not think I can count Mr. Owens as a suitable candidate for matrimony. I am still befuddled about it," Jory managed to fit into the conversation as Lady Winifred Kingston clasped an arm around her elbow and led them through the main hall toward the staircase. "I wasn't seriously considering him. I fear I barely know him except as a fellow villager, but I suppose I should ponder it, since I have no line of eager prospects to prevent me. A reply made in haste might cause me regret later, though I cannot even imagine it."

The duchess nodded, a smile playing on her lips. "That is wise. I have prayed for something to happen so that you could spend more time with Archer. Though the season will start in a few months, and the duke will be pestered by flocks of marriageable young ladies, it is the governess who will have his ear when it comes to matters of education concerning his children. So, you see, Providence has a hand in this matter."

"Perhaps," Jory mumbled, lifting her skirts as they climbed the staircase. Did Providence consider her plight? Why did it seem as if He had forgotten her? Had she been remiss in her prayers or done some horrible deed to find herself nearly on the shelf? "Do pardon me for speaking my mind." She paused on one of the steps to catch her breath, lifting her skirt so as not to trip on the hem. "I do not think the duke is interested in what you infer where I am concerned. He only wishes for a governess."

"Of course, he adores you, and for more than the role of a governess. Only he does not know it yet."

Jory could not imagine how the duchess knew this, but she spoke with great confidence.

"And he obviously remembers you quite well since he specifically asked for you. But he will soon know his heart after spending a little more time with you. Come along, Jory. We haven't a moment to waste." The duchess pulled her along. "Now you see, my favorite source for news of the Ton mentioned that the Duke of Pensford was seen in attendance at a few balls toward the end of the last season, but he almost always left very early and seldom danced with anyone, except for the daughter of a marquess. That made him a regrettable choice in marriage last season since he never came up to scratch, but I fear he was not ready to consider marrying anyone, being recently widowed only two years ago. But now…"

Jory leaned toward the duchess, taking in her words. Perhaps this was encouraging news …but why hadn't he written to her? He must have been quite taken with the daughter of the marquess. There lurked a rake inside the dandy for not writing to her even one time after raising her hopes as he had. She no longer trusted the man, even if the duchess praised him until the sun went down. Part of her couldn't blame him since she had no dowry, no lineage of great importance, and no courtesy title or otherwise to offer, but still…

Her Grace rambled on. "The writer of my favorite society column has recently declared him the most eligible bachelor of the coming season. She knows his period of mourning has ended and an extra year has passed for good measure, not to mention these many months since Christmas. *Now* is the time for you to embark upon this journey before all the mothers of the Ton send their daughters to secure his attention as the Marchioness of Colchester has done with Lady Flora, her daughter. You must have confidence in yourself and let the graciousness in your character shine. Everything else will fall into place."

Confidence? Graciousness? How about disappointment laced with a bit of disgust? Was there room for *that* in the duchess's favorite society column? But listening to Lady Kingston rattle on about the fact she would discard some of her new gowns and other fashionable items into Jory's trunk, she could see there would be no protesting the grand plans of the duchess.

"Lady Flora was last season's diamond of the first water, until the Marquess of Colchester, her father, made some unwise investments. To recover, he gambled away their fortune, along with her dowry, or so rumor has it. The scandal seems to have ruined her chances of obtaining a marriage proposal before the end of last season, but everyone expected Archer to have proposed by now. But he has not. So, it only makes sense that he is still considering you." They had reached the second floor and the Duchess of Gladdington paused, leaning against the railing. "Remember, dear Jory, you mustn't trust Lady Flora. Consider her your archenemy when you encounter her, for undoubtedly, her mother will insist she make every effort to obtain an offer of marriage from Archer."

"If she was last season's diamond, even without a dowry, she could have almost anyone…" Jory's brows furrowed as she considered the matter. "I cannot imagine him having any hopes for a governess."

"Yes, but surely, he has realized Lady Flora is digging for gold. And I have it on good authority from a friend that the marchioness wants the title of a duchess for her daughter *and* Lord Thornberry's fortune. In fact, I do not understand how the Marquess of Colchester continues to hold on to his country estate or his townhome in Mayfair after what he has done. But I think it is you who will ultimately make our duke happy. It was my intention to sponsor you for the coming season as a debutante since you are my protégée, but now this has happened beforehand. I believe it is our best course of action to guarantee you a chance with the duke. And, while you are in his care, dear Jory, always read the society columns when in London or engaging with any society in the countryside so that you can protect your reputation. Once lost, the Ton rarely accepts those it casts out."

Oh, dear! Archenemy? The Ton? She had only been to a few dances in London with the duchess, and only as her companion. What had the meddling duchess gotten her into? She was merely the daughter of a tenant farmer for the Duke of Gladdington, and her father had passed away long ago. She couldn't imagine being sponsored by the duchess, even if the duchess did consider her a protégée. She shouldn't get her hopes up concerning the duke. He had requested a governess, not a wife. Perhaps he would see her as wholly unsuited for the position and return her to Northampton at once. The fact she had only ever been an assistant to Mrs. Winthrop and a companion to the duchess was her saving grace.

In fact, she had all but given up on the idea of marriage. She did not seem to fit in anywhere. Not with the common man, nor those of the landed gentry, nor of the peerage. Would the Duke of Pensford continue to court last season's diamond while her benefactress forced her into the uncomfortable role of functioning as his governess? She simply had to find a way out of this impossible situation!

Chapter Two

Think not that I am come to send peace on earth: I came not to send peace, but a sword. For I am come to set a man at variance against his father, and the daughter against her mother, and the daughter in law against her mother in law. And a man's foes shall be they of his own household.

Matthew 10:34-36

27 Grosvenor Square, Mayfair, London

After three days of jostling inside the duchess's private traveling chariot, Jory was thankful when the drivers steered the chariot toward an old inn along the highway leading to London. She only wanted to stand and stretch, have a meal in the dining room, a hot bath, and collapse in a bed until the final leg of the journey, the following morning.

She placed her order for a bowl of hearty stew with the innkeeper's wife who informed them it was the day's special, as did Miss Matilda Davison, her maid. The waitress promised to return with a basket of piping hot bread, but she left them with a pot of steaming tea and two cups with saucers. Miss Davison sipped some tea and resumed knitting a scarf she'd worked on since they'd left Northampton. The latest edition of a newspaper from London lay nearby. Jory unfolded it, scanning it for the society column since Lady Kingston had said she should be mindful of what the papers printed.

Aghast after perusing the society column in the dim lighting of the Tudor-styled inn, the writer who'd penned it nearly sealed her opinion of the duke forever, relegating him to someone she would never want for a husband. She almost spit out her tea when she read a few lines about the duke--:

> *Ladies, beware the man who behaves like the handsome widower, the Duke of Pensford. Though a few weeks ago, it is true I deemed him the most eligible bachelor of the coming season, I have it on good authority from a most reliable source that at this very moment, he is moving his mistress—under the guise of some other role, no doubt—directly into his London residence before making an offer of matrimony to last season's diamond, Lady Flora. That is, if he will still have her, and if she will still have him. That aside, some of us might endure such a raging insult kept right under our noses for the size of such a fortune as the duke's, but don't most of us want true love? Tsk, tsk, I say, but can last season's diamond honestly expect to capture true love after surviving the scandal of one's father gambling away one's dowry?*

"Are you quite all right, Jory? You've lost all the color in your face." Miss Davison—Tilly to all who knew her well—peered at her with concern in her blue-gray eyes.

Jory folded the paper and slid it aside. "I'm fine, thank you." She closed her eyes and pressed a hand over half of her face. "Merely famished and weary of travel, but here comes our meal now." Was the gossip true?

Tilly eyed her warily and reached for the newspaper, suspicion in her expression. Jory could tell by her expression that she too now spotted the snippet of gossip. Sighing, she folded the paper and set it aside. "Mayhap 'tis not true. Most of this idle gossip is malice, waiting to destroy some other soul's life."

"Mayhap," Jory repeated, but when the innkeeper's wife brought them their warm bread and bowls of stew, she could barely enjoy the meal despite the protests of her empty stomach. Her mind swirled with confusion. Was it true that Lord Thornberry had taken a mistress into his household? And how often would she have to face Lady Flora, surely a beautiful debutante, the diamond of the first water from the last season?

Did Lord Thornberry, or his sisters perhaps, invite the daughter of the marquess to have tea or dine with them often? Did he dress in his finest cravat and waistcoat with tight fitting pantaloons, topping it off with his best beaver each week to attend dinner parties and the like with Lady Flora?

Tilly gulped down several bites of the stew and then reached for some bread to which she set about applying a generous amount of butter. "Ye don't suppose that news of his future governess has spread to the writer of this column before our arrival, do ye?"

Aghast, Jory swallowed her small bite of the stew. How shrewd of Miss Davison to discern that the very gossip they'd read might be written about none other than…*herself*…of all things! But no, it had to be about someone else. News couldn't travel that fast between servants that far apart and have time to reach the ears of some high society writer, could it? She shook her head. "Surely, it must be penned concerning some other victim of this horrid writer."

But the words of her travel companion nagged at her. And what of the duke's poor, dear children? When did he find time to give them the proper attention they deserved if he kept a mistress *and* courted a fine socialite everyone expected him to marry? The gall of it all had her blood nearly to boiling point by the time they arrived in London. She'd had the entirety of the final leg of their journey to consider it, convinced of her decision to plead with the duke that she might return to Northampton as the wisest course of action.

The traveling chariot finally arrived at the duke's fashionable townhome facing a square park. The park was a little piece of countryside in the middle of the townhomes facing it. She could only admire it from the front steps for a moment since the butler beckoned them inside. She squared her shoulders, intending to inform the duke that she was not suitable for the task and ask him to send her home.

Why waste a moment of his time or hers? The duchess would simply have to resign herself to defeat where her matchmaking plans for Lord Archer Thornberry were concerned. Surely her benefactress could think of someone better suited to the idea of a marriage with her if she insisted upon marrying her off to someone.

Only now, seated in the drawing room with Lord Thornberry's two sisters, she kept her hands folded and placed in her lap, occasionally sipping some of the tea his eldest sister had poured, waiting for the duke to return home from wherever he had gone. Perhaps he'd spent a customary day in his seat at the House of Lords, or maybe he'd dined with some important member of the Ton, engaging in a robust political discussion. Or worse, did he hide somewhere in the house with his mistress? The very thought made her gulp as she listened to his sisters bore her with a few remarks about their recent time in London and how the last season had gone for them.

Surely, wherever he was, she guessed even sitting in the House of Lords might be vastly more entertaining than the drole discussion she held with his sisters, who glanced at her with uneasy expressions upon their faces. Likely, they too had read the latest edition of the society column. In fact, Jory's keenly observant eyes spotted a newspaper tucked into the throw pillows on the end of the sofa where the sisters both sat, facing her. At least she could glance out of the front windows behind the sisters at the carriages passing by.

"Did I understand correctly that you have only ever been an assistant governess for the Duchess of Gladdington?" Lady Julia held her cup suspended above the saucer, peering at her with an arched brow, a low coffee table between them with the duke's finest tea service spread upon it.

Jory nodded unapologetically. If her plan were to succeed, she must be convincing to everyone in the duke's household that she simply lacked the experience and qualifications to become a governess in her own right. "You have understood me correctly. I'm sure the duke won't want me to stay when he could have someone far more qualified than myself. The

Duke and Duchess of Gladdington have only adopted me into their fold, treating me as if I were one of their daughters. In fact, the duchess is a kind benefactress and rather views me as one of her pet projects, her protégée if you will."

"I see. How very kind indeed and most fortunate for you." Lady Julia exchanged a wary glance with her younger sister, Lady Daphne.

Good. Her plan was already working. They seemed…wary. She could only pray they did not think *she* was the duke's mistress moving into his residence under the guise of governess.

The sisters resembled the duke, sharing the same dark hair and blue eyes. She learned a few things about them during the course of the tea, served with seedcakes, biscuits, and tiny cakes with butter icing. They were both "out," having been presented at court to Queen Charlotte, something Jory wouldn't need to worry about since she wasn't part of the aristocracy and the duchess had now put her forth as part of the respectable but nonetheless, working class. Julia, the same age as Jory at twenty and two years, had reluctantly admitted she was about to face her third season, and Daphne, about to enter her second, was twenty.

"Ah, being twenty-two, will the duchess perhaps sponsor you for a season, or apply to Almack's for vouchers for you?" Lady Julia tilted her head to one side.

Jory suspected she was on a fishing expedition, attempting to learn all she could about the new governess for her brother's children. "She did mention it for next season perhaps. I'm not entirely sure, so I do not raise my hopes. I suppose it is in the realm of possibilities for the future. Another reason why I do not think I would make for a good choice as the governess for the duke."

Lady Daphne patted the small poodle she called Mitzi, perched in her lap. "Although you are young as we are, it will be most refreshing to have a governess who can keep up with the energy of our nieces and nephews."

Voices clamored from the hall before Lady Julia could explore this topic any further. The noise caused her to squeeze her eyes shut and grimace. "An excellent point, Daphne."

"Ahoy, mates!" a young lad's voice echoed through the stairwell and into the drawing room.

Jory glanced through the open drawing room doors revealing the stairwell as a young boy slid down the banister. He did so while holding what appeared to be a toy sword. He carried out a boisterous landing onto both feet with great success, and a thud when his shoes hit the wooden floor.

She nearly called out bravo and resisted the urge to clap her hands for the performance, biting her lower lip instead. Cheering the young master of the house might be taking things a bit too far. Was he the oldest son? What if the duke wouldn't allow her to go home? She might be stuck in the household and expected to maintain some degree of dignity, not that she cared overmuch about maintaining one's dignity. But Lady Kingston said it was important.

Sliding down the banister immediately after the boy, a young girl hollered, "Move out of the way, Pirate Henry!" Her hands were tied together at the wrists with a bit of rope, but she managed to slide gracefully despite this predicament. A brightly colored pink crown of paper perched atop her dark curls.

'Pirate Henry' obeyed her command, jumping to one side in time for his sister to land where he'd stood seconds before. "Ho there, Princess Jane! Ye shall not escape my ship." He pointed his sword under her chin.

"Oh no! I am captured…" 'Princess Jane' adjusted the crown and swept the back of her hand in one smooth, dramatic action across her forehead. "I am doomed! Doomed, I say."

Lady Julia pressed a hand against her temple. Mitzi drooped her head on Lady Daphne's arm, appearing forlorn to have not been included in the action taking place out in the hall.

A smaller boy slid down the banister next, waving his sword about as he gripped the rail with his other hand, a small box tucked under his arm. "I've got the treasure! Ahoy! Make way for the pirate's loot!" The boy stopped sliding near the end of the banister. He eyed the space below and then jumped, landing squarely on his feet, the sound of his shoes hitting the polished flooring echoing through the hall.

"Well done, Pirate Charlie. Well done! Show me the treasure before we tie these princesses to the mast for their doomed fate." Henry flung part of his cape over one shoulder and held out his hand for the treasure box, but he kept a sword aimed at the one he'd called Princess Jane.

Before Pirate Charlie could comply, a fourth voice rang out. "Look out below, for here cometh a lady in distress! Make way for Princess Edith!" The smallest sister now slid down the same banister into Jory's view. She wore a paper crown to match her sister's and clutched a kitten who leapt from her arms, declaring it would have no more of sliding down banisters. Jory smothered a laugh. Edith was simply adorable, including her sweet lisp.

"Now you see what I meant about energy." Lady Daphne smiled warmly at Jory. "They are a lot to keep up with."

Lady Julia cleared her throat and elbowed her sister.

"But a happy lot, and very obedient," Daphne clarified.

Jory couldn't help but smile in response to Daphne's remarks and the delightful performance. The children were likely aware of her arrival and had decided to introduce themselves in their favorite type of play.

"Who shall rescue us now?" Princess Jane clung to Princess Edith, perhaps the same age as Lady Rosina, back in Northampton.

Yes, who indeed? They certainly needed rescuing, on account of their father. Jory sighed.

A door creaked open and closed. Floorboards creaked from somewhere down the hall, and a strong male voice called out. "I shall rescue you!"

Shrieks, squeals of delight, and greetings of *'Father!'* and *'Papa!'* ensued. Before the children and their onlookers could recover their surprise, the duke appeared amid them at the foot of the staircase. The culprit himself, offering to rescue them.

Jory guessed he had come inside through a private rear entrance. He swung Edith up into his arms, tweaked Jane on the nose, patted Charlie on the head, and ruffled Henry's hair as the children swarmed around him.

"Put me down, Father, or they shall have all the candy!" Edith wailed, to which Lord Thornberry complied so she could join in searching the pockets of his coat.

How could the duke seem so doting upon his children, if he was a reckless and womanizing rake? No, she wouldn't be so fooled by his title. Gentlemen with titles were supposed to be honorable men, but certainly not if they kept women in secret. When the maid who had brought the tea tray was accompanied by another maid who appeared to be new, judging by the lost look on her face, Jory guessed the servant could be the mistress the column had referred to. She had been pretty enough to be a mistress, even with her hair stuffed under a ruffled cap to match her white pinafore over its plain black dress.

A butler came into view, returning Jory to the present moment instead of her thoughts about the duke's new reputation, but he hung back after accepting His Grace's hat and cane, clearly waiting for the children to finish raiding pockets.

"Sugared almonds!" Jane squealed, her wrists still tied, though she managed to present a handful of the treats to her siblings.

"Candied jelly fruits!" Charlie held a sugary orange jelly up and popped it in his mouth, chewing it with a grin on his face as he handed some to the others.

When the children stood back to eye each other's treats and share their bounty, the butler stepped forward and accepted the coat Lord Thornberry held out. "Any news, Eddington?"

"Nothing that can't wait for later, but you do have a visitor in case you didn't see the carriage and drivers. The governess from Northampton, a Miss Pritchard, has arrived about half an hour ago." The butler, Mr. Eddington, nodded toward the drawing room.

Lord Thornberry spun around and peered in their direction. He connected with Jory's gaze at once. She looked away, decidedly peeved with him despite his delightful children.

Lady Jane stepped boldly into the drawing room. She gave Jory the once over, her eyes inspecting every inch, an impertinent expression in her face, as if deciding whether or not she was fit to be seated upon their sofa without a proper paper crown atop her head. "Are you to be our new governess?"

Honesty was always the best policy. "That depends," Jory replied, sipping some of her tea.

Henry stepped forward. "On what does it depend?"

"My decision. I haven't yet decided if I will stay." Jory returned her teacup to its saucer.

"Henry, Jane, take your brother and sister upstairs to the playroom and play quietly until supper." Lord Thornberry eyed his two eldest with a stern expression as he stepped inside the drawing room. His brows furrowed with concern as he glanced at Jory.

Jane tried to eat some of the sugared almonds, but with her hands tied, it did not have a very ladylike result.

"Perhaps someone should untie Jane…" Jory spoke softly, but she resumed drinking a sip of her tea as the children began filing toward the staircase.

The duke turned in time to see Jane's childish manners. "Untie your sister, Henry."

"Yes, sir." Henry, last to follow the others, untied Jane as they headed upstairs.

Jory made note of Henry's good manners, in case she truly had to take charge of the lively brood. She hadn't had to teach boys before, except if she counted her brothers. Hopefully the duke's children would not touch the banister and leave a trail of sticky sugar crumbs. Observing their ascent, she was pleasantly surprised to see none of the children touched the railing. Maybe they had been trained well thus far, but the duke's voice drew her attention.

"Ah! How good it is to see you again, Jory. I mean, Miss Pritchard. Do please forgive me for keeping you waiting. I trust your journey was enjoyable. Shall we have a private word in my study?" He stood only a few feet away, adjusting his waistcoat. Turning toward his sisters, he greeted them with a nod as Jory rose to follow him. "Good evening, Julia,

Daphne."

Lady Julia released a long sigh and sipped more tea. "I'm not sure if it is a good evening or not yet, but we are very glad you are here to install your new governess."

"Julia and I are heading to a rout this evening after dinner. Will you be joining us, dear brother?" Daphne angled toward him.

Anxious to be done speaking with him so she could either tell the postilion drivers waiting outside his stable behind the house to return her to Northampton or leave without her, Jory refrained from tapping an impatient foot. She'd already instructed Tilly—waiting upstairs in what was to be her London bedroom if she assumed the role the duke required—not to unpack a single thing.

He shook his head. "No, you know how I prefer to avoid those crowded parties like the plague, but Miss Pritchard and I will join you for dinner after our meeting. I assume you have escorts for the rout."

Waiting for the duke to lead the way to his study, Jory also resisted the urge to announce she would not be joining them for dinner. She'd rather dine at some London inn or tavern on the way back to Northampton or starve than remain in the duke's company for a moment longer than necessary.

"Yes, we do have an escort. Lord Leyton agreed to join us. And since the season has not begun, I doubt very much that this rout will be crowded overmuch. But very well then, we shall attend without you. However, I'm sure the earl will be disappointed once again." Lady Julia sighed and sipped more tea.

Lady Daphne patted the dejected poodle in her lap. "Don't worry, Mitzi. I shan't be out too late."

"He'll recover." Archer gazed at the dog. "The earl, I meant."

Jory gulped down a chuckle. At least the man had a sense of humor, though it did little to endear him to her at this point.

"Right this way, Miss Pritchard." He extended an arm toward the staircase and when she stepped forward, he led her upstairs to his study. He went around behind his desk while indicating she could choose one of the two leather chairs facing it. A warm fire crackled in the fireplace to their left, warding off the evening chill since fall had begun to turn the leaves and cooler weather was on its way. At least she had enjoyed the brilliant colors displaying God's handiwork along the way to London. Otherwise, in her opinion, the journey had been an utter waste.

A dog reclining before the fireplace caught her eye as she settled into a chair. A Great Dane, the well-groomed pet perked up at their intrusion into his domain, wagged his tail. Apparently, the doggie knew the master's routine, except oddly enough, it returned its head to rest upon the carpeted floor. Hmpf! Even the dog wanted little to do with his master. He did not even come around the desk for a pat on his head or a scratch between his ears. Ordinarily, she might have asked its name, but this was no pleasure visit. It was her best chance of escape.

Did he appear uncomfortable after she sat, taking little time to arrange her skirts? She hadn't said a word of greeting to the man who had uprooted her from everything she knew and loved. When he seated himself, she rather enjoyed the fact he shifted twice in his seat before finally settling and placing his large hands on the desk and folding them, unfolding them, and folding them again.

Perhaps it was good that he squirmed due to her silence. Why had he never resumed any contact with her? And if he had ever cared to know her more, why did he now find himself desperate enough for a governess to suddenly prevail upon *her* assistance, eight months after dancing with her twice, when all he had to do was place a discreet advertisement in the London newspapers or make a few local inquiries? Was there something to what the duchess had implied? And if so, how could there be if he courted last season's diamond *and* housed a mistress?

Chapter Three

Let us therefore follow after the things which make for peace,

and things wherewith one may edify another.

Romans 14:19

Gesturing toward the Great Dane who eyed them with curiosity but remained in his place, Lord Archer Thornberry offered a weak smile to Jory. Why did he have the distinct impression something was bothering her? "I should introduce you to Milo, but that can wait since we have more important matters to discuss."

She took in another glimpse of the dog at the mention of his name, turning her gaze upon him. "Yes, we do have important matters to discuss."

"I hope you didn't have too long of a wait before my arrival." Archer cleared his throat. "I was summoned to the palace to meet with the Prince Regent, an unavoidable request."

"I see." Miss Pritchard pressed her lips into a firm thin line.

Lips he might like to kiss one day, though he didn't know where that thought had come from. Presently, her chocolate eyes bored through him like flint. She did not look one bit happy with him about this arrangement, leaving him at a loss as to how to begin the conversation. He should tread cautiously.

Perhaps he could start by thanking her for coming to his rescue. "I must begin by thanking you for coming. I am in a dire predicament, Miss Pritchard."

"Begging your pardon, Your Grace, but you seem to have things well in hand, and I am not nearly experienced enough to become the governess for your children. I have only ever been an assistant governess. And in fact, other than looking after my brothers on occasion, I have never had any boys for students. So, you see, I confess I am not qualified to retain in your hire. You may return me to Hillbrook Hall at once and find someone more suitable." She maintained a stiff posture and kept her hands folded in her lap, staring straight ahead at something slightly above and beyond him.

So that was her problem. She doubted her qualifications, though he suspected there might be more to it than her admission of a lack in experience. He cleared his throat, again. "I am aware of your limited experience. The duchess has already written to explain. But it is my opinion and the good opinion of the Duchess of Gladdington, that you are perfectly suited for the position, though you may have doubts. I lack a governess, but here you are, and I am willing to give it a try." He paused. "Are you willing to give it a try?"

She shook her head. "I'm certain I would only be a great disappointment to Your Grace and his family."

"I care little about what my family thinks. What I need is your assistance and the expertise you have to offer." He leaned forward, but why did her eyes continue to stare above and behind him?

"Perhaps you could place an advertisement for a governess or make discreet inquiries for someone else, Your Grace. I fear this arrangement would only lead to regret." Her gaze remained solidly fixed on some object above his head. Perhaps the portrait of his wife…?

Maybe he should remove it in hopes of making eye contact. She seemed bent on avoiding not only the position but preventing connection. This wasn't the warm and friendly Jory he remembered. She had invited him to use her first name at Hillbrook Hall, but now she was so stiff and formal.

"Come now, Jory. I have no concerns since our first meeting at Christmas last. And I need someone now, not a few weeks hence. Finding someone else could take months, lengthy interviews, and perusing a great many reference letters. I prefer to hire my governesses through discreet inquiries from those whom I trust and know. In any case, it is *you* I am interested in for the position, not someone else." Why wouldn't she look at him directly? Ah, yes, the portrait.

He rose and removed the painting he'd commissioned of his dearly departed wife from the wall, leaning it against his desk but on the floor where she could no longer see it. Emma would forgive him if the good Lord happened to permit her to look down from heaven at this very moment, but she would be sorely disappointed if he did not find a governess to teach their children. He would return the portrait to its place later.

Settling into his seat again, he took in the same firm expression on her face. Lovely features to be sure, if only she would smile like when they'd first met. What had he done to upset her?

She sighed, her brows furrowing, a slightly puzzled expression appearing in those wide brown eyes. "Surely you are mistaken, my lord. I cannot possibly live up to your expectations."

Did she have some other reason behind her wish to return to Northampton? Perhaps a new beau? For how long she had been upset with him, he could not say. If he had lost her to some other gentleman, he had only himself to blame for making no attempt to write a letter to her since the Christmas ball. And he *had* been interested in writing to her, but he'd argued himself out of doing so.

'Twas likely she had expected a letter, and the lack of one had caused her to distance herself from him. But in his defense, he *had* been busy. Raising four children without a wife at his side took a great deal of his time, as did many other matters. And her station in life had given him some pause for concern once he'd returned home and had reflected on it. What would people say if he pursued a governess? Not that he hadn't enjoyed his encounters with her, but it just wasn't done.

"Live up to my expectations? Of course you can." He stumbled his way through a reply. "Y-you have already lived up to expectations, just by traveling all this way."

Seeing a slight grimace appear on her face, he guessed only pleading with her sensibility and mercy at this point could make a difference. Clearly, she did not wish to stay.

Perhaps he *should* have written to her. He *had* immensely enjoyed her company and dancing with her. It must have given rise to hopes of something more in her heart, but he wasn't sure if he was ready to begin such pursuits after losing Emma.

If he was honest, his mind had rehearsed their time together at Hillbrook Hall more times than he cared to admit. He had inquired about her as soon as his governess had packed up and fled with no notice. Perhaps he harbored something of a desire to know her more in his heart, too.

Only, he couldn't bring himself to say something so bold. A confession of that sort would not be well received, especially if she had another beau. And he wasn't sure that he was ready to admit such a preposterous thing. What if he had misjudged the situation? What if she didn't reciprocate his notion to get to know her a little more? Especially when he couldn't explain why he had allowed so much time to pass without writing to her.

Archer sighed and rose from his seat. Coming around the desk, he perched on the edge of the desk. He considered reaching out to place his hand over hers, but he dare not touch her or sit too close. She might fly out of the room faster than a hummingbird could flap its wings.

With everything he faced at stake, he simply had to find a way to convince her to stay. His former governess could not have chosen a worse time to leave. "Jory, if you will please allow me to explain."

She lowered her gaze to her hands. Her chest heaved when she drew in another sigh and released it, indicating her exasperation with him. "Go on."

Everyone wants something from a duke. How could he explain his troubles without sounding trite?

He began, keeping his pace measured. "First of all, while we are being honest with each other, I should admit that I am pressed by trouble on every side. I bear the burden of rearing four dearly spoiled and sometimes willful children. In addition, you have now met my two sisters, who are equally spoiled, just as demanding, and in want of husbands unless I wish to doom myself to living with them forever."

Her head tilted toward him, encouraging him to continue. He crossed his arms over his chest. "I also have a penniless—without blame that her jointure was unable to be met upon her husband's death—but opinionated and sometimes difficult mother-in-law. She too is dependent upon my generosity and resides in the dowager house at my ducal estate. I cannot cast her out. She is the only living grandparent for my children and has few relations. As if all of that were not enough, there is more. Much more."

She arched a brow.

Archer rested his hands on his knees. "Trouble is brewing in the village of Pensford, my principal seat. It began around the time of Peterloo, but I cannot put my finger on exactly what is amiss. I have been away, preventing my personal investigation of it. But I have a strong feeling that I should be there, looking into it. I had promised the children and my sisters that I would take them to the seaside for a brief summer respite. Now that we have returned, my two younger sisters, also entirely dependent upon me, are bored. They have pressed me relentlessly for a country house party."

"Oh." She spoke softly. "Country house parties do require a great deal of effort."

He nodded. But her response sounded a bit flat, as if she wasn't sure that anything he'd said thus far was reason enough for her to consider accepting the position.

All he'd admitted might even frighten her away if she did not wish to mingle with more members of the peerage, but he dove on so that she might understand his pressures. "I fear at this very moment they are planning to invite all sorts of imminent guests. I have only myself to blame. In a moment of weakness, I said yes to their wishes. Though I deeply regret it, I cannot bring myself to retract my own words."

She said nothing. He continued. "I grow more alarmed by the minute at the prospect of reviewing the guest list they are to present me with." He waved a hand. "The expense and trouble of it all. Feeding them, housing them, looking after them all...endless entertaining. The staff at Mulberry House, awaiting our imminent return, are in a dither according to a letter I've received from the housekeeper. As it turns out, perhaps the guests will be useful in keeping the prince occupied."

"The prince?" Her brows rose. "The prince is coming to your estate...to Mulberry House?"

"Yes. And if all that were not enough, a gossip columnist in London has pegged me as the coming season's most eligible bachelor and has said a great many dastardly things." He gestured toward a stack of correspondence on his desk. "I have spent many hours in the past eight months hiding from numerous callers and penning replies to decline a relentless mountain of invitations to soirées, balls, dinner parties, and the like. I am informed of a similar mountain of invitations and correspondence waiting for my arrival in the countryside."

Did he detect a faint but empathetic smile play upon her lips as she raised a brow and surveyed the toppling stack of correspondence? Yet another reason he hadn't had time of late for writing many other letters, namely to Miss Pritchard, which he now wished he had done despite his misgivings. "Bear in mind, I have recently discovered that my sisters and some of their friends whom I suspect they plan to invite to Mulberry House are in some sort of a war, pitted against each other, about who they each think I should marry. The farm manager has written to me, convinced we have a poacher. He refuses to let it go in principle, as if I should allow myself to care when so many are hungry because of the corn laws."

She nodded, sitting up straighter. "Not to mention the fact many are barely recovered from the crop failures of 1816, the year we had no summer."

He'd thrown that problem of the poacher into the discussion because he recalled the story she'd told him of how she'd been taken under his friend's wing after being caught poaching on his land. Who could forget that adorable detail about her background? He'd give almost anything to see her handle a shotgun. Perhaps she would appreciate his willingness to turn a blind eye to the matter on his own land.

But that aside, had he struck a chord about a matter she cared about? She'd perked up, even participating in the conversation. Maybe they were finally getting somewhere in their ability to communicate and see eye-to-eye on some topics. "In addition, I have joined forces with some other lords to repeal the blasted corn laws, but the opposition is fierce. It weighs upon all of us who oppose them. Meanwhile, people are starving and in peril and distress. As you say, barely recovered from the year without a summer. Hence, Peterloo. And against my wishes, many members of Parliament can only further stir up strife and unrest by creating more new laws to limit the rights of those who deserve better circumstances in life."

Her eyes widened. More nodding. She seemed to know all about the recent massacre that had taken place at Peterloo. Some eighteen deaths and numerous injuries…all because some local magistrates in Manchester had unleashed a yeoman's cavalry into a peaceful crowd gathered to protest their lack of voting rights and conditions of poverty.

He drew in one last breath, hoping to bring the ridiculous details of his troubles to an end lest he frighten her away, or say something trite before a lady of her intelligence. But he did have some silly problems to confess before leading up to more about the worst problem of all, the prince coming to his home. "Additionally, I am spending a small fortune in stockings for every member of the household because there remains an unsolved mystery as to how they keep disappearing. Baffling and most inconvenient matter."

Those rose red lips remained pressed together, brows furrowed.

He waved toward the Great Dane lying on the floor before the fireplace. "And Milo seems depressed. The children are obsessed with pirates and princesses. Then, the governess packed up and left with nary a word of explanation, and worst of all, the Prince Regent has informed me only an hour ago, for reasons which I cannot fathom since I have never considered myself a close friend, that he is coming for an extended stay at Mulberry House. That could mean weeks or months."

"Did he offer any reason for his sudden inclination to visit?" Jory's head tilted to one side, her lovely brown curls slipping over her shoulder.

He might like to caress that lovely shoulder one day, but he dare not think upon it. It was unlikely anything more could come of their friendship, even if he could salvage what remained of it. "It seems he wishes to flee London to escape morbid subjects like Peterloo. Maybe it is his wish to be close to visit Bath, but not to take up residence there. And he mentioned he needs a change of location from Carlton House. Something about how he is still mourning the loss of his daughter and it reminds him too much of her, before she married."

"Ah, yes. That explains it. He wants a new venue with peace and quiet, but not all of the time. A country house is just the thing for that. And I can hardly blame him for lamenting the loss of Princess Charlotte. It's only been two years and England has barely recovered from losing her, his only heir."

Archer nodded. He sank into his chair, his shoulders drooping. "In any case, I could not bring myself to deny him. To sum everything up, I could very much use an ally in the household to help me navigate all of these matters, but especially to look after my children so they are not lost in the shuffle. With the prince coming, I can't quite wrap my head around it all."

Would she agree to stay and help him when he needed her help most—even though he hadn't begun a correspondence with her after raising her hopes? Could she blame him when society imposed expectations upon men of his standing?

The Prince Regent coming for an extended stay…? How perfectly dreadful, especially on top of a country house party of more unwanted guests! Jory sucked in a breath when Lord Thornberry finished speaking. He certainly seemed to have a mountain of troubles.

He could have escaped to some other house with his children or stayed behind in London if not for the prince coming. But now he could not. In truth, he needed the country house party to entertain the prince, as he had said.

He was right. The children would be lost in the shuffle, not to mention the fact that if he had a mistress *and* Lady Flora to contend with, who would likely follow him to the countryside…those poor dear children would be sorely neglected.

And now, he waited for her answer. She bit her lower lip, considering all he had said.

Did he truly consider her an ally? Why did her heart flutter and begin to warm to him? She could see he had his hands full, and maybe he wasn't such an ill-mannered gentleman after all. He spoke of wanting to help people and feeling weighed down by the burden of it. He spoke of having concerns for the plight of the common man. At least these were admirable things, but he was still a rake if one shred of that society column was true, though he *had* called it dastardly.

Perhaps with all these matters pressing upon him, she could understand why he hadn't written her any letters. It might even be difficult finding a clear head to resolve the idea of pursuing a commoner and a mere assistant governess like herself.

His sisters likely had an agenda of their own, prioritizing their social calendars rather than assisting with the care of their nieces and nephews. The duke had so many dependents —including more than one household full of employees and relations to look after. And the dog lying on his floor in his study *did* appear supremely bored and more forlorn than the poodle. The poor thing had barely greeted them. Most dogs would jump to their feet and bound toward a guest unless kept back by the master or a servant.

But why had his former governess abandoned him? "Have you had many governesses before?"

Archer crossed his arms over his chest. "In truth, I fear this last one was the second since my wife's passing. Eliza leaving perplexes me, especially since the children were only studying literature for an hour each day and one French lesson each week for the duration of summer. I cannot think why that was so dreadful for her or the children. She had accompanied us to the seaside and seemed to enjoy it. She was greatly helpful in tending them through a period of mourning from the loss of their mother. They are not nearly as unruly or disturbed by nightmares or prone to bouts of melancholy as they were when she arrived. I suppose I must commend her on that count."

"That does seem perplexing…to be so caring and efficient, and then disappear." What else could she say? Perhaps the children had too much idle time on their hands. And if she'd had no assistant, four children could be a handful. Maybe the situation had become a nuisance to her. "It is puzzling indeed, since you do not know why she left." She drummed her fingers softly on the arm of the leather chair, her brows furrowing. Were his boys too energetic? This prompted her next question. "Would you at some point prefer to bring in a tutor for your sons? I suppose it is possible the boys are more of a handful than the governesses are prepared for."

"Emma and I had spoken of that very thing several times before her passing. It was our wish to hire a tutor a year from now, when Henry turns twelve. He'll then have two years to study at home with a private tutor before we give him the option to attend Eton, or some other fine school for boys."

She nodded since the plan made good sense. Not all boys were cut out for boarding school, and male tutors could be demanding in and of themselves. Twelve seemed a good age to begin that type of schooling. She'd heard many a story about unhappy youths who dreaded going away from home to obtain an education. Permitting his sons to choose their fate concerning boarding school was not necessarily a bad thing if they received plenty of discipline and a strict routine at home.

However, something else nagged at her. She didn't understand why he had removed the portrait hanging on the wall behind his desk. Obviously, he'd been trying to get her attention, since she'd fixed her eyes on it, determined to avoid making eye contact with him lest he peer inside her soul and discover how much she wished to return home because of his actions, or rather the lack thereof, or perhaps both. It did surprise her some to discover she bore an uncanny resemblance to his wife, or at least she assumed it was a portrait of her. Was he subconsciously stating the fact he was ready to pursue a relationship with someone else? If so, the Duchess of Gladdington would be thrilled, but she wasn't so sure it gave her any pause for such notions. Not if he were indeed a rake!

Still, the design of the plan the duchess had in mind lurked in the back of her thoughts. She found herself continually pushing these notions away. It was ridiculous to harbor such expectations of a man who surely must marry someone of his own class. And she wasn't so sure she wanted anything at all to do with him if that society column reflected his true character, though at this very moment, she struggled to see a resemblance between him and those rumors.

In any case, he now waited quite patiently for her decision while she drummed her fingers softly on the arm of the chair. She must decide to stay on and help him as a friend, or insist he allow her to return to Northampton. Clearly, Lord Thornberry was in great want of her help with a prince coming to stay for an indefinite amount of time, even if she did lack the experience his children deserved.

She sat up taller in her seat, a firm believer in displaying good posture. "I can see you are in a rather pressing dilemma with the Prince Regent coming, and dire straits without a governess. If I agree to stay on, it would *only* be with the understanding that you will make every effort to find my replacement within two months. I cannot stay longer since I am content in Northampton." Two months should be long enough to help him through his difficulties. Come November, she would be free to return home and forget about the duke. In the meantime, she could at least write to the duchess and say she had tried to make the best of the opportunity. If nothing else, she would perhaps gain a helpful reference, some experience, and make a better friend of Lord Thornberry and his family. Would her raised brow earn a reply of agreement?

A smile appeared on his face and he leaned toward her from his perch on the desk, holding out a hand to shake. "Splendid! Splendid indeed. Two months is better than nothing at all. Perhaps at the end of the two months, you'll decide to stay on. Nevertheless, to comply with your request, I'll place a discreet advertisement in the newspapers and will require several letters of reference from any future applicants. I'll also make some other inquiries, since I have little faith in newspaper advertisements when it comes to finding a suitable governess."

"Agreed, but I very much doubt come November that I will be inclined to stay on. Do be sure to place those advertisements." She gave him a stern look, refraining from accepting his outstretched hand for a shake until assured that he understood her position on the entire matter.

He nodded and Jory smiled. They shook hands. A satisfactory business arrangement had at last been reached. She could look forward to going home in two months.

Rising, Lord Thornberry straightened his waistcoat and stepped aside, but then turned to face her with some sort of last-minute thought. "Miss Pritchard, Jory, I insist you take meals and tea with the family while you are in my employ, just as you do at Hillbrook Hall."

"Mealtimes?" She repeated as she rose and bobbed a slight curtsey, unsure as to whether he deserved it. Her brow arched. At least he had considered something that gave her some semblance of belonging.

Or was he attempting to ensure they would have time together? He was nodding, but if that time included Lady Flora and a mistress afoot, she wasn't so sure she would attend many family meals, but for now, she would not refuse until she had a better idea of how things were going to go with the rake.

How dare he try to romance three women! If that was his plan, he had another thing coming. She would have no part of it. She'd take meals in her private quarters or with the children if necessary, to avoid him. But she held her tongue and managed a proper reply. "Thank you. Shall we speak about lessons and when they are to begin at our *next* meeting? Perhaps *after* we have arrived at Mulberry House, when I have had time to review your education materials, the grade ledgers, the school room, and have had a chance to get to know the children."

"Fine, fine. We shall depart tomorrow for the countryside, so you may wish to avoid fully unpacking. I will make an announcement at dinner about our plans." He glanced at the clock on his mantle rather than opening his pocket watch. "Ah, nearly seven o'clock, when dinner is generally served. I'll see you downstairs in the formal dining room then, after you've had a chance to freshen up from your journey."

"I assume you'll formally introduce me to the children at dinner then…?" She followed him to the door.

"Yes, of course. They'll be dining with us this evening. They usually do in the summertime." He bowed.

"Very good. I shall see you then."

He held the door open, and she slipped out into the hall and hurried away toward her room on the third floor. She would change her clothing for dinner, prevail upon Tilly to restyle her hair, and dismiss her postilion drivers so they could find lodgings for the night before making their long drive back to Northampton—sadly, without her.

But on the way upstairs, she bit her lower lip. Would she regret her decision? Would the duke be entangled with two women right under her nose? Could she keep her heart and hopes in check? Would her heart be torn apart?

Could she remember the rules of society and conduct herself properly to dine and mingle with the Prince Regent without putting a foot wrong? And if she did make a social blunder, could she forgive herself? More importantly, would the duke's scrutiny of her be kind and forgiving? Why did her heart beat a little faster around him? And what of Lord Thornberry's sisters, mother-in-law, children, friends, staff, not to mention *three* household pets? It seemed a daunting prospect to juggle interactions with all of them too. *Lord, help me.*

Chapter Four

These things I have spoken unto you, that in me ye might have peace. In the world ye shall have tribulation: but be of good cheer; I have overcome the world.

John 16:33

Archer didn't mind the jostling of the coach on the way to Somerset, not if it meant he might pass the time taking in the view of Jory's angelic, beautiful face. Did she realize how lovely and breathtaking she was? A shame to hide her away inside a classroom. He would see to it that she and his children had plenty of walks in the garden and horseback rides in the meadows surrounding Mulberry House.

He had insisted she ride with him and the children while her maid rode with his sisters and their maid in a second coach. Mitzi traveled with his sisters in Daphne's arms. Milo curled up at his feet inside his coach, and Kitty rode in Edith's lap. Jane and Edith sat on either side of Jory, and Henry and Charlie sat on his right and left. If they began to squabble, he'd relegate some of them to the other coaches.

A third coach full of household servants joined the caravan too, leaving a skeleton crew to look after his townhome in Mayfair. Three coaches made slow but steady progress, and hopefully they would arrive well in advance of the Prince Regent who had been vague about his estimated arrival, saying he had some matters to tend before his departure.

Jory frequently gazed out of the windows, her eyes appearing to take in the pleasant hills and vales they passed. He shifted in his seat, thinking of something to ask as a means of conversation now that the children had fallen asleep. "Are you enjoying the scenery along the journey? We'll stop at a tavern for a meal and a place to rest in a few hours."

"Oh yes, 'tis lovely." She nodded but returned her eyes to the long stretch of meadow they currently passed.

While he attempted to think of something else to say, she turned toward him, her face framed by a pretty bonnet with a big bow tied to one side of her graceful chin. "Perhaps you would like to tell me something more about each of your children."

"Ah, yes." What might he share of his brood of four? "Henry is obsessed with pirates as I mentioned before, and to my chagrin, Charlie follows in his footsteps. I would prefer they admired soldiers."

"At least it isn't Napoleon," she put in, causing him to smile.

"Our Lady Jane is obsessed with becoming a princess someday, only I don't think she understands what a princess should be. I would like her to understand the grace and charity and kindness of a true princess, but I do not know where to begin to help her understand. Edith, she loves her new kitten, and she wants to do everything Jane does. Charlie, Edith, and Jane have ponies. Henry has his first horse."

Jory rewarded him with one of her beautiful smiles, her eyes traveling from one sleeping child to the next. "It all sounds quite normal. They seem very well adjusted, from what I have seen thus far."

If she considered them normal, maybe he hadn't botched things up with them too badly then. "I suppose I lavish them with far too much leniency and indulge them with too many of their requests since the loss of their mother…" His voice faded in his attempt at explaining why they were so spoiled.

"Perfectly understandable." Her eyes continued to rest on each of the children briefly. What did she see? Perhaps she took in Henry's soft snores, Jane's eyelids that fluttered occasionally as she dreamed of something, Charlie's open mouth with his steady breathing, and Edith's curls resting against her own arm, already warming to the governess. They seemed to like Governess Pritchard, as they called her.

Even Milo rested his head on her feet, accustomed to the jostling of the coach and snoring occasionally, which made the governess laugh. Thankfully, Julia and Daphne had taken the urgent news about removing to Mulberry House on the day after Jory's arrival with a good deal of excitement and little complaining. In Julia's words, how grand the prince's visit would make their country house party. The discovery of his intention to visit had squashed any complaints they harbored about leaving London society behind, though most of the Ton would not return until November anyhow.

"I've noticed each of the children have your dark brown hair and big blue eyes," she remarked, her golden-brown curls bouncing alongside her graceful neck as the coach bobbed along.

She'd taken note of his eye and hair color? He sat up straighter, nodding silently, being careful not to wake his boys. What other details did Miss Jory Pritchard notice?

"How much interaction would you like them to have with the prince?" Jory tilted her head to one side.

His brows furrowed. "An excellent question. I'm sure they have need of deportment lessons when it comes to addressing the prince, curtseying, bowing, and the like. I would say that we should strive for minimal encounters and as few meals as possible with the prince or guests for now. Perhaps we could review that as we go farther along in the visit. But I do hope you will be at as many meals as possible with myself and the prince and our guests. I would expect your maid, Miss Matilda Davison, can assist you in the classroom and take meals with the children so that they are never left unattended. And we have servants who lend a hand with those sorts of things."

Jory's brow arched. "Oh, yes, I imagine Tilly would be most helpful in that regard."

Perhaps the arrangement would suit for the next few months. Only time would tell. As much as he regretted not attempting to get to know her better through letters and other visits, perhaps he could make up for that now. Did she think him a cad for his previous reclusive behavior, and if so, how might he turn that around? Or was it too late for that?

Mulberry House, near the village of Pensford, Somerset

Delighted to find white wallpaper with tiny peach and pink flowers and a four-poster canopy bed, Jory breathed a sigh of relief to be out of the coach. The wallpaper had begun to turn cream in a few places, a sign of its age, but she did not mind. She fell upon the bed and spread out her arms, staring at the underside of the canopy. The peach and pink striped coverlet and ruffled pillows, though also faded, contrasted surprisingly well with the wallpaper, cheering up her fourth-floor governess quarters.

She soon settled into unpacking her trunks with Tilly's assistance. The corner bedroom had a sitting area comprised of two wooden rocking chairs pulled up to the fireplace with a round tea table between them, a writing desk under a window facing the front lawn, and several mismatched furniture items consisting of a bureau, nightstand, vanity, and a wardrobe. More than sufficient, and as nice as the room she had at Hillbrook Hall.

Tilly's room was located across from hers on the corner of the west and south wing, directly across from the long schoolroom that faced the front lawn. The children each had their own bedroom beside her quarters, running along the same hall of the south wing. These went in order of age, with the youngest, Edith, closest to the governess. Since Jory's room faced the front lawn, she would be able to see all who came and went.

The other rooms on the fourth floor were sleeping quarters for household servants, but a spacious playroom beside the schoolroom faced the front. Past the stairwell and on the left was a pleasant sitting room for servants. She could imagine spending some of her evenings embroidering while mingling with the other employees. That is, if they did not despise her for having a lady's maid.

Thankfully, Lord Thornberry had introduced Tilly as the assistant governess to his household staff who had lined up at the door in the front hall to greet them. Jory had explained the duke's intentions for Tilly to act as her assistant one evening on the journey to Somerset when they had settled into a room at a comfortable inn. Her maid had seemed amenable to the idea.

The duke's valet had been among those riding in the third coach, and she had guessed the lady's maid who rode with Tilly and his sisters certainly wasn't the duke's mistress. She had also discounted the other maid riding beside the new one, for that maid had served in the duke's household at both London and Mulberry House for too long, or so she had learned.

"Tilly, might I ask a favor?" Jory placed both hands on her hips after placing her comb and brush set and toiletries on the vanity. She had also finished placing a stack of her clean, folded shifts into the bureau along with other necessities.

"That depends. What is this favor?" Tilly eyed her with a curious expression, but she continued hanging each of Jory's gowns on the hooks inside the worn and slightly faded wardrobe.

"You recall how I explained that the duke would like you to take all meals with the children and act in the capacity of an assistant governess while you are here so that they are never alone?"

Tilly nodded. "Aye, I remember."

"Well, it has me in a bit of a quandary. He is also insisting that I join the rest of his family for meals, as I did for the duchess. Perhaps you might continue to inform the other servants you are the assistant governess, rather than mentioning anything about functioning as my lady's maid too…" Jory sighed. There. She'd said it. Would Tilly understand?

Perhaps she did not wish to eat all of her meals with the children, and Jory would gladly trade with her if she thought she could get away with it. At some point, she expected Lady Flora to arrive and drive her from the family table. She didn't mean to offend the maid in any way. Acting as an assistant governess would certainly involve more duties than merely being a lady's maid, tending to her wardrobe and styling her hair. Tilly might even earn a fine reference letter out of the situation if she performed her duties well, but maybe she didn't care about obtaining a reference. Maybe she saw the whole situation as a bother.

"Of course, ma'am. I'd already told myself I would be helping ye in the classroom and with the children. With two boys, you've got your hands full, if ye ask me. 'Tis surely better than sitting around all day doin' next to nothing, waiting for me to tuck a strand of your hair in place or iron a dress." Tilly wore a smirk as she crossed to the trunk and pulled out another white muslin frock. "Of course, the other staff will figure I'm helping you with tending to your clothing when I carry items to and from the laundry house, when I iron anything, or when I lay out your garments. I suppose they'll realize I am authorized to assist you, but that can mean doing a lot of different tasks for ye. Can it not? And truth be told, I kind of like the title of assistant governess."

Jory released a long sigh and smiled. "Thank you, Tilly. I'm glad you are pleased. Let's try to continue in that vein lest the employees despise me. I nearly told the duchess not to send someone with me, but she didn't wish for me to travel unaccompanied, and she is so generous by nature."

Tilly waved a wrinkled hand showing signs of her age as she neared what Jory guessed to be her late forties or early fifties. "The staff won't despise you once they get to know you, but I will agree to what you've asked and what the duke would like fer me to do. Assistant governess is what we shall tell them if asked. Only his sisters know I was sent as your maid…and some of the servants from the London townhouse. Nothing we can do about that if rumors spread, but we'll nip it in the bud if we can."

"Thank you, Tilly. You are a Godsend." She offered a warm smile and placed her letter writing materials on the desk. She slid her worn Bible and the *Common Book of Prayer* inside the nightstand drawer.

Turning around, her maid held up the blunderbuss, having reached the bottom of the trunk containing most of her frocks and gowns. "And what shall I do with *this*?"

Jory gasped, laughing. "Oh, Tilly! You do make me laugh. Let us leave it in the trunk and lock them after we stack them and push them against the wall in this corner."

"Yes, ma'am. A wise thought indeed to lock them with children under our feet on this floor." Tilly did exactly as she requested, heaving a big sigh after handing her the keys when they'd finished pushing and stacking the trunks.

Jory opened the drawer of her nightstand and dropped the keys inside. "I think I've done all I can stand of unpacking for now. Would you mind if I explore the rest of the house and grounds? Since the duke sent some other servants to help the children unpack, now seems the perfect time."

Her assistant cocked her head to one side and put her hands on her hips. "Fine with me, but if they finish unpacking before you return, what shall I have them do? They be wide awake after sleeping for three days inside the coach. With all of these servants upstairs helping them, I fear they will be running amuck if I be without a plan."

Jory nodded but soon smiled, her eyes lighting up. "Ask them to go into the playroom until I return. There are plenty of toys for them to become reacquainted with. And do stay with them, please. I won't be too long, but I must see the layout of the grounds and inspect the gardens if I am to find my way around, not to mention the dining room. I feel quite lost in this grand old house."

"Yes, ma'am. I can do that. I'm about done here too, and I can start unpacking my things until the children need me attention."

"Very good." Jory hurried away, anxious to find her way around, and in want of exercise.

She'd already seen the front of the Georgian-style house and the vast lawn sprawling out before it as the coach had pulled up the long drive. The house itself sat atop a crest, overlooking everything below and the road that led to the village. She'd had a glimpse of the charming village and would eventually explore it too someday. The long stable and carriage house to the right of the manor house piqued her interest, and she'd seen several barns beyond the stable. But what else did the estate hide amongst its beautiful trees, meadows, shrubbery, and exquisite rear gardens she'd spotted through some of the windows?

And where had the duke scurried away to after directing some servants to lead them to their quarters? Perhaps to find his mother-in-law who hadn't been amongst the employees lined up in the hall to greet them, or maybe to barricade himself in his study as the Duke of Gladdington so often did.

Exploring the third floor, she encountered more guest rooms and not less than three drawing rooms and a parlor. Overlooking the gardens she could hardly wait to stroll through, she discovered an art room at the end of the east wing. Easels, canvases, paints of every color one could imagine, and brushes in every shape and size, along with many other art supplies were housed in the delightful room on tidy shelves.

Retracing her steps, she eventually found her way back to the main staircase and bounded down them to the second floor. She wouldn't explore too much of that floor, supposing it contained the family bedrooms and more drawing rooms or sitting rooms. Perhaps a second morning room like the duchess had in Northampton. She peeked into an open door facing the front lawn and found a red drawing room filled with red velvet furnishings, carpet, and brocade drapes. But it was the yellow sitting room near the staircase she liked best, guessing the cheerful room was indeed a morning room. But bursting into the hallway to head downstairs to the main floor as she came out of the yellow room, she ran directly into someone's chest and gasped.

As a decidedly male set of hands clasped her arms, steadying her before she toppled over after bouncing backwards a step, Jory took in the duke's amused face. Heat warmed her cheeks. How clumsy of her!

"Your Grace!" she sputtered. His chest was like a rock. How had she missed seeing him?

"Oh! I'm terribly sorry. I, uh, didn't see you there."

One of his brows lifted, but he kept a hold of her until sure of her recovery. "It does help if you are facing the way you are going."

The half smile on his face told her he was jesting, causing her to laugh. "Yes, I suppose it does." But why did her head spin? Did stars race about her eyes? Goodness, she'd nearly knocked herself out.

"Are you sure you are all right?" He did not seem convinced.

"I fear I am quite lost," she managed, pressing a hand to her temple. "I had been hoping to find the dining room, and p-perhaps a quick stroll through the gardens to help me get my bearings." The stars stopped swirling and the hallway seemed to settle, her vision returning to normal.

"Ah, yes. Please, permit me to give you a tour." He extended his elbow.

Unsure if she should accept it, she hesitated before giving in and placing her hand on his elbow. It might not be a bad idea, especially since she'd made herself dizzy running into him. Every hair on her arms stood up on end. If he wasn't so completely, entirely, ridiculously, utterly handsome. And strong! The man was pure iron under that cravat and waistcoat.

"Have you seen the rest of the second floor?" He extended a hand toward the hall on the other side of the staircase.

She shook her head. "Begging your pardon, but I didn't plan to venture any farther on this floor since I assumed this contains the family sleeping quarters. But I did enjoy the red drawing room, the yellow morning room, and the art room immensely."

He nodded. "Do you paint?"

"I do, though I am certain I am not very good at it," she confessed with a chuckle, "but I enjoy sketching too. The duchess and I often paint or sketch landscapes together. I did create a portrait of her children which she liked so well, she hung it in her morning room."

"You must have more talent than you realize, which does not surprise me." He led her to the staircase leading to the ground floor and nodded toward the far end of the hall she hadn't explored. "My quarters are on the corner at the end of this hall. Daphne's room is between the yellow morning room and the red drawing room. Julia's room is on the other side of the staircase, beside the room that used to...the room that connects to my chamber for my future duchess, if I ever remarry someday..." His voice faded.

Jory bit her lower lip. What a surprise that he pointed out the family personal quarters, much less *his*, or that he would make mention of his former or future wife's quarters. But then again, she hadn't expected to run directly into his chest. And she wasn't entirely sure she had recovered from the collision. It all made her head spin to consider what he'd shared. Did he seem lost, even perhaps lonely? Had he recovered from the loss of his wife? Why did she long to ask him? Was that why he had sought comfort in the arms of a mistress?

"The west wing on the second floor has the lilac drawing room, the nursery, and the hydrangea sitting room," he informed her. "But we'll save those rooms to explore for another day, since we must ensure your ability to find the main dining room and the gardens."

She nodded, eager to be outside in the fresh air. Maybe her head could stop spinning.

The nursery? She could hardly imagine having such a room for infant children after growing up in such a tiny two-room dwelling. But she had admired the nursery for Lady Celia, Lady Marcella, and Lady Rosina many times. She could not imagine him showing her these rooms. It didn't seem proper for him to walk her past his private quarters even if she would discover more drawing rooms. She held onto the railing with one hand and his elbow with her other as they descended the staircase to the ground floor.

"How long has Mulberry House been in your family, my lord?" Finally, she found her tongue as they approached the last few steps. Looking up, she could see all the way to the fourth-floor ceiling where a chandelier dangled far above, suspended over the foyer.

After the landing, he led them to the right at the foyer, and then down the main front hall toward the rear gardens. "Since the late 1600s."

"'Tis very beautiful, Your Grace." She admired a few marble-topped hall tables, elegant vases, gilt-framed mirrors, and lovely paintings.

"Thank you. It is beautiful and at the same time, a great deal to look after. With it comes much responsibility." He drew in a deep breath and released a sigh.

"It is nothing short of magnificent from what I have seen thus far," she confessed. "I hope that despite the enormous burden you bear to look after it, that you also take time to enjoy the fruit of your labor, and the labor of those who came before you."

"I do try, though it is sometimes easier said than done." He paused outside a set of double doors to their left and a set of French doors straight ahead, leading to a courtyard terrace with gardens beyond. "To your left, through these doors, is the main dining room. Dinner is served at seven as when we are in London. Straight ahead, the gardens and terrace. Would you like to see more of the first floor, or just the gardens for now?"

"I would love to see the gardens first, if you do not mind." Jory peeked up at him, and the smile on his face told her he was happy to lead her there.

Where was the new maid she'd seen accompanying them from London with the other employees? Didn't he prefer to spend time with his mistress instead of catering to the governess when he could assign a servant to show her around? Or was he trying to romance her, too?

He opened one of the French doors and she stepped onto the terrace. "An excellent choice. The gardens are one of my favorite things about this great big, old, drafty house."

She chuckled as he closed the door behind them and presented his elbow again. "The duchess says the same thing about Hillbrook Hall."

"Which part? The drafty house or the garden being her favorite?" He grinned.

"Both." She returned a smile as he led her across the stone terrace, her hand secure on his elbow. How was it that he could make her smile and enjoy his company? Only days ago, she could hardly wait to return to Northampton to escape his presence, but now, she found herself delighted to have encountered him on her exploration of his fine home. Maybe it was on account of finally being done with her travels, but the shift in her enjoyment of him surprised her. At the same time, she did not trust him. Not yet. Had he managed to fool the Duke and Duchess of Gladdington? Surely they would not wish to continue the bonds of a close friendship if Lord Thornberry had such a questionable character. Any day now, she supposed a letter would arrive from the duchess with word she would be required to return to Northampton, especially if Lady Kingston had seen the same society column she'd read.

Stepping down a few steps from the terrace onto stone paths leading through the garden, they strolled past a variety of flowers—including roses, lilies, rhododendrons, hollyhocks, cornflowers, Columbines, Sweet William, and lilacs. He pointed out some of his favorite plants while she breathed in the fresh air and scents emanating from delicate petals and woodsy timbers.

Row upon row of mounding shrubs and thick hedges in several shades of green made a pleasing perimeter before a northern border of oaks, beech trees, and pines extending their branches over wild strawberries, daisies, and berry bushes. Plum trees dotted the thick forest edge too. To the right and left of the woods in the distance beyond the garden, she saw more trails and paths leading to meadows, tall grasses, and fields. Yes, she would enjoy it here for the next few months, so long as she could walk these paths if only for a few minutes each day.

And if the duke behaved himself.

Pointing toward the east and the far right where a riding trail disappeared into the distance, he told her about more of the property. "That trail lined with all of those lilacs and shrubs leads to the dowager house, another wooded area, and a gazebo. The trail splits off and leads to a fishing and boating pond, the tea house, and the private family chapel. It eventually circles around to the barns, sheds, and the smokehouse."

She blocked the sun from her eyes with one hand over her brow, wishing she'd not been so hasty as to forget her bonnet and parasol. "It sounds lovely. And pray tell, what is in that direction, on the other side of the courtyard and garden?"

"To the left? There you will find the kitchen garden, laundry house, a creek, and the icehouse. Of course, beyond it, we are a few miles from the village."

"I see." She nodded, taking it all in, basking in the warm rays of sunshine. Turning back to the east, they spotted a matronly figure dressed in black, using a cane and walking toward them.

He stiffened. "I see you will have an opportunity to meet the countess, my mother-in-law."

She offered a weak smile, bracing herself for the encounter, remembering what he'd said about her before.

He led her forward to meet the countess, keeping her hand tucked into his elbow, his voice low. "Prepare thyself for scrutiny."

"Aye, aye, captain," she teased. Their jesting did alleviate her sense of foreboding.

He chuckled, eyeing her with amusement in his twinkling blue eyes. They soon closed the distance between them, the matron's bombazine skirts rustling over the garden path.

"Archer," the countess said without any smile when they reached her near the farthest point of the garden's edge. "I presumed you might have arrived by now. I hope you had a pleasant journey from London and a lovely time at the seaside."

"We did, thank you." He offered a curt nod. "And how is your health?"

"About the same as at the beginning of summer, but some mild improvement. And before I ask who is perched upon your arm, I must inquire about my grandchildren."

"They are full of all the energy we lack at our ages, not one bit weary from the journey, and they've brought you seashells," Lord Thornberry informed her.

"Very good. The children and I shall look forward to embellishing all sorts of things with those." Here, the countess offered him a half smile.

The duke turned toward Jory. "May I present our new governess, Miss Marjorie Pritchard, from Northampton, highly recommended by the Duchess of Gladdington. I was just giving her a tour of our gardens." He angled toward Jory. "Jory, this is Lady Rowans, the Countess of Foxhaven."

"Pleased to meet you, Lady Rowans." Jory bobbed a curtsey.

The countess stared long and hard at her through a quizzing glass. "Too young. Much too young to be the governess of my grandchildren."

Lord Thornberry lifted his chin. "I have chosen Miss Pritchard with great care, and I believe Emma would be pleased, especially since Eliza has abandoned us without notice."

His mother-in-law's mouth gaped. "What has happened to Eliza?"

"I wish I knew," he muttered.

Jory stepped back. Something she could not put her finger on gave her pause. Was it the duke's womanizing ways that drove away his former governesses?

The countess sighed, her chest heaving. "The children need stability, Archer."

He nodded. "Emma would agree."

"Yes, she would." Leaning heavily on her cane, the countess pressed her lips together into a thin line as a stern expression appeared on her face. "My daughter would want the very best for her children."

"Will you be joining us for dinner this evening? I am anxious to hear about the latest local news, Lady Rowans." The duke cocked his head to one side.

"Of course you are. No one else has a handle on any of the news around here except for myself, and that is because I am determined to look after you, Archer. And yes, I'll see you and your sisters at seven o'clock sharp for dinner. I assume Lady Julia and Lady Daphne have returned with you."

"They have and are resting from the journey, but I'm sure they'll dine with us this evening. I have invited Miss Pritchard to join us since she is accustomed to dining with the duke and duchess," he explained.

The countess peered at Jory through her quizzing glass one more time and released a harumph. Jory tried not to shrink despite her disdain. She wouldn't let the mean little quips, sarcasm, and jibes bother her any.

Archer cleared his throat and shifted his feet. "In any case, we are indebted to Jory. She has agreed to help us out of a great bind until I can find a permanent governess, since the prince is coming to Mulberry House."

Lady Rowans gasped. "The Prince Regent is coming here? When? And whatever for? To watch us squirm in our separate corners of the estate while we navigate the rumors spread about the Ton?"

Jory's brow shot up. The countess seemed well-informed and quick-witted. Then it occurred to her. Did the countess assume Jory was one of her son-in-law's mistresses? Jory snatched her hand away from the duke. Thankful she'd remembered her fan, she snapped it open and began fanning rapidly.

Archer fiddled with the buttons on one of his sleeves. "The prince is expected to join us by early next week. He mentioned a desire to take the waters at Bath. He seemed to want a countryside retreat where lords and ladies won't trouble him with more complaints about

Peterloo. I believe we have enough time to see that everything is well in hand while he tends to some other matters before departing London."

"Packing one or more of his mistresses off to some other destination, I would imagine. Heaven help us. I do hope we can be ready by then." The countess shook her head. "You do realize how much the prince consumes in lavish food and all of the entertaining he will require, do you not? You'll need a few more cooks if you do not wish to lose the one you have."

The duke stood up taller, his gaze traveling to some roses nearby, still blooming nicely for the end of summer upon them. "Yes, well the prince is likely sending his own team of cooks or chefs, but you will be most pleased to know I have hired a new maid. She will be of great assistance to us with the prince coming and all of the guests my sisters intend to invite to their country house party."

"Just what we need. One more helpless new maid. And a country house party too? You'll need more than one new maid for that." The countess clucked her tongue. "I think I shall go and have a lie down until dinner. I feel a great headache coming on." Muttering under her breath, she waved a hand and then spun around, relying on her cane as she did so, scurrying away much faster than she had arrived.

Did the duke often hire helpless new maids? No wonder the society column printed scandalous rumors. What if he had a string of mistresses like the prince reportedly had? What if he and the prince were better friends than Lord Thornberry had indicated?

At least he had prepared her well for the encounter with his mother-in-law, but Jory had the distinct impression 'twould be better to melt into the ground like snow or fade into the woods like a wilted flower than to cross the countess. In some ways, the elderly woman's demeanor was a tad refreshing and amusing. She certainly came right to the point.

If Lord Thornberry hadn't warned her, she might cower in fear or take the harsh words of Lady Rowans to heart. Clearly, the Countess of Foxhaven disapproved of her, and most everything else, too. She blamed Archer for not being able to keep a governess for any length of time.

Perhaps the duke's mother-in-law had good reason to be disappointed with her son-in-law. Did she know something more about his relationships with other women besides what the society column had printed? If so, maybe she was trying to lead him toward remembering his responsibility to his children. He needed to do better to protect his reputation, for their sakes. But some gossip was so maliciously planted that it could not be avoided. If he had poor hiring skills, she could see why it could lead to a problem. Servants often spoke with fellow servants in other households, and many a rumor began from such talk.

Dining with the duke's children began to hold greater appeal with every passing moment. At least she had enjoyed his garden and could now find her way to the dining room, but how would she win the countess over and dispel her nagging worries over the rumors swirling about everything concerning the duke?

Chapter Five

It is the glory of God to conceal a thing: but the honor of kings is to search out a matter.

Proverbs 25:2

Returning to her quarters, Jory found Tilly had finished unpacking her trunks. She spent the remainder of the afternoon taking inventory of the books and supplies in the schoolroom while Miss Davison kept a watchful eye on the children in the playroom, but one thing plagued her as she went about her work. She must get to the bottom of the truth behind those rumors.

After spending three days with the duke inside his coach, she could not deny an intense desire to discover the truth. She'd taken nearly all meals with him and his children at the various inns and taverns along the journey to Somerset, including the short time she'd spent at his London home in the fashionable Mayfair district. Something had begun to stir in her heart. She couldn't explain it, but something about Lord Archer Thornberry drew her toward him.

Maybe it was the way he made it seem as if she were the only female who existed in his world, the way he stole glances at her, the way she'd caught him studying her in the coach. He did not appear to behave as the society column portrayed him, but if there was any shred of truth to those rumors, she could not allow herself to become entangled and bamboozled by him.

She found the ledger where the former governesses had listed grades for each of the subjects the children had studied in the teacher's top desk drawer and pushed her concerns about the duke aside for the time being. After gathering the very best books for the various ages and on the topics she wished to teach and after gaining insight from the ledger with a history of the children's progress, she formulated a list of subjects for her students. Then she made another list of the supplies they would need after inspecting the supplies on hand.

She also took some time to observe the children at their leisure while Tilly watched over them. Jane and Edith played with their enormous dollhouse in one corner of the elegant playroom while Henry had his nose in a book, reading "Frankenstein" by Mary Shelley, lounging in a window seat, eating an apple. Advanced reading for a boy of his age. Charlie lay stretched out on the carpeted floor, sketching a ship on spare foolscap, a little plate of poppyseed cakes beside him. Tilly sat in a rocking chair with her knitting, appearing content with these circumstances, a cup of tea, and more of those cakes.

At five o'clock, a maid appeared on the fourth floor to inform Jory that the children's supper was ready for them in the small dining room near the kitchen where they customarily ate when not joining their father.

Jory asked Tilly to follow the maid and accompany the children downstairs for the meal while another maid appeared to clean the playroom. Perhaps she would have plenty of help after all. Had the duke sent the maid to assist them? How very kind of him, if so. Maybe he was acting in hopes of keeping her content through the two months of their agreement.

She began dressing for dinner at half past six when Tilly reappeared after settling the children into a bathing routine with yet another servant. Ahead of Tilly's plans for laying out her clothing, she'd settled on a pale pink dress with an empire waist embellished by a darker pink silk ribbon. She'd already laid it out upon the bed. Miss Davison ensured Jory's dark curls on each side of her hair had exactly the right amount of curl, bounce, and shine. She even added two pearl-edged combs to her hair—a Christmas gift from the Duke and Duchess of Gladdington—to help hold everything in place.

Tilly smiled at her completed appearance. "My, ye look lovely if I do say so myself, Jory."

"Thank you. Wish me well. My nerves are a bit rattled." She donned evening gloves and pale pink matching slippers suitable for her first dinner at Mulberry House, tucking her notes about school supplies and subjects to teach into her reticule in case the duke questioned her about lesson plans and such.

"Ye'll be fine, miss," Tilly encouraged. "I do hope ye enjoy the evening. This place is grand, and the food we ate earlier was divine."

"I'll try."

She hurried downstairs, thankful the duchess had employed the good sense to send Tilly along despite her own misgivings. She found herself anxious to interact with Lord Thornberry's family and to see the duke. Would it go well? Would he approve of her attire? Pfft! Why did she care? But to her amazement, as she entered the dining room, she found some part of her did care.

The duke's sisters were present. To Jory's relief, Lady Daphne greeted her with a warm smile, rising, carrying Mitzi under one arm. "There you are, Miss Pritchard. Archer did say you would be joining us for meals. Allow me to help you settle in, especially since I promised my brother I would make you feel comfortable."

"Oh, thank you." Her eyes widened. Had the duke thought of her amid the preparations weighing down upon him? "That would be most welcome."

"Please, come and sit beside the countess. She isn't here yet, but she'll sit there beside Archer at the head of the table." Daphne patted the back of the chair where she directed Jory. "My sister always sits at his other side, and I sit beside her, directly across from you if you need anything."

Lady Julia offered a warm smile too. "How nice to see you this evening, Miss Pritchard. I do hope you are settling in and finding everything you need. You will of course join us in the red drawing room after dinner each evening, won't you? 'Tis dreadfully boring around here in the countryside compared to London, but with you here, it cheers us a great deal."

"Yes, of course, and thank you, Lady Julia. It's nice to see you again too." Jory waited to sit since Daphne lingered nearby as if she had more to say.

"If the children dine with us, Henry and Jane sit beside their grandmother, the countess. Charlie and Edith generally sit beside me, and you may sit beside Edith on those occasions, since she is the youngest and may require the most attention from time to time. But with the prince coming, I doubt we'll have need of it. They'll likely dine well ahead of us until he returns to London, as our brother wishes."

Jory nodded. "Yes, of course. Thank you for your direction. I was nervous about where you would wish me to sit. It all makes perfect sense now."

Liveried footmen finished last-minute tasks and took their places as they spoke. They stiffened, ready to serve the meal as footsteps in the hall approached. The duke perhaps, or the countess? Maybe both?

"If we have other guests, you'll most likely be seated near me and the guests seated near the countess, or we'll find place cards with names," Lady Daphne explained while she returned to her seat on the other side of the long table. "My sister has become an expert at overseeing such matters since the passing of our dearly missed Emma."

Emma. The duke's departed wife. Jory nodded, placing a linen napkin in her lap.

The countess entered the dining room on the duke's arm, chatting away about something. Lord Thornberry led her to the empty seat beside Jory and took his at the head of the table. "How nice to see you, Miss Pritchard. Julia. Daphne. At last, we are all together again and done with our journey."

Jory nodded, as did his sisters and the countess, who added. "I have missed you all, but I am looking forward to the endless chatter you will surely subject me to and the joyful disturbance of pirates and princesses waving their swords at me in the garden when I least expect it. Jumping out of hiding in the sitting rooms. The dogs and the cat getting hair on my gowns…"

At this remark, Jory couldn't help but smile. The countess was the most interesting member of the duke's family, in her opinion.

"Yes, well, it is good to be home. Let us bow our heads in prayer." Archer glanced round the table, offering a brief smile at his family and Jory.

Was he going to remember to pray? It seemed he had forgotten or merely allowed everyone silent prayers on the journey. Would the Lord hear this man's prayer if those rumors were true? Nonetheless, she bowed her head while he rendered a prayer of thanks and blessing over the meal. After the short prayer, they began the first course of artichoke soup.

During this course, Lady Julia and her sister were up in the boughs, their faces alight with excitement about the guests who would soon join them. It became evident that they could hardly contain their glee about the prince coming while their guests would be in residence at Mulberry House. They rattled off names she wouldn't remember, both talking so much that no one else could hardly add a word.

The countess leaned toward Jory at one point. "Did I not tell you they would chatter?"

"You did, Lady Rowans, you did," she replied, surprised at this act of almost solidarity with her. Perhaps because she held her tongue, nodding and smiling throughout the meal.

Next came plates of haricot lamb served in a rich gravy with roasted carrots, cabbage, and asparagus. The duke instructed Lady Julia to bring her menu plans to him for the next few weeks by tomorrow morning so he could review them, to which she heartily agreed. Of course, Lady Julia served as his hostess for entertaining since he was widowed, and she fairly glowed at the prospect before her.

Slicing into his lamb, Archer glanced at Julia. "I have received a missive buried in my mail from Carlton House that Prince George will send two of his chefs and several helpers ahead with supplies from London. They will be happy to work with our menu plans, but they'll have many suggestions for items the prince prefers."

"In other words, the prince's personal chefs will be taking over the kitchen. To be sure, Julia and our cook will be deeply offended. The only question in my mind is who will be offended more." Lady Rowans tasted some of the cabbage and then reached for an elegant glass pepper shaker.

An expression of utter dejection and horror spread across Lady Julia's face. "I shall not have the prince's chefs think I am daft. They must receive my final approval before they change a single thing on my menu plans. I've spent three days in the coach from London to Somerset painstakingly penning those meals, searching through my mother's favorite recipe book. She once entertained King George and Queen Charlotte in this very house for a fortnight, you know."

"There, there, Julia. Do not let this vex you. I'm sure the prince's personal chefs will work things out with you and the cook to your satisfaction. Expect them to prepare a great deal many extra foods than what we are accustomed to serving," the duke advised.

Lady Julia managed to recover a smile, but she cast one last grimace toward the countess before turning back to Archer. "Yes, dear brother, I'm sure you are quite right. It will all work out in the end. I am most grateful the prince has thought to send some of his staff and supplies ahead."

The fish course of pickled mackerel alongside boiled potatoes served in a rich butter sauce was placed before them while Lady Daphne told them of some of the elaborate desserts Julia had in mind for the coming fête. She spoke with great animation on her face and sighed with great longing about the sweets to be presented before the prince and their guests, especially a towering, molded gelatin.

Daphne finished recounting her sister's ideas and shook her head. "We had best pray the prince does not overstay his welcome or our waistlines shall be so fattened, we shan't fit our gowns for the coming season."

"That is, if we aren't up the River Tick by the time the prince and all of our guests leave." The countess rolled her eyes and sliced into the savoury garden pie a footman placed before her.

Jory couldn't help but smile at the banter. She mainly listened and nodded, enjoying occasional moments when the duke's eyes met with hers. She also found the pie tasted superbly, reminding her of home and the one her mother made with leeks, turnips, and carrots smothered in a tasty white sauce under the flaky golden crust. The crust made her ponder about the skills the prince's pastry chef would surely have. She'd read about their elaborate creations in the newspapers.

"And Miss Pritchard, you must tell us about Northampton. I am remiss for having forgotten my manners to ask you before now," Lady Julia confessed as she used a fork to cut a bite of the slice of pie before her.

Perhaps the sisters were going to be kind to include and respect her after all, for they had largely ignored her at her first dinner with them in London, but Jory had assumed they were preoccupied with the rout they would attend later that evening. And the chatter of the children had kept her busy and amused at that meal. Perhaps being the daughter of a common tenant farmer made her somewhat wary of all interactions with anyone from the peerage or the gentry. But now she perked up. "Thank you. It is a beautiful area. We are mainly known for the production of boots for our military forces and have quite a large factory there, in my locality."

"Oh, how interesting. Do tell us more." Lady Julia tilted her head of dark curls, styled in much the same way Tilly had styled hers.

"Yes, do tell us more. Archer visits Northampton now and then. He and Emma used to visit together, you know, but Julia and I have never been." Lady Daphne leaned forward with a stemmed glass of orangeade in her hands.

In fact, the Duke of Gladdington had arranged it so her young brother, Christian, after only a few pleas, might obtain employment at the boot factory, but with the understanding he would continue attending the school in the village of Glad Crown since he was only fourteen. She wouldn't mention that detail though. Instead, she added, "We had quite a few militia and regiments come through Northampton during the war. In fact, two fine soldiers have married two of my younger sisters, Victoria and Regina, and one of them a young naval cadette." For this was perfectly acceptable with the upper classes, and Jory knew it to be true, for the duchess often spoke of it. Better if they were officers, and a naval cadette was a fine path to becoming an officer.

"Oh. I *am* sorry to hear they have married before you. My dear brother simply refuses to allow anyone to marry before my sister Julia marries, but for the life of me, I do not understand it." Daphne stabbed her pie with a regrettable expression.

Jory instantly wished she hadn't mentioned the fact her sisters were younger. She sat up straighter. "I do not mind, for I have not met anyone I wish to marry yet. They are very happy in their circumstances, and in fact, Victoria now lives quite near here in Bristol since her husband, the young officer in training, doesn't have an assignment to any particular ship. He has recently obtained a position in shipbuilding since he was highly recommended by his commanding officer when the war came to its end."

The duke pushed his plate back and a footman stepped forward at once, clearing it away. "We shall ensure sure you have a chance to visit your sister and her husband while you are here then."

"Thank you. I would like that very much." Would Victoria be pleased to see her? She would have to write and warn her of the possibility. She peeked at the duke as the next course of pickled figs came out. Had he heard her say she had not met anyone she wished to marry? Is that why he kept his eyes lowered and brows furrowed as he stared at his plate of figs while Daphne inquired about her other siblings and remarked upon what a large family she had? Then Julia said something about how sorry they were to hear her father had passed. Jory thanked her, for it had indeed been the darkest time in her entire life. Perhaps the duke could relate on some level after losing his wife. In fact, they had spoken of that very thing before, in Northampton.

Finally, dainty lemon cheesecakes were served next for dessert. During this course, Archer directed a question to her also. "How are you settling in, Jory? Have you found everything you require to put a curriculum together?"

She turned toward him. "Yes, Your Grace, if I may request a brief meeting at your soonest convenience to discuss your expectations, my lesson planning, and other questions?"

"Of course." The duke sipped some coffee from the cup served alongside his dessert. "I can offer you half an hour at nine o'clock each evening when tea is typically served in my study. I'm afraid tomorrow is proving to be rather full with other meetings and obligations, but we may begin this evening."

She nodded. "That would be fine. Thank you, my lord."

She supposed the meetings would provide a chance to speak with him about the needs of his children, and from the sounds of it, alone. Just as the duchess had said. Would he approve of her lesson plans? Would she be able to speak with him alone the entire time, or would the mysterious new maid she hadn't seen since their arrival reappear and interrupt their meeting at some point? Surely, if she were indeed his mistress, the maid would be afoot at all the wrong times.

But before she could finish considering the matter, the dining room doors which had been closed by a footman at the beginning of the meal burst open as a hefty man, huffing with indignation and the air of a country gentleman about him, flung the doors wide and marched forward, stopping at the far end of the long table. He stood near the empty seats, a scowl upon his face as he glared at the duke. On his heels came the butler, who had introduced himself as Jerome Reeds during the presentation of staff upon their arrival earlier in the day.

"Eee gads, Thornberry! You're back! I came as soon as I heard." He looked around while trying to catch his breath, as if surprised to find the duke having a meal with his family, and all ladies at that. Then he gulped. "Forgive the intrusion. Thank God, you are finally here. I told your man at the door I simply must speak with you."

Reeds caught up to him and cast the fellow a disapproving look. "I'm sorry, Your Grace. Squire Foley demanded to speak with you and marched right past me."

"What do you mean by charging in here like this unannounced, Foley?" Lord Thornberry returned his coffee cup to its saucer before he could take an intended sip and tossed the linen napkin from his lap aside. He leaned back in his chair, sitting up tall at the spectacle of the intrusion.

"A matter of utmost urgency, my lord." Foley clasped both lapels of his frock coat, his wide girth bulging forth in his kerseymere breeches as he rocked back on the heels of his shoes, peering round at them through his spectacles, and then back at the duke.

The gray ponytail dangling over one shoulder extended from under his tricorne hat, making him appear a bit fashionable in a classic sense, since it seemed to suit him, though the hat had begun to go out of style. He now swiped the hat from his head and nodded at the ladies, but his scowl remained. His breeches made of wool seemed perhaps too hot for early fall, but had he worn pantaloons, the vision gave Jory alarm that not only might he reveal more than anyone desired, but he might be unable to keep his stomach tucked into them.

"It's all right, Reeds." Thornberry leaned forward. "I am tired from the long journey, Foley. On what reason do you barge into my home and interrupt our dinner?"

The butler bowed and returned to the main hall after one last glare at the squire, bristled by the whole business.

"Well, since ye ask in the presence of the ladies…" Squire Foley cleared his throat and lifted his chin, appearing as if he now doubted that he should speak. Perhaps he expected the duke to dismiss the women and bring the meal to an abrupt end because of his grand entrance.

"Since you have disrupted the ladies and disrespected the man posted at my front doors, and disrespected me, and disrupted our otherwise pleasant meal, perhaps they deserve to know why," the duke replied with a frown as he fiddled with the buttons on his sleeve cuff, a tone of disgust Jory had never heard in his voice before. But he did make fine points.

"Trouble is brewing, Thornberry. Mark my words. Trouble is brewing." The squire stepped forward and tapped a stout finger on the linen tablecloth three times.

"Yes, I am aware. Trouble is always brewing somewhere," the duke said, but Jory knew he'd confided in her that he didn't know exactly what the trouble was. Nonetheless, he remained calm, his voice controlled, unmoved by the episode.

"Well, if that's how it shall be, maybe I should leave it for you to find out for yerself then. I needn't be disrespected when I've come all this way to warn ye." A bit of a Scottish accent laced the squire's words.

"So be it." The Duke of Pensford waved him away. "Have him escorted out, Franklin."

"Aye, Your Grace." Franklin, the eldest footman, nodded toward two tall and capable looking footmen. "White and Hill, see to it."

White and Hill went to work at once to escort their intruder out, who began bellowing as they dragged him toward the hall. "You'll regret this, Thornberry! You'll be sorry!"

"Of all the nerve…" The countess, observing the scuffle, spoke with as much indignation in her tone as the squire, only she wasn't bellowing.

But had the duke reacted in haste? Jory could not deny an interest in hearing what the squire had to say after making such an unusual disruption to their supper. Her mouth agape, her ears shrank in protest to the squire's madness and hollering which echoed under the tall ceilings in the great main hall while he attempted to wrestle himself free.

"Let go of me! Let go of me at once!" When he could not shrug them off, he applied a burst of strength by using his girth to smash up against one the duke's staff like a bull. Nonetheless, they did not release him, not even when the squire finally stood still and huffed, "I'll see myself out."

Pulling his sage green waistcoat down, the squire could no longer resist and the footmen carried him away. His dissents grew distant and in the formal dining room, Jory and the duke's family listened for the front doors to creak open. When they did, she supposed the footmen must have watched him ride away in whatever manner he'd come, for a minute or two passed before White and Hill returned.

While they waited for the footmen, the duke offered some words of reassurance and explanation. "Pay the squire no mind, ladies. He's merely disgruntled. I've heard a rumor or two from Crandall this very day, not long after my pleasant tour of the gardens with Miss Pritchard and finding the missive from the prince about the chefs."

He glanced at Jory, which made her cheeks warm, and she was sure they must be a bright pink color. But, aha! So that was why the duke had waved the squire away and had remained so calm. He had already learned something about the matter. Jory had to admit she admired the way he'd handled the interruption and had not given in to the fellow's demands.

"Is that so? And what did Finn have to say?" Julia leaned toward her brother, her blue eyes wide as she patted her curls.

"Yes, what indeed? I do hope he could shed some light on this ruffian behavior of the squire! I thought he was an old friend of your family. I've never seen him act so belligerently before." The countess wore an appalled expression and now slid her remaining dessert away, practically untouched, her appetite waned. "My Emma would have been appalled by this display."

Daphne sniffed, pressing a handkerchief to her nose. "Yes, she would have, Lady Rowans."

The duke sipped some of his coffee and set his cup in its saucer. "Finn believes the mayor and the squire have other plans for the same piece of land I have already put in a purchase offer upon. I hate to say it, but I suspected this could happen. Instead of Mayor Nicholson and Squire Foley setting an appointment and coming to discuss the matter like gentlemen of honor, Foley chooses to barge in here and throw his weight about to insist upon having his own way." He sighed. "I am left to believe that not only is Foley a fustian, but high up in a muddle with the mayor against me, presuming me guilty before they know my plans. I believe the squire is offering to finance the purchase. Maybe he even has investors."

The countess turned toward her son-in-law. "What? Do you mean this is all a fuss about the deceased Squire Curry Hopkins's land? I thought the land was to go to his estranged nephew as a country retreat and provide him some farming income. Were those only rumors I've heard then? I've heard none of the townsfolk have seen his nephew in years, not since he was a boy."

The duke nodded. "Yes, that is correct. In fact, I have gone to a great deal of trouble to track him down. Lawrence Hopkins, his nephew, did indeed inherit the land when Curry passed on, God rest his soul. There were no other descendants to pass the land onto. But after receiving my inquiry, it seems Lawrence may favor my offer, which was quite fair and reasonable. He has no intention of visiting or living there. He doesn't need the annual income which the land can produce in crops. He's a physician, living in Derbyshire. Quite content in his circumstances. In response to my inquiry and offer, he is sending a solicitor to meet with me, a Mr. Edgar Partridge, to finalize the sale. 'Tis a prime piece of land, being so close to the village, perfect for my development. But it appears we could enter a bidding war."

"And what do Mayor Nicholson and Squire Foley want this land for? Why are they against you?" Lady Julia inquired.

"That's what I want to know." The countess sipped some of her coffee.

"Phineas Crandall is still investigating that, but he believes it has something to do with the mayor's ambition to bring several factories to Pensford."

"Which could put more inhabitants to work," the countess pointed out. "Oh, good grief! The villagers will despise us indeed. But what kind of factories?"

"Dear me…" Lady Julia pressed a hand to her temples. "The countess is right. The villagers will despise you, dear brother, and us!"

"Now there, Julia. Don't go jumping to conclusions so hastily. There's more to this story than meets the eye. We need more housing before any new factories can move here. The mayor has gotten ahead of himself in my opinion." The duke sipped more of his coffee. "I'll need to find out exactly what the mayor has in mind before I make any further conjectures."

"Indeed. Well, in any case, I do hope you can restore peace and order before this gets too far out of hand, Archer. Squire Foley has been an ally to you these many years from what my darling Emma told me. I've not seen him so high in the instep before, not like this." The countess's brow furrowed as she reached for her cane. "Such fustian behavior indeed!"

"Yes, I'm afraid to admit that I quite agree. Let us withdraw to the drawing room and forget about this dreadful business," Julia suggested as a thoughtful footmen stepped forward to help pull her seat out so she might rise.

Daphne sniffled, nodding.

Jory nodded too. In her most soothing voice, adding, "A most agreeable suggestion, Lady Julia."

Chapter Six

Blessed are the peacemakers: for they shall be called the children of God.

Matthew 5:9

"Perhaps we should reconsider about inviting Miss Selina Foley to our country house party." Lady Julia set her book aside, turning it upside down on the red velvet sofa where she sat in the second-floor red drawing room once they had removed from the dining room.

"And exactly how would we withdraw our invitation at this point?" Lady Daphne's open mouth was a testament to her shock over the matter. She stopped patting Mitzi and looked around the room. "We finalized the invitations this afternoon and hers has been hand delivered by one of our footmen."

"Ah, then *that* is likely how the squire discovered we have returned," the countess put in as she patted Milo who looked up at her with adoring looks from where he sat on the floor beside her armchair. The Great Dane already appeared to have improved upon their first day in the countryside.

Jory had taken a few minutes of reprieve to poke her head in four doors, checking on each of the children. She'd found each one sound asleep and the boys snoring. She also obtained a satisfactory report about the bedtime routine from Tilly. None of the duke's offspring had protested going to bed, finally weary from the journey. Miss Davison relayed that she had indeed led them in prayers after a short bedtime story about pirates, after which, Edith had insisted the kitten be tucked in with her.

But now that Jory had returned to join the rest of the family, she realized she had pictured Foley hearing of their return over a pint of ale in the village tavern after the duke's caravan of coaches had roared into the village of Pensford, slowing down long enough to pass through safely. Daphne's question and Julia's suggestion seemed worthy of discussion in her opinion. She'd brought a book to read from her room, "Waverly" by Sir Walter Scott, a Christmas gift from her mother. And she found the red velvet armchair directly across from the duke's sisters quite comfortable for reading. But the duke did not look up from the book he read to comment on the remarks.

If Squire Foley had a daughter and he was in some sort of war against the duke, it did not seem good sense to include her as a guest. But she could not say for certain, for she had never met Miss Selina Foley. Glancing at the duke, he wore no discernable opinion in his expression regarding the matter.

The countess furrowed her brows and pressed her lips into a thin line. "You may very well be right not to invite Miss Selina Foley, Julia."

"Pray tell, what are your thoughts on the matter, Miss Pritchard?" Lady Julia tilted her head.

Jory, seated beside the countess's matching chair, peered over the edge of her book. "It has generally been my experience that honesty is usually the best policy. Perhaps you could write to Miss Foley and begin by saying how much you value her friendship, but that in view of this unexpected outburst by her father and his peculiar stance against your brother, perhaps a reprieve is necessary for a short time."

The countess lifted her quizzing glass to study Jory. "I do believe I may like this new governess." Turning toward Lady Julia, she continued. "Perhaps you could also say that the duke insists upon a reprieve, for if she has taken a side with her father and has an opinion on what should be done with the land, it may impact her behavior at this country house disturbance you call a party. Though I know my dear Emma did love parties."

Lady Daphne gasped and covered her mouth. "Oh dear! I shan't bear it if we cannot prevail upon our very dear friend and her companion to attend our party. Selina should be here. She has been our dearest of friends since childhood. You know that, Archer." She cast an imploring expression at her brother.

He shifted in the armchair where he sat facing the fireplace at the far end of the furniture grouping, reading the *Common Book of Prayer*, another thing that surprised Jory altogether. But he only paused long enough to glance up at Daphne and Julia before returning his attention to his book.

If those rumors were true, he very much needed to read those prayers. She almost wished they did not interrupt him, since it was her opinion that his very soul was at risk of being denied the right to an eternity in heaven with Jesus. Fornication was expressly forbidden, and Jory did everything she could to follow the Lord with all of her whole heart and soul. She was sure she could never marry a man involved in such a terrible deed.

And on top of this sordid affair with his mistress, it remained to be seen how involved he was with Lady Flora, who would soon appear at Mulberry House, no doubt. Was he dedicated to the daughter of the marquess too, all while romancing a maid, and shortly, right under Lady Flora's very nose? Though she would be going home to Northampton in two months, last season's diamond might face a lifetime of misery if she became engaged to the Duke of Pensford.

"Do you insist upon it, brother?" Julia's voice was just a hair above a whisper, her eyes wide, indicating she stood by her sister despite her doubts.

The duke cleared his throat. "No. I do not insist upon it. I leave it entirely up to you." He returned to reading his book.

"Ah. Thank heavens. Then all is well." Lady Julia exchanged a happy smile with her sister.

Daphne nodded vigorously. "Yes, all is well. Then it is decided. We shall ignore this little torrid display of indignation foisted upon us by the squire. After all, it is not Selina's fault her father has made a grave faux pas out of his own ignorance or that he is an arrogant fustian."

"That may very well be true," the countess said, "but I fear you may be in danger of making a grave mistake. The children almost always go the way of their parents in the end."

To this, no one responded, but Jory bit her lower lip. Was the countess correct? Would her words prove true? Would they regret having the daughter of the squire among the household and its guests? And what of her companion, whom they had said little about?

Jory couldn't help but admire the fact the duke did not give in to the countess. He hadn't even glanced at her during the discussion. But his sisters had feared the countess might sway him. Perhaps on some matters, the countess did sway the duke. She was, after all, older and wiser than his sisters. But the duke did not seem one bit daunted by the countess or her opinions. She was certainly opinionated as he had warned, and she had a knack for stirring an undercurrent of strife with her sometimes amusing and sometimes biased remarks.

Overall, she seemed to be a good example. She also exemplified someone who cared about their reputation and doing the right thing. Lady Rowans was a recipient of the duke's generosity, after all. Mulberry House was his family seat, not hers. She did not have the final say in any matters, except perhaps in the duke's absence if his sisters were not in residence. But she did seem to take it upon herself to look after them all and advise them, whether they desired her advice or not.

On the other hand, Jory counted the small strides she had made at dinner and in the drawing room with the countess and the duke's sisters as victories. If she were to live there for the next few months, peace with Lord Thornberry's family members meant something to her. It was the arrival of Lady Flora that she dreaded, and she had heard the sisters mention her in London and at one of the taverns on their journey to Mulberry House. They intended to invite her to the country house party, and when she arrived, then what? Especially since she had to admit since arriving that the duke stirred some part of her own heart. The idea of the diamond of the first water from last season being among them troubled her as much as trying to figure out the duke's character. What a quandary!

Nine o'clock soon saw Jory scratching upon the duke's door to his private study on the first floor. She had looked forward to this glimpse of his personal sanctuary, and the countess and the duke's sisters had retired for the evening. The door was open, and Lord Thornberry called out, "Come in, Jory!"

Stepping inside with her hands clasped behind her back, she spotted tea had been served on a round tea table situated between two chairs facing the fireplace.

"Please, make yourself comfortable." He gestured toward the seats as he rose from behind his magnificent desk where he surveyed a large map of sorts covering his entire desktop.

"Thank you, my lord." She settled into one of the armchairs. What would this meeting reveal about the man?

He stood beside the tea table, brows furrowed. "Now Jory, let us dispense with formalities. I thought we had accomplished that in Northampton, but appears we have both regressed, but especially you. Let us begin again on the right footing. May I call you, Jory, and will you call me Archer?"

She could agree. It was time they repaired this fracture in their relationship. "All right. From here on, I shall acquiesce except in the most formal situations, and yes, you may continue to call me Jory."

"Very good." He released a sigh. "Tea? Cream and sugar?"

"Yes, please. Both."

He poured two cups and handed her one. He moved the cream and sugar closer to her and then sat in the armchair on the other side of the tea table. "At our future meetings to discuss the progress of the education of my darling children, I confess I am terrible at pouring tea, so I shall rely upon you for that except for at this, our first of hopefully many enjoyable meetings."

She smiled. How charming the duke seemed. Was he always like this—so calm and charming, able to set her at ease? *Likeable even?* If so, she might begin to enjoy her time spent with him a great deal.

"I must apologize for that terrible intrusion at dinner this evening. That is not a reflection of how most of our dinners go at Mulberry House."

"Think nothing of it. I understand. Folks are often unpredictable."

"And have you come up with a plan for the children?" One of his brows arched.

Jory opened her reticule and withdrew the lists she'd made. Would he approve of her plans?

"I have made a plan, if it meets with your approval." Jory leaned toward him.

She bit her lower lip, and once again, Archer found himself thinking about kissing her. Straight out of the blue. He sat up taller, banishing the thought. Temporarily, of course. He might consider it at another opportune moment, and sooner rather than later. What was it about Jory that caused such passions to come to his mind? No one else had done that to him in a long while, not since Emma. But he'd been dreaming about Jory in the past eight months since meeting her in Northampton. He'd not noticed her before, when he'd attended other Christmas balls with his Emma, nor he supposed, had Jory noticed them. But now that he'd met her, he'd consider her unforgettable. How did she always seem to make him smile?

"I thought the children and I would take some exercise and fresh air each morning. Perhaps a vigorous stroll through the garden alternated with days of pony rides, horseback for Master Henry and me, of course. With a stable attendant on hand for the girls and their ponies."

"Very good." Archer nodded.

"Sometimes we might take our exercise by delivering bread or whatever the cook can spare for the poor or the tenant farmers. I thought you might make a list for me of the appropriate names with a map to their homes. This would be one way to teach the children grace and compassion. It would show Lady Jane and Lady Edith what a true princess is about." She paused to glance at him instead of her notes.

"Outstanding." Exactly what his girls needed, and it certainly wouldn't hurt his boys any to understand the plight of the homeless or less fortunate.

"Then mathematics, English grammar, and French in the mornings." She offered another glance in his direction. "About half an hour on each subject, for they are very young."

He nodded, unwilling to interrupt her.

"In the afternoon, we would study literature, geography, art, history, etiquette, and science." Here, she changed to the next list in her hands, but she glanced up at him, adding, "During etiquette, we will cover deportment."

"Excellent." He smiled, pleased with her conclusions. How lovely her chocolate eyes were when they danced as they did when she spoke of teaching! He could get lost in those big, warm, inquisitive, intelligent eyes.

"Before bed, I thought we would have prayers and a proper Bible reading. Another Scripture reading at breakfast each morning." Her brow arched. "Always a prayer before mealtimes. I wasn't sure if your previous governesses had given any other religious instruction to them but thought it safe to keep our readings to passages from God's Holy Word and the *Book of Common Prayer*. I had noticed they each have one on their nightstands, and their own Bibles."

Here again, he couldn't help but nod in approval. "Yes, Emma made sure of it. Birthday gifts." His heart soared to hear her speak of these things since he considered their spiritual upbringing of great importance. "And of course, we attend the village church each Sunday."

"Very good then. If that is satisfactory to you, may we have permission to use the art room when we are studying art? And do you find as I do, that thirty minutes is long enough for each subject at these ages?"

"Yes, I agree. So long as Henry and Jane are using age-appropriate books in comparison to Charlie and Edith," he added.

"I will be sure of it. We seem to have what we need regarding books, but here is a list of the supplies we need. I'll need it back after you review it." She handed him the other paper. "And I need to know when the dance master will come, and when the music teachers arrive for pianoforte and violin? I've heard the children speak of their lessons."

"These instructors come weekly when we are in residence. Usually on Friday mornings around ten. One week dance, the next music." Did she realize how lovely her cheekbones were…or the adorable structure of her nose?

"Very good. I'll add practices several times a week for their instruments after our usual school hours. I saw that the boys are taking violin lessons, and pianoforte for the girls." She tucked her remaining note inside her reticule.

He glanced at the items on the list she'd given him. Ink. Paper, Pencils. Candles. Chalk for the chalkboard. Notebooks. It all seemed reasonable. "I'll give you a letter affixed with my seal so that you may purchase whatever is needed in the village at the mercantile."

"Thank you, *Archer*."

It pleased him that she had used his name but troubled him that he would soon lose her during the day to the classroom and his children, but he had to put their needs above his own. He could look forward to similar meetings with her in the evenings, if she agreed to them. "Shall we meet each evening at nine o'clock for tea, here in my study, to discuss the progress you are making with the children?"

She nodded and sipped more of her tea. "Fine with me."

Did he detect a half smile and a crimson blush at the suggestion. He grinned, happy with her answer. He would cherish and look forward to those meetings at the end of each day.

He told her how to find the mercantile. Offered use of any of his conveyances or horses to travel to the village. They sipped their tea for a time in silence. "Jory, I should mention that the library is next door to my study. Please, feel free to borrow anything you need. Some books may be useful for the classroom as additional material."

Her eyes lit up, and he could see he'd hit a subject she appreciated by the way she smiled. This encouraged him. "I'd like to show you something else too. Come with me." He rose and crossing to his desk, in the corner behind where they currently sat, he motioned for her to follow. He could hardly wait to share his designs for the land Squire Hopkins had owned. Then he'd give her a tour of the library, after which they could finish their tea. Why did the time they shared seem to tick by all too fast? He could hardly wait to show her his plans for Pensford. Would she approve?

Chapter Seven

When the Lord takes pleasure in anyone's way,

He causes their enemies to make peace with them.

Proverbs 16:7, NIV

Three days hence, the prince's private chefs arrived with some additional security staff for the future king. This set the household in a frenzy, with everyone abuzz about whether the prince would arrive ahead of the other guests. Jory, busy settling into a daily routine with the children, had little time to concern herself with these matters.

She overheard some servants in the hall on the fourth floor speaking about a war brewing in the kitchen between the duke's cook, Mrs. Smithers, and the prince's chefs. But at dinner that evening, Julia implored her brother to come out of hiding and have a word with the cook to encourage her to get on well with the prince's staff, despite the fact Archer had largely remained behind closed doors in recent days.

The duke promised he would have a word with the cook. Smiling and chatty indeed, his sisters went to bed that night in the top of their boughs about the party, since guests would begin to arrive the very next day. Meanwhile, the rest of the household braced for impact.

Jory descended downstairs and came face to face with one of the guests after her classes finished the next afternoon. Guests had been arriving all day while she languished in the schoolroom teaching, unable to join the festivities, but she knew there'd be time to meet guests at dinner. Intent upon a brisk walk to the village to purchase the school supplies they needed, a letter in hand with the duke's seal, she looked forward to being out of the classroom. How helpful Miss Davison was to look after the children in her absence, though in truth, the children longed to spend time with their father, who always seemed so busy, though they saw him nearly every morning at breakfast when he visited the children's dining room. But her smile faded at once when she recognized the vivacious redhead Julia and Daphne welcomed in the foyer.

"We shall have so much fun now that you are here, Lady Flora," Julia gushed. "I can't wait for you to meet Miss Selina Foley and her companion, Miss Helena Parker. Lady Ivy will be here soon too. But she is coming all the way from Derbyshire and expected to arrive later this evening. Oh, and the Danforth sisters of Devonshire have arrived only half an hour ago; Lady Venezia, Lady Delphine, and Lady Vivienne."

Seven ladies! My, the duke's sisters had invited many guests. But how fleeting the calculation was, for now the redhead swung around with the duke's sisters on each arm to head up the grand staircase, blocked by Jory at present, who had stopped on the landing, aghast.

"*You* again!" the redhead hissed.

"I might say the same of you," Jory replied, lifting her chin as she placed two hands on her hips, her reticule dangling from one wrist.

Daphne looked from one to the other. "Dear me, am I to understand you already know each other?"

"Unfortunately." Lady Flora made no bones about her obvious disdain.

Though it pained her to do so, Jory stepped aside and spread an arm toward the staircase, allowing them to pass. "If you will excuse me, I am on an outing."

She lifted her chin, adjusted the long blue ribbons extending from each side of her fashionable straw bonnet, and hurried outside through the open doors. Passing Reeds on the way out, she left him to gaze after her, a perplexed look upon his face after witnessing the exchange.

Outside, she quickened her pace down the long drive, determined to get away from Mulberry House as quickly as possible. So *that* was Lady Flora! How utterly, absolutely, wretched! She was undone. Utterly undone.

As she progressed toward the main road, Jory recalled the same Christmas ball two years prior when she'd met the Earl of Dunmore, Lord Josephus Cunningham. On that same occasion, she'd had a miserable encounter with a younger Flora who had belittled her in front of a large group of other ladies of about the same age. Simply recalling the encounter made her gloved hands now ball into tight fists.

That same Flora had insisted Jory not be allowed to join them for a sleighride because, having arranged it herself with the Duke of Gladdington's stable hands, she declared there was room enough only for the ladies in her gathering, who all happened to be ladies of the peerage, except for herself. Why hadn't she connected *that* Flora to this one? Why, it had never crossed her mind that they might be one and the same person!

Jory had been invited at the last moment by Lady Cora, one of the other ladies who had risen to her defense, insisting that Jory should be welcome on the sleighride.

"I don't think so. As you can see, there are already twelve of us with room for exactly six in each sleigh," Lady Flora had said, keeping her hands inside her fur muff as she surveyed Jory.

"We can squeeze together to make room for one more," Lady Cora had urged.

"I don't know. The stable manager told me these two sleighs will comfortably hold only six in each. Who might you be, anyhow?" Lady Flora had inspected Jory's not so fashionable hand-me-down garments, her faded cloak, and scuffed boots, worn the Christmas season before as the group of ladies gathered around to do the same. "And, oh dear, where are your pattens?"

Jory had looked down at her walking boots, ashamed that she did not own any pattens. She didn't particularly like the contraptions, but she hadn't thought to say so, overwhelmed with shame for not wearing any. Nor had she thought to borrow any from the duchess. Ill-prepared for the event, she had it in mind to flee.

"She is the adopted daughter of the Duke of Gladdington," Lady Cora had tucked her arm around Jory. "If she cannot ride in the sleigh, I won't either. I'm sure the duchess won't be pleased if she hears of this."

"If anyone wishes to inform the duchess, I am quite sure she would only wish for our safety. Suit yourself if you prefer not to ride with us, Lady Cora. The miss can wait for the next sleighride, can she not?" Lady Flora had shrugged and turned away with a flounce, leaving Cora and Jory out of the festive ride.

Flora had treated Jory with sneers for the rest of the weekend and at the ball. Not even the kind introduction Cora had given extinguished her insolence. If this was who Archer contemplated marriage with, she felt sorry indeed for him and his children, but she refused to subject herself to more of Lady Flora's disdain.

She'd never mentioned the incident to the duchess, but without realizing it, Lady Catherine Edwina Kingston—Winnie, the duchess—had perhaps been right to warn her to consider last season's diamond an archenemy. How could anyone deem Lady Flora as a diamond of the first water when the opposite was true? Wouldn't a true diamond be kind and gracious?

Jory reached the road running in front of the manor house, aptly named King's Highway since it led to Pensford, connecting the village to the duke's home, and turned right. In her anger, she traipsed the five miles in what seemed no time at all. She had intended to head to the duke's stable and borrow a gig or a horse, but meeting Lady Flora had unnerved her so. She crossed over Bath Way, guessing the road connected to the road leading to Bath, and yielded to the left onto Lawn Avenue, heading into the village. This road was lined with charming houses and lodgings that led to the town square. All as Archer had said, but now she found herself even more anxious to discover how serious his relationship with the so-called diamond was.

Beyond the square, she caught a glimpse of River Road straight ahead, the River Chew in the distance. St. Thomas à Becket's Church rose up on her right as she turned left onto the square at River Road. Admiring the businesses on the riverbank to her right, she took note of the chandler shop, a bakery and cheese shop, the confectionary, and an assembly hall. The last building was the only tavern and inn in the village. On the west end of the square, just as the duke had said, she found the mercantile between the bank and the postal office.

There, she presented her letter and list to the cashier standing behind the till, the owner, she assumed since he had the air of one. He read through it and glanced at her with a perfunctory nod. "I'll have your items ready shortly if you'd care to browse, miss."

"Thank you." Jory turned away and began browsing the selections. Barrels of salt pork were stacked in one corner. A large jar of dill pickles upon the counter tempted patrons. Children might gaze at the peppermint candies in another jar. Sugared almonds too. Tins of tea and coffee did not stop their flavors from wafting. A few rolls and bolts of fabric occupied a table in one corner, a small selection of silk ribbons and colorful embroidery threads hanging above. Non-perishable items occupied numerous rows of shelving. She paused to admire the small display of bonnets and gloves to attract shoppers when she reached the front window.

A glance outside toward the square allowed her to feast her eyes upon the trees and their boughs of leaves turning into autumnal shades of red and gold. Glad for the cooler weather and the fact she'd worn her nicest spencer in a shade of blue over her muslin frock, for it not only kept her just warm enough but matched the blue ribbons streaming from her bonnet. At least this time, she felt better prepared to deal with Lady Flora. The duchess had seen to that, having showered her with so many newer items, various gifts, and increased attention since her first meeting with Flora. Mainly because Jory had now completed her training to step into a role as a fine lady, or so the duchess said.

Strong voices to her right caught her attention as she spotted the shopkeeper still filling her order from a storage room behind the till. Two men had entered the shop and now leaned over the far end of one of the counters near the front door of the establishment, involved in a hushed discussion that had begun before they entered.

"If you are as disgusted with things as I be, come to the Dragoniers next meeting. You shall not regret it. 'Tis the only way we shall see change," the taller burly man said, placing a hand on the other fellow's shoulder. "Are ye not sick of the way things be?"

"Aye, that I am." The other fellow nodded.

"Then we must join forces. Ridiculous prices. A man cannot afford to feed his family, all while the duke lives upon that hill in his fancy house. They feast to their heart's content while we watch our children starve and dress them in rags." The burly man gritted his teeth, handing him a pamphlet. "Time has come fer change."

"Something must be done. We cannot go on like it is for much longer. On that, we kin agree." The other fellow glanced at the pamphlet and folded it, tucking it in his breast pocket. He patted the pocket and in a low voice replied, "Saturday evenings at nine. The paper mill."

"Aye, but do not tell anyone who works for the duke." The burly man whispered, his beady eyes glancing round about as Jory ducked from view. "He is a selfish man who cares not fer the common man. Thinks he can own us all. Keep us in debt. Allows us to sink in our plight, doing little for Pensford townsfolk."

Jory hid behind a row of shelves with some shoes stacked upon it, but she peeked around the corner, barely breathing, her chest heaving. How these men hated the duke! Was he truly a selfish uncaring man? He did not seem so to her.

"'Tis all in secret, for the mayor and Squire Foley 'ave a jig. A plan if ye will. And it ain't no gammon either. We be dished up, but not fer long."

"A jig ye say?" The other fellow drew himself up taller.

"Aye. To bring in blunt for the common man. A real blunt-in-the-hand kind of jig. So's we won't be left to starve. A furniture manufacturer, a textile mill, *and* a garment factory. But the blasted duke stands in our way. Which is why the Dragoniers will take a stand against 'im."

"I am no arse. I won't be tellin' anyone loyal to the duke."

The Dragoniers? What and who exactly were the Dragoniers about? At least the duke had some folks loyal to him, or so the man inferred. But the shopkeeper had filled her order and summoned her to the till with a wave of his hand. Leaning toward her over the counter, he placed a hand on the package and in a low voice said, "You're new around here."

She nodded, unsure of what to expect from this remark. Maybe he was just being hospitable.

In an even lower voice, he added, "Pay them no mind. Archie is the finest, most caring, upstanding peer that Pensford could ever have. Have you seen the rectory orphanage he established beside the church?"

She shook her head no, but her mouth dropped open. An orphanage, established by the duke?

"Not only did he establish it, but he continues to provide for the orphans, not to mention the fine village school where he permits them to attend. Paid for the rebuilding of the church too. And no finer village school anywhere, thanks to his steady stream of donations. He permits girls to attend, as well." The man patted her package twice and pushed it toward her.

The duke had established an orphanage, rebuilt the church, financed the village school, *and* permitted girls to attend the village school? She thought the Lord Alexander Kingston was one of very few who permitted girls like herself to obtain a public education in Glad Crown. Many in England did not offer such privileges to females. But it was exceedingly nice to hear these things about the Duke of Pensford too, and most surprising after the society column she'd read.

"Thank you, kind sir. How nice to have met you." Jory gathered up her package, bid the man good day, and was careful to pass by the men near the door without glancing at them. She had much to ponder on the long walk home. But something must give. She could not remain in the duke's employee if Lady Flora remained under the same roof.

Reaching Mulberry House, Jory sighed as she climbed the staircase, thankful to slip inside unnoticed. Her mind reeled with the new information she'd heard in the village, but it mattered little at present. She must contend with the ordeal of Flora. And if the duke was indeed a pure and good man at heart as she was beginning to suspect, it only made matters worse. Losing him to Flora was more than her heart could take, though she didn't think she had allowed herself to fully consider him. Partly because of his rumored relationship with Flora. It was common knowledge that they had danced and dined together last season. The Ton expected them to marry.

She swiped tears from her eyes and sat down at her writing desk. She must implore upon the duchess to let her return to Northampton at once. This other information about the Dragoniers was the duke's battle, and everything surrounding him seemed in turmoil. But her heart pounded with its own kind of turmoil, fearing the further humiliation Lady Flora would surely heap upon her. And she still had the other matter to get to the bottom of, regarding the new maid she suspected, whom she had seen little of.

Pulling a sheet of foolscap from the desk, she penned her second letter to the duchess. Her first she had written from London to inform the duchess of her safe arrival. But in this correspondence, she must make the duchess understand her plight. As for dinners and evening meetings with the duke, she would take meals in her private quarters and forego the meetings, feigning a painful ache in her head, a chill, weariness, or other excuses until the duchess sent transportation to fetch her.

Some of the duke's male friends had begun to arrive over the course of the next few days, mainly to keep the ladies occupied and entertained, according to what Tilly shared with her at the end of one school day two days later. "A Viscount named Lord Edmund Dudley is among them," Miss Davison said while they tidied things and the children filed out to the playroom. "Everyone calls him 'Dud.' Lord Charles Leyton, the Earl of Woodbridge, and a close friend of the duke's is also here, and quite handsome. I saw him in the library when I returned a book."

Jory crossed the long room and began washing the chalkboard, recognizing the name of the gentleman Lady Julia had said would escort the sisters to the rout in London.

"Lord Leyton's younger brother, Jasper, arrived with Charles. And someone named 'Finn' is here now. He wants to become a physician, or so Beatrice says," Tilly informed her.

Jory remembered the mention of Finn at her first dinner. Phineas Crandall, a local friend of the duke. She had come to understand at some point that the Leyton brothers were also local when not in their London residence.

"She told me everything when I brought our clothing to the laundry house. And she said the duke is missing you. Asks about ye each evening at supper, according to one of the footmen. Beatrice has her eyes upon one of the footmen and they talk, or so she says."

"Is that so? And isn't Beatrice the new servant who accompanied us from London?" Jory spun around with her eyes wide. She'd hardly seen the new maid since arriving at Mulberry House, one of the reasons her investigation into the truth had failed.

"Aye."

"Well, the duke can keep missing me. I have no appetite for dining below stairs." Jory finished cleaning the chalkboard as Tilly gave her a pensive stare and then hurried away to tend the children in the playroom.

It *did* please her some to hear that Archer had mentioned her. Thankfully, she guessed he was too busy hiding in his study and avoiding the plethora of arriving guests to be overly concerned with her absence the past two days. And if the new maid had set her heart upon a footman, mayhap there was reason to rejoice. Could it be those rumors about the duke were unfounded Banbury Tales?

What had become of Miss Pritchard? Archer worried about the fact she hadn't made an appearance for dinner or their meetings, and allegedly on account of Lady Flora's arrival. Julia had privately informed him of their rocky greeting exchange. So, his strong and vivacious butterfly had a delicate side. She'd taken to hiding herself away in her quarters. What else could it be, unless she was genuinely ill? Should he send for the leech?

He'd even had breakfast in the children's dining room that very morning in hopes of seeing Jory since she always took breakfast with his four darlings. Edith had climbed onto his lap, and Charlie had hardly eaten a bite while telling him of his latest art project. Henry and Jane wanted to know when the prince would arrive. Could they meet him? Jane had even practiced her curtsey, proud of her newfound exercise in deportment. Edith had climbed down from his lap to mimic her, a wide smile on her sweet face and adorably pudgy cheeks. But he'd now learned the governess had asked for her third evening meal to be sent upstairs.

As the clock struck nine o'clock that evening, he heaved a sigh when Reeds delivered another note from Jory, excusing herself. How could she have acquired a chill? Unless it had developed from her walk to the village. He'd spotted her from a window in his study, walking up the drive with a package in hand the other day, but Julia had held him captive discussing the many card games like whist and other activities she'd planned for the prince's arrival. He'd heard the prince enjoyed such activities. Not his cup of tea, but he supposed the guests might enjoy it for a while.

He abandoned his study and took the stairs two at a time until he reached Miss Pritchard's door on the fourth floor. He drew in a deep breath and tapped with a knuckle. Would she answer? "Jory, 'tis Archer. I am concerned about you."

No reply. Only his own breathing.

"Shall I send for the physician?"

Finally, he heard a floorboard creak. Then her sweet, soft voice on the other side. "No, I am fine. Just under the weather is all."

He waited, his brows furrowing, unsure of what else to say. "All right. I am here for you if you require anything. Anything at all."

"Thank you, my lord." So, it was back to that, eh? He sighed and turned away. At least he had tried. Perhaps she would emerge in a day or two of her own accord. Until then, he must be patient.

Two more days passed before Jory finally received a reply from the duchess, delivered by Reeds to the schoolroom in the morning. "Miss Pritchard, the duke wanted me to inform you that the prince and his caravan of coaches and security arrived in the middle of the night. He is settled in the India Room on the third floor. The duke hopes to see you at dinner this evening…or tomorrow perhaps, if you are feeling better."

"Thank you, Reeds. I will consider it." Jory tore the letter open as soon as he left since the children were busy writing letters to their father in French. The duke could read them in one of their future meetings she supposed. The dance master had come that morning, and the children had finally settled down after their lessons in the ballroom. So far, she had managed to evade running into any of the guests during their early morning strolls in the gardens or their riding time at the stables. The few she had seen assumed she was busy with the children and had been so far away, neither she nor they had approached each other.

But the idea of attending church that weekend with the duke's family plagued her. Tilly had advised her to resume her routine by at least joining the duke and his guests for dinner rather than feigning illness. Not much got past her.

But what if Archer sat beside Lady Flora? It would irk her so. And what of Beatrice, the maid? How would the maid feel about this turn of events? But now, her hands trembled as she unfolded the letter from her benefactress. Would she send her chariot for Jory at once?

Dearest Jory,

Have no fear. As soon as I read the society column about the Duke of Pensford, I began to question my plans. What if I am wrong? This remains to be seen, but I do not believe a word of it. Not long after, I received a letter from the Earl of Dunmore. He asked about you and informed me he is to join the prince at Mulberry House. I wrote to him that you are helping the duke with his children, but he replied, excited to meet you once again in your new capacity of assisting the duke as his temporary governess. After speaking with my darling Xander, he said we shall place a fine dowry upon you. I shall indeed sponsor you during the coming season, if our plans come to naught. My husband will finance all of it. When the earl arrives, he will have read about your dowry in the society column, for I have leaked it out on purpose. Mark my words, either the duke or the earl will propose before the coming season. Perhaps both, so you may have your pick of husbands. Especially when they see your composure and grace under pressure, the true character of a diamond of the first water. And a lovely dowry to boot. Do your best to uncover the truth. Pray for guidance and wisdom.

Your Humble Friend and Benefactress,

Winnie

Jory buried her face in her hands. Not the answer she had expected at all. *What now?* Pray! She would pray fervently.

Easier said than done, she pushed herself to continue through lessons, but the children were in no mood for them. When she asked why they could not focus on their geography, Henry spoke up.

"The prince has arrived, and we'd like to meet him. And Charlie and I wish to play pirate games outside, as do Jane and Edith."

"I see. Well, let us push through our lessons. Maybe we can finish early. I fear I am not in much of a mood for our studies either. Let us move on to history. I shall give us a short reading about the Tudors and then, perhaps we shall take turns reading a few paragraphs from *Pumpernickel the Cat*."

The children clapped, and Edith did so vigorously, for she loved stories about Pumpernickel, the cat. Jory could hardly blame them for restlessness with so many guests about—and a prince among them! A dreadful distraction.

Nevertheless, she must carry on. But she had to reinforce her own resolve to not ride away on the next mail coach headed north when a glance out of the window offered a glimpse of Lady Flora strolling the grounds with Archer. At least he did not offer his arm, but her heart twinged with pangs of jealousy.

She announced the end of class and barely bothered to tidy a thing, hurrying to her quarters while Tilly herded the children into the playroom. Closing the door, Jory flung herself upon the bed, overset. A ninny she was! Such a fool's errand the duchess had sent her upon! She had turned into a wretched watering pot, her pillow soon soaked with tears. Reaching for her Bible, she cried out to the Lord silently, cradling the book to her chest.

See, I am doing a new thing. Before the rivers spring forth, I tell you of them…do you not see it? But this comforting whisper left her perplexed and full of hope all at once. Did the Lord command her attention so she could sort through the matter? He seemed to point to something good in her future, but what? Maybe the earl was her answer, after all. She did so enjoy his humor.

Staring out of the front window, she spied a large group of ladies and gentlemen walking toward the stable. Were they intent upon a horseback ride? She did not see the duke among them, but the heavyset older gentleman must be the prince, talking to Lady Flora, of course, red curls dangling from her veiled hat with its long scarf trailing down her back… and a scarf that matched her fashionable riding habit. Two of the prince's guards brought up the end of those among the riding party. Maybe she needed to dry her eyes and take a stroll in the rear gardens whilst they were away. Some fresh air might do her some good.

Fifteen minutes later, Jory had strolled far beyond the garden and veered off toward the pond with rowing boats which the duke had once pointed out to her. This led to a gazebo nearby, and as she drew closer, she realized Archer sat inside it, his head bowed over a notebook where he scribbled something. So, he hadn't joined the others. She should thank him for offering to send for a doctor.

She stepped onto the gazebo platform softly. He glanced up, surprise written in his expression.

"Jory!" He set his composition book and pencil aside, rising, bowing to acknowledge her.

"A beautiful day for a stroll," she replied, taking the seat beside him where he gestured for her to sit.

"How good it is to see you." He moved his book to sit closer.

"Are you writing poetry?" she mused after spying some of his words on the open page.

Archer nodded. "A hymn. I intend to set it to music, eventually. I can hear it, but then it escapes me, until I begin writing the words at the pianoforte."

So that was why he spent so much time in seclusion, for she had not seen him from the windows nearly as much as she had seen the guests amble about on the grounds. His children did not see much of him either. A hymn! His confession left her utterly speechless. Now she understood why she'd seen a pianoforte in a corner of his study. A writer and a composer! It began to make sense to her why he hid himself from his children and the household.

"I have another problem."

"Why am I not surprised by that?" She laughed, earning a sheepish grin. "Pray, do tell."

He drew out a list from inside the same book, handing it to her. A list of dates with activities, mostly card games, strolls, and horseback rides. "Julia seems to think this is our best course of action for entertaining the prince and our guests, but I beg to differ. While I agree he may enjoy a night of charades and another of riddles…it is sorely lacking, but I have been unable to convince her otherwise. Only I am at a loss as to what I should suggest instead. I only know the prince will surely seem bored after one night of whist."

"I see what you mean. This is dreadful for entertaining a royal prince, knowing what he is accustomed to from the things I have read about him in the newspapers. Hmm." Lady Julia did not seem to have applied much imagination to the list, something Jory used a great deal in the schoolroom, and perhaps a reason she enjoyed teaching so much. Ideas were already bursting in her mind.

She smiled and leaned toward him. "May I borrow your pencil? I think I know what we need to do. It would involve the children more too, who are simply dying to meet him and engage with our other guests. This is a historical and unique opportunity they should not miss, after all."

He cocked his head to one side, handing her the pencil. "I hadn't thought of it that way 'til now."

Jory wrote down her ideas beside some of the dates, pausing to brainstorm here and there. When satisfied, Archer smiled as he looked over her shoulder while she made revisions, crossed things off, and added other items. He kept nodding, his blue eyes dancing.

"What do you think? Too ponderous?" She handed him her completed revisions.

"Bravo! Marvelous!" he breathed. "You are a marvel, Jory. How I have missed you! An ache in my heart since I saw you last…" His voice faded.

She turned to look into his blue eyes, but he was so close. And then his lips brushed hers. His mouth returned to claim and crush hers with a strong, passionate kiss, his arm encircling her, drawing her against his chest until she heard his heartbeat.

When he withdrew, Jory pressed a hand to her lips, still warm from his breath. Her heart raced.

"You were born for this." His voice was low and husky. "To be my duchess."

"Then you approve?" she whispered, dizzy with excitement. *His duchess?*

"Oh, yes, I very much approve. But that's not why I kissed you. I kissed you because… you drive me mad with longing. Longing to hold you in my arms forever…"

Longing? She drove him *mad*? Did his kiss have nothing to do with love? Why hadn't he said he loved her? There was a distinct difference in her mind between longing and love! Hold her in his arms forever? Is that how he had enticed Beatrice, too? Perhaps he had used those exact words. If he'd first said he loved her and had then spoken those other words, she might have been able to open her heart to him, but with so many doubts swirling in her mind, she could not.

What did he mean exactly, and why couldn't she find her tongue to ask? *His duchess?* Is that what he had promised the maid and Lady Flora too? Bewildered and confused, Jory's mouth dropped open, and rising, she picked up her skirts, resisted the urge to stomp a foot, and fled.

Chapter Eight

Make every effort to live in peace with everyone and to be holy;

without holiness no one will see the Lord.

Hebrews 12:14, NIV

Three more days passed while she simmered. Only Jory did not leave her room to teach lessons. She had now missed two Sundays, a fact which grieved her so, but it could not be helped. She placed Miss Davison in charge and stayed in her quarters behind a locked door.

On the second Sunday she had missed, Tilly informed her that Lady Flora had not sat with the duke in his box when the vicar delivered his sermon. She also gave her the text of Proverbs 3:5-6, since Jory requested it to read what the vicar had preached on. She knew it at once to be on the topic of trusting the Lord, even when things made no sense, a passage she had never needed more than now.

But presently, she paced the floor of her room. She couldn't hide in her quarters any longer and must resume her teaching duties. And besides, despite the kiss, Archer had sent a note, apologizing for frightening her away. He pleaded with her that she make an appearance at dinner, by special request of the prince.

Special request of the prince? How absurd! She was only the governess. She read the note again from the beginning, trying to make sense of it.

Apparently, she had become quite the subject of interest among the guests, the duke wrote. Archer went on to say she was a mystery to the prince and had intrigued him with her absence, accustomed to everyone fussing over wanting to meet him. But only Lady Flora had seen her, of all the guests. The earl had arrived, and he wished for her to appear at dinner too. Would she please attend the dinner and prepare to sit beside the prince and the earl, near the head of the table with himself close at hand? "For you have become a kind of enigma to everyone. All the guests are dying of curiosity to meet you, even if only one time, to be able to say they have met you," Archer wrote.

Was this all some sort of lark? A nervous laugh released from her throat. Sit beside the prince himself? *And* the earl? *And* the duke? But she was nobody. Nobody special at all. A mere tenant farmer's daughter. A governess, too weak to appear because of a foe. And yet, she'd shot turkeys, rabbits, foxes, and hawks. Why fear Lady Flora? And yet, they called her a mystery. Of all things! An enigma!

But then she recalled the Lord's words to her. He was doing a new thing. So, it must be true. The Lord knew she was overset. The hand of the Lord must surely be upon her. He was orchestrating things to His satisfaction. She only wished He would let *her* in on the secret, but then what need would she have of faith? Faith demanded the belief that He was working on her behalf, in her best interest, and to carry out His plans. That whatever He did, it would be for her good, and not evil.

At seven o'clock, Jory appeared in the dining room, wearing a forest green evening gown of shimmery satin. If she were a mystery, she may as well play the part. Tilly had outdone herself making long curls in Jory's hair, styling it just so.

A hush fell on the room as she stood in the doorway, her cheeks flushed. There were almost no empty seats with so many guests in the house, and all of them turned to gaze at her. But Archer rose at once and strode to meet her. In seconds, he was at her side, drawing her gloved hand to his lips. Her brow arched, but he smiled, setting her at ease, putting an arm around her waist.

"Good evening," he whispered. She could not help but return an affectionate smile. Then he led her to sit beside the prince.

"Miss Pritchard, we are delighted you could join us this evening," Archer said, loud enough for his guests to hear.

Why did the prince and the earl stand too? And every gentleman in the room?

"Ah, here is our mystery lady! Finally! I am absolutely flummoxed. Thrilled to meet you. Utterly speechless, Miss Pritchard," the Regent gushed as the duke pulled out her chair.

"I am deeply pleased to meet you too, Your Royal Highness." Jory remembered to curtsey before taking her seat.

"How lovely to see you again, Miss Pritchard," the earl said before he took his seat on her other side. "It has been far too long."

"Lord Cunningham, how pleased I am to see you again, as well." Jory offered a warm smile in his direction.

Archer took his seat at the head of the table with the prince on one side, Lady Julia on his other. Beside Julia sat the countess, then Daphne, and *then* Lady Flora, who simmered, refusing to look in Jory's direction. The other gentlemen in the room who had risen when she entered sat once again, now that she was seated. Archer led them in prayer. Then, the prince rose to offer a toast.

"To Jory, our elegant mystery lady, and the most beautiful lady I believe I've ever laid eyes upon." He leaned toward her when he raised his glass higher, a wide smile upon his face.

"Here, here," the earl said, lifting his glass.

"To Jory," Archer said, smiling at her with his blue eyes twinkling.

"To Jory…" Others echoed around the table.

But worry lurked in Archer's sparkling eyes, too. As the evening progressed and polite conversation ensued, she could not help but ponder the meaning of Archer's kiss in the gazebo, a matter which still baffled her. She hadn't expected becoming a mystery to the guests, either.

She wasn't sure she liked being on such a display as the mystery lady, normally content to be in the background and lead a quiet life. In fact, she had not asked for any of this situation the duchess had gotten her into. All she could do now was her very best to muddle through.

By evening's end, Archer and his sisters had introduced her to each guest. The duke seldom left her side for more than a few minutes, and she had spent a great deal of time discussing artwork with the prince. Best of all, she had silenced Flora—and all was accomplished while the earl hovered nearby, gazing at her throughout the evening, seemingly happy to have conversed with her at dinner. Would the earl prove to be a better prospect? Or at least an ally amid her plight?

Jory chose to continue the aura of mystery surrounding her by not joining the ladies in the blue and white drawing room after dinner the next evening while the gentlemen lingered in the duke's study. Instead, she retreated to her quarters, anxious to steer clear of Lady Flora. She still found it hard to believe she may have won a battle concerning her value in Flora's warped estimations.

Around midnight, she yearned for another book to read after tossing and turning. She donned a wrapper and slid into her low-heeled slippers. Pulling her lace trimmed cap on more securely, she struck a match and lit a candle to illuminate her path down the staircase and through dimly lit halls. Reaching the library, she heard voices inside. Reconsidering, she nearly left, but with the door ajar, she caught her name mentioned.

Jory spun around and eyed the open door. She was able to slip inside and remain in the shadow the door cast. Her eyes narrowed, adjusting to the brighter candlelit streams of light in the library as she took in the scene.

"Do you not find Jory most fetching?" The Prince Regent wobbled in his seat as he leaned over a chess board at a game table. "I say, she is the most beautiful woman I've ever seen."

Jory covered her mouth. If the prince weren't so old, so clearly in his cups, and didn't have such a wretched reputation…but otherwise, she found his enamor with her rather sweet.

"Yes, I do find our dear Jory most fetching. Most fetching indeed! I've always thought so." Here, a large hiccup sounded, followed by an odious burp. "But 'tis Lady Julia has caught my roving eye with her plump pockets!" The Earl of Dunmore laughed hideously, and then the prince began to laugh.

Ugh! Jory doubted they could walk without falling based on their current state. The earl attempted to drink from an empty glass, holding it upside down over his upturned head. Her heart sank when she observed him shake the empty glass vigorously, but nary a drop landed on his tongue. He drew the glass over his eye, peering into it as if it were a spyglass.

"Empty!" The earl slammed it down on the chess table, knocking over several game pieces. "Ooopsie."

The men laughed with the giddiness of two silly girls. Clearly, deep in their cups!

"I say, yooo are more fickle than I, Joseee-phus. You r-rascal, you!" He rolled his r's, repeating rascal until the earl laughed. The prince then scooped up a bottle from the floor. "Here. Let me pour." He uncorked it and hiccupped.

The earl tried to hold his glass steady, but he wavered all over the place.

"Hold yer cup steady," the prince commanded.

"But under which bottle? I see three. No, two. Ope. Three again." The earl laughed, as did the prince, who ended up pouring a good deal of the bottle onto the chess game.

"But I am dished up before I've even begun. My father is deep in dun territory. I must therefore get leg-shackled to the highest bidder. Or so mother says." The earl slammed his fist onto the game table. "It has me in a dither. Topsy turvy. At sixes and sevens trying to guess whose pockets are plumpest. Is that a word?"

More laughter.

"I say, we are foxed, Dunmore. Foxed, I say." The prince's brows furrowed. "And who is the highest bidder? Julia, the duke's sister, or the mysterious Jory, rather adopted by a duke?"

My, how news traveled fast. She should have expected it though. It didn't bother her any. It didn't seem to bother the prince or the earl, but it did cause speculation about her worth.

"I cannot tell. I only know I am under the hatches. Dished up. Flummoxed. Doomed to gull one of them with toad flattery a plenty until I land myself in the parson's mousetrap." The earl laid his head on the chess game, scattering pieces all over the floor. "But I did see the gossip cit wrote that Jory has a right proper tidy sum upon her head, though Julia has me a thunking. Ope. Not sure if that be a word, either."

Incessant laughter, until the earl fell from his chair and lay on the floor laughing.

Jory shook her head and fled lest she be discovered. To think she'd had her heart broken by that vexing, detestable, drunk as a sailor bamboozler! If she were a man, she'd darken his daylights and plant a facer on him with all her might. He was nothing more than a fortune hunter!

Three days hence, Jory surveyed her desk in the schoolroom, her brows furrowing. The last few days had been distressing. First, she had discovered the earl's true intentions. That had caused her to retreat to having dinners alone in her quarters again, but she had attended one meeting with Archer the next evening after encountering the prince and the earl.

Meanwhile, she had been plagued by pranks in the schoolroom. She refused to consider her students to blame. She had not mentioned it to Archer yet, but tonight, she would. It had gotten out of hand now and had become a nuisance.

Her four darling students were seldom alone to commit such acts. Furthermore, her students were happy, knowing that they would soon be involved with some events with the guests and the prince. Besides this, she'd asked the duke at their last meeting if she and the children could have a little plot of land to make a children's garden. For the past two mornings, how much they had enjoyed planting flowers and playing in the soil in the lovely walled garden he'd shown her to the west of the house. But where was her new bottle of ink? She searched through her desk drawers and no ink anywhere!

First, the globe had gone missing before her meeting with Archer. Perhaps someone had borrowed it. Another reason why she hadn't mentioned it. But the next morning, the children complained more socks were missing. Later, after lunch, they found some of the pages inside *Pumpernickel the Cat* had been pasted together (another reason she did not blame the children who adored the story—even Henry, who saw how much joy it gave Edith). And only that morning when they first came to class after breakfast and time in the garden, to their horror, they'd found honey drizzled on the student's desks (another reason she did not blame the students, for had they done it, they would have drizzled it upon *her* desk). And now, finished cleaning the honey, she found her new inkwell missing! Stolen!

"I say, something is terribly amiss around here. My new bottle of ink is missing. And after this honey disaster…I am determined to discover who is behind all these pranks and shall have the duke hold the guilty party responsible when found." Jory rose from her seat. "Tilly, please take over our French lesson while I go in search of more ink. The children can write another letter to their father using their new vocabulary list."

Tilly stopped knitting from her corner in the classroom, for she usually knitted through a great many of their classes, only doing what Jory prevailed upon her to do or what seemed needful, which worked out well since she spent a great many afternoons and evenings with the children. "Oh dear! Would you like me to ask Miss Parker to purchase some at the stationer or the mercantile? She is spending part of every weekend with her parents in the village and will return on Monday next and leaves on Saturday by seven. I heard her say so at the tea break with all of the lady's maids and companions who have come with the other lady guests. We only have to ask her to leave early to stop at the stationer. Something about a quilting bee on Saturday night."

"Not necessary. I shall find some if you will take over until I return." But this remark concerning Miss Selina Foley's companion, Miss Helena Parker, stuck with Jory, nagging at her.

Her faithful assistant nodded, and Jory hurried downstairs to the art room, her mind a ramble. Did Miss Helena Parker plan to attend the Dragoniers' Saturday meetings in secret? Did they even allow women to attend? Was she influenced by Squire Foley to join forces with other villagers against the duke? Perhaps it was time to tell Archer what she had discovered, though she had attempted to push these matters aside, preferring not to become entangled in something she could not prove and knew little about.

Surely, she would find some ink in the art room. But when she didn't, she wandered down to the second floor, thinking perhaps she could borrow some from the desk she'd seen in the yellow morning room. Only she spotted Beatrice, at long last, scurrying down the far end of the hallway toward the duke's room, pushing a cart of linens.

Curiosity piqued, she caught up to the maid, following her inside the duke's chamber, tapping on the open door. "Hello there. May I come in?"

The maid shrugged and turned back to stripping the linen from the enormous four-poster bed. "Suit yourself."

Jory lingered near the door, hesitant. Then she stepped forward, hands on hips, one brow arching as she looked around at the elegant chamber decorated in sage green. "Do you come here often?"

The maid turned around with a linen sheet in hand and stared at her, blinking. "Oh no, ma'am. This is the first time Mrs. Rockport sent me to this 'ere floor *or* to change bed linens, for that matter. I've not been assigned to anything but drawing rooms for dustin' an' polishin' afore now. And a high mountain of kitchen duties be after that. Mrs. Rockport said I'm no good at much else. I'm a tad nervous and not sure whose chamber this is. I'm normally a parlor maid for half of each day. Then I go to the kitchen for the second half and wash a mountain of dishes until I can't stand at nightfall."

"Oh, I'm sorry to hear that." Jory bit her lower lip.

The maid stepped into the hall to retrieve some fresh linens from her cart and returned seconds later. "Makes my back ache for standing so long, but alas, me family needs me earnings, so I send whatever I kin to 'em. But with so many guests…things be topsy turvy around here lately. I kin barely keep up." Beatrice sighed and wiped her forehead with her forearm. "All I know is the housekeeper said to start with the corner rooms and work my way back down the hall to the staircase. Some other maid is on that side of the floor." She tossed the clean linens onto the stripped bed and began removing pillowcases.

"I see. I'm sure you are a fine and commendable employee." Jory nodded and looked around again, admiring the rest of the elegant room with its mahogany furnishings, fine velvet drapes, and lovely carpeting. "Have you met the duke?" She turned back to the maid and tilted her head to one side.

"I've seen 'im around a few times, and 'e seemed nice on the journey from London, but I've never spoken to 'im directly. I was told not to unless 'e speaks to me."

"Oh. Yes, of course."

Jory bit her lower lip again. If this were true, then how could Beatrice be the duke's mistress? "Well, I just came looking for some ink to borrow for the schoolroom. There wasn't any in the art room supplies."

The maid nodded toward the desk. "Help yerself, ma'am."

Surely the duke's mistress would have special privileges arranged for her so she wouldn't have to work so hard. And she'd most likely, most definitely, be familiar with his private chambers, sadly. The very idea made her sick to her stomach, excepting relations within the confines of a marriage (in which case she thought it all quite romantic and wonderful, from what little she knew of such things being innocent). But she'd suffered from a ponderous and essential, most pressing need to discover the truth before the duchess pushed her over a cliff with this plan she'd concocted to marry her off to someone of good standing in high society.

Jory only desired to marry a true gentleman, a pure gentleman, a kind gentleman, an honest, God-fearing man, if she must marry. More and more, it seemed to her that Archer was indeed that man. If what Tilly had said was true, and if Beatrice spoke truth, and it seemed she did, and if Beatrice had set her cap for a footman, the rumors simply made no sense. The news filled her with a great deal of relief. It didn't seem possible that the duke had a mistress. Beatrice had been the only new employee from London—except for Tilly and *herself*.

Maybe the gossip columnist *had* written to accuse *Jory* of being his mistress without mentioning her name or the title of her position. Maybe the columnist *had* heard something about the duke's new governess, just as she and Tilly had considered at the inn on the outskirts of London. But she knew *that* was balderdash, and in reality, Archer had behaved like a perfect gentleman around her, other than the one kiss…which now seemed romantic.

It all made her chuckle with glee as she spotted Archer's mahogany writing desk and crossed the room to it. The duke was innocent of the Banbury Tale! He *had* to be. And it made sense with everything else she had learned about his character. But did he have strong feelings for Lady Flora or an inclination to marry the daughter of the marquess?

That couldn't be the case, either. He had said she herself, Jory, was born to be his duchess. Had he not? What a silly girl she was for thinking those Banbury Tales held any truth! And how daft she was to have thought so. She only had to figure out how much Lady

Flora meant to Archer, but only a part of her questioned that now. She had seldom seen them together and rarely had seen them speak to each other, but then again, she had avoided him and had remained in hiding mainly upon the fourth floor…

Spying his fancy inkwell, she plucked it up. It couldn't be helped. She required ink to do her job, though it occurred to her just then that she might loan the schoolroom her own inkwell from her bedroom instead of the duke's. Except she had seen Beatrice and followed her here.

"There you are, Miss Pritchard. How nice to find you *here*."

A male voice laced with amusement caught her off guard as she stood there pondering Flora and Archer. No, no, no! And that male voice distinctly belonged to Archer himself. The duke! Why did her feet seem stuck to the floor? She squeezed her eyes shut. This could *not* be happening! She mustered every bit of her composure and spun around.

"Archer." A nervous laugh escaped her lips. "Good morning." She offered her most winning smile and leaned against his desk as if she always visited his chamber to… "Just borrowing some ink."

"Some ink," he repeated, a brow rising and a smile playing on his lips.

The maid bobbed a curtsey when he glanced in her direction as she fought with sliding a pillowcase onto a pillow.

Jory held the inkwell up, then fumbled it, tried to catch it, but missed, leaving the elegant lid in her hand. "Oh, dear!" And her mouth agape when some ink splattered upon his shirt, but Archer caught the bottle of black liquid just in time before it splattered elsewhere. He winced a little at seeing the few splatters on his shirt and fine waistcoat. But not nearly as much as Jory winced. Nonetheless, he held the ink out to her.

"Oh, dear me! I'm so sorry! What a clutter-budget I am today." She plucked it from his hand lest he spill more upon himself because of her clumsiness, accepting the precious inkwell, shaking. She replaced the lid, realizing there was no way to secure the elegant specially designed lid, for it was more like a vinaigrette bottle than an inkwell, and it bore his initials, 'A.T.' "How terribly clumsy of me…" Her voice faded.

He cleared his throat and began unbuttoning his waistcoat. "'Tis not a problem. I came to find my prayer book, but I have missed you at so many dinners and so many of our meetings over the past few weeks, it is a welcome sight to see you again. You have become another mystery, and I have thought of chasing you down in the schoolroom if only to see you for a moment, but then I thought I should not distract the children. I do hope the garden is coming along to your liking."

"The garden?" she repeated.

All the while, Archer untied his cravat, removed his vest, and unbuttoned his shirt, tossing them aside while she gasped. Her eyes were aghast at beholding that he had so quickly divested himself of his upper body clothing and now stood before her with a bare, muscular chest. She spun around to face away from him again, praying the maid did not leave her alone with the duke, or that perhaps she would. Oh, dear! That was not a right prayer. Not a right prayer at all. How beautiful a man he was, however.

"Oh, yes, the garden." Though for a second or two, Adam and Eve danced a vision in her mind. "It's turning into a lovely garden."

Had not God created females to be attracted to their male counterparts? And did she not appreciate him so much more, in light of the knowledge that it was extremely unlikely he was conducting any kind of impropriety with Beatrice? Furthermore, all the world seemed to know he had not yet proposed to Lady Flora, did it not? Perhaps he *was* a viable and honorable candidate for marriage, after all. Mayhap, she had been all too hasty to believe the fodder in that society column. For her deepest desire was to marry someone honorable, if she *were* to marry anyone.

Was he still dressing? Had she heard a bureau drawer open while he perhaps selected a clean shirt? "The a-art room did not seem to have any ink, Your Grace." She was sputtering but remained turned away. "And, well, ours seems to have gone missing. Along with our globe."

"The globe? You may turn around now."

She reluctantly turned around, heat warming her cheeks. Yes, the maid was still there, plumping the pillows. My, the duke must have worked on his land to earn those muscles as much as any tenant farmer! "And more socks."

"More socks missing? The prince was missing socks at breakfast." Archer held up a hand and shook his head. "No, that's not what I meant. He wore socks, but it was at breakfast that he said he was missing some. Not all, but some."

Did he seem, befuddled at her presence as much as she was with his, here in *this*, his personal chamber?

"How terrible!" But she could not hide a smile at this amusing turn of events. Someone had taken the *prince's* socks, too? How embarrassing for Archer. That was one mystery no one had been able to solve.

"Indeed," he agreed.

He fussed with his cravat, which she longed to tie properly for him, but which she did not know how to do. Perhaps he could find his valet.

On second thought, perhaps she would tell him about the other mysterious events another time. Glancing at Beatrice, whose arms were now laden with more linens to carry out, Jory picked up her skirt with one hand and made a beeline for the door.

Over her shoulder she called to him, "Pardon me for the interruption to your private chambers, but Beatrice here was most helpful and, well, we can discuss this some other time." She nodded at the maid as they nearly collided exiting into the hall. Jory flew past, careful not to spill the precious ink. She was sure her feet had never moved so fast as they did then. At least she had ink and had discovered the duke was innocent of those torrid accusations in the press. But…how peculiar and vexing an incident! Only it did cause her to laugh at herself.

Chapter Nine

May God Himself, the God of peace, sanctify you through and through. May your whole spirit, soul, and body be kept blameless at the coming of our Lord Jesus Christ. The one

who calls you is faithful, and He will do it.

I Thessalonians 5:23-24, NIV

Archer couldn't help but smile as his children bounded across the deck of a ship in Bristol's harbor. His boys had worn their swords and pirate garb for the ship's tour, and his daughters, their princess gowns and paper crowns. Even the prince appeared to have a grand time as he conversed with the vessel's captain. To think Jory's brother-in-law had arranged the whole tour, and now she lingered near her sister, catching up on whatever sisters did when reunited. Would she see that her sister seemed jubilant, even happy in her marriage to the shipbuilder? Would it help Jory any to consider him as a future husband to her? For Archer now found himself utterly besotted. Did she seem to glance in his direction with warm smiles a little more often than usual, as she did this very moment?

The other guests from Mulberry House seemed equally enthusiastic about the excursion, except for Miss Helena Parker, Miss Foley's companion, who could not join them on their travels since her family needed her at home. Otherwise, they were in a jovial mood after spending several days enjoying the pumps, the Roman baths, and assembly halls for dancing in Bath, a few miles to the south of Bristol. The prince had declared the baths restorative for his occasional flare-ups of gout. He also said he had immensely enjoyed the excursion and fine hotel where they had stayed.

In one of the assembly rooms, Archer had danced with Jory. He was drawn by her peace and contentment, her sensibility, compassion, warmth, easy temperament. The fact she did not have insatiable thirst for the finer things in life. Her love for books and the ways and things of God. And her vivacious nature reflected in her speech, mannerisms, and smile. Her eyes said more than her lips, though they too drew him. Her beauty was like an added reward for the man she might marry. Could it be him? He was finally sure he had found the right woman to become his wife and the next duchess.

And shortly after, he approached her to ask her to dance again. How could he resist when she looked resplendent in a shimmering gown the shade of midnight blue. He had bowed to her. "May I have this dance too, Jory?"

Her lovely cheekbones had turned a shade of deep crimson, like a blushing rose. "Why does it seem I cannot bring myself to refuse you anything, my lord?"

She had offered him her gloved hand, and raising more eyebrows, they had danced to a waltz. This had given him great pleasure, considering his governess still did not understand how much he adored her. And he had reached the point where he cared not what the world thought.

"I intend to come up to scratch with you, Jory, and very soon," he had whispered, earning pensive, wide eyes from her and a smile playing upon her sweet lips—lips he longed to kiss.

He was trying to let her know his intentions were honorable. But more scandalous than the two of them dancing twice, Lord Cunningham had danced with Lady Flora three times, and everyone assumed Flora was either "fast," or that the earl would propose to her, as well. Archer was glad he no longer fussed over Julia, since he suspected the earl was not up to his standards.

There had been a successful archery tournament at Mulberry House too, another of Jory's splendid ideas. His children had enjoyed the event, particularly his boys. But it was Jane who had surprised everyone with her natural prowess as an efficient archer, giving her brothers some healthy and fierce competition.

The picnic at the gazebo with rowing boats had been a favorite event of the ladies. Jory had seemed to take great pleasure when her boat with the earl capsized, dowsing him under water while Archer rowed the countess. Jory rose from the water, laughing with glee despite soaked garments. The prince had rowed Jane and Edith about the pond, saying it did his heart good, reminding him of happy memories with his daughter.

The pirate skit the children performed for the prince was another smashing success. Prince George had clapped profusely, laughing at every sweet line and adventurous action. Jory had written the skit and involved some of the footmen and other staff, assigning them parts. All participants were jovial. Even Reeds had a line and played the part of a pirate alongside his sons.

The prince enjoyed some afternoon fencing with the gentlemen before a clapping audience of delighted ladies who 'ooed' and 'awed' at all of the pivotal moments. How many times Leyton and Jasper let the prince win, he could not be sure. Lady Flora had largely left him alone, turning her attention upon Lord Cunningham. Jory said they deserved each other at their last meeting, something he did not doubt. He had never intended to propose to Lady Flora, and the gossip writer had exaggerated the few times he had danced with her to appease Flora's mother and his own sisters. But alas, the Ton and eager writers always misinterpreted his intentions.

Another of Archer's favorite moments had been the sinfonia performance, perhaps because he had been able to sit beside Jory while she held a sleepy Edith. After the sinfonia, his beautiful governess met with him in his study, informing him of the missing but vital piece of information no one in Pensford seemed willing to divulge concerning the nature of Squire Foley's plans, but Jory knew the details. And she told him all about the Dragoniers!

Not even his good friend Charles had been able to fish out this coveted information. How his governess had managed to discover it on her very first trip to the mercantile was remarkable. With only a day of painting planned for the guests at Mulberry House on Monday next and the Harvest Ball to come at the end of the week, after which the prince would return to London, Archer insisted Jory take the day off after the sinfonia to accompany him on a private excursion to see the land Squire Hopkins had willed to his nephew that he still intended to purchase.

She deserved the reward, having made the prince's visit and the country house party a huge success. Leaving the countess and his sisters in charge, they embarked upon a horseback ride, a picnic, and a day of exploring. He brought his valet to serve the meal and a groom to tend the horses so they would be properly chaperoned. The basket of food, consisting of cold roasted chicken, veal cutlets on biscuits, strawberries and grapes with a wedge of cheese, and a flagon of orangeade, looked tempting spread out on a comfortable blanket.

"I am not against the townsfolk at all," he explained to Jory, still amazed she had discovered the vital information he needed to find a resolution concerning the parcel of land everyone wanted. "We need both factories and housing, but I cannot fathom putting a textile mill on dry land without a powerful water source any more than I would build my hotel apart from this waterfall scenery it deserves. The mill should be closer to the River Chew, but in a place where it runs rapidly."

"You are on the right path with compromise, Archer. If anyone can find a solution, you can. Blessed are the peacemakers," Jory had encouraged him before the picnic when they'd sat astride horses, viewing the waterfall on Curry's nephew's land where he wished to build his fine hotel and charming but modest residential dwellings beyond. The dwellings would house up to forty or fifty new families, providing plenty of growth for the town. Only then could they attract enough inhabitants to make the mayor's plans a success for his three factories. She had turned to him after taking in the scenic waterfall splashing into a pool of water before them. "Seek peace, Archer, and pursue it."

Now he knew what he had to do. Find some land he already owned that he could offer the town for factory sites without financing, at a bargain of a rental or sale price. He had several prime locations in mind, far more suitable for manufacturing. This dreadful business about the Dragoniers…disturbing indeed! At least he had received a letter from Curry's nephew's solicitor. The gentleman had been delayed due to his father having a fit of apoplexy. Though he feared for that man's father, it gave him time to sort out this business with Nicholson and Foley.

But that afternoon, as they enjoyed the picnic, he fed her a strawberry and then kissed Jory again, the only matter on his mind at present. And this time, she did not flee.

But one thing remained amiss at Mulberry House. Who caused the petty mischief in the schoolroom? —a matter which Jory and Archer remained perplexed about after their picnic. The countess, encountering them in the rose garden after their return from the picnic, believed Miss Selina Foley had something to do with the events they divulged to her, but Jory remained unconvinced. Miss Foley had been nothing but delightful throughout her visit.

Jory did not share her opinion, but she held her tongue. Since their return from Bristol, no other events had occurred, though socks did continue to disappear, but that had been going on since before London. Where was the globe? Who had glued pages of Edith's favorite story together? Who had taken the ink and drizzled honey on the children's desks? And why?

She and Archer found most of their guests and his sisters and the prince strolling through the conservatory overlooking the rose garden and joined them there to admire the potted plants and many ferns in his collection of plants. Then the guests retreated to the olive-green drawing room on the first floor to pass the time until dinner with conversation and embroidery. But shortly after Jory had settled onto a sofa beside Archer as she listened to the Danforth sisters relate a riddle she was eager to help solve, Reeds interrupted to announce Miss Davison required Miss Pritchard in the hall on an urgent matter. This could only mean one thing: trouble concerning the children. The duke had only to see the alarm in Jory's eyes and he followed her out into the hall.

"Oh, Jory! Thank goodness you have returned from your outing. Come quickly…and Your Grace!" Tilly bobbed a curtsey seeing the duke on her heels, her eyes fearful. "Jane has fainted away, and so has Charlie! And I cannot seem to wake them. I have tried the smelling salts, to no avail. But Henry and Edith seem fine, because they didn't eat any…"

"Eat what, Tilly? What did they eat?" Jory held Tilly's hands to stop her from pressing them together so many times.

"Oh, I feel just wretched. But 'tis all my fault! Miss Helena gave me a gift of chocolates for them, and I thought it was a lovely gesture. But I fear, something is wrong! Can you please fetch the sawbones?"

"Where is Miss Parker now?" Jory inquired.

Tilly motioned toward the front doors. "I believe she was on her way to visit her parents. I really thought there was nothing wrong with those chocolates. But now, I'm not so sure. Something ain't right."

"Finn is here. He'll know what to do." The duke turned to Reeds. "Dispatch Thompson for the doctor in the village, and two of my best grooms, armed, to find Miss Helena Parker. Bring her to me. Do not harm her." Archer opened the drawing room door and poked his head inside. "Finn, your black bag. That one you always have on hand. We need you upstairs."

Reed sprang into motion. In what seemed like forever but only took a minute or two, Jory, Tilly, Archer, and Finn raced to the fourth floor. Finn took charge after Archer brought him up to speed, stopping in his room on the way to retrieve his medical bag. Jory and Tilly arrived first, despairing over the limp body of Charlie, and then Jane. They were breathing, but with shallow breaths.

"Oh, dear me…" Tilly began to cry. "I have done great harm."

"Do not cry, Miss Davison. Let us remain calm. It is not your fault. We may be more useful if we keep our heads. And pray." Jory began praying, taking hold of Jane's hand.

Tilly nodded, calming herself. "I'll try and wake Charlie in the next room."

Finn and Archer arrived seconds later, several maids following that Archer had gathered along the way on their heels, breathless and wide-eyed. Finn ordered Charlie brought to Jane's bed so he could tend them together. Archer nodded, rushed from Jane's room, and returned carrying Charlie, laying him alongside his sister. Henry and Edith hovered in the doorway, sniffling. Though he was not yet a physician, Jory could see Finn had a generous amount of knowledge stored in his brain as he checked pulses, listened for heartbeats, and checked their pupils.

"Bring me the chocolates if any are left," Finn barked. To Henry and Edith, he added sternly. "Do not eat any of those chocolates." Their eyes wide, they nodded.

Tilly and the maids sprang into action. Gathering all four tins, they handed them over. Finn began smelling the chocolate discs covered in nonpareils first. Then he began smelling some of the chocolate squares and a few of the marzipans, one by one. He wrinkled his nose. "Bitter almonds! Laurel water! She has brought them squares of chocolate poisoned with laurel water. They smell like bitter almonds. See for yourself, Archer." The duke smelled the bitter scent and his jaw clenched.

Finn turned to the maids. "Bring me some brandy and a solution of ammonia, two cups, and two teaspoons. And hurry!"

The maids sprang into action, disappearing at once. Archer held Charlie's hand, praying, while Jory held Jane's. Tilly knelt beside them too while they waited for the antidote Finn had ordered to arrive as he worked to wake the children out of their stupor. "Wake up, Jane. Wake up, Charlie." He shook their hands and arms gently but firmly.

"Come, Henry, Edith. Join us in prayer," Archer said, motioning his other children forward.

They all clasped hands, and Jory prayed with a fervent heart, regretting having left the children, yet unable to regret the day she had spent with their father. If anything happened to Jane and Charlie, how would she go on? *Please, Lord, help us!*

Chapter Ten

Deceit is in the hearts of those who plot evil,

but those who promote peace have joy.

Proverbs 12:20, NIV

Jane finally moaned, and a few minutes later, Charlie coughed. Archer's heart soared. Finn carefully mixed the brandy and drops of the ammonia solution into the glasses, while Jory and Archer helped the children reposition against their pillows to be able to drink some of the liquid. Every fifteen minutes, Finn administered more. An hour later, the children had recovered. They were weak, disoriented, and nauseated, but otherwise, strong and would pull through. The town doctor arrived, complimenting Phinneas Crandall for his actions, assuring them of a full recovery. Archer was elated, thankful to have Jory at his side, and grateful to Finn and the Lord.

"What would we have done without you, Finn?" Turning to a sniffling Miss Davison, he tried to assure her it wasn't her fault. He had other servants to thank too, and a drawing room full of worried guests to inform. Including the prince, pacing by the fireplace until he had delivered the good news.

Where had Jory disappeared to? Ah, there she was. Ready to follow him to his study, dressed rather oddly for her. Drab colors indeed. A faded brown frock. And interested to know if the grooms had arrived with Miss Helena Parker.

He turned in time to prevent running headlong into Reeds, who now informed them in the great entry hall that the despicable woman waited for him with her assailants at gunpoint in his study. "Shall I send for the constable or any of the royal guards to accompany you, Your Grace?"

"Yes. On both counts, though I will not wait for them. I may have other business to investigate. But I only trust Cornelius Poole's judgment on which constable to send. Have a rider stop at his house first to ask for an uncompromised constable. Trouble is afoot." He began heading down the hall to his study, Reeds at his side. "Then ask the royal guards to assist, when the constable arrives."

"I'm coming too." Jory caught up to them.

He paused outside his study, thinking the better of her following him inside as Reeds scrambled away. What if he lost his temper with Parker? Maybe Jory should not witness this, but how could he stop her? She'd proven to him time and again that she had a mind of her own and a strong will. It was one of the things he most loved about her. She was unlike any women he knew. "This may not be pleasant, but it will not be in any way violent unless she resists the arrest that is certain. Perhaps you would rather wait for the royal guards and the constable. I will not try to stop you from witnessing my questioning, but I must find out why she tried to retaliate against me by poisoning my children."

She reached for his arm. "And what of the Dragoniers? I believe she is one of them. They are reformers. What else are they planning? A revolt? Will they storm Mulberry House? We must find out and stop them, before a Peterloo occurs in Pensford. Before it is too late. If they harm innocent children, they will harm any of us. And the future king is here. We must stop them, Archer!"

"We should wait for the constable to decide this matter with the royal guards…" he argued, but he too thought of spying on the reformers by attending that evening's meeting.

"Ask her what she knows! Bargain with her. Tell her you will recommend a lighter sentence. Every minute wasted could mean our lives. The meeting is to begin in less than an hour. It is nearly eight o'clock." Jory crossed her arms over her chest.

He sighed, raking a hand through his hair. Did she intend to go to the reformer meeting too? "You may be right. Follow me." He burst through the door, barely nodding at his armed men, taking in the situation, restraining his temper for what his children had suffered at Miss Helena Parker's hands. Glaring at her, he only saw a stone-faced, coldhearted woman with no remorse seated between his men, her hands tied behind her back, a sneer upon her face.

"We had to tie her hands. She resisted," Johnson informed him, pistol in hand.

Archer crossed the room to stand behind his desk, glad to have the object between him and the woman who'd tried to murder his children. Jory perched on the edge of the desk and narrowed her eyes as she peered at the woman.

Archer leveled his gaze at Miss Parker too, planting his hands on his desk lest he think of strangling her. "I will give you one chance to tell me what you and the Dragoniers intend. In exchange for truth, I will recommend a lighter sentence than the lifetime in prison sentence I'm sure you will receive, that is, if the Prince Regent or powers that be do not ultimately decide to have you hanged for attempted murder."

Parker swallowed, staring at him. For a while, the sound of the ticking clock was the only noise filling his study. But then she heaved a sigh. "I will cooperate. Five men plan to assassinate the prince, to make a statement of protest against him, his monarchy, and his corn laws. I do not know the exact details yet. Those are to be finalized at tonight's meeting. They will be at the rear of the main floor in the paper mill, gathered behind the crowd. Five of them, the leaders Foley has chosen. Your children were to be the example for our outrage with the peerage and the voting laws."

Archer looked up at his men. "Do not take your eyes off of her for one minute until I return. When the constable arrives and they have gathered the royal guards, ask them to wait for my return. I will have valuable information by then. Do not release her into their custody without me. We do not know who we can trust. Understood?"

"Aye." Their nods told him his men would not let him down.

Jory stomped out of his study, and he followed, guessing her strange garb and scuffed walking boots meant she intended to slip into that meeting tonight. As she passed by Reeds, he handed her what appeared to be a worn cloak, and she winked at him. What were they up to?

"Thank you, Reeds," she said in a calm, pleasant tone.

What was she up to now as she headed outside the front doors toward the stables? He took long strides, finally catching up. The minx was unstoppable. He couldn't let her attend such a dangerous event, but he knew it was useless to talk her out of it. Instead, he tried, "Where are we headed?"

"The mill, of course." She swung around to stare at him, hands on her hips. "Have you forgotten everything you just said in there? Well done, Archer. You were perfect. Absolutely brilliant! But timing is everything. What is the matter? Why are you hesitating like this now, at this crucial moment, when every second counts? That woman nearly murdered your children! I'm kicking myself for not coming to you sooner with this information, but I was too much of a muddled mess myself. We haven't a moment to spare. Are you coming or not?"

"If there was any shred of brilliance to what I said, it was on account of your advice." He had hesitations of his own to grapple with, adding to his frustrations. "I have now known about these reformers since this afternoon, and I have wanted to go to tonight's meeting since you told me, but Jory…what if I can't forgive them after I see their faces? What if I can't live with myself after this? I feel as though I have failed them all by not informing villagers of my plans sooner. They do not realize I have been fighting for them to repeal these blasted corn laws, nor the care and thought and research I have put into the plans for the village."

"Look, you only need to make an example of these five men Parker mentioned and the bear leader, so to speak. Whoever that is! Squire Foley? Mayor Nicholson? Whoever is leading them." She waved her hand, clutching the cloak to her chest. "Once you know what the plan is against the prince, we can advise him to return to London, but at least we'll know if they are planning something worse. You can have arrests made by someone you trust. You can work with the ones willing to work with you. Hold a meeting with the squire or the mayor and see which is pliable. Whomever is the leader of the Dragoniers, that one must go. If there are several leaders or a group of men, they must be put behind bars. The villagers will come round. Many respect you. I know that much from the man behind the till and something another fellow said. Once they know you are on their side and that you have a plan to help them…they will fight to make the dream, that plan, a reality."

He clenched his jaw, set his face like flint, absorbing her words. "Yes. You are right. Always level-headed. A beacon of peace in the storm. I am ready."

"No, you are not. You cannot go dressed like that," she scoffed.

He glanced down, unsure of what she meant.

"Take off your fine frock coat."

Two stable hands stepped out of the stable while he did as she instructed.

Jory swung around to face them. "Hello, gentlemen. Will you please saddle two of the duke's fastest horses? We are on an errand of great importance requiring speed and endurance. We have not a moment to waste. No sidesaddle for me. A regular saddle."

Glancing at Archer, he nodded to the men. They sprang into action.

Jory reached down and picked up a handful of soil. "Hold still." She stood on the tips of her toes and smeared some dirt on his face, making him laugh. Now he clearly understood why she had dressed in drab garb.

"That's better. Now rub more dirt on your breeches, which *you* will have to do, until we are wed." A smile reached her lips, teasing him.

He grabbed her by the arms and held her still. "Did I hear you say that you will agree to marry me?"

She looked up at him with surprise in her eyes. "I suppose I did. Aye, my lord. You are the finest man I know, and…and I have not only fallen in love with you, but your children. If I don't marry you, I will be utterly lost and broken forever." Then she smiled, pleased with the realization evident in her expression.

Joy filled his heart, like air, making him able to truly breathe again. Perhaps for the first time since Tilly had brought them news that they were needed upstairs. He bent his head and pulled her to him, kissing her thoroughly. When he released her, she stood there, breathing heavily while he did his best to smear dirt on his breeches and appear more like those of a man who'd worked the fields all day.

"Here, now put this old work coat and tweed cap on and you will look more like a commoner." She handed him the items hidden in the folds of her cloak. "The cap will make you less recognizable. You can pull it over your eyes at the mill. I had Reeds prepare them for you after the doctor arrived when I went to change clothes. I had already decided to attend this meeting to find out what I could."

"I see this. Addle-brained girl," he teased, but he did all she suggested, even as a nervous laugh escaped her lips. She showed no fear, but he saw that her hands trembled, even as the stable hands brought two of his finest bay stallions to them on leads.

And that was how they ended up inside the paper mill, after listening from a hiding spot in the bushes outside the mill to others offering the code words, 'ten shillings,' before gaining entrance. Once inside, Archer was shocked to discover how many townsfolk had crowded inside the space. Squire Foley, that no-good weasel, led the crowd. He fired them up with his ill-chosen words and balderdash. Villagers clapped and cheered, women and children too. It tugged on his heart. He was sorely misunderstood by his own people, and Foley lied to them about his intentions. But as much as it made his heart ache, he thanked the good Lord for the angel by his side who had insisted upon attending the meeting despite his misgivings.

Blasted reformers! Not all were the bad kind. Some were the good kind he told himself, hoping to find better employment and put food on the table. Others, pure evil. For he and

Jory overheard some men gathered at the back of the crowd arguing about when to ambush Mulberry House, just as Miss Parker had said they would be. Word had naturally spread about the Prince Regent being in residence. They now concocted a plan to assassinate the prince, and all to make a statement of protest to all of England against the monarchy, in favor of reform to the corn laws and voting rights. Though he didn't disagree with the reforms they wanted, he didn't approve of their methods. One of the men, through gritted teeth, huffed about the duke's children being dead by now if Parker's plans had gone down as they hoped. Archer's jaw clenched.

"Where *is* Parker? I don't see her anywhere," one of the men growled.

"Probably laying low after she delivered the chocolates…" some other man said who Archer didn't recognize. In fact, he didn't recognize any of these men. Mayhap they weren't local but had joined forces with Foley to facilitate his plans.

"No matter. It is decided. Our ambush will go on as planned. In the afternoon, when the duke hosts this artistic event on his terrace for the prince and his blasted guests, as Parker said they intend. Around two o'clock, Monday. We take them by surprise. When the prince is dead, parliament will take notice, or we come after them next."

Archer's hands tightened into fists, but they must leave before the assembly ended. He'd heard enough. Miss Parker had obviously fed them the information they could not have known otherwise. Glad for the thick timber post to hide behind that held up one of the rafters, it kept them out of sight as they gleaned. Archer put an arm around Jory and nodded toward the door. He steered her outside the mill with a protective hand at the small of her back, keeping his head down lest someone recognize them.

Returning to Mulberry House, he summoned the prince and his royal guards, imploring George to return to London for his safety.

The prince refused. "I am no coward. Let us prepare for the ambush of our day of art in the garden, if that is what they intend. I need something to take my mind off losing my Charlotte. My men are trained. Their plan will not succeed. And I love sketching and shooting, though I admit I have not tried them together. But there is a first time for everything, is that not what they say?"

What could Archer say? The prince was braver than anyone credited him.

"Then we will need to build barricades around our easels, keep the women inside, and arm a few extra from among our men," Archer finally said.

Jory's eyes lit up. "We can use those columns and some of the potted palms from the conservatory to build barricades around and beside our easels. Easy to hide weapons behind those Greco-Roman pillars, and you have a plethora of them, Archer. But you'll need at least one lady with some of the men, or they will be suspicious. And since I know how to shoot, I will be one of them."

Archer cocked his head to one side. She had a good idea, and it was useless to argue with a woman like Jory with a mind of her own. "That might actually work, but some of their men may be up in the trees, waiting on us."

Jory crossed her arms. "We can post some of our armed men up in the trees before daybreak. The men involved in the ambush will come when it is still dark. We'll simply have to outsmart them; lie in wait."

And that was how he ended up having a front row seat to Jory aiming a blunderbuss at a

Dragonier hiding in the woods when he fired the first shot at the prince on the terrace. The shot blazed past them about half an hour after they had taken their places on the terrace, pretending to carry on with a day of painting and sketching. Archer pushed the prince behind the columns when the shot whizzed above their heads. He crouched low beside him but struggled to discern where the shot had come from exactly.

Meanwhile, Jory dove beside her easel, taking cover behind the stone columns and potted palms his footmen had dragged to the terrace the day before. She returned fire faster than the royal guards and aimed as well as any trained gentleman, shooting the attacker in the leg, disabling him from returning fire. With the columns placed near each easel, their attackers didn't stand a chance at success.

The man fell from the tree where he'd hidden, screaming like a ninny, laying on the ground in agony. But someone else tried to fire on the prince and Archer a few seconds later.

"I've got my eye on him," the prince said, taking a shot at about the same time as his guards returned gunfire.

More shots fired from their attackers, bouncing off the columns, causing plenty of stone to chip and fly about. Archer returned fire too, as did the prince, along with the Leyton brothers and Dud. Jory managed to fire another few shots, as well. Two bodies now lay on the ground near the perimeter, likely dead, and three men lay wounded, severely injured. One of the wounded finally lifted a limp hand, waving a white handkerchief, groaning from pain.

"White flag! Hold your fire!" One of the royal guards commanded.

"Clear," the other said when no shots had been fired for at least a minute of reprieve, waving two of the guards forward to inspect the area.

Archer blinked. It was hard to imagine all of this had transpired in his very own rose garden, but thankfully, a few minutes later, the royal guards declared they had achieved victory. No more attackers remained anywhere to be found. Jory and the prince were safe. He could breathe easy now. They were all safe. The injured could be taken into custody, and the deceased men turned over to the proper authorities.

The men had been no match for his preparations and the prince's security force, or Jory's skill, not even with the knowledge they had obtained aforehand.

The prince had fired a well-polished musket, and now appeared delighted to have hit his target. Archer had to inform him there were no more targets to shoot and urge him to put his rifle aside for a future hunting day as the prince reluctantly came to accept the fact they'd shot all five men.

"Pity. I was just getting warmed up." The Regent scrambled to his feet and muttered something about applying himself to signing letters waiting in his red box. "At least I've not cowered in fear, I am alive, and it was good fun. Good fun, I say. We shall continue this art tomorrow, when they've cleaned up this mess. Sorry about your beautiful columns."

"Easily replaced, Your Majesty. A good idea to continue our real day of art tomorrow. I would enjoy that, after we've all had a chance to recover from the excitement. Especially since most of the ladies had to wait this ambush out and were very much looking forward to a day of art." Archer and Jory exchanged a smile and followed George inside the house with the others. "Well done, everyone!"

It would have been of no use to prevent Jory from the fray, for she had wielded a gun since her poaching days, but she (and he) had insisted the children be kept safe upon the fourth floor. Henry now came running down the staircase, announcing he'd seen everything from his bedroom window overlooking the gardens. "Prince George, you are an excellent shot. You've wounded one of those attackers, as did Jory, and my father. I saw the whole thing," Henry declared, his eyes wide. "Two are dead, but it seems to me that it was one of the royal guards who shot them, though I cannot be entirely sure. It all happened so fast."

"Shall we dispatch some riders to send for the proper authorities, Your Grace?" Reeds inquired. "I have our best grooms standing by."

"Thank you, Reeds, that won't be necessary. I am told the royal guards will transfer the guilty to the infirmary and have them arrested until they recover and can be arraigned. Are you all right, Jory?" Archer searched her beautiful eyes.

"I am shaken and will require tea and a long nap, if you will send someone with a tray, Reeds. No classes today, Henry." Jory returned a weak smile as she passed Henry with her blunderbuss, patting his son on the shoulder. Reeds nodded and she headed toward the staircase and her quarters with Miss Davison, chattering away about the excitement.

"When will I be old enough to join a regiment, Father?" Henry asked.

A typical teenager, Archer mused as he patted Charles on the shoulder. "Well done, Charles. Jasper. Dud. Thank you for your help." He placed a hand on Henry's shoulder. "Hopefully you will never have to, son. But next year, I'll take you hunting if you continue to do well in your studies."

This pleased Henry and he stepped aside to the windows, eager to observe the royal guards in action as they handled their prisoners.

"No less than three of the ladies have fainted upon hearing the gunshots," the countess informed him as he turned toward the hall leading to his study. "Finn has been reviving them with my smelling salts. Tell me everyone is all right, Archer. What did I miss?"

"Everyone is fine, except our attackers, of course, who have surrendered. Three wounded, two dead. You may tell our guests not to worry," Archer replied.

"Horror of horrors! Two dead! May the Lord forgive us, but better them than us. Oh, Your Majesty, I am so happy to see you alive and well." Lady Rowans curtseyed and hobbled away with her cane, intent upon informing the ladies that they could come out of the drawing room.

"Yes, yes, your prince is alive. God has protected me. England prevails again. I shall be in the India room tending my red box. Will you send tea, Reeds?" The prince hurried toward the staircase.

"On its way, Your Majesty," Reeds called after him before turning toward the duke. "Your Grace, I will have tea and more of those lemon cakes sent to your study too. First, I must find someone to deliver a tray to the prince and Jory. She was spectacular."

Archer smiled. He couldn't argue with that.

"Jasper, Dud, and I shall help Finn calm the ladies. I wish to have a word with Lady Venezia, in case she saw my excellent shooting," Charles assured him as Jasper and Dud clapped him on the back.

"I'd say my shooting was better," Dud began. "Did you not see the way that reformer fell to the ground?"

Jasper bore an indignant expression. "Not to argue, but I'd say my shooting was the more accurate among us. I'm fairly certain it was my shot that took out that last fellow."

Archer chuckled and shook his head, retreating to his study to consider the entire array of events that had unfolded since spying upon the Dragoniers with his beautiful governess.

Reeds dashed away along with the others, all heading in various directions. At last, he was left to his study and blessed, quiet, beautiful *peace*. Nothing else sounded better, except perhaps the tea and cakes that rolled in on a cart pushed by a footman a short while later.

A cup of tea finally in his hands, he considered how the past few days had gone. Jory was visibly shaken, but a paragon of bravery. The children were well again, as if nothing had ever happened.

To think, they had all endured Miss Parker, a local spy and an anti-monarchist in their midst for weeks on end! The globe and the schoolroom ink had been found in her quarters too. She would of course, spend the rest of her life behind bars. Authorities would keep her in custody until a local, honest magistrate—far removed from the Dragoniers—could hear the case and arraign her to an assize court.

Hers would be an expedited arraignment, the justices of the peace and local magistrate had assured him. News traveled fast in Pensford, and the village justices greatly desired that peace be restored. The sooner arraigned, the better for all concerned. Rumors had stirred up conjecture and strife amongst villagers, and they wanted the matter of land disputes settled and secretly held reformer meetings done away with.

One of his biggest problems along those lines made him shudder even now to think that it might have all turned much worse—how to determine if the Pensford magistrates, constables, and justices were compromised? But the Lord had worked that out too. As the town's turmoil had heated to boiling point on the day before the ambush, after church on Sunday, the village leaders led by Cornelius Poole had appeared before him. They pledged their loyalty, having learned of the plan to harm the prince because of Miss Parker's arrest. Eager to assist if such an ordeal required more than barking irons too.

Archer was assured of their diligence to uphold and administer the law, and if necessary, protect all residents of Mulberry House. Assured of confidence in the defense formulated by the royal guards and himself, they agreed to remain out of the fray lest their ambushers suspect something, for everyone desired these men be placed behind bars. What better way than to permit the Dragoniers to proceed? Once they had attempted to fire upon the prince, they could be imprisoned. And now it had come to pass.

Meanwhile, Squire Foley was at this very moment, being arrested for forming and leading the reformers. Miss Selina Foley was distraught, but she would ultimately recover and brave on. Being the leader of the reformers, her father's arrest was crucial to restoring peace and order in Pensford. Now the dissenters would dissolve and dissipate, since examples had been made of their fiercest men and leader.

A glance out the window in his study revealed the three injured men being loaded into a wagon. The royal guards would accompany their transfer to the village infirmary. After recovery, these men would face arraignment. The constables and a handful of trusted men from the local militia would be posted to stand guard over them at the infirmary. All seemed well in hand as Archer watched the wagon rumble away from his window in the study.

Perhaps best of all, before the ambush, the solicitor arrived. After they finalized the transaction, making him the owner of Squire Hopkin's land, the mayor arrived. He'd taken great satisfaction in hearing the mayor's carriage drive away, for Nicholson had found out about the attempt to poison his children and the ambush. He'd confessed a desire to straighten these matters out and they'd come to an agreement, for he believed Foley had taken things too far.

When the townsfolk heard of the agreement, and in time for the news to spread before the coming Harvest Ball always hosted at Mulberry House, they would begin to rejoice. Their factories and housing would soon be in progress. And the day after the ball, he would host a fine picnic for the villagers. Then his guests would depart, including the prince.

To add to his surprises, Henry and Charlie had informed him on Sunday at luncheon, that they'd found a great pile of socks under a shelf in the library near where Milo sometimes lounged. Not only did it please him to know his sons occasionally used the library since Jory had encouraged them to make better use of it, but this solved the one remaining mystery that had disturbed him for so long. The prince had amazed everyone, running through the hallways with his boys, waving their socks in the air, rejoicing, making everyone laugh.

And Milo, now that he thought about it, sat beside his knee, letting him scratch him between the ears, quite recovered. Archer could not imagine how he would have survived any of it without Jory at his side. Could he finally return to writing hymns...and arranging the perfect ring and proposal for Miss Pritchard?

The evening of the Annual Harvest Ball arrived, and her time to return to Northampton had nearly come, but somehow, Jory had a strong sense that her return would perhaps be delayed. She spent time trying on several ballgowns the duchess had supplied her with in preparation for the exciting evening.

Settling on a gold empire-waisted gown with a long train, Jory marveled that the duchess had placed it inside her trunks. Her stomach fluttered with excitement as Tilly put the finishing touches on her cascade of curls, the ball only about an hour from beginning. Soon villagers would begin arriving at about dusk.

One last glance in the mirror revealed the way the fabric shimmered and sparkled in the light. Accompanied by a gauzy wrap in a softer shade of gold, she didn't feel one bit like a governess. More like a fine lady walking into a dream. How very kind of her benefactress to provide her with such a lovely gown to wear. Would Archer approve?

Best of all, the duke sent a note upstairs hand-delivered by Reeds, requesting her presence in the rose garden an hour before the ball. She met him there as requested, her heart pounding with excitement, her train flowing over the terrace behind her.

But upon arriving, nothing could have prepared her for finding the staff, their country house party guests, the children, the countess, Archer's sisters, the prince, and Archer himself on bended knee, waiting for her. Tilly found her way there too. Soon, the ballroom would be filled with music and dancing as villagers and guests from all over the area came to celebrate the annual harvest...but it was *this* moment that thrilled Jory to the core of her heart and soul.

How could a simple governess find such happiness and so many friends? The Lord had not let her down. Even Lady Flora smiled in her direction, seemingly happy for her, content with the earl at her side.

My, how well things had turned out for her and her handsome duke. She wasn't sure when she'd started thinking of him as *her* duke, but it was far better than anything she had ever expected. How good it was to trust the Lord! He had rewarded her handsomely.

Jory had seen Archer at his most vulnerable and as a strong leader, and she had fallen madly, deeply in love with him. She'd even written to the duchess (and her mother too) that an official engagement would be forthcoming. He'd indicated as much at the dance in Bath, but now it seemed he had chosen this moment to make it official. She and Archer could spend the season after they were married in London, together! He would need a new governess, but there was no hurry in finding one, though a few applicants had responded to his advertisement.

When she reached Archer, he took her hand in his and slid a lovely diamond ring upon her finger. "Darling Jory, a diamond I give to thy hand, for thou art truly my diamond of the first water. I love you so much, my heart will be forever undone if you say no. Please tell me once again, before our friends and family, say you will marry me that I may spend the rest of my life making you the happiest woman in all of England."

Had he perhaps said it before in a hundred different ways? But *this* time, she had clearly heard him say *he loved her*. How it melted her heart as she clasped his hands to hers! "Oh, my lord! You know I cannot refuse anything you ask. Yes, my wonderful, darling Archer, my heart belongs to you. Yes, yes, I will marry you! A thousand times over, I would marry you."

To thundering applause from their onlookers as the children surrounded them in an embrace, Archer rose and kissed her, his bride. The way her heart was singing with joy and pure bliss, she was of a great certainty they would live happily ever after!

The End

About the Author

Lisa M. Prysock is a *USA Today* Bestselling, Award-Winning Christian and Inspirational Author. She and her husband of more than twenty-five years reside in beautiful, rural Kentucky. They have five children, grown. Empty nesters, they are now slowly reclaiming the house.

She writes in the genres of both Historical Christian Romance and Contemporary Christian Romance, including a multi-author Western Christian Romance series, "Whispers in Wyoming." She is also the author of a devotional. Lisa enjoys sharing her faith in Jesus through her writing and has authored more than 50 published books in both Contemporary and Historical Christian Romance. She loves to make readers laugh and enjoys writing humor in her stories.

Discover more about this author at www.LisaPrysock.com where you'll find the links to purchase more of her books, free recipes, devotionals, author video interviews, book trailers, giveaways, blog posts, and much more, including an invitation to sign up for her free newsletter.

Links to Connect with Lisa:
Follow Lisa at her Official Facebook Page: https://www.facebook.com/LisaMPrysock
Follow Lisa at her Official Twitter Page: https://twitter.com/LPrysock
Lisa's Author Website: https://www.LisaPrysock.com
Lisa's Page at Amazon Author Central: https://www.amazon.com/-/e/B00J6MBC64
Author Page at Bookbub: https://www.bookbub.com/authors/lisa-m-prysock
Lisa's Facebook Reader & Friends Group: https://www.facebook.com/groups/500592113747995/
Follow Lisa on Goodreads: https://www.goodreads.com/author/show/7324280.Lisa_M_Prysock
Get a Free Book When You Sign Up for Lisa's FREE Newsletter: https://www.LisaPrysock.com/sign_up_for_my_newsletter
Follow Lisa on Instagram: https://www.instagram.com/lisaprysock

Mail-Order Millie

by Kit Morgan

Millie Scott has lost everything, so becoming a mail-order bride seemed like a viable option. Yes, she'd have to marry a stranger, but it was the only way she knew to survive. But when Millie meets and marries her groom, she gets more than she bargained for. A lot more!

A spy for the president, Bram Henry's next assignment is to arrest and then impersonate mild-mannered yet crooked bookkeeper Bill Krantz. But when the real Krantz meets with an untimely end, and his mail-order bride shows up earlier than expected, his plans of infiltrating a slaver's operation get thrown out the window. Now he's married to an unsuspecting mail-order bride who hasn't a clue he's not the real Bill Krantz. And wouldn't you know, she's not only pretty, but the sort of woman to make him want to quit his job and settle down. He just might. If he can keep them both alive long enough, that is.

Chapter One

Boston, September 1889

"I'm sorry Millie, but your father has passed."

Millie stared at Dr. Garrett, her heart in her throat. Her father's death didn't come as a shock. He'd been ill for some time now. Still, the fact he was gone hit hard.

She sank onto a sofa, a hand to her chest, and took in her meager surroundings. She'd spent everything they had on doctors to keep Father alive a little longer. But Gene Scott's time had finally run out.

"Miss Scott?" the doctor prompted.

Millie nodded and lifted her gaze to his. "Thank you, Dr. Garrett, for all you've done."

"I'm sorry I couldn't do more." He patted her on the shoulder, put a few stray items into his doctor's bag, and turned toward the front hall. "I'll settle with you later. I know you have arrangements to make."

She swallowed hard. "Thank you." Millie was already doing calculations in her head. There wasn't much more she could sell, and after she paid everyone, there would be nothing left. She'd be destitute.

The thought daunting, she headed for the kitchen when there came a knock on the front door.

Millie answered it. "Mr. Thornton." She stepped aside for her father's lawyer.

Mr. Thornton took off his hat. "I just spoke with Dr. Garrett. He told me the news. My condolences, Millie."

She nodded once as an odd numbness took hold. Father's passing wasn't a huge shock, but she didn't think it would affect her like this.

"Tea?" she managed to say.

"Yes, thank you." Mr. Thornton entered the parlor and sat. "I'll help you make all the necessary arrangements."

Millie caught his upward glance. "Poor Gene. I wish he'd have held on a little longer." He looked at Millie. "You realize you'll have to sell the house to pay his debts."

She closed her eyes. "Yes." Tears stung the backs of her eyes. "Can you help me..."

He held up a hand. "I'll take care of all of it. But... what will you do now? I know your father's financial situation. He left you nothing. I'm sorry..."

"Don't be," she said, cutting him off. "He gambled himself to death, one could say."

Mr. Thornton said nothing to that. Her father got shot for cheating at cards. The wound didn't heal right, and eventually he succumbed to an infection that ravaged his body.

"You know, my wife knows a woman who became a mail-order bride recently. We just heard from her. She's married now and starting a new life out west. Maybe you should consider..."

She looked at him, aghast. "Marry a stranger?"

"There are worse things." He stood. "I should go. Thank you for the offer of tea. Please make some for yourself. I'll send someone to gather your father."

Millie nodded and realized she hadn't been upstairs yet. She swallowed hard. "I want to say goodbye."

"Of course. But expect someone within the hour to take him away."

She nodded and looked at the staircase.

"I'll let myself out." Mr. Thornton left the parlor and headed for the door. When he reached it, he turned. "Think about what I said. There are plenty of advertisements for brides in the papers. You should at least peruse some."

She gave him a blank look and nodded. "Yes, of course."

Mr. Thornton gave her a nod and left.

Millie looked at the stairs, tears in her eyes. So, this was it. She was alone, destitute, with no place to go. What else could she do? Becoming a mail-order bride might be her only viable option. She didn't have money for another place just now. She had no relatives to stay with, and because of Father's poor reputation, who would take her in?

No money, soon no roof over her head, no job, no hope. Thank goodness Mr. Thornton was willing to help her with the arrangements. But, like everyone else, so long as he got his money, he'd be happy to do her a favor.

She trudged up the stairs. Boston was a big city; a change would do her good. There were lots of small towns out west. Maybe she'd wind up in one of them. There were large ones too. San Francisco, Seattle, Salem, and Portland to name a few.

She reached her father's door, straightened her shoulders and went inside. Dr. Garrett had covered her father with the bed's quilt.

Millie stared at the covered figure upon it. "So, you've left me. I hope and pray you're in a better place, Father."

She clasped her hands before her and caught sight of her reflection in the mirror over the dresser. Her dark hair was escaping its pins, and there were dark smudges under her brown eyes. Her creamy complexion made her brown eyes seem darker, and she noted how little color was in her cheeks.

"I'm going West, Father. I'll marry and start a family. All the things I've talked about. My husband will be kind and a good provider. He won't gamble or say the Lord's name in vain a hundred times a day. Yes, you were… difficult, Father. You… you cared more for your cards than you did for Mother and me. I imagine if she hadn't died a few years ago, she and I would have left you." She wrung her hands a few times. "I'm trying to think of nice things to say, but… the words won't come yet. You'll forgive me if it takes some time to forgive you."

She brought her clasped hands under her chin as tears stung the backs of her eyes. "So, this is goodbye. I'll have my husband and my children to keep me company. Eventually I'll have grandchildren too." She took a step toward the bed. "You realize you're forcing me to marry a stranger." She caught the bitterness in her voice and took a deep breath. "But I'll manage. I always do. He'll be honest, forthright, and again, he won't gamble. I'll make sure of that."

A tear slipped down her cheek, then another. She knew she had to forgive him, but the words still wouldn't come. Dr. Garrett warned her they might not. He knew her family and knew the strained relationship she had with her father. Though he was in his late twenties, the doctor knew her family well and told her to give it time, and when she was able, to tell Father she forgave him, no matter where she was or how long it took to get to that point. She had to speak the words.

"I'll tell you I forgive you when I'm good and ready, Father. Until then I'm afraid you'll just have to wait." She fixed her gaze on the quilt, and wiped tears from her eyes. "Goodbye."

Millie turned and left the room. She was numb, her heart empty, and Mr. Thornton had given her a way to fill it. Eventually. She just hoped her future husband, whomever he may be, was nothing like her father.

Chapter Two

"Have you got everything you need?"

Bramford Joseph Henry met the eyes of his boss, Jules Monroe. He and Dr. Rueben Newell led one of the biggest presidential spy operations in the country and did it all from a nothing little town in Montana. It was the perfect set up, and Bram was moving up the ranks quickly. "Yes, sir," he said.

"Now remember, you and our man from Boise are to capture Bill Krantz, turn him over to our other operative at the appointed place and time, and then you take Krantz's place. You and Krantz look enough alike that his new boss won't notice. He's also new to Baker City, so no one else should notice either. Our man keeping an eye on Krantz said he sent off for a mail-order bride. She's to meet Krantz in Baker City, so it's the perfect cover."

Bram rolled his eyes. "I'm not sure about this part. Do I have to marry some poor girl?"

"She'll be none the wiser," Jules said. "Besides, you won't really be married. Don't register the license. And she'll be well compensated when it's all over."

"And she won't be in danger?" Bram asked.

"She'll be fine. Remember, you're just gathering information. I want to know if the Double K Ranch is a cover for something else. If our old enemy Salim "Sal" Abiqua has anything to do with this, then this is bigger than we first thought." Jules paced to the other side of the church office and back. "Krantz just got hired on as the Double K's bookkeeper. If there's anything crooked going on, they'll try to butter you up right quick."

"Bribery, fine. I can handle that. Does this Krantz have a residence in town?"

"He does. Krantz rented a small house on a dead-end street." He slapped Bram on the back. "Don't worry, you'll be back dining in the finest restaurants and enjoying your townhouse in Washington soon enough."

"I understand sir," Bram said. "And don't get me wrong. I enjoy working in the field. If anyone on the Double K is up to no good, I'll find out what it is."

Jules patted his shoulder. "I know you will. Now, go to the hotel, get some rest, and be ready to leave for Bozeman at first light. Your train departs in two days. Once you get to Baker City, get to work. It's our guess that Krantz's bride will arrive a week or so after you do, so you'll have to move quickly."

"Understood." Bram shook Jules' hand. "May I ask a question, sir?"

"Of course."

Bram smiled. "Do you like living in Apple Blossom?"

"I do. And I like my cover as the town preacher. Just like Rueben likes being the town doctor. We get to do what we love and spy for the president all at the same time."

"But… do your wives know what you do?"

"They do now. One can only keep our line of work a secret for so long. But as far as the rest of the town is concerned, they haven't got a clue. Except for Captain Merriweather of course." He grinned.

Bram's eyes widened. He met him only once, and Captain Merriweather almost speared him with a harpoon!

"Best get going," Jules advised.

Bram put on his hat and left the church. He'd come to town posing as a distant relative of "Preacher Monroe's" and had been there a few days. Apple Blossom was a quaint little place and surrounded by apple orchards. It also had an odd history.

A little over ten years ago, outlaws came to town, robbed the bank and took off. A posse was formed to go after them but was ambushed. Only one of the posse members escaped the massacre. After the tragedy, the women had to fend for themselves. Which they did, and quite admirably too. The sheriff's daughter became the sheriff. The general store owner's daughter took over the store. The blacksmith's daughter took over his business, widows took over for their husbands and on it went. But the town struggled and would fade if they didn't get more people to move there. Lucky for Apple Blossom, six Englishmen came to town, stayed to help some of the women out, and wound up marrying them!

He sighed when he reached the hotel and trudged up the stairs to his room. Phileas Darlington—one of the Englishmen—and his wife Dora were wonderful, and he enjoyed listening to their stories of the town and some of its more colorful residents.

He packed and had some letters to write and should get them done so he could mail them when he got to Bozeman. He thought of his upcoming assignment and how to transport Bill Krantz to the meeting point. Once he handed him over, he was the other agent's problem.

"But what about his mail-order bride?" he mused aloud. "What am I going to do about her?"

Bram paced the room, thinking. The last thing he wanted was a woman underfoot. She'd get in the way for sure and probably get hurt. Women were curious creatures, and their curiosity often got them into trouble. What was Jules thinking telling him to go ahead and take Krantz's bride?

His eyes lit up as he got an idea. "I'll tell her I want to court first." He paced some more. "I can put her up in a hotel in town. Then she'd be out of my hair." He went to the window. "And I wouldn't have to go through the hassle of getting an annulment later."

He smiled and clasped his hands behind his back. It was a good plan, and he didn't think Jules would mind. After all, the last thing he needed was some poor woman following him around. A new bride often tried to please her new husband, and Heaven forbid she be pretty and tempt him.

Bram closed his eyes against the thought. It was best not to marry at all. Obviously, Jules Monroe didn't think this through. Unless he thought it a good way to get Bram a wife. Everyone figured he'd be married by now. But he enjoyed working in the field, and he couldn't have a wife while doing a lot of field work. It was too dangerous, and he didn't want to make some poor woman a widow.

He sighed, stepped away from the window and looked at his carpetbag. He should buy some extra ammunition before he left. If he was watched in Baker City, he didn't want anyone questioning why their new mild-mannered bookkeeper was buying up bullets. They especially didn't need to see a woman with him while he did it. She'd have a target on her back after that, and there were no guarantees he could protect her.

Chapter Three

Millie was a bundle of nerves as the train pulled into Baker City. She still couldn't believe she was doing this! What was she thinking coming to Oregon to marry a stranger? Was this Bill Krantz a drunkard like Father? What if he gambled as Father did? Would he be kind, upright, and have a strong moral character? All she really knew about him was that he was an accountant and would be as new to Baker City as she would.

"Baker City!" The conductor called. "Coming into Baker City!"

Millie fiddled with her careworn gloves and braced herself for her worst fear. Her groom not showing up. What little money was left from the sale of the house was enough to get her a room and feed her for a few days, but after that, she'd have nothing. For as much as she hated gambling, she was doing just that.

If her groom did show, she hoped they married quickly, and she could start her new life trying to… what? Try to please him like she had Father? How many years had she'd done that? And for what, she might add. Father never cared for anyone but himself.

She looked out the window as the train began to slow. Mr. Thornton said her new home had a population of about ten thousand. It wasn't Boston, but it also wasn't so small it wasn't on the map.

Millie gathered her meager belongings as the train came to a stop. She hoped she recognized Mr. Krantz when she saw him. He'd sent a photograph of a man with dark hair and a beard and mustache. He looked a little scruffy for a bookkeeper, but he was wearing a pair of spectacles. Besides, who knew when the picture was taken? She supposed he wouldn't look bad if he shaved and cleaned up a bit.

The train came to a stop, and she prepared to disembark along with the rest of the passengers. Millie tried peeking out the windows as she went but wasn't sure what good it would do. She'd have a better chance of spotting her groom once she was on the station's platform.

Millie stepped off the train and shaded her eyes against the afternoon sun. She moved across the platform, her carpetbag in one hand, a valise in the other, and began to search. She didn't see Mr. Krantz anywhere.

Her heart sank. She'd imagined every horrible scenario she could think of during her journey. After all she'd been through, she couldn't help it. Bad luck seemed to follow her everywhere.

More people left the platform and there was still no sign of him. "No…"

Panic crept up her spine, sending a chill through her body. He had to be around here somewhere. Maybe he was late?

She went to a bench near the ticket office and sat. "Yes, he's late, that's all. He'll be along any moment." She took a deep breath, held onto her luggage, and settled in to wait for her future husband.

Bram stared at Quincy Melbourne in shock. He was one of the best spies employed by the president. It was an honor to be working with him. Unfortunately, they had a problem. Bram looked at the kitchen table, then the overturned chair and drops of blood on the floor. "What happened?"

Quincy scratched the dark stubble covering his jaw. "I came by late last night and thought I'd check things out before we arrested Krantz tonight. I thought I heard some sort of scuffle inside, came in and there he was, slumped over the kitchen table, dead."

Bram couldn't believe it. Bill Krantz was dead? "How?"

"As far as I could tell, someone stabbed him in the back then took off," Quincy said. "I'll take care of Krantz while you search the house. We need to figure out who did this and why. If the murderer is still around, he thinks Krantz is dead. And Krantz is supposed to start work for the Double K any day now."

Bram ran his hand through his hair. What were they going to do? And what if whomever murdered Krantz caught sight of his victim walking through town?

"I'd better get going," Quincy said. "Find out what you can, and I'll do the same."

Before he could say a word, Quincy disappeared through the kitchen's back door. Bram heaved a sigh, then began to search for clues. He started in the bedroom. There was nothing hidden under the mattress, nothing in the drawers of the vanity. He turned, spied Krantz's spectacles on the dresser and put them in his pocket. He'd need them to pose as the man.

Bram noticed a folded newspaper on the dresser and picked it up. An envelope was beneath it. Bram looked at it. "Millie Scott of Boston. Could this be from his mail-order bride?" He took the letter out and read it. "What?! Great Scott!"

It was indeed a letter from Krantz's bride, and she was arriving on the afternoon train! Bram checked his pocket watch. "The train's already come through." He facepalmed. This wasn't going as planned!

"Great." He left the house and hadn't taken two steps when a couple of men approached him. "Looks like you're late, Krantz."

Bram stopped and stared at them. He hadn't contacted any of the men from the Double K Ranch yet. Had these men already met with Krantz? Did they know he was dead? "Yes, well, it's a big day."

"Whoowee! It sure is," the shorter of the two said. "Best not keep yer mail-order bride waiting." He scrutinized him. "Hey, don't ya wear spectacles?"

Krantz pulled them from his pocket and put them on.

"He's nervous, Charlie," the taller man said.

Charlie, Bram thought. Charlie Woolworth, one of the cowhands. He was buddies with a Mr. Montclair, the ranch foreman. That's who the taller of the two must be. His nickname was Monty.

"You clean up nice, Krantz," Monty said. "Boss said you were sort of scraggly when he met you the other day."

"Yes, well, it was quite the journey here, then getting the house and all." He glanced over his shoulder at the house. He didn't dare let them inside. "If you'll excuse me, gentlemen, I need to fetch my bride."

"You do that, Krantz," Monty said. "Once you've settled in with the new missus, Boss wants to see ya."

"Ah, have a heart, Monty. Tonight's his wedding night!" Charlie elbowed the man in the ribs.

Monty ignored him and slung an arm around Bram. "Come on, we'll see you to the train station." He practically dragged him down the front walk to the rickety gate. "Ya know, you might want to think about a bigger place for you and your bride. That shack ain't much."

Bram gave him a wan smile and mentally went over his role of Bill Krantz. He was a little mousy, though sly, and from what he knew, could be bought. He'd been guilty of petty theft but not much else. He also gambled a lot and for all Bram knew, got killed over cheating at cards. If that were the case, whomever murdered him might be long gone by now to avoid getting arrested by the local law. This meant he'd have to show up at the saloon a few nights a week to play cards to keep up his cover. Fine, he could do that.

By the time they got to the train station, it was empty.

"Are ya sure she was coming today?" Charlie asked. "You told the boss she was."

Bram scanned the platform, caught sight of a bit of blue skirt near one corner of the ticket office, and headed that way.

Charlie and Monty followed him. Sure enough, when he reached the end of the platform, he saw a woman leaning against the wall on the other side of the ticket office, dabbing her eyes with a handkerchief.

"Looks like ya got some apologizing to do," Charlie said with a frown.

Bram's eyebrows shot up at the look on the short man's face. "Yeah, looks that way."

"Well, don't just stand there," Monty said. "Go fetch the poor woman and take her to the church. We'll do our part."

He looked at them, his eyebrows shooting up again.

"Didn't the boss tell ya?" Charlie said. "We're yer witnesses!"

Bram gulped. "Witnesses?"

"Yeah, seeing as how you don't know anyone around here," Monty said.

The woman caught sight of him and stared at Bram with wide eyes. She was beautiful, even with a tear-stained face. "Mr. Krantz?" she asked, hopeful.

Bram stood stock still.

"Get a move one, ya big scaredy-cat!" Charlie said and gave him a shove.

He stumbled forward staring back. Her dark hair was piled on her head, her blue hat slightly askew. It matched her blue traveling outfit, and her dark eyes captured his.

"Mr. Krantz?" she repeated.

"Yes," he said as his eyes raked over her.

She smiled in relief. "Oh, thank goodness. I thought…"

"I apologize," he blurted. "I… I was…"

"Getting pretty!" Charlie chortled. "He done cleaned up nice, ma'am. Ya shoulda seen him before!"

Monty elbowed Charlie. "Leave him be." He smiled at her. "I'm Mr. Montclair, and this is Charlie."

Charlie chuckled. "You can call him Monty, everybody does."

She gave them a nod as Bram continued to stare at her. This beautiful creature was Bill Krantz's mail-order bride?! Oh boy…

"We'd best head for the church," Monty advised. "Charlie and me gotta get back to the ranch."

Bram blinked a few times. "Church?!"

"Yeah," Charlie said. "Yer gettin' married!"

Bram forced his gaze away from Krantz's bride. "Now?!"

"Yes, now," Monty said. He took Bram by the elbow and pulled him along. "Charlie, get the lady's bags."

"Yes, sir!"

Before he knew it, Monty and Charlie had taken him and Krantz's bride to a small nearby church where a preacher was waiting. If he backed out, he risked blowing his cover. So, he did what his boss Jules Monroe planned all along. He got married.

Chapter Four

Millie heard herself say the words, "I do," and almost fainted. She found it difficult to breathe, and Mr. Krantz grabbed her elbow to steady her.

"Are you okay?" he asked with concern.

Millie took a deep breath and nodded.

Preacher Barton, a wiry little bald man, grinned. "Now we've come to the good part." He cleared his throat. "I now pronounce you husband and wife. Mr. Krantz, you may kiss the bride."

Millie stared at her new husband. Her assumption was right, he looked much better without the beard and mustache. He had thick dark hair, piercing blue eyes, and was taller than she expected.

Mr. Krantz took her hands in his, bent to her, and gave her a quick peck on the lips.

When he straightened, he smiled.

At a loss for words, Millie smiled shyly back. She was married!

"Congratulations!" Charlie said.

Before she knew it, Preacher Barton was having everyone sign the license, and she noticed Mr. Krantz hesitate when it was his turn. "Is there a problem?" she asked.

He glanced between her and the license. "Not at all, just making sure everything is worded correctly."

Charlie laughed. "Hear that, Monty? Boss said he was a stickler for details!"

"Yeah," Monty said. "And speaking of details, we got some to see to before we leave town."

Mr. Krantz's head came up, and he looked at them.

"Sign the license, sir," Preacher Barton urged. "And you and your bride can be on your way."

Millie's new husband sighed like he was signing his death warrant rather than his marriage license, and her heart dropped. Did he not want to marry her? That would explain the shocked look on his face when he first laid eyes on her at the station.

Millie hid her disappointment by turning away from the men and pulling a handkerchief from her reticule. She quickly dabbed her eyes with it, then stuffed it back inside. She could do this. Millie drew in a deep breath and faced the men. "Is everything in order?"

Mr. Krantz shoved his spectacles up his nose. "Yes." He glanced at Charlie and Monty. "Thank you for all your help."

"Don't thank us," Monty said. "Thank the boss when you see him. He's giving you three days with your bride. Consider it a wedding present." He slapped him on the back and turned to leave.

"Enjoy your night!" Charlie giggled and followed.

Once they left the church, Millie turned back to him. "I suppose we should go home?"

He fixed his gaze on the marriage license, then looked at her. "Home?" He shook his head. "No... um, I have something special planned. You must be starving, for one, and tired from your journey."

"Well, yes, as a matter of fact..."

He took her by the arm, handed Preacher Barton some money, and ushered her from the church. "I thought a day or two at the hotel would be nice."

"The hotel? But your home..."

"Is a mess! I didn't have time to take care of things before you arrived. I need to do some cleaning before I take you home."

"How thoughtful, but I can take care of any cleaning..."

"There's a rat," he said with wide eyes. "A... big one. I need to get rid of it."

"Rat?" she said cringing. "Oh, please do."

Her new husband smiled at her. "I will. I want things safe for you."

He stopped and looked into her eyes with no small amount of concern. Millie's heart skipped a beat. "Thank you," she breathed.

He swallowed hard. "Don't mention it." He continued to the hotel, and soon he was checking them in as Mr. and Mrs. William Krantz.

He escorted her to their room, unlocked the door and went inside. "There, you'll be comfortable here."

She frowned. "Me? What about you?"

"I have that rat to take care of, remember?"

"Oh, yes." She watched him set her bags on the bed. "Are you hungry?"

He stood by the bed, his back to her. "I am. We could go to one of the restaurants in town or see if the dining room downstairs is open for dinner yet."

Millie studied him as he turned to face her. He was broader than she first thought, and she couldn't stop trying to take him in.

He took on a worried look. "What is it?"

Millie shook her head. "N-nothing. You surprised me, that's all."

He stepped toward her. "How so?"

When he reached her, she looked into his eyes. "You don't look anything like your photograph."

He rubbed his chin with a hand. "I shaved," he said in explanation.

Without thinking, she reached up and palmed one side of his face. "You look nice."

He swallowed as he gazed at her. "So do you."

Millie's cheeks heated, and she looked away. "We should check the dining room."

He reached up and put his hand over hers. "Yes, we should." He took her hand, held it, then led her to the door. In the hall, he let go her hand, locked the door, and handed her the key. "You'd best carry this."

She nodded and put the key in her reticule. Of all the scenarios she'd run through her head during her journey, this was not one of them. Her new husband was quiet, handsome, strong-looking, and tall. Maybe, just maybe, she could have a normal life now.

Downstairs they went into the dining room and were able to order dinner. While they waited for their food, Millie tried not to openly gawk at her new husband. "So tell me," she began. "What should I call you?"

He stared at her a moment. "Call me?"

"Yes. Should I call you William?"

He shook his head. "No, call me Bram." He stiffened as soon as he said it. "Or Bill…"

"Bram?" she said with a smile. "Is that a nickname?"

He gave her a tiny shrug. "My, um, mother used to call me that when I was younger."

She smiled again. "Bram. I like it. Is it short for anything?"

He drew in a breath and nodded. "Bramble. Because I was always getting stuck in the middle of something I didn't want to be stuck in."

"I see," she said with a laugh. "And did your mother have to pull you out of the bramble patch often?"

He gazed into her eyes before his eyes swept over her face. "No. I always got myself out." He gave her a heartfelt look, and for a moment, she thought she caught sympathy in his eyes. Why would he look at her like that?

Millie's eyes became downcast. Maybe he didn't want to marry her after all.

Chapter Five

What was he doing?! Bram never should have told her his real first name. Now he'd have to keep up the name ruse in case any of the Double K men or their boss, Mr. Kameyer, heard her use it.

After dinner, he escorted her back to the room and told her he had work to do on the house and the varmint to chase out. Thank goodness Quincy took care of Krantz and planned to give him a decent burial in another town somewhere.

But Bram still had to play his part. That meant making an appearance at the local saloons and looking for a game. So, if Bill Krantz was an avid gambler, then he'd be tempted to leave his new bride and try to find a card game, even on his wedding night.

Bram straightened things up at Krantz's house erasing any signs that a scuffle took place the night before, then headed for the nearest saloon. He'd start there, then work his way to the next and find out what he could about the last game Krantz took part in.

Bram got into a game right away and told the other players he couldn't remember the games he played the night before. As soon as he did, the other men started talking at once, and boy, did he get an earful! By the time he dragged himself to Krantz's house late in the evening, Bram pieced together what happened.

Krantz got caught cheating at cards. The man he cheated, a Mr. Winston, threatened revenge, and Bram and Quincy were the only ones that knew Winston got it. No one had seen him since, but it had only been twenty-four hours. Who knew if he was still in town or had vamoosed to the next? Bram figured this Winston was gone. What idiot sticks around long enough to get himself arrested?

Bram entered the bedroom, stared at the bed, then went into the kitchen and sat at the table. In the morning, he'd pull the bedding off and take it to a laundry service in town. It was the least he could do for Krantz's new bride.

"That poor woman," he muttered to himself. Mr. Kameyer gave him three days before he had to report to work. That was three days wasted, plus he'd have to pretend to be married! He thought of Millie's beautiful face and figure and cringed.

She would have to be one of the loveliest creatures he'd ever seen. He could have pulled off the whole "let's court first," ruse, then tell the young lady they wouldn't suit, make sure she was well compensated, then send her on her way. But now that they were "married," she'd expect them to do what married people did. Great Scott, if he so much as held her too long, he might have a problem. And if he kissed her?

Bram ran his hands through his hair and groaned. He supposed it couldn't be helped. Even if Charlie and Monty hadn't shown up when they did, Mr. Kameyer and his associates would expect him to marry at some point, and getting hitched was the only way to avoid suspicion.

He heaved a sigh. "Millie Krantz. What are you going to do when you find out I'm not Bill Krantz?" Bram closed his eyes in resignation. There was nothing he could do except avoid his new bride as much as possible.

His mind made up, he went into the small parlor, flopped onto the couch, and fell fast asleep.

Millie awoke the next morning to an empty bed. Where was her husband? Had he not returned last night?

She got up, went through her usual morning routine, then donned her favorite dress: a pale-yellow day dress with tiny blue flowers. It was the last thing her mother made for her. She hoped Bram liked it.

Millie checked herself in a mirror on the wall. At least she didn't look as tired as yesterday.

She left the room, went downstairs, and peeked in the dining room. There was no sign of Bram.

Millie found a small table, took a seat and ordered coffee and breakfast. If Bram didn't show up soon, she'd make a few inquiries and find out where he lived. For all she knew, he spent most of the night fixing up her new home. Between opening a new business in town, getting a place to live, and a new wife, she should give him some leeway. And she should help.

Her decision made, she enjoyed her breakfast, drank her coffee then left the hotel. She'd visit the church first. Surely Preacher Barton would know where to find him.

"Why yes," Preacher Barton said when she saw him. "Your husband got himself a little house at the other end of town. It's at the end of Second Street I believe. Last house on the right."

"Thank you, I do appreciate it."

Preacher Barton followed her to the church door. "We'd love to see the two of you here on Sundays, and as you're newly married, the missus and I understand how difficult starting out can be."

She sighed. "You mean the fact that I was a mail-order bride?"

"Yes," he said honestly. "If you ever need a listening ear or some advice, you know where to find us."

"Thank you. I'll keep that in mind." Millie gave him a nod and left the church.

She found the downtown area, cut through it, and soon found Second Street. The homes here were small, and she assumed workers from the sawmill outside of town lived here, along with other folks from Baker City's lower class. Well, Bram never said he was a man of means.

She walked to the end of the street where it dead ended and looked at the little white cottage. There was a picket fence around it that needed whitewashing. The house could use a new coat of paint, and she noticed one of the parlor windows had a crack in it.

Millie studied the weeds growing in what were once flowerbeds, and tried to imagine the house fixed up, the yard with fresh green grass and flowers. "Oh, Bram. There's a lot of work here."

She opened the rickety gate and went up the walk. Millie knocked on the door and waited.

No answer.

She knocked again.

Nothing.

She looked around, tried the doorknob. It turned, and she opened the door and stepped inside.

"Bram?" She went down the hall and peeked into the parlor. The furniture was old and dingy, and the curtains needed a good washing. Millie examined the rug. It would have to be taken out and beaten. She sighed and entered the dining room. A bay window let in plenty of light, as did the bay window in the parlor. With some new curtains, both rooms would look better.

She inspected the kitchen next. "Oh, dear, looks like he didn't get to this room yet." There were dirty dishes in the sink and the floor needed to be swept and mopped. At least the area around the kitchen table looked clean.

Millie went to inspect the bedroom. She knocked before entering and found it empty. There was a bed, but it had been stripped. A dresser graced one wall, an armoire another. There was also a small vanity. Millie sighed as she looked around. "Home sweet home."

She took off her hat, pulled off her gloves, and set them on the dresser. Out of curiosity, she opened the top drawer of the dresser. There were a few of Bram's shirts inside. She pulled one out, curious if anything needed mending, and held it up. "Hmmm, this looks awful small." She set it aside and pulled out another. "This one too."

Millie shrugged, folded the shirts, and put them away. Maybe Bram had put on weight. Did that mean he didn't have enough money to buy food at one time?

Millie pushed the thought aside, went into the kitchen, and decided to tackle the dishes first.

Chapter Six

Bram dropped off the laundry at a service near downtown, then went to the hotel. Millie wasn't there. Maybe she'd gone down to breakfast, and he didn't see her when he came in.

Downstairs he checked with the man at the front desk. "Your wife had breakfast over an hour ago. Then she left," he said.

Bram thanked him and hurried out the door. "Where could she be? And why would she leave the hotel? He scratched his head then it dawned on him. "The house."

Bram took off at a good clip. If he was in her shoes, and woke up to no husband in her bed, he'd go looking for said husband too.

He hurried to Krantz's house, saw that the front door was open, and went inside. "Millie?"

"In the kitchen," she called back.

Bram sighed in relief then frowned. What was he worried about? No one knew he was undercover, and just as Jules said, his new bride was none the wiser. She'd found out where he lived and went looking for him, that's all.

Bram smiled at the thought and headed for the kitchen. "Millie?"

She straightened and put a hand up to stop him. "I just mopped the floor. Don't you dare track any dirt across it."

Bram stood on the threshold to the kitchen, his hands up. "I'm staying put."

"See that you do." She wrung out the mop, picked up the bucket, and headed for the kitchen's back door.

"What are you doing?"

"Dumping the dirty water, of course."

"Let me do that for you." He started after her.

She spun on her heel wagging a finger at him. "Stop!"

He stood, several feet from the threshold, one foot in the air. "Sorry." He backed up. I'll go out the front door and come around to you." Bram hurried outside and met her at the back door. "Allow me." He took the bucket, walked a few feet away, and dumped it. There was a pump near the back porch, so he rinsed and re-filled the bucket for her. "There. Now you have fresh water to work with."

"Thank you." She brushed loose wisps of hair from her face and stared at him. "Where are your spectacles?"

"Oh, um, I only need them for reading." He plastered on a smile and tried to concentrate. She was so beautiful; it was making it hard to think. In fact, he was beginning to wonder if spending the next three days with her was such a good idea.

"Is something wrong?" she asked softly.

Bram closed his eyes. She had a sweet voice, and his chest warmed at the sound. "No," he said and opened his eyes. "Is there something I can do to help you?"

She gazed at him, her eyes roaming over his body. "Have you gained weight recently? I found shirts in the dresser, but they look too small for you."

Bram blinked in surprise. He'd forgotten to remove Krantz's things! But with her sudden arrival, and having to deal with Krantz, inspecting the dresser or armoire hadn't occurred to him. "Oh, um, yes," he finally said. "I'll need to get some new shirts. Nothing fits anymore."

She nodded. "That explains things. Then I won't bother mending them for you. Will you give them to the church? Preacher Barton asked if we'd come to Sunday service. We can ask if there's a donation box."

"Yes, of course." Why was his heart hammering in his chest?

She turned, and he noticed the lovely curve of her neck, not to mention a few other curves. He shut his eyes tight. *Hands off! She's not yours, never will be.*

Bram opened his eyes and watched her try to lift the bucket. "What are you doing?" he scolded. He picked it up. "Where do you want it?"

Her hands went to her hips, and she sighed. "Put it on the stove and we'll let the water heat. I'm sure I'll need it later." She eyed him. "Wipe your feet before you step on that floor."

Bram smiled. She was a feisty little thing. "Yes, ma'am." He carefully tipped toed through the kitchen, trying to step on the dry spots, and put the bucket on the stove. "Would you like me to start a fire?"

"Could you? I noticed there's some wood in the woodshed out back, but not much. Do you know where we might buy some?"

"I'll see what I can find out. I'm still learning my way around." He thought of her letter and where she was from. "Baker City must seem small to you."

"Much smaller." She smiled. "But I'll get used to it. Boston seems so far away now…"

His mind raced over the letter she'd sent Krantz. It was short, to the point, telling him when she'd arrive. "Why did you become a mail-order bride?"

Her shoulders slumped. "My father… he… died."

Bram closed the distance between them. "How, when?"

She stared at the floor. "He got shot, cheating at cards. He lived, but the wound never really healed. Eventually, he got an infection from it and died."

Bram cringed. "All because he was cheating at cards?"

She looked up at him. "Yes. He was a gambler. He… ruined our lives."

His heart went out to her. Unfortunately, there was nothing he could do for the poor thing. Bram's eyes widened. Oh no! A gambler?!

He caught the animosity in her eyes. "You hate gambling."

"I abhor it."

He fought the urge to clench his fists. This assignment kept getting better and better. After this he might never work in the field again.

"You don't gamble, do you?" she asked with narrowed eyes.

He gulped. "I have on occasion, same as any man." There, he hoped that was vague enough. He was going to have to rethink his strategy. But if he didn't show up at the saloon where Krantz played cards, someone might start asking questions. Had he played with Charlie or Monty? Would they expect to see him there?

Millie eyed him. "Do you still gamble?"

He looked her in the eyes, closed the distance between them, and did the only thing he could think of.

He kissed her.

Chapter Seven

Millie's eyes popped wide as soon as his lips touched hers. She thought her first kiss at the church was nice, but it was nothing like this.

Soon his arms came around her, and her eyes closed. She was enjoying this, perhaps too much. Yes, they were married, but the passion of his kiss was foreign, exciting, exhilarating! Who knew a kiss could do so much?

When he broke the kiss, she was pressed against his chest, trying to catch her breath.

"Wh-what…"

"I'm sorry," he said against her hair. "I… couldn't help myself." He drew back and gazed at her. "You're a beautiful woman, Millie. What man wouldn't want to kiss you in such a fashion?"

She took a deep breath, trying to get her brain to form words. "Y-you think I'm beautiful?"

He smiled, his eyes roaming her face. "I do."

She caught the sincerity in his eyes and her heart skipped a beat. "Thank you." Her cheeks heated with a blush, and she wasn't sure what else to say.

He gave her a heartfelt look that made her belly do a flip, then let her go. "Wood. Fire. Let me take care of that."

Millie nodded as he left for the woodshed. "Oh, my," she whispered, her brain still not working. What were they talking about? No matter, she'd just experienced her first real kiss, and it was wonderful!

She stared at the stove, then took in the rest of the kitchen. The room needed a lot of work, and she also hadn't gone through the hutch to see what sort of dishes there were or peeked in the pantry. Was there any food in the house?

Bram returned with an armful of wood and quickly built a fire in the cookstove. That done he gave her a guilty look. "I'm afraid we'll need a few supplies." He glanced around the room, then headed for a small door. He opened it. "Pantry," he stated. He went inside. "Not much here." He opened a jar and peeked inside. "Coffee?"

Millie smiled. "Yes, I'd love some."

He sniffed the contents of the jar. "It's even fresh."

She laughed. "Is it usually not?"

Bram grinned and gave her a playful shrug. "Sometimes."

"Well, best you leave the pantry supplies to me."

"Gladly." He handed her the jar then went to the hutch.

She watched him open both cupboards and pull out two cups and saucers. Millie joined him and noticed they were the *only* cups and saucers. "Oh dear. There's only one plate and bowl."

"Yes, um, I haven't had a chance to do much shopping yet. There's a place called The Emporium. I'm told they have a little of everything. Perhaps we can get a few things there."

"That would be wonderful, thank you." She took the cups and saucers from him and took them to the table. It was a simple thing. Make a pot of coffee, sit down and share some conversation. But she was about to do it with her new husband. A handsome man who seemed kind and attentive. So what if he was a little messy? He'd had a lot to deal with, and now that they were married, they'd have time to settle in.

Millie blushed. "I noticed the bed was stripped." She turned to him. "Where's the bedding?"

"I took it to a laundry service in town. I'll pick it up this evening."

Her blush deepened. "That's good. We can't very well sleep in a bed with no sheets or blankets."

He nodded then blanched. "Uh, of course not." He strode for the back door.

"Where are you going?" she asked.

"To get more wood. In case we want to build a fire tonight." He slipped out the back door and was gone.

Millie sighed in contentment and pictured the two of them sitting near the fire, reading. Maybe they'd talk instead, who knew? And when they finally went to bed, would he kiss her again, or would there be more? She wasn't completely ignorant when it came to such things. But she also didn't know everything.

After Bram's kiss, however, she was willing to learn.

Millie made the coffee while Bram busied himself in the backyard. Was he gathering more wood or seeing how much work there was to be done? Once they had the house and yards fixed up, the place would be charming. Millie had never had a place of her own, and she was excited to make the little house into something to be proud of.

When the coffee was done, she poured them each a cup and set everything on the table. She found some sugar in the pantry, but no cream. The ice box was empty and needed ice. She'd better start a list.

Millie went out the back door and watched Bram chop some kindling. After his kiss, she didn't know what to think! Now she was beginning to look at her husband with new eyes. He was more than a little handsome and, she sensed, a little shy. She liked that.

"The coffee's ready," she called to him.

He looked up from his work, put the ax in the woodshed, and started for her. When he reached the porch, she noticed how hot and sweaty he looked. "Goodness, how much wood did you chop?"

"As much as I could find." He went inside without another word, leaving her on the porch.

"My word," she said to herself. "Is he cranky?" Maybe he was tired after all that work.

She shook the thought off and went inside. Bram was already at the kitchen table sipping his coffee.

Millie sat across the table from him. "I'd like to make a list of things we need. Is that all right?"

He looked at her over the rim of his cup. "Of course. I'll leave some money."

She blinked a few times in surprise. "But… aren't you going with me? You mentioned The Emporium…"

"Oh, yes, I did…"

She tried not to gasp. Was that a hint of regret in his voice? Millie's heart sank as she studied the worn red and white checkered tablecloth. There were several moth holes in it. "What will you be doing?" She looked at him, not regretting the disappointment in her voice.

Bram stilled in his chair. "I… must see to my office. There are things I need to… arrange."

She cocked her head. "What things?"

He pressed his lips together and shook his head.

"It's a simple question," she pointed out.

"You're a curious little thing, aren't you?"

Millie shrugged. "I suppose." Truth be told, she was extremely curious. It came from years of wondering what gambling haunt her father was frequenting. Sometimes she'd leave the comfort of home to find out, if only to put her mother's mind at ease.

"When may I see your office?" she asked.

He almost spit out his coffee. "Wh-what?"

She watched him dab his mouth with a napkin. Was he nervous? "Your office," she repeated. "I'd love to see where you'll be working."

"Oh, yes. It's just past downtown near a tailor's shop." He looked at the front of his shirt and wiped at the coffee that spilled down his front.

Millie held her cup and tried not to smile. Was he ashamed to show her his office? Was it as ill kept as the house? Well, she'd find out with him or without him.

Chapter Eight

Bram was in so much trouble. What was he thinking kissing her like that? But… it did work. She forgot all about their conversation and it took her more than a little while to get her wits about her.

That kiss told Bram a lot, and unfortunately, she was more alluring than ever.

She was an innocent, for one, and that had to have been her first kiss. The one he gave her at their wedding hardly counted.

She had spunk and didn't pull away when he kissed her. Instead, she accepted what he had to offer. She was curious, and when she melted into his embrace, it was all he could do to break the kiss.

The sooner he got away from her the better. Problem was, she expected him to be a husband and do things with her. Like, go to The Emporium.

He sighed and eyed the coffee pot. "We could go this afternoon."

Millie blinked at him, as if she couldn't believe he'd acquiesced. "Really?" She eyed his cup. "Would you like more coffee?" She rose from her chair and went to the stove without waiting for an answer.

Bram watched as she refilled both their cups, returned the pot to the stove and sat. "You should… make a list."

"Yes." She sipped her coffee. "I'll do it now."

Bram watched her leave the table again, probably to search for some paper and a pencil, and quickly formed a plan. If he bought her everything she'd need to fix up the house, she'd be busy for days. He smiled. It was pure genius! What woman could resist the opportunity to decorate her very own home?

Millie returned to the table with a small notebook and pencil. "I found these in a drawer in the hutch." She sat and jotted a few things down. "Where shall we go first?"

"The Emporium. You'll want new curtains, table linens, maybe a new coverlet for the bed?"

Her eyes went wide. "All that?"

He looked around the kitchen. "I planned to purchase what I needed after I arrived. I'll let you pick everything out." He smiled. "How's that?"

Her entire face lit up. "Everything?"

His chest swelled at the excitement in her eyes. "Yes, sweetie, everything."

She blushed at his slip, and doggone if that didn't set off a tiny ache in his chest. *Uh oh...*

Bram drained his cup, not caring how hot the coffee was. The sooner he loaded her up with things for the house, the sooner she'd get to work. Then he could do his job. Besides, if she worked hard enough over the next few days, she'd be too exhausted at night for anything else. It was all the excuse he needed not to exercise his husbandly rights. He still had to figure out where he was going to sleep, and with any luck, that rickety bed was as weak as it looked. It would never hold them, and naturally he'd let her have it while he slept in the parlor. Perfect!

"Cream, eggs, flour?"

Bram jumped. "Huh?"

"Can you think of what else we need besides those three things?"

"Sugar," he blurted. "Whatever you think you'll need, write it on the list."

"Ice for the icebox," she jotted on the pad. Millie continued to write, and he realized he enjoyed watching her think. He wanted to tell her money was no object, but he didn't dare. How could a lowly accountant such as Krantz have enough money to say something like that?

His eyes darted around the room, and he thought of the condition of the front and back yards. He'd have to remember he was supposed to be from the lower classes instead of coming from Washington's high society.

Bram watched Millie, and for a moment, his heart went out to her. Her dress was old, he could tell by the thinness of the fabric. She'd had only one carpetbag and a valise with her. She needed clothes, shoes as well, he guessed. "We should get your things from the hotel," he said softly.

She stopped writing and raised her gaze to his. "Yes."

He swallowed hard. There was a breathlessness to her voice that almost did him in. "We'll go to the hotel, have lunch, get your things and bring them home?"

Millie smiled. "That sounds fine. Then can we go to The Emporium?"

"Yes. And anywhere else you'd like to go."

"We'll need the supplies I've written down," she said.

"There's a general store not far from my office."

She smiled and added a few more things to her list.

When she was done Millie stood and cleared away the dishes, took them to the sink and set them in the washtub. "I'm ready."

Bram slowly stood. Would she want to walk arm in arm as they went about their business?

He took a deep breath. Okay, how hard could it be? He'd escorted other women about town. Rich heiresses mostly who'd like nothing more than to marry him. Maybe that's why he agreed to work for Jules Monroe. It would get him away from women, and he needed a little adventure in his life. Here in the west, no one knew him, and he could pretend to be anyone Jules needed him to be. He still had his obligations of course, helping Father with his businesses and making an appearance now and then at social gatherings, but all in all, his life was a good one.

So, what was it about his so-called wife that made him feel like something was missing from his life? Was it time for him to take a wife? Did a part of him hanker for a woman to become the mother of his children?

"Are you okay?"

Bram blinked a few times. He'd been so deep in thought, he forgot what he was doing. "Of course." He headed for the back door. "I left my jacket outside. Let me fetch it."

"I'll get my hat and gloves," Millie said and disappeared into the bedroom.

Bram heaved another sigh, the small ache in his heart growing. After this assignment, he was going to have to take a long hard look at things.

He went outside, retrieved his jacket and hat, and put them on. When he returned to the kitchen, Millie was standing in the hall. Her hat looked old, as did her gloves, and his heart went out to her. "Since Mr. Kameyer gave me three days, I think we should use that time to spruce this place up."

"That's a wonderful idea," she gushed. "I was hoping you'd think so."

Bram smiled. This was going better than he planned. "So, while I get my office organized, you don't mind working on the house?"

Her face fell. "Oh, I thought we might do some of the work together."

"Of course, but I do have the office to contend with."

She smiled. "You'll help me with some of it then?"

"Certainly. There are things you might not be able to handle for one."

She blushed. "Thank you."

His smile broadened. "You're welcome. Now let's be on our way." He opened the front door and ushered her outside.

Chapter Nine

Millie walked arm in arm with her new husband and noticed the way people looked at them. She supposed they made a handsome couple, and the thought eased her mind about a few things. The more time she spent with Bram, the more she liked him. She couldn't imagine marrying a man after getting off the train only to discover he was horrid. But they'd been married less than twenty-four hours, so who knew what the future held? But so far, she sensed a bright one.

They reached the hotel, had lunch as planned then took her things back the house. Before leaving again, Bram had her look over the parlor, dining room and bedroom. The house even had a bathroom off the kitchen with a tub! They still had to heat their water, but she was used to that.

"Have you put everything on your list?" Bram asked when she came out of the bathroom.

She smiled. "I'm glad the house has some plumbing. That's a surprise."

"More and more people are putting it in." He looked at the notepad in her hand. "Your list?"

"Oh, yes." She perused it. "There are no towels, so we'll need some of those."

"Very well. You added them?"

"Yes." She stuffed the notebook and pencil into her reticule. "Shall we go?"

He smiled. "Yes. What do you think we should get today?"

"Towels, linens for the tables, and… curtains?" She asked with a blush.

He stopped them at the front door. "Millie, these are things we need, so don't worry about telling me. None of those things are frivolous. Besides, I've set some money aside for them."

She breathed a sigh of relief. "That's good to know."

He closed the distance between them and studied her a moment.

"What is it?" she asked. He held an intense look, as if he was trying to figure out some great mystery.

"Your father never let you have money for things you and your mother needed. He became upset when you asked for anything."

She gaped at him. "How did you know that?"

He shrugged. "It's not hard to figure out. You said he ruined your family. I assume that's financially?"

"Yes, but… there were other things…"

His face softened as he looked at her. "I'm sorry, Millie."

She returned his gaze. "For what?"

He took a step closer and traced her eyebrow with his thumb. "That your father didn't realize what a precious daughter he had." He lowered his hand and offered his arm.

She took it and they left the house, her heart beating like a hummingbird's at the gentleness of his simple touch. When they reached The Emporium, she couldn't wait to see what the store offered. She'd been in a few department stores in Boston, but never had the money to buy anything.

"The linens are this way," Bram said. He went left and led her down an aisle then into another.

Millie smiled at the amount of tablecloths, napkins, and curtains there were. "I don't know where to begin!"

He gave her a warm smile. "Why don't you go room by room? Start with the kitchen."

She looked at him and smiled. "Yes, that's a good idea." She went to the tablecloths and began to go through the stacks. Each was neatly folded, and she didn't want to ruin the display. She found a tablecloth for the kitchen, and as luck would have it, a matching pair of curtains!

"Get a pair for both kitchen windows, and something for the window in the back door," Bram suggested.

She jumped, not realizing he was right behind her. "Oh, you startled me."

He bent to her ear. "I didn't mean to."

His rich voice made her knees wobbly. "Will you hold these?" Millie handed him what she'd found so far, then fetched another pair of curtains, and a matching valance, along with a lace panel for the door. She turned to show her finds to Bram. "Won't these be pretty?"

He smiled as he met her gaze. "Very pretty."

She sensed he wasn't talking about the curtains, and blushed. Millie handed off the items, then returned to the tablecloths. "Now for the dining room."

She began to dig through the stack again, and sensed Bram's gaze on her. Millie gave him a side-long glance, and sure enough, he was watching her wearing a wide smile. Had she put it there? Did he enjoy the fact she was having a good time? For most, buying a few household items wouldn't be exciting. But Millie couldn't remember the last time she or Mother were allowed to purchase anything for the house. There was never enough money. Sometimes there wasn't enough for food.

Her shoulders slumped at the thought. Memories of her father, his horrible gambling, and the havoc it wreaked upon their lives was almost too much. Thank goodness that was no longer her life.

"Millie," Bram said gently behind her. "Is everything okay?"

She turned to him and nodded. "Yes, of course."

He smiled. "Find anything you like for the dining room?"

She was about to answer when several women walked past. "Did you hear about the Ruggles' ball?" one said. "Did you get an invitation?"

"I didn't," another said. "But I hear the Simpsons are going. Even Old Man Simpson is going and nothing gets him out of the house."

Bram watched them head down another aisle, his eyes narrowing slightly.

"Something wrong?" Millie asked.

"No, sweetie," he said, gently. "Go ahead and keep looking."

She smiled as her heart melted and returned to her task. She loved when he used little endearments. They made her feel special.

Soon she had curtains for the dining room's bay window, table linens, and remembered something she forgot to check. "Goodness me, is there silverware?"

"In the dining room?"

"Yes, did you check?"

"No. I never looked in the china cabinet or drawers."

"We should check when we get home. We do need some for the kitchen." She smiled. "We could use the same set for both."

He watched her a moment, his face an expressionless mask, then nodded. "That's fine."

She smiled. They could get by with one set. She didn't expect to be entertaining anyway. For one, she didn't know a soul in Baker City.

Millie pondered the conversation she overheard about a ball. She'd never been to a ball and wondered what it would be like. Where she grew up, there might be a dance held now and then, but she never attended one. Mother still taught her how to dance, often while they were waiting for Father to come home.

Millie pushed the thought aside and studied their surroundings. She'd been so caught up shopping, she didn't pay attention to anything else. She noted other women in their nice dresses, hats and gloves, and unconsciously reached up and touched her hat. It didn't match her dress, and her gloves were careworn.

"Millie…"

515

She let her hand drop and looked at Bram. "Yes?"

He bent to her. "Why don't you pick out a few dresses while we're here, then we'll go home."

A tiny gasp escaped. "Oh, no, I… I couldn't."

He straightened. "Why not, sweetie?"

Her heart fluttered at the endearment. "We're already getting so much."

He looked at the goods in his hands, then the things she held in hers. "Give those to me."

She did as he asked. "Are we leaving now?"

"We'll leave after you've picked out a few dresses. Why don't you find some, and I'll purchase these things?"

"But Bram…"

"Millie, I want you to have some new clothes." He leaned toward her. "Tomorrow, I'll get a few things for myself."

"You… you have clients to deal with. You need to look nice…"

"So do you, sweetie," he said with such tenderness, her heart melted, and tears stung the backs of her eyes. No one had spoken to her like that before. Not even her mother. "Okay," she whispered.

Bram smiled, kissed her on the cheek, then nodded in the direction of the women's clothes. "Go on."

Without thinking she stood on tiptoe and kissed him on the cheek. "Thank you."

Bram gave her a warm smile, then turned and walked away.

Chapter Ten

Bram paid for the things Millie picked out and waited for the store clerk to wrap his purchases. He leaned against the counter and watched Millie in the distance. She was going through the racks of dresses like a child opening present on Christmas. His heart went out to her and against his better judgement, he made up his mind to do what he could for her while she was with him. Millie was a huge part of his cover, and he didn't want to jeopardize her in any way. The best way to do that was to stay away from her. He'd give her money tomorrow to get more of what they needed. She could fix up the house the way she wanted it, and when the assignment was over, he'd purchase it for her. With the money she'd be compensated with, she'd have more than enough to live on for quite a while. She could find a job for extra money, maybe work here at The Emporium, or, if her sewing skills were good, get a job with one of the dressmakers in town.

He gathered their packages and joined her. "Find anything you like?"

She held a lovely, light blue day dress in her hands. "Yes, I like this one." Millie looked at the rack. "That green one is nice too."

"Get them both and pick out a third," Bram told her.

"Three?" She said with wide eyes.

"Four if you like, but I'm afraid that's my limit."

She blinked a few times, her mouth moving, but forming no words. Good grief, she was speechless!

Bram closed the distance between them. "Do you need to see if they fit?"

"I… I don't think so," she said in a soft voice.

"Millie?"

She met his gaze. "Thank you. You have no idea what this means to me."

Bram slowly nodded. "I believe I do. Now fetch the other dresses. Take your time."

Once again, she stood on tiptoe and kissed his cheek.

His chest swelled. He liked doing this for her. It was… fulfilling. Satisfaction grew inside of him the likes of which he'd never known. Great Scott, it was nothing but tablecloths, some curtains and a few dresses. But Millie appreciated them more than any woman he'd ever met. Of course, most of those were rich heiresses, and it didn't take long for him to figure out how hard they were to please. They wanted it all and more, and he wasn't willing to give them what they wanted. The women he knew were spoiled, haughty, and in general not very nice.

Bram sighed as he watched Millie sort through the racks, picking her four dresses with great care. "You have no idea how refreshing you are," he whispered.

Bram smiled as his chest warmed again. He was on dangerous ground and knew it. Millie was doing her best to take on the role of his wife, and had yet to realize that's all it was, just a role.

Bram hated the thought of disappointing her, but there was no help for it. Hopefully helping her to start a new life in Baker City would make up for it.

She brought her dresses to him, a big smile on her face, and showed him each one. She was so happy; he didn't know how to react.

"What do you think?" she asked. "Do you like them?"

"I'll like them better on you," he said with a grin. "Are you sure they'll fit?"

"Yes. I can tell by looking at them."

"You sew a lot?" he guessed.

"Oh, yes. I sew all my own clothes, so getting dresses without having to do the work is a luxury." She smiled again. "Would it be too much to get a petticoat?"

"No, sweetie. You go ahead." He gave her a warm smile, and she began to search for what she needed.

Bram took the dresses to the salesclerk that helped him earlier. He set everything down and told the clerk to wait.

When Millie found a petticoat, she handed it to the clerk. While he added up the total she gave Bram a shy smile. "Thank you so much. I've not had new things in years."

He stiffened, unable to help it. Who knows what her living conditions were like and for how long? If her father were still alive, he'd arrest him.

"You're welcome, sweetie. Now, help me carry some of these packages and let's go home." He paid for the dresses, and as soon as they were wrapped, picked up two and let Millie carry the others. They left, arms full, and went straight home. He liked the fact that Baker City was small enough for Millie to walk to everywhere she needed.

When they arrived, they placed everything on the dining room table. Bram pulled out his billfold, counted out some money, and set it next to the pile of packages.

"What's that for?" Millie asked.

"Food," he simply said.

Her face fell. "I thought we were getting supplies together. You said there's a general store not far from your office."

Drat, he did say that. "I thought you'd like to start dressing up the place."

"No, I…" she put her hand on his arm. "I want to spend time with you."

His heart warmed. *No, no, no!* "Oh, well…"

"I could help you straighten up your office. Get it ready for your meeting with your new client. Mr. Kameyer was it?"

"Erm, yes." Rats, what was he going to do now? He took in her big brown eyes and his resolve cracked. It was only today, then he'd avoid her as much as possible. "Fine, if that's what you want. I just thought…"

She gave his arm a squeeze. "You thought I only cared about the house? Bram, you're my husband. Of course I want to spend time with you."

He gulped. "Then we should get going." He put the money back in his billfold and they left.

"Are you tired?" he asked as they cut through the downtown area. His office was several blocks from here, and about two blocks from the general store he told her about.

"Not at all."

He smiled and wondered what she was going to think of his shabby little office. As it was part of his cover, Quincy didn't spend a lot of time seeking decent accommodations. No matter, he didn't plan on being in Baker City any longer than he had to. He wanted to make short work of this assignment and get back to Washington. Especially now.

They walked in silence the rest of the way, and he forgot Millie needed shoes. He'd take care of those tomorrow and see that she got several pairs. She'd need a sturdy pair of work shoes that she could wear for gardening and chores.

He was so busy thinking about what she'd need to start her new life, he didn't notice the small crowd gathered outside Springer's Tailors.

"What's going on?" Millie asked.

Bram stopped and looked at half a dozen women and even a few men trying to peek in the windows. "I don't know. Let's find out." They approached the shop and spoke to the nearest person. "Excuse me, but why are you all milling about?"

A plump woman with grey hair and an oversized hat smiled at him. "Mr. Springer and Mr. Merriweather are hosting Bella Weaver of Bella Designs. She's working on a ball gown!"

"Imagine, Bella Weaver in Baker City!" another gushed. "It's so exciting!"

"Who is Bella Weaver?" Millie asked.

Bram was about to answer then snapped his mouth shut. A man of Bill Krantz's ilk wouldn't have any idea whom the famous dressmaker was. Bram of course knew. He'd purchased a Bella designed gown for his mother last year for her birthday. But he couldn't let Millie know that.

"Why, Bella Weaver is one of the most famous dressmakers in the country!" a woman said.

He looked at Millie. She stood, wide eyed, taking in the small crowd, and still hadn't a clue whom they were talking about.

"Come on, sweetie, let's get to the office." He led her two doors down, unlocked the door and ushered her inside.

Chapter Eleven

Millie surveyed the cramped office, and her heart went out to Bram. "Is this what your other office was like?"

She ran a gloved finger over the desk. It was covered with dust. She wiped the finger on the skirt of her dress then gave him an expectant look.

Bram was staring back. "I… I know it's not much." He looked around. "But it was what I could afford." He stepped her way. "You won't think less of me?"

Her eyes rounded to saucers. "Of course not. I want to help you with your business. I could act as your secretary. I could write letters for you, help you with accounts. I'm very good with numbers, and the best part is you wouldn't have to pay me and…"

He took her by the hands and pulled her toward him. "No, I want you to fix up our home. Can you do that for me?"

He tugged her closer, until she stood flush against him. She could feel the heat of his body, and liked how he smelled of leather, soap, and a spicy scent she could not identify. "Yes, I can do that."

He lifted her hands to his lips and kissed them. "Good. But since you're here you can help me straighten the place up."

She looked around. "It could do with a good dusting."

He nodded as he looked her in the eyes. Millie wasn't sure if it was a look of admiration, or the fact his mere presence made her senses reel. But her heart did something in that moment, and she knew she was beginning to fall for him.

"Do you have a dust rag or a feather duster?" she asked in a soft voice.

He closed his eyes and made a small sound. When he opened them, he tucked a finger under her chin, tilted her face to his, and kissed her.

Millie immediately melted against him. She couldn't help it. He drew her like a moth to a flame, and she reveled in the fact she was married to this wonderful man.

When he broke the kiss he drew back, and her heart stopped. Was that regret in his eyes? "Bram?"

He shook his head. "We should get to work." He let her go and turned away. "I thought I saw a feather duster around here somewhere."

She swallowed hard as disappointment filled her. *It's not that he didn't like your kiss, Millie,* she silently scolded. *Nor is he disappointed in you. We have work to do, and he knows that. This is not the time or place for sparking!*

Millie licked her lips as he continued his search. She could still feel his lips on hers and

519

didn't want the sensation to go away. She could fall hard for this man, her husband, and wanted to let her heart have its way. But he was still a stranger, and she needed to take her time and get to know him. He also needed time to get to know her. She didn't want to try to please him at every turn the way she used to with Father. Nothing ever came of it. He still gambled his life away, just as he did hers and Mother's.

"Here," Bram said and handed her a feather duster. "I'm going to organize my bookshelves."

She took the feather duster from him and watched him go to a bookshelf. She noticed several crates of books on the floor and studied them. "Is that your library?"

He tapped a crate with his foot. "Yes, such as it is. Also the accounts of past clients I should bring to the house for storage. There's no use having them here." He picked up a stack of new ledger books. "These are for my future clients."

She smiled and started dusting the desk. "I'm sure you'll have many."

A group of people began to walk by. "Looks like the tailor shooed away all the people outside his shop." He joined her at the window. "Perhaps the shop is closing."

She gasped. "Really? What time is it?"

He pulled out his pocket watch. "Four-thirty."

"Oh, I'm sorry. I should have stayed home and gone for supplies."

"Ruggles & Son is only a couple of blocks away. We can get what we need there when we're done here."

"Will they still be open?"

"Yes, they don't close until six."

She smiled and got back to work. Millie noticed Bram glancing her way now and then. Sometimes she'd catch him smiling, the rest of the time, she couldn't read his expression. As if he didn't want her to know what he was thinking. She hoped he hadn't just spent all his money on her. One of her new dresses was more expensive than the others, and she hoped it wasn't something he considered an extravagance.

She thought of what the women from the tailor's shop said. If this Bella Weaver was a famous dressmaker, Millie could only imagine what she charged for a dress.

She tried not to think about it as she dusted the desk then started on a small bookshelf behind it.

Bram was removing books from the crates and stacking them on the desk. While he did that, she quickly dusted the other bookshelves for him. He smiled at her as she maneuvered around him and went to the windows. "I can wash these for you."

He smiled at her. "I won't argue if you do. There's a small bathroom in the back. You'll find a bucket there. I believe there's some soap and a rag too."

Millie smiled and got to work. Once she had some water in the bucket with a bit of soap, she started washing windows.

As she worked, a beautiful woman with dark hair with a bit of gray at the temples walked by outside. She was on the arm of a huge, good-looking man. Behind them walked another couple. This man was shorter than the other but no less handsome and wore a pair of spectacles. The woman he was with had red hair and was very pretty. The women's outfits were well made, and she wondered if one of them was the famous dressmaker. "Oh, my…"

"What is it?" Bram asked.

She got back to work on the windows. "I think the dressmaker just walked by." She craned her neck as she tried to see.

Bram laughed at her attempts. "Why not go outside?" He crossed the room to the door and stepped out.

Millie followed and stood beside him They watched the two couples as they continued down the boardwalk.

"I bet they're heading for the livery stable or the general store," Bram said.

"How do you know?"

He shrugged. "Other than a café, those are the only other business down that way."

She nodded but didn't say anything. She was too busy taking in the outfits of the two women. "Maybe you'll get to meet this famous dressmaker while she's here."

He looked at her and to her surprise, took one of her hands in his. "Would you like a fancy dress? Like the kind those women are wearing?"

Her heart skipped. Not because of the question, but because of the tender look he was giving her. "Pretty clothes are nice, but not what I need."

Bram cocked his head. "What do you mean?"

She gave him a tiny shrug. "There are the things I want, and then there are things I need. You are what I need, Bram. Not a fancy dress."

His eyes roamed her face a moment. "Mrs. Ruggles is holding a ball. What if I got us an invitation?"

She half laughed, half scoffed at the suggestion. "Us? At a fancy ball?"

"I could find a lot of potential clients at a ball like that."

Her jaw dropped. "You could?"

He nodded. "I could." He bent to her. "Would you care to go to a ball, milady?"

Her heart skipped and her belly flipped! "Yes."

Bram smiled, escorted her back inside, and kissed her like a prince kissing his princess. And that is when Millie vowed to herself to be the best wife she could possibly be.

Chapter Twelve

Bram was a heel for kissing her again. But he couldn't help himself. Millie was so appreciative of what he was doing for her and their home. Maybe he was getting too caught up in his role as her husband.

"Is that the general store up ahead?" she asked as they walked down the street.

"Yes. The Ruggles own the store and the livery stable. They have a decent selection of goods."

She smiled at him, the beginnings of trust in her eyes.

This was bad, oh so bad. He'd already gone too far. Now what was he going to do other than avoid her as much as possible until the assignment was complete?

They entered the general store and saw the two couples that passed by his office earlier.

Millie took one look at them then looked away. "We should give the storekeeper our list."

Bram put his hand to the small of her back and steered her to the counter at the back of the building. The younger Mr. Ruggles was there, speaking with the two couples. They stopped talking as he and Millie approached.

Bram smiled at them. "Mr. Ruggles. Can we trouble you to take care of our list?"

"Not at all," Mr. Ruggles said. "You rented the space a couple of doors down from Mr. Springer's tailor shop, didn't you?"

"That's right," Bram said. "I'm opening a bookkeeping service."

"How nice," the red-headed woman said.

"I work with Mr. Springer," the shorter of the two men said and offered Bram his hand. "Ives Merriweather. This is my wife, Lystra."

"Bill Krantz. And this is my wife, Millie." He looked at the other couple and smiled.

The woman, who had to be Bella Weaver, considering her clothes, was stunning. Her husband, a big, burly fellow, stepped toward him and extended his hand. "Calvin Weaver. This here is Bella. Nice to meet ya."

Bram took the hand offered, and Mr. Weaver gave it more than a healthy shake. Bram didn't wonder if the brute could rip his arm right off.

"It's a pleasure to meet you all," Bram said politely. "So, you were the cause of the crowd milling about on the boardwalk earlier?"

Calvin stuck his hands in his pockets. "Shucks, we're sorry about that. Happens whenever we go visitin' other towns and cities."

"That's quite alright," Bram said. "I'm not officially open for business yet."

"But you will be," Mr. Merriweather said. "And we'd hate to see the crowds outside the shop interrupt your work."

"How long are you planning to be here?" Bram asked. It was a logical question, all things considered, and he might be able to use it to his advantage.

"Until the Ruggles' ball," Bella said. "I am making a gown designed by Mr. Merriweather here."

Bram smiled at them. "You design for women as well?"

"I've just started," Mr. Merriweather said. "This is my first gown."

"And it will be stunning," Bella added with a smile.

"They're revealing it at my mother's ball," Mr. Ruggles said. "It's the talk of the town."

"We heard some women mention it at The Emporium earlier this afternoon," Millie said in a soft voice.

Bram glanced at her. She was blushing. He looped her arm around one of his. "Sounds like it will be quite the affair if it's stirring that much talk."

"Oh, trust me," Mr. Ruggles said. "It is."

Bram smiled and looked at the floor. "I'm afraid Millie and I are both new in town and don't know anyone yet. You'll excuse us if we're ignorant of the goings on around here."

Mr. Ruggles smiled. "Think nothing of it. In fact, why don't you come?"

Millie gasped. "T-to your ball?"

"Yes, since you're new it will give the two of you a wonderful opportunity to meet some people, have a nice evening, and even things out when it comes to my mother's guest list."

Bram's eyebrows shot up in question. "Guest list?"

Mr. Ruggles sighed. "Yes, my mother seems to think she's still in Baltimore." He gave them a playful eye roll. "It's a long story. Suffice to say, I'm extending both of you an invitation. After all, you're part of the neighborhood."

Millie looked at Bram with a big smile. "What do you think?"

I think you're the sweetest woman I know… "Um, of course we'll go."

"Wonderful," Mr. Ruggles said. "Now, about your list." He perused it and began to gather what he needed.

"Lystra and I should get going," Mr. Merriweather said. "James, we'll see you tomorrow. I'll hitch up Bobbin."

"If you give me a minute, I can do it for you," Mr. Ruggles called over his shoulder.

"No need. It's the least I can do." Mr. Merriweather steered his wife toward the door.

"Tomorrow then," Mr. Ruggles called after him.

Bram noted the Weavers hovering near the counter. It was obvious they were waiting to speak to Mr. Ruggles.

"Bram?" Millie said softly beside him.

"Yes, sweetie?"

"I… I'm afraid we didn't think this through."

He bent toward her. "What do you mean?"

She glanced at the Weavers and back. "Do you own any evening wear?"

He stiffened and also looked at the Weavers. Of course he owned evening wear. Unfortunately, it was all in Washington. "Oh, dear…"

She got closer. "And I haven't a ball gown."

Bella's eyes flicked her way. Bram caught her looking at Millie, then steered her toward the front entrance. "I'll see if I can catch Mr. Merriweather. Wait here." He handed her some money to pay for their supplies, then hurried out the door.

Mr. Merriweather was hitching up a buggy to a bay horse. "Excuse me, Mr. Merriweather?"

"Yes?" He stopped what he was doing and smiled at Bram. "Can I help you?"

"Yes, I'm afraid I need evening wear for the ball. Can you fit me into your schedule?"

He rubbed his chin thoughtfully then patted the horse on the neck. "Can you come by first thing in the morning so I can get some measurements?"

"Yes, of course."

"Good, I can squeeze in one more suit."

"Thank you." Bram glanced at the store. "Millie will need a gown. Is there any place other than The Emporium that might have something nice she can wear?"

"There are a couple of dressmakers in town," Mr. Merriweather said. "Mrs. Jones, and a Mrs. Fenton. I believe Mrs. Jones is still taking orders. The ball is a week from Saturday, so it will be cutting things close. I'd see if she's still at her shop. It's on Fourth Street."

"Thank you, we'll head there now." He tipped his hat and returned to the general store. He was making progress. Mr. Kameyer would be at the ball, and who knew how many of his associates? It would be the perfect place to gather information. In the meantime, he'd best make sure he got Millie a gown to wear.

523

Chapter Thirteen

Almost a week went by since Bram accepted Mr. Ruggles invitation. Millie was so nervous about going to the ball, she could barely concentrate on fixing things up around the house. Bram had been so busy getting his office ready and meeting with new clients, she barely saw him. No matter, things would settle down after the ball and maybe they'd have more time to themselves.

"Stand still, Mrs. Krantz," Mrs. Jones scolded. "I'm not done pinning the hem."

"Sorry," Millie said. She wrung her hands a few times. It was late afternoon, and she only had one more day to prepare. "Will my gown be ready in time?"

"Yes, now hold still." The dressmaker pinned another section of hem as Millie stared at the woman in the full-length mirror. She'd never seen herself look so beautiful. "I hope Bram likes it."

Mrs. Jones, who had to be sixty if she was a day, smiled up at her. "Trust me, my dear. You'll take his breath away."

She blushed and noted the red creeping up her neck into her cheeks. The off the shoulder gown was white with light pink lace. Tiny pink ribbons decorated the bodice and the front of the skirt. It was the prettiest thing she'd ever worn. Mercy, how was she going to style her hair? It was one more thing to figure out.

When Mrs. Jones was done, Millie thanked her, changed into the new blue day dress Bram purchased for her, and left the dressmaker's shop. She was only a few blocks from Bram's office and decided to pay him a visit. Neither of them really knew anyone in town yet, and she thought he might like some company for lunch.

When she arrived at the office, she noted two men seated on the other side of Bram's desk, so slipped into the tailor's a couple of doors down. She'd see if Bram's suit was ready, then report back to him.

"Mrs. Krantz," Mr. Merriweather said. "How lovely to see you. Are you here about your husband's suit?"

Millie didn't answer right away. The word "husband" hung in the air, and she smiled. "Yes. How is it coming along?"

"Splendidly. Do you think he can come before closing and try it on? I want to see if it needs any last-minute adjustments."

"Of course, I'll let him know." She heard voices come from the back of the shop, including several women's voices, and wondered how many people were back there.

Mr. Merriweather glanced over his shoulder. "It's a little crowded in the workroom. It's one of the reasons I'm up front." He cracked a smile. "Tell me, have you and Mr. Krantz ventured out to Fiddler's Gap?"

"Fiddler's Gap? Where is that?"

"About eight miles out of town, it's where I live. We have a town orchestra and are building an auditorium to hold concerts in."

"Really? How lovely. But eight miles…"

"We're working on getting the railroad to come through. It would connect Baker City and Fiddler's Gap, making the trip quick and easy."

"That would be wonderful. Is Fiddler's Gap very big?"

"Not exactly, but we're growing." He smiled again and sighed. "I should get back to work. Please tell your husband to come see me before he goes home."

"I will." She gave him a parting nod and left the shop. When she strolled back to Bram's office, he was alone. Good, she could deliver Mr. Merriweather's message, and join him for lunch.

"Millie," he said with a smile when she stepped inside. "What are you doing here?" He left his chair and came around the desk. "What a nice surprise." He pulled her into his arms. And kissed her.

She closed her eyes as he held her. Sometimes she didn't want him to let go. They had yet to consummate their marriage, and part of her worried about that, but the other part would scold her and tell her they were both tired.

"I just came from a fitting with Mrs. Jones. My gown will be ready tomorrow.

I also stopped in at the tailor shop. Mr. Merriweather wants you to come by after work and try on your suit."

He leaned against his desk and stared at her, as if seeing her for the first time.

"Is something wrong?" she asked.

Bram shook his head. "Other than you're so lovely?"

She swallowed hard. He'd been saying things like that more and more, and each time he did, she swore she saw regret in his eyes. "Are you… working late?"

"I might. I'm sorry I haven't been home with you in the evenings." He took her by the hand. "But we'll have the ball, and we can dance all night."

She blanched. "Dance?"

"It's a ball, silly, of course we'll dance."

"Oh… I… don't know a lot of dances."

He frowned. "You don't?"

"No, we never attended social functions." *Because Father had such a bad reputation*, but she wasn't going to tell him that. It was all in the past, and she wanted to keep moving forward in this new life of hers.

"Well, we'll dance all the ones you know, and maybe I can teach you a new one."

"How? The ball is the day after tomorrow?"

Before she could say anything, Charlie, one of the witnesses from their wedding popped through the door. "Krantz, boss wants to see ya."

"Now?" Bram said with a frown.

"Yep, wants ya to head out to the ranch and bring yer ledger with ya."

Bram sighed. "Very well." He gave his attention back to Millie. "I'm sorry. I must go."

"But your suit?" she reminded him.

"Yes, that also has to be taken care of." He turned to Charlie. "I'll need a few moments. There's something I need to take care of."

"Fine, but don't take too long," Charlie said. "I got the buckboard and need to pick a few things up at Ruggles & Son. Meet me there in twenty minutes."

Bram gave him a nod. "I will."

Millie watched Charlie leave then cocked her head. "He expects you to close up shop in the middle of the day and run out to the Double K Ranch?"

Bram shrugged. "Mr. Kameyer is my main client. I don't want to disappoint him." He kissed her on the cheek. "Don't wait up for me."

"What?" She gaped at him. "How long does it take to show the man how he's spending his money?"

Bram pulled a ledger off the bookshelf behind his desk. "Mr. Kameyer is a very particular man."

"Well, he's a little too particular if you ask me. Keeping you to himself all afternoon and into the night. Good heavens, what do you do out there?" This was the third time Bram had gone to the Double K since they married. Each time he didn't come home until late.

"Like I said, he's a particular man."

Millie crossed her arms. "I swear he spends more time with you than I do."

Bram smiled. "Not to worry. Now get on home. I'll see you tomorrow morning."

She let go a frustrated sigh. "We need to order a new bed…"

"Yes, and I told you I'd take care of it." He pulled another ledger book off the shelf and stuffed it into a leather satchel.

"Very well, but please don't forget again."

He gave her a wink and a smile. "I won't."

Millie nodded, kissed him on the cheek, then went out the door. She realized she didn't give him a chance to kiss her back, and turned around in time to see him sigh in relief through his office window.

Millie backed up as her heart sank. Was he glad she left? She turned and started up the boardwalk, passing Mr. Springer's tailor shop and several others before she got her wits about her. When she reached the end of the block she stopped and turned around. Bram left the shop and went into the tailor's.

"Well, at least he's doing what he said he would." Millie narrowed her eyes. She shouldn't have to convince herself that Bram wasn't up to no good. But old habits die hard, and she'd spent far too many nights being suspicious of her father's comings and goings, that she was doing the same thing with poor Bram.

"You are being ridiculous, Millie. Stop it." With a swish of skirt, she turned and started for home.

Chapter Fourteen

At home, Millie puttered around the house and worked on the dining room. She put up the new curtains, ironed the new tablecloth and spread it on the table, then took an inventory of what they still needed. They hadn't had a chance to do any more shopping, and she figured it was best to wait anyway. She hadn't discussed money with Bram yet, and didn't know how he handled his. She didn't know if he had money saved, or if he owned land or property anywhere. How many living relatives did he have? For Heaven's sake, she didn't even know if he had any siblings.

She sat at the dining room table, a frown on her face. Her new husband had been so busy they hadn't had time to have a decent conversation. And what was he doing out at the Double K that took so long? Surely Bram and Mr. Kameyer weren't going over the ranch's books this whole time?

Millie left her chair and paced. Why would Charlie come fetch Bram to the ranch, anyway? Oh, right. "Because Mr. Kameyer is particular," she said in a low voice. She sighed and retook her chair. She was bored and wondered if she should eat then take an evening stroll.

Millie fixed herself something for dinner, did the dishes, then went into the bedroom and looked at the rickety bed. Bram insisted it wouldn't hold both of them and had to be replaced. Well, fine. Now if he'd stop forgetting to order a new one, they could finally share a bed as husband and wife.

Out of pure frustration, she kicked the bed, stubbing her toe in the process. "Ouch!" She sat on the bed to rub her foot. The frame creaked and groaned, and she had to admit, Bram was right. The bed might not hold their combined weight.

She rubbed her foot through her shoe and to distract herself, wondered what sort of curtains would look good in the bedroom. She'd spent most of her time working on the kitchen and parlor, and today the dining room. She hadn't done much of anything in here.

Millie left the bed and opened the armoire. She'd dusted it before she hung up her new dresses, but wondered if she shouldn't give it a good polishing.

She bent to the drawer at the bottom and opened it. There were more old shirts of Bram's and a cigar box. She picked it up, opened it, and gasped. "What the…?"

She pulled out different folded pieces of paper. Several of which had IOU written on them, followed by a sum of money.

Millie dropped them like they were spiders and slammed the lid shut. "No." She got to her feet. "No, it can't be."

She shut her eyes and forced herself to think. "He's holding IOUs so someone owes him money?" Millie's hand flew to her mouth. What did it matter? Bram was gambling!

Her other hand went to her mouth to stifle a sob. How could he?!

Millie let her hands drop and took a deep breath, then another. "Don't panic, it might not be what you think."

She knelt on the floor and picked up the cigar box again. "Maybe they're old." She dumped the contents on the floor and picked out all the IOUs. She found a few notes about money Bram owed different men. The amounts and names written not only on the IOUs, but in a small notepad. "Ever the bookkeeper," she muttered. Millie looked at the notepad more closely. "This isn't Bram's handwriting," she mused aloud. "If it's not his, then whose is it?"

She leafed through the notebook, and saw more names, including the names of towns and cities. "Don't tell me this is a list of all the places you've gambled." Tears stung the backs of her eyes as she perused the list. "Oh, no. Please, not Bram. I can't lose anyone else to gambling, I just can't!"

Heartbroken, she tossed the notebook back in the box, shoved it into the drawer, and closed it.

Millie got to her feet, her heart in her throat, and did her best not to cry. She sat on the bed, ignoring the creaking springs, and stared at the wall. A familiar numbness took hold, and she wasn't sure what to do. She'd been married two weeks, and they'd been the best two weeks of her life. In part because she now *had a life*. One she could call her own and direct where she wanted it to go.

Or so she thought.

Millie shut her eyes against the tears that threatened. Father's gambling had destroyed everything she held dear, and she had to go and marry a man just like him!

She left the bed. "No!" she shook her head. "I won't go through that again. I won't!" For lack of a better idea, she stomped her foot in defiance.

But for all her bluster, the tears still came, and soon she found herself face down on her pillow unable to stop the flood of disappointment and anger that gripped her.

Chapter Fifteen

Bram entered the house well after midnight. Charlie brought him back to town before dark, but then insisted they play a few games at one of the local saloons. Thankfully, it wasn't the one where Krantz had been cheating at cards.

Unfortunately, two games turned into four, four into eight and so on. At least he won fair and square, and it made his cover stronger. A few men he'd played with at the other saloon joined their game and no one made any comments about cheating or otherwise. Well, he did receive a few congratulations on his recent marriage.

All in all, this assignment was coming along. Mr. Kameyer offered the expected bribe tonight, and Bram took it. The envelope with the bribe money was stashed in the inside pocket of his jacket, and he'd find a place to hide it when he got home. It was evidence, after all.

He gathered his winnings and looked at his pocket watch. It was almost midnight. "I'm afraid I must depart, gentlemen. Can't keep the wife waiting you know."

"You're departing with our money, Krantz," one of the players said. "The least you could do is give us a chance to win some of it back seeing as how you get to go home to a beautiful woman."

He smiled. "That she is." He stuffed his winnings in his pockets and stood. "Charlie, are you going to make it back to the ranch all right?"

"Sure, it's almost a full moon. Plenty of light to see by." Charlie left his chair. "I'd best mosey along too. Wish I had me a pretty gal to go home to. But wouldn't do to keep one in the bunkhouse."

The men laughed and a few even waved as they left. Outside Charlie peered up at him.

"The boss will be happy to know ya didn't gamble away all that money he done give ya."

Bram arched an eyebrow. "Why Charlie, did you get me to play to see if I'd gamble it all away?"

"Well, ya do have a reputation, Krantz."

He shrugged. "Fair point. But now that I'm a married man, I'm trying to be more respectable."

"Just so long as ya don't become too respectable," Charlie laughed and elbowed him in the ribs.

Bram frowned at him. "No, of course not. Mr. Kameyer and I came to a mutual understanding regarding my role as the ranch's bookkeeper."

Charlie eyed him. "Good. Cause the boss plans to add a few fillies to the stable. Can't have things looking suspicious."

Bram nodded. "So, Mr. Kameyer has branched into um… buying and selling horses?"

Charlie laughed. "More like breeding 'em, all depends on how ya look at it." He slapped Bram on the back and headed for the buckboard. "See ya later, Krantz. Best hide that money from the missus, or she'll be askin' where ya got it."

"I will." He gave Charlie a wave and headed in the other direction. Good grief! This was worse than he thought. There was money passing through the Double K all right, but it wasn't from cattle, and he could bet it had nothing to do with horses.

Jules was right. This was a slaver's operation. Was it that crazy Persian slaver Sal, or someone else?

He'd have to get word to Jules and Quincy. He was going to need help if it was Sal. The fiend often had a small army at his disposal.

He made it home and quietly entered the house. Hungry, he went to the kitchen, grabbed an apple from a bowl, and ate it. He was too frustrated to sleep, and wondered if Millie was still up. He doubted it, but he'd check anyway.

He peeked into the bedroom. She was sound asleep, her breathing even. He carefully closed the door. For some reason, he didn't like the look of her alone in the bed and reminded himself he'd have to order her a new one soon. He was running out of excuses not to. But if he timed things right, he could order one, and it would arrive as he was finishing up his assignment. Then she'd have a new bed.

He smiled at the thought, got ready for bed himself, and settled onto the sofa in the parlor. It took him a while to fall asleep, and right before he did, his last thoughts were of Millie sleeping.

The night of the ball had a slight chill to it but that was all right, Bram had purchased a cloak for Millie to wear so she wouldn't get cold. He rented a horse and buggy from James Ruggles, and again thanked him for the invitation. If his guess was right, Sal might have a man attending the ball tonight. One on the lookout for potential merchandise.

He narrowed his eyes at the thought as they pulled up in front of the Ruggles' home.

"Goodness," Millie breathed. "Such a big house."

"I've seen bigger," he said without thinking. He silently chastised himself, then realized she'd grown quiet. She'd been quiet all day, and hardly spoke a word to him as they readied themselves for the night's festivities.

"Are you okay?" he asked.

Millie stared straight ahead. "Of course. What makes you think something's wrong?"

"You're quiet this evening." He cocked his head. "Are you… mad about something?"

Her eyes darted to him and back. "I'd rather not discuss it."

He sighed. "Millie, I'm sorry I came home so late last night…"

She held up a hand. "I said I'd rather not talk about it. Now if you don't mind, I'd like to go inside."

"Of course." He drove past the house, found a place to park the buggy, and got out. After helping Millie down, he offered her his arm and escorted her to the front of the house. A woman in her forties stood with a younger woman at her side. They looked like a mother and daughter. Was that James Ruggles' mother?

"Good evening," the woman greeted. "We're so happy you could…" She stopped and looked them over. "I don't believe I know you."

"You don't," Bram stated. "Allow me to introduce myself. I'm Bill Krantz and this is my wife, Millie."

"How do you do," Millie said pleasantly.

The woman narrowed her eyes at them. "I'm sorry, but you're not familiar to me."

"We just moved here," Bram said. He wasn't going to explain they came to town separately then married.

"I see," the woman said as she scrutinized Millie's gown. "I'm Mrs. Thorndyke Hinkle, and this is my daughter, Alice. I'm sure you'll meet my husband inside."

Bram gave her a slight bow. "I look forward to it." He smiled at Millie then escorted her inside.

They entered the grand foyer, and Millie's eyes rounded to saucers. "It's so big."

"Indeed, it is." He thought of his town house. Its foyer was bigger.

He patted Millie's hand and followed several other couples up a grand staircase. They must have an attic ballroom.

On the third floor, Mr. and Mrs. Ruggles were greeting their guests. He recognized Mr. Ruggles from the livery stable and general store. Mr. Ruggles introduced him to his wife, and after the rest of the introductions were made, Bram and Millie entered the ballroom. It was time to get to work.

Chapter Sixteen

Millie took in her surroundings with no small amount of awe. She'd never seen such a pretty room. Flowers were festooned from one wall to the other overhead, while huge vases of flowers were placed atop white, sculpted flower stands spaced along each wall with the occasional refreshment table in between. Musicians were seated upon a dais at the far end of the room, and the dance floor was filled with guests milling about, talking. The entire scene made her forget how upset she was with Bram. But she wasn't ready to speak to him about what was in the armoire just yet. Still, she would have to confront him at some point. But tonight, she wanted to enjoy herself.

She watched the guests wandering about, talking and laughing. "Bram, why is no one dancing?"

He glanced at the entrance to the ballroom. "Because we're waiting for the mystery guests to arrive."

Her face screwed up with confusion. "What?"

He smiled. "Ives told me all about it."

"Mr. Merriweather?"

"Yes. Two of tonight's guests will be wearing the suit and gown Ives designed."

"Oh, I see. So, we're waiting on them."

"Exactly." He scanned the guests around them.

"Are you looking for someone?" she asked.

"No," he said quickly. "Just wondering if there are folks here I've seen around town."

Millie decided to look too. "I see Mrs. Jones over there, and the other dressmaker, Mrs. Fenton at a refreshment table."

"Of course they'd be here," he said.

The musicians played a fanfare, and all heads turned toward the ballroom's entrance. Bella Weaver swept in on the arm of her husband wearing a fabulous dark blue ball gown.

Millie's breath hitched. "Will you look at that? Isn't her gown beautiful?"

"Indeed." He bent to her. "And so is yours."

Mille couldn't help her shy smile or the blush creeping into her cheeks. She responded to him, always, and couldn't seem to help herself.

Another fanfare played and James Ruggles entered the ballroom with a young woman Millie had never seen before. She was petite like she was and wore an incredible gown of light pink. It was covered with tiny roses, had a scooped neck and short sleeves. It was a little like her own dress. "Oh, Bram. She looks like a princess!"

"That she does." He tightened his hold on her arm. "You're my princess."

Millie blushed again. Blast it, why was it so hard to stay mad at him? But if he was gambling, they had to talk. She swore to herself she'd never be with someone who gambled. But Bram was handsome, clean shaven, respectable looking. She wanted to marry him before he changed his mind. But now…

"Come on, let's see if we can get a closer look at that gown." Bram took her by the hand and used his tall frame to get through. People parted for them and soon they were near the couple.

Women were fawning over the young woman as men scrutinized the suit James Ruggles wore. "Fantastic," one man said. "I never would have thought a gold waistcoat would work, but it does."

"The gown is incredible!" a woman gushed. "You must be very proud to wear it, my dear."

The young lady wearing the gown blushed a deep red and nodded.

Millie smiled at her. "You're beautiful."

The woman's blushed deepened. "Th-thank you."

Millie looked over the gown and smiled at Bella Weaver as she came to stand beside the couple. She spied the Merriweathers nearby. Men were speaking to Ives and Mr. Springer, who stood a few feet away. From the sounds of their conversations, they were ordering suits.

Millie noticed some women making their way to Bella. Were they going to place orders for a gown?

"Magnificent," Bram said beside her. "Aren't you glad we came?"

She nodded as more people pressed in to get a look at the couple.

"Come, sweetie, we'd best let others get a look. Care for some punch?"

She nodded and let him lead them toward the nearest refreshment table. There were advantages to having a tall husband with broad shoulders.

As soon as they had their punch, she noticed James and his young lady had moved to the edge of the dance floor. "What's going on?"

"They'll dance the first dance to show off the gown, then the rest of us can join in."

The music started, a waltz, and James began dancing with the young lady. "Who is she?" Millie asked.

"Judging from the conversations around us, she's the daughter of the woman that greeted us outside the house. Mrs. Hinkle?"

She gazed up at him. "You learned that from eavesdropping?"

He gave her a playful eyeroll. "I wasn't eavesdropping. It's all anyone's talking about."

"I suppose…"

He drained his glass. "Finish your punch, and when the signal is given, we can dance."

She gasped. "Now?!"

"Don't worry, I'll help you."

"Oh, Bram… no…"

"Millie," he said softly. "You'll be fine. Besides, everyone's eyes will be on Miss Hinkle's gown."

She drew in a breath. "Very well." Millie finished her punch and set the glass down.

"That's my girl." Bram put his hand to the small of her back and steered her toward the edge of the dance floor. The music ended, and within moments, started again. "Ah, just as I thought," Bram said. "Another waltz. We'll dance along the outer part of the dance floor."

She nodded. If she stumbled, they might be less likely to bump into someone.

Bram gave her a quick lesson yesterday, so she knew a little of the waltz, but he was going to have to lead her carefully, or she would trip.

They began, and she concentrated on the steps, following his lead as best she could. Dancing with Bram was exhilarating, and she decided she wanted to learn how to dance properly. Even if they never attended another ball as long as they lived, they could always dance when the mood took them. Just as she and Mother used to do.

She blushed at the thought and pictured Bram dancing with her around the parlor and into the dining room. It would be fun!

Millie frowned when his blasted cigar box popped into her head. How much money did he owe? Who did he owe it to? Would the men come to collect? Would Bram come home battered and bruised like Father had on several occasions?

"Millie?"

She looked at him as the music ended and they stopped.

"Millie, what's wrong?" Bram asked.

Tears stung the backs of her eyes. How could he be like Father? So far, he'd been vastly different, but if he gambled, she knew what it could do to him over time.

"Millie, darling, you look upset…"

She shook her head. "I'll tell you later."

"You'll tell me now." He took her hand, and they left the dance floor. He guided her behind one of the decorative stands holding a huge vase of flowers. "Now, what has you looking so upset?"

She gulped. "I… well, I found…"

"Millie," he said gently, and her heart melted. Blast the man!

"Bram, I found your cigar box of IOUs." There, she said it.

He gaped at her. "Cigar box?"

Tears filled her eyes. "No, don't play dumb. Not with me. Please."

He looked at her in confusion. "Where did you find this cigar box?"

Millie told herself she'd remain calm. Then everything spilled out at once, and before she knew it, she was hurrying off to find the ladies' lounge area.

Chapter Seventeen

"Oh, Millie," Bram breathed as she made her escape. Unfortunately, she didn't let him get a word in edgewise. He'd hoped to keep the gambling side of his cover as far from her as possible. She was sensitive to the vice, as her father's gambling ruined her family. Now she thought his supposed gambling would ruin their marriage. But it wasn't a real marriage, and now he'd have to make the tough decision of whether to let her go on thinking he gambled or tell her the truth. Both would crush her, and he'd have to come up with something to get her through the rest of his assignment.

"I'll have to back off the card playing," he muttered.

"What was that Krantz?"

Bram turned to find Mr. Kameyer just behind him. "Good evening, sir."

"Evening," Mr. Kameyer said. "I didn't think I'd see you here."

Bram smiled at him. Mr. Kameyer was middle-aged, portly, with dark beady eyes. He wasn't looking at Bram with disdain, exactly, but was definitely surprised to see him. "James Ruggles extended my wife and me an invitation."

Mr. Kameyer's eyebrows rose. "That was nice of him. So, what do you think of Baker City's elite?"

Bram made a show of looking around. "They sure are fancy." Of course, where he was from, these people would be considered nothing but a bunch of country bumpkins.

"Ha, wait until I throw one of these shindigs at the ranch. I'll show this Mrs. Ruggles up and then some."

"And when might you be doing that?" Bram asked, curious.

"Not sure, but I'll get around to it. I've got too much business to take care of first. New fillies to be bought and sold."

Bram nodded and kept his mouth shut. Mr. Kameyer was watching him closely, and Bram decided he'd best change the subject. "What would Mrs. Kameyer have thought of Mrs. Ruggles' ball?"

The older man smiled. "She'd have loved it. She's been gone seven years now." He shook his head. "Such a shame."

"I'm sorry for your loss, sir," Bram said. He knew Mrs. Kameyer was killed when a gun misfired, but Bram didn't wonder if it was something more. He noticed Mr. Kameyer avoided telling him the details of his wife's death. Had he killed her? Did the woman find out about his little operation and threaten to tell the law? It was plausible.

"I suppose I'll take a gander at that suit," Mr. Kameyer said. He looked Bram in the eyes. "You play your cards right, and you'll be able to afford to buy that little wife of yours a gown like that." He winked at him and headed for James and Miss Hinkle, who were once again surrounded by admirers.

Bram sighed. He'd mention to Charlie and Monty that he was in trouble with his wife and would have to refrain from cards for a time. It was the easiest solution and would make Millie happy.

Bram made his way around the room before he checked on Millie. If Mr. Kameyer was here, then Sal might have a man here as well. He didn't think they'd be so bold as to target any of the young ladies, but one never knew.

It wasn't long before he ran into Monty. "Krantz!" Monty said and slapped him on him on the back. "What are you doing at this highfalutin party?"

He gave him a proud smile. "James Ruggles gave the wife and me a personal invitation."

"Well look at you, rubbing elbows with Baker City high society!"

Bram chuckled then plastered on a serious look. "Millie found my box of IOUs."

Monty's face fell. "What? Oh, that's too bad. What are you going to do?"

He frowned and gave him a helpless shrug. "The only thing I can do. I'm going to have to stop playing cards for a while until she settles down. Then I'll ease back into it." He winked at Monty.

"Ahhhh, I knew I liked you!" Monty put an arm around him. "Can't say I blame you though. Your Millie is a sweet looking thing. I'd hang onto that."

"I plan to."

Monty let his arm slide off Bram's shoulders. "Besides, you'll be making plenty of money with us." He gave him an exaggerated wink.

Bram smiled. "Yes, Charlie mentioned, as did Mr. Kameyer when I spoke to him a moment ago, about the fillies being bought and sold."

"Oh yeah," Monty said in a low voice. "We got a man here tonight making a transaction. But keep that to yourself. If the boss knew I told you, he'd have my head." He patted Bram on the chest. "I guess I'm a softie. No man ought to have to give up gambling for no woman. But seeing as how yours is such a pretty thing, you're the exception."

"Thanks, Monty. It's nice to know you understand."

He smacked his chest. "Sure I do!" He smiled and looked around. "Where is your wife?"

Bram gave him an exaggerated eye roll. "I suspect the ladies' lounge area. She informed me of her discovery, then took off."

Monty shook his head. "You did the right thing. Let the little lady blow off some steam first, then talk to her. Tell her you're sorry and all that and hope for the best." He shook his head again. "Me and Charlie are sure gonna miss having you in our games."

"It's only temporary," Bram assured.

Monty smacked his back again. "Thank goodness for that!"

Bram smiled and nodded as Monty sauntered off. As soon as he was gone, Bram surveyed the guests. So, one of Sal's men was here. He'd have to figure out who he was and fast. If the young lady being targeted was also in attendance, she might not make it home tonight. That is, if Sal's man planned on acquiring his target and moving her all in the same night.

He made his way around the room, listening to the different conversations going on, and caught sight of Ives and his wife Lystra speaking with James. There was no sign of Miss Hinkle. She was probably taking a little break from all the attention. Good, that meant she retreated to the ladies' lounge area as well. Maybe her gown would help take Millie's mind off things and she'd returned to the ball. He supposed the right thing to do would be to wait in the hall for her. But if he did that, he might miss something here. Still, the sooner she was on his arm again, the sooner he could get back to work. That, and he hated the thought of her getting so worked up, she caused herself a mischief.

Bram took one last look around the ballroom, noted James also leaving the ballroom, and left. He must be wondering what was taking Miss Hinkle so long. Had he said something to upset her?

Bram went to the second floor and followed the sound of women's voices. He stopped up short when he came upon a half dozen ladies sitting in chairs lining one side of the hallway. He didn't see Millie among them. "Excuse me, ladies. But I'm looking for my wife, Mrs. Krantz?"

One of the women sitting, looked at him. "She was here earlier, but said she needed some air."

"She went downstairs?" he clarified.

"Yes."

"Thank you." He started back down the hall. She was still angry. Worse, she might be wandering around alone outside, making her easy pickings for Sal's man.

Bram picked up the pace and hurried to the first floor and went out the front door.

A fancy carriage with a crest on the door was taking off, and he wondered to whom the carriage belonged. He pushed the thought aside and began to look for his wife. "Millie?" He went around the side of the house. Carriages and buggies were everywhere. "Millie!"

He came upon a gate, opened it, and followed a path to the backyard and gardens. Millie sat on a bench near a fountain. "Millie, sweetheart, what are you doing back here all by yourself?"

She glanced up at him, swallowed hard, then looked away.

Bram sighed. There was no help for it. He was going to have to kiss her worries away.

Chapter Eighteen

Millie sat, her throat tight. She'd worked herself up into a fine state. She was angry, hurt, and felt betrayed. She couldn't let this go.

"Millie…" Bram said gently and sat beside her. "What's wrong?"

"You know what's wrong." If he didn't, he was an idiot.

He took one of her hands in his. "Millie, darling, if this is about the IOUs…"

"Of course it is." She met his concerned gaze with agonized eyes. "You lied to me."

His eyebrows knit. "What?"

"When I asked if you gambled, you said you did no more than any other man. That answer was… vague. My father gambled to the point of his own detriment. It killed him and ruined us."

Regret filled his eyes, and he scooted closer. "Millie, I'll take care of my IOUs, then won't gamble anymore, if that's what you want."

She squeezed her eyes shut. How many times had she heard Father tell Mother the same thing? But he never stopped.

Millie shook her head. "It is what I want but…"

"Then consider it done, sweetheart." His voice was so gentle it was almost her undoing. But she had to stand her ground.

"Bram, how long have you been gambling?" She met his gaze again, tears in her eyes.

He swallowed hard as he looked at her, then took her in his arms. "I've gambled with more than cards, love. But I can't tell you anything more, not yet. But I promise I will. I can't stand seeing you like this. Your heart torn asunder." He pulled her closer, causing her head to tilt back. "Millie," he whispered against her mouth.

Her eyes closed, her heart hammering in her chest. Blast if her heart and everything else didn't respond to him. How could he affect her so?

"Millie," he said again, then kissed her.

Her body erupted with gooseflesh as he deepened the kiss, and before she knew it, she was kissing him back.

Millie's arms went around his neck, her fingers twining in his hair. A low moan escaped him, and he held her tighter, deepening the kiss.

Millie melted against him, seeking the safety of his arms. She needed this yet feared it. Was it all a ruse to fool her into thinking he'd stop? She didn't want to trust him, but her resolve was cracking.

When Bram finally broke the kiss, he looked into her eyes. "I'm sorry if I've caused you duress, Millie." His voice was a soft whisper against her cheek. "Forgive me."

Tears spilled from her eyes. She wanted to forgive him. But her fear of being disappointed was too great. "Prove it."

Bram drew away to look at her. "You don't believe me."

"No," she choked out. "I don't."

He cupped her face with both hands and wiped her tears away with his thumbs. "I can't say I blame you after all you've been through. But everything will work out, you'll see."

She blinked back tears. It was an odd statement, and she was unsure of what he meant by it. Before she could ask, he pulled her to her feet. "Did you wish to return inside, or shall I take you home?"

She sniffed back tears. "Please, take me home."

"Of course." He looped her arm through his and escorted her to their buggy. Once they were settled, they started for home. "I'll drop you off, then return the horse and buggy to the livery stable."

She nodded. "You'll come straight home?"

"Yes, Millie. You needn't worry." He put a hand on her leg and gave it a gentle pat. "I am not your father."

She sniffed, even though she had no tears, and wiped at her nose with the handkerchief she kept in her cloak's pocket. "I don't want you to be, Bram. That's the last thing I want."

"I know," he said.

They drove to the house in silence. When they arrived, he helped her down, escorted her inside, then left to return the horse and buggy.

Millie went into the bedroom and numbly got out of her gown and went through her nightly routine. Once again, she'd be sleeping alone in their bed, while Bram slept in the parlor. If she didn't know any better, she'd say he was avoiding sharing their bed with her. But it *was* rickety and might collapse with the two of them on it. Still, she couldn't help what she felt.

By the time she crawled into bed, fresh tears threatened. She thought of Bram's kisses, the way he held her, the safety she found in his arms. Everything felt so right, yet at the same time, something was off, and she couldn't figure out what it was.

Millie didn't know how long she slept before she awoke to the sound of men's voices outside her window. One of them sounded like Bram's. She didn't dare move, or the squeaking bed would alert Bram that she was awake. So, she lay there, quiet as a mouse, and tried to listen. He hadn't just come from a card game, had he?

"…you're going to have to figure something out, Bram."

"I know. I just can't stand to see such hurt in her eyes."

"She still knows nothing?"

"Yes. And I plan on keeping things that way until this is done. The less she knows the better, I don't want her to get hurt."

There was silence for a moment, and Millie wondered if they'd walked to the front of the house.

"You're falling for her," the other voice said.

More silence.

"You… might be right, Quincy. She's so… vulnerable. She needs a man to protect her. I…"

"She's to be compensated, remember. She'll be fine."

"Will she?" Bram said. "With Sal's men in the area? No, she's exactly the sort they take."

"We've put a stop to Sal's schemes before, we'll do it again. And this time, we'll keep those slavers from coming back to America. They'll not steal any more of our people."

Millie thought she heard Bram sigh, but her mind had latched onto one word. Slavers. She put a hand over her mouth to stifle the gasp threatening to escape.

"I hope you're right. Those vile fiends have caused enough trouble here."

"You're good then?" the other man asked. "You'll finish the assignment?"

"Yeah, I'm good. I just want to make sure Millie's protected. I don't want her getting wrapped up in this."

"Then keep quiet, don't blow your cover. I'm counting on you. So is Jules and the president."

"I'll do my best. Kameyer told me someone was at the ball tonight. An American associate is my guess. They have their sights on one of the young ladies attending. I'm sorry, but Millie was upset, and I had to take care of her…"

"Like I said," spoke the other man, cutting him off. "You're falling for her. Otherwise you would have tried to find out who it was."

Bram heaved a sigh. "You're right."

Millie's eyes widened. What was all this? Did Bram work for the president?

"Then when all this is over," the other man said, "do something about it. Court the woman, propose, get married for real. But you might have to give up field work."

Bram made a noise, but she couldn't figure out what it was. Was that a groan of disappointment?

"Thanks for all your help, Quincy. I'm sorry I messed up tonight."

"I understand, but if your feelings for Millie are getting in the way of your work, then I want you to quit. We'll bring in someone else."

"No, I want to finish this."

Millie fought the urge to get out of bed, go outside and see what they were talking about. But she stayed put, still trying to piece together their conversation.

"Oh, no…" she whispered, as realization dawned. "If Bram's a spy, not only are we not married. But he's not Bill Krantz."

Chapter Nineteen

Come Monday morning, Bram watched Millie scrambled some eggs for their breakfast. She was a decent cook, and for that he was grateful.

He watched her, eyebrows knit, and contemplated everything Quincy told him the other night.

The man was right, he was falling for Millie. In fact, he was falling faster than he'd like and contemplated pulling out of the assignment. But if he did that, there was only Quincy, and back up wasn't going to come in time. Unless Quincy had already arranged for some.

"Is the toast ready?" Millie asked and spooned eggs onto two plates.

"Yes." He took the toast out of the oven and brought it to the table. They sat, and after he said a quick blessing, began to eat. "What are your plans today?" he asked, trying to start a conversation.

She looked at the table. He noticed she'd been avoiding eye contact with him all morning.

"I thought I'd take a walk after my chores, and perhaps get a few things we need at Ruggles & Son."

He stared at her from across the table. "Are you planning on stopping in to see me?"

Her head came up. "I wasn't planning on it." Millie's eyes became downcast again. "Will you even be there?"

"Of course, why wouldn't I?"

She looked at him again, a hint of suspicion in her eyes. "Because Mr. Kameyer has a particular way of doing things."

"Ah, yes. That he does. I suppose I can't say if I'll be there or not. But if I am, and I'm not with a client, you should stop in and say hello."

She blinked a few times, and he swore her eyes were misting with tears. "I'll think about it."

He gave her a sage nod and finished his eggs and toast. When he was ready to leave, she met him at the front door. Bram looked into her big brown eyes and sighed. "Millie, I…"

She shook her head. "You should get going."

He stilled. Something was wrong. Yesterday she'd been much the same way. Except during church, but then, people would notice if she gave him the silent treatment there. "If you're still upset about the ball…"

She shook her head again. "I'm… confused." Millie looked into his eyes. "And yes, I'm angry."

"Then let's talk about it, sweetie." He ran his hands up and down her arms and felt her stiffen. "Millie, I don't like seeing you like this."

She stepped back. "I overheard you talking to someone the other night." Millie looked him in the eyes again. "Who are you?"

Drat! Bram took a deep breath. How much did she overhear? "I can explain…"

She held up a hand. "I'm… I'm not sure I'm ready to listen. But I do want to know one thing. Are we married?"

He gulped. "Um, well, sort of."

Her hands went to her hips. "Are we married or not?"

He heaved a sigh. "You're married to Bill Krantz."

"But that's not who you are, is it?"

Bram ran a hand through his hair. "Millie, sweetie…"

"Don't call me that," she snapped. "Who are you?"

He took her by the elbow, ignoring her squeak of alarm and her attempt to pull away, and led her into the parlor. He pulled her onto the sofa with him and looked her square in the eyes. "Millie, I work for a special branch of the government. I'm a spy."

Her eyes went wide, then narrowed on him. "For the president?"

"Yes, as a matter of fact. There's a white slavery operation we've been trying to thwart for years, and they have men operating here. We're trying to find out who is involved and shut them down."

She stared at him, wide eyed. "But… you married me!"

He took her by the hands. "Because the real Bill Krantz is a thief, a gambler, and easily bribed. My partner and I were to arrest him, and I was to take his place."

"So the real Bill Krantz is locked up somewhere?"

"No, honey. He's dead."

Her jaw dropped. "You killed him?!"

"No, no, sweetheart." Bram scooted closer. "He was murdered. Stabbed in the back for cheating a man at cards."

She shut her eyes tight and shook her head. "No…"

"I'm afraid so. And I understand how upset you must have been thinking I was a gambler. But I'm not. Bill Krantz was."

She opened her eyes. "Who are you?"

"Bramford Joseph Henry. Spy."

Millie gaped at him. "I… I… need some air." She tried to pull out of his grasp, but he didn't let go.

Bram pulled her close and held her against him. "Listen to me, Millie. What I'm doing can be dangerous. I don't want you drawing attention to yourself."

She laughed into his chest. "Attention? You're a spy! You've pulled me into this without telling me and you expect me to do what you want?" She squirmed out of his arms and stood. "You, you…" she pointed at him. "Oh!" She stomped her foot and marched from the room. "You lout!" she called over her shoulder.

Bram sighed in defeat. This was not going the way he wanted. But he couldn't blame her for being angry.

He stood and followed her into the bedroom. She was taking her dresses out of the armoire and tossing them on the bed. "Millie, what are you doing?"

"What does it look like?! I'm leaving!"

"No, sweetie. That's not a good idea. You'll be putting yourself in danger…"

"No!" She glared at him and poked his chest with a finger. "You already did that." Her jaw trembled. "You…" she swallowed hard. "You…"

Bram pulled her into his arms. "I'm so sorry, honey."

She struggled against him, trying to free herself. "Let me go, you cad!"

"No."

"What?!"

Bram's face softened. "I don't think I can ever let you go."

She stared at him with wide eyes. "Wh-what are you saying?"

He held her closer. He didn't have the time for this conversation. "I have to meet with Quincy."

"The man you were talking to the other night?"

"Yes, then go to the office. I have a meeting with some of Kameyer's men later. If my cover is blown, you will be in danger. Do you understand?"

She gaped at him. "And what happens when you're done with all of this?"

He gave her a heartfelt look. "Our marriage will be annulled, you'll get this house, and a good sum of money for your trouble."

Her jaw trembled again. "So that's it, you pay me off?"

He drew in a shuddering breath. "Yes."

She shoved him away. "I see. Because I'll no longer be needed."

Bram saw the hurt in her eyes. "Millie, it doesn't have to be that way…"

"Quiet," she snapped. She looked at the dresses on the bed and hugged herself. "Fine. I'll play along, then when all this is said and done, I never want to see you again."

"Millie…" his voice cracked, and he balled his hands into fists at his sides. How was he going to explain his feelings to her now? She'd never believe him. What a mess! "Very well, sweetheart…"

"Don't call me that." Her head turned in his direction, but she didn't look at him.

"I'll go now. Remember what I said. Be careful. Don't draw attention to yourself." Bram left the room, grabbed his hat off the coat rack near the door and put it on. He could hear soft crying coming from the bedroom and knew he was the cause of her tears.

Lord, help me. How am I going to convince her I'm in love?

Chapter Twenty

Millie wasn't sure how long she cried. All she knew was that her heart was breaking. Bram was a spy for the president? How could he use her like this? She should go to Washington and give President Harris a piece of her mind!

Millie wiped her eyes with her handkerchief. She should have made Bram stay and explain himself, but he left to meet with Mr. Kameyer's men. Did that mean Mr. Kameyer was involved with this so-called slavery operation? Is that why Bram was posing as Bill Krantz?

Millie sank onto the bed. "Oh, Bram…" She wasn't ignorant. Considering the sort of people Father used to surround himself with, she knew things. She'd heard Father talk about the darker side of things, but she never imagined it could stretch its ugly fingers into polite society.

She sniffed back more tears and thought about all he'd said. So, Bram had taken the real Bill Krantz's place, which included marrying her. Did he even know she was coming? He must have, why else would he have brought up compensating her for all her trouble? Millie looked around the bedroom. Did he say she'd get this house?

Millie stood and hung her dresses in the armoire one by one. She'd do what she'd planned today and talk to Bram again tonight. At least when all was said and done, she wouldn't be destitute, which is what she'd have become if Bram didn't use her as part of his cover. Still, it hurt.

"Oh no…" she breathed. "I haven't fallen in love, have I?" Indeed, why else would all of this hurt so much? It was bad enough she thought he was a gambler like her father, but this was far worse. At least if she thought he was a gambling fool, she'd have the hope that he would change. Actions spoke louder than words, and all she'd have to do was wait and see if Bram gave up gambling. But this was far worse. She was losing everything, including her heart. Oh, sure, she'd still have a roof over her head according to Bram, and money besides. But she wouldn't have Bram.

Millie buried her face in her hands a moment, expecting another round of tears. But none came, so she let her hands drop. "Very well. There's no use feeling sorry for myself." She stood, took a deep breath, then put on her hat and gloves. She had supplies to fetch and she might as well get them sooner than later.

She started for Ruggles & Son, and instead of walking by the office, she cut over one street and continued that way. When she reached the general store, she noticed a large buggy out front and a smaller one near the livery stable. Mr. Ruggles senior was unhitching the horse of the smaller buggy.

Millie went inside where several elderly couples were milling about.

"I say the poor girl needs some sense talked into her," a short, plump woman barked.

"Irene, she's had a horrible fright," a tall, thin woman said. "We'll take her some treats, maybe a good book, and let her have some time to herself. When she's ready to talk, she'll talk."

Millie skirted around the couples to the counter and set down her list. James Ruggles came through a door leading to the back of the building, saw her and gave her a weak smile. "Mrs. Krantz. What can I do for you this morning?"

She glanced at the couples and back. "I have a list."

"James," a petite, white-haired woman said. "Don't you think Verity needs some time to herself after what happened?"

Millie noted James' eyes narrowing. "I don't want her anymore upset than she already is. I hope that Mr. Crafton is found and put behind bars."

Millie glanced at the different couples, then stared at James. "Mr. Ruggles?"

He ran a hand through his hair. "It's nothing Mrs. Krantz. There was a little trouble with Miss Hinkle the night of the ball. She, um, left early with a headache."

"Headache," the short plump woman said. "Ha! Who knows what that cad had planned for her!"

Millie's eyes widened. Could this have anything to do with the assignment Bram and his partner have? "Cad?"

The tall, thin woman rolled her eyes. "It's nothing for you to worry about, child." She looked Millie over. "Say, you had on a might fine dress at that shindig. Did you have a nice time?"

Millie stared at her a moment, trying to collect her thoughts. "Yes. Thank you. But what happened to Miss Hinkle? I'm afraid I didn't know she left. My husband and I left early as well."

"You did?" the short, plump one said. "Some scoundrel didn't try to run off with you too, did he?"

"Irene, that's enough," one of the elderly men said. "We rescued her in time."

Millie gaped at this point. "What happened?"

James pinched the bridge of his nose. "Miss Hinkle's father was trying to arrange a marriage for her the night of the ball. Let's just say one of the candidates was an unsavory fellow who wasn't interested in marriage."

Her eyes went wide. "Oh, dear me. Who was this man?"

"Name's Crafton," one of the elderly gentlemen said. He had a spry build and from what she gathered, was married to the petite white-haired woman. "Nasty business, but we took care of him."

She looked over the three elderly gentlemen. Each wore a proud smile. "You… you rescued her?"

"We sure did," another said. He winked at the tall, thin woman then kissed her on the cheek.

Millie watched her blush and smiled, trying to think of what else to ask. Did Bram know any of this? "Where is this Crafton now?"

"We don't know," James said. "But when we find him, I'm going to …" he drew in a deep breath. "Never mind." He picked up her list. "I'll get this for you. Give me a few moments."

"Certainly." She stepped toward the couples. "I take it this Crafton attempted to… abduct Miss Hinkle?"

They stared at her a moment. "Well, that's one way of putting it," the tall, thin woman said. She held out a hand. "Call me Grandma, and this here is my husband Doc." Grandma nodded at the shorter, plump woman. "That's Irene and Wilfred Dunnigan, and next to them is Cyrus and Polly Van Cleet. We've been visiting folks and taking care of some business in Fiddler's Gap."

"I've heard of the town," Millie said and smiled. "Millie… Krantz." It was hard to say that now. She supposed she'd be Millie Scott again soon enough. Especially if this was a lead for Bram to follow. Maybe Mr. Crafton was the man they were looking for.

"Pleased to meet you Millie," Polly said. "I must say, you and your husband certainly made a handsome couple at the ball. Your gown was lovely."

Her throat grew thick. "Thank you." She looked at the floor. "How is Miss Hinkle?"

Grandma shook her head. "She had a horrible fright. Poor thing is afraid to come out of her room. She's staying with James and his family for now. Irene, Polly and I are heading that way in a few minutes."

"I'm sorry to hear that. Is there anything I can do?" Millie asked.

"I don't think so, dear," Polly said. "But thank you for offering."

Millie smiled. "Um, this might be an odd question, but… what does this Mr. Crafton look like?"

The couples exchanged the same look of curiosity. "Why do you ask?" Wilfred said.

Millie shrugged. There was nothing more for her to do other than help Bram get his man. "On account I think I know someone who might be able to help."

Chapter Twenty-one

Millie left Ruggles & Son with her purchases and no small amount of information. She headed straight for Bram's office, only to discover he wasn't alone. Monty was with him. Didn't Bram say she shouldn't come in unless he was alone?

She walked on, and didn't think Bram saw her. Part of her wanted to interrupt them, the other didn't want to do anything that might endanger Bram. Now that she knew what he was really doing, she began to see him in a new light. At least he wasn't the wastrel gambler she feared he was. If he was indeed a spy for the president, that said a lot about him. Not that marrying her wasn't wrong. It was. She should have been given a choice. Good grief, didn't these people take into consideration her feelings?

Obviously not.

She hurried home, put her supplies away, then went out the door again. She'd go to the Ruggles' home and see if she couldn't call on Verity Hinkle. But first, she picked a few wildflowers growing along the fence in the backyard.

She took them inside, tied a ribbon around them, put some cookies she'd baked yesterday in a small bag, and left the house. She wished she had more to offer, but this was the best she could do.

Millie wanted to speak to Verity and try to get more information before she saw Bram. For all she knew, this Mr. Crafton was no more than an unwanted suitor, and the elderly couples were exaggerating. But if not, then Bram and his partner might want to question Verity themselves and go after this Crafton fellow.

When she reached the Ruggles' home, she noted the large buggy she'd seen at Ruggles & Son was parked outside. A maid answered the door. "May I help you?"

Millie straightened. "I'm here to see Miss Hinkle."

"Who's there?" a woman snapped from behind the maid. She shoved the servant out of the way. "Who are you?"

Millie recognized her as the woman who greeted her and Bram outside at the ball. "Mrs. Hinkle?"

"What of it? Who are you?" She looked Millie up and down. "You were at the ball."

"Yes, I… heard your daughter Verity wasn't… feeling well. I came to see if she needed anything."

"She needs nothing from you," Mrs. Hinkle snapped. She heaved a sigh. "Besides, she doesn't want to see anyone right now."

"Who's at the door?" came a familiar voice.

Millie smiled at Mrs. Ruggles as she approached the door. "Ma'am, I'm … Mrs. Krantz, and I brought these for Verity." She held up the sprig of flowers and her bag of cookies.

Mrs. Ruggles smiled. "How kind, won't you come in?"

"Alma, do you know this woman?" Mrs. Hinkle asked.

"She went through the trouble of stopping by, which is more than I can say for Alice. She hasn't come by yet, and Verity her sister!" She stepped out of the way so Millie could enter. "I'm afraid Verity doesn't want any company."

"Humph!" Mrs. Hinkle huffed. "She won't even see her own mother."

"Can't say I blame her there," Mrs. Ruggles' quipped. "After all, it was you and Mr. Hinkle that did this."

"Can I help it if Thorndyke is a horrible judge of character?" Mrs. Hinkle stormed into the large parlor and paced.

"Don't mind her, dear. She's upset," Mrs. Ruggles said.

Millie smiled and nodded. "I'm sorry there was trouble, and I don't mean to be nosy, but why is Verity staying here?"

Mrs. Ruggles glanced at the parlor and back, then said in a low voice. "On account she doesn't want to be around her parents right now. They tried to arrange a marriage for Verity, and the man was quite impatient and tried to take her… well, we're not sure what happened. At any rate, she didn't care for him and refused, and now it's a big mess. She's not speaking to her parents and…" she glanced into the parlor again. "… I don't blame her."

Millie nodded. "Well, I hope she feels better soon, and everyone forgives each other."

"That's very kind of you to say, dear." She looked at the flowers and bag. "May I take those things up to Verity for you?"

"Would you?" She smiled. "And tell her I hope she's feeling better soon. She was so lovely in her gown at the ball, it was a shame she left early."

Mrs. Ruggles nodded her agreement. "It was." She gave Millie a smile. "Now run along dear, and with any luck, Verity will be up and about soon."

Millie backed to the door. "Thank you for letting me inquire after her." She opened the door and stepped outside.

"Thank you for stopping by." She gave Millie a parting smile then closed the door.

Millie faced the front walk. She should go home, wait for Bram, then tell him everything she discovered. When she reached the sidewalk, Millie noticed a man peeking around a tree in a neighbor's yard across the street. Hmm, was he watching the house? There was only one way to find out.

Millie boldly crossed the street and headed straight for him. She'd done the same thing when Mother sent her to track down Father. His friends often milled about outside the gambling hall, usually because they'd already lost their money, and were waiting on Father for whatever reason.

"Excuse me," she said politely.

The man was tall, his dark hair thinning. His eyes were just as dark, and he had a thin mustache. Millie took him in, memorizing his features.

"What do you want?" he snapped.

Before she could speak, he arched an eyebrow at her and looked her up and down as if assessing a horse. "Hmmm, well now," he purred. "What can I do for you?"

Millie forced a smile. She was growing uncomfortable. "Do you have the time?"

He pulled out his pocket watch and flipped it open. "Half past eleven," he said.

"Oh, dear, I was afraid of that. I'm late!" She lifted her skirt with both hands and hurried off. "Thank you," she called over one shoulder. He watched her with more than a little interest, and she picked up the pace. After she'd gone more than a block, she slowed, glancing over her shoulder once.

The man was following her. Oh no! What to do? She crossed the street, heading for the only place she knew she'd be safe.

Millie cut through downtown and headed straight for Bram's office.

Without bothering to look through the front window to see if he was alone, she burst inside, her heart in her throat, and stopped up short.

"Millie," Bram said and stood. "What are you doing here?" His eyes narrowed. "What's wrong?" He came around the desk and took her in his arms. "Millie?"

"Th-the man you're looking for. I think he's following me!"

Chapter Twenty-two

Bram went to the window, peeked out, then took Millie by the elbow. "I want you to hide in here. I'll tell you when it's safe to come out."

"What?" She didn't argue further as she was shoved into the bathroom. She heard the scrape of his chair as he retook his seat and likely pretended to work.

Her heart hammered in her chest as she listened for the office door to open. It didn't, and she wondered if the man stopped following her at some point. She tried not to look over her shoulder. Instead, she would stop, gaze at something in a shop window for a second or two, then continue. She caught sight of him a couple of times as she cut through downtown but hadn't looked to see if he followed her further.

Millie waited a long time before Bram stepped into the bathroom and closed the door "What are you doing?"

"My guess is he'll come back. I've locked the office door. It's lunch time, after all. He'll think I've gone somewhere to eat."

She looked up at him. The room was small, so they were standing close. "I... I'm sorry about this morning."

Bram looked into her eyes. "Ah, Millie, so am I. So sorry." He tucked a finger under her chin and tilted her face up to his. "Can you forgive me?"

Tears stung the backs of her eyes. She'd fallen for this man and hard. Her heart in her throat, she couldn't answer.

"Millie." He put his arms around her and kissed the top of her head.

She stiffened in his arms. "Don't do that."

He sighed, let go of her, then peeked out the door. "Come with me." He pulled her from the bathroom, took a few steps down the hall, and took her into a small storeroom.

"What are we doing in here?"

"I'm not going to tell you the sort of things I need to say in a bathroom."

She stared at him, perplexed. "Wh-what do you need to say?"

Bram pulled her into his arms again. "That these last few days have been torture."

"And whose fault is that?" she shot back.

He laughed. "Yours, if you must know."

"What?!"

He nodded. "It's true. You make it hard for me to eat, to sleep, and the most horrifying of all, to put together a coherent thought."

Millie blinked, trying to process what he was saying. "I don't understand."

Bram cupped her face with a hand. "My precious, Millie. I'm trying to tell you I love you."

She sucked in a breath as her knees wobbled. "Wh-what?!"

He said nothing. Instead, his lips were suddenly on hers, melding their mouths together in an incredible kiss. His arms tightened around her so possessively she thought she might swoon, his kiss full of hunger she couldn't begin to describe. And he was igniting the same sensation within her. But no, she couldn't let him fool her! He didn't really mean it, did he?

When Bram broke the kiss, they were breathless. "Millie," he gasped. "I've thought about this for two days. I can't give you up."

She tried to catch her breath. "What did you say?"

He lowered his face to hers again. "I can't, no… *won't* give you up. I know it sounds completely loco. But I've fallen for you these last couple of weeks."

Her lower lip trembled at his words. "You… love me?"

"Yes, honey, and I want you to become *my* wife. Not Bill Krantz's."

"But… what about your assignment?"

"As soon as it's done, which thanks to you, I believe it will be soon, then you and I are getting married."

"But… your job…"

"I can settle in one place. I have a home in Washington, not far from work."

"As in, the president?"

"Yes, honey."

"And… you… love me?"

He laughed. "I do! Quincy told me to marry you and be done with it. Because if I don't, I'm going to go loco."

"But you're a… a spy!"

"Not if you don't want me to be." He ran the back of his finger down one cheek. "I can work close to home. I have a rather nice one. But if you don't have any feelings toward me, then I understand. Especially after all the deception."

She continued to stare up at him. "You love me?"

He gave her a gentle smile. "Yes, honey. I love you."

She sucked in a breath. "I-I love you too."

He grinned ear to ear. "You do?"

She nodded and laughed. "I do!"

He held her tight. "Ah, Millie. You've just made me the happiest…" he pulled back and grinned again. "We have to make this official." He got down on one knee and took her hands in his. "Millie Scott, will you make an honest man out of me and become my wife?"

She almost choked as she laughed. "Oh, goodness. You're serious?!"

"Of course, I am. Marry me. Become Mrs. Bramford Henry."

Her heart pounded in her chest as she realized he was indeed serious! "Yes. Yes, I'll marry you!"

Bram stood, pulled her into his arms, and kissed her soundly. When he broke the kiss, he rested his head atop hers. "By the way, honey. I don't gamble. I don't really drink either."

Her shoulders shook with silent sobs. "Thank you for telling me."

She didn't know how long they stood in that storeroom holding each other, but in those moments, her fears began to disappear. Things made sense now, and though she was angry with him for his deception, she could also see the man he truly was. He worked for the president, for Pete's sake! That meant he was trustworthy, good at his job, a man of good moral character. He was steadfast, protective, and she could go on. But right now, she just wanted Bram to hold her.

Eventually he let go, and she told him about the man she confronted across the street from the Ruggles' house.

"I'll let Quincy know tonight, and he can send a telegraph message to send for help. Once we apprehend this Crafton, we can find out more about his involvement with Sal." He smiled at her. "What you did was very brave, but also very foolish. Promise me you'll never do anything like that again."

"But did it help?"

"You have no idea."

"I think he was at the ball," she said. "I passed a man that looked like him when I went to the ladies' lounge area. He and some other men surrounded Verity. I thought they were looking at her gown."

"No doubt it was him, and no doubt I missed seeing him take Verity from the ballroom when I ran into Monty. By the time I went downstairs to find you, a fancy carriage was pulling away. That might have been Crafton."

"Some elderly women and men were at the general store while I was there. They were going to see Verity earlier. They said they got Verity away from this Crafton the night of the ball. They can tell you what happened."

"And after hearing all that, you decided to pay her a visit too?"

She blushed. "To find out information for you."

Bram gave her a wide smile. "I appreciate it, darling, I really do. But don't do it again."

She gave him a sheepish shrug before he pulled her into his arms again and kissed her senseless.

Epilogue

As it turned out, after questioning the Dunnigans, Wallers, and Van Cleets, along with James Ruggles, Bram concluded the man that followed Millie to Bram's office was indeed Mr. Crafton. Millie was the only one to have seen him since the ball. No doubt he was making himself scarce so he wouldn't get caught. Which put Bram in a pickle. Did he stay in Baker City and see what else he could find out? Or should he head back to Washington? Either way, there was something he needed to take care of and told Millie it was going to be done today. And so, that's how she found herself in Fiddler's Gap, a tiny town eight miles out of Baker City, standing before their preacher reciting her wedding vows.

"And do you, Millie Ann Scott, take Bramford Joseph Henry to be your lawfully wedded husband?"

Millie gave the preacher a big smile. "I do."

"Then by the power vested in me by the great state of Oregon, I now pronounce you husband and wife. "Bramford, you may kiss the bride."

Bram lifted her veil, wrapped her in his arms, and kissed her soundly. This wasn't the first time they kissed, but it was the first time they kissed as a true husband and wife.

When Bram broke the kiss, he gazed into her eyes. "I love you."

She smiled. "I love you too."

Bram's eyes grew bright. "Now we're official."

She smiled back. "Does this mean you're going to order that new bed?"

He laughed. "No, but it does mean we're going to spend the night here in the hotel." He kept one arm around her as he faced the sheriff and his wife. "Thank you for standing in as witnesses."

"It was our pleasure," Sheriff Cole said. "And I want to hear all about this Crafton fellow when you have a chance. Cyrus Van Cleet told me about what happened at the ball. We were so caught up in dancing, we didn't pay any mind to Verity going home."

"I'll do that," Bram said. "But first, I'd like to spend time with my new bride." He looked at Millie. "My beautiful, wonderful, bride." He turned to the preacher. "Thank you, Reverend Murray. We appreciate you marrying us on such short notice."

"No problem son. Ellis and Arabella down at the hotel are making something special for your wedding supper." He gave them a wink.

Millie thanked Reverend Murray, along with the sheriff and his wife, Penelope, then let Bram escort her out of the church. She was no longer the wife of William "Bill" Krantz, but of Bramford Joseph Henry, and she couldn't be happier. He and his fellow spies still had work to do, and to keep her safe, Bram wanted her to stay in Fiddler's Gap under the watchful eye of Sheriff Aubrey Cole. As soon as they located Crafton and rounded him up, they would leave for Washington and her new home. Bram said it was a might bigger than their little cottage in Baker City, and he always smiled when he mentioned it. She had a strong feeling it was a lot bigger.

But she didn't want to think about that now. They were strolling down the street, Bram wearing the suit he wore to the ball, and she in her ballgown. It was the closest thing to a wedding dress she had, and Mrs. Murray had been able to fashion a veil for her in short order.

They entered the hotel, went up the stairs and down the hall to the last door on the right. Bram grinned at her, unlocked the door, then scooped her into his arms.

Millie giggled. "Bram!"

He looked down at her. "I have to carry you across the threshold. Didn't you notice I never did as Bill Krantz?"

Her eyes widened. "That's right, you didn't."

Bram looked into her eyes. "I couldn't because I knew we weren't really married."

"But we are now."

"Yes, sweetheart, we are." He carried her over the threshold into the room and smiled at her. "And now I can make you mine." He kissed her, closing the door with one foot, and did indeed, make her his.

THE END

About the Author

USA Today bestselling author Kit Morgan has written for fun all of her life. Whether she's writing contemporary or historical romance, her whimsical stories are fun, inspirational, sweet and clean, and depict a strong sense of family and community. Raised by a homicide detective, one would think she'd write suspense, (and yes, she plans to get around to those eventually, cozy mysteries too!) but Kit likes fun and romantic westerns! Kit resides in the beautiful Pacific Northwest in a little log cabin on Clear Creek, after which her fictional town that appears in many of her books is named.

Want to get in on the fun?

Find out about new releases, cover reveals, bonus content, fun times and more! Sign up for Kit's newsletter at www.authorkitmorgan.com

Leftover Mail-Order Bride

By Regina Scott

What's a mail-order bride to do when she's left at the altar?

Victoria Milford had spent much of her life caring for ailing relatives, so it wasn't a stretch to agree to marry a near-stranger in Washington Territory for a chance at a life of her own. But the man who had proposed marriage wed another while she was enroute. The local minister's wife assures her that bachelors abound on the frontier. Surely it isn't too much to ask that one might prefer Victoria?

The leader of the family ranch, Jack Willets is determined not to let his parents' insistence on finding true love sway him. What he needs in a bride is a lady who can work beside him. When the local minister's wife introduces him to Victoria, he's immediately drawn to her sweet nature. But can a city girl ever really feel comfortable in the country?

Between a boisterous, matchmaking family and dozens of other suitors chasing after Victoria, she and Jack may have their hands full as they discover being leftover just means the perfect love can come along.

If you like warm, witty historical romances, then you'll love this feel-good story set in the Pacific Northwest by an award-winning, bestselling author.

"I LOVE to read Regina Scott's books. They always feel comfortable. I honestly don't know how else to convey how 'at home' I feel when reading what she's written." Hott Book Reviews

Frontier Brides, taming the West one cowboy at a time.

To all who work to care for home and family—you are cherished! And to the Lord, who loves us all, no matter our calling.

Chapter One

Near Olympia, Washington Territory
Late April 1877

Did a mail-order bride necessarily require a groom?

The thought pushed Victoria Milford's fingers up and down the keys of the battered upright piano as she tried to focus on the Mozart sonata. Concentrating on the runs normally chased away any fretting, but today her problems crowded closer than the walls of the little frontier parlor.

Why hadn't he waited? It had only taken fourteen days to travel to Washington Territory from Albany. She had it on good authority few eligible ladies lived along Puget Sound. Had she been only a tool to make his former sweetheart jealous, despite the promises in his letters?

If that was the sum total of a gentleman's faithfulness, maybe having a husband wasn't worth the bother. She'd nursed for most of her life, first her father, then her mother, then Cousin Phyllis. The territorial capital and surrounding areas might not have a hospital yet, but surely some physician would appreciate a second pair of hands.

The doctor in nearby Puget City hadn't.

"Sorry, Miss Milford," Doctor Rawlins had said, rubbing his stubbled jaw with the back of one hand. "Much as I could use the help, I can't see bringing on an unmarried lady. It wouldn't be right. But never you fear. Someone as pretty and talented as you will have no trouble finding another groom."

No, just one she wanted.

She closed her eyes, let her fingers fly up and down the keys, and breathed in the final rousing movement of the music. *Show me Your will, Father. You must have had a reason for bringing me here.*

Beyond the pounding music, beyond her tumultuous thoughts, another noise intruded. She opened her eyes, expecting to find that her hostess had joined her. Instead, a man was standing in the parlor doorway, watching her. He stood tall and stocky in his rawhide coat and dusty trousers, gun at his hip, a dime novel frontiersman come to life.

She might not recognize him, but she recognized admiration when she saw it. The look on his handsome face was balm to her soul after being rejected practically at the altar. Her fingers slowed, stilled.

"Don't stop playing on my account," he said in a warm voice, removing his hat to reveal short-cut hair as fiery red as the feathers of a scarlet tanager. "It would be a shame to keep such beauty from the world."

Her mouth was turning up in a smile before she thought better of it. She pulled back her hands and folded them in the lap of her mauve silk gown. "Nonsense. You must have a purpose for coming to call. I wouldn't want to interfere."

He opened his mouth as if to explain, but Mrs. Dalrymple bustled in. The minister's wife was short, round, and quick in both action and speech, reminding Victoria of a house wren. If her interactions with Victoria and the few matrons who had come calling were any indication, she seemed to enjoy taking the helm and steering lives in a direction she considered better. Like Victoria, she wore the fine gowns expected of a parlor back East, not the more practical ginghams and calicos Victoria had seen when she'd come West. Mrs. Dalrymple's brown curls bobbed beside her face as she glanced between Victoria and the stranger.

"Oh, you've met," she said, rosebud mouth turning down. She sounded almost disappointed.

Why? Was this fellow someone she should avoid? Mrs. Dalrymple had certainly pointed out enough of those since Victoria had arrived three days ago. The clerk at the Egbert mercantile in Puget City with the nice smile had once given incorrect change and was not to be trusted with anything so important as a woman's heart. The rancher who'd offered them a cut of beef spoke unkindly to his horse and would likely treat his wife and children as badly. The farmer who brought the milk did not tithe to the church, and who wanted a tight-fisted husband?

Besides, Mrs. Dalrymple had confided, every bachelor in the area would think twice before courting someone's leftover mail-order bride. Victoria must study them carefully to know their intentions.

After all, she had little choice. She must either marry or find a position. She certainly couldn't live in the Dalrymples' spare bedroom for the rest of her life. The minister's wife had already erected a sign in the front yard saying *Room for Rent* as if she expected Victoria's tenure to be brief indeed.

"Miss Milford," Mrs. Dalrymple said now, pug nose up in the air as if she'd smelled day-old cabbage, "allow me to introduce Mr. Jack Willets. He's the second son of a local rancher."

Second son generally meant no inheritance was involved, but not always. With those broad shoulders and long limbs, Mr. Willets could likely work at anything he wanted.

"Mr. Willets," Victoria said, inclining her head.

"Miss Milford," he said with a nod that sent light rippling like flame through his hair. "I don't suppose you'd care to take a walk?" He glanced at Mrs. Dalrymple as if seeking her permission as well.

One look, and he wanted to walk out with her? Was he so impetuous, then? Would his interest cool as quickly as Charles' had?

The minister's wife heaved a martyred sigh that raised the ruffles on her generous bosom. "I suppose that would be suitable." She held up one finger. "Just to the end of the drive and back, mind you. Miss Milford has many obligations."

Miss Milford had had many obligations most of her life, from learning to be a lady and all the accomplishments that entailed to caring for her ailing family. At the moment, Miss Milford was blithefully free of obligations.

She rose from behind the piano. "I'll get my coat."

Mr. Willets stepped aside to let her pass, and she caught sight of his eyes. They were the smoky gray to match the fire of his hair. And they were gazing at her as if she were the most amazing person he had ever met. A woman could grow fond of such looks.

Something snagged her skirts, and she glanced back to find that Mrs. Dalrymple had followed her out of the parlor so closely she'd trod on Victoria's hem. The minister's wife tsked as she stepped aside.

"I'll watch from the porch," she murmured with a glance back at the waiting Mr. Willets.

"Is he not to be trusted then?" Victoria murmured back, spirits dipping as she shook out the flounces along her hem.

"He seems a very responsible gentleman," Mrs. Dalrymple assured her, going to pull Victoria's embroidered wool coat down from the hook by the door. "His parents dote on him. He tithes, and he's been leading the effort to erect our first church building. He does seem a bit bossy. He is in the market for a bride, but when I suggested he might write away for one, he refused." She shook her head as she helped Victoria into her coat. "'Pride goeth before destruction and a haughty spirit before a fall,' you know."

Humility. One more item to add to the list of characteristics Mrs. Dalrymple expected Victoria's husband to possess, along with patience, faithfulness, fiscal responsibility, kindness to animals, and frequent tithing. He would have to be an absolute paragon among men.

She'd never find a groom to match.

Jack slid his hat back on his head, only to pull it off again out of respect as the minister's wife sidled up to him.

"Walk if you like, but she's not a suitable bride for you," she murmured, gaze on Miss Milford's back.

Jack frowned, but Mrs. Dalrymple put on a smile and flapped her fingers, shooing him out of the house as if he were a recalcitrant chicken. Bemused, he followed Miss Milford down the front steps and onto the muddy track that ran out to the country road to Puget City.

He'd never accustomed himself to the house that was now being used as the parsonage. Everyone had shaken their heads when the former owner, Mr. Henshaw, had built the four-story narrow monstrosity and painted it a jaunty pink. With all the bric-a-brac edging the roof and windows, it might have graced the richest neighborhood in refined Port Townsend to the north, with other houses close on either side. It looked completely out of place standing alone on the edge of a plateau overlooking Puget Sound, surrounded by nothing but fields and forests.

But it fit the beauty walking beside him perfectly.

She was as unexpected as the house. That dusky red hair was smoothed back in a proper bun, but the arrangement couldn't hide the luster. How Ma would laugh if he brought home another red-head. Their family was filled with them.

And wouldn't Ma be pleased if she knew that he'd taken one look at the lady and toppled like a fir under his brother Jesse's two-handed ax?

Love at first sight? His parents claimed they'd married because of it. He'd thought it a fine story, something endearing to share with their children.

Until Victoria Milford had played that music, and all he could do was stand and stare.

He grimaced now and hoped she hadn't noticed. Love at first sight might be something his parents and the poets celebrated, but he wasn't looking for love. He wasn't looking for a bride only suited to the parlor either. He needed a wife who could be a helpmate, working beside him to care for his family. In a few years, three of his sisters would likely leave to marry and start their own families, and nothing said his brothers wouldn't do the same. Someone had to take charge of the ranch. Besides, if he'd wanted any old bride, he could have written away for a mail-order bride, like his younger brother Jeremy had.

Mrs. Dalrymple must know something about this woman that she hadn't been able to share with Jack to caution him against her. After all, he had asked her to help him find a lady to court. The minister's wife was sitting on the porch bench, knitting needles in her hands but gaze watchful. Perhaps she expected him to discover the flaw in this rose.

"Are the Dalrymples your family, then?" he asked.

Miss Milford picked up her skirts with one hand. Like the rest of her, they were dainty and elegant. His sisters Jenny and Joanna would have swooned at the number of rows of frilly ruffles that covered the bottom third of the dress. Jane would probably have laughed. She understood the need to be sensible.

"No," Miss Milford said. "They were kind enough to take me in after… I came West."

Single ladies didn't usually travel to the frontier alone, at least not ladies his mother would accept in her house.

"What brought you out this way?" he asked, frowning.

She turned to look at him and jerked to a stop, forcing him up as well. "What is that!"

Had she spotted a bear? A cougar? Jack whirled, hand to the revolver on his hip, but the fields rippled green into the distance, where the mountain rose in all her glory.

He smiled at his companion. "That's Mount Rainier. Is this the first you've seen her?"

She nodded, gaze on the mass of white snow and silvery rock rising beyond the Nisqually Delta.

"She likes to hide when it's rainy or there's any hint of a cloud between us and her," Jack explained, "but you have to admit she looks rather fine reigning over the area."

"She's beautiful," she said, voice hushed.

Yes, Miss Milford was. Her eyes were as brown as a walnut, with flecks of gold as if hinting of something fine, something precious inside. Her lips reminded him of the inside of the shells his sisters liked to gather from the shore, though they looked a lot softer and warmer. If he bent closer…

He reined in his thoughts with more difficulty than a runaway horse. He'd just met this woman! *He* wasn't the impetuous one in the family! He swallowed and forced his feet to move again. He was thankful she fell in beside him.

Still, he struggled to think of what to say next. Too soon to tell her his hopes for a match. Too intrusive to ask if she was itching to wed.

The area. That was a safe topic of conversation. He nodded to the northwest. "The forest is blocking the view, but if you get beyond it, you can see the Olympics across Puget Sound as well. Then there's Mount Saint Helens to the south and Mount Baker to the north. On a clear day, you can see all of them."

"You're ringed by grandeur," she said, shaking her head as if she could hardly believe such riches. "How do you get anything done without standing and shouting a hallelujah?"

He chuckled. "Well, you get used to it after a while."

"I hope I never do," she vowed.

So did he. It would be a shame to lose that light in her eyes.

Apparently, she had questions for him as well, for she cleared her throat and started asking. "Mrs. Dalrymple said you have a ranch nearby, I believe?"

"The Jumping J to the south of us." As soon as he said it, he felt foolish. "My littlest sister named it that. It's a busy ranch, and all our names start with the letter J."

"All?" she asked innocently.

Mrs. Dalrymple must not have mentioned that to her. Not everyone appreciated the size of his family. He'd heard the jokes for years.

Your pa sure must like pups 'cause he has a pack of them.

Why'd he stop at ten? Jesus had twelve apostles.

But any woman who married him had to marry into his family. Supporting them was non-negotiable.

"I'm one of ten," he told her. "My oldest brother, Jesse, lives up at Wallin Landing, near Seattle. Then there's me, Jeremy, Jacob, Jane, Jenny, Joanna, Jason, Joshua, and Joy."

"Joy, who named the ranch," she surmised.

She was quick. Not many would have followed that litany, particularly as he hadn't taken his time spitting it out. "That's right. She's the youngest at ten. Jesse is the oldest at one and thirty."

"What a time your mother must have had," she said, voice sounding awed again. "Ten live births is quite an accomplishment. She must have had a good midwife."

Funny. No one had ever talked about his mother's laying-ins before. Then again, most of the men in the area wouldn't have thought to question how hard it was to birth babies.

"Not many midwives in the area," Jack allowed. Not many wives of any kind, but if she hadn't figured that out, she would as soon as the other suitors started stampeding to her door.

She made a noise as if deploring the lack of medical care.

"Of course, we have a fine physician," he hurried to add. "Doctor Rawlins comes out whenever we send for him."

"Yes, I've met the good doctor," she said. She didn't sound particularly impressed.

In fact, aside from the view, she didn't seem impressed by much of anything in the area. Who could blame her? Not many were suited to live on the frontier. That's why so few traveled West.

Those who stayed in their big cities back East didn't know what they were missing. Freedom, purpose, a chance to make your own way.

The quiet to worship a God who had created all this for His children.

"You planning on staying in the area?" Jack asked.

She sighed. "Yes, I suppose so. There's nothing for me back home in Albany."

Albany. That was in New York state, if he remembered Ma's geography lessons right. Like Olympia to the southwest, it was the capital. Miss Milford might be used to dealing with governors and legislators, folks who lived in fancy houses and did important things.

Things more important than running a cattle ranch on Hawks Prairie.

The words popped out before he could stop them. "Are you fixing to marry, then?"

She flinched as if the question had taken a bite out of her.

"Sorry for the plain speaking," he said. "That's my way. Best you know now."

"I appreciate your candor, Mr. Willets," she said. "Allow me to offer the same. I am considering marriage as one option for my future, and Mrs. Dalrymple has encouraged me to look for a suitable groom, one who meets her criteria for a match."

Mrs. Dalrymple had criteria for husbands? He'd thought the minister's wife hesitant because of Miss Milford's qualifications, not his.

"Maybe I should talk with the lady," he said, glancing back at the porch.

Mrs. Dalrymple waved a plump hand at him, proving that she'd been watching them. Encouragement to continue his walk with Miss Milford?

Or encouragement to leave?

"That might be wise," she said. She seemed to think he'd want to do that right this moment, for she turned with a swirl of her frilly skirts and started back up the drive. "Marriage is an important endeavor. Too important to leave to chance."

"I couldn't agree more," he assured her. It was also too important to leave to letters through the mail or one glimpse across a crowded room.

Or even an uncrowded parlor.

True love is all that matters. He heard his mother's voice in his head. *The kind of love that lasts through thick and thin. The kind of love you can build a life around. That's what I want for all my children.*

He wouldn't have admitted it to any of his siblings, but he'd always hoped he might find a love like that. Oh, maybe it would start with a small seed, like the nubs that fell out of the fir cones, but it would grow into a tree that would shelter all those who came upon it.

Could a frontier rancher find that kind of love with a polished lady from a big city?

His heart seemed to be urging him to find out.

Chapter Two

He was a bit rough around the edges, like his clothing, but there seemed to be something honest and true about Jack Willets. Then again, she'd been fooled before.

Mrs. Dalrymple gathered her knitting and rose as they approached the parsonage. Victoria had seen the bundle of yarn and needles in her hands several times over the last few days, but the scarf never seemed to grow. She smiled at both of them now. "Well, it was very nice to see you again, Mr. Willets. I expect you'll be at services on Sunday."

Mr. Willets tipped his hat at her. "Yes, ma'am." He looked to Victoria. "Perhaps I could sit with you, Miss Milford."

He was still interested! Her heart fluttered, and she scolded herself. Hadn't she learned to take things slower this time? "That would be lovely, Mr. Willets. Until then."

He inclined his head and strode off across the fields toward where the land was being prepared for the new church.

Mrs. Dalrymple tsked. "Not a promising start."

"Why do you say that?" Victoria asked as she followed her hostess back into the house.

"Well, he is a *rancher*," Mrs. Dalrymple pointed out. "Living on a *ranch*, with *cows*."

Victoria held back her smile. "I do understand the two go together."

The minister's wife deposited her project in her work bag, then patted Victoria's arm. "You aren't used to ranching, dear. I have in mind a nice city boy for you."

She hadn't seen a city, nice or otherwise, since the train she'd ridden had passed the Rockies. "Oh?" she asked as they headed for the kitchen at the back of the house.

"Mr. Oscar Goodenough," she confided in a whisper, even though they were the only two occupants of the house at the moment. "A fine upstanding gentleman recently moved to the area. He keeps the books for the sawmill in Puget City." She nodded as if that were a very good accomplishment indeed. "He hasn't tithed yet, but I expect him to start shortly. He wears a stylish suit to services and is very respectful to Mr. Dalrymple and me."

Respectfulness she would be happy to add to the list of criteria, but she wasn't about to start judging men on whether their clothing was particularly stylish. Surely what was inside the suit mattered more.

Mr. Goodenough notwithstanding, Victoria paid particular attention when the Dalrymples drove her down to Puget City the next day. Mrs. Dalrymple had confided that the town had been platted when everyone thought the Northern Pacific Railroad would make Olympia its western terminus. When that honor had gone to Tacoma to the north, some citizens had left.

Now houses and other buildings crowded along a narrow valley between the towering forest at the edge of the plateau and the pebbled beach along Puget Sound. She spotted two mercantiles, a saloon, and a restaurant on the main street, which ran down to a dock sticking out into the blue-gray waters. The call of the gulls overhead was nearly drowned out by the whir of machinery at the sawmill near the dock.

"Where is the schoolhouse?" she asked as the minister drew the carriage to a stop in front of the Egbert mercantile. The white-washed box of a store had a wide, covered front porch that shaded the windows overlooking the street. Customers, mostly men in dusty clothes like Jack Willets had worn, moved in and out of the door to the tinkle of the shop bell.

"Puget City doesn't have a school," Mrs. Dalrymple confessed as her husband handed the reins to the boy who had come running at the sight of them. "Not enough children as yet, which is why more brides are so important."

Mr. Dalrymple chucked as he climbed down from the buggy. He was as sensible as his wife was whimsical. With his square jaw and squared shoulders, he looked as solid as the Word he preached. He seemed as concerned about fashion, however, for he wore a stylish double-breasted coat, and he'd slicked back his brown hair with pomade, which left it shining.

"I'm not sure I'll be a bride," Victoria demurred.

"Nonsense," he told her with a smile. "Any number of our young men would do well to marry. You might say you're a civilizing influence on the wilderness, Miss Milford."

From what she'd seen, the wilderness and its denizens had done quite well without any contribution from her, but she smiled back as he came around and helped first her and then his wife down.

"If there's no school and the doctor has no intention to hire a nurse, where else might I find employment?" she asked Mrs. Dalrymple as they followed her husband into the busy mercantile. Every manner of supply—from fishing hooks to flannel, tinned goods to tea—were piled along the worn plank floor, with more hanging from the rafters or on display behind the long counter at the back of the store. The air was so redolent with the scent of spices and liniment that Victoria nearly sneezed.

Mr. Dalrymple went straight to the counter to speak to the man on duty behind it. Mrs. Dalrymple wandered through the piles of offerings, which sometimes reached higher than Victoria's head.

"Oh, I wouldn't advise finding employment, dear," she said, picking up a tin of condensed milk and putting it down with a wrinkle of her nose. "There really isn't anything suitable here for a lady."

Most of the women Victoria had grown up with had had a similar attitude. Ladies managed their household, but much of the real work was done by hired staff—cooks, maids, laundresses. Ladies did good works, like visiting the sick and raising money to help the poor. A lady who found herself in the unfortunate position of having to support herself might do so as a governess, teacher, companion, or perhaps family nurse, but she would never scrub floors or clean clothes.

"I no longer have the luxury of being a lady," Victoria pointed out as they rounded a corner of kerosene cans. "I never learned to cook, but I could wash clothes. It seems to be a need here." She eyed another frontiersman in a gingham shirt and trousers caked in mud. He hurriedly tipped his broad-brimmed hat to her and grinned.

Mrs. Dalrymple tugged her in a different direction. "Now, you mustn't lose heart. I'm sure we'll find you the perfect match before you need to chafe your hands."

Better chafed hands than an empty belly. She wasn't about to turn down honest work.

Yet it sounded as if she'd have few opportunities in Puget City. As the territorial capital, Olympia likely held more. The legislature was due to meet later this year, she'd heard, swelling the population. But Charles' family had been keen to get his leftover mail-order bride out of town. Even if she ventured back, she'd have no place to stay. It would be the same in Tacoma and Seattle to the north. Having spent all her funds to reach Washington Territory, she had nothing left to start over.

So, what was a lady new to the frontier to do?

The bell chimed as Jack pushed through the door of the Egbert mercantile. His younger brothers would have stopped to peruse the new collection of fishhooks guaranteed to catch salmon, and his littlest sister would have been wheedling for a stick of candy from the jars lining one side of the counter. But he had a far more important mission. He needed to convince Bill Egbert to donate the nails, hinges, and doorknobs they'd need to build the new church.

So, he marched past the casks of flour and sugar and detoured around the bolts of bright gingham, determination lengthening his stride.

One look at the lady waiting beside Mrs. Dalrymple at the counter and every other thought vanished.

Victoria Milford's face was in profile to him, but that only made her cheekbones and delicate chin more obvious. Her coat hid much of her dress, but the plaid skirts were once more festooned with ruffles and lace. She held herself still, poised. Surrounded by tins of chewing tobacco and tubs of lard, she was a jewel in a brass setting.

"Be right with you, Jack," Bill Egbert, the proprietor, called over the ladies' heads.

Miss Milford turned with a welcoming smile that made him stand straighter. "Mr. Willets. How nice to see you again."

The minister's wife glanced between the two of them, then focused on her charge. "Will you wait for my order, dear? I need a word with Mr. Willets."

Miss Milford's smile dimmed, but she dutifully turned to the storekeeper again.

Mrs. Dalrymple motioned to him before mincing off behind a stack of furs someone must have brought in to trade. Mystified, Jack followed.

"Is this about the church building, ma'am?" he asked as they came to a stop and she put her hands on her hips.

"No, it's about your bride," she chided.

He couldn't stop himself from leaning back to look at the counter, where Miss Milford had her hand extended to accept the change Bill was counting into it. Jack had heard those hands bring forth beauty, joy.

"Ahem."

He returned his gaze to the minister's wife, whose foot now was tapping, if the movement of her navy skirts was any indication.

"You asked me to help you find a nice young lady to court," she reminded him. "Someone suitable to be a rancher's wife. Miss Milford, I fear, does not meet your requirements."

His heart howled in protest, and he widened his stance as if some part of him thought he'd have to fight for the right to stand at her side. Jack forced himself to relax. "I'd like to confirm that for myself."

She tsked. "I'm only trying to spare you both heartache. That poor girl has been through enough."

Victoria had faced heartache? When? From whom? How could he help?

Before he could ask, Mrs. Dalrymple's face brightened in a smile. "Ah, there you are, dear. Everything settled?"

"Mr. Egbert is having your purchases loaded into the buggy," Miss Milford said before turning to Jack. "I'm sorry if we delayed your shopping, Mr. Willets. When you walked up, you seemed to have an urgent purpose."

He did. He had a church to build, a ranch to run, and a bride to locate and court. But right then, nothing seemed more important than becoming better acquainted with Victoria Milford.

Mr. Willets was watching her with that mixture of awe and admiration again, as if she were a rare and precious rose he'd found budding among his turnips.

"Jack," Mr. Dalrymple greeted, joining them. "How is your family?"

"Well, sir," he said with a nod of his head.

Mr. Dalrymple waited a moment, but when nothing more was forthcoming, he smiled. "And how is the church coming along?"

"Well," Jack said. Then he seemed to realize he should embroider that word a little, for he stood taller, bringing his head even farther above the minister's. "I'm here to ask Bill about donating some supplies."

"An excellent suggestion." The minister winked at him. "We'll just go smooth the path for you." He took his wife's arm and led her back toward the counter. She frowned over her shoulder at Victoria.

"We came to purchase some supplies for the parsonage," Victoria explained. "What an interesting store! I don't think I've ever seen so many different items crammed into such a small space."

"I can't imagine this store can hold much of interest to you," he told her.

Did he think her such a snob? "Oh, I don't know," Victoria said. "I might end up needing fish hooks or a blade for a plow one day." She leaned closer. "But I will confess to being more tempted by the peppermint sticks."

His mouth turned up in a slow smile that set her pulse to fluttering. "Never said no to one of those myself."

Mrs. Dalrymple hurried back to her side. "I think you will find Mr. Egbert receptive to your suggestions, Mr. Willets. I hope you'll be receptive of mine."

He tipped his hat to them both. "I appreciate your concern, ma'am. Miss Milford."

Mrs. Dalrymple chivvied her out of the store, and Mr. Dalrymple handed them both back into the buggy before offering the boy who'd been holding the horses a coin.

"Good man, Jack Willets," he said as he gathered the reins to turn the buggy on the wide street. "I'm glad you could make his acquaintance, Miss Milford."

"And she'd be even gladder when she meets Mr. Goodenough tomorrow," his wife said with a smile to Victoria.

It seemed she was going to be on display at services. Given the way her quest to find a position was going, she should probably dress with care.

She'd had an extensive wardrobe when she'd moved in with her cousin, but Phyllis had insisted that it was unseemly for her to wear anything except the black of mourning until more time had passed after the deaths of Victoria's parents. Her cousin had seen fit to donate many of her dresses, substituting them with items from her own wardrobe, which had been far too big for Victoria. She'd been down to four dresses with color in them that fit and her riding habit, which was mercifully black, when she'd come West.

Sunday morning, she chose the rose-colored gown with the wider skirts and the red velvet jacket that fit over the bodice. With a lace-edged bonnet tied with a bow under her chin, she would likely win approval from Mrs. Dalrymple, at least.

While the Reverend Mr. Dalrymple's parishioners waited for their first church to be built, they took turns meeting in each other's homes. Mrs. Dalrymple had explained with a sniff that her parlor was entirely too small to accommodate so many. The parlor of the Hartley family, whose turn it was to host the meeting, didn't seem much bigger when Victoria followed the minister and his wife up the porch steps and into the long, white, single-story house.

"They call it the Lakeside Ranch," Mrs. Dalrymple had confided as they'd driven along the country road in the buggy, cool, moist air brushing their cheeks. "I haven't seen so much as a peek at a lake, but there are little ponds in every hollow along this prairie, it seems. That is, where there aren't trees." She'd wrinkled her nose at the cluster of firs they had been passing under a heavy sky.

"Good of you to host us, George," Mr. Dalrymple said now, shaking the hand of a strapping fellow with graying blond hair and a bushy beard to match.

"Pleasure," the fellow said, though his gaze went past the minister to Victoria.

"Miss Milford," Mr. Dalrymple said smoothly, "this is Mr. Hartley. He and his wife, Elma, are our hosts for today."

"*Miss* Milford?" Mr. Hartley's smile broadened, showing a gap between his two front teeth. "Well, I'll have to introduce you to my boy, Brett. He's looking for a wife."

"Aren't all the bachelors in the area?" Mrs. Dalrymple trilled. She pulled Victoria into the white-washed parlor, where ladder-backed chairs had been crowded in rows that were already mostly filled.

"Brett Hartley isn't suitable," the minister's wife murmured, steering her over to where several men were gathered by the stone hearth. "Far too young and untried." She raised her voice. "Ah, gentlemen, so good to see you today. Have you met my dear Victoria?"

They all stood taller and adjusted ties or collars as they murmured greetings.

Mrs. Dalrymple focused on the well-rounded one with the checkered coat and thick brown side whiskers. "Victoria, dear, I particularly wanted you to meet Mr. Goodenough. I'm sure you two have much in common."

"Certainly a love of the Lord and all His works," Mr. Goodenough said in a booming voice guaranteed to draw attention. His blue eyes crinkled at the corners. "A pleasure to meet a lady of quality, Miss Milford."

She offered him her hand, and he clasped it in both of his and held on as Mrs. Dalrymple herded the other bachelors into chairs.

Victoria would be expected to make some kind of conversation, but she didn't have to leave him in possession of her hand. "I understand you are recently arrived in Puget City, sir," she said, tugging back her fingers.

"I have a few months on you," he said with a bold wink. "But I wouldn't call myself a local." He laughed as if no one would ever want to make that claim.

"A shame," Victoria said, keeping her smile pleasant. "I wouldn't mind being considered a local, for I like the area quite well. Excuse me."

She purposely turned away, and there was Jack Willets, watching her again. Her heart started thumping an allegro tempo. His plain blue suit sat well on his broad shoulders, and she would have been proud to walk into any establishment in Albany on that arm.

They met each other at the back of the room.

"I see you're meeting other folks," he said with a nod toward Mr. Goodenough, who appeared to be considering them with a frown.

Victoria put her back to the fellow. "Mrs. Dalrymple was introducing me. Is your family here?"

For some reason, that made him drop his gaze, but he tipped his head toward the right side of the parlor. He'd said he had ten siblings, but she hadn't expected them all to have varying shades of red hair. With his mother and father, and another woman with coal black

563

hair, they now took up one entire side of the parlor.

"Excuse me!" Mrs. Dalrymple called from the top of the room. "Would you all take your places, please?" She caught Victoria's eye and nodded her toward a seat on the other side of the parlor, where Mr. Goodenough had already positioned himself. He glanced Victoria's way and patted the top of the chair beside him.

"I believe there's room here," Victoria said with a smile to Jack.

He led her to a spot on the last row and sat beside her just as Mr. Dalrymple stepped up to start the service.

Chapter Three

The last time Victoria had attended church had been before Phyllis' funeral. She had left Albany soon after and had been traveling until recently. Now she closed her eyes and listened to the words the minister read.

"'In thee, O Lord, do I put my trust: let me never be put to confusion. Deliver me in Thy righteousness and cause me to escape. Incline Thine ear unto me and save me. Be Thou my strong habitation, whereunto I may continually resort. Thou hast given commandment to save me, for Thou art my rock and my fortress.'"

She drew in a deep breath. That's what she needed to remember. When she was confused, when she was concerned, she had Someone waiting to save her.

She opened her eyes as Mr. Dalrymple continued with the service. Ahead of them, Mr. Goodenough glanced one way and the other, as if making sure at least some of the people were paying attention to him. Why the posturing? Did he think that highly of himself? Or did he feel the need to bolster a flagging consequence?

Beside her, Jack nodded slowly, as if agreeing with the minister's assertion that God could see them through any difficulty. How refreshing. A gentleman who wasn't here just for show. She settled back to listen, hope tiptoeing closer.

Miss Milford continued to impress. She had a way of tilting her head, one curl teasing her cheek, as she listened to the minister, as if considering every word. She was refined, polite, and polished as she greeted the others who came up to them after service. You didn't find that in a frontier parlor every day.

"You don't mind if I steal her away for a moment?" Mrs. Dalrymple asked Jack as she trotted up to them. Before he could respond, she latched onto Victoria's arm and dragged her across the parlor. Victoria glanced back at him and gave a regretful shrug.

Jack shook his head with a chuckle.

"Pretty little thing," Mr. Abercromby said, wandering up to Jack's side. A grizzle-haired farmer, he had the land closest to the Jumping J. "Too bad about her husband."

564

Jack started. "She's a widow?" He stared at the pretty rose-colored gown with its velvet jacket. Why wasn't she wearing black? Or had she married and lost him so young?

"A widow in a matter of speaking." The older man leaned closer and lowered his voice. "I heard she came West to be a mail-order bride to some fellow in Olympia. He turned tail at the last minute and found a local gal more to his liking."

Then she was well off without him, if that was his level of intelligence and faithfulness. He couldn't imagine anyone else in the area matching Victoria Milford for beauty, poise, or composure. But maybe, like him, the other man had decided he needed a bride more suited to the frontier.

"Seems Goodenough's set his sights on her," Mr. Abercromby said, nodding across the room to where Mrs. Dalrymple had ushered Victoria into the man's company. "Never figured him to be willing to accept someone else's leftovers."

Anger lit a fire inside. "I'd hardly call Miss Milford a leftover. If there's a fault in the situation, it doesn't lie with her. Excuse me."

He stalked across the room. Some of what he was feeling must have shown on his face, for his neighbors were quick to step aside, eyes widening.

"Miss Milford," he said, interrupting what the sawmill bookkeeper was saying, "I was wondering if you'd care to ride out to the Jumping J this afternoon with me."

Her lashes fluttered, and something inside him hitched. "Why, that sounds lovely, Mr. Willets. I do so enjoy riding."

She did? Well, that was to her favor.

Mrs. Dalrymple's little mouth was puckering. "It might be just the thing another day. I was hoping Mr. Goodenough could join us for dinner."

"Happy to oblige, dear lady," Goodenough assured her, shoving his way a little closer. He put his hand on Victoria's back, and she stiffened.

"I don't think it's very far," she said, stepping away from him. "I'm sure we'll be back in plenty of time." She turned to Jack with a brilliant smile that made him forget why he was even in the parlor to begin with. "If you'd meet me at the parsonage, Mr. Willets, I'll change into my riding habit."

He was vaguely aware of Mrs. Dalrymple huffing and Mr. Goodenough grumbling, but he nodded to Victoria, then went to tell his family.

His mother was watching the door as Victoria exited. "A new friend?" she asked, brows up. Not one of his siblings had inherited her brown hair, but more than one had her warm brown eyes and welcoming smile.

His two youngest brothers, standing next to her, elbowed each other.

"A new *sweetheart*," Jason, the second to the youngest at fifteen, teased.

It wasn't as if Jack had an old sweetheart running around somewhere. Single ladies in this neck of the woods were few and far between.

He focused on his mother though heat was climbing up his neck. "I'm going riding with Miss Milford. I thought I'd bring her by the ranch."

A chorus of oohs and ahs rose from among his four sisters.

Ma beamed at him. "I'd like that very much. I'll have lemonade and cookies waiting."

"Should I have the parson waiting?" his closest brother, Jeremy, teased. He had just married his mail-order bride, Caroline, who smiled at Jack in obvious approval from

Jeremy's side.

"Not just yet," Jack said. "But holding back the others so she doesn't get overwhelmed wouldn't hurt."

"We'll do whatever you need," Caroline promised with a look to Jeremy. Caroline was like that—always willing to lend a hand.

Jack nodded his thanks, but he did not like the amusement in his brother's green eyes.

He'd brought his own horse to services, so he rode Af over to the parsonage a short time later. Victoria was out in front, already up in the saddle. Her black skirts swept the flanks of a fine dun mare with black stockings, and jet buttons sparkled down the front of her tailored bodice. So that was a riding habit. He could see why a lady would favor them if they showed off her figure to such an advantage. With that black velvet hat edged in a net veil on her auburn hair, she looked mighty fetching.

His sisters would all want one the moment they laid eyes on the outfit.

"Perfect timing," she said with an easy smile. "I was about to take Myra here along the road to see how she fares. Mr. Dalrymple gave me leave to ride her, but I haven't had a chance until now."

"You saddle her yourself?" Jack asked. As far as he knew, the Dalrymples didn't have a hired hand, so he couldn't see how she might have saddled the horse otherwise.

Her smile stiffened. "Yes, I did. Should I have waited for you?"

"No, ma'am," Jack assured her. "I'm just impressed. Not many ladies from the East seem to know how to take care of their horses."

"Have you met all that many ladies from the East?" she asked, urging the horse forward.

Jack brought Af alongside, the skewbald gelding long used to dealing with other horses. "One or two. I don't think Mrs. Dalrymple could saddle her own horse."

"Doubtful," Victoria agreed. "But then, I take it she doesn't ride for pleasure."

Pleasure, she said, as if she relished her time in the saddle as much as he did. Sitting up high, gazing across the land, he could only feel a satisfaction, a pride. And when he and Af raced, well, that was pure power.

"You rode for pleasure, then?" he asked as they set off across the fields. Clumps of gray clouds hovered on the horizon, hiding any sight of Rainier, and he could smell rain in the cool air.

"As often as I could," she said. "My parents always had a riding horse or two, but once my father had his accident, there wasn't much time for anyone to ride." She sent him a sad smile that tugged on his heart like a rope on a steer. "He arranged and received shipments from the boats that travel the canal between Lake Erie and the Hudson. He was down at the river when a shipment in heavy casks broke free and rolled over him. He never walked again."

Small wonder Mrs. Dalrymple had said that Victoria had faced heartache. "What a blow to your family to have life upended like that," He shook his head.

"It was hard," she admitted with her usual composure, keeping her gaze on the fields stretching out before them. "My mother and I did what we could, but he just wasted away. And then not long after he'd gone, my mother contracted scarlet fever, and I lost her too."

He'd heard the bright red rash, fever, and sore throat could prove fatal. "I'm not sure what I'd do if I lost both Ma and Pa. Did other family take you in, then?"

Something crossed her face, like a chill wind bending the grasses. "My cousin, Phyllis. Mostly because she was already sickly, and she knew I could help. Between my father's accident and my mother's illness, I'd learned a great deal about nursing. And when it was clear Phyllis wouldn't be with us much longer, I knew I must look for alternatives."

And here was his opportunity to ask her about the story Mr. Abercromby had told him.

"Alternatives like marrying," he said, and she nodded.

"I agreed to become a mail-order bride, but my groom changed his mind while I was en route." Again she sent him a glance, as if wondering how he'd take this revelation. "Apparently, he already had a young lady he wanted to marry, but she was being courted by others. Hearing that she might have lost him made her jealous enough to accept his suit."

"Idiot," Jack said. "He had no business promising himself when his heart belonged elsewhere."

Her smile lifted. "My sentiments exactly. Unfortunately, his defection means I must either find a position or seek another groom. I'm not sure why Mrs. Dalrymple thought of Mr. Goodenough. After meeting him today, I don't think we'll ever suit."

He wasn't sure why he was grinning like a fool. "Shame."

Her lashes fluttered. "Terrible shame." Then she giggled, and the sound went straight to his heart.

Ahead, the ranch was coming into view, the twin barns rising to obscure the house behind them. In the fields alongside, the Red Ruby cattle ambled about as they grazed. Another horse and rider were trotting out to meet them: Jeremy and his dapple-gray, Quicksilver.

Jack must have made a face, for Victoria frowned. "Is something wrong?"

"No, ma'am," he said, although he wasn't sure why his brother thought they needed an escort, especially since Jack had asked him to keep the others back.

Jeremy pulled up in front of them and tipped his low-crowned hat. "Miss Milford. I'm Jeremy Willets. Allow me to be the first to welcome you to the Jumping J."

"Thank you, Mr. Willets," she said.

Jeremy laughed. His easy-going brother generally adapted to any situation. Jack was always the one who analyzed overly much.

"Oh, you can dispense with the Mr. and Miss Willets," his brother assured her. "We don't stand on ceremony. And there are a lot of us. I'm sure my brother would be pleased if you called him Jack."

"Jeremy…" he started in warning.

"No," Jeremy said with a wink. "Jack. I'm sure I was clear."

"What a very sensible suggestion, Jeremy," Victoria said. "I'd be happy to use your brother's first name. Perhaps you can all call me Victoria."

"That's real nice of you, Victoria," Jack managed, though he scowled at his brother.

Jeremy ignored him as he often did. "I like the way you ride, Victoria. Can you make that horse run?"

"Only one way to find out," she said, and she urged the mare forward.

Jack started as they shot past him, and Jeremy had to pull Quicksilver aside.

"Now look what you've done!" Jack shouted. "She's never ridden that horse before! She could be thrown!" Chest tightening, heart pounding, he drove his heels into Af's flank and tore after her.

Chapter Four

Oh, the thrill, the joy! She'd forgotten how much she loved racing—the wind tugging at her veil, the world flying past, and the power behind the reins. They sped across the grasses, veering around a stray bush and leaping little dips. She was an eagle! She was free!

The thud of more hoofbeats told her she had company even before Jack hove into view on her right. She sent him a grin before pressing her heels against Myra's flank and urging her faster. Ahead, the twin barns she'd spotted grew larger and larger, until they towered over the paddock beside them. She slowed the horse to a canter, a trot, a walk.

She stopped beside the wooden fence, and Jack reined in next to her. His hat had blown off along the way, and his red hair waved in wild abandon around his face. It was oddly appealing.

"Where," he started, "did you learn to ride like that?"

She might have bristled if she hadn't heard the admiration in his voice. "My father loved to ride. There was a track just outside our part of Albany with some fields and trees. We'd go out in the summer after he was done with work and ride."

With a whoop, his brother galloped past to wheel his mount in a cloud of dust.

"Now, that was a run! Jack, you should show her your skills." He tossed his brother's hat toward the brown and white patched horse, and Jack caught it with one hand even as color rose in his firm cheeks.

"Maybe another time," he said.

He had no reason to be so humble. They were becoming friends, after all. "I showed you my skills, sir," Victoria said with an encouraging smile.

He regarded her a moment, then nodded. "If you'd like." He handed her his hat. "Wait here."

She set the hat on her lap and patted Myra on the neck as he clucked to his horse and urged him out onto a track that ran between two fenced pastures toward the deep green wall of the forest beyond. Cows as red as his brother's hair raised their heads to watch him.

"That's Africa," Jeremy supplied as they waited.

"You brought the cows from so far away?" Victoria asked, surprised.

He chuckled. "No, ma'am. Africa is Jack's horse, though he tends to call him Af. Our brother Jacob named him. He thought that big white patch on the side looked like the continent. Jacob likes to read about geography and such." He shrugged as if it were an odd flaw.

"And Jack doesn't like to read?" she asked. The plaintive sound in her voice nearly made her wince.

568

"We all like to read," Jeremy assured her, watching as Jack turned the horse in the shadow of the trees. "But Jack's more of a problem solver than a deep thinker like Jacob. Here he comes!"

Victoria caught her breath as Africa thundered toward them, speed building with each stride. Jack slung one leg over the saddle. Surely he wouldn't dismount now. He'd be killed!

She clutched the reins so hard Myra shied, but she couldn't take her gaze off Jack. He dropped and bounced off the dusty track, then whipped his body over the other side and did it again. Hooking one knee into the stirrup, he hung so low to the ground the fingers on one hand skimmed the grass on the edge of the track.

Applause burst out of her as he righted himself in time to bring his horse to a stop beside her. With a gentle smile, he handed her a wildflower.

Victoria clutched it close. "That was amazing! Where did *you* learn to ride like that?"

He shrugged, reminding her of his brother. "Just takes practice."

"Lots and lots of practice," Jeremy told her. "Jacob and I can jump off the side, but only Jack can ride on the side."

"It was something we did when we were boys," Jack demurred. "Before we understood we had more important things to do on the ranch." He swung down from the saddle and stroked his mount's sweaty neck. "Let me help you, Miss… Victoria. Jeremy, since you have nothing better to do, see to the horses."

His brother saluted him as if he were a soldier. "Yes, sir! Serves me right for trying to get you to show off for a lady."

She offered Jack back his hat, then took her foot from the stirrup and let him lift her down beside him. Sheltered in his arms a moment, she gazed up into his face. The fierce joy she thought she'd seen while he'd been riding had gone, to be replaced with something that looked suspiciously like resignation.

How sad. She could almost see little Jack practicing and practicing with his brothers, cheering each other on, trying to be the best. It seemed work had stolen his joy, just as it had tried to steal hers.

As his brother led the horses away, Jack stepped back and offered her his arm. "How about I show you the ranch?"

Victoria looped up her skirts, tucked the wildflower behind a button, then put her hand on his arm. He led her along the track he'd just ridden. A cool breeze ruffled the veil on her riding hat, bringing with it the scent of something earthy and the sound of cattle lowing. Once again, some of the cows raised their heads, but they seemed to find Jack's company comforting, for they quickly returned to their grazing.

He stopped beside a split-rail fence, gaze going off across the pasture. "We have about one hundred head of cattle, give or take, every year, on three hundred and twenty acres. Mostly we raise them for beef, but we keep a few for milk."

"I haven't seen many cows," she admitted. "But I seem to recall them being black and white or tawny. How did you manage to find so many red ones?"

He smiled. "These are Red Rubies. Pa bought some off another settler when we first got to the territory. I think he liked the fact that they were redheads, like him."

"Like all of you, it seems," she said, remembering the rows of brothers and sisters sitting at the church service.

"All except Ma," he acknowledged. "And Caroline. She's Jeremy's wife. They live in the house with my parents and sisters. We're building a bunk house for my brothers and the hands we need when it comes time for branding and roundup."

Victoria looked back toward the barns. From this angle, she could make out the side of a white clapboard, two-story house. "Is the house so big, then?"

"Not big enough for another bride, if that's what you mean," he said. "I have rooms above the barn, but they won't be suitable for long either. I claimed a hundred and sixty acres of forest land. I was hoping to clear part of it and build my own home, after I'm done with the church and the bunkhouse."

That was a lot of work! Small wonder he didn't have time to practice his trick riding anymore.

He led her back toward the barns, pointing out the sheep in one of the pastures, the pigs in a pen, the chicken coop and hens hunting about the yard.

"We have to make sure the raccoons or foxes don't get them," he explained as if he'd seen her look. "My sisters generally gather the eggs, though all of us learned how as children."

She began to see why Mrs. Dalrymple had cautioned her away from being a ranch wife. She hadn't had many animals growing up, aside from the horses, but she knew they all required tending in one form or another. So many animals just meant more tending.

"And do you raise crops as well?" she asked as he turned for the house.

"Some hay," he allowed, "but we have a large garden beyond the house for the family. My brothers and I generally do the planting and help with the weeding, Ma and my sisters harvest and can."

Add all that to the usual activities of cooking, cleaning, and sewing, and Jack Willets and his family likely had their hands full.

"It must keep you busy," she mused as they approached what appeared to be the back of the house.

"Very busy," he confirmed. "Some days it's all I can do to keep everyone safe and fed."

The burden nearly bowed those broad shoulders. A wife would be expected to help carry it. Could she fill that role?

She could ride, and she'd showed a reasonable amount of interest in the ranch. But her back seemed stiffer as she lifted her skirts to climb the steps to the kitchen door.

The scent of baking ham met him as he stepped into the kitchen, molasses combined with the savory juices. Normally, Jenny would have been bustling about, one or more of his sisters or Caroline helping, to get everything else ready for dinner. Now the house seemed oddly quiet.

"Double oven," he felt compelled to point out to Victoria. "Good deep sink. I always like looking out the window when I'm helping with the dishes."

"How nice," she said, but she was using that polite, cool voice again, so she didn't sound particularly pleased.

He poked his head out the door from the kitchen into the hallway, half expecting to find his family lining the walls and eavesdropping. But the hardwood floor stretched between him and the front door, empty.

Victoria joined him by the door. He nodded across the hallway. "Ma and Pa have a room downstairs. We have four more bedrooms upstairs. Dining room and parlor are along here."

They passed the hooks where everyone in the family hung their coats. Most were missing. Funny. Ma usually insisted on more sedentary pursuits on Sundays except for the milking and egg gathering. Had they started some project they hadn't discussed with him?

He showed Victoria the dining room, where the table was already set for dinner. Fourteen seats rather than the usual thirteen. They were obviously hoping she'd stay. Tension gathering, he took her across to the parlor, expecting to find a crowd waiting.

She glanced around at the sofa and ladder-backed chairs, the stone hearth, and the bookcase filled with the family favorites. "Very cozy."

Also very empty.

She turned, gaze going out the big front window overlooking the porch. Shadows disappeared on either side. He could hear the thuds of people diving for cover. Alone on one of the chairs, his mother waved a hand regally as a duchess in one of Jacob's novels.

"Come meet my mother," he said, turning for the door.

She touched her hair, but he could have told her nothing was out of place, even after that pounding ride. Everything about Victoria was perfect.

Ma beamed at her as they came out the front door. A pitcher of lemonade, cups, and a platter of cookies waited on a side table next to her. "Oh, there you are, Jack."

"Ma," Jack said. "This is Miss Victoria Milford. She's a guest of the Dalrymples."

"I noticed you at services," Ma said, motioning Victoria into the chair nearest hers. His family had several scattered along the porch, which ran all across the front of the big ranch house. "New to the area?"

"Yes," Victoria said. "From Albany."

"And are you visiting or relocating?" his mother asked, pouring her a glass of lemonade.

"Relocating," Victoria said. "Jack was kind enough to show me some of your ranch. You must be very proud."

His mother straightened her shoulders. "We've worked hard, and it shows. Jack works hardest of all."

"I gathered that," Victoria said, pausing to take a sip.

His mother jerked her head at the plate of cookies, and Jack hurriedly offered it to Victoria.

She shook her head. "Thank you. Those look delicious, but I shouldn't spoil my appetite. I promised Mrs. Dalrymple I'd be back in time for dinner."

His mother's face fell. "Oh. We were hoping you could join us."

"I wish I could," Victoria told her regretfully. "But a guest has to honor her hostess' wishes." She set down the glass. "In fact, I should probably be going."

"Ride back with her, Jack," his mother ordered, rising with Victoria. "That's only gentlemanly."

As if he needed an excuse to spend more time with her. "I'll be back for dinner," he promised.

Ma reached out and pressed Victoria's hand. "I hope we have another opportunity to become acquainted, dear."

Victoria smiled at her. "I'd like that. Thank you again for your hospitality."

"Any time," Ma assured her with a look to Jack.

Jack saw Victoria back to the barn. A scuffle from the hayloft told him where at least some of his siblings were hiding. Jeremy had disappeared as well, so Jack brought out Af and Myra and helped Victoria back into the saddle. He'd helped his sisters mount on occasion when they were riding sidesaddle. Putting his hands to Victoria's waist was something else entirely. It reminded him it was his duty to protect, to cherish.

To love and honor.

His throat felt tight, and he wasn't sure what more to say, so he said nothing as they rode back to the parsonage. She didn't seem to need to fill the silence either. He could imagine walking, hands clasped, through the fields. And when they paused, he would take her in his arms and hold her close, letting his kiss tell her how much he valued her.

"May I call on you tomorrow?" he asked as he helped her down at the parsonage.

She glanced at him as she looped up her skirts. "I'd like that. Enjoy your evening, Mr. Willets."

Her smile was kind, but somehow, he felt as if he'd been demoted.

If only there was someone in the family he could trust to ask advice about courting. He'd always been close to their oldest brother, Jesse, but he was off at Wallin Landing with his own bride. Jeremy had just married Caroline, but theirs had been an unusual sort of courtship, with her showing up unexpectedly after answering an ad for a mail-order bride.

Of course, in their family, if you wanted to answer a question, you went to one person. As soon as he returned to the ranch, which had repopulated itself nicely in his absence, he found his brother Jacob holed up on one of the porch chairs, nose in a book.

"James Fenimore Cooper," Jack said, taking the chair next to his. "That's a new author."

Jacob glanced up, the glass in his spectacles glinting. "Ned sent it with Caroline's belongings."

Ned was Caroline's only brother. He'd been at the ranch a month ago, but he'd returned to their hometown of Cincinnati to take care of some family business and sent on her trunks as well.

"Mind if I interrupt a moment?" Jack asked. "I have a couple of questions for you."

Jacob set aside the book with obvious reluctance, then swiveled to face Jack more fully. Though his brother could look him in the eyes when they were standing, everything else about him was toned down—hair more russet than red, gray eyes lighter, and build leaner.

"You know I'm courting," Jack began.

"The elegant young lady from church this morning," his brother confirmed. "Jeremy insisted we all make ourselves scarce while she was here. Is she timid?"

By the way she'd ridden that dun neck for leather, he would never make that claim. "No. I just thought we might be a bit much all at once."

Jacob shook his head. "If you want her in the family, she'll have to get used to us at some point. And hiding us away might make her wonder if we're unsavory characters."

He hadn't thought of that. "Seems like I'm already failing."

"Courtship can be like that," Jacob said cheerfully, though Jack knew he had only attempted to court one young lady. "One moment, you're on top of the world. The next, you're six feet under."

"Well, that sounds dismal." Jack leaned back. "I was hoping you'd have examples you could offer from literature or history, particularly of couples who came from different backgrounds."

His brother stuck out his lower lip, as if thinking. "Well, there's Boaz and Ruth in the Bible. They seem to have fared well. I suppose you might consider Romeo and Juliet."

"What!" Jack sputtered. "They died!"

"A cautionary tale, to be sure," Jacob agreed. "But your family and hers aren't sworn enemies."

"Who's not a sworn enemy?" Pa asked, limping out onto the porch.

Jack shot to his feet to offer him his chair. Jacob frowned at Jack.

Sometimes, when he looked at his father, he thought he saw his own future. They were both stockily built, both dedicated to family and the ranch, in that order. But his father's hair was fading into gray, and he carried a bit more weight than when Jack had been younger.

Now Pa held up a hand, then leaned against the porch support as if to steady himself. "You fixing to fight someone, son?"

"No, sir," Jack said, remaining standing out of respect. "Jacob and I were just talking."

"About your gal?" Pa asked, brow up. "Should I be thinking about a cabin raising?"

"Not just yet," Jack allowed. "Seems I have a lot of competition."

His father barked a laugh, which turned into a cough. Jack had to fight to keep from patting his back. Pa didn't like folks fussing over him. Jack was the same way.

"I saw the looks Miss Milford was sending your way," his father said when he'd recovered. "And she didn't seem overly fond of that Goodenough fellow." He winked at Jack. "Seems he's not good enough after all."

Jack laughed despite his concerns. "Thanks, Pa."

His father pushed off from the support. "Dinner's about on the table. Don't be long."

"Right behind you," Jack said, but, as Pa entered the house, Jacob rose and put out a hand.

"What's going on?" he asked, gray eyes narrowing.

"Not sure what you mean," Jack said, keeping his voice neutral.

His brother ticked off the facts on his fingers. "Pa's limp is getting worse, and now he's coughing. Jeremy and Caroline decided to live in the house instead of building the cabin he wanted. You suddenly decide you need a bride. Now."

He should have known Jacob would notice. He was only surprised the others weren't asking similar questions. He glanced in the parlor window to make sure none of their siblings were listening, then took a step closer to his brother.

"A few months ago, Doc Rawlins told Pa his heart was failing him. Ma and I decided not to worry the rest of you. Jeremy and Caroline found out by accident and chose to stay close in case they were needed."

"And you decided we needed another pair of hands," Jacob reasoned. "That's why you're wondering about Victoria Milford."

Jack nodded. "She caught my eye the moment I met her, Jacob, just like Ma and Pa like to tell us. But can she contribute to the ranch?"

His brother shook his head again. "I think you're asking the wrong question, but, by all means, invite her to dinner. Just tell Ma in advance, ask everyone to be on their best behavior, and try to look as if you like her."

The last was the easiest. He liked Victoria all too well, from her quiet smiles to her polished demeanor and skills in the saddle. If only he could see her fitting in here and enjoying it.

Chapter Five

"And so I told him if he wanted me to keep working under those unsatisfactory conditions, he would have to raise my pay. And he did."

Victoria smiled politely over her turkey and dumplings. Who knew a sawmill could have so many trials and tribulations? Or perhaps it was Mr. Goodenough who had all the trials.

"Well, I'm sure you were pleased about that," Mrs. Dalrymple said with a bob of her head as she sat across the table from Victoria. "And now you have even more to offer a wife." She looked to Victoria.

She dabbed her mouth with her napkin as an excuse not to weigh in. She had worried Jack Willets might want merely another pair of hands for his ranch instead of a wife he could love and cherish, but she wasn't sure Mr. Goodenough had room in his heart for anyone but himself.

"I am in a most fortunate position," he declared now, mopping up the last of his second helping. "A steady job with good pay, a house right in town with the mercantiles only a few steps away, the admiration and respect of all my peers, though there are few enough of those, I admit. And I hope to purchase a buggy soon."

From what Victoria had seen, buggies were still somewhat rare here. Most families walked, rode, or drove in a wagon.

"How lovely," Mrs. Dalrymple enthused. "Isn't that lovely, Victoria?"

No room for excuses this time. She pasted on a smile. "Yes, very impressive. I hope those working to build the church will be as industrious as you are, Mr. Goodenough."

He puffed out his already thoroughly puffed chest, straining the buttons on his silk waistcoat. "What they need is motivation and good management." He turned to Mr. Dalrymple at the head of the table. "Speaking of which, I thought I would volunteer my skills to the task."

The minister nodded with a smile. "That would be very welcome. Many hands make light work. Talk to Jack Willets. He's leading the charge for us."

A little tingle went through her. Just at the mention of Jack's name? Where was her caution, her pride?

"Willets seems competent," Mr. Goodenough allowed, leaning back in the chair and setting it to creaking. "But I do wonder how much experience he has managing a task of this size. I'll see what I can do to help. At the very least, I can advise him on the budget."

Oh, Jack would love that. Victoria bit her lip and dropped her gaze to her nearly clean plate.

"Perhaps a walk after dinner," Mrs. Dalrymple suggested, rising. "Let's fetch our coats, Victoria, dear."

She rose, and the minister and Mr. Goodenough stood as well.

"I'd be delighted to join you," the latter said, holding her chair for her.

An interminable hour later, she finally stood on the porch as he rode off into the sunset toward Puget City.

"Successful fellow," Mrs. Dalrymple pointed out, turning for the door. "Well spoken."

"He certainly speaks well for himself," Victoria agreed, following her into the house.

The minister's wife pursed her lips. "I am beginning to get the impression you don't favor him."

She had to go carefully. The Dalrymples had done so much for her—taking her in when Charles had abandoned her, allowing her to live here free of charge, helping her find her way in this new community. She didn't want to insult the lady, but she couldn't lie to her.

"He isn't what I had hoped for in a husband," she tried as she pulled off her coat.

"Well, we can't always get everything we want," Mrs. Dalrymple said cheerfully. "What do you find lacking, dear?"

"A quieter, more contemplative nature?" she mused, helping the minister's wife off with her coat as well. "A focus on family rather than career? A dedication to helping others?"

Mrs. Dalrymple arched a brow. "You just described Jack Willets."

Victoria started, face heating. "Why, I suppose I did. But there's more." She glanced around as they came into the parlor and was relieved to find the minister hadn't joined them yet. Still, she lowered her voice. "I can't help thinking that I should feel something for the fellow I intend to marry. And I just can't find it in me to feel anything but annoyance with Mr. Goodenough."

Mrs. Dalrymple cocked her head. "And you felt something for Charles Bishop, who promised to marry you if you came all this way?"

The reminder still stung, as if she'd reopened a sore she'd thought healed.

"No, I suppose not," she said, dropping onto the sofa. "But look where that led me! It seems he used me merely to make his former sweetheart jealous. He never cared about me."

Mrs. Dalrymple perched beside her and reached out to pat her hands where she'd folded them tightly in her lap. "You were dealt a severe blow. There's no denying it. But it does not have to end tragically. Were there no young men in Albany who stirred your heart?"

She could not meet the woman's gaze. "I hadn't really settled on anyone before my father's accident and my mother's illness, and none saw fit to help with either. And afterward, my cousin wanted all my attention. I suppose I answered Mr. Bishop's ad because I needed to escape the daily reminders of what had been. And I certainly didn't want someone to marry me out of pity!"

"Still, I can see marrying Mr. Goodenough would not make you as happy as I'd hoped," Mrs. Dalrymple said. "Would marrying Mr. Willets be better?"

Hope leaped up, so strong she had to press her hand to her chest as if that would contain it. "I… I think so," she marveled, meeting her hostess' gaze at last. "But you were right. There's a lot about ranching I don't know. Can I be the wife Jack needs?"

The minister's wife smiled. "You leave everything to me, dear. With any luck, we'll have you engaged before Decoration Day at the end of May."

Jack wiped his brow with a kerchief before tucking it back into the pocket of his work trousers. The last day of April was sunnier and warmer than usual, and leveling the ground for the church wasn't the easiest task. The Hawks Prairie soil was thick and rich, but it grew rocks as well as it grew hay.

He'd taken on leadership for the effort, with their neighbors stopping by when they could to help. He probably should have left it to someone else, given all that was happening on the ranch, but everyone in his family had tried to contribute to the effort in some way.

Ma, Jane, Joanna, and Joy had donated various sewing projects like quilts, and Jenny and Caroline had baked pies and cobblers for the auction, that had helped raise money for the land and building materials. Jeremy, Jacob, and Pa had coordinated with the architect in Olympia to draw up plans. And Jason and Joshua had ridden miles carrying messages and donations. Jack knew how to get things done. Preparing the ground had seemed a logical task.

Now, across the thirty-foot square of cleared area, his oldest sister, Jane, raked some of the remaining rocks into a pile. Caroline had her own rake at the opposite corner. Joy and Joanna waited with their aprons tied in hammocks in front of them to pick up the stones and carry them off to one side, where they could be used for the foundation. Caroline and his sisters had all been far enough along on their chores for the week that he'd felt comfortable taking them away from the ranch.

"Is that your girl?" Jane asked with a nod toward the parsonage a little distance away.

Jack turned to find Victoria walking toward them. She was wearing that red-and-green plaid gown again. It shimmered as she moved, the lace at the hem and cuffs fluttering.

"What's she carrying?" Joanna asked, squinting.

Joy bounced on her feet, setting her apron to flapping. "I know, I know! That's a serving platter. She's bringing us tea!"

Lemonade, as it turned out. The silver platter held a pitcher of the yellow drink and several glasses.

"I thought you could use a break," Victoria said with a smile all around.

His heart started beating faster, and it wasn't at the thought of a drink of the cool lemonade. He set aside his shovel. "Here, let me hold that for you."

If anything, her grip tightened. "It isn't heavy. Perhaps you could introduce me, and someone else could pour?"

Where were his manners? Ma would be scolding him if she had been here. "Miss Victoria Milford, allow me to present my sisters, Jane…"

Jane nodded in greeting, hair as red as his glinting in the sunlight.

"Joanna…"

Joanna grinned, lighter-red curls already springing free of her bun.

"Caroline…"

Dark-haired Caroline waggled her fingers.

"And Joy."

Joy bobbed a wobbly curtsey, her own coppery curls swaying. "Very pleased to make your acquaintance, I'm sure."

"Very pleased to meet you as well," Victoria said. "In fact, you're some of the only young ladies I've met since arriving in Washington Territory."

Joanna put a hand on her hip. "Well, there aren't very many of us."

"Men still outnumber the women eight to one," Jane allowed. "And I'll pour." She reached for the pitcher as Caroline and Joy came to join them.

"Thank you," Victoria said. As Jane handed around glasses, Victoria glanced at the field. "This is where the church will stand?"

"Yes, ma'am," Jack said before taking a long swallow of the tart liquid.

"Would you like to see a drawing?" Joy asked. Before Victoria could even nod, she shoved her glass at Joanna and dug in her apron pocket. "This is what it's going to look like." She unfolded the piece of paper and held it up.

"I didn't know you'd sketched it, Joy," Jack said, eyeing his sister's handiwork. The square, white church showed two windows on a side, with a short steeple for the bell, capped with metal spikes surrounding the cross.

"I wanted a copy, so I took a likeness of the drawings the architect gave us," she said. She angled the paper so she could point at the top. "All those pointy pieces are called the crown of thorns, like what our Savior wore for us."

"Very fitting," Victoria said. "And a very good likeness, Miss Joy. Nicely done."

Joy folded her paper as she pressed up the shoulders of her gingham dress in obvious pleasure. "Thank you very kindly."

"How soon do you expect to finish?" Victoria asked as Jane, Joanna, and Caroline set their empty glasses back on the tray, and Joy began drinking.

"The first step is clearing and leveling the ground," Jack explained. "We should have that done shortly. Next, we'll set up the stones for the foundation and sink supports for the floor. The beams rest on those. Then we need to have all the materials delivered."

She cocked her head, and the breeze tugged a strand of hair free. He swallowed the longing to tuck it back.

"And did Mr. Egbert donate as you'd hoped?" she asked.

"Yes, ma'am. The kegs of nails and boxes of hinges and knobs will come with the lumber. I expect them later this week or early next. The weekend after, we'll have a church raising."

"Every man, woman, and child old enough to carry something will help," Jane confirmed. "You should come, Miss Milford."

"I'd be delighted to help wherever I can," she assured them, but her gaze went to Jack.

"Oh, good," Caroline said, stepping forward. "Jane and I about have piles ready. Maybe you could help Joanna and Joy carry them off the clearing."

Caroline and his sisters had on their work gowns, practical gingham, with aprons over the top. He wasn't sure what Victoria's gown was made of, but it certainly hadn't been designed for working.

"Of course," Victoria said. "Let me return this tray to the parsonage, and I'll be right back."

His gaze followed her figure, like she was water, and he was parched.

Jane came to nudge him with her shoulder. His sister was nearly as tall as him and her oldest brothers, making her tower over any other lady in the area and a good portion of the men. "I hear she rides well. Can she shoot?"

Jack gripped his shovel. "Never had call to ask."

"It's a handy trait," Joanna chimed in. "Fox in the henhouse, cougar going after one of the calves, rustlers."

"Joanna," Jack warned her, and his sister widened her eyes.

"What?" she asked innocently. "You had to fight off thieves only a month ago."

"Scare off more like," he reminded her.

She nodded to his hip. "You're still wearing your six-gun."

"That's just a precaution," Jack said.

"Like if we meet a bear or a wolf," Joy helpfully supplied.

Jack groaned. "Will you all keep that to yourselves? The last thing we need to do is scare her away."

Caroline patted his shoulder. "Oh, I don't think there's any chance of that. She seems eager to help." She nodded to where Victoria was already hurrying back toward them. Like his sisters, she now wore a voluminous apron over the top of her fancy gown.

Jane took her arm and led her over to the pile of rocks, explaining what was needed. Joanna paired herself with Caroline, and Joy stayed close to Jane and Victoria. He watched as Victoria bent and began picking up rocks. The sunlight outlined every curve. Mighty hard for a fellow to focus on work.

He gave himself a mental shake, then purposely put his back to the fetching sight and began plying his shovel again.

Their voices drifted to him across the space nonetheless.

"Did you have a school back East?" Joy asked.

"I had a governess," Victoria explained.

"What's that?" his littlest sister asked, sounding perplexed.

"It's a live-in teacher," Jane offered. "A woman trained in all manner of subjects who shows you how to become a lady."

"That's right," Victoria said. Did her voice sound strained? Jack chanced a glance, only to find her tottering toward the edge of the foundation with an armload of rocks. Everything in him urged him to go help. He shoved his blade down into the ground instead.

"I understand there's no school in Puget City," she said as she dumped her rocks near him with a clatter. "Do you have a schoolteacher on Hawks Prairie?" She smiled up at him, and somehow his shovel never moved.

"Not yet," Jane explained. "Though Jacob is hoping to start a school as soon as the church is built."

That was news to him, but it didn't surprise him, given his brother's great regard for learning. Victoria moved off, and he made himself keep working.

"Did she teach you to shoot, your governess?" Joy asked.

He nearly broke the shovel he gripped it so hard, but he thought for a moment that Jane was coming to the rescue.

"Ladies in cities don't need to shoot, Joy," she told the girl. "More likely Victoria's governess taught her to speak foreign languages and embroider and paint pretty pictures and such."

She made Victoria sound almost useless. Jack threw down the shovel. "I'll have you know that Victoria plays the piano. You never heard anything more beautiful."

Jane's face lit up with a grin. Had she been trying to provoke him?

"Thank you," Victoria said, and her smile warmed him more than the sunshine.

"You want me to take the shovel for a while, Jack?" his oldest sister asked, sweet as molasses.

Jack bent to retrieve it. "No. I'm fine. Best we keep working before the day gets any later."

Jane chuckled, but at least she stopped baiting him.

His sisters, Caroline, and Victoria continued to chat as they worked. The topics were benign enough that he could let the sound wash over him. When he was done here, he had to check on a cow that was about ready to calve and another that seemed to be having trouble eating enough. Then there was the planting for Ma's garden and preparing to brand the new calves. Joanna had been begging for a trip to the Sound to gather clams, even though it was a bit early in the season and they'd have to make sure there was no brackish water nearby. Everyone in the area knew that clams could turn deadly if they sat in the red-tinged water too long.

And then he had to build a church and a bunkhouse and his own cabin…

"I like it," Victoria said.

Jack looked up. She and Joy stood in the center of the space, rocks clustered around them. He nearly sagged. With a sigh, he tipped the shovel up on his shoulder and trudged over to them.

"The idea, Joy," he said, "is to clear the rocks. Not pile them up in a different place."

His little sister's face fell. "But Jack…"

"Move them," Jack said. "Now."

Victoria came up to him and put her hands on his shoulders. "Perhaps if you stood here, you might have a different perspective." She twisted him to one side.

Jack frowned at her. "I don't see…"

"Trust me," she murmured. "You will. Not everything has to be work, Jack. Look again."

He blinked as she stepped away, and his sister's handiwork came into focus. "Is that a heart?"

"And a cross inside," Joy said, scurrying around the design. "See, Jack?"

"Because our foundation is the Lord," Victoria murmured. "What better on which to build a church?"

Humbled, he lowered the shovel. "I'm sorry, Joy. That's beautiful. Thank you."

She swayed back and forth, skirts swishing. "Victoria helped."

"More than she knows," Jack said.

Victoria's lips turned up. "I'm glad you like it. Now, I should be going, alas. I promised Mrs. Dalrymple I'd help with the laundry." She glanced around. "It was very nice meeting you all."

"You too," Caroline called, and Joanna nodded.

She started away, and Jane tipped her head at Jack, mouthing *Go on!*

Jack dropped his shovel and hurried to pace Victoria.

"Thank you again," he said. "I can get too focused on work."

"I noticed," she said with a look in his direction. "But I'm glad you saw the beauty in what your sister created."

"It's easy to see beauty when you're standing by me."

Once more, color rose in her cheeks, until he had to fist his hands to keep from reaching out to touch them.

"Then I'm doubly glad I could help today," she said.

His throat was unaccountably tight. He cleared it. "I may not have a chance to call later today, as I'd hoped. Perhaps you'd be willing to come over to the ranch again on Saturday, even spend the night? Services will be at our place on Sunday. I'd love you to meet the rest of the family." He glanced back at his sisters and Caroline, who were all watching avidly. "I promise they'll be better behaved."

"Every member of your family I've met has been charming," she told him. "And I'd be delighted to join you on Saturday."

His head was bobbing like a horse about to be fed, but he saw her all the way to the door of the parsonage and stood for a moment even after the door had shut behind her.

Chapter Six

Mrs. Dalrymple bustled into the parlor the next morning as Victoria was playing the piano. "We should work in the kitchen today, dear," she said. "We want to make sure your cooking skills shine."

Victoria stilled her hands. "My cooking skills?"

The minister's wife snapped a nod. "Cooking, cleaning, washing, darning and mending, churning, all the wifely arts a rancher might expect from his bride. Except canning and preserving food. We don't have much of a harvest yet. But I intend to school you myself in the other areas."

She looked so very pleased that Victoria could hardly argue. And she was glad to be of assistance around the house. After all, the Dalrymples were giving her room and board. And if she ended up finding a position as a cook or a laundress, at least she'd have some skills. But she couldn't help thinking that the quality of her character ought to be more important than the work of her hands.

"Besides," Mrs. Dalrymple said as Victoria rose from the piano bench, "we have a better view of the church site from the kitchen window, so we can spot Mr. Willets when he arrives."

Sure enough, Jack, Jeremy, Caroline, and Joy drove up in a wagon as Mrs. Dalrymple was critiquing Victoria's ability to wash dishes (who knew glasses might spot if not dried with the proper towel?). The minister's wife hurried to set the clean glasses and a pitcher of water on her silver tray. "Take these out. Ask him questions. Men like that."

Jack hadn't seemed to appreciate idle conversation while he was working when she'd gone out yesterday. But she was curious about what he and his brother were doing unfurling that long line of twine, and she just wanted to spend time with him, so she carried the tray out once more.

The prairie seemed to know it was May Day. Wildflowers were beginning to pop up, rich reds, brilliant blues, and gorgeous golds. With a sharp cry, a gull wheeled overhead under a pale sky dotted with fluffy white clouds.

Caroline, gingham skirts pooling below her gray wool coat, was crouched at the side of the cleared space, now clutching one end of the twine, while Jack held the other end across from her. Jeremy took out a triangular wood frame with a lead-weighted string hanging from the top point and positioned the bottom of the triangle along the string.

"Level," he proclaimed, lifting the triangle. "Next."

Caroline advanced a few feet to the right. So did Jack.

"That's a plumb bob," Joy explained, skipping over to join Victoria. "They're making sure the ground is level so no one will slip in church."

"And Jack insists that the walls and roof actually be aligned," Jeremy teased with a wink to Victoria. "Imagine that."

"Good morning, Victoria!" Caroline called, waving her free hand.

Jack straightened as if noticing Victoria for the first time and yanked the hat off his head. "Victoria. Good morning. You didn't have to come out."

"I wanted to," she assured him. "Let me know when you're ready to take a break."

Jeremy set the plumb bob down on the ground. "How about now?"

Jack frowned at him. "We just got started."

"Good time to interrupt, then," his brother said. He tipped his head to his wife, who abandoned her end of the twine and came to join him.

With a sigh, Jack followed suit.

Soon, Jeremy and Caroline had moved to one side, heads close together. The smiles passing between them, the way Jeremy cradled her hand, raised such a longing in Victoria she had to grip the tray to keep from swaying. Could she ever have such a love?

"Honeymooners," Jack said, smiling as he shook his head.

"Every couple should be so fortunate," Victoria insisted.

He regarded her a moment, then took a cautious sip of water before commenting. "Is that what you hope for?"

Until she'd met him, it hadn't been. Perhaps the long days of toil caring for her parents and then Phyllis had done more damage to her hopes than she'd thought. Certainly Phyllis had had a dismal outlook on life. Whatever the cause, somewhere along the way, Victoria had given up on the idea of a love match. Now she couldn't stop the hope that was building.

"I suppose every girl wants a sweetheart who dotes on her," she told Jack. "My parents were affectionate."

"Mine too," he acknowledged. "They claim to have fallen in love at first sight." He shifted on his feet as if uncomfortable with the idea.

She couldn't claim to have been felled by love's first look, but every day she found more to admire about him. His quiet leadership, his dedication. The way his smile melted every concern.

"There must be as many paths to love as there are couples," she said. "Every courtship is unique in that regard."

He drew in a breath as if she'd eased a burden. "I agree. Any two people will bring something a little different to a relationship." He glanced across the foundation to where Jeremy was bending his head to kiss his bride. "I'm not sure how much work we're going to get out of those two today."

"Let's give them a few more moments," Victoria said with a smile. She set the tray down on a nearby rock, then perched on another. Jack came to sit on a third. It seemed he didn't mind conversation after all. Before she knew it, they were chatting about their childhoods. She learned he'd been born in Virginia, but his father had moved the growing family first to California and then progressively north before taking a claim on Hawks Prairie.

"We always had a house in town," she said, "with neighbors on every side. I can't imagine growing up first in a tent and then a cabin with no one around for miles!"

"It never felt hard to me," he said. "I suspect Ma and Pa took on more of the tasks then, but Jesse, our oldest brother, was born the biggest and strongest of us all, so he started lending a hand when he was pretty young."

Victoria smiled at him. "And you and your younger brothers learned those tricks in the saddle. What else did you do for fun?"

"Fun?" He blew out his cheeks as if the answer was hard to come by.

"Fun," she insisted. "Like me riding with my father. And in the winter, we'd ice skate on the pond near where we rode."

His gaze went off in the distance as if he peered back in time, and a smile teased the corners of his mouth.

"I remember one summer Pa had an extra wagon wheel rim. We used to roll that circle of iron up and down the drive, whacking it with sticks. I figured out that if I stayed in the middle of the track, between the ruts, I could keep the rim up the longest. Didn't take long for Jacob to notice what I was doing and copy me, even if he was smaller. He sulked when Pa took it back to put on the wagon, but I understood. Work has to come first."

"That's what Jack always says," Joy put in, coming to contribute a few stray rocks to the foundation. "May I have that agate by your foot, Victoria? It would look ever so nice at the point of the heart."

Victoria swung her skirts aside, but Jack seemed to have realized he was putting pleasure before work, for he rose and clapped his hands. "Break's over. We need to finish setting the foundation and get back to the ranch."

Jeremy broke away from Caroline with obvious reluctance, then jogged back to his plumb bob as she took up her place across from Jack again.

"You're welcome to stay and help, Victoria," Jeremy called as she reached for the tray. "I'm sure Caroline, Joy, and I would enjoy your company even if Jack doesn't."

Jack jerked upright. "Who says I don't enjoy her company?"

His brother arched a brow. "Oh, so you do favor her. My mistake."

Jack's face reddened. "Pay him no mind, Victoria. You are always welcome, but I'm sure you have things you'd rather be doing."

"Nothing more pressing than being with you," she assured him.

That slow smile sent her stomach into a flip.

In the center of the foundation, Jeremy bent to his tool. "Could we please focus on the task? Some of us have things to do."

Caroline giggled, but she bent to place the line.

Victoria stayed a while longer, helping Joy move rocks that were interfering with the leveling process. Mrs. Dalrymple nearly purred like a cat in the cream when Victoria finally returned to the house.

"Things are coming along well, I see," she said. "Tomorrow, we'll work on laundry and housekeeping."

Wednesday, Victoria was hanging out sheets on the clothesline behind the parsonage when Jack and Jane rode in to the church site. Another young man drove a buckboard wagon up beside them. Jane saw to the horses while the newcomer and Jack began unloading stump-like chunks of wood from the wagon bed. Did Jack look tired already? Were his movements a little stiff? Surely even those broad shoulders needed a rest once in a while! Everything in her itched to go talk to him, help him, but she could hardly leave wet things clumped in the wash basket. She might not have done laundry before—and what a hot, tiresome process it was!—but even she knew that.

The backdoor of the parsonage banged as Mrs. Dalrymple hurried down the steps, broad-brimmed hat in one hand.

"Here," she said, thrusting it at Victoria. "Take this. He needs something better to shield himself from the sun. Men like it when women fuss over them. I'll finish the laundry."

Bemused, Victoria accepted the hat and went to join the others at the worksite.

The men had already peeled off their coats and were taking up tools, a shovel for Jack and a heavy mallet for his helper, who had bright blond hair and light blue eyes.

He hastily lowered his tools and bobbed his head as she approached. "Ma'am. Can we help you?"

Jack turned and smiled, and the whole day brightened. "Victoria." He just gazed at her a moment, and she felt the color rising in her cheeks.

The other young man cleared his throat.

Jack collected himself. "Miss Milford, this is our neighbor, Mr. Hartley."

"Your family hosted services last Sunday," Victoria realized. "I believe I met your father."

"That's right," he said with a final nod. "Pa said he wanted me to meet you, but you were otherwise detained." He glanced at Jack as if he knew entirely who was to blame there.

"I'm new to the area," Victoria explained. "Mrs. Dalrymple is trying to introduce me to everyone. I'm very glad to see you here to help Mr. Willets today. This is a big project, and his family has been working so hard."

"Glad to be of assistance," Mr. Hartley said, raising his head and squaring his shoulders as if prepared to do battle.

Victoria turned to Jack and offered the hat. "Mrs. Dalrymple thought you might need this. I'm more curious about what you're doing today. Surely those logs are too small to start the walls."

"They're the supports," Jack said, accepting the hat and slipping it over his hair. "Hartley and I are going to pound them into the foundation, and Jane's going to check that they're level. We'll set the beams across them, then the floor joists over the beams before we put in the flooring."

"Fascinating," Victoria said.

Mr. Hartley flexed his arms, showing off the muscles along his shoulders. "Nothing gets the blood moving like a day with a mallet." He swung up his tool and strutted over to the foundation.

"I better help before he hurts himself," Jack said. "I'm not sure what you can do today, Victoria, but I appreciate you and Mrs. Dalrymple thinking of me."

She thought of him entirely too much! But she merely smiled as he went to dig a spot for the first support.

Jane came to join her. Her fiery hair was mostly hidden inside a plain straw bonnet that was fraying along one side. "Mr. Hartley is trying to impress, I see."

"So I gathered," Victoria said as he rolled one of the massive pegs into Jack's hole, then glanced up as if to make sure she was watching. "I thought maybe he was trying to get your attention."

"Not mine," Jane assured her with a laugh. "And I wouldn't be interested if he was. He needs a bit more time to cure. Besides, I don't think he likes having to look up into my eyes. Most men don't, it seems." She shrugged.

"Then they have far too fragile consequences," Victoria said. "I've heard of tall women who slumped to make men feel more comfortable. I'm glad you don't."

"Me too." Jane shared a smile with her. "Besides, I always thought it was more satisfying to be valued for who you are, not who others want you to be."

"That," Victoria said, gaze going back to Jack, "is what I'm coming to learn."

She wasn't afraid to work. Jack had to give Victoria that. Smart too. She'd only seen Jeremy use the plumb bob yesterday, as far as he knew, but she was using it to help Jane make sure the row of supports was level with each other, with no protest as to the amount of dust clinging to her flounced hem.

"Mighty pretty gal," Hartley said, pausing to wipe his brow with the back of his gloved hand. "You courting her?"

"I am," Jack said, and if he sounded proud of the fact, he was willing to acknowledge it.

Hartley sighed. "Figures. First Miss Cadhill marries your brother, and now you latch onto the next unmarried gal who shows up on Hawks Prairie."

Jack positioned the support in the hole and held it while Hartley brought the mallet down with a whack. "To be fair, Jeremy wrote away for Miss Cadhill, and I asked Mrs. Dalrymple to help me find a bride."

Hartley slammed down the mallet again. "Maybe I should do that, then, talk to the minister's wife."

Jack eyed him. Brett Hartley was young, having just turned one and twenty, but his father had entrusted him with more and more responsibility at the prosperous Lakeside Ranch, and he seemed to have a good head on his shoulders. "You know I have three sisters of marriageable age."

Hartley smacked the support, then nodded to Jack, who tried to wiggle it. It didn't move.

Hartley leaned closer and lowered his voice. "Jenny's sweet, but she never pays me the least mind. I hear Joanna has her heart set on Miss Cadhill's brother. And your sister Jane scares me."

Jack couldn't help his chuckle as Hartley straightened, cheeks reddening. "I reckon Jane scares a few fellows. She can out-ride and out-shoot most of them. But she's smart, and she's loyal, and she knows her way around a ranch. The man who wins her heart will be one lucky groom."

Hartley straightened and glanced at Jane again as if seeing her with new eyes. Then he shook his head and went to fetch the next support.

Jack looked to where his sister was pointing something out along the line of foundation rocks to Victoria. Aside from the red of their hair, they couldn't be more different. Victoria was daintier, more refined in her movements. Her clothes were tailored to her form and appeared to be chosen with care. Jane threw on whatever was handy, like that green gingham dress whose only tailoring was the cinch at her hips made by her gun belt.

His sister bent now and heaved on a rock. It must have proven too heavy even for her, for Victoria hurriedly crouched as if to help her. Jack tossed aside the shovel and strode toward them.

"Here," he said. "Allow me." He wrestled the boulder closer to the other stones until they fit snugly. As he straightened, he caught Victoria watching him. His shoulders came back, and his chest puffed out. What, was he posturing, like Hartley?

Her cheeks looked as hot as his felt, but maybe she had a better reason. He yanked off the hat and offered it to her. "Looks like the sun's kissed you. Maybe you need this more than I do."

"Maybe she's hoping for a kiss from someone other than the sun," Jane pointed out.

Victoria backed away. "No, no, you keep it. I should see about finishing the laundry. I hope everything goes well." She picked up her skirts and fled across the grass.

Jack shoved the hat back on his head. "You didn't have to frighten her off."

"You didn't have to strut around like a rooster," Jane countered. "And I don't think she's remotely afraid of you. More like you're afraid of her."

"What! Am not." Immediately, he felt like a boy again, arguing with his sister about who could ride faster, jump higher.

Jane didn't help. She stuck out her tongue at him. "Are too, or you would have proposed by now."

He closed the distance between them and lowered his voice, mindful of Hartley behind them. "I'm taking my time, making sure she's comfortable with me."

"Oh, I'd say she's comfortable," Jane said. "See how she keeps coming out like that every time we start working? See how she talks to you so easily, like you're old friends?"

"Maybe she's lonely," he hazarded. "She doesn't know many folks here yet."

"No offense, Jack, but a lot of other menfolk would be happy to talk with her, and more eloquently than you do."

He grimaced. "You don't have to rub salt in the wound."

"You know your limitations as well as I know mine," Jane said, cuffing him on the shoulder. "And I hope you know your stellar qualities as well. You love your family, you're a hard worker, and you're a born problem-solver. She'd be fortunate to have you. So, ask her."

"Not yet," Jack insisted. "Not 'til she's sure."

Jane shook her head. "Then you better do something to make her sure, because Hartley and Goodenough won't be the last fellows chasing after her. And they won't hesitate."

That's what he feared.

Chapter Seven

Thursday, Victoria was on the back steps of the parsonage, working the dasher on a butter churn. She'd been at it for more than a quarter hour and had only sighted a few stray specks when she'd lifted the lid of the tall wooden barrel to check. Already her shoulders ached.

"I will never take a buttered roll for granted again," she told Mrs. Dalrymple as the minister's wife poked her head out of the door.

"Never mind that," she said, coming to take the long rod of the dasher from her. "The lumber wagon is coming up the drive. I expect Mr. Willets will be here to meet it shortly." She studied Victoria critically. "You don't need to pinch your cheeks—you have an enviable amount of color at the moment."

Apparently churning was good for something more than making butter!

"Lick your lips," she advised. "Stand up tall. Go direct them on where to put everything. Men like a woman who's interested in their work."

There was interested, and there was interfering. She certainly had no intention of doing the latter. But she spotted Jack and Jeremy riding up, so she relinquished her spot at the churn with relief and gratitude and hurried out to meet them.

With a rattle and creak, the lumber wagon trundled around the parsonage. It was stacked high with long boards and beams and drawn by two stout oxen. She nearly cheered until she noticed Mr. Goodenough on the bench beside the driver. She certainly didn't want to give him the impression she was glad to see him.

Jack was glad to see the shipment. That was evident by the satisfied smile on his face as she approached. He nodded a welcome to her before focusing on the big wagon.

"Just there, I think," Mr. Goodenough ordered the driver. At least today he looked as if he was ready to work, for his coat was a more serviceable brown, and he'd pressed a derby to his head.

Jack waved him in a different direction. "Farther out. You're too close to the foundation."

Sure enough, the oxen had stepped over the even line of rocks, and now the front wheels were pressing against them, knocking a few out of place.

"All the better to distribute the boards," Mr. Goodenough countered.

"Whoa!" the driver commanded his team. "Stand!"

The oxen obediently came to a halt. Jeremy shook his head. Jack hurried forward even as Mr. Goodenough climbed down from the bench and surveyed the ground.

"I hope you're ready," he said. "That foundation looks unsteady to me."

Jack's jaw was tight. "We're ready. Help me unload this."

Mr. Goodenough held up both hands. "My task was to deliver the lumber and ensure that my owner is paid. No one said anything about manual labor." He must have noticed Victoria at last, for his round face broadened even further in a smile, and he snatched the hat from his head. "Miss Milford, what an unexpected pleasure! Come to see the good work we do at the sawmill?"

"And the good work Mr. Willets and his brother are doing on the church," Victoria said. "I believe you told Mr. Dalrymple that you were interested in helping too."

"I have helped," he said, patting the battered side of the rough-wood wagon. "I negotiated a very good price for these supplies. Speaking of which, I should see about my employer getting paid." He held out his arm. "Allow me to escort you back to the parsonage, Victoria, dear."

She had not given him leave to use her first name! "I believe I'll stay here."

His smile faded, and he pulled back his arm, but he turned and strode toward the parsonage.

"Presumptuous makebate," she muttered, turning to see how she might help. Jeremy was grinning at her, and Jack's cheek twitched, as if he was trying not to do the same.

While the driver saw to his oxen, the two brothers pulled the lumber from the bed and stacked it where the workers could use it for the church raising. Victoria couldn't very well help carry boards, but she found the small kegs of nails and hinges and the box of door knobs in the wagon and ferried those to the pile as well.

Mr. Goodenough returned in time to take one from her. "Now, then, what sort of gentleman allows a lady to work?" He shot Jack a scowl, then took Victoria's arm and led her off to one side. "I commend your spirit, my dear, but you'd be better suited to help Mrs. Dalrymple in the house. And I can assure you that my wife would never have to sully her hands in this sort of work."

But he certainly wouldn't sully his hands either, so she could only wonder at the truth of the statement. "I don't mind supporting a good cause, sir. If you'll excuse me, I'll go see if the Reverend Mr. Dalrymple might have a spare tarpaulin to cover the wood. It seems your employer neglected to send one."

He reddened, but Jack winked at her as she passed.

By the time she returned, the wagon, Mr. Goodenough, Jeremy, and the horses were gone. Jack helped her tuck the tarpaulin Mr. Dalrymple had provided around the precious lumber.

"That should do it," he said, stepping back. "We'll be ready whenever we have helpers."

"I see you decided to keep Joy's contribution," Victoria said, following his gaze out over the squared-up foundation.

He smiled. "We'll be laying the beams across it, so it won't hurt anything, and it was a nice thought." His gaze came back to hers, and something swirled in the smoke. "I wouldn't have seen it without you, Victoria. I didn't even realize Joy had a talent for drawing and such. You noticed, and you encouraged her. I hear from Jane you encouraged her to be herself too. That's a gift."

She felt warm all over, even with the cool breeze coming across the prairie. "Well, you certainly have the gift of perseverance! I've never met anyone who works as hard as you do."

"I expect anyone who ranches or farms has to work as hard," he allowed. "Though this is one of the busiest seasons of the year. You almost have time to hear yourself think between Christmas and Valentine's Day."

"Does it snow much here?" she asked, trying to imagine the undulating grasslands and forest covered in a coat of white.

"Not too bad most years. But you wait. The wildflowers are already starting to bloom, and in the next few weeks, the land will erupt in color." He licked his lips. "I don't suppose you have time to take a walk. There's something I'd like to show you."

Victoria grinned. "Intriguing! I'd be delighted to join you."

He gestured to the south, and she fell into step beside him. The grasses brushed her skirts, and the breeze brushed her cheeks.

Something brushed her fingers.

Glancing down, she found Jack's hand against her own. Easy enough to tuck her fingers into his grip. He smiled, and her heart sang.

She could hardly wait to see what more he wanted to show her.

They were holding hands. He couldn't stop grinning. It didn't matter that the clouds were dropping lower and getting blacker every moment. It didn't matter the amount of work waiting for him back home. Right now, he just wanted to be here, with her.

But he wasn't going to mention the significance of where he was taking her or honor its tradition.

The tradition of taking your sweetheart there for a kiss.

Jeremy had started it; Jesse had continued it. Everything in him wanted to pursue it. But a kiss was as good as a declaration, and he wasn't sure she was ready for that. He wasn't sure *he* was ready for that.

So, he led her along the fringe of trees that marked the edge of the plateau. An eagle soared above, then dove out of sight. Something larger rustled the bushes on the trees.

She must have heard it, for she moved a little closer to him.

"I won't let anything happen to you," he promised.

Her smile said she believed him. Was it possible for a man to feel any prouder or more humbled?

Ahead, the trees dropped off below the plateau, and the Nisqually Delta opened up in all its glory. Jack led her as close to the edge as was safe and heard her catch her breath.

It was a worthy sight. The green grasses of the delta stretched across the valley, threaded by silver streams and the darker Nisqually River. At the foot of the delta, forested islands rose from the blue of Puget Sound. On a clear day, at the head, Mount Rainier stood in all her glory.

Jack pointed with his free hand. "At high tide, the water comes all the way back to those trees. You could be looking at a river valley one hour and a few hours later, it's an inland sea."

"Amazing." She squinted at something moving along the nearest creek. "Is that a canoe?"

"Someone's likely fishing," he explained as the sleek bark canoe wove its way along the waters. "The tribes have the right by treaty to hunt and fish in their customary places. Some of us think they should have the right to live in their customary places too, but we weren't part of the treaty process."

She slanted him a glance. "Perhaps you should run for a seat in the legislature."

Jack snorted. "Not me. I have too much to do as it is." He glanced back to where the twin barns of the ranch were just visible. He could hear their call from here. "I should get you back."

With a sigh, she followed him back the way they had come. "You're a practical fellow, Jack Willets."

He wasn't sure whether that was a compliment. "Is practicality a trait you admire?"

"It is," she admitted. "I certainly didn't have much time to be anything less than practical when I was nursing. My parents' needs, Phyllis' needs, eclipsed almost everything."

He nodded. "That's how it is on the ranch right now. Growing up, I always thought my oldest brother, Jesse, would be leading us one day. When he decided to strike out on his own, I knew it was up to me to step in."

"Not Jeremy?" she asked, trailing her free hand along the tips of the grasses.

Jack chuckled. "Jeremy's not what you'd call practical. He'll be the first to see the humor, the first to offer help. But he struggles to make the hard decisions that come with running a ranch."

"But not everything is a hard decision," she protested as the parsonage rose up in the distance. "And no matter how hard the decision or the work involved, you have to find the joy where you can. It's like music—there are slow movements and fast, dark and light. Moving through one makes you appreciate the next more."

"'To everything there is a season, and a time to every purpose under the heaven,'" Jack remembered.

She smiled at him. "Exactly."

They were passing the church site now. A few more minutes, and he'd have to surrender her hand. Somehow, he thought that would be the hardest decision yet.

For a moment, when they had been standing looking over the magnificent Nisqually Delta, she'd thought he might kiss her, and every part of her had tingled with anticipation. But once again, work had won out over anything else. She understood duty better than some, but surely even he had a right to a few moments to himself!

They were nearly at the parsonage when something cold landed on her cheek, startling her. Darker spots appeared on her sleeves.

He tilted back his head. "Rain's coming on. Best you get back to the house."

Before she could even respond, the clouds opened, and rain pattered down across the fields, bending the grasses.

"Best you get under cover too!" she cried, tugging at his hand.

Taking off his hat, he held it over her head with his free hand as they made a run for the porch.

Once there, sheltered in front of the parsonage, she ducked out from under his hat.

"Thank you."

He set it on the bench where Mrs. Dalrymple often perched on a warm day. "We'll need to get you some heavier bonnets. It rains a lot here."

As he straightened, his gaze moved to her face. One hand came up to touch her cheek, feather soft. "Seems a raindrop wanted to get closer."

She couldn't look away as he brushed the water from her cheek. "Do you want to get closer, Jack?"

Perhaps that was the invitation he'd been waiting for, because he took a step, boots brushing the flounces of her skirt. "Yes, ma'am." Gaze on hers, as if giving her every opportunity to refuse, he lowered his lips to hers.

Her eyes drifted shut, and her breath hitched. His lips brushed hers gently, tenderly, almost reverently. She wanted to drink in the touch like water. Oh, to be so cherished every day!

A noise made her eyes pop open. He pulled back to glance at the parlor window. Mrs. Dalrymple waggled her fingers at them before disappearing from view.

"Will you be in trouble for this?" he asked with a frown.

"Doubtful," Victoria said, though her cheeks were heating. "But don't be surprised if she sends Mr. Dalrymple to ask your intentions. She might even ask you herself."

He held up his hands. "All honorable, I promise. May I call on you tomorrow?"

She nodded so rapidly she almost got dizzy. With a smile, he clapped his hat back on his head and strode off through the rain.

Victoria sighed. It wasn't the courtship she had expected, but then she hadn't expected any courtship at all when she'd come West as a mail-order bride. Now she found she couldn't complain in the slightest.

"Did he propose?" Mrs. Dalrymple asked, eyes hopeful, as Victoria floated into the house.

"Not yet," she allowed. "Perhaps tomorrow."

Mrs. Dalrymple beamed. "In that case, let's bake a pie or two. Never knew a man not to be pleased by a pie."

Victoria was waiting, along with a dried apple pie, the next afternoon when Jack arrived. The rain had dwindled to a steady drizzle, making it hard to see to the end of the drive. Mrs. Dalrymple had stationed her in the parlor in her best gown, a spring green concoction with a fitted long bodice edged in black braid and jet buttons, lace at the neck and sleeves, and seven rows of flounces along the hem. Victoria had had to tuck it at the very back of the wardrobe to keep Cousin Phyllis from having it dyed black.

"Why, Mr. Willets," the minister's wife warbled as she answered his knock, which was no louder than the pounding of Victoria's heart as she sat at the piano. "How nice to see you. And with flowers."

She ushered him into the parlor so quickly he nearly missed a step. He offered Victoria a bouquet of pale pink blossoms clustered on glossy green leaves that were still damp from the mist.

"Oh, how lovely," Victoria said. "Rhododendrons, I believe. Thank you." She grinned at him. "Did you have to ride on Africa's side to pick them?"

Mrs. Dalrymple glanced between them, clearly puzzled, but Jack gave Victoria that slow smile she felt to her toes.

"No, ma'am, but I'd do it if it meant seeing you happy."

Mrs. Dalrymple snatched the blossoms from her. "I'll just put these in water. You'll excuse me, I'm sure." She sent Victoria a look before hurrying for the kitchen.

Jack tipped his chin at the piano. "Seems I interrupted again."

"Not at all," she assured him. "I'd much rather spend time with you than the piano. Unless you play too?"

He shook his head. "We don't have any instruments at the ranch. We tend to sing together instead."

She could imagine the chorus. "That must be fun."

He studied the piano. "Would you miss having a piano in the house?"

Was he talking about when she came to be his bride? Her pulse quickened anew. "Perhaps, but I could always stop by the parsonage and ask Mrs. Dalrymple if I might play. If the church has a piano or organ, I could play that too."

"The church won't have one right away," he cautioned. "But I hear it's in the plans. Then again, there's not a lot of time for playing the piano and such things most days, I find."

After their conversation yesterday, was he still more interested in a worker than a wife? Disappointment nipped at her. Well, he valued plain speaking. She could honor that and address her concerns at the same time.

She went to sit on the sofa, and he settled himself beside her. "We should talk, Jack. You know I came West to marry. I've looked for a position, but I haven't had much luck. Mrs. Dalrymple is trying to find me a suitable husband."

He nodded. "She has her sights set on Goodenough."

They'd both set their sights, as he put it, on Jack, but she couldn't bring herself to expose her hopes so baldly. There was plain speaking, and there was revealing dreams too easily crushed.

"And if I were to marry you instead, what would you expect from your wife?"

He leaned back on the sofa, a slight frown drawing his russet brows together. "Someone who will work beside me, help me run the ranch. I don't think she needs to rope or brand, but being able to ride herd would be useful. Someone who could help Ma around the house and garden. Someone who will love and respect my family. Someone who actually *gets along* with my family."

Work and family. Not companionship. No mention of love. She had come all this way with little expectation of either. Was she wrong to want more now?

Chapter Eight

The rosy color in Victoria's cheeks was fading. The lips that had felt so warm and right against his were tightening. He was going to lose her, and who could blame her? He was making it sound like he wanted to hire a ranch hand or housekeeper, not marry a wife!

"You mentioned before that Mrs. Dalrymple has expectations for your husband too," he tried.

She rallied, head coming up. "According to her, he must be humble, patient, faithful, fiscally responsible, kind to animals, and supportive of the church."

His brothers and sisters complained he was too humble, so that was one tick in his favor. He kept his word, watched his expenses, and supported the church, so he might be able to check off several more of those requirements. But he wasn't known for his patience, and some might not think hunting very kind to animals, though he couldn't keep the family fed if he stopped.

"Not sure any man fully lives up to all that every day," he said, the collar of his shirt tighter than when he'd arrived.

"Agreed, and I'm not sure I'm all that patient," she admitted. "But I'm beginning to think I have other criteria. A love of family, a love for each other." She slanted him a glance and then quickly away.

Jack swallowed. "It would be easy to fall in love with you, Victoria. I'm more than halfway there already."

Her gaze came back, and he was certain the gleam in her eyes was hope. "Oh, Jack! I feel the same way about you."

There was nothing for it. He gathered her in his arms and held her close, pressing a kiss against the silk of her hair and inhaling the clean scent of it. She cuddled against him as if that was where she belonged.

"If I was anyone else, I'd be down on bended knee right now," he murmured. "But you haven't met everyone in my family yet, and you have a right to know what you're getting into."

She pulled back, brow puckered. "Are your father and other brothers so forbidding, then?"

"No, ma'am." He couldn't help his smile. "Pa is known for being the peacemaker in the family. Jacob will talk your ear off, but only if you ask him a question or show interest in the book he's reading. Jason and Joshua are still more boy than man. I just want to make sure you can be happy living like we do. My mother occasionally reminds us that marriage is for a lifetime, if you're fortunate."

She rested her head back against his shoulder. "A lifetime with you doesn't sound so bad to me, Jack."

He could only pray she'd feel the same way after her visit on Saturday.

Victoria stood in the little entry hall of the parsonage Saturday afternoon, tucking a stray strand of hair back into the bun at the nape of her neck.

"Here," Mrs. Dalrymple said, standing on tiptoe and reaching up to adjust the hat she'd insisted that Victoria borrow. She dropped back down on her feet and cocked her head. "Much better. They are all going to adore you, and you will come back here a bride-to-be. I just know it!"

Oh, but she hoped! She smoothed down her spring green skirts. She'd worn her best dress again. Jack had seen it, but the others wouldn't have. And just to make it seem a little different, she'd pinned her mother's ivory brooch at the neck. Still, her stomach fluttered, and her fingers tightened as she lowered her hands.

"I suppose it's possible they won't like me," she said, voicing one of her greatest fears about this visit.

Mrs. Dalrymple sniffed. "There's no accounting for taste. But take heart. Mr. Goodenough is still interested."

Victoria hid her shudder.

The sound of hooves and the rattle of tack heralded the arrival of Jack and the wagon.

"Pinch your cheeks," Mrs. Dalrymple advised, following her to the door. "Smile!" She threw open the door and waved at Jack and Jane, who sat next to him on the bench. "Be right out!"

She turned and put both hands on Victoria's shoulders. "Be strong and courageous."

"I'll try," Victoria promised. "And I'll see you tomorrow at services."

She picked up her case and started down the steps.

Jack jumped down and came to take the little case from her. "Thank you for coming. It means the world."

He looked so relieved, as if he'd thought she'd refuse in the end, that she could only smile at him. "Of course. It's an honor to be invited."

He stowed the case in the back of the wagon, then returned to her side. "Let me help you up."

Jane had slid over to one side and held the reins of a team of chestnut horses in one hand. Jack set his hands on Victoria's waist, and she fancied she could feel the strength, the determination, in them. Would she be holding those hands at a marriage ceremony soon?

Her breath stuttered as he lifted her up onto the bench.

As if she thought Victoria needed support, Jane patted her sky-blue gingham skirts. "Slide on over next to me."

Victoria obliged, and Jack jumped up on her other side. The wagon was narrow enough that she was pasted against each of them and warm as toast.

Clucking to the horses, Jane directed them out of the yard.

"You ride, you can drive a team, and you help build churches," Victoria said. "Is there nothing you can't do?"

His sister winked at her. "Well, I've never tried playing the piano. I hear you're very good."

Victoria sawed her fingers back and forth. "Middling."

"It didn't sound middling to me," Jack protested. "I'd travel to Olympia or even Seattle to hear you perform!"

Jane laughed. "I hope you like the ranch, Victoria, because my brother is clearly over the moon!"

Victoria blushed. So did Jack.

They managed to chat about this and that while the twin barns grew ahead of them, and Victoria's nerves kicked harder than a colt. A short while later, Jane pulled the team to a stop in front of the barns. Jack jumped down and handed Victoria to the ground.

"I'll bring in the case," his sister offered. "You know Ma doesn't want to wait another second."

Jack tucked Victoria's hand in his elbow and led her toward the house. "I asked them to take it slow again. We can be a lot at once."

Her stomach tightened as they came into the kitchen. One of his sisters was bending over an open oven, basting a roast. The sizzling scent filled the air. She straightened and smiled at Victoria, red hair sleeked back and blue eyes twinkling.

"Welcome to the Jumping J, Miss Milford," she said. "I hope you like venison."

"It smells delicious!" Victoria assured her. "And please, call me Victoria."

"I'm Jenny," she said. "I hear you already met Jane, Joanna, Joy, Jeremy, and Caroline. That just leaves the boys to go."

"I beg your pardon?" Another brother, who appeared to be a little younger and more slender than Jack, came into the kitchen and adjusted his spectacles. Like Jack, he wore sensible trousers and a cotton shirt covered by a brown coat. "I haven't considered myself a boy for more than a decade now."

"Victoria, this is my brother Jacob," Jack said. "He's next after Jeremy."

Jacob bowed. "A pleasure to meet you."

"And you as well," Victoria told him.

"He's the studious one in the family," Jenny explained. "Though I don't know that he's studied all that much about music, which I understand you enjoy."

Jacob raised his brows. "Mozart sonata? Beethoven's lullaby?"

Jenny laughed. "I stand corrected."

"You usually do," Jacob said. He spoiled the lofty attitude by winking at Victoria. "I'm sure you could teach me a great deal more."

Joy came into the kitchen, copper-colored curls bouncing. "I knew you were here, Victoria! Ma wants to know what's keeping you and Jack."

"That would be me," Jacob acknowledged, stepping aside. "I hope we have a chance to chat further, Victoria."

So did she, and she wasn't sure why that surprised her.

Jack led her down the short hallway to the parlor. His mother was sitting on the sofa, head high and serene, like a queen dispensing alms to her penitents. Her brown hair was parted in the middle and plaited on either side of her round face, and she'd added a lace collar to the pink gingham gown.

His father, seated on one of the ladder-back chairs near his wife, stood as Victoria and Jack entered. Like Jack, he was tall and well built, though his red hair was lighter and beginning to gray at the temples.

"Welcome, welcome," he heralded. "What a pleasure to meet you, Miss Milford. Jack's told us so much about you."

She shook the hand he offered.

"Yes, Jack sings your praises," Mrs. Willets said with a smile. "But he hasn't told us nearly all we'd like to know. Have a seat, and we can become better acquainted."

Victoria unpinned her hat and set it aside, then sat on one of the other chairs. Jack pulled up another beside her as if to protect her from all comers. Was this to be an inquisition, then?

Mrs. Willet's warm brown eyes focused on Victoria. "I was telling the family that you hail from Albany. What brought you West?"

Victoria swallowed. Jack apparently hadn't mentioned Charles. Would they think she must have some terrible flaw to be left at the altar?

"When my parents both died, there wasn't enough left to their estate to allow me to live on my own, if such a thing had been proper," she explained. "I nursed a cousin for two years, but I knew it was only a matter of time before I must find my future elsewhere. At that point, I just wanted a fresh start. So, I answered an ad for a mail-order bride."

"Jack! You didn't!" His mother rounded on him, shaking a finger. "Did you learn nothing from Jeremy and Caroline's courtship? I thought I made myself quite clear on how I felt about mail-order brides."

Victoria wanted to crawl under the rug. Instead, she knit her fingers together in her lap even as Jack bristled.

"To be clear, Jack didn't place the ad, Mrs. Willets," she forced herself to say. "Mr. Charles Bishop in Olympia did. We corresponded for a bit, and he proposed marriage. I came to Olympia to marry him, only to find he'd changed his mind and wed a local girl in the meantime. Everyone in his family was very embarrassed about the whole thing. I think they hoped I'd just go away quietly, but where was I to go? In the end, the minister's wife in Olympia contacted Mrs. Dalrymple, who agreed to take me in."

His mother's mouth turned down. "Oh, you poor thing! How cruel! Your heart must have been broken."

Her heart had never really been involved. "I was more disappointed and concerned. I know no one here, and my cousin has passed, so there's nothing for me to return to in Albany. I sought a way to support myself, but it's not easy for a single woman to find respectable work."

"I can imagine," Mrs. Willets said.

Jack reached out and took Victoria's hand. Could he feel the chill in it?

"You know I asked Mrs. Dalrymple to find me a local bride," Jack told his parents. "But I took one look at Victoria, and I suspected no other lady would ever match her."

Victoria stared at him. His gaze was fervent, his hand on hers firm. He looked ready to fight both mother and father if they suggested he find someone else. He'd claimed to be falling in love with her yesterday. Now he sounded as if he'd fallen the moment they'd met!

His mother must have believed him, for she clasped her hands. "Oh, Jack! That's exactly what I was hoping for."

His father smiled. "Sounds like we might have another wedding in our future."

"Victoria and I haven't reached any agreement," Jack cautioned, giving her hand a squeeze. "I thought it only fair that she meet you all first."

His mother waved a hand. "That's a formality. Of course she'll love it here. Everyone does."

Victoria could see why. They were so easy in each other's company, so ready to stand their ground yet give their love. She wanted to gather them all close in hopes they'd let her stay.

And Jack—that look, that touch, the warmth in his voice. Much more of this, and she'd be the one proposing to him!

The worst was over. He hadn't ever doubted that Pa would like Victoria. Pa made friends with rocks. But Ma accepted her, and that helped set his mind at ease. Now, if only Victoria liked them.

The smile on her pretty face encouraged him, but her fingers were still too cold, as if every muscle was tensed. Maybe Jacob was right; by limiting Victoria's contact with their family, Jack had painted a picture of people who would judge her, find her wanting.

As if anyone could find her wanting.

Ma rose. "I should help Jenny with dinner. Joe, I'm sure you had something you wanted to discuss with Jacob after the two of you and Joy visited the Abercrombys today."

Pa made a show of frowning, but Jack saw the twinkle in his eyes as he stood too. "Did I?"

Ma swatted his shoulder, and he chuckled, looping an arm about her waist as they left the room.

"I thought she might have more questions," Victoria said, gaze following them.

They didn't fool him. Like Mrs. Dalrymple, they expected Jack to propose. But not yet. Not until Victoria was as sure as he was.

"They can tell quality when they see it," Jack said. "I knew they would. I'm sorry if I made you feel you wouldn't be welcome. I was just trying to ease the way."

She swiveled to face him. "You didn't have to. Your family is wonderful! I always wanted a sister or brother. You're fortunate to have so many, and each one more talented than the last."

They'd all swell their chests if they heard her. "I'm glad you like them."

She glanced toward the door again. "I think there are still one or two I haven't met. Who's next?"

"I suppose that leaves Jason and Joshua, my youngest brothers. I'm not sure what they're up to at the moment."

As if in answer, a scuffling sounded in the hallway, and the two of them burst into the room. He remembered when he and Jesse were that age, all arms and legs and too much vinegar to sit still. Auburn-haired Jason couldn't wait to turn sixteen on his next birthday and receive the horse Pa usually gave each one of them then. He already rode better than most of them, and he was the family's best hunter, though he tended to hide his accomplishments behind a gruff manner and a ready complaint.

Joshua's hair was a deeper red and more unruly, for all he tended to be the more level-headed of the two. As the youngest boy, Ma had a special place in her heart for him, just as she did for Joy as the youngest girl. The two of them were still being tutored by their mother and Jacob.

Jack made the introductions, then Joshua thrust out a trillium he'd likely just picked from the shadows of the forest. "For you, Miss Milford."

"Why, thank you, Joshua," she said, accepting the tri-petaled white flower. "I see you're as thoughtful as your brother."

He ducked his head, but his ears were turning red.

Not to be outdone, Jason held out a sheath of papers. "Thought you might like these."

Jack took the flower so she could accept.

"New sheet music!" she cried, gaze devouring the pages. "Oh, how marvelous!"

Joshua shot him a look. "You tore those out of Joanna's magazine. She's going to tan your hide."

Jason raised his chin. "She can try."

Victoria lowered the pages, gaze going to Jack's. "Oh, I wouldn't want to take something from your sister."

"Joanna won't mind," Jack predicted. "Though you should have asked first, Jason."

Jason shrugged. "Ma said to do anything we could to help you get hitched. If all it takes is a few pages from a magazine, I call that a good trade."

Now Victoria's face was reddening.

Jacob came in then and shooed them out. "Ma wants your help setting the table."

Grumbling and jostling each other, they left.

"Sorry about that," Jack said. "They're still learning their manners."

"They both tried to make me feel welcome," she said. "I appreciate that."

Jacob made himself comfortable on the sofa. "We all want you to feel welcome. It's been a long time since we've seen Jack so happy. We'd like to keep it that way."

He almost sounded as if he was threatening Victoria to say yes! "Don't you have somewhere else to be too?" Jack demanded.

Jacob cocked a grin. "Not at the moment. Ma isn't the only one with questions about your sweetheart. I have to take the opportunity while I can." He leaned forward. "Jane tells me you had a governess in Albany. That sort of teaching usually qualifies a lady to be a teacher herself. I'm sure you could find a position, if you wanted."

Victoria blinked as if she hadn't considered that, and Jack could have cheerfully dropped his brother in the well. If Ma really had urged them all to help his courting, what was Jacob doing?

"But I understand there isn't a school on Hawks Prairie or Puget City," she said.

Jack nearly sagged with relief. At least she was still thinking about staying in the area.

"There isn't right now," Jacob admitted. "But I'm hoping to change that. Once the church is up, I'd like to see us start a school."

Jane had said something similar. But surely Jacob saw the difficulties.

"Where?" Jack asked. "We don't have any spare buildings on the ranch and neither does anyone else that I've seen. None of us will have money to buy another piece of property or bring in the lumber to erect a school for at least two more seasons."

Jacob eyed him. "There's the old block house. It's solid, it's in the middle of the area so everyone would be able to send their children, and there's room above for the teacher to sleep."

Jack leaned back, nodding. "That actually makes sense."

Jacob adjusted his spectacles. "I generally make sense, brother." He turned to Victoria. "So, would you be willing to consider being our teacher?"

Victoria smiled regretfully, and Jack wanted to get up and shout a hallelujah. "I have more experience with nursing. Especially for a new school, you'd be better served to find someone who'd been trained as a teacher and had some experience."

Jacob nodded thoughtfully. "Well, if Jeremy could write away for a mail-order bride, I suppose I can write for a mail-order teacher."

"And Ma might actually approve of that," Jack told him.

Joy darted into the room and took Victoria's hand. "Dinner is about on the table. Ma says come. You can sit by me, Victoria." She was tugging her out of the room before Jack could do more than climb to his feet.

"I like her," Jacob said, joining him. "I think you two could be very happy together. You both seem to understand your capabilities and how you can contribute to the world. There's a great blessing in that."

He couldn't argue as they joined the family for dinner. They'd seated Victoria near the top of the table between Jack and Joy, and Ma had brought out her best tablecloth, the soft blue linen Pa had given her for their tenth wedding anniversary. After Pa said the blessing, they passed around the roast, potatoes, and salad of miner's lettuce and watercress, and Jack served her. Conversation flew, and she seemed to have no trouble following it and interjecting her part. Every moment, Jack's hopes grew.

They all regrouped in the parlor after dinner, Jason and Joshua bringing in extra chairs from the dining room to fit everyone.

"I thought a musical night tonight, in honor of Victoria," Ma said. "And then we'll need to arrange the parlor for services tomorrow."

Pa shifted on the chair, hand to his stomach as if he'd eaten too much. "Why don't you start us off, Jack?"

He and Pa generally took the bass part to his brothers' tenors and baritones and sisters' altos and sopranos. He started a hymn, and everyone joined in. Victoria's sweet voice melded with his as if they'd been designed for each other.

As they finished, Pa rose. "Well, that winded me. Someone else take the next song. Excuse me a moment." He limped toward the door.

Ma was frowning at him. Jack could see why. His father was pale, and sweat stood out on his brow. The others didn't seem to notice, for they were advocating for this favorite and that.

Victoria leaned closer. "Your father doesn't look well."

As if he agreed, Pa stumbled and went down in a heap on the floor.

Chapter Nine

Victoria surged to her feet, but Jack reached his father first. "Pa!"

The others seemed to be in shock. Mrs. Willets had both hands pressed to her mouth, her eyes wide and frightened over the top. Jenny put an arm around Joy. Victoria didn't stop to think. She went to crouch beside Jack. "May I help?"

"I…" For the first time since she'd known him, for perhaps the first time in his life, this capable man seemed at a total loss. She put a hand on his shoulder, and he drew in a breath.

"Pat his cheek," Victoria advised, taking Mr. Willets' wrist in her hands. "Call to him."

"Pa?" Jack asked, cradling his father close. "Pa, can you hear me?"

"Oh, Joe!" Mrs. Willets sank down beside her husband, tears already staining her pale cheeks. She smoothed the hair back from his forehead. "Sweetheart, don't leave me."

The pulse fluttered against Victoria's fingers as she checked it, faster and more irregular than it should be. She pressed a hand to his chest and felt it rise and fall.

"Has he been ill long?" she murmured to Jack.

He and his mother met each other's gazes. With a nod, his mother rose.

"Jane, take Joy and Jenny upstairs," she ordered with brisk efficiency. "Joanna and Jacob, see to the milking. Jason and Joshua, start moving the benches from the barn to the parlor for services."

"But, Ma," Jason protested.

Her eyes flashed. "None of your sass now, young man. Move!"

They moved, until all that remained in the parlor were Jack, his mother and father, Jeremy, Caroline, and Victoria.

"Doctor Rawlins told him a few months ago that his heart was failing him," Mrs. Willets explained, wrapping an arm about her waist as if she needed the support. "Jack's been taking on more of the work, and Jeremy and Caroline decided to live in the house with us in case…" She sucked in a breath.

Caroline moved alongside her and patted her arm. "We're here. How can we help?"

"Anything you need, Ma," Jeremy agreed, for once with no teasing in his voice.

Victoria studied Mr. Willets' face. He was pale, and his mouth twitched, as if something inside tugged at it. "I don't think it's his heart, at least, not entirely. He clutched his stomach first."

"Ma!" Jenny's voice echoed down the stairs. "Joy's sick too!"

"What!" Mrs. Willets scrambled up and started toward the door, then jerked to a stop. She looked back at her husband, teeth worrying her lower lip.

Of course she would want to stay with the man she loved. "I'll go," Victoria said, gathering her skirts and rising. "Jack, it might be wise if you and your brother carried your father to his bed."

"Right away," he promised.

She was just thankful no one questioned her right or ability to step in. She might be a novice at the housewifely arts and running a ranch, but she knew how to take care of sick and injured people. Falling back into old patterns was easy.

She climbed the stairs to the door off the landing, where voices babbled. Joy was slumped on the floor, and her sisters were cleaning up the mess she'd made. The sour scent tainted the air.

"Dinner not set right?" Victoria asked, crouching beside her.

Like her father, the little girl's forehead was sweaty, and Victoria wouldn't have been surprised to find she was running a fever.

"My stomach hurts something awful," she said, rubbing it with one hand.

Footsteps on the stairs heralded the arrival of Joanna. "I don't think it's just Pa. Jacob's cast up his accounts in the barn."

Jane visibly swallowed. "I might join him." She hurried from the room.

Victoria straightened. "Jenny, Joanna? How are you feeling?"

"Fine," Joanna said.

"Aside from a little queasiness," Jenny agreed. "And that might be just because of everyone else. My stomach doesn't actually hurt."

"Good," Victoria said. "If it does, get yourself to a basin or porch if possible. The less cleaning we have to do, the more time we can spend helping others. Right now, will you boil some water for us?"

"On my way." She started for the door.

"What can I do?" Joanna begged, hands worrying in front of her gingham gown.

"Check with all your siblings and parents," Victoria said. "Find out who's sick and who's tending them and where. Then report back to me."

"Yes, ma'am." She hurried from the room.

Victoria bent beside Joy. "Can you get up onto your bed, honey?"

Joy nodded. Moving far slower than Victoria had ever seen her, she eased herself up and onto the nearest bed.

Victoria felt her pulse and listened to her breathing, then put a hand to her forehead. "If you have a fever, it's not high at the moment. Why don't you lie down on your side? I'm going to check on Jane."

She found Jack's oldest sister leaning against the wall down the corridor. Though her face was pale, and her hand pressed against her stomach, she didn't look as if she'd lost her dinner.

"How bad is it?" Victoria asked.

Jane straightened. "Livable. I think it might have been everyone else's problems that overset me."

"Completely understandable," Victoria assured her with a nod. "Will you sit with Joy? I'm going to see if I can help Jenny."

Jane went to her sister.

Downstairs, Jenny looked up as Victoria poked her head into the kitchen.

"Water's on the boil," she reported.

Joanna came through the back door. "I checked on everyone. Jeremy, Caroline, Jack, and

Ma are fine. They're with Ma and Pa in our parents' bedroom. Jason and Joshua got Jacob up the stairs to Jack's rooms in the barn. He's lying down. They're keeping an eye on him, but neither of them is showing any symptoms. They're more worried than anything."

"We all are," Jenny said.

"So, that's your father, Jacob, and Joy confirmed ill," Victoria said. "Jane says she's fine."

Joanna rolled her eyes. "Jane would. I say we keep an eye on her too."

"Will you go help her with Joy, then?" Victoria asked.

She hurried to comply.

Victoria took a step closer to Jenny. She had filled multiple small pots and pans and set them on each of the burners of the stove.

"I thought they'd heat faster than one big pot," she told Victoria as if she'd seen her look.

"Very smart," Victoria told her. "Am I right in thinking you do much of the cooking?"

Jenny nodded. "I've taken over a lot of Ma's duties in that area. Why?"

Victoria licked her lips. "Because I'm wondering whether this illness might have been caused by something they ate."

"What they ate!" Jenny drew herself up, two red spots blazing in her cheeks. "How dare you insinuate I'd make my own family sick!"

Victoria held up her hands. "I'm not implying you did it on purpose, Jenny. But the doctors I worked with when I was nursing my family told me that if it isn't a disease or accident that incapacitated someone, it was often something they ate or drank."

"But we all eat and drink the same things," Jenny reminded her. "You ate and drank at our table yourself, and you're not sick!"

There was that. "Then it might not have been food or drink served in this house," Victoria reasoned. "Did your father, brother, and sister go anywhere together in the last day or so that they might have eaten something? Picked the wrong mushroom from the field, perhaps?"

Jenny frowned. "No one's been mushroom picking that I've heard, and we all know the difference between ones that are edible and ones that are poisonous. As for eating something the rest of us didn't, Pa, Jacob, and Joy went to the Abercromby farm yesterday for a bit. Joy wants one of their pups so badly. I think she was trying to convince Pa to change his mind, and she brought Jacob along to help. Maybe they ate something there."

"Worth investigating," Victoria said, trying for a smile. "Thank you."

Jenny turned her attention to the stove once more, though her shoulders were still stiff. "Ma and Pa's room is across the hall, if you want to check on him."

"I'll do that, and thank you for your understanding. I just want to make sure we treat the right illness."

Jenny shrugged, and Victoria left her to her work.

The door was open across the hall, so she eased inside. Mr. Willets was resting on the four-poster bed in the center of the room, which had pink rosebuds on the wallpaper. Jeremy and Caroline were watching from one wall. Mrs. Willets sat on one side of her husband, holding his hand, and Jack sat on the other.

Lines she didn't remember crossed his forehead. He'd stepped up to lead the ranch after his older brother had left, but clearly his father's illness had added to the burden she so often imagined on his shoulders. He'd taken responsibility for them all, no matter the cost to himself. She just wanted to gather him in her arms, promise him all would be well.

But that was a promise she could not make.

Please, Lord, be with this family. Give Jack and me wisdom on how to help them during this time.

Jack looked up as Victoria ventured closer, then rose to join her.

"Thank you," he murmured, taking her hand. "I don't know what happened to me. I couldn't think, couldn't move."

And didn't like it. That was all too evident by his frown. Victoria reached up with her free hand and ran her fingers across his brow, as much to ease the lines as to check his temperature. His skin was warm to the touch, but not hot. Relief coursed through her.

"I'm used to being the one in charge," she said with a smile. "And being the nurse. I'm sorry if I overstepped."

"You're a godsend," he assured her. "How's Joy?"

"Resting," she said. "So is Jacob."

"Jacob too?" He directed his frown toward the bed. "What happened?"

"I'm guessing bad food," Victoria said. "But Jenny wasn't too pleased to hear that. It might have been something they ate at your neighbor's farm, the Abercrombys. Has your father regained consciousness?"

"Not yet." His gaze searched hers as if looking for any sign of hope. "Shouldn't he have?"

"If I'm right about the bad food, and his heart is weak, as you say, the effects might be harder for him to fight off than the others," Victoria allowed. "Keep an eye on him. I want to see if I can get everyone who's ill to take a few sips of water and whether they can keep it down. That might give us more of an idea as to what we're dealing with."

His mother roused herself to look at them. Like the others, she was pale, but she seemed more worried than ill.

"Jack, we should send word to Mrs. Dalrymple," she said. "Until we're certain this isn't contagious, we shouldn't hold services here."

Jeremy straightened away from the wall. "I'll ask Jason to ride."

As his brother left the room, Jack squeezed Victoria's hand. "I'm so glad you're here. This is just further proof that I need a wife."

The words landed like a blow. She pulled back from him and hurried into the corridor before he could see her reaction. With his declaration the other day and in front of his parents this afternoon, she'd been so sure he felt the stirrings of love as she did. What if he felt nothing for her but gratitude? Would he feel the same for any capable woman who could step in when he couldn't? Did he truly care about her only because she could help his family? Would work always be more important?

She'd thought she had a chance to marry for love, if not that moment, then growing surely over time.

Tears burned. Pressing her lips together, trying to hold the pain in, she leaned against the wall. The lament tumbled out anyway.

"Is that all I'll ever be worth, Lord?" she whispered. "To serve as a pair of hands to tend folks, only to be discarded or disregarded when they no longer need me? Am I never to be loved?

And we have known and believed the love that God hath to us. God is love; and he that dwelleth in love dwelleth in God, and God in him.

The remembered verse humbled her. No matter what happened in this world, her heavenly Father cared. Still, her heart ached. Her love for Jack had budded, and she felt as if it had just as surely been nipped before it could blossom.

Jack was never sure afterward how they made it through the night. Joanna and Jane watched over Joy, Joshua over Jacob until Jason returned from the Dalrymples, and Ma refused to leave Pa's side. Victoria moved among them, checking temperatures and pulses, administering the cooled, boiled water Jenny replenished. Under Victoria's direction, Jack, Jeremy, and Caroline cleaned up messes, helped Victoria carry water to the patients to sip when they woke, and debated what might have caused the illness to begin with. Joy had remembered eating some fresh-caught clams while at the Abercrombys' house, and Victoria thought they might have been the culprit, which meant no one else would be getting ill.

At least Pa woke near midnight, cast up his accounts, and smiled blearily at Ma. Victoria confided that his pulse was steadier than it had been, which gave them all hope that the worst was over.

Just in case, as light dawned, Jack sent Jason down to Puget City to request that Doctor Rawlins come out to the ranch.

"Though I don't think our local doctor could have done a better job than you," he told Victoria as they took a moment on the porch. The sunrise was a smudge of pink under a row of low-hanging clouds, and a cool breeze set the grasses to waving. After last night, it felt good against his cheeks.

"I should see how Joy's doing," she said, turning for the door.

Even though she'd been up all night, like him, her hair was still in its pins, and she moved with her usual composure. He had never been so thankful for another pair of competent hands. If he'd had any doubts that Victoria could fit among his family, could contribute to the ranch, this illness had wiped them all away like a storm sweeping across the prairie. She was the one.

Jane was coming down the stairs as he returned to the house.

"I'll make breakfast for those of us who can eat," she said. "Victoria says oatmeal, no ham, bacon, or sausage. Can you help?"

"Right behind you," Jack said.

Jenny pitched in too, though she hadn't had a lick of sleep that night either. Perhaps they could all nap once Doc Rawlins had seen to the patients.

The first person to knock at the door, however, wasn't the good doctor. Jack found their minister standing on the porch. Mr. Dalrymple whipped the hat from his pomaded hair.

"I wanted to check on how you're faring," he said. "We've relocated to the Abercromby farm for this morning. How's your father, your brother, and sister?" He peered around Jack. "Anyone else sick?"

"We're holding up," Jack reported. "No one else fell ill. But you need to know that Victoria thinks it could have been something Pa, Jacob, and Joy ate at the Abercromby's house, like those clams, that made them ill. You might warn the family."

He nodded. "I'll do that. Tactfully." He smiled.

Jack stepped out onto the porch and shut the door behind him. "There's another matter. I know Victoria's father has passed. You're the closest thing to a father she has here. I'd like your permission to propose to her."

Mr. Dalrymple's smile widened. "Given with pleasure. You'll make her an excellent husband."

"I promise to do my best every day of my life," Jack vowed.

The minister clapped him on the shoulder. "That's what marriage is about, son. I'll check on you all again after services."

Back inside the house, Jack squared his shoulders. A sickroom proposal wasn't exactly what he'd had in mind, but he didn't want to wait another minute to tell Victoria how he felt.

He found her in the barn, just coming down from the rooms his parents had fitted up as a bedroom and sitting room for him.

"Jacob is much improved," she told him, lifting her skirts to manage the last few narrow stairs. "He should be back to himself by evening."

"That's good news," he said, pacing her as she started across the straw-strewn dirt floor. The shadows of the barn receded as they stepped out into the light of morning.

He put a hand on her arm to stop her. "Victoria, I have to thank you again for all you've done for my family. I don't know how we would have gotten through the night without you."

"I'm sure you would have contrived," she said. "But I'm glad I could help."

She didn't smile, but he couldn't blame her. He wanted to curl up somewhere and sleep for a week.

"It's more than that," he said. "You're smart, you're talented, and you're just about the prettiest gal I've ever seen." He took her hand and held it to his heart. Could she feel it pounding? "Would you do me the honor of marrying me?"

She gazed into his eyes, as if she could see the hope and love shining there. Then she gently pulled away.

"No, Jack. I'm sorry. I'm glad you think I work hard, but I'd like to be appreciated for more than my hands. I've come to realize that that is not too much to ask in a marriage. Excuse me."

And she left him, taking his heart with her.

Chapter Ten

Victoria left with Mr. Dalrymple when he came to call after services. Jack didn't try to stop her. She'd already done so much for his family. Jacob had returned to the house and was resting in his room. Joy was nearly back to her bubbly self. And Pa was alive. They had much to be thankful for.

"You couldn't have slept much last night," Ma said when Jack came to check on her and Pa later that afternoon. "Why don't you rest?"

"Cows need milking, chickens feeding," he said.

"Cows always need something," his father said with his gentle smile. "That doesn't mean you should neglect your health."

His mother regarded him, brows raised.

He held up his hands with a chuckle that did Jack's heart good to hear. "All right, all right. But maybe I'd like my son to learn from my poor example."

His mother laid her hand over his. "He has learned a lot from your example, especially where love is concerned."

"And when should we expect to hear good news there?" Pa asked Jack.

His heart pinched. "Not for some time."

Immediately, his mother rounded on him. "Jack Hercules Willets, what have you done?"

He couldn't help his wince. When Ma used anyone's middle name, it was best to give up peaceably or run for cover.

"I proposed this morning, Ma," he said. "She declined."

His mother's eyes narrowed. "You proposed to a girl after a harrowing night in which she had no sleep and worked her fingers to the bone tending to *your* family? What did you expect her to do, dance a jig?"

Jack rubbed the back of his neck. "I told her how much I appreciated her work. I even said she was about the prettiest gal I'd ever met."

"*About* the prettiest!" his mother sputtered.

Pa patted her hand before focusing on Jack. "Do you love her, Jack?"

Throat tightening, he nodded. "Close enough I know what I feel will only grow with time. She's the one, Pa."

His mother's face softened. "Then you can't give up, Jack."

Pa nodded. "I'm real sorry if my illness came between you two. Is there anything I can do to help?"

Jack shook his head. "I wish I knew."

Ma rose and came to lay a hand on his shoulder. "If you truly feel she's the one God's called you to stand beside through life, talk to her, Jack. Tell her how you feel. Not here," she touched his forehead, then his chest, "here, from your heart. And don't focus so much on what she can do for you and the family, but what you can do for her to make your own family."

Hope pushed up, bright as a lily in summer. Jack enfolded his mother in a hug. "Thanks, Ma. I'll ride over as soon as I've seen to the milking."

Ma leaned back to eye him. "Now, if you please. You have eight brothers and sisters roaming around this place who are capable of milking a cow. You're the only one who can tell Victoria how much she's loved."

Victoria just wanted to retreat to her room in the parsonage and cry her eyes out. She was tired, and she hurt inside and out. But she couldn't give up her new dream. Somewhere, there must be a man who would love her for who she was, not for what she could do for him. Unfortunately, the man of her dreams wore Jack's slow smile.

"Never you fear," Mrs. Dalrymple said when Victoria explained she'd refused Jack's suit. "I invited Mr. Goodenough for dinner again, just to be on the safe side."

Oh, she would never survive another dinner with the fellow. "I didn't get any sleep last night," she told her hostess. "I'm not fit company."

"We all have our burdens to bear, dear," the minister's wife said. "I've had two gentlemen express interest in the spare room, so I really need you settled soon."

Her heart seemed to be shriveling. "Perhaps a nap before dinner," Victoria said.

Lord, where am I to go? If holding out for love truly is Your plan for me, please show me what to do.

When she rose a few hours later, she felt a little better. She changed into a fresh gown, her red and green plaid with her shawl over the top, washed her face, tidied her hair, and came downstairs to play the piano before her next suitor arrived. Next suitor. She shuddered at the thought.

Yet, she had to keep her hopes up. Jacob had suggested she might teach. Starting a new school still sounded daunting, but perhaps Mr. Dalrymple knew of some group who placed teachers in established schools. She was probably most qualified to teach music. Jack had certainly seemed awed by her talents. Unfortunately, with few instruments in the area, she likely couldn't support herself as a music teacher.

And there was always the possibility that another local man might show interest in marrying her. Falling for Jack, she hadn't given other men proper consideration. Not Mr. Goodenough, certainly, but there was Mr. Hartley. Her smile turned up remembering Jane's assessment of him. Jack would probably agree that the young man needed more time to grow into his potential before he looked for a bride.

And she really must break this habit of seeing the world through Jack's eyes!

She heard the knock at the front door and misplayed a note. Wincing, she finished the piece she was playing as Mrs. Dalrymple ushered Mr. Goodenough into the parlor.

"Isn't she a wonder?" the minister's wife warbled. "Why, if I was a gentleman, I'd snap her right up."

Mr. Goodenough's gaze remained on Victoria. "She's perfect."

Under that look, she didn't feel remotely close. In fact, she had to fight to keep from pulling her shawl closer or running from the room.

Mrs. Dalrymple didn't seem to notice, for she made her excuses and withdrew with a look to Victoria, who made herself go sit on the sofa.

To her surprise, instead of taking the upholstered chair nearby, Mr. Goodenough dropped down beside her and seized her hand. "Miss Milford, Victoria, I meant what I said a few moments ago. You would make the perfect wife for a man like me. You're pretty, poised, and capable of entertaining important people. I have dreams of rising here, first a seat in the legislature and then, dare I say, to the governor's house! Tell me you're willing to stand beside me as my bride."

He was offering prestige and power. As his wife, she likely would never need to fear she'd lack a place to live or pretty clothes to wear. A prudent woman might have accepted. *She* might have accepted before she'd met Jack. But now she just couldn't give up the dream in her heart.

"I'm so sorry to have raised your expectations, Mr. Goodenough," she said. "I cannot marry you."

He pulled back, eyes narrowing. "Holding out for someone wealthier, eh? Well, men like that can afford to be picky, and you can't. One fellow's already refused you, and it seems Willets decided to back off as well. I'm the best you're going to get."

She wasn't sure whether to argue or take herself off in high dudgeon. "Then I am surprised you'd even be interested."

He edged closer and slipped an arm around her waist. "Oh, I'm interested. Let me show you."

Victoria tried to recoil, but he pulled her closer. She put both hands to his chest. "Get away from me this minute!"

"You heard the lady," a voice growled from the doorway. "Get away from her. Now."

Jack! Relief and hope vied for first place inside her as Mr. Goodenough leaned away.

"I'm afraid you've interrupted a private moment, Willets," he said, keeping his arm securely around her. "Dear Victoria was just about to agree to be my bride."

"Never," she snapped, squirming out of his grip at last. "I would not marry you. On any day, under any circumstances. You have abused your hostess' hospitality, sir, along with my patience. Do not approach me again."

Shaking his head, Goodenough stood. "Fine. Your loss. I wish you luck with her, Willets. This is one filly who can't be tamed to the bridle."

"Let me see you to the door," Jack said. He grabbed the fellow by the collar and marched him protesting from the room.

Mrs. Dalrymple arrived with her tray of lemonade just in time to see them leave. "What's happening? Why is Mr. Willets treating Mr. Goodenough so shabbily?"

Before Victoria could answer, she set down the tray and clapped her hands together like a girl. "Oh, I see. You made him jealous, you clever thing!"

"I did no such thing!" Victoria protested, reminded all too forcefully of how Charles had treated her. "Mr. Goodenough attempted liberties when I refused to marry him. If Mr. Willets hadn't stepped in, I don't know what would have happened."

Jack came striding back. "Sorry to show up like this, ma'am. No one answered my knock, and I found I couldn't wait to speak with Victoria. And my apologies for taking over your housecleaning, but I didn't think you'd want trash dirtying up your parlor."

Mrs. Dalrymple put her hands on her ample hips, but her eyes sparkled with glee. "After such a display, Mr. Willets, I expect you to take action."

"I will."

He went down on one knee in front of Victoria. "Victoria, please forgive my poorly worded proposal this morning. You deserve so much better, so much more."

She wanted to cradle his dear face in her hands, but the minister's wife seemed glued to the carpet for once.

"It wasn't a bad proposal," Victoria told him. "Just not the one I wanted."

"It didn't come out the way I wanted either," he said. "I do appreciate your capabilities—nursing, playing the piano, encouraging people, helping others, but it wasn't your looks or your abilities that drew me to you. From the first day, I could see your determination and your devotion. Since then, I've come to admire how you can find the joy even when I'm too focused on the work. You inspire me. I'd marry you if you told me all you want to do is sit in the parlor and stare out the window all day."

She shook her head, smile breaking free. "Oh, Jack, you don't mean that."

"I do! I'd be lying if I said I didn't want a helpmate, a wife who can work beside me on the ranch. You are so much more than that. I'll spend the rest of my life showing you how much I value you. I'll bring you flowers every day. I'll ride to Olympia for sheet music. I'll find a way to get you a piano." He pulled back and dug in the pocket of his coat to produce a white paper packet.

Victoria blinked the tears that threatened to gather. "You remembered." Her fingers trembled as she accepted the peppermint stick from him.

"I remember everything you say to me. And I'm committed to doing whatever would make you happy."

She could hardly speak, for now her lips were trembling too. "I think I could be happy just being with you, if you truly want me."

"I don't ever want you to doubt that again. And you'll have a whole family of people who'll love and care about you too. Please marry me, Victoria. I don't think I'll be whole without you."

Joy surged up, wrapping itself around her heart. "I feel the same way. If you're sure, Jack."

"I'm sure."

In his gaze, in his smile, she saw the truth shining. He truly was falling in love with her just as she was with him. So long as they both kept working at it, there was no reason they couldn't have the future she dreamed of.

Thank You, Lord!

"Then, yes, Jack, I will marry you."

He rose and pulled her into his arms. The touch of his lips to hers, the tenderness of his arms around her, told her even more than his beautiful sentiments that she was valued and cherished.

Mrs. Dalrymple started applauding again. "Oh, wonderful! You must stay for dinner, Mr. Willets. I have plenty, and we have cause to celebrate!"

Jack kept his arms around Victoria's waist as if he would never let her go. "I'd be glad to, ma'am. Thank you."

"I must tell Richard," she said, trotting toward the door. "He'll be so pleased." She waved a hand. "Carry on!"

"She is the *worst* chaperone," Jack said with a shake of his head. "But you won't find me complaining."

"This time, me either," Victoria said, lifting her chin for another kiss.

Victoria returned with him to the ranch in the wagon after dinner so she could check on her patients. Jack indulged himself, holding the reins with one hand and slipping his other arm about her as she sat beside him on the bench. She rested her head against his shoulder, and all he could do was send a hallelujah heavenward. He would never deserve her, but he was more thankful than he could say that she'd agreed to be his bride. And to think anyone had once considered her a leftover!

Ma met them before they even started down the hall. She blocked the way forward, arms crossed over her chest. "Well?"

"We're engaged," Jack said. "Victoria is willing to take a chance on me."

"Not a very large risk," she pointed out as his mother dropped her arms and beamed. "I've watched you at work. I've seen you in times of cheer and times of trouble, sir."

"And I collapsed like a tent pole in a strong wind under the latter," he reminded her.

"You did no such thing," his mother protested. "You're the first one anyone calls when they need help, Jack. Now that you have someone you love to stand beside you, any trouble you face won't seem nearly as hard. You'll see."

Jack smiled. "Well, I won't wish for more trouble to test that theory, but I count myself the luckiest man alive."

"And I count myself the most fortunate woman," Victoria said, gazing at him in a way that made him want to stand taller, hold her closer.

His mother rubbed her hands together. "Now, we just need to find a nice girl for Jacob. Perhaps the new schoolmarm he's planning to engage." She laughed. "Who knows? It might be a different sort of engagement entirely."

"With our family," Jack said, "I wouldn't be surprised."

About the Author

Thank you for reading Jack and Victoria's story. If you're wondering how Jeremy and Caroline came to meet, look for *Sudden Mail-Order Bride*. And look for *Hideaway Frontier Bride* to learn how Jacob's quest to start a school led to a most unusual schoolmarm and the love of his life.

Regina Scott is a bestselling and award-winning author of warm, witty historical romance. Set in England and the Pacific Northwest, Regina's books seamlessly meld humor, history, and hijinks that have readers and reviewers raving. With more than 65 works and over 1,500,000 books read worldwide, she sweeps her readers into the romance of history with every richly envisioned happily ever after. She and her husband of 35 years reside in Washington State on the way to Mt. Rainier. Regina Scott has learned to fence, dressed as a Regency dandy, driven four in hand, and sailed on a tall ship, all in the name of research, of course.

Newsletter with exclusive stories: **https://subscribe.reginascott.com**
Website: **www.reginascott.com**
Facebook: **https://www.facebook.com/authorreginascott**
Instagram: **www.instagram.com/reginascottauthor/**
Goodreads: **www.goodreads.com/reginascott**
BookBub: **www.bookbub.com/authors/regina-scott**

Priscilla's Promise

by Teresa Slack

Priscilla Channing wants to honor her late father's wishes by marrying the man he chose for her years ago. But he's not the man of honor her father believed he was, and Priscilla isn't the same woman.

Priscilla's Promise by Award-Winning Author Teresa Slack
Book 1 of the Four Sisters Ranch Series

Chapter One

"Begging your pardon, miss. Are you all right?"

Priscilla Channing looked up toward the masculine voice. She couldn't make out details of the man save broad shoulders and a face concealed by the glare of the noonday sun and the brim of a wide slouch hat. While not familiar, the voice sounded benign enough. She was used to running into men on her uncle's ranch. What she wasn't used to was falling into a hole she was sure hadn't been there the last time she was in this field.

"Um, yes. I think so."

A scrape on her left hand burned where she'd tried to slow her descent as she fell into the hole that seemed to appear out of nowhere. A wet spot on her knee suggested broken skin. A shaft of pain shot up her leg as she shifted her weight. Despite the discomfort and embarrassment, none of the wounds appeared grave enough to be the end of her. Her dress, however, was another matter. She looked down in dismay and saw a large swath of dirt across her hip. Winona, the housekeeper would give her a good what-for when she got back to the house.

"Miss?"

"Yes," she called back, louder this time. Her cheeks colored with embarrassment. While she couldn't see him, he had a clear view of her in a very unladylike position in a hole. "Thank you for asking, but I'll live."

Who was asking, she couldn't yet tell. The unfamiliar voice was deep and resonating. Smooth with an inflection she couldn't identify as belonging to one of the ranch hands. She'd lived on her uncle's ranch since Papa's death three years ago. She knew this place as well as the back of her hand—was familiar with every gulley and depression. She cast her eyes around the small cylindrical hole. Where had it come from, and how had she fallen into it?

"I'm coming in to get you," the voice said.

"No! I mean, please, don't. It isn't necessary." Not to mention she was practically wedged into place. If he tried to climb in, he'd have to stand practically on top of her, and that surely wouldn't do. She stood and tested her sore knee. Tender but fine. She would survive. She wished the man would go back to whatever he'd been doing and leave her to rescue herself. Then she could shimmy out under her own steam, and no one need know what happened.

She took fistfuls of skirt and prepared to hike it up to her knees so she could lift her leg high enough to climb out. Until recently, she and her cousins wore trousers while riding around the ranch. Then, Winona woke up one morning and decided the girls were too old for traipsing around dressed like men.

"I've overlooked your foolishness for too long" she'd said. "You'll never find husbands by dressing like fieldhands."

Uncle Lucian didn't ordinarily put much stock in convention, but it could be that he was beginning to lament the absence of a son-in-law. In this matter, he stood with the housekeeper. None of the girls appreciated the new mandate, except maybe Clarissa, the oldest, who believed if a woman wanted to be respected and taken seriously in a man's world, she should follow the rules expected of one.

Priscilla missed wearing trousers today.

"Thank you kindly," she told her would-be rescuer. "I appreciate your concern, but I can get myself—"

"No, miss, I won't be doing that." She heard scuffling on the earth above her. A few clots of dirt clattered down the side of the hole and bounced off her shoulder. "I'm coming down."

Priscilla jumped away from the side of the hole and the loose clods of dirt and prairie soil. "I assure you, there's no room for the both of us. I can climb out if you'll just stand back a little."

"I'm sure you can, but since I'm the one who put this hole in your path, the least I can do is get you out of it."

A large, tanned hand reached toward her. "You get a toehold and I'll haul you out."

Priscilla studied the hand. She wasn't thrilled to put herself in the hands of a complete stranger, but it did seem the fastest, most efficient way out of the hole. The hand was calloused as expected from handling a shovel, but the nails were trimmed and even and relatively clean, which suggested he wasn't a simple ditchdigger.

She had ridden farther afield than normal today. Clarissa, who she worked with in the ranch office, knew she had gone riding, but she didn't know which direction Priscilla had taken. Darius, the stable manager, had seen her leave the barn on her mount, but he wouldn't begin to worry over her absence for hours yet. No one would have a reason to come looking for her if this man had nefarious plans in mind.

Stop thinking so much, she scolded. *You're fine. He's fine. Just get out of this hole.*

It wasn't likely a ne'er-do-well would've made it this far onto her uncle's vast property without detection. More than likely, he was a new hire, or one of the other riders had already seen her horse without a rider and was on his way across the prairie to see what had happened.

"Lord, I trust that You won't let him kill me," she prayed under her breath.

"Miss?"

"Nothing. Here I come."

She raised an arm skyward. He slid his hand to her elbow and took a firm grip. "Ready?"

She dug the toes of her boots into the freshly dug earth. "Quite."

He hefted with apparent ease. Her boots barely had time to skim the sides of the hole as she sailed upward. Halfway up, he let go of her elbow, grabbed her under the arms, and brought her the rest of the way to solid ground.

She landed unceremoniously on her hands and knees next to him in the trampled grass. "Oh, dear," she mumbled.

The man offered his hand, but she scrambled as gracefully as one could under such circumstances to her feet.

"Um, thank you...for that." She wagged her head in the direction of the hole. "Are you hurt?"

She flexed her sore ankle under her dress where he couldn't see. "I'm quite all right, thank you." Her hat hung down her back by the thin leather string that threatened to choke her. Strands of dark blond hair hung in her face. She took off the hat, slapped it into shape, then put it back on her head. She tucked her hair inside the hat.

The man tipped his hat at her. "Isaiah Paxton, owner of the hole."

She didn't recognize the name. Nor the man. She was sure she'd never seen him around here before, though nothing about him made her uncomfortable or desirous of her gun tucked in her saddlebag with her horse.

He didn't look like a fieldhand. His hands weren't rough enough, and though his clothes were covered with dust, they weren't in bad enough shape to be worn by a fieldhand. His chiseled square jaw was darkened by a few days-worth of growth and his white teeth did not show the evidence of chewing tobacco like most of the men under her uncle's employ. His hair, though mashed down by the hat, was thick and as black as night. His eyes were what captured her attention—a startling shade of green she'd never seen on a man.

"I'm sorry, but I don't know any Paxtons."

He smiled, lighting those captivating green eyes with amusement. "As far as I know there aren't any. I assume you're one of the Channing daughters. I met your father at a conference last fall and he invited me here. I'm an engineer under contract with the university in Lincoln."

Most of her tension slipped away. She remembered the conference last fall. And Uncle Lucian was a good judge of character. He wouldn't have invited this man here for something if he couldn't be trusted.

"I'm not one of the daughters. I'm their cousin Priscilla from Annapolis."

"It's nice to meet you, Priscilla from Annapolis. I'm from Palmyra, Nebraska myself. There are more Paxtons there than we know what to do with."

"I'm sorry. I don't know where that is."

"No one does." His smile widened.

He was charming, she'd give him that. And handsome. But she wasn't here to get acquainted with a man. Avoiding an entanglement with the opposite sex had been easy during the nearly three years since she moved here after Papa's death. She wouldn't entertain those thoughts now, though those green eyes were doing their best to pull at her.

"What is an engineer from Lincoln—or Palmyra—doing out here?" She gestured at the hole he'd just pulled her out of. "You came all this way to dig a hole in my uncle's field?"

His smile widened. She couldn't look away.

"I'm the lead on a team studying advances in irrigation. Your uncle attended one of my lectures. He's very interested in our research, as you may know."

She did not.

"He invited me to luncheon the next day, and we talked at length. He provided maps of his holdings for me to study. I saw right away this property is the perfect place for our research. We believe Nebraska sits atop some of the deepest and largest reserves of groundwater on the continent. Studying the water systems here can teach us how to access it while ensuring we preserve the resiliency of our resources."

They turned in a slow circle to survey the gently rolling landscape. It was late May. Though the month had been drier than any May Priscilla had experienced, the ground was green and vibrant. When she first arrived in Nebraska, the wide-open space had made her feel adrift, as if she walked too far, she'd drop off the earth. Now, her practiced eye noted the subtle undulation of the earth and patches of color of tilled ground, sagebrush, and natural fauna that kept her grounded.

"Where's the rest of your team?"

He cocked his head. "I suppose team is a generous term. There's only three of us here. The other men are working about two miles from here on another sector we've mapped out. We set up camp each night or use one of the ranch's old soddies, depending on where we're working, to discuss our findings and write our reports."

If she had to fall into a hole while musing and puzzling over her future, she was glad she had fallen into this one, so Isaiah Paxton was the one to pull her out.

"Your uncle was anxious to help in any way he could," he continued, thankfully unaware of the path her thoughts had taken. "He is astute enough to realize what we learn here will ensure his continued success as well. Water is the future of our state, or rather a way to manage it. Every agricultural department in every university west of the Mississippi is jockeying for top spot in this field to garner Washington's attention."

"Because that's where the money is."

"Exactly. Each department needs grants to continue the research, and we all believe ours will reap the best results to benefit a hungry nation."

She looked back at the hole. "Fascinating. I had no idea."

"It is fascinating work. If you're interested, you can come back out tomorrow or whenever you have time. I'll be working in this area the rest of the week. I'm easy to find." His lips quirked upward. "Now that you know where to look."

Was it her imagination or was he interested in more than just explaining the science of irrigation to a novice?

"Are you offering a private lecture?"

His green eyes flashed. "I am."

Her stomach twisted. She shouldn't come. She had no right to spend time alone with a man. She could easily go the rest of her life without understanding how groundwater reserves could change the face of the Great Plains. Despite the warning bells going off in her head telling her to ride back to the ranch and forget she'd met this handsome, intriguing engineer, she couldn't bring herself to say no.

"I work in the ranch office in the mornings with my cousin Clarissa. Perhaps after the noon meal, I can get away for a few hours."

He gave her a long look that warmed her all the way to her toes. "I'll be expecting you."

Chapter Two

The sun was sinking toward the horizon by the time Priscilla rode into the barnyard of her uncle's ranch house. The white painted house sat on a small knob, surrounded by tall trees Uncle Lucian and Aunt Grace had planted a generation ago. The outdoor pump was painted bright red and stood out in sharp contrast to the lush green grass of the yard.

Spanning the lane supported by two poles on either side was a wooden sign. For years the property had been referred to by the locals as *Channing Ranch*. As years passed and the elm trees matured, the property became more prosperous and outgrew its confines. Ten years ago, not long before Aunt Grace died, it became apparent no sons would be born to take over the property. Aunt Grace directed Uncle Lucian to erect a proper sign over the entrance to the expansive yard. From the second-floor window of what had become her sickroom, she watched the ranch hands erect a sign that immortalized her beloved daughters.

The ranch officially became *Four Sisters Ranch*.

Priscilla led her mount to the water trough inside the cool interior of the two-story barn. While the animal slaked her thirst, Priscilla removed the saddle and hung it over the stall wall. In the city, she only rode on horseback in parks or occasionally at a friend's country estate. She hadn't given a moment's thought to the care of the animal once she slid out of the saddle. Not so on her uncle's ranch. Though the ranch employed many ranch and stable hands, the girls were expected to care for the animals they used instead of passing the responsibility to someone else. The expectation was the same inside the house. If she made a mess or a decision that resulted in extra work, it was her duty to clean it up.

Footsteps approached and stopped outside the stall. She was bent over untangling a burr from the horse's fetlock, She peeked under her arm while she worked and saw her cousin Tara smiling in at her.

At twenty-one, Tara was the closest in age and appearance of the sisters to Priscilla. They shared the same oval face shape, delicate skin that freckled in the sun, and wide-set deep blue eyes. They were the same height and slender build. They each had long fingers and big feet they liked to tease the other about. Tara's thick blond hair was several shades lighter than Priscilla's honey blond locks. Per the usual for working on the ranch, Tara's was fashioned into a heavy braid that hung down to her waist.

"You sure were gone a long time," she observed as she stepped into the stall.

Priscilla straightened and pushed an errant lock of hair out of her eyes with the back of her arm. "I suppose I was."

Tara's gaze took in her soiled dress. "What happened?"

Priscilla had nearly forgotten her disheveled state. "Oh, um, it's nothing." She went back to brushing. She was nearly done. "I fell. In a hole."

Tara let out a one-syllable laugh. "You've ridden every inch of this ranch a thousand times. How did you find a hole to fall into?"

"It was a new hole."

"Excuse me?"

Priscilla tried not to smile but couldn't help it as she remembered her encounter with the handsome engineer. She rested her arm on the horse's smooth flank. "Did you know Uncle Lucian invited some men here from the university to study groundwater reservoirs?"

"I might've heard him say something about water. He's consumed with irrigation. Why?"

"I ran into one of them today. Actually, I fell into a hole he'd dug and he pulled me out."

Tara's azure eyes darkened with concern. Her gaze swept over Priscilla for signs of injury. "Are you hurt?"

"I twisted my knee a little. Don't tell Winona."

Tara smiled at the mention of the housekeeper, a tiny Indian woman from the Otoe tribe who had taken on the role of mothering the girls after Aunt Grace's death. She hadn't let up an inch even though Clarissa would turn twenty-four on her next birthday. "I won't. You'll have enough trouble explaining the state of that dress. Just tell me how you fell into a hole. Wasn't it marked or secured by a fence? I hope it wasn't in the pastures or where one of the animals can fall into it?"

The women exited the stall. Priscilla latched the door, then put the curry comb and brush in the tack box. "The hole will no longer be a threat to anyone or anything, and I'll watch better where I'm going."

Tara caught her hand and forced her to stand still. "Then tell me about the man who got you out."

Priscilla's stomach fluttered at the thought of Isaiah. A blush warmed her cheeks. "There's nothing to tell." She hoped the barn's shadows would keep Tara from noticing. They didn't.

Tara let out a cry of excitement and squeezed her hands tight. "I knew it! Tell me everything. Who is he? What does he look like?"

"I told you. He's one of the engineers from the university. He met Uncle at a conference last fall, and Uncle invited him and his team to come and study the property. We talked a little. He is very interesting."

"And?"

"And nothing. You can ask Uncle if you think he doesn't have a right to be on the property."

"I'm not worried about that. I'm worried about the effect he's had on you."

Priscilla couldn't stop thinking the same thing. She pulled her arm free and smiled gently. "He hasn't had an *effect*. He's just an interesting person. Did you know research teams all over the Great Plains are vying for federal funding to learn more about groundwater and irrigation projects?"

"Is he handsome?"

Priscilla felt her blush deepen. "Very."

"That's what I thought."

"What's that supposed to mean?"

Tara dipped her head and squinted at her as they stepped out of the barn and into the afternoon sunlight. "I hope you're not playing with fire, Cilla."

"I'm not playing with anything. I know what I'm doing." She immediately regretted the impatience in her voice. She just didn't want this afternoon to be ruined with thoughts of things that had already been decided and she couldn't change.

"I'm sorry. I didn't mean to snap."

"It was my fault. I shouldn't have said anything."

The cousins ambled toward the sprawling farmhouse. Uncle Lucian and Aunt Grace had built it over the years, adding on as means supplied and the size of the family dictated. Their first year on the prairie was lived in a soddy with a dirt floor on the ridge above the current house. Aunt Grace told the girls stories of the damp, spider-filled hovel. The girls loved to shriek and cringe at the images, but there were good stories, too, told laughingly as memories of rough times can be after the passage of time lessoned the horrors of the moment. Aunt Grace believed that year in the soddy and the hard lean years they shared had strengthened their union and closeness like nothing else could. Without that rough start, they wouldn't have built what they did.

When the cousins reached the porch that spanned the front of the house, Tara sat on the top step and pulled Priscilla down beside her. A soft breeze circled the house. Late Spring and early Fall were Priscilla's favorite times of year—before the relentless heat of a summer sun made the inside of the house nearly uninhabitable and before winter winds howled and piled snow often as high as the eaves.

Tara leaned her head against Priscilla's shoulder. "I don't want to see you get hurt."

"I appreciate that. I don't want to get hurt either."

Tara sat up and looked at her. "What is it you want, Cilla?"

"The same as everyone else, I suppose. Love. Romance."

"You don't have to go back to Annapolis to find it, you know."

Priscilla stiffened. She and Tara had had this conversation before. "It's not as simple as all that."

"You know you're free to make you own choices."

Priscilla pulled her hand free. "I am making my own decisions."

Tara pursed her lips and didn't speak for a moment. "A lot can change in three years. You want it to, don't you?"

Tears tickled Priscilla's nose. "It doesn't matter what I want. I made a promise. Papa wanted me to be happy and provided for. My future was his only concern on his deathbed. I've told you that. He said he could go in peace if he knew I was married to a successful man who would love me and provide for me the way he did Mama. How could I take that from him?"

Tara laid a hand on her knee. Priscilla didn't pull away. "You couldn't. But that doesn't mean Peter Hollister is the only man on earth who can give it to you. I never met your papa, but he was my papa's brother. I have to believe that means they were a lot alike. Your happiness was the most important thing to him. How can you be happy marrying a man you don't love?"

"I do love him." She heard the vehemence in her voice as if trying to convince herself. "Or I will learn to. He's smart and handsome and all the girls in our circle were so jealous that I was the one he chose."

"That was a long time ago. You were a girl."

To: "Old enough to know I had to stand by the word I gave Papa. Our fathers were business partners. They used to tease Peter and me about marrying." A gentle smile of remembrance softened her exasperation. "The older we got, they realized how suited we actually were and how we'd make a fitting union. Peter and I were agreeable. We weren't forced into anything. There's no reason why I should think about going back on my promise now."

"I don't mean to sound argumentative, but that was a long time ago. You were both children. You don't know anything about the man Peter is now. He's barely written in three years. He might've fallen in love or decided to chase after gold out west. Men aren't like us. They're no good at being on their own, especially men with money and position. And there's plenty of women willing to give them what they want."

"Not Peter." Priscilla wasn't sure why she was defending him so vehemently. Tara was right; she hadn't seen him in years. She knew next to nothing about him except that Papa always liked and respected him. Who knew if that was enough now.

To: "I'm just saying things might've changed for him too. Can you really say it would break your heart if you found out he had fallen in love and was marrying someone else?"

Priscilla chewed her lip, unsure how she felt about that possibility.

"You'd be released from your promise. Your papa couldn't hold you responsible for a vow if Peter was the one to break it." Tara leaned closer. "You'd be free," she whispered with a gleam in her eye.

Free.

Priscilla's heart surged at the thought, but what did it mean? Free to do what? She'd lived on this ranch for almost three years, and before today she'd not met one man who sparked her interest in the least. She had even begun to think of herself as an old maid. Everyone in the community of Channing already did. In these parts where men outnumbered women four to one, no woman reached the age of twenty-one without a man scooping her up unless something was wrong with her. The town blamed Uncle Lucian for allowing his girls to ride around in pants and rope cows and drive teams through the fields. He had practically turned them into men, the townspeople said. No wonder no one wanted them. Only Lucy and Marcia, the youngest sisters, were still considered marriageable, and their days were numbered if Lucian didn't rein them in quick, fast, and in a hurry.

She clasped her hands around one knee. "I wonder sometimes what my future will be like. Don't you? Do you ever think of what will become of us if…if no man wants us?"

Tara sniffed. "Not for a minute. I'd be happy if I lived here forever with Papa."

"He won't be here forever. But even then, it's easier for you. You have this place. This town. You belong. I always thought I belonged in Annapolis. After being here for so long with all of you, I'm not so sure anymore."

"You don't have to be sure, Cilla. You have us, and we have you. You don't need to worry one minute that you don't belong, or that you won't be complete without Peter in Annapolis."

"I appreciate you saying that, and I know you mean it, but everyone needs a place of their own."

Tara squeezed her hand. Priscilla resisted the urge to pull away. She didn't want Tara's pity. More even, she didn't want her charity. That's how she'd begun to feel. She knew her cousins loved her and considered her another sister, but she wasn't. As long as she stayed here—though none of them would ever say it or even think it—she'd be a charity case. The pitiful orphan cousin without a home who they graciously took in.

She loved them for all they'd done and appreciated every kindness, but she didn't want to be the one who didn't fit. The one without a life of her own.

Tara stood and smoothed the wrinkles out of her skirt. "I meant what I said, Cilla. You'll always be a part of this family whether you go back to Annapolis or stay right here."

The front door flung open. Both women whirled around to face it. Her youngest cousin Marcia rushed out the door. At seventeen, she was always rushing in a dozen directions at once like a prairie twister.

Her gaze slid past Tara to land on Priscilla. "Finally. I thought you'd never get here."

Tara and Priscilla exchanged amused glances. With Marcia, every matter was of utmost importance. "If I'd known you needed me so urgently, I wouldn't have left the house this morning."

Marcia wrinkled her pert little nose at the sarcasm in Priscilla's voice. She brandished a letter in her hand. "I would think not if you'd known this was coming."

A sick feeling in her stomach made Priscilla stand still. Tara reached for the heavy vellum envelope, but Marcia angled her body away and held the letter out of Tara's reach. "Huh uh. This is for Cilla's eyes only." She looked back at Priscilla, her blue eyes flashing with excitement. "It's from Annapolis. From Peter."

Chapter Three

Peter.

She hadn't received a letter from him in three months. Why now? Why after meeting the handsome engineer in the field? Was it a sign? Could Tara's prediction be coming true? He had found someone else and was marrying.

She was free. Free to…

Talk to Isaiah tomorrow.

Is that what she wanted? Yes, but at the same time, she wasn't sure. Since she was a girl, she knew she was going to become Mrs. Peter Hollister. Back then, the thought had thrilled her. Peter was everything the people in her social circle envied. Ambitious. Charming. Handsome. Intelligent. And she would be his wife.

During the six months of Papa's laying-up as he succumbed to his illness, Peter called on them less and less. He said he and his father were busy filling the gap and preparing the company for the eventual loss of her father. Priscilla had wished Peter were more available to offer a little support, to lean on as she grieved. She was never sure if he was needed as desperately at the firm as he claimed or if he wasn't good at offering solace and didn't know what to say or do to help her through the worst time of her life.

Or, worst of all, he didn't care all that much about her loss except for what Papa's absence would mean to the company. She had never let herself think about it too much.

In the nearly three full years she'd been in Nebraska she'd received less than a dozen letters. They were never letters of endearment one might expect from a fiancé. He seldom wrote anything personal, and she had a hard time thinking of things to write back. He made it no secret that he wasn't interested in the daily operation of Four Sisters Ranch or of her life here. Nor did he express love or affection for her. Even his valedictions included no term of endearment.

He closed each one: *With warmest regards, Peter Henry Hollister.* She knew for a fact he closed even business letters in the same manner, with the exception of *warmest*.

Marcia waved the letter more vigorously, clearly perplexed over why Priscilla hadn't jumped on it like a goose on a bug.

Tara snatched the letter out of her hand.

"Hey!" When Marcia saw that Priscilla didn't seem to care Tara had taken the letter, she lifted one shoulder, spun around, and went back inside.

Tara and Priscilla stared at each other. "It's been a while since you've heard from him," Tara observed.

Priscilla stared at the heavy envelope. She thought of how easy and natural her conversation had been with Isaiah today. Nothing like the stilted, awkward conversations with Peter where she spent the whole time wondering what he was really thinking behind that practiced smile.

It had been so long since they'd had a real conversation, she almost forgot what they found to talk about.

Peter liked to dress up and attend fancy parties and galas. He said it was important in business to present to the community as successful and prosperous. No one would invest in a company if the front men were not well established in the city. He had political aspirations as well. He was made for it since he could talk for hours and not say anything.

Tara held the letter out to her.

Priscilla didn't move. "I already know what it says."

"You still need to read it."

"No, I don't. He'll want to know how much longer until I come home. Until we get married."

"I thought that was the plan."

"It is, I guess."

She thought of Isaiah in the field, his eyes shining as he explained what he was doing here. She'd rather spend the whole evening talking to him about water and irrigation than think for one minute about Peter and his passionless letter.

She half turned away. "Read it to me. Please."

Tara hesitated a moment longer. Finally, she slipped two fingers between the flap and envelope to break the monogrammed seal. She pulled out one neatly folded page. "I shouldn't be doing this. Peter wrote it to you."

Her eyes scanned the page. "He misses you. His mother wants to start planning a wedding. His father wonders if you've gotten cold feet."

More like stone cold.

To: Tara thrust the letter and envelope into her hands. "I can't do this. It's betraying a trust. This is between you and him."

She was right. Priscilla had no right to ask her to read the words Peter had penned for her eyes only. She tried to steady her shaking hands as she quickly read the one-page letter, the whole time hoping against hope he would include one word of affection. That all this time apart had proven how much she meant to him. He couldn't bear one more day without her, and not just because his parents were getting impatient.

If he did, it might rekindle the feelings she once had for him. She remembered the breathless anticipation she felt as she dressed for a party where he would be in attendance. How hard it was to sit still as the maid fashioned her hair into an elegant up-do. How Mrs. Templeton brought fabric swatches and patterns to the house to help her design a spring wardrobe. All the time, she had thought of Peter and hoped if he would approve of the dress she chose with him in mind.

She no longer loved Peter but the idea of him. The successful, debonair husband who escorted her to fashionable society events. With the loss of Papa, she lost her love of that life too. It seemed so pointless. Boring. God forgive her, she now had the same feelings for Peter.

She reached the bottom of the letter. She gasped and nearly lost her hold on the paper. "He's coming. He's coming here."

Tara stepped forward, her horrified expression mirroring Priscilla's. "What for?"

Priscilla kept her eyes on the letter. "To fetch me. He's tired of waiting. He's coming to get me and take me back to the city to marry him."

"Not exactly a romantic proposal."

Priscilla pursed her lips and stared at the letter. "I suppose it could be perceived as one. He wants me home and he's willing to come all this way for me."

"How do you feel? You look shocked."

"I don't know…what to think. I…" She tried to imagine herself in a beautiful gown standing next to Peter with their family—well, his family since she had no one but the people on this ranch—and Peter's business associates in attendance as the minister pronounced them man and wife. She tried to conjure an image of herself in Peter's stately house residing over her own household staff. A staff that catered to her every desire but whispered and disrespected her behind her back.

The only image was of her on the back of a horse racing across an open field, the wind on her face and the pungent smell of grass and freshly tilled earth teasing her senses. A life lost to her once she went back to Annapolis.

She glanced toward the hills in the distance, green and lush and brimming with possibilities and freedom.

Tara touched her hand. "Did you hear me?"

Priscilla snapped out of her reverie. "I'm sorry. What?"

"You don't have to marry Peter," her cousin said gently. "You don't have to go back to Annapolis."

Irritation welled in her chest. They'd been over this so many times. "Yes, I do. Papa knew this was best for me. I trusted him then, and I trust him now. He knew Peter would give me the family he and Mother wanted me to have. I don't know Peter very well, but that will be remedied as soon as he gets here. The Bible says to find contentment in all things. All situations. That's what I'll do."

The more she talked, the more confident she became. "Papa didn't insist I make the promise to salve his pride. He knew what was best. I trust him. I have to."

Tara looked like she wanted to say more. Priscilla could almost read her mind. Love was what she wanted most. Not an arranged marriage with a man she didn't know. Had maybe never known.

Instead, she squeezed Priscilla's arm, then dropped her hand to her side. "We'll all miss you terribly when you go." Her blue eyes shone. "It won't be the same around here without you."

A longing to stay right here rose up in Priscilla, nearly bringing her to tears of panic. She pushed it aside. She would be content in her life with Peter like the Bible dictated. She ignored the knot in her stomach and pasted what she hoped was an optimistic smile on her face.

"I'm not leaving today." She flipped the heavy envelope over to read the postmark. "He sent this two weeks ago. He could be here anytime or not for a month. When he does arrive, he won't expect me to leave that moment. He'll want to visit with Uncle and get to know all of you."

She clasped the letter to her chest, determined to make the best of the situation. "I think I'd like a new dress for Peter's arrival. It won't do for him see me in a dirty torn dress that looks like I just got pulled out of a hole."

"It certainly would not." Tara laughed, and the morose mood dissipated. "I wish only the best for you, Cilla. Wherever that happens."

Priscilla returned the hug and hoped the best was in store for her. She pushed the lingering image of Isaiah and his captivating green eyes out of her head. It shouldn't be that hard to forget him, since she'd only known him for an hour. She'd known Peter and the future her parents designed for her all her life.

The next morning, Priscilla decided against hitching a buggy and riding into town to look at fabric and patterns for a new dress in which to greet Peter. Before she could talk herself out of it, she scrubbed her face until her pink cheeks glowed and took extra care with her hair. Her attempts wouldn't last once she mounted her horse and rode across the rolling prairie. Even if she arrived looking fit for a debutante ball, she had no reason to think Isaiah would notice. He was here on very important business, not to pay attention to an orphaned cousin living off the charity of her last living relatives.

She had no business seeking him out anyway. She was engaged—to a man she barely knew—but engaged, nonetheless. What she was doing wasn't fair to Isaiah or Peter. Or to herself.

Despite her good sense telling her to go to town for fabric and forget the engineer with the mossy green eyes, she saddled her favorite mount and headed out. She told herself she only wanted to learn a little more about the irrigation process and how it would impact Nebraska and her family's lives. That was all. Harmless interest. An interest that had nothing to do with the greenest eyes she'd ever seen, raven black hair, and an engaging smile that melted her insides.

As she rode, she tried to recall a time when she heard Peter laugh out loud. To be fair, three years ago he had just begun his career at the firm. He was focused on proving himself worthy to the company and to her. He hadn't had time for frivolity and horse play and idle chitchat.

Surely, he wasn't like that now. Even if he was, he possessed the qualities a woman needed in a husband. Security and stability were more important than joviality and horseback riding and watching the sun rise over an open prairie.

Wasn't it?

Was she wrong to want both?

She sighed. She wouldn't let thoughts of Peter and a long empty future of parties and volunteering for civic organizations she cared nothing about ruin her day. Once she and Peter got to know each other's adult selves, they would find things they both enjoyed. Instead of an open prairie, they would have the Atlantic Ocean. An awe-inspiring sight she sorely missed. They would awaken early while the rest of the city slept, take a carriage to the waterfront, and watch the sunrise.

Maybe he was ready for the same things in life she longed for, and that was what spurred his decision to come for her. Now that he was established in business, he recognized his need for a wife. His work and responsibilities wouldn't keep him from enjoying life's simple pleasures with her. The waves breaking on the beach or a baby's laugh. Their baby.

A bubble of excitement rose inside her. She would be a mother. She had put those feelings aside for a long time, but they were there, waiting for the right time.

Ahead, a smudge in the distance slowly morphed into the shape of a simple worksite with a man moving around. Isaiah.

All thoughts of Peter flew out of her head.

For a crazy, disconcerting moment the idea of her future child was held in Isaiah's arms. She shoved the thought away. She nearly wheeled the horse around and rode back to the house. Peter was her intended. Isaiah was a stranger. The thought of them together was nearly adulterous. He was here to do a job, not become part of her ridiculous fantasies. When he finished his research, he'd go back to the university, she'd go to Annapolis with Peter, and they would be nothing more to each other than a pleasant memory.

Isaiah straightened from where he knelt in the grass over some tools and directed his easy smile at her. Her breath caught and her stomach did a strange little somersault. It reminded her of the time in the ocean when a wave caught her unaware and tumbled her end over end before she got her feet under her again.

Was that interest she saw in his smile? Did she dare hope? And just why was she hoping for anything from this man?

She took a deep breath to calm her racing heart and slowed the horse. It wouldn't do to go tearing into camp, breathless and blushing like a schoolgirl. Especially when she harbored no romantic feelings for him.

His smile was still in place when she dismounted.

He tipped his hat, nodding politely. "Morning, Priscilla."

"Morning," she returned as casually as her pounding pulse would allow. "I hope I'm not interrupting anything."

"Not at all. I've been at it since first light. I was thinking of setting the coffeepot over the coals again. Now, I have an excuse." His smile widened and his green eyes warmed to the color of a late summer meadow. "Would you care for a cup?"

"I'd like that."

"Good." He reached for the reins, and she handed them over. He led the horse to where his grazed in the shade in a pen he'd made from sticks and fallen branches.

She waited until he returned, then followed him to the remains of an early morning fire. He poked the coals back to life.

"Shouldn't be but a minute."

"I don't mind waiting." She glanced around the campsite and hoped he wouldn't notice the effects his proximity had on her.

She thought of the centuries of men off making discoveries in parts unknown while the women waited at home, worrying and wondering. "How much longer do you think your project will keep you here?"

She hoped she didn't sound like she was asking for herself. She was just curious. It didn't matter to her if he was here for another day or a month.

Right?

"If all goes as planned, the rest of the summer,"

She kept her face impassive, despite the bloom of delight in her stomach. She reminded herself Peter was coming. She was just killing time until his arrival.

"I could probably work this area for the next five years and not discover all the secrets this land holds" His voice was awestruck. "I won't be on your uncle's property the entire summer. After I finish here, I'll move west toward the Sandhills. All the teams are hopping all over the Great Plains, hoping to learn as much as we can about the groundwater reserves. That knowledge and the ability to utilize it will change the prairie system's crop yield forever, affecting the entire nation."

Priscilla couldn't imagine thousands of acres of underground water waiting to be accessed. What other treasures were under her feet?

"Uncle loves this place. I've come to love it too. It would be wonderful to watch more acreage come alive with crop production and livestock."

Isaiah studied her with an appraising look. "It will be a wonderful thing indeed."

His intense gaze and quiet tone made her wonder if he was thinking of more than water. She glanced in the direction of the horses, wishing she could think of something to say. Something intelligent and thoughtful. She had attended the university for young women in Annapolis for nearly two years. She learned history, art, science, and literature. Most of the courses were designed to give young ladies from wealthy families just enough knowledge to participate in conversations with men smarter than themselves without taking over or showing off. The most substantial courses focused on running a household. The young ladies didn't take the science or history courses too seriously since the ultimate goal was to marry and have children.

Isaiah brushed his hands on the front of his shirt. "Would you like to sit while we wait for the coffee?"

"I'd like that, and you can tell me more about your work."

He turned toward the tent, then quickly back. "I trust, you're not suffering any affects from your fall yesterday."

"Oh, no. I mean, I'm not suffering…" She stopped talking. He must think her a dithering idiot.

"I'm glad. I worried about you last night."

Her heart warmed at his concern, though it shouldn't give her such pleasure. He was only thinking of her as one considerate person would think of another who may have suffered injury. He may have worried about his own situation as well. If she had been hurt by his failure to mark the hole properly, Uncle Lucian could've run him off the property and compromised his work. Still, she had been on his mind. Whatever the reason, she liked it.

"How do you know where to dig?" she asked. "Is it like witching for water?"

"You could say that, just on a much more scientific scale. We dig until we find high concentrations of moisture in the soil, like water in a sponge, then use the information to determine the extent of the aquifer. This system could extend all the way below Kansas and as far west as Colorado."

She gasped and peered into the hole. "Just this one system? That's incredible. And you can learn all that by digging holes?"

"By digging lots of holes. Other teams are doing the same thing as well as researching the most efficient ways to extract water from the soil. That's why it's important to learn as much as we can as quickly as we can. There's only so much federal funding available, and the government is incredibly slow at sending it. There are already too many lobbyists in D.C. vying for funds. I hope the university finds me integral to the work here, so when they're ready to send delegates to address a congressional committee, they'll consider me."

"Is that something you're interested in? Becoming a lobbyist?"

"Begging money from a bunch of Washington bureaucrats to benefit a part of the country they have no interest in seeing? Not really. But I believe in this project and the future of the Plains. I will be honored to be chosen."

"I'm sure they'll choose you. You're so…"

She stopped just before she said he was so handsome and articulate, he was the perfect candidate to plead the state's case in Washington.

"I appreciate your confidence," he said as her silence lengthened.

"You convinced me, and before yesterday, I had no idea this was even a thing," she amended.

He chuckled. "Shall we go back to the fire? I'm sure the coffee's hot."

Priscilla walked a few steps away from him so he wouldn't see the flush on her face.

She should go back to the house and get out of his way. She should tell him about Peter. But what was the point? He'd given her no indication he was even thinking of her in any way beyond an annoying woman keeping him from his work. What would he think if she blurted out; 'By the way, my fiancé is coming to fetch me any day, so don't go getting any ideas.'?

He would think she'd lost her mind. Besides, Peter wasn't here. He might not be for weeks. What was the harm in talking with Isaiah and learning about what he did.

It wasn't like she was going to fall in love with him or anything.

Chapter Four

Watching her there made Isaiah feel like he'd been punched in the gut. She was the prettiest thing to walk into his campsite in…well, forever. He gave himself a mental smack on the back of the head to stop staring and turned to his tent. He stuck his head and shoulders inside and brought out an armless, backless camp chair.

He set it down in front of her. "I wish I had something more comfortable."

She smiled her thanks and cautiously perched on the stool. He prayed it wouldn't collapse under her. Not because she was too heavy or gangly but because the chair was flimsy and the ground a little uneven. Her porcelain skin was flushed from the ride. Or maybe something more, but he wouldn't read too much into it.

Her deep blue eyes, the color of a dark sky, twinkled with life. She had a full mouth with deep pink lips that brought out the natural blush in her cheeks. She looked like she smiled and laughed a lot. He watched her situate her skirt around her legs, trying not to stare. She was so pretty. Her skin looked as smooth and soft as velvet. His fingers wrestled with the desire to touch her cheek to see for himself.

He gave himself an inward shake to thwart the direction his thoughts had taken. He took out a clean cup out of his satchel—thankfully he had an extra one—and glanced inside to make sure there was no lint or dust or spiders, before filling it with steaming black coffee from the pot. The only company he'd entertained around his fire were Lyle and Clayton, and they didn't count as company. They didn't look or smell as nice as Miss Channing either and didn't make him as nervous.

He'd been so focused on his work the last two years, he hadn't given more than a passing notice to those of the female persuasion. He attended plenty of dinners and symposiums at the university to drum up support and funds for various projects. The women in attendance were wives or guests of the professors, engineers, and dignitaries. He wouldn't have noticed them even if they'd all been eligible. His work came first. But something about Priscilla Channing piqued his interest. He couldn't decide if it was because meeting her had been so unexpected. Or something about her. Something that made him want to learn more.

He carefully handed her the cup with both hands. He tossed out the dregs of coffee from his previous cup into the tall grass and refilled it. He angled a hunk of log toward her and sat. He rested his forearms on his knees.

He blew away the steam rising off the coffee. "I'm not used to playing host. At the university, I spend most of my time in my office poring over maps and archaeological data. Out here it's even more solitary."

"What about your team?"

He chuckled appreciatively. "You mean Lyle and Clayton? They're not exactly the life of the party. I chose them because they're like me. Men who don't need much supervision. Last week I didn't see Lyle for three days. Anytime I see Clayton, he has his head bent over his charts and graphs. If not for their applications, I wouldn't even know their last names."

She laughed, her blue eyes dancing. "You should make an effort to know them better. You might get more out of them."

Isaiah looked at her for a long moment until he realized he was staring. He wanted to ask why she wasn't married. What she was doing on this remote section of ranch talking to him about water and irrigation. Did she have a man? If not, would she like one. His first priority was his work, though. He knew when he chose this line of work no woman would be interested in following him around Nebraska taking water readings, then back to his cramped, book-lined apartment while he worked to decipher the data.

"If they come into camp tonight, I'll ask where they're from."

She directed a dazzling smile at him. "That's a good place to start."

They smiled at each other and took cautious sips of coffee. Isaiah grimaced. The coffee had been strong and bitter when he first brewed it this morning. Now, it was practically undrinkable, but that's how every man drank his coffee—strong enough to take varnish off a floor.

"What do you do, Miss Channing?"

She blinked through the steam from her cup. "Do?"

He inwardly kicked himself. He needed to brush up on his conversation skills before he sat down across from a beautiful woman again. "At the ranch. All we've talked about is me. I'd rather talk about you?"

Surprise flashed across her face. He wondered how long it had been since a man asked about her. He knew from experience most men preferred to talk about themselves and the important things they were doing. How much did they miss out by not asking questions of beautiful women?

"I help my cousin Clarissa with the books."

He took another sip of coffee without taking his eyes off her, indicating she go on.

"Clarissa is my oldest cousin. She is the unofficial ranch manager, though everyone thinks Uncle handles it on his own. With Clarissa overseeing much of the day-to-day operations, Uncle is free to go on buying trips and attend conferences where he can meet men like you."

"When I first met him, I thought, now there's a man with a good staff at home to keep the place running in his absence."

"Clarissa definitely does that."

"And you, I'm sure."

"I do my part."

"I'm sure she couldn't do hers as well without you doing yours."

His response seemed to please her. He got the feeling she wasn't one to build herself up. "I've always been good with numbers. I suppose it's not very ladylike to admit. Bookkeeping is usually a man's game. Many people believe the female brain is incapable of complicated calculation."

He barked out a laugh before he could stop himself. "Whoever thinks that doesn't spend much time in a woman's company."

Priscilla smiled back. "Is that experience talking?"

He waved his free hand. "No, no, not me. It's just something I heard."

"Well, I live with five women, including the housekeeper, six in you count her daughter Rayen who helps with the housekeeping, especially on laundry day. I can attest that we can be quite calculating. Especially Winona when she's trying to teach us a lesson she thinks all young ladies should know."

"She sounds like my great-aunt. She never married and lived with us most of her adult life." He shook his head at the memory. "I loved that woman. Most opinionated person I ever met, but you know, she was usually proven right."

They sat in silence for a few moments. Isaiah wished he could think of something witty to say that would get the conversation back to what he really wanted to talk about. Priscilla.

She spoke first. "Is this what you always thought you'd do?" she asked, looking around the campsite.

"Digging holes all day, then sleeping on the hard ground at night?"

She laughed, a delightful sound he hoped he would hear again, and often.

"In some ways. I grew up on a farm. Nothing like this ranch but big enough to keep the seven of us busy and fed. Farming is hard work but noble. I knew the value of what I was doing. I knew if I could figure out ways to make the operation more efficient, we could produce more with less work. Traditional methods rely on the strength of a man's back. You can only get so far that way. Since I was big enough to follow my pa's plow, I imagined ways to ease his burden and keep the age off his face and hands."

"He must be very proud of you."

He glanced away, remembering Pa's disappointment the first time he mentioned his dream to get an education. The betrayal. After all this time, he still saw it on Pa's face whenever he went home to visit.

"They didn't understand how I thought a college education would do more good to homesteaders than staying at home where I was needed. Most farmers will never have a place like your uncle's, but what they do have is just as important to them and their families and to the future of this state."

Her eyes widened with the same look he got when standing behind a lectern addressing educators or engineers or farmers on the need for research and funding. He took a deep breath to tamp down his enthusiasm. He wasn't lecturing Priscilla. Simply enjoying a moment out of his lonely, focused existence to talk to a pretty girl.

"How did you end up here from Annapolis?"

She blinked at the sudden change of topic. "You remembered."

He simply smiled in return. Of course he remembered. He remembered everything about their interaction yesterday. Especially how nice she felt in his arms when he pulled her out of the hole. He hadn't been able to stop thinking about that.

"My father…um…passed away nearly three years ago."

He should've figured the only reason a beautiful young woman would leave a city like Annapolis to come here was a death or equally traumatic experience. figured the only reason a beautiful young woman would leave a city like Annapolis to come here was a death or equally traumatic experience. She continued, though, as if his question hadn't been insensitive at all. Maybe it was cathartic to talk.

Priscilla continued, though, as if his question hadn't been insensitive at all. Maybe it was cathartic to talk.

"My mother died when I was eleven. Papa became my best friend." She gave him a brief smile. "I guess that sounds strange, but I think it was our shared grief. Anyway, well, then he was gone. Uncle Lucian and Papa had chosen different paths in life. Papa was a businessman while Uncle wanted to tame the frontier. Once I came here, I realized he was just as much a businessman as Papa. Maybe even more so since he had to carve a business out of nothing but wide-open land. I'm always amazed at the ability of people like my uncle—and you—who can look at a blank canvas like this prairie and see the prosperous life they can build their families."

She bit her bottom lip and her cheeks colored. "I'm sorry. I kind of went on a tangent there, didn't I? You only asked what brought me here from Annapolis."

Isaiah bit back a smile. "I don't mind at all. You go on all the tangents you like."

Her shoulders rose and fell as she took a deep sigh. Again, Isaiah tried not to stare at this beautiful, passionate young woman. He couldn't ask her age. She looked to be in in her early twenties, nearly a decade younger than himself. She'd leave eventually and go back to whatever life she had in Annapolis. He wasn't sure why the thought of her leaving dismayed him. In a few weeks, his work would be done and he'd never see her again.

"After Papa…after he was gone," she continued, "Uncle invited me to come and stay for a while. I'd never been here or met my cousins. I had no idea what to expect."

"It must've been hard."

"It was, but it was nice having family to go to. I could've stayed in the city. I have friends there. But it was so lonely. It helped being here with people who loved Papa the way I did."

Her gaze scanned the gently rolling landscape. Isaiah was about to offer another round of condolences to fill the lengthening silence when her face cleared, and she looked back at him.

"It was strange at first, but I've come to love it. Even more than the city. It's so different from everything I knew. I guess that's an understatement and a half," she said with a laugh in her voice. "This land reminds me of the ocean. It goes on forever, ebbing and flowing, with so much potential and promise."

Isaiah's gaze swept the landscape. He had never seen the ocean, but he imagined she was exactly right. She had piqued his interest. If he was chosen to go to Washington, he would take a detour to Annapolis. Too bad she couldn't go with him and show him around. He shook his head to clear it. He was getting way ahead of himself. He hadn't been invited to represent the team in the nation's capitol, and it was scandalous to even think about taking her.

Only a wife would accompany a man on such a trip.

Wife? Where did that come from? He'd only known her for one day.

He loved what he did. He loved playing a role in changing the landscape of his state. At the same time, he sometimes wondered if his work was enough, especially in the last few years. After the project was finished, what would he do then?

There were enough jobs in this part of the country to keep him busy and employed for the rest of his life. But was that all he wanted out of his short time on earth? He wanted what his father and most of his friends at the university had. A strong union with a beautiful woman waiting for him at home.

"Do you plan to go back to the city?" he asked.

For an instant, her expression froze and the color drained from her face. She glanced down at her hands that had tightened around the tin cup.

"I'm sorry…" It was apparent she wasn't ready to think about going back to the place that brought so much heartache.

She set the cup on the rocks that surrounded the campfire and stood. "I should get back. I had planned to run some errands today, as well as my duties at the ranch. The reason I came, though…well, I wanted to invite you…" Her voice trailed off as if considering.

Isaiah stood. "Yes?"

"We're having a dinner on the ground after church service this Sunday. We do it often when the weather cooperates like it has lately. I'd love for you to come. We all would. Uncle will have plenty of questions about what you've learned so far. The rest of your team can come too. If you don't already have a place to worship, that is."

"No, we don't. That sounds nice."

"You don't have to bring anything." She laughed. "The women love to show off their cooking. Not that anyone shows off. I didn't mean…well, you know."

Isaiah laughed, too, secretly delighted that she was so nervous. Was it because of him? She didn't seem like the type who flustered easily. The thought pleased him very much.

"I know what you meant. The women in my church back home are the same way, including my pious mother. No pride in themselves except when it comes to who bakes the flakiest pie crust."

She seemed to relax a little. "I can answer that question for you around here. It's Winona. She's tried to teach me to master the art. I stick to cakes or cobblers. Anyway, there's always plenty of food. Our church is the big white one at the end of Channing's main street."

"The one with the huge cottonwood tree?"

"That's it. Perfect shade for a dinner on the ground."

He reached out to clasp her hand. "Thank you, Priscilla. I'll be there. I'm sure Lyle and Clayton will appreciate the invitation as well."

She snagged her bottom lip with perfect white teeth and gazed down at his tanned fingers covering hers. He quickly released his hold and stepped back. She blushed prettily as she looked at him from under the brim of her hat.

Isaiah tried not to flatter himself. The pink on her porcelain cheeks might not have anything to do with him. But he sure hoped it did.

Chapter Five

"I should've told him."

"Why didn't you?"

Priscilla dropped her face into her hands, then looked up at her cousin. Tara had been on the porch swing reading when she left the barn after brushing down her horse and leading it to the pasture to graze. She had dropped into the swing next to Tara and told her all about her morning with Isaiah.

She smoothed her hands through her hair and stared a moment at the porch ceiling. "I don't know. It seemed so...presumptuous. I wanted to say something, but I couldn't think of how without insinuating he was interested in me, which I know he isn't. He's only interested in work.

"The moment passed, and I couldn't say, 'Oh, and by the way, when you asked if I was going home to Annapolis, the answer is yes. As soon as my fiancé arrives, I'm moving back there, and we'll get married in a huge society wedding and I'll have babies and spend my life serving tea to other society wives.'"

Tara squeezed her hand. "You are interested in him, right? Isaiah?"

Priscilla jerked her hand free. "Certainly not. I barely know him. I told you he's here to work. He's not interested, and I'm not looking. I'm marrying Peter."

Tara's pale eyebrows arched in doubt. "If you weren't interested in him, you wouldn't care what he thought when you told him you were going to Annapolis to get married."

Priscilla opened her mouth to dispute it but stopped. Why hadn't she told him? Was she that worried he'd think she thought higher of herself than she ought? Or would telling him make Peter's arrival and their eventual wedding more real?

She had managed to put Peter and Annapolis out of her head for nearly three years. Three blissful years where she didn't have to worry about anything, especially the future. She couldn't do it forever. Her time here was transitional. She couldn't take advantage of her uncle's kindness indefinitely. Eventually she'd have to get back to her real life. A life as Mrs. Peter Hollister.

Before long he would show up on this very porch and she could no longer avoid fulfilling her vow to Papa. It wouldn't matter that her heart was falling for someone she couldn't have.

"Cilla, you know I love you and I only want the best for you."

Priscilla groaned inwardly. Tara was about to give her a big dose of truth. Truth she didn't want to hear right now.

"The way I see it, you have two choices. Either write to Peter and tell him not to come. Tell him you aren't ready. You're still grieving. Whatever you need to write until you're comfortable with whatever decision you make. Or tell Mr. Paxton you're committed to someone else. You appreciate his time in explaining his research. It's fascinating and very interesting, but you're busy preparing for your fiancé's arrival so you won't be back to the fields again."

Priscilla sank back into the wood slats of the porch swing. "The only problem is I'm not ready to do either. I don't want to go back to Annapolis, but I know I must. I don't want to stop spending time with Isaiah, but I know I have to do that too."

A soft breeze, heavy with the scent of lilac, teased the tendrils of hair at her temples. She brushed them back and set the swing in motion with her foot.

"Pray about it," Tara said softly. "God will give you wisdom and courage to do the right thing. You're not being fair to either of them by putting it off. Or to yourself."

Priscilla stood at the window and clutched Peter's letter with trembling fingers. She had hoped reading it for the fifth time would give her inspiration on how to respond. It could very well be too late to write anyway. By the time the letter reached his desk, he could be downstairs in the parlor waiting for her to greet him. She imagined herself hiding under the bed or shimmying down the flower trellis outside her window to avoid him.

Surely, she wouldn't resort to anything so childish. A big part of her wanted to do that very thing and he wasn't even here yet

Tara was right. Hiding or avoiding the inevitable wasn't fair to anyone. Isaiah might not have designs on her, but she needed to tell him her standing anyway so he didn't begin to develop feelings she could never reciprocate. How foolish he would feel if he did, only to discover she was engaged. She would feel terrible if that happened.

She looked down at Peter's tight, neat script. His letters had always been aloof and polite with no passion or words of affection. This one contained passion, just not the passion she dreamed of. His impatience had reached a new level. Now he was determined.

That was Peter in a nutshell. Ambitious. Even ruthless if he wanted something badly enough. Her stomach knotted. Is that how he saw her? A goal to achieve? Something to possess not because he loved her but because he was entitled?

She hadn't seen him in so long, she could nearly think of him as an apparition that floated through her dreams but whose image she forgot upon waking. Sometimes she had a hard time remembering the slope of his jaw, the shade of his hair, the sound of his voice.

Guilt swelled in her breast. He deserved better than that. He deserved a wife who loved him and thought of him fondly and sometimes whispered his name just to hear it on her lips.

The only problem was she didn't love him. She knew that now. She didn't miss him. She dreaded more than anticipated his arrival. But she couldn't go back on her vow to Papa. Love was a choice. A choice she would have to make.

How many times had Mother told her of how her grandparents came from the old country with only a few coins sewn into Grandmama's pantaloons. They had risked everything to give their children a future worthy of the name Channing. In Hertfordshire, they were poor farmers, taxed beyond measure with no hope of escaping a cycle of poverty and desperation.

Mother's voice always rose in admiration and her eyes shone with pride when she said, in America, people weren't trapped by the class system into which they'd been born. With grit and hard work, anyone could build a legacy to leave their children and their children's children.

Determined to build onto what his parents started, Papa created a prosperous business in Annapolis. Equally driven and adventurous, Uncle Lucian moved west to make a mark on the vast prairie. Who was Priscilla to dishonor that sacrifice? She would accept their gift with an open hand and a trusting heart.

If they believed Peter was the best for her, she would choose to believe it too.

She sat down several times that week to write to Peter. Within a few scribbled words, she wadded up the paper and walked away. The only thing she wanted to write was: *Don't come*, and she couldn't write that. He had every right to come. She was his betrothed. She'd put off setting a date for their wedding long enough. He probably wanted to start a family. So did she. She just wasn't sure she wanted to start one with him.

She stayed busy in the ranch office. Sometimes she worked with Clarissa but often alone. Every time a lilac scented breeze ruffled the papers on her desk, her gaze strayed to the window where she imagined Isaiah walking toward the house.

Not Peter.

Sunday morning, she sat at her dressing table and teased the curls at her temples into submission. The trains didn't run on Sunday, so she was confident Peter wouldn't arrive today. Last night, she had washed her hair and set it with strips of ribbon and now it shone like fresh honey as she combed her fingers through the soft curls.

"Cilla, what's taking so long?" Marcia called up the stairs. "We're going to be late."

"Coming."

She gave her reflection one last glance. Why *was* she taking so long? Peter wasn't coming so she needn't take extra care, but she couldn't stop herself. She snatched her straw hat off the dressing table and dashed out of the room.

Marcia passed her on the stairs as she was going down. "Where are *you* going?" she asked over her shoulder.

"I forgot something," Marcia said breathlessly, not slowing down. "I'll be right back."

Clarissa and Uncle waited in the foyer. "My, my, don't you look lovely," Uncle said before kissing her cheek.

Lucy came in, smoothing down her own flyaway strawberry hair. The only time it behaved was when she captured it into a braid, which she couldn't do on a Sunday morning. "Doesn't she, though?" she said with a teasing ring in her voice. "I don't know why you're wearing that coral-colored dress when we're eating on the ground. It'll show every grass stain."

Priscilla merely smiled in reply. She went to the mirror by the door to pin her hat in place.

"I know why she's wearing it," Tara said as she joined them. "She thinks it brings out the flush in her cheeks."

Priscilla found her cousin's gaze in the mirror's reflection and stuck out her tongue.

"Well, I think she's beautiful in everything she wears, as are all my girls." Uncle Lucian clasped his hands over his rounded stomach. "You remind me of a beautiful bouquet of wildflowers."

"Marcia, come on!" Lucy yelled up the stairs.

"Wild is right," Clarissa mumbled. She glanced at the watch fob pinned to her bodice.

Winona hurried into the foyer. "Lucy, stop shouting!" she scolded. "You'll scare the chickens out of laying eggs again."

"She knows I hate being late."

"We're not late," Clarissa soothed. "Yet."

"I'm coming. I'm coming." Marcia thundered down the stairs and skidded to a stop in front of Winona. Her own porcelain cheeks were flushed and her amethyst green eyes bright. She was the closest of all the sisters to a true redhead, though as she got older, the color had lost its brassiness and warmed with auburn highlights. She always took special care with her appearance on Sundays. It was the only day she could see her friends and every eligible man in the territory together in one place.

"Sorry," she said meekly before Winona could scold her for running.

Winona and her daughter attended the smaller Catholic church on the other end of the street, but the congregations usually blended for fellowship on the town's quiet streets after services. Especially with a dinner on the ground planned.

"We're all here and just in time," Uncle Lucian said as he opened the door. Jasper from the stables pulled the surrey to a stop at the foot of the steps.

He hopped out and tipped his hat at the ladies as they filed out. His graying hair was combed back from his forehead and his beard had been trimmed in honor of the Sabbath. He wore his Sunday-go-to-meeting gray shirt and black trousers. Priscilla was always amazed at how the wiry little man transformed on Sunday mornings. She wondered briefly if there had ever been a woman in his life. He was personable and industrious. She might ask him one of these days why some enterprising woman hadn't plucked him off the bachelor tree years ago.

They exchanged smiles as he took her hand and assisted her on board. Tara dropped onto the seat next to her. "I'm sure your engineer will notice how this color brings out your eyes."

"It's Sunday, and I don't think they have a regular place to worship. That's the only reason I invited him."

"I wasn't criticizing, just making an observation. Papa was right; you look lovely."

Priscilla plucked at the gauzy skirt. "This old thing."

Tara giggled and bumped her shoulder. "I just hope you're not setting yourself up for heartache."

Priscilla didn't answer. She looked out the other side of the surrey as it rocked into motion. She thought; *Me too.*

She almost didn't recognize Isaiah in his crisp dark suit and derby hat. He sat with two similarly dressed men she assumed were his teammates in the second to last pew. In case she missed him, Tara elbowed her and wagged her head in that direction. While not nearly as handsome as Isaiah, the other men—Lyle and Clayton—were presentable enough, and the group had attracted the attention of every unattached female and their mothers in the congregation.

Uncle Lucian strode purposefully to the front of the church like he always did, nodding and smiling, occasionally shaking the hands of friends, businessmen, and fellow ranchers as he passed. The girls stayed in line behind him, crowding each other two by two, the same as they did every Sunday. Once they reached the pew they typically occupied, Uncle Lucian remained standing in the aisle until the women filed in and took their seats. Only then did he step into the pew and take his seat on the end as if closing the door to a private club over which he was president and chairman. In not-so-subtle fashion, he was signaling to the girls and every man in town that until the pastor wrapped up the service there would be no fraternization. As long as he was in charge, everyone's mind was to remain on the Heavenly Father and why they'd assembled.

The Channing daughters knew the routine and didn't balk at it, though Marcia glanced around as she sidestepped along the pew and arranged her skirts just so before sitting. She managed to throw a coquettish smile at the young man who'd caught her eye this week—the son of a farmer with much less holdings than her father but was handsome enough to make up for being poor.

While it wasn't uncommon in the area for a seventeen-year-old to already be married, Uncle Lucian was of the belief that his youngest daughter was not free to begin paying court until at least one of her sisters had made the trip down the aisle. Preferably all three.

Priscilla caught Isaiah's eye. A brief smile flitted across her lips before she faced the front and sat down. She didn't get a good enough look to see if he returned the smile. She didn't want anyone to notice her gaze lingering on him, especially Uncle Lucian or Tara who was sliding into the pew next to her. She attributed the sudden warmth in her face to the temperature inside the stuffy building. Surely that's all it was.

When the congregation stood for the first hymn, she shot another glance over her shoulder but any view of the men at the back of the room was blocked by too many heads. Tara was staring at her, her lips pursed to contain her humor. Priscilla wrinkled her nose. There was no harm in looking as long as she kept her heart from getting involved.

The Channing daughters typically dispersed the moment a church elder uttered *Amen* to the closing prayer to find a friend and begin socializing. Priscilla discreetly stayed close to Uncle, smiling, murmuring hellos, and kissing a few cheeks of the older ladies in the congregation as they worked their way to the door.

Isaiah and his team had remained in their pew, exchanging greetings and introductions with parishioners as they waited for Uncle Lucian to reach them.

Uncle Lucian reached across the back of the pew to pump Isaiah's hand. "Good to see you, Mr. Paxton. How's the research? I'm sorry I haven't come out to see for myself how you fellows are proceeding. I truly intend to. The talk you gave at the conference in the fall was very intriguing."

"Nice to see you too, sir," Isaiah replied. "We're making great strides. The Sandhills team has made some interesting discoveries."

"I hope you don't mind if I introduce you around to the other landowners today. We need as many parties as possible involved in what you're doing here."

"I couldn't agree more." Isaiah looked past Uncle Lucian and nodded at Priscilla.

"Oh, yes, sorry about that," Uncle Lucian said. "Allow me to introduce my niece

Priscilla. I don't see any of my other girls at the moment."

"I've already had the pleasure, sir." His smile at Priscilla widened. "Miss Channing."

The smile seemed to hold more than polite greeting, but she was determined not to read too much into it. Even if she wanted his attention, she wasn't entitled to it.

"Mr. Paxton."

Uncle Lucian looked from her to Isaiah, confusion on his face. "You've already met? Well, I guess I should've known. It's hard to keep Priscilla in one place."

She squeezed his arm. "Uncle."

"Allow me to introduce my colleagues," Isaiah said. "Misters Lyle Gates and Clayton Hardesty." There were more hand-shaking and greetings. The blond Nordic-looking Mr. Gates had wide shoulders and ham-sized fists that seemed better suited for the other side of a plow than studying irrigation. A little older looking, though no more than thirty, Mr. Hardesty wore spectacles and was taller and leaner than the other men. His dark hair was combed straight back from his forehead. He had the bookish look she associated with a researcher.

"I hope you gentlemen will join us for dinner," Uncle Lucian said. "The women were baking and cooking all last night and this morning. We brought enough food to feed half the town."

Isaiah's lips twitched in Pricilla's direction. "We would like that very much, sir." No point in mentioning Priscilla had already invited them.

Uncle Lucian and Isaiah did most of the talking with the other two joining in only to answer a direct question as they moved toward the doors and the beckoning sunshine. Outside, the crowd milled around. Uncle Lucian motioned Isaiah and the others toward a group of men.

"Don't be long, Uncle," Priscilla gently reminded him before excusing herself to help set out the food.

Dorothy Grandell separated herself from her cloying mother and came over to grab Priscilla's arm. "My, my, my, who is that?" Her fingers dug into Priscilla's elbow as she eyed the engineers, her hungry gaze fixed on Isaiah.

Priscilla tactfully disengaged her arm from Dorothy's clutches. Though two years younger than Priscilla, Dorothy had been on the manhunt for as long as Priscilla had known her. She was very pretty with thick auburn hair, snapping blue eyes, and a rosebud mouth. Unfortunately, her looks could not cover her conniving nature. The men around Channing didn't suit her. Though she never spoke the words out loud, it was evident to everyone paying attention that she wasn't interested in a farmer or a rancher who'd move her to a 300-acre spread where she'd work the softness off her hands and the straightness out of her spine.

She wanted a life like her mother enjoyed as the wife of the town's banker with a two-story house in town with a wraparound porch and an icebox someone else kept filled.

"It's the team from the university who's come to study irrigation methods."

"The university. In Lincoln?" Dorothy breathed without taking her eyes off Isaiah. She tidied her hair and patted her bodice. "How long do they plan to stay?"

"I'm not certain," she hedged.

She could practically see Dorothy licking her lips. "I should go over and introduce myself."

Priscilla surveyed the crowd of men gathered around him dressed in attire ranging from jackets and ties to faded bib overalls or low-slung dungarees and scuffed boots. "Perhaps you should give him a chance to meet your father first."

Dorothy's full lips twisted in concentration. "That's probably a good idea. No need to appear overeager."

Too late, Priscilla thought.

"Is he committed?"

"I don't know anyone's situation."

"Apathy like that is why none of your girls are married yet."

The Channing girls' marital situation was grist for the rumor mills all through the community. Priscilla didn't care. Nor would she defend herself or her cousins to Dorothy or anyone. "We have better things to do than track every unsuspecting man who rides across the property. It was nice to see you, Dorothy. I must go and help my cousins set out our dinner."

Dorothy wrinkled her nose in disappointment that Priscilla hadn't offered any gossip before turning her attention back to the engineers.

Clarissa grinned when Priscilla reached the back of the wagon carrying their food that Pete had driven to church and parked in the shade. "Corralled by the man-hungry Dorothy again? I hope the men from the university know what they're up against." She set a crumb-top apple pie in Prisilla's hands.

"From what I understand, they've traveled all over the territory. I'm sure they're used to attention from unmarried women."

Clarissa looked over Priscilla's shoulder. "He's a handsome one. No denying that."

Priscilla didn't need to ask who she meant. "No denying it," she murmured.

"I see now why your head's been in the clouds the last few days."

Priscilla opened her mouth to tell her cousin her head hadn't been in the clouds. She closed it again. They worked together every day in the ranch office. Adamant denial would only prove Clarissa's point.

"I hope we have plenty of pie. The three of them are joining us for dinner."

At Clarissa's raised eyebrows, she added, "It's only neighborly." With a swish of skirts, she headed toward the checkered blankets that had been set out on the ground, ignoring her cousin's knowing glance.

Chapter Six

"How terrible that you have to spend your summer in Channing."

"Marcia!" Clarissa exclaimed.

Marcia gave her oldest sister an indignant look. "I just meant there are so many more exciting places to spend one's summer than here." Her gaze lingered on the broad-shouldered Lyle. "Don't you miss the city? Nothing ever happens in Channing."

"Actually, this assignment was quite sought after," Isaiah answered for the group.

The young woman's eyes bulged. "You mean out of all the places a person can be sent by the university, you wanted to come *here*?"

"Marcia," Uncle said in his gently warning voice. "You're speaking out of turn."

"I don't mean to. I'm just curious. I think it's a shame that if a person has to travel for work, the best his bosses could come up with is Channing."

The men smiled at the indignation on her young face. Marcia was very pretty and made even prettier with her sparkling blue eyes and effervescent smile. She glanced at Lyle, then coyly lowered her eyes. Priscilla sympathized with her uncle who would have his hands full in another year or two when his youngest daughter's beauty and headstrong personality reached full maturity.

Lucy was also watching the exchange. The freckles across her nose stood out in stark contrast to her porcelain cheeks as Robert caught her eye. Though she usually wore a large floppy hat over her reddish blond hair, the sun had bronzed her skin making her amethyst eyes sparkle. She was the only daughter without the Channing blue eyes. She was also the most fearless of the girls. Winona always said she was going to end up knocking her fool head off during her antics, but always with a sound of pride.

"There's another reason we wanted this assignment," Isaiah directed at Marcia. "It puts us one step closer to being chosen for the team to Washington."

Her eyes lit up. "Washington? D.C.?"

"I believe there's only one," Lucy said.

Priscilla hid a smile behind her hand.

"That's where the funding will come from," Uncle said. "You know, Isaiah, you planted a thought in my head last year when we talked at the conference."

"Sir?"

"Yes, about how I can impact the community out here even more than I already have. People have asked me over the years about running for elected office. After seeing what you young men are trying to accomplish, it's inspired me. This territory has been good to me and my family. I'd like to give back."

The women gasped in unison. Clarissa found her voice first. "Do you mean it, Papa? How could you serve from here?"

Marcia's eyes gleamed. "Would we move to Lincoln?"

He laughed at their reaction. "No, no, no. If I thought we had to move, I wouldn't consider it. There are a lot of elected positions that don't require a man live in the city. I would start with running for a county seat or even a state assemblyman. I'd only have to go to the capital a few times a year."

"Well, I'd go with you," Marcia said.

"Me, too," Lucy exclaimed. "I'm going."

Lucian dropped his hand onto Lucy's arm who was sitting closest to him. "I haven't even decided I'm going to run. But I'm glad to hear you're all in my corner."

"We are," Lucy said, "and we'd vote for you, too."

"Too bad women aren't allowed to vote."

"Yet!" Clarissa exclaimed. "Women have the vote in Wyoming. In no time Nebraska will catch up."

Lucian shook his head. "Now, daughter, don't talk nonsense. Only men are capable of decisions that affect a nation."

"Clarissa was nominated last cycle for a position on the Grange board," Tara put in. "If not for a few pig-headed businessmen, she would've been appointed."

"Don't call your neighbors pig-headed. And making decisions for the Grange can't be compared to voting for someone to run the state, let alone the country. I don't know what'll become of Wyoming with them giving women so much power. What were they thinking?"

"I don't know, sir," Isaiah said. "I'm sure you've heard the hand that rocks the cradle rules the world. I believe our nation will be better off when they get around to giving women the vote."

Uncle Lucian looked around the group. "I see I'm outnumbered. I suppose if you are given the vote, there's no way I can lose with all of you voting for me, should I decide to run."

After the meal, most of the men headed to where the horses were stabled to enjoy cigars and more conversation. Lucy and Marcia took off as soon as Clarissa turned her head. Tara and Clarissa carted empty dishes to the wagon. Priscilla grabbed a blanket off the ground and shook off the dried grass.

"Allow me." Isaiah reached past her to grab a corner. His tanned hand brushed hers.

She nearly jumped back at the pleasurable sensation from the contact. "Thank you," she murmured, suddenly tongue-tied. She kept her eyes on the blanket, hoping he wouldn't notice the furious blush on her cheeks.

He tugged on the end of the blanket, forcing her to look up. When she did, he smiled pleasantly. "Your cousins are a lively group."

Her awkwardness flitted away. "I'm afraid so." She thought of Dorothy Grandell and the other busybodies in town, who were often scandalized by their loud opinions. "I hope you didn't find their questions rude."

His smile widened. "As a matter of fact, I enjoyed it very much. I have three younger sisters. Spending time with all of you today made me realize how much I miss them."

Her heart sank. He thought of her as a little sister. It was just as well. As a betrothed woman, it shouldn't matter what he thought about anything.

They stepped closer and closer as the square of blanket became smaller and smaller. When he handed it to her, he didn't take his eyes off hers. He wasn't looking at her like one looked at a sister, but she wouldn't read too much into it.

She stepped back and hugged the blanket against her. "How did you get away?" She motioned with her head toward the group of men who had moved away from the church to keep the smoke from their cigars and pipes from offending the ladyfolk. "I thought they'd all want your attention."

"I was hoping you'd want some of my attention."

Her flush deepened. "Oh. I…" What was he saying?

He lifted a shoulder. "They were talking about what's on everyone's minds. Drought. Seed prices. Women. I don't think they'll miss me for a few minutes."

Why was he teasing her? And why did she enjoy it so much? "I...I'm glad you made it this morning. I hope you enjoyed the fellowship."

"Very much." He hadn't moved closer but still seemed to fill her space. The scent of bergamot soap teased her nose. Clean. Spicy. Masculine. She could scarcely breathe.

"Thank you for inviting us." He glanced past her toward the group of men whose voices drifted around them like a barely discernible wave. "My companions enjoyed it. Nearly as much as I did."

There was that look again. Interested. Intrigued.

"I'm glad you came. We all are." She looked directly into his green eyes. She felt like they were a magnet pulling her closer.

"The pie was delicious," he said, again with a teasing smile.

"That's because I didn't make it. Winona is the expert at anything you'd want to eat."

"Good to know. I'll have to figure out a way to finagle another dinner invitation out of you."

"You won't have to finagle one. Anytime you or your teammates feel like a home-cooked meal, come to the porch and someone…" Her voice drifted off as his smile widened.

"I might just do that, Or better yet, I'll take you into town this week to pay you back for the invitation and this delicious dinner. Even if you didn't prepare much of it yourself."

"That would be nice."

Even as the words came out of her mouth, she knew she couldn't have dinner with him at a restaurant. Sharing a dinner on the ground after church was one thing. But just the two of them. At a restaurant. Sharing food and intimate conversation—that was completely different. That's what couples did when they were courting. They certainly weren't courting.

"It really isn't necessary. We all loved having you. Uncle Lucian was anxious to talk with you about your research, as was everyone in town. Your work here could change our way of life."

Disappointment sobered the laugh in his green eyes. She knew he didn't want to talk about irrigation and everyone else. He wanted to talk about her.

"This has been a pleasant reprieve from our usual Sunday morning routine," he said. "We sit around the campfire. One of us opens in prayer and someone else reads from the Bible. We discuss it some using our own experiences if we have any. We sometimes sing a hymn or two."

"It sounds like a nice way to praise the Lord."

He chuckled. "You might not think so if you heard our croaking attempts at singing. I'm thankful the Lord hears the thoughts on the heart more than the sound we make."

She smiled back.

"The food today was a lot better than what we usually rustle up, and we all looked forward to sharing it with such pretty hostesses. That's what puzzles me about today." He moved a bit closer.

Priscilla's heart hitched at the intensity in his voice. Did he know? Had someone mentioned Peter to him? Not that hardly anyone in town knew. She should say it first. She should get it out there and over with.

"There are five of you Channing ladies. All quite lovely, if I may say so. What I didn't see was a man paying particular attention to any of you. There are plenty of unattached men in this town. I'm sure at least a few of them are looking for wives. I couldn't help wondering how all of you have avoided getting tied down by one of them."

Now was the time. She wouldn't bother to explain about her promise to Papa. She'd tell him she had a beau in Annapolis, who could very well be on his way here at this very moment. But then the easy banter would dry up and she'd go back to sitting alone and watching the breeze stir the grasses in the field while waiting for the life she loved to come to an end. She didn't want it to end. She especially didn't want her time with Isaiah to end. She wanted to enjoy it until he went back to Lincoln or Peter arrived, whichever happened first. They'd never see each other again and she'd have sweet memories to carry in her heart.

"Not that it's any of my business," he said hastily at her hesitation. "It looks like I'm the one speaking out of turn this time."

She waved away his concern. "You aren't the first one to wonder about the situation with the Channing women. Believe me, Uncle Lucian is quite perplexed by the situation as well. He worries about the future of the ranch if there's no son-in-law to run things after he's gone. I believe that's why Clarissa says she'll never marry. Her biggest fear is that an outsider will come in and try to change the way the ranch has been run all these years. She was thirteen when my aunt died. She stepped right in and learned how to manage the household and now the ranch. She's well suited for it. The last thing she wants is for a man to get in her way."

"I pity the one who tries."

Priscilla smiled. "You and me both. As for Tara, she likes the way her life is now. She hasn't made time to think about a husband. Lucy notices every single man she encounters, but she can't get off a horse long enough for proper courting. And Marcia, she'd get married tomorrow if Uncle allowed a man near her. It will be a long time before that happens."

She sobered. "Aunt Grace was sick for a long time before she passed. My cousins don't have experience with what a healthy marriage looks like. If they had, maybe they wouldn't be so gun-shy now."

His eyes darkened. "And you? Do you know what a healthy marriage looks like?"

"Oh, yes. I…"

He was asking for more than out of mere curiosity. Interest sparked in his green eyes. Interest she wished she was free to return. "My parents had a beautiful relationship. One I hope I can have myself someday."

With Peter? It seemed so distant.

He was looking at her again with that intense gaze that told her there was a lot more on his mind than he was saying. "I'll be working in the meadow on the south side of that craggy ridge of fir trees. You know the one I mean? The one with the light and dark rocks that looks like piano keys when the sun hits it right?"

She smiled. "I know just where you mean."

"Well, I'll be there all week if you—"

Laughter and running feet sounded behind her. Marcia and Lucy skidded to a stop. "There you are." Marcia frowned at Priscilla, then gave Isaiah a sidelong look. "We wondered what was taking so long."

Lucy grinned. "Now we know. Leaving us with all the work, so you could have Mr. Paxton to yourself."

Priscilla's cheeks flamed hot. "Lucy!"

Lucy smiled innocently and took the blanket from her.

Isaiah grinned while keeping his eyes on Priscilla. "I'll go join the men. I'm sure they have a lot of questions for me."

"Don't leave on our account," Marcia teased. "We didn't mean to interrupt anything." She nudged Lucy, and the two sisters burst into a fit of giggles.

Priscilla snatched the last blanket off the ground, rolled it in her arms and shoved it at her cousins. "That's the last of it. I'll join you at the surrey in a minute."

Lucy tucked the rolled blanket under her arm. "Don't be too long, Cilla. We don't want Papa to get the wrong idea about Mr. Paxton's integrity." The sisters hurried away, elbowing each other and nearly running which Uncle didn't approve of, especially on Sundays.

"I'm sorry about that," Priscilla mumbled. "Lucy doesn't usually act so immature. I'm afraid Marcia rubbed off on her."

"Don't give it a moment's thought. I have little sisters, remember?"

Chapter Seven

Besides the usual Monday morning invoices and paperwork in the ranch office, the first week of a new month meant audits of the previous month's expenses. Priscilla and Clarissa worked late and didn't get into the house until well after dark.

The late night and a problem-free Tuesday meant Priscilla was out of the office on Wednesday in time for a late midday meal. Instead of eating with Clarissa, she filled a satchel with bread, cheese, and thick slices of turkey and slid it into a saddlebag. She took a jar of lemonade she had left cooling in the well all morning and two slices of blueberry pie in a crock, wrapped them with a towel so they wouldn't bang together, and put them in the other saddlebag. To the west, dark clouds hung low in the sky. She drank deep of the cool breeze that stirred the strings of her hat against her cheeks. The skies hadn't given up more than a few sporadic showers throughout the month of May. Fields of struggling corn and beans looked as parched as the road on which she rode. She hoped the clouds carried rain, but she didn't want to get soaked either. They were far enough away she should have plenty of time to reach her destination, then make it home again.

It wasn't a wise errand. It was why she'd hurried through packing the food and riding off before Tara saw her and demanded to know just what she thought she was doing.

She wouldn't have had an answer. She had no future with Isaiah Paxton. She knew it, but it didn't stop her from wanting to see him again. Soon enough Peter would arrive and this girlish infatuation with a man she couldn't have would end. Once she got back to Annapolis, she'd settle into her life as wife and mistress of Peter's house. She assured herself there was no real harm in having a little fun before real life intruded on her daydreams of a mysterious, handsome man on a windswept prairie.

In the distance a flash of lightning lit up the low-hanging clouds. Heat lightning, she suspected. She picked up her pace just in case. Once she returned to Annapolis, her life would lose the spontaneity and independence she enjoyed here. She wouldn't work in a ranch office or anywhere. Her mathematic and organization skills would go no farther than organizing a party or raising money for a cause that Peter hoped would further his career. She planned to relish the freedom while she had it.

It wasn't long before she saw a marshy spot of water in the middle of a meadow with a man sticking out of it. There was a chance the man was Lyle or Clayton, but she didn't think so. Not this close to the ridge that looked like piano keys. She resisted the urge to pick up her pace. She didn't want to appear overeager, though she was. As she approached, Isaiah climbed out of the marsh, his progress slowed to barely a crawl by a pair of heavy rubber waders. By the time she reached him, he had slid the straps off his shoulders, climbed out of them, and replaced his boots.

She slid out of the saddle and landed a few feet in front of him. "I hope I'm not interrupting your work."

He shook his head, breathless from the struggle with the cumbersome rubber. "You're just in time. These things are hotter than blazes and weigh a ton, but they're better than getting my pants wet twenty times a day."

She stepped closer to the flooded marsh. "I've never seen water in this meadow."

"There's water all over this ranch if you know where to dig and how to access it."

"Amazing. It's a good thing you're here." She bit her lip as a blush warmed her face. She hoped he wouldn't read too much into it, though she meant it on several levels. "I hope you haven't eaten. I thought you might like something besides beans and jerky."

"I would, but I'm the one who owes you a meal."

She brushed aside his words. "You don't owe me anything. I thought we could eat in the shade while we watch to see if those clouds decide to grace us with their bounty."

"Sounds good to me. I'm curious to see what's in those saddlebags." He took the horse's reins and turned toward a stand of trees about a hundred yards from where he worked.

"Have you had much success this week?" she asked as they walked.

"I'm encouraged by the amount of groundwater in this meadow. Yesterday I received a telegram from our team in the Sandhills region. They've uncovered further evidence the aquifer is more massive than we predicted. It won't be long before we finish here. Clayton, Lyle, and I will probably be sent into Colorado."

Her heart sank. "Colorado?"

He was so excited by the discovery, he didn't seem to notice her consternation. "In the fall, the teams will meet back at the university to assemble our data, then decide who goes to Washington."

She tensed, wishing she could go too. How wonderful to see the Capitol again, but with a purpose, not as a tourist. Her feet felt heavy, knowing each step was taking him another step out of Nebraska and another step away from her. He wasn't walking out of her life, of course, since he'd never been in it. He was just an engineer she met last week when she fell into a hole. One tiny little moment in her life that would not affect the outcome one way or the other.

Her life was Mrs. Peter Hollister. She pictured him on a train car this very minute, reading the paper with a pipe clenched between his teeth. She could see him glancing at his watch, willing the train to move faster and bring him sooner to her. He'd always been impatient. He knew what he wanted and wasn't willing to stop before he got it. It was what made him so successful. Prosperous. Wasn't that the kind of husband every woman wanted? One who could give her a fine, comfortable life in a nice house filled with laughing, successful children.

Not one who dug in the dirt and dreamed only of water. One who may struggle financially and who didn't care about wealth and status. That wasn't what her parents and grandparents sacrificed to give her.

Was that what she wanted for her children? Wealth, position and ease? Or did she want them to find their own paths? To become who God destined them to be, even if it meant more sacrifice and never-ending hard work.

"Priscilla?"

She looked up to find him staring at her.

"Is everything all right?"

"Oh, yes. I'm sorry. I was…"

They had reached the trees. He took her hand and led her into the shade. "No, I'm sorry. I was talking too much. I do that. I talk and talk about what we've discovered, and I forget my audience isn't as excited about the subject as I am." He chuckled, though he still looked concerned at her appearance. "I looked over at you and your face had gone a little pale. You may have had too much sun or I bored you into a stupor. I hope it wasn't that."

She tried to laugh, but she barely heard a word he said. All she could focus on was his large, calloused hand engulfing hers. She resisted the temptation to curl her fingers around his. She liked the strength in his hands. This was how she imagined a man's hands to be—strong and confident, yet gentle.

"I'm fine, truly." She was far from fine. She let him sit her down on a log and fuss over her for a moment. It gave her time to collect her wits and remind herself this episode wasn't her life. Just a brief respite.

"Do you mind?" He wagged his head toward the saddlebags.

She was so flustered she'd nearly forgotten the food she brought. She drew in her legs to stand. "Oh, yes, I—"

"No, I've got it," he said with a teasing note in his deep voice. "It's the least I can do after you brought it all the way out here."

She settled back on the log and watched as he removed the first saddlebag and folded back the flap. He withdrew the jug, popped the cork, and sniffed. His mossy green eyes lit up. "Lemonade. And it's chilled. How did you know I've been pining for cold lemonade all day?"

Laughter bubbled out of her throat. "Who doesn't pine for lemonade after working in the sun all day?" She couldn't help herself. She jumped up and hurried around the horse for the other saddlebag.

Isaiah spread the saddle blanket on the ground. Within minutes, they had the food spread out and sat at opposite ends of the blanket. A rumble of thunder rolled toward them. They glanced skyward. "We should eat fast," he said. "We might get rained on."

"I wouldn't mind. It's been so dry. In the city, I never gave the rain a moment's thought unless I wanted to go riding. Now, I worry like an old woman."

He blessed the food, then they piled their plates and began to eat. "Do you miss it?" he asked after taking a bite of turkey.

"Hmm?" she asked around her own bite.

"The city. Do you miss it?"

She chewed thoughtfully for a moment. "I miss Papa. And my mother. Sometimes our house and my friends."

Not Peter. She didn't miss him. She seldom thought of him. But she was sure at the sight of him, she would remember afresh why she had been so enamored with him as a girl. It would all come back to her why her parents made the match, and they would work out whatever doubts she harbored now.

"I'm sure you miss your farm and family," she said to get the conversation off her.

"I do. In the last letter from Mama, she wrote that I have a new niece. That makes four and I've only met one of them. After I finish my research, and before I go to Washington—if I'm chosen—I'll go home for a few weeks. I enjoy what I do and get lost in my work, but I miss home. Meeting new people and experiencing new things makes it a fair trade."

Her heart leapt at the smoldering heat in his gaze.

His finger grazed hers. She looked back at him. "I've especially enjoyed getting to know you, Priscilla. I'd like to get to know you more."

What was he saying? What did he mean? "Uh, um…"

"I didn't mean to make you uncomfortable." The straight-forward look he gave her told her he wasn't sorry at all.

"I've enjoyed getting to know you too. Your work is so important. Selfless. I admire that. You remind me of Papa." She shook her head. "I don't mean you look like him or anything. Just that he always thought of the greater good. He wanted to help others. He wanted to teach them to help themselves."

He laid his hand on hers and kept it there. "I know what you meant."

She stared at his hand resting on hers. Tanned wide fingers. Scarred knuckles. Not what she would expect of an engineer who must spend much of his time behind a desk. He seemed to prefer to work outside in the heat and the weather making discoveries that could change the world. When she looked up, his eyes were still fixed on her. She moved her fingers slightly under his, caressing his palm. His gaze intensified. With his free hand, he moved his plate off his lap and slid closer to her.

Priscilla's breath froze in her throat. She didn't move her plate aside. She couldn't move a muscle. He lifted his hand from hers and ran it round the back of her neck. A delicious shiver ran through her like a jolt of electricity in the darkening sky. She couldn't think of anything but the calloused warmth.

He stared at her, seeming to measure her face, her cheeks, her lips with his eyes. Her throat went dry. She could scarcely breathe. A flash of lightning illuminated the western sky from horizon to horizon. A cool breeze rushed over them and ruffled the black hair at the nape of his neck. She reached out and smoothed it back into place. An exhalation erupted from between his parted lips as her fingernails raked over the rough skin. His hand tightened behind her neck. He leaned closer. Priscilla tensed, and her skin prickled in anticipation.

A crash of thunder sounded behind them and shook the ground. She was so wrapped up in Isaiah, she didn't know for a moment what happened. Then she became aware of the horses whinnying in alarm. Isaiah dropped his hand. They scrambled to their feet. Priscilla gripped his arm, her heart racing. The wind tugged at the underside of her hat. Flashes brightened the sky. A lightning bolt as wide as an oak tree struck the ground. Clouds boiled in the sky.

Her heartrate eased as she realized the storm was at least a mile away. "It felt so close."

He grunted in agreement. "I half expected to see a tree on the ground when I turned around." He looked at her mouth as though wishing they hadn't been interrupted. "The storm could turn this way fast. We'll gather your things and I'll ride with you to the ranch."

"You don't need—"

"I want to make sure you get there safely."

He was staring again. Priscilla couldn't look away.

Lightning flashed again. A huge bolt zigzagged across the sky. "Forget your things. We'll get them—" A terrific boom shook the ground. She shrieked and lunged into his arms. Flames leapt into the sky.

She screamed. "That's the Holcomb farm! It's been hit!"

Isaiah turned and ran for his horse. Priscilla ran after him. He had cinched his horse and was climbing into the saddle by the time she reached him. Her horse pranced against the tether holding it to the ground. It took her two tries before she was able to grab the reins and loose the tether.

"Go to the ranch and get help," Isaiah shouted over the rising wind.

"That'll take too long," she shouted back as she climbed into the saddle. "Others would've seen the explosion same as we did. They'll come. I'm going with you."

"It's too dangerous. Go to the ranch."

"They have children. I'm going with you."

She spurred her horse up the incline without waiting for an answer. By the time they reached the top, he had outpaced her and was moving ahead. Priscilla leaned over the front of the horse and squinted against the spray of dirt and grit in the air. Together they charged into the storm.

Chapter Eight

Black, acrid smoke filled the air surrounding the barnyard as they neared the farm. Priscilla's eyes burned and her lungs constricted. As if in response to her unasked question, the wind shifted, and the house came into view.

"Oh, thank God!" she exalted, though she knew Isaiah couldn't hear her. "It didn't hit the house."

Her relief was short-lived. A standing house didn't mean no one had been hurt or that the family hadn't suffered devastation. The biggest barn was engulfed in flames. Flames leapt into the sky and danced on the wind. She would've cried for the young family if her heart wasn't so filled with the possibilities of the damage beyond a burning barn.

A figure stood a few feet from the flames. It was Ivan Holcomb beating against the flames near the open door with his coat. The wind made it impossible to do much of anything to battle it. Two boys around ten and twelve years old ran from the pump carrying buckets of water. Coralee Holcomb stood at the well, shouting and gesturing at the boys, though whatever she was saying was drowned out by the wind and roar of the flames. Isaiah leapt off his horse, not bothering to secure it before running to help Ivan. The man had given up on beating the flame and had taken up a shovel to dig a trench in hopes of keeping the flames contained to the barn.

Priscilla dismounted and pulled both horses to the other side of the house where she tied them to a clothesline post.

"Is everyone safe?" she asked Coralee as she joined the bucket chain the woman and the two boys had formed from the well.

She nodded. "For now, thank God. Most of the animals were still afield. A cow and calf were in the barn. I don't think they got out." Her eyes were swollen with unshed tears, but she was too busy to give into them.

On the porch, the family's eight-year-old daughter Betty, who Priscilla had met once at church, held a squalling baby. Her free hand clung to the bib overalls of a little boy struggling to break free. She couldn't hold him in place much longer while holding the baby.

Priscilla grabbed the filled bucket from the woman. "Go to the children. If they get off the porch, they'll get in the way and get hurt."

The woman shook her head as she grabbed another bucket from her son. "I need to help."

It wasn't Priscilla's place to argue, but the situation would go from bad to worse if the little boy got away from his sister and ran into the fire.

A cloud of dust appeared on the horizon as thunder rumbled the ground around them. A few raindrops fell on Priscilla's face.

"Please, God, hurry up with the rain," Coralee cried in anguish.

Three horsemen came into view. Priscilla put her free hand on Mrs. Coralee's shoulder. "More help is coming. Go to your children and have Betty ring the life out of that bell."

The woman's terrified gaze ricocheted between the approaching riders and the burning barn. After another moment's hesitation, she ran to the porch. The little boy threw himself into his mother's arms. She kissed his head and took the baby from Betty. Betty scooted an upturned washtub to where the bell hung, climbed up, and began ringing it as hard as her little arms would swing. Everyone within earshot was already on their way, but ringing the bell let the little girl feel like she was doing her part while keeping her out of harm's way.

The rain never came. Two hours later Priscilla put a cup of coffee into Coralee's hands and sank onto the porch step beside her. The baby lay a few feet away in a laundry basket sound asleep. The little boy, whose name she had learned was Luther, was asleep next to his mother, his head in her lap. She absently stroked his fine brown hair with her free hand as she and Priscilla surveyed the barnyard. Three walls of the smoldering barn still stood but the structure was a complete ruin. Ivan Holcomb, Isaiah, and at least ten men from town including Uncle Lucian and the preacher moved around the perimeter, covering smoking places with shovels of dirt to make sure they didn't spark again as they discussed the damage in low tones.

"I don't know what we'll do," Coralee said wearily. "We moved here from Iowa. Put everything we had into this farm. The bank owns most of it. Ivan's about broke his back building it up."

Priscilla put her arm around her shoulders and drew her against her. "I'm sure you both did."

Silent tears streamed down Coralee's face. Her gaze drifted to the blackened fields behind the smoking hulk of the barn. "That was almost every stalk of corn we planted."

"It's still early. The community will help you replant."

Coralee sniffed mightily at the tears. "Ivan's proud. And stubborn. He might want to give it up and go back to Iowa. His father and brother are there. He talks about it some after a particularly hard season. He might be thinking of going back to work at the textile mill." The dejected slump of her shoulders told Priscilla that was the last thing she wanted her husband to do.

"Let's not worry about that right now. For now, we'll praise God that you're all safe. Most of your livestock was spared. The house wasn't touched. That's a lot to rebuild on."

Coralee looked toward a large oak west of the field. Not even a leaf had been singed. Under the tree was a leaning wooden marker in the shape of a cross. "I can't bear to leave Mary." A sad smile softened the lines on her face. "My firstborn. She would be fourteen this summer. We lost her three years ago. You never met a sweeter child. She was such a help to me. And company, too. She made me think with all her questions." The tears began again in earnest. "I don't want to leave her out here all alone."

She sighed again through her tears. "I know she's not under that tree. She's dancing on streets of gold without a care about lightning strikes and blizzards and bad growing seasons. My heart would still split wide open if I had to leave her. But I have to support Ivan in whatever he wants."

"I'm sure Ivan doesn't want to leave her either." It wasn't for Priscilla to say what Ivan was thinking. His immediate concern would be taking care of his children that were here, even if that meant going back to Iowa.

She hugged Coralee against her and rocked a little. "Uncle Lucian said my cousins and Winona are on their way with food. You'll feel better after you and the children have eaten. Then you can come to our house and get baths and some sleep. Give the men time to talk and work things out."

Coralee stiffened. "Ivan'll want me here."

Priscilla shook her head. "The children need you more than he does right now. He'll be relieved that he doesn't need to worry about any of you for a few hours."

"I appreciate that, Priscilla. I don't know what we'd've done if you and that irrigation fella hadn't showed up when you did. If one of these babies had gotten too close…"

"But they didn't." Priscilla squeezed her hard. "We're all thanking the good Lord for that."

Coralee looked down at the little boy and began to cry, deep silent sobs as tears rolled down her face. Priscilla rocked her back and forth until the tears slowly abated. Coralee dried her face on her apron, careful not to wake the little boy.

Priscilla disengaged herself and stood. "The food will be here any minute. I'll go direct the men to find some planks of wood to set up tables for everyone."

Coralee nodded absently, still stroking the little boy's head. Priscilla's heart ached for the family, especially Coralee. To not know what the next moment held must be terrifying. She supposed everyone was in that boat. No one knew the challenges the next moment held, even when all seemed to be going according to plan. She didn't know what her own life would look like once Peter arrived. All she knew was there was a life waiting in Annapolis that she didn't think she wanted anymore.

Her mind went to Isaiah. His hands on her neck. Her hands on him. Her breath quickened. He was what she wanted. Not just his kiss but everything. As quickly as the thought came to her, she knew it could never be. What happened today on this farm was proof; some things were out of a woman's control. There was no point in bemoaning the fact. Her life was already planned, and it didn't include Isaiah. She'd be better served getting that through her head and making the best of it. She would have a wonderful, fulfilling life, even if she couldn't see it yet.

Several men moved around the yard, digging and searching through the scorched boards for what could be salvaged. One of the family's older boys who had helped with the water chain lay on his back in the middle of the yard, staring at the sky, exhausted. Priscilla stopped next to him. "They're bringing food," she said gently. "Could you direct me to some planks of wood so we can set up tables for everyone?"

"Yes, ma'am." He pulled in his knees and stood. His soot-streaked face was careworn. He looked like he wanted to go cry somewhere but couldn't with the men milling about.

Isaiah came across the yard and laid a hand on the boy's shoulder. "That's all right, son. I'll take care of it. Why don't you fill a pitcher with water and go sit with your ma. I expect she needs you."

"Yes, sir," he mumbled and shuffled away.

Priscilla and Isaiah stepped together, watching him. Now that the rush of adrenaline from fighting the fire was over, Priscilla was completely spent. Her knees were weak, and her hands trembled. She almost wanted to drop onto the ground like the boy had done. She looked gratefully at Isaiah. "Thank you. He wants to be strong and brave for his ma's sake, but he's exhausted."

Isaiah studied her for a moment. He brushed aside a wisp of soot-streaked hair that clung to her cheek "So are you."

His voice was like a soothing balm. She wished she could lean into him. Rest for a moment. Or cry for a while.

He took her elbow. "Let's go sit for a few minutes. I think you could use a rest and some fresh water yourself."

She exhaled wearily, gathering her strength. "I need to set up some tables. The food'll be here soon."

He shook his head and turned her toward the well. "I doubt anybody's got the energy to gather around a table. They can fix themselves a plate off the back of the wagon and sit wherever they find a flat spot."

She looked toward the black smoke rising off the hulk of the barn. "I suppose."

With one hand on her elbow and the other around her waist, he guided her to the well. She allowed herself to relax just a little into him. She felt like she'd absorbed Coralee's despondency. She hated to think the family might give in to the tough conditions and go back to Iowa.

They reached the pump just as the boy began priming it with a skinny arm. Isaiah stopped him and took hold of his arm. The skin was pink and the red hair singed off. "You got any cold milk, son?" he asked, still holding the boy's arm.

The boy nodded and motioned with his head at the wooden cover over the well. "There's a pail hanging under there, sir."

Isaiah slid the wooden cover aside and pulled out a pail of milk where it was stored to keep cool and safe from the flies. He filled the dipper and poured it slowly over the boy's hand and arm. The tightness in his face lifted a degree. "Your ma can do this again for you tonight. Vinegar will help, too, if it starts bothering you."

"Thank you, sir."

Isaiah finished filling the water pitcher for the lad, then returned the milk to the hook inside the well. After the boy walked away, Isaiah rinsed out the dipper and gave Priscilla a long drink. They took turns drinking from the dipper until they'd had their fill. Then he guided her into the shade of the side of the house where Ivan had built a bench between two trees.

Despite her weariness, Priscilla was very aware of the weight of his hand in the middle of her back. They sat and she leaned against him. He put his arm around her shoulder. Neither spoke. She didn't know if, like her, he was too tired for talking or there was nothing to say in the moment.

The sun had begun to set, cloaking the yard in shadows. The black clouds had lifted and the smoke had been dispelled by the wind, replaced with long shadows of dusk. A few minutes later one of the Channing wagons rattled into the yard. A rider followed, probably one of the hands from the ranch. She stirred and sat up. "I should…"

Isaiah tightened his arm around her shoulder. "They'll be all right without you for a few minutes."

She watched the wagon creak to a stop, but the only thing on her mind was the steady rise and fall of his broad chest. "It could've been much worse," she said softly.

The bristle on his jaw rustled against her hair as he nodded. "One of your neighbors burned his hand. Another one got hit on the shoulder by a falling board. He'll be sore tomorrow, but no serious damage done."

"I'm glad," she murmured.

He smoothed his hand over the top of her head, then rested his cheek against it. "Now that it's over, I'm glad you came with me instead of going back to the ranch. It was dangerous, but Mrs. Holcomb needed a woman here."

Priscilla turned toward him. Her face was inches from his. She saw a few pink spots on his face where he'd been hit with ash and cinders. She touched one gingerly. He'd be sore tomorrow too. "I'm glad we were together when the lightning struck. I wouldn't have known what to do by myself…"

He was staring at her mouth. Suddenly, she wasn't thinking of the lightning strike or the fire or her exhaustion. She was thinking of his hands. The feel of his breath on her cheek. His solid arms around her. He laid a gentle hand against her cheek and smoothed her hair back from her face. He drew her close. She shifted so her body was facing him on the bench. He brushed his lips against hers as light as a butterfly landing. Her breath caught in her throat. She drew back to look into his eyes. She couldn't see the green in the shadows, but she saw longing. The same as she knew he saw in hers. She leaned in closer and let his mouth take hers.

"I hope I'm not interrupting anything."

Shock and embarrassment surged through her. She jerked back. Uncle Lucian, she thought, except the voice was too young. The timbre too deep.

Then she recognized the man in front of her, though she hadn't seen him in three years. "Peter!" She sprang to her feet and slapped absently at the soot on her dress.

He glanced past her to Isaiah. A sardonic smile curved his lips as he looked back at her. "Looks like I got here just in time."

Chapter Nine

"Peter," she repeated, her mind trying to catch up with what was happening. "I didn't expect…"

"I can see that. Now I know why you took so long in responding to my letters." He stepped around her and thrust out his hand at Isaiah who was getting to his feet. "Peter Hollister of Annapolis." He pumped Isaiah's hand, but his eyes remained fixed on Priscilla.

Isaiah's gaze ricocheted from one to the other. "Isaiah Paxton. I'm afraid you have me at a loss, sir."

Peter feigned remorse. "Quite sorry about that. I would've thought Priscilla would mention me since she and I are engaged."

"En…" Isaiah swung his head around to stare at her. "You're engaged?"

Priscilla wanted to run to the well, take the cover off, and jump in.

"Have been for quite a few years, haven't we, Priscilla? I'm quite flummoxed as to why she didn't tell the man she was…" His eyebrows arched in derision at the filth and grime covering Isaiah. "…keeping company with."

Priscilla was just as dirty and unkempt. Surely, she didn't need to remind him they'd been fighting a fire. "Peter, you mistook what you saw. We aren't keeping…"

He tilted his head and stared as if challenging her to go on. When she didn't speak, he took her hand and kissed her blackened knuckles. He managed to keep the distaste on his face to a minimum. "You look well, darling. Or as well as one can under the circumstances."

Priscilla's exhausted brain wouldn't allow her to make sense of the situation. Peter was here. Isaiah had kissed her. It was so ludicrous and upside down she nearly gave in to a fit of hysterical laughter.

Her weak knees could barely hold her, and she staggered a little. Isaiah grasped her elbow and steadied her. Peter's easy smile stiffened. Isaiah lowered his hand and took a nearly imperceptible step back.

"Um, when did you arrive?" she asked, her voice nearly as shaky as her legs. She didn't care about his travel itinerary, but social etiquette demanded that she ask.

Behind his smile, his jaw was tight. "About two hours ago. Your uncle and most of the men on the ranch had already come here. Your cousins were putting together a meal. Your housekeeper…" His upper lip curled in distaste before he could disguise it, "…was shouting orders at everyone. You'd think it was her house."

Peter had probably never seen an Indian woman except in newspaper articles. She wanted to commiserate with his ignorant prejudices, but she was too out of sorts. "It practically *is* her house. Winona's been there for twenty years. She's like a second mother to all us girls."

He made a sound in his throat. "I suppose I'm used to more subservient help, but it's not my call to make." He grasped her hands and pulled her closer as if to plant a kiss on her cheek. "It's so good to see you. It's been too long."

She stiffened and pulled her hands free. Even if Isaiah wasn't standing next to her and her lips still warm from his kiss, she wasn't comfortable with such an intimate greeting from a man she barely remembered. "I wish it could've been under better circumstances."

His gaze slid to Isaiah. "I'm sure."

She wanted to tell him he misunderstood. She wasn't talking about Isaiah. She meant the fire. The Holcomb family losing so much. Not everything was about him. But he'd never understand or believe her.

Isaiah dipped his head at her. "Priscilla, I've got to get back to work. It was nice meeting you, Mr…"

"Hollister."

"Yes." Isaiah's hand lifted as if to tip his hat but remembered he'd lost it at some point while battling the flames. He lowered his hand and walked away.

Peter reached for her hands again. Priscilla jerked away. "Why are you here?" she hissed.

He looked affronted. "I told you I stopped at the house."

"No, I mean *here*." She struggled to keep her voice low. "We haven't seen each other in almost three years. You should've waited for me to reply."

His dark eyes narrowed. His smile completely vanished. "It's time we move past this silly charade, Pricilla. Frankly, this long betrothal is beginning to look ridiculous. I knew if I didn't force your hand, you'd never come home. I need an heir, and you need a husband." He looked in the direction Isaiah had taken. "Apparently."

"Isaiah is here studying the aquifer under the ranch. We've become friends."

"I can see that."

"I don't appreciate your insinuation."

"I'm not insinuating anything. I saw him pawing you with my own two eyes."

"He wasn't—"

653

He went on as if she hadn't spoken. "The man is obviously interested in you. And you're interested in him. Or do you make a habit of kissing any number of men?"

"Peter! I don't…" What could she say? She'd been caught in the act. Isaiah. What would she tell him? That was more important to her at the moment. How could she explain when she hadn't found a way to mention Peter in the past week?

"I have to help with the food," she bit out. "You're welcome to join me."

"I believe I'll listen in on the men's discussion. I'm sure I'll have more input there. It'll make it easier to keep an eye on your cowboy."

Priscilla knew he was goading her. She spun around and hurried to the women milling around the wagon. What had she done? What was she going to do?

Despite her physical and emotional exhaustion, Priscilla slept fitfully. Every time she dozed off, she dreamed of flames, thundering horses, crashing timbers, and a crying baby. Isaiah stood on the periphery of each dream, his face etched with confusion and hurt.

Her muscles ached when she finally gave up on sleep and dragged herself out of bed before daybreak. Her heart ached worse. She drew back the curtains and gazed out at the barn and back pasture. She thanked the Lord for the time she had here. For the land. The sky. The smell of earth and grasses bending to the wind. Especially for making her a part of this sweet, funny, chaotic, loud, and loving family. She didn't want a single memory to fade.

A crash sounded across the hall. "Lucy!" Marcia cried.

"Keep your things out from under my feet," Lucy returned.

"Must every morning start this way?" Clarissa called from down the hall.

"Stop your hollering," Winona yelled from downstairs. "It's not ladylike. Now, get down here and eat before everything's cold and fit only for the hog trough."

Priscilla laughed as she hurried to the wardrobe to choose an outfit for the day. Something old since they had a lot of work to do.

The morning flew by, not giving Priscilla time to think about missing this place or Isaiah. She could always come back for a visit. And she had no right to miss Isaiah. She'd never see him again after what he learned last night. She didn't need to apologize for being engaged. But she should have told him. At least before he kissed her.

She tried not to think about the kiss. She had no right to that either, but she couldn't help herself. It was on her mind when Peter arrived just before noon in a carriage, dressed like he was going to a board meeting instead of work. He had so much to learn.

Marcia came to stand beside her as he rode into the yard. "He's so handsome," she whispered breathlessly.

Priscilla couldn't deny that.

"And so tall," Marcia noted as he climbed out of the carriage where his polished boots kicked up a cloud of dust.

Priscilla smiled. "You think everything in pants is handsome."

"I do not. All right, maybe I say that, but this time I really mean it. You're so lucky."

"Not lucky," Priscilla reminded her. "Blessed."

"I know. Papa says there's no such thing as luck."

Priscilla wrapped one arm around her and pulled her against her as Peter secured his horse. "I'm blessed to have all of you."

Marcia turned and leaned into Priscilla's arms. "Oh, Cilla, we're blessed to have you. I wish he wasn't here. He's going to take you away."

Priscilla hugged her tightly. "Don't cry. I'll come back and visit."

"Everyone says that and they never do. You'll go back East and we'll never see you again."

Priscilla stroked her hair. "I will come back. I promise."

One thing about her, she stood by her promises even when they broke her heart.

"Good morning, ladies," Peter said in his rich timbre.

Marcia pulled away and sniffed back her tears. "Morning," she murmured. She ducked her head and hurried toward the house.

"Is it something I said?" he asked with a teasing smile.

Priscilla sighed. Marcia could blame youth on any emotional outbursts. Though Priscilla was only twenty-one, she was supposed to be past unsightly, tearful eruptions. She sure felt like one now.

"She's just upset that I'm going away."

He shrugged. "Nothing stays the same forever. The sooner she learns that's how life works, the better off she'll be."

"Peter! She's just a girl."

"A girl who seems to have been given free rein from the looks of things." His straight, patrician nose crinkled as he ran his gaze down her faded gingham dress. "I wanted to take you to town for luncheon at the hotel restaurant. I rented the carriage for you. I had breakfast there a few hours ago. It's better than you'd think."

She wanted to remind him she already knew since she'd lived here almost three years.

"I can't go to town. We're putting things together for the Holcombs, then we're driving them home. Uncle and some men from the church are planning a barn raising for the end of the week. There's a lot to do to prepare, especially since Mr. Holcomb's fields also need replanted."

"A barn raising? I suppose that's some sort of pioneer tradition when a neighbor suffers calamity."

She brightened. "They're quite fun, actually. I mean, besides the work. People come from all over. The men compete to see which team can raise the fastest wall. Who hammers the most nails—things like that. The women get to show off new babies and their favorite recipes. And the children, oh, the children have a time running around and playing with the ones they haven't seen in forever."

"That's what people do around here for fun? Work?"

She couldn't keep from laughing at the disbelief on his face. "Why, yes. The work around here is endless, as I'm sure you've deduced, but it's more fun when it's shared. We can't go to the hotel to eat anyway. Winona will be insulted if we drive all the way to town for no special occasion after she's worked since before sunup to cook and bake for us and the Holcombs."

His gaze hardened. "You're worried about insulting an Indian woman who works for you? She's an employee, Priscilla. She doesn't have the right to be insulted."

She bit back a retort. It wasn't his fault that he didn't understand. He'd been raised in a different world where employees were meant to serve with no rights due them beyond their pay at the end of the week.

"Winona is more than an employee. I told you that last night. She practically raised my cousins. She's been nothing but generous and kind to me."

He exhaled and gave his head a slight shake. "Yes, I remember. I keep forgetting how the wants and whims of the women around here seem to run this ranch."

She swallowed her impatience. His lack of understanding was a cultural difference, not meanness. She hoped. He couldn't understand because he hadn't lived it. She wondered what all she wouldn't understand once she moved back East.

She brushed her hands down the front of her dress in case they were soiled from a morning chore and lifted them to him. He took them, pulled her closer, and kissed her offered cheek.

"It's nice to see you," she said sincerely. "I'm sorry today is so hectic. We've been rushing around all morning. With Mrs. Holcomb and her children here, that's seven extra people to get ready for the day. Uncle and a few of the hands have already headed to their farm to help Mr. Holcomb with clean up and to plan the barn raising."

"Your uncle certainly is generous with his time and resources."

"What do you mean?"

"I mean, a new barn will take a lot of lumber and supplies. From the looks of that place last night, Mr. Holcomb, or whatever his name is, doesn't have the money to repay any debt. Your uncle is shutting down his entire operation for the better part of a week and using his own hired men to drive out there and start work. He's either very generous, or maybe a little foolhardy."

Priscilla gasped. "I assure you Uncle is not foolhardy. That's what people do around here. They help each other without even thinking of the cost. They leave that to the Lord."

He gave her a placating smile. "And that, my dear, is what makes it foolhardy. I have no problem with helping out one's neighbor if the need is not preventable. But a man should be willing to take some responsibility for his bad luck. He knew the risks when he chose to build a farm in this…" He glanced around, and his jaw tightened. "He should've put some savings in the bank for this type of emergency. Heaven knows, it was just a matter of time before he'd need it."

"He has six children. It's hard to save money when every waking hour is spent keeping a roof over their heads."

"My point exactly. Maybe he should consider a less volatile career path. Or not having more children than he can afford to feed."

"Peter!" she gasped. "Families have children. That's the way it works."

"I'm just saying, a man should think about the tragedies and setbacks that could befall him before settling his family in this godforsaken land."

Priscilla couldn't believe what she was hearing. This land was anything but God-forsaken. He'd know that if he opened his eyes and looked around. As for a man preparing for inevitable tragedies and setbacks, she supposed he had a point, but it was an awful way to put it.

"If anything happened to any of us, Mr. Holcomb would be the first one in line to help. That's how these people are. It means they're kind and compassionate, not foolhardy."

He touched her flushed cheek. "I'm sorry, darling. I didn't mean to insult you or these people. They sound like hardy, salt-of-the-earth types. I just meant if a man can't handle the rigors of this life, he's better off accepting it sooner rather than later."

"I suppose." She moistened her dry lips. It was her turn to look up and down his clean, pressed clothes. "You're welcome to take the carriage, but it's easier to saddle a horse to ride out to their farm. You can go back to the hotel if you prefer, but the rest of us will be working there until late this evening. Their fields need turned before they can be replanted."

With effort, he managed not to grimace. "I suppose I can do my share. You said the barn raising is at the end of the week? I believe I can learn how to swing a hammer by then. If everyone's pitching in, I can too. Then you and I will be on our way home, and none of this will be your concern again."

Exactly, she thought. *It won't be my concern.*

Her heart fell like a rock in her chest.

Chapter Ten

"So what are you going to do?" Tara asked.

She was perched on the edge of Priscilla's bed. They'd both bathed and washed their hair. It had been a long day, but a satisfying one. The Holcomb family was back at home on their farm. Their fields had been turned by at least six teams of horses that had been brought from the whole area. The women had worked just as hard, washing and digging and hoeing the perimeters of the fields.

Peter had been a pleasant surprise. Wearing too-short, borrowed overalls from Uncle's closet, he had jumped right in and went to work with the other men who weren't driving plow horses.

"Peter is really trying," Priscilla replied, knowing what her cousin was asking. "When that Emerson boy hit him in the back with a dirt clod, he didn't even get mad."

Tara laughed afresh as she combed her fingers through her wet hair. "I laughed so hard I thought I'd have to run to the outhouse to change my bloomers."

"Tara!" Priscilla shrieked, then fell back onto the mattress laughing.

After they sobered, she sat up and moved to the dressing table to comb out her hair and braid it for the night. "You never answered my question," Tara said.

"What question?" though Priscilla knew exactly what she was talking about.

"What are you going to do about Mr. Hollister? He was a good sport today, and I imagine he'll work as hard as his city hands will allow at the barn raising." She paused as if measuring her next words. "I don't know him as well as you do, but you don't seem to have many similarities. He was gracious enough, but I got the feeling he thinks he's a little above us sodbusters."

"He didn't say sodbuster."

"He didn't have to. We could all tell that's what he was thinking."

"I'm sorry, Tara. I'm sure he didn't mean to insult anyone. It's just the way he was brought up. He doesn't understand our ways."

Tara arched her pale blond eyebrows. "If he doesn't understand our ways, how will he understand you?"

Priscilla had been wondering the same thing.

"I have to admit we don't know each other very well, Most couples don't know a lot about the other until they're living under the same roof. Many countries still have arranged marriages. Those work out."

"Do they? How do we know the couples are happy in those relationships? Especially the women. They always take the brunt of an unhappy union."

"Happiness is a choice. I won't be unhappy. My life will be different than it is here, I grant you, but I'll find things to love about it. The Apostle Paul said he found contentment in every situation. If he found it, that meant he had to look for it. That's what I'll do. I'll look for it."

She pulled the heavy braid over her shoulder and curled the end around her finger. She stared at her reflection in the mirror instead of Tara. She was afraid if she looked at her cousin, she'd burst into tears. It was easy to say, but she figured much harder to implement.

"This is what Papa wanted for me. He knew Peter could give me the kind of life he and Mother wanted me to have."

"I'm sure they wanted you to love your husband."

"And I will. I might not love Peter right now, but I'll learn to love him and I'll love our children. I'll love our life together."

"What about Isaiah?"

Priscilla's hands stilled. She didn't want to think about him "What about him? He seems perfectly content with his life. He travels all the time. After he leaves here, he's continuing his research in Colorado. Then on to Washington."

Tara slid down the mattress until she could reach Priscilla at the dressing table. "Oh, Cilla, you'd love that."

Priscilla shook her head and blinked away tears that threatened to form. "I love it here."

"Then don't leave. If Isaiah goes to Washington without you, you can live here forever with me and Clarissa and Winona and the other girls if they don't marry."

Priscilla smirked. "We know Lucy and Marcia will marry as soon as Uncle grants permission."

Tara squeezed her hand. "But you don't have to. You don't have to go back to Annapolis and marry a man you don't love. We love you and want you to be happy."

"I'll be happy as soon as I honor my promise to Papa. That's what I'm going to do, and I wish you'd stop giving me grief about it."

Tara picked at a broken fingernail. Priscilla couldn't help thinking that she doubted there was a single jagged fingernail on any lady's hands in Annapolis.

"You're right," Tara said at length. "It's your decision to make. I won't say anything more."

Priscilla wanted to apologize. She knew Tara wanted the best for her. That's all Papa had wanted too. The only problem was, when she thought of what that was, she pictured Isaiah. Not Peter.

The first day of the barn raising began well before daylight. Winona prepared mountains of biscuits and sausage patties, wrapped them in paper, and handed them out to the men headed to the Holcomb farm. She sent a pail of extras with Uncle Lucian in case anyone else arrived with an empty stomach. It wasn't likely, but no one would go hungry on her watch.

The Channing women wouldn't leave as early, but they were up and hard at work preparing food and supplies well before the men pulled out of the yard. The week had been a hectic one, riding back and forth between the two farms, hauling lumber and seeds and extra hand plows. The Holcombs' paddock fence had also been destroyed and needed rebuilt, along with a small shelter for the household stock until a proper barn was erected.

Priscilla was thankful for the activity. Peter continued to be a good sport and joined the men on several trips, pitching in and doing what he could. She hoped it would help him understand why she loved it here and would find it hard to leave. Best of all, it kept him out from under her feet. She knew they needed to get reacquainted before they headed East. Though they practically grew up together, she knew very little about him. What he found amusing. What he was passionate about. What disturbed him. What he expected from a wife, though she figured that was pretty much what every man expected.

She just couldn't work up much enthusiasm. She missed Isaiah.

In her head, she imagined excuses to get away from the house. She wanted to find him and explain why she hadn't told him about Peter. There was no excuse beyond enjoying his company without the bother of her obligations. That was a terrible reason she couldn't admit to anyone, especially him.

If only he hadn't come to mean so much to her. Which didn't make sense. She barely knew more about him than she did Peter. The only difference was she wanted to spend the rest of her life getting to know him.

Peter's rented carriage drove into the yard as the women and the hired hands who stayed behind were loading the last of the food and supplies into the wagons. His dark jacket and derby hat was replaced with denim trousers, a plaid shirt and an authentic cowboy hat.

"My, don't you look handsome?" she said.

He jumped to the ground and tipped his hat. "I heard you lovely ladies were raising a barn today. Thought I'd lend a hand"

His smile was youthful and carefree. Priscilla smiled as a flush warmed her cheeks. This was the charming Peter she remembered. "We can always use an extra hand. There's plenty of room in the wagons. You can stow your horse and rig and ride with us."

"I'd rather take the buggy so I can have you to myself."

He smiled teasingly. This was all her heart needed to get back in line. She might even fall in love with him.

Marcia barely nodded in response when she told them she was going with Peter. Every eligible young man in the area was already at the barn raising and she wanted to get there. Her chestnut red hair had been brushed to a glossy shine, and her new gingham bonnet brought out the blue in her eyes. She wanted to hurry up and get there.

Tara squeezed Priscilla's hand. "Don't get lost. We'll see you there."

She squeezed back. "We won't."

She felt a little giddy when Peter helped her into the carriage. He circled the back and climbed in beside her. She took note of his long legs and muscular frame. Marcia was right; he was handsome. And so dignified. In Annapolis he was quite a catch. Handsome. Successful. Ambitious. She was a bit surprised he hadn't become entangled with another woman while he was waiting for her mourning period to end. She studied him out of the corner of her eye. His commitment to her and his family must mean as much to him as it did to her. She could fall in love with him just for that.

They chatted and laughed all the way to the Holcombs'. It was good to feel so carefree. In no time, they arrived at the bustling barnyard. Peter jumped down and hurried around to her side. Priscilla tried not to, but she couldn't help looking for Isaiah in the crowd. The yard teemed with activity; men climbing up and down ladders, shouting orders, hammering trusses, and hurrying in every direction.

Then she saw him. Her heart stood still. He stood against the backdrop of the blackened field with another man. They lifted a finished truss off the ground and leaned it against the corner of a shed. He removed his brown slouch hat and combed his fingers through his thick black hair. Her breath caught in her throat as she willed him to look her way.

Below her, Peter cleared his throat. Priscilla let out a little squeak of surprise. He was standing below her with his hand extended. He followed her gaze. His jaw clenched when he spotted Isaiah. He gestured impatiently, all earlier humor gone. She meekly put her hand in his and let him help her to the ground.

"I'll go find where I'm needed," he said, his words clipped. "It obviously isn't here."

"Peter, wait," she began, but he was already stalking away. She felt bad for hurting his feelings. Nonetheless, her gaze drifted right back to Isaiah. She bit her bottom lip and watched him while she waited for the family wagons to arrive.

He didn't look like an engineer as he hefted two long boards and carried them to a clearing to begin fashioning another truss. She stared at the easy, confident way his back bent over his work and his long arms moved back and forth. He had grown up in a farming community. She shouldn't be surprised that he knew how to do nearly any chore.

She sighed at the futility of her thoughts. If she'd told him about Peter that first day—or better yet, gone straight home after he helped her out of that blasted hole and never given him a second thought—she wouldn't be in this pickle now, pining over a man she'd never see again once she went back to Annapolis. She wouldn't be missing his kisses or his arms around her.

A stew overseen by Winona and a few older women soon bubbled in a huge kettle, filling the air with a delicious spicy aroma of meat and vegetables. Work slowed and eventually stopped as men put down their hammers and saws and began drifting to the center of the yard for the noon meal. Two wagons had been pulled into the shade of an old pin oak where the women set out platters of ham, roast beef, pickled beets, and various beans and greens. The minister blessed the food, then the men moved from the bubbling stew to the wagons to fill their plates—most of them making more than one trip.

Priscilla and the other young women of the community moved through the crowd pouring refills of lemonade, water from the well, and hot coffee. They passed out biscuits and cornbread and hard-boiled eggs. The men laughed and teased each other about who was the slowest and which man was a force to keep up with. Peter took some good-natured ribbing about hitting his thumb with the hammer more often than the nail head. Because he was young and quick and had a strong back, they begrudgingly agreed that made up for his ineptitude with a hammer and saw.

Priscilla tried to avoid the side of the yard where Isaiah and a group of unattached men sat. Though she had no right to, her hackles went up at the sight of young ladies preening and giggling over them. Isaiah laughed and chatted right back. Her hands trembled around the water pitcher she carried. How could he openly flirt with those simpletons after kissing her the way he had?

She was so busy glaring at the spectacle he was making with those silly girls, she walked right into the side of the wagon. The empty pitcher clattered to the ground.

Tara reached out and steadied her. "Are you all right?"

Priscilla's cheeks colored. "Oh, sorry. I wasn't watching—"

Tara looked past her. "I see where you were watching." She picked up the water jug and put it in the wagon. She shoved a golden-brown cobbler into her hands. "This is Winona's juneberry cobbler. You know how Isaiah loves her baking."

Priscilla pulled back. "You take it."

"It'll taste better coming from you." She arched her blond eyebrows. "Sweeter."

"Oh, you."

"Hurry up. Once you cut into it, it'll disappear in thirty seconds and he won't get any. Seems a rough way to treat a man who's been working all day."

Priscilla sighed. She had been looking for an excuse to talk to him. This was as good a way as any to apologize without looking like she was paying him special attention. Tara stuck a long-handled serving spoon through the sugar-sprinkled crust and pushed Priscilla in his direction.

She pasted a neutral smile on her lips. Isaiah saw her coming and shook his head at Dorothy Grandell's offer of a cinnamon-topped bread pudding. "You won't turn me down, will you, Mr. Gates?" Dorothy asked Lyle with a plaintive pout in her voice.

Priscilla tried not to gag.

"No, ma'am. Go ahead and cut me a big piece out of there."

Dorothy beamed. "You men have certainly worked up healthy appetites. What have you got there, Priscilla?" she asked when Priscilla got close.

"Juneberry cobbler from last year's crop."

Dorothy eyed it critically. "Looks like Winona's. It's safe to eat," she announced to the men with a trilling laugh. "Priscilla isn't very adept at baking. She spends more time in the ranch's accounting office than in the kitchen." She wrinkled her nose.

Clayton signaled with his fork. "I'll have some."

She cut a large corner piece, then turned to Isaiah. "Care for a piece? She's right, it's

Winona's."

"Wouldn't miss it." His lips pulled upward. His mossy green eyes warmed as he looked directly into her eyes.

Priscilla's mouth went dry at the sight. Her hands trembled so much she could barely hold onto the spoon. She should say something about the other day. She should explain about Peter. She should tell him she was sorry she let him kiss her. Except she wasn't sorry. Looking down at him now, studying the curve of his lips and remembering the touch of them on hers, his eyes brimming with… What? Passion? Longing? The way he was looking at her now…

"Priscilla!" Dorothy shrieked.

She snapped to attention. Dorothy was at her elbow, a scoop of bread pudding extended toward Clayton. During her rumination, Priscilla had stepped onto the edge of Dorothy's skirt. Dorothy glared at her and jerked away.

Priscilla scrambled to move in the tight space between the two seated men. She bumped Dorothy's arm. The pudding landed upside down on Clayton's metal plate. As she tried to step off Dorothy's skirt, the pan of juneberry cobbler balanced precariously on her left arm tilted and hit Isaiah's shoulder.

"Oh!" she cried out. She kept hold of the pan but not before the cobbler slid out of the pan, onto his shoulder and down his back.

Isaiah dropped his plate onto the ground and leaped up.

"Cilla!" Dorothy scolded with a laugh in her voice. "You ruined his shirt."

"And a perfectly good cobbler," one of the men quipped.

Priscilla stared in shock at the back of Isaiah's shirt. Her face filled with heat. "I…"

Everyone on their side of the yard went silent as they stopped eating to look toward the cause for the noise. Then the afternoon filled with laughter.

"At least it wasn't just out of the oven," Isaiah said. He grabbed a fistful of fruit and crust off his shoulder and stuck it in his mouth. "Delicious," he announced to the crowd.

Some people applauded. Everyone went back to eating.

Priscilla set the nearly empty dish on the tree stump Isaiah had been using for a seat. "I am so sorry." She reached for him.

He shifted away from her. "Don't. You'll get it all over you."

"What a mess," Dorothy said. "You're so clumsy."

Priscilla wanted to remind her she wouldn't have dumped it on him if Dorothy would've waited until she moved before serving Clayton his bread pudding.

Isaiah kept swiping handfuls of mashed fruit off his shirt and dropping them on the ground. "I'm glad I wore an old shirt."

"I'll have it cleaned for you."

"Get down to the creek and get the worst of it out before it's beyond repair," Clayton advised.

"Good idea." Isaiah winked at Priscilla and turned toward the slope in the yard that led to the creek.

"I'll help you."

Priscilla wiped her sticky hands on her apron and hurried after him. She didn't look in Peter's direction to see if he'd heard what happened.

Chapter Eleven

By the time she reached the creek, Isaiah had pulled his shirttail out of his pants. He faced the water, giving her an unobstructed view of the muscles on his back straining against the fabric as he slid it off his shoulders. "Oh, my," she murmured under her breath before she got close enough for him to hear.

"Here, let me." With eyes averted, she reached for the shirt.

"It's just an old shirt."

"I know, but…"

It was hard to think with him standing there, the sun glinting off so much bare skin. She'd never seen the male form on such display. She'd never even considered such a thing. She certainly hadn't imagined so many hard angles and planes with taut muscles playing beneath the skin that beckoned to her fingers to touch.

She snatched the shirt away from him. "You've got it in your hair," she said brusquely. She almost reached over to comb it out with her fingers but pulled back just in time. "Wash your hair and I'll take care of the shirt."

"If you say so." He had a mischievous gleam in his eyes as knelt at the water. Was he amused by how flustered she was? Or did he know—God forbid—the forbidden path her mind had taken?

He scrubbed his wet hands through his hair. "My ma used to make juneberry jelly. She'd mix it with gooseberries and whatever else was in season."

Priscilla moved a few feet away and dipped the stained part of the shirt into the water. She didn't want to get the whole shirt wet since he'd have to put it back on. She swallowed hard before she spoke, hoping he wouldn't detect the tremor in her voice. "That's what Winona does with the cobbler. If there are no other varieties of berries, she just uses more sugar. I'm sorry you didn't get to taste much of it."

She stole a glance at him. He was pouring handfuls of water down his muscled back. *Oh, dear.* She hastily looked away.

"I'm more sorry about missing out on the cobbler than the shirt," he said with a laugh.

Like a moth to a flame, her gaze drifted back. His bare skin glistened in the sunlight. Her hand slipped and she dunked the biggest part of the shirt into the water. She jerked it out. "Oh, dear. I'm…uh…so sorry."

He laughed. "Don't be. The water feels great."

"I'm…um…glad you find this amusing."

"I've been wet before. Won't take no time to dry in this heat."

"I suppose not." She forced her focus onto the shirt and away from his bare back. She wasn't accomplishing much except spreading the wet. "I'm afraid it isn't getting any better without soap powder. I'll replace the shirt."

He scoffed and stood. "I told you it's an old shirt. I can use it to polish my boots when I get back to Lincoln."

Lincoln. How could she forget? He was leaving. Even if she wasn't, she wouldn't see him again after today.

She straightened beside him and focused her attention on wringing out the water as tightly as she could. "Isaiah, about the other night..." She glanced at him, then quickly away. The front of him was even more intriguing than the back. She wouldn't look. Much.

His smile stiffened. "You don't owe me an explanation."

Her heart sank at his expression. She had hurt him even if he was trying to minimize it. "I know, but I feel like I do. Peter and I have known each other since we were very young. Our fathers—"

He held up his hand. "Priscilla, please."

She lowered the shirt and looked directly at him. She tilted her chin to keep his chest out of her line of sight. "I should've told you the first time we met. Or I shouldn't have... Oh, I don't know. It wasn't fair of me to keep going out to the fields to talk with you and get to know you when..."

Her voice trailed off. What was there to say? She shouldn't have done any of it, but she really wanted to. She wanted to now, even knowing that Peter was sitting in the barnyard enjoying bread pudding and pie and Isaiah was going back to Lincoln, then Colorado, and maybe even Washington.

"Our fathers were business partners. They decided years ago Peter and I should marry. When Papa realized he wasn't going to be around, he wanted to make sure I was taken care of. That I had a good, secure life. It was so important to him."

Isaiah shook his head, interrupting her. "I'm glad I got to know you over the last few weeks. Don't apologize for that. I like talking to you. You're funny and interesting and smart. The kind of woman I always..."

He blew out a breath. "There was never an agreement between us. I'm not offended or mad if that's what you're worried about. Sometimes you meet someone and that's all it is. A pleasant experience you like to think on now and then."

Though relieved of her guilt, the words stung. That's all she was to him—a pleasurable memory that would fade with time.

Wasn't that the same way she had thought of him?

"Well, I'm glad I didn't offend you." She shoved the wadded-up shirt into his hands.

He let it fall to the ground between them. "I like you, Priscilla. I like you a lot. I want you to have everything you hope for in life. You do what you need to do, and I'll get back to doing what I was doing before I met you. There is one thing I need to do first, though."

He grabbed hold of her arms and jerked her against him. His lips landed forcefully on hers. A cry of exclamation escaped her lips before she gave herself to the kiss. This kiss wasn't tender and soothing like the other night. It was passionate. Exhilarating. Exploring. She put her hands on his shoulders and pulled him closer. Her fingers dug into his bare flesh.

Bare skin! On a man! She should pull away. She had no right. *He* had no right. She needed to stop this and go to the house. Still, she clung tighter and opened her mouth to his.

"Priscilla!"

The shrill, angry voice broke through her crashing emotions like a splash of water from the creek. She pushed away. Their heads swiveled toward the hill where gravity and rage propelled Winona toward them. Her ruddy face was stone-like and darker than Priscilla had ever seen it. Even from the distance, she saw those small black eyes flashing.

Isaiah snatched his shirt off the ground and struggled into it.

"Young lady! What do you think you're doing?"

"I was—trying to—"

"I can see what you were trying to do. And, young man, button that shirt!" Her eyes ricocheted from one to the other before settling on Priscilla. At an inch under five feet, she made a big presence on the creekbank. "You have a lot of explaining to do."

"I—"

Her work-worn hand snapped upward like a shield. "I don't want to hear it. I can't believe the two of you sneaking off like a couple of…" She shuddered. "I didn't know where you took off to until Lucy said you and he …" She exhaled so strongly it ruffled Priscilla's hair. "You get your little tail up that hill and back to work. And, young man, I better not lay eyes on you again unless you've got your hat in your hand with an apology and a request of Mr. Channing."

Priscilla's face darkened at what Winona was suggesting. "No, Winona, it isn't anything like that. We're not courting."

The Indian woman gaped at her. "Is that supposed to make me feel better? Why are you still standing here? I told you to get up that hill. You're not too old for me to take a switch to you. Or you either," she said, whirling around on Isaiah who had the wherewithal to button his shirt.

He held out his hands in surrender and backed up a step. "Yes, ma'am. I mean, no ma'am. I mean…" He cast a desperate look at Priscilla over the top of Winona's head. "I just meant—"

She set her hands on her hips and glared at him. "I know perfectly well what you meant. There's plenty of work waiting for you, too."

"Yes, ma'am."

"Then get to it. Priscilla, you heard me. Go!"

Without another word or glance at Isaiah, Priscilla hurried up the hill. Tears blurred her vision. Isaiah may have kissed her like a man possessed, but he didn't care that she was marrying Peter. He wouldn't lose a moment's sleep when she was back in Annapolis, and he was back at his research and his life.

He was right; they'd never had an agreement. He might not think of her as more than one passionate, earthshaking kiss, but her heart was breaking in two. A kiss wasn't enough. It never would be. She wanted more. She wanted him.

The last thing Priscilla wanted to do was ride back to the ranch with Peter, but there was no getting out of it. The carriage was barely in motion when he turned to her. "It's time we start planning our wedding."

Her heart sank. She didn't even want to think about a wedding.

"I need to tell you about Isaiah."

"It's nothing I need to hear. It's my own fault for allowing you to come here in the first place."

"Allowing me?"

He went on as if she hadn't spoken. "I should've insisted you observe your grieving period in Annapolis with Mother and my sisters. They would've been all the comfort you needed."

He patted her hand. "Don't worry, I don't blame you. You're a flighty young woman who hasn't been brought to task. You never had a mother to teach you what to expect from men who travel from place to place like that engineer." His face hardened. "She would've told you they're all the same. No, I blame your uncle. He encouraged you toward independence. Working in that accounting office and letting you believe you were as competent as a man. It's a quite unseemly attitude in a woman. One might overlook it under certain circumstances or when managing a household staff, but I won't tolerate it. Under Mother's tutelage, you'll learn the proper role of a lady."

She gasped. "Your mother? Peter, I don't need to be taught anything."

He smiled placatingly. "Of course not. I always knew you were of strong character. I like that in you. It's just that women are the gentler sex. They don't know what's best for them. That's why they need men. Your father did a fine job securing your future. Now that he's gone, I'll handle everything. You can focus on being beautiful like the Lord intended."

Priscilla stared into the distance. She didn't want to focus on being beautiful. She wanted freedom, peace, passionate kisses, independence. She wanted to keep learning things. She wanted to be challenged, not sit in a parlor and pour tea and listen to other women discussing their household staff or the latest fashions. Was she wrong for wanting more? Papa loved her and wanted the best for her. But what if he was wrong? What if the life Uncle Lucian offered his daughters was better? What if there was something more—someone else—the Lord designed specifically for her.

She hadn't asked God what *He* wanted in her situation. She hadn't considered anything beyond Papa's wants and her needs. She should've asked God. If she possessed the strong character Peter suggested, had she been given it for no other reason than managing a household? There had to be more to life. If she went back to Annapolis and became a dutiful wife and thoughtful daughter-in-law, she'd never know.

"We'll stay here a few more days," he was saying. "I know how important it is to you to see your neighbors' barn finished. Then after, we'll go home. Mother and Elizabeth have already done a lot in planning our wedding, but they can't finish without you. They need your approval of the small details like flowers. Time is of the essence. This is the season for roses."

"I don't care about roses," she interrupted. "I want to get married here. With my cousins watching and Uncle Lucian to give me away."

"You must be joking. Our wedding will be the social events of the season. It's already planned."

"I don't want to be a social event. I want something quiet and intimate with people who love me. We'll have plenty of years for society events to impress your business associates."

He looked at her like he'd never seen her before and swallowed back his impatience. "I don't think Mother will like it."

Priscilla bit her tongue. She didn't tell him she didn't care what his mother liked or didn't like. With an inward sigh, she realized she'd better start caring. Appearances were everything to people like the Hollisters. Civic organizations. Parties and political events. She certainly couldn't show up to those with her hair windblown and her nose sunburned.

She gathered her nerve. "Please, Peter. We can marry here as soon as you like." Her stomach dropped at the thought, but she kept talking. "You already said we've put it off too long. It's very important to share this moment with my family."

This moment.

The only moment she cared about was Isaiah's kiss. A stolen moment to last the rest of her life.

He sighed, then caught her hand and brought it to her lips. "I'll send Mother and Father a telegram and tell them what you want."

She gasped. "Oh, Peter, do you mean it? After we get back to the city, we can plan a banquet or reception or something so they can celebrate with us."

He stared at her. His gaze intensified and strayed to her lips. He leaned toward her. Priscilla looked away. She would have to kiss him someday. She just didn't want it to be today.

Chapter Twelve

Rain started during the night. Pounding rain that puddled on the hard ground. Priscilla watched it from her window. She should be happy. No one could work on the barn today. Or tomorrow if the rain kept falling. The longer it took to finish the barn, the longer she would have on Four Sisters Ranch with her cousins. But what difference did a few days make?

Today Peter was notifying his parents of her desire to marry here. He didn't know yet if they'd want to come to witness the ceremony. He doubted they'd be all that interested in boarding a dusty, crowded train to cross half the continent to see this union legalized. More than likely, they'd allow a fast ceremony and wait for the happy couple to get back to Annapolis. When they got his telegram, they would assume she was too anxious to marry their son to wait even one more day.

If they only knew.

Since Peter was telling his parents, she needed to tell the family. She hadn't even told Tara when Peter dropped her at the house last night. She'd gone straight to her room and fell across the bed trying to figure out how she felt about marrying Peter and knowing she would never kiss Isaiah again.

Isaiah. She missed him already and he wasn't even gone yet. She imagined looking into the faces of the children she would someday share with Peter and wondering what they would look like if Isaiah was their father. She was a terrible person. She wasn't fit to marry anyone.

None of that mattered. Papa's dying wish was for her to marry Peter, and she had promised that she would. She had her whole life to get to know him. Yes, he had a controlling and arrogant nature, but arrogant natures created strong, confident husbands. She would be a godly, submissive wife, and like she told Tara, she would choose to be content in her situation.

She and Clarissa worked all day in the ranch office as the rain tattooed on the roof over their heads. The barn raising had put them behind on their paperwork. With the rain keeping most people inside, there were limited distractions, so they caught up on nearly everything by the end of the day.

She didn't say anything about Peter or Isaiah to Clarissa and Clarissa didn't ask. Clarissa was a no-nonsense personwho kept her business to herself and didn't stick her nose into others'. Priscilla doubted she gave much thought to romance and kisses and the muscles that rippled across a man's back.

Priscilla did. A lot. But only since she met Isaiah.

They finished for the day with nearly an hour before suppertime. Clarissa went upstairs to freshen up. Priscilla wanted to. She wanted to go upstairs and have a good cry. She didn't have that luxury. It wasn't likely Peter would show up with the open skies, but it was possible. She needed to tell the family, especially her uncle, before he came and broke the news for her.

She found Uncle Lucian in his office bent over a ledger. "Priscilla, how are you, dear? I haven't seen much of you since your Mr. Hollister came to town."

She wanted to tell him Peter wasn't her Mr. Hollister, but he would be soon enough. She entered her uncle's home office and shut the door. The room was evident of him with its dark paneled walls and bookshelves on two walls, dusty and over-filled, the books in disarray since Uncle Lucian was always busy and rushing from one project to the next. Just like Papa. Her stomach lurched. She missed Papa so much. She missed home. She realized it wasn't the house or the city but the life she had there.

She clasped her hands in front of her. "I have something to tell you."

His faded blue eyes widened under a set of thinning eyebrows. He stood. "Of course. Have a seat. Is everything all right?"

"Oh, everything's fine. I didn't mean to worry you…" She took a deep breath and focused on relaxing her shoulders and neck. "I just wanted to ask, well, I want to tell you Peter and I are getting married."

The deep twin crease between his eyes smoothed out. He circled the desk and kissed her cheek. "I'm delighted to hear it, though I assumed that's why he was here."

"Yes, sir. What I wanted to ask, though, is if we could get married here? At the ranch. I thought a small affair with a few friends. I can't imagine getting married without all of you. And the ranch staff, of course. Winona and Rayen. Peter is sending a telegram to his parents. We'd like them to come if it's possible. I know it's short notice."

He finally cut her off. "Yes, yes, it's all right. I'd be delighted to host the ceremony. The girls will be so happy to hear you want to do it here. If you haven't told them already."

"No one knows. You're the first."

Uncle Lucian kissed her again, then took her hands and guided her into one of the leather chairs facing his desk. He lowered himself into the other one. "I'm honored that you want us to be part of your day, Cilla. You know I think of you as one of my own daughters."

A lump lodged in her throat. She opened her mouth to respond, but he kept going. "And as one of my own daughters, I'd like to ask you a question."

"Anything, Uncle."

"Why do you want to marry Mr. Hollister?"

She frowned. She must not have heard him correctly. "Sir?"

He leaned forward over his rounded belly and stared intently into her eyes. "If someone had asked me that question when I married my Grace, I could've given them a thousand reasons. Of course, they wouldn't have had to ask. It was written all over my face."

"Oh." Priscilla sat back in the chair. Why? Why was she marrying Peter? For Papa, of course. It's what he wanted. That was the only reason.

"It's been planned for—"

"For years. Yes, I know. It's what your parents wanted for you. I respect that, but I can't help noticing you've been a little…out of sorts since Mr. Hollister arrived. Not at all how I would expect a young lady to react at seeing her beau after a long absence."

She picked at a broken fingernail. It was a bad habit, and she stopped immediately. Peter's mother certainly wouldn't approve. "Yes, well, we haven't seen each other in a long time. I guess I don't know him very well."

"What about that engineer fellow, Mr. Paxton?"

The blood drained from her face. She thought of Isaiah's kiss. His taut arms holding her. His bare chest pressed against her. Did Uncle know? Had Winona told him? "Sir?"

"Well, I rather thought you were interested in him."

She swallowed hard, still unsure if he was preparing to scold her for yesterday's behavior. "No, Uncle. I mean, yes. He's very interesting. And intelligent. I enjoyed learning about his research. But I'm betrothed to Peter. Mother and Father wanted to make sure I was taken care of. They knew Peter's family could—"

"Are you unhappy here?"

"No! Not at all. I love it here."

"Do you believe you'll be as happy in Annapolis?"

"The Bible says a person is to be content wherever the Lord puts them."

"And you believe the Lord put you in this position?"

"Well, I don't know. I mean, He provided me with all of you after I lost Papa. I believe He directs my steps."

"Do you believe He put Mr. Hollister in your life?"

"Well…" She thought of her prayer the other day when she realized she hadn't prayed about what God wanted her to do with her life. She'd always done what everyone told her to do. She'd never actually had to make a decision on her own. She never had to completely seek the Lord for direction and guidance. She supposed she still hadn't.

"It's what Papa and Mother wanted. I trust them. They wanted the best for me. They gave up so much for me, just as your parents did for you. I heard all the stories about the sacrifices they made when they left Hertfordshire."

Uncle Lucian nodded as she talked. "I grew up hearing those same stories. Your grandparents and their parents before them gave up everything they had to build a successful life in America. They also raised us to fear the Lord first and seek His direction the way they did. That doesn't mean they knew what that life would look like when they stepped out in faith."

"But...they did. They wanted me to be safe and healthy and secure with a good man from a good family. It's all Papa talked about. He believed Peter was that man."

He tapped her leg with an envelope from the desk. "Priscilla, your papa loved you and wanted to ensure you had a good life after he wasn't here to take care of you. I want the same for my girls. That's why I raised them to be strong and self-sufficient." He sighed and slumped back in the leather chair. "Perhaps I did too good a job. I don't yet have a son-in-law, now do I?"

She smiled in response but was thinking of what Peter said about him giving his daughters too much freedom and making them unbecoming to men.

"If something happened to me," he went on, "or rather, *when* it happens to me, each of my girls is equipped to take care of herself and make the best choices to fulfill God's purpose for her. I don't expect them to live according to what they believe will make me happy.

"How do you think I ended up here? Annapolis was the right thing for your father. It wasn't for me. Maybe it isn't for you either. If your father were here, he'd see the changes in you the same as I do. I think he'd realize how strong you are, and he'd know you're capable of making your own decisions. I know he wouldn't want you to marry a man you don't love."

"But..." Priscilla's head spun. She didn't feel strong. She was more confused than ever. She'd lived her whole life for the day she married Peter. "I can learn to love Peter. People do it every day."

"Even when you love someone else?"

How did he know?

She wanted to tell him it didn't matter how she felt because Isaiah didn't love her. He was leaving. He was eager to get back to his life and his research. He'd given her no reason to think he wanted her. Except for a kiss she'd remember until her dying day.

"It's different for women," she said instead. "We don't have the luxury of independence the way men do. We can't earn a living. Papa knew I'd have a rough go of it if I were alone."

He squeezed her hand. "You're never alone. You have us. More than that, you have the Lord. All those years ago, when I struck out here without knowing anyone or anything about this land, I put myself completely in His hands. Your papa wanted to protect you the same way our parents wanted to protect me. But he would also want you to trust the Lord more than him. He couldn't have envisioned the life the Lord planned for you wasn't in Annapolis. That would've been as foreign to him as the idea of you meeting a young engineer in an irrigation ditch."

He chuckled and stroked his chin. "If I hadn't attended that young man's lecture at a conference last fall, he wouldn't have come here, and you never would've met him. Isn't the Lord funny that way? We make plans. We think we know which direction to turn and *Bam!*" He clapped his hands. "He drops a surprise into our laps and all those plans disappear as fast as a summer cloudburst."

Priscilla felt warmth rush to her face. Was she that transparent? Did everyone in the house know she loved Isaiah before she did?

"The last time I spoke to Papa all he talked about was my future. He looked into my eyes and begged me to promise I would marry Peter. I'll never forget the look on his face. I can't dishonor his wishes."

Uncle Lucian took her hands between his gnarled ones. "I would never ask you to do that. Nor will I try to talk you into anything. I know my brother. He truly believed he was doing right by you. Maybe Mr. Hollister is the right man for you. Maybe you'll have a beautiful life in Annapolis. Only God knows. Don't you owe it to yourself to ask Him before making what is probably the biggest decision of your life?"

He swung around to look at the window where sheets of rain pelted the panes. They could barely see that it was still daylight outside. "Looks like the rain has set in for the night. No one will be coming from town to disturb you. If you'd like, take your supper in your room. Do some thinking and praying. See what the Lord has to say about all this instead of just your cranky old uncle."

Priscilla got up and leaned over the man who reminded her so much of Papa and hugged him. "I love you, Uncle. Thank you for everything you've done for me."

He caught her hand and pulled her close to drop a kiss on her cheek. "I'd do it again a hundred times over."

Chapter Thirteen

Though it continued to rain the following day, things returned to normal on the ranch. Bad weather didn't keep the animals from needing fed or a hundred other chores from needing done. The roads from town remained swamped, so Priscilla wasn't too worried about Peter showing up unannounced. He was probably in town fretting over his parents' reaction to her request and annoyed and impatient that the weather had interfered with his schedule.

She knew she should use the time to pack and take care of things, so when he did come, they could exchange their vows and board the next train East. Instead, she helped Winona in the kitchen, worked in the office with Clarissa, and read in the study or wrote in her journal. And prayed. What did God want for her?

Friday night, the rain stopped. Saturday arrived bright and clear. If things dried out, the barn raising would continue on Monday. By Wednesday she could be a married woman. The thought of it made her sick to her stomach. Worse, she had no peace about the situation. That meant God was trying to speak to her. She just wasn't sure what He was saying.

Just after the noon meal, Peter's carriage drove under the signposts, the wheels throwing up rivers of muddy water. She wrapped her shawl around her shoulders and went out to wait for him on the veranda. He parked at the base of the stairs and climbed down.

"Have you eaten? We just finished up," she said as she descended the stairs to meet him.

His lips twitched upward in a distracted smile. "I ate before I left town, though I'm growing tired of the limited fare."

"They do the best with what they have," she said as cheerfully as she could muster.

He gazed at her from two steps below her. "I'll be glad to get back to the city and real restaurants. My cook at the house prepares better meals on her worst day than what I get here. Her name's Greta. She came highly recommended. You'll love her. Or you can hire someone else. You'll have complete control over the household staff with little input from me."

She supposed that was meant to flatter her. He'd fire Greta with no regard to what a loss of position would do to her if Priscilla deemed it so.

He stepped up to where she was standing and kissed her cheek. "It's good to see you."

"You as well." She wasn't sure she meant it, but she couldn't put off talking to him forever. "Let's take a walk."

He frowned and glanced at his boots. He clearly didn't want to ruin them in the mud. "It could rain again."

"If it does, we'll dash into one of the barns. I've been cooped up inside for three days, and the sun feels glorious."

He sighed discreetly. "Whatever you like."

She settled her shawl more securely around her shoulders as they set off. Normally, she would have him take the horse and carriage to the stable, but it wasn't a long ride from town, and he may not stay long.

"What do you think of Channing?" she asked conversationally.

He gave her a puzzled look. "It's your typical frontier town, I suppose, though more neat and orderly than some I traveled through."

"Uncle Lucian put a lot of money and energy into drawing businesses that would benefit the people who settled here. He and my Aunt Grace wanted it to be a town that would prosper and endure long after they were gone."

"Your uncle sounds a lot like his brother. Your father was also a wise businessman desirous of building a legacy that would last. A legacy to benefit you and me."

She nodded at his pointed look. She knew what he was getting at. She'd thought of nothing else since receiving his letter that he was coming for her. She'd also been thinking a lot about what Uncle Lucian said. Papa's greatest desire had been that she seek God's face and submit to His will above all else. What if doing so meant not fulfilling her vow?

If Papa were here, would he see that she wasn't designed for the life he created for her? Would that be all right with him?

"Why do you want to marry me, Peter?"

He stopped walking and gaped at her. "Why do I... Why wouldn't I? This is what our parents planned for us. It's what they always wanted. It will ensure stability and prosperity for our company that will enrich both our families for generations to come."

"Yes, but why do *you* want to marry me?"

"I'm afraid I don't understand."

She wasn't sure she understood either. This had always been the plan. Why wasn't it enough for her now? "Do you love me?"

"What kind of a question is that? I care about you a great deal. You know that."

"What about love? Don't you want that?"

"Of course, it would be optimal. But I know many successful marriages where the participants aren't exactly delirious over each other. Is that what you mean? I suppose it's nice, but I believe it's more important that a couple is compatible. Of similar breeding and manners. Most couples we know are…comfortable with each other. I believe that's what we should aspire to."

"Comfortable." She mulled the word over. A few months ago, that would've been enough. Now, she wanted more.

He stopped walking again and faced her full on. "What's this all about? I suppose living in a house with four other flighty females has filled your head with silly notions like romance and poetry and getting swept off your feet."

"My cousins are not flighty, Peter. Even if they were, don't men want those things? Love? Passion?"

She thought of Isaiah's passionate embrace. She wondered if Peter had experienced passion in his life.

"No man worth his salt wastes a minute on such frivolous thoughts. A man of power and reason goes into a marriage like he would any other business venture—measuring how it can propel him in the direction he wants to go and determined to make a success of it."

"I don't think I like the sound of that."

"You don't have to. That's why God put man over the woman. So you wouldn't have to worry about it."

The clouds covered the sun, casting the afternoon in shadows. Peter squeezed her hand. "Your father knew I would give you a good life. The feelings you're looking for may not come, but we can still make a good marriage. It worked for my parents. They're very happy. They each got what they wanted from their union. They complement each other and they're quite content with the way things are. If anything beyond that develops within a marriage, well, that's icing on the cake."

Priscilla focused on the ground, intent on avoiding mud puddles. She wished Papa were here. She would ask him what he wanted for her. A marriage likened to a successful business venture? Or one where she loved her husband and he adored her right back? She knew which one her parents had. She was sure he would want her to have the same.

A few drops of rain dotted her bare arms. She looked toward the darkening sky. "Looks like you were right about the rain."

They turned toward the house. Peter's brow had furrowed. He tightened his grip on her hand to slow her down. "I know what this is about, Priscilla. It's about that well digger you were kissing the other night?"

She jerked her hand free. "No, it isn't," she snapped, though she doubted she'd have these questions if she hadn't met Isaiah.

"All I know is you are not the woman you were when your father was alive."

"You're right. I'm not. I want love. I don't want to marry someone because it will make my business more prosperous."

"Well, you better consider those things. Life is more than living on dreams and feelings and the kindness of your neighbors if your barn burns down. A good husband is responsible and provides for his family."

Priscilla bristled. She wanted to defend Mr. Holcomb as a husband and provider, but Peter wouldn't listen, and it would only distract them.

He turned her toward him and took both her hands in his. "I can learn to love you, if that's what you want."

"I don't want you to learn anything, Peter. I don't think we can make each other happy. I don't believe we're compatible."

The intermittent raindrops turned to a steady drizzle. They ducked their heads and picked up their pace. They reached the bottom of the stairs. "Maybe you're right," Peter said. "We aren't compatible. I always wanted a beautiful woman on my arm at society function that other men would want. I thought it was you. Now, you would embarrass me with your ragged fingernails and the callouses on your hands. I haven't seen you in a decent dress or hat since I got here."

She burst out laughing. "I still have decent clothes. They're just impractical on horseback."

"Exactly," he bit out, not appreciating her mirth.

The rain began in earnest. They hurried up the porch steps. When they reached the top, they stopped to catch their breath.

She didn't want to leave him on a bad note, though when he left she may never have another chance at love or marriage. "We don't want the same things. It's nothing against either of us. We're just not a good match. It's better we figured it out now before we ended up making each other miserable in a very long marriage."

Out of the corner of her eye, she saw a figure with a hat pulled low and shoulders hunched against the rain running across the yard toward the house. She figured it was one of the hands headed to the back door and didn't pay him any mind. Peter didn't notice at all.

He sneered from under the brim of his dripping hat. "Your father would be so disappointed in the woman you've become."

Her mouth dropped at his cruelty. "No, he wouldn't. He loved me, and not just as a reflection of himself."

He stared at her as if she were speaking a different language. He took off his hat and slapped it against his leg before putting it back on. "If I leave here, I'm not coming back."

"I know."

The figure that had run across the yard dashed up the stairs. Halfway up, he lifted his head. It was Isaiah. He reached the top and stopped, looking awkward.

"You!" Peter bellowed. "You couldn't even wait until I was gone?"

"Wha—"

Peter launched into him. His feet slipped on the wet flagstones, and he hit Isaiah off center. Isaiah staggered but stayed on his feet. He pushed back, and Peter backpedaled to where Priscilla stood. She shrieked and leaped aside, coming close to the five-foot drop off the edge of the porch. The men grappled for each other. Their feet slipped and slid and neither could get a decent grip on the other in their wet clothes or steady themselves enough to land a punch.

"Stop!" Priscilla shouted. Her voice was drowned out by the rain pelting the roof of the veranda, not that they were listening anyway. "Stop it this instant."

Fear rose within her. She imagined them falling on the wet flagstones and busting their fool heads open. She grabbed at them but had no better luck in getting a grip on the wet fabric. The men kept scrabbling with each other and swinging their fists.

She exhaled in frustration. This was pointless. The rain had slacked off, but it wasn't likely anyone in the house had heard the fight. She needed help before someone got hurt.

Blasted men and their stubborn pride.

She headed to the door, though they were nearly against it. Isaiah threw a punch and caught Peter on the side of the head. Peter growled deep in his throat and threw his weight into Isaiah. Both men stumbled into her and pinned her against a porch post. Someone came down hard on her foot. She yowled in pain, now as mad as they were. She'd had enough. If she thought she could, she'd bang their heads together the way teachers used to do with brawling boys in the schoolyard.

Isaiah swung Peter around. He crashed into her. Her feet scrambled for purchase on the wet flagstones. She was propelled backward until there was nothing under her feet but air. She went off the side of the porch into the narrow space between the angle of the porch and where the bay window in the parlor jutted over a patch of grass. Pain shot through her ankle as she landed in an awkward heap in the mud. Above her the men went quiet.

The rain stopped falling and the clouds parted. An errant sunbeam landed on her rain-streaked face.

"Priscilla?"

"Are you hurt?"

She looked up into their red, panting, worried faces. If her ankle didn't hurt and she wasn't still mad, she would burst out laughing.

Isaiah recovered first. He dropped to his knees and stuck out a hand.

"I'm coming around," Peter said.

"There's no space," she called up to him. "Your horse is soaked and so are you. Just go."

He looked down at her for a moment, clearly not willing to accept defeat, but she saw in his eyes he was a little relieved he wouldn't have to take this muddy, disheveled woman home to meet his mother.

Isaiah eyed him warily from his knees, unsure if Peter would attack again with him in a compromised position. Peter looked from one to the other, then sighed heavily, straightened his coat, and hurried cautiously down the wet steps.

Isaiah looked back at her. "Why does this keep happening to you?"

She feigned a look of outrage. "This time you pushed me."

"It wasn't me. I'm helping you. As usual."

She stood and tested her weight on her ankle.

"Are you hurt?" he asked.

"No, no thanks to the two of you."

"Just give me your hand. Watch your head. Don't bang it on the underside of the window."

"I'm trying," she cried breathlessly as he lifted while her feet slipped and slid against the side of the porch. In no time she was sitting next to him on the wet flagstones. She brushed a smear of mud off her arm.

675

"Is that how grown men behave when their pride is wounded?"

He sat down beside her close enough that his long legs brushed against hers. "I was just coming to talk to your uncle. I had no idea I'd get bushwacked by your beau."

"He's not my beau." She looked away. He scooted a little closer. The heat from his body warmed her through her muddy dress.

He cupped his jaw and rotated it side to side. "Sure seemed to me like he thinks he is."

"We both realized we're not suited. I doubt we ever were. I just didn't know it."

He brushed a lock of wet hair from her face. "You should go inside and dry off."

"What did you need to see Uncle about?" she asked without moving.

"I came to tell him I'm leaving." He removed his hat and ran his hand through his wet hair, then put the hat back on. "We got a telegram from Lincoln this morning. They're satisfied with our research. They want us to pack up and head back."

She looked down at streaks of mud on her dress. "Are you going to Colorado?"

"Maybe. First, the teams need to meet at the university to compare data. A trip to Colorado may not be necessary."

Even though Peter was out of her life, Isaiah was still leaving. Her heart ached. She gingerly touched a small cut below his eye with her fingertip. He winced but didn't pull away. He was looking back with intensity burning in his green eyes.

She pulled in her legs to stand. "I'll tell Uncle you're here," she said around the catch in her throat.

He took her hands and held her in place. "I lied to you the other day."

"What?"

"Down at the creek when I told you I liked you and I liked talking to you."

That had been a lie? Then why had he kissed her? Was this a joke to him, or did he make women fall in love with him in every town he passed through?

"Even as I said it," he continued, "I knew it was a lie. I don't just like you."

His large hands closed around hers. "I love you, Priscilla. I don't want to go to Washington without you. I don't want to go anywhere without you. Even if it means staying right here on this ranch."

Tears sprang to her eyes. "What? I don't… You said you were leaving. Now you're not?"

He grinned, his white teeth in sharp contrast to the wet scruff of beard on his jaw. "You're not listening. I just told you I love you."

She opened her mouth to reply but no sound came out.

"I'll do whatever you want," he went on. "You can go with me to Lincoln. Or Washington. Or wherever they send me. Or we'll stay right here. Your uncle can hire me to…to muck out stalls or build barn trusses. Whatever he needs as long as I can do it with you."

She couldn't think. It was happening too fast. "Isaiah, I—"

"Marry me, Cilla. Right now."

She laughed. "We can't get married right now."

"Well, no. You'd probably want to change out of that dress."

She slapped his chest with both hands. "Oh, Isaiah. I love you."

He pulled her against him. After a long kiss that stole her breath, they broke apart. "Just so you know, I'm not going to spend the rest of my life pulling you out of tight spaces you manage to fall into."

"Yes, you will."

He heaved a beleaguered sigh. "I know."

Laughing, she combed her fingers through his thick black hair and knocked his hat off the back of his head. He caught hold of her wrists, pinned her arms against his chest, and drew her close for another long kiss.

The End

If you enjoyed Priscilla's story, please take a moment and leave a review on <u>Amazon</u> or any other marketplace or blog that allows reviews. Even a short review proves to Amazon there is interest in the Once Upon a Courtship compilation and they will display it to more readers.

The best way to support any author is still the old-fashioned method of recommending the book to a friend. Share my links on social media outlets. Follow me on Amazon, BookBub and GoodReads. Sign up for my newsletter if you haven't already and receive a free western romance *A Promise for Josie: A Willow Wood Brides Prequel*: https://teresaslack.com/join-newsletter/

I love hearing from readers. Email me at teresa@teresaslack.com anytime with your thoughts and input about my stories and series ideas you would love to read.

About Teresa

Teresa Slack loves reading, writing, and falling in love. Creating clean and wholesome western romances where cowboys still sweep spirited women off their feet was an easy choice for her.

She writes from her home in the beautiful southern Ohio hills, which she shares with her husband, rescue dog and rescue cats. Any errors and typos she blames on the cats, randomly running across her keyboard.

The Gilding of Minnie Tucker

by Marilyn Turk

Mountain girl Minnie Tucker, new maid at the Biltmore mansion, knows Mr. Vanderbilt's rule about the household staff not being seen. As one who loves to read, the Biltmore House library offers thousands of books, if she ever has the time. The secret door to the library gives her a chance, but running into a guest is not part of her plan.

Author Stanton Bardwell is a guest of the Vanderbilts at their mountain mansion, invited there to escort and hopefully, be attracted to, one of their female guests. However, when he has an unexpected meeting with charming Minnie Tucker, one of the parlor maids, he can't shake the attraction. But when he crosses barriers to be with her, the results are drastic for Minnie. How can he make things right between them and pursue the only woman who he's ever been drawn to love?

To my dear husband Chuck Turk, who patiently tolerates my writing anxiety.

I'm so thankful you're my happily-ever-after.

"Forgive, and you shall be forgiven." Luke 6:37

Chapter One

Biltmore House, North Carolina, 1899

"Minnie, quit fidgeting! She's coming."

Minnie stopped twisting her handkerchief in anxious anticipation of meeting famous Edith Vanderbilt, the highly esteemed mistress of the Biltmore House.

Her friend Sarah Beth peered down the corridor, then straightened as Mrs. Vanderbilt entered, followed by the housekeeper, Mrs. Emily King, who had hired the new maids.

Stuffing her handkerchief inside her sleeve, Minnie took a deep breath to control her nerves and sent a silent prayer skyward. *Dear Lord, help me calm down so Mrs. Vanderbilt will like me.*

Minnie was one of six maids standing in a straight line, all new employees of the grand Biltmore mansion, waiting to be introduced to Mrs. Vanderbilt. The maids had come from the surrounding area, small town girls vying for the well-paying, prestigious positions that were rare in the mountain community, and Minnie knew all of them, where they came from and who their families were. Looking like a row of penguins in their black dresses and white pinafore aprons, they kept their heads forward, casting nervous, sideways glances at the approaching ladies.

Sarah Beth told her they would be working alongside experienced maids from New York, England, and even France, who were accustomed to working for the well-to-do. Would they take a liking to her or look down on her because she was a poor mountain girl?

Standing as straight as she could, she hoped her new uniform looked properly starched and clean. Mrs. King and Mrs. Vanderbilt stopped in front of the first maid in the line.

"Mrs. Vanderbilt, this is Grace Smith." The tall Mrs. Vanderbilt towered over the petite girl. As she curtsied, Grace's white lace cap slipped to the side, defeated by the weight of her mass of wavy chestnut hair which defied the hairpins trying to hold it back.

"Nice to meet you, Grace," Mrs. Vanderbilt said, a warm smile on her face.

Next in line was Pauline Ross, a big-boned girl with thin light brown hair pulled into a bun. Pauline was close to Mrs. Vanderbilt's height and looked her straight in the eye before giving a jerky curtsy after being introduced

"Nice to meet you, Pauline."

When they reached Ruby Parks, Mrs. King introduced her in the same manner. Mrs. Vanderbilt smiled and said, "Might you be named for your hair color, Ruby?"

With flaming red hair, there was little doubt. "Yes, ma'am," Ruby nodded, glancing at the floor as she curtsied.

Alma Tate was the next in line, her face flushing as she was introduced. Terribly shy, Alma was a distant cousin of Minnie's, like most of the folks that lived near her family homestead in the mountains.

Mrs. Vanderbilt stopped in front of Sarah Beth next. Sarah Beth curtsied and smiled as if it were the most natural thing in the world. Sarah Beth displayed confidence, a trait Minnie wished she shared.

And then the most important woman in the world was standing in front of Minnie. She curtsied as Mrs. King said, "Minnie Tucker," fixing her eyes on the hem of Mrs. Vanderbilt's fashionable blue serge tailored skirt.

"Hello, Minnie. How nice to meet you."

Minnie's head popped up and she found herself looking into the cheerful hazel eyes of the woman in front of her. Mrs. Vanderbilt's clear rosy complexion and confident smile testified to health and strength. But unlike Minnie's expectations of somber royalty, the woman radiated kindness and warmth. If not for their distant positions in society, Minnie thought they could have been friends, so she smiled back with ease.

Minnie nodded, "The pleasure is mine, ma'am."

She felt all eyes on her as everyone else in the room glanced at her. What had she done? With warming cheeks, she realized she was the only maid to have said so much to Mrs. Vanderbilt. Oh dear. Had she misspoken?

But the gentle calm of her employer's face was nothing but friendly, so Minne quietly blew out a breath of relief.

Mrs. Vanderbilt then stepped back and let her gaze sweep the maids. "I'm sure Mrs. King has given you all the rules. She will instruct you and direct you in your tasks. She reports directly to me, and I trust her judgment implicitly. The fact that she chose you to work for Biltmore House is proof of your potential and something you can be proud of. Mrs. King will be able to answer any questions you have. Everyone who works here belongs to the exclusive family of the Biltmore Estate. I welcome you all and hope you enjoy being part of the family. Good day." Another smile and a nod, then she turned and left the room.

"She seems very nice," Minnie said to Sarah Beth.

"I heard she truly is. But the person we need to satisfy is Mrs. King. And she can be more difficult to please, so they say." Minnie had only met with the housekeeper the day she was hired and found her a no-nonsense person. With her gray-streaked brown hair pulled back and coiled into a bun at her neck, she could look stern. She came from England like the butler had, so she spoke in proper English, but Minnie thought her to be more like Granny, tough with a hidden soft side. She hoped she was right.

The girls chattered excitedly about their introductions until Mrs. King came back into the room, causing all voices to go silent.

"Grab your things and follow me to the fourth floor," Mrs. King said with a demanding expression. "I'll assign your rooms up there. You will each be sharing a room as well as sharing the two bathrooms in the hall."

Minnie and the others grabbed their carpet bags filled with the meager personal things brought from home and filed behind the matron as she climbed the backstairs up to the servants' quarters. At the top, they entered a hallway and followed her down it. Mrs. King stopped in front of a board with rows of buttons. "This is the annunciator. When Mr. or Mrs. Vanderbilt or any of their guests need anything, they push a button, and it rings on this board and one like it in the butler's pantry. You can see the location of each button written below, so we know exactly where to go to answer the call."

She continued on down the hall. "These rooms are for the female domestic help only. Men are housed in other areas, so you won't be running into each other."

Pausing in front of an open doorway, the matron motioned inside. "Grace and Ruby, you will share this room." The two girls exchanged glances, then entered.

At the next door, she said, "Alma and Pauline, this is your room." Mrs. King paused again before moving down the hall. "Sarah Beth and Minnie, this is your room," she said at the next open doorway. "You can bring a special piece of furniture or memento from home if you'd like, but there's not much space, and we want the rooms tidy."

"Thank you, ma'am," Minnie said, entering the room with Sarah Beth.

"Ladies, get your rooms in order and I'll see you in one hour in the basement for a tour of the house."

As soon as Mrs. King left the floor, Minnie and Sarah Beth plopped onto their wrought iron single beds.

"Our own beds!" Minnie said, falling back on hers. "I won't have to share a bed with my little sister anymore."

"And electricity, Minnie! We have electricity!" Sarah Beth said, hopping up to push a button on the wall. "Look. The white button makes the light come on, and the black button makes it go off."

"What is that noise?" Minnie asked.

Sarah Beth pushed the light buttons again. When the light was on, there was a humming noise emitted from the Edison bulb hanging from the ceiling. "I guess the Edison makes the noise." She pushed the black button again, and the room went silent.

"I think I can get used to the noise so we can have light," Minnie said.

In addition to the beds, each of them had a rush-seated rocker, an oak wardrobe and a dresser with all the linens they needed for their beds, as well as a towel and washcloth. "Sarah Beth, I could live here forever!"

"You can, as long as you do your job right and don't get married," Sarah Beth said.

Minnie was well aware of the rule against maids being married, but she wasn't worried about violating that rule.

"Married? Hah! Why would I want to do something like that?"

Sarah Beth laughed. "I can't think of a good reason, much less anyone who would offer a house this nice."

"Let's go look at the bathroom," Minnie's eagerness was shared by the other new maids who had never seen an indoor bathroom before. They gathered at the open doorway gaping at the shining, white-tiled room before taking tentative steps inside.

Pauline walked to the sink and turned one of the two white handles in the shape of daisies. When water came out, she jumped back. She looked with amazement at the others. "You don't even have to pump it."

Each of the girls ran over to feel the water. "What happens when you turn the other handle?" Alma said.

Minnie turned it and soon, the water got warm. "Hot water! Oh look, it says 'hot' in the middle of the knob, and the other one says 'cold.'" She couldn't wait to tell Granny about how she didn't even have to put a pot on the stove to get hot water.

The girls all giggled as Ruby went to the tub and turned the spigot there. Water gushed out and the girls screamed in delight.

"Oh my, I've died and gone to heaven," Grace said, a feeling they all shared.

None of them had houses with running water and electricity. In fact, they didn't even know anyone who did. The Biltmore House was unique, and almost too good to be true, like a castle in a fairy tale. Minnie knew, like the other girls, how fortunate it was to get such a job. Now that Pappy couldn't work anymore because of his bad back, the weight of responsibility to provide for her family rested on her shoulders. Minnie looked forward to sharing her good fortune with Granny and Pappy who'd taken care of her and Sissy since their parents died.

"We better hurry to meet Mrs. King," Sarah Beth said.

Minnie nodded and they rushed back to their room. Minnie put her extra pair of undies and nightclothes in the dresser and hung her dress in the shared wardrobe. She'd heard that Mrs. Vanderbilt had a room full of shelves for her fancy clothes and how her personal lady's maid had to be available everyday all day for whatever their mistress needed. Some of the other girls wanted to be lady's maids someday, but Minnie was content to be just a maid, something less demanding and something she couldn't mess up. How horrible to think she might scorch one of those exquisite dresses while ironing it!

After putting her things away, Minnie stood hands on hip and surveyed the room. It was about the same size as Granny's parlor, which also had the dining table in it. It almost didn't seem fair for her to have so much space for herself.

Sarah Beth put a small, framed picture on top of her dresser, standing back to admire it.

"Henry's going to keep an eye on us," she said.

Minnie wasn't too fond of knowing Sarah Beth's betrothed would be watching them, but couldn't begrudge her friend's photo, especially since Henry had gone out West to dig for gold. He'd been gone a year already, and Sarah Beth was probably the only person who thought he'd ever come back. Of course, if he did and they got married, Sarah Beth would have to leave Biltmore House.

Minnie didn't have a picture to put in the room, but she had a piece of a quilt her mama had made years ago when Minnie was little. That was all she had left from Mama, so she kept it on her bed like it was tucking her in at night the way Mama had.

"Come on, Minnie. Let's get downstairs."

Walking out, they closed the door behind them. As they climbed down the backstairs to the basement, they were joined by other servants, men and women, on their way down. At the bottom, Minnie followed the group to an assembly of about thirty servants.

Standing in front of the group, Mrs. King checked the time on the watch hanging from her chatelaine where multiple keys hung as well. Clearing her throat, she spoke up.

"Welcome ladies and gentlemen. I want to introduce you to our newest staff members. Please step forward, ladies."

Minnie felt like a crow in a flock of ducks as she stepped away from the wall. She was glad to have Sarah Beth's company, so she didn't have to stand out so much. Mrs. King introduced them to the others by name. Then the matron introduced the other female staff, including the parlor maids, and Mrs. Vanderbilt's French lady's maid, Mrs. Delacroix. She was the only person not in uniform, but in a fashionable blouse and skirt, a special privilege of her status. A tall man with gray hair at his temples and dressed in a formal suit, stepped forward and spoke in a fancy English accent, introducing himself as the head butler, Mr. Harvey. He then introduced the men who were hall boys, footmen, and underbutlers. He also introduced the head cook and her staff.

When the introductions were done, all but the new maids were dismissed.

"Ladies, as you can see, it takes a lot of people to maintain such a large place as the Biltmore House. With over 250 rooms on six levels, including 35 bedrooms and 43 bathrooms, there is much work to do. Our household staff consists of forty employees, while another 150 employees are gardeners, stable workers, and other workers. Consequently, Mr. and Mrs. Vanderbilt have very high standards and expectations. I expect you to become familiar with them."

Mrs. King continued. "You are expected to be at breakfast promptly at five o'clock in the morning and you will work eight to twelve hours, depending on whether the Vanderbilts are hosting guests. You will have two hours off each day and half a day on Sundays."

"Mr. Vanderbilt has one cardinal rule: the servants are not to be seen, so we must choose the best time for cleaning each area of the house. You will use the backstairs only the rest of the time."

Minnie considered what Mrs. King said. Not be seen? How could they do their work and not be seen? She pictured the servants like mice running around behind the walls. But if that's what was required of her, she'd gladly be a mouse so she could keep her job.

Chapter Two

After their introduction, Mr. Harvey started the tour of the Biltmore House in the basement. Minnie's head spun with the enormity of it all. A butler's pantry with a ladder to reach all the china in the two-story room. A dumbwaiter to transfer food upstairs to the dining room. A room for laundry and a room for ironing. An indoor watering hole, which Mr. Harvey called a swimming pool. Something called a bowling alley. While in awe of the extravagance of the Vanderbilts, Minnie preferred the simplicity of the tiny cabin in the mountains that she shared with Granny, Pappy, and Sissy

When they finished touring the basement, Mr. Harvey took them up the stairs to the first-floor landing where Mrs. King waited to conduct the next part of the tour. "Mr. and Mrs. Vanderbilt have gone out for the day, so now I will show you the rest of the house. You must know when they are otherwise engaged so you will be able to clear and polish everything while staying out of their sight. Sometimes that means getting up very early in the morning before they do."

Minnie was no stranger to getting up early. She often rose before the sun came up to do chores at home, gather eggs from the hen house and feed the other animals.

The tour upstairs was where the Vanderbilts lived and entertained guests, overwhelming in size and splendor. An atrium with a glass domed ceiling and exotic plants. A gentlemen's room with two billiard tables and walls adorned with hunting trophies. A banquet hall with tapestries, a pipe organ and a dining table with thirty-eight chairs. An elevator to take the guests upstairs. A Tapestry Room with a whole wall of ancient tapestries, velvet-upholstered furniture, family portraits and a grand piano.

"All of these items have to be dusted daily and the wood polished. I personally check to make sure it is all done adequately." Mrs. King said as they ogled the room. "There are thousands of items in the Vanderbilt collection, items from all over the world."

The responsibility was beginning to weigh on Minnie's shoulders. Would she be able to do her job sufficiently? What if she knocked something over and broke it? Terror grabbed her heart, and she barely registered the view of Mt. Pisgah, the highest peak in the mountains, as Mrs. King opened the doors to the terrace lined with a row of rocking chairs.

But all of Minnie's concerns faded when they entered the next room. An enormous room filled with books. "This is the Vanderbilts' personal library," Mrs. King said.

Minnie's mouth dropped open as she tried to take in the panorama of books surrounding her. A tremor of excitement coursed through her at the sight of more books than she'd ever seen in her whole life. The room had two stories of books, with a gorgeous, carved, spiral staircase leading to the second level. A massive fireplace centered one wall with the upper level walkway on either side of it which continued around the room. Oh, how she wanted to get a closer look at the books and see what the titles were.

Mrs. King pointed to the wall beside the fireplace above them. "There is a concealed door up there. Mr. Vanderbilt wanted his guests to feel free to come to the library if they felt like reading at night.

That way, they could access the library without walking through the main floor of the house.

"I know you're wondering. There are 20,000 books in Mr. Vanderbilt's library. He is an avid reader and collector. Mrs. Vanderbilt loves to read as well, and they encourage their staff to read when they have time."

"Do you mean we can read these books?" Minnie couldn't help but ask.

Mrs. King nodded. "Yes, if you have time. But you may be too tired when you're finished with your chores. However, if you do remove a book, you must be very careful to take care of it and return it to its proper place. And there are certain books, first editions, that Mr. Vanderbilt does not want touched. Those are over there." She pointed to one section.

Not have time? Minnie would rather read than sleep. She couldn't wait to see what stories this room contained waiting for her to read. Tonight, when everyone else was in bed, she'd come in here and find a book to borrow. Oh, but which one? There were so many to choose from!

Minnie would work her hardest, be the best maid she could be, if only to be able to visit this room and read these volumes. A smile pulled at her mouth. Yes, she was going to enjoy working in the Biltmore House.

After the house tour, Minnie was paired up with Louisa, who'd been hired by the Vanderbilts when they were in England. She told Minnie her previous employers had been the Lord and Lady Devonshire.

Minnie listened hard when Louisa spoke, trying to understand her rich British accent.

"We'll begin cleaning in the Tapestry room. It is the longest room in the house." Louise said early the next morning. "Mr. and Mrs. Vanderbilt are still sleeping. When they awake and dress, they go to breakfast in the breakfast room, so we have a couple of hours to clean before they enter the main house."

The two of them carried housemaid boxes which contained their cleaning supplies—polish of linseed oil, vinegar, turpentine and wine, plus cleaning cloths. When they reached the ornate room, Louisa showed her how to polish the furniture correctly. "Be sure to rub the rims and legs of the tables with vigor." She demonstrated on a nearby table. "Also, you must rub the backs and legs of the sofas and chairs." Louisa motioned to the area behind her. "You start on those."

Minnie rubbed the polish on every area of wood that was visible until the furniture shined. She glanced with yearning toward the door at the end of the room, the entrance to the library. "Will we be cleaning in the library as well?"

Louisa nodded. "Yes, we will go in there next. With so much woodwork in there, it'll take over an hour for us to polish it. Perhaps it will take less time with the two of us though."

Minnie worked hard and fast to speed up their entry into the next room. When Louisa finally stood and surveyed their work, it was time to go to the library. Excitement bubbled inside Minnie at the prospect of being near so many books. She went straight to the bookshelves and set to work, trying to read every title she could.

"Don't dawdle," Louisa said.

"Have you read any of these books?" Minnie asked, afraid Louisa would know how much she wanted to linger in the room.

"Yes, I've read a few."

"Which ones have you read?"

"I like books by Jane Austen. I've read *Pride and Prejudice, Sense and Sensibility*, and *Emma*."

"Those books are here?" Minnie glanced around.

"They are. I can show you where to find them after we finish cleaning."

Minnie suppressed a sigh. Looking around the room at all the wood in the furniture, shelves, ladders and walls, the task seemed enormous. Would they even finish today?

"Do we clean this room every day?" How could the room get that dusty so soon?

"No, every other day, unless guests are expected, then we're required to do an extra cleaning."

She could hear Granny's voice in her head telling her to look at the bright side and count her blessings while she worked, even when the chore was hard or dull. Minnie started saying thank you in her head for every object in the room, every book, every piece of furniture. She thanked God for the job, for the chance to learn more, read more and help her family. Minnie rubbed until her hands hurt. Mrs. King appeared in the doorway. "Finish up in here, ladies. Mr. Vanderbilt may be in here soon. They are on the first floor, so I suggest you leave by the upstairs door."

Panic seized her at the thought of running into Mr. Vanderbilt in person, the owner of this mansion and the man who didn't want to see the servants.

"Yes, ma'am," Louisa said.

She grabbed her things and made her way toward the spiral staircase leading to the second floor of the library.

"Louisa, could you please show me quickly where those books are you told me about?"

Louisa glanced around, then strode to a shelf and pulled out a book. She handed it to Minnie as she headed back to the staircase. "Make haste."

Minnie gathered her cleaning things and put them back into the box, then clutched the book and box to her chest as she hurried to follow Louisa. When they reached the second floor, they walked to the fireplace where Louisa pushed open a door hidden by the paneling and stepped behind the fireplace. From there, they found another door which opened into the second-floor hallway. They hurried down the hall, then found another hidden door that led to the backstairs area.

Louisa stopped and took a breath. "We never know for sure where they'll show up, so we have to be ready. Mrs. Vanderbilt is more tolerant if she sees us than he is."

"He dislikes servants that much?"

"Oh no. He's just used to things a certain way and each person has his or her place. He's actually a generous man, but he does like his privacy."

Minnie wondered if she'd ever see the man in person. But she could understand wanting privacy. If she were in his shoes, she'd tuck away somewhere nobody would bother her so she could read by herself.

"Go ahead and put your things away. It's getting close to lunchtime."

"Yes, ma'am," Minnie said.

"I am not your mistress, Minnie. Just a parlor maid like yourself, so you don't have to call me ma'am."

"I'm sorry, but that's the way my Granny raised me, to show respect."

Louisa laid her hand on Minnie's arm. "I appreciate your respect. You can show it by doing what I say. Is that understood? In the meantime, just call me Louisa."

"Yes, m…yes, Louisa."

Louisa smiled. "You'll do just fine. Just don't let yourself get lost in the library and neglect your chores. I think if you had the chance, you would."

Minnie's face warmed and she smiled. "You are probably right about that. But I can't think of a better place to get lost."

At lunchtime, Minnie sat alongside the table with the other maids across from the footmen and underbutlers while young servant girls known as tweenies rushed to put food in front of them. She tried to avoid staring at the men across from her, but listened to their conversations. The sensation of being watched made her look up from her food, and she found the footman named Jack gazing at her from down the table. When their gazes met, he grinned, and she quickly looked back down. Did he wink at her? It was suddenly very hot in the room. She grabbed her glass of milk to take a sip and cool off, thankful for the refrigeration of the Vanderbilts' coolers.

Jack's handsome image stayed in her mind, even though she wasn't looking at him anymore. Why did he have to look at her? There were plenty of other maids to look at. Another man said something at the end of the table, and the men started laughing. "Harold, you behave yourself," the maid named Mary said.

Minnie frowned and looked at Sarah Beth with raised eyebrows.

"Harold is Mary's brother," her friend said.

That explained the familiarity. Some of the other maids who had been there longer also conversed with the men, but Minnie had no intention of doing so. She planned to keep her distance from them, whether she was considered unfriendly or not.

Mr. Harvey stepped into the room, clearing his throat. Silence followed as talking stopped, as well as eating. Heads turned toward the head butler, giving him their full attention.

"Ladies and gentlemen, I have an important announcement for you. Mr. and Mrs. Vanderbilt will be entertaining guests for a week or so. They will be arriving in two days, so we must make sure everything is ready for them. Jack, one of the gentlemen, Mr. Bardwell, is not bringing a valet, so I'm appointing you to serve in that position while he is here."

Minnie felt a shift in the room as the staff exchanged looks spanning from excitement to nervousness at the anticipation of guests.

When Mr. Harvey left, Mrs. King addressed the maids. "We must work quickly, and that which is normally cleaned every other day will be cleaned today and tomorrow to ensure everything is perfectly prepared. I will be assigning the rooms to the guests after I meet with Mr. Harvey. Those rooms will get special attention. And there will be no time off until after the guests leave."

The servants looked at each other conveying their understanding of the demands. "Does that mean we won't have Sunday afternoon off while they're here?" Minnie asked. She had been looking forward to telling Granny, Pappy and Sissy all about her new job. Besides being disappointed to not see them, they'd be even more disappointed if they couldn't see her, since she'd never lived out of their house before.

"Probably not," Mrs. King said. "It will depend on the guests' plans."

A bell on the wall annunciator rang, and Mr. Harvey stepped to the door. "It's Mrs. Vanderbilt."

Mrs. King nodded. "It's time for me to discuss the menu with her." Glancing at the staff, she said, "You have your assignments." And then she hurried out the door.

For the next twenty-four hours, the house buzzed with activity. It seemed that the servants had doubled, as two or three could be seen in every room cleaning floors and polishing wood, metal and glass. The parlor maids worked alongside the footmen to make sure each room of the house was shining. Eventually, word got around about the guests that were coming.

The two couples were friends of the Vanderbilts from New York. One of the couples was Mrs. Vanderbilt's sister Natalie and her husband, Mr. John Brown. The other couple was the Duke and Duchess of Marlborough, the duchess being Mr. Vanderbilt's niece Consuelo. The unmarried man was Mr. Stanton Bardwell, a friend of the Vanderbilts. The unmarred woman was Miss Octavia Sloane, also a niece of Mr. Vanderbilt. Apparently, the Vanderbilts were playing matchmakers by inviting the two unmarried guests, hoping their friendship would blossom into something more.

The level of excitement and anticipation in the house created an air of tangible energy. Minnie was reminded of one of Granny's sayings about everyone running around like a stirred-up ant hill. Dinner was eaten in a hurry, and the staff spoke only briefly to each other until bedtime. Minnie had looked forward to reading *Sense and Sensibility*, the book from the library, after Sarah Beth went to sleep. But when she lay down that night and opened the book, her eyes wouldn't stay open. She was too tired. When had she ever been too tired to read? Maybe if she rested just a few minutes, she'd be able to complete a few chapters. Her eyes closed and the next thing she heard was a knock on the door telling her it was time to get up and start a new day again.

Chapter Three

Stanton Bardwell watched the scenery pass by the window of his private train car as he headed toward George Vanderbilt's new mansion in the south. He admired the vista of the mountains, some even with a bluish tint, in this part of the country. So these must be the so-called Blue Ridge Mountains. Why George had built a place so far from all their friends in the north, he didn't know, but if the view from the house was anything like what Stanton was seeing, perhaps that was the reason.

George had always been a little different, rather quiet and aloof to most people. But he and Stanton had met in college, and they shared their love of books. He had threatened to put George in one of his books, but George didn't care, as long as it wasn't a biography. "Just make me the hero who rescues the damsel in distress," he said.

But Stanton didn't write novels. He wrote poetry and essays which they both liked to read and discuss. They understood each other, each preferring quiet and solitude over parties and society. Stanton had been surprised when his friend George met and married Edith, expecting George to remain single. Yet, when Stanton met Edith, he saw that she, too, shared the enjoyment of literature. On some of their trips abroad, Stanton, George and Edith spent many an hour discussing books. Stanton counted Edith one of his friends now as well.

And that was why he was on this train. He had not yet visited their grand home, the one that was the talk of everyone in society, the largest house in the country. He chuckled. Good ole George, never the proud one, had outdone them all with his purchase of thousands of acres in North Carolina of all places, and his new American castle. Stanton had long promised George and Edith a visit, so here he was keeping his promise.

They'd also invited two other couples he knew, but George and Edith, the latter more likely, had thrown in an unexpected addition to his plans as well. Under the guise of keeping things balanced, they'd invited a woman, Octavia Sloane, no doubt expecting him to spend time with her. He had met her previously at parties in Newport, but there had been no attraction, at least on his part. She was George's niece, wealthy as well, but as yet unmarried. So now he'd have to be cordial. But anything more was not in his plans.

He was working on another book, one his publisher was waiting for, and he'd hoped this trip would inspire him. If he wanted to write, he'd have to spend time alone, which meant he wouldn't be very sociable. But he'd try. From what George told him about his vast library, Stanton planned to spend time exploring the room, whether reading or writing. George had told him there was even a secret door from the hallway to the library so he could go there without seeing other people, especially if he went at night. For that reason,

Stanton had asked for a room as close as possible to the library. He didn't know if Miss Sloane read or not and didn't really care. He was quite content to spend time with only a book to keep him company.

The sound of horses and carriages rolling down the driveway came through the open windows of the house, alerting the staff to the arrival of their special guests. Waiting in the servants' parlor, the maids hurried to peek out the windows overlooking the front of the house, hoping to spot the esteemed visitors without being seen themselves. Minnie stood on her tiptoes, looking between Sarah Beth and Pauline to see the guests. "Oohs" and "Aahs" whispered among the servants as glimpses were caught. Those who couldn't see were given descriptions by those who had a good view.

"That must be the duke and duchess," Pauline said, who, being the tallest, had the best view. "My, I've never seen such finery. She's wearing a white dress with a broad hat with something like feathers all over both of them. I think she'll fly away."

Snickers followed, then "shushes."

"Look at that top hat. Wonder how tall he is without the hat?" Ruby said.

"Probably half as tall as he is with the hat," Pauline said, and they all giggled.

That carriage moved away, then another one stopped. "So that's the other couple. They are dressed just as fine as the duke and duchess. The lady is wearing a blue dress with a stole. Lots of critters died to make that one," Pauline said.

When the next carriage stopped, she said, "The unmarried lady is here, Miss Octavia Stone. I can't see her face for the enormous hat, but her dress is a gorgeous shade of purple."

"And finally, the unmarried man, Mr. Bardwell, arrives." She stepped back. "Oh! He looked up. I wonder if he saw us?"

Minnie caught a glimpse of the gentleman when he gazed up at the house and was certain their gazes had met. She uttered a small gasp. She had never seen a man so attractive.

"Well, what did he look like?" Grace asked.

"From what I could see, he's a handsome one," Pauline said. "I wonder if he and Miss Stone will get on well?"

How could they not? Minnie could only imagine what Miss Stone would feel like being the center of the man's attention.

As the guests alighted from their carriages, they were greeted by Mr. and Mrs. Vanderbilt who stood in front of the main entrance. Then they all disappeared from view as they went inside.

Two more carriages arrived but went toward the stables instead of stopping.

"The valets and lady's maids are in those, along with their luggage," Louise said, the more experienced member of the maid staff. "That's everyone now."

The maids ran to their hallway, then ventured out on the back balcony to watch the carriages arrive behind the house near the stables. Each carriage stopped at the bottom of the servant stairs where the footmen unloaded the guests' steamer trunks from the carriage and then loaded them into the servants' elevator. Harold looked up and waved, and the maids waved back.

"Would you look at that? Are they moving in?" Alma said.

"Wonder how long they're staying?" Ruby asked.

Soon, they heard the whirring of the motor of the elevator as the contraption moved up. Because it stopped a floor below the maids' quarters, the maids couldn't see who was on the elevator. But they could hear them talking, as well as the grunts of the men who moved them. Minnie still hadn't learned exactly who did what yet. She just hoped she knew what she was supposed to do.

After the guests were settled in their rooms, they'd meet for afternoon tea. Louisa told Minnie the women would change clothes for tea, since they couldn't wear what they'd traveled in.

"Why not?" Minnie asked.

"It isn't done. How else will they show off their beautiful clothes? That's why they have so many trunks. They change clothes several times a day."

"My word. What a lot of trouble. I'm glad I don't have that many clothes," Minnie said.

"You might not say that if you could see the clothes. They're the finest, the latest styles from Paris," Louisa said. "Plus you don't have someone to help you get dressed."

"Help me get dressed? I haven't needed help with that since I was a very young child."

"Nor were you born in the privileged class as these people are. It's an entirely different world than you're used to."

Minnie was beginning to see that. She was not equal to the Vanderbilts and the people in their circles and never would be. But she didn't care. She was thankful to be employed here, sleep in a nice bed, have running water and good food. And she even got paid for it.

Before long, buttons lit up as the annunciator rang. "What shall we do?" Grace said.

Mrs. King strode in, looked at the board and gave orders to different maids – the chambermaids to the bedrooms, the parlor maids to other areas. Most of them had to gather something for her to take to the lady's maids of the female guests. Some of the other buttons would be answered by the butler's staff downstairs. "Mr. Harvey has met the servants that accompanied the guests and will help them if they need something from the kitchen."

"If I need your help, I'll come get you," she said. "For now, I'll go check on the mistress. Meanwhile, you can rest until they go down for tea at four. Then, get back to the guest rooms to make sure they're in order for the evening."

Minnie watched the matron walk away. "How does she stay so calm with so much going on?" she said to Sarah Beth.

Sarah Beth shook her head. "I don't know, but I don't envy her. Imagine what it's like when there are more guests."

"I don't think I can," Minnie said, glad she didn't have to worry about that. Instead, she could finally spend some time reading *Sense and Sensibility*. Soon she was lost in the world of the Dashwood family in England as they dealt with losing their home when their father died. It seemed that they would be poor unless one of the girls in the family married a rich man. How sad that they didn't have a Granny and Pappy to move in with, like she and Sissy did. And why couldn't the girls find jobs? Because they were rich or used to be and working was for servants? Well, Minnie was proud to be a servant. She certainly didn't need to marry someone just to provide for her. No, sir, she would work for her keep. And her family's too. She read quickly and had covered a third of the book when Mrs. King reappeared in the servants' quarters.

"They are downstairs in the parlor having tea now. Check on the bedrooms to make sure they are in order. Close the curtains and remove anything which appears soiled. You have one hour before your five o'clock supper where you will meet the visiting servants."

Visiting servants? What were they like? Minnie and the other Biltmore maids hurried downstairs to the third-floor guest rooms. They worked with haste, looking for anything that was out of place or needing cleaning. Afterwards, they freshened up and went down to supper. Five additional people waited to be introduced as they exchanged glances with the Biltmore staff, each sizing the others up. Mr. Harvey introduced the three lady's maids first, Mrs. Willingham who waited on the duchess, Mrs. Turnberry, whose mistress was Mrs. Natalie Brown, and Mrs. Parker, Miss Sloane's lady's maid. The lady's maids were all dressed in fine skirts and blouses, unlike the uniforms that the Biltmore maids wore.

The women nodded as their name was called. Minnie found the custom unusual to always address the lady's maids as "Mrs." like Mrs. King, even if they weren't married. In fact, none of the lady's maids were married because once servants got married, they usually lost their position. It stood to reason that only unmarried women would have the freedom to travel with their mistresses and spend as much time with them as they did.

The men were Mr. Bartholomew, the duke's valet, and Mr. Evans who was Mr. Brown's valet. The men also nodded at each other before Mr. Harvey invited them to sit down with the Biltmore staff. Mr. Bartholomew was English and acted aloof. But Mr. Evans was very friendly and attracted the attention of all the maids, except for Mrs. Parker who snubbed the maids and focused her attention on Jack. He lost no time charming her as he was prone to do around women, in Minnie's opinion. All of a sudden, he had risen above the rest of the staff, and frowns between the others relayed their mutual displeasure.

But Mr. Evans had him beat, as he smiled and entertained the other maids. He was very handsome, Minnie had to admit, easy on the eyes as Granny would say. One couldn't help but be drawn into his throng of admirers. Minnie wanted to laugh at the way Jack tried to regain some of the attention as if competing with him, like a rooster who had suddenly been faced with another rooster in the hen yard. Could it be possible that Jack was jealous of the new fellow?

Minnie listened to the conversation, hoping to learn more about the guests. The servants' dinner table was the place information was shared that might otherwise not be known. Granny would call it gossip, but like everyone else, Minnie wanted to hear more about the private lives of the well-to-do visitors. Here, the servants were more free to give their opinions, especially without Mr. Harvey and Mrs. King around, since they took their dinner in their own rooms instead of with the rest of the staff.

Mr. Bartholomew definitely had an air of superiority about him and gave opinions on topics of the day as if he were an expert. The visiting servants were very protective of their employers, trying not to cast dispersions on them. However, they weren't so protective of their employers' associates. Mrs. Parker let it be known that Miss Sloane and Mr. Bardwell had been especially invited so they would be thrown into each other's company as a match which would eventually lead to marriage. These families often played matchmaker and put people together based on title and wealth.

That revelation made Minnie even more certain that she did not wish to be part of the world that people like the Vanderbilts belonged to. If she ever did get married, it would be to someone she truly loved. Did these people ever marry for love? Even though Mr. and Mrs. Vanderbilt seemed to be well suited for each other, enjoying similar pastimes and beliefs, from what Minnie heard, the duke and duchess weren't so well-matched. Mrs. Parker seemed to think that she and Jack would be able to spend more time together, since their employers would be spending time together. Well, good for him. But a glance at Ruby told Minnie she was not in favor of the idea, since Mrs. Parker now claimed the attention he had recently been giving Ruby. In fact, Minnie thought she saw steam coming out of Ruby's ears.

Mr. Harvey stepped back into the room. "Time to prepare to serve dinner to the Vanderbilts and their guests." He sent two underbutlers to the dining room to make sure all the silverware and glasses were placed in the right position. Jack and the other valets excused themselves to go to their masters while the lady's maids left to tend to their mistresses.

"I'll see you upstairs," Mrs. Parker said to Jack with a coy smile.

"Actually, you won't." At her shocked expression, he said, "Mr. Bardwell asked to be put in one of the rooms on the second floor instead of one of the rooms on the third where the other guests are."

"Why would he do that?" she asked.

Jack shrugged. "He said something about liking to be in a quieter area. He's a writer, you know, so maybe he wants to write while he's here."

A writer? Minnie's heart leaped. A real writer who wrote books? What had he written? Were any of his books in the house library? She'd never seen a real writer before and really wanted to get a good look at the man to see what a writer looks like. But how could she without being seen herself? Could she hide in the servants' hall next to the formal dining room and steal a glimpse of him?

As they left the dining area, the servants dispersed to their assigned stations. Minnie didn't envy those who would be carrying food to the guests upstairs, the food that wouldn't go on the dumbwaiter. The kitchen maids would bring them up the stairs to the back hall of the dining room, and the male servants would serve the guests. Minnie didn't understand why, since where she grew up, the women always served the men. However, she wouldn't want to swap places with the male servants.

While the guests were at dinner, she hurried to help tidy the common areas while the chambermaids refreshed the bedrooms and got them ready for the guests to retire later. The mountain air was chilly at night, so they would start fires in the fireplaces and get the rooms warm. Who knew how long the guests would stay downstairs after dinner? They might play games or visit downstairs or perhaps visit upstairs in the third-floor guest sitting area. Minnie heard that the men often retired to the billiards room or smoking room after dinner. So until they all went to bed at night, the maids had to be ready to answer the annunciator bell if summoned.

After she helped prepare the sitting rooms and parlors, she and Sarah Beth went back to their room to wait. Sarah Beth enjoyed knitting to pass the time, but Minnie dove back into her book, not even hearing Sarah Beth while she chatted. Minnie simply had to find out what happened next to the characters in the book. A bell rang, and they hurried to the board. "It's the Louis XV room, where the duke and duchess are staying," Sarah Beth said. Should they answer or let one of the personal servants answer?

Mrs. King walked in and looked at the board. "They've asked for some warm milk, so the kitchen staff will prepare it and deliver it to their lady's maid."

Another bell rang, this time from Miss Sloane's room.

Mrs. King frowned. "I'm afraid Grace isn't feeling well, and that's her assigned room. I'll need to find someone else to cover for her."

"I'll go," Minnie said, curious about the unmarried woman who had her sights set on Mr. Bardwell. She checked her appearance in the mirror, then hurried down the stairs to the Madonna Room and tapped on the door. Mrs. Parker opened it, casting a disdainful glance at Minnie with her deep-set dark eyes, the kind of eyes that looked angry most of the time.

"Did you need something, Mrs. Parker?" Minnie asked, wishing she hadn't volunteered to answer the bell.

"Yes, it's chilly in here. Miss Sloane would like to have a larger fire in the fireplace."

Had Mrs. Parker never stoked a fire before?

"Yes, ma'am." Minnie hurried to the fireplace trying not to look at the other woman in the room. She picked up a couple of pieces of kindling and tossed them on the fire, then stoked it with the iron poker until flames rose. She set the fireplace screen back in place and looked up. "That should warm it up in here," she said, then noticed the curtains slightly open, so she walked over to pull them shut.

"Thank you," said the woman reclining on the bed.

Minnie looked at the woman briefly and smiled as she responded. "You're welcome, ma'am. Have a pleasant evening." She gave a quick curtsy, then went to the door that Mrs. Parker stood beside, her facial expression unchanged. At least her mistress was appreciative.

Hurrying back down the hall, Minnie reflected on Miss Sloane. Although she was dressed in her bed clothes, Minnie noticed how pale her skin was, almost the same color as her thin hair. Had the woman ever spent any time outside? Although women weren't supposed to show skin with sunspots, a little bit of color made one look so much better, even healthier, in her opinion. People she knew that were as pale as Miss Sloane were usually sick. Was Miss Sloane sick? Since she was supposedly at Biltmore to become more familiar with Mr. Bardwell, would she? Was the author interested in her? Maybe the other servants would share more gossip at breakfast.

Chapter Four

Stanton retired to the billiards room with George, the duke and John Brown. The men discussed politics and the economy until the duke and John said good night and left for their bedrooms. George and Stanton had some time to talk privately afterwards.

"So how do you like Octavia?" George said.

Stanton cut him a glance. "She's nice enough, George. Tell me, when did you and Edith become matchmakers?"

George laughed and sank a striped ball in the side pocket. "You know that was Edith's idea. She just wants you to be as happy as we are."

"I'm perfectly happy as I am. Unmarried."

"I used to say the same thing. Before I met Edith. So you're saying you're not attracted to Octavia?"

"Not especially, George. We haven't really talked much. But I wonder why she's so pale? She's either unhealthy or never goes outside. I may be bookish, but I do enjoy the outdoors."

George chuckled. "I assure you, she's healthy. And we'll get her outside tomorrow. I'm escorting all of you on a drive through the property. We'll stop by the French Broad River and have a picnic."

"Do I have to ride in a carriage? I prefer to ride horseback."

"You and I will. Not sure about the duke yet."

"I must say you have an impressive place here, George. You've got this place filled with treasures from all over the world."

George nodded. "It took several years to gather everything. Before I married Edith, Mother and I made several trips to Europe to purchase items."

"I'm sorry to hear about your mother's passing, George. I know you were very close."

"Thank you. Yes, we were, probably closer than she was to my brothers and sisters."

"No doubt because you were the baby of the family." Stanton shot and sank a solid ball into a corner pocket.

George smiled. "Privileged lot, aren't we?"

Stanton smiled, since he and George shared that position in the family.

"I'm really looking forward to spending some time in your library. I hope you don't plan to keep me so busy I can't."

"You know where it is. And with your room just down the hall from the secret door, you can access the library any time we don't have you scheduled for something else. Are you currently working on a book?"

"Yes, I am. Which is another reason I'd like to miss some of the activities if possible."

"There's a desk in the library as well, so you may write in there too."

"I might just do that."

George aimed and sank the final eight ball, and they downed the last sip of port.

"I'm ready to call it a day. Are you?" George said.

"Absolutely. I'll see you at breakfast tomorrow."

As they walked to the main staircase, George said, "How's the valet working out?"

"He's perfectly adequate, thank you."

At the top of the stairs, George said, "This is your floor. Mine's on the third, so I'll leave you here."

"Good night, then." Stanton said and turned down the hall to his room.

Back in her room again, Minnie saw that Sarah Beth was already asleep. But Minnie couldn't go to sleep yet. Not only was her mind still racing, she just had to finish the book first. She removed her uniform and laid it carefully over the back of her rocking chair. After putting on her nightgown, she unpinned her hair and let the long braid uncoil and fall down her back. Sitting in her bed, she turned on her bedside lamp and began reading. Time flew by as she reached the end of the story. She reflected on the way the story had turned out and the picture of English society it had painted, comparing the Vanderbilts. Louisa said there was more than one book by this author, Jane Austen, and now Minnie wanted to read another one.

Why not go get it now? After all, no one in the house was awake but her, and no one would see her go to the library. But what if she were caught? Would she be fired? No, she better not take the chance. However, if she used the backstairs to the second floor, she could slip into one of the unoccupied guest rooms, then come out into the hallway close to the library's secret second floor doorway. Her heart raced with anticipation. Or was it fear? But now she was convinced she could do it.

She pulled on her housecoat, tying it at the waist. Then she grabbed the book she had finished and crept out the door trying not to make a sound. She slipped down the hallway hearing someone snoring in one of the bedrooms. Thank goodness Sarah Beth wasn't a loud snorer. Pappy had wakened her in the night sometimes with his loud snorts. She hurried to the backstairs and went down two flights, grateful the library door was on the floor below the guest rooms so she wouldn't run into any if they were night walkers.

She tried to remember where Louisa had gotten the book, so she could return it to the same spot. Hopefully, another of Jane Austen's books would be in the same area. She found the servant entrance to one of the guest rooms and slipped in, walked through the room and out the door to the hallway. Moonlight shone through the large outside windows of the house giving her enough light to find her way through the dark house. She took a few steps and thought she heard, "Woof." She paused. Cedric. Mr. Vanderbilt's dog. Could he hear her moving around even though she was on the floor below theirs? What if he started barking and woke everyone in the house?

She froze, waiting while her heart pounded. After what seemed like a lifetime, there was no more noise, so she tiptoed to the end of the hallway. Finding the door, she carefully pushed it open and stepped inside, finding herself behind the fireplace on the second floor of the library. Safe. But it was too dark in here for her to find her way. No one would notice if she turned the light on, so she pushed the white button on the wall. The room lit up, revealing the gleaming patina of polished wood.

She mapped out her route to the place where the Jane Austen books were and carefully walked around to the spiral staircase. She took one step down before hearing the sound of a male voice.

"Hello there."

Minnie jumped and almost fell down the staircase. "Oh!" Her hand flew to her throat as she scanned the room for the source of the voice.

A gentleman in a brocade dressing gown stood up from the chair where he had been seated in front of the fireplace.

"I'm so sorry, sir. I didn't mean to disturb you! I didn't know anyone was here." She stepped back and turned to run out of the room.

"Wait. No harm done." He smiled and removed his eyeglasses, and she found herself looking at the handsome man she'd seen from the window when he arrived. His tousled dark hair accented a strong face with high cheekbones and a chiseled chin. "Perhaps I should introduce myself. I'm Stanton Bardwell."

She gulped. The author. Her voice left her.

"And you are …"

"M…Minnie. Minnie Tucker. I'm one of the parlor maids."

She glanced down, realizing she was in her bedclothes, and her hair was down. Her face flamed and she pulled her housecoat tightly around her. Oh my. Not only had she been seen, she'd been seen out of uniform. And he was in his dressing gown. She'd surely get fired. Or die. The latter was more favorable at this moment.

"Nice to meet you, Minnie Tucker. So do you suffer from insomnia too?"

"In… no. Unless I'm reading."

"Ah, so you enjoy reading, do you?"

She nodded. "Yes, sir. Ever since my mama taught my little sister and me to read when we were little girls, I've read everything I can get my hands on."

His lips parted in a warm smile. "Well, we have our love of reading in common. And what do you like to read, Minnie?"

"Anything. We don't have many books at home, so I borrow from anyone who does. We don't have a library in town, so I'd read everything in this room if I had the time."

Mr. Bardwell laughed, dimples in his face giving him the appearance of a happy youngster. "Well, then, Minnie Tucker. I share that feeling. Books are intriguing and comforting, don't you think? And aren't we glad George shares our love of reading?"

"George?"

He chuckled. "George Vanderbilt, the owner of this grand house." He glanced down at the book in her hand. "What is that you're reading now?"

She lifted the book to look, having just forgotten its title. "I just finished this one, *Sense and Sensibility.*"

"A Jane Austen fan. So have you read *Pride and Prejudice* yet?"

She shook her head. "No sir. This is the first book I've read by Jane Austen. I had hoped to get another one tonight when I put this one back."

"I see." He extended his arm and swept the room. "You know, Minnie. I love conversing with you, but my neck is tired of looking up. Would you please come down here so we can talk on the same level?"

She nodded, then hesitated. "Oh, I'm sorry. I'll return the book later." How foolish she was to have a conversation with him while looking down on him and he looking up at her.

"Minnie, please. Come on down and do what you came to do. Do not let me stand in your way."

"I don't mean to impose on your time in here, sir."

"Nonsense. Do return the book now while you're here. I won't tell." His warm smile was so inviting. "This is a wonderful library, and I don't blame you for wanting to enjoy it as I do."

She argued within herself, then nodded and proceeded down the staircase, taking each step gingerly. Trying to avoid his eyes, she glanced around the room when she reached the bottom before heading toward the area where she hoped to find the Austen books. She felt his gaze on her back as if he could see through her clothing. Granny would scold her and tell her how improper it was for a man and a woman to see each other in their bedclothes, especially if they were strangers, not to mention one was a servant and the other a guest of the Biltmore House.

She found *Pride and Prejudice* and slid the other book back on the bookshelf among the rest of the books. She hoped to have the time someday to read all the titles. Turning around, she glanced at him before crossing the room back to the staircase. She wanted to be invisible, to fly through the house like a ghost and disappear from his view. But this wasn't a fairy tale. It was an uncomfortable, terrible predicament to be in.

As she neared him, he stepped toward her, blocking her path. Her breath caught. He smiled, and his eyes twinkled as he fixed his gaze on hers, and she was undone.

"Minnie Tucker, please do not be afraid of me. I know you did not expect to find me here, so pretend you didn't, if it helps you feel better." He placed his hand on her arm and fire shot up to her shoulder. His warm brown eyes penetrated her to the core. "I do wish we could be friends and discuss books, but I understand how improbable that desire is. So, I'll say good night instead. I hope you enjoy your book."

She sighed and nodded, looking down at his hand on her arm.

"Yes, sir. I will, sir."

He stepped aside and she continued to the staircase, pausing at the bottom to turn around and look at him.

"You are an author, aren't you?"

"I am."

"I'd like to read what you write someday."

He smiled. "I'd love for you to."

She nodded and continued up the staircase. As she made her way back around to the secret door, he called out.

"Minnie?"

She looked down at him.

"Yes?"

"If you'd like to visit a little longer sometime when you can't sleep, you know where to find me." His smile this time was imploring, making her want to agree. "Perhaps I could even read some of my poetry to you."

Her face flamed and she couldn't get out of the room fast enough. Leaving through the secret door, she ran back to the guest room she'd come through and entered the servants' area, running back up the stairs to the fourth floor and back to her room. Sarah Beth was still sound asleep. Minnie pulled off her housecoat, then plopped down on her bed, lying on her back and staring at the ceiling. How could she go to sleep now? She lifted the new book, then dropped it back on the table. She couldn't even focus on reading now.

No, it didn't matter whether she closed her eyes or not, she couldn't shake the image of Stanton Bardwell from her mind. They were worlds apart but walking away from him left her with a yearning to see him again. They had only met briefly, yet the meeting felt intimate. How foolish she was. That a man like him would want to be friends with someone so far below himself was unthinkable. Improbable.

She wouldn't see him again. She'd make sure of it. Pale Miss Sloane's face came to her mind. She was the reason he was here, not to become friends with a lowly parlor maid. And she didn't dare tell Sarah Beth, much as she wanted to. She had to keep this accidental meeting secret and hoped Mr. Bardwell would too.

Chapter Five

Stanton mounted his horse and waited for George to mount his while the ladies were helped into an open carriage. He nodded and tipped his riding hat to Miss Sloane who looked his way and smiled, but he had other things on his mind.

"Stanton, are you ready?" George drew his horse alongside.

"Of course. Lead on."

George urged his horse in front of the others, and Stanton followed. The cool crisp mountain air refreshed his senses, helping to awaken him after his lack of sleep the night before. He gazed at the lush greenery, inhaling the scent of fir trees around them, as they followed the road George had had built through his property, taking advantage of the best views of the mountains.

"Stanton, can you hear me?"

Stanton jerked his head, abruptly noticing that George had stopped.

"I'm sorry, what did you say?"

George shook his head. "Crafting some entertaining prose, are you?"

Stanton frowned. "What do you mean?"

"You're so lost in thought, I was certain your creativity is spinning."

Stanton forced a chuckle. "Caught me."

George waved his arm out towards the expansive view. "No doubt you are being inspired by this gorgeous view. I do not blame you for that."

Stanton smiled and nodded. If George wanted to believe that was the case, so be it. His friend couldn't possibly know his mind was preoccupied by one beautiful parlor maid. George would not be pleased to know she and he had conversed. Alone. In the library and in their bedclothes, nonetheless. He chuckled again, this time recalling the unusual circumstances they had found themselves in. They hadn't talked very much, but he could tell Minnie Tucker had a bright mind. Add to that characteristic her flawless natural beauty — her hair the color of spun gold falling down her back, her eyes the color of a robin's egg.

Strength and character shone from those eyes and a determination to keep her principles. As she should. As he should. Why was he so drawn to her? Even though she was a servant, he wanted to know her better. However, he respected her wish to observe the rules of propriety. Still, her natural loveliness and pure honesty intrigued him in a way he'd never experienced before, inspiring him to write a poem about her. And then read it to her. If only he'd have the chance.

Behind him, he heard giggling. His reverie broken, he glanced at the women in the carriage. He smiled at them. "Ladies, what is it that amuses you so?"

"We were charmed by your serious expression as if you were miles away from here."

"A penny for your thoughts?" Miss Sloane said, giggling as if she had invented the worn phrase.

"How about a pound for your thoughts?" the foppish duke said laughing, as he pulled his horse up beside the carriage. "Aren't your thoughts worth more than a penny?"

Stanton couldn't help but notice the disdainful look Consuelo, the duchess, gave her husband. In fact, he had noticed the two shared a mutual dislike at other times too. Marital bliss did not appear to exist between them. But from what he understood, their marriage was one of convenience. Her parents had wanted her to marry the duke, so she had the fortune while he had the title. Rumor was that he needed her money to renovate his Blenheim Palace in England. Such marital arrangements were fairly common, but Stanton would never consider such a marriage. Thankfully, his inheritance was sufficient, even if his writing didn't provide wealth. And he'd rather live alone than with an unloving wife.

His thoughts returned to Minnie Tucker and their brief encounter in the library. George would scoff at his attraction, adamant about the separation of the servants from the upper class. But Stanton couldn't think of Minnie as lower-class. Didn't God make everyone equal? There once was a day when men thought they were superior to women, but wealth and title changed that idea for most men, especially when the woman had the title or the money or both.

"Well, which is it?" Miss Sloane said, smiling coyly as she held a lace parasol to shield her skin from the sun.

"Hmm?" Stanton pulled himself back into the current situation. He forced a laugh. "I'm afraid my thoughts aren't worth much at all. You may check with my publisher on that, though."

The rest of the party laughed along with him. He turned to George. "This is lovely countryside, George. I'm thoroughly enjoying the fresh air."

"Just imagine what it'll look like when all these new trees mature." George pointed to a hillside planted with young trees. "Unfortunately, the land was a mess due to haphazard logging, so we're trying to restore it to the way it should look naturally."

"You're referring to Olmstead, I assume?" Stanton was aware of the renown landscape architect George had hired to design the property.

"Yes, Fred believes in scientific forestry, a practice used in Europe. It's a method of managing the forests to improve its health and sustainability."

"That'll take some time, you know. And this is a bit larger than Central Park." Stanton referred to Olmstead's design in New York. "How many acres do you own here?"

"125,000."

Stanton gave a low whistle. "George, you practically own the whole state, don't you?"

"Not quite. But I'm definitely going to make sure it's all managed properly. We've even started a forestry school to teach others how to take care of the forests."

"Impressive. And Fred manages those? How's his health?"

George shook his head as they continued to trot along the new road. "No, Fred is a bit too old for camping. I have another man in charge of the school."

The party stopped on a stone bridge to enjoy the view of water rushing under.

"I recognize Fred's work," Stanton said, referring to the bridge.

"Yes, we have quite a few of these, very similar to the ones in Central Park."

The view from the bridge revealed the mountain range that bordered the property. "Those are the Blue Ridge Mountains, is that right?"

George nodded. "They do look blue in the shaded areas, don't they?"

"Oh, they are blue!" Miss Sloane said. "Are those trees blue?"

Edith Vanderbilt spoke up. "Not all of them. But there are some blue spruce which are blueish in color."

"How pretty!" Miss Sloane said. "Don't you think so, Mr. Bardwell?"

"Ah, yes. Yes, of course." What else was he supposed to say? Discuss the color blue?

"Well, George, I said I'd never return to the States, but I had to see this grand estate of yours. I'm glad I did. Someday, it may rival Blenheim!" The duke chuckled about his demeaning compliment comparing the Biltmore property to the centuries-old estate in England.

"And it won't take hundreds of years that Blenheim has existed either, I'm sure," Stanton said to counter the comment the duke asserted.

The consummate gentleman, George stayed silent. After admiring the view for a while, he motioned to the water beneath the bridge. "This is the French Broad River. It runs all through the property. And just a little ways further is a good spot alongside it for a picnic."

"Then let's make haste," the duke said, spurring his horse to trot faster. "I'm rather famished, aren't you all?"

"Chef has prepared an excellent picnic for us," Edith said. "I'm sure you'll be pleased."

They continued on around the bend, then George pointed to a place in the shade near the water. "Over there."

The footmen drew the carriage horses to a halt, then removed a stepstool from the rear of the carriage and placed it so the ladies could step down on it as they were helped out of the carriage. While one footman was helping the ladies, the other one was carrying supplies to the shaded area. Once there, he spread out gingham tablecloths on the ground. The other footman arrived carrying boxes and baskets which he began to arrange on the tablecloth while the first footman ran back to retrieve more baskets to supply the meal.

Silver, china, crystal and linen napkins were set out as if the occasion was a formal one. The baskets were placed strategically within arm's reach of the dinnerware.

"Please have a seat," George said, motioning to the spread. The women sat near each other, to Stanton's pleasure, and the men sat on the other side of the tablecloth. At every other meal, he was seated next to Miss Sloane, forcing him to make conversation with her.

Wine bottles were opened, and the glasses filled.

"Toast!" Stanton said, lifting a glass. "To George and Edith and their fabulous estate. May they continue to be blessed with such good fortune."

"Here, here," John Brown said, lifting his glass as well.

They all nodded and took a sip.

"George, I'm surprised you don't have a winery here," the duke said.

"Perhaps one day I will. Right now, we're focused on getting our dairy up and running."

"This is a lovely spot," the duchess said. "What a good choice for a picnic."

Everyone agreed as the baskets were passed around, and each person retrieved a portion of the contents. "Your chef is superb," Natalie Brown said. "This food is delicious!"

Stanton took a bite of a ham and cheese roll and nodded.

"Mr. Bardwell, doesn't this scenery evoke some prose?" the duchess said.

He swallowed and wiped his mouth with the napkin. "It does indeed."

"Please tell us some," Miss Sloane implored.

"Do you have a favorite author you like to read? A favorite piece?" he said. "Perhaps I can remember it."

Miss Sloane glanced around and blushed. "I don't really like to read, but I do like being read to."

"Would you say Mr. Bardwell is your favorite author?" the duke said, chuckling.

Miss Sloane's face turned crimson, and Stanton was more embarrassed for her than for himself. The duke was tactless and brash, and Stanton could see why the duchess might look askance. The man had put Miss Sloane in an uncomfortable position, and he doubted she had read anything he had written.

"I have one. From Keats. *'The poetry of earth is never dead,*" George said.

"That's an excellent line," Edith said, smiling. "*A thing of beauty is a joy forever,*" she quoted another of Keats' famous lines.

"I have one," John Brown said. "*Nothing ever becomes real 'til it is experienced.*"

"Stanton, surely you know one of Keats' lines." George urged his friend on.

"All right. *Beauty is truth and truth is beauty.*"

George nodded. "That's a good one."

"This is my favorite Keats' line," Natalie Brown said. "*Touch has a memory.*"

Immediately, Stanton's mind traveled to the evening before, and how he had touched Minnie on the arm. She had jumped in surprise. Perhaps he had been too forward, but he couldn't help himself. Would she remember his touch as he did?

"Anyone else?" George said, looking around the group.

"Here's another," Stanton said. "*If poetry comes not as naturally as the leaves to a tree, it had better not come at all.*"

Everyone laughed, nodding. "So you're saying your poetry is not coming naturally, Stanton?" George said.

"Right now, I'd say that's the case. Perhaps when we return to the house, and I have a few minutes to reflect on the day, the poetry will flow."

George removed his watch piece from his vest and looked at it. "We should be heading back now. The ladies might like to freshen up and play a game of bridge before tea. Which of you gentlemen will take me in a game of chess?"

"Is it true your chess set once belonged to Napoleon?" the duke asked.

George nodded. "That is true. It is an ivory set he played with when he was exiled on the island of St. Helena."

"Do tell. How did you acquire such a set?"

With a confident smile, George said. "Mother and I have been scouring the world for years looking for special pieces for this house. A collector in France possessed it until we paid him to part with it."

"That might make a nice addition to Blenheim," the duke said.

"It might," George said, "If I were willing to part with it."

The duke laughed at George's comment, but Stanton knew the truth. All of the money the duke acquired from his wife's dowry was being used to restore the duke's English palace to its former splendor, and Stanton highly doubted he could afford such treasures as Napoleon's chess set.

The footmen hurried to collect the picnic things and put them into the boot of the carriage as the men helped the women up from their seats on the tablecloth. Stanton extended a hand to Miss Sloane as well, seeing it was the gentlemanly thing to do, not to mention the other men helped their wives. She batted her eyelashes at him and smiled as if he'd done something special for her. How could he be cordial without conveying to her any interest in pursuing their relationship further? But he'd do what was expected as long as he was here, just to please George and Edith, nothing more. And after this time at the Biltmore, he wouldn't have to see Miss Sloane anymore.

Chapter Six

Minnie rushed around to get all the cleaning done and bedrooms in order while the Vanderbilts and their guests were out that day. She kept her hands busy, but she couldn't control her thoughts. What was Mr. Bardwell doing? Was he enjoying his time with Miss Sloane? Had she dreamed their encounter in the library? Surely, it couldn't have been real.

"Ladies, all is ready for our guests to return." Mrs. King surveyed the maids. "You may go to your rooms or the servants' parlor and rest until further notice."

Minnie couldn't wait to read the new book she'd gotten. She hadn't even opened it yet, she'd been so tired and distracted about last night. As she headed up the backstairs to her room, she ran into Jack and some of the other staff. She glanced away, but he stopped and grabbed her arm.

"Minnie, we're going up on the roof. Wouldn't you like to go too?"

No, she didn't want to go, but Ruby and Grace implored. "Come on, Minnie. Don't you want to see what it's like to be on top of the world?" Ruby said.

"Yes, for once we can look down on the guests when they return instead of them looking down on us," one of the male servants joked.

"Aw, come on, Minnie. You can't work all the time!" Ruby said.

Minnie let herself be swept up the stairs with the others, her curiosity overcoming her desire to go back to her room and read. As they stepped out into the fresh air onto the concrete room, she gazed wide-eyed around her. From one side of the room to the other, they ran to see the surrounding property from above. The atmosphere was other-worldly, a place invisible from below. Looking across to the peak of Mt. Pisgah, Minnie imagined herself being the same height.

The mountain people believed God walked on the mountaintops and from there could see everyone below. That's why they were called 'foothills,' Minnie had been told. From this rooftop, she believed she had the same God's eye view. She went to one side and tried to spot the location of Granny and Pappy's, but trees hid their little house from view. Not even their chimney was visible above the treetops. But here on the roof, she walked around the massive chimneys of the Biltmore house.

"You see?" Jack said, as he sidled up to her. "Pretty amazing view, isn't it?"

She nodded, then walked over to where the other maids stood on tiptoe to peer over the ledge. "Look! They're coming back!" Ruby said. "Will they see us?"

"Nah, they won't look up this high. Even if they did, they couldn't see us," Jack said, joining the group.

"Should we go back down?" Alma asked. "We better be ready."

"You won't be needed right away," Jack said. "I'll have to go first to see if Mr. Bardwell needs my assistance."

Minnie wanted so badly to ask about the man he was valeting for, but she couldn't let Jack or the others know she had too much interest in him. But she didn't have to.

"What's he like, Jack? Is he nice?" Ruby asked. Ruby had a tendency to share every thought that entered her mind, but this time it was a thought Minnie shared.

Jack shrugged. "He's all right. Not very demanding, thankfully. I'd hate to be the duke's valet. He can be quite the temperamental one, from what his valet says."

"I'd prefer Mr. Bardwell too," Ruby said. "He's such a handsome man!"

"Ruby!" Grace said, her eyes wide with shock.

"You would, Ruby? I've never heard of a woman being a valet," Jack said with a wink.

Ruby's face matched her hair. "You know what I mean, Jack."

"Look! There they are now," Pauline said, her height giving her an advantage.

Minnie strained to watch the three gentlemen on horseback ride up to the front of the house, with Mr. Vanderbilt's huge dog Cedric loping alongside Mr. Vanderbilt's horse, and the carriage arriving behind. She couldn't help but admire the way Stanton Bardwell sat tall in the saddle, regally, in her opinion. The men waited by the carriage until the footmen helped the women out, one at a time. Minnie watched to see if there was any interaction between Miss Sloane and Mr. Bardwell. From the direction of her head, Miss Sloane did indeed keep her eye on him, however, he was engrossed in conversation with Mr. Vanderbilt and didn't look her way. For some odd reason, Minnie was happy to see the lack of communication between Miss Sloane and Mr. Bardwell. As if she had any right to an opinion about them.

As the ladies stepped toward the front of the house, the men turned their horses toward the stables and trotted away. But Mr. Bardwell paused, glancing up at the house as if looking for something. Minnie stepped back. Could he see them that high up? Then he followed the others, moving out of view.

"Now we really must hurry," Alma said, running to the doorway leading down. Minnie followed along with the others. She had to admit to herself that she'd wanted to see Mr. Stanton Bardwell again, and she had. Keeping her distance from him was the best thing to do, even if she had to fight her heart's desire to do so.

Back in their room, Sarah Beth crossed her arms and studied Minnie.

"What's the matter, Minnie? You're not acting yourself."

Minnie gulped and looked away, tidying her bedcovers which didn't need tidying. "Hmm? Why, I don't know what you mean."

"Minnie, I know you, and you've been acting strangely all day. What happened?"

Oh, how she wanted to confide in her friend. But she just couldn't, knowing the scolding she'd get.

"I didn't get much sleep last night. Stayed up quite late reading." She faked a yawn. "What I really need is a nap."

"Uh huh." Sarah Beth walked over and picked up Minnie's book. "This doesn't look like the same one you were reading yesterday."

She was caught. "Okay, to be honest, I finished the other book last night and went to the library while everyone was asleep to get another one."

"You didn't!"

Minnie nodded. "I did." That was true, but she didn't have to tell her about seeing Stanton Bardwell in the library at the same time.

"But what if you'd been caught in the main house? And you were in your bedclothes, I assume?"

"Yes. But don't worry. I wasn't caught. I just got the book and came back." Unless Mr. Bardwell's hand on her arm was the same as being caught. "So you see why I'm tired."

Sarah Beth blew out an exasperated breath. "Minerva Mae Tucker! That reading habit of yours is going to be your downfall. I cannot believe getting a book was worth the risk."

Minnie questioned that fact herself. However, the deed was done. "You won't have to worry about my doing that again. It was rather frightening walking through this big house in the dark." She felt better confessing that much to her friend.

"I'm sure it is. Please promise me you won't to do that again. You could lose your job."

"I know. I won't try it again. I'll just get the next book when we go in there early to clean."

"All right. I hate to think of the uproar you could have caused."

"I thought I heard Cedric bark once, and that really scared me."

Sarah Beth covered her open mouth with her hands. "Oh my goodness, Minnie! What if that dog had gotten loose and attacked you? That's a huge dog!"

"I know. Thankfully, he only barked once, so nobody stirred." Besides the fact that Minnie didn't think the big friendly St. Bernard would attack anyone.

"Minnie Tucker! What am I going to do with you?"

Minnie gave her a sheepish grin. "Be my friend?"

Sarah Beth shook her head. "I'll still be your friend as long as your escapades don't get me in trouble too."

"They won't."

Sarah Beth lifted an eyebrow.

"I mean, there won't be anymore."

A bell rang on the annunciator, and the girls went into the hall to see where it came from.

"It's Miss Sloane's room," Pauline said. "Grace is feeling better, so she'll go."

A few minutes later, an exasperated Grace returned.

"I can't do it! She wants me to do her hair. I'm not a lady's maid!"

Minnie groaned. "I went last time. I don't think her lady's maid likes me. Maybe someone else can go this time?"

"I'll go," Sarah Beth said, casting a warning look at Minnie.

"Good. Thank you."

The last person she wanted to see right now was the lady who was supposed to be escorted by Mr. Bardwell. She went back into her room and waited to hear what Sarah Beth was asked to do. She didn't have to wait long because her friend came back shortly afterward.

"You're back already? What did she want?"

"She wants you."

"What? Why? She doesn't even know my name."

"Perhaps not, but when I showed up, she said she wanted that other maid who had come the last time."

"How do you know she meant me?"

"She said, 'I want that pretty blond maid to come do my hair like she does hers.'"

Minnie gaped. "But what about her lady's maid? She's the one who's supposed to fix her hair."

"Apparently, she's angry with her lady's maid because she can't fix her hair like yours."

"Heaven help me. Miss Sloane's hair isn't like mine. It's way too thin to fix like mine."

"Well you have to try."

Minnie's stomach clenched. Why did she answer the call to Miss Sloane's room before?

Mrs. King came into the servants' corridor. "Who answered Miss Sloane's call?"

Sarah Beth and Minnie exchanged glances.

"Well, first, Grace answered her, but when Miss Sloane asked her to do her hair, she panicked and said she didn't know how because she was just a chambermaid. So I went," Sarah Beth said.

"And were you able to help her?"

Sarah Beth glanced at Minnie. "No, ma'am. She wanted Minnie to do her hair done because she wanted it to look like Minnie's."

"Minnie?" The matron looked at Minnie. "Have you done hair before?"

Minnie explained why she had previously been in Miss Sloane's room. "Apparently, she took a liking to my hair and wanted hers fixed the same way."

"Why are you still standing here? Aren't you going to do it?"

"Mrs. King, I will try. But Miss Sloane's hair is thin and won't work like mine. She needs a hairpiece to get this style."

"Then improvise. You have to try. And if she doesn't like it, at least you tried."

"Yes, ma'am." Minnie nodded and hurried away.

When she knocked at Miss Sloane's door, the woman called out. "Come in."

Surprised that Mrs. Parker was not present, she walked in and found Miss Sloane sitting at the bench in front of the dressing table. The woman huffed.

"There you are. Come here and fix my hair. I want it to look like yours."

What should she say? That it was impossible with her hair? No, Minnie knew the woman would have a hissy fit as Granny would say, if she was told that. She walked to the back of the woman who sat rigidly, hairbrush in hand. Minnie took the brush and ran it through Miss Sloane's hair. Then she pulled the hair back and braided it the way she did her own hair, the result being a very thin braid, more than half the thickness of her own. Then she pulled the braid up as high as she could to coil it on top of Miss Sloane's head. But the result was a flat pile of hair. She finished and looked in the mirror for the woman's reaction.

"That's it? You're finished? That does not look like your hair at all. You must redo it."

"Ma'am, I fixed it the way I do my own hair, but our hair is different, so the result is not the same. I think you need a hairpiece to get the look you want."

"And where am I supposed to get one of those now? I must be prepared for dinner so Mr. Bardwell will notice. I want hair like yours!"

Minnie's heart was heavy as a stone, while her mind battled between her own desires and the truth of the situation. She reminded herself why she was here, what her job was, and whom she should please. She choked back a sigh.

"I have an idea, ma'am. I have plenty of hair and can spare some, so I will cut off enough to make you a hairpiece. Our hair color is almost the same, so I think it will blend. It will take me a little time, but I'm sure I can have it ready for you before your engagements today."

"Fine! Please make haste."

"Yes, ma'am."

Minnie hurried out of the room and back to her own. When she didn't find Sarah Beth there, she went into the servants' sitting room and saw Sarah Beth at a table with three of the other maids. Each of them worked on some sewing.

"Sarah Beth, please come quickly. Bring your sewing kit."

Everyone looked at Minnie, and Sarah Beth's brow creased with a frown. "What happened?"

"Please. I'll explain when we get to our room."

Sarah Beth grabbed her things and followed Minnie. In the room, Minnie closed the door behind them.

"I need to make a hairpiece for Miss Sloane out of my hair."

"You are?" Sarah Beth gaped. "Do you really think that's necessary? But you have such lovely thick hair."

"Exactly. That's why I can spare some. Besides, it grows quickly so I won't miss it. So what I need you to do is cut off about ten inches of it."

"Ten?"

Minnie unpinned her hair, and her braid fell below her waist. "Yes. I think that's enough to make a suitable hairpiece. Just cut the braid and it'll be easier to shape into a ball we can sew together."

"Are you sure you want to do this?"

"Yes, and please hurry. I promised her I'd have it ready in time for her to go to tea."

"All right. But I think Mrs. Vanderbilt should know what a sacrifice you're making for her guest."

"That's not important. I'm just solving a problem. Miss Sloane wants to impress Mr. Bardwell, so I'm helping her."

"That's mighty kind of you," Sarah Beth said as she cut through the braid. "I don't think I would do something like this."

"Don't worry. This is just a special situation. Are you finished?"

"Yes." Sarah Beth held up the ten-inch piece of braid.

Minnie reached behind her and felt where her hair stopped, abut five inches above her waist. She didn't need that missing hair anyway.

She took the piece of braid from Sarah Beth and began to work with it and shape it into a little mound. "Do you have a needle threaded that I can use?"

Sarah Beth handed her one, and watched as Minnie began to sew the hair together. She pointed to an area. "Better put some stitches there too."

Minnie complied and soon she held a hairpiece that would stay together. "How does it look?"

"It looks like an acceptable hairpiece. I hope she appreciates your effort."

Minnie shrugged. "Well, I appreciate it, and you do too, so that's enough." She lay the hairpiece down on the dresser, then rebraided her own hair and repinned it in place before pinning her cap back on. Glancing at her reflection, she nodded. "You can't even tell there's less hair."

"No, you can't." Sarah Beth crossed her arms. "I can't wait to hear how this works out. Good luck."

Minnie took the piece in both her hands, holding it discreetly so no one would know what she carried if she ran into anyone else in the hall. She knocked on Miss Sloane's door. "It's me, Miss Sloane. Minnie Tucker."

"Come in."

Minnie carried the hairpiece over to the woman who lounged on a chaise for her inspection.

"Hmm. It better work." She got up and walked to the dressing table and sat before the mirror again.

Minnie set to work placing the hairpiece on top of Miss Sloane's hair, then pulling up the sides of her hair to give the woman the popular Gibson girl look. Using as many hairpins as she could, she managed to create a flattering hairstyle on the woman. She stepped back when she was finished. "Is this satisfactory, Miss Sloane?"

A slow smile eased across her face as Miss Sloane held the hand mirror up and looked at her hair from different angles. "Yes, it is. I dare say my hair has never looked better!"

Minnie smiled. "I'm happy you're pleased, ma'am." She turned to leave.

"Wait. Where are you going? Are you going to dress me?"

Minnie's jaw dropped. She was not a lady's maid. "Ma'am? I thought Mrs. Parker was your lady's maid. Shouldn't she help you dress? She is more experience than I am."

"I don't know where she is."

"I can go find her." She took a step toward the door. "Or you can ring the bell."

"I don't have time to wait for her and you're here. Surely, you know how to dress."

Minnie knew how to dress herself, but she'd never worn all the things women of Miss Sloane's class wore.

"Don't worry. I'll tell you what to do."

Chapter Seven

Minnie paused, then decided she might as well try, since the woman was so determined. After an hour, some waist-cinching, and a cacophony of huffing, puffing and exasperated sighs, the woman was finally dressed. Minnie appraised the finished result as Miss Sloane inspected herself in the mirror. The woman looked better than Minnie had seen her so far but thought the glamorous gold satin dress with puff sleeves trimmed in pearls, was not a good color for the pale woman.

"Isn't this gown gorgeous? Charles Frederick Worth designed it for me."

Minnie had no idea who that was, but she was no student of fashion. "It's lovely, ma'am, and you look lovely too."

"I think so too," Miss Sloane said.

"Ma'am, your dinner is not until later. What will you do until then?"

Miss Sloane glanced around. "What time is it?"

"It's almost five o'clock, ma'am."

"Why didn't you tell me? I missed tea!"

How could Minnie tell her working on her hair had taken up so much time?

"I'm sorry, ma'am. I thought you knew when you asked me to make your hairpiece."

"Well, I didn't. You'll have to give Mrs. Vanderbilt my apologies. Tell her I had a headache from being in the sun and needed to lie down."

Minnie was getting a headache too. There was no pleasing this lady. "What will you do until dinner then?"

"I think I will take a nap now."

"In your gown, ma'am?"

"Of course not. Come, undress me. Then come back before I need to dress for dinner."

There was no way out of it. Minnie's stomach growled reminding her it was time for the staff supper. Now she would be late. However, now that she knew how everything went on, Minnie was quick to get all the clothes off. She laid the pieces across the settee in the room.

"Ma'am, you might try to sleep sitting up so you don't muss your hair. It might take too long to redo if you sleep on it."

Miss Sloane pursed her lips. "You're right. I'll just recline on the chaise and rest my eyes."

"Then I'll return and redress you later, unless you want me to find Mrs. Parker before then."

Miss Sloane waved her hand as if batting a fly. "No, you do it. You know how now. But if you see Mrs. Parker, tell her she can assist me when I retire tonight." With a sly smile, she said, "And who knows when that will be if a certain gentleman wants to escort me for a moonlight walk in the garden?"

Minnie left the room wanting to scream. She never wanted to be a lady's maid. She hurried down to the staff dining room arriving late. "Sorry," she said, as she slid into a chair.

"So did you take a long nap?" Harold asked, grinning.

"Are you feeling all right?" Sweet Grace asked with a look of compassion.

"She's been taking over my position, that's what she's been doing!" Mrs. Parker said from the other end of the table.

All eyes turned to face her.

"What do you mean by that?" Ruby asked, ready to defend her friend.

"She can tell you how she weaseled her way into Miss Sloane's favor." Mrs. Parker glared at Minnie, her slicked-back, coal-black hair adding a severity to her expression.

Minnie's face heated and she was tired, but she did not want to be falsely accused.

"She asked for me to fix her hair, so I did." She left out *because Mrs. Parker couldn't do it well enough to meet her mistress's expectations.*

"And when I came back to check on her, you were still there, helping her dress!"

Minnie had no idea Mrs. Parker had looked in the door, so caught up was she with trying to appease Miss Sloane.

"Well, if you would've come in, you could've taken that task over. I never planned to do that, but Miss Sloane insisted, since I was there." And you weren't, she wanted to say.

"So now she wants you to be her lady's maid, is that right? Well, isn't that convenient?"

"No, that is not true. I'd rather be a parlor maid."

Hungry as she was, her appetite had vanished. "Excuse me." She pushed her chair back and stood. As she was passing by Mrs. Parker, she said, "Miss Sloane told me to tell you she expects to see you tonight when she returns after dinner so you can help her undress."

Minnie hurried back upstairs but Sarah Beth caught up to her. "You barely ate, Minnie."

"I know, but I had no desire to stay in the same room with that woman and be accused of doing something I didn't do. As if I'd want to be Miss Sloane's lady's maid!"

"Mrs. Parker is just afraid she'll lose her position. You know how temperamental Miss Sloane can be."

"Oh yes, I certainly know!" Minnie went on to tell Sarah Beth about dressing the woman only to discover it was too soon and had to be undressed. And in a little while, she'd have to go back and dress her again.

"Oh my. I'm sorry about all this. From what I've heard the other lady's maids say, not all the mistresses are so difficult to please. In fact, it seems the others are more like friends."

Minnie considered what Sarah Beth said. It would be impossible for her and Miss Sloane to be friends. If only Mrs. Parker could fix her hair the way Minnie did. Was she going to be summoned every time Miss Sloane needed her hair done? She prayed not.

"So tonight once they've started their dinner, I'll run straighten and clean her room to get it ready for her to go to bed, then I don't plan to see her again for a long time. Mrs. Parker will put her to bed as usual. That is her job, not mine."

Minnie went back to her and Sarah Beth's room where she sat up on her bed and opened her book from the library. Keeping an eye on the clock, she closed her book when it was time to go redress Miss Sloane. Back in the lady's room, Minnie thankfully discovered she hadn't ruined her hair. Minnie helped her back into her clothes, then Miss Sloane extended her arm out straight. What did that mean?

"Well, put my gloves on, silly girl!"

Glancing around, Minnie found the creamy satin elbow-length gloves and pulled them onto Miss Sloane's arms. She adjusted the hairpiece slightly and made sure it was secure. As soon as the woman left the room, Minnie hurried to clean and straighten the room by picking up the clothes Miss Sloane had worn that day—which Mrs. Parker would have to clean and freshen—folded them loosely and set them in a stack on the dresser. Then she fluffed the pillows and turned down the bedcovers. She started a fire in the fireplace so the room would be warm when Miss Sloane returned. When she finished, she straightened and surveyed the room. Everything appeared to be in order, so she left the room and returned to her own room. She sat back against her headboard and picked up her book.

The next thing she knew, Mrs. King was shaking her shoulders. "Minnie, wake up."

Minnie opened her eyes and focused on the stern face of the matron.

"Yes, ma'am?"

"Minnie, you fell asleep before taking care of Miss Sloane's room. When she returned tonight, it was a mess. Mrs. Parker had to clean it herself."

Minnie sat up straight, fully awake. "But that's not true. I set the room aright as soon as Mrs. Sloane left for dinner."

"How did you know when she left?"

"Because I'm the one who dressed her. She asked me to after I did her hair."

"So you're telling me Mrs. Parker is lying?"

"Yes, ma'am. She has to be because I promise I cleaned the room as usual."

Sarah Beth was awake now, so she sat up too. "Mrs. King, I think Mrs. Parker is mad at Minnie for fixing Miss Sloane's hair. Remember, she *asked* Minnie to do it?"

"Yes, I do. I'll tell Mrs. Vanderbilt. Let's hope she believes you. Sorry to disturb you. We'll see you in the morning."

Sarah Beth fell back on her bed. "It'll work out, Minnie. Don't worry." Soon her soft snores told Minnie she was asleep again.

Minnie stood to undress, but now she couldn't stop thinking about Mrs. Parker's accusation. She needed some fresh air. It was past midnight so the guests were in bed. And if Mr. Bardwell was in the library again, she'd be sure not to go there. Instead of undressing, she quietly left the room and tiptoed down the hall to the backstairs, descending to the first floor. When she entered the door to the main parlor, she paused and listened to see if anyone was still in the area. After a few moments of silence, she was assured no one was awake. She crossed through the house to the main parlor and on to the terrace doors. She quietly opened the door and stepped outside where the full moon shone bright in the sky.

The chilly night air was refreshing as she inhaled the scent of the evergreen trees and listened to the croak of frogs. She stood still, soaking in the peaceful view of the world around her bathed in the evening light. The peace and calm relaxed her, quieting the turmoil inside her as she struggled with the way things had turned out that night. How could her efforts to do her best turn out this way? Who would Mrs. Vanderbilt believe? How could she prove her innocence? Only God had seen her tidy the room. Surely, he would vouch for her somehow.

Rustling from one of the chairs on the terrace stole her attention, and she jerked her head to see what it was. Someone was sitting out there. Had they seen her? She turned to leave quietly.

"Minnie, is that you?"

She knew that voice. Mr. Bardwell. Oh no, not again. If she didn't answer, maybe she could steal away. Her brain told her feet to move, but her heart made her stay rooted in place.

Then he was standing next to her, and she could smell a spicy lavender scent. He touched her hand. "Minnie?"

"Yes, it's me. I'm sorry. I'll leave."

"Don't." He grasped her hand. "Having trouble sleeping again?"

"I, I just needed some fresh air."

He chuckled. "At this time of night? Well, to be honest, I did too. It's beautiful out here, isn't it?"

She nodded. "I love the moonlight."

"So do I. It caresses the world in a soft blanket of light."

"I hear the poet speaking," she said.

He chuckled again, and she could see his smile without looking at him. "Ah, you noticed." He stroked the back of her hand with his thumb. "So you couldn't read tonight? Is something else on your mind?"

She couldn't tell him what happened. He wouldn't understand, nor did he need to know. "Yes, I think I've been too busy and now I can't rest."

"I know what you mean. I've had a lot on my mind, too."

"Are you writing another book?"

"I'm supposed to be, but other things are on my mind too, other people."

Of course he was talking about Miss Sloane. Who else would he be talking about? She shivered as a brisk wind blew across the terrace penetrating her blouse. She wrapped her arms around herself. But then his arm was around her.

"Are you cold, Minnie?" He removed his jacket and put it on her. She inhaled the aroma of his clothing and drew in the warmth of him. "Is that better?"

She nodded, not knowing if he could see her or not. "Much better. Thank you."

"Minnie Tucker, what do you do with your free time, besides read?"

"I take walks on the mountain around my Granny's cabin. Sometimes Sissy, my little sister, goes with me. Other times, I go alone."

"And when you're alone, what do think about?"

"I pray or try to recite Bible verses."

"That's a worthy use of your time."

"When I'm by myself on the mountain, I know I'm not really alone because God is there with me, and it comforts me."

"And do you ever hear His voice?"

"Sometimes I think I do, especially if I've been asking questions and need an answer. He told me I was going to work here."

"He did?"

"Yes, I'm sure of it."

"And did He tell you you'd meet me?"

Minnie startled. No, meeting Stanton Bardwell was completely unexpected.

He lifted her hand to his lips and kissed it. "I'm sorry. I shouldn't have asked you that. But if God had anything to do with our meeting, I thank Him for it."

"I have to go," she said, slipping out of his coat and letting go of his hand.

"I understand. Thank you for talking with me. Our visits are short, but they are meaningful to me."

Minnie hurried back to her room, quickly undressed and lay down in her bed. That had not happened. It was just a dream. So maybe if she went to sleep she'd dream it again. That's the only way she could be with Stanton Bardwell in the future.

Chapter Eight

At breakfast the next morning, Mr. Harvey told the servants that the guests would be gone for most of the day, as Mr. Vanderbilt wanted to take them to see the Biltmore Village, the model town he had created beyond the gates of the Biltmore estate. The absence of the guests gave the servants a chance to roam the rooms freely and get their work done without the adding pressure of avoiding the guests.

Minnie was relieved to know she wouldn't run into Mr. Bardwell again. After last night's encounter, she was more determined than ever to avoid him.

When Mr. Harvey left, the servants chatted among themselves candidly without the presence of the valets and lady's maids of the guests overhearing them, since the guests had taken their attendants with them.

"Can't get used to calling the place Biltmore Village," Jack said. "When I grew up, it was the town of Best."

The others nodded in agreement.

"But Best didn't have everything the Biltmore Village does. In fact, it didn't have much at all," Pauline said. "Now it's got cottages for the workers who come to work on the estate, plus it has a train station and a post office."

"And it's supposed to look like an English village," Alma said. "I've never been to England, so I don't know what that looks like."

"I'm glad Mr. Vanderbilt built a new school. I know lots of workers whose children attend it now," Harold said.

"That church is going to be beautiful when it's finished," Sarah Beth said. "I hear it's going to be called "All Soul's Church.""

"You think those rich folks will be impressed? I bet that duke won't be," Ruby said.

"If he is, he probably won't admit it, from what the other valets say about him," Jack said.

Mrs. King stepped into the room. "Time to get to work. The guests will be back sometime after lunch, so let's take advantage of this time. They'll be here for dinner, so there's still much to do."

The servants scattered to their assigned areas. Minnie was glad she hadn't needed to move as quickly as she had the previous day, so she had a chance to rest. But she hadn't had time to read. Maybe she'd have a chance to before the guests returned.

She and Louisa worked in the Tapestry Room as usual, opening the doors to the terrace to allow fresh air to circulate. As Minnie looked outside, last night's encounter with Mr. Bardwell replayed in her mind. Thankfully, no one knew about it besides herself and him. She would be in so much trouble. She shuddered at the thought. No more wandering the house at night for her. She had learned her lesson.

As they walked into the library, Louisa pointed to the chairs in front of the fireplace.

"Looks like they played chess in here last night." She walked over to the area and began rearranging the chairs surrounding the treasured chess set Minnie had heard about. She had no doubt Mr. Bardwell had been one of those who'd played.

"I wonder how you play that game?" Minnie asked.

"I think it's kind of like checkers," Louisa said, wiping off the glass case the game was stored in.

"Then why do they have all those special pieces like horses and such?" Minnie asked.

Louisa shrugged. "So you want to play?" She laughed. "When would you do that and who would teach you? I'm certain Mr. Vanderbilt doesn't want the servants to play with this game. Books are one thing, this game is quite another. "

"Oh, I wouldn't dare touch that one," Minnie said. Louisa was right. She'd never have time to play such a game. That was for the well-to-do who didn't have to work like she did.

By noon, the servants were finished, so after lunch, several of the men went outside to walk around, while most of the maids sat in the servants' parlor mending or just sitting around and talking. Minnie went to her room to read in privacy. After an hour of reading, she wanted to stretch her legs too. She peeked into the servants' parlor to see where Sarah Beth was.

"She's gone out back," Grace said, looking up from some needlework. "Harold was going to give her and Ruby a tour of the stables. They're supposed to be much nicer than an average barn," Grace said, looking up from some needlework.

Minnie had hoped Sarah Beth would go with her to the library, because she wanted her friend's company when she went in to look at the huge globe and find some places she'd read about. But she didn't want to go out to the stables to get her, so she went downstairs by herself, thankful the guests had not returned yet.

She walked into the room that welcomed her as if it were an old friend and went over to the globe, examining the surface of the shiny varnished ball. Shapes of countries all over the world were printed on it, along with names of cities, rivers and oceans. She found the United States, then North Carolina, then traced her finger from there to England. Louisa was from England and so was the duke, but she didn't know what part of England they had lived in.

"Good afternoon." A male voice she recognized startled her from behind.

She spun around and faced Stanton Bardwell, her heart doing a flip. What was he doing here? Her hand covered her mouth.

"You're back. I'm sorry, I didn't realize you had returned." She moved away from the globe.

"The others haven't returned yet. I left them in the village. Please don't leave, Minnie. I can't say I'm sorry to see you, because on the contrary, I had hoped to. In the daylight." He smiled with a light of mischief in his eyes.

She glanced around, peering behind him. "I must get back to my station. Mr. Vanderbilt prefers the servants are not seen by the guests."

"That may be what George prefers but I like to make decisions for myself about whom I'd like to see. And you, dear lady, I very much want to see."

He called her a lady? Oh my, what was she to do? Why did he want to see her? What about Miss Sloane?

"Sir, I do not know why you would waste your time talking with me, a parlor maid, when there are others who would prefer your attention."

He chuckled and his eyes lit up in an endearing way. "Hmm. I think I know who you're referring to. Let me assure you, I did not arrange the meeting in question, but my hosts did, so I am being cordial to show them my respect."

Minnie thought she understood what he said, but he wasn't very direct.

"So Minnie, have you enjoyed *Pride and Prejudice*?"

"I have, so far, but I've been too busy and too tired to finish it."

"Or go to sleep, of course. But that's entirely unfair, dear Minnie. You should be able to read whenever you wish."

Dear Minnie? "I do not get paid to read, sir."

He chuckled again, this time showing his dimples. Her hands yearned to touch those dimples, so she clasped her hands behind her back to control the urge. He strode over to the globe. "I noticed you were looking at this. Would you like to see any of those places in person?"

"Sir, I'll never leave North Carolina, but I'm amazed by all the people who have seen other parts of the world. People like yourself."

"And if you could go anyplace else, where would you go?"

She stepped toward the globe. After studying it, she pointed to England. "I think because the books I'm reading are set in England, I'd like to see the places firsthand, to find out if they look in reality the way they look in my mind."

He moved closer to her and placed his hand over hers, his face near hers and whispered. "Minnie, I'd like to take you there."

She could smell his familiar scent, he was so close. Too close. Her heart pounded in her chest. Could he hear it? How could she draw her hand back with his trapping it?

"Mr. Bardwell…I do not understand your attention to me. It isn't…isn't…" She made the mistake of turning to face him and found him impossibly close. She searched his eyes as he focused on her lips. No, this can't happen.

But despite her need to protest, his lips brushed hers, and she knew she was done for. The touch was brief, but the sensation made her head swim.

She jerked back. "No. You, we, mustn't. Please."

He straightened. "I do apologize for making you uncomfortable. I've been wanting to kiss you ever since I last saw you. I couldn't help myself." Giving her a warm smile and fixing his gaze on her eyes, he said, "Minnie, some day I predict we will be together. I don't know how or when, but I'm sure of it. Maybe because I want it to be so. But it will happen, I promise you."

"Well, look at this! Minnie Tucker, now you're trying to seduce the guests!" Mrs. Parker stood in the doorway, hands on her hips.

"I assure you, that is not the case," Stanton Bardwell stated, moving to stand in front of Minnie as if he could block the accusation.

"We'll just see about that. Just wait until Mrs. Vanderbilt hears about this!" Mrs. Parker spun and marched away.

Mr. Bardwell turned around to face Minnie as tears gathered in her eyes. "I'm so sorry, Minnie. I will vouch for your character. You have done nothing untowards."

Minnie shook her head as tears trickled down her cheeks. "No one will believe me, and when Mrs. Parker tells Miss Sloane, Miss Sloane will be indignant and call for my termination."

Minnie ran from the room, leaving him behind.

Chapter Nine

Minnie stepped up onto the sagging porch of her grandparents' cabin, the carpet bag in her hands heavy as if she carried an anvil. What was she going to tell Granny and Pappy? She'd been thinking about what to tell them ever since Mrs. King had told her that her behavior was out of line for a parlor maid.

They had believed Mrs. Parker's accusations, telling her they'd talk later. Meanwhile, she had to go home at least until the guests left. After that, Mrs. King told Minnie they would give her another chance to explain herself. Meanwhile, she needed to leave, go home. She'd hoped to go back home to Granny's beaming with pride and excited to share details of her job and the Biltmore House.

But instead, she'd come home in disgrace. The dogs started barking and made Granny come to the door to *Shhh* them.

"Minnie, is that you, child?" Granny shuffled out the door with her arms open, letting the screen door slam behind her.

"Yes, Granny, it's me," Minnie said, choking to hold back tears. But the tears fell anyway, streaming down her cheeks. Granny opened her arms and Minnie fell into them.

"Now, now, honey," Granny said, patting her back. "You just take a deep breath and tell me all about it."

Minnie took a deep breath, then released a sigh. She sank onto a cane rocking chair as Granny brought her a glass of tea. Minnie took a long sip, then gathered herself together and began telling Granny all about what had happened. "Granny, I'm such a failure. I worked so hard and was looking forward to sharing my good fortune with you and Pappy, but…" She started sobbing again.

Granny hugged her. "Minnie, you done nothing wrong, and I'm proud of you for trying to do right by them folks. That Mr. Bardwell, he's the problem, as I see it."

"No, Granny, he's not. He's really a very nice man, it's just that we ran into each other in the library and well…"

Granny studied Minnie's face. "You have feelings for that man, don't you?"

Minnie nodded. "I know I shouldn't, but I couldn't help but be attracted to him. I know there would never be a future for us, but if fairy tales came true, he'd be mine."

"Maybe it's God will that you had to leave. Maybe it's best you are separated from Mr. Bardwell. Have you thought of that?"

Minnie shook her head. "No, I just thought God's punishing me for being attracted to the man. But Granny, if God didn't want us together, why did we have to run into each other and stir up these feelings in me? Why would God do that?"

Shaking her head, Granny said, "The Good Book says His ways aren't our ways and our ways aren't His ways. We just can't always figure out why God does what He does."

Minnie sniffed, then reached into her pocket and pulled out an envelope Mrs. Vanderbilt had given her when Minnie left. She handed the envelope to Granny. "This is all I've got to give you, Granny. I wasn't there long enough to make much, but I want you to have what I got."

Granny took the envelope and peeked inside, eyes widening. "Minnie, this is a right lot of money for the little time you were there."

"Really? I didn't even look. Maybe she felt sorry for me. She didn't act mad, just disappointed. She really is a nice person, Granny, not haughty like some of her guests."

"So, there. You can be thankful to have met her and learned how to be a maid in one of those grand places. Maybe you can find work like that in Asheville."

"But then I'd be farther away from you."

"And you could come visit when you're not working. It's just a train ride away."

Sissy came running up to the house. "Minnie, what are you doing here?"

Minnie and Granny exchanged glances as her little sister looked between the two of them. Sissy seemed to know Minnie's homecoming had not been a happy one, so she quieted, then asked, "What's it like up there?" redirecting her question.

Minnie spent the rest of the afternoon telling Sissy and Granny about the Biltmore House and the staff. Her mood lifted as she watched Granny and Sissy's reaction to the amazing modern conveniences of the house.

"Ooh. I wish I could see a real bathroom!" Sissy said with a faraway look in her eyes.

"Oh, Sissy. I wish you could see the amazing library in the house. Mr. Vanderbilt loves to read and has over 22,000 books in it!"

Sissy's eyes widened. "Are there that many books in the world? Would he let you read any of them?"

"Yes, he did allow his servants to borrow them, so I read a couple, but of course, they can't leave the house. I wish I'd been able to read more." Minnie's voice caught as she realized she'd never have access to those books again. She changed the subject and talked about the electricity in the house.

"You say the lights go on and off when you push buttons? My goodness," Granny said. "I want me some of those buttons!"

Minnie laughed at Granny's reaction. "It's called electricity. There are lots of things in the house that use electricity." She went on to talk about the dumb waiter and the elevators.

At the lifted eyebrow on Granny's face, Minnie could tell she didn't quite believe what she was hearing. Some things you had to see to believe, and the Biltmore House was certainly one of them. How Minnie wished she could show it to Granny and Sissy.

She had heard that families were invited to the Vanderbilt Christmas party for the employees. But her heart pinched knowing she wouldn't be included, much less her family. Despite her short time at the house, she was thankful she'd experienced working for the Vanderbilts.

Over the next few days, Minnie reflected on the various people she'd met or worked with at the Biltmore House. Weren't they her friends? Couldn't anyone vouch for her? But if the same thing had happened to Sarah Beth, would Minnie have tried to stand up for her friend? The next weekend, Sarah Beth showed up at Granny's.

Minnie ran to hug her friend. "I've missed you so!" Minnie said.

"I've missed my roommate too," Sarah Beth said. "In fact, we've all missed you."

"Come and sit with me," Minnie said, pointing to the porch swing.

Sarah nodded and joined Minnie on the swing.

Minnie reflected on what Sarah Beth had said about being missed. The sentiment was a small consolation but appreciated. "And life goes on at the Biltmore House without me," Minnie said. "Are the guests still there?" She wanted to hear about Stanton Bardwell without appearing overly curious.

"Oh no," Sarah Beth said, waving her hand. "They left a couple of days after you did."

"They all left together?" Minnie said but was mostly interested in whether Mr. Bardwell left with Miss Sloane. The thought of the two being together saddened her, but so did the thought that she would never see him again.

"Actually, Mr. Bardwell stayed a couple more days. I heard that he was quite upset that you were let go because of him."

"Is that so?" And well he should be. She wanted to blame him, yet wasn't she as guilty for desiring his company?

"Oh, and you'll never guess," Sarah Beth leaned toward Minnie as she lowered her voice as if anyone from the Biltmore estate was lurking in the shadows.

"What?"

"Miss Sloane and Mrs. Parker had another argument and a huge falling out." Lowering her voice even more, Sarah Beth said, "Miss Sloane told her she wanted you to be her lady's maid instead."

Minnie clasped her hand over her mouth. "She did?"

Sarah Beth nodded. "However, Mrs. Parker told her she found you and Mr. Bardwell in an intimate situation in the library, so Miss Sloane changed her mind."

"Of course she would."

"And then Mr. Bardwell told Miss Sloane he knew of a better lady's maid back in New York that she should hire."

"He did? Why would he do that?"

Sarah Beth shrugged. "Maybe he was telling the truth. Or maybe he was trying to pacify her. Or maybe he wanted to spare you from working for the woman. You know how demanding she is."

Minnie nodded, looking down at her feet. "I know that for a fact."

"Minnie, would you really want to be Miss Sloane's lady's maid? I know it would pay a lot."

"No, I wouldn't." Minnie wouldn't even consider the possibility. Not because the offer was yanked away before she'd even learned of it, but because she couldn't fathom being in Miss Sloane's employ. "Miss Sloane only thought of herself. I'd rather be here where I'm treated with respect, even though we're poor."

"What will you do now, Minnie? Will you get another job?"

"Yes, I'm planning on going to Asheville and applying for a position at one of the fine houses there or maybe that new Kenilworth Inn."

"I wish you could come back to the Biltmore House." Sarah Beth's voice trembled. "I miss my roommate."

Minnie shook her head. "I've burned that bridge."

Sarah Beth put her hand on Minnie's. "I heard that Mrs. King went to Mrs. Vanderbilt to speak on your behalf. She knows what a good worker you are, Minnie."

"Mrs. King would do that for me?"

Sarah Beth nodded. "Well, she hired you, so she wants to prove her choice was good."

"Oh. Yet nothing has changed. I'm still here. Unemployed."

"It still could happen, Minnie."

Minnie shook her head. Another fairy tale. It was time she focused on fact.

"You must miss reading the books in the Biltmore library, since you enjoy reading so much," Sarah Beth said.

"Actually, I haven't read much since I left. I've kind of lost my interest in reading since that's one of the reasons I got in this mess." She hadn't finished *Pride and Prejudice*, but she had read enough to see how similar Miss Sloane was to some of the snobby people in the book who looked down on people like Elizabeth Bennett, like herself. No wonder Mr. Darcy and Miss Bennett couldn't be together.

"Oh, Minnie! It was that awful Mrs. Parker who wanted to get you in trouble. She was jealous of you."

"That's so silly. She was a lady's maid, and I was just a parlor maid."

"But you pleased her mistress when she couldn't. And I have another idea. I think she was jealous of the way Jack looked at you."

"Jack? Oh my word. He looks at all the women. In fact, I remember how he flirted with her," Minnie said. A memory flashed through her mind. "Sarah Beth, remember when I was accused of not preparing Miss Sloane's room? I know I did. Do you think Mrs. Parker messed the room up so I'd get in trouble?"

Sarah Beth nodded. "I sure do."

"Well, she got her wish. I got in trouble and lost my job."

"She's a spiteful woman. And it's simply not fair that she made you lose your job."

Minnie looked around her at the small unpainted cabin she had grown up in. When Ma and Pa had caught the fever and both passed, she and Sissy became orphans. Was that fair? And Granny and Pappy had two young'uns to raise again at their age? That wasn't fair either. No life wasn't fair, but it was life. She knew a lot of people who were bitter because of the way their life had turned out, and they weren't pleasant people to be around. Minnie didn't want to be like them. Didn't the good Lord say to be joyful? How can you be joyful and bitter at the same time? You couldn't. It was a choice, and Minnie chose to be joyful, even if it meant ignoring the pain that pricked her heart every time a thought of Stanton Bardwell stole a place in her mind.

Chapter Ten

Stanton gazed up at the stone building in front of him, its turrets reminding him of the original Carnegie Library he'd visited in Dunfermline, Scotland, Andrew Carnegie's birthplace. This one in Braddock, Pennsylvania, was built in a similar style, although larger. Ever since Stanton had heard of the steel magnate's quest to donate part of his fortune to building libraries, he'd been impressed by the man's philanthropy.

The idea had piqued his interest, but now had become a quest of his own. Ever since leaving the Biltmore House, a piece of his heart was missing. He carried the burden of guilt for putting Minnie in a compromising situation, resulting in her losing her job, and he was determined to set things right. He couldn't interfere in George and Edith's affairs and make them rehire Minnie, but he also wanted to apologize to her. He'd been racking his brain to find a way to do that in a way she'd accept, something more than mere words.

He knew now that he had fallen in love with her. In fact, if love at first sight was true, he was proof. From Minnie's reaction, especially the look in her eyes, Stanton thought she had been attracted to him as well. But love? She was a practical woman, he could tell, and knowing the differences in their stations might prohibit her from having feelings for him. Perhaps they would not live happily ever after together like in a fairy tale, but maybe he could still make her happy.

Their mutual love of books was the key he was pinning his hopes on. Today, he had a meeting with Andrew Carnegie to learn more about his library plan. He took a carriage to the Carnegie Building in downtown Pittsburg, alighting in front of the fourteen-story building that housed the headquarters of the Pittsburgh Steel Company. Taking the elevator to the top floor, he was then ushered into the impressive office of Andrew Carnegie, one of the wealthiest men in the world.

Seated in a padded leather chair behind a massive mahogany desk, Andrew rose and extended his hand. "Nice to see you, Stanton. How are your parents doing? I haven't seen them for a while."

Shaking the man's hand, Stanton smiled. "Thank you, sir. They are fine. Thank you for asking. Father and Mother don't travel as much as they used to, preferring to stay at their country place in Connecticut. Father goes into the city only if necessary."

"Hmm. Sounds like a nice, relaxed life. Someday, I plan to have one of those too." He opened a cigar box on the desk and offered one to Stanton before taking one himself.

Stanton shook his head. "No, thank you, sir. I've never acquired the taste."

"You're probably better off for it." Carnegie snipped off the end of the cigar, lit it, then took a couple of puffs before leaning back in his chair. "How's your writing going?"

"It's going well, sir. My latest book of prose was published two months ago."

Nodding, Carnegie said, "Good. Good. I'm working on a new book myself, but I'm afraid it's much more political in nature."

"I read *The Gospel of Wealth*, sir, and I find your philosophy agreeable," Stanton said.

"Ha! You may be in the minority of those who are wealthy that agree with my ideas. Selfish, that's what we are. Selfish."

"I agree. And I applaud your beliefs that those of us who are fortunate enough to have wealth should use it to help the general public who have less."

Carnegie stood and looked out the large window behind his desk. "So you heard that I have decided to take an annual income no greater than $50,000. More than that, I do not need to earn or make any effort to increase my fortune. Instead, I spend the surplus each year for benevolent purposes."

"I greatly admire your unselfish contributions to society," Stanton said.

Carnegie turned around to face Stanton. "I've spent years amassing a fortune, and now I have more than I need to adequately live on. Starting in Scotland and then in London, I have focused my wealth on education and improvement of the poorer classes. Stanton, did you know the amassing of wealth is one of the worst forms of idolatry? And God condemns worshipping anything besides Himself! No idol is more debasing than the worship of money!"

Andrew Carnegie was not a tall man, but to Stanton, he was a giant, a powerful man who was passionate about helping others. He had seen this trait in George Vanderbilt as well, but not to the extent of Carnegie. Stanton's own life had been that of luxury with access to anything he wanted, be it material possessions or travel. Being around people like the Duke of Marlborough and his obsession with wealth had left a bitter taste in Stanton's mouth.

"You are correct, sir. We have become too obsessed with our wealth, ignoring the needs of the less fortunate."

Carnegie sat back down and puffed on his cigar.

"I apologize for getting carried away, standing on my soapbox. Now, what can I help you with?"

"No apology is necessary. Your beliefs are why I came to see you. You and I share a great love of the written word, and we are privy to every form of reading material we can get our hands on. I think people in our position often think everyone has the same access and those that don't must lack intelligence. But I recently met someone who opened my eyes to reality. There are many people who like to read or want to read and don't have access to written material, especially books. That's why your free public libraries have caught my interest."

Carnegie leaned forward. "I'm glad to hear you approve of my efforts to help educate the public."

Stanton nodded. "I know you donate a large sum of money for the libraries, but will you please explain how the process works? How do you decide where to put these libraries?"

"Certainly. I'm happy to provide funds to build and equip the libraries, but only on the condition that the local authority provide the land and a budget to operate and maintain the library."

"Sounds like an equitable plan."

Carnegie nodded. "I've learned that people appreciate things better when they have a stake in it as well. Up until a couple of years ago, we'd only built libraries in this state, Pennsylvania, since this is where our headquarters are, and we wanted to do something for the people here. We've built fifteen libraries in as many states so far, with two more being built this year. We also have several more applications to consider."

"That's very admirable. So many towns don't have libraries. Do you have a set limit as to how many you're planning to build?"

Carnegie puffed on the cigar. "No. As long as I have money to give, I'll give to worthy organizations. Some of these libraries are part of colleges, and not just towns." He leaned back. "So Stanton, is there a certain place you're considering putting a library?"

"I'm thinking about it. It's not an area I live in, so I need to find out if the locals want one and can meet the criteria."

"All right. You just let me know what I can do to help. I can introduce you to James Bertram, my personal assistant. I've given him charge of fielding requests from municipalities and overseeing the dispensing of grants for libraries. When he receives a request for a library, he sends the applicant a questionnaire inquiring about the town's population, whether it has other libraries, how large its book collection is, and what its circulation figures are. If they meet these requirements, he asked how much the town is willing to pledge for the library's annual maintenance, whether a site is being provided, and the amount of money already available."

"I look forward to meeting Mr. Bertram," Stanton said.

"One of the reasons we're building more libraries now is due to the women's clubs that have flourished since the last war. They're the ones getting behind the drive for more libraries. You get some women behind the project, and it'll get done!"

Stanton knew at least one woman who would be a strong advocate for the libraries, if only he had the chance to speak to her about it. But first, he needed to have a conversation with George and Edith and see what they were willing to do. Maybe George would want to follow Mr. Carnegie's example. He had his own marvelous library. But no one benefitted from it besides his guests and employees. No one else who lived in the vicinity would ever see the library, much less have access to its books.

"Thank you, sir." Stanton stood to leave.

Andrew Carnegie stood as well. Stanton shook his hand. "I will be in touch with you, soon, I hope."

Carnegie lifted an eyebrow. "You said you met someone who opened your eyes to reality. Was that someone a woman? The way your face lit up when you mentioned this someone leads me to think so." He gave a knowing smile.

Stanton's face heated and he nodded, hat in hand. "Yes, sir, she is."

"Then I congratulate you on meeting someone who shares my desire to offer opportunities to the less fortunate."

"Yes, sir. Thank you, sir. She undoubtedly does."

"I've never met any women in our social circles with that desire."

"No, sir. Besides Edith Vanderbilt, I don't know any others myself."

"Hmm. Could she possibly not be in our social circles?"

Stanton paused. Would Carnegie condemn him if he admitted the woman on his mind was outside their class? Would he be as open-minded to appreciate her opinions?

"She is not, sir. She's in a class all her own." Stanton lifted his chest as he stated his support for her, deciding he didn't care if Carnegie approved of her or not. But Carnegie's next statement took him by surprise.

"Perhaps you will introduce me to her someday?"

Stanton relaxed his shoulders. "I'd love to. Indeed, I would."

Stanton put his hat on and strode out of Andrew Carnegie's office with a determination to rectify several situations. First he would go back to the Biltmore House and meet with George Vanderbilt. Then he would find Minnie and hope she would share his new vision.

Chapter Eleven

"How do I look?" Minnie smoothed her skirt and tried to see her reflection in the window.

"You look very nice, like a person that would be a good employee," Granny said.

Minnie had sewn a new blouse similar to the one Mrs. Vanderbilt had worn when they first met, a high-necked white blouse with puffed shoulders and long sleeves buttoned at the wrist.

"I'm sure you'll come home with a new job," Sissy said.

Minnie placed her hat on her head and grabbed her pocketbook. Placing a cheek on Granny's cheek, she said. "Well, I better hurry so I won't miss the train."

Sissy gave her a quick hug, then Minnie began the two-mile trek to the train station.

Minnie had convinced herself she needed a new start after what had happened at the Biltmore House. She'd made peace with the false accusations, knowing she was innocent of any wrongdoings. After church yesterday, she'd realized she needed to forgive her accusers, namely, Mrs. Parker. That was hard, but the preacher had reminded them that if Jesus could forgive His enemies, so could she. At least the woman hadn't tried to kill her. But in some ways, the betrayal had tried to kill part of her by stealing her joy.

She had been so happy to get the job at the Biltmore House and was willing to put in the hard work and long hours. In a way, she felt sorry for Mrs. Parker. If she was so jealous that she had to hurt other people, then she was a sad person, maybe even unloved. Minnie didn't know about her family or what she had gone through, so Minnie was not in a position to judge her, even though she wanted to. No, as Granny had often told her, she needed to love her enemies and pray for them.

As Minnie walked down the road, she mulled over those words. Love her enemies? She wasn't sure she could do that, but she could pray for them and ask God to show His love to her, especially if she felt unloved. Wasn't love supposed to be for people who love you too? She loved Granny and Pappy and Sissy. She loved Sarah Beth too. Stanton Bardwell popped back into her mind. Would she ever be able to forget him? They had barely kissed, but if what she felt at that moment was love, then she loved him. But she accepted the fact that their encounter was only brief and only once, not a forever kind of love.

Her eyes moistened, and she wiped them with the back of her hand. No. She mustn't cry. There would be no good to come of it. Who wants to hire a sniveling mess? Minnie sucked in a deep breath and exhaled. Forget Stanton Bardwell. He was in the past, and she needed a future.

As she approached the train station, she heard its whistle through the mountains. She hurried to the ticket window and purchased her ticket to Asheville. She was on her way to the Battery Park Hotel. The hotel was just a few years older than the Biltmore House, yet was the first hotel in the south to have an electric elevator as well as electric lighting. Famous people from all over the country had come to Asheville since the trains arrived ten years ago to enjoy the mountain air and they had all stayed at the Battery Park Hotel. Minnie looked forward to seeing it in person after all she'd heard about it, but she was nervous about applying for a job. What if they asked about what happened at the Biltmore House, why she wasn't there anymore? If she told the truth, would it hurt her chances of being hired?

The train pulled into the station with a deafening screech as it stopped. She waited for all of those departing the train to get off before she stepped on and began looking for a seat. Finding one by the window, she slipped into it, watching the activity as people sought their luggage and friends. Her car began to fill up, and she wondered who would be sitting next to her. She wasn't afraid of strangers, but preferred them to keep their distance, which was quite impossible on the leather benches of the railroad car.

"All aboard!" shouted the conductor, and everyone scrambled to sit down. The space on the seat beside her remained empty. Would she have it all to herself? If only she had a book to read. She'd probably never know how *Pride and Prejudice* ended, since she had to leave the book at the Biltmore House.

The train began to move, and Minnie breathed a sigh of relief that she would be able to ride the thirty minutes to Asheville without company.

But a rustle of material and crush of a garment beside her interrupted her thoughts as a woman plopped down onto the seat beside her. Minnie averted her eyes as the woman huffed and sighed. But when she started complaining about the people at the station, the train and the people onboard, Minnie recognize the voice. Reluctantly, she turned toward Mrs. Parker.

When their eyes met, Mrs. Parker's brimmed with anger. "You!"

"Hello, Mrs. Parker."

The woman looked around as if looking for an escape. "Of all the…"

Minnie forced herself to remain calm and not respond to Mrs. Parker's rudeness. This was a person she had to forgive, someone she had prayed for, but love her? She had to work up to that if it were possible. As civilly as she could muster, she said, "I'm surprised to see you here."

"I'm sure you are!" Mrs. Parker snapped. "After you made me lose my job!"

Minnie made *her* lose her job? Was the woman confused?

"I don't know what you mean. I lost *my* job."

"As you should have! But before you left, you got me in trouble with my mistress, Miss Sloane."

Minnie glanced around to see if other people were watching since Mrs. Parker was practically yelling. The conductor came down the aisle collecting tickets providing a brief lull in the conversation.

Should she defend herself? No, there was no point. What was there to be gained by arguing? She breathed a silent prayer for help.

"I'm sorry that happened to you. It was not my intention to come between you and Miss Sloane. I am not qualified to be a lady's maid like you are. I think Miss Sloane made a mistake."

Mrs. Parker deflated a little and seemed confused about how to react to Minnie's apology.

"You're right. You are not qualified to be a lady's maid. You shouldn't have pretended to be."

Bitterness rose in Minnie's throat, but she pushed it back down. "So now Miss Sloane is without a lady's maid."

"Hmph! Oh, she has one. She took one of those other maids from the Vanderbilts with her when she left."

Who on earth would that have been? "Oh? I didn't know there were any other lady's maids on the staff."

"There weren't. This one, Louisa, I think is her name, isn't a real lady's maid, but she's from England, and Miss Sloane seemed to think that made her better than American maids."

Louisa? Poor lady. Minnie would have to pray for her. So why was Mrs. Parker on this train? Dared she ask?

"I'm sure you'll find another position as a lady's maid soon, that is, if you haven't already. I hear a lot of well-to-do people go to Asheville."

Mrs. Parker didn't respond. Instead, she glanced in the other direction as if something on the other side of the aisle had caught her attention. Since she apparently had lost interest in talking, Minnie turned to look out the window. Had she done or said the right thing? At least the woman had calmed down. Minnie let herself relax. She hadn't won the argument, but she felt like she had won the battle, the battle that had raged inside herself ever since she had been let go at the Biltmore House. Maybe now they were even with no one having an upper hand. However, Minnie was finally at peace, but cutting a glance at her seatmate, she saw the clenched jaw of Mrs. Parker and knew the woman did not have the same peace.

They rode the rest of the way in silence, except for the occasional snore coming from Mrs. Parker who had succumbed to sleep. As the train rolled into Asheville, and the conductor called out the name of the place, the passengers stirred and began collecting their things. When the whistle blew, Mrs. Parker jumped in her seat, then sat up straight, looking around her.

"Are we in Asheville?" she asked Minnie.

Minnie glanced out the window where Asheville was written across the sign displayed in front of the station. She pointed. "Yes."

Mrs. Parker looked away, then down at her bag. When the train stopped, she stood and pushed her way through the other departing customers. What was her hurry? Was her next boss waiting outside for her?

Minnie stepped off the train and looked around. She followed the crowd to the street on the other side of the station and glanced both ways. A carriage was parked alongside the station, so Minnie stopped and asked the driver where the Battery Park Hotel was.

"About a mile up the street, ma'am. I can take you there."

"Thank you, but I'd rather walk after sitting on the train so long," she said, which was true, but it was also true that she couldn't afford to pay him anything for the ride.

As she climbed the steep hill, the green roofs of the hotel came into view. Finally, she reached the top of the hill and stood before the ornate colorful hotel. Built in what was called the Victorian style, the hotel was comprised of several buildings that stretched across the property. In addition to the green roofs, the first two floors were painted yellow, while the floors above were painted deep red. The main building had a cone-shaped pointed roof while the other tall building had a dome-shaped roof. Green awnings covered windows in dormers on the top floors. Tall chimneys and balconies filled the spaces between.

Minnie gaped at the ornate décor of the hotel, so unlike the white limestone of the Biltmore House. The overall impression reminded her of a circus which she'd gone to with her parents so long ago. But this property didn't have rides and sell boiled peanuts. She followed a lady wearing fashionable clothes carrying a lacy parasol to the entrance of the building. As she stepped inside, she waited her turn to get to the front desk.

"May I help you, ma'am?" The man behind the counter with his hair parted down the middle and stuck to his head with pomade asked.

"Yes, sir. I'd like to apply for a job."

He lifted his eyebrows, then pointed down a corridor. "The hotel manager's office is right down there. Good luck!"

Minnie followed the hallway to an office door with the name "Manager" on a brass plaque. She tapped on the door. "Come in," a woman's voice said.

Stepping inside, she found a secretary sitting at a desk. "May I help you?"

"Yes, I'd like to apply for a job."

The woman handed Minnie a piece of paper and a pencil. "Write your name, where you're from, where you worked before, what you did there, and what position you're applying for. You may sit over there." She nodded to a row of four chairs along the wall.

Minnie sat down and wrote, "Minnie Tucker, Best—the name the area by Biltmore Village used to be called—North Carolina, Biltmore House parlor maid, and maid," then handed it back to the woman.

"Mr. Murphy will be with you in a moment. He's with someone else now."

Muted voices came from the other side of the door. A few minutes later, the door and Mrs. Parker rushed out, her face flushed. Her eyes widened as she saw Minnie, opening her mouth if to say something, then clamping it shut and hurrying out the office.

"You may go in now," the secretary said.

Minnie stepped into the office where a portly gentleman with thinning brown hair stood and motioned her to sit in the chair opposite the desk.

Minnie forced a polite smile and sat. "Thank you," she said.

"Well, young lady. What is your name and what can I do for you?" He reached for the paper in her hand, then sat down behind the desk.

She handed it to him. "I'm Minnie Tucker. I last worked at the Biltmore House as a parlor maid. I would like to apply for the position of a maid here at your hotel."

"Hmm. The Biltmore House? Why would you leave there? I understand the Vanderbilts are very nice to their employees."

"They are, sir. However, I believe working in your hotel would be a better position for me."

"And why do you think that?"

"I think I'd rather be an employee than a servant."

He studied her. "I think I know what you're saying. There's too many levels in a manor house, I think. We're not in Europe and don't have butlers, footmen, etc. We're mostly locals, mountain people who want to work. Is that right?"

"Yes, sir."

"When can you start?"

"Tomorrow?"

Mr. Murphy smiled. "Excellent." He stood, rubbing his chin. "Would you be opposed to being a waitress instead of a maid? Someone as pretty as you should meet our guests."

Her face heated at his comment, and she was a little uncomfortable hearing it. Was she being hired on her appearance? She needed to prove herself, regardless. "I can try, sir. I've never been a waitress, but I can learn."

"Good." He walked to the door and opened it. "Helen, please take Miss Tucker here to the uniform room and give a waitress uniform."

"Yes, sir." The lady at the desk stood and came around. "Follow me," she said.

"Can you be here at eight in the morning, Miss Tucker?" Mr. Murphy stood in the doorway to his office, arms crossed. "You will report to the kitchen manager for training."

"If the train runs early enough, I can be here then. But I do not know the train schedule well."

"Do the best you can. We'll work out the details tomorrow." He went back into his office and Minnie followed Helen to a room filled with uniforms. She handed Minnie a long green skirt, white blouse and white pinafore apron. "Wear black stockings and black shoes if you have them. And your hair is fine like that, but you need to tie this ribbon in it." She handed Minnie a green grosgrain ribbon. "Good luck."

Minnie took the stack of clothes and rolled them into a bundle to carry. She was elated to have landed the job so easily. Now, if only the train schedule will cooperate.

As she left the building, she rounded a corner where a woman sat on a bench inside a garden area. A quick glance told her the woman was Mrs. Parker. A closer glance told her Mrs. Parker was crying.

Chapter Twelve

Stanton stepped down from the carriage, studying the exterior of the Biltmore House again. It looked unchanged, and yet there were changes.

He would be the only guest of Edith and George this time with no one else to try to impress or focus attention on. As a result, there would be no grand dinners or parties, as he had requested to join the Vanderbilts in their smaller, more intimate breakfast room for meals. In such a relaxed setting, it would be easier to converse.

Another difference in this visit and the last was the fact that Minnie would not be there. How he wished he could run into her in the library again. But he had to present his idea to the Vanderbilts without appearing overly emotional or self-interested. He blew out a breath as he climbed the steps to the front door where Mr. Harvey stood waiting to greet him.

"Good day, Mr. Bardwell. I hope your trip was pleasant. Mr. Vanderbilt is waiting for you in the billiards room. I'll put your bags in the same room you had before, as you requested."

"Thank you, Mr. Harvey." Stanton removed his hat and handed it to the butler, then walked past the sunlit atrium with the marble floors to the Bachelor's Wing on the far side of the foyer. Stanton chuckled to himself about the name of the wing given to the area when the house was built and before he married Edith. Might she want that wing renamed? But Edith was a good sport and didn't care about things like that. She had her ladies' sitting area as well. They were united on both subjects, something Stanton was counting on this time.

He pressed open the door to the billiards room and found George playing a game of billiards by himself. He glanced up from his stance of aiming the ball and straightened, extending a hand.

"Good to see you again so soon, old chap. You missed us, did you?" George Vanderbilt laughed. "Or was it the house?"

Stanton grinned as he shook George's hand. "I must admit it was the house I've missed."

The two laughed, while Stanton picked up a pool cue and waited for George to rack the balls.

"So where have you been since you left? Traveling?"

"Some, but mostly here in the states. Although I did take a little trip to Scotland."

"A *little* trip? Last I checked, that's a bit far away from the States."

"Maybe I should have said, short, as I wasn't there long."

George broke the balls, then stepped back for Stanton to have a turn. "A man of mystery, huh?"

"I'll tell you and Edith more about it at dinner. I'd like to talk to both of you at once."

"All right. Well, things are progressing around here. We're still working on the Biltmore Village for the townspeople."

"Is that right? What are you planning to build there?"

"First, a school. Edith has some ideas for teaching a course to train young ladies on how to be household help, make them more employable so they can get work outside of town, like Asheville. We can't hire everyone, you know."

Stanton nodded. "I'm glad to hear you want to help the community.'

"We're part of it, and we want to encourage good relationships."

Stanton was glad to hear George shared some of Andrew's thoughts about helping the community and providing education. Hopefully, George would want to extend his resources even more for the benefit of others. They finished their game, and George offered him a drink on the terrace.

"I don't care for any alcohol, but I'd love a glass of that wonderful iced tea you had last time I was here."

"Ah yes, it's quite refreshing. Having ice is vital to making the drink. That's why we have our own ice plant. Even thought the mountains stay pretty cool, it can get hot during the daytime in the summer."

George pushed a button on the wall of the billiards room, and Mr. Harper appeared in the doorway.

"Yes, sir?"

"Would you please bring Mr. Bardwell and myself a pitcher of iced tea out on the terrace?"

The butler bowed slightly. "Yes, sir."

George and Stanford walked through the first floor to the Tapestry room where the doors were open to the terrace. Cool air blew through as the men settled into rocking chairs looking toward the mountains. Stanton looked around as they passed through the house. Where did the help keep themselves hidden?

"Are you looking for something, Stanton?" George asked.

"Not really. It just occurred to me how many servants you must have to keep this place maintained."

"We have 65 inside servants at this time."

"Yet, you cannot see any, except for Mr. Harvey, as if they are invisible."

"I prefer it that way. Which reminds me…the maid that was accused of flirting with you, she is no longer here."

"Yes, I heard. But I do not think the accusation was just. She was in the library cleaning, and I happened in at the same time."

"She should've been finished before you arrived."

"George. It was 5:30 in the morning. I believe she was there so early to avoid running into any guests, including myself."

"Mrs. Harper said the two of you were very close. Tell me, Stanton, was that an accident? Shouldn't she have left the room when you came in?"

"I asked her to stay, George. I wanted to talk to her."

George lifted his eyebrows as the butler brought a tray with a pitcher of tea and two filled glasses out to them.

George took a glass and drank some. "Is that right? Why would you want to talk with her?"

"She likes to read as do I, so we talked about books."

"Hmm. I thought you might like to talk with Octavia Sloane about books instead of with a parlor maid."

Stanton rolled his eyes. "George, Miss Sloane does not read. Didn't you notice how ignorant she was of Keats when we discussed his work at the picnic? She was completely bored. Don't tell me you didn't notice."

George stared out toward Mt. Pisgah. "I noticed. I just find it difficult to understand that you had more in common with a parlor maid."

"You know, George, reading can be a universal enterprise. Everyone should be allowed to appreciate books like you and I do. Don't you agree?"

George didn't answer, but Stanton knew he was pondering the question since he allowed his servants to read books from his library. Good. He'd pursue the subject again at dinner.

***

Minnie wanted to hurry past and ignore Mrs. Parker, but something told her to go to the woman instead. Reluctantly, she slowly approached the woman.

"Mrs. Parker? Is anything wrong?"

The woman looked up, eyes red. Minnie expected a tongue-lashing for intruding, but the sorrowful look on her face was not Mrs. Parker's usual demeanor. She sniffed, so Minnie pulled her handkerchief from her bag and handed it to the woman. Taking a glance at Minnie, then the handkerchief, Mrs. Parker took it and blew her nose. "Thank you," she said softly.

"Is there anything I can do for you, Mrs. Parker?"

A big tear rolled down the woman's face and she shook her head. Minnie had never seen her look so vulnerable, didn't even think she was capable of being vulnerable.

"Florence. My name is Florence, but I go by Flo. You don't need to call me Mrs. Parker anymore. I'm not your superior anymore." She sniffed again.

Minnie had never thought of her as a superior, but she was glad to hear she had a shorter name. "Flo, how can I help you?"

"You can't."

Minnie took a bold step and sat down beside Flo. "Can you tell me about it? I saw you in the manager's office. Was he rude to you?"

Shaking her head, Flo said, "No. But he didn't hire me either. He wants someone who can read." Almost in a whisper she said, "And I can't." Flo looked up at Minnie. "I can't read. And I can't write. I didn't go to school."

What should she say? "Your parents didn't read?"

"I don't have any parents. They died when I was very young and I was put in an orphanage. An old lady adopted me to be her maid, so I got out. But I didn't go to school."

"But how did you become a lady's maid?" Minnie thought all the lady's maids had more education than parlor maids.

"I pretended. I was hired as a maid like you, but when I heard how much more the pay was for a lady's maid, I watched other lady's maids and copied them. I was pretty good at it, I think. But I couldn't fix Miss Sloane's hair. Didn't know anything about hairpieces or where to get one."

"And that was why you were let go?"

"No. We argued about other things too, like her clothes. Then she saw me with Jack and got really mad, saying she wasn't paying me to cavort with the male servants. I got mad back at her, so she fired me. And now I can't get another job."

Minnie was shocked to hear the truth coming from Flo. But Flo didn't care who knew anymore. She'd given up hope.

"So you didn't get a job here because you can't read?"

Flo shook her head. "I don't know what to do now. Maybe I'm doomed to working in a brothel like my mother did, so I've been told."

"Oh, no! You don't have to do that. I'll help you. Where are you staying?"

"In a boarding house in Best until my money runs out."

"Good. That's not far from where I live. I can teach you how to read and write."

Flo drew back and considered Minnie. "You can? You would do that for me after how mean I've been to you?"

"Yes." But Minnie hadn't figured out when she would have time to teach Flo. "You and I are both starting over."

Flo looked at her in disbelief. "I can't believe you would do that for me."

"The Good Book says to treat others the way you'd want to be treated, not the way they treated you. If I were in your shoes, I would like for someone to teach me to read. And once you learn, you'll love it. Reading will open up all new worlds to you."

"You sound excited."

"I am." Minnie realized she was, surprising herself.

"When we get back to Best, come to my house and we'll start right away."

"Today?"

"Yes. You need to be able to read and write to get a job, so there's no time to waste. Are you ready to learn?"

"Why yes, I suppose so."

"Then let's go catch that train!"

Chapter Thirteen

Stanton waited for the dishes to be removed at dinner. When the table was cleared, he learned forward, looking from Edith Vanderbilt to George.

"I wanted to talk with you two about something I have become very passionate about. When I was last here, I had the opportunity to converse with a very smart young lady in your employ." Edith and George exchanged glances.

"Minnie Tucker?" Edith said.

"Yes. Before then, I had never had a conversation with a servant beyond asking them to attend to my needs. But that was very ignorant of me, very arrogant. I discovered that she loved to read and loved your library about as much as you do, with a hunger to read books like you and I share. She was fortunate to be taught by her mother, which is rare for mountain people. I've learned that there are many less fortunate like her that would also love to read but haven't had the education or the access to books to do so.

"So I went to visit Andrew Carnegie and learned about his philanthropic program to share his wealth with the less fortunate by providing funds for libraries and schools. Have you heard of his program?"

Edith and George shook their heads as the butler brought them tea and cake for dessert.

"Carnegie gives money to build a library or even a college building if the recipient's application meets his criteria. They are required to provide the land and a budget plan for how they will manage the facility once it is built. First, he built a library in his hometown in Scotland, but now he's building them all over the United States. He, like many of us, is now comfortable enough financially to be generous and help others. I think it's a wonderful plan, don't you?"

The two people across the table from him nodded in agreement.

"And you are telling us this because you'd like us to do the same?" George said.

"Yes. George, you said you have built a school for the village, and Edith, I know you're interested in training domestic servants, which are both worthy endeavors. But I'd like to see you build a library for the area as well. You can teach people to read in your school, but they will need books to read. I'm not talking about a lavish library such as yours. No, I'm talking about something with enough variety that would benefit the whole community on a smaller scale. I'm willing to go in with you."

George learned back in his chair. "A library? I hadn't considered a library for the village. First, we built All Soul's Church designed by my good friend Richard Hunt, who passed away before it was finished. Next we built the school. But I understand the need for the library as well."

"Since you own all the land around here, you wouldn't have to ask anyone else to supply the site. But maybe you can ask some people in town to help manage it. What do you think?"

"I think it's quite feasible." He turned to Edith. "What do you think, Edith?"

"I agree. We should build a library for the townspeople to use. I require that those who enter my training school for domestics know how to read. Perhaps the library can stock some books on cooking, cleaning, and so forth."

"Excellent. So when can we get started?" Stanton said.

"You're in a hurry, Stanton?" Edith asked, her eyebrows lifted.

"I must admit I'm eager to see the project through. Do you know where you would put it? If not, I can go with you tomorrow and help choose a spot if you don't."

George rubbed his chin. "I've got an idea. But certainly, let's ride into town tomorrow and look around."

"Stanton, have you seen Minnie Tucker since she left our employ?" Edith asked.

"No, I haven't. I don't even know where to find her. She may not even speak to me."

"Why wouldn't she?"

"Because I believe it's my fault she was fired. She was completely innocent of wrongdoing, but I imposed on her to talk with me."

"From what I remember, it was Mrs. Parker that accused her of being improper. And now I realize that Mrs. Parker was not trustworthy. I should hire Minnie back."

"You would do that?"

"She was a good worker, so yes, I would."

Stanton tried to imagine Minnie's response if she were offered the opportunity to come back to work at the Biltmore House. Would she be happy about it? What if she had gotten another position elsewhere?

"Stanton, I know it's highly irregular for someone of your status to associate with a servant, but I also know what love looks like, and I see it on your face. If you want to find her, I can ask her best friend who works here," Edith said.

Stanton's face heated. Was it so obvious that he was in love with Minnie Tucker? "Would you please ask her? She may not want to see me, but I know she'd be happy to know about the library. I'm looking forward to choosing the site tomorrow, so I can tell her about it."

Minnie and Flo had spent the rest of the day going over the alphabet, writing it, and making words. Flo was eager to learn, even though she got confused often. When Sissy and Granny learned who she was, they were shocked to know Minnie was helping her. But this Flo was nothing like the woman Minnie had worked with before. She was humble and thankful for the kindness. Granny invited her to dinner, and although Flo protested at first, Minnie insisted, wondering what the woman would have to eat at the boarding house.

After dinner, Flo left, passing Sarah Beth on the way out. Sarah Beth's eyes grew wide as saucers as she hurried to the house.

"What was she doing here?" Sarah Beth asked.

"Learning how to read and write," Minnie said.

"She doesn't know how?"

"No, she doesn't. Never even went to school." Minnie explained to her friend what she'd learned about Flo and how Minnie had ended up teaching her.

"You're a better person than I am, Minnie Tucker," Sarah Beth said. "After what she did to you."

Minnie shrugged. "I've forgiven her. All that's in the past now." She grabbed Sarah Beth's hand. "I have a new job now! I'll be working as a waitress at the Battery Park Hotel in Asheville!"

"You will? As a waitress? Do you know how to do that?"

"I'll learn. You serve food to customers."

"Well, that's wonderful news, Minnie." Sarah Beth didn't sound very excited though.

"Why aren't you happy about that, Sarah Beth?" Minnie let go of Sarah Beth's hand.

"Well, Mrs. Vanderbilt came looking for me today. She wanted to know your address."

"She did?" What had she done now? "Why?"

"She plans to offer your position back to you. She said you were a good worker and falsely accused."

"She did? Are you sure?"

Sarah Beth nodded. "So what will you do? Will you go to work at the hotel or come back to the Biltmore House?"

"I don't know." Minnie bit her lip, considering the possibility. "What if I don't take the waitress job and then Mrs. Vanderbilt changes her mind?"

"I don't think she would have told me if she wasn't sure."

"I'll have to pray about it, Sarah Beth. This is a hard decision"

Sarah Beth nodded. "I know. I don't know what to tell you to do. You have to make that decision."

Minnie mulled over the choices. It would be difficult to catch the train back and forth every day, but she'd do it if she needed the job. But if she could go back to the Biltmore House with her name cleared, well, that might be even better. And then there was that library and the chance to read more books.

"I need to tell you something else," Sarah Beth said.

"What? Did something else happen?"

"Mr. Bardwell has returned to Biltmore. By himself."

Minnie's heart skipped a beat. He was back. Would she see him again? Would she take the job at Biltmore just to see him? But no, that was what got her in her situation, innocent or not. She still had feelings for him, and he was still out of reach and always would be. Maybe she shouldn't accept her former job.

No, the decision had been made for her. She couldn't return, couldn't jeopardize her job again. She'd have to go to work at the hotel in Asheville, convenient or not.

Chapter Fourteen

"It's perfect," Stanton said, when George showed him his suggestion for a library site.

"Good." George surveyed the flat green land from the back of his horse. "Then I'll have my architect draw up plans."

"George, I know you want a masterpiece, but let's not make it such a work of art that it will take a long time to build." Stanton knew George's tendency toward the elaborate, as well as how much longer it took to build more extravagant buildings. But Stanton was eager to see his plan come to fruition.

George chuckled. "We'll see."

They turned their horses around and headed back to Biltmore. "Wait," Stanton said.

George paused. "What?"

Stanton swallowed past a lump in his throat, his heart quickening like a schoolboy seeing his first infatuation. "I have an errand to run, that is, someone to see."

George nodded. "I think I know who that is."

"You'd be right. I have the directions to her house, so I want to go see her and tell her about the library now."

"All right. I'll see you back at the house." George urged his horse, and they trotted away.

Stanton pulled a sheet of paper from his pocket and read the directions. Looking around to get his bearings, he followed the instructions that led away from town and into the woods as the road climbed up. When he spotted the cabin in the woods, he brought his horse to a stop. Was this where Minnie lived? Such a humble place, but it didn't matter. The woman he loved lived there, and he had to see her.

He rode up toward the house, then dismounted and tied the reins around a fence post. Glancing around, he wondered what kind of reception he'd get. He walked over and stepped up on the front porch, then tapped on the screen door.

An elderly, gray-haired woman with blue eyes the color of Minnie's came to the door and opened it. Peering up at him, she said, "Sir? Are you lost?"

He shook his head. "I don't think so. Does Minnie Tucker live here?"

"She sure does."

A young girl with golden hair like Minnie's came running up behind the woman.

"Who...?" Her big blue eyes rounded as she saw him. "You're him."

He cocked his head. "I apologize for not introducing myself. My name is Stanton Bardwell. And you must be Sissy."

Her face turned crimson. "I am. I'm Minnie's sister."

He turned toward the older woman. "And I suppose you're Granny?"

She grinned and her eyes crinkled at the corners. "I sure am!"

He looked around. "Is Minnie here?"

The two women shook their heads. "No. She's gone to work in Asheville. She works at the Battery Park Hotel. Her train won't be back until later."

His heart fell. "Please tell her I came by."

They nodded. "We will," they said in unison.

He walked back to his horse, disappointment in every step as he walked away. Climbing on the horse, he started back down the mountain, the horse plodding along with the heaviness he felt. He had been so excited to see her, to tell her about the library, even offering her a position there when it was finished, but maybe it was too late. As the trees opened up toward the road, he glimpsed golden hair climbing uphill towards him. He stopped his horse, his heart thumping in his chest. She was focused on the path and didn't see him at first. Then she lifted her gaze, and their eyes met.

He climbed down off the horse and began walking toward her. Somehow, he forgot all the things he'd planned to tell her as he got closer to her. Her eyes were wide with wonder, but then he saw something else in them. Love. They closed the gap between them, and he wrapped his arms around her, lifting her off her feet.

Setting her down, he leaned toward her and pressed his lips to hers. She responded and nothing else in the world existed. Finally, they separated, staring at each other.

"I love you, Minnie Tucker."

Her eyes filled with tears. "I love you too, Stanton Bardwell."

"I have so much to tell you," he said. "But first, I have something to give you." He reached inside his coat and pulled out a copy of *Pride and Prejudice*. Handing it to her, he said, "I don't think you had a chance to finish this."

Minnie took the book and smiled up at him, eyes glistening. "I just want to know if they lived happily ever after."

Stanton smiled and wrapped his arms around her waist. "They did."

Reaching up and pulling his face toward hers, she said, "Starting now."

THE END

About the Author

Award-winning author Marilyn Turk writes historical and contemporary novels laced with suspense and romance. She especially likes finding little-known historical tidbits to include in her books. In addition to fiction, Marilyn is a contributor to Guideposts' Walking in Grace and other anthologies. She and her husband are lighthouse enthusiasts, have visited over 100 lighthouses, and served as volunteer lighthouse caretakers at Little River Light off the coast of Maine.

When not writing or visiting lighthouses, Marilyn enjoys reading, walking, kayaking, fishing, gardening and playing tennis. She also sings in the choir at her church and leads a women's Bible study group.

She is a member of ACFW, Faith, Hope and Love Christian Writers, AWSA, Word Weavers International and the United States Lighthouse Society.

Facebook – https://www.facebook.com/marilyn.turk.9/
Twitter – @marilynturk.com
Pinterest - https://www.pinterest.com/bluewaterbayou.
Website – Pathways of the Heart, https://pathwayheart.com/. Two blogs: Lighthouse blog and The Writers Path blog. Sign up for newsletter and blogs on this site.
Bookbub - https://www.bookbub.com/profile/marilyn-turk
Goodreads - https://www.goodreads.com/author/show/9791210.Marilyn_Turk
Amazon author page - https://www.amazon.com/Marilyn-Turk/e/B017Y76L9A

Milton Keynes UK
Ingram Content Group UK Ltd.
UKHW030905191024
449758UK00008B/63